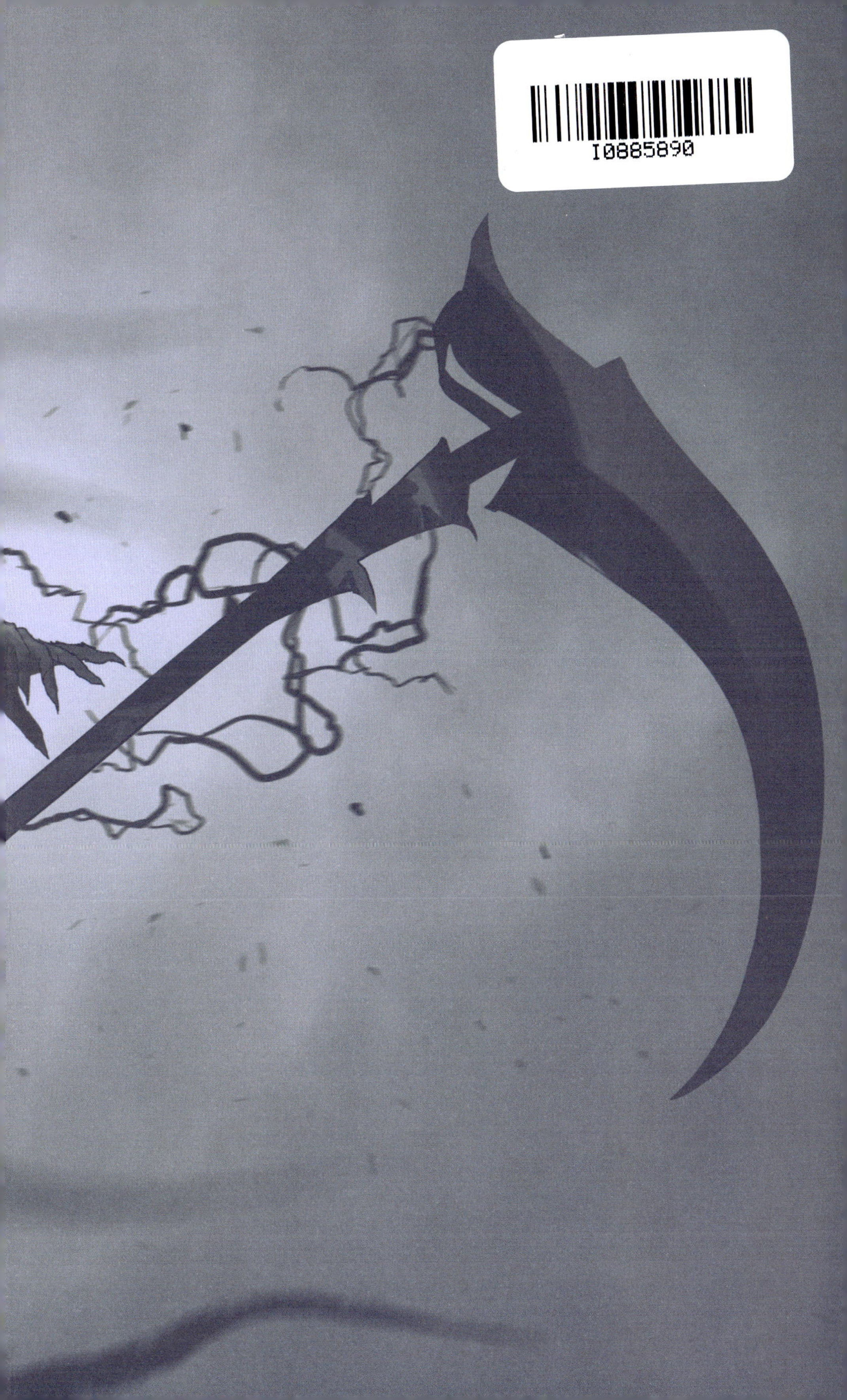

THE CLASSIC

HORROR

COLLECTION

THE CLASSIC HORROR COLLECTION

SIRIUS

SIRIUS

This edition published in 2025 by Sirius Publishing, a division of
Arcturus Publishing Limited,
26/27 Bickels Yard, 151–153 Bermondsey Street,
London SE1 3HA

Cover design: Peter Ridley
Cover illustration: Tithi Luadthong

ISBN: 978-1-3988-6098-8
AD006076NT

Printed in China

Contents

Introduction

Terror is a hard emotion to evoke in a book. Unlike a movie, there is no sight of the impending horror. There is no soundtrack to ratchet up the suspense. There are only the words on the page and your own imagination. Yet, without fail, the authors in this volume achieve this feat with ease and provide a more chilling experience than you could ever encounter elsewhere. They do not rely on cheap thrills or making you jump. Instead, the horror they provide is an all-encompassing, all-pervading atmosphere from which there is no escape. Put down the book and a sense of apprehension will remain with you for hours.

Nineteenth-century pioneers drew on traditions of Gothic literature and folklore to create new ways to terrify their readers. Vampires, a longstanding feature of superstitions across Europe, found their way into popular literature through the works of Joseph Sheridan Le Fanu, Bram Stoker and others.

Authors better known for their other classic works, such as Mary Shelley and Robert Louis Stevenson, also dabbled in short works of horror fiction. Deals with supernatural beings gone wrong were a common theme. In Stevenson's "The Bottle Imp," a disquieting curse surrounds the bottle containing an imp that will grant its owner three wishes. In W. W. Jacobs' "The Monkey's Paw," the artefact has three wishes to give, but only for an enormous cost. Mary Shelley's "The Mortal Immortal" subverts the reader's expectations by showing the torturous effects immortality can convey on a man. Cursed artefacts continued to be a popular theme. Pearl Norton Swet's "The Medici Boots" features a cursed pair of 500-year-old ladies' boots acquired by an unwary American family.

Francis Marion Crawford's "The Screaming Skull" tells the tale of an elderly sailor who discovers a skull in a house he has recently inherited. As his peaceful retirement is disturbed by piercing screams that he can attribute only to the skull, he finds the gruesome artefact is more dangerous than it first appears. "For the Blood is the Life" is a classic vampire tale featuring a woman whose love continues from beyond the grave. Unusually for such stories, Crawford evokes a measure of sympathy for the vampire. We are introduced to a young woman who is cruelly murdered, and then, after death, becomes the bloodsucking protagonist of the tale and a danger to unfortunate passers-by.

Other writers understood that the real world could provide just as terrifying an inspiration as any magical powers. Ambrose Bierce was an American Civil War veteran who used his experiences of that terrible conflict to inform his writing. "An Occurrence at Owl Creek Bridge" has been described as one of the most famous works of American literature. It is the story of a plantation owner awaiting his own hanging.

Sometimes, it is not the visible terrors that have the greatest impact but the threat of something dreadful which is just out of sight. Many 19th-century writers were masters at the subtle manipulation of their readers' minds.

The pessimism of Guy de Maupassant pervades his classic stories such as "Diary of a Madman" and "He?". The slowly deteriorating minds of his protagonists create an entirely different type of fear than stories of vampires, ghosts or evil spirits. Unlike the works of Stoker or Poe, there is little hope of escape from the terrors he presents—and we are only too aware of how such madness could one day embrace any of us.

Edgar Allan Poe was one of the first truly great writers of American horror. "The Tell-Tale Heart" is a masterpiece of suspense, recounting the story of a murderer in the moments after the deed has been committed. In the grandiose "The Fall of the House of Usher," the sinister "The Masque of the Red Death," and the unnerving "The Black Cat," Edgar Allan Poe creates a range of disturbing atmospheres, elaborate horrors and deeply unsettling experiences.

By the 20th century, a new fascination with the supernatural took hold. The growth of the pulp magazines during the interwar period provided a new outlet for imaginative stories that were too unconventional for traditional publishers.

William Hope Hodgson's "The Thing Invisible" and "The Gateway of the Monster" feature the occult detective Carnacki. Combining the appeal of the detective story with the fascinations of supernatural phenomena and the frights of the horror genre, these stories entertained and terrified in equal measure. First appearing in the *Idler* magazine in 1910, Carnacki's adventures are refreshing in presenting a protagonist as ordinary and fearful as any one of us.

Arthur Machen, the influential Welsh novelist best known for the controversial *The Great God Pan*, was a leading short story writer, too. "The Red Hand" features a ritual murder and the gradual unravelling of the mystery. "The Terror" was Machen's attempts to respond to the trauma of World War I in which a rash of mysterious deaths beset England's small towns and farming communities.

One of Machen's devotees was H. P. Lovecraft, who looked to horrors on a cosmic scale, with ancient and unknowable gods who mercilessly toy with the protagonists. The Cthulhu mythos that he created, with its tales of psychological deterioration in the face of unknowable terrors, has fascinated readers for generations. The tales of Arkham, the Miskatonic university, and the Great Old Ones have inspired writers, artists, screenwriters and video game designers since "The Call of Cthulhu" was first published in 1928.

"The Thing from—Outside" was one of George Allan England's few forays into horror. Following in the tradition of Lovecraft, it features utterly alien beings who toyed with humans for their own unknowable reasons. In a similar vein were M. P. Shiel's stories. Combining creeping insanity with supernatural dangers, Shiel's elaborate prose created a sense of existential horror. Edgar Allan Poe's influence shines through in his writing. Part tribute to the American literary master's "The Fall of the House of Usher," "Vaila" is the story of a pair of students, a dark past and a haunted house, while "Xélucha" draws upon the themes of Poe's story "Ligea."

No collection of horror stories would be complete without a few ghost stories. People have tended to believe there is something childish about ghost stories. The friendly ghost has become a fixture of popular culture. The stories of E. F. Benson and M. R. James remind us that ghosts can be just as terrifying a subject as any other. In these tales, suspense continues to build until a frightful twist is suddenly revealed. The elegant writing and accomplished plotting provides these stories with the power to shock. Hinting at the terrors that hide in the darkness, these tales of the undead evoke an atmosphere of discomfort and the sense that something is not right. Charlotte Riddell was one of the most popular Victorian writers, and in "The Open Door" she demonstrates her mastery of the classic ghost story. After a clerk is fired, he stays in an old manor house where one door refuses to remain closed, pointing to a supernatural entity behind the disturbance.

In these stories, there are rarely happy endings. Prepare yourself for the horrors that follow—there is no turning back now.

The Tell-Tale Heart

by Edgar Allan Poe

True!—nervous—very, very dreadfully nervous I had been and am; but why will you say that I am mad? The disease had sharpened my senses—not destroyed—not dulled them. Above all was the sense of hearing acute. I heard all things in the heaven and in the earth. I heard many things in hell. How, then, am I mad? Hearken! and observe how healthily—how calmly I can tell you the whole story.

It is impossible to say how first the idea entered my brain; but once conceived, it haunted me day and night. Object there was none. Passion there was none. I loved the old man. He had never wronged me. He had never given me insult. For his gold I had no desire. I think it was his eye! yes, it was this! He had the eye of a vulture—a pale blue eye, with a film over it. Whenever it fell upon me, my blood ran cold; and so by degrees—very gradually—I made up my mind to take the life of the old man, and thus rid myself of the eye for ever.

Now this is the point. You fancy me mad. Madmen know nothing. But you should have seen me. You should have seen how wisely I proceeded—with what caution—with what foresight—with what dissimulation I went to work! I was never kinder to the old man than during the whole week before I killed him. And every night, about midnight, I turned the latch of his door and opened it—oh, so gently! And then, when I had made an opening sufficient for my head,

I put in a dark lantern, all closed, closed, so that no light shone out, and then I thrust in my head. Oh, you would have laughed to see how cunningly I thrust it in! I moved it slowly—very, very slowly, so that I might not disturb the old man's sleep. It took me an hour to place my whole head within the opening so far that I could see him as he lay upon his bed. Ha!—would a madman have been so wise as this? And then, when my head was well in the room, I undid the lantern cautiously—oh, so cautiously—cautiously (for the hinges creaked)—I undid it just so much that a single thin ray fell upon the vulture eye. And this I did for seven long nights—every night just at midnight—but I found the eye always closed; and so it was impossible to do the work; for it was not the old man who vexed me, but his Evil Eye. And every morning, when the day broke, I went boldly into the chamber, and spoke courageously to him, calling him by name in a hearty tone, and inquiring how he had passed the night. So you see he would have been a very profound old man, indeed, to suspect that every night, just at twelve, I looked in upon him while he slept.

Upon the eighth night I was more than usually cautious in opening the door. A watch's minute-hand moves more quickly than did mine. Never before that night, had I felt the extent of my own powers—of my sagacity. I could scarcely contain my feelings of triumph. To think that there I was, opening the door, little by little, and he not even to dream of my secret deeds or thoughts. I fairly chuckled at the idea; and perhaps he heard me; for he moved on the bed suddenly, as if startled. Now you may think that I drew back—but no. His room was as black as pitch with the thick darkness (for the shutters were close fastened, through fear of robbers), and so I knew that he could not see the opening of the door, and I kept pushing it on steadily, steadily.

I had my head in, and was about to open the lantern, when my thumb slipped upon the tin fastening, and the old man sprang up in bed, crying out—"Who's there?"

I kept quite still and said nothing. For a whole hour I did not move a muscle, and in the meantime I did not hear him lie down. He was still sitting up in the bed listening;—just as I have done, night after night, hearkening to the death-watches in the wall.

Presently I heard a slight groan, and I knew it was the groan of mortal terror. It was not a groan of pain or of grief—oh, no!—it was the low stifled sound that arises from the bottom of the soul when overcharged with awe. I knew the sound well. Many a night, just at midnight, when all the world slept, it has welled up from my own bosom, deepening, with its dreadful echo, the terrors that distracted me. I say I knew it well. I knew what the old man felt, and pitied him, although I chuckled at heart. I knew that he had been lying awake ever since the first slight noise, when he had turned in the bed. His fears had been ever since growing upon him. He had been trying to fancy them causeless, but could not. He had been saying to himself—"It is nothing but the wind in the chimney—it is only a mouse crossing the floor," or "it is merely a cricket which has made a single chirp." Yes, he had been trying to comfort himself with these suppositions: but he had found all in vain. All in vain; because Death, in approaching him had stalked with his black shadow before him, and enveloped the victim. And it was the mournful influence of the unperceived shadow that caused him to feel—although he neither saw nor heard—to feel the presence of my head within the room.

When I had waited a long time, very patiently, without hearing him lie down, I resolved to open a little—a very, very little crevice in the lantern. So I opened it—you cannot imagine how stealthily, stealthily—until, at length a single dim ray, like the thread of the spider, shot from out the crevice and fell full upon the vulture eye.

It was open—wide, wide open—and I grew furious as I gazed upon it. I saw it with perfect distinctness—all a dull blue, with a hideous veil over it that chilled the very marrow in my bones; but I could see nothing else of the old man's face or person: for I had directed the ray, as if by instinct, precisely upon the damned spot.

And have I not told you that what you mistake for madness is but overacuteness of the senses?—now, I say, there came to my ears a low, dull, quick sound, such as a watch makes when enveloped in cotton. I knew that sound well, too. It was the beating of the old man's heart. It increased my fury, as the beating of a drum stimulates the soldier into courage.

But even yet I refrained and kept still. I scarcely breathed. I held the lantern motionless. I tried how steadily I could maintain the ray upon the eye. Meantime the hellish tattoo of the heart increased. It grew quicker and quicker, and louder and louder every instant. The old man's terror must have been extreme! It grew louder, I say, louder every moment!—do you mark me well? I have told you that I am nervous: so I am. And now at the dead hour of the night, amid the dreadful silence of that old house, so strange a noise as this excited me to uncontrollable terror. Yet, for some minutes longer I refrained and stood still. But the beating grew louder, louder! I thought the heart must burst. And now a new anxiety seized me—the sound would be heard by a neighbor! The old man's hour had come! With a loud yell, I threw open the lantern and leaped into the room. He shrieked once—once only. In an instant I dragged him to the floor, and pulled the heavy bed over him. I then smiled gaily, to find the deed so far done. But, for many minutes, the heart beat on with a muffled sound. This, however, did not vex me; it would not be heard through the wall. At length it ceased. The old man was dead. I removed the bed and examined the corpse. Yes, he was stone, stone dead. I placed my hand upon the heart and held it there many minutes. There was no pulsation. He was stone dead. His eye would trouble me no more.

If still you think me mad, you will think so no longer when I describe the wise precautions I took for the concealment of the body. The night waned, and I worked hastily, but in silence. First of all I dismembered the corpse. I cut off the head and the arms and the legs.

I then took up three planks from the flooring of the chamber, and deposited all between the scantlings. I then replaced the boards so cleverly, so cunningly, that no human eye—not even his—could have detected anything wrong. There was nothing to wash out—no stain of any kind—no blood-spot whatever. I had been too wary for that. A tub had caught all—ha! ha!

When I had made an end of these labors, it was four o'clock—still dark as midnight. As the bell sounded the hour, there came a knocking at the street door. I went down to open it with a light heart,—for what had I now to fear? There entered three men, who introduced themselves, with perfect suavity, as officers of the police. A shriek had been heard by a neighbor during the night; suspicion of foul play had been aroused; information had been lodged at the police office, and they (the officers) had been deputed to search the premises.

I smiled,—for what had I to fear? I bade the gentlemen welcome. The shriek, I said, was my own in a dream. The old man, I mentioned, was absent in the country. I took my visitors all over the house. I bade them search—search well. I led them, at length, to his chamber. I showed them his treasures, secure, undisturbed. In the enthusiasm of my confidence, I brought chairs into the room, and desired them here to rest from their fatigues, while I myself, in the wild audacity of my perfect triumph, placed my own seat upon the very spot beneath which reposed the corpse of the victim.

The officers were satisfied. My manner had convinced them. I was singularly at ease. They sat, and while I answered cheerily, they chatted of familiar things. But, ere long, I felt myself getting pale and wished them gone. My head ached, and I fancied a ringing in my ears: but still they sat and still chatted. The ringing became more distinct:—it continued and became more distinct: I talked more freely to get rid of the feeling: but it continued and gained definiteness—until, at length, I found that the noise was not within my ears.

No doubt I now grew very pale;—but I talked more fluently, and with a heightened voice. Yet the sound increased—and what could I do? It was a low, dull, quick sound—much such a sound as a watch makes when enveloped in cotton. I gasped for breath—and yet the officers heard it not. I talked more quickly—more vehemently; but the noise steadily increased. I arose and argued about trifles, in a high key and with violent gesticulations; but the noise steadily increased. Why would they not be gone? I paced the floor to and fro with heavy strides, as if excited to fury by the observations of the men—but the noise steadily increased. Oh God! what could I do? I foamed—I raved—I swore! I swung the chair upon which I had been sitting, and grated it upon the boards, but the noise arose over all and continually increased. It grew louder—louder—louder! And still the men chatted pleasantly, and smiled. Was it possible they heard not? Almighty God!—no, no! They heard!—they suspected!—they knew!—they were making a mockery of my horror!—this I thought, and this I think. But anything was better than this agony! Anything was more tolerable than this derision! I could bear those hypocritical smiles no longer! I felt that I must scream or die! and now—again!—hark! louder! louder! louder! louder!

"Villains!" I shrieked, "dissemble no more! I admit the deed!—tear up the planks! here, here!—it is the beating of his hideous heart!"

The Fall of the House of Usher

by Edgar Allan Poe

Son cœur est un luth suspendu;
Sitôt qu'on le touche il résonne.
De Béranger

During the whole of a dull, dark, and soundless day in the autumn of the year, when the clouds hung oppressively low in the heavens, I had been passing alone, on horseback, through a singularly dreary tract of country; and at length found myself, as the shades of the evening drew on, within view of the melancholy House of Usher. I know not how it was—but, with the first glimpse of the building, a sense of insufferable gloom pervaded my spirit. I say insufferable; for the feeling was unrelieved by any of that half-pleasureable, because poetic, sentiment, with which the mind usually receives even the sternest natural images of the desolate or terrible. I looked upon the scene before me—upon the mere house, and the simple landscape features of the domain—upon the bleak walls—upon the vacant eye-like windows—upon a few rank sedges—and upon a few white trunks of decayed trees—with an utter depression of soul which I can compare to no earthly sensation more properly than to the after-dream of the reveler upon opium—the bitter lapse into everyday life—the hideous dropping off of the veil. There was an iciness, a sinking, a sickening of the heart—an unredeemed dreariness of thought which no goading of the imagination could torture into aught of the sublime. What was it—I paused to think—what was it that so unnerved me in the contemplation of the House of Usher? It was a mystery all insoluble; nor could I grapple with the shadowy fancies that crowded upon me as I pondered. I was forced to fall back upon the unsatisfactory conclusion, that while, beyond doubt, there are combinations of very simple natural objects which have the power of thus affecting us, still the analysis of this power lies among considerations beyond our depth. It was possible, I reflected, that a mere different arrangement of the particulars of the scene, of the details of the picture, would be sufficient to modify, or perhaps to annihilate its capacity for sorrowful impression; and, acting upon this idea, I reined my horse to the precipitous brink of a black and lurid tarn that lay in unruffled luster by the dwelling, and gazed down—but with a shudder even more thrilling than before—upon the remodeled and inverted images of the gray sedge, and the ghastly tree-stems, and the vacant and eye-like windows.

Nevertheless, in this mansion of gloom I now proposed to myself a sojourn of some weeks. Its proprietor, Roderick Usher, had been one of my boon companions in boyhood; but many years had elapsed since our last meeting. A letter, however, had lately reached me in a distant part of the country—a letter from him—which, in its wildly importunate nature, had admitted of no other than a personal reply. The MS. gave evidence of nervous agitation. The writer spoke of acute bodily illness—of a mental disorder which oppressed him—and of an earnest desire to see me, as his best, and indeed his only personal friend, with a view of attempting, by the cheerfulness of my society, some alleviation of his malady. It was the manner in which all this, and much more, was said—it was the apparent heart that went with his request—which allowed me no room for hesitation; and I accordingly obeyed forthwith what I still considered a very singular summons.

Although, as boys, we had been even intimate associates, yet I really knew little of my friend. His reserve had been always excessive and habitual. I was aware, however, that his very ancient family had been noted, time out of mind, for a peculiar sensibility of temperament, displaying itself, through long ages, in many works of exalted art, and manifested, of late, in repeated deeds of munificent yet unobtrusive charity, as well as in a passionate devotion to the intricacies, perhaps even more than to the orthodox and easily recognizable beauties, of musical science. I had learned, too, the very remarkable fact, that the stem of the Usher race, all time-honored as it was, had put forth, at no period, any enduring branch; in other words, that the entire family lay in the direct line of descent, and had always, with very trifling and very temporary variation, so lain. It was this deficiency, I considered, while running over in thought the perfect keeping of the character of the premises with the accredited character of the people, and while speculating upon the possible influence which the one, in the long lapse of centuries, might have exercised upon the other—it was this deficiency, perhaps, of collateral issue, and the consequent undeviating transmission, from sire to son, of the patrimony with the name, which had, at length, so identified the two as to merge the original title of the estate in the quaint and equivocal appellation of the "House of Usher"—an appellation which seemed to include, in the minds of the peasantry who used it, both the family and the family mansion.

I have said that the sole effect of my somewhat childish experiment—that of looking down within the tarn—had been to deepen the first singular impression. There can be no doubt that the consciousness of the rapid increase of my superstition—for why should I not so term it?—served mainly to accelerate the increase itself. Such, I have long known, is the paradoxical law of all sentiments having terror as a basis. And it might have been for this reason only, that, when I again uplifted my eyes to the house itself, from its image in the pool, there grew in my mind a strange fancy—a fancy so ridiculous, indeed, that I but mention it to show the vivid force of the sensations which oppressed me. I had so worked upon my imagination as really to believe that about the whole mansion and domain there hung an atmosphere peculiar to themselves and their immediate vicinity—an atmosphere which had no affinity with the air of heaven, but which had reeked up from the decayed trees, and the gray wall, and the silent tarn—a pestilent and mystic vapor, dull, sluggish, faintly discernible, and leaden-hued.

Shaking off from my spirit what must have been a dream, I scanned more narrowly the real aspect of the building. Its principal feature seemed to be that of an excessive antiquity. The discoloration of ages had been great. Minute fungi overspread the whole exterior, hanging in a fine tangled web-work from the eaves.

Yet all this was apart from any extraordinary dilapidation. No portion of the masonry had fallen; and there appeared to be a wild inconsistency between its still perfect adaptation of parts, and the crumbling condition of the individual stones. In this there was much that reminded me of the specious totality of old woodwork which has rotted for long years in some neglected vault, with no disturbance from the breath of the external air. Beyond this indication of extensive decay, however, the fabric gave little token of instability. Perhaps the eye of a scrutinizing observer might have discovered a barely perceptible fissure, which, extending from the roof of the building in front, made its way down the wall in a zigzag direction, until it became lost in the sullen waters of the tarn.

Noticing these things, I rode over a short causeway to the house. A servant in waiting took my horse, and I entered the Gothic archway of the hall. A valet, of stealthy step, thence conducted me, in silence, through many dark and intricate passages in my progress to the studio of his master. Much that I encountered on the way contributed, I know not how, to heighten the vague sentiments of which I have already spoken. While the objects around me—while the carvings of the ceilings, the somber tapestries of the walls, the ebon blackness of the floors, and the phantasmagoric armorial trophies which rattled as I strode, were but matters to which, or to such as which, I had been accustomed from my infancy—while I hesitated not to acknowledge how familiar was all this—I still wondered to find how unfamiliar were the fancies which ordinary images were stirring up. On one of the staircases, I met the physician of the family. His countenance, I thought, wore a mingled expression of low cunning and perplexity. He accosted me with trepidation and passed on. The valet now threw open a door and ushered me into the presence of his master.

The room in which I found myself was very large and lofty. The windows were long, narrow, and pointed, and at so vast a distance from the black oaken floor as to be altogether inaccessible from within. Feeble gleams of encrimsoned light made their way through the trellised panes, and served to render sufficiently distinct the more prominent objects around; the eye, however, struggled in vain to reach the remoter angles of the chamber, or the recesses of the vaulted and fretted ceiling. Dark draperies hung upon the walls. The general furniture was profuse, comfortless, antique, and tattered. Many books and musical instruments lay scattered about, but failed to give any vitality to the scene. I felt that I breathed an atmosphere of sorrow. An air of stern, deep, and irredeemable gloom hung over and pervaded all.

Upon my entrance, Usher arose from a sofa on which he had been lying at full length, and greeted me with a vivacious warmth which had much in it, I at first thought, of an overdone cordiality—of the constrained effort of the ennuyé man of the world. A glance, however, at his countenance, convinced me of his perfect sincerity. We sat down; and for some moments, while he spoke not, I gazed upon him with a feeling half of pity, half of awe. Surely, man had never before so terribly altered, in so brief a period, as had Roderick Usher! It was with difficulty that I could bring myself to admit the identity of the wan being before me with the companion of my early boyhood. Yet the character of his face had been at all times remarkable. A cadaverousness of complexion; an eye large, liquid, and luminous beyond comparison; lips somewhat thin and very pallid, but of a surpassingly beautiful curve; a nose of a delicate Hebrew model, but with a breadth of nostril unusual in similar formations; a finely-molded chin, speaking, in its want of prominence, of a want of moral energy; hair of a more than web-like softness and tenuity; these features, with an inordinate expansion above the regions of the temple, made up altogether a countenance not easily to be forgotten. And now in the mere exaggeration of the prevailing character of these features, and of the expression they were wont to convey, lay so much of change that I doubted to whom I spoke. The now ghastly pallor of the skin, and the now miraculous luster of the eye, above all things startled and even awed me. The silken hair, too, had been suffered to grow all unheeded, and as, in its wild gossamer texture, it floated rather than fell about the face, I could not, even with effort, connect its arabesque expression with any idea of simple humanity.

In the manner of my friend I was at once struck with an incoherence—an inconsistency; and I soon found this to arise from a series of feeble and futile struggles to overcome an habitual trepidancy—an excessive nervous agitation. For something of this nature I had indeed been prepared, no less by his letter, than by reminiscences of certain boyish traits, and by conclusions deduced from his peculiar physical conformation and temperament. His action was alternately vivacious and sullen. His voice varied rapidly from a tremulous indecision (when the animal spirits seemed utterly in abeyance) to that species of energetic concision—that abrupt, weighty, unhurried, and hollow-sounding enunciation—that leaden, self-balanced and perfectly modulated guttural utterance, which may be observed in the lost drunkard, or the irreclaimable eater of opium, during the periods of his most intense excitement.

It was thus that he spoke of the object of my visit, of his earnest desire to see me, and of the solace he expected me to afford him. He entered, at some length, into what he conceived to be the nature of his malady. It was, he said, a constitutional and a family evil, and one for which he despaired to find a remedy—a mere nervous affection, he immediately added, which would undoubtedly soon pass off. It displayed itself in a host of unnatural sensations. Some of these, as he detailed them, interested and bewildered me; although, perhaps, the terms, and the general manner of the narration had their weight. He suffered much from a morbid acuteness of the senses; the most insipid food was alone endurable; he could wear only garments of certain texture; the odors of all flowers were oppressive; his eyes were tortured by even a faint light; and there were but peculiar sounds, and these from stringed instruments, which did not inspire him with horror.

To an anomalous species of terror I found him a bounden slave. "I shall perish," said he, "I must perish in this deplorable folly. Thus, thus, and not otherwise, shall I be lost. I dread the events of the future, not in themselves, but in their results. I shudder at the thought of any, even the most trivial, incident, which may operate upon this intolerable agitation of soul. I have, indeed, no abhorrence of danger, except in its absolute effect—in terror. In this unnerved—in this pitiable condition—I feel that the period will sooner or later arrive when I must abandon life and reason together, in some struggle with the grim phantasm, Fear."

I learned, moreover, at intervals, and through broken and equivocal hints, another singular feature of his mental condition. He was enchained by certain superstitious impressions in regard to the dwelling which he tenanted, and whence, for many years, he had never ventured forth—in regard to an influence whose supposititious force was conveyed in terms too shadowy here to be restated—an influence which some peculiarities in the mere form and substance of his family mansion, had, by dint of long sufferance, he said, obtained over his spirit—an effect which the physique of the gray walls and turrets, and of the dim tarn into which they all looked down, had, at length, brought about upon the morale of his existence.

He admitted, however, although with hesitation, that much of the peculiar gloom which thus afflicted him could be traced to a more natural and far more palpable origin—to the severe and long-continued illness—indeed to the evidently approaching dissolution—of a tenderly beloved sister—his sole companion for long years—his last and only relative on earth. "Her decease," he said, with a bitterness which I can never forget, "would leave him (him the hopeless and the frail) the last of the ancient race of the Ushers." While he spoke, the Lady Madeline (for so was she called) passed slowly through a remote portion of the apartment, and, without having noticed my presence, disappeared. I regarded her with an utter astonishment not unmingled with dread—and yet I found it impossible to account for such feelings. A sensation of stupor oppressed me, as my eyes followed her retreating steps. When a door, at length, closed upon her, my glance sought instinctively and eagerly the countenance of the brother—but he had buried his face in his hands, and I could only perceive that a far more than ordinary wanness had overspread the emaciated fingers through which trickled many passionate tears.

The disease of the Lady Madeline had long baffled the skill of her physicians. A settled apathy, a gradual wasting away of the person, and frequent although transient affections of a partially cataleptical character, were the unusual diagnosis. Hitherto she had steadily borne up against the pressure of her malady, and had not betaken herself finally to bed; but, on the closing in of the evening of my arrival at the house, she succumbed (as her brother told me at night with inexpressible agitation) to the prostrating power of the destroyer; and I learned that the glimpse I had obtained of her person would thus probably be the last I should obtain—that the lady, at least while living, would be seen by me no more.

For several days ensuing, her name was unmentioned by either Usher or myself: and during this period I was busied in earnest endeavors to alleviate the melancholy of my friend. We painted and read together; or I listened, as if in a dream, to the wild improvisations of his speaking guitar. And thus, as a closer and still closer intimacy admitted me more unreservedly into the recesses of his spirit, the more bitterly did I perceive the futility of all attempt at cheering a mind from which darkness, as if an inherent positive quality, poured forth upon all objects of the moral and physical universe, in one unceasing radiation of gloom.

I shall ever bear about me a memory of the many solemn hours I thus spent alone with the master of the House of Usher. Yet I should fail in any attempt to convey an idea of the exact character of the studies, or of the occupations, in which he involved me, or led me the way. An excited and highly distempered ideality threw a sulfureous luster over all. His long improvised dirges will ring for ever in my ears. Among other things, I hold painfully in mind a certain singular perversion and amplification of the wild air of the last waltz of Von

Weber. From the paintings over which his elaborate fancy brooded, and which grew, touch by touch, into vagueness at which I shuddered the more thrillingly, because I shuddered knowing not why;—from these paintings (vivid as their images now are before me) I would in vain endeavor to educe more than a small portion which should lie within the compass of merely written words. By the utter simplicity, by the nakedness of his designs, he arrested and overawed attention. If ever mortal painted an idea, that mortal was Roderick Usher. For me at least—in the circumstances then surrounding me—there arose out of the pure abstractions which the hypochondriac contrived to throw upon his canvas, an intensity of intolerable awe, no shadow of which felt I ever yet in the contemplation of the certainly glowing yet too concrete reveries of Fuseli.

One of the phantasmagoric conceptions of my friend, partaking not so rigidly of the spirit of abstraction, may be shadowed forth, although feebly, in words. A small picture presented the interior of an immensely long and rectangular vault or tunnel, with low walls, smooth, white, and without interruption or device. Certain accessory points of the design served well to convey the idea that this excavation lay at an exceeding depth below the surface of the earth. No outlet was observed in any portion of its vast extent, and no torch, or other artificial source of light was discernible; yet a flood of intense rays rolled throughout, and bathed the whole in a ghastly and inappropriate splendor.

I have just spoken of that morbid condition of the auditory nerve which rendered all music intolerable to the sufferer, with the exception of certain effects of stringed instruments. It was, perhaps, the narrow limits to which he thus confined himself upon the guitar, which gave birth in great measure, to the fantastic character of his performances. But the fervid facility of his impromptus could not be so accounted for. They must have been, and were, in the notes, as well as in the words of his wild fantasias (for he not unfrequently accompanied himself with rhymed verbal improvisations), the result of that intense mental collectedness and concentration to which I have previously alluded as observable only in particular moments of the highest artificial excitement. The words of one of these rhapsodies I have easily remembered. I was, perhaps, the more forcibly impressed with it, as he gave it, because, in the under or mystic current of its meaning, I fancied that I perceived, and for the first time, a full consciousness on the part of Usher, of the tottering of his lofty reason upon her throne. The verses, which were entitled "The Haunted Palace," ran very nearly, if not accurately, thus:

I
In the greenest of our valleys,
  By good angels tenanted,
Once a fair and stately palace—
  Radiant palace—reared its head.
In the monarch Thought's dominion—
  It stood there!
Never seraph spread a pinion
  Over fabric half so fair.

II
Banners yellow, glorious, golden,
  On its roof did float and flow;
(This—all this—was in the olden
  Time long ago)
And every gentle air that dallied,
  In that sweet day,
Along the ramparts plumed and pallid,
  A winged odor went away.

III
Wanderers in that happy valley
  Through two luminous windows saw
Spirits moving musically
  To a lute's well tuned law,
Round about a throne, where sitting
  (Porphyrogene!)
In state his glory well befitting,
  The ruler of the realm was seen.

IV
And all with pearl and ruby glowing
  Was the fair palace door,
Through which came flowing, flowing, flowing
  And sparkling evermore,
A troop of echoes whose sweet duty

Was but to sing,
In voices of surpassing beauty,
The wit and wisdom of their king.

V
But evil things, in robes of sorrow,
Assailed the monarch's high estate;
(Ah, let us mourn, for never morrow
Shall dawn upon him, desolate!)
And, round about his home, the glory
That blushed and bloomed
Is but a dim-remembered story
Of the old time entombed.

VI
And travelers now within that valley,
Through the red-litten windows, see
Vast forms that move fantastically
To a discordant melody;
While, like a rapid ghastly river,
Through the pale door,
A hideous throng rush out forever,
And laugh—but smile no more.

I well remember that suggestions arising from this ballad, led us into a train of thought wherein there became manifest an opinion of Usher's which I mention not so much on account of its novelty (for other men have thought thus), as on account of the pertinacity with which he maintained it. This opinion, in its general form, was that of the sentience of all vegetable things. But, in his disordered fancy, the idea had assumed a more daring character, and trespassed, under certain conditions, upon the kingdom of inorganization. I lack words to express the full extent, or the earnest abandon of his persuasion. The belief, however, was connected (as I have previously hinted) with the gray stones of the home of his forefathers. The conditions of the sentience had been here, he imagined, fulfilled in the method of collocation of these stones—in the order of their arrangement, as well as in that of the many fungi which overspread them, and of the decayed trees which stood around—above all, in the long undisturbed endurance of this arrangement, and in its reduplication in the still waters of the tarn. Its evidence—the evidence of the sentience—was to be seen, he said (and I here started as he spoke) in the gradual yet certain condensation of an atmosphere of their own about the waters and the walls. The result was discoverable, he added, in that silent, yet importunate and terrible influence which for centuries had molded the destinies of his family, and which made him what I now saw him—what he was. Such opinions need no comment, and I will make none.

Our books—the books which, for years, had formed no small portion of the mental existence of the invalid—were, as might be supposed, in strict keeping with this character of phantasm. We pored together over such works as the *Ververt et Chartreuse* of Gresset; the *Belphegor* of Machiavelli; the *Heaven and Hell* of Swedenborg; the *Subterranean Voyage of Nicholas Klimm* by Holberg; the *Chiromancy* of Robert Flud, of Jean D'Indaginé, and of De la Chambre; the *Journey into the Blue Distance* of Tieck; and the *City of the Sun* of Campanella. One favorite volume was a small octavo edition of the *Directorium Inquisitorum*, by the Dominican Eymeric de Gironne; and there were passages in *Pomponius Mela*, about the old African Satyrs and Ægipans, over which Usher would sit dreaming for hours. His chief delight, however, was found in the perusal of an exceedingly rare and curious book in quarto Gothic—the manual of a forgotten church—the *Vigiliae Mortuorum secundum Chorum Ecclesiae Maguntinae*.

I could not help thinking of the wild ritual of this work, and of its probable influence upon the hypochondriac, when, one evening, having informed me abruptly that the Lady Madeline was no more, he stated his intention of preserving her corpse for a fortnight (previously to its final interment), in one of the numerous vaults within the main walls of the building. The worldly reason, however, assigned for this singular proceeding, was one which I did not feel at liberty to dispute. The brother had been led to his resolution (so he told me) by consideration of the unusual character of the malady of the deceased, of certain obtrusive and eager inquiries on the part of her medical men, and of the remote and exposed situation of the burial ground of the family. I will not deny that when I called to mind the sinister countenance of the person whom I met upon the staircase, on the day of my arrival at the house, I had no desire to oppose what I regarded as at best but a harmless, and by no means an unnatural, precaution.

At the request of Usher, I personally aided him in the arrangements for the temporary entombment. The body having been encoffined, we two alone bore it to its rest. The vault in which we placed it (and which had been so long unopened that our torches, half smothered in its oppressive atmosphere, gave us little opportunity for investigation) was small, damp, and entirely without means of admission for light; lying, at great depth, immediately beneath that portion of the building in which was my own sleeping apartment. It had been used, apparently, in remote feudal times, for the worst purpose of a donjon-keep, and, in later days, as a place of deposit for powder, or some other highly combustible substance, as a portion of its floor, and the whole interior of a long archway through which we reached it, were carefully sheathed with copper. The door, of massive iron, had been, also, similarly protected. Its immense weight caused an unusually sharp grating sound, as it moved upon its hinges.

Having deposited our mournful burden upon trestles within this region of horror, we partially turned aside the yet unscrewed lid of the coffin, and looked upon the face of the tenant. A striking similitude between the brother and sister now first arrested my attention; and Usher, divining, perhaps, my thoughts, murmured out some few words from which I learned that the deceased and himself had been twins, and that sympathies of a scarcely intelligible nature had always existed between them. Our glances, however, rested not long upon the dead—for we could not regard her unawed. The disease which had thus entombed the lady in the maturity of youth, had left, as usual in all maladies of a strictly cataleptical character, the mockery of a faint blush upon the bosom and the face, and that suspiciously lingering smile upon the lip which is so terrible in death. We replaced and screwed down the lid, and, having secured the door of iron, made our way, with toil, into the scarcely less gloomy apartments of the upper portion of the house.

And now, some days of bitter grief having elapsed, an observable change came over the features of the mental disorder of my friend. His ordinary manner had vanished. His ordinary occupations were neglected or forgotten. He roamed from chamber to chamber with hurried, unequal, and objectless step. The pallor of his countenance had assumed, if possible, a more ghastly hue—but the luminousness of his eye had utterly gone out. The once occasional huskiness of his tone was heard no more; and a tremulous quaver, as if of extreme terror, habitually characterized his utterance. There were times, indeed, when I thought his unceasingly agitated mind was laboring with some oppressive secret, to divulge which he struggled for the necessary courage. At times, again, I was obliged to resolve all into the mere inexplicable vagaries of madness, for I beheld him gazing upon vacancy for long hours, in an attitude of the profoundest attention, as if listening to some imaginary sound. It was no wonder that his condition terrified—that it infected me. I felt creeping upon me, by slow yet certain degrees, the wild influences of his own fantastic yet impressive superstitions.

It was, especially, upon retiring to bed late in the night of the seventh or eighth day after the placing of the Lady Madeline within the donjon, that I experienced the full power of such feelings. Sleep came not near my couch—while the hours waned and waned away. I struggled to reason off the nervousness which had dominion over me. I endeavored to believe that much, if not all of what I felt, was due to the bewildering influence of the gloomy furniture of the room—of the dark and tattered draperies, which, tortured into motion by the breath of a rising tempest, swayed fitfully to and fro upon the walls, and rustled uneasily about the decorations of the bed. But my efforts were fruitless. An irrepressible tremor gradually pervaded my frame; and, at length, there sat upon my very heart an incubus of utterly causeless alarm. Shaking this off with a gasp and a struggle, I uplifted myself upon the pillows, and, peering earnestly within the intense darkness of the chamber, hearkened—I know not why, except that an instinctive spirit prompted me—to certain low and indefinite sounds which came, through the pauses of the storm, at long intervals, I knew not whence. Overpowered by an intense sentiment of horror, unaccountable yet unendurable, I threw on my clothes with haste (for I felt that I should sleep no more during the night), and endeavored to arouse myself from the pitiable condition into which I had fallen, by pacing rapidly to and fro through the apartment.

I had taken but few turns in this manner, when a light step on an adjoining staircase arrested my attention. I presently recognized it as that of Usher. In an instant afterward he rapped, with a gentle touch, at my door, and entered, bearing a lamp. His countenance was, as usual cadaverously wan—but, moreover, there was a species of mad hilarity in his eyes—an evident restrained hysteria in his whole demeanor. His air appalled me—but anything was preferable to the solitude which I had so long endured, and I even welcomed his presence as a relief.

"And you have not seen it?" he said abruptly, after having stared about him for some moments in silence—"you have not then seen it?—but, stay! you shall." Thus speaking, and having carefully shaded his lamp, he hurried to one of the casements, and threw it freely open to the storm.

The impetuous fury of the entering gust nearly lifted us from our feet. It was, indeed, a tempestuous yet sternly beautiful night, and one wildly singular in its terror and its beauty. A whirlwind had apparently collected its force in our vicinity; for there were frequent and violent alterations in the direction of the wind; and the exceeding density of the clouds (which hung so low as to press upon the turrets of the house) did not prevent our perceiving the lifelike velocity with which they flew careering from all points against each other, without passing away into the distance. I say that even their exceeding density did not prevent our perceiving this—yet we had no glimpse of the moon or stars—nor was there any flashing forth of the lighting. But the under surfaces of the huge masses of agitated vapor, as well as all terrestrial objects immediately around us, were glowing in the unnatural light of a faintly luminous and distinctly visible gaseous exhalation which hung about and enshrouded the mansion.

"You must not—you shall not behold this!" said I, shudderingly, to Usher, as I led him, with a gentle violence, from the window to a seat. "These appearances, which bewilder you, are merely electrical phenomena not uncommon—or it may be that they have their ghastly origin in the rank miasma of the tarn. Let us close this casement;—the air is chilling and dangerous to your frame. Here is one of your favorite romances. I will read, and you shall listen;—and so we will pass away this terrible night together."

The antique volume which I had taken up was the *Mad Trist* of Sir Launcelot Canning; but I had called it a favorite of Usher's more in sad jest than in earnest; for, in truth, there is little in its uncouth and unimaginative prolixity which could have had interest for the lofty and spiritual ideality of my friend. It was, however, the only book immediately at hand; and I indulged a vague hope that the excitement which now agitated the hypochondriac, might find relief (for the history of mental disorder is full of similar anomalies) even in the extremeness of the folly which I should read. Could I have judged, indeed, by the wild overstrained air of vivacity with which he hearkened, or apparently hearkened, to the words of the tale, I might well have congratulated myself upon the success of my design.

I had arrived at that well-known portion of the story where Ethelred, the hero of the *Trist*, having sought in vain for peaceable admission into the dwelling of the hermit, proceeds to make good an entrance by force. Here, it will be remembered, the words of the narrative run thus:

"And Ethelred, who was by nature of a doughty heart, and who was now mighty withal, on account of the powerfulness of the wine which he had drunken, waited no longer to hold parley with the hermit, who in sooth, was of an obstinate and maliceful turn, but, feeling the rain upon his shoulders, and fearing the rising of the tempest, uplifted his mace outright, and, with blows, made quickly room in the plankings of the door for his gauntleted hand; and now pulling therewith sturdily, he so cracked, and ripped, and tore all asunder, that the noise of the dry and hollow-sounding wood alarmed and reverberated throughout the forest."

At the termination of this sentence I started, and for a moment, paused; for it appeared to me (although I at once concluded that my excited fancy had deceived me)—it appeared to me that, from some very remote portion of the mansion, there came, indistinctly, to my ears, what might have been, in its exact similarity of character, the echo (but a stifled and dull one certainly) of the very cracking and ripping sound which Sir Launcelot had so particularly described. It was, beyond doubt, the coincidence alone which had arrested my attention; for, amid the rattling of the sashes of the casements, and the ordinary commingled noises of the still increasing storm, the sound, in itself, had nothing, surely, which should have interested or disturbed me. I continued the story:

"But the good champion Ethelred, now entering within the door, was sore enraged and amazed to perceive no signal of the maliceful hermit; but, in the stead thereof, a dragon of a scaly and prodigious demeanor, and of a fiery tongue, which sate in guard before a palace of gold, with a floor of silver; and upon the wall there hung a shield of shining brass with this legend enwritten—

Who entereth herein, a conqueror hath bin;
Who slayeth the dragon, the shield he shall win;

and Ethelred uplifted his mace, and struck upon the head of the dragon, which fell before him, and gave up his pesty breath, with a shriek so horrid and harsh, and withal so piercing, that Ethelred had fain to close his ears with his hands against the dreadful noise of it, the like whereof was never before heard."

Here again I paused abruptly, and now a feeling of wild amazement—for there could be no doubt whatever that, in this instance, I did actually hear (although from what direction it proceeded I found it impossible to say) a low and apparently distant, but harsh, protracted, and most unusual screaming or grating sound—the exact counterpart of what my fancy had already conjured up for the dragon's unnatural shriek as described by the romancer.

Oppressed, as I certainly was, upon the occurrence of the second and most extraordinary coincidence, by a thousand conflicting sensations, in which wonder and extreme terror were predominant, I still retained sufficient presence of mind to avoid exciting, by any observation, the sensitive nervousness of my companion. I was by no means certain that he had noticed the sounds in question; although, assuredly, a strange alteration had, during the last few minutes, taken place in his demeanor. From a position fronting my own, he had gradually brought round his chair, so as to sit with his face to the door of the chamber; and thus I could but partially perceive his features, although I saw that his lips trembled as if he were murmuring inaudibly. His head had dropped upon his breast—yet I knew that he was not asleep, from the wide and rigid opening of the eye as I caught a glance of it in profile. The motion of his body, too, was at variance with this idea—for he rocked from side to side with a gentle yet constant and uniform sway. Having rapidly taken notice of all this, I resumed the narrative of Sir Launcelot, which thus proceeded:

"And now, the champion, having escaped from the terrible fury of the dragon, bethinking himself of the brazen shield, and of the breaking up of the enchantment which was upon it, removed the carcass from out of the way before him, and approached valorously over the silver pavement of the castle to where the shield was upon the wall; which in sooth tarried not for his full coming, but fell down at his feet upon the silver floor, with a mighty great and terrible ringing sound."

No sooner had these syllables passed my lips, than—as if a shield of brass had indeed, at the moment, fallen heavily upon a floor of silver—I became aware of a distinct, hollow, metallic, and clangorous, yet apparently muffled reverberation. Completely unnerved, I leaped to my feet; but the measured rocking movement of Usher was undisturbed. I rushed to the chair in which he sat. His eyes were bent fixedly before him, and throughout his whole countenance there reigned a stony rigidity. But, as I placed my hand upon his shoulder, there came a strong shudder over his whole person; a sickly smile quivered about his lips; and I saw that he spoke in a low, hurried, and gibbering murmur, as if unconscious of my presence. Bending closely over him, I at length drank in the hideous import of his words.

"Not hear it?—yes, I hear it, and have heard it. Long—long—long—many minutes, many hours, many days, have I heard it—yet I dared not—oh, pity me, miserable wretch that I am!—I dared not—I dared not speak! We have put her living in the tomb! Said I not that my senses were acute? I now tell you that I heard her first feeble movements in the hollow coffin. I heard them—many, many days ago—yet I dared not—I dared not speak! And now—tonight—Ethelred—ha! ha!—the breaking of the hermit's door, and the death-cry of the dragon, and the clangour of the shield!—say, rather, the rending of her coffin, and the grating of the iron hinges of her prison, and her struggles within the coppered archway of the vault! Oh whither shall I fly? Will she not be here anon? Is she not hurrying to upbraid me for my haste? Have I not heard her footstep on the stair? Do I not distinguish that heavy and horrible beating of her heart? Madman!" here he sprang furiously to his feet, and shrieked out his syllables, as if in the effort he were giving up his soul—"Madman! I tell you that she now stands without the door!"

As if in the superhuman energy of his utterance there had been found the potency of a spell—the huge antique panels to which the speaker pointed, threw slowly back, upon the instant, their ponderous and ebony jaws. It was the work of the rushing gust—but then without those doors there did stand the lofty and enshrouded figure of the Lady Madeline of Usher. There was blood upon her white robes, and the evidence of some bitter struggle upon every portion of her emaciated frame. For a moment she remained trembling and reeling to and fro upon the threshold, then, with a low moaning cry, fell heavily inward upon the person of her brother, and in her violent and now final death-agonies, bore him to the floor a corpse, and a victim to the terrors he had anticipated.

From that chamber, and from that mansion, I fled aghast. The storm was still abroad in all its wrath as I found myself crossing the old causeway. Suddenly there shot along the path a wild light, and I turned to see whence a gleam so unusual could have issued; for the vast house and its shadows were alone behind me. The radiance was that of the full, setting, and blood-red moon which now shone vividly through that once barely discernible fissure of which I have before spoken as extending from the roof of the building, in a zigzag direction, to the base. While I gazed, this fissure rapidly widened—there came a fierce breath of the whirlwind—the entire orb of the satellite burst at once upon my sight—my brain reeled as I saw the mighty walls rushing asunder—there was a long tumultuous shouting sound like the voice of a thousand waters—and the deep and dank tarn at my feet closed sullenly and silently over the fragments of the "House of Usher."

The Masque of the Red Death

by Edgar Allan Poe

The "Red Death" had long devastated the country. No pestilence had ever been so fatal, or so hideous. Blood was its Avatar and its seal—the redness and horror of blood. There were sharp pains, and sudden dizziness, and then profuse bleeding at the pores, with dissolution. The scarlet stains upon the body and especially upon the face of the victim, were the pest ban which shut him out from the aid and from the sympathy of his fellow-men. And the whole seizure, progress, and termination of the disease, were the incidents of half an hour.

But the Prince Prospero was happy and dauntless and sagacious. When his dominions were half-depopulated, he summoned to his presence a thousand hale and light-hearted friends from among the knights and dames of his court, and with these retired to the deep seclusion of one of his castellated abbeys. This was an extensive and magnificent structure, the creation of the prince's own eccentric yet august taste. A strong and lofty wall girdled it in. This wall had gates of iron. The courtiers, having entered, brought furnaces and massy hammers and welded the bolts. They resolved to leave means neither of ingress nor egress to the sudden impulses of despair or of frenzy from within. The abbey was amply provisioned.

With such precautions the courtiers might bid defiance to contagion. The external world could take care of itself. In the meantime it was folly to grieve, or to think. The prince had provided all the appliances of pleasure. There were buffoons, there were improvisatori, there were ballet-dancers, there were musicians, there was Beauty, there was wine. All these and security were within. Without was the "Red Death."

It was toward the close of the fifth or sixth month of his seclusion, and while the pestilence raged most furiously abroad, that the Prince Prospero entertained his thousand friends at a masked ball of the most unusual magnificence.

It was a voluptuous scene, that masquerade. But first let me tell of the rooms in which it was held. There were seven—an imperial suite. In many palaces, however, such suites form a long and straight vista, while the folding doors slide back nearly to the walls on either hand, so that the view of the whole extent is scarcely impeded. Here the case was very different, as might have been expected from the duke's love of the bizarre. The apartments were so irregularly disposed that the vision embraced but little more than one at a time. There was a sharp turn at every twenty or thirty yards, and at each turn a novel effect. To the right and left, in the middle of each wall, a tall and narrow Gothic window looked out upon a closed corridor which pursued the windings of the suite. These windows were of stained glass whose color varied in accordance with the prevailing hue of the decorations of the chamber into which it opened. That at the eastern extremity was hung, for example, in blue—and vividly blue were its windows. The second chamber was purple in its ornaments and tapestries, and here the panes were purple. The third was green throughout, and so were the casements. The fourth was furnished and lighted with orange—the fifth with white—the sixth with violet. The seventh apartment was closely shrouded in black velvet tapestries that hung all over the ceiling and down the walls, falling in heavy folds upon a carpet of the same material and hue. But in this chamber only, the color of the windows failed to correspond with the decorations. The panes here were scarlet—a deep blood color. Now in no one of the seven apartments was there any lamp or candelabrum, amid the profusion of golden ornaments that lay scattered to and fro or depended from the roof. There was no light of any kind emanating from lamp or candle within the suite of chambers. But in the corridors that followed the suite there stood, opposite to each window, a heavy tripod, bearing a brazier of fire, that projected its rays through the tinted glass and so glaringly illumined the room. And thus were produced a multitude of gaudy and fantastic appearances. But in the western or black chamber the effect of the firelight that streamed upon the dark hangings through the blood-tinted panes was ghastly in the extreme, and produced so wild a look upon the countenances of those who entered, that there were few of the company bold enough to set foot within its precincts at all.

It was in this apartment, also, that there stood against the western wall, a gigantic clock of ebony. Its pendulum swung to and fro with a dull, heavy, monotonous clang; and when the minute-hand made the circuit of the face, and the hour was to be stricken, there came from the brazen lungs of the clock a sound which was clear and loud and deep and exceedingly musical, but of so peculiar a note and emphasis that, at each lapse of an hour, the musicians of the orchestra were constrained to pause, momentarily, in their performance, to harken to the sound; and thus the waltzers perforce ceased their evolutions; and there was a brief disconcert of the whole gay company; and, while the chimes of the clock yet rang, it was observed that the giddiest grew pale, and the more aged and sedate passed their hands over their brows as if in confused reverie or meditation. But when the echoes had fully ceased, a light laughter at once pervaded the assembly; the musicians looked at each other and smiled as if at their own nervousness and folly, and made whispering vows, each to the other, that the next chiming of the clock should produce in them no similar emotion; and then, after the lapse of sixty minutes (which embrace three thousand and six hundred seconds of the Time that flies), there came yet another chiming of the clock, and then were the same disconcert and tremulousness and meditation as before.

But, in spite of these things, it was a gay and magnificent revel. The tastes of the duke were peculiar. He had a fine eye for colors and effects. He disregarded the decora of mere fashion. His plans were bold and fiery, and his conceptions glowed with barbaric luster. There are some who would have thought him mad. His followers felt that he was not. It was necessary to hear and see and touch him to be sure that he was not.

He had directed, in great part, the movable embellishments of the seven chambers, upon occasion of this great fête; and it was his own guiding taste which had given character to the masqueraders. Be sure they were grotesque. There were much glare and glitter and piquancy and phantasm—much of what has been since seen in Hernani. There were arabesque figures with unsuited limbs and appointments. There were delirious fancies such as the madman fashions. There were much of the beautiful, much of the wanton, much of the bizarre, something of the terrible, and not a little of that which might have excited disgust. To and fro in the seven chambers there stalked, in fact, a multitude of dreams. And these—the dreams—writhed in and about, taking hue from the rooms, and causing the wild music of the orchestra to seem as the echo of their steps. And, anon, there strikes the ebony clock which stands in the hall of the velvet. And then, for a moment, all is still, and all is silent save the voice of the clock. The dreams are stiff-frozen as they stand. But the echoes of the chime die away—they have endured but an instant—and a light, half-subdued laughter floats after them as they depart. And now again the music swells, and the dreams live, and writhe to and fro more merrily than ever, taking hue from the many-tinted windows through which stream the rays from the tripods. But to the chamber which lies most westwardly of the seven there are now none of the maskers who venture; for the night is waning away; and there flows a ruddier light through the blood-colored panes; and the blackness of the sable drapery appals; and to him whose foot falls upon the sable carpet, there comes from the near clock of ebony a muffled peal more solemnly emphatic than any which reaches their ears who indulged in the more remote gaieties of the other apartments.

But these other apartments were densely crowded, and in them beat feverishly the heart of life. And the revel went whirlingly on, until at length there commenced the sounding of midnight upon the clock. And then the music ceased, as I have told; and the evolutions of the waltzers were quieted; and there was an uneasy cessation of all things as before. But now there were twelve strokes to be sounded by the bell of the clock; and thus it happened, perhaps, that more of thought crept, with more of time, into the meditations of the thoughtful among those who reveled. And thus too, it happened, perhaps, that before the last echoes of the last chime had utterly sunk into silence, there were many individuals in the crowd who had found leisure to become aware of the presence of a masked figure which had arrested the attention of no single individual before. And the rumor of this new presence having spread itself whisperingly around, there arose at length from the whole company a buzz, or murmur, expressive of disapprobation and surprise—then finally, of terror, of horror, and of disgust.

In an assembly of phantasms such as I have painted, it may well be supposed that no ordinary appearance could have excited such sensation. In truth the masquerade license of the night was nearly unlimited; but the figure in question had out-Heroded Herod, and gone beyond the bounds of even the prince's indefinite decorum. There are chords in the hearts of the most reckless which cannot be touched without emotion. Even with the utterly lost, to whom life and death are equally jests, there are matters of which no jest can be made. The whole company, indeed, seemed now deeply to feel that in the costume and bearing of the stranger neither wit nor propriety existed. The figure was tall and gaunt, and shrouded from head to foot in the habiliments of the grave. The mask which concealed the visage was made so nearly to resemble the countenance of a stiffened corpse that the closest scrutiny must have had difficulty in detecting the cheat. And yet all this might have been endured, if not approved, by the mad revelers around. But the mummer had gone so far as to assume the type of the Red Death. His vesture was dabbled in blood—and his broad brow, with all the features of the face, was be-sprinkled with the scarlet horror.

When the eyes of Prince Prospero fell upon this spectral image (which, with a slow and solemn movement, as if more fully to sustain its rôle, stalked to and fro among the waltzers) he was seen to be convulsed in the first moment with a strong shudder either of terror or distaste; but, in the next, his brow reddened with rage.

"Who dares,"—he demanded hoarsely of the courtiers who stood near him—"who dares insult us with this blasphemous mockery? Seize him and unmask him—that we may know whom we have to hang, at sunrise, from the battlements!"

It was in the eastern or blue chamber in which stood the Prince Prospero as he uttered these words. They rang throughout the seven rooms loudly and clearly—for the prince was a bold and robust man, and the music had become hushed at the waving of his hand.

It was in the blue room where stood the prince, with a group of pale courtiers by his side. At first, as he spoke, there was a slight rushing movement of this group in the direction of the intruder, who at the moment was also near at hand, and now, with deliberate and stately step, made closer approach to the speaker. But from a certain nameless awe with which the mad assumptions of the mummer had inspired the whole party, there were found none who put forth hand to seize him; so that, unimpeded, he passed within a yard of the prince's person; and, while the vast assembly, as if with one impulse, shrank from the centers of the rooms to the walls, he made his way uninterruptedly, but with the same solemn and measured step which had distinguished him from the first, through the blue chamber to the purple—through the purple to the green—through the green to the orange—through this again to the white—and even thence to the violet, ere a decided movement had been made to arrest him. It was then, however, that the Prince Prospero, maddening with rage and the shame of his own momentary cowardice, rushed hurriedly through the six chambers, while none followed him on account of a deadly terror that had seized upon all. He bore aloft a drawn dagger, and had approached, in rapid impetuosity, to within three or four feet of the retreating figure, when the latter, having attained the extremity of the velvet apartment, turned suddenly and confronted his pursuer. There was a sharp cry—and the dagger dropped gleaming upon the sable carpet, upon which, instantly afterward, fell prostrate in death the Prince Prospero. Then, summoning the wild courage of despair, a throng of the revelers at once threw themselves into the black apartment, and, seizing the mummer, whose tall figure stood erect and motionless within the shadow of the ebony clock, gasped in unutterable horror at finding the grave cerements and corpse-like mask, which they handled with so violent a rudeness, untenanted by any tangible form.

And now was acknowledged the presence of the Red Death. He had come like a thief in the night. And one by one dropped the revelers in the blood-bedewed halls of their revel, and died each in the despairing posture of his fall. And the life of the ebony clock went out with that of the last of the gay. And the flames of the tripods expired. And Darkness and Decay and the Red Death held illimitable dominion over all.

The Black Cat

by Edgar Allan Poe

For the most wild, yet most homely narrative which I am about to pen, I neither expect nor solicit belief. Mad indeed would I be to expect it, in a case where my very senses reject their own evidence. Yet—mad am I not—and very surely do I not dream. But tomorrow I die, and today I would unburden my soul. My immediate purpose is to place before the world plainly, succinctly, and without comment, a series of mere household events. In their consequences these events have terrified—have tortured—have destroyed me. Yet I will not attempt to expound them. To me they have presented little but horror—to many they will seem less terrible than *barroques*. Hereafter, perhaps, some intellect may be found which will reduce my phantasm to the common-place—some intellect more calm, more logical, and far less excitable than my own, which will perceive in the circumstances I detail with awe, nothing more than an ordinary succession of very natural causes and effects.

From my infancy I was noted for the docility and humanity of my disposition. My tenderness of heart was even so conspicuous as to make me the jest of my companions. I was especially fond of animals, and was indulged by my parents with a great variety of pets. With these I spent most of my time, and never was so happy as when feeding and caressing them. This peculiarity of character grew with my growth, and in my manhood I derived from it one of my principal sources of pleasure. To those who have cherished an affection for a faithful and sagacious dog, I need hardly be at the trouble of explaining the nature or the intensity of the gratification thus derivable. There is something in the unselfish and self-sacrificing love of a brute which goes directly to the heart of him who has had frequent occasion to test the paltry friendship and gossamer fidelity of mere *Man.*

I married early, and was happy to find in my wife a disposition not uncongenial with my own. Observing my partiality for domestic pets, she lost no opportunity of procuring those of the most agreeable kind. We had birds, goldfish, a fine dog, rabbits, a small monkey, and *a cat.*

This latter was a remarkably large and beautiful animal, entirely black, and sagacious to an astonishing degree. In speaking of his intelligence, my wife, who at heart was not a little tinctured with superstition, made frequent allusion to the ancient popular notion which regarded all black cats as witches in disguise. Not that she was ever serious upon this point, and I mention the matter at all for no better reason than that it happens just now to be remembered.

Pluto—this was the cat's name—was my favorite pet and playmate. I alone fed him, and he attended me wherever I went about the house. It was even with difficulty that I could prevent him from following me through the streets.

Our friendship lasted in this manner for several years, during which my general temperament and character—through the instrumentality of the Fiend Intemperance—had (I blush to confess it) experienced a radical alteration for the worse. I grew, day by day, more moody, more irritable, more regardless of the feelings of others. I suffered myself to use intemperate language to my wife. At length, I even offered her personal violence. My pets of course were made to feel the change in my disposition. I not only neglected, but ill-used them. For Pluto, however, I still retained sufficient regard to restrain me from maltreating him, as I made no scruple of maltreating the rabbits, the monkey, or even the dog, when by accident, or through affection, they came in my way. But my disease grew upon me—for what disease is like Alcohol?—and at length even Pluto, who was now becoming old, and consequently somewhat peevish—even Pluto began to experience the effects of my ill-temper.

One night, returning home much intoxicated, from one of my haunts about town, I fancied that the cat avoided my presence. I seized him; when, in his fright at my violence, he inflicted a slight wound upon my hand with his teeth. The fury of a demon instantly possessed me. I knew myself no longer. My original soul seemed at once to take its flight from my body, and a more than fiendish malevolence, gin-nurtured, thrilled every fibre of my frame. I took from my waistcoat-pocket a penknife, opened it, grasped the poor beast by the throat, and deliberately cut one of its eyes from the socket! I blush, I burn, I shudder, while I pen the damnable atrocity.

When reason returned with the morning—when I had slept off the fumes of the night's debauch—I experienced a sentiment half of horror, half of remorse, for the crime of which I had been guilty; but it was, at best, a feeble and equivocal feeling, and the soul remained untouched. I again plunged into excess, and soon drowned in wine all memory of the deed.

In the meantime the cat slowly recovered. The socket of the lost eye presented, it is true, a frightful appearance, but he no longer appeared to suffer any pain. He went about the house as usual, but, as might be expected, fled in extreme terror at my approach. I had so much of my old heart left as to be at first grieved by this evident dislike on the part of a creature which had once so loved me. But this feeling soon gave place to irritation. And then came, as if to my final and irrevocable overthrow, the spirit of Perverseness. Of this spirit philosophy takes no account. Yet I am not more sure that my soul lives, than I am that perverseness is one of the primitive impulses of the human heart—one of the indivisible primary faculties, or sentiments, which gives direction to the character of Man. Who has not, a hundred times, found himself committing a vile or a silly action for no other reason than because he knows he should not! Have we not a perpetual inclination, in the teeth of our best judgment, to violate that which is *Law*, merely because we understand it to be such? This spirit of perverseness, I say, came to my final overthrow. It was this unfathomable longing of the soul *to vex itself*—to offer violence to its own nature—to do wrong for the wrong's sake only—that urged me to continue and finally to consummate the injury I had inflicted upon the unoffending brute. One morning, in cold blood, I slipped a noose about its neck and hung it to the limb of a tree;—hung it with the tears streaming from my eyes; and with the bitterest remorse at my heart;—hung it *because* I knew that it had loved me, and *because* I felt it had given me no reason of offense;—hung it *because* I knew that in so doing I was committing a sin—a deadly sin that would so jeopardize my immortal soul as to place it, if such a thing were possible, even beyond the reach of the infinite mercy of the Most Merciful and Most Terrible God.

On the night of the day on which this cruel deed was done, I was aroused from sleep by the cry of fire. The curtains of my bed were in flames. The whole house was blazing. It was with great difficulty that my wife, a servant, and myself, made our escape from the conflagration. The destruction was complete. My entire worldly wealth was swallowed up, and I resigned myself thenceforward to despair.

I am above the weakness of seeking to establish a sequence of cause and effect, between the disaster and the atrocity. But I am detailing a chain of facts, and wish not to leave even a possible link imperfect. On the day succeeding the fire, I visited the ruins. The walls, with one exception, had fallen in. This exception was found in a compartment wall, not very thick, which stood about the middle of the house, and against which had rested the head of my bed. The plastering had here, in great measure, resisted the action of the fire, a fact which I attributed to its having been recently spread. About this wall a dense crowd were collected and many persons seemed to be examining a particular portion of it with very minute and eager attention. The words "strange!" "singular!" and other similar expressions, excited my curiosity. I approached, and saw, as if graven in bas-relief upon the white surface, the figure of a gigantic *cat*. The impression was given with an accuracy truly marvelous. There was a rope about the animal's neck.

When I first beheld this apparition—for I could scarcely regard it as less—my wonder and my terror were extreme. But at length reflection came to my aid. The cat, I remembered, had been hung in a garden adjacent to the house. Upon the alarm of fire, this garden had been immediately filled by the crowd, by some one of whom the animal must have been cut from the tree and thrown, through an open window, into my chamber. This had probably been done with the view of arousing me from sleep. The falling of the other walls had compressed the victim of my cruelty into the substance of the freshly spread plaster; the lime of which, with the flames and the *ammonia* from the carcass, had then accomplished the portraiture as I saw it.

Although I thus readily accounted to my reason, if not altogether to my conscience, for the startling fact just detailed, it did not the less fail to make a deep impression upon my fancy. For months I could not rid myself of the phantasm of the cat; and during this period there came back into my spirit a half-sentiment that seemed, but was not, remorse. I went so far as to regret the loss of the animal, and to look about me, among the vile haunts which I now habitually frequented, for another pet of the same species, and of somewhat similar appearance, with which to supply its place.

One night as I sat half stupefied in a den of more than infamy, my attention was suddenly drawn to some black object reposing upon the head of one of the immense hogsheads of gin or of rum which constituted the chief furniture of the apartment. I had been looking steadily at the top of this hogshead for some minutes, and what now caused me surprise was the fact that I had not sooner perceived the object thereupon. I approached it, and touched it with my hand. It was a black cat, a very large one, fully as large as Pluto, and closely resembling him in every respect but one. Pluto had not a white hair upon any portion of his body; but this cat had a large, although indefinite, splotch of white, covering nearly the whole region of the breast.

Upon my touching him, he immediately arose, purred loudly, rubbed against my hand, and appeared delighted with my notice. This, then, was the very creature of which I was in search. I at once offered to purchase it of the landlord; but this person made no claim to it—knew nothing of it—had never seen it before.

I continued my caresses; and when I prepared to go home, the animal evinced a disposition to accompany me. I permitted it to do so, occasionally stooping and patting it as I proceeded. When it reached the house it domesticated itself at once, and became immediately a great favorite with my wife.

For my own part, I soon found a dislike to it arising within me. This was just the reverse of what I had anticipated; but—I know not how or why it was—its evident fondness for myself rather disgusted and annoyed. By slow degrees these feelings of disgust and annoyance rose into the bitterness of hatred. I avoided the creature; a certain sense of shame, and the remembrance of my former deed of cruelty, preventing me from physically abusing it. I did not for some weeks strike or otherwise violently ill-use it; but gradually—very gradually—I came to look upon it with unutterable loathing, and to flee silently from its odious presence, as from the breath of a pestilence.

What added, no doubt, to my hatred of the beast, was the discovery, on the morning after I brought it home, that, like Pluto, it also had been deprived of one of its eyes. This circumstance, however, only endeared it to my wife, who, as I have already said, possessed, in a high degree, that humanity of feeling which had once been my distinguishing trait, and the source of many of my simplest and purest pleasures.

With my aversion to this cat, however, its partiality for myself seemed to increase. It followed my footsteps with a pertinacity which it would be difficult to make the reader comprehend. Whenever I sat, it would crouch beneath my chair, or spring upon my knees, covering me with its loathsome caresses. If I arose to walk it would get between my feet, and thus nearly throw me down; or, fastening its long and sharp claws in my dress, clamber in this manner to my breast. At such times, although I longed to destroy it with a blow, I was yet withheld from so doing, partly by a memory of my former crime, but chiefly—let me confess it at once—by absolute dread of the beast.

This dread was not exactly a dread of physical evil—and yet I should be at a loss how otherwise to define it. I am almost ashamed to own—yes, even in this felon's cell I am almost ashamed to own—that the terror and horror with which the animal inspired me had been heightened by one of the merest chimeras it would be possible to conceive. My wife had called my attention more than once to the character of the mark of white hair of which I have spoken, and which constituted the sole visible difference between the strange beast and the one I had destroyed. The reader will remember that this mark, although large, had been originally very indefinite; but by slow degrees—degrees nearly imperceptible, and which for a long time my Reason struggled to reject as fanciful—it had at length assumed a rigorous distinctness of outline. It was now the representation of an object that I shudder to name—and for this, above all, I loathed and dreaded and would have rid myself of the monster *had I dared*—it was now, I say, the image of a hideous—of a ghastly thing—of the Gallows!—O mournful and terrible engine of Horror and of Crime—of Agony and of Death!

And now was I indeed wretched beyond the wretchedness of mere Humanity. And *a brute beast*—whose fellow I had contemptuously destroyed—*a brute beast* to work out for *me*—for me, a man fashioned in the image of the High God—so much of insufferable woe! Alas! neither by day nor by night knew I the blessing of rest any more! During the former the creature left me no moment alone; and, in the latter, I started hourly from dreams of unutterable fear, to find the hot breath of *the thing* upon my face, and its vast weight an incarnate Nightmare that I had no power to shake off—incumbent eternally upon my *heart*!

Beneath the pressure of torments such as these, the feeble remnant of the good within me succumbed. Evil thoughts became my sole intimates—the darkest and most evil of thoughts. The moodiness of my usual temper increased to hatred of all things and of all mankind; while, from the sudden, frequent, and ungovernable outbursts of a fury to which I now blindly abandoned myself, my uncomplaining wife, alas! was the most usual and the most patient of sufferers.

One day she accompanied me, upon some household errand, into the cellar of the old building which our poverty compelled us to inhabit. The cat followed me down the steep stairs, and, nearly throwing me headlong, exasperated me to madness. Uplifting an ax, and, forgetting in my wrath the childish dread which had hitherto stayed my mind, I aimed a blow at the animal, which of course would have proved instantly fatal had it descended as I wished. But this blow was arrested by the hand of my wife. Goaded, by the interference, into a rage more than demoniacal, I withdrew my arm from her grasp, and buried the ax in her brain. She fell dead upon the spot, without a groan.

This hideous murder accomplished, I set myself forthwith, and with entire deliberation, to the task of concealing the body. I knew that I could not remove it from the house, either by day or by night, without the risk of being observed by the neighbors. Many projects entered my mind. At one period I thought of cutting the corpse into minute fragments and destroying them by fire. At another, I resolved to dig a grave for it in the floor of the cellar. Again, I deliberated about casting it in the well in the yard—about packing it in a box, as if merchandise, with the usual arrangements, and so getting a porter to take it from the house. Finally I hit upon what I considered a far better expedient than either of these. I determined to wall it up in the cellar—as the monks of the Middle Ages are recorded to have walled up their victims.

For a purpose such as this the cellar was well adapted. Its walls were loosely constructed, and had lately been plastered throughout with rough plaster, which the dampness of the atmosphere had prevented from hardening. Moreover, in one of the walls was a projection, caused by a false chimney, or fireplace, that had been filled up, and made to resemble the rest of the cellar. I made no doubt that I could readily displace the bricks at this point, insert the corpse, and wall the whole up as before, so that no eye could detect anything suspicious.

And in this calculation I was not deceived. By means of a crowbar I easily dislodged the bricks; and, having carefully deposited the body against the inner wall, I propped it in that position, while with little trouble I relaid the whole structure as it originally stood. Having procured mortar, sand, and hair, with every possible precaution, I prepared a plaster which could not be distinguished from the old, and with this I very carefully went over the new brickwork. When I had finished, I felt satisfied that all was right. The wall did not present the slightest appearance of having been disturbed. The rubbish on the floor was picked up with the minutest care. I looked around triumphantly, and said to myself, "Here at last, then, my labor has not been in vain."

My next step was to look for the beast which had been the cause of so much wretchedness; for I had at length firmly resolved to put it to death. Had I been able to meet with it at the moment there could have been no doubt of its fate, but it appeared that the crafty animal had been alarmed at the violence of my previous anger, and forbore to present itself in my present mood. It is impossible to describe or to imagine the deep, the blissful sense of relief which the absence of the detested creature occasioned in my bosom. It did not make its appearance during the night; and thus for one night at least since its introduction into the house, I soundly and tranquilly slept—ay, slept even with the burden of murder upon my soul!

The second and third day passed, and still my tormentor came not. Once again I breathed as a free man. The monster, in terror, had fled the premises for ever! I should behold it no more! My happiness was supreme! The guilt of my dark deed disturbed me but little. Some few inquiries had been made, but these had been readily answered. Even a search had been instituted; but of course nothing was to be discovered. I looked upon my future felicity as secured.

Upon the fourth day of the assassination, a party of the police came over unexpectedly into the house, and proceeded again to make rigorous investigation of the premises. Secure, however, in the inscrutability of my place of concealment, I felt no embarrassment whatever. The officers bade me accompany them in their search. They left no nook or corner unexplored. At length, for the third or fourth time, they descended into the cellar. I quivered not in a muscle. My heart beat calmly as that of one who slumbers in innocence. I walked the cellar from end to end. I folded my arms upon my bosom, and roamed easily to and fro. The police were thoroughly satisfied, and prepared to depart. The glee of my heart was too strong to be restrained. I burned to say, if but one word, by way of triumph, and to render doubly sure their assurance of my guiltlessness.

"Gentlemen," I said at last, as the party ascended the steps, "I delight to have allayed your suspicions. I wish you all health, and a little more courtesy. By the by, gentlemen, this—this is a very well constructed house." (In the rabid desire to say something easily, I scarcely knew what I uttered at all.) "I may say an *excellently* well constructed house. These walls—are you going, gentlemen?—these walls are solidly put together"; and here, through the mere frenzy of bravado, I rapped heavily, with a cane which I held in my hand, upon that very portion of the brickwork behind which stood the corpse of the wife of my bosom.

But may God shield and deliver me from the fangs of the Arch-Fiend! No sooner had the reverberation of my blows sunk into silence than I was answered by a voice from within the tomb!—by a cry, at first muffled and broken, like the sobbing of a child, and then quickly swelling into one long, loud, and continuous scream, utterly anomalous and inhuman—a howl—a wailing shriek, half of horror and half of triumph, such as might have arisen only out of hell, conjointly from the throats of the damned in their agony and of the demons that exult in the damnation.

Of my own thoughts it is folly to speak. Swooning, I staggered to the opposite wall. For one instant the party upon the stairs remained motionless, through extremity of terror and of awe. In the next, a dozen stout arms were toiling at the wall. It fell bodily. The corpse, already greatly decayed and clotted with gore, stood erect before the eyes of the spectators. Upon its head, with red extended mouth and solitary eye of fire, sat the hideous beast whose craft had seduced me into murder, and whose informing voice had consigned me to the hangman. I had walled the monster up within the tomb!

The Call of Cthulhu

by H. P. Lovecraft

(FOUND AMONG THE PAPERS OF
THE LATE FRANCIS WAYLAND THURSTON,
OF BOSTON)

"Of such great powers or beings there may be conceivably a survival . . . a survival of a hugely remote period when . . . consciousness was manifested, perhaps, in shapes and forms long since withdrawn before the tide of advancing humanity . . . forms of which poetry and legend alone have caught a flying memory and called them gods, monsters, mythical beings of all sorts and kinds . . ."
—Algernon Blackwood

I. THE HORROR IN CLAY

The most merciful thing in the world, I think, is the inability of the human mind to correlate all its contents. We live on a placid island of ignorance in the midst of black seas of infinity, and it was not meant that we should voyage far. The sciences, each straining in its own direction, have hitherto harmed us little; but some day the piecing together of dissociated knowledge will open up such terrifying vistas of reality, and of our frightful position therein, that we shall either go mad from the revelation or flee from the deadly light into the peace and safety of a new dark age.

Theosophists have guessed at the awesome grandeur of the cosmic cycle wherein our world and human race form transient incidents. They have hinted at strange survivals in terms which would freeze the blood if not masked by a bland optimism. But it is not from them that there came the single glimpse of forbidden eons which chills me when I think of it and maddens me when I dream of it. That glimpse, like all dread glimpses of truth, flashed out from an accidental piecing together of separated things—in this case an old newspaper item and the notes of a dead professor. I hope that no one else will accomplish this piecing out; certainly, if I live, I shall never knowingly supply a link in so hideous a chain. I think that the professor, too, intended to keep silent regarding the part he knew, and that he would have destroyed his notes had not sudden death seized him.

My knowledge of the thing began in the winter of 1926–27 with the death of my great-uncle George Gammell Angell, Professor Emeritus of Semitic Languages in Brown University, Providence, Rhode Island. Professor Angell was widely known as an authority on ancient inscriptions, and had frequently been resorted to by the heads of prominent museums; so that his passing at the age of ninety-two may be recalled by many. Locally, interest was intensified by the obscurity of the cause of death. The professor had been stricken whilst returning from the Newport boat; falling suddenly, as witnesses said, after having been jostled by a nautical looking negro who had come from one of the queer dark courts on the precipitous hillside which formed a short cut from the waterfront to the deceased's home in Williams Street. Physicians were unable to find any visible disorder, but concluded after perplexed debate that some obscure lesion of the heart, induced by the brisk ascent of so steep a hill by so elderly a man, was responsible for the end. At the time I saw no reason to dissent from this dictum, but latterly I am inclined to wonder—and more than wonder.

As my great-uncle's heir and executor, for he died a childless widower, I was expected to go over his papers with some thoroughness; and for that purpose moved his entire set of files and boxes to my quarters in Boston. Much of the material which I correlated will be later published by the American Archaeological Society, but there was one box which I found exceedingly puzzling, and which

I felt much averse from showing to other eyes. It had been locked, and I did not find the key till it occurred to me to examine the personal ring which the professor carried always in his pocket. Then indeed I succeeded in opening it, but when I did so seemed only to be confronted by a greater and more closely locked barrier. For what could be the meaning of the queer clay bas-relief and the disjointed jottings, ramblings, and cuttings which I found? Had my uncle, in his latter years, become credulous of the most superficial impostures? I resolved to search out the eccentric sculptor responsible for this apparent disturbance of an old man's peace of mind.

The bas-relief was a rough rectangle less than an inch thick and about five by six inches in area; obviously of modern origin. Its designs, however, were far from modern in atmosphere and suggestion; for although the vagaries of cubism and futurism are many and wild, they do not often reproduce that cryptic regularity which lurks in prehistoric writing. And writing of some kind the bulk of these designs seemed certainly to be; though my memory, despite much familiarity with the papers and collections of my uncle, failed in any way to identify this particular species, or even to hint at its remotest affiliations.

Above these apparent hieroglyphics was a figure of evidently pictorial intent, though its impressionistic execution forbade a very clear idea of its nature. It seemed to be a sort of monster, or symbol representing a monster, of a form which only a diseased fancy could conceive. If I say that my somewhat extravagant imagination yielded simultaneous pictures of an octopus, a dragon, and a human caricature, I shall not be unfaithful to the spirit of the thing. A pulpy, tentacled head surmounted a grotesque and scaly body with rudimentary wings; but it was the *general outline* of the whole which made it most shockingly frightful. Behind the figure was a vague suggestion of a Cyclopean architectural background.

The writing accompanying this oddity was, aside from a stack of press cuttings, in Professor Angell's most recent hand; and made no pretence to literary style. What seemed to be the main document was headed "CTHULHU CULT" in characters painstakingly printed to avoid the erroneous reading of a word so unheard of. The manuscript was divided into two sections, the first of which was headed "1925—Dream and Dream Work of H. A. Wilcox, 7 Thomas St, Providence, RI," and the second, "Narrative of Inspector John R. Legrasse, 121 Bienville St, New Orleans, La, at 1908 A. A. S. Mtg—Notes on Same, & Prof. Webb's Acct." The other manuscript papers were all brief notes, some of them accounts of the queer dreams of different persons, some of them citations from theosophical books and magazines (notably W. Scott-Elliot's *Atlantis and the Lost Lemuria*), and the rest comments on long surviving secret societies and hidden cults, with references to passages in such mythological and anthropological source books as Frazer's *Golden Bough* and Miss Murray's *Witch-Cult in Western Europe.* The cuttings largely alluded to *outré* mental illnesses and outbreaks of group folly or mania in the spring of 1925.

The first half of the principal manuscript told a very peculiar tale. It appears that on March 1st, 1925, a thin, dark young man of neurotic and excited aspect had called upon Professor Angell bearing the singular clay bas-relief, which was then exceedingly damp and fresh. His card bore the name of Henry Anthony Wilcox, and my uncle had recognized him as the youngest son of an excellent family slightly known to him, who had latterly been studying sculpture at the Rhode Island School of Design and living alone at the Fleur-de-Lys Building near that institution. Wilcox was a precocious youth of known genius but great eccentricity, and had from childhood excited attention through the strange stories and odd dreams he was in the habit of relating. He called himself "psychically hypersensitive," but the staid folk of the ancient commercial city dismissed him as merely "queer." Never mingling much with his kind, he had dropped gradually from social visibility, and was now known only to a small group of aesthetes from other towns. Even the Providence Art Club, anxious to preserve its conservatism, had found him quite hopeless.

On the occasion of the visit, ran the professor's manuscript, the sculptor abruptly asked for the benefit of his host's archaeological knowledge in identifying the hieroglyphics on the bas-relief. He spoke in a dreamy, stilted manner which suggested pose and alienated sympathy; and my uncle showed some sharpness in replying, for the conspicuous freshness of the tablet implied kinship with anything but archaeology. Young Wilcox's rejoinder, which impressed my uncle enough to make him recall and record it verbatim, was of a fantastically poetic cast which must have typified his whole conversation, and which I have since found highly characteristic of him. He said, "It is new, indeed, for I made it last night in a dream of strange cities; and dreams are older than brooding Tyre, or the contemplative Sphinx, or garden-girdled Babylon."

It was then that he began that rambling tale which suddenly played upon a sleeping memory and won the fevered interest of my uncle. There had been a slight earthquake tremor the night before, the most considerable felt in New England for some years; and Wilcox's imagination had been keenly affected. Upon retiring, he had had an unprecedented dream of great Cyclopean cities of titan blocks and sky-flung monoliths, all dripping with green ooze and sinister with latent horror. Hieroglyphics had covered the walls and pillars, and from some undetermined point below had come a voice that was not a voice; a chaotic sensation which only fancy could transmute into sound, but which he attempted to render by the almost unpronounceable jumble of letters "*Cthulhu fhtagn.*"

This verbal jumble was the key to the recollection which excited and disturbed Professor Angell. He questioned the sculptor with scientific minuteness; and studied with almost frantic intensity the bas-relief on which the youth had found himself working, chilled and clad only in his night clothes, when waking had stolen bewilderingly over him. My uncle blamed his old age, Wilcox afterward said, for his slowness in recognizing both hieroglyphics and pictorial design. Many of his questions seemed highly out of place to his visitor, especially those which tried to connect the latter with strange cults or societies; and Wilcox could not understand the repeated promises of silence which he was offered in exchange for an admission of membership in some widespread mystical or paganly religious body. When Professor Angell became convinced that the sculptor was indeed ignorant of any cult or system of cryptic lore, he besieged his visitor with demands for future reports of dreams. This bore regular fruit, for after the first interview the manuscript records daily calls of the young man, during which he related startling fragments of nocturnal imagery whose burden was always some terrible Cyclopean vista of dark and dripping stone, with a subterrene voice or intelligence shouting monotonously in enigmatical sense impacts uninscribable save as gibberish. The two sounds most frequently repeated are those rendered by the letters "*Cthulhu*" and "*R'lyeh.*"

On March 23rd, the manuscript continued, Wilcox failed to appear; and inquiries at his quarters revealed that he had been stricken with an obscure sort of fever and taken to the home of his family in Waterman Street. He had cried out in the night, arousing several other artists in the building, and had manifested since then only alternations of unconsciousness and delirium. My uncle at once telephoned the family, and from that time forward kept close watch of the case; calling often at the Thayer Street office of Dr. Tobey, whom he learned to be in charge. The youth's febrile mind, apparently, was dwelling on strange things; and the doctor shuddered now and then as he spoke of them. They included not only a repetition of what he had formerly dreamed, but touched wildly on a gigantic thing "miles high" which walked or lumbered about.

He at no time fully described this object, but occasional frantic words, as repeated by Dr. Tobey, convinced the professor that it must be identical with the nameless monstrosity he had sought to depict in his dream sculpture. Reference to this object, the doctor added, was invariably a prelude to the young man's subsidence into lethargy. His temperature, oddly enough, was not greatly above normal; but his whole condition was otherwise such as to suggest true fever rather than mental disorder.

On April 2nd at about 3 p.m. every trace of Wilcox's malady suddenly ceased. He sat upright in bed, astonished to find himself at home and completely ignorant of what had happened in dream or reality since the night of March 22nd. Pronounced well by his physician, he returned to his quarters in three days; but to Professor Angell he was of no further assistance. All traces of strange dreaming had vanished with his recovery, and my uncle kept no record of his night thoughts after a week of pointless and irrelevant accounts of thoroughly usual visions.

Here the first part of the manuscript ended, but references to certain of the scattered notes gave me much material for thought—so much, in fact, that only the ingrained skepticism then forming my philosophy can account for my continued distrust of the artist. The notes in question were those descriptive of the dreams of various persons covering the same period as that in which young Wilcox had had his strange visitations. My uncle, it seems, had quickly instituted a prodigiously far-flung body of inquiries amongst nearly all the friends whom he could question without impertinence, asking for nightly reports of their dreams, and the dates of any notable visions for some time past. The reception of his request seems to have been varied; but he must, at the very least, have received more responses than any ordinary man could have handled without a secretary. This original correspondence was not preserved, but his notes formed a thorough and really significant digest. Average people in society and business—New England's traditional "salt of the earth"—gave an almost completely negative result, though scattered cases of uneasy but formless nocturnal impressions appear here and there, always between March 23rd and April 2nd—the period of young Wilcox's delirium. Scientific men were little more affected, though four cases of vague description suggest fugitive glimpses of strange landscapes, and in one case there is mentioned a dread of something abnormal.

It was from the artists and poets that the pertinent answers came, and I know that panic would have broken loose had they been able to compare notes. As it was, lacking their original letters, I half suspected the compiler of having asked leading questions, or of having edited the correspondence in corroboration of what he had latently resolved to see. That is why I continued to feel that Wilcox, somehow cognizant of the old data which my uncle had possessed, had been imposing on the veteran scientist. These responses from aesthetes told a disturbing tale. From February 28th to April 2nd a large proportion of them had dreamed very bizarre things, the intensity of the dreams being immeasurably the stronger during the period of the sculptor's delirium. Over a fourth of those who reported anything, reported scenes and half-sounds not unlike those which Wilcox had described; and some of the dreamers confessed acute fear of the gigantic nameless thing visible toward the last. One case, which the note describes with emphasis, was very sad. The subject, a widely known architect with leanings toward theosophy and occultism, went violently insane on the date of young Wilcox's seizure, and expired several months later after incessant screamings to be saved from some escaped denizen of hell. Had my uncle referred to these cases by name instead of merely by number, I should have attempted some corroboration and personal investigation; but as it was, I succeeded in tracing down only a few. All of these, however, bore out the notes in full. I have often wondered if all the objects of the professor's questioning felt as puzzled as did this fraction. It is well that no explanation shall ever reach them.

The press cuttings, as I have intimated, touched on cases of panic, mania, and eccentricity during the given period. Professor Angell must have employed a cuttings bureau, for the number of extracts was tremendous and the sources scattered throughout the globe. Here was a nocturnal suicide in London, where a lone sleeper had leaped from a window after a shocking cry. Here likewise a rambling letter to the editor of a paper in South America, where a fanatic deduces a dire future from visions he has seen. A dispatch from California describes a theosophist colony as donning white robes en masse for some "glorious fulfillment" which never arrives, whilst items from India speak guardedly of serious native unrest toward the end of March. Voodoo orgies multiply in Haiti, and African outposts report ominous mutterings. American officers in the Philippines find certain tribes bothersome about this time, and New York policemen are mobbed by hysterical Levantines on the night of March 22nd–23rd. The west of Ireland, too, is full of wild rumor and legendry, and a fantastic painter named Ardois-Bonnot hangs a blasphemous "Dream Landscape" in the Paris spring salon of 1926. And so numerous are the recorded troubles in insane asylums, that only a miracle can have stopped the medical fraternity from noting strange parallelisms and drawing mystified conclusions. A weird bunch of cuttings, all told; and I can at this date scarcely envisage the callous rationalism with which I set them aside. But I was then convinced that young Wilcox had known of the older matters mentioned by the professor.

II. THE TALE OF INSPECTOR LEGRASSE

The older matters which had made the sculptor's dream and bas-relief so significant to my uncle formed the subject of the second half of his long manuscript. Once before, it appears, Professor Angell had seen the hellish outlines of the nameless monstrosity, puzzled over the unknown hieroglyphics, and heard the ominous syllables which can be rendered only as "*Cthulhu*;" and all this in so stirring and horrible a connection that it is small wonder he pursued young Wilcox with queries and demands for data.

The earlier experience had come in 1908, seventeen years before, when the American Archaeological Society held its annual meeting in St. Louis. Professor Angell, as befitted one of his authority and attainments, had had a prominent part in all the deliberations; and was one of the first to be approached by the several outsiders who took advantage of the convocation to offer questions for correct answering and problems for expert solution.

The chief of these outsiders, and in a short time the focus of interest for the entire meeting, was a commonplace-looking middle-aged man who had traveled all the way from New Orleans for certain special information unobtainable from any local source. His name was John Raymond Legrasse, and he was by profession an Inspector of Police. With him he bore the subject of his visit, a grotesque, repulsive, and apparently very ancient stone statuette whose origin he was at a loss to determine. It must not be fancied that Inspector Legrasse had the least interest in archaeology. On the contrary, his wish for enlightenment was prompted by purely professional considerations. The statuette, idol, fetish, or whatever it was, had been captured some months before in the wooded swamps south of New Orleans during a raid on a supposed voodoo meeting; and so singular and hideous were the rites connected with it, that the police could not but realize that they had stumbled on a dark cult totally unknown to them, and infinitely more diabolic than even the blackest of the African voodoo circles. Of its origin, apart from the erratic and unbelievable tales extorted from the captured members, absolutely nothing was to be discovered; hence the anxiety of the police for any antiquarian lore which might help them to place the frightful symbol, and through it track down the cult to its fountain head.

Inspector Legrasse was scarcely prepared for the sensation which his offering created. One sight of the thing had been enough to throw the assembled men of science into a state of tense excitement, and they lost no time in crowding around him to gaze at the diminutive figure whose utter strangeness and air of genuinely abysmal antiquity hinted so potently at unopened and archaic vistas. No recognized school of sculpture had animated this terrible object, yet centuries and even thousands of years seemed recorded in its dim and greenish surface of unplaceable stone.

The figure, which was finally passed slowly from man to man for close and careful study, was between seven and eight inches in height, and of exquisitely artistic workmanship. It represented a monster of vaguely anthropoid outline, but with an octopus-like head whose face was a mass of feelers, a scaly, rubbery-looking body, prodigious claws on hind and fore feet, and long, narrow wings behind. This thing, which seemed instinct with a fearsome and unnatural malignancy, was of a somewhat bloated corpulence, and squatted evilly on a rectangular block or pedestal covered with undecipherable characters. The tips of the wings touched the back edge of the block, the seat occupied the center, whilst the long, curved claws of the doubled-up, crouching hind legs gripped the front edge and extended a quarter of the way down toward the bottom of the pedestal. The cephalopod head was bent forward, so that the ends of the facial feelers brushed the backs of huge fore paws which clasped the croucher's elevated knees. The aspect of the whole was abnormally life like, and the more subtly fearful because its source was so totally unknown. Its vast, awesome, and incalculable age was unmistakable; yet not one link did it show with any known type of art belonging to civilization's youth—or indeed to any other time. Totally separate and apart, its very material was a mystery; for the soapy, greenish-black stone with its golden or iridescent flecks and striations resembled nothing familiar to geology or mineralogy. The characters along the base were equally baffling; and no member present, despite a representation of half the world's expert learning in this field, could form the least notion of even their remotest linguistic kinship. They, like the subject and material, belonged to something horribly remote and distinct from mankind as we know it; something frightfully suggestive of old and unhallowed cycles of life in which our world and our conceptions have no part.

And yet, as the members severally shook their heads and confessed defeat at the Inspector's problem, there was one man in that gathering who suspected a touch of bizarre familiarity in the monstrous shape and writing, and who presently told with some diffidence of the odd trifle he knew. This person was the late William Channing Webb, Professor of Anthropology in Princeton University, and an explorer of no slight note. Professor Webb had been engaged, forty-eight years before, in a tour of Greenland and Iceland in search of some runic inscriptions which he failed to unearth; and whilst high up on the West Greenland coast had encountered a singular tribe or cult of degenerate Eskimos whose religion, a curious form of devil worship, chilled him with its deliberate bloodthirstiness and repulsiveness. It was a faith of which other Eskimos knew little, and which they mentioned only with shudders, saying that it had come down from horribly ancient eons before ever the world was made. Besides nameless rites and human sacrifices, there were certain queer hereditary rituals addressed to a supreme elder devil or *tornasuk;* and of this Professor Webb had taken a careful phonetic copy from an aged *angekok* or wizard-priest, expressing the sounds in Roman letters as best he knew how. But just now of prime significance was the fetish which this cult had cherished, and around which they danced when the aurora leaped high over the ice cliffs. It was, the professor stated, a very crude bas-relief of stone, comprising a hideous picture and some cryptic writing. And so far as he could tell, it was a rough parallel in all essential features of the bestial thing now lying before the meeting.

This data, received with suspense and astonishment by the assembled members, proved doubly exciting to Inspector Legrasse; and he began at once to ply his informant with questions. Having noted and copied an oral ritual among the swamp cult worshippers his men had arrested, he besought the professor to remember as best he might the syllables taken down amongst the diabolist Eskimos. There then followed an exhaustive comparison of details, and a moment of really awed silence when both detective and scientist agreed on the virtual identity of the phrase common to two hellish rituals so many worlds of distance apart. What, in substance, both the Eskimo wizards and the Louisiana swamp-priests had chanted to their kindred idols was something very like this—the word divisions being guessed at from traditional breaks in the phrase as chanted aloud:

"Ph'nglui mglw'nafh Cthulhu R'lyeh wgah'nagl fhtagn."

Legrasse had one point in advance of Professor Webb, for several among his mongrel prisoners had repeated to him what older celebrants had told them the words meant. This text, as given, ran something like this:

"In his house at R'lyeh dead Cthulhu waits dreaming."

And now, in response to a general and urgent demand, Inspector Legrasse related as fully as possible his experience with the swamp worshippers; telling a story to which I could see my uncle attached profound significance. It savored of the wildest dreams of myth maker and theosophist, and disclosed an astonishing degree of cosmic imagination among such half-castes and pariahs as might be least expected to possess it.

On November 1st, 1907, there had come to the New Orleans police a frantic summons from the swamp and lagoon country to the south. The squatters there, mostly primitive but good-natured descendants of Lafitte's men, were in the grip of stark terror from an unknown thing which had stolen upon them in the night. It was voodoo, apparently, but voodoo of a more terrible sort than they had ever known; and some of their women and children had disappeared since the malevolent tom-tom had begun its incessant beating far within the black haunted woods where no dweller ventured. There were insane shouts and harrowing screams, soul-chilling chants and dancing devil flames; and, the frightened messenger added, the people could stand it no more.

So a body of twenty police, filling two carriages and an automobile, had set out in the late afternoon with the shivering squatter as a guide. At the end of the passable road they alighted, and for miles splashed on in silence through the terrible cypress woods where day never came. Ugly roots and malignant hanging nooses of Spanish moss beset them, and now and then a pile of dank stones or fragment of a rotting wall intensified by its hint of morbid habitation a depression which every malformed tree and every fungous islet combined to create. At length the squatter settlement, a miserable huddle of huts, hove in sight; and hysterical dwellers ran out to cluster around the group of bobbing lanterns. The muffled beat of tom-toms was now faintly audible far, far ahead; and a curdling shriek came at infrequent intervals when the wind shifted. A reddish glare, too, seemed to filter through the pale undergrowth beyond endless avenues of forest night. Reluctant even to be left alone again, each one of the cowed squatters refused point-blank to advance another inch toward the scene of unholy worship, so Inspector Legrasse and his nineteen colleagues plunged on unguided into black arcades of horror that none of them had ever trod before.

The region now entered by the police was one of traditionally evil repute, substantially unknown and untraversed by white men. There were legends of a hidden lake unglimpsed by mortal sight, in which dwelt a huge, formless white polypous thing with luminous eyes; and squatters whispered that bat-winged devils flew up out of caverns in inner earth to worship it at midnight. They said it had been there before D'Iberville, before La Salle, before the Indians, and before even the wholesome beasts and birds of the woods. It was nightmare itself, and to see it was to die. But it made men dream, and so they knew enough to keep away. The present voodoo orgy was, indeed, on the merest fringe of this abhorred area, but that location was bad enough; hence perhaps the very place of the worship had terrified the squatters more than the shocking sounds and incidents.

Only poetry or madness could do justice to the noises heard by Legrasse's men as they plowed on through the black morass toward the red glare and the muffled tom-toms. There are vocal qualities peculiar to men, and vocal qualities peculiar to beasts; and it is terrible to hear the one when the source should yield the other. Animal fury and orgiastic license here whipped themselves to demoniac heights by howls and squawking ecstasies that tore and reverberated through those nighted woods like pestilential tempests from the gulfs of hell. Now and then the less organized ululation would cease, and from what seemed a well-drilled chorus of hoarse voices would rise in sing-song chant that hideous phrase or ritual:

"Ph'nglui mglw'nafh Cthulhu R'lyeh wgah'nagl fhtagn."

Then the men, having reached a spot where the trees were thinner, came suddenly in sight of the spectacle itself. Four of them reeled, one fainted, and two were shaken into a frantic cry which the mad cacophony of the orgy fortunately deadened. Legrasse dashed swamp water on the face of the fainting man, and all stood trembling and nearly hypnotized with horror.

In a natural glade of the swamp stood a grassy island of perhaps an acre's extent, clear of trees and tolerably dry. On this now leaped and twisted a more indescribable horde of human abnormality than any but a Sime or an Angarola could paint. Void of clothing, this hybrid spawn were braying, bellowing, and writhing about a monstrous ring-shaped bonfire; in the center of which, revealed by occasional rifts in the curtain of flame, stood a great granite monolith some eight feet in height; on top of which, incongruous with its diminutiveness, rested the noxious carven statuette. From a wide circle of ten scaffolds set up at regular intervals with the flame-girt monolith as a center hung, head downward, the oddly marred bodies of the helpless squatters who had disappeared. It was inside this circle that the ring of worshippers jumped and roared, the general direction of the mass motion being from left to right in endless bacchanal between the ring of bodies and the ring of fire.

It may have been only imagination and it may have been only echoes which induced one of the men, an excitable Spaniard, to fancy he heard antiphonal responses to the ritual from some far and unillumined spot deeper within the wood of ancient legendry and horror. This man, Joseph D. Galvez, I later met and questioned; and he proved distractingly imaginative. He indeed went so far as to hint of the faint beating of great wings, and of a glimpse of shining eyes and a mountainous white bulk beyond the remotest trees—but I suppose he had been hearing too much native superstition.

Actually, the horrified pause of the men was of comparatively brief duration. Duty came first; and although there must have been nearly a hundred mongrel celebrants in the throng, the police relied on their firearms and plunged determinedly into the nauseous rout. For five minutes the resultant din and chaos were beyond description. Wild blows were struck, shots were fired, and escapes were made; but in the end Legrasse was able to count some forty-seven sullen prisoners, whom he forced to dress in haste and fall into line between two rows of policemen. Five of the worshippers lay dead, and two severely wounded ones were carried away on improvised stretchers by their fellow prisoners. The image on the monolith, of course, was carefully removed and carried back by Legrasse.

Examined at headquarters after a trip of intense strain and weariness, the prisoners all proved to be men of a very low, mixed-blooded, and mentally aberrant type. Most were seamen, and a sprinkling of negroes and mulattoes, largely West Indians or Brava Portuguese from the Cape Verde Islands, gave a coloring of voodooism to the heterogeneous cult. But before many questions were asked, it became manifest that something far deeper and older than negro fetishism was involved. Degraded and ignorant as they were, the creatures held with surprising consistency to the central idea of their loathsome faith.

They worshipped, so they said, the Great Old Ones who lived ages before there were any men, and who came to the young world out of the sky. Those Old Ones were gone now, inside the earth and under the sea; but their dead bodies had told their secrets in dreams to the first men, who formed a cult which had never died. This was that cult, and the prisoners said it had always existed and always would exist, hidden in distant wastes and dark places all over the world until the time when the great priest Cthulhu, from his dark house in the mighty city of R'lyeh under the waters, should rise and bring the earth again beneath his sway. Some day he would call, when the stars were ready, and the secret cult would always be waiting to liberate him.

Meanwhile, no more must be told. There was a secret which even torture could not extract. Mankind was not absolutely alone among the conscious things of earth, for shapes came out of the dark to visit the faithful few. But these were not the Great Old Ones. No man had ever seen the Old Ones. The carven idol was great Cthulhu, but none might say whether or not the others were precisely like him. No one could read the old writing now, but things were told by word of mouth. The chanted ritual was not the secret—that was never spoken aloud, only whispered. The chant meant only this: "In his house at R'lyeh dead Cthulhu waits dreaming."

Only two of the prisoners were found sane enough to be hanged, and the rest were committed to various institutions. All denied a part in the ritual murders, and averred that the killing had been done by Black Winged Ones, which had come to them from their immemorial meeting-place in the haunted wood. But of those mysterious allies no coherent account could ever be gained. What the police did extract, came mainly from an immensely aged mestizo named Castro, who claimed to have sailed to strange ports and talked with undying leaders of the cult in the mountains of China.

Old Castro remembered bits of hideous legend that paled the speculations of theosophists and made man and the world seem recent and transient indeed. There had been eons when other Things ruled on the earth, and They had had great cities. Remains of Them, he said the deathless Chinamen had told him, were still to be found as Cyclopean stones on islands in the Pacific. They all died vast epochs of time before men came, but there were arts which could revive Them when the stars had come round again to the right positions in the cycle of eternity. They had, indeed, come themselves from the stars, and brought Their images with Them.

These Great Old Ones, Castro continued, were not composed altogether of flesh and blood. They had shape—for did not this star-fashioned image prove it?—but that shape was not made of matter. When the stars were right, They could plunge from world to world through the sky; but when the stars were wrong, They could not live. But although They no longer lived, They would never really die. They all lay in stone houses in Their great city of R'lyeh, preserved by the spells of mighty Cthulhu for a glorious resurrection when the stars and the earth might once more be ready for Them. But at that time some force from outside must serve to liberate Their bodies. The spells that preserved Them intact likewise prevented Them from making an initial move, and They could only lie awake in the dark and think whilst uncounted millions of years rolled by. They knew all that was occurring in the universe, but Their mode of speech was transmitted thought. Even now They talked in Their tombs. When, after infinities of chaos, the first men came, the Great Old Ones spoke to the sensitive among them by molding their dreams; for only thus could Their language reach the fleshly minds of mammals.

Then, whispered Castro, those first men formed the cult around small idols which the Great Ones shewed them; idols brought in dim eras from dark stars. That cult would never die till the stars came right again, and the secret priests would take great Cthulhu from His tomb to revive His subjects and resume His rule of earth. The time would be easy to know, for then mankind would have become as the Great Old Ones; free and wild and beyond good and evil, with laws and morals thrown aside and all men shouting and killing and reveling in joy. Then the liberated Old Ones would teach them new ways to shout and kill and revel and enjoy themselves, and all the earth would flame with a holocaust of ecstasy and freedom. Meanwhile the cult, by appropriate rites, must keep alive the memory of those ancient ways and shadow forth the prophecy of their return.

In the elder time chosen men had talked with the entombed Old Ones in dreams, but then something had happened. The great stone city R'lyeh, with its monoliths and sepulchers, had sunk beneath the waves; and the deep waters, full of the one primal mystery through which not even thought can pass, had cut off the spectral intercourse. But memory never died, and high priests said that the city would rise again when the stars were right. Then came out of the earth the black spirits of earth, moldy and shadowy, and full of dim rumors picked up in caverns beneath forgotten sea-bottoms. But of them old Castro dared not speak much. He cut himself off hurriedly, and no amount of persuasion or subtlety could elicit more in this direction. The *size* of the Old Ones, too, he curiously declined to mention. Of the cult, he said that he thought the center lay amid the pathless deserts of Arabia, where Irem, the City of Pillars, dreams hidden and untouched. It was not allied to the European witch cult, and was virtually unknown beyond its members. No book had ever really hinted of it, though the deathless Chinamen said that there were double meanings in the *Necronomicon* of the mad Arab Abdul Alhazred which the initiated might read as they chose, especially the much-discussed couplet:

"That is not dead which can eternal lie,
And with strange eons even death may die."

Legrasse, deeply impressed and not a little bewildered, had inquired in vain concerning the historic affiliations of the cult. Castro, apparently, had told the truth when he said that it was wholly secret. The authorities at Tulane University could shed no light upon either cult or image, and now the detective had come to the highest authorities in the country and met with no more than the Greenland tale of Professor Webb.

The feverish interest aroused at the meeting by Legrasse's tale, corroborated as it was by the statuette, is echoed in the subsequent correspondence of those who attended; although scant mention occurs in the formal publications of the society. Caution is the first care of those accustomed to face occasional charlatanry and imposture. Legrasse for some time lent the image to Professor Webb, but at the latter's death it was returned to him and remains in his possession, where I viewed it not long ago. It is truly a terrible thing, and unmistakably akin to the dream sculpture of young Wilcox.

That my uncle was excited by the tale of the sculptor I did not wonder, for what thoughts must arise upon hearing, after a knowledge of what Legrasse had learned of the cult, of a sensitive young man who had *dreamed* not only the figure and exact hieroglyphics of the swamp-found image and the Greenland devil tablet, but had come *in his dreams* upon at least three of the precise words of the formula uttered alike by Eskimo diabolists and mongrel Louisianans? Professor Angell's instant start on an investigation of the utmost thoroughness was eminently natural; though privately I suspected young Wilcox of having heard of the cult in some indirect way, and of having invented a series of dreams to heighten and continue the mystery at my uncle's expense. The dream narratives and cuttings collected by the professor were, of course, strong corroboration; but the rationalism of my mind and the extravagance of the whole subject led me to adopt what I thought the most sensible conclusions. So, after thoroughly studying the manuscript again and correlating the theosophical and anthropological notes with the cult narrative of Legrasse, I made a trip to Providence to see the sculptor and give him the rebuke I thought proper for so boldly imposing upon a learned and aged man.

Wilcox still lived alone in the Fleur-de-Lys Building in Thomas Street, a hideous Victorian imitation of seventeenth-century Breton architecture which flaunts its stuccoed front amidst the lovely colonial houses on the ancient hill, and under the very shadow of the finest Georgian steeple in America. I found him at work in his rooms, and at once conceded from the specimens scattered about that his genius is indeed profound and authentic. He will, I believe, some time be heard from as one of the great decadents; for he has crystallized in clay and will one day mirror in marble those nightmares and fantasies which Arthur Machen evokes in prose, and Clark Ashton Smith makes visible in verse and in painting.

Dark, frail, and somewhat unkempt in aspect, he turned languidly at my knock and asked me my business without rising. When I told him who I was, he displayed some interest; for my uncle had excited his curiosity in probing his strange dreams, yet had never explained the reason for the study. I did not enlarge his knowledge in this regard, but sought with some subtlety to draw him out. In a short time I became convinced of his absolute sincerity, for he spoke of the dreams in a manner none could mistake. They and their subconscious residuum had influenced his art profoundly, and he shewed me a morbid statue whose contours almost made me shake with the potency of its black suggestion. He could not recall having seen the original of this thing except in his own dream bas-relief, but the outlines had formed themselves insensibly under his hands. It was, no doubt, the giant shape he had raved of in delirium. That he really knew nothing of the hidden cult, save from what my uncle's relentless catechism had let fall, he soon made clear; and again I strove to think of some way in which he could possibly have received the weird impressions.

He talked of his dreams in a strangely poetic fashion, making me see with terrible vividness the damp Cyclopean city of slimy green stone—whose *geometry,* he oddly said, was *all wrong*—and hear with frightened expectancy the ceaseless, half-mental calling from underground: "*Cthulhu fhtagn,*" "*Cthulhu fhtagn.*" These words had formed part of that dread ritual which told of dead Cthulhu's dream-vigil in his stone vault at R'lyeh, and I felt deeply moved despite my rational beliefs. Wilcox, I was sure, had heard of the cult in some casual way, and had soon forgotten it amidst the mass of his equally weird reading and imagining. Later, by virtue of its sheer impressiveness, it had found subconscious expression in dreams, in the bas-relief, and in the terrible statue I now beheld; so that his imposture upon my uncle had been a very innocent one. The youth was of a type, at once slightly affected and slightly ill-mannered, which I could never like; but I was willing enough now to admit both his genius and his honesty. I took leave of him amicably, and wish him all the success his talent promises.

The matter of the cult still remained to fascinate me, and at times I had visions of personal fame from researches into its origin and connections. I visited New Orleans, talked with Legrasse and others of that old-time raiding party, saw the frightful image, and even questioned such of the mongrel prisoners as still survived. Old Castro, unfortunately, had been dead for some years. What I now heard so graphically at first hand, though it was really no more than a detailed confirmation of what my uncle had written, excited me afresh; for I felt sure that I was on the track of a very real, very secret, and very ancient religion whose discovery would make me an anthropologist of note. My attitude was still one of absolute materialism, as I wish it still were, and I discounted with almost inexplicable perversity the coincidence of the dream notes and odd cuttings collected by Professor Angell.

One thing I began to suspect, and which I now fear I *know,* is that my uncle's death was far from natural. He fell on a narrow hill street leading up from an ancient waterfront swarming with foreign mongrels, after a careless push from a negro sailor. I did not forget the mixed blood and marine pursuits of the cult members in Louisiana, and would not be surprised to learn of secret methods and poison needles as ruthless and as anciently known as the cryptic rites and beliefs. Legrasse and his men, it is true, have been let alone; but in Norway a certain seaman who saw things is dead. Might not the deeper inquiries of my uncle after encountering the sculptor's data have come to sinister ears? I think Professor Angell died because he knew too much, or because he was likely to learn too much. Whether I shall go as he did remains to be seen, for I have learned much now.

III. THE MADNESS FROM THE SEA

If heaven ever wishes to grant me a boon, it will be a total effacing of the results of a mere chance which fixed my eye on a certain stray piece of shelf paper. It was nothing on which I would naturally have stumbled in the course of my daily round, for it was an old number of an Australian journal, the *Sydney Bulletin* for April 18th, 1925. It had escaped even the cutting bureau which had at the time of its issuance been avidly collecting material for my uncle's research.

I had largely given over my inquiries into what Professor Angell called the "Cthulhu Cult," and was visiting a learned friend in Paterson, New Jersey; the curator of a local museum and a mineralogist of note. Examining one day the reserve specimens roughly set on the storage shelves in a rear room of the museum, my eye was caught by an odd picture in one of the old papers spread beneath the stones. It was the *Sydney Bulletin* I have mentioned, for my friend has wide affiliations in all conceivable foreign parts; and the picture was a half-tone cut of a hideous stone image almost identical with that which Legrasse had found in the swamp.

Eagerly clearing the sheet of its precious contents, I scanned the item in detail; and was disappointed to find it of only moderate length. What it suggested, however, was of portentous significance to my flagging quest; and I carefully tore it out for immediate action. It read as follows:

MYSTERY DERELICT FOUND AT SEA

Vigilant Arrives With Helpless Armed New Zealand Yacht in Tow. One Survivor and Dead Man Found Aboard. Tale of Desperate Battle and Deaths at Sea. Rescued Seaman Refuses Particulars of Strange Experience. Odd Idol Found in His Possession. Inquiry to Follow.

The Morrison Co.'s freighter Vigilant, *bound from Valparaiso, arrived this morning at its wharf in Darling Harbour, having in tow the battled and disabled but heavily armed steam yacht* Alert *of Dunedin, NZ, which was sighted April 12th in S. Latitude 34° 21', W. Longitude 152° 17' with one living and one dead man aboard.*

The Vigilant *left Valparaiso March 25th, and on April 2nd was driven considerably south of her course by exceptionally heavy storms and monster waves. On April 12th the derelict was sighted; and though apparently deserted, was found upon boarding to contain one survivor in a half-delirious condition and one man who had evidently been dead for more than a week. The living man was clutching a horrible stone idol of unknown origin, about a foot in height, regarding whose nature authorities at Sydney University, the Royal Society, and the Museum in College Street all profess complete bafflement, and which the survivor says he found in the cabin of the yacht, in a small carved shrine of common pattern.*

This man, after recovering his senses, told an exceedingly strange story of piracy and slaughter. He is Gustaf Johansen, a Norwegian of some intelligence, and had been second mate of the two-masted schooner Emma *of Auckland, which sailed for Callao February 20th with a complement of eleven men. The* Emma*, he says, was delayed and thrown widely south of her course by the* *great storm of March 1st, and on March 22nd, in S. Latitude 49° 51', W. Longitude 128° 34', encountered the* Alert, *manned by a queer and evil-looking crew of Kanakas and half-castes. Being ordered peremptorily to turn back, Capt. Collins refused; whereupon the strange crew began to fire savagely and without warning upon the schooner with a peculiarly heavy battery of brass cannon forming part of the yacht's equipment. The* Emma's *men shewed fight, says the survivor, and though the schooner began to sink from shots beneath the waterline they managed to heave alongside their enemy and board her, grappling with the savage crew on the yacht's deck, and being forced to kill them all, the number being slightly superior, because of their particularly abhorrent and desperate though rather clumsy mode of fighting.*

Three of the Emma's *men, including Capt. Collins and First Mate Green, were killed; and the remaining eight under Second Mate Johansen proceeded to navigate the captured yacht, going ahead in their original direction to see if any reason for their ordering back had existed. The next day, it appears, they raised and landed on a small island, although none is known to exist in that part of the ocean; and six of the men somehow died ashore, though Johansen is queerly reticent about this part of his story, and speaks only of their falling into a rock chasm. Later, it seems, he and one companion boarded the yacht and tried to manage her, but were beaten about by the storm of April 2nd. From that time till his rescue on the 12th the man remembers little, and he does not even recall when William Briden, his companion, died. Briden's death reveals no apparent cause, and was probably due to excitement or exposure. Cable advices from Dunedin report that the* Alert *was well known there as an island trader, and bore an evil reputation along the waterfront. It was owned by a curious group of half-castes whose frequent meetings and night trips to the woods attracted no little curiosity; and it had set sail in great haste just after the storm and earth tremors of March 1st. Our Auckland correspondent gives the* Emma *and her crew an excellent reputation, and Johansen is described as a sober and worthy man. The admiralty will institute an inquiry on the whole matter beginning tomorrow, at which every effort will be made to induce Johansen to speak more freely than he has done hitherto.*

This was all, together with the picture of the hellish image; but what a train of ideas it started in my mind! Here were new treasuries of data on the Cthulhu

Cult, and evidence that it had strange interests at sea as well as on land. What motive prompted the hybrid crew to order back the *Emma* as they sailed about with their hideous idol? What was the unknown island on which six of the *Emma*'s crew had died, and about which the mate Johansen was so secretive? What had the vice-admiralty's investigation brought out, and what was known of the noxious cult in Dunedin? And most marvelous of all, what deep and more than natural linkage of dates was this which gave a malign and now undeniable significance to the various turns of events so carefully noted by my uncle?

March 1st—our February 28th according to the International Date Line—the earthquake and storm had come. From Dunedin the *Alert* and her noisome crew had darted eagerly forth as if imperiously summoned, and on the other side of the earth poets and artists had begun to dream of a strange, dank Cyclopean city whilst a young sculptor had molded in his sleep the form of the dreaded Cthulhu. March 23d the crew of the *Emma* landed on an unknown island and left six men dead; and on that date the dreams of sensitive men assumed a heightened vividness and darkened with dread of a giant monster's malign pursuit, whilst an architect had gone mad and a sculptor had lapsed suddenly into delirium! And what of this storm of April 2nd—the date on which all dreams of the dank city ceased, and Wilcox emerged unharmed from the bondage of strange fever? What of all this—and of those hints of old Castro about the sunken, star-born Old Ones and their coming reign; their faithful cult *and their mastery of dreams?* Was I tottering on the brink of cosmic horrors beyond man's power to bear? If so, they must be horrors of the mind alone, for in some way April 2nd had put a stop to whatever monstrous menace had begun its siege of mankind's soul.

That evening, after a day of hurried cabling and arranging, I bade my host adieu and took a train for San Francisco. In less than a month I was in Dunedin; where, however, I found that little was known of the strange cult members who had lingered in the old sea taverns. Waterfront scum was far too common for special mention; though there was vague talk about one inland trip these mongrels had made, during which faint drumming and red flame were noted on the distant hills. In Auckland I learned that Johansen had returned *with yellow hair turned white* after a perfunctory and inconclusive questioning at Sydney, and had thereafter sold his cottage in West Street and sailed with his wife to his old home in Oslo. Of his stirring experience he would tell his friends no more than he had told the admiralty officials, and all they could do was to give me his Oslo address.

After that I went to Sydney and talked profitlessly with seamen and members of the vice-admiralty court. I saw the *Alert*, now sold and in commercial use, at Circular Quay in Sydney Cove, but gained nothing from its noncommittal bulk. The crouching image with its cuttlefish head, dragon body, scaly wings, and hieroglyphed pedestal, was preserved in the Museum at Hyde Park; and I studied it long and well, finding it a thing of balefully exquisite workmanship, and with the same utter mystery, terrible antiquity, and unearthly strangeness of material which I had noted in Legrasse's smaller specimen. Geologists, the curator told me, had found it a monstrous puzzle; for they vowed that the world held no rock like it. Then I thought with a shudder of what old Castro had told Legrasse about the primal Great Ones: "They had come from the stars, and had brought Their images with Them."

Shaken with such a mental revolution as I had never before known, I now resolved to visit Mate Johansen in Oslo. Sailing for London, I reembarked at once for the Norwegian capital; and one autumn day landed at the trim wharves in the shadow of the Egeberg. Johansen's address, I discovered, lay in the Old Town of King Harold Haardrada, which kept alive the name of Oslo during all the centuries that the greater city masqueraded as "Christiana." I made the brief trip by taxicab, and knocked with palpitant heart at the door of a neat and ancient building with plastered front. A sad-faced woman in black answered my summons, and I was stung with disappointment when she told me in halting English that Gustaf Johansen was no more.

He had not survived his return, said his wife, for the doings at sea in 1925 had broken him. He had told her no more than he had told the public, but had left a long manuscript—of "technical matters" as he said—written in English, evidently in order to safeguard her from the peril of casual perusal. During a walk through a narrow lane near the Gothenburg dock, a bundle of papers falling from an attic window had knocked him down. Two Lascar sailors at once helped him to his feet, but before the ambulance could reach him he was dead. Physicians found no adequate cause for the end, and laid it to heart trouble and a weakened constitution.

I now felt gnawing at my vitals that dark terror which will never leave me till I, too, am at rest; "accidentally" or otherwise. Persuading the widow that my connection with her husband's "technical matters" was sufficient to entitle me to his manuscript, I bore the document away and began to read it on the London boat. It was a simple, rambling thing—a naive sailor's effort at a *post-facto* diary—and strove to recall day by day that last awful voyage. I cannot attempt to transcribe it verbatim in all its cloudiness and redundance, but I will tell its gist enough to show why the sound of the water against the vessel's sides became so unendurable to me that I stopped my ears with cotton.

Johansen, thank God, did not know quite all, even though he saw the city and the Thing, but I shall never sleep calmly again when I think of the horrors that lurk ceaselessly behind life in time and in space, and of those unhallowed blasphemies from elder stars which dream beneath the sea, known and favored by a nightmare cult ready and eager to loose them on the world whenever another earthquake shall heave their monstrous stone city again to the sun and air.

Johansen's voyage had begun just as he told it to the vice-admiralty. The *Emma,* in ballast, had cleared Auckland on February 20th, and had felt the full force of that earthquake-born tempest which must have heaved up from the sea bottom the horrors that filled men's dreams. Once more under control, the ship was making good progress when held up by the *Alert* on March 22nd, and I could feel the mate's regret as he wrote of her bombardment and sinking. Of the swarthy cult fiends on the *Alert* he speaks with significant horror. There was some peculiarly abominable quality about them which made their destruction seem almost a duty, and Johansen shows ingenuous wonder at the charge of ruthlessness brought against his party during the proceedings of the court of inquiry. Then, driven ahead by curiosity in their captured yacht under Johansen's command, the men sight a great stone pillar sticking out of the sea, and in S. Latitude 47° 9', W. Longitude 123° 43' come upon a coastline of mingled mud, ooze, and weedy Cyclopean masonry which can be nothing less than the tangible substance of earth's supreme terror—the nightmare corpse-city of R'lyeh, that was built in measureless eons behind history by the vast, loathsome shapes that seeped down from the dark stars. There lay great Cthulhu and his hordes, hidden in green slimy vaults and sending out at last, after cycles incalculable, the thoughts that spread fear to the dreams of the sensitive and called imperiously to the faithful to come on a pilgrimage of liberation and restoration. All this Johansen did not suspect, but God knows he soon saw enough!

I suppose that only a single mountaintop, the hideous monolith-crowned citadel whereon great Cthulhu was buried, actually emerged from the waters. When I think of the extent of all that may be brooding down there I almost wish to kill myself forthwith. Johansen and his men were awed by the cosmic majesty of this dripping Babylon of elder demons, and must have guessed without guidance that it was nothing of this or of any sane planet. Awe at the unbelievable size of the greenish stone blocks, at the dizzying height of the great carven monolith, and at the stupefying identity of the colossal statues and bas-reliefs with the queer image found in the shrine on the *Alert,* is poignantly visible in every line of the mate's frightened description.

Without knowing what futurism is like, Johansen achieved something very close to it when he spoke of the city; for instead of describing any definite structure or building, he dwells only on broad impressions of vast angles and stone surfaces—surfaces too great to belong to any thing right or proper for this earth, and impious with horrible images and hieroglyphs. I mention his talk about *angles* because it suggests something Wilcox had told me of his awful dreams. He had said that the *geometry* of the dream-place he saw was abnormal, non-Euclidean, and loathsomely redolent of spheres and dimensions apart from ours. Now an unlettered seaman felt the same thing whilst gazing at the terrible reality.

Johansen and his men landed at a sloping mudbank on this monstrous Acropolis, and clambered slipperily up over titan oozy blocks which could have been no mortal staircase. The very sun of heaven seemed distorted when viewed through the polarizing miasma welling out from this sea-soaked perversion, and twisted menace and suspense lurked leeringly in those crazily elusive angles of carven rock, where a second glance showed concavity after the first showed convexity.

Something very like fright had come over all the explorers before anything more definite than rock and ooze and weed was seen. Each would have fled had he not feared the scorn of the others, and it was only half heartedly that they searched—vainly, as it proved—for some portable souvenir to bear away.

It was Rodriguez the Portuguese who climbed up the foot of the monolith and shouted of what he had found. The rest followed him, and looked curiously at the immense carved door with the now familiar squid dragon bas-relief. It was, Johansen said, like a great barn door; and they all felt that it was a door because of the ornate lintel, threshold, and jambs around it, though they could not decide whether it lay flat like a trapdoor or slantwise like an outside cellar door. As Wilcox would have said, the geometry of the place was all wrong. One could not be sure that the sea and the ground were horizontal, hence the relative position of everything else seemed phantasmally variable.

Briden pushed at the stone in several places without result. Then Donovan felt over it delicately around the edge, pressing each point separately as he went. He climbed interminably along the grotesque stone molding—that is, one would call it climbing if the thing was not after all horizontal—and the men wondered how any door in the universe could be so vast. Then, very softly and slowly, the acre-great panel began to give inward at the top; and they saw that it was balanced. Donovan slid or somehow propelled himself down or along the jamb and rejoined his fellows, and everyone watched the queer recession of the monstrously carven portal. In this fantasy of prismatic distortion it moved anomalously in a diagonal way, so that all the rules of matter and perspective seemed upset.

The aperture was black with a darkness almost material. That tenebrousness was indeed a *positive quality;* for it obscured such parts of the inner walls as ought to have been revealed, and actually burst forth like smoke from its eon-long imprisonment, visibly darkening the sun as it slunk away into the shrunken and gibbous sky on flapping membranous wings. The odor arising from the newly opened depths was intolerable, and at length the quick-eared Hawkins thought he heard a nasty, slopping sound down there. Everyone listened, and everyone was listening still when It lumbered slobberingly into sight and gropingly squeezed Its gelatinous green immensity through the black doorway into the tainted outside air of that poison city of madness.

Poor Johansen's handwriting almost gave out when he wrote of this. Of the six men who never reached the ship, he thinks two perished of pure fright in that accursed instant. The Thing cannot be described—there is no language for such abysms of shrieking and immemorial lunacy, such eldritch contradictions of all matter, force, and cosmic order. A mountain walked or stumbled. God! What wonder that across the earth a great architect went mad, and poor Wilcox raved with fever in that telepathic instant? The Thing of the idols, the green, sticky spawn of the stars, had awaked to claim his own. The stars were right again, and what an age-old cult had failed to do by design, a band of innocent sailors had done by accident. After vigintillions of years great Cthulhu was loose again, and ravening for delight.

Three men were swept up by the flabby claws before anybody turned. God rest them, if there be any rest in the universe. They were Donovan, Guerrera, and Ångstrom. Parker slipped as the other three were plunging frenziedly over endless vistas of green-crusted rock to the boat, and Johansen swears he was swallowed up by an angle of masonry which shouldn't have been there; an angle which was acute, but behaved as if it were obtuse. So only Briden and Johansen reached the boat, and pulled desperately for the *Alert* as the mountainous monstrosity flopped down the slimy stones and hesitated floundering at the edge of the water.

Steam had not been suffered to go down entirely, despite the departure of all hands for the shore; and it was the work of only a few moments of feverish rushing up and down between wheel and engines to get the *Alert* under way. Slowly, amidst the distorted horrors of that indescribable scene, she began to churn the lethal waters; whilst on the masonry of that charnel shore that was not of earth the titan Thing from the stars slavered and gibbered like Polypheme cursing the fleeing ship of Odysseus. Then, bolder than the storied Cyclops, great Cthulhu slid greasily into the water and began to pursue with vast wave-raising strokes of cosmic potency. Briden looked back and went mad, laughing shrilly as he kept on laughing at intervals till death found him one night in the cabin whilst Johansen was wandering deliriously.

But Johansen had not given out yet. Knowing that the Thing could surely overtake the *Alert* until steam was fully up, he resolved on a desperate chance; and, setting the engine for full speed, ran lightning-like on deck and reversed the wheel. There was a mighty eddying and foaming in the noisome brine, and as the steam mounted higher and higher the brave Norwegian drove his vessel head on against the pursuing jelly which rose above the unclean froth like the stern of a demon galleon. The awful squid-head with writhing feelers came nearly up to the bowsprit of the sturdy yacht, but Johansen drove on relentlessly. There was a bursting as of an exploding bladder, a slushy nastiness as of a cloven sunfish, a stench as of a thousand opened graves, and a sound that the chronicler would not put on paper. For an instant the ship was befouled by an acrid and blinding green cloud, and then there was only a venomous seething astern; where—God in heaven!—the scattered plasticity of that nameless sky-spawn was nebulously *recombining* in its hateful original form, whilst its distance widened every second as the *Alert* gained impetus from its mounting steam.

That was all. After that Johansen only brooded over the idol in the cabin and attended to a few matters of food for himself and the laughing maniac by his side. He did not try to navigate after the first bold flight, for the reaction had taken something out of his soul. Then came the storm of April 2nd, and a gathering of the clouds about his consciousness. There is a sense of spectral whirling through liquid gulfs of infinity, of dizzying rides through reeling universes on a comet's tail, and of hysterical plunges from the pit to the moon and from the moon back again to the pit, all livened by a cachinnating chorus of the distorted, hilarious elder gods and the green, bat-winged mocking imps of Tartarus.

Out of that dream came rescue—the *Vigilant,* the vice-admiralty court, the streets of Dunedin, and the long voyage back home to the old house by the Egeberg. He could not tell—they would think him mad. He would write of what he knew before death came, but his wife must not guess. Death would be a boon if only it could blot out the memories.

That was the document I read, and now I have placed it in the tin box beside the bas-relief and the papers of Professor Angell. With it shall go this record of mine—this test of my own sanity, wherein is pieced together that which I hope may never be pieced together again. I have looked upon all that the universe has to hold of horror, and even the skies of spring and the flowers of summer must ever afterward be poison to me. But I do not think my life will be long. As my uncle went, as poor Johansen went, so I shall go. I know too much, and the cult still lives.

Cthulhu still lives, too, I suppose, again in that chasm of stone which has shielded him since the sun was young. His accursed city is sunken once more, for the *Vigilant* sailed over the spot after the April storm; but his ministers on earth still bellow and prance and slay around idol-capped monoliths in lonely places. He must have been trapped by the sinking whilst within his black abyss, or else the world would by now be screaming with fright and frenzy. Who knows the end? What has risen may sink, and what has sunk may rise. Loathsomeness waits and dreams in the deep, and decay spreads over the tottering cities of men. A time will come—but I must not and cannot think! Let me pray that, if I do not survive this manuscript, my executors may put caution before audacity and see that it meets no other eye.

The Color Out of Space

by H. P. Lovecraft

West of Arkham the hills rise wild, and there are valleys with deep woods that no axe has ever cut. There are dark narrow glens where the trees slope fantastically, and where thin brooklets trickle without ever having caught the glint of sunlight. On the gentler slopes there are farms, ancient and rocky, with squat, moss-coated cottages brooding eternally over old New England secrets in the lee of great ledges; but these are all vacant now, the wide chimneys crumbling and the shingled sides bulging perilously beneath low gambrel roofs.

The old folk have gone away, and foreigners do not like to live there. French-Canadians have tried it, Italians have tried it, and the Poles have come and departed. It is not because of anything that can be seen or heard or handled, but because of something that is imagined. The place is not good for the imagination, and does not bring restful dreams at night. It must be this which keeps the foreigners away, for old Ammi Pierce has never told them of anything he recalls from the strange days. Ammi, whose head has been a little queer for years, is the only one who still remains, or who ever talks of the strange days; and he dares to do this because his house is so near the open fields and the traveled roads around Arkham.

There was once a road over the hills and through the valleys, that ran straight where the blasted heath is now; but people ceased to use it and a new road was laid curving far toward the south. Traces of the old one can still be found amidst the weeds of a returning wilderness, and some of them will doubtless linger even when half the hollows are flooded for the new reservoir. Then the dark woods will be cut down and the blasted heath will slumber far below blue waters whose surface will mirror the sky and ripple in the sun. And the secrets of the strange days will be one with the deep's secrets; one with the hidden lore of old ocean, and all the mystery of primal earth.

When I went into the hills and vales to survey for the new reservoir they told me the place was evil. They told me this in Arkham, and because that is a very old town full of witch legends I thought the evil must be something which grandams had whispered to children through centuries. The name "blasted heath" seemed to me very odd and theatrical, and I wondered how it had come into the folklore of a Puritan people. Then I saw that dark westward tangle of glens and slopes for myself, and ceased to wonder at anything besides its own elder mystery. It was morning when I saw it, but shadow lurked always there. The trees grew too thickly, and their trunks were too big for any healthy New England wood. There was too much silence in the dim alleys between them, and the floor was too soft with the dank moss and mattings of infinite years of decay.

In the open spaces, mostly along the line of the old road, there were little hillside farms; sometimes with all the buildings standing, sometimes with only one or two, and sometimes with only a lone chimney or fast-filling cellar. Weeds and briers reigned, and furtive wild things rustled in the undergrowth. Upon everything was a haze of restlessness and oppression; a touch of the unreal and the grotesque, as if some vital element of perspective or chiaroscuro were awry. I did not wonder that the foreigners would not stay, for this was no region to sleep in. It was too much like a landscape of Salvator Rosa; too much like some forbidden woodcut in a tale of terror.

But even all this was not so bad as the blasted heath. I knew it the moment I came upon it at the bottom of a spacious valley; for no other name could fit such a thing, or any other thing fit such a name. It was as if the poet had coined the phrase from having seen this one particular region. It must, I thought as I viewed it, be the outcome of a fire; but why had nothing new ever grown over those five acres of gray desolation that sprawled open to the sky like a great spot eaten by acid in the woods and fields? It lay largely to the north of the ancient road line, but encroached a little on the other side. I felt an odd reluctance about approaching, and did so at last only because my business took me through and past it. There was no vegetation of any kind on that broad expanse, but only a fine gray dust or ash which no wind seemed ever to blow about. The trees near it were sickly and stunted, and many dead trunks stood or lay rotting at the rim. As I walked hurriedly by I saw the tumbled bricks and stones of an old chimney and cellar on my right, and the yawning black maw of an abandoned well whose stagnant vapors played strange tricks with the hues of the sunlight. Even the long, dark woodland climb beyond seemed welcome in contrast, and I marveled no more at the frightened whispers of Arkham people. There had been no house or ruin near; even in the old days the place must have been lonely and remote. And at twilight, dreading to repass that ominous spot, I walked circuitously back to the town by the curving road on the south. I vaguely wished some clouds would gather, for an odd timidity about the deep skyey voids above had crept into my soul.

In the evening I asked old people in Arkham about the blasted heath, and what was meant by that phrase "strange days" which so many evasively muttered. I could not, however, get any good answers, except that all the mystery was much more recent than I had dreamed. It was not a matter of old legendry at all, but something within the lifetime of those who spoke. It had happened in the 'eighties, and a family had disappeared or was killed. Speakers would not be exact; and because they all told me to pay no attention to old Ammi Pierce's crazy tales, I sought him out the next morning, having heard that he lived alone in the ancient tottering cottage where the trees first begin to get very thick. It was a fearsomely archaic place, and had begun to exude the faint miasmal odor which clings about houses that have stood too long. Only with persistent knocking could I rouse the aged man, and when he shuffled timidly to the door I could tell he was not glad to see me. He was not so feeble as I had expected; but his eyes drooped in a curious way, and his unkempt clothing and white beard made him seem very worn and dismal. Not knowing just how he could best be launched on his tales, I feigned a matter of business; told him of my surveying, and asked vague questions about the district. He was far brighter and more educated than I had been led to think, and before I knew it had grasped quite as much of the subject as any man I had talked with in Arkham. He was not like other rustics I had known in the sections where reservoirs were to be. From him there were no protests at the miles of old wood and farmland to be blotted out, though perhaps there would have been had not his home lain outside the bounds of the future lake.

Relief was all that he shewed; relief at the doom of the dark ancient valleys through which he had roamed all his life. They were better under water now—better under water since the strange days. And with this opening his husky voice sank low, while his body leaned forward and his right forefinger began to point shakily and impressively.

It was then that I heard the story, and as the rambling voice scraped and whispered on I shivered again and again despite the summer day. Often I had to recall the speaker from ramblings, piece out scientific points which he knew only by a fading parrot memory of professors' talk, or bridge over gaps where his sense of logic and continuity broke down. When he was done I did not wonder that his mind had snapped a trifle, or that the folk of Arkham would not speak much of the blasted heath. I hurried back before sunset to my hotel, unwilling to have the stars come out above me in the open; and the next day returned to Boston to give up my position. I could not go into that dim chaos of old forest and slope again, or face another time that gray blasted heath where the black well yawned deep beside the tumbled bricks and stones. The reservoir will soon be built now, and all those elder secrets will be safe forever under watery fathoms. But even then I do not believe I would like to visit that country by night—at least, not when the sinister stars are out; and nothing could bribe me to drink the new city water of Arkham.

It all began, old Ammi said, with the meteorite. Before that time there had been no wild legends at all since the witch trials, and even then these western woods were not feared half so much as the small island in the Miskatonic where the devil held court beside a curious stone altar older than the Indians. These were not haunted woods, and their fantastic dusk was never terrible till the strange days. Then there had come that white noontide cloud, that string of explosions in the air, and that pillar of smoke from the valley far in the wood. And by night all Arkham had heard of the great rock that fell out of the sky and bedded itself in the ground beside the well at the Nahum Gardner place. That was the house which had stood where the blasted heath was to come—the trim white Nahum Gardner house amidst its fertile gardens and orchards.

Nahum had come to town to tell people about the stone, and had dropped in at Ammi Pierce's on the way. Ammi was forty then, and all the queer things were fixed very strongly in his mind. He and his wife had gone with the three professors from Miskatonic University who hastened out the next morning to see the weird visitor from unknown stellar space, and had wondered why Nahum had called it so large the day before. It had shrunk, Nahum said as he pointed out the big brownish mound above the ripped earth and charred grass near the archaic well-sweep in his front yard; but the wise men answered that stones do not shrink. Its heat lingered persistently, and Nahum declared it had glowed faintly in the night. The professors tried it with a geologist's hammer and found it was oddly soft. It was, in truth, so soft as to be almost plastic; and they gouged rather than chipped a specimen to take back to the college for testing. They took it in an old pail borrowed from Nahum's kitchen, for even the small piece refused to grow cool. On the trip back they stopped at Ammi's to rest, and seemed thoughtful when Mrs. Pierce remarked that the fragment was growing smaller and burning the bottom of the pail. Truly, it was not large, but perhaps they had taken less than they thought.

The day after that—all this was in June of '82—the professors had trooped out again in a great excitement. As they passed Ammi's they told him what queer things the specimen had done, and how it had faded wholly away when they put it in a glass beaker. The beaker had gone, too, and the wise men talked of the strange stone's affinity for silicon. It had acted quite unbelievably in that well-ordered laboratory; doing nothing at all and shewing no occluded gases when heated on charcoal, being wholly negative in the borax bead, and soon proving itself absolutely non-volatile at any producible temperature, including that of the oxy-hydrogen blowpipe. On an anvil it appeared highly malleable, and in the dark its luminosity was very marked. Stubbornly refusing to grow cool, it soon had the college in a state of real excitement; and when upon heating before the spectroscope it displayed shining bands unlike any known colors of the normal spectrum there was much breathless talk of new elements, bizarre optical properties, and other things which puzzled men of science are wont to say when faced by the unknown.

Hot as it was, they tested it in a crucible with all the proper reagents. Water did nothing. Hydrochloric acid was the same. Nitric acid and even aqua regia merely hissed and spattered against its torrid invulnerability. Ammi had difficulty in recalling all these things, but recognized some solvents as I mentioned them in the usual order of use. There were ammonia and caustic soda, alcohol and ether, nauseous carbon disulphide and a dozen others; but although the weight grew steadily less as time passed, and the fragment seemed to be slightly cooling, there was no change in the solvents to shew that they had attacked the substance at all. It was a metal, though, beyond a doubt. It was magnetic, for one thing;

and after its immersion in the acid solvents there seemed to be faint traces of the Widmannstätten figures found on meteoric iron. When the cooling had grown very considerable, the testing was carried on in glass; and it was in a glass beaker that they left all the chips made of the original fragment during the work. The next morning both chips and beaker were gone without trace, and only a charred spot marked the place on the wooden shelf where they had been.

All this the professors told Ammi as they paused at his door, and once more he went with them to see the stony messenger from the stars, though this time his wife did not accompany him. It had now most certainly shrunk, and even the sober professors could not doubt the truth of what they saw. All around the dwindling brown lump near the well was a vacant space, except where the earth had caved in; and whereas it had been a good seven feet across the day before, it was now scarcely five. It was still hot, and the sages studied its surface curiously as they detached another and larger piece with hammer and chisel. They gouged deeply this time, and as they pried away the smaller mass they saw that the core of the thing was not quite homogeneous.

They had uncovered what seemed to be the side of a large colored globule imbedded in the substance. The color, which resembled some of the bands in the meteor's strange spectrum, was almost impossible to describe; and it was only by analogy that they called it color at all. Its texture was glossy, and upon tapping it appeared to promise both brittleness and hollowness. One of the professors gave it a smart blow with a hammer, and it burst with a nervous little pop. Nothing was emitted, and all trace of the thing vanished with the puncturing. It left behind a hollow spherical space about three inches across, and all thought it probable that others would be discovered as the enclosing substance wasted away.

Conjecture was vain; so after a futile attempt to find additional globules by drilling, the seekers left again with their new specimen—which proved, however, as baffling in the laboratory as its predecessor had been. Aside from being almost plastic, having heat, magnetism, and slight luminosity, cooling slightly in powerful acids, possessing an unknown spectrum, wasting away in air, and attacking silicon compounds with mutual destruction as a result, it presented no identifying features whatsoever; and at the end of the tests the college scientists were forced to own that they could not place it. It was nothing of this earth, but a piece of the great outside; and as such dowered with outside properties and obedient to outside laws.

That night there was a thunderstorm, and when the professors went out to Nahum's the next day they met with a bitter disappointment. The stone, magnetic as it had been, must have had some peculiar electrical property; for it had "drawn the lightning," as Nahum said, with a singular persistence. Six times within an hour the farmer saw the lightning strike the furrow in the front yard, and when the storm was over nothing remained but a ragged pit by the ancient well-sweep, half-choked with caved-in earth. Digging had borne no fruit, and the scientists verified the fact of the utter vanishment. The failure was total; so that nothing was left to do but go back to the laboratory and test again the disappearing fragment left carefully cased in lead. That fragment lasted a week, at the end of which nothing of value had been learned of it. When it had gone, no residue was left behind, and in time the professors felt scarcely sure they had indeed seen with waking eyes that cryptic vestige of the fathomless gulfs outside; that lone, weird message from other universes and other realms of matter, force, and entity.

As was natural, the Arkham papers made much of the incident with its collegiate sponsoring, and sent reporters to talk with Nahum Gardner and his family. At least one Boston daily also sent a scribe, and Nahum quickly became a kind of local celebrity. He was a lean, genial person of about fifty, living with his wife and three sons on the pleasant farmstead in the valley. He and Ammi exchanged visits frequently, as did their wives; and Ammi had nothing but praise for him after all these years. He seemed slightly proud of the notice his place had attracted, and talked often of the meteorite in the succeeding weeks. That July and August were hot, and Nahum worked hard at his haying in the ten-acre pasture across Chapman's Brook; his rattling wain wearing deep ruts in the shadowy lanes between. The labor tired him more than it had in other years, and he felt that age was beginning to tell on him.

Then fell the time of fruit and harvest. The pears and apples slowly ripened, and Nahum vowed that his orchards were prospering as never before. The fruit was growing to phenomenal size and unwonted gloss, and in such abundance that extra barrels were ordered to handle the future crop. But with the ripening came sore disappointment; for of all that gorgeous array of specious lusciousness not one single jot was fit to eat. Into the fine flavor of the pears and apples had crept a stealthy bitterness and sickishness, so that even the smallest of bites induced a lasting disgust. It was the same with the melons and tomatoes, and Nahum sadly saw that his entire crop was lost. Quick to connect events, he declared that the meteorite had poisoned the soil, and thanked heaven that most of the other crops were in the upland lot along the road.

Winter came early, and was very cold. Ammi saw Nahum less often than usual, and observed that he had begun to look worried. The rest of his family, too, seemed to have grown taciturn; and were far from steady in their churchgoing or their attendance at the various social events of the countryside. For this reserve or melancholy no cause could be found, though all the household confessed now and then to poorer health and a feeling of vague disquiet. Nahum himself gave the most definite statement of anyone when he said he was disturbed about certain footprints in the snow. They were the usual winter prints of red squirrels, white rabbits, and foxes, but the brooding farmer professed to see something not quite right about their nature and arrangement. He was never specific, but appeared to think that they were not as characteristic of the anatomy and habits of squirrels and rabbits and foxes as they ought to be. Ammi listened without interest to this talk until one night when he drove past Nahum's house in his sleigh on the way back from Clark's Corners. There had been a moon, and a rabbit had run across the road, and the leaps of that rabbit were longer than either Ammi or his horse liked. The latter, indeed, had almost run away when brought up by a firm rein. Thereafter Ammi gave Nahum's tales more respect, and wondered why the Gardner dogs seemed so cowed and quivering every morning. They had, it developed, nearly lost the spirit to bark.

In February the McGregor boys from Meadow Hill were out shooting woodchucks, and not far from the Gardner place bagged a very peculiar specimen. The proportions of its body seemed slightly altered in a queer way impossible to describe, while its face had taken on an expression which no one ever saw in a woodchuck before. The boys were genuinely frightened, and threw the thing away at once, so that only their grotesque tales of it ever reached the people of the countryside. But the shying of the horses near Nahum's house had now become an acknowledged thing, and all the basis for a cycle of whispered legend was fast taking form.

People vowed that the snow melted faster around Nahum's than it did anywhere else, and early in March there was an awed discussion in Potter's general store at Clark's Corners. Stephen Rice had driven past Gardner's in the morning, and had noticed the skunk-cabbages coming up through the mud by the woods across the road. Never were things of such size seen before, and they held strange colors that could not be put into any words. Their shapes were monstrous, and the horse had snorted at an odor which struck Stephen as wholly unprecedented. That afternoon several persons drove past to see the abnormal growth, and all agreed that plants of that kind ought never to sprout in a healthy world. The bad fruit of the fall before was freely mentioned, and it went from mouth to mouth that there was poison in Nahum's ground. Of course it was the meteorite; and remembering how strange the men from the college had found that stone to be, several farmers spoke about the matter to them.

One day they paid Nahum a visit; but having no love of wild tales and folklore were very conservative in what they inferred. The plants were certainly odd, but all skunk-cabbages are more or less odd in shape and odor and hue. Perhaps some mineral element from the stone had entered the soil, but it would soon be washed away. And as for the footprints and frightened horses—of course this was mere country talk which such a phenomenon as the aërolite would be certain to start. There was really nothing for serious men to do in cases of wild gossip, for superstitious rustics will say and believe anything. And so all through the strange days the professors stayed away in contempt. Only one of them, when given two phials of dust for analysis in a police job over a year and a half later, recalled that the queer color of that skunk-cabbage had been very like one of the anomalous bands of light shewn by the meteor fragment in the college spectroscope, and like the brittle globule found imbedded in the stone from the abyss. The samples in this analysis case gave the same odd bands at first, though later they lost the property.

The trees budded prematurely around Nahum's, and at night they swayed ominously in the wind. Nahum's second son Thaddeus, a lad of fifteen, swore that they swayed also when there was no wind; but even the gossips would not credit this. Certainly, however, restlessness was in the air. The entire Gardner family developed the habit of stealthy listening, though not for any sound which they could consciously name. The listening was, indeed, rather a product of moments when consciousness seemed half to slip away. Unfortunately such moments increased week by week, till it became common speech that "something was wrong with all Nahum's folks." When the early saxifrage came out it had another strange color; not quite like that of the skunk-cabbage, but plainly related and equally unknown to anyone who saw it. Nahum took some blossoms to Arkham and shewed them to the editor of the *Gazette,* but that dignitary did no more than write a humorous article about them, in which the dark fears of rustics were held up to polite ridicule. It was a mistake of Nahum's to tell a stolid city man about the way the great, overgrown mourning-cloak butterflies behaved in connexion with these saxifrages.

April brought a kind of madness to the country folk, and began that disuse of the road past Nahum's which led to its ultimate abandonment. It was the vegetation. All the orchard trees blossomed forth in strange colors, and through the stony soil of the yard and adjacent pasturage there sprang up a bizarre growth which only a botanist could connect with the proper flora of the region. No sane wholesome colors were anywhere to be seen except in the green grass and leafage; but everywhere those hectic and prismatic variants of some diseased, underlying primary tone without a place among the known tints of earth. The Dutchman's breeches became a thing of sinister menace, and the bloodroots grew insolent in their chromatic perversion. Ammi and the Gardners thought that most of the colors had a sort of haunting familiarity, and decided that they reminded one of the brittle globule in the meteor. Nahum plowed and sowed the ten-acre pasture and the upland lot, but did nothing with the land around the house. He knew it would be of no use, and hoped that the summer's strange growths would draw all the poison from the soil. He was prepared for almost anything now, and had grown used to the sense of something near him waiting to be heard. The shunning of his house by neighbors told on him, of course; but it told on his wife more. The boys were better off, being at school each day; but they could not help being frightened by the gossip. Thaddeus, an especially sensitive youth, suffered the most.

In May the insects came, and Nahum's place became a nightmare of buzzing and crawling. Most of the creatures seemed not quite usual in their aspects and motions, and their nocturnal habits contradicted all former experience. The Gardners took to watching at night—watching in all directions at random for something . . . they could not tell what. It was then that they all owned that Thaddeus had been right about the trees. Mrs. Gardner was the next to see it from the window as she watched the swollen boughs of a maple against a moonlit sky. The boughs surely moved, and there was no wind. It must be the sap. Strangeness had come into everything growing now. Yet it was none of Nahum's family at all who made the next discovery. Familiarity had dulled them, and what they could not see was glimpsed by a timid windmill salesman from Bolton who drove by one night in ignorance of the country legends. What he told in Arkham was given a short paragraph in the *Gazette;* and it was there that all the farmers, Nahum included, saw it first. The night had been dark and the buggy-lamps faint, but around a farm in the valley which everyone knew from the account must be Nahum's the darkness had been less thick. A dim though distinct luminosity seemed to inhere in all the vegetation, grass, leaves, and blossoms alike, while at one moment a detached piece of the phosphorescence appeared to stir furtively in the yard near the barn.

The grass had so far seemed untouched, and the cows were freely pastured in the lot near the house, but toward the end of May the milk began to be bad. Then Nahum had the cows driven to the uplands, after which the trouble ceased. Not long after this the change in grass and leaves became apparent to the eye. All the verdure was going gray, and was developing a highly singular quality of brittleness. Ammi was now the only person who ever visited the place, and his visits were becoming fewer and fewer. When school closed the Gardners were virtually cut off from the world, and sometimes let Ammi do their errands in town. They were failing curiously both physically and mentally, and no one was surprised when the news of Mrs. Gardner's madness stole around.

It happened in June, about the anniversary of the meteor's fall, and the poor woman screamed about things in the air which she could not describe. In her raving there was not a single specific noun, but only verbs and pronouns. Things moved and changed and fluttered, and ears tingled to impulses which were not wholly sounds. Something was taken away—she was being drained of something—something was fastening itself on her that ought not to be—someone must make it keep off—nothing was ever still in the night—the walls and windows shifted. Nahum did not send her to the county asylum, but let her wander about the house as long as she was harmless to herself and others. Even when her expression changed he did nothing. But when the boys grew afraid of her, and Thaddeus nearly fainted at the way she made faces at him, he decided to keep her locked in the attic. By July she had ceased to speak and crawled on all fours, and before that month was over Nahum got the mad notion that she was slightly luminous in the dark, as he now clearly saw was the case with the nearby vegetation.

It was a little before this that the horses had stampeded. Something had aroused them in the night, and their neighing and kicking in their stalls had been terrible. There seemed virtually nothing to do to calm them, and when Nahum opened the stable door they all bolted out like frightened woodland deer. It took a week to track all four, and when found they were seen to be quite useless and unmanageable. Something had snapped in their brains, and each one had to be shot for its own good. Nahum borrowed a horse from Ammi for his haying, but found it would not approach the barn. It shied, balked, and whinnied, and in the end he could do nothing but drive it into the yard while the men used their own strength to get the heavy wagon near enough the hayloft for convenient pitching.

And all the while the vegetation was turning gray and brittle. Even the flowers whose hues had been so strange were graying now, and the fruit was coming out gray and dwarfed and tasteless. The asters and goldenrod bloomed gray and distorted, and the roses and zinneas and hollyhocks in the front yard were such blasphemous-looking things that Nahum's oldest boy Zenas cut them down. The strangely puffed insects died about that time, even the bees that had left their hives and taken to the woods.

By September all the vegetation was fast crumbling to a grayish powder, and Nahum feared that the trees would die before the poison was out of the soil. His wife now had spells of terrific screaming, and he and the boys were in a constant state of nervous tension. They shunned people now, and when school opened the boys did not go. But it was Ammi, on one of his rare visits, who first realized that the well water was no longer good. It had an evil taste that was not exactly fetid nor exactly salty, and Ammi advised his friend to dig another well on higher ground to use till the soil was good again. Nahum, however, ignored the warning, for he had by that time become calloused to strange and unpleasant things. He and the boys continued to use the tainted supply, drinking it as listlessly and mechanically as they ate their meager and ill-cooked meals and did their thankless and monotonous chores through the aimless days. There was something of stolid resignation about them all, as if they walked half in another world between lines of nameless guards to a certain and familiar doom.

Thaddeus went mad in September after a visit to the well. He had gone with a pail and had come back empty-handed, shrieking and waving his arms, and sometimes lapsing into an inane titter or a whisper about "the moving colors down there." Two in one family was pretty bad, but Nahum was very brave about it. He let the boy run about for a week until he began stumbling and hurting himself, and then he shut him in an attic room across the hall from his mother's. The way they screamed at each other from behind their locked doors was very terrible, especially to little Merwin, who fancied they talked in some terrible language that was not of earth. Merwin was getting frightfully imaginative, and his restlessness was worse after the shutting away of the brother who had been his greatest playmate.

Almost at the same time the mortality among the livestock commenced. Poultry turned grayish and died very quickly, their meat being found dry and noisome upon cutting. Hogs grew inordinately fat, then suddenly began to undergo loathsome changes which no one could explain. Their meat was of course useless, and Nahum was at his wit's end. No rural veterinary would approach his place, and the city veterinary from Arkham was openly baffled. The swine began growing gray and brittle and falling to pieces before they died, and their eyes and muzzles developed singular alterations. It was very inexplicable, for they had never been fed from the tainted vegetation. Then something struck the cows. Certain areas or sometimes the whole body would be uncannily shriveled or compressed, and atrocious collapses or disintegrations were common. In the last stages—and death was always the result—there would be a graying and turning brittle like that which beset the hogs. There could be no question of poison, for all the cases occurred in a locked and undisturbed barn. No bites of prowling things could have brought the virus, for what live beast of earth can pass through solid obstacles? It must be only natural disease—yet what disease could wreak such results was beyond any mind's guessing. When the harvest came there was not an animal surviving on the place, for the stock and poultry were dead and the dogs had run away. These dogs, three in number, had all vanished one night and were never heard of again. The five cats had left some time before, but their going was scarcely noticed since there now seemed to be no mice, and only Mrs. Gardner had made pets of the graceful felines.

On the nineteenth of October Nahum staggered into Ammi's house with hideous news. The death had come to poor Thaddeus in his attic room, and it had come in a way which could not be told. Nahum had dug a grave in the railed family plot behind the farm, and had put therein what he found. There could have been nothing from outside, for the small barred window and locked door were intact; but it was much as it had been in the barn. Ammi and his wife consoled the stricken man as best they could, but shuddered as they did so. Stark terror seemed to cling round the Gardners and all they touched, and the very presence of one in the house was a breath from regions unnamed and unnamable. Ammi accompanied Nahum home with the greatest reluctance, and did what he might to calm the hysterical sobbing of little Merwin. Zenas needed no calming. He had come of late to do nothing but stare into space and obey what his father told him; and Ammi thought that his fate was very merciful. Now and then Merwin's screams were answered faintly from the attic, and in response to an inquiring look Nahum said that his wife was getting very feeble. When night approached, Ammi managed to get away; for not even friendship could make him stay in that spot when the faint glow of the vegetation began and the trees may or may not have swayed without wind. It was really lucky for Ammi that he was not more imaginative. Even as things were, his mind was bent ever so slightly; but had he been able to connect and reflect upon all the portents around him he must inevitably have turned a total maniac. In the twilight he hastened home, the screams of the mad woman and the nervous child ringing horribly in his ears.

Three days later Nahum lurched into Ammi's kitchen in the early morning, and in the absence of his host stammered out a desperate tale once more, while Mrs. Pierce listened in a clutching fright. It was little Merwin this time. He was gone. He had gone out late at night with a lantern and pail for water, and had never come back. He'd been going to pieces for days, and hardly knew what he was about. Screamed at everything. There had been a frantic shriek from the yard then, but before the father could get to the door, the boy was gone. There was no glow from the lantern he had taken, and of the child himself no trace. At the time Nahum thought the lantern and pail were gone too; but when dawn came, and the man had plodded back from his all-night search of the woods and fields, he had found some very curious things near the well. There was a crushed and apparently somewhat melted mass of iron which had certainly been the lantern; while a bent bail and twisted iron hoops beside it, both half-fused, seemed to hint at the remnants of the pail. That was all. Nahum was past imagining, Mrs. Pierce was blank, and Ammi, when he had reached home and heard the tale, could give no guess. Merwin was gone, and there would be no use in telling the people around, who shunned all Gardners now. No use, either, in telling the city people at Arkham who laughed at everything. Thad was gone, and now Merwin was gone. Something was creeping and creeping and waiting to be seen and felt and heard. Nahum would go soon, and he wanted Ammi to look after his wife and Zenas if they survived him. It must all be a judgment of some sort; though he could not fancy what for, since he had always walked uprightly in the Lord's ways so far as he knew.

For over two weeks Ammi saw nothing of Nahum; and then, worried about what might have happened, he overcame his fears and paid the Gardner place a visit. There was no smoke from the great chimney, and for a moment the visitor was apprehensive of the worst. The aspect of the whole farm was shocking—grayish withered grass and leaves on the ground, vines falling in brittle wreckage from archaic walls and gables, and great bare trees clawing up at the gray November sky with a studied malevolence which Ammi could not but feel had come from some subtle change in the tilt of the branches. But Nahum was alive, after all.

He was weak, and lying on a couch in the low-ceiled kitchen, but perfectly conscious and able to give simple orders to Zenas. The room was deadly cold; and as Ammi visibly shivered, the host shouted huskily to Zenas for more wood. Wood, indeed, was sorely needed; since the cavernous fireplace was unlit and empty, with a cloud of soot blowing about in the chill wind that came down the chimney. Presently Nahum asked him if the extra wood had made him any more comfortable, and then Ammi saw what had happened. The stoutest cord had broken at last, and the hapless farmer's mind was proof against more sorrow.

Questioning tactfully, Ammi could get no clear data at all about the missing Zenas. "In the well—he lives in the well—" was all that the clouded father would say. Then there flashed across the visitor's mind a sudden thought of the mad wife, and he changed his line of inquiry. "Nabby? Why, here she is!" was the surprised response of poor Nahum, and Ammi soon saw that he must search for himself. Leaving the harmless babbler on the couch, he took the keys from their nail beside the door and climbed the creaking stairs to the attic. It was very close and noisome up there, and no sound could be heard from any direction. Of the four doors in sight, only one was locked, and on this he tried various keys on the ring he had taken. The third key proved the right one, and after some fumbling Ammi threw open the low white door.

It was quite dark inside, for the window was small and half-obscured by the crude wooden bars; and Ammi could see nothing at all on the wide-planked floor. The stench was beyond enduring, and before proceeding further he had to retreat to another room and return with his lungs filled with breathable air. When he did enter he saw something dark in the corner, and upon seeing it more clearly he screamed outright. While he screamed he thought a momentary cloud eclipsed the window, and a second later he felt himself brushed as if by some hateful current of vapor. Strange colors danced before his eyes; and had not a present horror numbed him he would have thought of the globule in the meteor that the geologist's hammer had shattered, and of the morbid vegetation that had sprouted in the spring. As it was he thought only of the blasphemous monstrosity which confronted him, and which all too clearly had shared the nameless fate of young Thaddeus and the livestock. But the terrible thing about this horror was that it very slowly and perceptibly moved as it continued to crumble.

Ammi would give me no added particulars to this scene, but the shape in the corner does not reappear in his tale as a moving object. There are things which cannot be mentioned, and what is done in common humanity is sometimes cruelly judged by the law. I gathered that no moving thing was left in that attic room, and that to leave anything capable of motion there would have been a deed so monstrous as to damn any accountable being to eternal torment. Anyone but a stolid farmer would have fainted or gone mad, but Ammi walked conscious through that low doorway and locked the accursed secret behind him. There would be Nahum to deal with now; he must be fed and tended, and removed to some place where he could be cared for.

Commencing his descent of the dark stairs, Ammi heard a thud below him. He even thought a scream had been suddenly choked off, and recalled nervously the clammy vapor which had brushed by him in that frightful room above. What presence had his cry and entry started up? Halted by some vague fear, he heard still further sounds below. Indubitably there was a sort of heavy dragging, and a most detestably sticky noise as of some fiendish and unclean species of suction. With an associative sense goaded to feverish heights, he thought unaccountably of what he had seen upstairs. Good God! What eldritch dream-world was this into which he had blundered? He dared move neither backward nor forward, but stood there trembling at the black curve of the boxed-in staircase. Every trifle of the scene burned itself into his brain. The sounds, the sense of dread expectancy, the darkness, the steepness of the narrow steps—and merciful heaven! . . . the faint but unmistakable luminosity of all the woodwork in sight; steps, sides, exposed laths, and beams alike!

Then there burst forth a frantic whinny from Ammi's horse outside, followed at once by a clatter which told of a frenzied runaway. In another moment horse and buggy had gone beyond earshot, leaving the frightened man on the dark stairs to guess what had sent them. But that was not all. There had been another sound out there. A sort of liquid splash—water—it must have been the well. He had left Hero untied near it, and a buggy-wheel must have brushed the coping and knocked in a stone. And still the pale phosphorescence glowed in that detestably ancient woodwork. God! how old the house was! Most of it built before 1670, and the gambrel roof not later than 1730.

A feeble scratching on the floor downstairs now sounded distinctly, and Ammi's grip tightened on a heavy stick he had picked up in the attic for some purpose. Slowly nerving himself, he finished his descent and walked boldly toward the kitchen. But he did not complete the walk, because what he sought was no longer there. It had come to meet him, and it was still alive after a fashion. Whether it had crawled or whether it had been dragged by any external force, Ammi could not say; but the death had been at it. Everything had happened in the last half-hour, but collapse, graying, and disintegration were already far advanced. There was a horrible brittleness, and dry fragments were scaling off. Ammi could not touch it, but looked horrifiedly into the distorted parody that had been a face. "What was it, Nahum—what was it?" he whispered, and the cleft, bulging lips were just able to crackle out a final answer.

"Nothin' . . . nothin' . . . the color . . . it burns . . . cold an' wet . . . but it burns . . . it lived in the well . . . I seen it . . . a kind o' smoke . . . jest like the flowers last spring . . . the well shone at night . . . Thad an' Mernie an' Zenas . . . everything alive . . . suckin' the life out of everything . . . in that stone . . . it must a' come in that stone . . . pizened the whole place . . . dun't know what it wants . . . that round thing them men from the college dug outen the stone . . . they smashed it . . . it was that same color . . . jest the same, like the flowers an' plants . . . must a' ben more of 'em . . . seeds . . . seeds . . . they growed . . . I seen it the fust time this week . . . must a' got strong on Zenas . . . he was a big boy, full o' life . . . it beats down your mind an' then gits ye . . . burns ye up . . . in the well water . . . you was right about that . . . evil water . . . Zenas never come back from the well . . . can't git away . . . draws ye . . . ye know summ'at's comin', but 'tain't no use . . . I seen it time an' agin senct Zenas was took . . . whar's Nabby, Ammi? . . . my head's no good . . . dun't know how long senct I fed her . . . it'll git her ef we ain't keerful . . . jest a color . . . her face is gettin' to hev that color sometimes towards night . . . an' it burns an' sucks . . . it come from some place whar things ain't as they is here . . . one o' them professors said so . . . he was right . . . look out, Ammi, it'll do suthin' more . . . sucks the life out . . ."

But that was all. That which spoke could speak no more because it had completely caved in. Ammi laid a red checked tablecloth over what was left and reeled out the back door into the fields. He climbed the slope to the ten-acre pasture and stumbled home by the north road and the woods. He could not pass that well from which his horse had run away. He had looked at it through the window, and had seen that no stone was missing from the rim. Then the lurching buggy had not dislodged anything after all—the splash had been something else—something which went into the well after it had done with poor Nahum . . .

When Ammi reached his house the horse and buggy had arrived before him and thrown his wife into fits of anxiety. Reassuring her without explanations, he set out at once for Arkham and notified the authorities that the Gardner family was no more. He indulged in no details, but merely told of the deaths of Nahum and Nabby, that of Thaddeus being already known, and mentioned that the cause seemed to be the same strange ailment which had killed the livestock. He also stated that Merwin and Zenas had disappeared. There was considerable questioning at the police station, and in the end Ammi was compelled to take three officers to the Gardner farm, together with the coroner, the medical examiner, and the veterinary who had treated the diseased animals. He went much against his will, for the afternoon was advancing and he feared the fall of night over that accursed place, but it was some comfort to have so many people with him.

The six men drove out in a democrat-wagon, following Ammi's buggy, and arrived at the pest-ridden farmhouse about four o'clock. Used as the officers were to gruesome experiences, not one remained unmoved at what was found in the attic and under the red checked tablecloth on the floor below. The whole aspect of the farm with its gray desolation was terrible enough, but those two crumbling objects were beyond all bounds. No one could look long at them, and even the medical examiner admitted that there was very little to examine. Specimens could be analyzed, of course, so he busied himself in obtaining them—and here it develops that a very puzzling aftermath occurred at the college laboratory where the two phials of dust were finally taken. Under the spectroscope both samples gave off an unknown spectrum, in which many of the baffling bands were precisely like those which the strange meteor had yielded in the previous year. The property of emitting this spectrum vanished in a month, the dust thereafter consisting mainly of alkaline phosphates and carbonates.

Ammi would not have told the men about the well if he had thought they meant to do anything then and there. It was getting toward sunset, and he was anxious to be away. But he could not help glancing nervously at the stony curb by the great sweep, and when a detective questioned him he admitted that Nahum had feared something down there—so much so that he had never even thought of searching it for Merwin or Zenas. After that nothing would do but that they empty and explore the well immediately, so Ammi had to wait trembling while pail after pail of rank water was hauled up and splashed on the soaking ground outside. The men sniffed in disgust at the fluid, and toward the last held their noses against the fetor they were uncovering. It was not so long a job as they had feared it would be, since the water was phenomenally low. There is no need to speak too exactly of what they found. Merwin and Zenas were both there, in part, though the vestiges were mainly skeletal. There were also a small deer and a large dog in about the same state, and a number of bones of smaller animals. The ooze and slime at the bottom seemed inexplicably porous and bubbling, and a man who descended on hand-holds with a long pole found that he could sink the wooden shaft to any depth in the mud of the floor without meeting any solid obstruction.

Twilight had now fallen, and lanterns were brought from the house. Then, when it was seen that nothing further could be gained from the well, everyone went indoors and conferred in the ancient sitting-room while the intermittent light of a spectral half-moon played wanly on the gray desolation outside. The men were frankly nonplussed by the entire case, and could find no convincing common element to link the strange vegetable conditions, the unknown disease of livestock and humans, and the unaccountable deaths of Merwin and Zenas in the tainted well. They had heard the common country talk, it is true; but could not believe that anything contrary to natural law had occurred. No doubt the meteor had poisoned the soil, but the illness of persons and animals who had eaten nothing grown in that soil was another matter. Was it the well water? Very possibly. It might be a good idea to analyze it. But what peculiar madness could have made both boys jump into the well? Their deeds were so similar—and the fragments shewed that they had both suffered from the gray brittle death. Why was everything so gray and brittle?

It was the coroner, seated near a window overlooking the yard, who first noticed the glow about the well. Night had fully set in, and all the abhorrent grounds seemed faintly luminous with more than the fitful moonbeams; but this new glow was something definite and distinct, and appeared to shoot up from the black pit like a softened ray from a searchlight, giving dull reflections in the little ground pools where the water had been emptied. It had a very queer color, and as all the men clustered round the window Ammi gave a violent start. For this strange beam of ghastly miasma was to him of no unfamiliar hue. He had seen that color before, and feared to think what it might mean. He had seen it in the nasty brittle globule in that aërolite two summers ago, had seen it in the crazy vegetation of the springtime, and had thought he had seen it for an instant that very morning against the small barred window of that terrible attic room where nameless things had happened. It had flashed there a second, and a clammy and hateful current of vapor had brushed past him—and then poor Nahum had been taken by something of that color. He had said so at the last—said it was the globule and the plants. After that had come the runaway in the yard and the splash in the well—and now that well was belching forth to the night a pale insidious beam of the same daemoniac tint.

It does credit to the alertness of Ammi's mind that he puzzled even at that tense moment over a point which was essentially scientific. He could not but wonder at his gleaning of the same impression from a vapor glimpsed in the daytime, against a window opening on the morning sky, and from a nocturnal exhalation seen as a phosphorescent mist against the black and blasted landscape. It wasn't right—it was against Nature—and he thought of those terrible last words of his stricken friend, "It come from some place whar things ain't as they is here . . . one o' them professors said so . . ."

All three horses outside, tied to a pair of shriveled saplings by the road, were now neighing and pawing frantically. The wagon driver started for the door to do something, but Ammi laid a shaky hand on his shoulder. "Dun't go out thar," he whispered. "They's more to this nor what we know. Nahum said somethin' lived in the well that sucks your life out. He said it must be some'at growed from a round ball like one we all seen in the meteor stone that fell a year ago June. Sucks an' burns, he said, an' is jest a cloud of color like that light out thar now, that ye can hardly see an' can't tell what it is. Nahum thought it feeds on everything livin' an' gits stronger all the time. He said he seen it this last week. It must be somethin' from away off in the sky like the men from the college last year says the meteor stone was. The way it's made an' the way it works ain't like no way o' God's world. It's some'at from beyond."

So the men paused indecisively as the light from the well grew stronger and the hitched horses pawed and whinnied in increasing frenzy. It was truly an awful moment; with terror in that ancient and accursed house itself, four monstrous sets of fragments—two from the house and two from the well—in the woodshed behind, and that shaft of unknown and unholy iridescence from the slimy depths in front. Ammi had restrained the driver on impulse, forgetting how uninjured he himself was after the clammy brushing of that colored vapor in the attic room, but perhaps it is just as well that he acted as he did. No one will ever know what was abroad that night; and though the blasphemy from beyond had not so far hurt any human of unweakened mind, there is no telling what it might not have done at that last moment, and with its seemingly increased strength and the special signs of purpose it was soon to display beneath the half-clouded moonlit sky.

All at once one of the detectives at the window gave a short, sharp gasp. The others looked at him, and then quickly followed his own gaze upward to the point at which its idle straying had been suddenly arrested. There was no need for words. What had been disputed in country gossip was disputable no longer, and it is because of the thing which every man of that party agreed in whispering later on that the strange days are never talked about in Arkham. It is necessary to premise that there was no wind at that hour of the evening. One did arise not long afterward, but there was absolutely none then. Even the dry tips of the lingering hedge-mustard, gray and blighted, and the fringe on the roof of the standing democrat-wagon were unstirred. And yet amid that tense, godless calm the high bare boughs of all the trees in the yard were moving. They were twitching morbidly and spasmodically, clawing in convulsive and epileptic madness at the moonlit clouds; scratching impotently in the noxious air as if jerked by some alien and bodiless line of linkage with subterrene horrors writhing and struggling below the black roots.

Not a man breathed for several seconds. Then a cloud of darker depth passed over the moon, and the silhouette of clutching branches faded out momentarily. At this there was a general cry; muffled with awe, but husky and almost identical from every throat. For the terror had not faded with the silhouette, and in a fearsome instant of deeper darkness the watchers saw wriggling at that treetop height a thousand tiny points of faint and unhallowed radiance, tipping each bough like the fire of St. Elmo or the flames that came down on the apostles' heads at Pentecost. It was a monstrous constellation of unnatural light, like a glutted swarm of corpse-fed fireflies dancing hellish sarabands over an accursed marsh; and its color was that same nameless intrusion which Ammi had come to recognize and dread. All the while the shaft of phosphorescence from the well was getting brighter and brighter, bringing to the minds of the huddled men a sense of doom and abnormality which far outraced any image their conscious minds could form. It was no longer *shining* out, it was *pouring* out; and as the shapeless stream of unplaceable color left the well it seemed to flow directly into the sky.

The veterinary shivered, and walked to the front door to drop the heavy extra bar across it. Ammi shook no less, and had to tug and point for lack of a controllable voice when he wished to draw notice to the growing luminosity of the trees. The neighing and stamping of the horses had become utterly frightful, but not a soul of that group in the old house would have ventured forth for any earthly reward. With the moments the shining of the trees increased, while their restless branches seemed to strain more and more toward verticality. The wood of the well-sweep was shining now, and presently a policeman dumbly pointed to some wooden sheds and bee-hives near the stone wall on the west. They were commencing to shine, too, though the tethered vehicles of the visitors seemed so far unaffected. Then there was a wild commotion and clopping in the road, and as Ammi quenched the lamp for better seeing they realized that the span of frantic grays had broke their sapling and run off with the democrat-wagon.

The shock served to loosen several tongues, and embarrassed whispers were exchanged. "It spreads on everything organic that's been around here," muttered the medical examiner. No one replied, but the man who had been in the well gave a hint that his long pole must have stirred up something intangible. "It was awful," he added. "There was no bottom at all. Just ooze and bubbles and the feeling of something lurking under there." Ammi's horse still pawed and screamed deafeningly in the road outside, and nearly drowned its owner's faint quaver as he mumbled his formless reflections. "It come from that stone . . . it growed down thar . . . it got everything livin' . . . it fed itself on 'em, mind and body . . . Thad an' Mernie, Zenas an' Nabby . . . Nahum was the last . . . they all drunk the water . . . it got strong on 'em . . . it come from beyond, whar things ain't like they be here . . . now it's goin' home . . ."

At this point, as the column of unknown color flared suddenly stronger and began to weave itself into fantastic suggestions of shape which each spectator later described differently, there came from poor tethered Hero such a sound as no man before or since ever heard from a horse. Every person in that low-pitched sitting room stopped his ears, and Ammi turned away from the window in horror and nausea. Words could not convey it—when Ammi looked out again the hapless beast lay huddled inert on the moonlit ground between the splintered shafts of the buggy. That was the last of Hero till they buried him next day. But the present was no time to mourn, for almost at this instant a detective silently called attention to something terrible in the very room with them. In the absence of the lamplight it was clear that a faint phosphorescence had begun to pervade the entire apartment. It glowed on the broad-planked floor and the fragment of rag carpet, and shimmered over the sashes of the small-paned windows. It ran up and down the exposed corner-posts, coruscated about the shelf and mantel, and infected the very doors and furniture. Each minute saw it strengthen, and at last it was very plain that healthy living things must leave that house.

Ammi shewed them the back door and the path up through the fields to the ten-acre pasture. They walked and stumbled as in a dream, and did not dare look back till they were far away on the high ground. They were glad of the path, for they could not have gone the front way, by that well. It was bad enough passing the glowing barn and sheds, and those shining orchard trees with their gnarled, fiendish contours; but thank heaven the branches did their worst twisting high up. The moon went under some very black clouds as they crossed the rustic bridge over Chapman's Brook, and it was blind groping from there to the open meadows.

When they looked back toward the valley and the distant Gardner place at the bottom they saw a fearsome sight. All the farm was shining with the hideous unknown blend of color; trees, buildings, and even such grass and herbage as had not been wholly changed to lethal gray brittleness. The boughs were all straining skyward, tipped with tongues of foul flame, and lambent tricklings of the same monstrous fire were creeping about the ridgepoles of the house, barn, and sheds. It was a scene from a vision of Fuseli, and over all the rest reigned that riot of luminous amorphousness, that alien and undimensioned rainbow of cryptic poison from the well—seething, feeling, lapping, reaching, scintillating, straining, and malignly bubbling in its cosmic and unrecognizable chromaticism.

Then without warning the hideous thing shot vertically up toward the sky like a rocket or meteor, leaving behind no trail and disappearing through a round and curiously regular hole in the clouds before any man could gasp or cry out. No watcher can ever forget that sight, and Ammi stared blankly at the stars of Cygnus, Deneb twinkling above the others, where the unknown color had melted into the Milky Way. But his gaze was the next moment called swiftly to earth by the crackling in the valley. It was just that. Only a wooden ripping and crackling, and not an explosion, as so many others of the party vowed. Yet the outcome was the same, for in one feverish, kaleidoscopic instant there burst up from that doomed and accursed farm a gleamingly eruptive cataclysm of unnatural sparks and substance; blurring the glance of the few who saw it, and sending forth to the zenith a bombarding cloudburst of such colored and fantastic fragments as our universe must needs disown. Through quickly re-closing vapors they followed the great morbidity that had vanished, and in another second they had vanished too. Behind and below was only a darkness to which the men dared not return, and all about was a mounting wind which seemed to sweep down in black, frore gusts from interstellar space. It shrieked and howled, and lashed the fields and distorted woods in a mad cosmic frenzy, till soon the trembling party realized it would be no use waiting for the moon to shew what was left down there at Nahum's.

Too awed even to hint theories, the seven shaking men trudged back toward Arkham by the north road. Ammi was worse than his fellows, and begged them to see him inside his own kitchen, instead of keeping straight on to town. He did not wish to cross the nighted, wind-whipped woods alone to his home on the main road. For he had had an added shock that the others were spared, and was crushed forever with a brooding fear he dared not even mention for many years to come. As the rest of the watchers on that tempestuous hill had stolidly set their faces toward the road, Ammi had looked back an instant at the shadowed valley of desolation so lately sheltering his ill-starred friend. And from that stricken, far-away spot he had seen something feebly rise, only to sink down again upon the place from which the great shapeless horror had shot into the sky. It was just a color—but not any color of our earth or heavens. And because Ammi recognized that color, and knew that this last faint remnant must still lurk down there in the well, he has never been quite right since.

Ammi would never go near the place again. It is over half a century now since the horror happened, but he has never been there, and will be glad when the new reservoir blots it out. I shall be glad, too, for I do not like the way the sunlight changed color around the mouth of that abandoned well I passed. I hope the water will always be very deep—but even so, I shall never drink it. I do not think I shall visit the Arkham country hereafter. Three of the men who had been with Ammi returned the next morning to see the ruins by daylight, but there were not any real ruins. Only the bricks of the chimney, the stones of the cellar, some mineral and metallic litter here and there, and the rim of that nefandous well. Save for Ammi's dead horse, which they towed away and buried, and the buggy which they shortly returned to him, everything that had ever been living had gone. Five eldritch acres of dusty gray desert remained, nor has anything ever grown there since. To this day it sprawls open to the sky like a great spot eaten by acid in the woods and fields, and the few who have ever dared glimpse it in spite of the rural tales have named it "the blasted heath."

The rural tales are queer. They might be even queerer if city men and college chemists could be interested enough to analyze the water from that disused well, or the gray dust that no wind seems ever to disperse. Botanists, too, ought to study the stunted flora on the borders of that spot, for they might shed light on the country notion that the blight is spreading—little by little, perhaps an inch a year. People say the color of the neighboring herbage is not quite right in the spring, and that wild things leave queer prints in the light winter snow. Snow never seems quite so heavy on the blasted heath as it is elsewhere. Horses—the few that are left in this motor age—grow skittish in the silent valley; and hunters cannot depend on their dogs too near the splotch of grayish dust.

They say the mental influences are very bad, too. Numbers went queer in the years after Nahum's taking, and always they lacked the power to get away. Then the stronger-minded folk all left the region, and only the foreigners tried to live in the crumbling old homesteads. They could not stay, though; and one sometimes wonders what insight beyond ours their wild, weird stores of whispered magic have given them. Their dreams at night, they protest, are very horrible in that grotesque country; and surely the very look of the dark realm is enough to stir a morbid fancy. No traveler has ever escaped a sense of strangeness in those deep ravines, and artists shiver as they paint thick woods whose mystery is as much of the spirit as of the eye. I myself am curious about the sensation I derived from my one lone walk before Ammi told me his tale. When twilight came I had vaguely wished some clouds would gather, for an odd timidity about the deep skyey voids above had crept into my soul.

Do not ask me for my opinion. I do not know—that is all. There was no one but Ammi to question; for Arkham people will not talk about the strange days, and all three professors who saw the aërolite and its colored globule are dead. There were other globules—depend upon that. One must have fed itself and escaped, and probably there was another which was too late. No doubt it is still down the well—I know there was something wrong with the sunlight I saw above that miasmal brink. The rustics say the blight creeps an inch a year, so perhaps there is a kind of growth or nourishment even now. But whatever daemon hatchling is there, it must be tethered to something or else it would quickly spread. Is it fastened to the roots of those trees that claw the air? One of the current Arkham tales is about fat oaks that shine and move as they ought not to do at night.

What it is, only God knows. In terms of matter I suppose the thing Ammi described would be called a gas, but this gas obeyed laws that are not of our cosmos. This was no fruit of such worlds and suns as shine on the telescopes and photographic plates of our observatories. This was no breath from the skies whose motions and dimensions our astronomers measure or deem too vast to measure. It was just a color out of space—a frightful messenger from unformed realms of infinity beyond all Nature as we know it; from realms whose mere existence stuns the brain and numbs us with the black extra-cosmic gulfs it throws open before our frenzied eyes.

I doubt very much if Ammi consciously lied to me, and I do not think his tale was all a freak of madness as the townfolk had forewarned. Something terrible came to the hills and valleys on that meteor, and something terrible—though I know not in what proportion—still remains. I shall be glad to see the water come. Meanwhile I hope nothing will happen to Ammi. He saw so much of the thing—and its influence was so insidious. Why has he never been able to move away? How clearly he recalled those dying words of Nahum's—"can't git away . . . draws ye . . . ye know summ'at's comin', but 'tain't no use . . ." Ammi is such a good old man—when the reservoir gang gets to work I must write the chief engineer to keep a sharp watch on him. I would hate to think of him as the gray, twisted, brittle monstrosity which persists more and more in troubling my sleep.

The Hound

by H. P. Lovecraft

I.

In my tortured ears there sounds unceasingly a nightmare whirring and flapping, and a faint, distant baying as of some gigantic hound. It is not dream—it is not, I fear, even madness—for too much has already happened to give me these merciful doubts. St. John is a mangled corpse; I alone know why, and such is my knowledge that I am about to blow out my brains for fear I shall be mangled in the same way. Down unlit and illimitable corridors of eldritch phantasy sweeps the black, shapeless Nemesis that drives me to self-annihilation.

May heaven forgive the folly and morbidity which led us both to so monstrous a fate! Wearied with the commonplaces of a prosaic world, where even the joys of romance and adventure soon grow stale, St. John and I had followed enthusiastically every aesthetic and intellectual movement which promised respite from our devastating ennui. The enigmas of the Symbolists and the ecstasies of the pre-Raphaelites all were ours in their time, but each new mood was drained too soon of its diverting novelty and appeal. Only the somber philosophy of the Decadents could hold us, and this we found potent only by increasing gradually the depth and diabolism of our penetrations. Baudelaire and Huysmans were soon exhausted of thrills, till finally there remained for us only the more direct stimuli of unnatural personal experiences and adventures. It was this frightful emotional need which led us eventually to that detestable course which even in my present fear I mention with shame and timidity—that hideous extremity of human outrage, the abhorred practice of grave-robbing.

I cannot reveal the details of our shocking expeditions, or catalog even partly the worst of the trophies adorning the nameless museum we prepared in the great stone house where we jointly dwelt, alone and servantless. Our museum was a blasphemous, unthinkable place, where with the satanic taste of neurotic virtuosi we had assembled an universe of terror and decay to excite our jaded sensibilities. It was a secret room, far, far underground; where huge winged daemons carven of basalt and onyx vomited from wide grinning mouths weird green and orange light, and hidden pneumatic pipes ruffled into kaleidoscopic dances of death the lines of red charnel things hand in hand woven in voluminous black hangings. Through these pipes came at will the odors our moods most craved; sometimes the scent of pale funeral lilies, sometimes the narcotic incense of imagined Eastern shrines of the kingly dead, and sometimes—how I shudder to recall it!—the frightful, soul-upheaving stenches of the uncovered grave.

Around the walls of this repellent chamber were cases of antique mummies alternating with comely, life-like bodies perfectly stuffed and cured by the taxidermist's art, and with headstones snatched from the oldest churchyards of the world. Niches here and there contained skulls of all shapes, and heads preserved in various stages of dissolution. There one might find the rotting, bald pates of famous noblemen, and the fresh and radiantly golden heads of new-buried children. Statues and paintings there were, all of fiendish subjects and some executed by St. John and myself. A locked portfolio, bound in tanned human skin, held certain unknown and unnamable drawings which it was rumored Goya had perpetrated but dared not acknowledge. There were nauseous musical instruments, stringed, brass, and wood-wind, on which St. John and I sometimes produced dissonances of exquisite morbidity and cacodaemoniacal ghastliness; whilst in a multitude of inlaid ebony cabinets reposed the most incredible and unimaginable variety of tomb-loot ever assembled by human madness and perversity. It is of this loot in particular that I must not speak—thank God I had the courage to destroy it long before I thought of destroying myself.

The predatory excursions on which we collected our unmentionable treasures were always artistically memorable events. We were no vulgar ghouls, but worked only under certain conditions of mood, landscape, environment, weather, season, and moonlight. These pastimes were to us the most exquisite form of aesthetic expression, and we gave their details a fastidious technical care. An inappropriate hour, a jarring lighting effect, or a clumsy manipulation of the damp sod, would almost totally destroy for us that ecstatic titillation which followed the exhumation of some ominous, grinning secret of the earth. Our quest for novel scenes and piquant conditions was feverish and insatiate—St. John was always the leader, and he it was who led the way at last to that mocking, that accursed spot which brought us our hideous and inevitable doom.

By what malign fatality were we lured to that terrible Holland churchyard? I think it was the dark rumor and legendry, the tales of one buried for five centuries, who had himself been a ghoul in his time and had stolen a potent thing from a mighty sepulcher. I can recall the scene in these final moments—the pale autumnal moon over the graves, casting long horrible shadows; the grotesque trees, drooping sullenly to meet the neglected grass and the crumbling slabs; the vast legions of strangely colossal bats that flew against the moon; the antique ivied church pointing a huge spectral finger at the livid sky; the phosphorescent insects that danced like death-fires under the yews in a distant corner; the odors of mold, vegetation, and less explicable things that mingled feebly with the night-wind from over far swamps and seas; and worst of all, the faint deep-toned baying of some gigantic hound which we could neither see nor definitely place. As we heard this suggestion of baying we shuddered, remembering the tales of the peasantry; for he whom we sought had centuries before been found in this self-same spot, torn and mangled by the claws and teeth of some unspeakable beast.

I remembered how we delved in this ghoul's grave with our spades, and how we thrilled at the picture of ourselves, the grave, the pale watching moon, the horrible shadows, the grotesque trees, the titanic bats, the antique church, the dancing death-fires, the sickening odors, the gently moaning night-wind, and the strange, half-heard, directionless baying, of whose objective existence we could scarcely be sure. Then we struck a substance harder than the damp mold, and beheld a rotting oblong box crusted with mineral deposits from the long undisturbed ground. It was incredibly tough and thick, but so old that we finally pried it open and feasted our eyes on what it held.

Much—amazingly much—was left of the object despite the lapse of five hundred years. The skeleton, though crushed in places by the jaws of the thing that had killed it, held together with surprising firmness, and we gloated over the clean white skull and its long, firm teeth and its eyeless sockets that once had glowed with a charnel fever like our own. In the coffin lay an amulet of curious and exotic design, which had apparently been worn around the sleeper's neck. It was the oddly conventionalized figure of a crouching winged hound, or sphinx with a semi-canine face, and was exquisitely carved in antique Oriental fashion from a small piece of green jade. The expression on its features was repellent in the extreme, savoring at once of death, bestiality, and malevolence. Around the base was an inscription in characters which neither St. John nor I could identify; and on the bottom, like a maker's seal, was graven a grotesque and formidable skull.

Immediately upon beholding this amulet we knew that we must possess it; that this treasure alone was our logical pelf from the centuried grave. Even had its outlines been unfamiliar we would have desired it, but as we looked more closely we saw that it was not wholly unfamiliar. Alien it indeed was to all art and literature which sane and balanced readers know, but we recognized it as the thing hinted of in the forbidden *Necronomicon* of the mad Arab Abdul Alhazred; the ghastly soul-symbol of the corpse-eating cult of inaccessible Leng, in Central Asia. All too well did we trace the sinister lineaments described by the old Arab daemonologist; lineaments, he wrote, drawn from some obscure supernatural manifestation of the souls of those who vexed and gnawed at the dead.

Seizing the green jade object, we gave a last glance at the bleached and cavern-eyed face of its owner and closed up the grave as we found it. As we hastened from that abhorrent spot, the stolen amulet in St. John's pocket, we thought we saw the bats descend in a body to the earth we had so lately rifled, as if seeking for some cursed and unholy nourishment. But the autumn moon shone weak and pale, and we could not be sure. So, too, as we sailed the next day away from Holland to our home, we thought we heard the faint distant baying of some gigantic hound in the background. But the autumn wind moaned sad and wan, and we could not be sure.

II.

Less than a week after our return to England, strange things began to happen. We lived as recluses; devoid of friends, alone, and without servants in a few rooms of an ancient manor-house on a bleak and unfrequented moor; so that our doors were seldom disturbed by the knock of the visitor. Now, however, we were troubled by what seemed to be frequent fumblings in the night, not only around the doors but around the windows also, upper as well as lower. Once we fancied that a large, opaque body darkened the library window when the moon was shining against it, and another time we thought we heard a whirring or flapping sound not far off. On each occasion investigation revealed nothing, and we began to ascribe the occurrences to imagination alone—that same curiously disturbed imagination which still prolonged in our ears the faint far baying we thought we had heard in the Holland churchyard. The jade amulet now reposed in a niche in our museum, and sometimes we burned strangely scented candles before it. We read much in Alhazred's *Necronomicon* about its properties, and about the relation of ghouls' souls to the objects it symbolized; and were disturbed by what we read. Then terror came.

On the night of September 24, 19—, I heard a knock at my chamber door. Fancying it St. John's, I bade the knocker enter, but was answered only by a shrill laugh. There was no one in the corridor. When I aroused St. John from his sleep, he professed entire ignorance of the event, and became as worried as I. It was that night that the faint, distant baying over the moor became to us a certain and dreaded reality. Four days later, whilst we were both in the hidden museum, there came a low, cautious scratching at the single door which led to the secret library staircase. Our alarm was now divided, for besides our fear of the unknown, we had always entertained a dread that our grisly collection might be discovered. Extinguishing all lights, we proceeded to the door and threw it suddenly open; whereupon we felt an unaccountable rush of air, and heard as if receding far away a queer combination of rustling, tittering, and articulate chatter. Whether we were mad, dreaming, or in our senses, we did not try to determine. We only realized, with the blackest of apprehensions, that the apparently disembodied chatter was beyond a doubt *in the Dutch language.*

After that we lived in growing horror and fascination. Mostly we held to the theory that we were jointly going mad from our life of unnatural excitements, but sometimes it pleased us more to dramatize ourselves as the victims of some creeping and appalling doom. Bizarre manifestations were now too frequent to count. Our lonely house was seemingly alive with the presence of some malign being whose nature we could not guess, and every night that daemoniac baying rolled over the windswept moor, always louder and louder. On October 29 we found in the soft earth underneath the library window a series of footprints utterly impossible to describe. They were as baffling as the hordes of great bats which haunted the old manor-house in unprecedented and increasing numbers.

The horror reached a culmination on November 18, when St. John, walking home after dark from the distant railway station, was seized by some frightful carnivorous thing and torn to ribbons. His screams had reached the house, and I had hastened to the terrible scene in time to hear a whir of wings and see a vague black cloudy thing silhouetted against the rising moon. My friend was dying when I spoke to him, and he could not answer coherently. All he could do was to whisper, "The amulet—that damned thing—." Then he collapsed, an inert mass of mangled flesh.

I buried him the next midnight in one of our neglected gardens, and mumbled over his body one of the devilish rituals he had loved in life. And as I pronounced the last daemoniac sentence I heard afar on the moor the faint baying of some gigantic hound. The moon was up, but I dared not look at it. And when I saw on the dim-litten moor a wide nebulous shadow sweeping from mound to mound, I shut my eyes and threw myself face down upon the ground. When I arose trembling, I know not how much later, I staggered into the house and made shocking obeisances before the enshrined amulet of green jade.

Being now afraid to live alone in the ancient house on the moor, I departed on the following day for London, taking with me the amulet after destroying by fire and burial the rest of the impious collection in the museum. But after three nights I heard the baying again, and before a week was over felt strange eyes upon me whenever it was dark. One evening as I strolled on Victoria Embankment for some needed air, I saw a black shape obscure one of the reflections of the lamps in the water. A wind stronger than the night-wind rushed by, and I knew that what had befallen St. John must soon befall me.

The next day I carefully wrapped the green jade amulet and sailed for Holland. What mercy I might gain by returning the thing to its silent, sleeping owner I knew not; but I felt that I must at least try any step conceivably logical. What the hound was, and why it pursued me, were questions still vague; but I had first heard the baying in that ancient churchyard, and every subsequent event including St. John's dying whisper had served to connect the curse with the stealing of the amulet. Accordingly I sank into the nethermost abysses of despair when, at an inn in Rotterdam, I discovered that thieves had despoiled me of this sole means of salvation.

The baying was loud that evening, and in the morning I read of a nameless deed in the vilest quarter of the city. The rabble were in terror, for upon an evil tenement had fallen a red death beyond the foulest previous crime of the neighborhood. In a squalid thieves' den an entire family had been torn to shreds by an unknown thing which left no trace, and those around had heard all night above the usual clamor of drunken voices a faint, deep, insistent note as of a gigantic hound.

So at last I stood again in that unwholesome churchyard where a pale winter moon cast hideous shadows, and leafless trees drooped sullenly to meet the withered, frosty grass and cracking slabs, and the ivied church pointed a jeering finger at the unfriendly sky, and the night-wind howled maniacally from over frozen swamps and frigid seas. The baying was very faint now, and it ceased altogether as I approached the ancient grave I had once violated, and frightened away an abnormally large horde of bats which had been hovering curiously around it.

I know not why I went thither unless to pray, or gibber out insane pleas and apologies to the calm white thing that lay within; but, whatever my reason, I attacked the half-frozen sod with a desperation partly mine and partly that of a dominating will outside myself. Excavation was much easier than I expected, though at one point I encountered a queer interruption; when a lean vulture darted down out of the cold sky and pecked frantically at the grave-earth until I killed him with a blow of my spade. Finally I reached the rotting oblong box and removed the damp nitrous cover. This is the last rational act I ever performed.

For crouched within that centuried coffin, embraced by a close-packed nightmare retinue of huge, sinewy, sleeping bats, was the bony thing my friend and I had robbed; not clean and placid as we had seen it then, but covered with caked blood and shreds of alien flesh and hair, and leering sentiently at me with phosphorescent sockets and sharp ensanguined fangs yawning twistedly in mockery of my inevitable doom. And when it gave from those grinning jaws a deep, sardonic bay as of some gigantic hound, and I saw that it held in its gory, filthy claw the lost and fateful amulet of green jade, I merely screamed and ran away idiotically, my screams soon dissolving into peals of hysterical laughter.

Madness rides the star-wind . . . claws and teeth sharpened on centuries of corpses . . . dripping death astride a Bacchanale of bats from night-black ruins of buried temples of Belial . . . Now, as the baying of that dead, fleshless monstrosity grows louder and louder, and the stealthy whirring and flapping of those accursed web-wings circles closer and closer, I shall seek with my revolver the oblivion which is my only refuge from the unnamed and unnamable.

The Rats in the Walls

by H. P. Lovecraft

On July 16, 1923, I moved into Exham Priory after the last workman had finished his labors. The restoration had been a stupendous task, for little had remained of the deserted pile but a shell-like ruin; yet because it had been the seat of my ancestors I let no expense deter me. The place had not been inhabited since the reign of James the First, when a tragedy of intensely hideous, though largely unexplained, nature had struck down the master, five of his children, and several servants; and driven forth under a cloud of suspicion and terror the third son, my lineal progenitor and the only survivor of the abhorred line. With this sole heir denounced as a murderer, the estate had reverted to the crown, nor had the accused man made any attempt to exculpate himself or regain his property. Shaken by some horror greater than that of conscience or the law, and expressing only a frantic wish to exclude the ancient edifice from his sight and memory, Walter de la Poer, eleventh Baron Exham, fled to Virginia and there founded the family which by the next century had become known as Delapore.

Exham Priory had remained untenanted, though later allotted to the estates of the Norrys family and much studied because of its peculiarly composite architecture; an architecture involving Gothic towers resting on a Saxon or Romanesque substructure, whose foundation in turn was of a still earlier order or blend of orders—Roman, and even Druidic or native Cymric, if legends speak truly. This foundation was a very singular thing, being merged on one side with the solid limestone of the precipice from whose brink the priory overlooked a desolate valley three miles west of the village of Anchester. Architects and antiquarians loved to examine this strange relic of forgotten centuries, but the country folk hated it. They had hated it hundreds of years before, when my ancestors lived there, and they hated it now, with the moss and mold of abandonment on it. I had not been a day in Anchester before I knew I came of an accursed house. And this week workmen have blown up Exham Priory, and are busy obliterating the traces of its foundations.

The bare statistics of my ancestry I had always known, together with the fact that my first American forbear had come to the colonies under a strange cloud. Of details, however, I had been kept wholly ignorant through the policy of reticence always maintained by the Delapores. Unlike our planter neighbors, we seldom boasted of crusading ancestors or other medieval and Renaissance heroes; nor was any kind of tradition handed down except what may have been recorded in the sealed envelope left before the Civil War by every squire to his eldest son for posthumous opening. The glories we cherished were those achieved since the migration; the glories of a proud and honorable, if somewhat reserved and unsocial Virginia line.

During the war our fortunes were extinguished and our whole existence changed by the burning of Carfax, our home on the banks of the James. My grandfather, advanced in years, had perished in that incendiary outrage, and with him the envelope that bound us all to the past. I can recall that fire today as I saw it then at the age of seven, with the Federal soldiers shouting, the women screaming, and the negroes howling and praying. My father was in the army, defending Richmond, and after many formalities my mother and I were passed through the lines to join him. When the war ended we all moved north, whence my mother had come; and I grew to manhood, middle age, and ultimate wealth as a stolid Yankee. Neither my father nor I ever knew what our hereditary envelope had contained, and as I merged into the grayness of Massachusetts business life I lost all interest in the mysteries which evidently lurked far back in my family tree. Had I suspected their nature, how gladly I would have left Exham Priory to its moss, bats, and cobwebs!

My father died in 1904, but without any message to leave me, or to my only child, Alfred, a motherless boy of ten. It was this boy who reversed the order of family information; for although I could give him only jesting conjectures about the past, he wrote me of some very interesting ancestral legends when the late war took him to England in 1917 as an aviation officer. Apparently the Delapores had a colorful and perhaps sinister history, for a friend of my son's, Capt. Edward Norrys of the Royal Flying Corps, dwelt near the family seat at Anchester and related some peasant superstitions which few novelists could equal for wildness and incredibility. Norrys himself, of course, did not take them seriously; but they amused my son and made good material for his letters to me. It was this legendry which definitely turned my attention to my transatlantic heritage, and made me resolve to purchase and restore the family seat which Norrys shewed to Alfred in its picturesque desertion, and offered to get for him at a surprisingly reasonable figure, since his own uncle was the present owner.

I bought Exham Priory in 1918, but was almost immediately distracted from my plans of restoration by the return of my son as a maimed invalid. During the two years that he lived I thought of nothing but his care, having even placed my business under the direction of partners. In 1921, as I found myself bereaved and aimless, a retired manufacturer no longer young, I resolved to divert my remaining years with my new possession. Visiting Anchester in December, I was entertained by Capt. Norrys, a plump, amiable young man who had thought much of my son, and secured his assistance in gathering plans and anecdotes to guide in the coming restoration. Exham Priory itself I saw without emotion, a jumble of tottering medieval ruins covered with lichens and honeycombed with rooks' nests, perched perilously upon a precipice, and denuded of floors or other interior features save the stone walls of the separate towers.

As I gradually recovered the image of the edifice as it had been when my ancestor left it over three centuries before, I began to hire workmen for the reconstruction. In every case I was forced to go outside the immediate locality, for the Anchester villagers had an almost unbelievable fear and hatred of the place. This sentiment was so great that it was sometimes communicated to the outside laborers, causing numerous desertions; whilst its scope appeared to include both the priory and its ancient family.

My son had told me that he was somewhat avoided during his visits because he was a de la Poer, and I now found myself subtly ostracized for a like reason until I convinced the peasants how little I knew of my heritage. Even then they sullenly disliked me, so that I had to collect most of the village traditions through the mediation of Norrys. What the people could not forgive, perhaps, was that

I had come to restore a symbol so abhorrent to them; for, rationally or not, they viewed Exham Priory as nothing less than a haunt of fiends and werewolves.

Piecing together the tales which Norrys collected for me, and supplementing them with the accounts of several savants who had studied the ruins, I deduced that Exham Priory stood on the site of a prehistoric temple; a Druidical or ante-Druidical thing which must have been contemporary with Stonehenge. That indescribable rites had been celebrated there, few doubted; and there were unpleasant tales of the transference of these rites into the Cybele-worship which the Romans had introduced. Inscriptions still visible in the sub-cellar bore such unmistakable letters as "DIV . . . OPS . . . MAGNA. MAT . . ." sign of the Magna Mater whose dark worship was once vainly forbidden to Roman citizens. Anchester had been the camp of the third Augustan legion, as many remains attest, and it was said that the temple of Cybele was splendid and thronged with worshipers who performed nameless ceremonies at the bidding of a Phrygian priest. Tales added that the fall of the old religion did not end the orgies at the temple, but that the priests lived on in the new faith without real change. Likewise was it said that the rites did not vanish with the Roman power, and that certain among the Saxons added to what remained of the temple, and gave it the essential outline it subsequently preserved, making it the center of a cult feared through half the heptarchy. About 1000 A.D. the place is mentioned in a chronicle as being a substantial stone priory housing a strange and powerful monastic order and surrounded by extensive gardens which needed no walls to exclude a frightened populace. It was never destroyed by the Danes, though after the Norman Conquest it must have declined tremendously; since there was no impediment when Henry the Third granted the site to my ancestor, Gilbert de la Poer, First Baron Exham, in 1261.

Of my family before this date there is no evil report, but something strange must have happened then. In one chronicle there is a reference to a de la Poer as "cursed of God" in 1307, whilst village legendry had nothing but evil and frantic fear to tell of the castle that went up on the foundations of the old temple and priory. The fireside tales were of the most grisly description, all the ghastlier because of their frightened reticence and cloudy evasiveness. They represented my ancestors as a race of hereditary daemons beside whom Gilles de Retz and the Marquis de Sade would seem the veriest tyros, and hinted whisperingly at their responsibility for the occasional disappearance of villagers through several generations.

The worst characters, apparently, were the barons and their direct heirs; at least, most was whispered about these. If of healthier inclinations, it was said, an heir would early and mysteriously die to make way for another more typical scion. There seemed to be an inner cult in the family, presided over by the head of the house, and sometimes closed except to a few members. Temperament rather than ancestry was evidently the basis of this cult, for it was entered by several who married into the family. Lady Margaret Trevor from Cornwall, wife of Godfrey, the second son of the fifth baron, became a favorite bane of children all over the countryside, and the daemon heroine of a particularly horrible old ballad not yet extinct near the Welsh border. Preserved in balladry, too, though not illustrating the same point, is the hideous tale of Lady Mary de la Poer, who shortly after her marriage to the Earl of Shrewsfield was killed by him and his mother, both of the slayers being absolved and blessed by the priest to whom they confessed what they dared not repeat to the world.

These myths and ballads, typical as they were of crude superstition, repelled me greatly. Their persistence, and their application to so long a line of my ancestors, were especially annoying; whilst the imputations of monstrous habits proved unpleasantly reminiscent of the one known scandal of my immediate forbears—the case of my cousin, young Randolph Delapore of Carfax, who went among the negroes and became a voodoo priest after he returned from the Mexican War.

I was much less disturbed by the vaguer tales of wails and howlings in the barren, windswept valley beneath the limestone cliff; of the graveyard stenches after the spring rains; of the floundering, squealing white thing on which Sir John Clave's horse had trod one night in a lonely field; and of the servant who had gone mad at what he saw in the priory in the full light of day. These things were hackneyed spectral lore, and I was at that time a pronounced skeptic. The accounts of vanished peasants were less to be dismissed, though not especially significant in view of medieval custom. Prying curiosity meant death, and more than one severed head had been publicly shewn on the bastions—now effaced—around Exham Priory.

A few of the tales were exceedingly picturesque, and made me wish I had learnt more of comparative mythology in my youth. There was, for instance, the belief that a legion of bat-winged devils kept Witches' Sabbath each night at the priory—a legion whose sustenance might explain the disproportionate abundance of coarse vegetables harvested in the vast gardens. And, most vivid of all, there was the dramatic epic of the rats—the scampering army of obscene vermin which had burst forth from the castle three months after the tragedy that doomed it to desertion—the lean, filthy, ravenous army which had swept all before it and devoured fowl, cats, dogs, hogs, sheep, and even two hapless human beings before its fury was spent. Around that unforgettable rodent army a whole separate cycle of myths revolves, for it scattered among the village homes and brought curses and horrors in its train.

Such was the lore that assailed me as I pushed to completion, with an elderly obstinacy, the work of restoring my ancestral home. It must not be imagined for a moment that these tales formed my principal psychological environment. On the other hand, I was constantly praised and encouraged by Capt. Norrys and the antiquarians who surrounded and aided me. When the task was done, over two years after its commencement, I viewed the great rooms, wainscotted walls, vaulted ceilings, mullioned windows, and broad staircases with a pride which fully compensated for the prodigious expense of the restoration. Every attribute of the Middle Ages was cunningly reproduced, and the new parts blended perfectly with the original walls and foundations. The seat of my fathers was complete, and I looked forward to redeeming at last the local fame of the line which ended in me. I would reside here permanently, and prove that a de la Poer (for I had adopted again the original spelling of the name) need not be a fiend. My comfort was perhaps augmented by the fact that, although Exham Priory was medievally fitted, its interior was in truth wholly new and free from old vermin and old ghosts alike.

As I have said, I moved in on July 16, 1923. My household consisted of seven servants and nine cats, of which latter species I am particularly fond. My eldest cat, "Nigger-Man," was seven years old and had come with me from my home in Bolton, Massachusetts; the others I had accumulated whilst living with Capt. Norrys' family during the restoration of the priory. For five days our routine proceeded with the utmost placidity, my time being spent mostly in the codification of old family data. I had now obtained some very circumstantial accounts of the final tragedy and flight of Walter de la Poer, which I conceived to be the probable contents of the hereditary paper lost in the fire at Carfax. It appeared that my ancestor was accused with much reason of having killed all the other members of his household, except four servant confederates, in their sleep, about two weeks after a shocking discovery which changed his whole demeanor, but which, except by implication, he disclosed to no one save perhaps the servants who assisted him and afterward fled beyond reach.

This deliberate slaughter, which included a father, three brothers, and two sisters, was largely condoned by the villagers, and so slackly treated by the law that its perpetrator escaped honored, unharmed, and undisguised to Virginia; the general whispered sentiment being that he had purged the land of an immemorial curse. What discovery had prompted an act so terrible, I could scarcely even conjecture. Walter de la Poer must have known for years the sinister tales about his family, so that this material could have given him no fresh impulse. Had he, then, witnessed some appalling ancient rite, or stumbled upon some frightful and revealing symbol in the priory or its vicinity? He was reputed to have been a shy, gentle youth in England. In Virginia he seemed not so much hard or bitter as harassed and apprehensive. He was spoken of in the diary of another gentleman-adventurer, Francis Harley of Bellview, as a man of unexampled justice, honor, and delicacy.

On July 22 occurred the first incident which, though lightly dismissed at the time, takes on a preternatural significance in relation to later events. It was so simple as to be almost negligible, and could not possibly have been noticed under the circumstances; for it must be recalled that since I was in a building practically fresh and new except for the walls, and surrounded by a well-balanced staff of servitors, apprehension would have been absurd despite the locality. What I afterward remembered is merely this—that my old black cat, whose moods I know so well, was undoubtedly alert and anxious to an extent wholly out of keeping with his natural character. He roved from room to room, restless and disturbed, and sniffed constantly about the walls which formed part of the old Gothic structure. I realize how trite this sounds—like the inevitable dog in the ghost story, which always growls before his master sees the sheeted figure—yet I cannot consistently suppress it.

The following day a servant complained of restlessness among all the cats in the house. He came to me in my study, a lofty west room on the second story, with groined arches, black oak paneling, and a triple Gothic window overlooking the limestone cliff and desolate valley; and even as he spoke I saw the jetty form of Nigger-Man creeping along the west wall and scratching at the new panels which overlaid the ancient stone. I told the man that there must be some singular odor or emanation from the old stonework, imperceptible to human senses, but affecting the delicate organs of cats even through the new woodwork. This I truly believed, and when the fellow suggested the presence of mice or rats, I mentioned that there had been no rats there for three hundred years, and that even the field mice of the surrounding country could hardly be found in these high walls, where they had never been known to stray. That afternoon I called on Capt. Norrys, and he assured me that it would be quite incredible for field mice to infest the priory in such a sudden and unprecedented fashion.

That night, dispensing as usual with a valet, I retired in the west tower chamber which I had chosen as my own, reached from the study by a stone staircase and short gallery—the former partly ancient, the latter entirely restored. This room was circular, very high, and without wainscotting, being hung with arras which I had myself chosen in London. Seeing that Nigger-Man was with me, I shut the heavy Gothic door and retired by the light of the electric bulbs which so cleverly counterfeited candles, finally switching off the light and sinking on the carved and canopied four-poster, with the venerable cat in his accustomed place across my feet. I did not draw the curtains, but gazed out at the narrow north window which I faced. There was a suspicion of aurora in the sky, and the delicate traceries of the window were pleasantly silhouetted.

At some time I must have fallen quietly asleep, for I recall a distinct sense of leaving strange dreams, when the cat started violently from his placid position. I saw him in the faint auroral glow, head strained forward, fore feet on my ankles, and hind feet stretched behind. He was looking intensely at a point on the wall somewhat west of the window, a point which to my eye had nothing to mark it, but toward which all my attention was now directed. And as I watched, I knew that Nigger-Man was not vainly excited. Whether the arras actually moved I cannot say. I think it did, very slightly. But what I can swear to is that behind it I heard a low, distinct scurrying as of rats or mice. In a moment the cat had jumped bodily on the screening tapestry, bringing the affected section to the floor with his weight, and exposing a damp, ancient wall of stone; patched here and there by the restorers, and devoid of any trace of rodent prowlers. Nigger-Man raced up and down the floor by this part of the wall, clawing the fallen arras and seemingly trying at times to insert a paw between the wall and the oaken floor. He found nothing, and after a time returned wearily to his place across my feet. I had not moved, but I did not sleep again that night.

In the morning I questioned all the servants, and found that none of them had noticed anything unusual, save that the cook remembered the actions of a cat which had rested on her windowsill. This cat had howled at some unknown hour of the night, awaking the cook in time for her to see him dart purposefully out of the open door down the stairs. I drowsed away the noontime, and in the afternoon called again on Capt. Norrys, who became exceedingly interested in what I told him. The odd incidents—so slight yet so curious—appealed to his sense of the picturesque, and elicited from him a number of reminiscences of local ghostly lore. We were genuinely perplexed at the presence of rats, and Norrys lent me some traps and Paris green, which I had the servants place in strategic localities when I returned.

I retired early, being very sleepy, but was harassed by dreams of the most horrible sort. I seemed to be looking down from an immense height upon a twilit grotto, knee-deep with filth, where a white-bearded daemon swineherd drove about with his staff a flock of fungous, flabby beasts whose appearance filled me with unutterable loathing. Then, as the swineherd paused and nodded over his task, a mighty swarm of rats rained down on the stinking abyss and fell to devouring beasts and man alike.

From this terrific vision I was abruptly awaked by the motions of Nigger-Man, who had been sleeping as usual across my feet. This time I did not have to question the source of his snarls and hisses, and of the fear which made him sink his claws into my ankle, unconscious of their effect; for on every side of the chamber the walls were alive with nauseous sound—the verminous slithering of ravenous, gigantic rats. There was now no aurora to shew the state of the arras—the fallen section of which had been replaced—but I was not too frightened to switch on the light.

As the bulbs leapt into radiance I saw a hideous shaking all over the tapestry, causing the somewhat peculiar designs to execute a singular dance of death. This motion disappeared almost at once, and the sound with it. Springing out of bed, I poked at the arras with the long handle of a warming-pan that rested near, and lifted one section to see what lay beneath. There was nothing but the patched stone wall, and even the cat had lost his tense realization of abnormal presences. When I examined the circular trap that had been placed in the room, I found all of the openings sprung, though no trace remained of what had been caught and had escaped.

Further sleep was out of the question, so, lighting a candle, I opened the door and went out in the gallery toward the stairs to my study, Nigger-Man following at my heels. Before we had reached the stone steps, however, the cat darted ahead of me and vanished down the ancient flight. As I descended the stairs myself, I became suddenly aware of sounds in the great room below; sounds of a nature which could not be mistaken. The oak-paneled walls were alive with rats, scampering and milling, whilst Nigger-Man was racing about with the fury of a baffled hunter. Reaching the bottom, I switched on the light, which did not this time cause the noise to subside. The rats continued their riot, stampeding with such force and distinctness that I could finally assign to their motions a definite direction. These creatures, in numbers apparently inexhaustible, were engaged in one stupendous migration from inconceivable heights to some depth conceivably, or inconceivably, below.

I now heard steps in the corridor, and in another moment two servants pushed open the massive door. They were searching the house for some unknown source of disturbance which had thrown all the cats into a snarling panic and caused them to plunge precipitately down several flights of stairs and squat, yowling, before the closed door to the sub-cellar. I asked them if they had heard the rats, but they replied in the negative. And when I turned to call their attention to the sounds in the panels, I realized that the noise had ceased. With the two men, I went down to the door of the sub-cellar, but found the cats already dispersed. Later I resolved to explore the crypt below, but for the present I merely made a round of the traps. All were sprung, yet all were tenantless. Satisfying myself that no one had heard the rats save the felines and me, I sat in my study till morning; thinking profoundly, and recalling every scrap of legend I had unearthed concerning the building I inhabited.

I slept some in the forenoon, leaning back in the one comfortable library chair which my medieval plan of furnishing could not banish. Later I telephoned to Capt. Norrys, who came over and helped me explore the sub-cellar. Absolutely nothing untoward was found, although we could not repress a thrill at the knowledge that this vault was built by Roman hands. Every low arch and massive pillar was Roman—not the debased Romanesque of the bungling Saxons, but the severe and harmonious classicism of the age of the Caesars; indeed, the walls abounded with inscriptions familiar to the antiquarians who had repeatedly explored the place—things like "P.GETAE. PROP . . . TEMP . . . DONA . . ." and "L. PRAEC . . . VS . . . PONTIFI . . . ATYS . . ."

The reference to Atys made me shiver, for I had read Catullus and knew something of the hideous rites of the Eastern god, whose worship was so mixed with that of Cybele. Norrys and I, by the light of lanterns, tried to interpret the odd and nearly effaced designs on certain irregularly rectangular blocks of stone generally held to be altars, but could make nothing of them. We remembered that one pattern, a sort of rayed sun, was held by students to imply a non-Roman origin, suggesting that these altars had merely been adopted by the Roman priests from some older and perhaps aboriginal temple on the same site. On one of these blocks were some brown stains which made me wonder. The largest, in the center of the room, had certain features on the upper surface which indicated its connexion with fire—probably burned offerings.

Such were the sights in that crypt before whose door the cats had howled, and where Norrys and I now determined to pass the night. Couches were brought down by the servants, who were told not to mind any nocturnal actions of the cats, and Nigger-Man was admitted as much for help as for companionship. We decided to keep the great oak door—a modern replica with slits for ventilation—tightly closed; and, with this attended to, we retired with lanterns still burning to await whatever might occur.

The vault was very deep in the foundations of the priory, and undoubtedly far down on the face of the beetling limestone cliff overlooking the waste valley. That it had been the goal of the scuffling and unexplainable rats I could not doubt, though why, I could not tell. As we lay there expectantly, I found my vigil occasionally mixed with half-formed dreams from which the uneasy motions of the cat across my feet would rouse me. These dreams were not wholesome, but horribly like the one I had had the night before. I saw again the twilit grotto, and the swineherd with his unmentionable fungous beasts wallowing in filth, and as I looked at these things they seemed nearer and more distinct—so distinct that I could almost observe their features. Then I did observe the flabby features of one of them—and awaked with such a scream that Nigger-Man started up, whilst Capt. Norrys, who had not slept, laughed considerably. Norrys might have laughed more—or perhaps less—had he known what it was that made me scream. But I did not remember myself till later. Ultimate horror often paralyzes memory in a merciful way.

Norrys waked me when the phenomena began. Out of the same frightful dream I was called by his gentle shaking and his urging to listen to the cats. Indeed, there was much to listen to, for beyond the closed door at the head of the stone steps was a veritable nightmare of feline yelling and clawing, whilst Nigger-Man, unmindful of his kindred outside, was running excitedly around the bare stone walls, in which I heard the same babel of scurrying rats that had troubled me the night before.

An acute terror now rose within me, for here were anomalies which nothing normal could well explain. These rats, if not the creatures of a madness which I shared with the cats alone, must be burrowing and sliding in Roman walls I had thought to be of solid limestone blocks . . . unless perhaps the action of water through more than seventeen centuries had eaten winding tunnels which rodent bodies had worn clear and ample . . . But even so, the spectral horror was no less; for if these were living vermin why did not Norrys hear their disgusting commotion? Why did he urge me to watch Nigger-Man and listen to the cats outside, and why did he guess wildly and vaguely at what could have aroused them?

By the time I had managed to tell him, as rationally as I could, what I thought I was hearing, my ears gave me the last fading impression of the scurrying; which had retreated *still downward,* far underneath this deepest of sub-cellars till it seemed as if the whole cliff below were riddled with questing rats. Norrys was not as skeptical as I had anticipated, but instead seemed profoundly moved. He motioned to me to notice that the cats at the door had ceased their clamor, as if giving up the rats for lost; whilst Nigger-Man had a burst of renewed restlessness, and was clawing frantically around the bottom of the large stone altar in the center of the room, which was nearer Norrys' couch than mine.

My fear of the unknown was at this point very great. Something astounding had occurred, and I saw that Capt. Norrys, a younger, stouter, and presumably more naturally materialistic man, was affected fully as much as myself—perhaps because of his lifelong and intimate familiarity with local legend. We could for the moment do nothing but watch the old black cat as he pawed with decreasing fervor at the base of the altar, occasionally looking up and mewing to me in that persuasive manner which he used when he wished me to perform some favor for him.

Norrys now took a lantern close to the altar and examined the place where Nigger-Man was pawing; silently kneeling and scraping away the lichens of centuries which joined the massive pre-Roman block to the tesselated floor. He did not find anything, and was about to abandon his effort when I noticed a trivial circumstance which made me shudder, even though it implied nothing more than I had already imagined. I told him of it, and we both looked at its almost imperceptible manifestation with the fixedness of fascinated discovery and acknowledgment. It was only this—that the flame of the lantern set down near the altar was slightly but certainly flickering from a draft of air which it had not before received, and which came indubitably from the crevice between floor and altar where Norrys was scraping away the lichens.

We spent the rest of the night in the brilliantly lighted study, nervously discussing what we should do next. The discovery that some vault deeper than the deepest known masonry of the Romans underlay this accursed pile—some vault unsuspected by the curious antiquarians of three centuries—would have been sufficient to excite us without any background of the sinister. As it was, the fascination became twofold; and we paused in doubt whether to abandon our search and quit the priory forever in superstitious caution, or to gratify our sense of adventure and brave whatever horrors might await us in the unknown depths. By morning we had compromised, and decided to go to London to gather a group of archeologists and scientific men fit to cope with the mystery. It should be mentioned that before leaving the sub-cellar we had vainly tried to move the central altar which we now recognized as the gate to a new pit of nameless fear. What secret would open the gate, wiser men than we would have to find.

During many days in London Capt. Norrys and I presented our facts, conjectures, and legendary anecdotes to five eminent authorities, all men who could be trusted to respect any family disclosures which future explorations might develop. We found most of them little disposed to scoff, but instead intensely interested and sincerely sympathetic. It is hardly necessary to name them all, but I may say that they included Sir William Brinton, whose excavations in the Troad excited most of the world in their day. As we all took the train for Anchester I felt myself poised on the brink of frightful revelations, a sensation symbolized by the air of mourning among the many Americans at the unexpected death of the President on the other side of the world.

On the evening of August 7th we reached Exham Priory, where the servants assured me that nothing unusual had occurred. The cats, even old Nigger-Man, had been perfectly placid; and not a trap in the house had been sprung. We were to begin exploring on the following day, awaiting which I assigned well-appointed rooms to all my guests. I myself retired in my own tower chamber, with Nigger-Man across my feet. Sleep came quickly, but hideous dreams assailed me. There was a vision of a Roman feast like that of Trimalchio, with a horror in a covered platter. Then came that damnable, recurrent thing about the swineherd and his filthy drove in the twilit grotto. Yet when I awoke it was full daylight, with normal sounds in the house below. The rats, living or spectral, had not troubled me; and Nigger-Man was quietly asleep. On going down, I found that the same tranquility had prevailed elsewhere; a condition which one of the assembled savants—a fellow named Thornton, devoted to the psychic—rather absurdly laid to the fact that I had now been shewn the thing which certain forces had wished to shew me.

All was now ready, and at 11 a.m. our entire group of seven men, bearing powerful electric searchlights and implements of excavation, went down to the sub-cellar and bolted the door behind us. Nigger-Man was with us, for the investigators found no occasion to despise his excitability, and were indeed anxious that he be present in case of obscure rodent manifestations. We noted the Roman inscriptions and unknown altar designs only briefly, for three of the savants had already seen them, and all knew their characteristics. Prime attention was paid to the momentous central altar, and within an hour Sir William Brinton had caused it to tilt backward, balanced by some unknown species of counterweight.

There now lay revealed such a horror as would have overwhelmed us had we not been prepared. Through a nearly square opening in the tiled floor, sprawling on a flight of stone steps so prodigiously worn that it was little more than an inclined plane at the center, was a ghastly array of human or semi-human bones. Those which retained their collocation as skeletons shewed attitudes of panic fear, and over all were the marks of rodent gnawing. The skulls denoted nothing short of utter idiocy, cretinism, or primitive semi-apedom. Above the hellishly littered steps arched a descending passage seemingly chiseled from the solid rock, and conducting a current of air. This current was not a sudden and noxious rush as from a closed vault, but a cool breeze with something of freshness in it. We did not pause long, but shiveringly began to clear a passage down the steps. It was then that Sir William, examining the hewn walls, made the odd observation that the passage, according to the direction of the strokes, must have been chiseled *from beneath.*

I must be very deliberate now, and choose my words.

After plowing down a few steps amidst the gnawed bones we saw that there was light ahead; not any mystic phosphorescence, but a filtered daylight which could not come except from unknown fissures in the cliff that overlooked the waste valley. That such fissures had escaped notice from outside was hardly remarkable, for not only is the valley wholly uninhabited, but the cliff is so high and beetling that only an aëronaut could study its face in detail. A few steps more, and our breaths were literally snatched from us by what we saw; so literally that Thornton, the psychic investigator, actually fainted in the arms of the dazed man who stood behind him. Norrys, his plump face utterly white and flabby, simply cried out inarticulately; whilst I think that what I did was to gasp or hiss, and cover my eyes. The man behind me—the only one of the party older than I—croaked the hackneyed "My God!" in the most cracked voice I ever heard. Of seven cultivated men, only Sir William Brinton retained his composure; a thing more to his credit because he led the party and must have seen the sight first.

It was a twilit grotto of enormous height, stretching away farther than any eye could see; a subterraneous world of limitless mystery and horrible suggestion. There were buildings and other architectural remains—in one terrified glance I saw a weird pattern of tumuli, a savage circle of monoliths, a low-domed Roman ruin, a sprawling Saxon pile, and an early English edifice of wood—but all these were dwarfed by the ghoulish spectacle presented by the general surface of the ground. For yards about the steps extended an insane tangle of human bones, or bones at least as human as those on the steps. Like a foamy sea they stretched, some fallen apart, but others wholly or partly articulated as skeletons; these latter invariably in postures of daemoniac frenzy, either fighting off some menace or clutching other forms with cannibal intent.

When Dr. Trask, the anthropologist, stooped to classify the skulls, he found a degraded mixture which utterly baffled him. They were mostly lower than the Piltdown man in the scale of evolution, but in every case definitely human. Many were of higher grade, and a very few were the skulls of supremely and sensitively developed types. All the bones were gnawed, mostly by rats, but somewhat by others of the half-human drove. Mixed with them were many tiny bones of rats—fallen members of the lethal army which closed the ancient epic.

I wonder that any man among us lived and kept his sanity through that hideous day of discovery. Not Hoffmann or Huysmans could conceive a scene more wildly incredible, more frenetically repellent, or more Gothically grotesque than the twilit grotto through which we seven staggered; each stumbling on revelation after revelation, and trying to keep for the nonce from thinking of the events which must have taken place there three hundred years, or a thousand, or two thousand, or ten thousand years ago. It was the antechamber of hell, and poor Thornton fainted again when Trask told him that some of the skeleton things must have descended as quadrupeds through the last twenty or more generations.

Horror piled on horror as we began to interpret the architectural remains. The quadruped things—with their occasional recruits from the biped class—had been kept in stone pens, out of which they must have broken in their last delirium of hunger or rat-fear. There had been great herds of them, evidently fattened on the coarse vegetables whose remains could be found as a sort of poisonous ensilage at the bottom of huge stone bins older than Rome. I knew now why my ancestors had had such excessive gardens—would to heaven I could forget! The purpose of the herds I did not have to ask.

Sir William, standing with his searchlight in the Roman ruin, translated aloud the most shocking ritual I have ever known; and told of the diet of the antediluvian cult which the priests of Cybele found and mingled with their own. Norrys, used as he was to the trenches, could not walk straight when he came out of the English building. It was a butcher shop and kitchen—he had expected that—but it was too much to see familiar English implements in such a place, and to read familiar English *graffiti* there, some as recent as 1610. I could not go in that building—that building whose daemon activities were stopped only by the dagger of my ancestor Walter de la Poer.

What I did venture to enter was the low Saxon building, whose oaken door had fallen, and there I found a terrible row of ten stone cells with rusty bars. Three had tenants, all skeletons of high grade, and on the bony forefinger of one I found a seal ring with my own coat-of-arms. Sir William found a vault with far older cells below the Roman chapel, but these cells were empty. Below them was a low crypt with cases of formally arranged bones, some of them bearing terrible parallel inscriptions carved in Latin, Greek, and the tongue of Phrygia. Meanwhile, Dr. Trask had opened one of the prehistoric tumuli, and brought to light skulls which were slightly more human than a gorilla's, and which bore indescribable ideographic carvings. Through all this horror my cat stalked unperturbed. Once I saw him monstrously perched atop a mountain of bones, and wondered at the secrets that might lie behind his yellow eyes.

Having grasped to some slight degree the frightful revelations of this twilit area—an area so hideously foreshadowed by my recurrent dream—we turned to that apparently boundless depth of midnight cavern where no ray of light from the cliff could penetrate. We shall never know what sightless Stygian worlds yawn beyond the little distance we went, for it was decided that such secrets are not good for mankind. But there was plenty to engross us close at hand, for we had not gone far before the searchlights shewed that accursed infinity of pits in which the rats had feasted, and whose sudden lack of replenishment had driven the ravenous rodent army first to turn on the living herds of starving things, and then to burst forth from the priory in that historic orgy of devastation which the peasants will never forget.

God! those carrion black pits of sawed, picked bones and opened skulls! Those nightmare chasms choked with the pithecanthropoid, Celtic, Roman, and English bones of countless unhallowed centuries! Some of them were full, and none can say how deep they had once been. Others were still bottomless to our searchlights, and peopled by unnamable fancies. What, I thought, of the hapless rats that stumbled into such traps amidst the blackness of their quests in this grisly Tartarus?

Once my foot slipped near a horribly yawning brink, and I had a moment of ecstatic fear. I must have been musing a long time, for I could not see any of the party but the plump Capt. Norrys. Then there came a sound from that inky, boundless, farther distance that I thought I knew; and I saw my old black cat dart past me like a winged Egyptian god, straight into the illimitable gulf of the unknown. But I was not far behind, for there was no doubt after another second. It was the eldritch scurrying of those fiend-born rats, always questing for new horrors, and determined to lead me on even unto those grinning caverns of earth's center where Nyarlathotep, the mad faceless god, howls blindly to the piping of two amorphous idiot flute-players.

My searchlight expired, but still I ran. I heard voices, and yowls, and echoes, but above all there gently rose that impious, insidious scurrying; gently rising, rising, as a stiff bloated corpse gently rises above an oily river that flows under endless onyx bridges to a black, putrid sea. Something bumped into me—something soft and plump. It must have been the rats; the viscous, gelatinous, ravenous army that feast on the dead and the living . . . Why shouldn't rats eat a de la Poer as a de la Poer eats forbidden things? . . . The war ate my boy, damn them all . . . and the Yanks ate Carfax with flames and burned Grandsire Delapore and the secret . . . No, no, I tell you, I am *not* that daemon swineherd in the twilit grotto! It was *not* Edward Norrys' fat face on that flabby, fungous thing! Who says I am a de la Poer? He lived, but my boy died! . . . Shall a Norrys hold the lands of a de la Poer? . . . It's voodoo, I tell you . . . that spotted snake . . . Curse you, Thornton, I'll teach you to faint at what my family do! . . . 'Sblood, thou stinkard, I'll learn ye how to gust . . . wolde ye swynke me thilke wys? . . . *Magna Mater! Magna Mater!* . . . *Atys* . . . *Dia ad aghaidh 's ad aodann* . . . *agus bas dunach ort! Dhonas's dholas ort, agus leat-sa!* . . . *Ungl* . . . *ungl* . . . *rrrlh* . . . *chchch* . . .

That is what they say I said when they found me in the blackness after three hours; found me crouching in the blackness over the plump, half-eaten body of Capt. Norrys, with my own cat leaping and tearing at my throat. Now they have blown up Exham Priory, taken my Nigger-Man away from me, and shut me into this barred room at Hanwell with fearful whispers about my heredity and experiences. Thornton is in the next room, but they prevent me from talking to him. They are trying, too, to suppress most of the facts concerning the priory. When I speak of poor Norrys they accuse me of a hideous thing, but they must know that I did not do it. They must know it was the rats; the slithering, scurrying rats whose scampering will never let me sleep; the daemon rats that race behind the padding in this room and beckon me down to greater horrors than I have ever known; the rats they can never hear; the rats, the rats in the walls.

The Outsider

by H. P. Lovecraft

That night the Baron dreamt of many a woe;
And all his warrior-guests, with shade and form
Of witch, and demon, and large coffin-worm,
Were long be-nightmared.
—*Keats*

Unhappy is he to whom the memories of childhood bring only fear and sadness. Wretched is he who looks back upon lone hours in vast and dismal chambers with brown hangings and maddening rows of antique books, or upon awed watches in twilight groves of grotesque, gigantic, and vine-encumbered trees that silently wave twisted branches far aloft. Such a lot the gods gave to me—to me, the dazed, the disappointed; the barren, the broken. And yet I am strangely content, and cling desperately to those sere memories, when my mind momentarily threatens to reach beyond to *the other.*

I know not where I was born, save that the castle was infinitely old and infinitely horrible; full of dark passages and having high ceilings where the eye could find only cobwebs and shadows. The stones in the crumbling corridors seemed always hideously damp, and there was an accursed smell everywhere, as of the piled-up corpses of dead generations. It was never light, so that I used sometimes to light candles and gaze steadily at them for relief; nor was there any sun outdoors, since the terrible trees grew high above the topmost accessible tower. There was one black tower which reached above the trees into the unknown outer sky, but that was partly ruined and could not be ascended save by a well-nigh impossible climb up the sheer wall, stone by stone.

I must have lived years in this place, but I cannot measure the time. Beings must have cared for my needs, yet I cannot recall any person except myself; or anything alive but the noiseless rats and bats and spiders. I think that whoever nursed me must have been shockingly aged, since my first conception of a living person was that of something mockingly like myself, yet distorted, shriveled, and decaying like the castle. To me there was nothing grotesque in the bones and skeletons that strowed some of the stone crypts deep down among the foundations. I fantastically associated these things with every-day events, and thought them more natural than the colored pictures of living beings which I found in many of the moldy books. From such books I learned all that I know. No teacher urged or guided me, and I do not recall hearing any human voice in all those years—not even my own; for although I had read of speech, I had never thought to try to speak aloud. My aspect was a matter equally unthought of, for there were no mirrors in the castle, and I merely regarded myself by instinct as akin to the youthful figures I saw drawn and painted in the books. I felt conscious of youth because I remembered so little.

Outside, across the putrid moat and under the dark mute trees, I would often lie and dream for hours about what I read in the books; and would longingly picture myself amidst gay crowds in the sunny world beyond the endless forest. Once I tried to escape from the forest, but as I went farther from the castle the shade grew denser and the air more filled with brooding fear; so that I ran frantically back lest I lose my way in a labyrinth of nighted silence.

So through endless twilights I dreamed and waited, though I knew not what I waited for. Then in the shadowy solitude my longing for light grew so frantic that I could rest no more, and I lifted entreating hands to the single black ruined tower that reached above the forest into the unknown outer sky. And at last I resolved to scale that tower, fall though I might; since it were better to glimpse the sky and perish, than to live without ever beholding day.

In the dank twilight I climbed the worn and aged stone stairs till I reached the level where they ceased, and thereafter clung perilously to small footholds leading upward. Ghastly and terrible was that dead, stairless cylinder of rock; black, ruined, and deserted, and sinister with startled bats whose wings made no noise. But more ghastly and terrible still was the slowness of my progress; for climb as I might, the darkness overhead grew no thinner, and a new chill as of haunted and venerable mold assailed me. I shivered as I wondered why I did not reach the light, and would have looked down had I dared. I fancied that night had come suddenly upon me, and vainly groped with one free hand for a window embrasure, that I might peer out and above, and try to judge the height I had attained.

All at once, after an infinity of awesome, sightless crawling up that concave and desperate precipice, I felt my head touch a solid thing, and I knew I must have gained the roof, or at least some kind of floor. In the darkness I raised my free hand and tested the barrier, finding it stone and immovable. Then came a deadly circuit of the tower, clinging to whatever holds the slimy wall could give; till finally my testing hand found the barrier yielding, and I turned upward again, pushing the slab or door with my head as I used both hands in my fearful ascent. There was no light revealed above, and as my hands went higher I knew that my climb was for the nonce ended; since the slab was the trap-door of an aperture leading to a level stone surface of greater circumference than the lower tower, no doubt the floor of some lofty and capacious observation chamber. I crawled through carefully, and tried to prevent the heavy slab from falling back into place; but failed in the latter attempt. As I lay exhausted on the stone floor I heard the eerie echoes of its fall, but hoped when necessary to pry it open again.

Believing I was now at a prodigious height, far above the accursed branches of the wood, I dragged myself up from the floor and fumbled about for windows, that I might look for the first time upon the sky, and the moon and stars of which I had read. But on every hand I was disappointed; since all that I found were vast shelves of marble, bearing odious oblong boxes of disturbing size. More and more I reflected, and wondered what hoary secrets might abide in this high apartment so many eons cut off from the castle below. Then unexpectedly my hands came upon a doorway, where hung a portal of stone, rough with strange chiseling. Trying it, I found it locked; but with a supreme burst of strength I overcame all obstacles and dragged it open inward. As I did so there came to me the purest ecstasy I have ever known; for shining tranquilly through an ornate grating of iron, and down a short stone passageway of steps that ascended from the newly found doorway, was the radiant full moon, which I had never before seen save in dreams and in vague visions I dared not call memories.

Fancying now that I had attained the very pinnacle of the castle, I commenced to rush up the few steps beyond the door; but the sudden veiling of the moon by a cloud caused me to stumble, and I felt my way more slowly in the dark. It was still very dark when I reached the grating—which I tried carefully and found unlocked, but which I did not open for fear of falling from the amazing height to which I had climbed. Then the moon came out.

Most daemoniacal of all shocks is that of the abysmally unexpected and grotesquely unbelievable. Nothing I had before undergone could compare in terror with what I now saw; with the bizarre marvels that sight implied. The sight itself was as simple as it was stupefying, for it was merely this: instead of a dizzying prospect of treetops seen from a lofty eminence, there stretched around me on a level through the grating nothing less than *the solid ground,* decked and diversified by marble slabs and columns, and overshadowed by an ancient stone church, whose ruined spire gleamed spectrally in the moonlight.

Half unconscious, I opened the grating and staggered out upon the white gravel path that stretched away in two directions. My mind, stunned and chaotic as it was, still held the frantic craving for light; and not even the fantastic wonder which had happened could stay my course. I neither knew nor cared whether my experience was insanity, dreaming, or magic; but was determined to gaze on brilliance and gaiety at any cost. I knew not who I was or what I was, or what my surroundings might be; though as I continued to stumble along I became conscious of a kind of fearsome latent memory that made my progress not wholly fortuitous. I passed under an arch out of that region of slabs and columns, and wandered through the open country; sometimes following the visible road, but sometimes leaving it curiously to tread across meadows where only occasional ruins bespoke the ancient presence of a forgotten road. Once I swam across a swift river where crumbling, mossy masonry told of a bridge long vanished.

Over two hours must have passed before I reached what seemed to be my goal, a venerable ivied castle in a thickly wooded park; maddeningly familiar, yet full of perplexing strangeness to me. I saw that the moat was filled in, and that some of the well-known towers were demolished; whilst new wings existed to confuse the beholder. But what I observed with chief interest and delight were the open windows—gorgeously ablaze with light and sending forth sound of the gayest revelry. Advancing to one of these I looked in and saw an oddly dressed company, indeed; making merry, and speaking brightly to one another. I had never, seemingly, heard human speech before; and could guess only vaguely what was said. Some of the faces seemed to hold expressions that brought up incredibly remote recollections; others were utterly alien.

I now stepped through the low window into the brilliantly lighted room, stepping as I did so from my single bright moment of hope to my blackest convulsion of despair and realization. The nightmare was quick to come; for as I entered, there occurred immediately one of the most terrifying demonstrations I had ever conceived. Scarcely had I crossed the sill when there descended upon the whole company a sudden and unheralded fear of hideous intensity, distorting every face and evoking the most horrible screams from nearly every throat. Flight was universal, and in the clamor and panic several fell in a swoon and were dragged away by their madly fleeing companions. Many covered their eyes with their hands, and plunged blindly and awkwardly in their race to escape; overturning furniture and stumbling against the walls before they managed to reach one of the many doors.

The cries were shocking; and as I stood in the brilliant apartment alone and dazed, listening to their vanishing echoes, I trembled at the thought of what might be lurking near me unseen. At a casual inspection the room seemed deserted, but when I moved toward one of the alcoves I thought I detected a presence there—a hint of motion beyond the golden-arched doorway leading to another and somewhat similar room. As I approached the arch I began to perceive the presence more clearly; and then, with the first and last sound I ever uttered—a ghastly ululation that revolted me almost as poignantly as its noxious cause—I beheld in full, frightful vividness the inconceivable, indescribable, and unmentionable monstrosity which had by its simple appearance changed a merry company to a herd of delirious fugitives.

I cannot even hint what it was like, for it was a compound of all that is unclean, uncanny, unwelcome, abnormal, and detestable. It was the ghoulish shade of decay, antiquity, and desolation; the putrid, dripping eidolon of unwholesome revelation; the awful baring of that which the merciful earth should always hide. God knows it was not of this world—or no longer of this world—yet to my horror I saw in its eaten-away and bone-revealing outlines a leering, abhorrent travesty on the human shape; and in its moldy, disintegrating apparel an unspeakable quality that chilled me even more.

I was almost paralyzed, but not too much so to make a feeble effort toward flight; a backward stumble which failed to break the spell in which the nameless, voiceless monster held me. My eyes, bewitched by the glassy orbs which stared loathsomely into them, refused to close; though they were mercifully blurred, and shewed the terrible object but indistinctly after the first shock. I tried to raise my hand to shut out the sight, yet so stunned were my nerves that my arm could not fully obey my will. The attempt, however, was enough to disturb my balance; so that I had to stagger forward several steps to avoid falling. As I did so I became suddenly and agonizingly aware of the *nearness* of the carrion thing, whose hideous hollow breathing I half fancied I could hear. Nearly mad, I found myself yet able to throw out a hand to ward off the fetid apparition which pressed so close; when in one cataclysmic second of cosmic nightmarishness and hellish accident *my fingers touched the rotting outstretched paw of the monster beneath the golden arch.*

I did not shriek, but all the fiendish ghouls that ride the night-wind shrieked for me as in that same second there crashed down upon my mind a single and fleeting avalanche of soul-annihilating memory. I knew in that second all that had been; I remembered beyond the frightful castle and the trees, and recognized the altered edifice in which I now stood; I recognized, most terrible of all, the unholy abomination that stood leering before me as I withdrew my sullied fingers from its own.

But in the cosmos there is balm as well as bitterness, and that balm is nepenthe. In the supreme horror of that second I forgot what had horrified me, and the burst of black memory vanished in a chaos of echoing images. In a dream I fled from that haunted and accursed pile, and ran swiftly and silently in the moonlight. When I returned to the churchyard place of marble and went down the steps I found the stone trap-door immovable; but I was not sorry, for I had hated the antique castle and the trees. Now I ride with the mocking and friendly ghouls on the night-wind, and play by day amongst the catacombs of Nephren-Ka in the sealed and unknown valley of Hadoth by the Nile. I know that light is not for me, save that of the moon over the rock tombs of Neb, nor any gaiety save the unnamed feasts of Nitokris beneath the Great Pyramid; yet in my new wildness and freedom I almost welcome the bitterness of alienage.

For although nepenthe has calmed me, I know always that I am an outsider; a stranger in this century and among those who are still men. This I have known ever since I stretched out my fingers to the abomination within that great gilded frame; stretched out my fingers and touched *a cold and unyielding surface of polished glass.*

Carmilla

by Joseph Sheridan Le Fanu

PROLOGUE

Upon a paper attached to the Narrative which follows, Doctor Hesselius has written a rather elaborate note, which he accompanies witha reference to his Essay on the strange subject which the MS. illuminates.

This mysterious subject he treats, in that Essay, with his usual learning and acumen, and with remarkable directness and condensation. It will form but one volume of the series of that extraordinary man's collected papers.

As I publish the case, in this volume, simply to interest the "laity," I shall forestall the intelligent lady, who relates it, in nothing; and after due consideration, I have determined, therefore, to abstain from presenting any précis of the learned Doctor's reasoning, or extract from his statement on a subject which he describes as "involving, not improbably, some of the profoundest arcana of our dual existence, and its intermediates."

I was anxious on discovering this paper, to reopen the correspondence commenced by Doctor Hesselius, so many years before, with a person so clever and careful as his informant seems to have been. Much to my regret, however, I found that she had died in the interval.

She, probably, could have added little to the Narrative which she communicates in the following pages, with, so far as I can pronounce, such conscientious particularity.

I. AN EARLY FRIGHT

In Styria, we, though by no means magnificent people, inhabit a castle, or schloss. A small income, in that part of the world, goes a great way. Eight or nine hundred a year does wonders. Scantily enough ours would have answered among wealthy people at home. My father is English, and I bear an English name, although I never saw England. But here, in this lonely and primitive place, where everything is so marvelously cheap, I really don't see how ever so much more money would at all materially add to our comforts, or even luxuries.

My father was in the Austrian service, and retired upon a pension and his patrimony, and purchased this feudal residence, and the small estate on which it stands, a bargain.

Nothing can be more picturesque or solitary. It stands on a slight eminence in a forest. The road, very old and narrow, passes in front of its drawbridge, never raised in my time, and its moat, stocked with perch, and sailed over by many swans, and floating on its surface white fleets of water lilies.

Over all this the schloss shows its many-windowed front; its towers, and its Gothic chapel.

The forest opens in an irregular and very picturesque glade before its gate, and at the right a steep Gothic bridge carries the road over a stream that winds in deep shadow through the wood. I have said that this is a very lonely place. Judge whether I say truth. Looking from the hall door towards the road, the forest in which our castle stands extends fifteen miles to the right, and twelve to the left. The nearest inhabited village is about seven of your English miles to the left. The nearest inhabited schloss of any historic associations, is that of old General Spielsdorf, nearly twenty miles away to the right.

I have said "the nearest *inhabited* village," because there is, only three miles westward, that is to say in the direction of General Spielsdorf's schloss, a ruined village, with its quaint little church, now roofless, in the aisle of which are the moldering tombs of the proud family of Karnstein, now extinct, who once owned the equally desolate chateau which, in the thick of the forest, overlooks the silent ruins of the town.

Respecting the cause of the desertion of this striking and melancholy spot, there is a legend which I shall relate to you another time.

I must tell you now, how very small is the party who constitute the inhabitants of our castle. I don't include servants, or those dependents who occupy rooms in the buildings attached to the schloss. Listen, and wonder! My father, who is the kindest man on earth, but growing old; and I, at the date of my story, only nineteen. Eight years have passed since then.

I and my father constituted the family at the schloss. My mother, a Styrian lady, died in my infancy, but I had a good-natured governess, who had been with me from, I might almost say, my infancy. I could not remember the time when her fat, benignant face was not a familiar picture in my memory.

This was Madame Perrodon, a native of Berne, whose care and good nature now in part supplied to me the loss of my mother, whom I do not even remember, so early I lost her. She made a third at our little dinner party. There was a fourth, Mademoiselle De Lafontaine, a lady such as you term, I believe, a "finishing governess." She spoke French and German, Madame Perrodon French and broken English, to which my father and I added English, which, partly to prevent its becoming a lost language among us, and partly from patriotic motives, we spoke every day. The consequence was a Babel, at which strangers used to laugh, and which I shall make no attempt to reproduce in this narrative. And there were two or three young lady friends besides, pretty nearly of my own age, who were occasional visitors, for longer or shorter terms; and these visits I sometimes returned.

These were our regular social resources; but of course there were chance visits from "neighbours" of only five or six leagues distance. My life was, notwithstanding, rather a solitary one, I can assure you.

My gouvernantes had just so much control over me as you might conjecture such sage persons would have in the case of a rather spoiled girl, whose only parent allowed her pretty nearly her own way in everything.

The first occurrence in my existence, which produced a terrible impression upon my mind, which, in fact, never has been effaced, was one of the very earliest incidents of my life which I can recollect. Some people will think it so trifling that it should not be recorded here. You will see, however, by-and-by, why I mention it. The nursery, as it was called, though I had it all to myself, was a large room in the upper story of the castle, with a steep oak roof. I can't have been more than six years old, when one night I awoke, and looking round the room from my bed, failed to see the nursery maid. Neither was my nurse there; and I thought myself alone. I was not frightened, for I was one of those happy children who are studiously kept in ignorance of ghost stories, of fairy tales, and of all such lore as makes us cover up our heads when the door cracks suddenly, or the flicker of an expiring candle makes the shadow of a bedpost dance upon the wall, nearer to our faces. I was vexed and insulted at finding myself, as I conceived, neglected, and I began to whimper, preparatory to a hearty bout of roaring; when to my surprise, I saw a solemn, but very pretty face looking at me from the side of the bed. It was that of a young lady who was kneeling, with her hands under the coverlet. I looked at her with a kind of pleased wonder, and ceased whimpering. She caressed me with her hands, and lay down beside me on the bed, and drew me towards her, smiling; I felt immediately delightfully soothed, and fell asleep again. I was wakened by a sensation as if two needles ran into my breast very deep at the same moment, and I cried loudly. The lady started back, with her eyes fixed on me, and then slipped down upon the floor, and, as I thought, hid herself under the bed.

I was now for the first time frightened, and I yelled with all my might and main. Nurse, nursery maid, housekeeper, all came running in, and hearing my story, they made light of it, soothing me all they could meanwhile. But, child as I was, I could perceive that their faces were pale with an unwonted look of anxiety, and I saw them look under the bed, and about the room, and peep under tables and pluck open cupboards; and the housekeeper whispered to the nurse: "Lay your hand along that hollow in the bed; someone *did* lie there, so sure as you did not; the place is still warm."

I remember the nursery maid petting me, and all three examining my chest, where I told them I felt the puncture, and pronouncing that there was no sign visible that any such thing had happened to me.

The housekeeper and the two other servants who were in charge of the nursery, remained sitting up all night; and from that time a servant always sat up in the nursery until I was about fourteen.

I was very nervous for a long time after this. A doctor was called in, he was pallid and elderly. How well I remember his long saturnine face, slightly pitted with smallpox, and his chestnut wig. For a good while, every second day, he came and gave me medicine, which of course I hated.

The morning after I saw this apparition I was in a state of terror, and could not bear to be left alone, daylight though it was, for a moment.

I remember my father coming up and standing at the bedside, and talking cheerfully, and asking the nurse a number of questions, and laughing very heartily at one of the answers; and patting me on the shoulder, and kissing me, and telling me not to be frightened, that it was nothing but a dream and could not hurt me.

But I was not comforted, for I knew the visit of the strange woman was *not* a dream; and I was *awfully* frightened.

I was a little consoled by the nursery maid's assuring me that it was she who had come and looked at me, and lain down beside me in the bed, and that I must have been half-dreaming not to have known her face. But this, though supported by the nurse, did not quite satisfy me.

I remembered, in the course of that day, a venerable old man, in a black cassock, coming into the room with the nurse and housekeeper, and talking a little to them, and very kindly to me; his face was very sweet and gentle, and he told me they were going to pray, and joined my hands together, and desired me to say, softly, while they were praying, "Lord hear all good prayers for us, for Jesus' sake." I think these were the very words, for I often repeated them to myself, and my nurse used for years to make me say them in my prayers.

I remembered so well the thoughtful sweet face of that white-haired old man, in his black cassock, as he stood in that rude, lofty, brown room, with the clumsy furniture of a fashion three hundred years old about him, and the scanty light entering its shadowy atmosphere through the small lattice. He kneeled, and the three women with him, and he prayed aloud with an earnest quavering voice for, what appeared to me, a long time. I forget all my life preceding that event, and for some time after it is all obscure also, but the scenes I have just described stand out vivid as the isolated pictures of the phantasmagoria surrounded by darkness.

II. A GUEST

I am now going to tell you something so strange that it will require all your faith in my veracity to believe my story. It is not only true, nevertheless, but truth of which I have been an eyewitness.

It was a sweet summer evening, and my father asked me, as he sometimes did, to take a little ramble with him along that beautiful forest vista which I have mentioned as lying in front of the schloss.

"General Spielsdorf cannot come to us so soon as I had hoped," said my father, as we pursued our walk.

He was to have paid us a visit of some weeks, and we had expected his arrival next day. He was to have brought with him a young lady, his niece and ward, Mademoiselle Rheinfeldt, whom I had never seen, but whom I had heard described as a very charming girl, and in whose society I had promised myself many happy days. I was more disappointed than a young lady living in a town, or a bustling neighborhood can possibly imagine. This visit, and the new acquaintance it promised, had furnished my day dream for many weeks.

"And how soon does he come?" I asked.

"Not till autumn. Not for two months, I dare say," he answered. "And I am very glad now, dear, that you never knew Mademoiselle Rheinfeldt."

"And why?" I asked, both mortified and curious.

"Because the poor young lady is dead," he replied. "I quite forgot I had not told you, but you were not in the room when I received the General's letter this evening."

I was very much shocked. General Spielsdorf had mentioned in his first letter, six or seven weeks before, that she was not so well as he would wish her, but there was nothing to suggest the remotest suspicion of danger.

"Here is the General's letter," he said, handing it to me. "I am afraid he is in great affliction; the letter appears to me to have been written very nearly in distraction."

We sat down on a rude bench, under a group of magnificent lime trees. The sun was setting with all its melancholy splendor behind the sylvan horizon, and the stream that flows beside our home, and passes under the steep old bridge I have mentioned, wound through many a group of noble trees, almost at our feet, reflecting in its current the fading crimson of the sky. General Spielsdorf's letter was so extraordinary, so vehement, and in some places so self-contradictory, that I read it twice over—the second time aloud to my father—and was still unable to account for it, except by supposing that grief had unsettled his mind.

It said "I have lost my darling daughter, for as such I loved her. During the last days of dear Bertha's illness I was not able to write to you.

"Before then I had no idea of her danger. I have lost her, and now learn *all*, too late. She died in the peace of innocence, and in the glorious hope of a blessed futurity. The fiend who betrayed our infatuated hospitality has done it all. I thought I was receiving into my house innocence, gaiety, a charming companion for my lost Bertha. Heavens! what a fool have I been!

"I thank God my child died without a suspicion of the cause of her sufferings. She is gone without so much as conjecturing the nature of her illness, and the accursed passion of the agent of all this misery. I devote my remaining days to tracking and extinguishing a monster. I am told I may hope to accomplish my righteous and merciful purpose. At present there is scarcely a gleam of light to guide me. I curse my conceited incredulity, my despicable affectation of superiority, my blindness, my obstinacy—all—too late. I cannot write or talk collectedly now. I am distracted. So soon as I shall have a little recovered, I mean to devote myself for a time to enquiry, which may possibly lead me as far as Vienna. Some time in the autumn, two months hence, or earlier if I live, I will see you—that is, if you permit me; I will then tell you all that I scarce dare put upon paper now. Farewell. Pray for me, dear friend."

In these terms ended this strange letter. Though I had never seen Bertha Rheinfeldt my eyes filled with tears at the sudden intelligence; I was startled, as well as profoundly disappointed.

The sun had now set, and it was twilight by the time I had returned the General's letter to my father.

It was a soft clear evening, and we loitered, speculating upon the possible meanings of the violent and incoherent sentences which I had just been reading. We had nearly a mile to walk before reaching the road that passes the schloss in front, and by that time the moon was shining brilliantly. At the drawbridge we met Madame Perrodon and Mademoiselle De Lafontaine, who had come out, without their bonnets, to enjoy the exquisite moonlight.

We heard their voices gabbling in animated dialogue as we approached. We joined them at the drawbridge, and turned about to admire with them the beautiful scene.

The glade through which we had just walked lay before us. At our left the narrow road wound away under clumps of lordly trees, and was lost to sight amid the thickening forest. At the right the same road crosses the steep and picturesque bridge, near which stands a ruined tower which once guarded that pass; and beyond the bridge an abrupt eminence rises, covered with trees, and showing in the shadows some grey ivy-clustered rocks.

Over the sward and low grounds a thin film of mist was stealing like smoke, marking the distances with a transparent veil; and here and there we could see the river faintly flashing in the moonlight.

No softer, sweeter scene could be imagined. The news I had just heard made it melancholy; but nothing could disturb its character of profound serenity, and the enchanted glory and vagueness of the prospect.

My father, who enjoyed the picturesque, and I, stood looking in silence over the expanse beneath us. The two good governesses, standing a little way behind us, discoursed upon the scene, and were eloquent upon the moon.

Madame Perrodon was fat, middle-aged, and romantic, and talked and sighed poetically. Mademoiselle De Lafontaine—in right of her father who was a German, assumed to be psychological, metaphysical, and something of a mystic—now declared that when the moon shone with a light so intense it was well known that it indicated a special spiritual activity. The effect of the full moon in such a state of brilliancy was manifold. It acted on dreams, it acted on lunacy, it acted on nervous people, it had marvelous physical influences connected with life. Mademoiselle related that her cousin, who was mate of a merchant ship, having taken a nap on deck on such a night, lying on his back, with his face full in the light on the moon, had wakened, after a dream of an old woman clawing him by the cheek, with his features horribly drawn to one side; and his countenance had never quite recovered its equilibrium.

"The moon, this night," she said, "is full of idyllic and magnetic influence—and see, when you look behind you at the front of the schloss how all its windows flash and twinkle with that silvery splendor, as if unseen hands had lighted up the rooms to receive fairy guests."

There are indolent styles of the spirits in which, indisposed to talk ourselves, the talk of others is pleasant to our listless ears; and I gazed on, pleased with the tinkle of the ladies' conversation.

"I have got into one of my moping moods tonight," said my father, after a silence, and quoting Shakespeare, whom, by way of keeping up our English, he used to read aloud, he said:

"'In truth I know not why I am so sad.
It wearies me: you say it wearies you;
But how I got it—came by it.'

"I forget the rest. But I feel as if some great misfortune were hanging over us. I suppose the poor General's afflicted letter has had something to do with it."

At this moment the unwonted sound of carriage wheels and many hoofs upon the road, arrested our attention.

They seemed to be approaching from the high ground overlooking the bridge, and very soon the equipage emerged from that point. Two horsemen first crossed the bridge, then came a carriage drawn by four horses, and two men rode behind.

It seemed to be the traveling carriage of a person of rank; and we were all immediately absorbed in watching that very unusual spectacle. It became, in a few moments, greatly more interesting, for just as the carriage had passed the summit of the steep bridge, one of the leaders, taking fright, communicated his panic to the rest, and after a plunge or two, the whole team broke into a wild gallop together, and dashing between the horsemen who rode in front, came thundering along the road towards us with the speed of a hurricane.

The excitement of the scene was made more painful by the clear, long-drawn screams of a female voice from the carriage window.

We all advanced in curiosity and horror; me rather in silence, the rest with various ejaculations of terror.

Our suspense did not last long. Just before you reach the castle drawbridge, on the route they were coming, there stands by the roadside a magnificent lime tree, on the other stands an ancient stone cross, at sight of which the horses, now going at a pace that was perfectly frightful, swerved so as to bring the wheel over the projecting roots of the tree.

I knew what was coming. I covered my eyes, unable to see it out, and turned my head away; at the same moment I heard a cry from my lady friends, who had gone on a little.

Curiosity opened my eyes, and I saw a scene of utter confusion. Two of the horses were on the ground, the carriage lay upon its side with two wheels in the air; the men were busy removing the traces, and a lady with a commanding air and figure had got out, and stood with clasped hands, raising the handkerchief that was in them every now and then to her eyes.

Through the carriage door was now lifted a young lady, who appeared to be lifeless. My dear old father was already beside the elder lady, with his hat in his hand, evidently tendering his aid and the resources of his schloss. The lady did not appear to hear him, or to have eyes for anything but the slender girl who was being placed against the slope of the bank.

I approached; the young lady was apparently stunned, but she was certainly not dead. My father, who piqued himself on being something of a physician, had just had his fingers on her wrist and assured the lady, who declared herself her mother, that her pulse, though faint and irregular, was undoubtedly still distinguishable. The lady clasped her hands and looked upward, as if in a momentary transport of gratitude; but immediately she broke out again in that theatrical way which is, I believe, natural to some people.

She was what is called a fine looking woman for her time of life, and must have been handsome; she was tall, but not thin, and dressed in black velvet, and looked rather pale, but with a proud and commanding countenance, though now agitated strangely.

"Who was ever being so born to calamity?" I heard her say, with clasped hands, as I came up. "Here am I, on a journey of life and death, in prosecuting which to lose an hour is possibly to lose all. My child will not have recovered sufficiently to resume her route for who can say how long. I must leave her: I cannot, dare not, delay. How far on, sir, can you tell, is the nearest village? I must leave her there; and shall not see my darling, or even hear of her till my return, three months hence."

I plucked my father by the coat, and whispered earnestly in his ear: "Oh! papa, pray ask her to let her stay with us—it would be so delightful. Do, pray."

"If Madame will entrust her child to the care of my daughter, and of her good gouvernante, Madame Perrodon, and permit her to remain as our guest, under my charge, until her return, it will confer a distinction and an obligation upon us, and we shall treat her with all the care and devotion which so sacred a trust deserves."

"I cannot do that, sir, it would be to task your kindness and chivalry too cruelly," said the lady, distractedly.

"It would, on the contrary, be to confer on us a very great kindness at the moment when we most need it. My daughter has just been disappointed by a cruel misfortune, in a visit from which she had long anticipated a great deal of happiness. If you confide this young lady to our care it will be her best consolation. The nearest village on your route is distant, and affords no such inn as you could think of placing your daughter at; you cannot allow her to continue her journey for any considerable distance without danger. If, as you say, you cannot suspend your journey, you must part with her tonight, and nowhere could you do so with more honest assurances of care and tenderness than here."

There was something in this lady's air and appearance so distinguished and even imposing, and in her manner so engaging, as to impress one, quite apart from the dignity of her equipage, with a conviction that she was a person of consequence.

By this time the carriage was replaced in its upright position, and the horses, quite tractable, in the traces again.

The lady threw on her daughter a glance which I fancied was not quite so affectionate as one might have anticipated from the beginning of the scene; then she beckoned slightly to my father, and withdrew two or three steps with him out of hearing; and talked to him with a fixed and stern countenance, not at all like that with which she had hitherto spoken.

I was filled with wonder that my father did not seem to perceive the change, and also unspeakably curious to learn what it could be that she was speaking, almost in his ear, with so much earnestness and rapidity.

Two or three minutes at most I think she remained thus employed, then she turned, and a few steps brought her to where her daughter lay, supported by Madame Perrodon. She kneeled beside her for a moment and whispered, as Madame supposed, a little benediction in her ear; then hastily kissing her she stepped into her carriage, the door was closed, the footmen in stately liveries jumped up behind, the outriders spurred on, the postilions cracked their whips, the horses plunged and broke suddenly into a furious canter that threatened soon again to become a gallop, and the carriage whirled away, followed at the same rapid pace by the two horsemen in the rear.

III. WE COMPARE NOTES

We followed the *cortège* with our eyes until it was swiftly lost to sight in the misty wood; and the very sound of the hoofs and the wheels died away in the silent night air.

Nothing remained to assure us that the adventure had not been an illusion of a moment but the young lady, who just at that moment opened her eyes. I could not see, for her face was turned from me, but she raised her head, evidently looking about her, and I heard a very sweet voice ask complainingly, "Where is mamma?"

Our good Madame Perrodon answered tenderly, and added some comfortable assurances.

I then heard her ask:

"Where am I? What is this place?" and after that she said, "I don't see the carriage; and Matska, where is she?"

Madame answered all her questions in so far as she understood them; and gradually the young lady remembered how the misadventure came about, and was glad to hear that no one in, or in attendance on, the carriage was hurt; and on learning that her mamma had left her here, till her return in about three months, she wept.

I was going to add my consolations to those of Madame Perrodon when Mademoiselle De Lafontaine placed her hand upon my arm, saying:

"Don't approach, one at a time is as much as she can at present converse with; a very little excitement would possibly overpower her now."

As soon as she is comfortably in bed, I thought, I will run up to her room and see her.

My father in the meantime had sent a servant on horseback for the physician, who lived about two leagues away; and a bedroom was being prepared for the young lady's reception.

The stranger now rose, and leaning on Madame's arm, walked slowly over the drawbridge and into the castle gate.

In the hall, servants waited to receive her, and she was conducted forthwith to her room. The room we usually sat in as our drawing room is long, having four windows, that looked over the moat and drawbridge, upon the forest scene I have just described.

It is furnished in old carved oak, with large carved cabinets, and the chairs are cushioned with crimson Utrecht velvet. The walls are covered with tapestry, and surrounded with great gold frames, the figures being as large as life, in ancient and very curious costume, and the subjects represented are hunting, hawking, and generally festive. It is not too stately to be extremely comfortable; and here we had our tea, for with his usual patriotic leanings he insisted that the national beverage should make its appearance regularly with our coffee and chocolate.

We sat here this night, and with candles lighted, were talking over the adventure of the evening.

Madame Perrodon and Mademoiselle De Lafontaine were both of our party. The young stranger had hardly lain down in her bed when she sank into a deep sleep; and those ladies had left her in the care of a servant.

"How do you like our guest?" I asked, as soon as Madame entered. "Tell me all about her?"

"I like her extremely," answered Madame, "she is, I almost think, the prettiest creature I ever saw; about your age, and so gentle and nice."

"She is absolutely beautiful," threw in Mademoiselle, who had peeped for a moment into the stranger's room.

"And such a sweet voice!" added Madame Perrodon.

"Did you remark a woman in the carriage, after it was set up again, who did not get out," enquired Mademoiselle, "but only looked from the window?"

"No, we had not seen her."

Then she described a hideous black woman, with a sort of colored turban on her head, and who was gazing all the time from the carriage window, nodding and grinning derisively towards the ladies, with gleaming eyes and large white eyeballs, and her teeth set as if in fury.

"Did you remark what an ill-looking pack of men the servants were?" asked Madame.

"Yes," said my father, who had just come in, "ugly, hang-dog looking fellows as ever I beheld in my life. I hope they mayn't rob the poor lady in the forest. They are clever rogues, however; they got everything to rights in a minute."

"I dare say they are worn out with too long traveling," said Madame.

"Besides looking wicked, their faces were so strangely lean, and dark, and sullen. I am very curious, I own; but I dare say the young lady will tell you all about it tomorrow, if she is sufficiently recovered."

"I don't think she will," said my father, with a mysterious smile, and a little nod of his head, as if he knew more about it than he cared to tell us.

This made us all the more inquisitive as to what had passed between him and the lady in the black velvet, in the brief but earnest interview that had immediately preceded her departure.

We were scarcely alone, when I entreated him to tell me. He did not need much pressing.

"There is no particular reason why I should not tell you. She expressed a reluctance to trouble us with the care of her daughter, saying she was in delicate health, and nervous, but not subject to any kind of seizure—she volunteered that—nor to any illusion; being, in fact, perfectly sane."

"How very odd to say all that!" I interpolated. "It was so unnecessary."

"At all events it *was* said," he laughed, "and as you wish to know all that passed, which was indeed very little, I tell you. She then said, 'I am making a long journey of *vital* importance—she emphasized the word—rapid and secret; I shall return for my child in three months; in the meantime, she will be silent as to who we are, whence we come, and whither we are traveling.' That is all she said. She spoke very pure French. When she said the word 'secret,' she paused for a few seconds, looking sternly, her eyes fixed on mine. I fancy she makes a great point of that. You saw how quickly she was gone. I hope I have not done a very foolish thing, in taking charge of the young lady."

For my part, I was delighted. I was longing to see and talk to her; and only waiting till the doctor should give me leave. You, who live in towns, can have no idea how great an event the introduction of a new friend is, in such a solitude as surrounded us.

The doctor did not arrive till nearly one o'clock; but I could no more have gone to my bed and slept, than I could have overtaken, on foot, the carriage in which the princess in black velvet had driven away.

When the physician came down to the drawing room, it was to report very favorably upon his patient. She was now sitting up, her pulse quite regular, apparently perfectly well. She had sustained no injury, and the little shock to her nerves had passed away quite harmlessly. There could be no harm certainly in my seeing her, if we both wished it; and, with this permission I sent, forthwith, to know whether she would allow me to visit her for a few minutes in her room.

The servant returned immediately to say that she desired nothing more.

You may be sure I was not long in availing myself of this permission.

Our visitor lay in one of the handsomest rooms in the schloss. It was, perhaps, a little stately. There was a somber piece of tapestry opposite the foot of the bed, representing Cleopatra with the asps to her bosom; and other solemn classic scenes were displayed, a little faded, upon the other walls. But there was gold carving, and rich and varied color enough in the other decorations of the room, to more than redeem the gloom of the old tapestry.

There were candles at the bedside. She was sitting up; her slender pretty figure enveloped in the soft silk dressing gown, embroidered with flowers, and lined with thick quilted silk, which her mother had thrown over her feet as she lay upon the ground.

What was it that, as I reached the bedside and had just begun my little greeting, struck me dumb in a moment, and made me recoil a step or two from before her? I will tell you.

I saw the very face which had visited me in my childhood at night, which remained so fixed in my memory, and on which I had for so many years so often ruminated with horror, when no one suspected of what I was thinking.

It was pretty, even beautiful; and when I first beheld it, wore the same melancholy expression.

But this almost instantly lighted into a strange fixed smile of recognition.

There was a silence of fully a minute, and then at length she spoke; I could not.

"How wonderful!" she exclaimed. "Twelve years ago, I saw your face in a dream, and it has haunted me ever since."

"Wonderful indeed!" I repeated, overcoming with an effort the horror that had for a time suspended my utterances. "Twelve years ago, in vision or reality,

I certainly saw you. I could not forget your face. It has remained before my eyes ever since."

Her smile had softened. Whatever I had fancied strange in it, was gone, and it and her dimpling cheeks were now delightfully pretty and intelligent.

I felt reassured, and continued more in the vein which hospitality indicated, to bid her welcome, and to tell her how much pleasure her accidental arrival had given us all, and especially what a happiness it was to me.

I took her hand as I spoke. I was a little shy, as lonely people are, but the situation made me eloquent, and even bold. She pressed my hand, she laid hers upon it, and her eyes glowed, as, looking hastily into mine, she smiled again, and blushed.

She answered my welcome very prettily. I sat down beside her, still wondering; and she said:

"I must tell you my vision about you; it is so very strange that you and I should have had, each of the other so vivid a dream, that each should have seen, I you and you me, looking as we do now, when of course we both were mere children. I was a child, about six years old, and I awoke from a confused and troubled dream, and found myself in a room, unlike my nursery, wainscoted clumsily in some dark wood, and with cupboards and bedsteads, and chairs, and benches placed about it. The beds were, I thought, all empty, and the room itself without anyone but myself in it; and I, after looking about me for some time, and admiring especially an iron candlestick with two branches, which I should certainly know again, crept under one of the beds to reach the window; but as I got from under the bed, I heard someone crying; and looking up, while I was still upon my knees, I saw you—most assuredly you—as I see you now; a beautiful young lady, with golden hair and large blue eyes, and lips—your lips—you as you are here.

"Your looks won me; I climbed on the bed and put my arms about you, and I think we both fell asleep. I was aroused by a scream; you were sitting up screaming. I was frightened, and slipped down upon the ground, and, it seemed to me, lost consciousness for a moment; and when I came to myself, I was again in my nursery at home. Your face I have never forgotten since. I could not be misled by mere resemblance. *You are* the lady whom I saw then."

It was now my turn to relate my corresponding vision, which I did, to the undisguised wonder of my new acquaintance.

"I don't know which should be most afraid of the other," she said, again smiling—"If you were less pretty I think I should be very much afraid of you, but being as you are, and you and I both so young, I feel only that I have made your acquaintance twelve years ago, and have already a right to your intimacy; at all events it does seem as if we were destined, from our earliest childhood, to be friends. I wonder whether you feel as strangely drawn towards me as I do to you; I have never had a friend—shall I find one now?" She sighed, and her fine dark eyes gazed passionately on me.

Now the truth is, I felt rather unaccountably towards the beautiful stranger. I did feel, as she said, "drawn towards her," but there was also something of repulsion. In this ambiguous feeling, however, the sense of attraction immensely prevailed. She interested and won me; she was so beautiful and so indescribably engaging.

I perceived now something of languor and exhaustion stealing over her, and hastened to bid her good night.

"The doctor thinks," I added, "that you ought to have a maid to sit up with you tonight; one of ours is waiting, and you will find her a very useful and quiet creature."

"How kind of you, but I could not sleep, I never could with an attendant in the room. I shan't require any assistance—and, shall I confess my weakness, I am haunted with a terror of robbers. Our house was robbed once, and two servants murdered, so I always lock my door. It has become a habit—and you look so kind I know you will forgive me. I see there is a key in the lock."

She held me close in her pretty arms for a moment and whispered in my ear, "Good night, darling, it is very hard to part with you, but good night; tomorrow, but not early, I shall see you again."

She sank back on the pillow with a sigh, and her fine eyes followed me with a fond and melancholy gaze, and she murmured again "Good night, dear friend."

Young people like, and even love, on impulse. I was flattered by the evident, though as yet undeserved, fondness she showed me. I liked the confidence with which she at once received me. She was determined that we should be very near friends.

Next day came and we met again. I was delighted with my companion; that is to say, in many respects.

Her looks lost nothing in daylight—she was certainly the most beautiful creature I had ever seen, and the unpleasant remembrance of the face presented in my early dream, had lost the effect of the first unexpected recognition.

She confessed that she had experienced a similar shock on seeing me, and precisely the same faint antipathy that had mingled with my admiration of her. We now laughed together over our momentary horrors.

IV. HER HABITS—A SAUNTER

I told you that I was charmed with her in most particulars.

There were some that did not please me so well.

She was above the middle height of women. I shall begin by describing her. She was slender, and wonderfully graceful. Except that her movements were languid—very languid—indeed, there was nothing in her appearance to indicate an invalid. Her complexion was rich and brilliant; her features were small and beautifully formed; her eyes large, dark, and lustrous; her hair was quite wonderful, I never saw hair so magnificently thick and long when it was down about her shoulders; I have often placed my hands under it, and laughed with wonder at its weight. It was exquisitely fine and soft, and in color a rich very dark brown, with something of gold. I loved to let it down, tumbling with its own weight, as, in her room, she lay back in her chair talking in her sweet low voice, I used to fold and braid it, and spread it out and play with it. Heavens! If I had but known all!

I said there were particulars which did not please me. I have told you that her confidence won me the first night I saw her; but I found that she exercised with respect to herself, her mother, her history, everything in fact connected with her life, plans, and people, an ever wakeful reserve. I dare say I was unreasonable, perhaps I was wrong; I dare say I ought to have respected the solemn injunction laid upon my father by the stately lady in black velvet. But curiosity is a restless and unscrupulous passion, and no one girl can endure, with patience, that hers should be baffled by another. What harm could it do anyone to tell me what I so ardently desired to know? Had she no trust in my good sense or honour? Why would she not believe me when I assured her, so solemnly, that I would not divulge one syllable of what she told me to any mortal breathing.

There was a coldness, it seemed to me, beyond her years, in her smiling melancholy persistent refusal to afford me the least ray of light.

I cannot say we quarreled upon this point, for she would not quarrel upon any. It was, of course, very unfair of me to press her, very ill-bred, but I really could not help it; and I might just as well have let it alone.

What she did tell me amounted, in my unconscionable estimation—to nothing.

It was all summed up in three very vague disclosures:

First—Her name was Carmilla.

Second—Her family was very ancient and noble.

Third—Her home lay in the direction of the west.

She would not tell me the name of her family, nor their armorial bearings, nor the name of their estate, nor even that of the country they lived in.

You are not to suppose that I worried her incessantly on these subjects. I watched opportunity, and rather insinuated than urged my enquiries. Once or twice, indeed, I did attack her more directly. But no matter what my tactics, utter failure was invariably the result. Reproaches and caresses were all lost upon her. But I must add this, that her evasion was conducted with so pretty a melancholy and deprecation, with so many, and even passionate declarations of her liking for me, and trust in my honor, and with so many promises that I should at last know all, that I could not find it in my heart long to be offended with her.

She used to place her pretty arms about my neck, draw me to her, and laying her cheek to mine, murmur with her lips near my ear, "Dearest, your little heart is wounded; think me not cruel because I obey the irresistible law of my strength and weakness; if your dear heart is wounded, my wild heart bleeds with yours. In the rapture of my enormous humiliation I live in your warm life, and you shall die—die, sweetly die—into mine. I cannot help it; as I draw near to you, you, in your turn, will draw near to others, and learn the rapture of that cruelty, which yet is love; so, for a while, seek to know no more of me and mine, but trust me with all your loving spirit."

And when she had spoken such a rhapsody, she would press me more closely in her trembling embrace, and her lips in soft kisses gently glow upon my cheek.

Her agitations and her language were unintelligible to me.

From these foolish embraces, which were not of very frequent occurrence, I must allow, I used to wish to extricate myself; but my energies seemed to fail me. Her murmured words sounded like a lullaby in my ear, and soothed my resistance into a trance, from which I only seemed to recover myself when she withdrew her arms.

In these mysterious moods I did not like her. I experienced a strange tumultuous excitement that was pleasurable, ever and anon, mingled with a vague sense of fear and disgust. I had no distinct thoughts about her while such scenes lasted, but I was conscious of a love growing into adoration, and also of abhorrence. This I know is paradox, but I can make no other attempt to explain the feeling.

I now write, after an interval of more than ten years, with a trembling hand, with a confused and horrible recollection of certain occurrences and situations, in the ordeal through which I was unconsciously passing; though with a vivid and very sharp remembrance of the main current of my story.

But, I suspect, in all lives there are certain emotional scenes, those in which our passions have been most wildly and terribly roused, that are of all others the most vaguely and dimly remembered.

Sometimes after an hour of apathy, my strange and beautiful companion would take my hand and hold it with a fond pressure, renewed again and again; blushing softly, gazing in my face with languid and burning eyes, and breathing so fast that her dress rose and fell with the tumultuous respiration. It was like the ardor of a lover; it embarrassed me; it was hateful and yet over-powering; and with gloating eyes she drew me to her, and her hot lips traveled along my cheek in kisses; and she would whisper, almost in sobs, "You are mine, you *shall* be mine, you and I are one for ever." Then she had thrown herself back in her chair, with her small hands over her eyes, leaving me trembling.

"Are we related," I used to ask; "what can you mean by all this? I remind you perhaps of someone whom you love; but you must not, I hate it; I don't know you—I don't know myself when you look so and talk so."

She used to sigh at my vehemence, then turn away and drop my hand.

Respecting these very extraordinary manifestations I strove in vain to form any satisfactory theory—I could not refer them to affectation or trick. It was unmistakably the momentary breaking out of suppressed instinct and emotion. Was she, notwithstanding her mother's volunteered denial, subject to brief visitations of insanity; or was there here a disguise and a romance? I had read in old storybooks of such things. What if a boyish lover had found his way into the house, and sought to prosecute his suit in masquerade, with the assistance of a clever old adventuress. But there were many things against this hypothesis, highly interesting as it was to my vanity.

I could boast of no little attentions such as masculine gallantry delights to offer. Between these passionate moments there were long intervals of commonplace, of gaiety, of brooding melancholy, during which, except that I detected her eyes so full of melancholy fire, following me, at times I might have been as nothing to her. Except in these brief periods of mysterious excitement her ways were girlish; and there was always a languor about her, quite incompatible with a masculine system in a state of health.

In some respects her habits were odd. Perhaps not so singular in the opinion of a town lady like you, as they appeared to us rustic people. She used to come down very late, generally not till one o'clock, she would then take a cup of chocolate, but eat nothing; we then went out for a walk, which was a mere saunter, and she seemed, almost immediately, exhausted, and either returned to the schloss or sat on one of the benches that were placed, here and there, among the trees. This was a bodily languor in which her mind did not sympathize. She was always an animated talker, and very intelligent.

She sometimes alluded for a moment to her own home, or mentioned an adventure or situation, or an early recollection, which indicated a people of strange manners, and described customs of which we knew nothing. I gathered from these chance hints that her native country was much more remote than I had at first fancied.

As we sat thus one afternoon under the trees a funeral passed us by. It was that of a pretty young girl, whom I had often seen, the daughter of one of the rangers of the forest. The poor man was walking behind the coffin of his darling; she was his only child, and he looked quite heartbroken.

Peasants walking two-and-two came behind, they were singing a funeral hymn.

I rose to mark my respect as they passed, and joined in the hymn they were very sweetly singing.

My companion shook me a little roughly, and I turned surprised.

She said brusquely, "Don't you perceive how discordant that is?"

"I think it very sweet, on the contrary," I answered, vexed at the interruption, and very uncomfortable, lest the people who composed the little procession should observe and resent what was passing.

I resumed, therefore, instantly, and was again interrupted. "You pierce my ears," said Carmilla, almost angrily, and stopping her ears with her tiny fingers. "Besides, how can you tell that your religion and mine are the same; your forms wound me, and I hate funerals. What a fuss! Why you must die—*everyone* must die; and all are happier when they do. Come home."

"My father has gone on with the clergyman to the churchyard. I thought you knew she was to be buried today."

"She? I don't trouble my head about peasants. I don't know who she is," answered Carmilla, with a flash from her fine eyes.

"She is the poor girl who fancied she saw a ghost a fortnight ago, and has been dying ever since, till yesterday, when she expired."

"Tell me nothing about ghosts. I shan't sleep tonight if you do."

"I hope there is no plague or fever coming; all this looks very like it," I continued. "The swineherd's young wife died only a week ago, and she thought something seized her by the throat as she lay in her bed, and nearly strangled her. Papa says such horrible fancies do accompany some forms of fever. She was quite well the day before. She sank afterwards, and died before a week."

"Well, *her* funeral is over, I hope, and *her* hymn sung; and our ears shan't be tortured with that discord and jargon. It has made me nervous. Sit down here, beside me; sit close; hold my hand; press it hard-hard-harder."

We had moved a little back, and had come to another seat.

She sat down. Her face underwent a change that alarmed and even terrified me for a moment. It darkened, and became horribly livid; her teeth and hands were clenched, and she frowned and compressed her lips, while she stared down upon the ground at her feet, and trembled all over with a continued shudder as irrepressible as ague. All her energies seemed strained to suppress a fit, with which she was then breathlessly tugging; and at length a low convulsive cry of suffering broke from her, and gradually the hysteria subsided. "There! That comes of strangling people with hymns!" she said at last. "Hold me, hold me still. It is passing away."

And so gradually it did; and perhaps to dissipate the somber impression which the spectacle had left upon me, she became unusually animated and chatty; and so we got home.

This was the first time I had seen her exhibit any definable symptoms of that delicacy of health which her mother had spoken of. It was the first time, also, I had seen her exhibit anything like temper.

Both passed away like a summer cloud; and never but once afterwards did I witness on her part a momentary sign of anger. I will tell you how it happened.

She and I were looking out of one of the long drawing room windows, when there entered the courtyard, over the drawbridge, a figure of a wanderer whom I knew very well. He used to visit the schloss generally twice a year.

It was the figure of a hunchback, with the sharp lean features that generally accompany deformity. He wore a pointed black beard, and he was smiling from ear to ear, showing his white fangs. He was dressed in buff, black, and scarlet, and crossed with more straps and belts than I could count, from which hung all manner of things. Behind, he carried a magic lantern, and two boxes, which I well knew, in one of which was a salamander, and in the other a mandrake. These monsters used to make my father laugh. They were compounded of parts of monkeys, parrots, squirrels, fish, and hedgehogs, dried and stitched together with great neatness and startling effect. He had a fiddle, a box of conjuring apparatus, a pair of foils and masks attached to his belt, several other mysterious cases dangling about him, and a black staff with copper ferrules in his hand. His companion was a rough spare dog, that followed at his heels, but stopped short, suspiciously at the drawbridge, and in a little while began to howl dismally.

In the meantime, the mountebank, standing in the midst of the courtyard, raised his grotesque hat, and made us a very ceremonious bow, paying his compliments very volubly in execrable French, and German not much better.

Then, disengaging his fiddle, he began to scrape a lively air to which he sang with a merry discord, dancing with ludicrous airs and activity, that made me laugh, in spite of the dog's howling.

Then he advanced to the window with many smiles and salutations, and his hat in his left hand, his fiddle under his arm, and with a fluency that never took breath, he gabbled a long advertisement of all his accomplishments, and the resources of the various arts which he placed at our service, and the curiosities and entertainments which it was in his power, at our bidding, to display.

"Will your ladyships be pleased to buy an amulet against the oupire, which is going like the wolf, I hear, through these woods," he said dropping his hat on the pavement. "They are dying of it right and left and here is a charm that never fails; only pinned to the pillow, and you may laugh in his face."

These charms consisted of oblong slips of vellum, with cabalistic ciphers and diagrams upon them.

Carmilla instantly purchased one, and so did I.

He was looking up, and we were smiling down upon him, amused; at least, I can answer for myself. His piercing black eye, as he looked up in our faces, seemed to detect something that fixed for a moment his curiosity. In an instant he unrolled a leather case, full of all manner of odd little steel instruments.

"See here, my lady," he said, displaying it, and addressing me, "I profess, among other things less useful, the art of dentistry. Plague take the dog!" he interpolated. "Silence, beast! He howls so that your ladyships can scarcely hear a word. Your noble friend, the young lady at your right, has the sharpest tooth,—long, thin, pointed, like an awl, like a needle; ha, ha! With my sharp and long sight, as I look up, I have seen it distinctly; now if it happens to hurt the young lady, and I think it must, here am I, here are my file, my punch, my nippers; I will make it round and blunt, if her ladyship pleases; no longer the tooth of a fish, but of a beautiful young lady as she is. Hey? Is the young lady displeased? Have I been too bold? Have I offended her?"

The young lady, indeed, looked very angry as she drew back from the window.

"How dares that mountebank insult us so? Where is your father? I shall demand redress from him. My father would have had the wretch tied up to the pump, and flogged with a cart whip, and burnt to the bones with the cattle brand!"

She retired from the window a step or two, and sat down, and had hardly lost sight of the offender, when her wrath subsided as suddenly as it had risen, and she gradually recovered her usual tone, and seemed to forget the little hunchback and his follies.

My father was out of spirits that evening. On coming in he told us that there had been another case very similar to the two fatal ones which had lately occurred. The sister of a young peasant on his estate, only a mile away, was very ill, had been, as she described it, attacked very nearly in the same way, and was now slowly but steadily sinking.

"All this," said my father, "is strictly referable to natural causes. These poor people infect one another with their superstitions, and so repeat in imagination the images of terror that have infested their neighbours."

"But that very circumstance frightens one horribly," said Carmilla.

"How so?" enquired my father.

"I am so afraid of fancying I see such things; I think it would be as bad as reality."

"We are in God's hands: nothing can happen without his permission, and all will end well for those who love him. He is our faithful creator; He has made us all, and will take care of us."

"Creator! *Nature!*" said the young lady in answer to my gentle father. "And this disease that invades the country is natural. Nature. All things proceed from Nature—don't they? All things in the heaven, in the earth, and under the earth, act and live as Nature ordains? I think so."

"The doctor said he would come here today," said my father, after a silence. "I want to know what he thinks about it, and what he thinks we had better do."

"Doctors never did me any good," said Carmilla.

"Then you have been ill?" I asked.

"More ill than ever you were," she answered.

"Long ago?"

"Yes, a long time. I suffered from this very illness; but I forget all but my pain and weakness, and they were not so bad as are suffered in other diseases."

"You were very young then?"

"I dare say, let us talk no more of it. You would not wound a friend?"

She looked languidly in my eyes, and passed her arm round my waist lovingly, and led me out of the room. My father was busy over some papers near the window.

"Why does your papa like to frighten us?" said the pretty girl with a sigh and a little shudder.

"He doesn't, dear Carmilla, it is the very furthest thing from his mind."

"Are you afraid, dearest?"

"I should be very much if I fancied there was any real danger of my being attacked as those poor people were."

"You are afraid to die?"

"Yes, every one is."

"But to die as lovers may—to die together, so that they may live together.

"Girls are caterpillars while they live in the world, to be finally butterflies when the summer comes; but in the meantime there are grubs and larvae, don't you see—each with their peculiar propensities, necessities and structure. So says Monsieur Buffon, in his big book, in the next room."

Later in the day the doctor came, and was closeted with papa for some time.

He was a skilful man, of sixty and upwards, he wore powder, and shaved his pale face as smooth as a pumpkin. He and papa emerged from the room together, and I heard papa laugh, and say as they came out:

"Well, I do wonder at a wise man like you. What do you say to hippogriffs and dragons?"

The doctor was smiling, and made answer, shaking his head—

"Nevertheless life and death are mysterious states, and we know little of the resources of either."

And so they walked on, and I heard no more. I did not then know what the doctor had been broaching, but I think I guess it now.

V. A WONDERFUL LIKENESS

This evening there arrived from Gratz the grave, dark-faced son of the picture cleaner, with a horse and cart laden with two large packing cases, having many pictures in each. It was a journey of ten leagues, and whenever a messenger arrived at the schloss from our little capital of Gratz, we used to crowd about him in the hall, to hear the news.

This arrival created in our secluded quarters quite a sensation. The cases remained in the hall, and the messenger was taken charge of by the servants till he had eaten his supper. Then with assistants, and armed with hammer, ripping chisel, and turnscrew, he met us in the hall, where we had assembled to witness the unpacking of the cases.

Carmilla sat looking listlessly on, while one after the other the old pictures, nearly all portraits, which had undergone the process of renovation, were brought to light. My mother was of an old Hungarian family, and most of these pictures, which were about to be restored to their places, had come to us through her.

My father had a list in his hand, from which he read, as the artist rummaged out the corresponding numbers. I don't know that the pictures were very good, but they were, undoubtedly, very old, and some of them very curious also. They had, for the most part, the merit of being now seen by me, I may say, for the first time; for the smoke and dust of time had all but obliterated them.

"There is a picture that I have not seen yet," said my father. "In one corner, at the top of it, is the name, as well as I could read, 'Marcia Karnstein,' and the date '1698'; and I am curious to see how it has turned out."

I remembered it; it was a small picture, about a foot and a half high, and nearly square, without a frame; but it was so blackened by age that I could not make it out.

The artist now produced it, with evident pride. It was quite beautiful; it was startling; it seemed to live. It was the effigy of Carmilla!

"Carmilla, dear, here is an absolute miracle. Here you are, living, smiling, ready to speak, in this picture. Isn't it beautiful, Papa? And see, even the little mole on her throat."

My father laughed, and said "Certainly it is a wonderful likeness," but he looked away, and to my surprise seemed but little struck by it, and went on talking to the picture cleaner, who was also something of an artist, and discoursed with intelligence about the portraits or other works, which his art had just brought into light and color, while I was more and more lost in wonder the more I looked at the picture.

"Will you let me hang this picture in my room, papa?" I asked.

"Certainly, dear," said he, smiling, "I'm very glad you think it so like. It must be prettier even than I thought it, if it is."

The young lady did not acknowledge this pretty speech, did not seem to hear it. She was leaning back in her seat, her fine eyes under their long lashes gazing on me in contemplation, and she smiled in a kind of rapture.

"And now you can read quite plainly the name that is written in the corner. It is not Marcia; it looks as if it was done in gold. The name is Mircalla, Countess Karnstein, and this is a little coronet over and underneath A.D. 1698. I am descended from the Karnsteins; that is, mamma was."

"Ah!" said the lady, languidly, "so am I, I think, a very long descent, very ancient. Are there any Karnsteins living now?"

"None who bear the name, I believe. The family were ruined, I believe, in some civil wars, long ago, but the ruins of the castle are only about three miles away."

"How interesting!" she said, languidly. "But see what beautiful moonlight!" She glanced through the hall door, which stood a little open. "Suppose you take a little ramble round the court, and look down at the road and river."

"It is so like the night you came to us," I said.

She sighed; smiling.

She rose, and each with her arm about the other's waist, we walked out upon the pavement.

In silence, slowly we walked down to the drawbridge, where the beautiful landscape opened before us.

"And so you were thinking of the night I came here?" she almost whispered.

"Are you glad I came?"

"Delighted, dear Carmilla," I answered.

"And you asked for the picture you think like me, to hang in your room," she murmured with a sigh, as she drew her arm closer about my waist, and let her pretty head sink upon my shoulder. "How romantic you are, Carmilla," I said. "Whenever you tell me your story, it will be made up chiefly of some one great romance."

She kissed me silently.

"I am sure, Carmilla, you have been in love; that there is, at this moment, an affair of the heart going on."

"I have been in love with no one, and never shall," she whispered, "unless it should be with you."

How beautiful she looked in the moonlight!

Shy and strange was the look with which she quickly hid her face in my neck and hair, with tumultuous sighs, that seemed almost to sob, and pressed in mine a hand that trembled.

Her soft cheek was glowing against mine. "Darling, darling," she murmured, "I live in you; and you would die for me, I love you so."

I started from her.

She was gazing on me with eyes from which all fire, all meaning had flown, and a face colorless and apathetic.

"Is there a chill in the air, dear?" she said drowsily. "I almost shiver; have I been dreaming? Let us come in. Come; come; come in."

"You look ill, Carmilla; a little faint. You certainly must take some wine," I said.

"Yes. I will. I'm better now. I shall be quite well in a few minutes. Yes, do give me a little wine," answered Carmilla, as we approached the door.

"Let us look again for a moment; it is the last time, perhaps, I shall see the moonlight with you."

"How do you feel now, dear Carmilla? Are you really better?" I asked.

I was beginning to take alarm, lest she should have been stricken with the strange epidemic that they said had invaded the country about us.

"Papa would be grieved beyond measure," I added, "if he thought you were ever so little ill, without immediately letting us know. We have a very skilful doctor near us, the physician who was with papa today."

"I'm sure he is. I know how kind you all are; but, dear child, I am quite well again. There is nothing ever wrong with me, but a little weakness.

"People say I am languid; I am incapable of exertion; I can scarcely walk as far as a child of three years old: and every now and then the little strength I have falters, and I become as you have just seen me. But after all I am very easily set up again; in a moment I am perfectly myself. See how I have recovered."

So, indeed, she had; and she and I talked a great deal, and very animated she was; and the remainder of that evening passed without any recurrence of what I called her infatuations. I mean her crazy talk and looks, which embarrassed, and even frightened me.

But there occurred that night an event which gave my thoughts quite a new turn, and seemed to startle even Carmilla's languid nature into momentary energy.

VI. A VERY STRANGE AGONY

When we got into the drawing room, and had sat down to our coffee and chocolate, although Carmilla did not take any, she seemed quite herself again, and Madame, and Mademoiselle De Lafontaine, joined us, and made a little card party, in the course of which papa came in for what he called his "dish of tea."

When the game was over he sat down beside Carmilla on the sofa, and asked her, a little anxiously, whether she had heard from her mother since her arrival.

She answered "No."

He then asked whether she knew where a letter would reach her at present.

"I cannot tell," she answered ambiguously, "but I have been thinking of leaving you; you have been already too hospitable and too kind to me. I have given you an infinity of trouble, and I should wish to take a carriage tomorrow, and post in pursuit of her; I know where I shall ultimately find her, although I dare not yet tell you."

"But you must not dream of any such thing," exclaimed my father, to my great relief. "We can't afford to lose you so, and I won't consent to your leaving us, except under the care of your mother, who was so good as to consent to your remaining with us till she should herself return. I should be quite happy if I knew that you heard from her: but this evening the accounts of the progress of the mysterious disease that has invaded our neighbourhood, grow even more alarming; and my beautiful guest, I do feel the responsibility, unaided by advice from your mother, very much. But I shall do my best; and one thing is certain, that you must not think of leaving us without her distinct direction to that effect. We should suffer too much in parting from you to consent to it easily."

"Thank you, sir, a thousand times for your hospitality," she answered, smiling bashfully. "You have all been too kind to me; I have seldom been so happy in all my life before, as in your beautiful chateau, under your care, and in the society of your dear daughter."

So he gallantly, in his old-fashioned way, kissed her hand, smiling and pleased at her little speech.

I accompanied Carmilla as usual to her room, and sat and chatted with her while she was preparing for bed.

"Do you think," I said at length, "that you will ever confide fully in me?"

She turned round smiling, but made no answer, only continued to smile on me.

"You won't answer that?" I said. "You can't answer pleasantly; I ought not to have asked you."

"You were quite right to ask me that, or anything. You do not know how dear you are to me, or you could not think any confidence too great to look for. But I am under vows, no nun half so awfully, and I dare not tell my story yet, even to you. The time is very near when you shall know everything. You will think me cruel, very selfish, but love is always selfish; the more ardent the more selfish. How jealous I am you cannot know. You must come with me, loving me, to death; or else hate me and still come with me, and *hating* me through death and after. There is no such word as indifference in my apathetic nature."

"Now, Carmilla, you are going to talk your wild nonsense again," I said hastily.

"Not I, silly little fool as I am, and full of whims and fancies; for your sake I'll talk like a sage. Were you ever at a ball?"

"No; how you do run on. What is it like? How charming it must be."

"I almost forget, it is years ago."

I laughed.

"You are not so old. Your first ball can hardly be forgotten yet."

"I remember everything about it—with an effort. I see it all, as divers see what is going on above them, through a medium, dense, rippling, but transparent. There occurred that night what has confused the picture, and made its colours faint. I was all but assassinated in my bed, wounded here," she touched her breast, "and never was the same since."

"Were you near dying?"

"Yes, very—a cruel love—strange love, that would have taken my life. Love will have its sacrifices. No sacrifice without blood. Let us go to sleep now; I feel so lazy. How can I get up just now and lock my door?"

She was lying with her tiny hands buried in her rich wavy hair, under her cheek, her little head upon the pillow, and her glittering eyes followed me wherever I moved, with a kind of shy smile that I could not decipher.

I bid her good night, and crept from the room with an uncomfortable sensation.

I often wondered whether our pretty guest ever said her prayers. I certainly had never seen her upon her knees. In the morning she never came down until long after our family prayers were over, and at night she never left the drawing room to attend our brief evening prayers in the hall.

If it had not been that it had casually come out in one of our careless talks that she had been baptised, I should have doubted her being a Christian. Religion was a subject on which I had never heard her speak a word. If I had known the world better, this particular neglect or antipathy would not have so much surprised me.

The precautions of nervous people are infectious, and persons of a like temperament are pretty sure, after a time, to imitate them. I had adopted Carmilla's habit of locking her bedroom door, having taken into my head all her whimsical alarms about midnight invaders and prowling assassins. I had also adopted her precaution of making a brief search through her room, to satisfy herself that no lurking assassin or robber was "ensconced."

These wise measures taken, I got into my bed and fell asleep. A light was burning in my room. This was an old habit, of very early date, and which nothing could have tempted me to dispense with.

Thus fortified I might take my rest in peace. But dreams come through stone walls, light up dark rooms, or darken light ones, and their persons make their exits and their entrances as they please, and laugh at locksmiths.

I had a dream that night that was the beginning of a very strange agony.

I cannot call it a nightmare, for I was quite conscious of being asleep.

But I was equally conscious of being in my room, and lying in bed, precisely as I actually was. I saw, or fancied I saw, the room and its furniture just as I had seen it last, except that it was very dark, and I saw something moving round the foot of the bed, which at first I could not accurately distinguish. But I soon saw that it was a sooty-black animal that resembled a monstrous cat. It appeared to me about four or five feet long for it measured fully the length of the hearthrug as it passed over it; and it continued to-ing and fro-ing with the lithe, sinister restlessness of a beast in a cage. I could not cry out, although as you may suppose, I was terrified. Its pace was growing faster, and the room rapidly darker and darker, and at length so dark that I could no longer see anything of it but its eyes. I felt it spring lightly on the bed. The two broad eyes approached my face, and suddenly I felt a stinging pain as if two large needles darted, an inch or two apart, deep into my breast. I waked with a scream. The room was lighted by the candle that burnt there all through the night, and I saw a female figure standing at the foot of the bed, a little at the right side. It was in a dark loose dress, and its hair was down and covered its shoulders. A block of stone could not have been more still. There was not the slightest stir of respiration. As I stared at it, the figure appeared to have changed its place, and was now nearer the door; then, close to it, the door opened, and it passed out.

I was now relieved, and able to breathe and move. My first thought was that Carmilla had been playing me a trick, and that I had forgotten to secure my door. I hastened to it, and found it locked as usual on the inside. I was afraid to open it—I was horrified. I sprang into my bed and covered my head up in the bedclothes, and lay there more dead than alive till morning.

VII. DESCENDING

It would be vain my attempting to tell you the horror with which, even now, I recall the occurrence of that night. It was no such transitory terror as a dream leaves behind it. It seemed to deepen by time, and communicated itself to the room and the very furniture that had encompassed the apparition.

I could not bear next day to be alone for a moment. I should have told papa, but for two opposite reasons. At one time I thought he would laugh at my story, and I could not bear its being treated as a jest; and at another I thought he might fancy that I had been attacked by the mysterious complaint which had invaded our neighbourhood. I had myself no misgiving of the kind, and as he had been rather an invalid for some time, I was afraid of alarming him.

I was comfortable enough with my good-natured companions, Madame Perrodon, and the vivacious Mademoiselle Lafontaine. They both perceived that I was out of spirits and nervous, and at length I told them what lay so heavy at my heart.

Mademoiselle laughed, but I fancied that Madame Perrodon looked anxious.

"By-the-by," said Mademoiselle, laughing, "the long lime tree walk, behind Carmilla's bedroom window, is haunted!"

"Nonsense!" exclaimed Madame, who probably thought the theme rather inopportune, "and who tells that story, my dear?"

"Martin says that he came up twice, when the old yard gate was being repaired, before sunrise, and twice saw the same female figure walking down the lime tree avenue."

"So he well might, as long as there are cows to milk in the river fields," said Madame.

"I daresay; but Martin chooses to be frightened, and never did I see fool more frightened."

"You must not say a word about it to Carmilla, because she can see down that walk from her room window," I interposed, "and she is, if possible, a greater coward than I."

Carmilla came down rather later than usual that day.

"I was so frightened last night," she said, so soon as were together, "and I am sure I should have seen something dreadful if it had not been for that charm I bought from the poor little hunchback whom I called such hard names. I had a dream of something black coming round my bed, and I awoke in a perfect horror, and I really thought, for some seconds, I saw a dark figure near the chimney-piece, but I felt under my pillow for my charm, and the moment my fingers touched it, the figure disappeared, and I felt quite certain, only that I had it by me, that something frightful would have made its appearance, and, perhaps, throttled me, as it did those poor people we heard of.

"Well, listen to me," I began, and recounted my adventure, at the recital of which she appeared horrified.

"And had you the charm near you?" she asked, earnestly.

"No, I had dropped it into a china vase in the drawing room, but I shall certainly take it with me tonight, as you have so much faith in it."

At this distance of time I cannot tell you, or even understand, how I overcame my horror so effectually as to lie alone in my room that night. I remember distinctly that I pinned the charm to my pillow. I fell asleep almost immediately, and slept even more soundly than usual all night.

Next night I passed as well. My sleep was delightfully deep and dreamless.

But I wakened with a sense of lassitude and melancholy, which, however, did not exceed a degree that was almost luxurious.

"Well, I told you so," said Carmilla, when I described my quiet sleep, "I had such delightful sleep myself last night; I pinned the charm to the breast of my nightdress. It was too far away the night before. I am quite sure it was all fancy, except the dreams. I used to think that evil spirits made dreams, but our doctor told me it is no such thing. Only a fever passing by, or some other malady, as they often do, he said, knocks at the door, and not being able to get in, passes on, with that alarm."

"And what do you think the charm is?" said I.

"It has been fumigated or immersed in some drug, and is an antidote against the malaria," she answered.

"Then it acts only on the body?"

"Certainly; you don't suppose that evil spirits are frightened by bits of ribbon, or the perfumes of a druggist's shop? No, these complaints, wandering in the air, begin by trying the nerves, and so infect the brain, but before they can seize upon you, the antidote repels them. That I am sure is what the charm has done for us. It is nothing magical, it is simply natural."

I should have been happier if I could have quite agreed with Carmilla, but I did my best, and the impression was a little losing its force.

For some nights I slept profoundly; but still every morning I felt the same lassitude, and a languor weighed upon me all day. I felt myself a changed girl. A strange melancholy was stealing over me, a melancholy that I would not have interrupted. Dim thoughts of death began to open, and an idea that I was slowly sinking took gentle, and, somehow, not unwelcome, possession of me. If it was sad, the tone of mind which this induced was also sweet.

Whatever it might be, my soul acquiesced in it.

I would not admit that I was ill, I would not consent to tell my papa, or to have the doctor sent for.

Carmilla became more devoted to me than ever, and her strange paroxysms of languid adoration more frequent. She used to gloat on me with increasing ardor the more my strength and spirits waned. This always shocked me like a momentary glare of insanity.

Without knowing it, I was now in a pretty advanced stage of the strangest illness under which mortal ever suffered. There was an unaccountable fascination in its earlier symptoms that more than reconciled me to the incapacitating effect of that stage of the malady. This fascination increased for a time, until it reached a certain point, when gradually a sense of the horrible mingled itself with it, deepening, as you shall hear, until it discolored and perverted the whole state of my life.

The first change I experienced was rather agreeable. It was very near the turning point from which began the descent of Avernus.

Certain vague and strange sensations visited me in my sleep. The prevailing one was of that pleasant, peculiar cold thrill which we feel in bathing, when we move against the current of a river. This was soon accompanied by dreams that seemed interminable, and were so vague that I could never recollect their scenery and persons, or any one connected portion of their action. But they left an awful impression, and a sense of exhaustion, as if I had passed through a long period of great mental exertion and danger.

After all these dreams there remained on waking a remembrance of having been in a place very nearly dark, and of having spoken to people whom I could not see; and especially of one clear voice, of a female's, very deep, that spoke as if at a distance, slowly, and producing always the same sensation of indescribable solemnity and fear. Sometimes there came a sensation as if a hand was drawn softly along my cheek and neck. Sometimes it was as if warm lips kissed me, and longer and longer and more lovingly as they reached my throat, but there the caress fixed itself. My heart beat faster, my breathing rose and fell rapidly and full drawn; a sobbing, that rose into a sense of strangulation, supervened, and turned into a dreadful convulsion, in which my senses left me and I became unconscious.

It was now three weeks since the commencement of this unaccountable state.

My sufferings had, during the last week, told upon my appearance. I had grown pale, my eyes were dilated and darkened underneath, and the languor which I had long felt began to display itself in my countenance.

My father asked me often whether I was ill; but, with an obstinacy which now seems to me unaccountable, I persisted in assuring him that I was quite well.

In a sense this was true. I had no pain, I could complain of no bodily derangement. My complaint seemed to be one of the imagination, or the nerves, and, horrible as my sufferings were, I kept them, with a morbid reserve, very nearly to myself.

It could not be that terrible complaint which the peasants called the oupire, for I had now been suffering for three weeks, and they were seldom ill for much more than three days, when death put an end to their miseries.

Carmilla complained of dreams and feverish sensations, but by no means of so alarming a kind as mine. I say that mine were extremely alarming. Had I been capable of comprehending my condition, I would have invoked aid and advice on my knees. The narcotic of an unsuspected influence was acting upon me, and my perceptions were benumbed.

I am going to tell you now of a dream that led immediately to an odd discovery.

One night, instead of the voice I was accustomed to hear in the dark, I heard one, sweet and tender, and at the same time terrible, which said, "Your mother warns you to beware of the assassin." At the same time a light unexpectedly sprang up, and I saw Carmilla, standing, near the foot of my bed, in her white nightdress, bathed, from her chin to her feet, in one great stain of blood.

I wakened with a shriek, possessed with the one idea that Carmilla was being murdered. I remember springing from my bed, and my next recollection is that of standing on the lobby, crying for help.

Madame and Mademoiselle came scurrying out of their rooms in alarm; a lamp burned always on the lobby, and seeing me, they soon learned the cause of my terror.

I insisted on our knocking at Carmilla's door. Our knocking was unanswered.

It soon became a pounding and an uproar. We shrieked her name, but all was vain.

We all grew frightened, for the door was locked. We hurried back, in panic, to my room. There we rang the bell long and furiously. If my father's room had been at that side of the house, we would have called him up at once to our aid. But, alas! he was quite out of hearing, and to reach him involved an excursion for which we none of us had courage.

Servants, however, soon came running up the stairs; I had got on my dressing gown and slippers meanwhile, and my companions were already similarly furnished. Recognizing the voices of the servants on the lobby, we sallied out together; and having renewed, as fruitlessly, our summons at Carmilla's door, I ordered the men to force the lock. They did so, and we stood, holding our lights aloft, in the doorway, and so stared into the room.

We called her by name; but there was still no reply. We looked round the room. Everything was undisturbed. It was exactly in the state in which I had left it on bidding her good night. But Carmilla was gone.

VIII. SEARCH

At sight of the room, perfectly undisturbed except for our violent entrance, we began to cool a little, and soon recovered our senses sufficiently to dismiss the men. It had struck Mademoiselle that possibly Carmilla had been wakened by the uproar at her door, and in her first panic had jumped from her bed, and hid herself in a press, or behind a curtain, from which she could not, of course, emerge until the majordomo and his myrmidons had withdrawn. We now recommenced our search, and began to call her name again.

It was all to no purpose. Our perplexity and agitation increased. We examined the windows, but they were secured. I implored of Carmilla, if she had concealed herself, to play this cruel trick no longer—to come out and to end our anxieties. It was all useless. I was by this time convinced that she was not in the room, nor in the dressing room, the door of which was still locked on this side. She could not have passed it. I was utterly puzzled. Had Carmilla discovered one of those secret passages which the old housekeeper said were known to exist in the schloss, although the tradition of their exact situation had been lost? A little time would, no doubt, explain all—utterly perplexed as, for the present, we were.

It was past four o'clock, and I preferred passing the remaining hours of darkness in Madame's room. Daylight brought no solution of the difficulty.

The whole household, with my father at its head, was in a state of agitation next morning. Every part of the chateau was searched. The grounds were explored. No trace of the missing lady could be discovered. The stream was about to be dragged; my father was in distraction; what a tale to have to tell the poor girl's mother on her return. I, too, was almost beside myself, though my grief was quite of a different kind.

The morning was passed in alarm and excitement. It was now one o'clock, and still no tidings. I ran up to Carmilla's room, and found her standing at her dressing table. I was astounded. I could not believe my eyes. She beckoned me to her with her pretty finger, in silence. Her face expressed extreme fear.

I ran to her in an ecstasy of joy; I kissed and embraced her again and again. I ran to the bell and rang it vehemently, to bring others to the spot who might at once relieve my father's anxiety.

"Dear Carmilla, what has become of you all this time? We have been in agonies of anxiety about you," I exclaimed. "Where have you been? How did you come back?"

"Last night has been a night of wonders," she said.

"For mercy's sake, explain all you can."

"It was past two last night," she said, "when I went to sleep as usual in my bed, with my doors locked, that of the dressing room, and that opening upon the gallery. My sleep was uninterrupted, and, so far as I know, dreamless; but I woke just now on the sofa in the dressing room there, and I found the door between the rooms open, and the other door forced. How could all this have happened without my being wakened? It must have been accompanied with a great deal of noise, and I am particularly easily wakened; and how could I have been carried out of my bed without my sleep having been interrupted, I whom the slightest stir startles?"

By this time, Madame, Mademoiselle, my father, and a number of the servants were in the room. Carmilla was, of course, overwhelmed with enquiries, congratulations, and welcomes. She had but one story to tell, and seemed the least able of all the party to suggest any way of accounting for what had happened.

My father took a turn up and down the room, thinking. I saw Carmilla's eye follow him for a moment with a sly, dark glance.

When my father had sent the servants away, Mademoiselle having gone in search of a little bottle of valerian and salvolatile, and there being no one now in the room with Carmilla, except my father, Madame, and myself, he came to her thoughtfully, took her hand very kindly, led her to the sofa, and sat down beside her.

"Will you forgive me, my dear, if I risk a conjecture, and ask a question?"

"Who can have a better right?" she said. "Ask what you please, and I will tell you everything. But my story is simply one of bewilderment and darkness. I know absolutely nothing. Put any question you please, but you know, of course, the limitations mamma has placed me under."

"Perfectly, my dear child. I need not approach the topics on which she desires our silence. Now, the marvel of last night consists in your having been removed from your bed and your room, without being wakened, and this removal having occurred apparently while the windows were still secured, and the two doors locked upon the inside. I will tell you my theory and ask you a question."

Carmilla was leaning on her hand dejectedly; Madame and I were listening breathlessly.

"Now, my question is this. Have you ever been suspected of walking in your sleep?"

"Never, since I was very young indeed."

"But you did walk in your sleep when you were young?"

"Yes; I know I did. I have been told so often by my old nurse."

My father smiled and nodded.

"Well, what has happened is this. You got up in your sleep, unlocked the door, not leaving the key, as usual, in the lock, but taking it out and locking it on the outside; you again took the key out, and carried it away with you to some one of the five-and-twenty rooms on this floor, or perhaps upstairs or downstairs. There are so many rooms and closets, so much heavy furniture, and such accumulations of lumber, that it would require a week to search this old house thoroughly. Do you see, now, what I mean?"

"I do, but not all," she answered.

"And how, papa, do you account for her finding herself on the sofa in the dressing room, which we had searched so carefully?"

"She came there after you had searched it, still in her sleep, and at last awoke spontaneously, and was as much surprised to find herself where she was as any one else. I wish all mysteries were as easily and innocently explained as yours, Carmilla," he said, laughing. "And so we may congratulate ourselves on the certainty that the most natural explanation of the occurrence is one that involves no drugging, no tampering with locks, no burglars, or poisoners, or witches—nothing that need alarm Carmilla, or anyone else, for our safety."

Carmilla was looking charmingly. Nothing could be more beautiful than her tints. Her beauty was, I think, enhanced by that graceful languor that was peculiar to her. I think my father was silently contrasting her looks with mine, for he said:

"I wish my poor Laura was looking more like herself"; and he sighed.

So our alarms were happily ended, and Carmilla restored to her friends.

IX. THE DOCTOR

As Carmilla would not hear of an attendant sleeping in her room, my father arranged that a servant should sleep outside her door, so that she would not attempt to make another such excursion without being arrested at her own door.

That night passed quietly; and next morning early, the doctor, whom my father had sent for without telling me a word about it, arrived to see me.

Madame accompanied me to the library; and there the grave little doctor, with white hair and spectacles, whom I mentioned before, was waiting to receive me.

I told him my story, and as I proceeded he grew graver and graver.

We were standing, he and I, in the recess of one of the windows, facing one another. When my statement was over, he leaned with his shoulders against the wall, and with his eyes fixed on me earnestly, with an interest in which was a dash of horror.

After a minute's reflection, he asked Madame if he could see my father.

He was sent for accordingly, and as he entered, smiling, he said:

"I dare say, doctor, you are going to tell me that I am an old fool for having brought you here; I hope I am."

But his smile faded into shadow as the doctor, with a very grave face, beckoned him to him.

He and the doctor talked for some time in the same recess where I had just conferred with the physician. It seemed an earnest and argumentative conversation. The room is very large, and I and Madame stood together, burning with curiosity, at the farther end. Not a word could we hear, however, for they spoke in a very low tone, and the deep recess of the window quite concealed the doctor from view, and very nearly my father, whose foot, arm, and shoulder only could we see; and the voices were, I suppose, all the less audible for the sort of closet which the thick wall and window formed.

After a time my father's face looked into the room; it was pale, thoughtful, and, I fancied, agitated.

"Laura, dear, come here for a moment. Madame, we shan't trouble you, the doctor says, at present."

Accordingly I approached, for the first time a little alarmed; for, although I felt very weak, I did not feel ill; and strength, one always fancies, is a thing that may be picked up when we please.

My father held out his hand to me, as I drew near, but he was looking at the doctor, and he said:

"It certainly is very odd; I don't understand it quite. Laura, come here, dear; now attend to Doctor Spielsberg, and recollect yourself."

"You mentioned a sensation like that of two needles piercing the skin, somewhere about your neck, on the night when you experienced your first horrible dream. Is there still any soreness?"

"None at all," I answered.

"Can you indicate with your finger about the point at which you think this occurred?"

"Very little below my throat—here," I answered.

I wore a morning dress, which covered the place I pointed to.

"Now you can satisfy yourself," said the doctor. "You won't mind your papa's lowering your dress a very little. It is necessary, to detect a symptom of the complaint under which you have been suffering."

I acquiesced. It was only an inch or two below the edge of my collar.

"God bless me!—so it is," exclaimed my father, growing pale.

"You see it now with your own eyes," said the doctor, with a gloomy triumph.

"What is it?" I exclaimed, beginning to be frightened.

"Nothing, my dear young lady, but a small blue spot, about the size of the tip of your little finger; and now," he continued, turning to papa, "the question is what is best to be done?"

"Is there any danger?" I urged, in great trepidation.

"I trust not, my dear," answered the doctor. "I don't see why you should not recover. I don't see why you should not begin immediately to get better. That is the point at which the sense of strangulation begins?"

"Yes," I answered.

"And—recollect as well as you can—the same point was a kind of center of that thrill which you described just now, like the current of a cold stream running against you?"

"It may have been; I think it was."

"Ay, you see?" he added, turning to my father. "Shall I say a word to Madame?"

"Certainly," said my father.

He called Madame to him, and said:

"I find my young friend here far from well. It won't be of any great consequence, I hope; but it will be necessary that some steps be taken, which I will explain by-and-by; but in the meantime, Madame, you will be so good as not to let Miss Laura be alone for one moment. That is the only direction I need give for the present. It is indispensable."

"We may rely upon your kindness, Madame, I know," added my father.

Madame satisfied him eagerly.

"And you, dear Laura, I know you will observe the doctor's direction."

"I shall have to ask your opinion upon another patient, whose symptoms slightly resemble those of my daughter, that have just been detailed to you—very much milder in degree, but I believe quite of the same sort. She is a young lady—our guest; but as you say you will be passing this way again this evening, you can't do better than take your supper here, and you can then see her. She does not come down till the afternoon."

"I thank you," said the doctor. "I shall be with you, then, at about seven this evening."

And then they repeated their directions to me and to Madame, and with this parting charge my father left us, and walked out with the doctor; and I saw them pacing together up and down between the road and the moat, on the grassy platform in front of the castle, evidently absorbed in earnest conversation.

The doctor did not return. I saw him mount his horse there, take his leave, and ride away eastward through the forest.

Nearly at the same time I saw the man arrive from Dranfield with the letters, and dismount and hand the bag to my father.

In the meantime, Madame and I were both busy, lost in conjecture as to the reasons of the singular and earnest direction which the doctor and my father had concurred in imposing. Madame, as she afterwards told me, was afraid the doctor apprehended a sudden seizure, and that, without prompt assistance, I might either lose my life in a fit, or at least be seriously hurt.

The interpretation did not strike me; and I fancied, perhaps luckily for my nerves, that the arrangement was prescribed simply to secure a companion, who would prevent my taking too much exercise, or eating unripe fruit, or doing any of the fifty foolish things to which young people are supposed to be prone.

About half an hour after my father came in—he had a letter in his hand—and said:

"This letter had been delayed; it is from General Spielsdorf. He might have been here yesterday, he may not come till tomorrow or he may be here today."

He put the open letter into my hand; but he did not look pleased, as he used when a guest, especially one so much loved as the General, was coming.

On the contrary, he looked as if he wished him at the bottom of the Red Sea. There was plainly something on his mind which he did not choose to divulge.

"Papa, darling, will you tell me this?" said I, suddenly laying my hand on his arm, and looking, I am sure, imploringly in his face.

"Perhaps," he answered, smoothing my hair caressingly over my eyes.

"Does the doctor think me very ill?"

"No, dear; he thinks, if right steps are taken, you will be quite well again, at least, on the high road to a complete recovery, in a day or two," he answered, a little dryly. "I wish our good friend, the General, had chosen any other time; that is, I wish you had been perfectly well to receive him."

"But do tell me, papa," I insisted, "what does he think is the matter with me?"

"Nothing; you must not plague me with questions," he answered, with more irritation than I ever remember him to have displayed before; and seeing that I looked wounded, I suppose, he kissed me, and added, "You shall know all about it in a day or two; that is, all that I know. In the meantime you are not to trouble your head about it."

He turned and left the room, but came back before I had done wondering and puzzling over the oddity of all this; it was merely to say that he was going to Karnstein, and had ordered the carriage to be ready at twelve, and that I and Madame should accompany him; he was going to see the priest who lived near those picturesque grounds, upon business, and as Carmilla had never seen them, she could follow, when she came down, with Mademoiselle, who would bring materials for what you call a picnic, which might be laid for us in the ruined castle.

At twelve o'clock, accordingly, I was ready, and not long after, my father, Madame and I set out upon our projected drive.

Passing the drawbridge we turn to the right, and follow the road over the steep Gothic bridge, westward, to reach the deserted village and ruined castle of Karnstein.

No sylvan drive can be fancied prettier. The ground breaks into gentle hills and hollows, all clothed with beautiful wood, totally destitute of the comparative formality which artificial planting and early culture and pruning impart.

The irregularities of the ground often lead the road out of its course, and cause it to wind beautifully round the sides of broken hollows and the steeper sides of the hills, among varieties of ground almost inexhaustible.

Turning one of these points, we suddenly encountered our old friend, the General, riding towards us, attended by a mounted servant. His portmanteaus were following in a hired wagon, such as we term a cart.

The General dismounted as we pulled up, and, after the usual greetings, was easily persuaded to accept the vacant seat in the carriage and send his horse on with his servant to the schloss.

X. BEREAVED

It was about ten months since we had last seen him: but that time had sufficed to make an alteration of years in his appearance. He had grown thinner; something of gloom and anxiety had taken the place of that cordial serenity which used to characterize his features. His dark blue eyes, always penetrating, now gleamed with a sterner light from under his shaggy grey eyebrows. It was not such a change as grief alone usually induces, and angrier passions seemed to have had their share in bringing it about.

We had not long resumed our drive, when the General began to talk, with his usual soldierly directness, of the bereavement, as he termed it, which he had sustained in the death of his beloved niece and ward; and he then broke out in a tone of intense bitterness and fury, inveighing against the "hellish arts" to which she had fallen a victim, and expressing, with more exasperation than piety, his wonder that Heaven should tolerate so monstrous an indulgence of the lusts and malignity of hell.

My father, who saw at once that something very extraordinary had befallen, asked him, if not too painful to him, to detail the circumstances which he thought justified the strong terms in which he expressed himself.

"I should tell you all with pleasure," said the General, "but you would not believe me."

"Why should I not?" he asked.

"Because," he answered testily, "you believe in nothing but what consists with your own prejudices and illusions. I remember when I was like you, but I have learned better."

"Try me," said my father; "I am not such a dogmatist as you suppose. Besides which, I very well know that you generally require proof for what you believe, and am, therefore, very strongly predisposed to respect your conclusions."

"You are right in supposing that I have not been led lightly into a belief in the marvelous—for what I have experienced is marvelous—and I have been forced by extraordinary evidence to credit that which ran counter, diametrically, to all my theories. I have been made the dupe of a preternatural conspiracy."

Notwithstanding his professions of confidence in the General's penetration, I saw my father, at this point, glance at the General, with, as I thought, a marked suspicion of his sanity.

The General did not see it, luckily. He was looking gloomily and curiously into the glades and vistas of the woods that were opening before us.

"You are going to the Ruins of Karnstein?" he said. "Yes, it is a lucky coincidence; do you know I was going to ask you to bring me there to inspect them. I have a special object in exploring. There is a ruined chapel, ain't there, with a great many tombs of that extinct family?"

"So there are—highly interesting," said my father. "I hope you are thinking of claiming the title and estates?"

My father said this gaily, but the General did not recollect the laugh, or even the smile, which courtesy exacts for a friend's joke; on the contrary, he looked grave and even fierce, ruminating on a matter that stirred his anger and horror.

"Something very different," he said, gruffly. "I mean to unearth some of those fine people. I hope, by God's blessing, to accomplish a pious sacrilege here, which will relieve our earth of certain monsters, and enable honest people to sleep in their beds without being assailed by murderers. I have strange things to tell you, my dear friend, such as I myself would have scouted as incredible a few months since."

My father looked at him again, but this time not with a glance of suspicion—with an eye, rather, of keen intelligence and alarm.

"The house of Karnstein," he said, "has been long extinct: a hundred years at least. My dear wife was maternally descended from the Karnsteins. But the name and title have long ceased to exist. The castle is a ruin; the very village is deserted; it is fifty years since the smoke of a chimney was seen there; not a roof left."

"Quite true. I have heard a great deal about that since I last saw you; a great deal that will astonish you. But I had better relate everything in the order in which it occurred," said the General. "You saw my dear ward—my child, I may call her. No creature could have been more beautiful, and only three months ago none more blooming."

"Yes, poor thing! when I saw her last she certainly was quite lovely," said my father. "I was grieved and shocked more than I can tell you, my dear friend; I knew what a blow it was to you."

He took the General's hand, and they exchanged a kind pressure. Tears gathered in the old soldier's eyes. He did not seek to conceal them. He said:

"We have been very old friends; I knew you would feel for me, childless as I am. She had become an object of very near interest to me, and repaid my care by an affection that cheered my home and made my life happy. That is all gone. The years that remain to me on earth may not be very long; but by God's mercy I hope to accomplish a service to mankind before I die, and to subserve the vengeance of Heaven upon the fiends who have murdered my poor child in the spring of her hopes and beauty!"

"You said, just now, that you intended relating everything as it occurred," said my father. "Pray do; I assure you that it is not mere curiosity that prompts me."

By this time we had reached the point at which the Drunstall road, by which the General had come, diverges from the road which we were traveling to Karnstein.

"How far is it to the ruins?" enquired the General, looking anxiously forward.

"About half a league," answered my father. "Pray let us hear the story you were so good as to promise."

XI. THE STORY

"With all my heart," said the General, with an effort; and after a short pause in which to arrange his subject, he commenced one of the strangest narratives I ever heard.

"My dear child was looking forward with great pleasure to the visit you had been so good as to arrange for her to your charming daughter." Here he made me a gallant but melancholy bow. "In the meantime we had an invitation to my old friend the Count Carlsfeld, whose schloss is about six leagues to the other side of Karnstein. It was to attend the series of fetes which, you remember, were given by him in honor of his illustrious visitor, the Grand Duke Charles."

"Yes; and very splendid, I believe, they were," said my father.

"Princely! But then his hospitalities are quite regal. He has Aladdin's lamp. The night from which my sorrow dates was devoted to a magnificent masquerade. The grounds were thrown open, the trees hung with coloured lamps. There was such a display of fireworks as Paris itself had never witnessed. And such music—music, you know, is my weakness—such ravishing music! The finest instrumental band, perhaps, in the world, and the finest singers who could be collected from all the great operas in Europe. As you wandered through these fantastically illuminated grounds, the moon-lighted chateau throwing a rosy light from its long rows of windows, you would suddenly hear these ravishing voices stealing from the silence of some grove, or rising from boats upon the lake. I felt myself, as I looked and listened, carried back into the romance and poetry of my early youth.

"When the fireworks were ended, and the ball beginning, we returned to the noble suite of rooms that were thrown open to the dancers. A masked ball, you know, is a beautiful sight; but so brilliant a spectacle of the kind I never saw before.

"It was a very aristocratic assembly. I was myself almost the only 'nobody' present.

"My dear child was looking quite beautiful. She wore no mask. Her excitement and delight added an unspeakable charm to her features, always lovely. I remarked a young lady, dressed magnificently, but wearing a mask, who appeared to me to be observing my ward with extraordinary interest. I had seen her, earlier in the evening, in the great hall, and again, for a few minutes, walking near us, on the terrace under the castle windows, similarly employed. A lady, also masked, richly and gravely dressed, and with a stately air, like a person of rank, accompanied her as a chaperon.

"Had the young lady not worn a mask, I could, of course, have been much more certain upon the question whether she was really watching my poor darling.

"I am now well assured that she was.

"We were now in one of the salons. My poor dear child had been dancing, and was resting a little in one of the chairs near the door; I was standing near. The two ladies I have mentioned had approached and the younger took the chair next my ward; while her companion stood beside me, and for a little time addressed herself, in a low tone, to her charge.

"Availing herself of the privilege of her mask, she turned to me, and in the tone of an old friend, and calling me by my name, opened a conversation with me, which piqued my curiosity a good deal. She referred to many scenes where she had met me—at Court, and at distinguished houses. She alluded to little incidents which I had long ceased to think of, but which, I found, had only lain in abeyance in my memory, for they instantly started into life at her touch.

"I became more and more curious to ascertain who she was, every moment. She parried my attempts to discover very adroitly and pleasantly. The knowledge she showed of many passages in my life seemed to me all but unaccountable; and she appeared to take a not unnatural pleasure in foiling my curiosity, and in seeing me flounder in my eager perplexity, from one conjecture to another.

"In the meantime the young lady, whom her mother called by the odd name of Millarca, when she once or twice addressed her, had, with the same ease and grace, got into conversation with my ward.

"She introduced herself by saying that her mother was a very old acquaintance of mine. She spoke of the agreeable audacity which a mask rendered practicable; she talked like a friend; she admired her dress, and insinuated very prettily her admiration of her beauty. She amused her with laughing criticisms upon the people who crowded the ballroom, and laughed at my poor child's fun. She was very witty and lively when she pleased, and after a time they had grown very good friends, and the young stranger lowered her mask, displaying a remarkably beautiful face. I had never seen it before, neither had my dear child. But though it was new to us, the features were so engaging, as well as lovely, that it was impossible not to feel the attraction powerfully. My poor girl did so. I never saw anyone more taken with another at first sight, unless, indeed, it was the stranger herself, who seemed quite to have lost her heart to her.

"In the meantime, availing myself of the license of a masquerade, I put not a few questions to the elder lady.

"'You have puzzled me utterly,' I said, laughing. 'Is that not enough? Won't you, now, consent to stand on equal terms, and do me the kindness to remove your mask?'

"'Can any request be more unreasonable?' she replied. 'Ask a lady to yield an advantage! Beside, how do you know you should recognize me? Years make changes.'

"'As you see,' I said, with a bow, and, I suppose, a rather melancholy little laugh.

"'As philosophers tell us,' she said; 'and how do you know that a sight of my face would help you?'

"'I should take chance for that,' I answered. 'It is vain trying to make yourself out an old woman; your figure betrays you.'

"'Years, nevertheless, have passed since I saw you, rather since you saw me, for that is what I am considering. Millarca, there, is my daughter; I cannot then be young, even in the opinion of people whom time has taught to be indulgent, and I may not like to be compared with what you remember me. You have no mask to remove. You can offer me nothing in exchange.'

"'My petition is to your pity, to remove it.'

"'And mine to yours, to let it stay where it is,' she replied.

"'Well, then, at least you will tell me whether you are French or German; you speak both languages so perfectly.'

"'I don't think I shall tell you that, General; you intend a surprise, and are meditating the particular point of attack.'

"'At all events, you won't deny this,' I said, 'that being honoured by your permission to converse, I ought to know how to address you. Shall I say Madame la Comtesse?'

"She laughed, and she would, no doubt, have met me with another evasion—if, indeed, I can treat any occurrence in an interview every circumstance of which was prearranged, as I now believe, with the profoundest cunning, as liable to be modified by accident.

"'As to that,' she began; but she was interrupted, almost as she opened her lips, by a gentleman, dressed in black, who looked particularly elegant and distinguished, with this drawback, that his face was the most deadly pale I ever saw, except in death. He was in no masquerade—in the plain evening dress of a gentleman; and he said, without a smile, but with a courtly and unusually low bow:—

"'Will Madame la Comtesse permit me to say a very few words which may interest her?'

"The lady turned quickly to him, and touched her lip in token of silence; she then said to me, 'Keep my place for me, General; I shall return when I have said a few words.'

"And with this injunction, playfully given, she walked a little aside with the gentleman in black, and talked for some minutes, apparently very earnestly. They then walked away slowly together in the crowd, and I lost them for some minutes.

"I spent the interval in cudgeling my brains for a conjecture as to the identity of the lady who seemed to remember me so kindly, and I was thinking of turning about and joining in the conversation between my pretty ward and the Countess's daughter, and trying whether, by the time she returned, I might not have a surprise in store for her, by having her name, title, chateau, and estates at my fingers' ends. But at this moment she returned, accompanied by the pale man in black, who said:

"'I shall return and inform Madame la Comtesse when her carriage is at the door.'

"He withdrew with a bow."

XII. A PETITION

"'Then we are to lose Madame la Comtesse, but I hope only for a few hours,' I said, with a low bow.

"'It may be that only, or it may be a few weeks. It was very unlucky his speaking to me just now as he did. Do you now know me?'

"I assured her I did not.

"'You shall know me,' she said, 'but not at present. We are older and better friends than, perhaps, you suspect. I cannot yet declare myself. I shall in three weeks pass your beautiful schloss, about which I have been making enquiries. I shall then look in upon you for an hour or two, and renew a friendship which I never think of without a thousand pleasant recollections. This moment a piece of news has reached me like a thunderbolt. I must set out now, and travel by a devious route, nearly a hundred miles, with all the dispatch I can possibly make. My perplexities multiply. I am only deterred by the compulsory reserve I practice as to my name from making a very singular request of you. My poor child has not quite recovered her strength. Her horse fell with her, at a hunt which she had ridden out to witness, her nerves have not yet recovered the shock, and our physician says that she must on no account exert herself for some time to come. We came here, in consequence, by very easy stages—hardly six leagues a day. I must now travel day and night, on a mission of life and death—a mission the critical and momentous nature of which I shall be able to explain to you when we meet, as I hope we shall, in a few weeks, without the necessity of any concealment.'

"She went on to make her petition, and it was in the tone of a person from whom such a request amounted to conferring, rather than seeking a favour.

"This was only in manner, and, as it seemed, quite unconsciously. Than the terms in which it was expressed, nothing could be more deprecatory. It was simply that I would consent to take charge of her daughter during her absence.

"This was, all things considered, a strange, not to say, an audacious request. She in some sort disarmed me, by stating and admitting everything that could be urged against it, and throwing herself entirely upon my chivalry. At the same moment, by a fatality that seems to have predetermined all that happened, my poor child came to my side, and, in an undertone, besought me to invite her new friend, Millarca, to pay us a visit. She had just been sounding her, and thought, if her mamma would allow her, she would like it extremely.

"At another time I should have told her to wait a little, until, at least, we knew who they were. But I had not a moment to think in. The two ladies assailed me together, and I must confess the refined and beautiful face of the young lady, about which there was something extremely engaging, as well as the elegance and fire of high birth, determined me; and, quite overpowered, I submitted, and undertook, too easily, the care of the young lady, whom her mother called Millarca.

"The Countess beckoned to her daughter, who listened with grave attention while she told her, in general terms, how suddenly and peremptorily she had been summoned, and also of the arrangement she had made for her under my care, adding that I was one of her earliest and most valued friends.

"I made, of course, such speeches as the case seemed to call for, and found myself, on reflection, in a position which I did not half like.

"The gentleman in black returned, and very ceremoniously conducted the lady from the room.

"The demeanor of this gentleman was such as to impress me with the conviction that the Countess was a lady of very much more importance than her modest title alone might have led me to assume.

"Her last charge to me was that no attempt was to be made to learn more about her than I might have already guessed, until her return. Our distinguished host, whose guest she was, knew her reasons.

"'But here,' she said, 'neither I nor my daughter could safely remain for more than a day. I removed my mask imprudently for a moment, about an hour ago, and, too late, I fancied you saw me. So I resolved to seek an opportunity of talking a little to you. Had I found that you had seen me, I would have thrown myself on your high sense of honour to keep my secret some weeks. As it is, I am satisfied that you did not see me; but if you now suspect, or, on reflection, should suspect, who I am, I commit myself, in like manner, entirely to your honour. My daughter will observe the same secrecy, and I well know that you will, from time to time, remind her, lest she should thoughtlessly disclose it.'

"She whispered a few words to her daughter, kissed her hurriedly twice, and went away, accompanied by the pale gentleman in black, and disappeared in the crowd.

"'In the next room,' said Millarca, 'there is a window that looks upon the hall door. I should like to see the last of mamma, and to kiss my hand to her.'

"We assented, of course, and accompanied her to the window. We looked out, and saw a handsome old-fashioned carriage, with a troop of couriers and footmen. We saw the slim figure of the pale gentleman in black, as he held a thick velvet cloak, and placed it about her shoulders and threw the hood over her head. She nodded to him, and just touched his hand with hers. He bowed low repeatedly as the door closed, and the carriage began to move.

"'She is gone,' said Millarca, with a sigh.

"'She is gone,' I repeated to myself, for the first time—in the hurried moments that had elapsed since my consent—reflecting upon the folly of my act.

"'She did not look up,' said the young lady, plaintively.

"'The Countess had taken off her mask, perhaps, and did not care to show her face,' I said; 'and she could not know that you were in the window.'

"She sighed, and looked in my face. She was so beautiful that I relented. I was sorry I had for a moment repented of my hospitality, and I determined to make her amends for the unavowed churlishness of my reception.

"The young lady, replacing her mask, joined my ward in persuading me to return to the grounds, where the concert was soon to be renewed. We did so, and walked up and down the terrace that lies under the castle windows.

"Millarca became very intimate with us, and amused us with lively descriptions and stories of most of the great people whom we saw upon the terrace. I liked her more and more every minute. Her gossip without being ill-natured, was extremely diverting to me, who had been so long out of the great world. I thought what life she would give to our sometimes lonely evenings at home.

"This ball was not over until the morning sun had almost reached the horizon. It pleased the Grand Duke to dance till then, so loyal people could not go away, or think of bed.

"We had just got through a crowded saloon, when my ward asked me what had become of Millarca. I thought she had been by her side, and she fancied she was by mine. The fact was, we had lost her.

"All my efforts to find her were vain. I feared that she had mistaken, in the confusion of a momentary separation from us, other people for her new friends, and had, possibly, pursued and lost them in the extensive grounds which were thrown open to us.

"Now, in its full force, I recognized a new folly in my having undertaken the charge of a young lady without so much as knowing her name; and fettered as I was by promises, of the reasons for imposing which I knew nothing, I could not even point my inquiries by saying that the missing young lady was the daughter of the Countess who had taken her departure a few hours before.

"Morning broke. It was clear daylight before I gave up my search. It was not till near two o'clock next day that we heard anything of my missing charge.

"At about that time a servant knocked at my niece's door, to say that he had been earnestly requested by a young lady, who appeared to be in great distress, to make out where she could find the General Baron Spielsdorf and the young lady his daughter, in whose charge she had been left by her mother.

"There could be no doubt, notwithstanding the slight inaccuracy, that our young friend had turned up; and so she had. Would to heaven we had lost her!

"She told my poor child a story to account for her having failed to recover us for so long. Very late, she said, she had got to the housekeeper's bedroom in despair of finding us, and had then fallen into a deep sleep which, long as it was, had hardly sufficed to recruit her strength after the fatigues of the ball.

"That day Millarca came home with us. I was only too happy, after all, to have secured so charming a companion for my dear girl."

XIII. THE WOODMAN

"There soon, however, appeared some drawbacks. In the first place, Millarca complained of extreme languor—the weakness that remained after her late illness—and she never emerged from her room till the afternoon was pretty far advanced. In the next place, it was accidentally discovered, although she always locked her door on the inside, and never disturbed the key from its place till she admitted the maid to assist at her toilet, that she was undoubtedly sometimes absent from her room in the very early morning, and at various times later in the day, before she wished it to be understood that she was stirring. She was repeatedly seen from the windows of the schloss, in the first faint grey of the morning, walking through the trees, in an easterly direction, and looking like a person in a trance. This convinced me that she walked in her sleep. But this hypothesis did not solve the puzzle. How did she pass out from her room, leaving the door locked on the inside? How did she escape from the house without unbarring door or window?

"In the midst of my perplexities, an anxiety of a far more urgent kind presented itself.

"My dear child began to lose her looks and health, and that in a manner so mysterious, and even horrible, that I became thoroughly frightened.

"She was at first visited by appalling dreams; then, as she fancied, by a specter, sometimes resembling Millarca, sometimes in the shape of a beast, indistinctly seen, walking round the foot of her bed, from side to side.

"Lastly came sensations. One, not unpleasant, but very peculiar, she said, resembled the flow of an icy stream against her breast. At a later time, she felt something like a pair of large needles pierce her, a little below the throat, with a very sharp pain. A few nights after, followed a gradual and convulsive sense of strangulation; then came unconsciousness."

I could hear distinctly every word the kind old General was saying, because by this time we were driving upon the short grass that spreads on either side of the road as you approach the roofless village which had not shown the smoke of a chimney for more than half a century.

You may guess how strangely I felt as I heard my own symptoms so exactly described in those which had been experienced by the poor girl who, but for the catastrophe which followed, would have been at that moment a visitor at my father's chateau. You may suppose, also, how I felt as I heard him detail habits and mysterious peculiarities which were, in fact, those of our beautiful guest, Carmilla!

A vista opened in the forest; we were on a sudden under the chimneys and gables of the ruined village, and the towers and battlements of the dismantled castle, round which gigantic trees are grouped, overhung us from a slight eminence.

In a frightened dream I got down from the carriage, and in silence, for we had each abundant matter for thinking; we soon mounted the ascent, and were among the spacious chambers, winding stairs, and dark corridors of the castle.

"And this was once the palatial residence of the Karnsteins!" said the old General at length, as from a great window he looked out across the village, and saw the wide, undulating expanse of forest. "It was a bad family, and here its bloodstained annals were written," he continued. "It is hard that they should, after death, continue to plague the human race with their atrocious lusts. That is the chapel of the Karnsteins, down there."

He pointed down to the grey walls of the Gothic building partly visible through the foliage, a little way down the steep. "And I hear the axe of a woodman," he added, "busy among the trees that surround it; he possibly may give us the information of which I am in search, and point out the grave of Mircalla, Countess of Karnstein. These rustics preserve the local traditions of great families, whose stories die out among the rich and titled so soon as the families themselves become extinct."

"We have a portrait, at home, of Mircalla, the Countess Karnstein; should you like to see it?" asked my father.

"Time enough, dear friend," replied the General. "I believe that I have seen the original; and one motive which has led me to you earlier than I at first intended, was to explore the chapel which we are now approaching."

"What! see the Countess Mircalla," exclaimed my father; "why, she has been dead more than a century!"

"Not so dead as you fancy, I am told," answered the General.

"I confess, General, you puzzle me utterly," replied my father, looking at him, I fancied, for a moment with a return of the suspicion I detected before. But although there was anger and detestation, at times, in the old General's manner, there was nothing flighty.

"There remains to me," he said, as we passed under the heavy arch of the Gothic church—for its dimensions would have justified its being so styled—"but one object which can interest me during the few years that remain to me on earth, and that is to wreak on her the vengeance which, I thank God, may still be accomplished by a mortal arm."

"What vengeance can you mean?" asked my father, in increasing amazement.

"I mean, to decapitate the monster," he answered, with a fierce flush, and a stamp that echoed mournfully through the hollow ruin, and his clenched hand was at the same moment raised, as if it grasped the handle of an axe, while he shook it ferociously in the air.

"What?" exclaimed my father, more than ever bewildered.

"To strike her head off."

"Cut her head off!"

"Aye, with a hatchet, with a spade, or with anything that can cleave through her murderous throat. You shall hear," he answered, trembling with rage. And hurrying forward he said:

"That beam will answer for a seat; your dear child is fatigued; let her be seated, and I will, in a few sentences, close my dreadful story."

The squared block of wood, which lay on the grass-grown pavement of the chapel, formed a bench on which I was very glad to seat myself, and in the meantime the General called to the woodman, who had been removing some boughs which leaned upon the old walls; and, axe in hand, the hardy old fellow stood before us.

He could not tell us anything of these monuments; but there was an old man, he said, a ranger of this forest, at present sojourning in the house of the priest, about two miles away, who could point out every monument of the old Karnstein family; and, for a trifle, he undertook to bring him back with him, if we would lend him one of our horses, in little more than half an hour.

"Have you been long employed about this forest?" asked my father of the old man.

"I have been a woodman here," he answered in his patois, "under the forester, all my days; so has my father before me, and so on, as many generations as I can count up. I could show you the very house in the village here, in which my ancestors lived."

"How came the village to be deserted?" asked the General.

"It was troubled by revenants, sir; several were tracked to their graves, there detected by the usual tests, and extinguished in the usual way, by decapitation, by the stake, and by burning; but not until many of the villagers were killed.

"But after all these proceedings according to law," he continued—"so many graves opened, and so many vampires deprived of their horrible animation—the village was not relieved. But a Moravian nobleman, who happened to be traveling this way, heard how matters were, and being skilled—as many people are in his country—in such affairs, he offered to deliver the village from its tormentor. He did so thus: There being a bright moon that night, he ascended, shortly after sunset, the towers of the chapel here, from whence he could distinctly see the churchyard beneath him; you can see it from that window. From this point he watched until he saw the vampire come out of his grave, and place near it the linen clothes in which he had been folded, and then glide away towards the village to plague its inhabitants.

"The stranger, having seen all this, came down from the steeple, took the linen wrappings of the vampire, and carried them up to the top of the tower, which he again mounted. When the vampire returned from his prowlings and missed his clothes, he cried furiously to the Moravian, whom he saw at the summit of the tower, and who, in reply, beckoned him to ascend and take them. Whereupon the vampire, accepting his invitation, began to climb the steeple, and so soon as he had reached the battlements, the Moravian, with a stroke of his sword, clove his skull in twain, hurling him down to the churchyard, whither, descending by the winding stairs, the stranger followed and cut his head off, and next day delivered it and the body to the villagers, who duly impaled and burnt them.

"This Moravian nobleman had authority from the then head of the family to remove the tomb of Mircalla, Countess Karnstein, which he did effectually, so that in a little while its site was quite forgotten."

"Can you point out where it stood?" asked the General, eagerly.

The forester shook his head, and smiled.

"Not a soul living could tell you that now," he said; "besides, they say her body was removed; but no one is sure of that either."

Having thus spoken, as time pressed, he dropped his axe and departed, leaving us to hear the remainder of the General's strange story.

XIV. THE MEETING

"My beloved child," he resumed, "was now growing rapidly worse. The physician who attended her had failed to produce the slightest impression on her disease, for such I then supposed it to be. He saw my alarm, and suggested a consultation. I called in an abler physician, from Gratz.

"Several days elapsed before he arrived. He was a good and pious, as well as a learned man. Having seen my poor ward together, they withdrew to my library to confer and discuss. I, from the adjoining room, where I awaited their summons, heard these two gentlemen's voices raised in something sharper than a strictly philosophical discussion. I knocked at the door and entered. I found the old physician from Gratz maintaining his theory. His rival was combating it with undisguised ridicule, accompanied with bursts of laughter. This unseemly manifestation subsided and the altercation ended on my entrance.

"'Sir,' said my first physician, 'my learned brother seems to think that you want a conjuror, and not a doctor.'

"'Pardon me,' said the old physician from Gratz, looking displeased, 'I shall state my own view of the case in my own way another time. I grieve, Monsieur le General, that by my skill and science I can be of no use. Before I go I shall do myself the honor to suggest something to you.'

"He seemed thoughtful, and sat down at a table and began to write.

"Profoundly disappointed, I made my bow, and as I turned to go, the other doctor pointed over his shoulder to his companion who was writing, and then, with a shrug, significantly touched his forehead.

"This consultation, then, left me precisely where I was. I walked out into the grounds, all but distracted. The doctor from Gratz, in ten or fifteen minutes, overtook me. He apologized for having followed me, but said that he could not conscientiously take his leave without a few words more. He told me that he could not be mistaken; no natural disease exhibited the same symptoms; and that death was already very near. There remained, however, a day, or possibly two, of life. If the fatal seizure were at once arrested, with great care and skill her strength might possibly return. But all hung now upon the confines of the irrevocable. One more assault might extinguish the last spark of vitality which is, every moment, ready to die.

"'And what is the nature of the seizure you speak of?' I entreated.

"'I have stated all fully in this note, which I place in your hands upon the distinct condition that you send for the nearest clergyman, and open my letter in his presence, and on no account read it till he is with you; you would despise it else, and it is a matter of life and death. Should the priest fail you, then, indeed, you may read it.'

"He asked me, before taking his leave finally, whether I would wish to see a man curiously learned upon the very subject, which, after I had read his letter, would probably interest me above all others, and he urged me earnestly to invite him to visit him there; and so took his leave.

"The ecclesiastic was absent, and I read the letter by myself. At another time, or in another case, it might have excited my ridicule. But into what quackeries will not people rush for a last chance, where all accustomed means have failed, and the life of a beloved object is at stake?

"Nothing, you will say, could be more absurd than the learned man's letter.

"It was monstrous enough to have consigned him to a madhouse. He said that the patient was suffering from the visits of a vampire! The punctures which she described as having occurred near the throat, were, he insisted, the insertion of those two long, thin, and sharp teeth which, it is well known, are peculiar to vampires; and there could be no doubt, he added, as to the well-defined presence of the small livid mark which all concurred in describing as that induced by the demon's lips, and every symptom described by the sufferer was in exact conformity with those recorded in every case of a similar visitation.

"Being myself wholly skeptical as to the existence of any such portent as the vampire, the supernatural theory of the good doctor furnished, in my opinion, but another instance of learning and intelligence oddly associated with some one hallucination. I was so miserable, however, that, rather than try nothing, I acted upon the instructions of the letter.

"I concealed myself in the dark dressing room, that opened upon the poor patient's room, in which a candle was burning, and watched there till she was fast asleep. I stood at the door, peeping through the small crevice, my sword laid on the table beside me, as my directions prescribed, until, a little after one, I saw a large black object, very ill-defined, crawl, as it seemed to me, over the foot of the bed, and swiftly spread itself up to the poor girl's throat, where it swelled, in a moment, into a great, palpitating mass.

"For a few moments I had stood petrified. I now sprang forward, with my sword in my hand. The black creature suddenly contracted towards the foot of the bed, glided over it, and, standing on the floor about a yard below the foot of the bed, with a glare of skulking ferocity and horror fixed on me, I saw Millarca. Speculating I know not what, I struck at her instantly with my sword; but I saw her standing near the door, unscathed. Horrified, I pursued, and struck again. She was gone; and my sword flew to shivers against the door.

"I can't describe to you all that passed on that horrible night. The whole house was up and stirring. The spectre Millarca was gone. But her victim was sinking fast, and before the morning dawned, she died."

The old General was agitated. We did not speak to him. My father walked to some little distance, and began reading the inscriptions on the tombstones; and thus occupied, he strolled into the door of a side chapel to prosecute his researches. The General leaned against the wall, dried his eyes, and sighed heavily. I was relieved on hearing the voices of Carmilla and Madame, who were at that moment approaching. The voices died away.

In this solitude, having just listened to so strange a story, connected, as it was, with the great and titled dead, whose monuments were moldering among the dust and ivy round us, and every incident of which bore so awfully upon my own mysterious case—in this haunted spot, darkened by the towering foliage that rose on every side, dense and high above its noiseless walls—a horror began to steal over me, and my heart sank as I thought that my friends were, after all, not about to enter and disturb this triste and ominous scene.

The old General's eyes were fixed on the ground, as he leaned with his hand upon the basement of a shattered monument.

Under a narrow, arched doorway, surmounted by one of those demoniacal grotesques in which the cynical and ghastly fancy of old Gothic carving delights, I saw very gladly the beautiful face and figure of Carmilla enter the shadowy chapel.

I was just about to rise and speak, and nodded smiling, in answer to her peculiarly engaging smile; when with a cry, the old man by my side caught up the woodman's hatchet, and started forward. On seeing him a brutalized change came over her features. It was an instantaneous and horrible transformation, as she made a crouching step backwards. Before I could utter a scream, he struck at her with all his force, but she dived under his blow, and unscathed, caught him in her tiny grasp by the wrist. He struggled for a moment to release his arm, but his hand opened, the axe fell to the ground, and the girl was gone.

He staggered against the wall. His grey hair stood upon his head, and a moisture shone over his face, as if he were at the point of death.

The frightful scene had passed in a moment. The first thing I recollect after, is Madame standing before me, and impatiently repeating again and again, the question, "Where is Mademoiselle Carmilla?"

I answered at length, "I don't know—I can't tell—she went there," and I pointed to the door through which Madame had just entered; "only a minute or two since."

"But I have been standing there, in the passage, ever since Mademoiselle Carmilla entered; and she did not return."

She then began to call "Carmilla," through every door and passage and from the windows, but no answer came.

"She called herself Carmilla?" asked the General, still agitated.

"Carmilla, yes," I answered.

"Aye," he said; "that is Millarca. That is the same person who long ago was called Mircalla, Countess Karnstein. Depart from this accursed ground, my poor child, as quickly as you can. Drive to the clergyman's house, and stay there till we come. Begone! May you never behold Carmilla more; you will not find her here."

XV. ORDEAL AND EXECUTION

As he spoke one of the strangest looking men I ever beheld entered the chapel at the door through which Carmilla had made her entrance and her exit. He was tall, narrow-chested, stooping, with high shoulders, and dressed in black. His face was brown and dried in with deep furrows; he wore an oddly-shaped hat with a broad leaf. His hair, long and grizzled, hung on his shoulders. He wore a pair of gold spectacles, and walked slowly, with an odd shambling gait, with his face sometimes turned up to the sky, and sometimes bowed down towards the ground, seemed to wear a perpetual smile; his long thin arms were swinging, and his lank hands, in old black gloves ever so much too wide for them, waving and gesticulating in utter abstraction.

"The very man!" exclaimed the General, advancing with manifest delight. "My dear Baron, how happy I am to see you, I had no hope of meeting you so soon." He signed to my father, who had by this time returned, and leading the fantastic old gentleman, whom he called the Baron to meet him. He introduced him formally, and they at once entered into earnest conversation. The stranger took a roll of paper from his pocket, and spread it on the worn surface of a tomb that stood by. He had a pencil case in his fingers, with which he traced imaginary lines from point to point on the paper, which from their often glancing from it, together, at certain points of the building, I concluded to be a plan of the chapel. He accompanied, what I may term, his lecture, with occasional readings from a dirty little book, whose yellow leaves were closely written over.

They sauntered together down the side aisle, opposite to the spot where I was standing, conversing as they went; then they began measuring distances by paces, and finally they all stood together, facing a piece of the sidewall, which they began to examine with great minuteness; pulling off the ivy that clung over it, and rapping the plaster with the ends of their sticks, scraping here, and knocking there. At length they ascertained the existence of a broad marble tablet, with letters carved in relief upon it.

With the assistance of the woodman, who soon returned, a monumental inscription, and carved escutcheon, were disclosed. They proved to be those of the long lost monument of Mircalla, Countess Karnstein.

The old General, though not I fear given to the praying mood, raised his hands and eyes to heaven, in mute thanksgiving for some moments.

"Tomorrow," I heard him say; "the commissioner will be here, and the Inquisition will be held according to law."

Then turning to the old man with the gold spectacles, whom I have described, he shook him warmly by both hands and said:

"Baron, how can I thank you? How can we all thank you? You will have delivered this region from a plague that has scourged its inhabitants for more than a century. The horrible enemy, thank God, is at last tracked."

My father led the stranger aside, and the General followed. I know that he had led them out of hearing, that he might relate my case, and I saw them glance often quickly at me, as the discussion proceeded.

My father came to me, kissed me again and again, and leading me from the chapel, said:

"It is time to return, but before we go home, we must add to our party the good priest, who lives but a little way from this; and persuade him to accompany us to the schloss."

In this quest we were successful: and I was glad, being unspeakably fatigued when we reached home. But my satisfaction was changed to dismay, on discovering that there were no tidings of Carmilla. Of the scene that had occurred in the ruined chapel, no explanation was offered to me, and it was clear that it was a secret which my father for the present determined to keep from me.

The sinister absence of Carmilla made the remembrance of the scene more horrible to me. The arrangements for the night were singular. Two servants, and Madame were to sit up in my room that night; and the ecclesiastic with my father kept watch in the adjoining dressing room.

The priest had performed certain solemn rites that night, the purport of which I did not understand any more than I comprehended the reason of this extraordinary precaution taken for my safety during sleep.

I saw all clearly a few days later.

The disappearance of Carmilla was followed by the discontinuance of my nightly sufferings.

You have heard, no doubt, of the appalling superstition that prevails in Upper and Lower Styria, in Moravia, Silesia, in Turkish Serbia, in Poland, even in Russia; the superstition, so we must call it, of the Vampire.

If human testimony, taken with every care and solemnity, judicially, before commissions innumerable, each consisting of many members, all chosen for integrity and intelligence, and constituting reports more voluminous perhaps than exist upon any one other class of cases, is worth anything, it is difficult to deny, or even to doubt the existence of such a phenomenon as the Vampire.

For my part I have heard no theory by which to explain what I myself have witnessed and experienced, other than that supplied by the ancient and well-attested belief of the country.

The next day the formal proceedings took place in the Chapel of Karnstein. The grave of the Countess Mircalla was opened; and the General and my father recognized each his perfidious and beautiful guest, in the face now disclosed to view. The features, though a hundred and fifty years had passed since her funeral, were tinted with the warmth of life. Her eyes were open; no cadaverous smell exhaled from the coffin. The two medical men, one officially present, the other on the part of the promoter of the inquiry, attested the marvelous fact that there was a faint but appreciable respiration, and a corresponding action of the heart. The limbs were perfectly flexible, the flesh elastic; and the leaden coffin floated with blood, in which to a depth of seven inches, the body lay immersed.

Here then, were all the admitted signs and proofs of vampirism. The body, therefore, in accordance with the ancient practice, was raised, and a sharp stake driven through the heart of the vampire, who uttered a piercing shriek at the moment, in all respects such as might escape from a living person in the last agony. Then the head was struck off, and a torrent of blood flowed from the severed neck. The body and head was next placed on a pile of wood, and reduced to ashes, which were thrown upon the river and borne away, and that territory has never since been plagued by the visits of a vampire.

My father has a copy of the report of the Imperial Commission, with the signatures of all who were present at these proceedings, attached in verification of the statement. It is from this official paper that I have summarized my account of this last shocking scene.

XVI. CONCLUSION

I write all this you suppose with composure. But far from it; I cannot think of it without agitation. Nothing but your earnest desire so repeatedly expressed, could have induced me to sit down to a task that has unstrung my nerves for months to come, and reinduced a shadow of the unspeakable horror which years after my deliverance continued to make my days and nights dreadful, and solitude insupportably terrific.

Let me add a word or two about that quaint Baron Vordenburg, to whose curious lore we were indebted for the discovery of the Countess Mircalla's grave.

He had taken up his abode in Gratz, where, living upon a mere pittance, which was all that remained to him of the once princely estates of his family, in Upper Styria, he devoted himself to the minute and laborious investigation of the marvelously authenticated tradition of Vampirism. He had at his fingers' ends all the great and little works upon the subject.

"*Magia Posthuma*," "*Phlegon de Mirabilibus*," "*Augustinus de cura pro Mortuis*," "*Philosophicae et Christianae Cogitationes de Vampiris*," by John Christofer Herenberg; and a thousand others, among which I remember only a few of those which he lent to my father. He had a voluminous digest of all the judicial cases, from which he had extracted a system of principles that appear to govern—some always, and others occasionally only—the condition of the vampire. I may mention, in passing, that the deadly pallor attributed to that sort of revenants, is a mere melodramatic fiction. They present, in the grave, and when they show themselves in human society, the appearance of healthy life. When disclosed to light in their coffins, they exhibit all the symptoms that are enumerated as those which proved the vampire-life of the long-dead Countess Karnstein.

How they escape from their graves and return to them for certain hours every day, without displacing the clay or leaving any trace of disturbance in the state of the coffin or the cerements, has always been admitted to be utterly inexplicable. The amphibious existence of the vampire is sustained by daily renewed slumber in the grave. Its horrible lust for living blood supplies the vigor of its waking existence. The vampire is prone to be fascinated with an engrossing vehemence, resembling the passion of love, by particular persons. In pursuit of these it will exercise inexhaustible patience and stratagem, for access to a particular object may be obstructed in a hundred ways. It will never desist until it has satiated its passion, and drained the very life of its coveted victim. But it will, in these cases, husband and protract its murderous enjoyment with the refinement of an epicure, and heighten it by the gradual approaches of an artful courtship. In these cases it seems to yearn for something like sympathy and consent. In ordinary ones it goes direct to its object, overpowers with violence, and strangles and exhausts often at a single feast.

The vampire is, apparently, subject, in certain situations, to special conditions. In the particular instance of which I have given you a relation, Mircalla seemed to be limited to a name which, if not her real one, should at least reproduce, without the omission or addition of a single letter, those, as we say, anagrammatically, which compose it.

Carmilla did this; so did Millarca.

My father related to the Baron Vordenburg, who remained with us for two or three weeks after the expulsion of Carmilla, the story about the Moravian nobleman and the vampire at Karnstein churchyard, and then he asked the Baron how he had discovered the exact position of the long-concealed tomb of the Countess Mircalla? The Baron's grotesque features puckered up into a mysterious smile; he looked down, still smiling on his worn spectacle case and fumbled with it. Then looking up, he said:

"I have many journals, and other papers, written by that remarkable man; the most curious among them is one treating of the visit of which you speak, to Karnstein. The tradition, of course, discolours and distorts a little. He might have been termed a Moravian nobleman, for he had changed his abode to that territory, and was, beside, a noble. But he was, in truth, a native of Upper Styria. It is enough to say that in very early youth he had been a passionate and favoured lover of the beautiful Mircalla, Countess Karnstein. Her early death plunged him into inconsolable grief. It is the nature of vampires to increase and multiply, but according to an ascertained and ghostly law.

"Assume, at starting, a territory perfectly free from that pest. How does it begin, and how does it multiply itself? I will tell you. A person, more or less wicked, puts an end to himself. A suicide, under certain circumstances, becomes a vampire. That specter visits living people in their slumbers; they die, and almost invariably, in the grave, develop into vampires. This happened in the case of the beautiful Mircalla, who was haunted by one of those demons. My ancestor, Vordenburg, whose title I still bear, soon discovered this, and in the course of the studies to which he devoted himself, learned a great deal more.

"Among other things, he concluded that suspicion of vampirism would probably fall, sooner or later, upon the dead Countess, who in life had been his idol. He conceived a horror, be she what she might, of her remains being profaned by the outrage of a posthumous execution. He has left a curious paper to prove that the vampire, on its expulsion from its amphibious existence, is projected into a far more horrible life; and he resolved to save his once beloved Mircalla from this.

"He adopted the stratagem of a journey here, a pretended removal of her remains, and a real obliteration of her monument. When age had stolen upon him, and from the vale of years, he looked back on the scenes he was leaving, he considered, in a different spirit, what he had done, and a horror took possession of him. He made the tracings and notes which have guided me to the very spot, and drew up a confession of the deception that he had practiced. If he had intended any further action in this matter, death prevented him; and the hand of a remote descendant has, too late for many, directed the pursuit to the lair of the beast."

We talked a little more, and among other things he said was this:

"One sign of the vampire is the power of the hand. The slender hand of Mircalla closed like a vice of steel on the General's wrist when he raised the hatchet to strike. But its power is not confined to its grasp; it leaves a numbness in the limb it seizes, which is slowly, if ever, recovered from."

The following Spring my father took me a tour through Italy. We remained away for more than a year. It was long before the terror of recent events subsided; and to this hour the image of Carmilla returns to memory with ambiguous alternations—sometimes the playful, languid, beautiful girl; sometimes the writhing fiend I saw in the ruined church; and often from a reverie I have started, fancying I heard the light step of Carmilla at the drawing room door.

Dickon the Devil

by Joseph Sheridan Le Fanu

About thirty years ago I was selected by two rich old maids to visit a property in that part of Lancashire which lies near the famous forest of Pendle, with which Mr Ainsworth's 'Lancashire Witches' has made us so pleasantly familiar. My business was to make partition of a small property, including a house and demesne, to which they had a long time before succeeded as co-heiresses.

The last forty miles of my journey I was obliged to post, chiefly by cross-roads, little known, and less frequented, and presenting scenery often extremely interesting and pretty. The picturesqueness of the landscape was enhanced by the season, the beginning of September, at which I was travelling.

I had never been in this part of the world before; I am told it is now a great deal less wild, and, consequently, less beautiful.

At the inn where I had stopped for a relay of horses and some dinner- for it was then past five o'clock—I found the host, a hale old fellow of five-and-sixty, as he told me, a man of easy and garrulous benevolence, willing to accommodate his guests with any amount of talk, which the slightest tap sufficed to set flowing, on any subject you pleased.

I was curious to learn something about Barwyke, which was the name of the demesne and house I was going to. As there was no inn within some miles of it,

I had written to the steward to put me up there, the best way he could, for a night.

The host of the 'Three Nuns,' which was the sign under which he entertained wayfarers, had not a great deal to tell. It was twenty years, or more, since old Squire Bowes died, and no one had lived in the Hall ever since, except the gardener and his wife.

"Tom Wyndsour will be as old a man as myself but he's a bit taller, and not so much in flesh, quite," said the fat innkeeper.

"But there were stories about the house," I repeated, "that they said, prevented tenants from coming into it?"

"Old wives' tales; many years ago, that will be, sir; I forget 'em; I forget 'em all. Oh yes, there always will be, when a house is left so; foolish folk will always be talkin'; but I hadn't heard a word about it this twenty year."

It was vain trying to pump him; the old landlord of the 'Three Nuns,' for some reason, did not choose to tell tales of Barwyke Hall, if he really did, as I suspected, remember them.

I paid my reckoning, and resumed my journey, well pleased with the good cheer of that old-world inn, but a little disappointed.

We had been driving for more than an hour, when we began to cross a wild common; and I knew that, this passed, a quarter of an hour would bring me to the door of Barwyke Hall.

The peat and furze were pretty soon left behind; we were again in the wooded scenery that I enjoyed so much, so entirely natural and pretty, and so little disturbed by traffic of any kind. I was looking from the chaise-window, and soon detected the object of which, for some time, my eye had been in search. Barwyke Hall was a large, quaint house, of that cage-work fashion known as 'black-and-white,' in which the bars and angles of an oak framework contrast, black as ebony, with the white plaster that overspreads the masonry built into its interstices. This steep-roofed Elizabethan house stood in the midst of park-like grounds of no great extent, but rendered imposing by the noble stature of the old trees that now cast their lengthening shadows eastward over the sward, from the declining sun.

The park-wall was grey with age, and in many places laden with ivy. In deep grey shadow, that contrasted with the dim fires of evening reflected on the foliage above it, in a gentle hollow, stretched a lake that looked cold and black, and seemed, as it were, to skulk from observation with a guilty knowledge.

I had forgot that there was a lake at Barwyke; but the moment this caught my eye, like the cold polish of a snake in the shadow, my instinct seemed to recognize something dangerous, and I knew that the lake was connected, I could not remember how, with the story I had heard of this place in my boyhood.

I drove up a grass-grown avenue, under the boughs of these noble trees, whose foliage, dyed in autumnal red and yellow, returned the beams of the western sun gorgeously.

We drew up at the door. I got out, and had a good look at the front of the house; it was a large and melancholy mansion, with signs of long neglect upon it; great wooden shutters, in the old fashion, were barred, outside, across the windows; grass, and even nettles, were growing thick on the courtyard, and a thin moss streaked the timber beams; the plaster was discoloured by time and weather, and bore great russet and yellow stains. The gloom was increased by several grand old trees that crowded close about the house.

I mounted the steps, and looked round; the dark lake lay near me now, a little to the left. It was not large; it may have covered some ten or twelve acres; but it added to the melancholy of the scene. Near the centre of it was a small island, with two old ash trees, leaning toward each other, their pensive images reflected in the stirless water. The only cheery influence in this scene of antiquity, solitude, and neglect was that the house and landscape were warmed with the ruddy western beams. I knocked, and my summons resounded hollow and ungenial in my ear; and the bell, from far away, returned a deep-mouthed and surly ring, as if it resented being roused from a score years' slumber.

A light-limbed, jolly-looking old fellow, in a barracan jacket and gaiters, with a smile of welcome, and a very sharp, red nose, that seemed to promise good cheer, opened the door with a promptitude that indicated a hospitable expectation of my arrival.

There was but little light in the hall, and that little lost itself in darkness in the background. It was very spacious and lofty, with a gallery running round it, which, when the door was open, was visible at two or three points. Almost in the dark my new acquaintance led me across this wide hall into the room destined for my reception. It was spacious, and wainscoted up to the ceiling. The furniture of this capacious chamber was old-fashioned and clumsy. There were curtains still to the windows, and a piece of Turkey carpet lay upon the floor; those windows were two in number, looking out, through the trunks of the trees close to the house, upon the lake. It needed all the fire, and all the pleasant associations of my entertainer's red nose, to light up this melancholy chamber. A door at its farther end admitted to the room that was prepared for my sleeping apartment. It was wainscoted, like the other. It had a four-post bed, with heavy tapestry curtains, and in other respects was furnished in the same old-world and ponderous style as the other room. Its window, like those of that apartment, looked out upon the lake.

Sombre and sad as these rooms were, they were yet scrupulously clean. I had nothing to complain of but the effect was rather dispiriting. Having given some directions about supper—a pleasant incident to look forward to—and made a rapid toilet, I called on my friend with the gaiters and red nose (Tom Wyndsour) whose occupation was that of a 'bailiff' or under-steward, of the property, to accompany me, as we had still an hour or so of sun and twilight, in a walk over the grounds.

It was a sweet autumn evening, and my guide, a hardy old fellow, strode at a pace that tasked me to keep up with.

Among clumps of trees at the northern boundary of the demesne we lighted upon the little antique parish church. I was looking down upon it, from an eminence, and the park-wall interposed; but a little way down was a stile affording access to the road, and by this we approached the iron gate of the churchyard. I saw the church door open; the sexton was replacing his pick, shovel, and spade, with which he had just been digging a grave in the churchyard, in their little repository under the stone stair of the tower. He was a polite, shrewd little hunchback, who was very happy to show me over the church. Among the monuments was one that interested me; it was erected to commemorate the very Squire Bowes from whom my two old maids had inherited the house and estate of Barwyke. It spoke of him in terms of grandiloquent eulogy, and informed the Christian reader that he had died, in the bosom of the Church of England, at the age of seventy-one.

I read this inscription by the parting beams of the setting sun, which disappeared behind the horizon just as we passed out from under the porch.

"Twenty years since the Squire died," said I, reflecting as I loitered still in the churchyard.

"Ay, sir; 'twill be twenty year the ninth o' last month."

"And a very good old gentleman?"

"Good-natured enough, and an easy gentleman he was, sir; I don't think while he lived he ever hurt a fly," acquiesced Tom Wyndsour. "It ain't always easy sayin' what's in 'em though, and what they may take or turn to afterwards; and some o' them sort, I think, goes mad."

"You don't think he was out of his mind?" I asked.

"He? La! No; not he, sir; a bit lazy, mayhap, like other old fellows; but a knew devilish well what he was about."

Tom Wyndsour's account was a little enigmatical; but, like old Squire Bowes, I was "a bit lazy" that evening, and asked no more questions about him.

We got over the stile upon the narrow road that skirts the churchyard. It is overhung by elms more than a hundred years old, and in the twilight, which now prevailed, was growing very dark. As side-by-side we walked along this road, hemmed in by two loose stone-like walls, something running towards us in a zig-zag line passed us at a wild pace, with a sound like a frightened laugh or a shudder, and I saw, as it passed, that it was a human figure. I may confess now, that I was a little startled. The dress of this figure was, in part, white: I know I mistook it at first for a white horse coming down the road at a gallop. Tom Wyndsour turned about and looked after the retreating figure.

"He'll be on his travels tonight," he said, in a low tone. "Easy served with a bed, *that* lad be; six foot o' dry peat or heath, or a nook in a dry ditch. That lad hasn't slept once in a house this twenty year, and never will while grass grows."

"Is he mad?" I asked.

"Something that way, sir; he's an idiot, an awpy; we call him "Dickon the devil," because the devil's almost the only word that's ever in his mouth."

It struck me that this idiot was in some way connected with the story of old Squire Bowes.

"Queer things are told of him, I dare say?" I suggested.

"More or less, sir; more or less. Queer stories, some."

"Twenty years since he slept in a house? That's about the time the Squire died," I continued.

"So it will be, sir; and not very long after."

"You must tell me all about that, Tom, tonight, when I can hear it comfortably after supper."

Tom did not seem to like my invitation; and looking straight before him as we trudged on, he said,

"You see, sir, the house has been quiet, and nout's been troubling folk inside the walls or out, all round the woods of Barwyke, this ten year, or more; and my old woman, down there, is clear against talking about such matters, and thinks it best—and so do I—to let sleepin' dogs be."

He dropped his voice towards the close of the sentence, and nodded significantly.

We soon reached a point where he unlocked a wicket in the park wall, by which we entered the grounds of Barwyke once more.

The twilight deepening over the landscape, the huge and solemn trees, and the distant outline of the haunted house, exercised a sombre influence on me, which, together with the fatigue of a day of travel, and the brisk walk we had had, disinclined me to interrupt the silence in which my companion now indulged.

A certain air of comparative comfort, on our arrival, in great measure dissipated the gloom that was stealing over me. Although it was by no means a cold night, I was very glad to see some wood blazing in the grate; and a pair of candles aiding the light of the fire, made the room look cheerful. A small table, with a very white cloth, and preparations for supper, was also a very agreeable object.

I should have liked very well, under these influences, to have listened to Tom Wyndsour's story; but after supper I grew too sleepy to attempt to lead him to the subject; and after yawning for a time, I found there was no use in contending against my drowsiness, so I betook myself to my bedroom, and by ten o'clock was fast asleep.

What interruption I experienced that night I shall tell you presently. It was not much, but it was very odd.

By next night I had completed my work at Barwyke. From early morning till then I was so incessantly occupied and hard-worked, that I had not time to think over the singular occurrence to which I have just referred. Behold me, however, at length once more seated at my little supper-table, having ended a comfortable meal. It had been a sultry day, and I had thrown one of the large windows up as high as it would go. I was sitting near it, with my brandy and water at my elbow, looking out into the dark. There was no moon, and the trees that are grouped about the house make the darkness round it supernaturally profound on such nights.

"Tom," said I, so soon as the jug of hot punch I had supplied him with began to exercise its genial and communicative influence; "you must tell me who beside your wife and you and myself slept in the house last night."

Tom, sitting near the door, set down his tumbler, and looked at me askance, while you might count seven, without speaking a word.

"Who else slept in the house?" he repeated, very deliberately. "Not a living soul, sir;' and he looked hard at me, still evidently expecting something more.

"That *is* very odd," I said returning his stare, and feeling really a little odd. "You are sure *you* were not in my room last night?"

"Not till I came to call you, sir, this morning; *I* can make oath of that."

"Well," said I, "there was some one there, *I* can make oath of that. I was so tired I could not make up my mind to get up; but I was waked by a sound that I thought was some one flinging down the two tin boxes in which my papers were locked up violently on the floor. I heard a slow step on the ground, and there was light in the room, although I remembered having put out my candle. I thought it must have been you, who had come in for my clothes, and upset the boxes by accident. Whoever it was, he went out and the light with him. I was about to settle again, when, the curtain being a little open at the foot of the bed, I saw a light on the wall opposite; such as a candle from outside would cast if the door were very cautiously opening. I started up in the bed, drew the side curtain, and saw that the door *was* opening, and admitting light from outside. It is close, you know, to the head of the bed. A hand was holding on the edge of the door and pushing it open; not a bit like yours; a very singular hand. Let me look at yours."

He extended it for my inspection.

'Oh no; there's nothing wrong with your hand. This was differently shaped; fatter; and the middle finger was stunted, and shorter than the rest, looking as if it had once been broken, and the nail was crooked like a claw I called out "Who's there?" and the light and the hand were withdrawn, and I saw and heard no more of my visitor.'

"So sure as you're a living man, that was him!" exclaimed Tom Wyndsour, his very nose growing pale, and his eyes almost starting out of his head.

"Who?" I asked.

"Old Squire Bowes; 'twas *his* hand you saw; the Lord a' mercy on us!" answered Tom. "The broken finger, and the nail bent like a hoop. Well for you, sir, he didn't come back when you called, that time. You came here about them Miss Dymocks' business, and he never meant they should have a foot o' ground in Barwyke; and he was making a will to give it away quite different, when death took him short. He never was uncivil to no one; but he couldn't abide them ladies. My mind misgave me when I heard 'twas about their business you were coming; and now you see how it is; he'll be at his old tricks again!"

With some pressure and a little more punch, I induced Tom Wyndsour to explain his mysterious allusions by recounting the occurrences which followed the old Squire's death.

"Squire Bowes of Barwyke died without making a will, as you know," said Tom. "And all the folk round were sorry; that is to say, sir, as sorry as folk will be for an old man that has seen a long tale of years, and has no right to grumble that death has knocked an hour too soon at his door. The Squire was well liked; he was never in a passion, or said a hard word; and he would not hurt a fly; and that made what happened after his decease the more surprising.

"The first thing these ladies did, when they got the property, was to buy stock for the park.

"It was not wise, in any case, to graze the land on their own account. But they little knew all they had to contend with.

"Before long something went wrong with the cattle; first one, and then another, took sick and died, and so on, till the loss began to grow heavy. Then, queer stories, little by little, began to be told. It was said, first by one, then by another, that Squire Bowes was seen, about evening time, walking, just as he used to do when he was alive, among the old trees, leaning on his stick; and, sometimes when he came up with the cattle, he would stop and lay his hand kindly like on the back of one of them; and that one was sure to fall sick next day, and die soon after.

"No one ever met him in the park, or in the woods, or ever saw him, except a good distance off. But they knew his gait and his figure well, and the clothes he used to wear; and they could tell the beast he laid his hand on by its colour—white, dun, or black; and that beast was sure to sicken and die. The neighbours grew shy of taking the path over the park; and no one liked to walk in the woods, or come inside the bounds of Barwyke: and the cattle went on sickening and dying as before.

"At that time there was one Thomas Pyke; he had been a groom to the old Squire; and he was in care of the place, and was the only one that used to sleep in the house.

"Tom was vexed, hearing these stories; which he did not believe the half on 'em; and more especial as he could not get man or boy to herd the cattle; all being afeared. So he wrote to Matlock in Derbyshire, for his brother, Richard Pyke, a clever lad, and one that knew nout o' the story of the old Squire walking.

'Dick came; and the cattle was better; folk said they could still see the old

Squire, sometimes, walking, as before, in openings of the wood, with his stick in his hand; but he was shy of coming nigh the cattle, whatever his reason might be, since Dickon Pyke came; and he used to stand a long bit off, looking at them, with no more stir in him than a trunk o' one of the old trees, for an hour at a time, till the shape melted away, little by little, like the smoke of a fire that burns out.

"Tom Pyke and his brother Dickon, being the only living souls in the house, lay in the big bed in the servants' room, the house being fast barred and locked, one night in November.

"Tom was lying next the wall, and he told me, as wide awake as ever he was at noonday. His brother Dickon lay outside, and was sound asleep.

"Well, as Tom lay thinking, with his eyes turned toward the door, it opens slowly, and who should come in but old Squire Bowes, his face lookin' as dead as he was in his coffin.

"Tom's very breath left his body; he could not take his eyes off him; and he felt the hair rising up on his head.

"The Squire came to the side of the bed, and put his arms under Dickon, and lifted the boy—in a dead sleep all the time—and carried him out so, at the door.

"Such was the appearance, to Tom Pyke's eyes, and he was ready to swear to it, anywhere.

"When this happened, the light, wherever it came from, all on a sudden went out, and Tom could not see his own hand before him.

"More dead than alive, he lay till daylight.

"Sure enough his brother Dickon was gone. No sign of him could he discover about the house; and with some trouble he got a couple of the neighbours to help him to search the woods and grounds. Not a sign of him anywhere.

"At last one of them thought of the island in the lake; the little boat was moored to the old post at the water's edge. In they got, though with small hope of finding him there. Find him, nevertheless, they did, sitting under the big ash tree, quite out of his wits; and to all their questions he answered nothing but one cry—'Bowes, the devil! See him; see him; Bowes, the devil!' An idiot they found him; and so he will be till God sets all things right. No one could ever get him to sleep under roof-tree more. He wanders from house to house while daylight lasts; and no one cares to lock the harmless creature in the workhouse. And folk would rather not meet him after nightfall, for they think where he is there may be worse things near."

A silence followed Tom's story. He and I were alone in that large room; I was sitting near the open window, looking into the dark night air. I fancied I saw something white move across it; and I heard a sound like low talking that swelled into a discordant shriek—"Hoo-oo-oo! Bowes, the devil! Over your shoulder. Hoo-oo-oo! Ha! Ha! Ha!" I started up, and saw, by the light of the candle with which Tom strode to the window, the wild eyes and blighted face of the idiot, as, with a sudden change of mood, he drew off, whispering and tittering to himself, and holding up his long fingers, and looking at the tips like a 'hand of glory'

Tom pulled down the window. The story and its epilogue were over. I confess I was rather glad when I heard the sound of the horses' hoofs on the court-yard, a few minutes later; and still gladder when, having bidden Tom a kind farewell, I had left the neglected house of Barwyke a mile behind me.

The Screaming Skull

by Francis Marion Crawford

I have often heard it scream. No, I am not nervous, I am not imaginative, and I never believed in ghosts, unless that thing is one. Whatever it is, it hates me almost as much as it hated Luke Pratt, and it screams at me.

If I were you, I would never tell ugly stories about ingenious ways of killing people, for you never can tell but that some one at the table may be tired of his or her nearest and dearest. I have always blamed myself for Mrs. Pratt's death, and I suppose I was responsible for it in a way, though heaven knows I never wished her anything but long life and happiness. If I had not told that story she might be alive yet. That is why the thing screams at me, I fancy.

She was a good little woman, with a sweet temper, all things considered, and a nice gentle voice; but I remember hearing her shriek once when she thought her little boy was killed by a pistol that went off though everyone was sure that it was not loaded. It was the same scream; exactly the same, with a sort of rising quaver at the end; do you know what I mean? Unmistakable.

The truth is, I had not realized that the doctor and his wife were not on good terms. They used to bicker a bit now and then when I was here, and I often noticed that little Mrs. Pratt got very red and bit her lip hard to keep her temper, while Luke grew pale and said the most offensive things. He was that sort when he was in the nursery, I remember, and afterwards at school. He was my cousin, you know; that is how I came by this house; after he died, and his boy Charley was killed in South Africa, there were no relations left. Yes, it's a pretty little property, just the sort of thing for an old sailor like me who has taken to gardening.

One always remembers one's mistakes much more vividly than one's cleverest things, doesn't one? I've often noticed it. I was dining with the Pratts one night, when I told them the story that afterwards made so much difference. It was a wet night in November, and the sea was moaning. Hush!—if you don't speak you will hear it now . . .

Do you hear the tide? Gloomy sound, isn't it? Sometimes, about this time of year—hallo!—there it is! Don't be frightened, man—it won't eat you—it's only a noise, after all! But I'm glad you've heard it, because there are always people who think it's the wind, or my imagination, or something. You won't hear it again tonight, I fancy, for it doesn't often come more than once. Yes—that's right. Put another stick on the fire, and a little more stuff into that weak mixture you're so fond of. Do you remember old Blauklot the carpenter, on that German ship that picked us up when the *Clontarf* went to the bottom? We were hove to in a howling gale one night, as snug as you please, with no land within five hundred miles, and the ship coming up and falling off as regularly as clockwork—"Biddy te boor beebles ashore tis night, poys!" old Blauklot sang out, as he went off to his quarters with the sail-maker. I often think of that, now that I'm ashore for good and all.

Yes, it was on a night like this, when I was at home for a spell, waiting to take the *Olympia* out on her first trip—it was on the next voyage that she broke the record, you remember—but that dates it. Ninety-two was the year, early in November. The weather was dirty, Pratt was out of temper, and the dinner was bad, very bad indeed, which didn't improve matters, and cold, which made it worse. The poor little lady was very unhappy about it, and insisted on making a Welsh rarebit on the table to counteract the raw turnips and the half-boiled mutton. Pratt must have had a hard day. Perhaps he had lost a patient. At all events, he was in a nasty temper.

"My wife is trying to poison me, you see!" he said. "She'll succeed some day." I saw that she was hurt, and I made believe to laugh, and said that Mrs. Pratt was much too clever to get rid of her husband in such a simple way; and then I began to tell them about Japanese tricks with spun glass and chopped horsehair and the like.

Pratt was a doctor, and knew a lot more than I did about such things, but that only put me on my mettle, and I told a story about a woman in Ireland who did for three husbands before anyone suspected foul play.

Did you never hear that tale? The fourth husband managed to keep awake and caught her, and she was hanged. How did she do it? She drugged them, and poured melted lead into their ears through a little horn funnel when they were asleep… No—that's the wind whistling. It's backing up to the southward again. I can tell by the sound. Besides, the other thing doesn't often come more than once in an evening even at this time of year—when it happened. Yes, it was in November. Poor Mrs. Pratt died suddenly in her bed not long after I dined here. I can fix the date, because I got the news in New York by the steamer that followed the *Olympia* when I took her out on her first trip. You had the Leofric the same year? Yes, I remember. What a pair of old buffers we are coming to be, you and I. Nearly fifty years since we were apprentices together on the *Clontarf.* Shall you ever forget old Blauklot? "Biddy te boor beebles ashore, poys!" Ha, ha! Take a little more, with all that water. It's the old Hulstkamp I found in the cellar when this house came to me, the same I brought Luke from Amsterdam five-and-twenty years ago. He had never touched a drop of it. Perhaps he's sorry now, poor fellow.

Where did I leave off? I told you that Mrs. Pratt died suddenly—yes. Luke must have been lonely here after she was dead, I should think; I came to see him now and then, and he looked worn and nervous, and told me that his practice was growing too heavy for him, though he wouldn't take an assistant on any account. Years went on, and his son was killed in South Africa, and after that he began to be queer. There was something about him not like other people. I believe he kept his senses in his profession to the end; there was no complaint of his having made mad mistakes in cases, or anything of that sort, but he had a look about him—

Luke was a red-headed man with a pale face when he was young, and he was never stout; in middle age he turned a sandy grey, and after his son died he grew thinner and thinner, till his head looked like a skull with parchment stretched over it very tight, and his eyes had a sort of glare in them that was very disagreeable to look at.

He had an old dog that poor Mrs. Pratt had been fond of, and that used to follow her everywhere. He was a bulldog, and the sweetest tempered beast you ever saw, though he had a way of hitching his upper lip behind one of his fangs that frightened strangers a good deal. Sometimes, of an evening, Pratt and

Bumble—that was the dog's name—used to sit and look at each other a long time, thinking about old times, I suppose, when Luke's wife used to sit in that chair you've got. That was always her place, and this was the doctor's, where I'm sitting. Bumble used to climb up by the footstool—he was old and fat by that time, and could not jump much, and his teeth were getting shaky. He would look steadily at Luke, and Luke looked steadily at the dog, his face growing more and more like a skull with two little coals for eyes; and after about five minutes or so, though it may have been less, old Bumble would suddenly begin to shake all over, and all on a sudden he would set up an awful howl, as if he had been shot, and tumble out of the easy-chair and trot away, and hide himself under the sideboard, and lie there making odd noises.

Considering Pratt's looks in those last months, the thing is not surprising, you know. I'm not nervous or imaginative, but I can quite believe he might have sent a sensitive woman into hysterics—his head looked so much like a skull in parchment.

At last I came down one day before Christmas, when my ship was in dock and I had three weeks off. Bumble was not about, and I said casually that I supposed the old dog was dead.

"Yes," Pratt answered, and I thought there was something odd in his tone even before he went on after a little pause. "I killed him," he said presently. "I could stand it no longer."

I asked what it was that Luke could not stand, though I guessed well enough. "He had a way of sitting in her chair and glaring at me, and then howling," Luke shivered a little. "He didn't suffer at all, poor old Bumble," he went on in a hurry, as if he thought I might imagine he had been cruel. "I put dionine into his drink to make him sleep soundly, and then I chloroformed him gradually, so that he could not have felt suffocated even if he was dreaming. It's been quieter since then."

I wondered what he meant, for the words slipped out as if he could not help saying them. I've understood since. He meant that he did not hear that noise so often after the dog was out of the way. Perhaps he thought at first that it was old Bumble in the yard howling at the moon, though it's not that kind of noise, is it? Besides, I know what it is, if Luke didn't. It's only a noise after all, and a noise never hurt anybody yet. But he was much more imaginative than I am. No doubt there really is something about this place that I don't understand; but when I don't understand a thing, I call it a phenomenon, and I don't take it for granted that it's going to kill me, as he did. I don't understand everything, by long odds, nor do you, nor does any man who has been to sea. We used to talk of tidal waves, for instance, and we could not account for them; now we account for them by calling them submarine earthquakes, and we branch off into fifty theories, any one of which might make earthquakes quite comprehensible if we only knew what they were. I fell in with one of them once, and the inkstand flew straight up from the table against the ceiling of my cabin. The same thing happened to Captain Lecky—I dare say you've read about it in his 'Wrinkles'. Very good. If that sort of thing took place ashore, in this room for instance, a nervous person would talk about spirits and levitation and fifty things that mean nothing, instead of just quietly setting it down as a 'phenomenon' that has not been explained yet. My view of that voice, you see.

Besides, what is there to prove that Luke killed his wife? I would not even suggest such a thing to anyone but you. After all, there was nothing but the coincidence that poor little Mrs. Pratt died suddenly in her bed a few days after I told that story at dinner. She was not the only woman who ever died like that. Luke got the doctor over from the next parish, and they agreed that she had died of something the matter with her heart Why not? It's common enough.

Of course, there was the ladle. I never told anybody about that, and, it made me start when I found it in the cupboard in the bedroom. It was new, too—a little tinned iron ladle that had not been in the fire more than once or twice, and there was some lead in it that had been melted, and stuck to the bottom of the bowl, all grey, with hardened dross on it. But that proves nothing. A country doctor is generally a handy man, who does everything for himself, and Luke may have had a dozen reasons for melting a little lead in a ladle. He was fond of sea-fishing, for instance, and he may have cast a sinker for a night-line; perhaps it was a weight for the hall clock, or something like that. All the same, when I found it I had a rather queer sensation, because it looked so much like the thing I had described when I told them the story. Do you understand? It affected me unpleasantly, and I threw it away; it's at the bottom of the sea a mile from the Spit, and it will be jolly well rusted beyond recognizing if it's ever washed up by the tide.

You see, Luke must have bought it in the village, years ago, for the man sells just such ladles still. I suppose they are used in cooking. In any case, there was no reason why an inquisitive housemaid should find such a thing lying about, with lead in it, and wonder what it was, and perhaps talk to the maid who heard me tell the story at dinner—for that girl married the plumber's son in the village, and may remember the whole thing.

You understand me, don't you? Now that Luke Pratt is dead and gone, and lies buried beside his wife, with an honest man's tombstone at his head, I should not care to stir up anything that could hurt his memory. They are both dead, and their son, too. There was trouble enough about Luke's death, as it was.

How? He was found dead on the beach one morning, and there was a coroner's inquest. There were marks on his throat, but he had not been robbed. The verdict was that he had come to his end 'By the hands or teeth of some person or animal unknown,' for half the jury thought it might have been a big dog that had thrown him down and gripped his windpipe, though the skin of his throat was not broken. No one knew at what time he had gone out, nor where he had been. He was found lying on his back above high-water mark, and an old cardboard bandbox that had belonged to his wife lay under his hand, open. The lid had fallen off. He seemed to have been carrying home a skull in the box—doctors are fond of collecting such things. It had rolled out and lay near his head, and it was a remarkably fine skull, rather small, beautifully shaped and very white, with perfect teeth. That is to say, the upper jaw was perfect, but there was no lower one at all, when I first saw it.

Yes, I found it here when I came. You see, it was very white and polished, like a thing meant to be kept under a glass case, and the people did not know where it came from, nor what to do with it; so they put it back into the bandbox and set it on the shelf of the cupboard in the best bedroom, and of course they showed it to me when I took possession. I was taken down to the beach, too, to be shown the place where Luke was found, and the old fisherman explained just how he was lying, and the skull beside him. The only point he could not explain was why the skull had rolled up the sloping sand towards Luke's head instead of rolling downhill to his feet. It did not seem odd to me at the time, but I have often thought of it since, for the place is rather steep. I'll take you there tomorrow if you like—I made a sort of cairn of stones there afterwards.

When he fell down, or was thrown down—whichever happened—the bandbox struck the sand, and the lid came off, and the thing came out and ought to have rolled down. But it didn't. It was close to his head almost touching it, and turned with the face towards it. I say it didn't strike me as odd when the man told me; but I could not help thinking about It afterwards, again and again, till I saw a picture of it all when I closed my eyes; and then I began to ask myself why the plaguey thing had rolled up instead of down, and why it had stopped near Luke's head instead of anywhere else, a yard away, for instance.

You naturally want to know what conclusion I reached, don't you? None that at all explained the rolling, at all events. But I got something else into my head, after a time, that made me feel downright uncomfortable.

Oh, I don't mean as to anything supernatural! There may be ghosts, or there may not be. If there are, I'm not inclined to believe that they can hurt living people except by frightening them, and, for my part, I would rather face any shape of ghost than a fog in the Channel when it's crowded. No. What bothered me was just a foolish idea, that's all, and I cannot tell how it began, nor what made it grow till it turned into a certainty.

I was thinking about Luke and his poor wife one evening over my pipe and a dull book, when it occurred to me that the skull might possibly be hers, and I have never got rid of the thought since.

You'll tell me there's no sense in it, no doubt, that Mrs. Pratt was buried like a Christian and is lying in the churchyard where they put her, and that it's perfectly monstrous to suppose her husband kept her skull in her old bandbox in his bedroom. All the same, in the face of reason, and common sense, and probability, I'm convinced that he did. Doctors do all sorts of queer things that would make men like you and me feel creepy, and those are Just the things that don't seem probable, nor logical, nor sensible to us.

Then, don't you see?—if it really was her skull, poor woman, the only way of accounting for his having it is that he really killed her, and did it in that way, as the woman killed her husbands in the story, and that he was afraid there might be an examination some day which would betray him. You see, I told that too, and I believe it had really happened some fifty or sixty years ago.

They dug up the three skulls, you know, and there was a small lump of lead rattling about in each one. That was what hanged the woman. Luke remembered that, I'm sure. I don't want to know what he did when he thought of it; my taste never ran in the direction of horrors, and I don't fancy you care for them either, do you? No. If you did, you might supply what is wanting to the story.

It must have been rather grim, eh? I wish I did not see the whole thing so distinctly, just as everything must have happened. He took it the night before she was buried, I'm sure, after the coffin had been shut, and when the servant girl was asleep. I would bet anything, that when he'd got it, he put something under the sheet in its place, to fill up and look like it. What do you suppose he put there, under the sheet?

I don't wonder you take me up on what I'm saying! First I tell you that I don't want to know what happened, and that I hate to think about horrors, and then I describe the whole thing to you as if I had seen it. I'm quite sure that it was her work-bag that he put there. I remember the bag very well, for she always used it of an evening; it was made of brown plush, and when it was stuffed full it was about the size of—you understand. Yes, there I am, at it again! You may laugh at me, but you don't live here alone, where it was done, and you didn't tell Luke the story about the melted lead. I'm not nervous, I tell you, but sometimes I begin to feel that I understand why some people are. I dwell on all this when I'm alone, and I dream of it, and when that thing screams—well, frankly, I don't like the noise any more than you do, though I should be used to it by this time.

I ought not to be nervous. I've sailed in a haunted ship. There was a Man in the Top, and two-thirds of the crew died of the West Coast fever inside of ten days after we anchored; but I was all right, then and afterwards. I have seen some ugly sights, too, just as you have, and all the rest of us. But nothing ever stuck in my head in the way this does.

You see, I've tried to get rid of the thing, but it doesn't like that. It wants to be there in its place, in Mrs. Pratt's bandbox in the cupboard in the best bedroom. It's not happy anywhere else. How do I know that? Because I've tried it. You don't suppose that I've not tried, do you? As long as it's there it only screams now and then, generally at this time of year, but if I put it out of the house it goes on all night, and no servant will stay here twenty-four hours. As it is, I've often been left alone and have been obliged to shift for myself for a fortnight at a time. No one from the village would ever pass a night under the roof now, and as for selling the place, or even letting it, that's out of the question. The old women say that if I stay here I shall come to a bad end myself before long.

I'm not afraid of that. You smile at the mere idea that anyone could take such nonsense seriously. Quite right. It's utterly blatant nonsense, I agree with you. Didn't I tell you that it's only a noise after all when you started and looked round as if you expected to see a ghost standing behind your chair?

I may be all wrong about the skull, and I like to think that I am when I can. It may be just a fine specimen which Luke got somewhere long ago, and what rattles about inside when you shake it may be nothing but a pebble, or a bit of hard clay, or anything. Skulls that have lain long in the ground generally have something inside them that rattles don't they? No, I've never tried to get it out, whatever it is; I'm afraid it might be lead, don't you see? And if it is, I don't want to know the fact, for I'd much rather not be sure. If it really is lead, I killed her quite as much as if I had done the deed myself. Anybody must see that, I should think. As long as I don't know for certain, I have the consolation of saying that it's all utterly ridiculous nonsense, that Mrs. Pratt died a natural death and that the beautiful skull belonged to Luke when he was a student in London. But if I were quite sure, I believe I should have to leave the house; indeed I do, most certainly. As it is, I had to give up trying to sleep in the best bedroom where the cupboard is.

You ask me why I don't throw it into the pond—yes, but please don't call it a 'confounded bugbear'—it doesn't like being called names.

There! Lord, what a shriek! I told you so! You're quite pale, man. Fill up your pipe and draw your chair nearer to the fire, and take some more drink. Old Hollands never hurt anybody yet. I've seen a Dutchman in Java drink half a jug of Hulstkamp in a morning without turning a hair. I don't take much rum myself, because it doesn't agree with my rheumatism, but you are not rheumatic and it won't damage you. Besides, it's a very damp night outside. The wind is howling again, and it will soon be in the south-west; do you hear how the windows rattle? The tide must have turned too, by the moaning.

We should not have heard the thing again if you had not said that. I'm pretty sure we should not. Oh yes, if you choose to describe it as a coincidence, you are quite welcome, but I would rather that you should not call the thing names again, if you don't mind. It may be that the poor little woman hears, and perhaps it hurts her, don't you know? Ghosts? No! You don't call anything a ghost that you can take in your hands and look at in broad daylight, and that rattles when you shake it do you, now? But it's something that hears and understands; there's no doubt about that.

I tried sleeping in the best bedroom when I first came to the house just because it was the best and most comfortable, but I had to give it up It was their room, and there's the big bed she died in, and the cupboard is in the thickness of the wall, near the head, on the left. That's where it likes to be kept, in its bandbox. I only used the room for a fortnight after I came, and then I turned out and took the little room downstairs, next to the surgery, where Luke used to sleep when he expected to be called to a patient during the night.

I was always a good sleeper ashore; eight hours is my dose, eleven to seven when I'm alone, twelve to eight when I have a friend with me. But I could not sleep after three o'clock in the morning in that room—a quarter past, to be accurate—as a matter of fact, I timed it with my old pocket chronometer, which still keeps good time, and it was always at exactly seventeen minutes past three. I wonder whether that was the hour when she died?

It was not what you have heard. If it had been that, I could not have stood it two nights. It was just a start and a moan and hard breathing for a few seconds in the cupboard, and it could never have waked me under ordinary circumstances, I'm sure. I suppose you are like me in that, and we are just like other people who have been to sea. No natural sounds disturb us at all, not all the racket of a square-rigger hove to in a heavy gale, or rolling on her beam ends before the wind. But if a lead pencil gets adrift and rattles in the drawer of your cabin table you are awake in a moment. Just so—you always understand. Very well, the noise in the cupboard was no louder than that, but it waked me instantly.

I said it was like a 'start'. I know what I mean, but it's hard to explain without seeming to talk nonsense. Of course you cannot exactly 'hear' a person 'start'; at the most, you might hear the quick drawing of the breath between the parted lips and closed teeth, and the almost imperceptible sound of clothing that moved suddenly though very slightly. It was like that.

You know how one feels what a sailing vessel is going to do, two or three seconds before she does it, when one has the wheel. Riders say the same of a horse, but that's less strange, because the horse is a live animal with feelings of its own, and only poets and landsmen talk about a ship being alive, and all that. But I have always felt somehow that besides being a steaming machine or a sailing machine for carrying weights, a vessel at sea is a sensitive instrument, and a means of communication between nature and man, and most particularly the man at the wheel, if she is steered by hand. She takes her impressions directly from wind and sea, tide and stream, and transmits them to the man's hand, just as the wireless telegraphy picks up the interrupted currents aloft and turns them out below in the form of a message.

You see what I am driving at; I felt that something started in the cupboard, and I felt it so vividly that I heard it, though there may have been nothing to hear, and the sound inside my head waked me suddenly. But I really heard the other noise. It was as if it were muffled inside a box, as far away as if it came through a long-distance telephone; and yet I knew that it was inside the cupboard near the head of my bed. My hair did not bristle and my blood did not run cold that time. I simply resented being waked up by something that had no business to make a noise, any more than a pencil should rattle in the drawer of my cabin table on board ship. For I did not understand; I just supposed that the cupboard had some communication with the outside air, and that the wind had got in and was moaning through it with a sort of very faint screech. I struck a light and looked at my watch, and it was seventeen minutes past three. Then I turned over and went to sleep on my right ear. That's my good one; I'm pretty deaf with the other, for I struck the water with it when I was a lad in diving from the fore-topsail yard. Silly thing to do, it was, but the result is very convenient when I want to go to sleep when there's a noise.

That was the first night, and the same thing happened again and several times afterwards, but not regularly, though it was always at the same time, to a second; perhaps I was sometimes sleeping on my good ear, and sometimes not. I overhauled the cupboard and there was no way by which the wind could get in, or anything else, for the door makes a good fit, having been meant to keep out moths, I suppose; Mrs. Pratt must have kept her winter things in it, for it still smells of camphor and turpentine.

After about a fortnight I had had enough of the noises. So far I had said to myself that it would be silly to yield to it and take the skull out of the room. Things always look differently by daylight, don't they? But the voice grew louder—I suppose one may call it a voice—and it got inside my deaf ear, too, one night. I realized that when I was wide awake, for my good ear was jammed down on the pillow, and I ought not to have heard a foghorn in that position. But I heard that, and it made me lose my temper, unless it scared me, for sometimes the two are not far apart. I struck a light and got up, and I opened the cupboard, grabbed the bandbox and threw it out of the window, as far as I could.

Then my hair stood on end. The thing screamed in the air, like a shell from a twelve-inch gun. It fell on the other side of the road. The night was very dark, and I could not see it fall, but I know it fell beyond the road The window is just over the front door, it's fifteen yards to the fence, more or less, and the road is ten yards wide. There's a thick-set hedge beyond, along the glebe that belongs to the vicarage.

I did not sleep much more than night. It was not more than half an hour after I had thrown the bandbox out when I heard a shriek outside—like what we've had tonight, but worse, more despairing, I should call it; and it may have been my imagination, but I could have sworn that the screams came nearer and nearer each time. I lit a pipe, and walked up and down for a bit, and then took a book and sat up reading, but I'll be hanged if I can remember what I read nor even what the book was, for every now and then a shriek came up that would have made a dead man turn in his coffin.

A little before dawn someone knocked at the front door. There was no mistaking that for anything else, and I opened my window and looked down, for I guessed that someone wanted the doctor, supposing that the new man had taken Luke's house. It was rather a relief to hear a human knock after that awful noise.

You cannot see the door from above, owing to the little porch. The knocking came again, and I called out, asking who was there, but nobody answered, though the knock was repeated. I sang out again, and said that the doctor did not live here any longer. There was no answer, but it occurred to me that it might be some old countryman who was stone deaf. So I took my candle and went down to open the door. Upon my word, I was not thinking of the thing yet, and I had almost forgotten the other noises. I went down convinced that I should find somebody outside, on the doorstep, with a message. I set the candle on the hall table, so that the wind should not blow it out when I opened. While I was drawing the old-fashioned bolt I heard the knocking again. It was not loud, and it had a queer, hollow sound, now that I was close to it, I remember, but I certainly thought it was made by some person who wanted to get in.

It wasn't. There was nobody there, but as I opened the door inward, standing a little on one side, so as to see out at once, something rolled across the threshold and stopped against my foot.

I drew back as I felt it, for I knew what it was before I looked down. I cannot tell you how I knew, and it seemed unreasonable, for I am still quite sure that I had thrown it across the road. It's a French window, that opens wide, and I got a good swing when I flung it out. Besides, when I went out early in the morning, I found the bandbox beyond the thick hedge.

You may think it opened when I threw it, and that the skull dropped out; but that's impossible, for nobody could throw an empty cardboard box so far. It's out of the question; you might as well try to fling a ball of paper twentyfive yards, or a blown bird's egg.

To go back, I shut and bolted the hall door, picked the thing up carefully, and put it on the table beside the candle. I did that mechanically, as one instinctively does the right thing in danger without thinking at all—unless one does the opposite. It may seem odd, but I believe my first thought had been that somebody might come and find me there on the threshold while it was resting against my foot, lying a little on its side, and turning one hollow eye up at my face, as if it meant to accuse me. And the light and shadow from the candle played in the hollows of the eyes as it stood on the table, so that they seemed to open and shut at me. Then the candle went out quite unexpectedly, though the door was fastened and there was not the least draught; and I used up at least half a dozen matches before it would burn again.

I sat down rather suddenly, without quite knowing why. Probably I had been badly frightened, and perhaps you will admit there was no great shame in being scared. The thing had come home, and it wanted to go upstairs, back to its cupboard. I sat still and stared at it for a bit till I began to feel very cold; then I took it and carried it up and set it in its place, and I remember that I spoke to it, and promised that it should have its bandbox again in the morning.

You want to know whether I stayed in the room till daybreak? Yes but I kept a light burning, and sat up smoking and reading, most likely out of fright; plain, undeniable fear, and you need not call it cowardice either, for that's not the same thing. I could not have stayed alone with that thing in the cupboard; I should have been scared to death, though I'm not more timid than other people. Confound it all, man, it had crossed the road alone, and had got up the doorstep and had knocked to be let in.

When the dawn came, I put on my boots and went out to find the bandbox. I had to go a good way round, by the gate near the high road, and I found the box open and hanging on the other side of the hedge. It had caught on the twigs by the string, and the lid had fallen off and was lying on the ground below it. That shows that it did not open till it was well over; and if it had not opened as soon as it left my hand, what was inside it must have gone beyond the road too.

That's all. I took the box upstairs to the cupboard, and put the skull back and locked it up. When the girl brought me my breakfast she said she was sorry, but that she must go, and she did not care if she lost her month's wages. I looked at her, and her face was a sort of greenish yellowish white. I pretended to be surprised, and asked what was the matter; but that was of no use, for she just turned on me and wanted to know whether I meant to stay in a haunted house, and how long I expected to live if I did, for though she noticed I was sometimes a little hard of hearing, she did not believe that even I could sleep through those screams again—and if I could, why had I been moving about the house and opening and shutting the front door, between three and four in the morning? There was no answering that, since she had heard me, so off she went, and I was left to myself. I went down to the village during the morning and found a woman who was willing to come and do the little work there is and cook my dinner, on condition that she might go home every night. As for me, I moved downstairs that day, and I have never tried to sleep in the best bedroom since. After a little while I got a brace of middle-aged Scotch servants from London, and things were quiet enough for a long time. I began by telling them that the house was in a very exposed position, and that the wind whistled round it a good deal in the autumn and winter, which had given it a bad name in the village, the Cornish people being inclined to superstition and telling ghost stories. The two hard-faced, sandyhaired sisters almost smiled, and they answered with great contempt that they had no great opinion of any Southern bogey whatever, having been in service in two English haunted houses, where they had never seen so much as the Boy in Grey, whom they reckoned no very particular rarity in Forfarshire.

They stayed with me several months, and while they were in the house we had peace and quiet. One of them is here again now, but she went away with her sister within the year. This one—she was the cook—married the sexton, who works in my garden. That's the way of it. It's a small village and he has not much to do, and he knows enough about flowers to help me nicely, besides doing most of the hard work; for though I'm fond of exercise, I'm getting a little stiff in the hinges. He's a sober, silent sort of fellow, who minds his own business, and he was a widower when I came here—Trehearn is his name, James Trehearn. The Scottish sisters would not admit that there was anything wrong about the house, but when November came they gave me warning that they were going, on the ground that the chapel was such a long walk from here, being in the next parish, and that they could not possibly go to our church. But the younger one came back in the spring, and as soon as the banns could be published she was married to James Trehearn by the vicar, and she seems to have had no scruples about hearing him preach since then. I'm quite satisfied, if she is! The couple live in a small cottage that looks over the churchyard.

I suppose you are wondering what all this has to do with what I was talking about. I'm alone so much that when an old friend comes to see me, I sometimes go on talking just for the sake of hearing my own voice. But in this case there is really a connection of ideas. It was James Trehearn who buried poor Mrs. Pratt, and her husband after her in the same grave, and it's not far from the back of his cottage. That's the connection in my mind, you see. It's plain enough. He knows something; I'm quite sure that he does, though he's such a reticent beggar.

Yes, I'm alone in the house at night now, for Mrs. Trehearn does everything herself, and when I have a friend the sexton's niece comes in to wait on the table. He takes his wife home every evening in winter, but in summer, when there's light, she goes by herself. She's not a nervous woman, but she's less sure than she used to be that there are no bogies in England worth a Scotchwoman's notice. Isn't it amusing, the idea that Scotland has a monopoly of the supernatural? Odd sort of national pride, I call that, don't you?

That's a good fire, isn't it? When driftwood gets started at last there's nothing like it, I think. Yes, we get lots of it, for I'm sorry to say there are still a great many wrecks about here. It's a lonely coast, and you may have all the wood you want for the trouble of bringing it in. Trehearn and I borrow a cart now and then, and load it between here and the Spit. I hate a coal fire when I can get wood of any sort. A log is company, even if it's only a piece of a deck beam or timber sawn off, and the salt in it makes pretty sparks. See how they fly, like Japanese hand-fireworks! Upon my word, with an old friend and a good fire and a pipe, one forgets all about that thing upstairs, especially now that the wind has moderated. It's only a lull, though, and it will blow a gale before morning.

You think you would like to see the skull? I've no objection. There's no reason why you shouldn't have a look at it, and you never saw a more perfect one in your life, except that there are two front teeth missing in the lower jaw.

Oh yes—I had not told you about the jaw yet. Trehearn found it in the garden last spring when he was digging a pit for a new asparagus bed. You know we make asparagus beds six or eight feet deep here. Yes, yes—I had forgotten to tell you that. He was digging straight down, just as he digs a grave; if you want a good asparagus bed made, I advise you to get a sexton to make it for you. Those fellows have a wonderful knack at that sort of digging.

Trehearn had got down about three feet when he cut into a mass of white lime in the side of the trench. He had noticed that the earth was a little looser there, though he says it had not been disturbed for a number of years. I suppose he thought that even old lime might not be good for asparagus, so he broke it out and threw it up. It was pretty hard, he says, in biggish lumps, and out of sheer force of habit he cracked the lumps with his spade as they lay outside the pit beside him; the jaw bone of the skull dropped out of one of the pieces. He thinks he must have knocked out the two front teeth in breaking up the lime, but he did not see them anywhere. He's a very experienced man in such things, as you may imagine, and he said at once that the jaw had probably belonged to a young woman, and that the teeth had been complete when she died. He brought it to me, and asked me if I wanted to keep it; if I did not, he said he would drop it into the next grave he made in the churchyard, as he supposed it was a Christian jaw, and ought to have decent burial, wherever the rest of the body might be. I told him that doctors often put bones into quicklime to whiten them nicely, and that I supposed Dr Pratt had once had a little lime pit in the garden for that purpose, and had forgotten the jaw. Trehearn looked at me quietly.

"Maybe it fitted that skull that used to be in the cupboard upstairs, sir," he said. "Maybe Dr Pratt had put the skull into the lime to clean it, or something, and when he took it out he left the lower jaw behind. There's some human hair sticking in the lime, sir."

I saw there was, and that was what Trehearn said. If he did not suspect something, why in the world should he have suggested that the jaw might fit the skull? Besides, it did. That's proof that he knows more than he cares to tell. Do you suppose he looked before she was buried? Or perhaps—when he buried Luke in the same grave—

Well, well, it's of no use to go over that, is it? I said I would keep the jaw with the skull, and I took it upstairs and fitted it into its place. There's not the slightest doubt about the two belonging together, and together they are.

Trehearn knows several things. We were talking about plastering the kitchen a while ago, and he happened to remember that it had not been done since the very week when Mrs. Pratt died. He did not say that the mason must have left some lime on the place, but he thought it, and that it was the very same lime he had found in the asparagus pit. He knows a lot. Trehearn is one of your silent beggars who can put two and two together. That grave is very near the back of his cottage, too, and he's one of the quickest men with a spade I ever saw. If he wanted to know the truth, he could, and no one else would ever be the wiser unless he chose to tell. In a quiet village like ours, people don't go and spend the night in the churchyard to see whether the sexton potters about by himself between ten o'clock and daylight.

What is awful to think of, is Luke's deliberation, if he did it; his cool certainty that no one would find him out; above all, his nerve, for that must have been extraordinary. I sometimes think it's bad enough to live in the place where it was done, if it really was done. I always put in the condition, you see, for the sake of his memory, and a little bit for my own sake, too.

I'll go upstairs and fetch the box in a minute. Let me light my pipe; there's no hurry! We had supper early, and it's only half-past nine o'clock. I never let a friend go to bed before twelve, or with less than three glasses—you may have as many more as you like, but you shan't have less, for the sake of old times.

It's breezing up again, do you hear? That was only a lull just now, and we are going to have a bad night.

A thing happened that made me start a little when I found that the jaw fitted exactly. I'm not very easily startled in that way myself, but I have seen people make a quick movement, drawing their breath sharply, when they had thought they were alone and suddenly turned and saw someone very near them. Nobody can call that fear. You wouldn't, would you? No. Well, just when I had set the jaw in its place under the skull, the teeth closed sharply on my finger. It felt exactly as if it were biting me hard, and I confess that I jumped before I realized that I had been pressing the jaw and the skull together with my other hand. I assure you I was not at all nervous. It was broad daylight, too, and a fine day, and the sun was streaming into the best bedroom. It would have been absurd to be nervous, and it was only a quick mistaken impression, but it really made me feel queer. Somehow it made me think of the funny verdict of the coroner's jury on Luke's death, 'by the hand or teeth of some person or animal unknown'. Ever since that I've wished I had seen those marks on his throat, though the lower jaw was missing then.

I have often seen a man do insane things with his hands that he does not realize at all. I once saw a man hanging on by an old awning stop with one hand, leaning backward, outboard, with all his weight on it, and he was just cutting the stop with the knife in his other hand when I got my arms round him. We were in mid-ocean, going twenty knots. He had not the smallest idea what he was doing; neither had I when I managed to pinch my finger between the teeth of that thing. I can feel it now. It was exactly as if it were alive and were trying to bite me. It would if it could, for I know it hates me, poor thing! Do you suppose that what rattles about inside is really a bit of lead? Well, I'll get the box down presently, and if whatever it is happens to drop out into your hands, that's your affair. If it's only a clod of earth or a pebble, the whole matter would be off my mind, and I don't believe I should ever think of the skull again; but somehow I cannot bring myself to shake out the bit of hard stuff myself. The mere idea that it may be lead makes me confoundedly uncomfortable, yet I've got the conviction that I shall know before long. I shall certainly know. I'm sure Trehearn knows, but he's such a silent beggar.

I'll go upstairs now and get it. What? You had better go with me? Ha, ha! do you think I'm afraid of a bandbox and a noise? Nonsense!

Bother the candle, it won't light! As if the ridiculous thing understood what it's wanted for! Look at that—the third match. They light fast enough for my pipe. There, do you see? It's a fresh box, just out of the tin safe where I keep the supply on account of the dampness. Oh, you think the wick of the candle may be damp, do you? All right, I'll light the beastly thing in the fire. That won't go out, at all events. Yes, it sputters a bit, but it will keep lighted now. It burns just like any other candle, doesn't it? The fact is, candles are not very good about here. I don't know where they come from, but they have a way of burning low occasionally, with a greenish flame that spits tiny sparks, and I'm often annoyed by their going out of themselves. It cannot be helped, for it will be long before we have electricity in our village. It really is rather a poor light, isn't it?

You think I had better leave you the candle and take the lamp, do you? I don't like to carry lamps about, that's the truth. I never dropped one in my life, but I have always thought I might, and it's so confoundedly dangerous if you do. Besides, I am pretty well used to these rotten candles by this time.

You may as well finish that glass while I'm getting it, for I don't mean to let you off with less than three before you go to bed. You won't have to go upstairs, either, for I've put you in the old study next to the surgery—that's where I live myself. The fact is, I never ask a friend to sleep upstairs now. The last man who did was Crackenthorpe, and he said he was kept awake all night. You remember old Crack, don't you? He stuck to the Service, and they've just made him an admiral. Yes, I'm off now— unless the candle goes out. I couldn't help asking if you remembered Crackenthorpe. If anyone had told us that the skinny little idiot he used to be was to turn out the most successful of the lot of us, we should have laughed at the idea, shouldn't we? You and I did not do badly, it's true—but I'm really going now. I don't mean to let you think that I've been putting it off by talking! As if there were anything to be afraid of! If I were scared, I should tell you so quite frankly, and get you to go upstairs with me.

Here's the box. I brought it down very carefully, so as not to disturb it, poor thing. You see, if it were shaken, the jaw might get separated from it again, and I'm sure it wouldn't like that. Yes, the candle went out as I was coming downstairs, but that was the draught from the leaky window on the landing. Did you hear anything? Yes, there was another scream. Am I pale, do you say? That's nothing. My heart is a little queer sometimes, and I went upstairs too fast. In fact, that's one reason why I really prefer to live altogether on the ground floor.

Wherever the shriek came from, it was not from the skull, for I had the box in my hand when I heard the noise, and here it is now; so we have proved definitely that the screams are produced by something else. I've no doubt I shall find out some day what makes them. Some crevice in the wall, of course, or a crack in a chimney, or a chink in the frame of a window. That's the way all ghost stories end in real life. Do you know, I'm jolly glad I thought of going up and bringing it down for you to see, for that last shriek settles the question. To think that I should have been so weak as to fancy that the poor skull could really cry out like a living thing!

Now I'll open the box, and we'll take it out and look at it under the bright light. It's rather awful to think that the poor lady used to sit there, in your chair, evening after evening, in just the same light, isn't it? But then—I've made up my mind that it's all rubbish from beginning to end, and that it's just an old skull that Luke had when he was a student and perhaps he put it into the lime merely to whiten it, and could not find the jaw.

I made a seal on the string, you see, after I had put the jaw in its place, and I wrote on the cover. There's the old white label on it still, from the milliner's, addressed to Mrs. Pratt when the hat was sent to her, and as there was room I wrote on the edge: 'A skull, once the property of the late Luke Pratt, MD.' I don't quite know why I wrote that, unless it was with the idea of explaining how the thing happened to be in my possession. I cannot help wondering sometimes what sort of hat it was that came in the bandbox. What colour was it, do you think? Was it a gay spring hat with a bobbing feather and pretty ribands? Strange that the very same box should hold the head that wore the finery—perhaps. No—we made up our minds that it just came from the hospital in London where Luke did his time. It's far better to look at it in that light, isn't it? There's no more connection between that skull and poor Mrs. Pratt than there was between my story about the lead and—

Good Lord! Take the lamp—don't let it go out, if you can help it—I'll have the window fastened again in a second—I say, what a gale! There, it's out! I told you so! Never mind, there's the firelight—I've got the window shut—the bolt was only half down. Was the box blown off the table? Where the deuce is it?

There! That won't open again, for I've put up the bar. Good dodge, an old-fashioned bar—there's nothing like it. Now, you find the bandbox while I light the lamp. Confound those wretched matches! Yes, a pipe spill is better—it must light in the fire—hadn't thought of it—thank you—there we are again. Now, where's the box? Yes, put it back on the table, and we'll open it.

That's the first time I have ever known the wind to burst that window open; but it was partly carelessness on my part when I last shut it. Yes, of course I heard the scream. It seemed to go all round the house before it broke in at the window. That proves that it's always been the wind and nothing else, doesn't it? When it was not the wind, it was my imagination I've always been a very imaginative man: I must have been, though I did not know it. As we grow older we understand ourselves better, don't you know?

I'll have a drop of the Hulstkamp neat, by way of an exception, since you are filling up your glass. That damp gust chilled me, and with my rheumatic tendency I'm very much afraid of a chill, for the cold sometimes seems to stick in my joints all winter when it once gets in.

By George, that's good stuff! I'll just light a fresh pipe, now that everything is snug again, and then we'll open the box. I'm so glad we heard that last scream together, with the skull here on the table between us, for a thing cannot possibly be in two places at the same time, and the noise most certainly came from outside, as any noise the wind makes must. You thought you heard it scream through the room after the window was burst open? Oh yes, so did I, but that was natural enough when everything was open. Of course we heard the wind. What could one expect?

Look here, please. I want you to see that the seal is intact before we open the box together. Will you take my glasses? No, you have your own. All right. The seal is sound, you see, and you can read the words of the motto easily. 'Sweet and low'—that's it—because the poem goes on 'Wind of the Western Sea', and says, 'blow him again to me', and all that. Here is the seal on my watch chain, where it's hung for more than forty years. My poor little wife gave it to me when I was courting, and I never had any other. It was just like her to think of those words—she was always fond of Tennyson.

It's no use to cut the string, for it's fastened to the box, so I'll just break the wax and untie the knot, and afterwards we'll seal it up again. You see, I like to feel that the thing is safe in its place, and that nobody can take it out. Not that I should suspect Trehearn of meddling with it, but I always feel that he knows a lot more than he tells. You see, I've managed it without breaking the string, though when I fastened it I never expected to open the bandbox again. The lid comes off easily enough. There! Now look!

What! Nothing in it! Empty! It's gone, man, the skull is gone!

No, there's nothing the matter with me. I'm only trying to collect my thoughts. It's so strange. I'm positively certain that it was inside when I put on the seal last spring. I can't have imagined that: it's utterly impossible. If I ever took a stiff glass with a friend now and then, I would admit that I might have made some idiotic mistake when I had taken too much. But I don't, and I never did. A pint of ale at supper and half a go of rum at bedtime was the most I ever took in my good days. I believe it's always we sober fellows who get rheumatism and gout! Yet there was my seal, and there is the empty bandbox. That's plain enough.

I say, I don't half like this. It's not right. There's something wrong about it, in my opinion. You needn't talk to me about supernatural manifestations, for I don't believe in them, not a little bit! Somebody must have tampered with the seal and stolen the skull. Sometimes, when I go out to work in the garden in summer, I leave my watch and chain on the table. Trehearn must have taken the seal then, and used it, for he would be quite sure that I should not come in for at least an hour. If it was not Trehearn—oh, don't talk to me about the possibility that the thing has got out by itself! If it has, it must be somewhere about the house, in some out-of-the-way corner, waiting. We may come upon it anywhere, waiting for us, don't you know?—just waiting in the dark. Then it will scream at me; it will shriek at me in the dark, for it hates me, I tell you!

The bandbox is quite empty. We are not dreaming, either of us. There, I turn it upside down.

What's that? Something fell out as I turned it over. It's on the floor, it s near your feet. I know it is, and we must find it. Help me to find it, man. Have you got it? For God's sake, give it to me, quickly!

Lead! I knew it when I heard it fall. I knew it couldn't be anything else by the little thud it made on the hearthrug. So it was lead after all and Luke did it.

I feel a little bit shaken up—not exactly nervous, you know, but badly shaken up, that's the fact. Anybody would, I should think. After all, you cannot say that it's fear of the thing, for I went up and brought it down—at least, I believed I was bringing it down, and that's the same thing, and by George, rather than give in to such silly nonsense, I'll take the box upstairs again and put it back in its place. It's not that. It's the certainty that the poor little woman came to her end in that way, by my fault, because I told the story. That's what is so dreadful. Somehow, I had always hoped that I should never be quite sure of it, but there is no doubting it now. Look at that!

Look at it! That little lump of lead with no particular shape. Think of what it did, man! Doesn't it make you shiver? He gave her something to make her sleep, of course, but there must have been one moment of awful agony. Think of having boiling lead poured into your brain. Think of it. She was dead before she could scream, but only think of—oh! there it is again—it's just outside—I know it's just outside—I can't keep it out of my head!—oh!—oh!

You thought I had fainted? No, I wish I had, for it would have stopped sooner. It's all very well to say that it's only a noise, and that a noise never hurt anybody—you're as white as a shroud yourself. There's only one thing to be done, if we hope to close an eye tonight. We must find it and put it back into its The Screaming Skull 65 bandbox and shut it up in the cupboard, where it likes to be I don't know how it got out, but it wants to get in again. That's why it screams so awfully tonight—it was never so bad as this—never since I first—

Bury it? Yes, if we can find it, we'll bury it, if it takes us all night. We'll bury it six feet deep and ram down the earth over it, so that it shall never get out again, and if it screams, we shall hardly hear it so deep down. Quick, we'll get the lantern and look for it. It cannot be far away; I'm sure it's just outside—it was coming in when I shut the window, I know it.

Yes, you're quite right. I'm losing my senses, and I must get hold of myself. Don't speak to me for a minute or two; I'll sit quite still and keep my eyes shut and repeat something I know. That's the best way.

"Add together the altitude, the latitude, and the polar distance, divide by two and subtract the altitude from the half-sum; then add the logarithm of the secant of the latitude, the cosecant of the polar distance, the cosine of the half-sum and the sine of the half-sum minus the altitude"—there! Don't say that I'm out of my senses, for my memory is all right, isn't it?

Of course, you may say that it's mechanical, and that we never forget the things we learned when we were boys and have used almost every day for a lifetime. But that's the very point. When a man is going crazy, it's the mechanical part of his mind that gets out of order and won't work right; he remembers things that never happened, or he sees things that aren't real, or he hears noises when there is perfect silence. That's not what is the matter with either of us, is it?

Come, we'll get the lantern and go round the house. It's not raining—only blowing like old boots, as we used to say. The lantern is in the cupboard under the stairs in the hall, and I always keep it trimmed in case of a wreck.

No use to look for the thing? I don't see how you can say that. It was nonsense to talk of burying it, of course, for it doesn't want to be buried; it wants to go back into its bandbox and be taken upstairs, poor thing! Trehearn took it out, I know, and made the seal over again. Perhaps he took it to the churchyard, and he may have meant well. I dare say he thought that it would not scream any more if it were quietly laid in consecrated ground, near where it belongs. But it has come home. Yes, that's it. He's not half a bad fellow, Trehearn, and rather religiously inclined, I think. Does not that sound natural, and reasonable, and well meant? He supposed it screamed because it was not decently buried—with the rest. But he was wrong. How should he know that it screams at me because it hates me, and because it's my fault that there was that little lump of lead in it?

No use to look for it, anyhow? Nonsense! I tell you it wants to be found—Hark! what's that knocking? Do you hear it? Knock—knock—knock—three times, then a pause, and then again. It has a hollow sound, hasn't it?

It has come home. I've heard that knock before. It wants to come in and be taken upstairs in its box. It's at the front door.

Will you come with me? We'll take it in. Yes, I own that I don't like to go alone and open the door. The thing will roll in and stop against my foot, just as it did before, and the light will go out. I'm a good deal shaken by finding that bit of lead, and, besides, my heart isn't quite right—too much strong tobacco, perhaps. Besides, I'm quite willing to own that I'm a bit nervous tonight, if I never was before in my life.

That's right, come along! I'll take the box with me, so as not to come back. Do you hear the knocking? It's not like any other knocking I ever heard. If you will hold this door open, I can find the lantern under the stairs by the light from this room without bringing the lamp into the hall—it would only go out.

The thing knows we are coming—hark! It's impatient to get in. Don't shut the door till the lantern is ready, whatever you do. There will be the usual trouble with the matches, I suppose—no, the first one, by Jove! I tell you it wants to get in, so there's no trouble. All right with that door now; shut it, please. Now come and hold the lantern, for it's blowing so hard outside that I shall have to use both hands. That's it, hold the light low. Do you hear the knocking still? Here goes—I'll open just enough with my foot against the bottom of the door—now!

Catch it! it's only the wind that blows it across the floor, that's all—there's half a hurricane outside, I tell you! Have you got it? The bandbox is on the table. One minute, and I'll have the bar up. There!

Why did you throw it into the box so roughly? It doesn't like that, you know.

What do you say? Bitten your hand? Nonsense, man! You did just what I did. You pressed the jaws together with your other hand and pinched yourself. Let me see. You don't mean to say you have drawn blood? You must have squeezed hard by Jove, for the skin is certainly torn. I'll give you some carbolic solution for it before we go to bed, for they say a scratch from a skull's tooth may go bad and give trouble.

Come inside again and let me see it by the lamp. I'll bring the bandbox—never mind the lantern, it may just as well burn in the hall for I shall need it presently when I go up the stairs. Yes, shut the door if you will; it makes it more cheerful and bright. Is your finger still bleeding? I'll get you the carbolic in an instant; just let me see the thing.

Ugh! There's a drop of blood on the upper jaw. It's on the eyetooth. Ghastly, isn't it? When I saw it running along the floor of the hall, the strength almost went out of my hands, and I felt my knees bending, then I understood that it was the gale, driving it over the smooth boards. You don't blame me? No, I should think not! We were boys together, and we've seen a thing or two, and we may just as well own to each other that we were both in a beastly funk when it slid across the floor at you. No wonder you pinched your finger picking it up, after that, if I did the same thing out of sheer nervousness, in broad daylight, with the sun streaming in on me.

Strange that the jaw should stick to it so closely, isn't it? I suppose it's the dampness, for it shuts like a vice—I have wiped off the drop of blood, for it was not nice to look at. I'm not going to try to open the jaws, don't be afraid! I shall not play any tricks with the poor thing, but I'll just seal the box again, and we'll take it upstairs and put it away where it wants to be. The wax is on the writing table by the window. Thank you. It will be long before I leave my seal lying about again, for Trehearn to use, I can tell you. Explain? I don't explain natural phenomena, but if you choose to think that Trehearn had hidden it somewhere in the bushes, and that the gale blew it to the house against the door, and made it knock, as if it wanted to be let in, you're not thinking the impossible, and I'm quite ready to agree with you.

Do you see that? You can swear that you've actually seen me seal it this time, in case anything of the kind should occur again. The wax fastens the strings to the lid, which cannot possibly be lifted, even enough to get in one finger. You're quite satisfied, aren't you? Yes. Besides, I shall lock the cupboard and keep the key in my pocket hereafter.

Now we can take the lantern and go upstairs. Do you know? I'm very much inclined to agree with your theory that the wind blew it against the house. I'll go ahead, for I know the stairs; just hold the lantern near my feet as we go up. How the wind howls and whistles! Did you feel the sand on the floor under your shoes as we crossed the hall?

Yes—this is the door of the best bedroom. Hold up the lantern, please. This side, by the head of the bed. I left the cupboard open when I got the box. Isn't it queer how the faint odour of women's dresses will hang about an old closet for years? This is the shelf. You've seen me set the box there, and now you see me turn the key and put it into my pocket. So that's done!

Goodnight. Are you sure you're quite comfortable? It's not much of a room, but I dare say you would as soon sleep here as upstairs tonight. If you want anything, sing out; there's only a lath and plaster partition between us. There's not so much wind on this side by half. There's the Hollands on the table, if you'll have one more nightcap. No? Well, do as you please. Goodnight again, and don't dream about that thing, if you can.

The following paragraph appeared in the Penraddon News, 23rd November 1906:

MYSTERIOUS DEATH OF A RETIRED SEA CAPTAIN

The village of Tredcombe is much disturbed by the strange death of Captain Charles Braddock, and all sorts of impossible stories are circulating with regard to the circumstances, which certainly seem difficult of explanation. The retired captain, who had successfully commanded in his time the largest and fastest liners belonging to one of the principal transatlantic steamship companies, was found dead in his bed on Tuesday morning in his own cottage, a quarter of a mile from the village. An examination was made at once by the local practitioner, which revealed the horrible fact that the deceased had been bitten in the throat by a human assailant, with such amazing force as to crush the windpipe and cause death. The marks of the teeth of both jaws were so plainly visible on the skin that they could be counted, but the perpetrator of the deed had evidently lost the two lower middle incisors. It is hoped that this peculiarity may help to identify the murderer, who can only be a dangerous escaped maniac. The deceased, though over sixty-five years of age, is said to have been a hale man of considerable physical strength, and it is remarkable that no signs of any struggle were visible in the room, nor could it be ascertained how the murderer had entered the house. Warning has been sent to all the insane asylums in the United Kingdom, but as yet no information has been received regarding the escape of any dangerous patient. The coroner's Jury returned the somewhat singular verdict that Captain Braddock came to his death "by the hands or teeth of some person unknown". The local surgeon is said to have expressed privately the opinion that the maniac is a woman, a view he deduces from the small size of the jaws, as shown by the marks of the teeth. The whole affair is shrouded in mystery. Captain Braddock was a widower, and lived alone. He leaves no children.

* * * * *

(AUTHOR'S NOTE.—Students of ghost lore and haunted houses will find the foundation of the foregoing story in the legends about a skull which is still preserved in the farmhouse called Bettiscombe Manor, situated, I believe, on the Dorsetshire coast.)

For the Blood is the Life

by M. R. James

We had dined at sunset on the broad roof of the old tower, because it was cooler there during the great heat of summer. Besides, the little kitchen was built at one corner of the great square platform, which made it more convenient than if the dishes had to be carried down the steep stone steps broken in places and everywhere worn with age. The tower was one of those built all down the west coast of Calabria by the Emperor Charles V early in the sixteenth century, to keep off the Barbary pirates, when the unbelievers were allied with Francis I against the Emperor and the Church. They have gone to ruin, a few still stand intact, and mine is one of the largest. How it came into my possession ten years ago, and why I spend a part of each year in it, are matters which do not concern this tale. The tower stands in one of the loneliest spots in Southern Italy, at the extremity of a curving, rocky promontory, which forms a small but safe natural harbour at the southern extremity of the Gulf of Policastro, and just north of Cape Scalea, the birthplace of Judas Iscariot, according to the old local legend. The tower stands alone on this hooked spur of the rock, and there is not a house to be seen within three miles of it. When I go there I take a couple of sailors, one of whom is a fair cook, and when I am away it is in charge of a gnome-like little being who was once a miner and who attached himself to me long ago.

My friend, who sometimes visits me in my summer solitude, is an artist by profession, a Scandinavian by birth, and a cosmopolitan by force of circumstances.

We had dined at sunset; the sunset glow had reddened and faded again, and the evening purple steeped the vast chain of the mountains that embrace the deep gulf to eastward and rear themselves higher and higher towards the south. It was hot, and we sat at the landward corner of the platform, waiting for the night breeze to come down from the lower hills. The colour sank out of the air, there was a little interval of deep-grey twilight, and a lamp sent a yellow streak from the open door of the kitchen, where the men were getting their supper.

Then the moon rose suddenly above the crest of the promontory, flooding the platform and lighting up every little spur of rock and knoll of grass below us, down to the edge of the motionless water. My friend lighted his pipe and sat looking at a spot on the hillside. I knew that he was looking at it, and for a long time past I had wondered whether he would ever see anything there that would fix his attention. I knew that spot well. It was clear that he was interested at last, though it was a long time before he spoke. Like most painters, he trusts to his own eyesight, as a lion trusts his strength and a stag his speed, and he is always disturbed when he cannot reconcile what he sees with what he believes that he ought to see.

"It's strange," he said. "Do you see that little mound just on this side of the boulder?"

"Yes," I said, and I guessed what was coming.

"It looks like a grave," observed Holger.

"Very true. It does look like a grave."

"Yes," continued my friend, his eyes still fixed on the spot. "But the strange thing is that I see the body lying on the top of it. Of course," continued Holger, turning his head on one side as artists do, "it must be an effect of light. In the first place, it is not a grave at all. Secondly, if it were, the body would be inside and not outside. Therefore, it's an effect of the moonlight. Don't you see it?"

"Perfectly; I always see it on moonlight nights."

"It doesn't seem it interest you much," said Holger.

"On the contrary, it does interest me, though I am used to it. You're not so far wrong, either. The mound is really a grave."

"Nonsense!" cried Holger incredulously. "I suppose you'll tell me that what I see lying on it is really a corpse!"

"No," I answered, "it's not. I know, because I have taken the trouble to go down and see."

"Then what is it?" asked Holger.

"It's nothing."

"You mean that it's an effect of light, I suppose?"

"Perhaps it is. But the inexplicable part of the matter is that it makes no difference whether the moon is rising or setting, or waxing or waning. If there's any moonlight at all, from east or west or overhead, so long as it shines on the grave you can see the outline of the body on top."

Holger stirred up his pipe with the point of his knife, and then used his finger for a stopper. When the tobacco burned well, he rose from his chair.

"If you don't mind," he said, "I'll go down and take a look at it."

He left me, crossed the roof, and disappeared down the dark steps. I did not move, but sat looking down until he came out of the tower below. I heard him humming an old Danish song as he crossed the open space in the bright moonlight, going straight to the mysterious mound. When he was ten paces from it, Holger stopped short, made two steps forward, and then three or four backward, and then stopped again. I know what that meant. He had reached the spot where the Thing ceased to be visible—where, as he would have said, the effect of light changed.

Then he went on till he reached the mound and stood upon it. I could see the Thing still, but it was no longer lying down; it was on its knees now, winding its white arms round Holger's body and looking up into his face. A cool breeze stirred my hair at that moment, as the night wind began to come down from the hills, but it felt like a breath from another world.

The Thing seemed to be trying to climb to its feet helping itself up by Holger's body while he stood upright, quite unconcious of it and apparently looking toward the tower, which is very picturesque when the moonlight falls upon it on that side.

"Come along!" I shouted. "Don't stay there all night!"

It seemed to me that he moved reluctantly as he stepped from the mound, or else with difficulty. That was it. The Thing's arms were still round his waist, but its feet could not leave the grave. As he came slowly forward it was drawn and lengthened like a wreath of mist, thin and white, till I saw distinctly that Holger shook himself, as a man does who feels a chill. At the same instant a little wail of pain came to me on the breeze—it might have been the cry of the small owl that lives amongst the rocks—and the misty presence floated swiftly back from Holger's advancing figure and lay once more at its length upon the mound.

Again I felt the cool breeze in my hair, and this time an icy thrill of dread ran down my spine. I remembered very well that I had once gone down there alone in the moonlight; that presently, being near, I had seen nothing; that, like Holger, I had gone and had stood upon the mound; and I remembered how when I came back, sure that there was nothing there, I had felt the sudden conviction that there was something after all if I would only look back, a temptation I had resisted as unworthy of a man of sense, until, to get rid of it, I had shaken myself just as Holger did.

And now I knew that those white, misty arms had been round me, too; I knew it in a flash, and I shuddered as I remembered that I had heard the night owl then, too. But it had not been the night owl. It was the cry of the Thing.

I refilled my pipe and poured out a cup of strong southern wine; in less than a minute Holger was seated beside me again.

"Of course there's nothing there," he said, "but it's creepy, all the same. Do you know, when I was coming back I was so sure that there was something behind me that I wanted to turn around and look? It was an effort not to."

He laughed a little, knocked the ashes out of his pipe, and poured himself out some wine. For a while neither of us spoke, and the moon rose higher and we both looked at the Thing that lay on the mound.

"You might make a story about that," said Holger after a long time.

"There is one," I answered. "If you're not sleepy, I'll tell it to you."

"Go ahead," said Holger, who likes stories.

Old Aderio was dying up there in the village beyond the hill. You remember him, I have no doubt. They say that he made his money by selling sham jewelry in South America, and escaped with his gains when he was found out. Like all those fellows, if they bring anything back with them, he at once set to work to enlarge his house, and as there are no masons here, he sent all the way to Paola for two workmen. They were a rough-looking pair of scoundrels—a Neapolitan who had lost one eye and a Sicilian with an old scar half an inch deep across his left cheek. I often saw them, for on Sundays they used to come down here and fish off the rocks. When Alario caught the fever that killed him the masons were still at work. As he had agreed that part of their pay should be their board and lodging, he made them sleep in the house. His wife was dead, and he had an only son called Angelo, who was a much better sort than himself. Angelo was to marry the daughter of the richest man in the village, and, strange to say, though the marriage was arranged by their parents, the young people were said to be in love with each other.

For that matter, the whole village was in love with Angelo, and among the rest a wild, good-looking creature called Cristina, who was more like a gipsy than any girl I ever saw about here. She had very red lips and very black eyes, she was built like a greyhound, and had the tongue of the devil. But Angelo did not care a straw for her. He was rather a simpleminded fellow, quite different from his old scoundrel of a father, and under what I should call normal circumstances I really believe that he would never have looked at any girl except the nice plump little creature, with a fat dowry, whom his father meant him to marry. But things turned up which were neither normal nor natural.

On the other hand, a very handsome young shepherd from the hills above Maratea was in love with Cristina, who seems to have been quite indifferent to him. Cristina had no regular means of subsistence, but she was a good girl and willing to do any work or go on errands to any distance for the sake of a loaf of bread or a mess of beans, and permission to sleep under cover. She was especially glad when she could get something to do about the house of Angelo's father. There is no doctor in the village, and when the neighbours saw that old Alario was dying they sent Cristina to Scalea to fetch one. That was late in the afternoon, and if they had waited so long it was because the dying miser refused to allow any such extravagance while he was able to speak. But while Cristina was gone matters grew rapidly worse, the priest was brought to the bedside, and when he had done what he could he gave it as his opinion to the bystanders that the old man was dead, and left the house.

You know these people. They have a physical horror of death. Until the priest spoke, the room had been full of people. The words were hardly out of his mouth before it was empty. It was night now. They hurried down the dark steps and out into the street.

Angelo, as I have said, was away, Cristina had not come back—the simple woman-servant who had nursed the sick man fled with the rest, and the body was left alone in the flickering light of the earthen oil lamp.

Five minutes later two men looked in cautiously and crept forward toward the bed. They were the one-eyed Neapolitan mason and his Sicilian companion. They knew what they wanted. In a moment they had dragged from under the bed a small but heavy iron-bound box, and long before anyone thought of coming back to the dead man they had left the house and the village under cover of darkness. It was easy enough, for Alario's house is the last toward the gorge which leads down here, and the thieves merely went out by the back door, got over the stone wall, and had nothing to risk after that except that possibility of meeting some belated countryman, which was very small indeed, since few of the people use that path. They had a mattock and shovel, and they made their way without accident.

I am telling you this story as it must have happened, for, of course, there were no witnesses to this part of it. The men brought the box down by the gorge, intending to bury it on the beach in the wet sand, where it would have been much safer. But the paper would have rotted if they had been obliged to leave it there long, so they dug their hole down there, close to that boulder. Yes, just where the mound is now.

Cristina did not find the doctor in Scalea, for he had been sent for from a place up the valley, half-way to San Domenico. If she had found him we would have come on his mule by the upper road, which is smoother but much longer. But Cristina took the short cut by the rocks, which passes about fifty feet above the mound, and goes round that corner. The men were digging when she passed, and she heard them at work. It would not have been like her to go by without finding out what the noise was, for she was never afraid of anything in her life, and, besides, the fishermen sometimes come ashore here at night to get a stone for an anchor or to gather sticks to make a little fire. The night was dark and Cristina probably came close to the two men before she could see what they were doing. She knew them, of course, and they knew her, and understood instantly that they were in her power. There was only one thing to be done for their safety, and they did it. They knocked her on the head, they dug the hole deep, and they buried her quickly with the iron-bound chest. They must have understood that their only chance of escaping suspicion lay in getting back to the village before their absence was noticed, for they returned immediately, and were found half and hour later gossiping quietly with the man who was making Alario's coffin. He was a crony of theirs, and had been working at the repairs in the old man's house. So far as I have been able to make out, the only persons who were supposed to know where Alario kept his treasure were Angelo and the one woman-servant I have mentioned. Angelo was away; it was the woman who discovered the theft.

It was easy enough to understand why no one else knew where the money was. The old man kept his door locked and the key in his pocket when he was out, and did not let the woman enter to clean the place unless he was there himself. The whole village knew that he had money somewhere, however, and the masons had probably discovered the whereabouts of the chest by climbing in at the window in his absence. If the old man had not been delirious until he lost conciousness he would have been in frightful agony of mind for his riches. The faithful woman-servant forgot their existence only for a few moments when she fled with the rest, overcome by the horror of death. Twenty minutes had not passed before she returned with the two hideous old hags who are always called in to prepare the dead for burial. Even then she had not at first the courage to go near the bed with them, but she made a pretence of dropping something, went down on her knees as if to find it, and looked under the bedstead. The walls of the room were newly whitewashed down to the floor and she saw at a glance that the chest was gone. It had been there in the afternoon, it had therefore been stolen in the short interval since she had left the room.

There are no carabineers stationed in the village; there is not so much as a municipal watchman, for there is no municipality. There never was such a place, I believe. Scalea is supposed to look after it in some mysterious way, and it takes a couple of hours to get anybody from there. As the old woman had lived in the village all her life, it did not even occur to her to apply to any civil authority for help. She simply set up a howl and ran through the village in the dark, screaming out that her dead master's house had been robbed. Many of the people looked out, but at first no one seemed inclined to help her. Most of them, judging her by themselves, whispered to each other that she had probably stolen the money herself. The first man to move was the father of the girl whom Angelo was to marry; having collected his household, all of whom felt a personal interest in the wealth which was to have come into the family, he declared it to be his opinion that the chest had been stolen by the two journeymen masons who lodged in the house. He headed a search for them, which naturally began in Alario's house and ended in the carpenter's workshop, where the thieves were found discussing a measure of wine with the carpenter over the half-finished coffin, by the light of one earthen lamp filled with oil and tallow. The search-party at once accused the delinquents of the crime, and threatened to lock them up in the cellar till the carabineers could be fetched from Scalea. The two men looked at each other for one moment, and then without the slightest hesitation they put out the single light, seized the unfinished coffin between them, and using it as a sort of battering ram, dashed upon their assailants in the dark. In a few moments they were beyond pursuit.

That is the end of the first part of the story. The tresure had disappeared, and as no trace of it could be found the people supposed that the thieves had succeeded in carrying it off. The old man was buried, and when Angelo came back at last he had to borrow money to pay for the miserable funeral, and had some difficulty in doing so. He hardly needed to be told that in losing his inheritance he had lost his bride. In this part of the world marriages are made on strictly business principles, and if the promised cash is not forthcoming on the appointed day, the bride or the bridegroom whose parents have failed to produce it may as well take themselves off, for there will be no wedding. Poor Angelo knew that well enough. His father had been possessed of hardly any land, and now that the hard cash which he had brought from South America was gone, there was nothing left but debts for the building materials that were to have been used for enlarging and improving the old house. Angelo was beggared, and the nice plump little creature who was to have been his, turned up her nose at him in the most approved fashion. As for Cristina, it was several days before she was missed, for no one remembered that she had been sent to Scalea for the doctor, who had never come. She often disappeared in the same way for days together, when she could find a little work here and there at the distant farms among the hills. But when she did not come back at all, people began to wonder, and at last made up their minds that she had connived with the masons and had escaped with them.

I paused and emptied my glass.

"That sort of thing could not happen anywhere else," observed Holger, filling his everlasting pipe again. "It is wonderful what a natural charm there is about murder and sudden death in a romantic country like this. Deeds that would be simply brutal and disgusting anywhere else become dramatic and mysterious because this is Italy, and we are living in a genuine tower of Charles V built against Barbary pirates."

"There's something in that," I admitted. Holger is the most romantic man in the world inside of himself, but he always thinks it necessary to explain why he feels anything.

"I suppose they found the poor girl's body with the box," he said presently.

"As it seems to interest you," I answered, "I'll tell you the rest of the story."

The mood had risen by this time; the outline of the Thing on the mound was clearer to our eyes than before.

The village very soon settled down to its small dull life. No one missed old

Alario, who had been away so much on his voyages to South America that he had never been a familiar figure in his native place. Angelo lived in the half-finished house, and because he had no money to pay the old woman-servant, she would not stay with him, but once in a long time she would come and wash a shirt for him for old acquaintance' sake. Besides the house, he had inherited a small patch of ground at some distance from the village; he tried to cultivate it, but he had no heart in the work, for he knew he could neer pay the taxes on it and on the house, which would certainly be confiscated by the Government, or seized for the debt of the building material, which the man who had supplied it refused to take back.

Angelo was very unhappy. So long as his father had been alive and rich, every girl in the village had been in love with him; but that was all changed now. It had been pleasant to be admired and courted, and invited to drink wine by fathers who had girls to marry. It was hard to be stared at coldly, and sometimes laughed at because he had been robbed of his inheritance. He cooked his miserable meals for himself, and from being sad became melancholy and morose.

At twilight, when the day's work was done, instead of hanging about in the open space before the church with young fellows of his own age, he took to wandering in lonely places on the outskirts of the village till it was quite dark. Then he slunk home and went to bed to save the expense of a light. But in those lonely twilight hours he began to have strange waking dreams. He was not always alone, for often when he sat on the stump of a tree, where the narrow path turns down the gorge, he was sure that a woman came up noiselessly over the rough stones, as if her feet were bare; and she stood under a clump of chestnut trees only half a dozen yards down the path, and beckoned to him without speaking. Though she was in the shadow he knew that her lips were red, and that when they parted a little and smiled at him she showed two small sharp teeth. He knew this at first rather than saw it, and he knew that it was Cristina, and that she was dead. Yet he was not afraid; he only wondered whether it was a dream, for he thought that if he had been awake he should have been frightened.

Besides, the dead woman had red lips, and that could only happen in a dream. Whenever he went near the gorget after sunset she was already there waiting for him, or else she very soon appeared, and he began to be sure of her blood-red mouth, but now each feature grew distinct, and the pale face looked at him with deep and hungry eyes.

It was the eyes that grew dim. Little by little he came to know that someday the dream would not end when he turned away to go home, but would lead him down the gorge out of which the vision rose. She was nearer now when she beckoned to him. Her cheeks were not livid like those of the dead, but pale with starvation, with the furious and unappeased physical hunger of her eyes that devoured him. They feasted on his soul and cast a spell over him, and at last they were close to his own and held him. He could not tell whether her breath was as hot as fire, or as cold as ice; he could not tell whether her red lips burned his or froze them, or whether her five fingers on his wrists seared scorching scars or bit his flesh like frost; he could not tell whether he was awake or asleep, whether she was alive or dead, but he knew that she loved him, she alone of all creatures, earthly or unearthly, and her spell had power over him.

When the moon rose high that night the shadow of that Thing was not alone down there upon the mound.

Angelo awoke in the cool dawn, drenched with dew and chilled through flesh, and blood, and bone. He opened his eyes to the faint grey light, and saw the stars were still shining overhead. He was very weak, and his heart was beating so slowly that he was almost like a man fainting. Slowly he turned his head on the mound, as on a pillow, but the other face was not there. Fear seized him suddenly, a fear unspeakable and unknown; he sprang to his feet and fled up the gorge, and he never looked behind him until he reached the door of the house on the outskirts of the village. Drearily he went to his work that day, and wearily the hours dragged themselves after the sun, till at last it touched the sea and sank, and the great sharp hills above Maratea turned purple against the dove-coloured eastern sky.

Angelo shouldered his heavy hoe and left the field. He felt less tired now than in the morning when he had begun to work, but he promised himself that he would go home without lingering by the gorge, and eat the best supper he could get himself, and sleep all night in his bed like a Christian man. Not again would he be tempted down the narrow way by a shadow with red lips and icy breath; not again would he dream that dream of terror and delight. He was near the village now; it was half an hour since the sun had set, and the cracked church bell sent little discordant echoes across the rocks and ravines to tell all good people that the day was done. Angelo stood still a moment where the path forked, where it led toward the village on the left, and down to the gorge on the right, where a clump of chestnut trees overhung the narrow way. He stood still a minute, lifting his battered hat from his head and gazing at the fast-fading sea westward, and his lips moved as he silently repeated the familiar evening prayer. His lips moved, but the words that followed them in his brain lost their meaning and turned into others, and ended in a name that he spoke aloud—Cristina! With the name, the tension of his will relaxed suddenly, reality went out and the dream took him again, and bore him on swiftly and surely like a man walking in his sleep, down, down, by the steep path in the gathering darkness. And as she glided beside him, Cristina whispered strange, sweet things in his ear, which somehow, if he had been awake, he knew that he could not quite have understood; but now they were the most wonderful words he had ever heard in his life. And she kissed him also, but not upon his mouth. He felt her sharp kisses upon his white throat, and he knew that her lips were red. So the wild dream sped on through twilight and darkness and moonrise, and all the glory of the summer's night. But in the chilly dawn he lay as one half dead upon the mound down there, recalling and not recalling, drained of his blood, yet strangely longing to give those red lips more. Then came the fear, the awful nameless panic, the mortal horror that guards the confines of the world we see not, neither know of as we know of other things, but which we feel when its icy chill freezes our bones and stirs our hair with the touch of a ghostly hand. Once more Angelo sprang from the mound and fled up the gorge in the breaking day, but his step was less sure this time, and he panted for breath as he ran; and when he came to the bright spring of water that rises half way up the hillside, he dropped upon his knees and hands and plunged his whole face in and drank as he had never drunk before—for it was the thirst of the wounded man who has lain bleeding all night upon the battle-field.

She had him fast now, and he could not escape her, but would come to her every evening at dusk until she had drained him of his last drop of blood. It was in vain that when the day was done he tried to take another turning and to go home by a path that did not lead near the gorge. It was in vain that he made promises to himself each morning at dawn when he climbed the lonely way up from the shore to the village. It was all in vain, for when the sun sank burning into the sea, and the coolness of the evening stole out as from a hiding-place to delight the weary world, his feet turned toward the old way, and she was waiting for him in the shadow under the chestnut trees; and then all happened as before, and she fell to kissing his white throat even as she flitted lightly down the way, winding one arm about him. And as his blood failed, she grew more hungry and more thirsty every day, and every day when he awoke in the early dawn it was harder to rouse himself to the effort of climbing the steep path to the village; and when he went to his work his feet dragged painfully, and there was hardly strength in his arms to wield the heavy hoe. He scarcely spoke to anyone now, but the people said he was "consuming himself" for love of the girl he was to have married when he lost his inheritance; and they laughed heartily at the thought, for this is not a very romantic country. At this time Antonio, the man who stays here to look after the tower, returned from a visit to his people, who live near Salerno. He had been away all the time since before Alario's death and knew nothing of what had happened. He has told me that he came back late in the afternoon and shut himself up in the tower to eat and sleep, for he was very tired. It was past midnight when he awoke, and when he looked out toward the mound, and he saw something, and he did not sleep again that night. When he went out again in the morning it was broad daylight, and there was nothing to be seen on the mound but loose stones and driven sand. Yet he did not go very near it; he went straight up the path to the village and directly to the house of the old priest.

"I have seen an evil thing this night," he said; "I have seen how the dead drink the blood of the living. And the blood is the life."

"Tell me what you have seen," said the priest in reply.

Antonio told him everything he had seen.

"You must bring your book and your holy water tonight," he added. "I will be here before sunset to go down with you, and if it pleases your reverence to sup with me while we wait, I will make ready."

"I will come," the priest answered, "for I have read in old books of these strange beings which are neither quick nor dead, and which lie ever fresh in their graves, stealing out in the dusk to taste life and blood."

Antonio cannot read, but he was glad to see that the priest understood the business; for, of course, the books must have been instructed him as to the best means of quieting the half-living Thing for ever.

So Antonio went away to his work, which consists largely in sitting on the shady side of the tower, when he is not perched upon a rock with a fishing-line catching nothing. But on that day he went twice to look at the mound in the bright sunlight, and he searched round and round it for some hole through which the being might get in and out; but he found none. When the sun began to sink and the air was cooler in the shadows, he went up to fetch the old priest, carrying a little wicker basket with him; and in this they placed a bottle of holy water, and the basin, and sprinkler, and the stole which the priest would need; and they came down and waited in the door of the tower till it should be dark. But while the light still lingered very grey and faint, they saw something moving, just there, two figures, a man's that walked, and a woman's that flitted beside him, and while her head lay on his shoulder she kissed his throat. The priest has told me that, too, and that his teeth chattered and he grasped Antonio's arm. The vision passed and disappeared into the shadow. Then Antonio got the leathern flask of strong liquor, which he kept for great occasions, and poured such a draught as made the old man feel almost young again; and gave the priest his stole to put on and the holy water to carry, and they went out together toward the spot where the work was to be done. Antonio says that in spite of the rum his own knees shook together, and the priest stumbled over his Latin. For when they were yet a few yards from the mound the flickering light of the lantern fell upon Angelo's white face, unconscious as if in sleep, and on his upturned throat, over which a very thin red line of blood trickled down into his collar; and the flickering light of the lantern played upon another face that looked up from the feast, upon two deep, dead eyes that saw in spite of death—upon parted lips, redder than life itself—upon two gleaming teeth on which glistened a rosy drop. Then the priest, good old man, shut his eyes tight and showered holy water before him, and his cracked voice rose almost to a scream; and then Antonio, who is no coward after all, raised his pick in one hand and the lantern in the other, as he sprang forward, not knowing what the end should be; and then he swears that he heard a woman's cry, and the Thing was gone, and Angelo lay alone on the mound unconscious, with the red line on his throat and the beads of deathly sweat on his cold forehead. They lifted him, half-dead as he was, and laid him on the ground close by; then Antonio went to work, and the priest helped him, thought he was old and could not do much; and they dug deep, and at last Antonio, standing in the grave, stooped down with his lantern to see what he might see.

His hair used to be dark brown, with grizzled streaks about the temples; in less than a month from that day he was as grey as a badger. He was a miner when he was young, and most of these fellows have seen ugly sights now and then, when accidents have happened, but he had never seen what he saw that night—that Thing which is neither alive nor dead, that Thing that will abide neither above ground nor in the grave. Antonio had brought something with him which the priest had not noticed—a sharp stake shaped from a piece of tough old driftwood. He had it with him now, and he had his heavy pick, and he had taken the lantern down into the grave. I don't think any power on earth could make him speak of what happened then, and the old priest was too frightened to look in. He says he heard Antonio breathing like a wild beast, and moving as if he were fighting with something almost as strong as himself; and he heard an evil sound also, with blows, as of something violently driven through flesh and bone; and then, the most awful sound of all—a woman's shriek, the unearthly scream of a woman neither dead nor alive, but buried deep for many days. And he, the poor old priest, could only rock himself as he knelt there in the sand, crying aloud his prayers and exorcisms to drown these dreadful sounds. Then suddenly a small iron-bound chest was thrown up and rolled over against the old man's knee, and in a moment more Antonio was beside him, his face as white as tallow in the flickering light of the lantern, shoveling the sand and pebbles into the grave with furious haste, and looking over the edge till the pit was half full; and the priest said that there was much fresh blood on Antonio's hands and on his clothes.

I had come to the end of my story. Holger finished his wine and leaned back in his chair.

"So Angelo got his own again." he said. "Did he marry the prim and plump young person to whom he had been betrothed?"

"No; he had been badly frightened. He went to South America, and has not been heard of since."

"And that poor thing's body is there still, I suppose," said Holger. "Is it quite dead yet, I wonder?"

I wonder, too. But whether it be dead or alive, I should hardly care to see it, even in broad daylight. Antonio is as grey as a badger, and he has never been quite the same man since that night.

The Mortal Immortal

by Mary Shelley

July 16, 1833. —This is a memorable anniversary for me; on it I complete my three hundred and twenty-third year!

The Wandering Jew?—certainly not. More than eighteen centuries have passed over his head. In comparison with him, I am a very young Immortal.

Am I, then, immortal? This is a question which I have asked myself, by day and night, for now three hundred and three years, and yet cannot answer it. I detected a grey hair amidst my brown locks this very day— that surely signifies decay. Yet it may have remained concealed there for three hundred years—for some persons have become entirely white headed before twenty years of age.

I will tell my story, and my reader shall judge for me. I will tell my story, and so contrive to pass some few hours of a long eternity, become so wearisome to me. For ever! Can it be? to live for ever! I have heard of enchantments, in which the victims were plunged into a deep sleep, to wake, after a hundred years, as fresh as ever: I have heard of the Seven Sleepers—thus to be immortal would not be so burthensome: but, oh! the weight of never-ending time—the tedious passage of the still-succeeding hours! How happy was the fabled Nourjahad!—But to my task.

All the world has heard of Cornelius Agrippa. His memory is as immortal as his arts have made me. All the world has also heard of his scholar, who, unawares, raised the foul fiend during his master's absence, and was destroyed by him. The report, true or false, of this accident, was attended with many inconveniences to the renowned philosopher. All his scholars at once deserted him—his servants disappeared. He had no one near him to put coals on his ever-burning fires while he slept, or to attend to the changeful colours of his medicines while he studied. Experiment after experiment failed, because one pair of hands was insufficient to complete them: the dark spirits laughed at him for not being able to retain a single mortal in his service.

I was then very young—very poor—and very much in love. I had been for about a year the pupil of Cornelius, though I was absent when this accident took place. On my return, my friends implored me not to return to the alchymist's abode. I trembled as I listened to the dire tale they told; I required no second warning; and when Cornelius came and offered me a purse of gold if I would remain under his roof, I felt as if Satan himself tempted me. My teeth chattered—my hair stood on end:—I ran off as fast as my trembling knees would permit.

My failing steps were directed whither for two years they had every evening been attracted,—a gently bubbling spring of pure living waters, beside which lingered a dark-haired girl, whose beaming eyes were fixed on the path I was accustomed each night to tread. I cannot remember the hour when I did not love Bertha; we had been neighbours and playmates from infancy—her parents, like mine, were of humble life, yet respectable—our attachment had been a source of pleasure to them. In an evil hour, a malignant fever carried off both her father and mother, and Bertha became an orphan. She would have found a home beneath my paternal roof, but, unfortunately, the old lady of the near castle, rich, childless, and solitary, declared her intention to adopt her. Henceforth Bertha was clad in silk—inhabited a marble palace—and was looked on as being highly favoured by fortune. But in her new situation among her new associates, Bertha remained true to the friend of her humbler days; she often visited the cottage of my father, and when forbidden to go thither, she would stray towards the neighbouring wood, and meet me beside its shady fountain.

She often declared that she owed no duty to her new protectress equal in sanctity to that which bound us. Yet still I was too poor to marry, and she grew weary of being tormented on my account. She had a haughty but an impatient spirit, and grew angry at the obstacles that prevented our union. We met now after an absence, and she had been sorely beset while I was away; she complained bitterly, and almost reproached me for being poor. I replied hastily,—

"I am honest, if I am poor!—were I not, I might soon become rich!"

This exclamation produced a thousand questions. I feared to shock her by owning the truth, but she drew it from me; and then, casting a look of disdain on me, she said—

"You pretend to love, and you fear to face the Devil for my sake!"

I protested that I had only dreaded to offend her;—while she dwelt on the magnitude of the reward that I should receive. Thus encouraged— shamed by her—led on by love and hope, laughing at my late fears, with quick steps and a light heart, I returned to accept the offers of the alchymist, and was instantly installed in my office.

A year passed away. I became possessed of no insignificant sum of money. Custom had banished my fears. In spite of the most painful vigilance, I had never detected the trace of a cloven foot; nor was the studious silence of our abode ever disturbed by demoniac howls. I still continued my stolen interviews with Bertha, and Hope dawned on me—Hope—but not perfect joy; for Bertha fancied that love and security were enemies, and her pleasure was to divide them in my bosom. Though true of heart, she was somewhat of a coquette in manner; and I was jealous as a Turk. She slighted me in a thousand ways, yet would never acknowledge herself to be in the wrong. She would drive me mad with anger, and then force me to beg her pardon. Sometimes she fancied that I was not sufficiently submissive, and then she had some story of a rival, favoured by her protectress. She was surrounded by silk-clad youths—the rich and gay—What chance had the sad-robed scholar of Cornelius compared with these?

On one occasion, the philosopher made such large demands upon my time, that I was unable to meet her as I was wont. He was engaged in some mighty work, and I was forced to remain, day and night, feeding his furnaces and watching his chemical preparations. Bertha waited for me in vain at the fountain. Her haughty spirit fired at this neglect; and when at last I stole out during the few short minutes allotted to me for slumber, and hoped to be consoled by her, she received me with disdain, dismissed me in scorn, and vowed that any man should possess her hand rather than he who could not be in two places at once for her sake. She would be revenged!—And truly she was. In my dingy retreat I heard that she had been hunting, attended by Albert Hoffer. Albert Hoffer was favoured by her protectress, and the three passed in cavalcade before my smoky window. Methought that they mentioned my name—it was followed by a laugh of derision, as her dark eyes glanced contemptuously towards my abode.

Jealousy, with all its venom, and all its misery, entered my breast. Now I shed a torrent of tears, to think that I should never call her mine; and, anon, I imprecated a thousand curses on her inconstancy. Yet, still I must stir the fires of the alchymist, still attend on the changes of his unintelligible medicines.

Cornelius had watched for three days and nights, nor closed his eyes. The progress of his alembics was slower than he expected: in spite of his anxiety, sleep weighed upon his eyelids. Again and again he threw off drowsiness with more than human energy; again and again it stole away his senses. He eyed his crucibles wistfully. "Not ready yet," he murmured; "will another night pass before the work is accomplished? Winzy, you are vigilant—you are faithful—you have slept, my boy—you slept last night. Look at that glass vessel. The liquid it contains is of a soft rose-colour: the moment it begins to change its hue, awaken me—till then I may close my eyes. First, it will turn white, and then emit golden flashes; but wait not till then; when the rose-colour fades, rouse me." I scarcely heard the last words, muttered, as they were, in sleep. Even then he did not quite yield to nature. "Winzy, my boy," he again said, "do not touch the vessel—do not put it to your lips; it is a philter—a philter to cure love; you would not cease to love your Bertha—beware to drink!"

And he slept. His venerable head sunk on his breast, and I scarce heard his regular breathing. For a few minutes I watched the vessel—the rosy hue of the liquid remained unchanged. Then my thoughts wandered—they visited the fountain, and dwelt on a thousand charming scenes never to be renewed—never! Serpents and adders were in my heart as the word "Never!" half formed itself on my lips. False girl!—false and cruel! Never more would she smile on me as that evening she smiled on Albert. Worthless, detested woman! I would not remain unrevenged—she should see Albert expire at her feet—she should die beneath my vengeance. She had smiled in disdain and triumph—she knew my wretchedness and her power. Yet what power had she?—the power of exciting my hate—my utter scorn—my—oh, all but indifference! Could I attain that—could I regard her with careless eyes, transferring my rejected love to one fairer and more true, that were indeed a victory!

A bright flash darted before my eyes. I had forgotten the medicine of the adept; I gazed on it with wonder: flashes of admirable beauty, more bright than those which the diamond emits when the sun's rays are on it, glanced from the surface of the liquid; an odour the most fragrant and grateful stole over my sense; the vessel seemed one globe of living radiance, lovely to the eye, and most inviting to the taste. The first thought, instinctively inspired by the grosser sense, was, I will—I must drink. I raised the vessel to my lips. "It will cure me of love—of torture!" Already I had quaffed half of the most delicious liquor ever tasted by the palate of man, when the philosopher stirred. I started—I dropped the glass—the fluid flamed and glanced along the floor, while I felt Cornelius's gripe at my throat, as he shrieked aloud, "Wretch! you have destroyed the labour of my life!"

The philosopher was totally unaware that I had drunk any portion of his drug. His idea was, and I gave a tacit assent to it, that I had raised the vessel from curiosity, and that, frighted at its brightness, and the flashes of intense light it gave forth, I had let it fall. I never undeceived him. The fire of the medicine was quenched—the fragrance died away—he grew calm, as a philosopher should under the heaviest trials, and dismissed me to rest.

I will not attempt to describe the sleep of glory and bliss which bathed my soul in paradise during the remaining hours of that memorable night. Words would be faint and shallow types of my enjoyment, or of the gladness that possessed my bosom when I woke. I trod air—my thoughts were in heaven. Earth appeared heaven, and my inheritance upon it was to be one trance of delight. "This it is to be cured of love," I thought; "I will see Bertha this day, and she will find her lover cold and regardless: too happy to be disdainful, yet how utterly indifferent to her!"

The hours danced away. The philosopher, secure that he had once succeeded, and believing that he might again, began to concoct the same medicine once more. He was shut up with his books and drugs, and I had a holiday. I dressed myself with care; I looked in an old but polished shield, which served me for a mirror; methought my good looks had wonderfully improved. I hurried beyond the precincts of the town, joy in my soul, the beauty of heaven and earth around me. I turned my steps towards the castle—I could look on its lofty turrets with lightness of heart, for I was cured of love. My Bertha saw me afar off, as I came up the avenue. I know not what sudden impulse animated her bosom, but at the sight, she sprung with a light fawn-like bound down the marble steps, and was hastening towards me. But I had been perceived by another person. The old high-born hag, who called herself her protectress, and was her tyrant, had seen me, also; she hobbled, panting, up the terrace; a page, as ugly as herself, held up her train, and fanned her as she hurried along, and stopped my fair girl with a "How, now, my bold mistress? whither so fast? Back to your cage—hawks are abroad!"

Bertha clasped her hands—her eyes were still bent on my approaching figure. I saw the contest. How I abhorred the old crone who checked the kind impulses of my Bertha's softening heart. Hitherto, respect for her rank had caused me to avoid the lady of the castle; now I disdained such trivial considerations. I was cured of love, and lifted above all human fears; I hastened forwards, and soon reached the terrace. How lovely Bertha looked! her eyes flashing fire, her cheeks glowing with impatience and anger, she was a thousand times more graceful and charming than ever—I no longer loved—Oh! no, I adored—worshipped—idolized her!

She had that morning been persecuted, with more than usual vehemence, to consent to an immediate marriage with my rival. She was reproached with the encouragement that she had shown him—she was threatened with being turned out of doors with disgrace and shame. Her proud spirit rose in arms at the threat; but when she remembered the scorn that she had heaped upon me, and how, perhaps, she had thus lost one whom she now regarded as her only friend, she wept with remorse and rage. At that moment I appeared. "O, Winzy!" she exclaimed, "take me to your mother's cot; swiftly let me leave the detested luxuries and wretchedness of this noble dwelling—take me to poverty and happiness."

I clasped her in my arms with transport. The old lady was speechless with fury, and broke forth into invective only when we were far on our road to my natal cottage. My mother received the fair fugitive, escaped from a gilt cage to nature and liberty, with tenderness and joy; my father, who loved her, welcomed her heartily; it was a day of rejoicing, which did not need the addition of the celestial potion of the alchymist to steep me in delight.

Soon after this eventful day, I became the husband of Bertha. I ceased to be the scholar of Cornelius, but I continued his friend. I always felt grateful to him for having, unawares, procured me that delicious draught of a divine elixir, which, instead of curing me of love (sad cure! solitary and joyless remedy for evils which seem blessings to the memory), had inspired me with courage and resolution, thus winning for me an inestimable treasure in my Bertha.

I often called to mind that period of trance-like inebriation with wonder. The drink of Cornelius had not fulfilled the task for which he affirmed that it had been prepared, but its effects were more potent and blissful than words can express.

They had faded by degrees, yet they lingered long—and painted life in hues of splendour. Bertha often wondered at my lightness of heart and unaccustomed gaiety; for, before, I had been rather serious, or even sad, in my disposition. She loved me the better for my cheerful temper, and our days were winged by joy.

Five years afterwards I was suddenly summoned to the bedside of the dying Cornelius. He had sent for me in haste, conjuring my instant presence. I found him stretched on his pallet, enfeebled even to death; all of life that yet remained animated his piercing eyes, and they were fixed on a glass vessel, full of a roseate liquid.

"Behold," he said, in a broken and inward voice, "the vanity of human wishes! a second time my hopes are about to be crowned, a second time they are destroyed. Look at that liquor—you remember five years ago I had prepared the same, with the same success;—then, as now, my thirsting lips expected to taste the immortal elixir—you dashed it from me! and at present it is too late."

He spoke with difficulty, and fell back on his pillow. I could not help saying,—

"How, revered master, can a cure for love restore you to life?"

A faint smile gleamed across his face as I listened earnestly to his scarcely intelligible answer. "A cure for love and for all things—the Elixir of Immortality. Ah! if now I might drink, I should live for ever!"

As he spoke, a golden flash gleamed from the fluid; a well-remembered fragrance stole over the air; he raised himself, all weak as he was— strength seemed miraculously to re-enter his frame—he stretched forth his hand—a loud explosion startled me—a ray of fire shot up from the elixir, and the glass vessel which contained it was shivered to atoms! I turned my eyes towards the philosopher; he had fallen back—his eyes were glassy—his features rigid—he was dead!

But I lived, and was to live for ever! So said the unfortunate alchymist, and for a few days I believed his words. I remembered the glorious drunkenness that had followed my stolen draught. I reflected on the change I had felt in my frame—in my soul. The bounding elasticity of the one—the buoyant lightness of the other. I surveyed myself in a mirror, and could perceive no change in my features during the space of the five years which had elapsed. I remembered the radiant hues and grateful scent of that delicious beverage—worthy the gift it was capable of bestowing—I was, then, IMMORTAL!

A few days after I laughed at my credulity. The old proverb, that "a prophet is least regarded in his own country," was true with respect to me and my defunct master. I loved him as a man—I respected him as a sage—but I derided the notion that he could command the powers of darkness, and laughed at the superstitious fears with which he was regarded by the vulgar. He was a wise philosopher, but had no acquaintance with any spirits but those clad in flesh and blood. His science was simply human; and human science, I soon persuaded myself, could never conquer nature's laws so far as to imprison the soul for ever within its carnal habitation. Cornelius had brewed a soul-refreshing drink—more inebriating than wine—sweeter and more fragrant than any fruit: it possessed probably strong medicinal powers, imparting gladness to the heart and vigor to the limbs; but its effects would wear out; already were they diminished in my frame. I was a lucky fellow to have quaffed health and joyous spirits, and perhaps long life, at my master's hands; but my good fortune ended there: longevity was far different from immortality.

I continued to entertain this belief for many years. Sometimes a thought stole across me—Was the alchymist indeed deceived? But my habitual credence was, that I should meet the fate of all the children of Adam at my appointed time—a little late, but still at a natural age. Yet it was certain that I retained a wonderfully youthful look. I was laughed at for my vanity in consulting the mirror so often, but I consulted it in vain—my brow was untrenched—my cheeks—my eyes—my whole person continued as untarnished as in my twentieth year.

I was troubled. I looked at the faded beauty of Bertha—I seemed more like her son. By degrees our neighbours began to make similar observations, and I found at last that I went by the name of the Scholar bewitched. Bertha herself grew uneasy. She became jealous and peevish, and at length she began to question me. We had no children; we were all in all to each other; and though, as she grew older, her vivacious spirit became a little allied to ill-temper, and her beauty sadly diminished, I cherished her in my heart as the mistress I had idolized, the wife I had sought and won with such perfect love.

At last our situation became intolerable: Bertha was fifty—I twenty years of age. I had, in very shame, in some measure adopted the habits of a more advanced age; I no longer mingled in the dance among the young and gay, but my heart bounded along with them while I restrained my feet; and a sorry figure I cut among the Nestors of our village. But before the time I mention, things were altered—we were universally shunned; we were—at least, I was—reported to have kept up an iniquitous acquaintance with some of my former master's supposed friends. Poor Bertha was pitied, but deserted. I was regarded with horror and detestation.

What was to be done? we sat by our winter fire—poverty had made itself felt, for none would buy the produce of my farm; and often I had been forced to journey twenty miles, to some place where I was not known, to dispose of our property. It is true we had saved something for an evil day—that day was come.

We sat by our lone fireside—the old-hearted youth and his antiquated wife. Again Bertha insisted on knowing the truth; she recapitulated all she had ever heard said about me, and added her own observations. She conjured me to cast off the spell; she described how much more comely grey hairs were than my chestnut locks; she descanted on the reverence and respect due to age—how preferable to the slight regard paid to mere children: could I imagine that the despicable gifts of youth and good looks outweighed disgrace, hatred, and scorn? Nay, in the end I should be burnt as a dealer in the black art, while she, to whom I had not deigned to communicate any portion of my good fortune, might be stoned as my accomplice. At length she insinuated that I must share my secret with her, and bestow on her like benefits to those I myself enjoyed, or she would denounce me—and then she burst into tears.

Thus beset, methought it was the best way to tell the truth. I revealed it as tenderly as I could, and spoke only of a very long life, not of immortality—which representation, indeed, coincided best with my own ideas. When I ended, I rose and said,

"And now, my Bertha, will you denounce the lover of your youth? —You will not, I know. But it is too hard, my poor wife, that you should suffer from my ill-luck and the accursed arts of Cornelius. I will leave you—you have wealth enough, and friends will return in my absence. I will go; young as I seem, and strong as I am, I can work and gain my bread among strangers, unsuspected and unknown. I loved you in youth; God is my witness that I would not desert you in age, but that your safety and happiness require it."

I took my cap and moved towards the door; in a moment Bertha's arms were round my neck, and her lips were pressed to mine. "No, my husband, my Winzy," she said, "you shall not go alone—take me with you; we will remove from this place, and, as you say, among strangers we shall be unsuspected and safe. I am not so very old as quite to shame you, my Winzy; and I dare say the charm will soon wear off, and, with the blessing of God, you will become more elderly-looking, as is fitting; you shall not leave me."

I returned the good soul's embrace heartily. "I will not, my Bertha; but for your sake I had not thought of such a thing. I will be your true, faithful husband while you are spared to me, and do my duty by you to the last."

The next day we prepared secretly for our emigration. We were obliged to make great pecuniary sacrifices—it could not be helped. We realised a sum sufficient, at least, to maintain us while Bertha lived; and, without saying adieu to any one, quitted our native country to take refuge in a remote part of western France.

It was a cruel thing to transport poor Bertha from her native village, and the friends of her youth, to a new country, new language, new customs. The strange secret of my destiny rendered this removal immaterial to me; but I compassionated her deeply, and was glad to perceive that she found compensation for her misfortunes in a variety of little ridiculous circumstances. Away from all tell-tale chroniclers, she sought to decrease the apparent disparity of our ages by a thousand feminine arts—rouge, youthful dress, and assumed juvenility of manner. I could not be angry— Did not I myself wear a mask? Why quarrel with hers, because it was less successful? I grieved deeply when I remembered that this was my Bertha, whom I had loved so fondly, and won with such transport—the dark eyed, dark-haired girl, with smiles of enchanting archness and a step like a fawn—this mincing, simpering, jealous old woman. I should have revered her grey locks and withered cheeks; but thus!—It was my, work, I knew; but I did not the less deplore this type of human weakness.

Her jealousy never slept. Her chief occupation was to discover that, in spite of outward appearances, I was myself growing old. I verily believe that the poor soul loved me truly in her heart, but never had woman so tormenting a mode of displaying fondness. She would discern wrinkles in my face and decrepitude in my walk, while I bounded along in youthful vigour, the youngest looking of twenty youths. I never dared address another woman: on one occasion, fancying that the belle of the village regarded me with favouring eyes, she bought me a grey wig. Her constant discourse among her acquaintances was, that though I looked so young, there was ruin at work within my frame; and she affirmed that the worst symptom about me was my apparent health. My youth was a disease, she said, and I ought at all times to prepare, if not for a sudden and awful death, at least to awake some morning white-headed, and bowed down with all the marks of advanced years. I let her talk—I often joined in her conjectures. Her warnings chimed in with my never-ceasing speculations concerning my state, and I took an earnest, though painful, interest in listening to all that her quick wit and excited imagination could say on the subject.

Why dwell on these minute circumstances? We lived on for many long years. Bertha became bed-rid and paralytic: I nursed her as mother might a child. She grew peevish, and still harped upon one string—of how long I should survive her. It has ever been a source of consolation to me, that I performed my duty scrupulously towards her. She had been mine in youth, she was mine in age, and at last, when I heaped the sod over her corpse, I wept to feel that I had lost all that really bound me to humanity.

Since then how many have been my cares and woes, how few and empty my enjoyments! I pause here in my history—I will pursue it no further. A sailor without rudder or compass, tossed on a stormy sea—a traveller lost on a wide-spread heath, without landmark or star to him—such have I been: more lost, more hopeless than either. A nearing ship, a gleam from some far cot, may save them; but I have no beacon except the hope of death.

Death! mysterious, ill-visaged friend of weak humanity! Why alone of all mortals have you cast me from your sheltering fold? O, for the peace of the grave! the deep silence of the iron-bound tomb! that thought would cease to work in my brain, and my heart beat no more with emotions varied only by new forms of sadness!

Am I immortal? I return to my first question. In the first place, is it not more probable that the beverage of the alchymist was fraught rather with longevity than eternal life? Such is my hope. And then be it remembered that I only drank half of the potion prepared by him. Was not the whole necessary to complete the charm? To have drained half the Elixir of Immortality is but to be half immortal—my For-ever is thus truncated and null.

But again, who shall number the years of the half of eternity? I often try to imagine by what rule the infinite may be divided. Sometimes I fancy age advancing upon me. One grey hair I have found. Fool! Do I lament? Yes, the fear of age and death often creeps coldly into my heart; and the more I live, the more I dread death, even while I abhor life. Such an enigma is man—born to perish—when he wars, as I do, against the established laws of his nature.

But for this anomaly of feeling surely I might die: the medicine of the alchymist would not be proof against fire—sword—and the strangling waters. I have gazed upon the blue depths of many a placid lake, and the tumultuous rushing of many a mighty river, and have said, peace inhabits those waters; yet I have turned my steps away, to live yet another day. I have asked myself, whether suicide would be a crime in one to whom thus only the portals of the other world could be opened. I have done all, except presenting myself as a soldier or duellist, an object of destruction to my—no, not my fellow-mortals, and therefore I have shrunk away. They are not my fellows. The inextinguishable power of life in my frame, and their ephemeral existence, place us wide as the poles asunder. I could not raise a hand against the meanest or the most powerful among them.

Thus I have lived on for many a year—alone, and weary of myself— desirous of death, yet never dying—a mortal immortal. Neither ambition nor avarice can enter my mind, and the ardent love that gnaws at my heart, never to be returned—never to find an equal on which to expend itself—lives there only to torment me.

This very day I conceived a design by which I may end all—without self-slaughter, without making another man a Cain—an expedition, which mortal frame can never survive, even endued with the youth and strength that inhabits mine. Thus I shall put my immortality to the test, and rest for ever—or return, the wonder and benefactor of the human species.

Before I go, a miserable vanity has caused me to pen these pages. I would not die, and leave no name behind. Three centuries have passed since I quaffed the fatal beverage: another year shall not elapse before, encountering gigantic dangers—warring with the powers of frost in their home—beset by famine, toil, and tempest—I yield this body, too tenacious a cage for a soul which thirsts for freedom, to the destructive elements of air and water—or, if I survive, my name shall be recorded as one of the most famous among the sons of men; and, my task achieved, I shall adopt more resolute means, and, by scattering and annihilating the atoms that compose my frame, set at liberty the life imprisoned within, and so cruelly prevented from soaring from this dim earth to a sphere more congenial to its immortal essence.

The Monkey's Paw

by W. W. Jacobs

I.

Without, the night was cold and wet, but in the small parlour of Laburnam Villa the blinds were drawn and the fire burned brightly. Father and son were at chess, the former, who possessed ideas about the game involving radical changes, putting his king into such sharp and unnecessary perils that it even provoked comment from the white-haired old lady knitting placidly by the fire.

"Hark at the wind," said Mr White, who, having seen a fatal mistake after it was too late, was amiably desirous of preventing his son from seeing it.

"I'm listening," said the latter, grimly surveying the board as he stretched out his hand. "Check."

"I should hardly think that he'd come tonight," said his father, with his hand poised over the board.

"Mate," replied the son.

"That's the worst of living so far out," bawled Mr White, with sudden and unlooked-for violence; "of all the beastly, slushy, out-of-the-way places to live in, this is the worst. Pathway's a bog, and the road's a torrent. I don't know what people are thinking about. I suppose because only two houses on the road are let, they think it doesn't matter."

"Never mind, dear," said his wife soothingly; "perhaps you'll win the next one."

Mr White looked up sharply, just in time to intercept a knowing glance between mother and son. The words died away on his lips, and he hid a guilty grin in his thin grey beard.

"There he is," said Herbert White, as the gate banged to loudly and heavy footsteps came toward the door.

The old man rose with hospitable haste, and opening the door, was heard condoling with the new arrival. The new arrival also condoled with himself, so that Mrs. White said, "Tut, tut!" and coughed gently as her husband entered the room, followed by a tall burly man, beady of eye and rubicund of visage.

"Sergeant-Major Morris," he said, introducing him.

The sergeant-major shook hands, and taking the proffered seat by the fire, watched contentedly while his host got out whisky and tumblers and stood a small copper kettle on the fire.

At the third glass his eyes got brighter, and he began to talk, the little family circle regarding with eager interest this visitor from distant parts, as he squared his broad shoulders in the chair and spoke of strange scenes and doughty deeds; of wars and plagues and strange peoples.

"Twenty-one years of it," said Mr White, nodding at his wife and son. "When he went away he was a slip of a youth in the warehouse. Now look at him."

"He don't look to have taken much harm," said Mrs. White, politely.

"I'd like to go to India myself," said the old man, "just to look round a bit, you know."

"Better where you are," said the sergeant-major, shaking his head. He put down the empty glass, and sighing softly, shook it again.

"I should like to see those old temples and fakirs and jugglers," said the old man. "What was that you started telling me the other day about a monkey's paw or something, Morris?"

"Nothing," said the soldier hastily. "Leastways, nothing worth hearing."

"Monkey's paw?" said Mrs. White curiously.

"Well, it's just a bit of what you might call magic, perhaps," said the sergeant-major off-handedly.

His three listeners leaned forward eagerly. The visitor absentmindedly put his empty glass to his lips and then set it down again. His host filled it for him.

"To look at," said the sergeant-major, fumbling in his pocket, "it's just an ordinary little paw, dried to a mummy."

He took something out of his pocket and proffered it. Mrs. White drew back with a grimace, but her son, taking it, examined it curiously.

"And what is there special about it?" inquired Mr White, as he took it from his son and, having examined it, placed it upon the table.

"It had a spell put on it by an old fakir," said the sergeant-major, "a very holy man. He wanted to show that fate ruled people's lives, and that those who interfered with it did so to their sorrow. He put a spell on it so that three separate men could each have three wishes from it."

His manner was so impressive that his hearers were conscious that their light laughter jarred somewhat.

"Well, why don't you have three, sir?" said Herbert White cleverly.

The soldier regarded him in the way that middle age is wont to regard presumptuous youth. "I have," he said quietly, and his blotchy face whitened.

"And did you really have the three wishes granted?" asked Mrs. White.

"I did," said the sergeant-major, and his glass tapped against his strong teeth.

"And has anybody else wished?" inquired the old lady.

"The first man had his three wishes, yes," was the reply. "I don't know what the first two were, but the third was for death. That's how I got the paw."

His tones were so grave that a hush fell upon the group.

"If you've had your three wishes, it's no good to you now, then, Morris," said the old man at last. "What do you keep it for?"

The soldier shook his head. "Fancy, I suppose," he said slowly.

"If you could have another three wishes," said the old man, eyeing him keenly, "would you have them?"

"I don't know," said the other. "I don't know."

He took the paw, and dangling it between his front finger and thumb, suddenly threw it upon the fire. White, with a slight cry, stooped down and snatched it off.

"Better let it burn," said the soldier solemnly.

"If you don't want it, Morris," said the old man, "give it to me."

"I won't," said his friend doggedly. "I threw it on the fire. If you keep it, don't blame me for what happens. Pitch it on the fire again, like a sensible man."

The other shook his head and examined his new possession closely. "How do you do it?" he inquired.

"Hold it up in your right hand and wish aloud,' said the sergeant-major, "but I warn you of the consequences."

"Sounds like the Arabian Nights," said Mrs White, as she rose and began to set the supper. "Don't you think you might wish for four pairs of hands for me?"

Her husband drew the talisman from his pocket and then all three burst into laughter as the sergeant-major, with a look of alarm on his face, caught him by the arm.

"If you must wish," he said gruffly, "wish for something sensible."

Mr White dropped it back into his pocket, and placing chairs, motioned his friend to the table. In the business of supper the talisman was partly forgotten, and afterward the three sat listening in an enthralled fashion to a second instalment of the soldier's adventures in India.

"If the tale about the monkey paw is not more truthful than those he has been telling us," said Herbert, as the door closed behind their guest, just in time for him to catch the last train, "we shan't make much out of it."

"Did you give him anything for it, father?" inquired Mrs. White, regarding her husband closely.

"A trifle," said he, colouring slightly. "He didn't want it, but I made him take it. And he pressed me again to throw it away."

"Likely," said Herbert, with pretended horror. "Why, we're going to be rich, and famous, and happy. Wish to be an emperor, father, to begin with; then you can't be henpecked."

He darted round the table, pursued by the maligned Mrs. White armed with an antimacassar.

Mr White took the paw from his pocket and eyed it dubiously. "I don't know what to wish for, and that's a fact," he said slowly. "It seems to me I've got all I want."

"If you only cleared the house, you'd be quite happy, wouldn't you?" said Herbert, with his hand on his shoulder. "Well, wish for two hundred pounds, then; that'll just do it."

His father, smiling shamefacedly at his own credulity, held up the talisman, as his son, with a solemn face somewhat marred by a wink at his mother, sat down at the piano and struck a few impressive chords.

"I wish for two hundred pounds," said the old man distinctly.

A fine crash from the piano greeted the words, interrupted by a shuddering cry from the old man. His wife and son ran toward him.

"It moved, he cried, with a glance of disgust at the object as it lay on the floor. "As I wished it twisted in my hands like a snake."

"Well, I don't see the money," said his son, as he picked it up and placed it on the table, "and I bet I never shall."

"It must have been your fancy, father," said his wife, regarding him anxiously.

He shook his head. "Never mind, though; there's no harm done, but it gave me a shock all the same."

They sat down by the fire again while the two men finished their pipes. Outside, the wind was higher than ever, and the old man started nervously at the sound of a door banging upstairs. A silence unusual and depressing settled upon all three, which lasted until the old couple rose to retire for the night.

"I expect you'll find the cash tied up in a big bag in the middle of your bed," said Herbert, as he bade them good-night, "and something horrible squatting up on top of the wardrobe watching you as you pocket your ill-gotten gains."

He sat alone in the darkness, gazing at the dying fire, and seeing faces in it. The last face was so horrible and so simian that he gazed at it in amazement. It got so vivid that, with a little uneasy laugh, he felt on the table for a glass containing a little water to throw over it. His hand grasped the monkey's paw, and with a little shiver he wiped his hand on his coat and went up to bed.

II.

In the brightness of the wintry sun next morning as it streamed over the breakfast table Herbert laughed at his fears. There was an air of prosaic wholesomeness about the room which it had lacked on the previous night, and the dirty, shrivelled little paw was pitched on the sideboard with a carelessness which betokened no great belief in its virtues.

"I suppose all old soldiers are the same," said Mrs White. "The idea of our listening to such nonsense! How could wishes be granted in these days? And if they could, how could two hundred pounds hurt you, father?"

"Might drop on his head from the sky," said the frivolous Herbert.

"Morris said the things happened so naturally," said his father, "that you might if you so wished attribute it to coincidence."

"Well, don't break into the money before I come back," said Herbert, as he rose from the table. "I'm afraid it'll turn you into a mean, avaricious man, and we shall have to disown you."

His mother laughed, and following him to the door, watched him down the road, and returning to the breakfast table, was very happy at the expense of her husband's credulity. All of which did not prevent her from scurrying to the door at the postman's knock, nor prevent her from referring somewhat shortly to retired sergeant-majors of bibulous habits when she found that the post brought a tailor's bill.

"Herbert will have some more of his funny remarks, I expect, when he comes home," she said, as they sat at dinner.

"I dare say," said Mr White, pouring himself out some beer; "but for all that, the thing moved in my hand; that I'll swear to."

"You thought it did," said the old lady soothingly.

"I say it did," replied the other. "There was no thought about it; I had just—What's the matter?"

His wife made no reply. She was watching the mysterious movements of a man outside, who, peering in an undecided fashion at the house, appeared to be trying to make up his mind to enter. In mental connection with the two hundred pounds, she noticed that the stranger was well dressed and wore a silk hat of glossy newness. Three times he paused at the gate, and then walked on again. The fourth time he stood with his hand upon it, and then with sudden resolution flung it open and walked up the path. Mrs. White at the same moment placed her hands behind her, and hurriedly unfastening the strings of her apron, put that useful article of apparel beneath the cushion of her chair.

She brought the stranger, who seemed ill at ease, into the room. He gazed at her furtively, and listened in a preoccupied fashion as the old lady apologized for the appearance of the room, and her husband's coat, a garment which he usually reserved for the garden. She then waited as patiently as her sex would permit, for him to broach his business, but he was at first strangely silent.

"I—was asked to call," he said at last, and stooped and picked a piece of cotton from his trousers. "I come from Maw and Meggins."

The old lady started. "Is anything the matter?" she asked breathlessly. "Has anything happened to Herbert? What is it? What is it?"

Her husband interposed. "There, there, mother," he said hastily. "Sit down, and don't jump to conclusions. You've not brought bad news, I'm sure, sir" and he eyed the other wistfully.

"I'm sorry—" began the visitor.

"Is he hurt?" demanded the mother.

The visitor bowed in assent. "Badly hurt," he said quietly, "but he is not in any pain."

"Oh, thank God!" said the old woman, clasping her hands. "Thank God for that! Thank—"

She broke off suddenly as the sinister meaning of the assurance dawned upon her and she saw the awful confirmation of her fears in the other's averted face. She caught her breath, and turning to her slower-witted husband, laid her trembling old hand upon his. There was a long silence.

"He was caught in the machinery," said the visitor at length, in a low voice.

"Caught in the machinery," repeated Mr White, in a dazed fashion, "yes."

He sat staring blankly out at the window, and taking his wife's hand between his own, pressed it as he had been wont to do in their old courting days nearly forty years before.

"He was the only one left to us," he said, turning gently to the visitor. "It is hard."

The other coughed, and rising, walked slowly to the window. "The firm wished me to convey their sincere sympathy with you in your great loss," he said, without looking round. "I beg that you will understand I am only their servant and merely obeying orders."

There was no reply; the old woman's face was white, her eyes staring, and her breath inaudible; on the husband's face was a look such as his friend the sergeant might have carried into his first action.

"I was to say that Maw and Meggins disclaim all responsibility," continued the other. "They admit no liability at all, but in consideration of your son's services they wish to present you with a certain sum as compensation."

Mr White dropped his wife's hand, and rising to his feet, gazed with a look of horror at his visitor. His dry lips shaped the words, "How much?"

"Two hundred pounds," was the answer.

Unconscious of his wife's shriek, the old man smiled faintly, put out his hands like a sightless man, and dropped, a senseless heap, to the floor.

III.

In the huge new cemetery, some two miles distant, the old people buried their dead, and came back to a house steeped in shadow and silence. It was all over so quickly that at first they could hardly realize it, and remained in a state of expectation as though of something else to happen—something else which was to lighten this load, too heavy for old hearts to bear.

But the days passed, and expectation gave place to resignation—the hopeless resignation of the old, sometimes miscalled, apathy. Sometimes they hardly exchanged a word, for now they had nothing to talk about, and their days were long to weariness.

It was about a week after that that the old man, waking suddenly in the night, stretched out his hand and found himself alone. The room was in darkness, and the sound of subdued weeping came from the window. He raised himself in bed and listened.

"Come back," he said tenderly. "You will be cold."

"It is colder for my son," said the old woman, and wept afresh.

The sound of her sobs died away on his ears. The bed was warm, and his eyes heavy with sleep. He dozed fitfully, and then slept until a sudden wild cry from his wife awoke him with a start.

"The paw!" she cried wildly. "The monkey's paw!"

He started up in alarm. "Where? Where is it? What's the matter?"

She came stumbling across the room toward him. "I want it," she said quietly. "You've not destroyed it?"

"It's in the parlour, on the bracket," he replied, marvelling. "Why?"

She cried and laughed together, and bending over, kissed his cheek.

"I only just thought of it," she said hysterically. "Why didn't I think of it before? Why didn't you think of it?"

"Think of what?" he questioned.

"The other two wishes," she replied rapidly. "We've only had one."

"Was not that enough?" he demanded fiercely.

"No," she cried, triumphantly; "we'll have one more. Go down and get it quickly, and wish our boy alive again."

The man sat up in bed and flung the bedclothes from his quaking limbs. "Good God, you are mad!" he cried aghast.

"Get it," she panted; "get it quickly, and wish— Oh, my boy, my boy!"

Her husband struck a match and lit the candle. "Get back to bed," he said, unsteadily. "You don't know what you are saying."

"We had the first wish granted," said the old woman, feverishly; "why not the second."

"A coincidence," stammered the old man.

"Go and get it and wish," cried the old woman, quivering with excitement.

The old man turned and regarded her, and his voice shook. "He has been dead ten days, and besides he—I would not tell you else, but—I could only recognize him by his clothing. If he was too terrible for you to see then, how now?"

"Bring him back," cried the old woman, and dragged him toward the door. "Do you think I fear the child I have nursed?"

He went down in the darkness, and felt his way to the parlour, and then to the mantelpiece. The talisman was in its place, and a horrible fear that the unspoken wish might bring his mutilated son before him ere he could escape from the room seized upon him, and he caught his breath as he found that he had lost the direction of the door. His brow cold with sweat, he felt his way round the table, and groped along the wall until he found himself in the small passage with the unwholesome thing in his hand.

Even his wife's face seemed changed as he entered the room. It was white and expectant, and to his fears seemed to have an unnatural look upon it. He was afraid of her.

"Wish!" she cried, in a strong voice.

"It is foolish and wicked," he faltered.

"Wish!" repeated his wife.

He raised his hand. "I wish my son alive again."

The talisman fell to the floor, and he regarded it fearfully. Then he sank trembling into a chair as the old woman, with burning eyes, walked to the window and raised the blind.

He sat until he was chilled with the cold, glancing occasionally at the figure of the old woman peering through the window. The candle end, which had burnt below the rim of the china candlestick, was throwing pulsating shadows on the ceiling and walls, until, with a flicker larger than the rest, it expired. The old man, with an unspeakable sense of relief at the failure of the talisman, crept back to his bed, and a minute or two afterward the old woman came silently and apathetically beside him.

Neither spoke, but both lay silently listening to the ticking of the clock. A stair creaked, and a squeaky mouse scurried noisily through the wall. The darkness was oppressive, and after lying for some time screwing up his courage, the husband took the box of matches, and striking one, went downstairs for a candle.

At the foot of the stairs the match went out, and he paused to strike another, and at the same moment a knock, so quiet and stealthy as to be scarcely audible, sounded on the front door.

The matches fell from his hand. He stood motionless, his breath suspended until the knock was repeated. Then he turned and fled swiftly back to his room, and closed the door behind him. A third knock sounded through the house.

"What's that?" cried the old woman, starting up.

"A rat," said the old man, in shaking tones—"a rat. It passed me on the stairs."

His wife sat up in bed listening. A loud knock resounded through the house.

"It's Herbert!" she screamed. "It's Herbert!"

She ran to the door, but her husband was before her, and catching her by the arm, held her tightly.

"What are you going to do?" he whispered hoarsely.

"It's my boy; it's Herbert!" she cried, struggling mechanically. "I forgot it was two miles away. What are you holding me for? Let go. I must open the door."

"For God's sake, don't let it in," cried the old man trembling.

"You're afraid of your own son," she cried, struggling. "Let me go. I'm coming, Herbert; I'm coming."

There was another knock, and another. The old woman with a sudden wrench broke free and ran from the room. Her husband followed to the landing, and called after her appealingly as she hurried downstairs. He heard the chain rattle back and the bottom bolt drawn slowly and stiffly from the socket. Then the old woman's voice, strained and panting.

"The bolt," she cried loudly. "Come down. I can't reach it."

But her husband was on his hands and knees groping wildly on the floor in search of the paw. If he could only find it before the thing outside got in. A perfect fusillade of knocks reverberated through the house, and he heard the scraping of a chair as his wife put it down in the passage against the door. He heard the creaking of the bolt as it came slowly back, and at the same moment he found the monkey's paw, and frantically breathed his third and last wish.

The knocking ceased suddenly, although the echoes of it were still in the house. He heard the chair drawn back and the door opened. A cold wind rushed up the staircase, and a long loud wail of disappointment and misery from his wife gave him courage to run down to her side, and then to the gate beyond. The street lamp flickering opposite shone on a quiet and deserted road.

The Diary of a Madman

by Guy de Maupassant

He was dead—the head of a high tribunal, the upright magistrate whose irreproachable life was a proverb in all the courts of France. Advocates, young counsellors, judges had greeted him at sight of his large, thin, pale face lighted up by two sparkling deep-set eyes, bowing low in token of respect.

He had passed his life in pursuing crime and in protecting the weak. Swindlers and murderers had no more redoubtable enemy, for he seemed to read the most secret thoughts of their minds.

He was dead, now, at the age of eighty-two, honoured by the homage and followed by the regrets of a whole people. Soldiers in red trousers had escorted him to the tomb and men in white cravats had spoken words and shed tears that seemed to be sincere beside his grave.

But here is the strange paper found by the dismayed notary in the desk where he had kept the records of great criminals! It was entitled: WHY?

20th June, 1851. I have just left court. I have condemned Blondel to death! Now, why did this man kill his five children? Frequently one meets with people to whom the destruction of life is a pleasure. Yes, yes, it should be a pleasure, the greatest of all, perhaps, for is not killing the next thing to creating? To make and to destroy! These two words contain the history of the universe, all the history of worlds, all that is, all! Why is it not intoxicating to kill?

25th June. To think that a being is there who lives, who walks, who runs. A being? What is a being? That animated thing, that bears in it the principle of motion and a will ruling that motion. It is attached to nothing, this thing. Its feet do not belong to the ground. It is a grain of life that moves on the earth, and this grain of life, coming I know not whence, one can destroy at one's will. Then nothing—nothing more. It perishes, it is finished.

26th June. Why then is it a crime to kill? Yes, why? On the contrary, it is the law of nature. The mission of every being is to kill; he kills to live, and he kills to kill. The beast kills without ceasing, all day, every instant of his existence. Man kills without ceasing, to nourish himself; but since he needs, besides, to kill for pleasure, he has invented hunting! The child kills the insects he finds, the little birds, all the little animals that come in his way. But this does not suffice for the irresistible need to massacre that is in us. It is not enough to kill beasts; we must kill man too. Long ago this need was satisfied by human sacrifices. Now the requirements of social life have made murder a crime. We condemn and punish the assassin! But as we cannot live without yielding to this natural and imperious instinct of death, we relieve ourselves, from time to time, by wars. Then a whole nation slaughters another nation. It is a feast of blood, a feast that maddens armies and that intoxicates civilians, women and children, who read, by lamplight at night, the feverish story of massacre.

One might suppose that those destined to accomplish these butcheries of men would be despised! No, they are loaded with honours. They are clad in gold and in resplendent garments; they wear plumes on their heads and ornaments on their breasts, and they are given crosses, rewards, titles of every kind. They are proud, respected, loved by women, cheered by the crowd, solely because their mission is to shed human blood; They drag through the streets their instruments of death, that the passer-by, clad in black, looks on with envy. For to kill is the great law set by nature in the heart of existence! There is nothing more beautiful and honourable than killing!

30th June. To kill is the law, because nature loves eternal youth. She seems to cry in all her unconscious acts: "Quick! quick! quick!" The more she destroys, the more she renews herself.

2nd July. A human being—what is a human being? Through thought it is a reflection of all that is; through memory and science it is an abridged edition of the universe whose history it represents, a mirror of things and of nations, each human being becomes a microcosm in the macrocosm.

3rd July. It must be a pleasure, unique and full of zest, to kill; to have there before one the living, thinking being; to make therein a little hole, nothing but a little hole, to see that red thing flow which is the blood, which makes life; and to have before one only a heap of limp flesh, cold, inert, void of thought!

5th August. I, who have passed my life in judging, condemning, killing by the spoken word, killing by the guillotine those who had killed by the knife, I, I, if I should do as all the assassins have done whom I have smitten, I—I—who would know it?

10th August. Who would ever know? Who would ever suspect me, me, me, especially if I should choose a being I had no interest in doing away with?

15th August. The temptation has come to me. It pervades my whole being; my hands tremble with the desire to kill.

22nd August. I could resist no longer. I killed a little creature as an experiment, for a beginning. Jean, my servant, had a goldfinch in a cage hung in the office window. I sent him on an errand, and I took the little bird in my hand, in my hand where I felt its heart beat. It was warm. I went up to my room. From time to time I squeezed it tighter; its heart beat faster; this was atrocious and delicious. I was near choking it. But I could not see the blood.

Then I took scissors, short-nail scissors, and I cut its throat with three slits, quite gently. It opened its bill, it struggled to escape me, but I held it, oh! I held it—I could have held a mad dog—and I saw the blood trickle.

And then I did as assassins do—real ones. I washed the scissors, I washed my hands. I sprinkled water and took the body, the corpse, to the garden to hide it. I buried it under a strawberry-plant. It will never be found. Every day I shall eat a strawberry from that plant. How one can enjoy life when one knows how!

My servant cried; he thought his bird flown. How could he suspect me? Ah! ah!

25th August. I must kill a man! I must—

30th August. It is done. But what a little thing! I had gone for a walk in the forest of Vernes. I was thinking of nothing, literally nothing. A child was in the road, a little child eating a slice of bread and butter.

He stops to see me pass and says, "Good-day, Mr President."

And the thought enters my head, "Shall I kill him?"

I answer: "You are alone, my boy?"

"Yes, sir."

"All alone in the wood?"

"Yes, sir."

The wish to kill him intoxicated me like wine. I approached him quite softly, persuaded that he was going to run away. And, suddenly, I seized him by the throat. He looked at me with terror in his eyes—such eyes! He held my wrists in his little hands and his body writhed like a feather over the fire. Then he moved no more. I threw the body in the ditch, and some weeds on top of it. I returned home, and dined well. What a little thing it was! In the evening I was very gay, light, rejuvenated; I passed the evening at the Prefect's. They found me witty. But I have not seen blood! I am tranquil.

31st August. The body has been discovered. They are hunting for the assassin. Ah! ah!

1st September. Two tramps have been arrested. Proofs are lacking.

2nd September. The parents have been to see me. They wept! Ah! ah!

6th October. Nothing has been discovered. Some strolling vagabond must have done the deed. Ah! ah! If I had seen the blood flow, it seems to me I should be tranquil now! The desire to kill is in my blood; it is like the passion of youth at twenty.

20th October. Yet another. I was walking by the river, after breakfast. And I saw, under a willow, a fisherman asleep. It was noon. A spade was standing in a potato-field near by, as if expressly, for me.

I took it. I returned; I raised it like a club, and with one blow of the edge I cleft the fisherman's head. Oh! he bled, this one! Rose-coloured blood. It flowed into the water, quite gently. And I went away with a grave step. If I had been seen! Ah! ah! I should have made an excellent assassin.

25th October. The affair of the fisherman makes a great stir. His nephew, who fished with him, is charged with the murder.

26th October. The examining magistrate affirms that the nephew is guilty. Everybody in town believes it. Ah! ah!

27th October. The nephew makes a very poor witness. He had gone to the village to buy bread and cheese, he declared. He swore that his uncle had been killed in his absence! Who would believe him?

28th October. The nephew has all but confessed, they have badgered him so. Ah! ah! justice!

15th November. There are overwhelming proofs against the nephew, who was his uncle's heir. I shall preside at the sessions.

25th January. To death! to death! to death! I have had him condemned to death! Ah! ah! The advocate-general spoke like an angel! Ah! ah! Yet another! I shall go to see him executed!

10th March. It is done. They guillotined him this morning. He died very well! very well! That gave me pleasure! How fine it is to see a man's head cut off!

Now, I shall wait, I can wait. It would take such a little thing to let myself be caught.

The manuscript contained yet other pages, but without relating any new crime.

Alienist physicians to whom the awful story has been submitted declare that there are in the world many undiscovered madmen as adroit and as much to be feared as this monstrous lunatic.

He?

by Guy de Maupassant

My dear friend, you cannot understand it by any possible means, you say, and I perfectly believe you. You think I am going mad? It may be so, but not for the reasons which you suppose.

Yes, I am going to get married, and I will give you what has led me to take that step.

My ideas and my convictions have not changed at all. I look upon all legalized cohabitation as utterly stupid, for I am certain that nine husbands out of ten are cuckolds; and they get no more than their deserts for having been idiotic enough to fetter their lives, and renounce their freedom in love, the only happy and good thing in the world, and for having clipped the wings of fancy, which continually drives us on towards all women, &c., &c., &c. You know what I mean. More than ever I feel that I am incapable of loving one woman alone, because I shall always adore all the others too much. I should like to have a thousand arms, a thousand mouths, and a thousand—*temperaments*, to be able to strain an army of these charming creatures in my embrace at the same moment.

And yet I am going to get married!

I may add that I know very little of the girl who is going to become my wife tomorrow; I have only seen her four or five times. I know that there is nothing unpleasing about her, and that is enough for my purpose. She is small, fair, and stout; so of course the day after tomorrow I shall ardently wish for a tall, dark, thin woman.

She is not rich, and belongs to the middle-classes. She is a girl such as you may find by the gross, well adapted for matrimony, without any apparent faults, and with no particularly striking qualities. People say of her:

"Mlle. Lajolle is a very nice girl," and tomorrow they will say: "What a very nice woman Madame Raymon is." She belongs, in a word, to that immense number of girls whom one is glad to have for one's wife till the moment comes, when one discovers that one happens to prefer all the other women to that particular woman whom one has married.

"Well," you will say to me, "what on earth did you get married for?"

I hardly like to tell you the strange and seemingly improbable reason that urged me on to this senseless act; the fact, however, is that I am frightened of being alone!

I don't know how to tell you or to make you understand me, but my state of mind is so wretched that you will pity me and despise me.

I do not want to be alone any longer at night; I want to feel that there is someone close to me, touching me, a being who can speak and say something, no matter what it be.

I wish to be able to awaken somebody by my side, so that I may be able to ask some sudden question, a stupid question even if I feel inclined, so that I may hear a human voice, and feel that there is some waking soul close to me, someone whose reason is at work; so that when I hastily light the candle I may see some human face by my side—because—because—I am ashamed to confess it—because I am afraid of being alone.

Oh! you don't understand me yet.

I am not afraid of any danger; if a man were to come into the room I should kill him without trembling. I am not afraid of ghosts, nor do I believe in the supernatural. I am not afraid of dead people, for I believe in the total annihilation of every being that disappears from the face of this earth.

Well,—yes, well, it must be told; I am afraid of myself, afraid of that horrible sensation of incomprehensible fear.

You may laugh, if you like. It is terrible, and I cannot get over it. I am afraid of the walls, of the furniture, of the familiar objects, which are animated, as far as I am concerned, by a kind of animal life. Above all, I am afraid of my own dreadful thoughts, of my reason, which seems as if it were about to leave me, driven away by a mysterious and invisible agony.

At first I feel a vague uneasiness in my mind which causes a cold shiver to run all over me. I look round, and of course nothing is to be seen, and I wish there were something there, no matter what, as long as it were something tangible: I am frightened, merely because I cannot understand my own terror.

If I speak, I am afraid of my own voice. If I walk, I am afraid of I know not what, behind the door, behind the curtains, in the cupboard, or under my bed, and yet all the time I know there is nothing anywhere, and I turn round suddenly because I am afraid of what is behind me, although there is nothing there, and I know it.

I get agitated; I feel that my fear increases, and so I shut myself up in my own room, get into bed, and hide under the clothes, and there, cowering down rolled into a ball, I close my eyes in despair, and remain thus for an indefinite time, remembering that my candle is alight on the table by my bedside, and that I ought to put it out, and yet—I dare not do it!

It is very terrible, is it not, to be like that?

Formerly I felt nothing of all that; I came home quite comfortably, and went up and down in my rooms without anything disturbing my calmness of mind. Had anyone told me that I should be attacked by a malady—for I can call it nothing else—of most improbable fear, such a stupid and terrible malady as it is, I should have laughed outright. I was certainly never afraid of opening the door in the dark; I went to bed slowly without locking it, and never got up in the middle of the night to make sure that everything was firmly closed.

It began last year in a very strange manner, on a damp autumn evening. When my servant had left the room, after I had dined, I asked myself what I was going to do. I walked up and down my room for some time, feeling tired without any reason for it, unable to work, and even without energy to read. A fine rain was falling, and I felt unhappy, a prey to one of those fits of despondency, without any apparent cause which makes us feel inclined to cry, or to talk, no matter to whom, so as to shake off our depressing thoughts.

I felt that I was alone, and my rooms seemed to me to be more empty than they had ever done before, while I was surrounded by a sensation of infinite and overwhelming solitude. What was I to do? I sat down, but then a kind of nervous impatience agitated my legs, so I got up and began to walk about again. I was rather feverish, for my hands, which I had clasped behind me, as one often does when walking slowly, almost seemed to burn one another. Then suddenly a cold shiver ran down my back, and I thought the damp air might have penetrated into my room, so I lit the fire for the first time that year, and sat down again and looked at the flames. But soon I felt that I could not possibly remain quiet, and so I got up again and determined to go out, to pull myself together, and to find a friend to bear me company.

I could not find anyone, so I went on to the boulevards to try and meet some acquaintance or other there.

It was wretched everywhere, and the wet pavement glistened in the gaslight, while the oppressive warmth of the almost impalpable rain lay heavily over the streets and seemed to obscure the light from the lamps.

I went on slowly, saying to myself, "I shall not find a soul to talk to."

I glanced into several cafés, from the Madeleine as far as the Faubourg Poissonière, and saw many unhappy-looking individuals sitting at the tables, who did not seem even to have enough energy left to finish the refreshments they had ordered.

For a long time I wandered aimlessly up and down, and about midnight I started off for home; I was very calm and very tired. My concierge* opened the door at once, which was quite unusual for him, and I thought that another lodger had no doubt just come in.

When I go out I always double-lock the door of my room, and I found it merely closed, which surprised me; but I supposed that some letters had been brought up for me in the course of the evening.

I went in, and found my fire still burning, so that it lighted up the room a little, and, in the act of taking up a candle, I noticed somebody sitting in my armchair by the fire, warming his feet, with his back towards me.

I was not in the slightest degree frightened. I thought very naturally that some friend or other had come to see me. No doubt the porter, whom I had told when I went out, had lent him his own key. In a moment I remembered all the circumstances of my return, how the street door had been opened immediately, and that my own door was only latched, and not locked.

I could see nothing of my friend but his head, and he had evidently gone to sleep while waiting for me, so I went up to him to rouse him. I saw him quite clearly; his right arm was hanging down and his legs were crossed, while his head, which was somewhat inclined to the left of the armchair, seemed to indicate that

* Hall-porter.

he was asleep. "Who can it be?" I asked myself. I could not see clearly, as the room was rather dark, so I put out my hand to touch him on the shoulder, and it came in contact with the back of the chair. There was nobody there; the seat was empty.

I fairly jumped with fright. For a moment I drew back as if some terrible danger had suddenly appeared in my way; then I turned round again, impelled by some imperious desire of looking at the armchair again, and I remained standing upright, panting with fear, so upset that I could not collect my thoughts, and ready to drop.

But I am a cool man, and soon recovered myself. I thought: "It is a mere hallucination, that is all," and I immediately began to reflect about this phenomenon. Thoughts fly very quickly at such moments.

I had been suffering from a hallucination, that was an incontestable fact. My mind had been perfectly lucid and had acted regularly and logically, so there was nothing the matter with the brain. It was only my eyes that had been deceived; they had had a vision, one of those visions which lead simple folk to believe in miracles. It was a nervous accident to the optical apparatus, nothing more; the eyes were rather congested, perhaps.

I lit my candle, and when I stooped down to the fire in so doing, I noticed that I was trembling, and I raised myself up with a jump, as if somebody had touched me from behind.

I was certainly not by any means quiet.

I walked up and down a little, and hummed a tune or two.

Then I double-locked my door, and felt rather reassured; now, at any rate, nobody could come in.

I sat down again, and thought over my adventure for a long time; then I went to bed, and blew out my light.

For some minutes all went well; I lay quietly on my back, but then an irresistible desire seized me to look round the room, and I turned on to my side.

My fire was nearly out, and the few glowing embers threw a faint light on to the floor by the chair, where I fancied I saw the man sitting again.

I quickly struck a match, but I had been mistaken, for there was nothing there; I got up, however, and hid the chair behind my bed, and tried to get to sleep as the room was now dark, but I had not forgotten myself for more than five minutes when in my dream I saw all the scene which I had witnessed as clearly as if it were reality. I woke up with a start, and having lit the candle, I sat up in bed, without venturing even to try and go to sleep again.

Twice, however, sleep overcame me for a few moments in spite of myself, and twice I saw the same thing again, till I fancied I was going mad; when day broke, however, I thought that I was cured, and slept peacefully till noon.

It was all past and over. I had been feverish, had had the nightmare; I don't know what. I had been ill, in a word, but yet I thought that I was a great fool.

I enjoyed myself thoroughly that evening; I went and dined at a restaurant; afterwards I went to the theatre, and then started home. But as I got near the house I was seized by a strange feeling of uneasiness once more; I was afraid of *seeing* him again. I was not afraid of him, not afraid of his presence, in which I did not believe; but I was afraid of being deceived again; I was afraid of some fresh hallucination, afraid lest fear should take possession of me.

Far more than an hour I wandered up and down the pavement; then I thought that I was really too foolish, and at last I returned home. I panted so that I could scarcely get upstairs, and I remained standing outside my door for more than ten minutes; then suddenly I took courage, and screwed myself together. I inserted my key into the lock, and went in with a candle in my hand. I kicked open my half-open bedroom door, and gave a frightened look towards the fireplace; there was nothing there. A—h!

What a relief and what a delight! What a deliverance! I walked up and down briskly and boldly, but I was not altogether reassured, and kept turning round with a jump; the very shadows in the corner disquieted me.

I slept badly, and was constantly disturbed by imaginary noises, but I did not see *him*; no, that was all over.

Since that time I have been afraid of being alone at night. I feel that the specter is there, close to me, around me; but it has not appeared to me again. And supposing it did, what would it matter, since I do not believe in it, and know that it is nothing?

It still worries me, however, because I am constantly thinking of it: *his right arm hanging down and his head inclined to the left like a man who was asleep . . .* Enough of that, in Heaven's name! I don't want to think about it!

Why, however, am I so persistently possessed with this idea? His feet were close to the fire!

He haunts me; it is very stupid, but so it is. Who and what is HE? I know that he does not exist except in my cowardly imagination, in my fears, and in my agony! There—enough of that! . . .

Yes, it is all very well for me to reason with myself, *to stiffen myself,* so to say;

but I cannot remain at home, because I know he is there. I know I shall not see him again; he will not show himself again; that is all over. But he is there all the same in my thoughts. He remains invisible, but that does not prevent his being there. He is behind the doors, in the closed cupboards, in the wardrobe, under the bed, in every dark corner. If I open the door or the cupboard, if I take the candle to look under the bed and throw a light on to the dark places, he is there no longer, but I feel that he is behind me. I turn round, certain that I shall not see him, that I shall never see him again; but he is, for all that, none the less behind me.

It is very stupid, it is dreadful; but what am I to do? I cannot help it.

But if there were two of us in the place, I feel certain that he would not be there any longer, for he is there just because I am alone; simply and solely because I am alone!

The Hand

by Guy de Maupassant

All were crowding around M. Bermutier, the judge, who was giving his opinion about the Saint-Cloud mystery. For a month this inexplicable crime had been the talk of Paris. Nobody could make head or tail of it.

M. Bermutier, standing with his back to the fireplace, was talking, citing the evidence, discussing the various theories, but arriving at no conclusion.

Some women had risen, in order to get nearer to him, and were standing with their eyes fastened on the clean shaven face of the judge, who was saying such weighty things. They, were shaking and trembling, moved by fear and curiosity, and by the eager and insatiable desire for the horrible, which haunts the soul of every woman. One of them, paler than the others, said during a pause:

"It's terrible. It verges on the supernatural. The truth will never be known."

The judge turned to her:

"True, madame, it is likely that the actual facts will never be discovered. As for the word 'supernatural' which you have just used, it has nothing to do with the matter. We are in the presence of a very cleverly conceived and executed crime, so well enshrouded in mystery that we cannot disentangle it from the involved circumstances which surround it. But once I had to take charge of an affair in which the uncanny seemed to play a part. In fact, the case became so confused that it had to be given up."

Several women exclaimed at once:

"Oh! Tell us about it!"

M. Bermutier smiled in a dignified manner, as a judge should, and went on:

"Do not think, however, that I, for one minute, ascribed anything in the case to supernatural influences. I believe only in normal causes. But if, instead of using the word 'supernatural' to express what we do not understand, we were simply to make use of the word 'inexplicable,' it would be much better. At any rate, in the affair of which I am about to tell you, it is especially the surrounding, preliminary circumstances which impressed me. Here are the facts:

"I was, at that time, a judge at Ajaccio, a little white city on the edge of a bay which is surrounded by high mountains.

"The majority of the cases which came up before me concerned vendettas. There are some that are superb, dramatic, ferocious, heroic. We find there the most beautiful causes for revenge of which one could dream, enmities hundreds of years old, quieted for a time but never extinguished; abominable stratagems, murders becoming massacres and almost deeds of glory. For two years I heard of nothing but the price of blood, of this terrible Corsican prejudice which compels revenge for insults meted out to the offending person and all his descendants and relatives. I had seen old men, children, cousins murdered; my head was full of these stories.

"One day I learned that an Englishman had just hired a little villa at the end of the bay for several years. He had brought with him a French servant, whom he had engaged on the way at Marseilles.

"Soon this peculiar person, living alone, only going out to hunt and fish, aroused a widespread interest. He never spoke to any one, never went to the town, and every morning he would practice for an hour or so with his revolver and rifle.

"Legends were built up around him. It was said that he was some high personage, fleeing from his fatherland for political reasons; then it was affirmed that he was in hiding after having committed some abominable crime. Some particularly horrible circumstances were even mentioned.

"In my judicial position I thought it necessary to get some information about this man, but it was impossible to learn anything. He called himself Sir John Rowell.

"I therefore had to be satisfied with watching him as closely as I could, but I could see nothing suspicious about his actions.

"However, as rumours about him were growing and becoming more widespread, I decided to try to see this stranger myself, and I began to hunt regularly in the neighbourhood of his grounds.

"For a long time I watched without finding an opportunity. At last it came to me in the shape of a partridge which I shot and killed right in front of the Englishman. My dog fetched it for me, but, taking the bird, I went at once to Sir John Rowell and, begging his pardon, asked him to accept it.

"He was a big man, with red hair and beard, very tall, very broad, a kind of calm and polite Hercules. He had nothing of the so-called British stiffness, and in a broad English accent he thanked me warmly for my attention. At the end of a month we had had five or six conversations.

"One night, at last, as I was passing before his door, I saw him in the garden, seated astride a chair, smoking his pipe. I bowed and he invited me to come in and have a glass of beer. I needed no urging.

"He received me with the most punctilious English courtesy, sang the praises of France and of Corsica, and declared that he was quite in love with this country.

"Then, with great caution and under the guise of a vivid interest, I asked him a few questions about his life and his plans. He answered without embarrassment, telling me that he had travelled a great deal in Africa, in the Indies, in America. He added, laughing:

"'I have had many adventures.'

"Then I turned the conversation on hunting, and he gave me the most curious details on hunting the hippopotamus, the tiger, the elephant, and even the gorilla.

"I said:

"'Are all these animals dangerous?'

"He smiled:

"'Oh, no! Man is the worst.'

"And he laughed a good broad laugh, the wholesome laugh of a contented Englishman.

"'I have also frequently been man-hunting.'

"Then he began to talk about weapons, and he invited me to come in and see different makes of guns.

"His parlour was draped in black, black silk embroidered in gold. Big yellow flowers, as brilliant as fire, were worked on the dark material.

"He said:

"'It is a Japanese material.'

"But in the middle of the widest panel a strange thing attracted my attention. A black object stood out against a square of red velvet. I went up to it; it was a hand, a human hand. Not the clean white hand of a skeleton, but a dried black hand, with yellow nails, the muscles exposed and traces of old blood on the bones, which were cut off as clean as though it had been chopped off with an axe, near the middle of the forearm.

"Around the wrist, an enormous iron chain, riveted and soldered to this unclean member, fastened it to the wall by a ring, strong enough to hold an elephant in leash.

"I asked:

"'What is that?'

"The Englishman answered quietly:

"'That is my best enemy. It comes from America, too. The bones were severed by a sword and the skin cut off with a sharp stone and dried in the sun for a week.'

"I touched these human remains, which must have belonged to a giant. The uncommonly long fingers were attached by enormous tendons which still had pieces of skin hanging to them in places. This hand was terrible to see; it made one think of some savage vengeance.

"I said:

"'This man must have been very strong.'

"The Englishman answered quietly:

"'Yes, but I was stronger than he. I put on this chain to hold him.'

"I thought that he was joking. I said:

"'This chain is useless now, the hand won't run away.'

"Sir John Rowell answered seriously:

"'It always wants to go away. This chain is needed.'

"I glanced at him quickly, questioning his face, and I asked myself:

"'Is he an insane man or a practical joker?'

"But his face remained inscrutable, calm and friendly. I turned to other subjects, and admired his rifles.

"However, I noticed that he kept three loaded revolvers in the room, as though constantly in fear of some attack.

"I paid him several calls. Then I did not go any more. People had become used to his presence; everybody had lost interest in him.

"A whole year rolled by. One morning, toward the end of November, my servant awoke me and announced that Sir John Rowell had been murdered during the night.

"Half an hour later I entered the Englishman's house, together with the police commissioner and the captain of the gendarmes. The servant, bewildered and in despair, was crying before the door. At first I suspected this man, but he was innocent.

"The guilty party could never be found.

"On entering Sir John's parlour, I noticed the body, stretched out on its back, in the middle of the room.

"His vest was torn, the sleeve of his jacket had been pulled off, everything pointed to, a violent struggle.

"The Englishman had been strangled! His face was black, swollen and frightful, and seemed to express a terrible fear. He held something between his teeth, and his neck, pierced by five or six holes which looked as though they had been made by some iron instrument, was covered with blood.

"A physician joined us. He examined the finger marks on the neck for a long time and then made this strange announcement:

"'It looks as though he had been strangled by a skeleton.'

"A cold chill seemed to run down my back, and I looked over to where I had formerly seen the terrible hand. It was no longer there. The chain was hanging down, broken.

"I bent over the dead man and, in his contracted mouth, I found one of the fingers of this vanished hand, cut—or rather sawed off by the teeth down to the second knuckle.

"Then the investigation began. Nothing could be discovered. No door, window or piece of furniture had been forced. The two watch dogs had not been aroused from their sleep.

"Here, in a few words, is the testimony of the servant:

"For a month his master had seemed excited. He had received many letters, which he would immediately burn.

"Often, in a fit of passion which approached madness, he had taken a switch and struck wildly at this dried hand riveted to the wall, and which had disappeared, no one knows how, at the very hour of the crime.

"He would go to bed very late and carefully lock himself in. He always kept weapons within reach. Often at night he would talk loudly, as though he were quarrelling with some one.

"That night, somehow, he had made no noise, and it was only on going to open the windows that the servant had found Sir John murdered. He suspected no one.

"I communicated what I knew of the dead man to the judges and public officials. Throughout the whole island a minute investigation was carried on. Nothing could be found out.

"One night, about three months after the crime, I had a terrible nightmare. I seemed to see the horrible hand running over my curtains and walls like an immense scorpion or spider. Three times I awoke, three times I went to sleep again; three times I saw the hideous object galloping round my room and moving its fingers like legs.

"The following day the hand was brought me, found in the cemetery, on the grave of Sir John Rowell, who had been buried there because we had been unable to find his family. The first finger was missing.

"Ladies, there is my story. I know nothing more."

The women, deeply stirred, were pale and trembling. One of them exclaimed:

"But that is neither a climax nor an explanation! We will be unable to sleep unless you give us your opinion of what had occurred."

The judge smiled severely:

"Oh! Ladies, I shall certainly spoil your terrible dreams. I simply believe that the legitimate owner of the hand was not dead, that he came to get it with his remaining one. But I don't know how. It was a kind of vendetta."

One of the women murmured:

"No, it can't be that."

And the judge, still smiling, said:

"Didn't I tell you that my explanation would not satisfy you?"

The Inn

by Guy de Maupassant

Resembling in appearance all the wooden hostelries of the High Alps situated at the foot of glaciers in the barren rocky gorges that intersect the summits of the mountains, the Inn of Schwarenbach serves as a resting place for travellers crossing the Gemini Pass.

It remains open for six months in the year and is inhabited by the family of Jean Hauser; then, as soon as the snow begins to fall and to fill the valley so as to make the road down to Loeche impassable, the father and his three sons go away and leave the house in charge of the old guide, Gaspard Hari, with the young guide, Ulrich Kunsi, and Sam, the great mountain dog.

The two men and the dog remain till the spring in their snowy prison, with nothing before their eyes except the immense white slopes of the Balmhorn, surrounded by light, glistening summits, and are shut in, blocked up and buried by the snow which rises around them and which envelops, binds and crushes the little house, which lies piled on the roof, covering the windows and blocking up the door.

It was the day on which the Hauser family were going to return to Loeche, as winter was approaching, and the descent was becoming dangerous. Three mules started first, laden with baggage and led by the three sons. Then the mother, Jeanne Hauser, and her daughter Louise mounted a fourth mule and set off in their turn and the father followed them, accompanied by the two men in charge, who were to escort the family as far as the brow of the descent. First of all they passed round the small lake, which was now frozen over, at the bottom of the mass of rocks which stretched in front of the inn, and then they followed the valley, which was dominated on all sides by the snow-covered summits.

A ray of sunlight fell into that little white, glistening, frozen desert and illuminated it with a cold and dazzling flame. No living thing appeared among this ocean of mountains. There was no motion in this immeasurable solitude and no noise disturbed the profound silence.

By degrees the young guide, Ulrich Kunsi, a tall, long-legged Swiss, left old man Hauser and old Gaspard behind, in order to catch up the mule which bore the two women. The younger one looked at him as he approached and appeared to be calling him with her sad eyes. She was a young, fair-haired little peasant girl, whose milk-white cheeks and pale hair looked as if they had lost their colour by their long abode amid the ice. When he had got up to the animal she was riding he put his hand on the crupper and relaxed his speed. Mother Hauser began to talk to him, enumerating with the minutest details all that he would have to attend to during the winter. It was the first time that he was going to stay up there, while old Hari had already spent fourteen winters amid the snow, at the inn of Schwarenbach.

Ulrich Kunsi listened, without appearing to understand and looked incessantly at the girl. From time to time he replied: "Yes, Madame Hauser," but his thoughts seemed far away and his calm features remained unmoved.

They reached Lake Daube, whose broad, frozen surface extended to the end of the valley. On the right one saw the black, pointed, rocky summits of the Daubenhorn beside the enormous moraines of the Lommern glacier, above which rose the Wildstrubel. As they approached the Gemmi pass, where the descent of Loeche begins, they suddenly beheld the immense horizon of the Alps of the Valais, from which the broad, deep valley of the Rhone separated them.

In the distance there was a group of white, unequal, flat, or pointed mountain summits, which glistened in the sun; the Mischabel with its two peaks, the huge group of the Weisshorn, the heavy Brunegghorn, the lofty and formidable pyramid of Mount Cervin, that slayer of men, and the Dent-Blanche, that monstrous coquette.

Then beneath them, in a tremendous hole, at the bottom of a terrific abyss, they perceived Loeche, where houses looked as grains of sand which had been thrown into that enormous crevice that is ended and closed by the Gemmi and which opens, down below, on the Rhone.

The mule stopped at the edge of the path, which winds and turns continually, doubling backward, then, fantastically and strangely, along the side of the mountain as far as the almost invisible little village at its feet. The women jumped into the snow and the two old men joined them. "Well," father Hauser said, "goodbye, and keep up your spirits till next year, my friends," and old Hari replied: "Till next year."

They embraced each other and then Madame Hauser in her turn offered her cheek, and the girl did the same.

When Ulrich Kunsi's turn came, he whispered in Louise's ear, "Do not forget those up yonder," and she replied, "No," in such a low voice that he guessed what she had said without hearing it. "Well, adieu," Jean Hauser repeated, "and don't fall ill." And going before the two women, he commenced the descent, and soon all three disappeared at the first turn in the road, while the two men returned to the inn at Schwarenbach.

They walked slowly, side by side, without speaking. It was over, and they would be alone together for four or five months. Then Gaspard Hari began to relate his life last winter. He had remained with Michael Canol, who was too old now to stand it, for an accident might happen during that long solitude. They had not been dull, however; the only thing was to make up one's mind to it from the first, and in the end one would find plenty of distraction, games and other means of whiling away the time.

Ulrich Kunsi listened to him with his eyes on the ground, for in his thoughts he was following those who were descending to the village. They soon came in sight of the inn, which was, however, scarcely visible, so small did it look, a black speck at the foot of that enormous billow of snow, and when they opened the door Sam, the great curly dog, began to romp round them.

"Come, my boy," old Gaspard said, "we have no women now, so we must get our own dinner ready. Go and peel the potatoes." And they both sat down on wooden stools and began to prepare the soup.

The next morning seemed very long to Kunsi. Old Hari smoked and spat on the hearth, while the young man looked out of the window at the snow-covered mountain opposite the house.

In the afternoon he went out, and going over yesterday's ground again, he looked for the traces of the mule that had carried the two women. Then when he had reached the Gemmi Pass, he laid himself down on his stomach and looked at Loeche.

The village, in its rocky pit, was not yet buried under the snow, from which it was sheltered by the pine woods which protected it on all sides. Its low houses looked like paving stones in a large meadow from above. Hauser's little daughter was there now in one of those grey-coloured houses. In which? Ulrich Kunsi was too far away to be able to make them out separately. How he would have liked to go down while he was yet able!

But the sun had disappeared behind the lofty crest of the Wildstrubel and the young man returned to the chalet. Daddy Hari was smoking, and when he saw his mate come in he proposed a game of cards to him, and they sat down opposite each other, on either side of the table. They played for a long time a simple game called brisque and then they had supper and went to bed.

The following days were like the first, bright and cold, without any fresh snow. Old Gaspard spent his afternoons in watching the eagles and other rare birds which ventured on those frozen heights, while Ulrich returned regularly to the Gemmi Pass to look at the village. Then they played cards, dice or dominoes and lost and won a trifle, just to create an interest in the game.

One morning Hari, who was up first, called his companion. A moving, deep and light cloud of white spray was falling on them noiselessly and was by degrees burying them under a thick, heavy coverlet of foam. That lasted four days and four nights. It was necessary to free the door and the windows, to dig out a passage and to cut steps to get over this frozen powder, which a twelve hours' frost had made as hard as the granite of the moraines.

They lived like prisoners and did not venture outside their abode. They had divided their duties, which they performed regularly. Ulrich Kunsi undertook the scouring, washing and everything that belonged to cleanliness. He also chopped up the wood while Gaspard Hari did the cooking and attended to the fire. Their regular and monotonous work was interrupted by long games at cards or dice, and they never quarrelled, but were always calm and placid. They were never seen impatient or ill-humoured, nor did they ever use hard words, for they had laid in a stock of patience for their wintering on the top of the mountain.

Sometimes old Gaspard took his rifle and went after chamois, and occasionally he killed one. Then there was a feast in the inn at Schwarenbach and they revelled in fresh meat. One morning he went out as usual. The thermometer outside marked eighteen degrees of frost, and as the sun had not yet risen, the hunter hoped to surprise the animals at the approaches to the Wildstrubel, and Ulrich, being alone, remained in bed until ten o'clock. He was of a sleepy nature, but he would not have dared to give way like that to his inclination in the presence of the old guide, who was ever an early riser. He breakfasted leisurely with Sam, who also spent his days and nights in sleeping in front of the fire; then he felt low-spirited and even frightened at the solitude, and was seized by a longing for his daily game of cards, as one is by the craving of a confirmed habit, and so he went out to meet his companion, who was to return at four o'clock.

The snow had levelled the whole deep valley, filled up the crevasses, obliterated all signs of the two lakes and covered the rocks, so that between the high summits there was nothing but an immense, white, regular, dazzling, and frozen surface. For three weeks Ulrich had not been to the edge of the precipice from which he had looked down on the village, and he wanted to go there before climbing the slopes which led to Wildstrubel. Loeche was now also covered by the snow and the houses could scarcely be distinguished, covered as they were by that white cloak.

Then, turning to the right, he reached the Loemmern glacier. He went along with a mountaineer's long strides, striking the snow, which was as hard as a rock, with his iron-pointed stick, and with his piercing eyes he looked for the little black, moving speck in the distance, on that enormous, white expanse.

When he reached the end of the glacier he stopped and asked himself whether the old man had taken that road, and then he began to walk along the moraines with rapid and uneasy steps. The day was declining, the snow was assuming a rosy tint, and a dry, frozen wind blew in rough gusts over its crystal surface. Ulrich uttered a long, shrill, vibrating call. His voice sped through the deathlike silence in which the mountains were sleeping; it reached the distance, across profound and motionless waves of glacial foam, like the cry of a bird across the waves of the sea. Then it died away and nothing answered him.

He began to walk again. The sun had sunk yonder behind the mountain tops, which were still purple with the reflection from the sky, but the depths of the valley were becoming grey, and suddenly the young man felt frightened. It seemed to him as if the silence, the cold, the solitude, the winter death of these mountains were taking possession of him, were going to stop and to freeze his blood, to make his limbs grow stiff and to turn him into a motionless and frozen object, and he set off running, fleeing toward his dwelling. The old man, he thought, would have returned during his absence. He had taken another road; he would, no doubt, be sitting before the fire, with a dead chamois at his feet. He soon came in sight of the inn, but no smoke rose from it. Ulrich walked faster and opened the door. Sam ran up to him to greet him, but Gaspard Hari had not returned. Kunsi, in his alarm, turned round suddenly, as if he had expected to find his comrade hidden in a corner. Then he relighted the fire and made the soup, hoping every moment to see the old man come in. From time to time he went out to see if he were not coming. It was quite night now, that wan, livid night of the mountains, lighted by a thin, yellow crescent moon, just disappearing behind the mountain tops.

Then the young man went in and sat down to warm his hands and feet, while he pictured to himself every possible accident. Gaspard might have broken a leg, have fallen into a crevasse, taken a false step and dislocated his ankle. And, perhaps, he was lying on the snow, overcome and stiff with the cold, in agony of mind, lost and, perhaps, shouting for help, calling with all his might in the silence of the night. But where? The mountain was so vast, so rugged, so dangerous in places, especially at that time of the year, that it would have required ten or twenty guides to walk for a week in all directions to find a man in that immense space. Ulrich Kunsi, however, made up his mind to set out with Sam if Gaspard did not return by one in the morning, and he made his preparations.

He put provisions for two days into a bag, took his steel climbing iron, tied a long, thin, strong rope round his waist, and looked to see that his iron-shod stick and his axe, which served to cut steps in the ice, were in order. Then he waited. The fire was burning on the hearth, the great dog was snoring in front of it, and the clock was ticking, as regularly as a heart beating, in its resounding wooden case. He waited, with his ears on the alert for distant sounds, and he shivered when the wind blew against the roof and the walls. It struck twelve and he trembled. Then, frightened and shivering, he put some water on the fire, so that he might have some hot coffee before starting, and when the clock struck one he got up, woke Sam, opened the door and went off in the direction of the Wildstrubel. For five hours he mounted, scaling the rocks by means of his climbing irons, cutting into the ice, advancing continually, and occasionally hauling up the dog, who remained below at the foot of some slope that was too steep for him, by means of the rope. It was about six o'clock when he reached one of the summits to which old Gaspard often came after chamois, and he waited till it should be daylight.

The sky was growing pale overhead, and a strange light, springing nobody could tell whence, suddenly illuminated the immense ocean of pale mountain summits, which extended for a hundred leagues around him. One might have said that this vague brightness arose from the snow itself and spread abroad in space. By degrees the highest distant summits assumed a delicate, pink flesh colour, and the red sun appeared behind the ponderous giants of the Bernese Alps.

Ulrich Kunsi set off again, walking like a hunter, bent over, looking for tracks, and saying to his dog: "Seek, old fellow, seek!"

He was descending the mountain now, scanning the depths closely, and from time to time shouting, uttering aloud, prolonged cry, which soon died away in that silent vastness. Then he put his ear to the ground to listen. He thought he could distinguish a voice, and he began to run and shouted again, but he heard nothing more and sat down, exhausted and in despair. Toward midday he breakfasted and gave Sam, who was as tired as himself, something to eat also, and then he recommenced his search.

When evening came he was still walking, and he had walked more than thirty miles over the mountains. As he was too far away to return home and too tired to drag himself along any further, he dug a hole in the snow and crouched in it with his dog under a blanket which he had brought with him. And the man and the dog lay side by side, trying to keep warm, but frozen to the marrow nevertheless. Ulrich scarcely slept, his mind haunted by visions and his limbs shaking with cold.

Day was breaking when he got up. His legs were as stiff as iron bars and his spirits so low that he was ready to cry with anguish, while his heart was beating so that he almost fell over with agitation, when he thought he heard a noise.

Suddenly he imagined that he also was going to die of cold in the midst of this vast solitude, and the terror of such a death roused his energies and gave him renewed vigor. He was descending toward the inn, falling down and getting up again, and followed at a distance by Sam, who was limping on three legs, and they did not reach Schwarenbach until four o'clock in the afternoon. The house was empty and the young man made a fire, had something to eat and went to sleep, so worn out that he did not think of anything more.

He slept for a long time, for a very long time, an irresistible sleep. But suddenly a voice, a cry, a name, "Ulrich!" aroused him from his profound torpor and made him sit up in bed. Had he been dreaming? Was it one of those strange appeals which cross the dreams of disquieted minds? No, he heard it still, that reverberating cry-which had entered his ears and remained in his flesh-to the tips of his sinewy fingers. Certainly somebody had cried out and called "Ulrich!" There was somebody there near the house, there could be no doubt of that, and he opened the door and shouted, "Is it you, Gaspard?" with all the strength of his lungs. But there was no reply, no murmur, no groan, nothing. It was quite dark and the snow looked wan.

The wind had risen, that icy wind that cracks the rocks and leaves nothing alive on those deserted heights, and it came in sudden gusts, which were more parching and more deadly than the burning wind of the desert, and again Ulrich shouted: "Gaspard! Gaspard! Gaspard." And then he waited again. Everything was silent on the mountain.

Then he shook with terror and with a bound he was inside the inn, when he shut and bolted the door, and then he fell into a chair trembling all over, for he felt certain that his comrade had called him at the moment he was expiring.

He was sure of that, as sure as one is of being alive or of eating a piece of bread. Old Gaspard Hari had been dying for two days and three nights somewhere, in some hole, in one of those deep, untrodden ravines whose whiteness is more sinister than subterranean darkness. He had been dying for two days and three nights and he had just then died, thinking of his comrade. His soul, almost before it was released, had taken its flight to the inn where Ulrich was sleeping, and it had called him by that terrible and mysterious power which the spirits of the dead have to haunt the living. That voiceless soul had cried to the worn-out soul of the sleeper; it had uttered its last farewell, or its reproach, or its curse on the man who had not searched carefully enough.

And Ulrich felt that it was there, quite close to him, behind the wall, behind the door which he had just fastened. It was wandering about, like a night bird which lightly touches a lighted window with his wings, and the terrified young man was ready to scream with horror. He wanted to run away, but did not dare to go out; he did not dare, and he should never dare to do it in the future, for that phantom would remain there day and night, round the inn, as long as the old man's body was not recovered and had not been deposited in the consecrated earth of a churchyard.

When it was daylight Kunsi recovered some of his courage at the return of the bright sun. He prepared his meal, gave his dog some food and then remained motionless on a chair, tortured at heart as he thought of the old man lying on the snow, and then, as soon as night once more covered the mountains, new terrors assailed him. He now walked up and down the dark kitchen, which was scarcely lighted by the flame of one candle, and he walked from one end of it to the other with great strides, listening, listening whether the terrible cry of the other night would again break the dreary silence outside. He felt himself alone, unhappy man, as no man had ever been alone before! He was alone in this immense desert of Snow, alone five thousand feet above the inhabited earth, above human habitation, above that stirring, noisy, palpitating life, alone under an icy sky! A mad longing impelled him to run away, no matter where, to get down to Loeche by flinging himself over the precipice; but he did not even dare to open the door, as he felt sure that the other, the dead man, would bar his road, so that he might not be obliged to remain up there alone.

Toward midnight, tired with walking, worn out by grief and fear, he at last fell into a doze in his chair, for he was afraid of his bed as one is of a haunted spot. But suddenly the strident cry of the other evening pierced his ears, and it was so shrill that Ulrich stretched out his arms to repulse the ghost, and he fell backward with his chair.

Sam, who was awakened by the noise, began to howl as frightened dogs do howl, and he walked all about the house trying to find out where the danger came from. When he got to the door, he sniffed beneath it, smelling vigorously, with his coat bristling and his tail stiff, while he growled angrily. Kunsi, who was terrified, jumped up, and, holding his chair by one leg, he cried: "Don't come in, don't come in, or I shall kill you." And the dog, excited by this threat, barked angrily at that invisible enemy who defied his master's voice. By degrees, however, he quieted down and came back and stretched himself in front of the fire, but he was uneasy and kept his head up and growled between his teeth.

Ulrich, in turn, recovered his senses, but as he felt faint with terror, he went and got a bottle of brandy out of the sideboard, and he drank off several glasses, one after another, at a gulp. His ideas became vague, his courage revived and a feverish glow ran through his veins.

He ate scarcely anything the next day and limited himself to alcohol, and so he lived for several days, like a drunken brute. As soon as he thought of Gaspard Hari, he began to drink again, and went on drinking until he fell to the ground, overcome by intoxication. And there he remained lying on his face, dead drunk, his limbs benumbed, and snoring loudly. But scarcely had he digested the maddening and burning liquor than the same cry, "Ulrich!" woke him like a bullet piercing his brain, and he got up, still staggering, stretching out his hands to save himself from falling, and calling to Sam to help him. And the dog, who appeared to be going mad like his master, rushed to the door, scratched it with his claws and gnawed it with his long white teeth, while the young man, with his head thrown back drank the brandy in draughts, as if it had been cold water, so that it might by and by send his thoughts, his frantic terror, and his memory to sleep again.

In three weeks he had consumed all his stock of ardent spirits. But his continual drunkenness only lulled his terror, which awoke more furiously than ever as soon as it was impossible for him to calm it. His fixed idea then, which had been intensified by a month of drunkenness, and which was continually increasing in his absolute solitude, penetrated him like a gimlet. He now walked about the house like a wild beast in its cage, putting his ear to the door to listen if the other were there and defying him through the wall. Then, as soon as he dozed, overcome by fatigue, he heard the voice which made him leap to his feet.

At last one night, as cowards do when driven to extremities, he sprang to the door and opened it, to see who was calling him and to force him to keep quiet, but such a gust of cold wind blew into his face that it chilled him to the bone, and he closed and bolted the door again immediately, without noticing that Sam had rushed out. Then, as he was shivering with cold, he threw some wood on the fire and sat down in front of it to warm himself, but suddenly he started, for somebody was scratching at the wall and crying. In desperation he called out: "Go away!" but was answered by another long, sorrowful wail.

Then all his remaining senses forsook him from sheer fright. He repeated: "Go away!" and turned round to try to find some corner in which to hide, while the other person went round the house still crying and rubbing against the wall. Ulrich went to the oak sideboard, which was full of plates and dishes and of provisions, and lifting it up with superhuman strength, he dragged it to the door, so as to form a barricade. Then piling up all the rest of the furniture, the mattresses, palliasses and chairs, he stopped up the windows as one does when assailed by an enemy.

But the person outside now uttered long, plaintive, mournful groans, to which the young man replied by similar groans, and thus days and nights passed without their ceasing to howl at each other. The one was continually walking round the house and scraped the walls with his nails so vigorously that it seemed as if he wished to destroy them, while the other, inside, followed all his movements, stooping down and holding his ear to the walls and replying to all his appeals with terrible cries. One evening, however, Ulrich heard nothing more, and he sat down, so overcome by fatigue, that he went to sleep immediately and awoke in the morning without a thought, without any recollection of what had happened, just as if his head had been emptied during his heavy sleep, but he felt hungry, and he ate.

The winter was over and the Gemmi Pass was practicable again, so the Hauser family started off to return to their inn. As soon as they had reached the top of the ascent the women mounted their mule and spoke about the two men whom they would meet again shortly. They were, indeed, rather surprised that neither of them had come down a few days before, as soon as the road was open, in order to tell them all about their long winter sojourn. At last, however, they saw the inn, still covered with snow, like a quilt. The door and the window were closed, but a little smoke was coming out of the chimney, which reassured old Hauser. On going up to the door, however, he saw the skeleton of an animal which had been torn to pieces by the eagles, a large skeleton lying on its side.

They all looked close at it and the mother said:

"That must be Sam," and then she shouted: "Hi, Gaspard!" A cry from the interior of the house answered her and a sharp cry that one might have thought some animal had uttered it. Old Hauser repeated, "Hi, Gaspard!" and they heard another cry similar to the first.

Then the three men, the father and the two sons, tried to open the door, but it resisted their efforts. From the empty cow-stall they took a beam to serve as a battering-ram and hurled it against the door with all their might. The wood gave way and the boards flew into splinters. Then the house was shaken by a loud voice, and inside, behind the side board which was overturned, they saw a man standing upright, with his hair falling on his shoulders and a beard descending to his breast, with shining eyes, and nothing but rags to cover him. They did not recognize him, but Louise Hauser exclaimed:

"It is Ulrich, mother." And her mother declared that it was Ulrich, although his hair was white.

He allowed them to go up to him and to touch him, but he did not reply to any of their questions, and they were obliged to take him to Loeche, where the doctors found that he was mad, and nobody ever found out what had become of his companion.

Little Louise Hauser nearly died that summer of decline, which the physicians attributed to the cold air of the mountains.

The Bottle Imp

by Robert Louis Stevenson

There was a man of the Island of Hawaii, whom I shall call Keawe; for the truth is, he still lives, and his name must be kept secret; but the place of his birth was not far from Honaunau, where the bones of Keawe the Great lie hidden in a cave. This man was poor, brave, and active; he could read and write like a schoolmaster; he was a first-rate mariner besides, sailed for some time in the island steamers, and steered a whaleboat on the Hamakua coast. At length it came in Keawe's mind to have a sight of the great world and foreign cities, and he shipped on a vessel bound to San Francisco.

This is a fine town, with a fine harbour, and rich people uncountable; and in particular, there is one hill which is covered with palaces. Upon this hill Keawe was one day taking a walk with his pocket full of money, viewing the great houses upon either hand with pleasure. "What fine houses these are!" he was thinking, "and how happy must those people be who dwell in them, and take no care for the morrow!" The thought was in his mind when he came abreast of a house that was smaller than some others, but all finished and beautified like a toy; the steps of that house shone like silver, and the borders of the garden bloomed like garlands, and the windows were bright like diamonds; and Keawe stopped and wondered at the excellence of all he saw. So stopping, he was aware of a man that looked forth upon him through a window so clear that Keawe could see him as you see a fish in a pool upon the reef. The man was elderly, with a bald head and a black beard; and his face was heavy with sorrow, and he bitterly sighed. And the truth of it is, that as Keawe looked in upon the man, and the man looked out upon Keawe, each envied the other.

All of a sudden, the man smiled and nodded, and beckoned Keawe to enter, and met him at the door of the house.

"This is a fine house of mine," said the man, and bitterly sighed. "Would you not care to view the chambers?"

So he led Keawe all over it, from the cellar to the roof, and there was nothing there that was not perfect of its kind, and Keawe was astonished.

"Truly," said Keawe, "this is a beautiful house; if I lived in the like of it I should be laughing all day long. How comes it, then, that you should be sighing?"

"There is no reason," said the man, "why you should not have a house in all points similar to this, and finer, if you wish. You have some money, I suppose?"

"I have fifty dollars," said Keawe; "but a house like this will cost more than fifty dollars."

The man made a computation. "I am sorry you have no more," said he, "for it may raise you trouble in the future; but it shall be yours at fifty dollars."

"The house?" asked Keawe.

"No, not the house," replied the man; "but the bottle. For, I must tell you, although I appear to you so rich and fortunate, all my fortune, and this house itself and its garden, came out of a bottle not much bigger than a pint. This is it."

And he opened a lockfast place, and took out a round-bellied bottle with a long neck; the glass of it was white like milk, with changing rainbow colours in the grain. Withinsides something obscurely moved, like a shadow and a fire.

"This is the bottle," said the man; and, when Keawe laughed, "You do not believe me?" he added. "Try, then, for yourself. See if you can break it."

So Keawe took the bottle up and dashed it on the floor till he was weary; but it jumped on the floor like a child's ball, and was not injured.

"This is a strange thing," said Keawe. "For by the touch of it, as well as by the look, the bottle should be of glass."

"Of glass it is," replied the man, sighing more heavily than ever; "but the glass of it was tempered in the flames of hell. An imp lives in it, and that is the shadow we behold there moving; or so I suppose. If any man buy this bottle the imp is at his command; all that he desires—love, fame, money, houses like this house, ay, or a city like this city—all are his at the word uttered. Napoleon had this bottle, and by it he grew to be the king of the world; but he sold it at the last, and fell. Captain Cook had this bottle, and by it he found his way to so many islands; but he, too sold it, and was slain upon Hawaii. For, once it is sold, the power goes and the protection; and unless a man remain content with what he has, ill will befall him."

"And yet you talk of selling it yourself?" Keawe said.

"I have all I wish, and I am growing elderly," replied the man. "There is one thing the imp cannot do—he cannot prolong life; and, it would not be fair to conceal from you, there is a drawback to the bottle; for if a man die before he sells it, he must burn in hell for ever."

"To be sure, that is a drawback and no mistake," cried Keawe. "I would not meddle with the thing. I can do without a house, thank God; but there is on thing I could not be doing with one particle, and that is to be damned."

"Dear me, you must not run away with things, " returned the man. "All you have to do is to use the power of the imp in moderation, and then sell it to someone else, as I do to you, and finish your life in comfort."

"Well, I observe two things," said Keawe. "All the time you keep sighing like a maid in love, that is one; and, for the other, you sell this bottle very cheap."

"I have told you already why I sigh," said the man. "It is because I fear my health is breaking up; and, as you said yourself, to die and go to the devil is a pity for anyone. As for why I sell so cheap, I must explain to you there is a peculiarity about the bottle. Long ago, when the devil brought it first upon earth, it was extremely expensive, and was sold first of all to Prester John for many millions of dollars; but it cannot be sold at all, unless sold at a loss. If you sell it for as much as you paid for it, back it comes to you again like a homing pigeon. It follows that the price has kept falling in these centuries, and the bottle is now remarkably cheap. I bought it myself from one of my great neighbours on this hill, and the price I paid was only ninety dollars. I could sell it for as high as eighty-nine dollars and ninety-nine cents, but not a penny dearer, or back the thing must come to me. Now, about this there are two bothers. First, when you offer a bottle so singular for eighty odd dollars, people suppose you to be jesting. And second—but there is no hurry about that—and I need not go into it. Only remember it must be coined money that you sell it for."

"How am I to know that this is all true?" asked Keawe.

"Some of it you can try at once," replied the man. "Give me your fifty dollars, take the bottle, and wish your fifty dollars back into your pocket. If that does not happen, I pledge you my honour I will cry off the bargain and restore your money."

"You are not deceiving me?" said Keawe.

The man bound himself with a great oath.

"Well, I will risk that much," said Keawe, "for that can do no harm." And he paid over his money to the man, and the man handed him the bottle.

"Imp of the bottle," said Keawe, "I want my fifty dollars back." And sure enough he had scarce said the word before his pocket was as heavy as ever.

"To be sure this is a wonderful bottle," said Keawe.

"And now, good morning to you, my fine fellow, and the devil go with you for me!" said the man.

"Hold on," said Keawe, "I don't want any more of this fun. Here, take your bottle back."

"You have bought it for less than I paid for it," replied the man, rubbing his hands. "It is yours now; and, for my part, I am only concerned to see the back of you." And with that he rang for his Chinese servant, and had Keawe shown out of the house.

Now, when Keawe was in the street, with the bottle under his arm, he began to think. "If all is true about this bottle, I may have made a losing bargain," thinks he. "But perhaps the man was only fooling me." The first thing he did was to count his money; the sum was exact—forty-nine dollars American money, and one Chili piece. "That looks like the truth," said Keawe. "Now I will try another part."

The streets in that part of the city were as clean as a ship's decks, and though it was noon, there were no passengers. Keawe set the bottle in the gutter and walked away. Twice he looked back, and there was the milky, round-bellied bottle where he left it. A third time he looked back, and turned a corner; but he had scarce done so, when something knocked upon his elbow, and behold! it was the long neck sticking up; and as for the round belly, it was jammed into the pocket of his pilot-coat.

"And that looks like the truth," said Keawe.

The next thing he did was to buy a cork-screw in a shop, and go apart into a secret place in the fields. And there he tried to draw the cork, but as often as he put the screw in, out it came again, and the cork as whole as ever.

"This is some new sort of cork," said Keawe, and all at once he began to shake and sweat, for he was afraid of that bottle.

On his way back to the port-side, he saw a shop where a man sold shells and clubs from the wild islands, old heathen deities, old coined money, pictures from China and Japan, and all manner of things that sailors bring in their sea-chests. And here he had an idea. So he went in and offered the bottle for a hundred dollars. The man of the shop laughed at him at the first, and offered him five; but indeed, it was a curious bottle—such glass was never blown in any human glass-works, so prettily the colours shown under the milky white, and so strangely the shadow hovered in the midst; so, after he had disputed awhile after the manner of his kind, the shopman gave Keawe sixty silver dollars for the thing, and set it on a shelf in the midst of his window.

"Now," said Keawe, "I have sold that for sixty which I bought for fifty—so, to say truth, a little less, because one of my dollars was from Chili. Now I shall know the truth upon another point."

So he went back on board his ship, and, when he opened his chest, there was the bottle, and had come more quickly than himself. Now Keawe had a mate on board whose name was Lopaka.

"What ails you?" said Lopaka, "that you stare in your chest?"

They were alone in the ship's forecastle, and Keawe bound him to secrecy, and told all.

"This is a very strange affair," said Lopaka; "and I fear you will be in trouble about this bottle. But there is one point very clear—that you are sure of the trouble, and you had better have the profit in the bargain. Make up your mind what you want with it; give the order, and if it is done as you desire, I will buy the bottle myself; for I have an idea of my own to get a schooner, and go trading through the islands."

"That is not my idea," said Keawe; "but to have a beautiful house and garden on the Kona Coast, where I was born, the sun shining in at the door, flowers in the garden, glass in the windows, pictures on the walls, and toys and fine carpets on the tables, for all the world like the house I was in this day—only a storey higher, and with balconies all about like the king's palace; and to live there without care and make merry with my friends and relatives."

"Well," said Lopaka, "let us carry it back with us to Hawaii, and if all comes true, as you suppose, I will buy the bottle, as I said, and ask a schooner."

Upon that they were agreed, and it was not long before the ship returned to Honolulu, carrying Keawe and Lopaka, and the bottle. They were scarce come ashore when they met a friend upon the beach, who began at once to condole with Keawe.

"I do not know what I am to be condoled about," said Keawe.

"Is it possible you have not heard," said the friend, "your uncle—that good old man—is dead, and your cousin—that beautiful boy—was drowned at sea?"

Keawe was filled with sorrow, and, beginning to weep and to lament he forgot about the bottle. But Lopaka was thinking to himself, and presently, when Keawe's grief was a little abated, "I have been thinking," said Lopaka. "Had not your uncle lands in Hawaii, in the district of Kau?"

"No," said Keawe, "not in Kau; they are on the mountain-side—a little way south of Hookena."

"These lands will now be yours?" asked Lopaka.

"And so they will," says Keawe, and began again to lament for his relatives.

"No," said Lopaka, "do not lament at present. I have a thought in my mind. How if this should be the doing of the bottle? For here is the place ready for your house."

"If this be so," cried Keawe, "it is a very ill way to serve me by killing my relatives. But it may be, indeed; for it was in just such a station that I saw the house with my mind's eye."

"The house, however, is not yet built," said Lopaka.

"No, nor like to be!" said Keawe, "for though my uncle has some coffee and ava and bananas, it will not be more than will keep me in comfort; and the rest of that land is the black lava."

"Let us go to the lawyer," said Lopaka; "I have still this idea in my mind."

Now, when they came to the lawyer's, it appeared Keawe's uncle had grown monstrous rich in the last days, and there was a fund of money.

"And here is the money for the house!" cried Lopaka.

"If you are thinking of a new house," said the lawyer, "here is the card of a new architect, of whom they tell me great things."

"Better and better!" cried Lopaka. "Here is all made plain for us. Let us continue to obey orders."

So they went to the architect, and he had drawings of houses on his table.

"You want something out of the way," said the architect. "How do you like this?" and he handed a drawing to Keawe.

Now, when Keawe set eyes on the drawing, he cried out aloud, for it was the picture of his thought exactly drawn.

"I am for this house," thought he. "Little as I like the way it comes to me, I am in for it now, and I may as well take the good along with the evil."

So he told the architect all that he wished, and how he would have that house furnished, and about the pictures on the wall and the knick-knacks on the tables; and he asked the man plainly for how much he would undertake the whole affair.

The architect put many questions, and took his pen and made a computation; and when he had done he named the very sum that Keawe had inherited.

Lopaka and Keawe looked at one another and nodded.

"It is quite clear," thought Keawe, "that I am to have this house, whether or no. It comes from the devil, and I fear I will get little good by that; and of one thing I am sure, I will make no more wishes as long as I have this bottle. But with the house I am saddled, and I may as well take the good along with the evil."

So he made his terms with the architect, and they signed a paper; and Keawe and Lopaka took ship again and sailed to Australia; for it was concluded between them they should not interfere at all, but leave the architect and the bottle imp to build and to adorn that house at their own pleasure.

The voyage was a good voyage, only all the time Keawe was holding in his breath, for he had sworn he would utter no more wishes, and take no more favours from the devil. The time was up when they go back. The architect told them that the house was ready, and Keawe and Lopaka took a passage in the Hall, and went down Kona way to view the house, and see if all had been done fitly according to the thought that was in Keawe's mind.

Now, the house stood on the mountain-side, visible to ships. Above, the forest ran up into the clouds of rain; below, the black lava fell in cliffs, where the kings of old lay buried. A garden bloomed about that house with every hue of flowers; and there was an orchard of papaia on the one hand and an orchard of breadfruit on the other, and right in front, toward the sea, a ship's mast had been rigged up and bore a flag. As for the house, it was three storeys high, with great chambers and broad balconies on each. The windows were of glass, so excellent that it was as clear as water and as bright as day. All manner of furniture adorned the chambers. Pictures hung upon the wall in golden frames: pictures of ships, and men fighting, and of the most beautiful women, and of singular places; nowhere in the world are there pictures of so bright a colour as those Keawe found hanging in his house. As for the knick-knacks, they were extraordinary fine; chiming clocks and musical boxes, little men with nodding heads, books filled with pictures, weapons of price from all quarters of the world, and the most elegant puzzles to entertain the leisure of a solitary man. And as no one would care to live in such chambers, only to walk through and view them, the balconies were made so broad that a whole town might have lived upon them in delight; and Keawe knew not which to prefer, whether the back porch, where you got the land breeze, and looked upon the orchards and the flowers, or the front balcony, where you could drink the wind of the sea, and look down the steep wall of the mountain and see the Hall going by once a week or so between Kookena and the hills of Pele, or the schooners plying up the coast for wood and ava and bananas.

When they had viewed all, Keawe and Lopaka sat on the porch.

"Well," asked Lopaka, "is it all as you designed?"

"Words cannot utter it," said Keawe. "It is better than I dreamed, and I am sick with satisfaction."

"There is but one thing to consider," said Lopaka; "all this may be quite natural, and the bottle imp have nothing whatever to say to it. If I were to buy the bottle, and got no schooner after all, I should have put my hand in the fire for nothing. I gave you my word, I know; but yet I think you would not grudge me one more proof."

"I have sworn I would take no more favours," said Keawe. "I have gone already deep enough."

"This is no favour I am thinking of," replied Lopaka. "It is only to see the imp himself. There is nothing to be gained by that, and so nothing to be ashamed of; and yet, if I once saw him, I should be sure of the whole matter. So indulge me so far, and let me see the imp; and, after that, here is the money in my hand, and I will buy it."

"There is only one thing I am afraid of," said Keawe. "The imp may be very ugly to view; and if you once set eyes upon him you might be very undesirous of the bottle."

"I am a man of my word," said Lopaka. "And here is the money betwixt us."

"Very well," replied Keawe. "I have a curiosity myself. So come, let us have one look at you, Mr Imp."

Now as soon as that was said, the imp looked out of the bottle, and in again, swift as a lizard; and there sat Keawe and Lopaka turned to stone. The night had quite come, before either found a thought to say or voice to say it with; and then Lopaka pushed the money over and took the bottle.

"I am a man of my word," said he, "and had need to be so, or I would not touch this bottle with my foot. Well, I shall get my schooner and a dollar or two for my pocket; and then I will be rid of this devil as fast as I can. For to tell you the plain truth, the look of him has cast me down."

"Lopaka," said Keawe, "do not you think any worse of me than you can help; I know it is night, and the roads had, and the pass by the tombs an ill place to go by so late, but I declare since I have seen that little face, I cannot eat or sleep or pray till it is gone from me. I will give you a lantern, and a basket to put the bottle in, and any picture or fine thing in all my house that takes your fancy;—and be gone at once, and go sleep at Hookena with Nahinu."

"Keawe," said Lopaka, "many a man would take this ill; above all, when I am doing you a turn so friendly, as to keep my word and buy the bottle; and for that matter, the night and the dark, and the way by the tombs, must be all tenfold more dangerous to a man with such a sin upon his conscience, and such a bottle under his arm. But for my part, I am so extremely terrified myself, I have not the heart to blame you. Here I go then; and I pray God you may be happy in your house, and I fortunate with my schooner, and both get to heaven in the end in spite of the devil and his bottle."

So Lopaka went down the mountain; and Keawe stood in his front balcony, and listened to the clink of the horse's shoes, and watched the lantern go shining down the path, and along the cliff of caves where the old dead are buried; and all the time he trembled and clasped his hands, and prayed for his friend, and gave glory to God that he himself had escaped out of that trouble.

But the next day came very brightly, and that new house of his was so delightful to behold that he forgot his terrors. One day followed another, and Keawe dwelt there in perpetual joy. He had his place on the back porch; it was there he ate and lived, and read the stories in the Honolulu newspapers; but when anyone came by they would go in and view the chambers and the pictures. And the fame of the house went far and wide; it was called Ka-Hale Nui—the Great House—in all Kona; and sometimes the Bright House, for Keawe kept a Chinaman, who was all day dusting and furbishing; and the glass and the gilt, and the fine stuffs, and the pictures, shown as bright as the morning. As for Keawe himself, he could not walk in the chambers without singing, his heart was so enlarged; and when ships sailed by upon the sea, he would fly his colours on the mast.

So time went by, until one day Keawe went upon a visit as far as Kailua to certain of his friends. There he was well feasted; and left as soon as he could the next morning, and rode hard, for he was impatient to behold his beautiful house; and, besides, the night then coming on was the night in which the dead of old days go abroad in the sides of Kona; and having already meddled with the devil, he was the more chary of meeting with the dead. A little beyond Honaunau, looking far ahead, he was aware of a woman bathing in the edge of the sea; and she seemed a well grown girl, but he thought no more of it. Then he saw her white shift flutter as she put it on, and then her red holoku; and by the time he came abreast of her she was done with her toilet, and had come up from the sea, and stood by the track-side in her red holoku, and she was all freshened with the bath, and her eyes shone and were kind. Now Keawe no sooner beheld her than he drew rein.

"I thought I knew everyone in this country," said he. "How comes it that I do not know you?"

"I am Kokua, daughter of Kiano," said the girl, "and I have just returned from Oahu. Who are you?"

"I will tell you who I am in a little," said Keawe, dismounting from his horse, "but not now. For I have a thought in my mind, and if you knew who I was, you might have heard of me, and would not give me a true answer. But tell me, first of all, one thing: Are you married?"

At this Kokua laughed out aloud. "It is you who ask questions," said she. "Are you married yourself?"

"Indeed, Kokua, I am not," repled Keawe, "and never thought to be until this hour. But here is the plain truth. I have met you here at the roadside, and I saw your eyes, which are like the stars, and my heart went to you as swift as a bird. And so now, if you want none of me, say so, and I will go on to my own place; but if you think me no worse than any other young man, say so, too, and I will turn aside to your father's for the night, and tomorrow I will talk with the good man."

Kokua said never a word, but she looked at the sea and laughed.

"Kokua," said Keawe, "if you say nothing, I will take that for the good answer; so let us be stepping to your father's door."

She went on ahead of him, still without speech; only sometimes she glanced back and glanced away again, and she kept the string of her hat in her mouth.

Now, when they had come to the door, Kiano came out on his verandah, and cried out and welcomed Keawe by name. At that the girl looked over, for the fame of the great house had come to her ears; and, to be sure, it was a great temptation. All that evening they were very merry together; and the girl was as bold as brass under the eyes of her parents, and made a mock of Keawe, for she had a quick wit. The next day he had a word with Kiano, and found the girl alone.

"Kokua," said he, "you made a mock of me all the evening; and it is still time to bid me go. I would not tell you who I was, because I have so fine a house, and I feared you would think too much of that house and too little of the man that loves you. Now you know all, and if you wish to have seen the last of me, say so at once."

"No," said Kokua; but this time she did not laugh, nor did Keawe ask for more.

This was the wooing of Keawe; things had gone quickly; but so an arrow goes, and the ball of a rifle swifter still, and yet both may strike the target. Things had gone fast, but they had gone far also, and the thought of Keawe rang in the maiden's head; she heard his voice in the breach of the surf upon the lava, and for this young man that she had seen but twice she would have left father and mother and her native islands. As for Keawe himself, his horse flew up the path of the mountain under the cliff of tombs, and the sound of the hoofs, and the sound of Keawe singing to himself for pleasure echoed in the caverns of the dead. He came to the Bright House, and still he was singing. He sat and ate in the broad balcony, and the Chinaman wondered at his master, to hear how he sang between the mouthfuls. The sun went down into the sea, and the night came; and Keawe walked the balconies by lamplight, high on the mountains, and the voice of his singing startled men on ships.

"Here am I now upon my high place," he said to himself. "Life may be no better; this is the mountain top; and all shelves about me towards the worse. For the first time I will light up the chambers, and bathe in my fine bath with the hot water and the cold, and sleep alone in the bed of my bridal chamber."

So the Chinaman had word, and he must rise from sleep and light the furnaces; and as he wrought below, beside the boilers, he heard his master singing and rejoicing above him in the lighted chambers. When the water began to be hot the Chinaman cried to his master; and Keawe went into the bathroom; and the Chinaman heard him sing as he filled the marble basin; and heard him sing, and the signing broken, as he undressed; until of a sudden, the song ceased. The Chinaman listened, and listened; he called up the house to Keawe to ask if all were well, and Keawe answered him "Yes," and bad him go to bed; but there was no more singing in the Bright House; and all night long, the Chinaman heard his master's feet go round and round the balconies without repose.

Now the truth of it was this: as Keawe undressed for his bath, he spied upon his flesh a patch like a patch of lichen on a rock, and it was then that he stopped singing. For he knew the likeness of that patch, and knew that he was fallen in the Chinese Evil.* Now, it is a sad thing for any man to fall into this sickness. And it would be a sad thing for anyone to leave a house so beautiful and so commodious, and depart from all his friends to the north coast of Molokai between the mighty cliff and the sea-breakers. But what was that the case of the man Keawe, he who had met his love but yesterday, and won her but that morning, and now saw all his hopes break, in a moment, like a piece of glass?

Awhile he sat upon the edge of the bath; then sprang, with a cry and ran outside; and to and fro, to and fro, along the balcony, like one despairing.

"Very willingly could I leave Hawaii, the home of my fathers," Keawe was thinking. "Very lightly could I leave my house, the high-placed, the many-windowed, here upon the mountains. Very bravely could I go to Molokai, to Kalaupapa by the cliffs, to live with the smitten and to sleep there, far from my fathers. But what wrong have I done, what sin lies upon my soul, that I should have encountered Kokua coming cool from the sea-water in the evening? Kokua, the soul ensnarer! Kokua, the light of my life! Her may I never wed, her may I look upon no longer, her may I no more handle with my living hand; and it is for this, it is for you, O Kokua! that I pour my lamentations!"

Now you are to observe what sort of a man Keawe was, for he might have dwelt there in the Bright House for years, and no one been the wiser of his sickness; but he reckoned nothing of that, if he must lose Kokua. And again, he might have wed Kokua even as he was; and so many would have done, because they have the souls of pigs; but Keawe loved the maid manfully, and he would do her no hurt and bring her in no danger.

A little beyond the midst of the night, there came in his mind the recollection of that bottle. He went round to the back porch, and called to memory the day when the devil had looked forth; and at the thought ice ran in his veins.

"A dreadful thing is the bottle," thought Keawe, "and dreadful is the imp, and it is a dreadful thing to risk the flames of hell. But what other hope have I to cure the sickness or to wed Kokua? What!" he thought, "would I beard the devil once, only to get me a house, and not face him again to win Kokua?"

---

* Leprosy

Thereupon he called to mind it was the next day the Hall went by on her return to Honolulu. "There must I go first," he thought, "and see Lopaka. For the best hope that I have now is to find that same bottle I was so please to be rid of."

Never a wink could he sleep; the food stuck in his throat; but he sent a letter to Kiano, and about the time when the steamer would be coming, rode down beside the cliff of the tombs. It rained; his horse went heavily; he looked up at the black mouths of the caves, and he envied the dead that slept there and were done with trouble; and called to mind how he had galloped by the day before, and was astonished. So he came down to Hookena, and there was all the country gathered for the steamer as usual. In the shed before the store they sat and jested and passed the news; but there was no matter of speech in Keawe's bosom, and he sat in their midst and looked without on the rain falling on the houses, and the surf beating among the rocks, and the sighs arose in his throat.

"Keawe of the Bright House is out of spirits," said one to another. Indeed, and so he was, and little wonder.

Then the Hall came, and the whaleboat carried him on board. The after-part of the ship was full of Haoles [footnote: Whites] who had been to visit the volcano, as their custom is; and the midst was crowded with Kanakas, and the forepart with wild bulls from Hilo and horses from Kau; but Keawe sat apart from all in his sorrow, and watched for the house of Kiano. There is sat, low upon the shore in the black rocks and shaded by the cocoa palms, and there by the door was a red holoku, no greater than a fly, and going to and fro with a fly's busyness.

"Ah, queen of my heart," he cried, "I'll venture my dear soul to win you!"

Soon after, darkness fell, and the cabins were lit up, and the Haoles sat and played at the cards and drank whisky as their custom is; but Keawe walked the deck all night; and all the next day, as they steamed under the lee of Maui or of Molokai, he was still pacing to and from like a wild animal in a menagerie.

Towards evening they passed Diamond Head, and came to the pier of Honolulu. Keawe stepped out among the crowd and began to ask for Lopaka. It seemed he had become the owner of a schooner—none better in the islands—and was gone upon an adventure as far as Pola-Pola or Kahiki; so there was no help to be looked for from Lopaka. Keawe called to mind a friend of his, a lawyer in the town (I must not tell his name), and inquired of him. They said he was grown suddenly rich, and had a fine new house upon Waikiki shore; and this put a thought in Keawe's head, and he called a hack and drove to the lawyer's house.

The house was all brand new, and the trees in the garden no greater than walking-sticks, and the lawyer, when he came, had the air of a man well pleased.

"What can I do to serve you?" said the lawyer.

"You are a friend of Lopaka's," replied Keawe, "and Lopaka purchased from me a certain piece of goods that I thought you might enable me to trace."

The lawyer's face became very dark. "I do not profess to misunderstand you, Mr Keawe," said he, "though this is an ugly business to be stirring in. You maybe sure I know nothing, but yet I have a guess, and if you would apply in a certain quarter I think you might have news."

And he named the name of a man, which, again, I had better not repeat. So it was for days, and Keawe went from one to another, finding everywhere new clothes and carriages, and fine new houses and men everywhere in great contentment, although, to be sure, when he hinted at his business their faces would cloud over.

"No doubt I am upon the track," thought Keawe. "These new clothes and carriages are all the gifts of the little imp, and these glad faces are the faces of men who have taken their profit and got rid of the accursed thing in safety. When I see pale cheeks and hear sighing, I shall know that I am near the bottle."

So it befell at last that he was recommended to a Haole in Beritania Street. When he came to the door, about the hour of the evening meal, there were the usual marks of the new house, and the young garden, and the electric light shining in the windows; but when the owner came, a shock of hope and fear ran through Keawe; for here was a young man, white as a corpse, and black about the eyes, the hair shedding from his head, and such a look in his countenance as a man may have when he is waiting for the gallows.

"Here it is, to be sure," thought Keawe, and so with this man he no ways veiled his errand. "I am come to buy the bottle," said he.

At the word, the young Haole of Beritania Street reeled against the wall.

"The bottle!" he gasped. "To buy the bottle!" Then he seemed to choke, and seizing Keawe by the arm carried him into a room and poured out wine in two glasses.

"Here is my respects," said Keawe, who had been much about with Haoles in his time. "Yes," he added, "I am come to buy the bottle. What is the price by now?"

At that word the young man let his glass slip through his fingers, and looked upon Keawe like a ghost.

"The price," says he; "the price! you do not know the price?"

"It is for that I am asking you," returned Keawe. "But why are you so much concerned? Is there anything wrong about the price?"

"It has dropped a great deal in value since your time, Mr Keawe," said the young man, stammering.

"Well, well, I shall have the less to pay for it," said Keawe. "How much did it cost you?"

The young man was as white as a sheet. "Two cents," said he.

"What?" cried Keawe, "two cents? Why, then, you can only sell it for one. And he who buys it—" The words died upon Keawe's tongue; he who bought it could never sell it again, the bottle and the bottle imp must abide with him until he died, and when he died must carry him to the red end of hell.

The young man of Beritania Street fell upon his knees. "For God's sake buy it!" he cried. "You can have all my fortune in the bargain. I was mad when I bought it at that price. I had embezzled money at my store; I was lost else; I must have gone to jail."

"Poor creature," said Keawe, "you would risk your soul upon so desperate an adventure, and to avoid the proper punishment of your own disgrace; and you think I could hesitate with love in front of me. Give me the bottle, and the change which I make sure you have all ready. Here is a five-cent piece."

It was as Keawe supposed; the young man had the change ready in a drawer; the bottle changed hands, and Keawe's fingers were no sooner clasped upon the stalk than he had breathed his wish to be a clean man. And, sure enough, when he got home to his room and stripped himself before a glass, his flesh was whole like an infant's. And here was the strange thing: he had no sooner seen this miracle, than his mind was changed within him, and he cared naught for the Chinese Evil, and little enough for Kokua; and had but the one thought, that here he was bound to the bottle imp for time and for eternity, and had no better hope but to be a cinder for ever in the flames of hell. Away ahead of him he saw them blaze with his mind's eye, and his soul shrank, and darkness fell upon the light.

When Keawe came to himself a little, he was aware it was the night when the band played at the hotel. Thither he went, because he feared to be alone; and there, among happy faces, walked to and fro, and heard the tunes go up and down, and saw Berger beat the measure, and all the while he heard the flames crackle, and saw the red fire burning in the bottomless pit. Of a sudden the band played Hiki-ao-ao; that was a song that he had sung with Kokua, and at the strain courage returned to him.

"It is done now," he thought, "and once more let me take the good along with the evil."

So it befell that he returned to Hawaii by the first steamer, and as soon as it could be managed he was wedded to Kokua, and carried her up the mountain side to the Bright House.

Now it was so with these two, that when they ere together, Keawe's heart was stilled; but so soon has he was alone he fell into a brooding horror, and heard the flames crackle, and saw the red fire burn in the bottomless pit. The girl, indeed, had come to him wholly; her heart leapt in her side at sight of him, her hand clung to his; and she was so fashioned from the hair upon her head to the nails upon her toes that none could see her without joy. She was pleasant in her nature. She had the good word always. Full of song she was, and went to and fro in the Bright House, the brightest thing in its three storeys, carolling like the birds. And Keawe beheld and heard her with delight, and then must shrink upon one side, and weep and groan to think upon the price that he had paid for her; and then he must dry his eyes, and wash his face, and go and sit with her on the broad balconies joining in her songs, and, with a sick spirit, answering her smiles.

There came a day when her feet began to be heavy and her songs more rare; and now it was not Keawe only that would weep apart, but each would sunder from the other and sit in opposite balconies with the whole width of the Bright House betwixt. Keawe was so sunk in his despair, he scarce observed the change, and was only glad he had more hours to sit alone and brood upon his destiny and was not so frequently condemned to pull a smiling face on a sick heart. But one day, coming softly through the house, he heard the sound of a child sobbing, and there was Kokua rolling her face upon the balcony floor, and weeping like the lost.

"You do well to weep in this house, Kokua," he said. "And yet I would give the head off my body that you (at least) might have been happy."

"Happy!" she cried. "Keawe, when you lived alone in your Bright House, you were the word of the island for a happy man; laughter and song were in your mouth, and your face was as bright as the sunrise. Then you wedded pour Kokua; and the good God knows what is amiss in her—but from that day you have not smiled. Ah!" she cried, "what ails me? I thought I was pretty, and I knew I loved him. What ails me that I throw this cloud upon my husband?"

"Poor Kokua," said Keawe. He sat down by her side, and sought to take her hand; but that she plucked away. "Poor Kokua," he said, again. "My poor child—

my pretty. And I thought all this while to spare you! Well, you shall know all. Then, at least, you will pity poor Keawe; then you will understand how much he loved you in the past—that he dared hell for your possession—and how much he loves you still (the poor condemned one), that he can yet call up a smile when he beholds you."

With that, he told her all, even from the beginning.

"You have done this for me?" she cried. "Ah, well then what do I care!"—and she clasped and wept upon him.

"Ah, child!" said Keawe, "and yet, when I consider of the fire of hell, I care a good deal!"

"Never tell me," said she; "no man can be lost because he loved Kokua, and no other fault. I tell you, Keawe, I shall save you with these hands, or perish in your company. What! you loved me, and gave your soul, and you think I will not die to save you in return?"

"Ah, my dear! you might die a hundred times, and what difference would that make?" he cried, "except to leave me lonely till the time comes of my damnation?"

"You know nothing," said she. "I was educated in a school in Honolulu; I am no common girl. And I tell you, I shall save my lover. What is this you say about a cent? But all the world is not American. In England they have a piece they call a farthing, which is about half a cent. Ah! sorrow!" she cried, "that makes it scarcely better, for the buyer must be lost, and we shall find none so brave as my Keawe! But, then, there is France; they have a small coin there which they call a centime, and these go five to the cent or thereabout. We could not do better. Come, Keawe, let us go to the French islands; let us go to Tahiti, as fast as ships can bear us. There we have four centimes, three centimes, two centimes one centime; four possible sales to come and go on; and two of us to push the bargain. Come, my Keawe! kiss me, and banish care. Kokua will defend you."

"Gift of God!" he cried. "I cannot think that God will punish me for desiring aught so good! Be it as you will, then; take me where you please: I put my life and my salvation in your hands."

Early the next day Kokua was about her preparations. She took Keawe's chest that he went with sailoring; and first she put the bottle in a corner; and then packed it with the richest of the clothes and the bravest of the knick-knacks in the house. "For," said she, "we must seem to be rich folks, or who will believe in the bottle?" All the time of her preparation she was as gay as a bird; only when she looked upon Keawe, the tears would spring in her eye, and she must run and kiss him. As for Keawe, a weight was off his soul; now that he had his secret shared, and some hope in front of him, he seemed like a new man, his feet went lightly on the earth, and his breath was good to him again. Yet was terror still at his elbow; and ever and again, as the wind blows out a taper, hope died in him, and he saw the flames toss and the red fire burn in hell.

It was given out in the country they were gone pleasuring to the States, which was thought a strange thing, and yet not so strange as the truth, if any could have guessed it. So they went to Honolulu in the Hall, and thence in the Umatilla to San Francisco with a crowd of Haoles, and at San Francisco took their passage by the mail brigantine, the Tropic Bird for Papeete, the chief place of the French in the south islands. Thither they came, after a pleasant voyage, on a fair day of the Trade Wind, and saw the reef with the surf breaking, and Motuiti with its palms, and the schooner riding within-side, and the white houses of the town low down along the shore among green trees, and overhead the mountains and the clouds of Tahiti, the wise island.

It was judged the most wise to hire a house, which they did accordingly, opposite the British Consul's, to make a great parade of money, and themselves conspicuous with carriages and horses. This it was very easy to do, so long as they had the bottle in their possession; for Kokua was more bold than Keawe, and whenever she had a mind, called on the imp for twenty or a hundred dollars. At this rate they soon grew to be remarked in the town; and the strangers from Hawaii, their riding and their driving, the fine holokus and the rich lace of Kokua, became the matter of much talk.

They got on well after the first with the Tahitian language, which is indeed like to the Hawaiian, with a change of certain letters; and as soon as they had any freedom of speech, began to push the bottle. You are to consider it was not an easy subject to introduce; it was not easy to persuade people you were in earnest, when you offered so sell them for four centimes the spring of health and riches inexhaustible. It was necessary besides to explain the dangers of the bottle; and either people disbelieved the whole thing and laughed or they thought the more of the darker part, became overcast with gravity, and drew away from Keawe and Kokua, as from persons who had dealings with the devil. So far from gaining ground, these two began to find they were avoided in the town; the children ran away from them screaming, a thing intolerable to Kokua; Catholics crossed themselves as they went by; and all persons began with one accord to disengage themselves from their advances.

Depression fell upon their spirits. They would sit at night in their new house, after a day's weariness, and not exchange one word, or the silence would be broken by Kokua bursting suddenly into sobs. Sometimes they would pray together; sometimes they would have the bottle out upon the floor, and sit all evening watching how the shadow hovered in the midst. At such times they would be afraid to go to rest. It was long ere slumber came to them, and if either dozed off, it would be to wake and find the other silently weeping in the dark, or perhaps, to wake alone, the other having fled from the house and the neighbourhood of that bottle, to pace under the bananas in the little garden, or to wander on the beach by moonlight.

One night it was so when Kokua awoke. Keawe was gone. She felt in the bed and his place was cold. Then fear fell upon her, and she sat up in bed. A little moonshine filtered through the shutters. The room was bright, and she could spy the bottle on the floor. Outside it blew high, the great trees of the avenue cried aloud, and the fallen leaves rattled in the verandah. In the midst of this Kokua was aware of another sound; whether of a beast or of a man she could scarce tell, but it was as sad as death, and cut her to the soul. Softly she arose, set the door ajar, and looked forth in the moonlit yard. There, under the bananas, lay Keawe, his mouth in the dust, and as he lay he moaned.

It was Kokua's first thought to run forward and console him; her second potently withheld her. Keawe had borne himself before his wife like a brave man; it became her little in the hour of weakness to intrude upon his shame. With the thought she drew back into the house.

"Heavens!" she thought, "how careless have I been—how weak! It is he, not I that stands in this eternal peril; it was he, not I, that took the curse upon his soul. It is for my sake, and for the love of a creature of so little worth and such poor help, that he now beholds so close to him the flames of hell—ay, and smells the smoke of it, lying without there in the wind and moonlight. Am I so dull of spirit that never till now I have surmised my duty, or have I seen it before and turned aside? But now, at least, I take upon my soul in both the hands of my affection; now I say farewell to the white steps of heaven and the waiting faces of my friends. A love for a love, and let mine be equalled with Keawe's! A soul for a soul, and be it mine to perish!"

She was a deft woman with her hands, and was soon apparelled. She took in her hands the change—the precious centimes they kept ever at their side; for this coin is little used, and they had made provision at a Government office. When she was forth in the avenue clouds came on the wind, and the moon was blackened. The town slept, and she knew not whither to turn till she heard one coughing in the shadow of the trees.

"Old man," said Kokua, "what do you here abroad in the cold night?"

The old man could scarce express himself for coughing, but she made out that he was old and poor, and a stranger in the island.

"Will you do me a service?" said Kokua. "As one stranger to another, and as an old man to a young woman, will you help a daughter of Hawaii?"

"Ah," said the old man. "So you are the witch from the eight islands, and even my old soul you seek to entangle. But I have heard of you, and defy your wickedness."

"Sit down here," said Kokua, "and let me tell you a tale." And she told him the story of Keawe from the beginning to the end.

"And now," said she, "I am his wife, whom he bought with his soul's welfare. And what should I do? If I went to him myself and offered to buy it, he would refuse. But if you go, he will sell it eagerly; I will await you here; you will buy it for four centimes, and I will buy it again for three. And the Lord strengthen a poor girl!"

"If you meant falsely," said the old man, "I think God would strike you dead."

"He would!" cried Kokua. "Be sure he would. I could not be so treacherous—God would not suffer it."

"Give me the four centimes and await me here," said the old man.

Now, when Kokua stood alone in the street, her spirit died. The wind roared in the trees, and it seemed to her the rushing of the flames of hell; the shadows tossed in the light of the street lamp, and they seemed to her the snatching hands of evil ones. If she had had the strength, she must have run away, and if she had had the breath she must have screamed aloud; but, in truth, she could do neither, and stood trembled in the avenue, like an affrighted child.

Then she saw the old man returning, and he had the bottle in his hand.

"I have done your bidding," said he. "I left your husband weeping like a child; tonight he will sleep easy." And he held the bottle forth.

"Before you give it me," Kokua panted, "take the good with the evil—ask to be delivered from your cough."

"I am an old man," replied the other, "and too near the gate of the grave to take a favour from the devil. But what is this? Why do you not take the bottle? Do you hesitate?"

"Not hesitate!" cried Kokua. "I am only weak. Give me a moment. It is my hand resists, my flesh shrinks back from the accursed thing. One moment only!"

The old man looked upon Kokua kindly. "Poor child!" said he, "you fear; your soul misgives you. Well, let me keep it. I am old and can never more be happy in this world, and as for the next—"

"Give it me!" gasped Kokua. "There is your money. Do you think I am so base as that? Give me the bottle."

"God bless you, child," said the old man.

Kokua concealed the bottle under her holoku, said farewell to the old man, and walked off along the avenue, she cared not whither. For all roads were not the same to her, and led equally to hell. Sometimes she walked, and sometimes ran; sometimes she screamed out loud in the night, and sometimes lay by the wayside in the dust and wept. All that she had heard of hell came back to her; she saw the flames blaze, and she smelt the smoke, and her flesh withered on the coals.

Near the day she came to her mind again, and returned to the house. It was even as the old man said— Keawe slumbered like a child. Kokua stood and gazed upon his face.

"Now, my husband," said she, "it is your turn to sleep. When you wake it will be your turn to sing and laugh. But for poor Kokua, alas! that meant no evil—for poor Kokua no more sleep, no more singing, no more delight, whether in earth or heaven."

With that she lay down int he bed by his side, and her misery was so extreme that she fell in a deep slumber instantly.

Late in the morning her husband woke her and gave her the good news. It seemed he was silly with delight, for he paid no heed to her distress, ill though she dissembled it. The words stuck in her mouth, it mattered not; Keawe did the speaking. She ate not a bite, but who was to observe it? For Keawe cleared the dish. Kokua saw and heard him, like some strange thing in a dream; there were times when she forgot or doubted, and put her hands to her brow; to know herself doomed and hear her husband babble, seemed so monstrous.

All the while Keawe was eating and talking, and planning the time of their return, and thanking her for saving him, and fondling her, and calling her the true help er after all. He laughed at the old man that was fool enough to buy that bottle.

"A worthy old man he seemed," Keawe said. "But no one can judge by appearances. For why did the old reprobate require the bottle?"

"My husband," said Kokua, humbly, "his purpose may have been good."

Keawe laughed like an angry man.

"Fiddle-de-dee!" cried Keawe. "An old rogue, I tell you; and an old ass to boot. For the bottle was hard enough to sell at four centimes; and at three it will be quite impossible. The margin is not broad enough, the thing begins to smell of scorching—brrr!" said he, and shuddered. "It is true I bought it myself at a cent, when I knew not there were smaller coins. I was a fool for my pains; there will never be found another: and whoever has that bottle now will carry it to the pit."

"O my husband!" said Kokua. "It is not a terrible thing to save oneself by the eternal ruin of another? It seems to me I could not laugh. I would be humbled. I would be filled with melancholy. I would pray for the poor holder."

Then Keawe, because he felt the truth of what she said, grew the more angry. "Heighty-teighty!" cried he. "You maybe filled with melancholy if you please. It is not the mind of a good wife. If you thought at all of me, you would sit shamed."

Thereupon he went out, and Kokua was alone.

What chance had she to sell that bottle at two centimes? None, she perceived. And if she had any, here was her husband hurrying her away to a country where there was nothing lower than a cent. And here—on the morrow of her sacrifice—was her husband leaving her and blaming her.

She would not even try to profit by what time she had, but sat in the house, and now had the bottle out and viewed it with unutterable fear, and now, with loathing, hid it out of sight.

By-and-by, Keawe came back, and would have her take a drive.

"My husband, I am ill," she said. "I am out of heart. Excuse me, I can take no pleasure."

Then was Keawe more wroth than ever. With her, because he thought she was brooding over the case of the old man; and with himself, because he thought she was right, and was ashamed to be so happy.

"This is your truth," cried he, "and this your affection! Your husband is just saved from eternal ruin, which he encountered for the love of you—and you take no pleasure! Kokua, you have a disloyal heart."

He went forth again furious, and wandered in the town all day. He met friends, and drank with them; they hired a carriage and drove into the country, and there drank again. All the time Keawe was ill at ease, because he was taking this pastime while his wife was sad, and because he knew in his heart that she was more right than he; and the knowledge made him drink the deeper.

Now there was an old brutal Haole drinking with him, one that had been a boatswain of a whaler, a runaway, a digger in gold mines, a convict in prisons. He had a low mind and a foul mouth; he loved to drink and to see other drunken; and he pressed the glass upon Keawe. Soon there was no more money in the company.

"Here, you!" says the boatswain, "you are rich, you have been always saying. You have a bottle or some foolishness."

"Yes," says Keawe, "I am rich; I will go back and get some money from my wife, who keeps it."

"That's a bad idea, mate," said the boatswain. "Never you trust a petticoat with dollars. They're all as false as water; you keep an eye on her."

Now, this word struck in Keawe's mind; for he was muddled with what he had been drinking.

"I should not wonder but she was false, indeed," thought he. "Why else should she be so cast down at my release? But I will show her I am not the man to be fooled, I will catch her in the act."

Accordingly, when they were back in town, Keawe bade the boatswain wait for him at the corner, by the old calaboose, and went forward up the avenue alone to the door of his house. The night had come again; there was a light within, but never a sound; and Keawe crept about the corner, opened the back door softly, and looked in.

There was Kokua on the floor, the lamp at her side, before her was a milk-white bottle, with a round belly and a long neck; and as she viewed it, Kokua wrong her hands.

A long time Keawe stood and looked in the doorway. At first he was struck stupid; and then fear fell upon him that the bargain had been made amiss, and the bottle had come back to him as it came at San Francisco; and at that his knees were loosened, and the fumes of the wine departed from his head like mists off a river in the morning. And then he had another thought; and it was a strange one, that made his cheeks to burn.

"I must make sure of this," thought he.

So he closed the door, and went softly round the corner again, and then came noisily in, as though he were but now returned. And, lo! by the time he opened the front door no bottle was to be seen; and Kokua sat in a chair and started up like one awakened out of sleep.

"I have been drinking all day and making merry," said Keawe. "I have been with good companions, and now I only come back for money, and return to drink and carouse with them again."

Both his face and voice were as stern as judgement, but Kokua was too troubled to observe.

"You do well to use your own, my husband," said she, and her words trembled.

"O, I do well in all things," said Keawe, and he went straight to the chest and took out money. But he looked besides in the corner where they kept the bottle, and there was no bottle there.

At that the chest heaved upon the floor like a sea-billow, and the house span about him like a wreath of smoke, for he saw he was lost now, and there was no escape. "It is what I feared," he thought. "It is she who bought it."

And then he came to himself a little and rose up; but the sweat streamed on his face as thick as the rain and as cold as the well-water.

"Kokua," said he, "I said to you today what ill became me. Now I return to carouse with my jolly companions," and at that he laughed a little quietly. "I will take more pleasure in the cup if you forgive me."

She clasped his knees in a moment; she kissed his knees with flowing tears.

"O," she cried, "I asked but a kind word!"

"Let us never one think hardly of the other," said Keawe, and was gone out of the house.

Now, the money that Keawe had taken was only some of that store of centime piece they had laid in at their arrival. It was very sure he had no mind to be drinking. His wife had given her soul for him, now he must give his for hers; no other thought was in the world with him.

At the corner, by the old calaboose, there was the boatswain waiting.

"My wife has the bottle," said Keawe, "and, unless you help me to recover it, there can be no more money and no more liquor tonight."

"You do not mean to say you are serious about that bottle?" cried the boatswain.

"There is the lamp," said Keawe. "Do I look as if I was jesting?"

"That is so," said the boatswain. "You look as serious as a ghost."

"Well, then," said Keawe, "here are two centimes; you must go to my wife in the house, and offer her these for the bottle, which (if I am not much mistaken) she will give you instantly. Bring it to me here, and I will buy it back from you for one; for that is the law with this bottle, that it still must be sold for a less sum. But whatever you do, never breathe a word to her that you have come from me."

"Mate, I wonder are you making a fool of me?" asked the boatswain.

"It will do you no harm if I am," returned Keawe.

"That is so, mate," said the boatswain.

"And if you doubt me," added Keawe, "you can try. As soon as you are clear of the house, wish to have your pocket full of money, or a bottle of the best rum, or what you please, and you will see the virtue of the thing."

"Very well, Kanaka," says the boatswain. "I will try; but if you are having your fun out of me, I will take my fun out of you with a belaying pin."

So the whaler-man went off upon the avenue; and Keawe stood and waited. It was near the same spot where Kokua had waited the night before; but Keawe was more resolved, and never faltered in his purpose; only his soul was bitter with despair.

It seemed a long time he had to wait before he heard a voice singing in the darkness of the avenue. He knew the voice to be the boatswain's; but it was strange how drunken it appeared upon a sudden.

Next, the man himself came stumbling into the light of the lamp. He had the devil's bottle buttoned in his coat; another bottle was in his hand; and even as he came in view he raised it to his mouth and drank.

"You have it," said Keawe. "I see that."

"Hands off!" cried the boatswain, jumping back. "Take a step near me, and I'll smash your mouth. You thought you could make a cat's-paw of me, did you?"

"What do you mean?" cried Keawe.

"Mean?" cried the boatswain. "This is a pretty good bottle, this is; that's what I mean. How I got it for two centimes I can't make out; but I'm sure you shan't have it for one."

"You mean you won't sell?" gasped Keawe.

"No, sir!" cried the boatswain. "But I'll give you a drink of the rum, if you like."

"I tell you," said Keawe, "the man who has that bottle goes to hell."

"I reckon I'm going anyway," returned the sailor; "and this bottle's the best thing to go with I've struck yet. No, sir!" he cried again, "this is my bottle now, and you can go and fish for another."

"Can this be true?" Keawe cried. "For your own sake, I beseech you, sell it me!"

"I don't value any of your talk," replied the boatswain. "You thought I was a flat; now you see I'm not; and there's an end. If you won't have a swallow of the rum, I'll have one myself. Here's your health, and goodnight to you!"

So off he went down the avenue toward town, and there goes the bottle out of the story.

But Keawe ran to Kokua light as the wind; and great was their joy that night; and great, since then has been the peace of all their days in the Bright House.

The Body Snatcher

by Robert Louis Stevenson

Every night in the year, four of us sat in the small parlour of the George at Debenham—the undertaker, and the landlord, and Fettes, and myself. Sometimes there would be more; but blow high, blow low, come rain or snow or frost, we four would be each planted in his own particular arm-chair. Fettes was an old drunken Scotchman, a man of education obviously, and a man of some property, since he lived in idleness. He had come to Debenham years ago, while still young, and by a mere continuance of living had grown to be an adopted townsman. His blue camlet cloak was a local antiquity, like the church-spire. His place in the parlour at the George, his absence from church, his old, crapulous, disreputable vices, were all things of course in Debenham. He had some vague Radical opinions and some fleeting infidelities, which he would now and again set forth and emphasise with tottering slaps upon the table. He drank rum—five glasses regularly every evening; and for the greater portion of his nightly visit to the George sat, with his glass in his right hand, in a state of melancholy alcoholic saturation. We called him the Doctor, for he was supposed to have some special knowledge of medicine, and had been known, upon a pinch, to set a fracture or reduce a dislocation; but beyond these slight particulars, we had no knowledge of his character and antecedents.

One dark winter night—it had struck nine some time before the landlord joined us—there was a sick man in the George, a great neighbouring proprietor suddenly struck down with apoplexy on his way to Parliament; and the great man's still greater London doctor had been telegraphed to his bedside. It was the first time that such a thing had happened in Debenham, for the railway was but newly open, and we were all proportionately moved by the occurrence.

"He's come," said the landlord, after he had filled and lighted his pipe.

"He?' said I. "Who?—not the doctor?"

"Himself," replied our host.

"What is his name?"

"Doctor Macfarlane," said the landlord.

Fettes was far through his third tumbler, stupidly fuddled, now nodding over, now staring mazily around him; but at the last word he seemed to awaken, and repeated the name 'Macfarlane' twice, quietly enough the first time, but with sudden emotion at the second.

"Yes," said the landlord, "that's his name, Doctor Wolfe Macfarlane."

Fettes became instantly sober; his eyes awoke, his voice became clear, loud, and steady, his language forcible and earnest. We were all startled by the transformation, as if a man had risen from the dead.

"I beg your pardon," he said, "I am afraid I have not been paying much attention to your talk. Who is this Wolfe Macfarlane?" And then, when he had heard the landlord out, "It cannot be, it cannot be," he added; "and yet I would like well to see him face to face."

"Do you know him, Doctor?" asked the undertaker, with a gasp.

"God forbid!" was the reply. "And yet the name is a strange one; it were too much to fancy two. Tell me, landlord, is he old?"

"Well," said the host, 'he's not a young man, to be sure, and his hair is white; but he looks younger than you."

"He is older, though; years older. But," with a slap upon the table, "it's the rum you see in my face—rum and sin. This man, perhaps, may have an easy conscience and a good digestion. Conscience! Hear me speak. You would think I was some good, old, decent Christian, would you not? But no, not I; I never canted. Voltaire might have canted if he'd stood in my shoes; but the brains"—with a rattling fillip on his bald head—'the brains were clear and active, and I saw and made no deductions."

"If you know this doctor," I ventured to remark, after a somewhat awful pause, "I should gather that you do not share the landlord's good opinion."

Fettes paid no regard to me.

"Yes," he said, with sudden decision, "I must see him face to face."

There was another pause, and then a door was closed rather sharply on the first floor, and a step was heard upon the stair.

"That's the doctor," cried the landlord. "Look sharp, and you can catch him."

It was but two steps from the small parlour to the door of the old George Inn; the wide oak staircase landed almost in the street; there was room for a Turkey rug and nothing more between the threshold and the last round of the descent; but this little space was every evening brilliantly lit up, not only by the light upon the stair and the great signal-lamp below the sign, but by the warm radiance of the bar-room window. The George thus brightly advertised itself to passers-by in the cold street. Fettes walked steadily to the spot, and we, who were hanging behind, beheld the two men meet, as one of them had phrased it, face to face. Dr. Macfarlane was alert and vigorous. His white hair set off his pale and placid, although energetic, countenance. He was richly dressed in the finest of broadcloth and the whitest of linen, with a great gold watch-chain, and studs and spectacles of the same precious material. He wore a broad—folded tie, white and speckled with lilac, and he carried on his arm a comfortable driving-coat of fur. There was no doubt but he became his years, breathing, as he did, of wealth and consideration; and it was a surprising contrast to see our parlour sot—bald, dirty, pimpled, and robed in his old camlet cloak—confront him at the bottom of the stairs.

"Macfarlane!" he said somewhat loudly, more like a herald than a friend.

The great doctor pulled up short on the fourth step, as though the familiarity of the address surprised and somewhat shocked his dignity.

"Toddy Macfarlane!" repeated Fettes.

The London man almost staggered. He stared for the swiftest of seconds at the man before him, glanced behind him with a sort of scare, and then in a startled whisper, "Fettes!" he said, "You!"

"Ay," said the other, "me! Did you think I was dead too? We are not so easy shut of our acquaintance."

"Hush, hush!" exclaimed the doctor. "Hush, hush! this meeting is so unexpected—I can see you are unmanned. I hardly knew you, I confess, at first; but I am overjoyed—overjoyed to have this opportunity. For the present it must be how-d'ye-do and good-bye in one, for my fly is waiting, and I must not fail the train; but you shall—let me see—yes—you shall give me your address, and you can count on early news of me. We must do something for you, Fettes. I fear you are out at elbows; but we must see to that for auld lang syne, as once we sang at suppers."

"Money!" cried Fettes; "money from you! The money that I had from you is lying where I cast it in the rain."

Dr. Macfarlane had talked himself into some measure of superiority and confidence, but the uncommon energy of this refusal cast him back into his first confusion.

A horrible, ugly look came and went across his almost venerable countenance. "My dear fellow," he said, "be it as you please; my last thought is to offend you. I would intrude on none. I will leave you my address, however—"

"I do not wish it—I do not wish to know the roof that shelters you," interrupted the other. "I heard your name; I feared it might be you; I wished to know if, after all, there were a God; I know now that there is none. Begone!"

He still stood in the middle of the rug, between the stair and doorway; and the great London physician, in order to escape, would be forced to step to one side. It was plain that he hesitated before the thought of this humiliation. White as he was, there was a dangerous glitter in his spectacles; but while he still paused uncertain, he became aware that the driver of his fly was peering in from the street at this unusual scene and caught a glimpse at the same time of our little body from the parlour, huddled by the corner of the bar. The presence of so many witnesses decided him at once to flee. He crouched together, brushing on the wainscot, and made a dart like a serpent, striking for the door. But his tribulation was not yet entirely at an end, for even as he was passing Fettes clutched him by the arm and these words came in a whisper, and yet painfully distinct, "Have you seen it again?"

The great rich London doctor cried out aloud with a sharp, throttling cry; he dashed his questioner across the open space, and, with his hands over his head, fled out of the door like a detected thief. Before it had occurred to one of us to make a movement the fly was already rattling toward the station. The scene was over like a dream, but the dream had left proofs and traces of its passage. Next day the servant found the fine gold spectacles broken on the threshold, and that very night we were all standing breathless by the bar—room window, and Fettes at our side, sober, pale, and resolute in look.

"God protect us, Mr Fettes!" said the landlord, coming first into possession of his customary senses. 'What in the universe is all this? These are strange things you have been saying."

Fettes turned toward us; he looked us each in succession in the face. "See if you can hold your tongues," said he. "That man Macfarlane is not safe to cross; those that have done so already have repented it too late."

And then, without so much as finishing his third glass, far less waiting for the other two, he bade us good-bye and went forth, under the lamp of the hotel, into the black night.

We three turned to our places in the parlour, with the big red fire and four clear candles; and as we recapitulated what had passed, the first chill of our surprise soon changed into a glow of curiosity. We sat late; it was the latest session I have known in the old George. Each man, before we parted, had his theory that he was bound to prove; and none of us had any nearer business in this world than to track out the past of our condemned companion, and surprise the secret that he shared with the great London doctor. It is no great boast, but I believe I was a better hand at worming out a story than either of my fellows at the George; and perhaps there is now no other man alive who could narrate to you the following foul and unnatural events.

In his young days Fettes studied medicine in the schools of Edinburgh. He had talent of a kind, the talent that picks up swiftly what it hears and readily retails it for its own. He worked little at home; but he was civil, attentive, and intelligent in the presence of his masters. They soon picked him out as a lad who listened closely and remembered well; nay, strange as it seemed to me when I first heard it, he was in those days well favoured, and pleased by his exterior. There was, at that period, a certain extramural teacher of anatomy, whom I shall here designate by the letter K. His name was subsequently too well known. The man who bore it skulked through the streets of Edinburgh in disguise, while the mob that applauded at the execution of Burke called loudly for the blood of his employer. But Mr K— was then at the top of his vogue; he enjoyed a popularity due partly to his own talent and address, partly to the incapacity of his rival, the university professor. The students, at least, swore by his name, and Fettes believed himself, and was believed by others, to have laid the foundations of success when he had acquired the favour of this meteorically famous man. Mr K— was a *bon vivant* as well as an accomplished teacher; he liked a sly illusion no less than a careful preparation. In both capacities Fettes enjoyed and deserved his notice, and by the second year of his attendance he held the half-regular position of second demonstrator or sub—assistant in his class.

In this capacity the charge of the theatre and lecture-room devolved in particular upon his shoulders. He had to answer for the cleanliness of the premises and the conduct of the other students, and it was a part of his duty to supply, receive, and divide the various subjects. It was with a view to this last—at that time very delicate—affair that he was lodged by Mr K— in the same wynd, and at last in the same building, with the dissecting-rooms. Here, after a night of turbulent pleasures, his hand still tottering, his sight still misty and confused, he would be called out of bed in the black hours before the winter dawn by the unclean and desperate interlopers who supplied the table. He would open the door to these men, since infamous throughout the land. He would help them with their tragic burden, pay them their sordid price, and remain alone, when they were gone, with the unfriendly relics of humanity. From such a scene he would return to snatch another hour or two of slumber, to repair the abuses of the night, and refresh himself for the labours of the day.

Few lads could have been more insensible to the impressions of a life thus passed among the ensigns of mortality. His mind was closed against all general considerations. He was incapable of interest in the fate and fortunes of another, the slave of his own desires and low ambitions. Cold, light, and selfish in the last resort, he had that modicum of prudence, miscalled morality, which keeps a man from inconvenient drunkenness or punishable theft. He coveted, besides, a measure of consideration from his masters and his fellow-pupils, and he had no desire to fail conspicuously in the external parts of life. Thus he made it his pleasure to gain some distinction in his studies, and day after day rendered unimpeachable eye-service to his employer, Mr K—. For his day of work he indemnified himself by nights of roaring, blackguardly enjoyment; and when that balance had been struck, the organ that he called his conscience declared itself content.

The supply of subjects was a continual trouble to him as well as to his master. In that large and busy class, the raw material of the anatomists kept perpetually running out; and the business thus rendered necessary was not only unpleasant in itself, but threatened dangerous consequences to all who were concerned. It was the policy of Mr K— to ask no questions in his dealings with the trade. "They bring the body, and we pay the price," he used to say, dwelling on the alliteration—'*quid pro quo*.' And, again, and somewhat profanely, "Ask no questions," he would tell his assistants, "for conscience' sake." There was no understanding that the subjects were provided by the crime of murder. Had that idea been broached to him in words, he would have recoiled in horror; but the lightness of his speech upon so grave a matter was, in itself, an offence against good manners, and a temptation to the men with whom he dealt. Fettes, for instance, had often remarked to himself upon the singular freshness of the bodies. He had been struck again and again by the hang-dog, abominable looks of the ruffians who came to him before the dawn;

and putting things together clearly in his private thoughts, he perhaps attributed a meaning too immoral and too categorical to the unguarded counsels of his master. He understood his duty, in short, to have three branches: to take what was brought, to pay the price, and to avert the eye from any evidence of crime.

One November morning this policy of silence was put sharply to the test. He had been awake all night with a racking toothache—pacing his room like a caged beast or throwing himself in fury on his bed—and had fallen at last into that profound, uneasy slumber that so often follows on a night of pain, when he was awakened by the third or fourth angry repetition of the concerted signal. There was a thin, bright moonshine; it was bitter cold, windy, and frosty; the town had not yet awakened, but an indefinable stir already preluded the noise and business of the day. The ghouls had come later than usual, and they seemed more than usually eager to be gone. Fettes, sick with sleep, lighted them upstairs. He heard their grumbling Irish voices through a dream; and as they stripped the sack from their sad merchandise he leaned dozing, with his shoulder propped against the wall; he had to shake himself to find the men their money. As he did so his eyes lighted on the dead face. He started; he took two steps nearer, with the candle raised.

"God Almighty!" he cried. "That is Jane Galbraith!"

The men answered nothing, but they shuffled nearer the door.

"I know her, I tell you," he continued. "She was alive and hearty yesterday. It's impossible she can be dead; it's impossible you should have got this body fairly."

"Sure, sir, you're mistaken entirely," said one of the men.

But the other looked Fettes darkly in the eyes, and demanded the money on the spot.

It was impossible to misconceive the threat or to exaggerate the danger. The lad's heart failed him. He stammered some excuses, counted out the sum, and saw his hateful visitors depart. No sooner were they gone than he hastened to confirm his doubts. By a dozen unquestionable marks he identified the girl he had jested with the day before. He saw, with horror, marks upon her body that might well betoken violence. A panic seized him, and he took refuge in his room. There he reflected at length over the discovery that he had made; considered soberly the bearing of Mr K-'s instructions and the danger to himself of interference in so serious a business, and at last, in sore perplexity, determined to wait for the advice of his immediate superior, the class assistant.

This was a young doctor, Wolfe Macfarlane, a high favourite among all the reckless students, clever, dissipated, and unscrupulous to the last degree. He had travelled and studied abroad. His manners were agreeable and a little forward. He was an authority on the stage, skilful on the ice or the links with skate or golf-club; he dressed with nice audacity, and, to put the finishing touch upon his glory, he kept a gig and a strong trotting-horse. With Fettes he was on terms of intimacy; indeed, their relative positions called for some community of life; and when subjects were scarce the pair would drive far into the country in Macfarlane's gig, visit and desecrate some lonely graveyard, and return before dawn with their booty to the door of the dissecting-room.

On that particular morning Macfarlane arrived somewhat earlier than his wont. Fettes heard him, and met him on the stairs, told him his story, and showed him the cause of his alarm. Macfarlane examined the marks on her body.

"Yes," he said with a nod, "it looks fishy."

"Well, what should I do?" asked Fettes.

"Do?" repeated the other. "Do you want to do anything? Least said soonest mended, I should say."

"Some one else might recognise her," objected Fettes. "She was as well known as the Castle Rock."

"We'll hope not," said Macfarlane, "and if anybody does—well, you didn't, don't you see, and there's an end. The fact is, this has been going on too long. Stir up the mud, and you'll get K— into the most unholy trouble; you'll be in a shocking box yourself. So will I, if you come to that. I should like to know how any one of us would look, or what the devil we should have to say for ourselves, in any Christian witness-box. For me, you know there's one thing certain—that, practically speaking, all our subjects have been murdered."

"Macfarlane!" cried Fettes.

"Come now!" sneered the other. "As if you hadn't suspected it yourself!"

"Suspecting is one thing—"

"And proof another. Yes, I know; and I'm as sorry as you are this should have come here," tapping the body with his cane. "The next best thing for me is not to recognise it; and," he added coolly, "I don't. You may, if you please. I don't dictate, but I think a man of the world would do as I do; and I may add, I fancy that is what K— would look for at our hands. The question is, Why did he choose us two for his assistants? And I answer, because he didn't want old wives."

This was the tone of all others to affect the mind of a lad like Fettes. He agreed to imitate Macfarlane. The body of the unfortunate girl was duly dissected, and no one remarked or appeared to recognise her.

One afternoon, when his day's work was over, Fettes dropped into a popular tavern and found Macfarlane sitting with a stranger. This was a small man, very pale and dark, with coal-black eyes. The cut of his features gave a promise of intellect and refinement which was but feebly realised in his manners, for he proved, upon a nearer acquaintance, coarse, vulgar, and stupid. He exercised, however, a very remarkable control over Macfarlane; issued orders like the Great Bashaw; became inflamed at the least discussion or delay, and commented rudely on the servility with which he was obeyed. This most offensive person took a fancy to Fettes on the spot, plied him with drinks, and honoured him with unusual confidences on his past career. If a tenth part of what he confessed were true, he was a very loathsome rogue; and the lad's vanity was tickled by the attention of so experienced a man.

"I'm a pretty bad fellow myself," the stranger remarked, "but Macfarlane is the boy—Toddy Macfarlane I call him. "Toddy, order your friend another glass." Or it might be, "Toddy, you jump up and shut the door." "Toddy hates me," he said again. "Oh yes, Toddy, you do!"

"Don't you call me that confounded name," growled Macfarlane.

"Hear him! Did you ever see the lads play knife? He would like to do that all over my body," remarked the stranger.

"We medicals have a better way than that," said Fettes. "When we dislike a dead friend of ours, we dissect him."

Macfarlane looked up sharply, as though this jest were scarcely to his mind.

The afternoon passed. Gray, for that was the stranger's name, invited Fettes to join them at dinner, ordered a feast so sumptuous that the tavern was thrown into commotion, and when all was done commanded Macfarlane to settle the bill. It was late before they separated; the man Gray was incapably drunk. Macfarlane, sobered by his fury, chewed the cud of the money he had been forced to squander and the slights he had been obliged to swallow. Fettes, with various liquors singing in his head, returned home with devious footsteps and a mind entirely in abeyance. Next day Macfarlane was absent from the class, and Fettes smiled to himself as he imagined him still squiring the intolerable Gray from tavern to tavern. As soon as the hour of liberty had struck he posted from place to place in quest of his last night's companions. He could find them, however, nowhere; so returned early to his rooms, went early to bed, and slept the sleep of the just.

At four in the morning he was awakened by the well-known signal. Descending to the door, he was filled with astonishment to find Macfarlane with his gig, and in the gig one of those long and ghastly packages with which he was so well acquainted.

"What?" he cried. "Have you been out alone? How did you manage?"

But Macfarlane silenced him roughly, bidding him turn to business. When they had got the body upstairs and laid it on the table, Macfarlane made at first as if he were going away. Then he paused and seemed to hesitate; and then, "You had better look at the face," said he, in tones of some constraint. "You had better," he repeated, as Fettes only stared at him in wonder.

"But where, and how, and when did you come by it?" cried the other.

"Look at the face," was the only answer.

Fettes was staggered; strange doubts assailed him. He looked from the young doctor to the body, and then back again. At last, with a start, he did as he was bidden. He had almost expected the sight that met his eyes, and yet the shock was cruel. To see, fixed in the rigidity of death and naked on that coarse layer of sackcloth, the man whom he had left well clad and full of meat and sin upon the threshold of a tavern, awoke, even in the thoughtless Fettes, some of the terrors of the conscience. It was a *cras tibi* which re-echoed in his soul, that two whom he had known should have come to lie upon these icy tables. Yet these were only secondary thoughts. His first concern regarded Wolfe. Unprepared for a challenge so momentous, he knew not how to look his comrade in the face. He durst not meet his eye, and he had neither words nor voice at his command.

It was Macfarlane himself who made the first advance. He came up quietly behind and laid his hand gently but firmly on the other's shoulder.

"Richardson," said he, "may have the head."

Now Richardson was a student who had long been anxious for that portion of the human subject to dissect. There was no answer, and the murderer resumed: "Talking of business, you must pay me; your accounts, you see, must tally."

Fettes found a voice, the ghost of his own: "Pay you!" he cried. "Pay you for that?"

"Why, yes, of course you must. By all means and on every possible account, you must," returned the other. "I dare not give it for nothing, you dare not take it for nothing; it would compromise us both. This is another case like Jane Galbraith's. The more things are wrong the more we must act as if all were right. Where does old K— keep his money?"

"There," answered Fettes hoarsely, pointing to a cupboard in the corner.

"Give me the key, then," said the other, calmly, holding out his hand.

There was an instant's hesitation, and the die was cast. Macfarlane could not suppress a nervous twitch, the infinitesimal mark of an immense relief, as he felt the key between his fingers. He opened the cupboard, brought out pen and ink and a paper-book that stood in one compartment, and separated from the funds in a drawer a sum suitable to the occasion.

"Now, look here," he said, "there is the payment made—first proof of your good faith: first step to your security. You have now to clinch it by a second. Enter the payment in your book, and then you for your part may defy the devil."

The next few seconds were for Fettes an agony of thought; but in balancing his terrors it was the most immediate that triumphed. Any future difficulty seemed almost welcome if he could avoid a present quarrel with Macfarlane. He set down the candle which he had been carrying all this time, and with a steady hand entered the date, the nature, and the amount of the transaction.

"And now," said Macfarlane, "it's only fair that you should pocket the lucre. I've had my share already. By the bye, when a man of the world falls into a bit of luck, has a few shillings extra in his pocket—I'm ashamed to speak of it, but there's a rule of conduct in the case. No treating, no purchase of expensive class-books, no squaring of old debts; borrow, don't lend."

"Macfarlane," began Fettes, still somewhat hoarsely, "I have put my neck in a halter to oblige you."

"To oblige me?" cried Wolfe. "Oh, come! You did, as near as I can see the matter, what you downright had to do in self-defence. Suppose I got into trouble, where would you be? This second little matter flows clearly from the first. Mr Gray is the continuation of Miss Galbraith. You can't begin and then stop. If you begin, you must keep on beginning; that's the truth. No rest for the wicked."

A horrible sense of blackness and the treachery of fate seized hold upon the soul of the unhappy student.

"My God!" he cried, "but what have I done? and when did I begin? To be made a class assistant—in the name of reason, where's the harm in that? Service wanted the position; Service might have got it. Would *he* have been where I am now?"

"My dear fellow," said Macfarlane, "what a boy you are! What harm *has* come to you? What harm *can* come to you if you hold your tongue? Why, man, do you know what this life is? There are two squads of us—the lions and the lambs. If you're a lamb, you'll come to lie upon these tables like Gray or Jane Galbraith; if you're a lion, you'll live and drive a horse like me, like K—, like all the world with any wit or courage. You're staggered at the first. But look at K—! My dear fellow, you're clever, you have pluck. I like you, and K— likes you. You were born to lead the hunt; and I tell you, on my honour and my experience of life, three days from now you'll laugh at all these scarecrows like a High School boy at a farce."

And with that Macfarlane took his departure and drove off up the wynd in his gig to get under cover before daylight. Fettes was thus left alone with his regrets. He saw the miserable peril in which he stood involved. He saw, with inexpressible dismay, that there was no limit to his weakness, and that, from concession to concession, he had fallen from the arbiter of Macfarlane's destiny to his paid and helpless accomplice. He would have given the world to have been a little braver at the time, but it did not occur to him that he might still be brave. The secret of Jane Galbraith and the cursed entry in the day-book closed his mouth.

Hours passed; the class began to arrive; the members of the unhappy Gray were dealt out to one and to another, and received without remark. Richardson was made happy with the head; and before the hour of freedom rang Fettes trembled with exultation to perceive how far they had already gone toward safety.

For two days he continued to watch, with increasing joy, the dreadful process of disguise.

On the third day Macfarlane made his appearance. He had been ill, he said; but he made up for lost time by the energy with which he directed the students. To Richardson in particular he extended the most valuable assistance and advice, and that student, encouraged by the praise of the demonstrator, burned high with ambitious hopes, and saw the medal already in his grasp.

Before the week was out Macfarlane's prophecy had been fulfilled. Fettes had outlived his terrors and had forgotten his baseness. He began to plume himself upon his courage, and had so arranged the story in his mind that he could look back on these events with an unhealthy pride. Of his accomplice he saw but little. They met, of course, in the business of the class; they received their orders together from Mr K—. At times they had a word or two in private, and Macfarlane was from first to last particularly kind and jovial. But it was plain that he avoided any reference to their common secret; and even when Fettes whispered to him that he had cast in his lot with the lions and foresworn the lambs, he only signed to him smilingly to hold his peace.

At length an occasion arose which threw the pair once more into a closer union. Mr K— was again short of subjects; pupils were eager, and it was a part of this teacher's pretensions to be always well supplied. At the same time there came the news of a burial in the rustic graveyard of Glencorse. Time has little changed the place in question. It stood then, as now, upon a cross road, out of call of human habitations, and buried fathom deep in the foliage of six cedar trees. The cries of the sheep upon the neighbouring hills, the streamlets upon either hand, one loudly singing among pebbles, the other dripping furtively from pond to pond, the stir of the wind in mountainous old flowering chestnuts, and once in seven days the voice of the bell and the old tunes of the precentor, were the only sounds that disturbed the silence around the rural church. The Resurrection Man—to use a byname of the period—was not to be deterred by any of the sanctities of customary piety. It was part of his trade to despise and desecrate the scrolls and trumpets of old tombs, the paths worn by the feet of worshippers and mourners, and the offerings and the inscriptions of bereaved affection. To rustic neighbourhoods, where love is more than commonly tenacious, and where some bonds of blood or fellowship unite the entire society of a parish, the body-snatcher, far from being repelled by natural respect, was attracted by the ease and safety of the task. To bodies that had been laid in earth, in joyful expectation of a far different awakening, there came that hasty, lamp-lit, terror-haunted resurrection of the spade and mattock. The coffin was forced, the cerements torn, and the melancholy relics, clad in sackcloth, after being rattled for hours on moonless byways, were at length exposed to uttermost indignities before a class of gaping boys.

Somewhat as two vultures may swoop upon a dying lamb, Fettes and Macfarlane were to be let loose upon a grave in that green and quiet resting-place. The wife of a farmer, a woman who had lived for sixty years, and been known for nothing but good butter and a godly conversation, was to be rooted from her grave at midnight and carried, dead and naked, to that far-away city that she had always honoured with her Sunday's best; the place beside her family was to be empty till the crack of doom; her innocent and almost venerable members to be exposed to that last curiosity of the anatomist.

Late one afternoon the pair set forth, well wrapped in cloaks and furnished with a formidable bottle. It rained without remission—a cold, dense, lashing rain. Now and again there blew a puff of wind, but these sheets of falling water kept it down. Bottle and all, it was a sad and silent drive as far as Penicuik, where they were to spend the evening. They stopped once, to hide their implements in a thick bush not far from the churchyard, and once again at the Fisher's Tryst, to have a toast before the kitchen fire and vary their nips of whisky with a glass of ale. When they reached their journey's end the gig was housed, the horse was fed and comforted, and the two young doctors in a private room sat down to the best dinner and the best wine the house afforded. The lights, the fire, the beating rain upon the window, the cold, incongruous work that lay before them, added zest to their enjoyment of the meal. With every glass their cordiality increased. Soon Macfarlane handed a little pile of gold to his companion.

"A compliment," he said. "Between friends these little d—d accommodations ought to fly like pipe-lights."

Fettes pocketed the money, and applauded the sentiment to the echo. "You are a philosopher," he cried. "I was an ass till I knew you. You and K— between you, by the Lord Harry! but you'll make a man of me."

"Of course we shall," applauded Macfarlane. "A man? I tell you, it required a man to back me up the other morning. There are some big, brawling, forty-year-old cowards who would have turned sick at the look of the d-d thing; but not you—you kept your head. I watched you."

"Well, and why not?" Fettes thus vaunted himself. "It was no affair of mine. There was nothing to gain on the one side but disturbance, and on the other I could count on your gratitude, don't you see?" And he slapped his pocket till the gold pieces rang.

Macfarlane somehow felt a certain touch of alarm at these unpleasant words. He may have regretted that he had taught his young companion so successfully, but he had no time to interfere, for the other noisily continued in this boastful strain:—

"The great thing is not to be afraid. Now, between you and me, I don't want to hang—that's practical; but for all cant, Macfarlane, I was born with a contempt. Hell, God, Devil, right, wrong, sin, crime, and all the old gallery of curiosities—they may frighten boys, but men of the world, like you and me, despise them. Here's to the memory of Gray!"

It was by this time growing somewhat late. The gig, according to order, was brought round to the door with both lamps brightly shining, and the young men had to pay their bill and take the road. They announced that they were bound for Peebles, and drove in that direction till they were clear of the last houses of the town; then, extinguishing the lamps, returned upon their course, and followed a by-road toward Glencorse. There was no sound but that of their own passage, and the incessant, strident pouring of the rain. It was pitch dark; here and there a white gate or a white stone in the wall guided them for a short space across the night; but for the most part it was at a foot pace, and almost groping, that they picked their way through that resonant blackness to their solemn and isolated destination. In the sunken woods that traverse the neighbourhood of the burying—ground the last glimmer failed them, and it became necessary to kindle a match and re-illumine one of the lanterns of the gig. Thus, under the dripping trees, and environed by huge and moving shadows, they reached the scene of their unhallowed labours.

They were both experienced in such affairs, and powerful with the spade; and they had scarce been twenty minutes at their task before they were rewarded by a dull rattle on the coffin lid. At the same moment Macfarlane, having hurt his hand upon a stone, flung it carelessly above his head. The grave, in which they now stood almost to the shoulders, was close to the edge of the plateau of the graveyard; and the gig lamp had been propped, the better to illuminate their labours, against a tree, and on the immediate verge of the steep bank descending to the stream. Chance had taken a sure aim with the stone. Then came a clang of broken glass; night fell upon them; sounds alternately dull and ringing announced the bounding of the lantern down the bank, and its occasional collision with the trees. A stone or two, which it had dislodged in its descent, rattled behind it into the profundities of the glen; and then silence, like night, resumed its sway; and they might bend their hearing to its utmost pitch, but naught was to be heard except the rain, now marching to the wind, now steadily falling over miles of open country.

They were so nearly at an end of their abhorred task that they judged it wisest to complete it in the dark. The coffin was exhumed and broken open; the body inserted in the dripping sack and carried between them to the gig; one mounted to keep it in its place, and the other, taking the horse by the mouth, groped along by wall and bush until they reached the wider road by the Fisher's Tryst. Here was a faint, diffused radiancy, which they hailed like daylight; by that they pushed the horse to a good pace and began to rattle along merrily in the direction of the town.

They had both been wetted to the skin during their operations, and now, as the gig jumped among the deep ruts, the thing that stood propped between them fell now upon one and now upon the other. At every repetition of the horrid contact each instinctively repelled it with the greater haste; and the process, natural although it was, began to tell upon the nerves of the companions. Macfarlane made some ill-favoured jest about the farmer's wife, but it came hollowly from his lips, and was allowed to drop in silence. Still their unnatural burden bumped from side to side; and now the head would be laid, as if in confidence, upon their shoulders, and now the drenching sack-cloth would flap icily about their faces. A creeping chill began to possess the soul of Fettes. He peered at the bundle, and it seemed somehow larger than at first. All over the country-side, and from every degree of distance, the farm dogs accompanied their passage with tragic ululations; and it grew and grew upon his mind that some unnatural miracle had been accomplished, that some nameless change had befallen the dead body, and that it was in fear of their unholy burden that the dogs were howling.

"For God's sake," said he, making a great effort to arrive at speech, "for God's sake, let's have a light!"

Seemingly Macfarlane was affected in the same direction; for, though he made no reply, he stopped the horse, passed the reins to his companion, got down, and proceeded to kindle the remaining lamp. They had by that time got no farther than the cross-road down to Auchenclinny. The rain still poured as though the deluge were returning, and it was no easy matter to make a light in such a world of wet and darkness. When at last the flickering blue flame had been transferred to the wick and began to expand and clarify, and shed a wide circle of misty brightness round the gig, it became possible for the two young men to see each other and the thing they had along with them. The rain had moulded the rough sacking to the outlines of the body underneath; the head was distinct from the trunk, the shoulders plainly modelled; something at once spectral and human riveted their eyes upon the ghastly comrade of their drive.

For some time Macfarlane stood motionless, holding up the lamp. A nameless dread was swathed, like a wet sheet, about the body, and tightened the white skin upon the face of Fettes; a fear that was meaningless, a horror of what could not be, kept mounting to his brain. Another beat of the watch, and he had spoken. But his comrade forestalled him.

"That is not a woman," said Macfarlane, in a hushed voice.

"It was a woman when we put her in," whispered Fettes.

"Hold that lamp," said the other. "I must see her face."

And as Fettes took the lamp his companion untied the fastenings of the sack and drew down the cover from the head. The light fell very clear upon the dark, well-moulded features and smooth-shaven cheeks of a too familiar countenance, often beheld in dreams of both of these young men. A wild yell rang up into the night; each leaped from his own side into the roadway: the lamp fell, broke, and was extinguished; and the horse, terrified by this unusual commotion, bounded and went off toward Edinburgh at a gallop, bearing along with it, sole occupant of the gig, the body of the dead and long-dissected Gray.

An Occurrence at Owl Creek Bridge

by Ambrose Bierce

I.

A man stood upon a railroad bridge in northern Alabama, looking down into the swift water twenty feet below. The man's hands were behind his back, the wrists bound with a cord. A rope closely encircled his neck. It was attached to a stout cross-timber above his head and the slack fell to the level of his knees. Some loose boards laid upon the ties supporting the rails of the railway supplied a footing for him and his executioners—two private soldiers of the Federal army, directed by a sergeant who in civil life may have been a deputy sheriff. At a short remove upon the same temporary platform was an officer in the uniform of his rank, armed. He was a captain. A sentinel at each end of the bridge stood with his rifle in the position known as 'support,' that is to say, vertical in front of the left shoulder, the hammer resting on the forearm thrown straight across the chest—a formal and unnatural position, enforcing an erect carriage of the body. It did not appear to be the duty of these two men to know what was occurring at the center of the bridge; they merely blockaded the two ends of the foot planking that traversed it.

Beyond one of the sentinels nobody was in sight; the railroad ran straight away into a forest for a hundred yards, then, curving, was lost to view. Doubtless there was an outpost farther along. The other bank of the stream was open ground—a gentle slope topped with a stockade of vertical tree trunks, loopholed for rifles, with a single embrasure through which protruded the muzzle of a brass cannon commanding the bridge. Midway up the slope between the bridge and fort were the spectators—a single company of infantry in line, at 'parade rest,' the butts of their rifles on the ground, the barrels inclining slightly backward against the right shoulder, the hands crossed upon the stock. A lieutenant stood at the right of the line, the point of his sword upon the ground, his left hand resting upon his right. Excepting the group of four at the center of the bridge, not a man moved. The company faced the bridge, staring stonily, motionless. The sentinels, facing the banks of the stream, might have been statues to adorn the bridge. The captain stood with folded arms, silent, observing the work of his subordinates, but making no sign. Death is a dignitary who when he comes announced is to be received with formal manifestations of respect, even by those most familiar with him. In the code of military etiquette silence and fixity are forms of deference.

The man who was engaged in being hanged was apparently about thirty-five years of age. He was a civilian, if one might judge from his habit, which was that of a planter. His features were good—a straight nose, firm mouth, broad forehead, from which his long, dark hair was combed straight back, falling behind his ears to the collar of his well fitting frock coat. He wore a moustache and pointed beard, but no whiskers; his eyes were large and dark gray, and had a kindly expression which one would hardly have expected in one whose neck was in the hemp. Evidently this was no vulgar assassin. The liberal military code makes provision for hanging many kinds of persons, and gentlemen are not excluded.

The preparations being complete, the two private soldiers stepped aside and each drew away the plank upon which he had been standing. The sergeant turned to the captain, saluted and placed himself immediately behind that officer, who in turn moved apart one pace. These movements left the condemned man and the sergeant standing on the two ends of the same plank, which spanned three of the cross-ties of the bridge. The end upon which the civilian stood almost, but not quite, reached a fourth. This plank had been held in place by the weight of the captain; it was now held by that of the sergeant. At a signal from the former the latter would step aside, the plank would tilt and the condemned man go down between two ties. The arrangement commended itself to his judgement as simple and effective. His face had not been covered nor his eyes bandaged. He looked a moment at his 'unsteadfast footing,' then let his gaze wander to the swirling water of the stream racing madly beneath his feet. A piece of dancing driftwood caught his attention and his eyes followed it down the current. How slowly it appeared to move! What a sluggish stream!

He closed his eyes in order to fix his last thoughts upon his wife and children. The water, touched to gold by the early sun, the brooding mists under the banks at some distance down the stream, the fort, the soldiers, the piece of drift—all had distracted him. And now he became conscious of a new disturbance. Striking through the thought of his dear ones was sound which he could neither ignore nor understand, a sharp, distinct, metallic percussion like the stroke of a blacksmith's hammer upon the anvil; it had the same ringing quality. He wondered what it was, and whether immeasurably distant or near by—it seemed both. Its recurrence was regular, but as slow as the tolling of a death knell. He awaited each new stroke with impatience and—he knew not why—apprehension. The intervals of silence grew progressively longer; the delays became maddening. With their greater infrequency the sounds increased in strength and sharpness. They hurt his ear like the thrust of a knife; he feared he would shriek. What he heard was the ticking of his watch.

He unclosed his eyes and saw again the water below him. "If I could free my hands," he thought, "I might throw off the noose and spring into the stream. By diving I could evade the bullets and, swimming vigorously, reach the bank, take to the woods and get away home. My home, thank God, is as yet outside their lines; my wife and little ones are still beyond the invader's farthest advance."

As these thoughts, which have here to be set down in words, were flashed into the doomed man's brain rather than evolved from it the captain nodded to the sergeant. The sergeant stepped aside.

II.

Peyton Farquhar was a well to do planter, of an old and highly respected Alabama family. Being a slave owner and like other slave owners a politician, he was naturally an original secessionist and ardently devoted to the Southern cause. Circumstances of an imperious nature, which it is unnecessary to relate here, had prevented him from taking service with that gallant army which had fought the disastrous campaigns ending with the fall of Corinth, and he chafed under the inglorious restraint, longing for the release of his energies, the larger life of the soldier, the opportunity for distinction. That opportunity, he felt, would come, as it comes to all in wartime. Meanwhile he did what he could. No service was too humble for him to perform in the aid of the South, no adventure too perilous for him to undertake if consistent with the character of a civilian who was at heart a soldier, and who in good faith and without too much qualification assented to at least a part of the frankly villainous dictum that all is fair in love and war.

One evening while Farquhar and his wife were sitting on a rustic bench near the entrance to his grounds, a gray-clad soldier rode up to the gate and asked for a drink of water. Mrs. Farquhar was only too happy to serve him with her own white hands. While she was fetching the water her husband approached the dusty horseman and inquired eagerly for news from the front.

"The Yanks are repairing the railroads," said the man, "and are getting ready for another advance. They have reached the Owl Creek bridge, put it in order and built a stockade on the north bank. The commandant has issued an order, which is posted everywhere, declaring that any civilian caught interfering with the railroad, its bridges, tunnels, or trains will be summarily hanged. I saw the order."

"How far is it to the Owl Creek bridge?" Farquhar asked.

"About thirty miles."

"Is there no force on this side of the creek?"

"Only a picket post half a mile out, on the railroad, and a single sentinel at this end of the bridge."

"Suppose a man—a civilian and student of hanging—should elude the picket post and perhaps get the better of the sentinel," said Farquhar, smiling, "what could he accomplish?"

The soldier reflected. "I was there a month ago," he replied. "I observed that the flood of last winter had lodged a great quantity of driftwood against the wooden pier at this end of the bridge. It is now dry and would burn like tinder."

The lady had now brought the water, which the soldier drank. He thanked her ceremoniously, bowed to her husband and rode away. An hour later, after nightfall, he repassed the plantation, going northward in the direction from which he had come. He was a Federal scout.

III.

As Peyton Farquhar fell straight downward through the bridge he lost consciousness and was as one already dead. From this state he was awakened—ages later, it seemed to him—by the pain of a sharp pressure upon his throat, followed by a sense of suffocation. Keen, poignant agonies seemed to shoot from his neck downward through every fiber of his body and limbs. These pains appeared to flash along well defined lines of ramification and to beat with an inconceivably rapid periodicity. They seemed like streams of pulsating fire heating him to an intolerable temperature. As to his head, he was conscious of nothing but a feeling of fullness—of congestion. These sensations were unaccompanied by thought. The intellectual part of his nature was already effaced; he had power only to feel, and feeling was torment. He was conscious of motion. Encompassed in a luminous cloud, of which he was now merely the fiery heart, without material substance, he swung through unthinkable arcs of oscillation, like a vast pendulum. Then all at once, with terrible suddenness, the light about him shot upward with the noise of a loud splash; a frightful roaring was in his ears, and all was cold and dark. The power of thought was restored; he knew that the rope had broken and he had fallen into the stream. There was no additional strangulation; the noose about his neck was already suffocating him and kept the water from his lungs. To die of hanging at the bottom of a river!—the idea seemed to him ludicrous. He opened his eyes in the darkness and saw above him a gleam of light, but how distant, how inaccessible! He was still sinking, for the light became fainter and fainter until it was a mere glimmer. Then it began to grow and brighten, and he knew that he was rising toward the surface—knew it with reluctance, for he was now very comfortable. "To be hanged and drowned," he thought, "that is not so bad; but I do not wish to be shot. No; I will not be shot; that is not fair."

He was not conscious of an effort, but a sharp pain in his wrist apprised him that he was trying to free his hands. He gave the struggle his attention, as an idler might observe the feat of a juggler, without interest in the outcome. What splendid effort!—what magnificent, what superhuman strength! Ah, that was a fine endeavor! Bravo! The cord fell away; his arms parted and floated upward, the hands dimly seen on each side in the growing light. He watched them with a new interest as first one and then the other pounced upon the noose at his neck. They tore it away and thrust it fiercely aside, its undulations resembling those of a water snake. "Put it back, put it back!" He thought he shouted these words to his hands, for the undoing of the noose had been succeeded by the direst pang that he had yet experienced. His neck ached horribly; his brain was on fire, his heart, which had been fluttering faintly, gave a great leap, trying to force itself out at his mouth. His whole body was racked and wrenched with an insupportable anguish! But his disobedient hands gave no heed to the command. They beat the water vigorously with quick, downward strokes, forcing him to the surface. He felt his head emerge; his eyes were blinded by the sunlight; his chest expanded convulsively, and with a supreme and crowning agony his lungs engulfed a great draught of air, which instantly he expelled in a shriek!

He was now in full possession of his physical senses. They were, indeed, preternaturally keen and alert. Something in the awful disturbance of his organic system had so exalted and refined them that they made record of things never before perceived. He felt the ripples upon his face and heard their separate sounds as they struck. He looked at the forest on the bank of the stream, saw the individual trees, the leaves and the veining of each leaf—he saw the very insects upon them: the locusts, the brilliant bodied flies, the gray spiders stretching their webs from twig to twig. He noted the prismatic colors in all the dewdrops upon a million blades of grass. The humming of the gnats that danced above the eddies of the stream, the beating of the dragon flies' wings, the strokes of the water spiders' legs, like oars which had lifted their boat—all these made audible music. A fish slid along beneath his eyes and he heard the rush of its body parting the water.

He had come to the surface facing down the stream; in a moment the visible world seemed to wheel slowly round, himself the pivotal point, and he saw the bridge, the fort, the soldiers upon the bridge, the captain, the sergeant, the two privates, his executioners. They were in silhouette against the blue sky. They shouted and gesticulated, pointing at him. The captain had drawn his pistol, but did not fire; the others were unarmed. Their movements were grotesque and horrible, their forms gigantic.

Suddenly he heard a sharp report and something struck the water smartly within a few inches of his head, spattering his face with spray. He heard a second report, and saw one of the sentinels with his rifle at his shoulder, a light cloud of blue smoke rising from the muzzle. The man in the water saw the eye of the man on the bridge gazing into his own through the sights of the rifle. He observed that it was a gray eye and remembered having read that gray eyes were keenest, and that all famous marksmen had them. Nevertheless, this one had missed.

A counter-swirl had caught Farquhar and turned him half round; he was again looking at the forest on the bank opposite the fort. The sound of a clear, high voice in a monotonous singsong now rang out behind him and came across the water with a distinctness that pierced and subdued all other sounds, even the beating of the ripples in his ears. Although no soldier, he had frequented camps enough to know the dread significance of that deliberate, drawling, aspirated chant; the lieutenant on shore was taking a part in the morning's work. How coldly and pitilessly—with what an even, calm intonation, presaging, and enforcing tranquility in the men—with what accurately measured interval fell those cruel words:

"Company! ... Attention! ... Shoulder arms! ... Ready! ... Aim! ... Fire!"

Farquhar dived—dived as deeply as he could. The water roared in his ears like the voice of Niagara, yet he heard the dull thunder of the volley and, rising again toward the surface, met shining bits of metal, singularly flattened, oscillating slowly downward. Some of them touched him on the face and hands, then fell away, continuing their descent. One lodged between his collar and neck; it was uncomfortably warm and he snatched it out.

As he rose to the surface, gasping for breath, he saw that he had been a long time under water; he was perceptibly farther downstream—nearer to safety. The soldiers had almost finished reloading; the metal ramrods flashed all at once in the sunshine as they were drawn from the barrels, turned in the air, and thrust into their sockets. The two sentinels fired again, independently and ineffectually.

The hunted man saw all this over his shoulder; he was now swimming vigorously with the current. His brain was as energetic as his arms and legs; he thought with the rapidity of lightning:

"The officer," he reasoned, "will not make that martinet's error a second time. It is as easy to dodge a volley as a single shot. He has probably already given the command to fire at will. God help me, I cannot dodge them all!"

An appalling splash within two yards of him was followed by a loud, rushing sound, *diminuendo*, which seemed to travel back through the air to the fort and died in an explosion which stirred the very river to its deeps! A rising sheet of water curved over him, fell down upon him, blinded him, strangled him! The cannon had taken an hand in the game. As he shook his head free from the commotion of the smitten water he heard the deflected shot humming through the air ahead, and in an instant it was cracking and smashing the branches in the forest beyond.

"They will not do that again," he thought; "the next time they will use a charge of grape. I must keep my eye upon the gun; the smoke will apprise me—the report arrives too late; it lags behind the missile. That is a good gun."

Suddenly he felt himself whirled round and round—spinning like a top. The water, the banks, the forests, the now distant bridge, fort and men, all were commingled and blurred. Objects were represented by their colors only; circular horizontal streaks of color—that was all he saw. He had been caught in a vortex and was being whirled on with a velocity of advance and gyration that made him giddy and sick. In few moments he was flung upon the gravel at the foot of the left bank of the stream—the southern bank—and behind a projecting point which concealed him from his enemies. The sudden arrest of his motion, the abrasion of one of his hands on the gravel, restored him, and he wept with delight. He dug his fingers into the sand, threw it over himself in handfuls and audibly blessed it. It looked like diamonds, rubies, emeralds; he could think of nothing beautiful which it did not resemble. The trees upon the bank were giant garden plants; he noted a definite order in their arrangement, inhaled the fragrance of their blooms. A strange roseate light shone through the spaces among their trunks and the wind made in their branches the music of Aeolian harps. He had no wish to perfect his escape—he was content to remain in that enchanting spot until retaken.

A whiz and a rattle of grapeshot among the branches high above his head roused him from his dream. The baffled cannoneer had fired him a random farewell. He sprang to his feet, rushed up the sloping bank, and plunged into the forest.

All that day he traveled, laying his course by the rounding sun. The forest seemed interminable; nowhere did he discover a break in it, not even a woodman's road. He had not known that he lived in so wild a region. There was something uncanny in the revelation.

By nightfall he was fatigued, footsore, famished. The thought of his wife and children urged him on. At last he found a road which led him in what he knew to be the right direction. It was as wide and straight as a city street, yet it seemed untraveled. No fields bordered it, no dwelling anywhere. Not so much as the barking of a dog suggested human habitation. The black bodies of the trees formed a straight wall on both sides, terminating on the horizon in a point, like a diagram in a lesson in perspective. Overhead, as he looked up through this rift in the wood, shone great golden stars looking unfamiliar and grouped in strange constellations. He was sure they were arranged in some order which had a secret and malign significance. The wood on either side was full of singular noises, among which—once, twice, and again—he distinctly heard whispers in an unknown tongue.

His neck was in pain and lifting his hand to it found it horribly swollen. He knew that it had a circle of black where the rope had bruised it. His eyes felt congested; he could no longer close them. His tongue was swollen with thirst; he relieved its fever by thrusting it forward from between his teeth into the cold air. How softly the turf had carpeted the untraveled avenue—he could no longer feel the roadway beneath his feet!

Doubtless, despite his suffering, he had fallen asleep while walking, for now he sees another scene—perhaps he has merely recovered from a delirium. He stands at the gate of his own home. All is as he left it, and all bright and beautiful in the morning sunshine. He must have traveled the entire night. As he pushes open the gate and passes up the wide white walk, he sees a flutter of female garments; his wife, looking fresh and cool and sweet, steps down from the veranda to meet him. At the bottom of the steps she stands waiting, with a smile of ineffable joy, an attitude of matchless grace and dignity. Ah, how beautiful she is! He springs forwards with extended arms. As he is about to clasp her he feels a stunning blow upon the back of the neck; a blinding white light blazes all about him with a sound like the shock of a cannon—then all is darkness and silence!

Peyton Farquhar was dead; his body, with a broken neck, swung gently from side to side beneath the timbers of the Owl Creek bridge.

The Haunted Valley

by Ambrose Bierce

I. HOW TREES ARE FELLED IN CHINA

A half-mile north from Jo. Dunfer's, on the road from Hutton's to Mexican Hill, the highway dips into a sunless ravine which opens out on either hand in a half-confidential manner, as if it had a secret to impart at some more convenient season. I never used to ride through it without looking first to the one side and then to the other, to see if the time had arrived for the revelation. If I saw nothing—and I never did see anything—there was no feeling of disappointment, for I knew the disclosure was merely withheld temporarily for some good reason which I had no right to question. That I should one day be taken into full confidence I no more doubted than I doubted the existence of Jo. Dunfer himself, through whose premises the ravine ran.

It was said that Jo. had once undertaken to erect a cabin in some remote part of it, but for some reason had abandoned the enterprise and constructed his present hermaphrodite habitation, half residence and half groggery, at the roadside, upon an extreme corner of his estate; as far away as possible, as if on purpose to show how radically he had changed his mind.

This Jo. Dunfer—or, as he was familiarly known in the nalysingood, Whisky Jo.—was a very important personage in those parts. He was apparently about forty years of age, a long, shock-headed fellow, with a corded face, a gnarled arm and a knotty hand like a bunch of prison-keys. He was a hairy man, with a stoop in his walk, like that of one who is about to spring upon something and rend it.

Next to the peculiarity to which he owed his local appellation, Mr Dunfer's most obvious characteristic was a deep-seated antipathy to the Chinese. I saw him once in a towering rage because one of his herdsmen had permitted a travel-heated Asian to slake his thirst at the horse-trough in front of the saloon end of Jo.'s establishment. I ventured faintly to remonstrate with Jo. for his unchristian spirit, but he merely explained that there was nothing about Chinamen in the New Testament, and strode away to wreak his displeasure upon his dog, which also, I suppose, the inspired scribes had overlooked.

Some days afterward, finding him sitting alone in his barroom, I cautiously approached the subject, when, greatly to my relief, the habitual austerity of his expression visibly softened into something that I took for condescension.

"You young Easterners," he said, "are a mile-and-a-half too good for this country, and you don't catch on to our play. People who don't know a Chileno from a Kanaka can afford to hang out liberal ideas about Chinese immigration, but a fellow that has to fight for his bone with a lot of mongrel coolies hasn't any time for foolishness."

This long consumer, who had probably never done an honest day's-work in his life, sprung the lid of a Chinese tobacco-box and with thumb and forefinger forked out a wad like a small haycock. Holding this reinforcement within supporting distance he fired away with renewed confidence.

"They're a flight of devouring locusts, and they're going for everything green in this God blest land, if you want to know."

Here he pushed his reserve into the breach and when his gabble-gear was again disengaged resumed his uplifting discourse.

"I had one of them on this ranch five years ago, and I'll tell you about it, so that you can see the nub of this whole question. I didn't pan out particularly well those days—drank more whisky than was prescribed for me and didn't seem to care for my duty as a patriotic American citizen; so I took that pagan in, as a kind of cook. But when I got religion over at the Hill and they talked of running me for the Legislature it was given to me to see the light. But what was

I to do? If I gave him the go somebody else would take him, and mightn't treat him white. *What* was I to do? What would any good Christian do, especially one new to the trade and full to the neck with the brotherhood of Man and the fatherhood of God?"

Jo. paused for a reply, with an expression of unstable satisfaction, as of one who has solved a problem by a distrusted method. Presently he rose and swallowed a glass of whisky from a full bottle on the counter, then resumed his story.

"Besides, he didn't count for much—didn't know anything and gave himself airs. They all do that. I said him nay, but he muled it through on that line while he lasted; but after turning the other cheek seventy and seven times I doctored the dice so that he didn't last forever. And I'm almighty glad I had the sand to do it."

Jo.'s gladness, which somehow did not impress me, was duly and ostentatiously celebrated at the bottle.

"About five years ago I started in to stick up a shack. That was before this one was built, and I put it in another place. I set Ah Wee and a little cuss named Gopher to cutting the timber. Of course I didn't expect Ah Wee to help much, for he had a face like a day in June and big black eyes—I guess maybe they were the damn'dest eyes in this neck o' woods."

While delivering this trenchant thrust at common sense Mr Dunfer absently regarded a knot-hole in the thin board partition separating the bar from the living-room, as if that were one of the eyes whose size and color had incapacitated his servant for good service.

"Now you Eastern galoots won't believe anything against the yellow devils," he suddenly flamed out with an appearance ofearnestness not altogether convincing, "but I tell you that Chink was the perversest scoundrel outside San Francisco. The miserable pig-tail Mongolian went to hewing away at the saplings all round the stems, like a worm o' the dust gnawing a radish. I pointed out his error as patiently as I knew how, and showed him how to cut them on two sides, so as to make them fall right; but no sooner would I turn my back on him, like this"—and he turned it on me, amplifying the illustration by taking some more liquor—"than he was at it again. It was just this way: while I looked at him, *so*"—regarding me rather unsteadily and with evident complexity of vision—"he was all right; but when I looked away, *so*"—taking a long pull at the bottle—"he defied me. Then I'd gaze at him reproachfully, *so*, and butter wouldn't have melted in his mouth."

Doubtless Mr Dunfer honestly intended the look that he fixed upon me to be merely reproachful, but it was singularly fit to arouse the gravest apprehension in any unarmed person incurring it; and as I had lost all interest in his pointless and interminable narrative, I rose to go. Before I had fairly risen, he had again turned to the counter, and with a barely audible "so," had emptied the bottle at a gulp.

Heavens! What a yell! It was like a Titan in his last, strong agony. Jo. staggered back after emitting it, as a cannon recoils from its own thunder, and then dropped into his chair, as if he had been "knocked in the head" like a beef—his eyes drawn sidewise toward the wall, with a stare of terror. Looking in the same direction, I saw that the knot-hole in the wall had indeed become a human eye—a full, black eye, that glared into my own with an entire lack of expression more awful than the most devilish glitter. I think I must have covered my face with my hands to shut out the horrible illusion, if such it was, and Jo.'s little white man-of-all-work coming into the room broke the spell, and I walked out of the house with a sort of dazed fear that *delirium tremens* might be infectious. My horse was hitched at the watering-trough, and untying him I mounted and gave him his head, too much troubled in mind to note whither he took me.

I did not know what to think of all this, and like every one who does not know what to think I thought a great deal, and to little purpose. The only reflection that seemed at all satisfactory, was, that on the morrow I should be some miles away, with a strong probability of never returning.

A sudden coolness brought me out of my abstraction, and looking up I found myself entering the deep shadows of the ravine. The day was stifling; and this transition from the pitiless, visible heat of the parched fields to the cool gloom, heavy with pungency of cedars and vocal with twittering of the birds that had been driven to its leafy asylum, was exquisitely refreshing. I looked for my mystery, as usual, but not finding the ravine in a communicative mood, dismounted, led my sweating animal into the undergrowth, tied him securely to a tree and sat down upon a rock to meditate.

I began bravely by nalysing my pet superstition about the place. Having resolved it into its constituent elements I arranged them in convenient troops and squadrons, and collecting all the forces of my logic bore down upon them from impregnable premises with the thunder of irresistible conclusions and a great noise of chariots and general intellectual shouting. Then, when my big mental guns had overturned all opposition, and were growling almost inaudibly away on the horizon of pure speculation, the routed enemy straggled in upon their rear, massed silently into a solid phalanx, and captured me, bag and baggage. An indefinable dread came upon me. I rose to shake it off, and began threading the narrow dell by an old, grass-grown cow-path that seemed to flow along the bottom, as a substitute for the brook that Nature had neglected to provide.

The trees among which the path straggled were ordinary, well-behaved plants, a trifle perverted as to trunk and eccentric as to bough, but with nothing unearthly in their general aspect. A few loose bowlders, which had detached themselves from the sides of the depression to set up an independent existence at the bottom, had dammed up the pathway, here and there, but their stony repose had nothing in it of the stillness of death. There was a kind of death-chamber hush in the valley, it is true, and a mysterious whisper above: the wind was just fingering the tops of the trees—that was all.

I had not thought of connecting Jo. Dunfer's drunken narrative with what I now sought, and only when I came into a clear space and stumbled over the level trunks of some small trees did I have the revelation. This was the site of the abandoned "shack." The discovery was verified by noting that some of the rotting stumps were hacked all round, in a most unwoodmanlike way, while others were cut straight across, and the butt ends of the corresponding trunks had the blunt wedge-form given by the axe of a master.

The opening among the trees was not more than thirty paces across. At one side was a little knoll—a natural hillock, bare of shrubbery but covered with wild grass, and on this, standing out of the grass, the headstone of a grave!

I do not remember that I felt anything like surprise at this discovery. I viewed that lonely grave with something of the feeling that Columbus must have had when he saw the hills and headlands of the new world. Before approaching it I leisurely completed my survey of the surroundings. I was even guilty of the affectation of winding my watch at that unusual hour, and with needless care and deliberation. Then I approached my mystery.

The grave—a rather short one—was in somewhat better repair than was consistent with its obvious age and isolation, and my eyes, I dare say, widened a trifle at a clump of unmistakable garden flowers showing evidence of recent watering. The stone had clearly enough done duty once as a doorstep. In its front was carved, or rather dug, an inscription. It read thus:

Ah Wee—Chinaman.

Age unknown. Worked for Jo. Dunfer.
This monument is erected by him to keep the Chink's memory green.
Likewise as a warning to Celestials not to take on airs. Devil take 'em!
She Was a Good Egg.

I cannot adequately relate my astonishment at this uncommon inscription! The meagre but sufficient identification of the deceased; the impudent candor of confession; the brutal anathema; the ludicrous change of sex and sentiment—all marked this record as the work of one who must have been at least as much demented as bereaved. I felt that any further disclosure would be a paltry anticlimax, and with an unconscious regard for dramatic effect turned squarely about and walked away. Nor did I return to that part of the county for four years.

II. WHO DRIVES SANE OXEN SHOULD HIMSELF BE SANE

"Gee-up, there, old Fuddy-Duddy!"

This unique adjuration came from the lips of a queer little man perched upon a wagonful of firewood, behind a brace of oxen that were hauling it easily along with a simulation of mighty effort which had evidently not imposed on their lord and master. As that gentleman happened at the moment to be staring me squarely in the face as I stood by the roadside it was not altogether clear whether he was addressing me or his beasts; nor could I say if they were named Fuddy and Duddy and were both subjects of the imperative verb "to gee-up." Anyhow the command produced no effect on us, and the queer little man removed his eyes from mine long enough to spear Fuddy and Duddy alternately with a long pole, remarking, quietly but with feeling: "Dern your skin," as if they enjoyed that integument in common. Observing that my request for a ride took no attention, and finding myself falling slowly astern, I placed one foot upon the inner circumference of a hind wheel and was slowly elevated to the level of the hub, whence I boarded the concern, *sans cérémonie*, and scrambling forward seated myself beside the driver who took no notice of me until he had administered another indiscriminate castigation to his cattle, accompanied with the advice to "buckle down, you derned Incapable!" Then, the master of the outfit (or rather the former master, for I could not suppress a whimsical feeling that the entire establishment was my lawful prize) trained his big, black eyes upon me with an expression strangely, and somewhat unpleasantly, familiar, laid down his rod—which neither blossomed nor turned into a serpent, as I half expected—folded his arms, and gravely demanded, "W'at did you do to W'isky?"

My natural reply would have been that I drank it, but there was something about the query that suggested a hidden significance, and something about the man that did not invite a shallow jest. And so, having no other answer ready, I merely held my tongue, but felt as if I were resting under an imputation of guilt, and that my silence was being construed into a confession.

Just then a cold shadow fell upon my cheek, and caused me to look up. We were descending into my ravine! I can not describe the sensation that came upon me: I had not seen it since it unbosomed itself four years before, and now I felt like one to whom a friend has made some sorrowing confession of crime long past, and who has basely deserted him in consequence. The old memories of Jo. Dunfer, his fragmentary revelation, and the unsatisfying explanatory note by the headstone, came back with singular distinctness. I wondered what had become of Jo., and—I turned sharply round and asked my prisoner. He was intently watching his cattle, and without withdrawing his eyes replied:

"Gee-up, old Terrapin! He lies aside of Ah Wee up the gulch. Like to see it? They always come back to the spot—I've been expectin' you. H-woa!"

At the enunciation of the aspirate, Fuddy-Duddy, the incapable terrapin, came to a dead halt, and before the vowel had died away up the ravine had folded up all his eight legs and lain down in the dusty road, regardless of the effect upon his derned skin. The queer little man slid off his seat to the ground and started up the dell without deigning to look back to see if I was following. But I was.

It was about the same season of the year, and at near the same hour of the day, of my last visit. The jays clamored loudly, and the trees whispered darkly, as before; and I somehow traced in the two sounds a fanciful analogy to the open boastfulness of Mr Jo. Dunfer's mouth and the mysterious reticence of his manner, and to the mingled hardihood and tenderness of his sole literary production—the epitaph. All things in the valley seemed unchanged, excepting the cowpath, which was almost wholly overgrown with weeds. When we came out into the "clearing," however, there was change enough. Among the stumps and trunks of the fallen saplings, those that had been hacked "China fashion" were no longer distinguishable from those that were cut "'Melican way." It was as if the Old-World barbarism and the New-World civilization had reconciled their differences by the arbitration of an impartial decay—as is the way of civilizations. The knoll was there, but the Hunnish brambles had overrun and all but obliterated its effete grasses; and the patrician garden-violet had capitulated to his plebeian brother—perhaps had merely reverted to his original type. Another grave—a long, robust mound—had been made beside the first, which seemed to shrink from the comparison; and in the shadow of a new headstone the old one lay prostrate, with its marvelous inscription illegible by accumulation of leaves and soil. In point of literary merit the new was inferior to the old—was even repulsive in its terse and savage jocularity:

JO. DUNFER. DONE FOR.

I turned from it with indifference, and brushing away the leaves from the tablet of the dead pagan restored to light the mocking words which, fresh from their long neglect, seemed to have a certain pathos. My guide, too, appeared to take on an added seriousness as he read it, and I fancied that I could detect beneath his whimsical manner something of manliness, almost of dignity. But while I looked at him his former aspect, so subtly unhuman, so tantalizingly familiar, crept back into his big eyes, repellant and attractive. I resolved to make an end of the mystery if possible.

"My friend," I said, pointing to the smaller grave, "did Jo. Dunfer murder that Chinaman?"

He was leaning against a tree and looking across the open space into the top of another, or into the blue sky beyond. He neither withdrew his eyes, nor altered his posture as he slowly replied:

"No, sir; he justifiably homicided him."

"Then he really did kill him."

"Kill 'im? I should say he did, rather. Doesn't everybody know that? Didn't he stan' up before the coroner's jury and confess it? And didn't they find a verdict of 'Came to 'is death by a wholesome Christian sentiment workin' in the Caucasian breast'? An' didn't the church at the Hill turn W'isky down for it? And didn't the sovereign people elect him Justice of the Peace to get even on the gospelers? I don't know where you were brought up."

"But did Jo. do that because the Chinaman did not, or would not, learn to cut down trees like a white man?"

"Sure!—it stan's so on the record, which makes it true an' legal. My knowin' better doesn't make any difference with legal truth; it wasn't my funeral and I wasn't invited to deliver an oration. But the fact is, W'isky was jealous o' *me*"—and the little wretch actually swelled out like a turkeycock and made a pretense of adjusting an imaginary neck-tie, noting the effect in the palm of his hand, held up before him to represent a mirror.

"Jealous of *you!*" I repeated with ill-mannered astonishment.

"That's what I said. Why not?—don't I look all right?"

He assumed a mocking attitude of studied grace, and twitched the wrinkles out of his threadbare waistcoat. Then, suddenly dropping his voice to a low pitch of singular sweetness, he continued:

"W'isky thought a lot o' that Chink; nobody but me knew how 'e doted on 'im. Couldn't bear 'im out of 'is sight, the derned protoplasm! And w'en'e came down to this clearin' one day an' found him an' me neglectin' our work—him asleep an' me grapplin a tarantula out of 'is sleeve—W'isky laid hold of my axe and let us have it, good an' hard! I dodged just then, for the spider bit me, but Ah Wee got it bad in the side an' tumbled about like anything. W'isky was just weighin' me out one w'en 'e saw the spider fastened on my finger; then 'e knew he'd made a jack ass of 'imself. He threw away the axe and got down on 'is knees alongside of Ah Wee, who gave a last little kick and opened 'is eyes—he had eyes like mine—an' puttin' up 'is hands drew down W'isky's ugly head and held it there w'ile 'e stayed. That wasn't long, for a tremblin' ran through 'im and 'e gave a bit of a moan an' beat the game."

During the progress of the story the narrator had become transfigured. The comic, or rather, the sardonic element was all out of him, and as he painted that strange scene it was with difficulty that I kept my composure. And this consummate actor had somehow so managed me that the sympathy due to his *dramatis personæ* was given to himself. I stepped forward to grasp his hand, when suddenly a broad grin danced across his face and with a light, mocking laugh he continued:

"W'en W'isky got 'is nut out o' that 'e was a sight to see! All his fine clothes he dressed mighty blindin' those days—were spoiled everlastin''! 'Is hair was towsled and his face—what I could see of it—was whiter than the ace of lilies. 'E stared once at me, and looked away as if I didn't count; an' then there were shootin' pains chasm' one another from my bitten finger into my head, and it was Gopher to the dark. That's why I wasn't at the inquest."

"But why did you hold your tongue afterward?" I asked.

"It's that kind of tongue," he replied, and not another word would he say about it.

"After that W'isky took to drinkin' harder an' harder, and was rabider an' rabider anti-coolie, but I don't think 'e was ever particularly glad that 'e dispelled Ah Wee. He didn't put on so much dog about it w'en we were alone as w'en he had the ear of a denied Spectacular Extravaganza like you. 'E put up that headstone and gouged the inscription accordin' to his varyin' moods. It took 'im three weeks, workin' between drinks. I gouged his in one day."

"When did Jo. die?" I asked rather absently. The answer took my breath:

"Pretty soon after I looked at him through that knot-hole, w'en you had put something in his w'isky, you derned Borgia!"

Recovering somewhat from my surprise at this astounding charge, I was half-minded to throttle the audacious accuser, but was restrained by a sudden conviction that came to me in the light of a revelation. I fixed a grave look upon him and asked, as calmly as I could: "And when did you go luny?"

"Nine years ago!" he shrieked, throwing out his clenched hands—"nine years ago, w'en that big brute killed the woman who loved him better than she did me!—me who had followed 'er from San Francisco, where 'e won 'er at draw poker!—me who had watched over 'er for years w'en the scoundrel she belonged to was ashamed to acknowledge 'er and treat 'er white!—me who for her sake kept 'is cussed secret till it ate 'im up!—me who w'en you poisoned the beast fulfilled 'is last request to lay 'im alongside 'er and give 'im a stone to the head of 'im! And I've never since seen 'er grave till now, for I didn't want to meet 'im here."

"Meet him? Why, Gopher, my poor fellow, he is dead!"

"That's why I'm afraid of 'im."

I followed the little wretch back to his wagon and wrung his hand at parting. It was now nightfall, and as I stood there at the roadside in the deepening gloom, watching the blank outlines of the receding wagon, a sound was borne to me on the evening wind—a sound as of a series of vigorous thumps—and a voice came out of the night:

"Gee-up, there, you derned old Geranium."

The Death of Halpin Frayser

Ambrose Bierce

I.

For by death is wrought greater change than hath been shown. Whereas in general the spirit that removed cometh back upon occasion, and is sometimes seen of those in flesh (appearing in the form of the body it bore) yet it hath happened that the veritable body without the spirit hath walked. And it is attested of those encountering who have lived to speak thereon that a lich so raised up hath no natural affection, nor remembrance thereof, but only hate. Also, it is known that some spirits which in life were benign become by death evil altogether.

—*Hali.*

One dark night in midsummer a man waking from a dreamless sleep in a forest lifted his head from the earth, and staring a few moments into the blackness, said: "Catherine Larue." He said nothing more; no reason was known to him why he should have said so much.

The man was Halpin Frayser. He lived in St. Helena, but where he lives now is uncertain, for he is dead. One who practices sleeping in the woods with nothing under him but the dry leaves and the damp earth, and nothing over him but the branches from which the leaves have fallen and the sky from which the earth has fallen, cannot hope for great longevity, and Frayser had already attained the age of thirty-two. There are persons in this world, millions of persons, and far and away the best persons, who regard that as a very advanced age. They are the children. To those who view the voyage of life from the port of departure the bark that has accomplished any considerable distance appears already in close approach to the farther shore. However, it is not certain that Halpin Frayser came to his death by exposure.

He had been all day in the hills west of the Napa Valley, looking for doves and such small game as was in season. Late in the afternoon it had come on to be cloudy, and he had lost his bearings; and although he had only to go always downhill—everywhere the way to safety when one is lost—the absence of trails had so impeded him that he was overtaken by night while still in the forest. Unable in the darkness to penetrate the thickets of manzanita and other undergrowth, utterly bewildered and overcome with fatigue, he had lain down near the root of a large madroño and fallen into a dreamless sleep. It was hours later, in the very middle of the night, that one of God's mysterious messengers, gliding ahead of the incalculable host of his companions sweeping westward with the dawn line, pronounced the awakening word in the ear of the sleeper, who sat upright and spoke, he knew not why, a name, he knew not whose.

Halpin Frayser was not much of a philosopher, nor a scientist. The circumstance that, waking from a deep sleep at night in the midst of a forest, he had spoken aloud a name that he had not in memory and hardly had in mind did not arouse an enlightened curiosity to investigate the phenomenon. He thought it odd, and with a little perfunctory shiver, as if in deference to a seasonal presumption that the night was chill, he lay down again and went to sleep. But his sleep was no longer dreamless.

He thought he was walking along a dusty road that showed white in the gathering darkness of a summer night. Whence and whither it led, and why he traveled it, he did not know, though all seemed simple and natural, as is the way in dreams; for in the Land Beyond the Bed surprises cease from troubling and the judgment is at rest. Soon he came to a parting of the ways; leading from the highway was a road less traveled, having the appearance, indeed, of having been long abandoned, because, he thought, it led to something evil; yet he turned into it without hesitation, impelled by some imperious necessity.

As he pressed forward he became conscious that his way was haunted by invisible existences whom he could not definitely figure to his mind. From among the trees on either side he caught broken and incoherent whispers in a strange tongue which yet he partly understood. They seemed to him fragmentary utterances of a monstrous conspiracy against his body and soul.

It was now long after nightfall, yet the interminable forest through which he journeyed was lit with a wan glimmer having no point of diffusion, for in its mysterious lumination nothing cast a shadow. A shallow pool in the guttered depression of an old wheel rut, as from a recent rain, met his eye with a crimson gleam. He stooped and plunged his hand into it. It stained his fingers; it was blood! Blood, he then observed, was about him everywhere. The weeds growing rankly by the roadside showed it in blots and splashes on their big, broad leaves. Patches of dry dust between the wheelways were pitted and spattered as with a red rain. Defiling the trunks of the trees were broad maculations of crimson, and blood dripped like dew from their foliage.

All this he observed with a terror which seemed not incompatible with the fulfillment of a natural expectation. It seemed to him that it was all in expiation of some crime which, though conscious of his guilt, he could not rightly remember. To the menaces and mysteries of his surroundings the consciousness was an added horror. Vainly he sought by tracing life backward in memory, to reproduce the moment of his sin; scenes and incidents came crowding tumultuously into his mind, one picture effacing another, or commingling with it in confusion and obscurity, but nowhere could he catch a glimpse of what he sought. The failure augmented his terror; he felt as one who has murdered in the dark, not knowing whom nor why. So frightful was the situation—the mysterious light burned with so silent and awful a menace; the noxious plants, the trees that by common consent are invested with a melancholy or baleful character, so openly in his sight conspired against his peace; from overhead and all about came so audible and startling whispers and the sighs of creatures so obviously not of earth—that he could endure it no longer, and with a great effort to break some malign spell that bound his faculties to silence and inaction, he shouted with the full strength of his lungs! His voice broken, it seemed, into an infinite multitude of unfamiliar sounds, went babbling and stammering away into the distant reaches of the forest, died into silence, and all was as before. But he had made a beginning at resistance and was encouraged. He said:

"I will not submit unheard. There may be powers that are not malignant traveling this accursed road. I shall leave them a record and an appeal. I shall relate my wrongs, the persecutions that I endure—I, a helpless mortal, a penitent, an unoffending poet!" Halpin Frayser was a poet only as he was a penitent: in his dream.

Taking from his clothing a small red-leather pocketbook, one-half of which was leaved for memoranda, he discovered that he was without a pencil. He broke a twig from a bush, dipped it into a pool of blood and wrote rapidly. He had hardly touched the paper with the point of his twig when a low, wild peal of laughter broke out at a measureless distance away, and growing ever louder, seemed approaching ever nearer; a soulless, heartless, and unjoyous laugh, like that of the loon, solitary by the lakeside at midnight; a laugh which culminated in an unearthly shout close at hand, then died away by slow gradations, as if the accursed being that uttered it had withdrawn over the verge of the world whence it had come. But the man felt that this was not so—that it was near by and had not moved.

A strange sensation began slowly to take possession of his body and his mind. He could not have said which, if any, of his senses was affected; he felt it rather as a consciousness—a mysterious mental assurance of some overpowering presence—some supernatural malevolence different in kind from the invisible existences that swarmed about him, and superior to them in power. He knew that it had uttered that hideous laugh. And now it seemed to be approaching him; from what direction he did not know—dared not conjecture. All his former fears were forgotten or merged in the gigantic terror that now held him in thrall. Apart from that, he had but one thought: to complete his written appeal to the benign powers who, traversing the haunted wood, might some time rescue him if he should be denied the blessing of annihilation. He wrote with terrible rapidity, the twig in his fingers rilling blood without renewal; but in the middle of a sentence his hands denied their service to his will, his arms fell to his sides, the book to the earth; and powerless to move or cry out, he found himself staring into the sharply drawn face and blank, dead eyes of his own mother, standing white and silent in the garments of the grave!

II.

In his youth Halpin Frayser had lived with his parents in Nashville, Tennessee. The Fraysers were well-to-do, having a good position in such society as had survived the wreck wrought by civil war. Their children had the social and educational opportunities of their time and place, and had responded to good associations and instruction with agreeable manners and cultivated minds. Halpin being the youngest and not over robust was perhaps a trifle "spoiled." He had the double disadvantage of a mother's assiduity and a father's neglect. Frayser *père* was what no Southern man of means is not—a politician. His country, or rather his section and State, made demands upon his time and attention so exacting that to those of his family he was compelled to turn an ear partly deafened by the thunder of the political captains and the shouting, his own included.

Young Halpin was of a dreamy, indolent, and rather romantic turn, somewhat more addicted to literature than law, the profession to which he was bred. Among those of his relations who professed the modern faith of heredity it was well understood that in him the character of the late Myron Bayne, a maternal great-grandfather, had revisited the glimpses of the moon—by which orb Bayne had in his lifetime been sufficiently affected to be a poet of no small Colonial distinction. If not specially observed, it was observable that while a Frayser who was not the proud possessor of a sumptuous copy of the ancestral "poetical works" (printed at the family expense, and long ago withdrawn from an inhospitable market) was a rare Frayser indeed, there was an illogical indisposition to honor the great deceased in the person of his spiritual successor. Halpin was pretty generally deprecated as an intellectual black sheep who was likely at any moment to disgrace the flock by bleating in meter. The Tennessee Fraysers were a practical folk—not practical in the popular sense of devotion to sordid pursuits, but having a robust contempt for any qualities unfitting a man for the wholesome vocation of politics.

In justice to young Halpin it should be said that while in him were pretty faithfully reproduced most of the mental and moral characteristics ascribed by history and family tradition to the famous Colonial bard, his succession to the gift and faculty divine was purely inferential. Not only had he never been known to court the muse, but in truth he could not have written correctly a line of verse to save himself from the Killer of the Wise. Still, there was no knowing when the dormant faculty might wake and smite the lyre.

In the meantime the young man was rather a loose fish, anyhow. Between him and his mother was the most perfect sympathy, for secretly the lady was herself a devout disciple of the late and great Myron Bayne, though with the tact so generally and justly admired in her sex (despite the hardy calumniators who insist that it is essentially the same thing as cunning) she had always taken care to conceal her weakness from all eyes but those of him who shared it. Their common guilt in respect of that was an added tie between them. If in Halpin's youth his mother had "spoiled" him, he had assuredly done his part toward being spoiled. As he grew to such manhood as is attainable by a Southerner who does not care which way elections go the attachment between him and his beautiful mother—whom from early childhood he had called Katy—became yearly stronger and more tender. In these two romantic natures was manifest in a signal way that neglected phenomenon, the dominance of the sexual element in all the relations of life, strengthening, softening, and beautifying even those of consanguinity. The two were nearly inseparable, and by strangers observing their manner were not infrequently mistaken for lovers.

Entering his mother's boudoir one day Halpin Frayser kissed her upon the forehead, toyed for a moment with a lock of her dark hair which had escaped from its confining pins, and said, with an obvious effort at calmness:

"Would you greatly mind, Katy, if I were called away to California for a few weeks?"

It was hardly needful for Katy to answer with her lips a question to which her telltale cheeks had made instant reply. Evidently she would greatly mind; and the tears, too, sprang into her large brown eyes as corroborative testimony.

"Ah, my son," she said, looking up into his face with infinite tenderness, "I should have known that this was coming. Did I not lie awake a half of the night weeping because, during the other half, Grandfather Bayne had come to me in a dream, and standing by his portrait—young, too, and handsome as that—pointed to yours on the same wall? And when I looked it seemed that I could not see the features; you had been painted with a face cloth, such as we put upon the dead. Your father has laughed at me, but you and I, dear, know that such things are not for nothing. And I saw below the edge of the cloth the marks of hands on your throat—forgive me, but we have not been used to keep such things from each other. Perhaps you have another interpretation. Perhaps it does not mean that you will go to California. Or maybe you will take me with you?"

It must be confessed that this ingenious interpretation of the dream in the light of newly discovered evidence did not wholly commend itself to the son's more logical mind; he had, for the moment at least, a conviction that it foreshadowed a more simple and immediate, if less tragic, disaster than a visit to the Pacific Coast. It was Halpin Frayser's impression that he was to be garroted on his native heath.

"Are there not medicinal springs in California?" Mrs. Frayser resumed before he had time to give her the true reading of the dream—"places where one recovers from rheumatism and neuralgia? Look—my fingers feel so stiff; and I am almost sure they have been giving me great pain while I slept."

She held out her hands for his inspection. What diagnosis of her case the young man may have thought it best to conceal with a smile the historian is unable to state, but for himself he feels bound to say that fingers looking less stiff, and showing fewer evidences of even insensible pain, have seldom been submitted for medical inspection by even the fairest patient desiring a prescription of unfamiliar scenes.

The outcome of it was that of these two odd persons having equally odd notions of duty, the one went to California, as the interest of his client required, and the other remained at home in compliance with a wish that her husband was scarcely conscious of entertaining.

While in San Francisco Halpin Frayser was walking one dark night along the water front of the city, when, with a suddenness that surprised and disconcerted him, he became a sailor. He was in fact 'shanghaied' aboard a gallant, gallant ship, and sailed for a far countree. Nor did his misfortunes end with the voyage; for the ship was cast ashore on an island of the South Pacific, and it was six years afterward when the survivors were taken off by a venturesome trading schooner and brought back to San Francisco.

Though poor in purse, Frayser was no less proud in spirit than he had been in the years that seemed ages and ages ago. He would accept no assistance from strangers, and it was while living with a fellow survivor near the town of St. Helena, awaiting news and remittances from home, that he had gone gunning and dreaming.

III.

The apparition confronting the dreamer in the haunted wood—the thing so like, yet so unlike his mother—was horrible! It stirred no love nor longing in his heart; it came unattended with pleasant memories of a golden past—inspired no sentiment of any kind; all the finer emotions were swallowed up in fear. He tried to turn and run from before it, but his legs were as lead; he was unable to lift his feet from the ground. His arms hung helpless at his sides; of his eyes only he retained control, and these he dared not remove from the lusterless orbs of the apparition, which he knew was not a soul without a body, but that most dreadful of all existences infesting that haunted wood—a body without a soul! In its blank stare was neither love, nor pity, nor intelligence—nothing to which to address an appeal for mercy. "An appeal will not lie," he thought, with an absurd reversion to professional slang, making the situation more horrible, as the fire of a cigar might light up a tomb.

For a time, which seemed so long that the world grew gray with age and sin, and the haunted forest, having fulfilled its purpose in this monstrous culmination of its terrors, vanished out of his consciousness with all its sights and sounds, the apparition stood within a pace, regarding him with the mindless malevolence of a wild brute; then thrust its hands forward and sprang upon him with appalling ferocity! The act released his physical energies without unfettering his will; his mind was still spellbound, but his powerful body and agile limbs, endowed with a blind, insensate life of their own, resisted stoutly and well. For an instant he seemed to see this unnatural contest between a dead intelligence and a breathing mechanism only as a spectator—such fancies are in dreams; then he regained his identity almost as if by a leap forward into his body, and the straining automaton had a directing will as alert and fierce as that of its hideous antagonist.

But what mortal can cope with a creature of his dream? The imagination creating the enemy is already vanquished; the combat's result is the combat's cause. Despite his struggles—despite his strength and activity, which seemed wasted in a void, he felt the cold fingers close upon his throat. Borne backward to the earth, he saw above him the dead and drawn face within a hand's breadth of his own, and then all was black. A sound as of the beating of distant drums—a murmur of swarming voices, a sharp, far cry signing all to silence, and Halpin Frayser dreamed that he was dead.

IV.

A warm, clear night had been followed by a morning of drenching fog. At about the middle of the afternoon of the preceding day a little whiff of light vapor—a mere thickening of the atmosphere, the ghost of a cloud—had been observed clinging to the western side of Mount St. Helena, away up along the barren altitudes near the summit. It was so thin, so diaphanous, so like a fancy made visible, that one would have said: "Look quickly! in a moment it will be gone."

In a moment it was visibly larger and denser. While with one edge it clung to the mountain, with the other it reached farther and farther out into the air above the lower slopes. At the same time it extended itself to north and south, joining small patches of mist that appeared to come out of the mountain-side on exactly the same level, with an intelligent design to be absorbed. And so it grew and grew until the summit was shut out of view from the valley, and over the valley itself was an ever-extending canopy, opaque and gray. At Calistoga, which lies near the head of the valley and the foot of the mountain, there were a starless night and a sunless morning. The fog, sinking into the valley, had reached southward, swallowing up ranch after ranch, until it had blotted out the town of St. Helena, nine miles away. The dust in the road was laid; trees were adrip with moisture; birds sat silent in their coverts; the morning light was wan and ghastly, with neither color nor fire.

Two men left the town of St. Helena at the first glimmer of dawn, and walked along the road northward up the valley toward Calistoga. They carried guns on their shoulders, yet no one having knowledge of such matters could have mistaken them for hunters of bird or beast. They were a deputy sheriff from Napa and a detective from San Francisco—Holker and Jaralson, respectively. Their business was man-hunting.

"How far is it?" inquired Holker, as they strode along, their feet stirring white the dust beneath the damp surface of the road.

"The White Church? Only a half mile farther," the other answered. "By the way," he added, "it is neither white nor a church, it is an abandoned schoolhouse, gray with age and neglect. Religious services were once held in it when it—was white, and there is a graveyard that would delight a poet. Can you guess why I sent for you, and told you to come heeled?"

"Oh, I never have bothered you about things of that kind. I've always found you communicative when the time came. But if I may hazard a guess, you want me to help you arrest one of the corpses in the graveyard."

"You remember Branscom?" said Jaralson, treating his companion's wit with the inattention that it deserved.

"The chap who cut his wife's throat? I ought; I wasted a week's work on him and had my expenses for my trouble. There is a reward of five hundred dollars, but none of us ever got a sight of him. You don't mean to say—"

"Yes, I do. He has been under the noses of you fellows all the time. He comes by night to the old graveyard at the White Church."

"The devil! That's where they buried his wife."

"Well, you fellows might have had sense enough to suspect that he would return to her grave some time."

"The very last place that anyone would have expected him to return to."

"But you had exhausted all the other places. Learning your failure at them, I 'laid for him' there."

"And you found him?"

"Damn it! he found *me*. The rascal got the drop on me—regularly held me up and made me travel. It's God's mercy that he didn't go through me. Oh, he's a good one, and I fancy the half of that reward is enough for me if you're needy."

Holker laughed good humoredly, and explained that his creditors were never more importunate.

"I wanted merely to show you the ground, and arrange a plan with you," the detective explained. "I thought it as well for us to be heeled, even in daylight."

"The man must be insane," said the deputy sheriff. "The reward is for his capture and conviction. If he's mad he won't be convicted."

Mr Holker was so profoundly affected by that possible failure of justice that he involuntarily stopped in the middle of the road, then resumed his walk with abated zeal.

"Well, he looks it," assented Jaralson. "I'm bound to admit that a more unshaven, unshorn, unkempt, and uneverything wretch I never saw outside the ancient and honorable order of tramps. But I've gone in for him, and can't make up my mind to let go. There's glory in it for us, anyhow. Not another soul knows that he is this side of the Mountains of the Moon."

"All right," Holker said; "we will go and view the ground," and he added, in the words of a once favorite inscription for tombstones: " 'where you must shortly lie'—I mean, if old Branscom ever gets tired of you and your impertinent intrusion. By the way, I heard the other day that 'Branscom' was not his real name."

"What is?"

"I can't recall it. I had lost all interest in the wretch, and it did not fix itself in my memory—something like Pardee. The woman whose throat he had the bad taste to cut was a widow when he met her. She had come to California to look up some relatives—there are persons who will do that sometimes. But you know all that."

"Naturally."

"But not knowing the right name, by what happy inspiration did you find the right grave? The man who told me what the name was said it had been cut on the headboard."

"I don't know the right grave." Jaralson was apparently a trifle reluctant to admit his ignorance of so important a point of his plan. "I have been watching about the place generally. A part of our work this morning will be to identify that grave. Here is the White Church."

For a long distance the road had been bordered by fields on both sides, but now on the left there was a forest of oaks, madroños, and gigantic spruces whose lower parts only could be seen, dim and ghostly in the fog. The udergrowth was, in places, thick, but nowhere impenetrable. For some moments Holker saw nothing of the building, but as they turned into the woods it revealed itself in faint gray outline through the fog, looking huge and far away. A few steps more, and it was within an arm's length, distinct, dark with moisture, and insignificant in size. It had the usual country-schoolhouse form—belonged to the packing-box order of architecture; had an underpinning of stones, a moss-grown roof, and blank window spaces, whence both glass and sash had long departed. It was ruined, but not a ruin—a typical Californian substitute for what are known to guide-bookers abroad as "monuments of the past." With scarcely a glance at this uninteresting structure Jaralson moved on into the dripping undergrowth beyond.

"I will show you where he held me up," he said. "This is the graveyard."

Here and there among the bushes were small inclosures containing graves, sometimes no more than one. They were recognized as graves by the discolored stones or rotting boards at head and foot, leaning at all angles, some prostrate; by the ruined picket fences surrounding them; or, infrequently, by the mound itself showing its gravel through the fallen leaves. In many instances nothing marked the spot where lay the vestiges of some poor mortal—who, leaving "a large circle of sorrowing friends," had been left by them in turn—except a depression in the earth, more lasting than that in the spirits of the mourners. The paths, if any paths had been, were long obliterated; trees of a considerable size had been permitted to grow up from the graves and thrust aside with root or branch the inclosing fences. Over all was that air of abandonment and decay which seems nowhere so fit and significant as in a village of the forgotten dead.

As the two men, Jaralson leading, pushed their way through the growth of young trees, that enterprising man suddenly stopped and brought up his shotgun to the height of his breast, uttered a low note of warning, and stood motionless, his eyes fixed upon something ahead. As well as he could, obstructed by brush, his companion, though seeing nothing, imitated the posture and so stood, prepared for what might ensue. A moment later Jaralson moved cautiously forward, the other following.

Under the branches of an enormous spruce lay the dead body of a man. Standing silent above it they noted such particulars as first strike the attention—the face, the attitude, the clothing; whatever most promptly and plainly answers the unspoken question of a sympathetic curiosity.

The body lay upon its back, the legs wide apart. One arm was thrust upward, the other outward; but the latter was bent acutely, and the hand was near the throat. Both hands were tightly clenched. The whole attitude was that of desperate but ineffectual resistance to—what?

Near by lay a shotgun and a game bag through the meshes of which was seen the plumage of shot birds. All about were evidences of a furious struggle; small sprouts of poison-oak were bent and denuded of leaf and bark; dead and rotting leaves had been pushed into heaps and ridges on both sides of the legs by the action of other feet than theirs; alongside the hips were unmistakable impressions of human knees.

The nature of the struggle was made clear by a glance at the dead man's throat and face. While breast and hands were white, those were purple—almost black. The shoulders lay upon a low mound, and the head was turned back at an angle otherwise impossible, the expanded eyes staring blankly backward in a direction opposite to that of the feet. From the froth filling the open mouth the tongue protruded, black and swollen. The throat showed horrible contusions; not mere finger-marks, but bruises and lacerations wrought by two strong hands that must have buried themselves in the yielding flesh, maintaining their terrible grasp until long after death. Breast, throat, face, were wet; the clothing was saturated; drops of water, condensed from the fog, studded the hair and mustache.

All this the two men observed without speaking—almost at a glance. Then Holker said:

"Poor devil! he had a rough deal."

Jaralson was making a vigilant circumspection of the forest, his shotgun held in both hands and at full cock, his finger upon the trigger.

"The work of a maniac," he said, without withdrawing his eyes from the inclosing wood. "It was done by Branscom—Pardee."

Something half hidden by the disturbed leaves on the earth caught Holker's attention. It was a red-leather pocketbook. He picked it up and opened it. It contained leaves of white paper for memoranda, and upon the first leaf was the name "Halpin Frayser." Written in red on several succeeding leaves—scrawled as if in haste and barely legible—were the following lines, which Holker read aloud, while his companion continued scanning the dim gray confines of their narrow world and hearing matter of apprehension in the drip of water from every burdened branch:

"Enthralled by some mysterious spell, I stood
 In the lit gloom of an enchanted wood.
The cypress there and myrtle twined their boughs,
 Significant, in baleful brotherhood.

"The brooding willow whispered to the yew;
 Beneath, the deadly nightshade and the rue,
With immortelles self-woven into strange
 Funereal shapes, and horrid nettles grew.

"No song of bird nor any drone of bees,
 Nor light leaf lifted by the wholesome breeze:
The air was stagnant all, and Silence was
 A living thing that breathed among the trees.

"Conspiring spirits whispered in the gloom,
 Half-heard, the stilly secrets of the tomb.
With blood the trees were all adrip; the leaves
 Shone in the witch-light with a ruddy bloom.

"I cried aloud!—the spell, unbroken still,
 Rested upon my spirit and my will.
Unsouled, unhearted, hopeless and forlorn,
 I strove with monstrous presages of ill!

"At last the viewless—"

Holker ceased reading; there was no more to read. The manuscript broke off in the middle of a line.

"That sounds like Bayne," said Jaralson, who was something of a scholar in his way. He had abated his vigilance and stood looking down at the body.

"Who's Bayne?" Holker asked rather incuriously.

"Myron Bayne, a chap who flourished in the early years of the nation—more than a century ago. Wrote mighty dismal stuff; I have his collected works. That poem is not among them, but it must have been omitted by mistake."

"It is cold," said Holker; "let us leave here; we must have up the coroner from Napa."

Jaralson said nothing, but made a movement in compliance. Passing the end of the slight elevation of earth upon which the dead man's head and shoulders lay, his foot struck some hard substance under the rotting forest leaves, and he took the trouble to kick it into view. It was a fallen headboard, and painted on it were the hardly decipherable words, "Catharine Larue."

"Larue, Larue!" exclaimed Holker, with sudden animation. "Why, that is the real name of Branscom—not Pardee. And—bless my soul! how it all comes to me—the murdered woman's name had been Frayser!"

"There is some rascally mystery here," said Detective Jaralson. "I hate anything of that kind."

There came to them out of the fog—seemingly from a great distance—the sound of a laugh, a low, deliberate, soulless laugh, which had no more of joy than that of a hyena night-prowling in the desert; a laugh that rose by slow gradation, louder and louder, clearer, more distinct and terrible, until it seemed barely outside the narrow circle of their vision; a laugh so unnatural, so unhuman, so devilish, that it filled those hardy man-hunters with a sense of dread unspeakable! They did not move their weapons nor think of them; the menace of that horrible sound was not of the kind to be met with arms. As it had grown out of silence, so now it died away; from a culminating shout which had seemed almost in their ears, it drew itself away into the distance, until its failing notes, joyless and mechanical to the last, sank to silence at a measureless remove.

The Eyes of the Panther

by Ambrose Bierce

I. ONE DOES NOT ALWAYS MARRY WHEN INSANE

A man and a woman—nature had done the grouping—sat on a rustic seat, in the late afternoon. The man was middle-aged, slender, swarthy, with the expression of a poet and the complexion of a pirate—a man at whom one would look again. The woman was young, blonde, graceful, with something in her figure and movements suggesting the word "lithe." She was habited in a gray gown with odd brown markings in the texture. She may have been beautiful; one could not readily say, for her eyes denied attention to all else. They were gray-green, long and narrow, with an expression defying analysis. One could only know that they were disquieting. Cleopatra may have had such eyes.

The man and the woman talked.

"Yes," said the woman, "I love you, God knows! But marry you, no. I cannot, will not."

"Irene, you have said that many times, yet always have denied me a reason.

I've a right to know, to understand, to feel and prove my fortitude if I have it. Give me a reason."

"For loving you?"

The woman was smiling through her tears and her pallor. That did not stir any sense of humor in the man.

"No; there is no reason for that. A reason for not marrying me. I've a right to know. I must know. I will know!"

He had risen and was standing before her with clenched hands, on his face a frown—it might have been called a scowl. He looked as if he might attempt to learn by strangling her. She smiled no more—merely sat looking up into his face with a fixed, set regard that was utterly without emotion or sentiment. Yet it had something in it that tamed his resentment and made him shiver.

"You are determined to have my reason?" she asked in a tone that was entirely mechanical—a tone that might have been her look made audible.

"If you please—if I'm not asking too much."

Apparently this lord of creation was yielding some part of his dominion over his co-creature.

"Very well, you shall know: I am insane."

The man started, then looked incredulous and was conscious that he ought to be amused. But, again, the sense of humor failed him in his need and despite his disbelief he was profoundly disturbed by that which he did not believe. Between our convictions and our feelings there is no good understanding.

"That is what the physicians would say," the woman continued—"if they knew. I might myself prefer to call it a case of 'possession.' Sit down and hear what I have to say."

The man silently resumed his seat beside her on the rustic bench by the wayside. Over-against them on the eastern side of the valley the hills were already sunset-flushed and the stillness all about was of that peculiar quality that foretells the twilight. Something of its mysterious and significant solemnity had imparted itself to the man's mood. In the spiritual, as in the material world, are signs and presages of night. Rarely meeting her look, and whenever he did so conscious of the indefinable dread with which, despite their feline beauty, her eyes always affected him, Jenner Brading listened in silence to the story told by Irene Marlowe. In deference to the reader's possible prejudice against the artless method of an unpractised historian the author ventures to substitute his own version for hers.

II. A ROOM MAY BE TOO NARROW FOR THREE, THOUGH ONE IS OUTSIDE

In a little log house containing a single room sparely and rudely furnished, crouching on the floor against one of the walls, was a woman, clasping to her breast a child. Outside, a dense unbroken forest extended for many miles in every direction. This was at night and the room was black dark: no human eye could have discerned the woman and the child. Yet they were observed, narrowly, vigilantly, with never even a momentary slackening of attention; and that is the pivotal fact upon which this narrative turns.

Charles Marlowe was of the class, now extinct in this country, of woodmen pioneers—men who found their most acceptable surroundings in sylvan solitudes that stretched along the eastern slope of the Mississippi Valley, from the Great Lakes to the Gulf of Mexico. For more than a hundred years these men pushed ever westward, generation after generation, with rifle and ax, reclaiming from Nature and her savage children here and there an isolated acreage for the plow, no sooner reclaimed than surrendered to their less venturesome but more thrifty successors. At last they burst through the edge of the forest into the open country and vanished as if they had fallen over a cliff. The woodman pioneer is no more; the pioneer of the plains—he whose easy task it was to subdue for occupancy two-thirds of the country in a single generation—is another and inferior creation. With Charles Marlowe in the wilderness, sharing the dangers, hardships and privations of that strange, unprofitable life, were his wife and child, to whom, in the manner of his class, in which the domestic virtues were a religion, he was passionately attached. The woman was still young enough to be comely, new enough to the awful isolation of her lot to be cheerful. By withholding the large capacity for happiness which the simple satisfactions of the forest life could not have filled, Heaven had dealt honorably with her. In her light household tasks, her child, her husband and her few foolish books, she found abundant provision for her needs.

One morning in midsummer Marlowe took down his rifle from the wooden hooks on the wall and signified his intention of getting game.

"We've meat enough," said the wife; "please don't go out today. I dreamed last night, O, such a dreadful thing! I cannot recollect it, but I'm almost sure that it will come to pass if you go out."

It is painful to confess that Marlowe received this solemn statement with less of gravity than was due to the mysterious nature of the calamity foreshadowed. In truth, he laughed.

"Try to remember," he said. "Maybe you dreamed that Baby had lost the power of speech."

The conjecture was obviously suggested by the fact that Baby, clinging to the fringe of his hunting-coat with all her ten pudgy thumbs was at that moment uttering her sense of the situation in a series of exultant goo-goos inspired by sight of her father's raccoon-skin cap.

The woman yielded: lacking the gift of humor she could not hold out against his kindly badinage. So, with a kiss for the mother and a kiss for the child, he left the house and closed the door upon his happiness forever.

At nightfall he had not returned. The woman prepared supper and waited. Then she put Baby to bed and sang softly to her until she slept. By this time the fire on the hearth, at which she had cooked supper, had burned out and the room was lighted by a single candle. This she afterward placed in the open window as a sign and welcome to the hunter if he should approach from that side. She had thoughtfully closed and barred the door against such wild animals as might prefer it to an open window—of the habits of beasts of prey in entering a house uninvited she was not advised, though with true female prevision she may have considered the possibility of their entrance by way of the chimney. As the night wore on she became not less anxious, but more drowsy, and at last rested her arms upon the bed by the child and her head upon the arms. The candle in the window burned down to the socket, sputtered and flared a moment and went out unobserved; for the woman slept and dreamed.

In her dreams she sat beside the cradle of a second child. The first one was dead. The father was dead. The home in the forest was lost and the dwelling in which she lived was unfamiliar. There were heavy oaken doors, always closed, and outside the windows, fastened into the thick stone walls, were iron bars, obviously (so she thought) a provision against Indians. All this she noted with an infinite self-pity, but without surprise—an emotion unknown in dreams. The child in the cradle was invisible under its coverlet which something impelled her to remove. She did so, disclosing the face of a wild animal! In the shock of this dreadful revelation the dreamer awoke, trembling in the darkness of her cabin in the wood.

As a sense of her actual surroundings came slowly back to her she felt for the child that was not a dream, and assured herself by its breathing that all was well with it; nor could she forbear to pass a hand lightly across its face. Then, moved by some impulse for which she probably could not have accounted, she rose and took the sleeping babe in her arms, holding it close against her breast. The head of the child's cot was against the wall to which the woman now turned her back as she stood. Lifting her eyes she saw two bright objects starring the darkness with a reddish-green glow. She took them to be two coals on the hearth, but with her returning sense of direction came the disquieting consciousness that they were not in that quarter of the room, moreover were too high, being nearly at the level of the eyes—of her own eyes. For these were the eyes of a panther.

The beast was at the open window directly opposite and not five paces away. Nothing but those terrible eyes was visible, but in the dreadful tumult of her feelings as the situation disclosed itself to her understanding she somehow knew that the animal was standing on its hinder feet, supporting itself with its paws on the window-ledge. That signified a malign interest—not the mere gratification of an indolent curiosity. The consciousness of the attitude was an added horror, accentuating the menace of those awful eyes, in whose steadfast fire her strength and courage were alike consumed. Under their silent questioning she shuddered and turned sick. Her knees failed her, and by degrees, instinctively striving to avoid a sudden movement that might bring the beast upon her, she sank to the floor, crouched against the wall and tried to shield the babe with her trembling body without withdrawing her gaze from the luminous orbs that were killing her. No thought of her husband came to her in her agony—no hope nor suggestion of rescue or escape. Her capacity for thought and feeling had narrowed to the dimensions of a single emotion—fear of the animal's spring, of the impact of its body, the buffeting of its great arms, the feel of its teeth in her throat, the mangling of her babe. Motionless now and in absolute silence, she awaited her doom, the moments growing to hours, to years, to ages; and still those devilish eyes maintained their watch.

Returning to his cabin late at night with a deer on his shoulders Charles Marlowe tried the door. It did not yield. He knocked; there was no answer. He laid down his deer and went round to the window. As he turned the angle of the building he fancied he heard a sound as of stealthy footfalls and a rustling in the undergrowth of the forest, but they were too slight for certainty, even to his practised ear. Approaching the window, and to his surprise finding it open, he threw his leg over the sill and entered. All was darkness and silence. He groped his way to the fire-place, struck a match and lit a candle.

Then he looked about. Cowering on the floor against a wall was his wife, clasping his child. As he sprang toward her she rose and broke into laughter, long, loud, and mechanical, devoid of gladness and devoid of sense—the laughter that is not out of keeping with the clanking of a chain. Hardly knowing what he did he extended his arms. She laid the babe in them. It was dead—pressed to death in its mother's embrace.

III. THE THEORY OF THE DEFENSE

That is what occurred during a night in a forest, but not all of it did Irene Marlowe relate to Jenner Brading; not all of it was known to her. When she had concluded the sun was below the horizon and the long summer twilight had begun to deepen in the hollows of the land. For some moments Brading was silent, expecting the narrative to be carried forward to some definite connection with the conversation introducing it; but the narrator was as silent as he, her face averted, her hands clasping and unclasping themselves as they lay in her lap, with a singular suggestion of an activity independent of her will.

"It is a sad, a terrible story," said Brading at last, "but I do not understand. You call Charles Marlowe father; that I know. That he is old before his time, broken by some great sorrow, I have seen, or thought I saw. But, pardon me, you said that you—that you—"

"That I am insane," said the girl, without a movement of head or body.

"But, Irene, you say—please, dear, do not look away from me—you say that the child was dead, not demented."

"Yes, that one—I am the second. I was born three months after that night, my mother being mercifully permitted to lay down her life in giving me mine."

Brading was again silent; he was a trifle dazed and could not at once think of the right thing to say. Her face was still turned away. In his embarrassment he reached impulsively toward the hands that lay closing and unclosing in her lap, but something—he could not have said what—restrained him. He then remembered, vaguely, that he had never altogether cared to take her hand.

"Is it likely," she resumed, "that a person born under such circumstances is like others—is what you call sane?"

Brading did not reply; he was preoccupied with a new thought that was taking shape in his mind—what a scientist would have called an hypothesis; a detective, a theory. It might throw an added light, albeit a lurid one, upon such doubt of her sanity as her own assertion had not dispelled.

The country was still new and, outside the villages, sparsely populated. The professional hunter was still a familiar figure, and among his trophies were heads and pelts of the larger kinds of game. Tales variously credible of nocturnal meetings with savage animals in lonely roads were sometimes current, passed through the customary stages of growth and decay, and were forgotten. A recent addition to these popular apocrypha, originating, apparently, by spontaneous generation in several households, was of a panther which had frightened some of their members by looking in at windows by night. The yarn had caused its little ripple of excitement—had even attained to the distinction of a place in the local newspaper; but Brading had given it no attention. Its likeness to the story to which he had just listened now impressed him as perhaps more than accidental. Was it not possible that the one story had suggested the other—that finding congenial conditions in a morbid mind and a fertile fancy, it had grown to the tragic tale that he had heard?

Brading recalled certain circumstances of the girl's history and disposition, of which, with love's incuriosity, he had hitherto been heedless—such as her solitary life with her father, at whose house no one, apparently, was an acceptable visitor and her strange fear of the night, by which those who knew her best accounted for her never being seen after dark. Surely in such a mind imagination once kindled might burn with a lawless flame, penetrating and enveloping the entire structure. That she was mad, though the conviction gave him the acutest pain, he could no longer doubt; she had only mistaken an effect of her mental disorder for its cause, bringing into imaginary relation with her own personality the vagaries of the local myth-makers. With some vague intention of testing his new "theory," and no very definite notion of how to set about it he said, gravely, but with hesitation:

"Irene, dear, tell me—I beg you will not take offence, but tell me—"

"I have told you," she interrupted, speaking with a passionate earnestness that he had not known her to show—"I have already told you that we cannot marry; is anything else worth saying?"

Before he could stop her she had sprung from her seat and without another word or look was gliding away among the trees toward her father's house. Brading had risen to detain her; he stood watching her in silence until she had vanished in the gloom. Suddenly he started as if he had been shot; his face took on an expression of amazement and alarm: in one of the black shadows into which she had disappeared he had caught a quick, brief glimpse of shining eyes! For an instant he was dazed and irresolute; then he dashed into the wood after her, shouting: "Irene, Irene, look out! The panther! The panther!"

In a moment he had passed through the fringe of forest into open ground and saw the girl's gray skirt vanishing into her father's door. No panther was visible.

IV. AN APPEAL TO THE CONSCIENCE OF GOD

Jenner Brading, attorney-at-law, lived in a cottage at the edge of the town. Directly behind the dwelling was the forest. Being a bachelor, and therefore, by the Draconian moral code of the time and place denied the services of the only species of domestic servant known thereabout, the "hired girl," he boarded at the village hotel, where also was his office. The woodside cottage was merely a lodging maintained—at no great cost, to be sure—as an evidence of prosperity and respectability. It would hardly do for one to whom the local newspaper had pointed with pride as "the foremost jurist of his time" to be "homeless," albeit he may sometimes have suspected that the words "home" and "house" were not strictly synonymous. Indeed, his consciousness of the disparity and his will to harmonize it were matters of logical inference, for it was generally reported that soon after the cottage was built its owner had made a futile venture in the direction of marriage—had, in truth, gone so far as to be rejected by the beautiful but eccentric daughter of Old Man Marlowe, the recluse. This was publicly believed because he had told it himself and she had not—a reversal of the usual order of things which could hardly fail to carry conviction.

Brading's bedroom was at the rear of the house, with a single window facing the forest.

One night he was awakened by a noise at that window; he could hardly have said what it was like. With a little thrill of the nerves he sat up in bed and laid hold of the revolver which, with a forethought most commendable in one addicted to the habit of sleeping on the ground floor with an open window, he had put under his pillow. The room was in absolute darkness, but being unterrified he knew where to direct his eyes, and there he held them, awaiting in silence what further might occur. He could now dimly discern the aperture—a square of lighter black. Presently there appeared at its lower edge two gleaming eyes that burned with a malignant lustre inexpressibly terrible! Brading's heart gave a great jump, then seemed to stand still. A chill passed along his spine and through his hair; he felt the blood forsake his cheeks. He could not have cried out—not to save his life; but being a man of courage he would not, to save his life, have done so if he had been able. Some trepidation his coward body might feel, but his spirit was of sterner stuff. Slowly the shining eyes rose with a steady motion that seemed an approach, and slowly rose Brading's right hand, holding the pistol. He fired!

Blinded by the flash and stunned by the report, Brading nevertheless heard, or fancied that he heard, the wild, high scream of the panther, so human in sound, so devilish in suggestion. Leaping from the bed he hastily clothed himself and, pistol in hand, sprang from the door, meeting two or three men who came running up from the road. A brief explanation was followed by a cautious search of the house. The grass was wet with dew; beneath the window it had been trodden and partly leveled for a wide space, from which a devious trail, visible in the light of a lantern, led away into the bushes. One of the men stumbled and fell upon his hands, which as he rose and rubbed them together were slippery. On examination they were seen to be red with blood.

An encounter, unarmed, with a wounded panther was not agreeable to their taste; all but Brading turned back. He, with lantern and pistol, pushed courageously forward into the wood. Passing through a difficult undergrowth he came into a small opening, and there his courage had its reward, for there he found the body of his victim. But it was no panther. What it was is told, even to this day, upon a weather-worn headstone in the village churchyard, and for many years was attested daily at the graveside by the bent figure and sorrow-seamed face of Old Man Marlowe, to whose soul, and to the soul of his strange, unhappy child, peace. Peace and reparation.

Visions of the Night

by Ambrose Bierce

For there be divers sorts of death—some wherein the body remaineth; and in some it vanisheth quite away with the spirit. This commonly occurreth only in solitude (such is God's will) and, none seeing the end, we say the man is lost, or gone on a long journey - which indeed he hath; but sometimes it hath happened in sight of many, as abundant testimony showeth. In one kind of death the spirit also dieth, and this it hath been known to do while yet the body was in vigor for many years. Sometimes, as is veritably attested, it dieth with the body, but after a season is raised up again in that place where the body did decay.

Pondering these words of Hali (whom God rest) and questioning their full meaning, as one who, having an intimation, yet doubts if there be not something behind, other than that which he has discerned, I noted not whither I had strayed until a sudden chill wind striking my face revived in me a sense of my surroundings. I observed with astonishment that everything seemed unfamiliar. On every side of me stretched a bleak and desolate expanse of plain, covered with a tall overgrowth of sere grass, which rustled and whistled in the autumn wind with heaven knows what mysterious and disquieting suggestion. Protruded at long intervals above it, stood strangely shaped and somber-colored rocks, which seemed to have an understanding with one another and to exchange looks of uncomfortable significance, as if they had reared their heads to watch the issue of some foreseen event. A few blasted trees here and there appeared as leaders in this malevolent conspiracy of silent expectation.

The day, I thought, must be far advanced, though the sun was invisible; and although sensible that the air was raw and chill my consciousness of that fact was rather mental than physical—I had no feeling of discomfort. Over all the dismal landscape a canopy of low, lead-colored clouds hung like a visible curse. In all this there were a menace and a portent—a hint of evil, an intimation of doom. Bird, beast, or insect there was none. The wind sighed in the bare branches of the dead trees and the gray grass bent to whisper its dread secret to the earth; but no other sound nor motion broke the awful repose of that dismal place.

I observed in the herbage a number of weather-worn stones, evidently shaped with tools. They were broken, covered with moss and half sunken in the earth. Some lay prostrate, some leaned at various angles, none was vertical. They were obviously headstones of graves, though the graves themselves no longer existed as either mounds or depressions; the years had leveled all. Scattered here and there, more massive blocks showed where some pompous tomb or ambitious monument had once flung its feeble defiance at oblivion. So old seemed these relics, these vestiges of vanity and memorials of affection and piety, so battered and worn and stained—so neglected, deserted, forgotten the place, that I could not help thinking myself the discoverer of the burial-ground of a prehistoric race of men whose very name was long extinct.

Filled with these reflections, I was for some time heedless of the sequence of my own experiences, but soon I thought, "How came I hither?" A moment's reflection seemed to make this all clear and explain at the same time, though in a disquieting way, the singular character with which my fancy had invested all that I saw or heard. I was ill. I remembered now that I had been prostrated by a sudden fever, and that my family had told me that in my periods of delirium I had constantly cried out for liberty and air, and had been held in bed to prevent my escape out-of-doors. Now I had eluded the vigilance of my attendants and had wandered hither to—to where? I could not conjecture. Clearly I was at a considerable distance from the city where I dwelt—the ancient and famous city of Carcosa.

No signs of human life were anywhere visible nor audible; no rising smoke, no watch-dog's bark, no lowing of cattle, no shouts of children at play—nothing but that dismal burial-place, with its air of mystery and dread, due to my own disordered brain. Was I not becoming again delirious, there beyond human aid? Was it not indeed all an illusion of my madness? I called aloud the names of my wives and sons, reached out my hands in search of theirs, even as I walked among the crumbling stones and in the withered grass.

A noise behind me caused me to turn about. A wild animal—a lynx—was approaching. The thought came to me: If I break down here in the desert—if the fever return and I fail, this beast will be at my throat. I sprang toward it, shouting. It trotted tranquilly by within a hand's breadth of me and disappeared behind a rock.

A moment later a man's head appeared to rise out of the ground a short distance away. He was ascending the farther slope of a low hill whose crest was hardly to be distinguished from the general level. His whole figure soon came into view against the background of gray cloud. He was half naked, half clad in skins. His hair was unkempt, his beard long and ragged. In one hand he carried a bow and arrow; the other held a blazing torch with a long trail of black smoke. He walked slowly and with caution, as if he feared falling into some open grave concealed by the tall grass. This strange apparition surprised but did not alarm, and taking such a course as to intercept him I met him almost face to face, accosting him with the familiar salutation, "God keep you."

He gave no heed, nor did he arrest his pace.

"Good stranger," I continued, "I am ill and lost. Direct me, I beseech you, to Carcosa."

The man broke into a barbarous chant in an unknown tongue, passing on and away.

An owl on the branch of a decayed tree hooted dismally and was answered by another in the distance. Looking upward, I saw through a sudden rift in the clouds Aldebaran and the Hyades! In all this there was a hint of night—the lynx, the man with the torch, the owl. Yet I saw—I saw even the stars in absence of the darkness. I saw, but was apparently not seen nor heard. Under what awful spell did I exist?

I seated myself at the root of a great tree, seriously to consider what it were best to do. That I was mad I could no longer doubt, yet recognized a ground of doubt in the conviction. Of fever I had no trace. I had, withal, a sense of exhilaration and vigor altogether unknown to me—a feeling of mental and physical exaltation. My senses seemed all alert; I could feel the air as a ponderous substance; I could hear the silence.

A great root of the giant tree against whose trunk I leaned as I sat held inclosed in its grasp a slab of stone, a part of which protruded into a recess formed by another root. The stone was thus partly protected from the weather, though greatly decomposed. Its edges were worn round, its corners eaten away, its surface deeply furrowed and scaled. Glittering particles of mica were visible in the earth about it—vestiges of its decomposition. This stone had apparently marked the grave out of which the tree had sprung ages ago. The tree's exacting roots had robbed the grave and made the stone a prisoner.

A sudden wind pushed some dry leaves and twigs from the uppermost face of the stone; I saw the low-relief letters of an inscription and bent to read it. God in Heaven! my name in full!—the date of *my* birth!—the date of *my* death!

A level shaft of light illuminated the whole side of the tree as I sprang to my feet in terror. The sun was rising in the rosy east. I stood between the tree and his broad red disk—no shadow darkened the trunk!

A chorus of howling wolves saluted the dawn. I saw them sitting on their haunches, singly and in groups, on the summits of irregular mounds and tumuli filling a half of my desert prospect and extending to the horizon. And then I knew that these were ruins of the ancient and famous city of Carcosa.

Such are the facts imparted to the medium Bayrolles by the spirit Hoseib Alar Robardin.

The Red Hand

by Arthur Machen

I. THE PROBLEM OF THE FISH–HOOKS

"There can be no doubt whatever," said Mr Phillipps, "that my theory is the true one; these flints are prehistoric fish-hooks."

"I dare say; but you know that in all probability the things were forged the other day with a door-key."

"Stuff!" said Phillipps; "I have some respect, Dyson, for your literary abilities, but your knowledge of ethnology is insignificant, or rather non-existent. These fish-hooks satisfy every test; they are perfectly genuine."

"Possibly, but as I said just now, you go to work at the wrong end. You neglect the opportunities that confront you and await you, obvious, at every corner; you positively shrink from the chance of encountering primitive man in this whirling and mysterious city, and you pass the weary hours in your agreeable retirement of Red Lion Square fumbling with bits of flint, which are, as I said, in all probability, rank forgeries."

Phillipps took one of the little objects, and held it up in exasperation.

"Look at that ridge," he said. "Did you ever see such a ridge as that on a forgery?"

Dyson merely grunted and lit his pipe and the two sat smoking in rich silence, watching through the open window the children in the square as they flitted to and fro in the twilight of the lamps, as elusive as bats flying on the verge of a dark wood.

"Well,' said Phillipps at last, "it is really a long time since you have been round. I suppose you have been working at your old task."

"Yes," said Dyson, "always the chase of the phrase. I shall grow old in the hunt. But it is a great consolation to meditate on the fact that there are not a dozen people in England who know what style means."

"I suppose not; for the matter of that, the study of ethnology is far from popular. And the difficulties! Primitive man stands dim and very far off across the great bridge of years."

"By the way," he went on after a pause, "what was that stuff you were talking just now about shrinking from the chance of encountering primitive man at the corner, or something of the kind? There are certainly people about here whose ideas are very primitive."

"I wish, Phillipps, you would not rationalize my remarks. If, I recollect the phrases correctly, I hinted that you shrank from the chance of encountering primitive man in this whirling and mysterious city, and I meant exactly what I said. Who can limit the age of survival? The troglodyte and the lake-dweller, perhaps representatives of yet darker races, may very probably be lurking in our midst, rubbing shoulders with frock-coated and finely draped humanity, ravening like wolves at heart and boiling with the foul passions of the swamp and the black cave. Now and then as I walk in Holborn or Fleet Street I see a face which I pronounce abhorred, and yet I could not give a reason for the thrill of loathing that stirs within me."

"My dear Dyson, I refuse to enter myself in your literary 'trying-on' department. I know that survivals do exist, but all things have a limit, and your speculations are absurd. You must catch me your troglodyte before I will believe in him."

"I agree to that with all my heart," said Dyson, chuckling at the ease with which he had succeeded in 'drawing' Phillipps. "Nothing could be better. It's a fine night for a walk," he added taking up his hat.

"What nonsense you are talking, Dyson!" said Phillipps. "However, I have no objection to taking a walk with you: as you say, it is a pleasant night."

"Come along then," said Dyson, grinning, "but remember our bargain."

The two men went out into the square, and threading one of the narrow passages that serve as exits, struck towards the north-east. As they passed along a flaring causeway they could hear at intervals between the clamour of the children and the triumphant *Gloria* played on a piano-organ the long deep hum and roll of the traffic in Holborn, a sound so persistent that it echoed like the turning of everlasting wheels. Dyson looked to the right and left and conned the way, and presently they were passing through a more peaceful quarter, touching on deserted squares and silent streets black as midnight. Phillipps had lost all count of direction, and as by degrees the region of faded respectability gave place to the squalid, and dirty stucco offended the eye of the artistic observer, he merely ventured the remark that he had never seen a neighbourhood more unpleasant or more commonplace.

"More mysterious, you mean," said Dyson. "I warn you, Phillipps, we are now hot upon the scent."

They dived yet deeper into the maze of brickwork; some time before they had crossed a noisy thoroughfare running east and west, and now the quarter seemed all amorphous, without character; here a decent house with sufficient garden, here a faded square, and here factories surrounded by high, blank walls, with blind passages and dark corners; but all ill-lighted and unfrequented and heavy with silence.

Presently, as they paced down a forlorn street of two-story houses, Dyson caught sight of a dark and obscure turning.

"I like the look of that," he said; "it seems to me promising." There was a street lamp at the entrance, and another, a mere glimmer, at the further end. Beneath the lamp, on the pavement, an artist had evidently established his academy in the daytime, for the stones were all a blur of crude colours rubbed into each other, and a few broken fragments of chalk lay in a little heap beneath the wall.

"You see people do occasionally pass this way," said Dyson, pointing to the ruins of the screever's work. "I confess I should not have thought it possible. Come, let us explore."

On one side of this byway of communication was a great timber-yard, with vague piles of wood looming shapeless above the enclosing wall; and on the other side of the road a wall still higher seemed to enclose a garden, for there were shadows like trees, and a faint murmur of rustling leaves broke the silence. It was a moonless night, and clouds that had gathered after sunset had blackened, and midway between the feeble lamps the passage lay all dark and formless, and when one stopped and listened, and the sharp echo of reverberant footsteps ceased, there came from far away, as from beyond the hills, a faint roll of the noise of London. Phillipps was bolstering up his courage to declare that he had had enough of the excursion, when a loud cry from Dyson broke in upon his thoughts.

"Stop, stop, for Heaven's sake, or you will tread on it! There! almost under your feet!" Phillipps looked down, and saw a vague shape, dark, and framed in surrounding darkness, dropped strangely on the pavement, and then a white cuff glimmered for a moment as Dyson lit a match, which went out directly.

"It's a drunken man," said Phillipps very coolly.

"It's a murdered man," said Dyson, and he began to call for police with all his might, and soon from the distance running footsteps echoed and grew louder, and cries sounded.

A policeman was the first to come up.

"What's the matter?" he said, as he drew to a stand, panting. "Anything amiss here?" for he had not seen what was on the pavement.

"Look!" said Dyson, speaking out of the gloom. "Look there! My friend and I came down this place three minutes ago, and that is what we found."

The man flashed his light on the dark shape and cried out.

"Why, it's murder," he said; "there's blood all about him, and a puddle of it in the gutter there. He's not dead long, either. Ah! there's the wound! It's in the neck."

Dyson bent over what was lying there. He saw a prosperous gentleman, dressed in smooth, well-cut clothes. The neat whiskers were beginning to grizzle a little; he might have been forty-five an hour before; and a handsome gold watch had half slipped out of his waistcoat pocket. And there in the flesh of the neck, between chin and ear, gaped a great wound, clean cut, but all clotted with drying blood, and the white of the cheeks shone like a lighted lamp above the red.

Dyson turned, and looked curiously about him; the dead man lay across the path with his head inclined towards the wall, and the blood from the wound streamed away across the pavement, and lay a dark puddle, as the policeman had said, in the gutter. Two more policemen had come up, the crowd gathered, humming from all quarters, and the officers had as much as they could do to keep the curious at a distance. The three lanterns were flashing here and there, searching for more evidence, and in the gleam of one of them Dyson caught sight of an object in the road, to which he called the attention of the policeman nearest to him.

"Look, Phillipps," he said, when the man had secured it and held it up. "Look, that should be something in your way!"

It was a dark flinty stone, gleaming like obsidian, and shaped to a broad edge something after the manner of an adze. One end was rough, and easily grasped in the hand, and the whole thing was hardly five inches long. The edge was thick with blood.

"What is that, Phillipps?" said Dyson; and Phillipps looked hard at it.

"It's a primitive flint knife," he said. "It was made about ten thousand years ago. One exactly like this was found near Abury, in Wiltshire, and all the authorities gave it that age."

The policeman stared astonished at such a development of the case; and Phillipps himself was all aghast at his own words. But Mr Dyson did not notice him. An inspector who had just come up and was listening to the outlines of the case, was holding a lantern to the dead man's head. Dyson, for his part, was staring with a white heat of curiosity at something he saw on the wall, just above where the man was lying; there were a few rude marks done in red chalk.

"This is a black business," said the inspector at length: "does anybody know who it is?"

A man stepped forward from the crowd. "I do, governor," he said, "he's a big doctor, his name's Sir Thomas Vivian; I was in the 'orspital abart six months ago, and he used to come round; he was a very kind man."

"Lord," cried the inspector, "this is a bad job indeed. Why, Sir Thomas Vivian goes to the Royal Family. And there's a watch worth a hundred guineas in his pocket, so it isn't robbery."

Dyson and Phillipps gave their cards to the authority, and moved off, pushing with difficulty through the crowd that was still gathering, gathering fast; and the alley that had been lonely and desolate now swarmed with white staring faces and hummed with the buzz of rumour and horror, and rang with the commands of the officers of police. The two men once free from this swarming curiosity stepped out briskly, but for twenty minutes neither spoke a word.

"Phillipps," said Dyson, as they came into a small but cheerful street, clean and brightly lit, "Phillipps, I owe you an apology. I was wrong to have spoken as I did tonight. Such infernal jesting," he went on, with heat, "as if there were no wholesome subjects for a joke. I feel as if I had raised an evil spirit."

"For Heaven's sake say nothing more,' said Phillipps, choking down horror with visible effort. 'You told the truth to me in my room; the troglodyte, as you said, is still lurking about the earth, and in these very streets around us, slaying for mere lust of blood."

"I will come up for a moment," said Dyson, when they reached Red Lion

Square, "I have something to ask you. I think there should be nothing hidden between us at all events."

Phillipps nodded gloomily, and they went up to the room, where everything hovered indistinct in the uncertain glimmer of the light from without.

When the candle was lighted and the two men sat facing each other, Dyson spoke.

"Perhaps," he began, "you did not notice me peering at the wall just above the place where the head lay. The light from the inspector's lantern was shining full on it, and I saw something that looked queer to me, and I examined it closely. I found that some one had drawn in red chalk a rough outline of a hand—a human hand—upon the wall. But it was the curious position of the fingers that struck me; it was like this"; and he took a pencil and a piece of paper and drew rapidly, and then handed what he had done to Phillipps. It was a rough sketch of a hand seen from the back, with the fingers clenched, and the top of the thumb protruded between the first and second fingers, and pointed downwards, as if to something below.

"It was just like that," said Dyson, as he saw Phillipps's face grow still whiter. "The thumb pointed down as if to the body; it seemed almost a live hand in ghastly gesture. And just beneath there was a small mark with the powder of the chalk lying on it—as if someone had commenced a stroke and had broken the chalk in his hand. I saw the bit of chalk lying on the ground. But what do you make of it?"

"It's a horrible old sign," said Phillipps—"one of the most horrible signs connected with the theory of the evil eye. It is used still in Italy, but there can be no doubt that it has been known for ages. It is one of the survivals; you must look for the origin of it in the black swamp whence man first came."

Dyson took up his hat to go.

"I think, jesting apart," said he, "that I kept my promise, and that we were and are hot on the scent, as I said. It seems as if I had really shown you primitive man, or his handiwork at all events."

II. INCIDENT OF THE LETTER

About a month after the extraordinary and mysterious murder of Sir Thomas Vivian, the well-known and universally respected specialist in heart disease, Mr Dyson called again on his friend Mr Phillipps, whom he found, not as usual, sunk deep in painful study, but reclining in his easy-chair in an attitude of relaxation. He welcomed Dyson with cordiality.

"I am very glad you have come," he began; "I was thinking of looking you up. There is no longer the shadow of a doubt about the matter."

"You mean the case of Sir Thomas Vivian?"

"Oh, no, not at all. I was referring to the problem of the fish-hooks. Between ourselves, I was a little too confident when you were here last, but since then other facts have turned up; and only yesterday I had a letter from a distinguished F.R.S. which quite settles the affair. I have been thinking what I should tackle next; and I am inclined to believe that there is a good deal to be done in the way of so-called undecipherable inscriptions."

"Your line of study pleases me," said Dyson, "I think it may prove useful. But in the meantime, there was surely something extremely mysterious about the case of Sir Thomas Vivian."

"Hardly, I think. I allowed myself to be frightened that night; but there can be no doubt that the facts are patient of a comparatively commonplace explanation."

"Really! What is your theory then?"

"Well, I imagine that Vivian must have been mixed up at some period of his life in an adventure of a not very creditable description, and that he was murdered out of revenge by some Italian whom he had wronged."

"Why Italian?"

"Because of the hand, the sign of the *mano in fica*. That gesture is now only used by Italians. So you see that what appeared the most obscure feature in the case turns out to be illuminant."

"Yes, quite so. And the flint knife?"

"That is very simple. The man found the thing in Italy, or possibly stole it from some museum. Follow the line of least resistance, my dear fellow, and you will see there is no need to bring up primitive man from his secular grave beneath the hills."

"There is some justice in what you say," said Dyson. "As I understand you, then, you think that your Italian, having murdered, Vivian, kindly chalked up that hand as a guide to Scotland Yard?"

"Why not? Remember a murderer is always a madman. He may plot and contrive nine-tenths of his scheme with the acuteness and the grasp of a chess-player or a pure mathematician; but somewhere or other his wits leave him and he behaves like a fool. Then you must take into account the insane pride or vanity of the criminal; he likes to leave his mark, as it were, upon his handiwork."

"Yes, it is all very ingenious; but have you read the reports of the inquest?"

"No, not a word. I simply gave my evidence, left the court, and dismissed the subject from my mind."

"Quite so. Then if you don't object I should like to give you an account of the case. I have studied it rather deeply, and I confess it interests me extremely."

"Very good. But I warn you I have done with mystery. We are to deal with facts now."

"Yes, it is fact that I wish to put before you. And this is fact the first. When the police moved Sir Thomas Vivian's body they found an open knife beneath him. It was an ugly-looking thing such as sailors carry, with a blade that the mere opening rendered rigid, and there the blade was all ready, bare and gleaming, but without a trace of blood on it, and the knife was found to be quite new; it had never been used. Now, at the first glance it looks as if your imaginary Italian were just the man to have such a tool. But consider a moment. Would he be likely to buy a new knife expressly to commit murder? And, secondly, if he had such a knife, why didn't he use it, instead of that very odd flint instrument?

"And I want to put this to you. You think the murderer chalked up the hand after the murder as a sort of 'melodramatic Italian assassin his mar'" touch. Passing over the question as to whether the real criminal ever does such a thing, I would point out that, on the medical evidence, Sir Thomas Vivian hadn't been dead for more than an hour; That would place the stroke at about a quarter to ten, and you know it was perfectly dark when we went out at 9.30. And that passage was singularly gloomy and ill-lighted, and the hand was drawn roughly, it is true, but correctly and without the bungling of strokes and the bad shots that are inevitable when one tries to draw in the dark or with shut eyes. Just try to draw such a simple figure as a square without looking at the paper, and then ask me to conceive that your Italian, with the rope waiting for his neck, could draw the hand on the wall so firmly and truly, in the black shadow of that alley. It is absurd. By consequence, then, the hand was drawn early in the evening, long before any murder was committed; or else—mark this, Phillipps—it was drawn by some one to whom darkness and gloom were familiar and habitual; by some one to whom the common dread of the rope was unknown!

"Again: a curious note was found in Sir Thomas Vivian's pocket. Envelope and paper were of a common make, and the stamp bore the West Central postmark. I will come to the nature of the contents later on, but it is the question of the handwriting that is so remarkable. The address on the outside was neatly written in a small clear hand, but the letter itself might have been written by a Persian who had learnt the English script. It was upright, and the letters were curiously contorted, with an affectation of dashes and backward curves which really reminded me of an Oriental manuscript, though it was all perfectly legible. But—and here comes the poser—on searching the dead man's waistcoat pockets a small memorandum book was found; it was almost filled with pencil jottings. These memoranda related chiefly to matters of a private as distinct from a professional nature; there were appointments to meet friends, notes of theatrical first-nights, the address of a good hotel in Tours, and the title of a new novel—nothing in any way intimate. And the whole of these jottings were written in a hand nearly identical with the writing of the note found in the dead man's coat pocket! There was just enough difference between them to enable the expert to swear that the two were not written by the same person. I will just read you so much of Lady Vivian's evidence as bears on this point of the writing; I have the printed slip with me. Here you see she says: 'I was married to my late husband seven years ago; I never saw any letter addressed to him in a hand at all resembling that on the envelope produced, nor have I ever seen writing like that in the letter before me. I never saw my late husband using the memorandum book, but I am sure he did write everything in it; I am certain of that because we stayed last May at the Hotel du Faisan, Rue Royale, Tours, the address of which is given in the book; I remember his getting the novel *A Sentinel* about six weeks ago. Sir Thomas Vivian never liked to miss the first-nights at the theatres. His usual hand was perfectly different from that used in the note-book.'

"And now, last of all, we come back to the note itself. Here it is in facsimile. My possession of it is due to the kindness of Inspector Cleeve, who is pleased to be amused at my amateur inquisitiveness. Read it, Phillipps; you tell me you are interested in obscure inscriptions; here is something for you to decipher."

Mr Phillipps, absorbed in spite of himself in the strange circumstances Dyson had related, took the piece of paper, and scrutinized it closely. The handwriting was indeed bizarre in the extreme, and, as Dyson had noted, not unlike the Persian character in its general effect, but it was perfectly legible.

"Read it aloud," said Dyson, and Phillipps obeyed.

"'Hand did not point in vain. The meaning of the stars is no longer obscure. Strangely enough, the black heaven vanished, or was stolen yesterday, but that does not matter in the least, as I have a celestial globe. Our old orbit remains unchanged; you have not forgotten the number of my sign, or will you appoint some other house? I have been on the other side of the moon, and can bring something to show you.'"

"And what do you make of that?" said Dyson.

"It seems to me mere gibberish," said Phillipps; "you suppose it has a meaning?"

"Oh, surely; it was posted three days before the murder; it was found in the murdered man's pocket; it is written in a fantastic hand which the murdered man himself used for his private memoranda. There must be purpose under all this, and to my mind there is something ugly enough hidden under the circumstances of this case of Sir Thomas Vivian."

"But what theory have you formed?"

"Oh, as to theories, I am still in a very early stage; it is too soon to state conclusions. But I think I have demolished your Italian. I tell you, Phillipps, again the whole thing has an ugly look to my eyes. I cannot do as you do, and fortify myself with cast-iron propositions to the effect that this or that doesn't happen, and never has happened. You note that the first word in the letter is 'hand'. That seems to me, taken with what we know about the hand on the wall, significant enough, and what you yourself told me of the history and meaning of the symbol, its connection with a world-old belief and faiths of dim far-off years, all this speaks of mischief, for me at all events. No; I stand pretty well to what I said to you half in joke that night before we went out. There are sacraments of evil as well as of good about us, and we live and move to my belief in an unknown world, a place where there are caves and shadows and dwellers in twilight. It is possible that man may sometimes return on the track of evolution, and it is my belief that an awful lore is not yet dead."

"I cannot follow you in all this," said Phillipps; "it seems to interest you strangely. What do you propose to do?"

"My dear, Phillipps," replied Dyson, speaking in a lighter tone, "I am afraid I shall have to go down a little in the world. I have a prospect of visits to the pawnbrokers before me, and the publicans must not be neglected. I must cultivate a taste for four ale; shag tobacco I already love and esteem with all my heart."

III. SEARCH FOR THE VANISHED HEAVEN

For many days after the discussion with Phillipps. Mr Dyson was resolute in the line of research he had marked out for himself. A fervent curiosity and an innate liking for the obscure were great incentives, but especially in this case of Sir Thomas Vivian's death (for Dyson began to boggle a little at the word 'murder') there seemed to him an element that was more than curious. The sign of the red hand upon the wall, the tool of flint that had given death, the almost identity between the handwriting of the note and the fantastic script reserved religiously, as it appeared, by the doctor for trifling jottings, all these diverse and variegated threads joined to weave in his mind a strange and shadowy picture, with ghastly shapes dominant and deadly, and yet ill-defined, like the giant figures wavering in an ancient tapestry. He thought he had a clue to the meaning of the note, and in his resolute search for the 'black heaven', which had vanished, he beat furiously about the alleys and obscure streets of central London, making himself a familiar figure to the pawnbroker, and a frequent guest at the more squalid pot-houses.

For a long time he was unsuccessful, and he trembled at the thought that the 'black heaven' might be hid in the coy retirements of Peckham, or lurk perchance in distant Willesden, but finally, improbability, in which he put his trust, came to the rescue. It was a dark and rainy night, with something in the unquiet and stirring gusts that savoured of approaching winter, and Dyson, beating up a narrow street not far from the Gray's Inn Road, took shelter in an extremely dirty 'public', and called for beer, forgetting for the moment his preoccupations, and only thinking of the sweep of the wind about the tiles and the hissing of the rain through the black and troubled air. At the bar there gathered the usual company: the frowsy women and the men in shiny black, those who appeared to mumble secretly together, others who wrangled in interminable argument, and a few shy drinkers who stood apart, each relishing his dose, and the rank and biting flavour of cheap spirit. Dyson was wondering at the enjoyment of it all, when suddenly there came a sharper accent. The folding-doors swayed open, and a middle-aged woman staggered towards the bar, and clutched the pewter rim as if she stepped a deck in a roaring gale. Dyson glanced at her attentively as a pleasing specimen of her class; she was decently dressed in black, and carried a black bag of somewhat rusty leather, and her intoxication was apparent and far advanced. As she swayed at the bar, it was evidently all she could do to stand upright, and the barman, who had looked at her with disfavour, shook his head in reply to her thick-voiced demand for a drink. The woman glared at him, transformed in a moment to a fury, with bloodshot eyes, and poured forth a torrent of execration, a stream of blasphemies and early English phraseology.

"Get out of this," said the man; "shut up and be off, or I'll send for the police."

"Police, you—" bawled the woman 'I'll—well give you something to fetch the police for!' and with a rapid dive into her bag she pulled out some object which she hurled furiously at the barman's head.

The man ducked down, and the missile flew over his head and smashed a bottle to fragments, while the woman with a peal of horrible laughter rushed to the door, and they could hear her steps pattering fast over the wet stones.

The barman looked ruefully about him.

"Not much good going after her," he said, "and I'm afraid what she's left won't pay for that bottle of whisky." He fumbled amongst the fragments of broken glass, and drew out something dark, a kind of square stone it seemed, which he held up.

"Valuable cur'osity," he said, "any gent like to bid?"

The habitues had scarcely turned from their pots and glasses during these exciting incidents; they gazed a moment, fishily, when the bottle smashed, and that was all, and the mumble of the confidential was resumed and the jangle of the quarrelsome, and the shy and solitary sucked in their lips and relished again the rank flavour of the spirit.

Dyson looked quickly at what the barman held before him.

"Would you mind letting me see it?" he said; "it's a queer-looking old thing, isn't it?"

It was a small black tablet, apparently of stone, about four inches long by two and a half broad, and as Dyson took it he felt rather than saw that he touched the secular with his flesh. There was some kind of carving on the surface, and, most conspicuous, a sign that made Dyson's heart leap.

"I don't mind taking it," he said quietly. "Would two shillings be enough?"

"Say half a dollar," said the man, and the bargain was concluded. Dyson drained his pot of beer, finding it delicious, and lit his pipe, and went out deliberately soon after. When he reached his apartment he locked the door, and placed the tablet on his desk, and then fixed himself in his chair, as resolute as an army in its trenches before a beleaguered city. The tablet was full under the light of the shaded candle, and scrutinizing it closely, Dyson saw first the sign of the hand with the thumb protruding between the fingers; it was cut finely and firmly on the dully black surface of the stone, and the thumb pointed downward to what was beneath.

"It is mere ornament," said Dyson to himself, 'perhaps symbolical ornament, but surely not an inscription, or the signs of any words ever spoken.'

The hand pointed at a series of fantastic figures, spirals and whorls of the finest, most delicate lines, spaced at intervals over the remaining surface of the tablet. The marks were as intricate and seemed almost as much without design as the pattern of a thumb impressed upon a pane of glass.

"Is it some natural marking?" thought Dyson; 'there have been queer designs, likenesses of beasts and flowers, in stones with which man's hand had nothing to do; and he bent over the stone with a magnifier, only to be convinced that no hazard of nature could have delineated these varied labyrinths of line. The whorls were of different sizes; some were less than the twelfth of an inch in diameter, and the largest was a little smaller than a sixpence, and under the glass the regularity and accuracy of the cutting were evident, and in the smaller spirals the lines were graduated at intervals of a hundredth of an inch. The whole thing had a marvellous and fantastic look, and gazing at the mystic whorls beneath the hand, Dyson became subdued with an impression of vast and far-off ages, and of a living being that had touched the stone with enigmas before the hills were formed, when the hard rocks still boiled with fervent heat.

"The 'black heaven' is found again," he said, "but the meaning of the stars is likely to be obscure for everlasting so far as I am concerned."

London stilled without, and a chill breath came into the room as Dyson sat gazing at the tablet shining duskily under the candle-light; and at last as he closed the desk over the ancient stone, all his wonder at the case of Sir Thomas Vivian increased tenfold, and he thought of the well-dressed prosperous gentleman lying dead mystically beneath the sign of the hand, and the insupportable conviction seized him that between the death of this fashionable West End doctor and the weird spirals of the tablet there were most secret and unimaginable links.

For days he sat before his desk gazing at the tablet, unable to resist its lodestone fascination, and yet quite helpless, without even the hope of solving the symbols so secretly inscribed. At last, desperate he called in Mr Phillipps in consultation, and told in brief the story of the finding the stone.

"Dear me!" said Phillipps, "this is extremely curious; you have had a find indeed. Why, it looks to me even more ancient than the Hittite seal. I confess the character, if it is a character, is entirely strange to me. These whorls are really very quaint."

"Yes, but I want to know what they mean. You must remember this tablet is the 'black heaven' of the letter found in Sir Thomas Vivian's pocket; it bears directly on his death."

"Oh, no, that is nonsense! This is, no doubt, an extremely ancient tablet, which has been stolen from some collection. Yes, the hand makes an odd coincidence, but only a coincidence after all."

"My dear Phillipps, you are a living example of the truth of the axiom that extreme scepticism is mere credulity. But can you decipher the inscription?"

"I undertake to decipher anything," said Phillipps. "I do not believe in the insoluble. These characters are curious, but I cannot fancy them to be inscrutable."

"Then take the thing away with you and make what you can of it. It has begun to haunt me; I feel as if I had gazed too long into the eyes of the Sphinx."

Phillipps departed with the tablet in an inner pocket. He had not much doubt of success, for he had evolved thirty-seven rules for the solution of inscriptions. Yet when a week had passed and he called to see Dyson there was no vestige of triumph on his features. He found his friend in a state of extreme irritation, pacing up and down in the room like a man in a passion. He turned with a start as the door opened.

"Well," said Dyson, "you have got it? What is it all about?"

"My dear fellow, I am sorry to say I have completely failed. I have tried every known device in vain. I have even been so officious as to submit it to a friend at the Museum, but he, though a man of prime authority on the subject, tells me he is quite at fault. It must be some wreckage of a vanished race, almost, I think—a fragment of another world than ours. I am not a superstitious man, Dyson, and you know that I have no truck with even the noble delusions, but I confess I yearn to be rid of this small square of blackish stone. Frankly, it has given me an ill week; it seems to me troglodytic and abhorred."

Phillipps drew out the tablet and laid it on the desk before Dyson.

"By the way," he went on, "I was right at all events in one particular; it has formed part of some collection. There is a piece of grimy paper on the back that must have been a label."

"Yes, I noticed that," said Dyson, who had fallen into deepest disappointment; "no doubt the paper is a label. But as I don't much care where the tablet originally came from, and only wish to know what the inscription means, I paid no attention to the paper. The thing is a hopeless riddle, I suppose, and yet it must surely be of the greatest importance."

Phillipps left soon after, and Dyson, still despondent, took the tablet in his hand and carelessly turned it over. The label had so grimed that it seemed merely a dull stain, but as Dyson looked at it idly, and yet attentively, he could see pencil-marks, and he bent over it eagerly, with his glass to his eye. To his annoyance, he found that part of the paper had been torn away, and he could only with difficulty make out odd words and pieces of words. First he read something that looked like 'inroad', and then beneath, 'stony-hearted step —' and a tear cut off the rest. But in an instant a solution suggested itself, and he chuckled with huge delight.

"Certainly," he said out loud, "this is not only the most charming but the most convenient quarter in all London; here I am, allowing for the accidents of side streets, perched on a tower of observation."

He glanced triumphant out of the window across the street to the gate of the British Museum. Sheltered by the boundary wall of that agreeable institution, a 'screever', or artist in chalks, displayed his brilliant impressions on the pavement, soliciting the approval and the coppers of the gay and serious.

"This," said Dyson, "is more than delightful! An artist is provided to my hand."

IV. THE ARTIST OF THE PAVEMENT

Mr Phillipps, in spite of all disavowals—in spite of the wall of sense of whose enclosure and limit he was wont to make his boast—yet felt in his heart profoundly curious as to the case of Sir Thomas Vivian. Though he kept a brave face for his friend, his reason could not decently resist the conclusion that Dyson had enunciated, namely, that the whole affair had a look both ugly and mysterious. There was the weapon of a vanished race that had pierced the great arteries; the red hand, the symbol of a hideous faith, that pointed to the slain man; and then the tablet which Dyson declared he had expected to find, and had certainly found, bearing the ancient impress of the hand of malediction, and a legend written beneath in a character compared with which the most antique cuneiform was a thing of yesterday. Besides all this, there were other points that tortured and perplexed. How to account for the bare knife found unstained beneath the body? And the hint that the red hand upon the wall must have been drawn by some one whose life was passed in darkness thrilled him with a suggestion of dim and infinite horror. Hence he was in truth not a little curious as to what was to come, and some ten days after he had returned the tablet he again visited the 'mystery-man', as he privately named his friend.

Arrived in the grave and airy chambers in Great Russell Street, he found the moral atmosphere of the place had been transformed. All Dyson's irritation had disappeared, his brow was smoothed with complacency, and he sat at a table by the window gazing out into the street with an expression of grim enjoyment, a pile of books and papers lying unheeded before him.

"My dear Phillipps, I am delighted to see you! Pray excuse my moving. Draw your chair up here to the table, and try this admirable shag tobacco."

"Thank you," said Phillipps, "judging by the flavour of the smoke, I should think it is a little strong. But what on earth is all this? What are you looking at?"

"I am on my watch-tower. I assure you that the time seems short while I contemplate this agreeable street and the classic grace of the Museum portico."

"Your capacity for nonsense is amazing," replied Phillipps, "but have you succeeded in deciphering the tablet? It interests me."

"I have not paid much attention to the tablet recently," said Dyson. "I believe the spiral character may wait."

"Really! And how about the Vivian murder?"

"Ah, you do take an interest in that case? Well, after all, we cannot deny that it was a queer business. But is not 'murder' rather a coarse word? It smacks a little, surely, of the police poster. Perhaps I am a trifle decadent, but I cannot help believing in the splendid word; 'sacrifice', for example, is surely far finer than 'murder'."

"I am all in the dark," said Phillipps. "I cannot even imagine by what track you are moving in this labyrinth."

"I think that before very long the whole matter will be a good deal clearer for us both, but I doubt whether you will like hearing the story."

Dyson lit his pipe afresh and leant back, not relaxing, however, in his scrutiny of the street. After a somewhat lengthy pause, he startled Phillipps by a loud breath of relief as he rose from the chair by the window and began to pace the floor.

"It's over for the day," he said, "and, after all, one gets a little tired."

Phillipps looked with inquiry into the street. The evening was darkening, and the pile of the Museum was beginning to loom indistinct before the lighting of the lamps, but the pavements were thronged and busy. The artist in chalks across the way was gathering together his materials, and blurring all the brilliance of his designs, and a little lower down there was the clang of shutters being placed in position. Phillipps could see nothing to justify Mr Dyson's sudden abandonment of his attitude of surveillance, and grew a little irritated by all these thorny enigmas.

"Do you know, Phillipps," said Dyson, as he strolled at ease up and down the room, "I will tell you how I work. I go upon the theory of improbability. The theory is unknown to you? I will explain. Suppose I stand on the steps of St. Paul's and look out for a blind man lame of the left leg to pass me, it is evidently highly improbable that I shall see such a person by waiting for an hour. If I wait two hours the improbability is diminished, but is still enormous, and a watch of a whole day would give little expectation of success. But suppose I take up the same position day after day, and week after week, don't you perceive that the improbability is lessening constantly—growing smaller day after day. Don't you see that two lines which are not parallel are gradually approaching one another, drawing nearer and nearer to a point of meeting, till at last they do meet, and improbability has vanished altogether. That is how I found the black tablet: I acted on the theory of improbability. It is the only scientific principle I know of which can enable one to pick out an unknown man from amongst five million."

"And you expect to find the interpreter of the black tablet by this method?"

"Certainly."

"And the murderer of Sir Thomas Vivian also?"

"Yes, I expect to lay my hands on the person concerned in the death of Sir Thomas Vivian in exactly the same way."

The rest of the evening after Phillipps had left was devoted by Dyson to sauntering in the streets, and afterwards, when the night grew late, to his literary labours, or the chase of the phrase, as he called it. The next morning the station by the window was again resumed. His meals were brought to him at the table, and he ate with his eyes on the street. With briefest intervals, snatched reluctantly from time to time, he persisted in his survey throughout the day, and only at dusk, when the shutters were put up and the 'screever' ruthlessly deleted all his labour of the day, just before the gas-lamps began to star the shadows, did he feel at liberty to quit his post. Day after day this ceaseless glance upon the street continued, till the landlady grew puzzled and aghast at such a profitless pertinacity.

But at last, one evening, when the play of lights and shadows was scarce beginning, and the clear cloudless air left all distinct and shining, there came the moment. A man of middle age, bearded and bowed, with a touch of grey about the ears, was strolling slowly along the northern pavement of Great Russell Street from the eastern end. He looked up at the Museum as he went by, and then glanced involuntarily at the art of the 'screever', and at the artist himself, who sat beside his pictures, hat in hand. The man with the beard stood still an instant, swaying slightly to and fro as if in thought, and Dyson saw his fists shut tight, and his back quivering, and the one side of his face in view twitched and grew contorted with the indescribable torment of approaching epilepsy. Dyson drew a soft hat from his pocket, and dashed the door open, taking the stair with a run.

When he reached the street, the person he had seen so agitated had turned about, and, regardless of observation, was racing wildly towards Bloomsbury Square, with his back to his former course. Mr Dyson went up to the artist of the pavement and gave him some money, observing quietly, "You needn't trouble to draw that thing again."

Then he, too, turned about, and strolled idly down the street in the opposite direction to that taken by the fugitive. So the distance between Dyson and the man with the bowed head grew steadily greater.

V. STORY OF THE TREASURE-HOUSE

"There are many reasons why I chose your rooms for the meeting in preference to my own. Chiefly, perhaps because I thought the man would be more at his ease on neutral ground."

"I confess, Dyson,' said Phillipps, 'that I feel both impatient and uneasy. You know my standpoint: hard matter of fact, materialism if you like, in its crudest form. But there is something about all this affair of Vivian that makes me a little restless. And how did you induce the man to come?"

"He has an exaggerated opinion of my powers. You remember what I said about the doctrine of improbability? When it does work out, it gives results which seem very amazing to a person who is not in the secret. That is eight striking, isn't it? And there goes the bell."

They heard footsteps on the stair, and presently the door opened, and a middle-aged man, with a bowed head, bearded, and with a good deal of grizzling hair about his ears, came into the room. Phillipps glanced at his features, and recognised the lineaments of terror.

"Come in, Mr Selby," said Dyson. "This is Mr Phillipps, my intimate friend and our host for this evening. Will you take anything? Then perhaps we had better hear your story—a very singular one, I am sure."

The man spoke in a voice hollow and a little quavering, and a fixed stare that never left his eyes seemed directed to something awful that was to remain before him by day and night for the rest of his life.

"You will, I am sure, excuse preliminaries," he began; "what I have to tell is best told quickly. I will say, then, that I was born in a remote part of the west of England, where the very outlines of the woods and hills, and the winding of the streams in the valleys, are apt to suggest the mystical to any one strongly gifted with imagination. When I was quite a boy there were certain huge and rounded hills, certain depths of hanging wood, and secret valleys bastioned round on every side that filled me with fancies beyond the bourne of rational expression, and as I grew older and began to dip into my father's books, I went by instinct, like the bee, to all that would nourish fantasy. Thus, from a course of obsolete and occult reading, and from listening to certain wild legends in which the older people still secretly believed, I grew firmly convinced of the existence of treasure, the hoard of a race extinct for ages, still hidden beneath the hills, and my every thought was directed to the discovery of the golden heaps that lay, as I fancied within a few feet of the green turf. To one spot, in especial, I was drawn as if by enchantment; it was a tumulus, the domed memorial of some forgotten people, crowning the crest of a vast mountain range; and I have often lingered there on summer evenings, sitting on the great block of limestone at the summit, and looking out far over the yellow sea towards the Devonshire coast. One day as I dug heedlessly with the ferrule of my stick at the mosses and lichens which grew rank over the stone, my eye was caught by what seemed a pattern beneath the growth of green; there was a curving line, and marks that did not look altogether the work of nature. At first I thought I had bared some rarer fossil, and I took out my knife and scraped away at the moss till a square foot was uncovered. Then I saw two signs which startled me; first, a closed hand, pointing downwards, the thumb protruding between the fingers, and beneath the hand a whorl or spiral, traced with exquisite accuracy in the hard surface of the rock. Here I persuaded myself, was an index to the great secret, but I chilled at the recollection of the fact that some antiquarians had tunnelled the tumulus through and through, and had been a good deal surprised at not finding so much as an arrowhead within. Clearly, then, the signs on the limestone had no local significance; and I made up my mind that I must search abroad. By sheer accident I was in a measure successful in my quest. Strolling by a cottage, I saw some children playing by the roadside; one was holding up some object in his hand, and the rest were going through one of the many forms of elaborate pretence which make up a great part of the mystery of a child's life. Something in the object held by the little boy attracted me, and I asked him to let me see it. The plaything of these children consisted of an oblong tablet of black stone; and on it was inscribed the hand pointing downwards, just as I had seen it on the rock, while beneath, spaced over the tablet, were a number of whorls and spirals, cut, as it seemed to me, with the utmost care and nicety. I bought the toy for a couple of shillings; the woman of the house told me it had been lying about for years; she thought her husband had found it one day in the brook which ran in front of the cottage: it was a very hot summer, and the stream was almost dry, and he saw it amongst the stones. That day I tracked the brook to a well of water gushing up cold and clear at the head of a lonely glen in the mountain. That was twenty years ago, and I only succeeded in deciphering the mysterious inscription last August. I must not trouble you with irrelevant details of my life; it is enough for me to say that I was forced, like many another man, to leave my old home and come to London. Of money I had very little, and I was glad to find a cheap room in a squalid street off the Gray's Inn Road. The late Sir Thomas Vivian, then far poorer and more wretched than myself, had a garret in the same house, and before many months we became intimate friends, and I had confided to him the object of my life. I had at first great difficulty in persuading him that I was not giving my days and my nights to an inquiry altogether hopeless and chimerical; but when he was convinced he grew keener than myself, and glowed at the thought of the riches which were to be the prize of some ingenuity and patience. I liked the man intensely, and pitied his case; he had a strong desire to enter the medical profession, but he lacked the means to pay the smallest fees, and indeed he was, not once or twice, but often reduced to the very verge of starvation. I freely and solemnly promised, that under whatever chances, he should share in my heaped fortune when it came, and this promise to one who had always been poor, and yet thirsted for wealth and pleasure in a manner unknown to me, was the strongest incentive. He threw himself into the task with eager interest, and applied a very acute intellect and unwearied patience to the solution of the characters on the tablet. I, like other ingenious young men, was curious in the matter of handwriting, and I had invented or adapted a fantastic script which I used occasionally, and which took Vivian so strongly that he was at the pains to imitate it. It was arranged between us that if we were ever parted, and had occasion to write on the affair that was so close to our hearts, this queer hand of my invention was to be used, and we also contrived a semi-cypher for the same purpose. Meanwhile we exhausted ourselves in efforts to get at the heart of the mystery, and after a couple of years had gone by I could see that Vivian begall to sicken a little of the adventure, and one night he told me with some emotion that he feared both our lives were being passed away in idle and hopeless endeavour. Not many months afterwards he was so happy as to receive a considerable legacy from an aged and distant relative whose very existence had been almost forgotten by him; and with money at the bank, he became at once a stranger to me. He had passed his preliminary examination many years before, and forthwith decided to enter at St. Thomas's Hospital, and he told me that he must look out for a more convenient lodging. As we said good-bye, I reminded him of the promise I had given, and solemnly renewed it; but Vivian laughed with something between pity and contempt in his voice and expression as he thanked me. I need not dwell on the long struggle and misery of my existence, now doubly lonely; I never wearied or despaired of final success, and every day saw me at work, the tablet before me, and only at dusk would I go out and take my daily walk along Oxford Street, which attracted me, I think, by the noise and motion and glitter of lamps.

"This walk grew with me to a habit; every night, and in all weathers, I crossed the Gray's Inn Road and struck westward, sometimes choosing a northern track, by the Euston Road and Tottenham Court Road, sometimes I went by Holborn, and I sometimes by way of Great Russell Street. Every night I walked for an hour to and fro on the northern pavement of Oxford Street, and the tale of De Quincey and his name for the Street, 'Stony-hearted step mother', often recurred to my memory. Then I would return to my grimy den and spend hours more in endless analysis of the riddle before me.

"The answer came to me one night a few weeks; ago; it flashed into my brain in a moment, and I read the inscription, and saw that after all I had not wasted my days. 'The place of the treasure-house of them that dwell below,' were the first words I read, and then followed minute indications of the spot in my own country where the great works of gold were to be kept for ever. Such a track was to be followed, such a pitfall avoided; here the way narrowed almost to a fox's hole, and there it broadened, and so at last the chamber would be reached. I determined to lose no time in verifying my discovery—not that I doubted at that great moment, but I would not risk even the smallest chance of disappointing my old friend Vivian, now a rich and prosperous man. I took the train for the West, and one night, with chart in hand, traced out the passage of the hills, and went so far that I saw the gleam of gold before me. I would not go on; I resolved that Vivian must be with me; and I only brought away a strange knife of flint which lay on the path, as confirmation of what I had to tell. I returned to London, and was a good deal vexed to find the stone tablet had disappeared from my rooms. My landlady, an inveterate drunkard, denied all knowledge of the fact, but I have little doubt she had stolen the thing for the sake of the glass of whisky it might fetch. However, I knew what was written on the tablet by heart, and I had also made an exact facsimile of the characters, so the loss was not severe. Only one thing annoyed me: when I first came into possession of the stone, I had pasted a piece of paper on the back and had written down the date and place of finding, and later on I had scribbled a word or two, a trivial sentiment, the name of my street, and such-like idle pencillings on the paper; and these memories of days that had seemed so hopeless were dear to me: I had thought they would help to remind me in the future of the hours when I had hoped against despair. However, I wrote at once to Sir Thomas Vivian, using the handwriting I have mentioned and also the quasi-cypher. I told him of my success, and after mentioning the loss of the tablet and the fact that I had a copy of the inscription, I reminded him once more of my promise, and asked him either to write or call. He replied that he would see me in a certain obscure passage in Clerkenwell well known to us both in the old days, and at seven o'clock one evening I went to meet him. At the corner of this by way, as I was walking to and fro, I noticed the blurred pictures of some street artist, and I picked up a piece of chalk he had left behind him, not much thinking what I was doing. I paced up and down the passage, wondering a good deal, as you may imagine, as to what manner of man I was to meet after so many years of parting, and the thoughts of the buried time coming thick upon me, I walked mechanically without raising my eyes from the ground. I was startled out of my reverie by an angry voice and a rough inquiry why I didn't keep to the right side of the pavement, and looking up I found I had confronted a prosperous and important gentleman, who eyed my poor appearance with a look of great dislike and contempt. I knew directly it was my old comrade, and when I recalled myself to him, he apologized with some show of regret, and began to thank me for my kindness, doubtfully, as if he hesitated to commit himself, and, as I could see, with the hint of a suspicion as to my sanity. I would have engaged him at first in reminiscences of our friendship, but I found Sir Thomas viewed those days with a good deal of distaste, and replying politely to my remarks, continually edged in 'business matters', as he called them. I changed my topics, and told him in greater detail what I have told you. Then I saw his manner suddenly change; as I pulled out the flint knife to prove my journey 'to the other side of the moon', as we called it in our jargon, there came over him a kind of choking eagerness, his features were somewhat discomposed, and I thought I detected a shuddering horror, a clenched resolution, and the effort to keep quiet succeed one another in a manner that puzzled me. I had occasion to be a little precise in my particulars, and it being still light enough, I remembered the red chalk in my pocket, and drew the hand on the wall. 'Here, you see, is the hand', I said, as I explained its true meaning, 'note where the thumb issues from between the first and second fingers', and I would have gone on, and had applied the chalk to the wall to continue my diagram, when he struck my hand down much to my surprise. 'No, no,' he said, 'I do not want all that. And this place is not retired enough; let us walk on, and do you explain everything to me minutely.' I complied readily enough, and he led me away choosing the most unfrequented by-ways, while I drove in the plan of the hidden house word by word. Once or twice as I raised my eyes I caught Vivian looking strangely about him; he seemed to give a quick glint up and down, and glance at the houses; and there was a furtive and anxious air about him that displeased me. 'Let us walk on to the north,' he said at length, 'we shall come to some pleasant lanes where we can discuss these matters, quietly; my night's rest is at your service.' I declined, on the pretext that I could not dispense with my visit to Oxford Street, and went on till he understood every turning and winding and the minutest detail as well as myself. We had returned on our footsteps, and stood again in the dark passage, just where I had drawn the red hand on the wall, for I recognized the vague shape of the trees whose branches hung above us. 'We have come back to our starting-point,' I said; 'I almost think I could put my finger on the wall where I drew the hand. And I am sure you could put your finger on the mystic hand in the hills as well as I. Remember between stream and stone.'

"I was bending down, peering at what I thought must be my drawing, when I heard a sharp hiss of breath, and started up, and saw Vivian with his arm uplifted and a bare blade in his hand, and death threatening in his eyes. In sheer self-defence I caught at the flint weapon in my pocket, and dashed at him in blind fear of my life, and the next instant he lay dead upon the stones.

"I think that is all," Mr Selby continued after a pause, "and it only remains for me to say to you, Mr Dyson, that I cannot conceive what means enabled you to run me down."

"I followed many indications," said Dyson, "and I am bound to disclaim all credit for acuteness, as I have made several gross blunders. Your celestial cypher did not, I confess, give me much trouble; I saw at once that terms of astronomy were substituted for common words and phrases. You had lost something black, or something black had been stolen from you; a celestial globe is a copy of the heavens, so I knew you meant you had a copy of what you had lost. Obviously, then, I came to the conclusion that you had lost a black object with characters or symbols written or inscribed on it, since the object in question certainly contained valuable information and all information must be written or pictured. 'Our old orbit remains unchanged'; evidently our old course or arrangement. 'The number of my sign' must mean the number of my house, the allusion being to the signs of the zodiac. I need not say that 'the other side of the moon' can stand for nothing but some place where no one else has been; and 'some other house' is some other place of meeting, the 'house' being the old term "house of the heavens." Then my next step was to find the 'black heaven' that had been stolen, and by a process of exhaustion I did so."

"You have got the tablet?"

"Certainly. And on the back of it, on the slip of paper you have mentioned, I read 'inroad,' which puzzled me a good deal, till I thought of Gray's Inn Road; you forgot the second *n*. 'Stony-hearted step—' immediately suggested the phrase of De Quincey you have alluded to; and I made the wild but correct shot, that you were a man who lived in or near the Gray's Inn Road, and had the habit of walking in Oxford Street, for you remember how the opium-eater dwells on his wearying promenades along that thoroughfare. On the theory of improbability, which I have explained to my friend here, I concluded that occasionally, at all events, you would choose the way by Guildford Street, Russell Square, and Great Russell Street, and I knew that if I watched long enough I should see you. But how was I to recognize my man? I noticed the screever opposite my rooms, and got him to draw every day a large hand, in the gesture so familiar to us all, upon the wall behind him. I thought that when the unknown person did pass he would certainly betray some emotion at the sudden vision of the sign, to him the most terrible of symbols. You know the rest. Ah, as to catching you an hour later, that was, I confess, a refinement. From the fact of your having occupied the same rooms for so many years, in a neighbourhood moreover where lodgers are migratory to excess, I drew the conclusion that you were a man of fixed habit, and I was sure that after you had got over your fright you would return for the walk down Oxford Street. You did, by way of New Oxford Street, and I was waiting at the corner."

"Your conclusions are admirable," said Mr Selby. "I may tell you that I had my stroll down Oxford Street the night Sir Thomas Vivian died. And I think that is all I have to say."

"Scarcely," said Dyson. "How about the treasure?"

"I had rather we did not speak of that," said Mr Selby, with a whitening of the skin about the temples.

"Oh, nonsense, sir, we are not blackmailers. Besides, you know you are in our power."

"Then, as you put it like that, Mr Dyson, I must tell you I returned to the place. I went on a little farther than before."

The man stopped short; his mouth began to twitch, his lips moved apart, and he drew in quick breaths, sobbing.

"Well, well," said Dyson, "I dare say you have done comfortably."

"Comfortably," Selby went on, constraining himself with an effort, "yes, so comfortably that hell burns hot within me for ever. I only brought one thing away from that awful house within the hills; it was lying just beyond the spot where I found the flint knife."

"Why did you not bring more?"

The whole bodily frame of the wretched man visibly shrank and wasted; his face grew yellow as tallow, and the sweat dropped from his brows. The spectacle was both revolting and terrible, and when the voice came it sounded like the hissing of a snake.

"Because the keepers are still there, and I saw them, and because of this," and he pulled out a small piece of curious gold-work and held it up.

"There," he said, "that is the Pain of the Goat."

Phillipps and Dyson cried out together in horror at the revolting obscenity of the thing.

"Put it away, man; hide it, for Heaven's sake, hide it!"

"I brought that with me; that is all," he said. "You do not wonder that I did not stay long in a place where those who live are a little higher than the beasts, and where what you have seen is surpassed a thousandfold?"

"Take this," said Dyson, "I brought it with me in case it might be useful; and he drew out the black tablet, and handed it to the shaking, horrible man.

"And now," said Dyson, "will you go out?"

The two friends sat silent a little while, facing one another with restless eyes and lips that quivered.

"I wish to say that I believe him," said Phillipps.

"My dear Phillipps," said Dyson as he threw the windows wide open, "I do not know that, after all, my blunders in this queer case were so very absurd."

The Terror

by Arthur Machen

I. THE COMING OF THE TERROR

After two years we are turning once more to the morning's news with a sense of appetite and glad expectation. There were thrills at the beginning of the war; the thrill of horror and of a doom that seemed at once incredible and certain; this was when Namur fell and the German host swelled like a flood over the French fields, and drew very near to the walls of Paris. Then we felt the thrill of exultation when the good news came that the awful tide had been turned back, that Paris and the world were safe; for awhile at all events.

Then for days we hoped for more news as good as this or better. Has Von Kluck been surrounded? Not today, but perhaps he will be surrounded tomorrow. But the days became weeks, the weeks drew out to months; the battle in the West seemed frozen. Now and again things were done that seemed hopeful, with promise of events still better. But Neuve Chapelle and Loos dwindled into disappointments as their tale was told fully; the lines in the West remained, for all practical purposes of victory, immobile. Nothing seemed to happen; there was nothing to read save the record of operations that were clearly trifling and insignificant. People speculated as to the reason of this inaction; the hopeful said that Joffre had a plan, that he was "nibbling," others declared that we were short of munitions, others again that the new levies were not yet ripe for battle. So the months went by, and almost two years of war had been completed before the motionless English line began to stir and quiver as if it awoke from a long sleep, and began to roll onward, overwhelming the enemy.

The secret of the long inaction of the British Armies has been well kept. On the one hand it was rigorously protected by the censorship, which severe, and sometimes severe to the point of absurdity—"the captains and the ... depart," for instance—became in this particular matter ferocious. As soon as the real significance of that which was happening, or beginning to happen, was perceived by the authorities, an underlined circular was issued to the newspaper proprietors of Great Britain and Ireland. It warned each proprietor that he might impart the contents of this circular to one other person only, such person being the responsible editor of his paper, who was to keep the communication secret under the severest penalties. The circular forbade any mention of certain events that had taken place, that might take place; it forbade any kind of allusion to these events or any hint of their existence, or of the possibility of their existence, not only in the Press, but in any form whatever. The subject was not to be alluded to in conversation, it was not to be hinted at, however obscurely, in letters; the very existence of the circular, its subject apart, was to be a dead secret.

These measures were successful. A wealthy newspaper proprietor of the North, warmed a little at the end of the Throwsters' Feast (which was held as usual, it will be remembered), ventured to say to the man next to him: "How awful it would be, wouldn't it, if...." His words were repeated, as proof, one regrets to say, that it was time for "old Arnold" to "pull himself together;" and he was fined a thousand pounds. Then, there was the case of an obscure weekly paper published in the county town of an agricultural district in Wales. The *Meiros Observer* (we will call it) was issued from a stationer's back premises, and filled its four pages with accounts of local flower shows, fancy fairs at vicarages, reports of parish councils, and rare bathing fatalities. It also issued a visitors' list, which has been known to contain six names.

This enlightened organ printed a paragraph, which nobody noticed, which was very like paragraphs that small country newspapers have long been in the habit of printing, which could hardly give so much as a hint to any one—to any one, that is, who was not fully instructed in the secret. As a matter of fact, this piece of intelligence got into the paper because the proprietor, who was also the editor, incautiously left the last processes of this particular issue to the staff, who was the Lord-High-Every-thing-Else of the establishment; and the staff put in a bit of gossip he had heard in the market to fill up two inches on the back page. But the result was that the *Meiros Observer* ceased to appear, owing to "untoward circumstances" as the proprietor said; and he would say no more. No more, that is, by way of explanation, but a great deal more by way of execration of "damned, prying busybodies."

Now a censorship that is sufficiently minute and utterly remorseless can do amazing things in the way of hiding … what it wants to hide. Before the war, one would have thought otherwise; one would have said that, censor or no censor, the fact of the murder at X or the fact of the bank robbery at Y would certainly become known; if not through the Press, at all events through rumour and the passage of the news from mouth to mouth. And this would be true—of England three hundred years ago, and of savage tribelands of today. But we have grown of late to such a reverence for the printed word and such a reliance on it, that the old faculty of disseminating news by word of mouth has become atrophied. Forbid the Press to mention the fact that Jones has been murdered, and it is marvelous how few people will hear of it, and of those who hear how few will credit the story that they have heard. You meet a man in the train who remarks that he has been told something about a murder in Southwark; there is all the difference in the world between the impression you receive from such a chance communication and that given by half a dozen lines of print with name, and street and date and all the facts of the case. People in trains repeat all sorts of tales, many of them false; newspapers do not print accounts of murders that have not been committed.

Then another consideration that has made for secrecy. I may have seemed to say that the old office of rumor no longer exists; I shall be reminded of the strange legend of "the Russians" and the mythology of the "Angels of Mons." But let me point out, in the first place, that both these absurdities depended on the papers for their wide dissemination. If there had been no newspapers or magazines Russians and Angels would have made but a brief, vague appearance of the most shadowy kind—a few would have heard of them, fewer still would have believed in them, they would have been gossiped about for a bare week or two, and so they would have vanished away.

And, then, again, the very fact of these vain rumors and fantastic tales having been so widely believed for a time was fatal to the credit of any stray mutterings that may have got abroad. People had been taken in twice; they had seen how grave persons, men of credit, had preached and lectured about the shining forms that had saved the British Army at Mons, or had testified to the trains, packed with grey-coated Muscovites, rushing through the land at dead of night: and now there was a hint of something more amazing than either of the discredited legends. But this time there was no word of confirmation to be found in daily paper, or weekly review, or parish magazine, and so the few that heard either laughed, or, being serious, went home and jotted down notes for essays on "War-time Psychology: Collective Delusions."

I followed neither of these courses. For before the secret circular had been issued my curiosity had somehow been aroused by certain paragraphs concerning a "Fatal Accident to Well-known Airman." The propeller of the airplane had been shattered, apparently by a collision with a flight of pigeons; the blades had been broken and the machine had fallen like lead to the earth. And soon after I had seen this account, I heard of some very odd circumstances relating to an explosion in a great munition factory in the Midlands. I thought I saw the possibility of a connection between two very different events.

It has been pointed out to me by friends who have been good enough to read this record, that certain phrases I have used may give the impression that I ascribe all the delays of the war on the Western front to the extraordinary circumstances which occasioned the issue of the Secret Circular. Of course this is not the case, there were many reasons for the immobility of our lines from October 1914 to July 1916. These causes have been evident enough and have been openly discussed and deplored. But behind them was something of infinitely greater moment. We lacked men, but men were pouring into the new army; we were short of shells, but when the shortage was proclaimed the nation set itself to mend this matter with all its energy. We could undertake to supply the defects of our army both in men and munitions—*if* the new and incredible danger could be overcome. It has been overcome; rather, perhaps, it has ceased to exist; and the secret may now be told.

I have said my attention was attracted by an account of the death of a well-known airman. I have not the habit of preserving cuttings, I am sorry to say, so that I cannot be precise as to the date of this event. To the best of my belief it was either towards the end of May or the beginning of June 1915. The newspaper paragraph announcing the death of Flight-Lieutenant Western-Reynolds was brief enough; accidents, and fatal accidents, to the men who are storming the air for us are, unfortunately, by no means so rare as to demand an elaborated notice.

But the manner in which Western-Reynolds met his death struck me as extraordinary, inasmuch as it revealed a new danger in the element that we have lately conquered. He was brought down, as I said, by a flight of birds; of pigeons, as appeared by what was found on the bloodstained and shattered blades of the propeller. An eye-witness of the accident, a fellow-officer, described how Western-Reynolds set out from the aerodrome on a fine afternoon, there being hardly any wind. He was going to France; he had made the journey to and fro half a dozen times or more, and felt perfectly secure and at ease.

"'Wester' rose to a great height at once, and we could scarcely see the machine. I was turning to go when one of the fellows called out, 'I say! What's this?' He pointed up, and we saw what looked like a black cloud coming from the south at a tremendous rate. I saw at once it wasn't a cloud; it came with a swirl and a rush quite different from any cloud I've ever seen. But for a second I couldn't make out exactly what it was. It altered its shape and turned into a great crescent, and wheeled and veered about as if it was looking for something. The man who had called out had got his glasses, and was staring for all he was worth. Then he shouted that it was a tremendous flight of birds, 'thousands of them.' They went on wheeling and beating about high up in the air, and we were watching them, thinking it was interesting, but not supposing that they would make any difference to 'Wester,' who was just about out of sight. His machine was just a speck. Then the two arms of the crescent drew in as quick as lightning, and these thousands of birds shot in a solid mass right up there across the sky, and flew away somewhere about nor'-nor'-by-west. Then Henley, the man with the glasses, called out, 'He's down!' and started running, and I went after him. We got a car and as we were going along Henley told me that he'd seen the machine drop dead, as if it came out of that cloud of birds. He thought then that they must have mucked up the propeller somehow. That turned out to be the case. We found the propeller blades all broken and covered with blood and pigeon feathers, and carcasses of the birds had got wedged in between the blades, and were sticking to them."

This was the story that the young airman told one evening in a small company. He did not speak "in confidence," so I have no hesitation in reproducing what he said. Naturally, I did not take a verbatim note of his conversation, but I have something of a knack of remembering talk that interests me, and I think my reproduction is very near to the tale that I heard. And let it be noted that the flying man told his story without any sense or indication of a sense that the incredible, or all but the incredible, had happened. So far as he knew, he said, it was the first accident of the kind. Airmen in France had been bothered once or twice by birds—he thought they were eagles—flying viciously at them, but poor old "Wester" had been the first man to come up against a flight of some thousands of pigeons.

"And perhaps I shall be the next," he added, "but why look for trouble? Anyhow, I'm going to see *Toodle-oo* tomorrow afternoon."

Well, I heard the story, as one hears all the varied marvels and terrors of the air; as one heard some years ago of "air pockets," strange gulfs or voids in the atmosphere into which airmen fell with great peril; or as one heard of the experience of the airman who flew over the Cumberland mountains in the burning summer of 1911, and as he swam far above the heights was suddenly and vehemently blown upwards, the hot air from the rocks striking his plane as if it had been a blast from a furnace chimney. We have just begun to navigate a strange region; we must expect to encounter strange adventures, strange perils. And here a new chapter in the chronicles of these perils and adventures had been opened by the death of Western-Reynolds; and no doubt invention and contrivance would presently hit on some way of countering the new danger.

It was, I think, about a week or ten days after the airman's death that my business called me to a northern town, the name of which, perhaps, had better remain unknown. My mission was to inquire into certain charges of extravagance which had been laid against the working people, that is, the munition workers of this especial town. It was said that the men who used to earn £2 10s. a week were now getting from seven to eight pounds, that "bits of girls" were being paid two pounds instead of seven or eight shillings, and that, in consequence, there was an orgy of foolish extravagance. The girls, I was told, were eating chocolates at four, five, and six shillings a pound, the women were ordering thirty-pound pianos which they couldn't play, and the men bought gold chains at ten and twenty guineas apiece.

I dived into the town in question and found, as usual, that there was a mixture of truth and exaggeration in the stories that I had heard. Gramophones, for example: they cannot be called in strictness necessaries, but they were undoubtedly finding a ready sale, even in the more expensive brands. And I thought that there were a great many very spick and span perambulators to be seen on the pavement; smart perambulators, painted in tender shades of color and expensively fitted.

"And how can you be surprised if people will have a bit of a fling?" a worker said to me. "We're seeing money for the first time in our lives, and it's bright. And we work hard for it, and we risk our lives to get it. You've heard of explosion yonder?"

He mentioned certain works on the outskirts of the town. Of course, neither the name of the works nor of the town had been printed; there had been a brief notice of "Explosion at Munition Works in the Northern District: Many Fatalities." The working man told me about it, and added some dreadful details.

"They wouldn't let their folks see bodies; screwed them up in coffins as they found them in shop. The gas had done it."

"Turned their faces black, you mean?"

"Nay. They were all as if they had been bitten to pieces."

This was a strange gas.

I asked the man in the northern town all sorts of questions about the extraordinary explosion of which he had spoken to me. But he had very little more to say. As I have noted already, secrets that may not be printed are often deeply kept; last summer there were very few people outside high official circles who knew anything about the "Tanks," of which we have all been talking lately, though these strange instruments of war were being exercised and tested in a park not far from London. So the man who told me of the explosion in the munition factory was most likely genuine in his profession that he knew nothing more of the disaster. I found out that he was a smelter employed at a furnace on the other side of the town to the ruined factory; he didn't know even what they had been making there; some very dangerous high explosive, he supposed. His information was really nothing more than a bit of gruesome gossip, which he had heard probably at third or fourth or fifth hand. The horrible detail of faces "as if they had been bitten to pieces" had made its violent impression on him, that was all.

I gave him up and took a tram to the district of the disaster; a sort of industrial suburb, five miles from the center of the town. When I asked for the factory, I was told that it was no good my going to it as there was nobody there. But I found it; a raw and hideous shed with a walled yard about it, and a shut gate. I looked for signs of destruction, but there was nothing. The roof was quite undamaged; and again it struck me that this had been a strange accident. There had been an explosion of sufficient violence to kill workpeople in the building, but the building itself showed no wounds or scars.

A man came out of the gate and locked it behind him. I began to ask him some sort of question, or rather, I began to "open" for a question with "A terrible business here, they tell me," or some such phrase of convention. I got no farther. The man asked me if I saw a policeman walking down the street. I said I did, and I was given the choice of getting about my business forthwith or of being instantly given in charge as a spy. "Th'ast better be gone and quick about it," was, I think, his final advice, and I took it.

Well, I had come literally up against a brick wall. Thinking the problem over, I could only suppose that the smelter or his informant had twisted the phrases of the story. The smelter had said the dead men's faces were "bitten to pieces"; this might be an unconscious perversion of "eaten away." That phrase might describe well enough the effect of strong acids, and, for all I knew of the processes of munition-making, such acids might be used and might explode with horrible results in some perilous stage of their admixture.

It was a day or two later that the accident to the airman, Western-Reynolds, came into my mind. For one of those instants which are far shorter than any measure of time there flashed out the possibility of a link between the two disasters. But here was a wild impossibility, and I drove it away. And yet I think that the thought, mad as it seemed, never left me; it was the secret light that at last guided me through a somber grove of enigmas.

It was about this time, so far as the date can be fixed, that a whole district, one might say a whole county, was visited by a series of extraordinary and terrible calamities, which were the more terrible inasmuch as they continued for some time to be inscrutable mysteries. It is, indeed, doubtful whether these awful events do not still remain mysteries to many of those concerned; for before the inhabitants of this part of the country had time to join one link of evidence to another the circular was issued, and thenceforth no one knew how to distinguish undoubted fact from wild and extravagant surmise.

The district in question is in the far west of Wales; I shall call it, for convenience, Meirion. In it there is one seaside town of some repute with holiday-makers for five or six weeks in the summer, and dotted about the county there are three or four small old towns that seem drooping in a slow decay, sleepy and gray with age and forgetfulness. They remind me of what I have read of towns in the west of Ireland. Grass grows between the uneven stones of the pavements, the signs above the shop windows decline, half the letters of these signs are missing, here and there a house has been pulled down, or has been allowed to slide into ruin, and wild greenery springs up through the fallen stones, and there is silence in all the streets. And, it is to be noted, these are not places that were once magnificent. The Celts have never had the art of building, and so far as I can see, such towns as Towy and Merthyr Tegveth and Meiros must have been always much as they are now, clusters of poorish, meanly-built houses, ill-kept and down at heel.

And these few towns are thinly scattered over a wild country where north is divided from south by a wilder mountain range. One of these places is sixteen miles from any station; the others are doubtfully and deviously connected by single-line railways served by rare trains that pause and stagger and hesitate on their slow journey up mountain passes, or stop for half an hour or more at lonely sheds called stations, situated in the midst of desolate marshes. A few years ago I traveled with an Irishman on one of these queer lines, and he looked to right and saw the bog with its yellow and blue grasses and stagnant pools, and he looked to left and saw a ragged hillside, set with gray stone walls. "I can hardly believe," he said, "that I'm not still in the wilds of Ireland."

Here, then, one sees a wild and divided and scattered region a land of outland hills and secret and hidden valleys. I know white farms on this coast which must be separate by two hours of hard, rough walking from any other habitation, which are invisible from any other house. And inland, again, the farms are often ringed about by thick groves of ash, planted by men of old days to shelter their roof-trees from rude winds of the mountain and stormy winds of the sea; so that these places, too, are hidden away, to be surmised only by the wood smoke that rises from the green surrounding leaves. A Londoner must see them to believe in them; and even then he can scarcely credit their utter isolation.

Such, then in the main is Meirion, and on this land in the early summer of last year terror descended—a terror without shape, such as no man there had ever known.

It began with the tale of a little child who wandered out into the lanes to pick flowers one sunny afternoon, and never came back to the cottage on the hill.

II. DEATH IN THE VILLAGE

The child who was lost came from a lonely cottage that stands on the slope of a steep hillside called the Allt, or the height. The land about it is wild and ragged; here the growth of gorse and bracken, here a marshy hollow of reeds and rushes, marking the course of the stream from some hidden well, here thickets of dense and tangled undergrowth, the outposts of the wood. Down through this broken and uneven ground a path leads to the lane at the bottom of the valley; then the land rises again and swells up to the cliffs over the sea, about a quarter of a mile away. The little girl, Gertrude Morgan, asked her mother if she might go down to the lane and pick the purple flowers—these were orchids—that grew there, and her mother gave her leave, telling her she must be sure to be back by tea-time, as there was apple-tart for tea.

She never came back. It was supposed that she must have crossed the road and gone to the cliff's edge, possibly in order to pick the sea-pinks that were then in full blossom. She must have slipped, they said, and fallen into the sea, two hundred feet below. And, it may be said at once, that there was no doubt some truth in this conjecture, though it stopped very far short of the whole truth. The child's body must have been carried out by the tide, for it was never found.

The conjecture of a false step or of a fatal slide on the slippery turf that slopes down to the rocks was accepted as being the only explanation possible. People thought the accident a strange one because, as a rule, country children living by the cliffs and the sea become wary at an early age, and Gertrude Morgan was almost ten years old. Still, as the neighbors said, "that's how it must have happened, and it's a great pity, to be sure." But this would not do when in a week's time a strong young laborer failed to come to his cottage after the day's work. His body was found on the rocks six or seven miles from the cliffs where the child was supposed to have fallen; he was going home by a path that he had used every night of his life for eight or nine years, that he used of dark nights in perfect security, knowing every inch of it. The police asked if he drank, but he was a teetotaler; if he were subject to fits, but he wasn't. And he was not murdered for his wealth, since agricultural laborers are not wealthy. It was only possible again to talk of slippery turf and a false step; but people began to be frightened. Then a woman was found with her neck broken at the bottom of a disused quarry near Llanfihangel, in the middle of the county. The "false step" theory was eliminated here, for the quarry was guarded with a natural hedge of gorse bushes. One would have to struggle and fight through sharp thorns to destruction in such a place as this; and indeed the gorse bushes were broken as if some one had rushed furiously through them, just above the place where the woman's body was found. And this was strange: there was a dead sheep lying beside her in the pit, as if the woman and the sheep together had been chased over the brim of the quarry. But chased by whom, or by what? And then there was a new form of terror.

This was in the region of the marshes under the mountain. A man and his son, a lad of fourteen or fifteen, set out early one morning to work and never reached the farm where they were bound. Their way skirted the marsh, but it was broad, firm and well metalled, and it had been raised about two feet above the bog. But when search was made in the evening of the same day Phillips and his son were found dead in the marsh, covered with black slime and pondweed. And they lay some ten yards from the path, which, it would seem, they must have left deliberately. It was useless of course, to look for tracks in the black ooze, for if one threw a big stone into it a few seconds removed all marks of the disturbance. The men who found the two bodies beat about the verges and purlieus of the marsh in hope of finding some trace of the murderers; they went to and fro over the rising ground where the black cattle were grazing, they searched the alder thickets by the brook; but they discovered nothing.

Most horrible of all these horrors, perhaps, was the affair of the Highway, a lonely and unfrequented by-road that winds for many miles on high and lonely land. Here, a mile from any other dwelling, stands a cottage on the edge of a dark wood. It was inhabited by a laborer named Williams, his wife, and their three children. One hot summer's evening, a man who had been doing a day's gardening at a rectory three or four miles away, passed the cottage, and stopped for a few minutes to chat with Williams, the labourer, who was pottering about his garden, while the children were playing on the path by the door. The two talked of their neighbors and of the potatoes till Mrs. Williams appeared at the doorway and said supper was ready, and Williams turned to go into the house. This was about eight o'clock, and in the ordinary course the family would have their supper and be in bed by nine, or by half-past nine at latest. At ten o'clock that night the local doctor was driving home along the Highway. His horse shied violently and then stopped dead just opposite the gate to the cottage. The doctor got down, frightened at what he saw; and there on the roadway lay Williams, his wife, and the three children, stone dead, all of them. Their skulls were battered in as if by some heavy iron instrument; their faces were beaten into a pulp.

III. THE DOCTOR'S THEORY

It is not easy to make any picture of the horror that lay dark on the hearts of the people of Meirion. It was no longer possible to believe or to pretend to believe that these men and women and children had met their deaths through strange accidents. The little girl and the young laborer might have slipped and fallen over the cliffs, but the woman who lay dead with the dead sheep at the bottom of the quarry, the two men who had been lured into the ooze of the marsh, the family who were found murdered on the Highway before their own cottage door; in these cases there could be no room for the supposition of accident. It seemed as if it were impossible to frame any conjecture or outline of a conjecture that would account for these hideous and, as it seemed, utterly purposeless crimes. For a time people said that there must be a madman at large, a sort of country variant of Jack the Ripper, some horrible pervert who was possessed by the passion of death, who prowled darkling about that lonely land, hiding in woods and in wild places, always watching and seeking for the victims of his desire.

Indeed, Dr. Lewis, who found poor Williams, his wife and children miserably slaughtered on the Highway, was convinced at first that the presence of a concealed madman in the countryside offered the only possible solution to the difficulty.

"I felt sure," he said to me afterwards, "that the Williams's had been killed by a homicidal maniac. It was the nature of the poor creatures' injuries that convinced me that this was the case. Some years ago thirty-seven or thirty-eight years ago as a matter of fact—I had something to do with a case which on the face of it had a strong likeness to the Highway murder. At that time I had a practice at Usk, in Monmouthshire. A whole family living in a cottage by the roadside were murdered one evening; it was called, I think, the Llangibby murder; the cottage was near the village of that name. The murderer was caught in Newport; he was a Spanish sailor, named Garcia, and it appeared that he had killed father, mother, and the three children for the sake of the brass works of an old Dutch clock, which were found on him when he was arrested.

"Garcia had been serving a month's imprisonment in Usk Jail for some small theft, and on his release he set out to walk to Newport, nine or ten miles away; no doubt to get another ship. He passed the cottage and saw the man working in his garden. Garcia stabbed him with his sailor's knife. The wife rushed out; he stabbed her. Then he went into the cottage and stabbed the three children, tried to set the place on fire, and made off with the clockworks. That looked like the deed of a madman, but Garcia wasn't mad—they hanged him, I may say—he was merely a man of a very low type, a degenerate who hadn't the slightest value for human life. I am not sure, but I think he came from one of the Spanish islands, where the people are said to be degenerates, very likely from too much inter-breeding.

"But my point is that Garcia stabbed to kill and did kill, with one blow in each case. There was no senseless hacking and slashing. Now those poor people on the Highway had their heads smashed to pieces by what must have been a storm of blows. Any one of them would have been fatal, but the murderer must have gone on raining blows with his iron hammer on people who were already stone dead. And *that* sort of thing is the work of a madman, and nothing but a madman. That's how I argued the matter out to myself just after the event.

"I was utterly wrong, monstrously wrong. But who could have suspected the truth?"

Thus Dr. Lewis, and I quote him, or the substance of him, as representative of most of the educated opinion of the district at the beginnings of the terror. People seized on this theory largely because it offered at least the comfort of an explanation, and any explanation, even the poorest, is better than an intolerable and terrible mystery. Besides, Dr. Lewis's theory was plausible; it explained the lack of purpose that seemed to characterize the murders. And yet—there were difficulties even from the first. It was hardly possible that a strange madman should be able to keep hidden in a countryside where any stranger is instantly noted and noticed; sooner or later he would be seen as he prowled along the lanes or across the wild places. Indeed, a drunken, cheerful, and altogether harmless tramp was arrested by a farmer and his man in the fact and act of sleeping off beer under a hedge; but the vagrant was able to prove complete and undoubted alibis, and was soon allowed to go on his wandering way.

Then another theory, or rather a variant of Dr. Lewis's theory, was started. This was to the effect that the person responsible for the outrages was, indeed, a madman; but a madman only at intervals. It was one of the members of the Porth Club, a certain Mr Remnant, who was supposed to have originated this more subtle explanation. Mr Remnant was a middle-aged man, who, having nothing particular to do, read a great many books by way of conquering the hours. He talked to the club—doctors, retired colonels, parsons, lawyers—about "personality," quoted various psychological textbooks in support of his contention that personality was sometimes fluid and unstable, went back to "Dr. Jekyll and Mr Hyde" as good evidence of this proposition, and laid stress on Dr. Jekyll's speculation that the human soul, so far from being one and indivisible, might, possibly turn out to be a mere polity, a state in which dwelt many strange and incongruous citizens, whose characters were not merely unknown but altogether unsurmised by that form of consciousness which so rashly assumed that it was not only the president of the republic but also its sole citizen.

"The long and the short of it is," Mr Remnant concluded, "that any one of us may be the murderer, though he hasn't the faintest notion of the fact. Take Llewelyn there."

Mr Payne Llewelyn was an elderly lawyer, a rural Tulkinghorn. He was the hereditary solicitor to the Morgans of Pentwyn. This does not sound anything tremendous to the Saxons of London; but the style is far more than noble to the Celts of West Wales; it is immemorial; Teilo Sant was of the collaterals of the first known chief of the race. And Mr Payne Llewelyn did his best to look like the legal adviser of this ancient house. He was weighty, he was cautious, he was sound, he was secure. I have compared him to Mr Tulkinghorn of Lincoln's Inn Fields; but Mr Llewelyn would most certainly never have dreamed of employing his leisure in peering into the cupboards where the family skeletons were hidden. Supposing such cupboards to have existed, Mr Payne Llewelyn would have risked large out-of-pocket expenses to furnish them with double, triple, impregnable locks. He was a new man, an *advena*, certainly; for he was partly of the Conquest, being descended on one side from Sir Payne Turberville; but he meant to stand by the old stock.

"Take Llewelyn now," said Mr Remnant. "Look here, Llewelyn, can you produce evidence to show where you were on the night those people were murdered on the Highway? I thought not."

Mr Llewelyn, an elderly man, as I have said, hesitated before speaking.

"I thought not," Remnant went on. "Now I say that it is perfectly possible that Llewelyn may be dealing death throughout Meirion, although in his present personality he may not have the faintest suspicion that there is another Llewelyn within him, a Llewelyn who follows murder as a fine art."

Mr Payne Llewelyn did not at all relish Mr Remnant's suggestion that he might well be a secret murderer, ravening for blood, remorseless as a wild beast. He thought the phrase about his following murder as a fine art was both nonsensical and in the worst taste, and his opinion was not changed when Remnant pointed out that it was used by De Quincey in the title of one of his most famous essays.

"If you had allowed me to speak," he said with some coldness of manner, "I would have told you that on Tuesday last, the night on which those unfortunate people were murdered on the Highway I was staying at the Angel Hotel, Cardiff. I had business in Cardiff, and I was detained till Wednesday afternoon."

Having given this satisfactory alibi, Mr Payne Llewelyn left the club, and did not go near it for the rest of the week.

Remnant explained to those who stayed in the smoking room that, of course, he had merely used Mr Llewelyn as a concrete example of his theory, which, he persisted, had the support of a considerable body of evidence.

"There are several cases of double personality on record," he declared. "And I say again that it is quite possible that these murders may have been committed by one of us in his secondary personality. Why, I may be the murderer in my Remnant B. state, though Remnant A. knows nothing whatever about it, and is perfectly convinced that he could not kill a fowl, much less a whole family. Isn't it so, Lewis?"

Dr. Lewis said it was so, in theory, but he thought not in fact.

"Most of the cases of double or multiple personality that have been investigated," he said, "have been in connection with the very dubious experiments of hypnotism, or the still more dubious experiments of spiritualism. All that sort of thing, in my opinion, is like tinkering with the works of a clock—amateur tinkering, I mean. You fumble about with the wheels and cogs and bits of mechanism that you don't really know anything about; and then you find your clock going backwards or striking 240 at tea-time. And I believe it's just the same thing with these psychical research experiments; the secondary personality is very likely the result of the tinkering and fumbling with a very delicate apparatus that we know nothing about. Mind, I can't say that it's impossible for one of us to be the Highway murderer in his B. state, as Remnant puts it. But I think it's extremely improbable. Probability is the guide of life, you know, Remnant," said Dr. Lewis, smiling at that gentleman, as if to say that he also had done a little reading in his day. "And it follows, therefore, that improbability is also the guide of life. When you get a very high degree of probability, that is, you are justified in taking it as a certainty; and on the other hand, if a supposition is highly improbable, you are justified in treating it as an impossible one. That is, in nine hundred and ninety-nine cases out of a thousand."

"How about the thousandth case?" said Remnant. "Supposing these extraordinary crimes constitute the thousandth case?"

The doctor smiled and shrugged his shoulders, being tired of the subject. But for some little time highly respectable members of Porth society would look suspiciously at one another wondering whether, after all, there mightn't be "something in it." However, both Mr Remnant's somewhat crazy theory and Dr. Lewis's plausible theory became untenable when two more victims of an awful and mysterious death were offered up in, sacrifice, for a man was found dead in the Llanfihangel quarry, where the woman had been discovered. And on the same day a girl of fifteen was found broken on the jagged rocks under the cliffs near Porth. Now, it appeared that these two deaths must have occurred at about the same time, within an hour of one another, certainly; and the distance between the quarry and the cliffs by Black Rock is certainly twenty miles.

"A motor could do it," one man said.

But it was pointed out that there was no high road between the two places; indeed, it might be said that there was no road at all between them. There was a network of deep, narrow, and tortuous lands that wandered into one another at all manner of queer angles for, say, seventeen miles; this in the middle, as it were, between Black Rock and the quarry at Llanfihangel. But to get to the high land of the cliffs one had to take a path that went through two miles of fields; and the quarry lay a mile away from the nearest by-road in the midst of gorse and bracken and broken land. And, finally, there was no track of motor-car or motor-bicycle in the lanes which must have been followed to pass from one place to the other.

"What about an airplane, then?" said the man of the motor-car theory. Well, there was certainly an aerodrome not far from one of the two places of death; but somehow, nobody believed that the Flying Corps harboured a homicidal maniac. It seemed clear, therefore, that there must be more than one person concerned in the terror of Meirion. And Dr. Lewis himself abandoned his own theory.

"As I said to Remnant at the Club," he remarked, "improbability is the guide of life. I can't believe that there are a pack of madmen or even two madmen at large in the country. I give it up."

And now a fresh circumstance or set of circumstances became manifest to confound judgment and to awaken new and wild surmises. For at about this time people realized that none of the dreadful events that were happening all about them was so much as mentioned in the Press. I have already spoken of the fate of the *Meiros Observer*. This paper was suppressed by the authorities because it had inserted a brief paragraph about some person who had been "found dead under mysterious circumstances;" I think that paragraph referred to the first death of Llanfihangel quarry. Thenceforth, horror followed on horror, but no word was printed in any of the local journals. The curious went to the newspaper offices—there were two left in the county—but found nothing save a firm refusal to discuss the matter. And the Cardiff papers were drawn and found blank; and the London Press was apparently ignorant of the fact that crimes that had no parallel were terrorizing a whole countryside. Everybody wondered what could have happened, what was happening; and then it was whispered that the coroner would allow no inquiry to be made as to these deaths of darkness.

"In consequence of instructions received from the Home Office," one coroner was understood to have said, "I have to tell the jury that their business will be to hear the medical evidence and to bring in a verdict immediately in accordance with that evidence. I shall disallow all questions."

One jury protested. The foreman refused to bring in any verdict at all.

"Very good," said the coroner. "Then I beg to inform you, Mr Foreman and gentlemen of the jury, that under the Defense of the Realm Act, I have power to supersede your functions, and to enter a verdict according to the evidence which has been laid before the Court as if it had been the verdict of you all."

The foreman and jury collapsed and accepted what they could not avoid. But the rumours that got abroad of all this, added to the known fact that the terror was ignored in the Press, no doubt by official command, increased the panic that was now; arising, and gave it a new direction. Clearly, people reasoned, these Government restrictions and prohibitions could only refer to the war, to some great danger in connection with the war. And that being so, it followed that the outrages which must be kept so secret were the work of the enemy, that is of concealed German agents.

IV. THE SPREAD OF THE TERROR

It is time, I think, for me to make one point clear. I began this history with certain references to an extraordinary accident to an airman whose machine fell to the ground after collision with a huge flock of pigeons; and then to an explosion in a northern munition factory, an explosion, as I noted, of a very singular kind. Then I deserted the neighborhood of London, and the northern district, and dwelt on a mysterious and terrible series of events which occurred in the summer of 1915 in a Welsh county, which I have named, for convenience, Meirion.

Well, let it be understood at once that all this detail that I have given about the occurrences in Meirion does not imply that the county in the far west was alone or especially afflicted by the terror that was over the land. They tell me that in the villages about Dartmoor the stout Devonshire hearts sank as men's hearts used to sink in the time of plague and pestilence. There was horror, too, about the Norfolk Broads, and far up by Perth no one would venture on the path that leads by Scone to the wooded heights above the Tay. And in the industrial districts: I met a man by chance one day in an odd London corner who spoke with horror of what a friend had told him.

"'Ask no questions, Ned,' he says to me, 'but I tell yow a' was in Bairnigan t'other day, and a' met a pal who'd seen three hundred coffins going out of a works not far from there.'"

And then the ship that hovered outside the mouth of the Thames with all sails set and beat to and fro in the wind, and never answered any hail, and showed no light! The forts shot at her and brought down one of the masts, but she went suddenly about with a change of wind under what sail still stood, and then veered down Channel, and drove ashore at last on the sandbanks and pinewoods of Arcachon, and not a man alive on her, but only rattling heaps of bones! That last voyage of the *Semiramis* would be something horribly worth telling; but I only heard it at a distance as a yarn, and only believed it because it squared with other things that I knew for certain.

This, then, is my point; I have written of the terror as it fell on Meirion, simply because I have had opportunities of getting close there to what really happened. Third or fourth or fifth hand in the other places; but round about Porth and Merthyr Tegveth I have spoken with people who have seen the tracks of the terror with their own eyes.

Well, I have said that the people of that far western county realized, not only that death was abroad in their quiet lanes and on their peaceful hills, but that for some reason it was to be kept all secret. Newspapers might not print any news of it, the very juries summoned to investigate it were allowed to investigate nothing. And so they concluded that this veil of secrecy must somehow be connected with the war; and from this position it was not a long way to a further inference: that the murderers of innocent men and women and children were either Germans or agents of Germany. It would be just like the Huns, everybody agreed, to think out such a devilish scheme as this; and they always thought out their schemes beforehand. They hoped to seize Paris in a few weeks, but when they were beaten on the Marne they had their trenches on the Aisne ready to fall back on: it had all been prepared years before the war. And so, no doubt, they had devised this terrible plan against England in case they could not beat us in open fight: there were people ready, very likely, all over the country, who were prepared to murder and destroy everywhere as soon as they got the word. In this way the Germans intended to sow terror throughout England and fill our hearts with panic and dismay, hoping so to weaken their enemy at home that he would lose all heart over the war abroad. It was the Zeppelin notion, in another form; they were committing these horrible and mysterious outrages thinking that we should be frightened out of our wits.

It all seemed plausible enough; Germany had by this time perpetrated so many horrors and had so excelled in devilish ingenuities that no abomination seemed too abominable to be probable, or too ingeniously wicked to be beyond the tortuous malice of the Hun. But then came the questions as to who the agents of this terrible design were, as to where they lived, as to how they contrived to move unseen from field to field, from lane to lane. All sorts of fantastic attempts were made to answer these questions; but it was felt that they remained unanswered. Some suggested that the murderers landed from submarines, or flew from hiding places on the West Coast of Ireland, coming and going by night; but there were seen to be flagrant impossibilities in both these suggestions. Everybody agreed that the evil work was no doubt the work of Germany; but nobody could begin to guess how it was done. Somebody at the Club asked Remnant for his theory.

"My theory," said that ingenious person, "is that human progress is simply a long march from one inconceivable to another. Look at that airship of ours that came over Porth yesterday: ten years ago that would have been an inconceivable sight. Take the steam engine, stake printing, take the theory of gravitation: they were all inconceivable till somebody thought of them. So it is, no doubt, with this infernal dodgery that we're talking about: the Huns have found it out, and we haven't; and there you are. We can't conceive how these poor people have been murdered, because the method's inconceivable to us."

The club listened with some awe to this high argument. After Remnant had gone, one member said:

"Wonderful man, that." "Yes," said Dr. Lewis. "He was asked whether he knew something. And his reply really amounted to 'No, I don't.' But I have never heard it better put."

It was, I suppose, at about this time when the people were puzzling their heads as to the secret methods used by the Germans or their agents to accomplish their crimes that a very singular circumstance became known to a few of the Porth people. It related to the murder of the Williams family on the Highway in front of their cottage door. I do not know that I have made it plain that the old Roman road called the Highway follows the course of a long, steep hill that goes steadily westward till it slants down and droops towards the sea. On either side of the road the ground falls away, here into deep shadowy woods, here to high pastures, now and again into a field of corn, but for the most part into the wild and broken land that is characteristic of Arfon. The fields are long and narrow, stretching up the steep hillside; they fall into sudden dips and hollows, a well springs up in the midst of one and a grove of ash and thorn bends over it, shading it; and beneath it the ground is thick with reeds and rushes. And then may come on either side of such a field territories glistening with the deep growth of bracken, and rough with gorse and rugged with thickets of blackthorn, green lichen hanging strangely from the branches; such are the lands on either side of the Highway.

Now on the lower slopes of it, beneath the Williams's cottage, some three or four fields down the hill, there is a military camp. The place has been used as a camp for many years, and lately the site has been extended and huts have been erected. But a considerable number of the men were under canvas here in the summer of 1915.

On the night of the Highway murder this camp, as it appeared afterwards, was the scene of the extraordinary panic of the horses.

A good many men in the camp were asleep in their tents soon after 9:30, when the Last Post was sounded. They woke up in panic. There was a thundering sound on the steep hillside above them, and down upon the tents came half a dozen horses, mad with fright, trampling the canvas, trampling the men, bruising dozens of them and killing two.

Everything was in wild confusion, men groaning and screaming in the darkness, struggling with the canvas and the twisted ropes, shouting out, some of them, raw lads enough, that the Germans had landed, others wiping the blood from their eyes, a few, roused suddenly from heavy sleep, hitting out at one another, officers coming up at the double roaring out orders to the sergeants, a party of soldiers who were just returning to camp from the village seized with fright at what they could scarcely see or distinguish, at the wildness of the shouting and cursing and groaning that they could not understand, bolting out of the camp again and racing for their lives back to the village: everything in the maddest confusion of wild disorder.

Some of the men had seen the horses galloping down the hill as if terror itself was driving them. They scattered off into the darkness, and somehow or another found their way back in the night to their pasture above the camp. They were grazing there peacefully in the morning, and the only sign of the panic of the night before was the mud they had scattered all over themselves as they pelted through a patch of wet ground. The farmer said they were as quiet a lot as any in Meirion; he could make nothing of it.

"Indeed," he said, "I believe they must have seen the devil himself to be in such a fright as that: save the people!"

Now all this was kept as quiet as might be at the time when it happened; it became known to the men of the Porth Club in the days when they were discussing the difficult question of the German outrages, as the murders were commonly called. And this wild stampede of the farm horses was held by some to be evidence of the extraordinary and unheard of character of the dreadful agency that was at work. One of the members of the club had been told by an officer who was in the camp at the time of the panic that the horses that came charging down were in a perfect fury of fright, that he had never seen horses in such a state, and so there was endless speculation as to the nature of the sight or the sound that had driven half a dozen quiet beasts into raging madness.

Then, in the middle of this talk, two or three other incidents, quite as odd and incomprehensible, came to be known, borne on chance trickles of gossip that came into the towns from outland farms, or were carried by cottagers tramping into Porth on market day with a fowl or two and eggs and garden stuff; scraps and fragments of talk gathered by servants from the country folk and repeated—to their mistresses. And in such ways it came out that up at Plas Newydd there had been a terrible business over swarming the bees; they had turned as wild as wasps and much more savage. They had come about the people who were taking the swarms like a cloud. They settled on one man's face so that you could not see the flesh for the bees crawling all over it, and they had stung him so badly that the doctor did not know whether he would get over it, and they had chased a girl who had come out to see the swarming, and settled on her and stung her to death. Then they had gone off to a brake below the farm and got into a hollow tree there, and it was not safe to go near it, for they would come out at you by day or by night.

And much the same thing had happened, it seemed, at three or four farms and cottages where bees were kept. And there were stories, hardly so clear or so credible, of sheep dogs, mild and trusted beasts, turning as savage as wolves and injuring the farm boys in a horrible manner—in one case it was said with fatal results. It was certainly true that old Mrs. Owen's favorite Brahma-Dorking cock had gone mad; she came into Porth one Saturday morning with her face and her neck all bound up and plastered. She had gone out to her bit of a field to feed the poultry the night before, and the bird had flown at her and attacked her most savagely, inflicting some very nasty wounds before she could beat it off.

"There was a stake handy, lucky for me," she said, "and I did beat him and beat him till the life was out of him. But what is come to the world, whatever?"

Now Remnant, the man of theories, was also a man of extreme leisure. It was understood that he had succeeded to ample means when he was quite a young man, and after tasting the savours of the law, as it were, for half a dozen terms at the board of the Middle Temple, he had decided that it would be senseless to bother himself with passing examinations for a profession which he had not the faintest intention of practising. So he turned a deaf ear to the call of "Manger" ringing through the Temple Courts, and set himself out to potter amiably through the world. He had pottered all over Europe, he had looked at Africa, and had even put his head in at the door of the East, on a trip which included the Greek isles and Constantinople. Now getting into the middle fifties, he had settled at Porth for the sake, as he said, of the Gulf Stream and the fuchsia hedges, and pottered over his books and his theories and the local gossip. He was no more brutal than the general public, which revels in the details of mysterious crime; but it must be said that the terror, black though it was, was a boon to him. He peered and investigated and poked about with the relish of a man to whose life a new zest has been added. He listened attentively to the strange tales of bees and dogs and poultry that came into Porth with the country baskets of butter, rabbits, and green peas; and he evolved at last a most extraordinary theory.

Full of this discovery, as he thought it, he went one night to see Dr. Lewis and take his view of the matter.

"I want to talk to you," said Remnant to the doctor, "about what I have called provisionally, the Z Ray."

V. THE INCIDENT OF THE UNKNOWN TREE

Dr. Lewis, smiling indulgently, and quite prepared for some monstrous piece of theorizing, led Remnant into the room that overlooked the terraced garden and the sea.

The doctor's house, though it was only a ten minutes' walk from the center of the town, seemed remote from all other habitations. The drive to it from the road came through a deep grove of trees and a dense shrubbery, trees were about the house on either side, mingling with neighboring groves, and below, the garden fell down, terrace by green terrace, to wild growth, a twisted path amongst red rocks, and at last to the yellow sand of a little cove. The room to which the doctor took Remnant looked over these terraces and across the water to the dim boundaries of the bay. It had French windows that were thrown wide open, and the two men sat in the soft light of the lamp—this was before the days of severe lighting regulations in the Far West—and enjoyed the sweet odors and the sweet vision of the summer evening. Then Remnant began:

"I suppose, Lewis, you've heard these extraordinary stories of bees and dogs and things that have been going about lately?"

"Certainly I have heard them. I was called in at Plas Newydd, and treated Thomas Trevor, who's only just out of danger, by the way. I certified for the poor child, Mary Trevor. She was dying when I got to the place. There was no doubt she was stung to death by bees, and I believe there were other very similar cases at Llantarnam and Morwen; none fatal, I think. What about them?"

"Well: then there are the stories of good-tempered old sheepdogs turning wicked and 'savaging' children?"

"Quite so. I haven't seen any of these cases professionally; but I believe the stories are accurate enough."

"And the old woman assaulted by her own poultry?"

"That's perfectly true. Her daughter put some stuff of their own concoction on her face and neck, and then she came to me. The wounds seemed going all right, so I told her to continue the treatment, whatever it might be."

"Very good," said Mr Remnant. He spoke now with an italic impressiveness. "*Don't you see the link between all this and the horrible things that have been happening about here for the last month?*"

Lewis stared at Remnant in amazement. He lifted his red eyebrows and lowered them in a kind of scowl. His speech showed traces of his native accent.

"Great burning!" he exclaimed. "What on earth are you getting at now? It is madness. Do you mean to tell me that you think there is some connection between a swarm or two of bees that have turned nasty, a cross dog, and a wicked old barn-door cock and these poor people that have been pitched over the cliffs and hammered to death on the road? There's no sense in it, you know."

"I am strongly inclined to believe that there is a great deal of sense in it," replied Remnant, with extreme calmness. "Look here, Lewis, I saw you grinning the other day at the club when I was telling the fellows that in my opinion all these outrages had been committed, certainly by the Germans, but by some method of which we have no conception. But what I meant to say when I talked about inconceivables was just this: that the Williams's and the rest of them have been killed in some way that's not in theory at all, not in our theory, at all events, some way we've not contemplated, not thought of for an instant. Do you see my point?"

"Well, in a sort of way. You mean there's an absolute originality in the method? I suppose that is so. But what next?"

Remnant seemed to hesitate, partly from a sense of the portentous nature of what he was about to say, partly from a sort of half-unwillingness to part with so profound a secret.

"Well," he said, "you will allow that we have two sets of phenomena of a very extraordinary kind occurring at the same time. Don't you think that it's only reasonable to connect the two sets with one another."

"So the philosopher of Tenterden steeple and the Goodwin Sands thought, certainly," said Lewis. "But what is the connection? Those poor folks on the Highway weren't stung by bees or worried by a dog. And horses don't throw people over cliffs or stifle them in marshes."

"No; I never meant to suggest anything so absurd. It is evident to me that in all these cases of animals turning suddenly savage the cause has been terror, panic, fear. The horses that went charging into the camp were mad with fright, we know. And I say that in the other instances we have been discussing the cause was the same. The creatures were exposed to an infection of fear, and a frightened beast or bird or insect uses its weapons, whatever they may be. If, for example, there had been anybody with those horses when they took their panic they would have lashed out at him with their heels."

"Yes, I dare say that that is so. Well."

"Well; my belief is that the Germans have made an extraordinary discovery. I have called it the Z Ray. You know that the ether is merely an hypothesis; we have to suppose that it's there to account for the passage of the Marconi current from one place to another. Now, suppose that there is a psychic ether as well as a material ether, suppose that it is possible to direct irresistible impulses across this medium, suppose that these impulses are towards murder or suicide; then I think that you have an explanation of the terrible series of events that have been happening in Meirion for the last few weeks. And it is quite clear to my mind that the horses and the other creatures have been exposed to this Z Ray, and that it has produced on them the effect of terror, with ferocity as the result of terror. Now what do you say to that? Telepathy, you know, is well established; so is hypnotic suggestion. You have only to look in the *Encyclopaedia Britannica* to see that, and suggestion is so strong in some cases as to be an irresistible imperative. Now don't you feel that putting telepathy and suggestion together, as it were, you have more than the elements of what I call the Z Ray? I feel myself that I have more to go on in making my hypothesis than the inventor of the steam engine had in making his hypothesis when he saw the lid of the kettle bobbing up and down. What do you say?"

Dr. Lewis made no answer. He was watching the growth of a new, unknown tree in his garden.

The doctor made no answer to Remnant's question. For one thing, Remnant was profuse in his eloquence—he has been rigidly condensed in this history—and Lewis was tired of the sound of his voice. For another thing, he found the Z Ray theory almost too extravagant to be bearable, wild enough to tear patience to tatters. And then as the tedious argument continued Lewis became conscious that there was something strange about the night.

It was a dark summer night. The moon was old and faint, above the Dragon's Head across the bay, and the air was very still. It was so still that Lewis had noted that not a leaf stirred on the very tip of a high tree that stood out against the sky; and yet he knew that he was listening to some sound that he could not determine or define. It was not the wind in the leaves, it was not the gentle wash of the water of the sea against the rocks; that latter sound he could distinguish quite easily. But there was something else. It was scarcely a sound; it was as if the air itself trembled and fluttered, as the air trembles in a church when they open the great pedal pipes of the organ.

The doctor listened intently. It was not an illusion, the sound was not in his own head, as he had suspected for a moment; but for the life of him he could not make out whence it came or what it was. He gazed down into the night over the terraces of his garden, now sweet with the scent of the flowers of the night; tried to peer over the tree-tops across the sea towards the Dragon's Head. It struck him suddenly that this strange fluttering vibration of the air might be the noise of a distant aeroplane or airship; there was not the usual droning hum, but this sound might be caused by a new type of engine. A new type of engine? Possibly it was an enemy airship; their range, it had been said, was getting longer; and Lewis was just going to call Remnant's attention to the sound, to its possible cause, and to the possible danger that might be hovering over them, when he saw something that caught his breath and his heart with wild amazement and a touch of terror.

He had been staring upward into the sky, and, about to speak to Remnant, he had let his eyes drop for an instant. He looked down towards the trees in the garden, and saw with utter astonishment that one had changed its shape in the few hours that had passed since the setting of the sun. There was a thick grove of ilexes bordering the lowest terrace, and above them rose one tall pine, spreading its head of sparse, dark branches dark against the sky.

As Lewis glanced down over the terraces he saw that the tall pine tree was no longer there. In its place there rose above the ilexes what might have been a greater ilex; there was the blackness of a dense growth of foliage rising like a broad and far-spreading and rounded cloud over the lesser trees.

Here, then was a sight wholly incredible, impossible. It is doubtful whether the process of the human mind in such a case has ever been analyzed and registered; it is doubtful whether it ever can be registered. It is hardly fair to bring in the mathematician, since he deals with absolute truth (so far as mortality can conceive absolute truth); but how would a mathematician feel if he were suddenly confronted with a two-sided triangle? I suppose he would instantly become a raging madman; and Lewis, staring wide-eyed and wild-eyed at a dark and spreading tree which his own experience informed him was not there, felt for an instant that shock which should affront us all when we first realize the intolerable antinomy of Achilles and the Tortoise. Common sense tells us that Achilles will flash past the tortoise almost with the speed of the lightning; the inflexible truth of mathematics assures us that till the earth boils and the heavens cease to endure the Tortoise must still be in advance; and thereupon we should, in common decency, go mad. We do not go mad, because, by special grace, we are certified that, in the final: court of appeal, all science is a lie, even the highest science of all; and so we simply grin at Achilles and the Tortoise, as we grin at Darwin, deride Huxley, and laugh at Herbert Spencer.

Dr. Lewis did not grin. He glared into the dimness of the night, at the great spreading tree that he knew could not be there. And as he gazed he saw that what at first appeared the dense blackness of foliage was fretted and starred with wonderful appearances of lights and colors.

Afterwards he said to me: "I remember thinking to myself: 'Look here, I am not delirious; my temperature is perfectly normal. I am not drunk; I only had a pint of Graves with my dinner, over three hours ago. I have not eaten any poisonous fungus; I have not taken *Anhelonium Lewinii* experimentally. So, now then! What is happening?'"

The night had gloomed over; clouds obscured the faint moon and the misty stars. Lewis rose, with some kind of warning and inhibiting gesture to Remnant, who, he was conscious was gaping at him in astonishment. He walked to the open French window, and took a pace forward on to the path outside, and looked, very intently, at the dark shape of the tree, down below the sloping garden, above the washing of the waves. He shaded the light of the lamp behind him by holding his hands on each side of his eyes.

The mass of the tree—the tree that couldn't be there—stood out against the sky, but not so clearly, now that the clouds had rolled up. Its edges, the limits of its leafage, were not so distinct. Lewis thought that he could detect some sort of quivering movement in it; though the air was at a dead calm. It was a night on which one might hold up a lighted match and watch it burn without any wavering or inclination of the flame.

"You know," said Lewis, "how a bit of burnt paper will sometimes hang over the coals before it goes up the chimney, and little worms of fire will shoot through it. It was like that, if you should be standing some distance away. Just threads and hairs of yellow light I saw, and specks and sparks of fire, and then a twinkling of a ruby no bigger than a pin point, and a green wandering in the black, as if an emerald were crawling, and then little veins of deep blue. 'Woe is me!' I said to myself in Welsh, 'What is all this colour and burning?'

"And, then, at that very moment there came a thundering rap at the door of the room inside, and there was my man telling me that I was wanted directly up at the Garth, as old Mr Trevor Williams had been taken very bad. I knew his heart was not worth much, so I had to go off directly, and leave Remnant to make what he could of it all."

VI. MR REMNANT'S Z RAY

Dr. Lewis was kept some time at the Garth. It was past twelve when he got back to his house.

He went quickly to the room that overlooked the garden and the sea and threw open the French window and peered into the darkness. There, dim indeed against the dim sky but unmistakable, was the tall pine with its sparse branches, high above the dense growth of the ilex trees. The strange boughs which had amazed him had vanished; there was no appearance now of colours or of fires.

He drew his chair up to the open window and sat there gazing and wondering far into the night, till brightness came upon the sea and sky, and the forms of the trees in the garden grew clear and evident. He went up to his bed at last filled with a great perplexity, still asking questions to which there was no answer.

The doctor did not say anything about the strange tree to Remnant. When they next met, Lewis said that he had thought there was a man hiding amongst the bushes—this in explanation of that warning gesture he had used, and of his going out into the garden and staring into the night. He concealed the truth because he dreaded the Remnant doctrine that would undoubtedly be produced; indeed, he hoped that he had heard the last of the theory of the Z Ray. But Remnant firmly reopened this subject.

"We were interrupted just as I was putting my case to you," he said. "And to sum it all up, it amounts to this: that the Huns have made one of the great leaps of science. They are sending 'suggestions' (which amount to irresistible commands) over here, and the persons affected are seized with suicidal or homicidal mania. The people who were killed by falling over the cliffs or into the quarry probably committed suicide; and so with the man and boy who were found in the bog. As to the Highway case, you remember that Thomas Evans said that he stopped and talked to Williams on the night of the murder. In my opinion Evans was the murderer. He came under the influence of the Ray, became a homicidal maniac in an instant, snatched Williams's spade from his hand and killed him and the others."

"The bodies were found by me on the road."

"It is possible that the first impact of the Ray produces violent nervous excitement, which would manifest itself externally. Williams might have called to his wife to come and see what was the matter with Evans. The children would naturally follow their mother. It seems to me simple. And as for the animals—the horses, dogs, and so forth, they as I say, were no doubt panic stricken by the Ray, and hence driven to frenzy."

"Why should Evans have murdered Williams instead of Williams murdering Evans? Why should the impact of the Ray affect one and not the other?"

"Why does one man react violently to a certain drug, while it makes no impression on another man? Why is A able to drink a bottle of whisky and remain sober, while B is turned into something very like a lunatic after he has drunk three glasses?"

"It is a question of idiosyncrasy," said the doctor.

"Is idiosyncrasy Greek for 'I don't know'?" asked Remnant.

"Not at all," said Lewis, smiling blandly. "I mean that in some diatheses whisky—as you have mentioned whisky—appears not to be pathogenic, or at all events not immediately pathogenic. In other cases, as you very justly observed, there seems to be a very marked cachexia associated with the exhibition of the spirit in question, even in comparatively small doses."

Under this cloud of professional verbiage Lewis escaped from the Club and from Remnant. He did not want to hear any more about that Dreadful Ray, because he felt sure that the Ray was all nonsense. But asking himself why he felt this certitude in the matter he had to confess that he didn't know. An aeroplane, he reflected, was all nonsense before it was made; and he remembered talking in the early nineties to a friend of his about the newly discovered X Rays. The friend laughed incredulously, evidently didn't believe a word of it, till Lewis told him that there was an article on the subject in the current number of the *Saturday Review*; whereupon the unbeliever said, "Oh, is that so? Oh, really. I *see*," and was converted on the X Ray faith on the spot. Lewis, remembering this talk, marveled at the strange processes of the human mind, its illogical and yet all-compelling *ergos*, and wondered whether he himself was only waiting for an article on the Z Ray in the *Saturday Review* to become a devout believer in the doctrine of Remnant.

But he wondered with far more fervour as to the extraordinary thing he had seen in his own garden with his own eyes. The tree that changed all its shape for an hour or two of the night, the growth of strange boughs, the apparition of secret fires among them, the sparkling of emerald and ruby lights: how could one fail to be afraid with great amazement at the thought of such a mystery?

Dr. Lewis's thoughts were distracted from the incredible adventure of the tree by the visit of his sister and her husband. Mr and Mrs. Merritt lived in a well-known manufacturing town of the Midlands, which was now, of course, a centre of munition work. On the day of their arrival at Porth, Mrs. Merritt, who was tired after the long, hot journey, went to bed early, and Merritt and Lewis went into the room by the garden for their talk and tobacco. They spoke of the year that had passed since their last meeting, of the weary dragging of the war, of friends that had perished in it, of the hopelessness of an early ending of all this misery. Lewis said nothing of the terror that was on the land. One does not greet a tired man who is come to a quiet, sunny place for relief from black smoke and work and worry with a tale of horror. Indeed, the doctor saw that his brother-in-law looked far from well. And he seemed "jumpy"; there was an occasional twitch of his mouth that Lewis did not like at all.

"Well," said the doctor, after an interval of silence and port wine, "I am glad to see you here again. Porth always suits you. I don't think you're looking quite up to your usual form. But three weeks of Meirion air will do wonders."

"Well, I hope it will," said the other. "I am not up to the mark. Things are not going well at Midlingham."

"Business is all right, isn't it?"

"Yes. Business is all right. But there are other things that are all wrong. We are living under a reign of terror. It comes to that."

"What on earth do you mean?"

"Well, I suppose I may tell you what I know. It's not much. I didn't dare write it. But do you know that at every one of the munition works in Midlingham and all about it there's a guard of soldiers with drawn bayonets and loaded rifles day and night? Men with bombs, too. And machine-guns at the big factories."

"German spies?"

"You don't want Lewis guns to fight spies with. Nor bombs. Nor a platoon of men. I woke up last night. It was the machine-gun at Benington's Army Motor Works. Firing like fury. And then bang! bang! bang! That was the hand bombs."

"But what against?"

"Nobody knows."

"Nobody knows what is happening," Merritt repeated, and he went on to describe the bewilderment and terror that hung like a cloud over the great industrial city in the Midlands, how the feeling of concealment, of some intolerable secret danger that must not be named, was worst of all.

"A young fellow I know," he said, "was on short leave the other day from the front, and he spent it with his people at Belmont—that's about four miles out of Midlingham, you know. 'Thank God,' he said to me, 'I am going back tomorrow. It's no good saying that the Wipers salient is nice, because it isn't. But it's a damned sight better than this. At the front you know what you're up against anyhow.' At Midlingham everybody has the feeling that we're up against something awful and we don't know what; it's that that makes people inclined to whisper. There's terror in the air."

Merritt made a sort of picture of the great town cowering in its fear of an unknown danger.

"People are afraid to go about alone at nights in the outskirts. They make up parties at the stations to go home together if it's anything like dark, or if there are any lonely bits on their way."

"But why? I don't understand. What are they afraid of?"

"Well, I told you about my being awakened up the other night with the machine-guns at the motor works rattling away, and the bombs exploding and making the most terrible noise. That sort of thing alarms one, you know. It's only natural."

"Indeed, it must be very terrifying. You mean, then, there is a general nervousness about, a vague sort of apprehension that makes people inclined to herd together?"

"There's that, and there's more. People have gone out that have never come back. There were a couple of men in the train to Holme, arguing about the quickest way to get to Northend, a sort of outlying part of Holme where they both lived. They argued all the way out of Midlingham, one saying that the high road was the quickest though it was the longest way. 'It's the quickest going because it's the cleanest going,' he said."

"The other chap fancied a short cut across the fields, by the canal. 'It's half the distance,' he kept on. 'Yes, if you don't lose your way,' said the other. Well, it appears they put an even half-crown on it, and each was to try his own way when they got out of the train. It was arranged that they were to meet at the 'Wagon' in Northend. 'I shall be at the 'Wagon' first,' said the man who believed in the short cut, and with that he climbed over the stile and made off across the fields. It wasn't late enough to be really dark, and a lot of them thought he might win the stakes. But he never turned up at the Wagon—or anywhere else for the matter of that."

"What happened to him?"

"He was found lying on his back in the middle of a field—some way from the path. He was dead. The doctors said he'd been suffocated. Nobody knows how. Then there have been other cases. We whisper about them at Midlingham, but we're afraid to speak out."

Lewis was ruminating all this profoundly. Terror in Meirion and terror far away in the heart of England; but at Midlingham, so far as he could gather from these stories of soldiers on guard, of crackling machine-guns, it was a case of an organized attack on the munitioning of the army. He felt that he did not know enough to warrant his deciding that the terror of Meirion and of Stratfordshire were one.

Then Merritt began again:

"There's a queer story going about, when the door's shut and the curtain's drawn, that is, as to a place right out in the country over the other side of Midlingham; on the opposite side to Dunwich. They've built one of the new factories out there, a great red brick town of sheds they tell me it is, with a tremendous chimney. It's not been finished more than a month or six weeks. They plumped it down right in the middle of the fields, by the line, and they're building huts for the workers as fast as they can but up to the present the men are billeted all about, up and down the line.

"About two hundred yards from this place there's an old footpath, leading from the station and the main road up to a small hamlet on the hillside. Part of the way this path goes by a pretty large wood, most of it thick undergrowth. I should think there must be twenty acres of wood, more or less. As it happens, I used this path once long ago; and I can tell you it's a black place of nights.

"A man had to go this way one night. He got along all right till he came to the wood. And then he said his heart dropped out of his body. It was awful to hear the noises in that wood. Thousands of men were in it, he swears that. It was full of rustling, and pattering of feet trying to go dainty, and the crack of dead boughs lying on the ground as some one trod on them, and swishing of the grass, and some sort of chattering speech going on, that sounded, so he said, as if the dead sat in their bones and talked! He ran for his life, anyhow; across fields, over hedges, through brooks. He must have run, by his tale, ten miles out of his way before he got home to his wife, and beat at the door, and broke in, and bolted it behind him."

"There is something rather alarming about any wood at night," said Dr. Lewis.

Merritt shrugged his shoulders.

"People say that the Germans have landed, and that they are hiding in underground places all over the country."

VII. THE CASE OF THE HIDDEN GERMANS

Lewis gasped for a moment, silent in contemplation of the magnificence of rumour. The Germans already landed, hiding underground, striking by night, secretly, terribly, at the power of England! Here was a conception which made the myth of 'The Russians' a paltry fable; before which the Legend of Mons was an ineffectual thing.

It was monstrous. And yet—

He looked steadily at Merritt; a square-headed, black-haired, solid sort of man. He had symptoms of nerves about him for the moment, certainly, but one could not wonder at that, whether the tales he told were true, or whether he merely believed them to be true. Lewis had known his brother-in-law for twenty years or more, and had always found him a sure man in his own small world. "But then," said the doctor to himself, "those men, if they once get out of the ring of that little world of theirs, they are lost. Those are the men that believed in Madame Blavatsky."

"Well," he said, "what do you think yourself? The Germans landed and hiding somewhere about the country: there's something extravagant in the notion, isn't there?"

"I don't know what to think. You can't get over the facts. There are the soldiers with their rifles and their guns at the works all over Stratfordshire, and those guns go off. I told you I'd heard them. Then who are the soldiers shooting at? That's what we ask ourselves at Midlingham."

"Quite so; I quite understand. It's an extraordinary state of things."

"It's more than extraordinary; it's an awful state of things. It's terror in the dark, and there's nothing worse than that. As that young fellow I was telling you about said, 'At the front you do know what you're up against.'"

"And people really believe that a number of Germans have somehow got over to England and have hid themselves underground?"

"People say they've got a new kind of poison-gas. Some think that they dig underground places and make the gas there, and lead it by secret pipes into the shops; others say that they throw gas bombs into the factories. It must be worse than anything they've used in France, from what the authorities say."

"The authorities? Do *they* admit that there are Germans in hiding about Midlingham?"

"No. They call it 'explosions.' But we know it isn't explosions. We know in the Midlands what an explosion sounds like and looks like. And we know that the people killed in these 'explosions' are put into their coffins in the works. Their own relations are not allowed to see them."

"And so you believe in the German theory?"

"If I do, it's because one must believe in something. Some say they've seen the gas. I heard that a man living in Dunwich saw it one night like a black cloud with sparks of fire in it floating over the tops of the trees by Dunwich Common."

The light of an ineffable amazement came into Lewis's eyes. The night of Remnant's visit, the trembling vibration of the air, the dark tree that had grown in his garden since the setting of the sun, the strange leafage that was starred with burning, with emerald and ruby fires, and all vanished away when he returned from his visit to the Garth; and such a leafage had appeared as a burning cloud far in the heart of England: what intolerable mystery, what tremendous doom was signified in this? But one thing was clear and certain: that the terror of Meirion was also the terror of the Midlands.

Lewis made up his mind most firmly that if possible all this should be kept from his brother-in-law. Merritt had come to Porth as to a city of refuge from the horrors of Midlingham; if it could be managed he should be spared the knowledge that the cloud of terror had gone before him and hung black over the western land. Lewis passed the port and said in an even voice:

"Very strange, indeed; a black cloud with sparks of fire?"

"I can't answer for it, you know; it's only a rumour."

"Just so; and you think or you're inclined to think that this and all the rest you've told me is to be put down to the hidden Germans?"

"As I say; because one must think something.

"I quite see your point. No doubt, if it's true, it's the most awful blow that has ever been dealt at any nation in the whole history of man. The enemy established in our vitals! But is it possible, after all? How could it have been worked?"

Merritt told Lewis how it had been worked, or rather, how people said it had been worked. The idea, he said, was that this was a part, and a most important part, of the great German plot to destroy England and the British Empire.

The scheme had been prepared years ago, some thought soon after the Franco-Prussian War. Moltke had seen that the invasion of England (in the ordinary sense of the term invasion) presented very great difficulties. The matter was constantly in discussion in the inner military and high political circles, and the general trend of opinion in these quarters was that at the best, the invasion of England would involve Germany in the gravest difficulties, and leave France in the position of the *tertius gaudens*. This was the state of affairs when a very high Prussian personage was approached by the Swedish professor, Huvelius.

Thus Merritt, and here I would say in parenthesis that this Huvelius was by all accounts an extraordinary man. Considered personally and apart from his writings he would appear to have been a most amiable individual. He was richer than the generality of Swedes, certainly far richer than the average university professor in Sweden. But his shabby, green frock-coat, and his battered, furry hat were notorious in the university town where he lived. No one laughed, because it was well known that Professor Huvelius spent every penny of his private means and a large portion of his official stipend on works of kindness and charity. He hid his head in a garret, some one said, in order that others might be able to swell on the first floor. It was told of him that he restricted himself to a diet of dry bread and coffee for a month in order that a poor woman of the streets, dying of consumption, might enjoy luxuries in hospital.

And this was the man who wrote the treatise *De Facinore Humano*; to prove the infinite corruption of the human race.

Oddly enough, Professor Huvelius wrote the most cynical book in the world—Hobbes preaches rosy sentimentalism in comparison—with the very highest motives. He held that a very large part of human misery, misadventure, and sorrow was due to the false convention that the heart of man was naturally and in the main well disposed and kindly, if not exactly righteous. "Murderers, thieves, assassins, violators, and all the host of the abominable," he says in one passage, "are created by the false pretense and foolish credence of human virtue. A lion in a cage is a fierce beast, indeed; but what will he be if we declare him to be a lamb and open the doors of his den? Who will be guilty of the deaths of the men, women and children whom he will surely devour, save those who unlocked the cage?" And he goes on to show that kings and the rulers of the peoples could decrease the sum of human misery to a vast extent by acting on the doctrine of human wickedness. "War," he declares, "which is one of the worst of evils, will always continue to exist. But a wise king will desire a brief war rather than a lengthy one, a short evil rather than a long evil. And this not from the benignity of his heart towards his enemies, for we have seen that the human heart is naturally malignant, but because he desires to conquer, and to conquer easily, without a great expenditure of men or of treasure, knowing that if he can accomplish this feat his people will love him and his crown will be secure. So he will wage brief victorious wars, and not only spare his own nation, but the nation of the enemy, since in a short war the loss is less on both sides than in a long war. And so from evil will come good."

And how, asks Huvelius, are such wars to be waged? The wise prince, he replies, will begin by assuming the enemy to be infinitely corruptible and infinitely stupid, since stupidity and corruption are the chief characteristics of man. So the prince will make himself friends in the very councils of his enemy, and also amongst the populace, bribing the wealthy by proffering to them the opportunity of still greater wealth, and winning the poor by swelling words. "For, contrary to the common opinion, it is the wealthy who are greedy of wealth; while the populace are to be gained by talking to them about liberty, their unknown god. And so much are they enchanted by the words liberty, freedom, and such like, that the wise can go to the poor, rob them of what little they have, dismiss them with a hearty kick, and win their hearts and their votes for ever, if only they will assure them that the treatment which they have received is called liberty."

Guided by these principles, says Huvelius, the wise prince will entrench himself in the country that he desires to conquer; "nay, with but little trouble, he may actually and literally throw his garrisons into the heart of the enemy country before war has begun."

This is a long and tiresome parenthesis; but it is necessary as explaining the long tale which Merritt told his brother-in-law, he having received it from some magnate of the Midlands, who had traveled in Germany. It is probable that the story was suggested in the first place by the passage from Huvelius which I have just quoted.

Merritt knew nothing of the real Huvelius, who was all but a saint; he thought of the Swedish professor as a monster of iniquity, "worse," as he said, "than Neech"—meaning, no doubt, Nietzsche.

So he told the story of how Huvelius had sold his plan to the Germans; a plan for filling England with German soldiers. Land was to be bought in certain suitable and well-considered places, Englishmen were to be bought as the apparent owners of such land, and secret excavations were to be made, till the country was literally undermined. A subterranean Germany, in fact, was to be dug under selected districts of England; there were to be great caverns, underground cities, well drained, well ventilated, supplied with water, and in these places vast stores both of food and of munitions were to be accumulated, year after year, till 'the Day' dawned. And then, warned in time, the secret garrison would leave shops, hotels, offices, villas, and vanish underground, ready to begin their work of bleeding England at the heart.

"That's what Henson told me," said Merritt at the end of his long story. "Henson, head of the Buckley Iron and Steel Syndicate. He has been a lot in Germany."

"Well," said Lewis, "of course, it may be so. If it is so, it is terrible beyond words."

Indeed, he found something horribly plausible in the story. It was an extraordinary plan, of course; an unheard of scheme; but it did not seem impossible. It was the Trojan Horse on a gigantic scale; indeed, he reflected, the story of the horse with the warriors concealed within it which was dragged into the heart of Troy by the deluded Trojans themselves might be taken as a prophetic parable of what had happened to England—if Henson's theory were well founded. And this theory certainly squared with what one had heard of German preparations in Belgium and in France: emplacements for guns ready for the invader, German manufactories which were really German forts on Belgian soil, the caverns by the Aisne made ready for the cannon; indeed, Lewis thought he remembered something about suspicious concrete tennis-courts on the heights commanding London. But a German army hidden under English ground! It was a thought to chill the stoutest heart.

And it seemed from that wonder of the burning tree, that the enemy mysteriously and terribly present at Midlingham, was present also in Meirion. Lewis, thinking of the country as he knew it, of its wild and desolate hillsides, its deep woods, its wastes and solitary places, could not but confess that no more fit region could be found for the deadly enterprise of secret men. Yet, he thought again, there was but little harm to be done in Meirion to the armies of England or to their munitionment. They were working for panic terror? Possibly that might be so; but the camp under the Highway? That should be their first object, and no harm had been done there.

Lewis did not know that since the panic of the horses men had died terribly in that camp; that it was now a fortified place, with a deep, broad trench, a thick tangle of savage barbed wire about it, and a machine-gun planted at each corner.

VIII. WHAT MR MERRITT FOUND

Mr Merritt began to pick up his health and spirits a good deal. For the first morning or two of his stay at the doctor's he contented himself with a very comfortable deck chair close to the house, where he sat under the shade of an old mulberry tree beside his wife and watched the bright sunshine on the green lawns, on the creamy crests of the waves, on the headlands of that glorious coast, purple even from afar with the imperial glow of the heather, on the white farmhouses gleaming in the sunlight, high over the sea, far from any turmoil, from any troubling of men.

The sun was hot, but the wind breathed all the while gently, incessantly, from the east, and Merritt, who had come to this quiet place, not only from dismay, but from the stifling and oily airs of the smoky Midland town, said that that east wind, pure and clear and like well water from the rock, was new life to him. He ate a capital dinner, at the end of his first day at Porth and took rosy views. As to what they had been talking about the night before, he said to Lewis, no doubt there must be trouble of some sort, and perhaps bad trouble; still, Kitchener would soon put it all right.

So things went on very well. Merritt began to stroll about the garden, which was full of the comfortable spaces, groves, and surprises that only country gardens know. To the right of one of the terraces he found an arbor or summer-house covered with white roses, and he was as pleased as if he had discovered the Pole. He spent a whole day there, smoking and lounging and reading a rubbishy sensational story, and declared that the Devonshire roses had taken many years off his age. Then on the other side of the garden there was a filbert grove that he had never explored on any of his former visits; and again there was a find. Deep in the shadow of the filberts was a bubbling well, issuing from rocks, and all manner of green, dewy ferns growing about it and above it, and an angelica springing beside it. Merritt knelt on his knees, and hollowed his hand and drank the well water. He said (over his port) that night that if all water were like the water of the filbert well the world would turn to teetotalism. It takes a townsman to relish the manifold and exquisite joys of the country.

It was not till he began to venture abroad that Merritt found that something was lacking of the old rich peace that used to dwell in Meirion. He had a favourite walk which he never neglected, year after year. This walk led along the cliffs towards Meiros, and then one could turn inland and return to Porth by deep winding lanes that went over the Allt. So Merritt set out early one morning and got as far as a sentry-box at the foot of the path that led up to the cliff. There was a sentry pacing up and down in front of the box, and he called on Merritt to produce his pass, or to turn back to the main road. Merritt was a good deal put out, and asked the doctor about this strict guard. And the doctor was surprised.

"I didn't know they had put their bar up there," he said. "I suppose it's wise. We are certainly in the far West here; still, the Germans might slip round and raid us and do a lot of damage just because Meirion is the last place we should expect them to go for."

"But there are no fortifications, surely, on the cliff?"

"Oh, no; I never heard of anything of the kind there."

"Well, what's the point of forbidding the public to go on the cliff, then? I can quite understand putting a sentry on the top to keep a look-out for the enemy. What I don't understand is a sentry at the bottom who can't keep a look-out for anything, as he can't see the sea. And why warn the public off the cliffs? I couldn't facilitate a German landing by standing on Pengareg, even if I wanted to."

"It is curious," the doctor agreed. "Some military reasons, I suppose."

He let the matter drop, perhaps because the matter did not affect him. People who live in the country all the year round, country doctors certainly, are little given to desultory walking in search of the picturesque.

Lewis had no suspicion that sentries whose object was equally obscure were being dotted all over the country. There was a sentry, for example, by the quarry at Llanfihangel, where the dead woman and the dead sheep had been found some weeks before. The path by the quarry was used a good deal, and its closing would have inconvenienced the people of the neighborhood very considerably. But the sentry had his box by the side of the track and had his orders to keep everybody strictly to the path, as if the quarry were a secret fort.

It was not known till a month or two ago that one of these sentries was himself a victim of the terror. The men on duty at this place were given certain very strict orders, which from the nature of the case, must have seemed to them unreasonable. For old soldiers, orders are orders; but here was a young bank clerk, scarcely in training for a couple of months, who had not begun to appreciate the necessity of hard, literal obedience to an order which seemed to him meaningless. He found himself on a remote and lonely hillside, he had not the faintest notion that his every movement was watched; and he disobeyed a certain instruction that had been given him. The post was found deserted by the relief; the sentry's dead body was found at the bottom of the quarry.

This by the way; but Mr Merritt discovered again and again that things happened to hamper his walks and his wanderings. Two or three miles from Porth there is a great marsh made by the Afon river before it falls into the sea, and here Merritt had been accustomed to botanize mildly. He had learned pretty accurately the causeways of solid ground that lead through the sea of swamp and ooze and soft yielding soil, and he set out one hot afternoon determined to make a thorough exploration of the marsh, and this time to find that rare Bog Bean, that he felt sure, must grow somewhere in its wide extent.

He got into the by-road that skirts the marsh, and to the gate which he had always used for entrance.

There was the scene as he had known it always, the rich growth of reeds and flags and rushes, the mild black cattle grazing on the 'islands' of firm turf, the scented procession of the meadowsweet, the royal glory of the loosestrife, flaming pennons, crimson and golden, of the giant dock.

But they were bringing out a dead man's body through the gate.

A labouring man was holding open the gate on the marsh. Merritt, horrified, spoke to him and asked who it was, and how it had happened.

"They do say he was a visitor at Porth. Somehow he has been drowned in the marsh, whatever."

"But it's perfectly safe. I've been all over it a dozen times."

"Well, indeed, we did always think so. If you did slip by accident, like, and fall into the water, it was not so deep; it was easy enough to climb out again. And this gentleman was quite young, to look at him, poor man; and he has come to Meirion for his pleasure and holiday and found his death in it!"

"Did he do it on purpose? Is it suicide?"

"They say he had no reasons to do that."

Here the sergeant of police in charge of the party interposed, according to orders, which he himself did not understand.

"A terrible thing, sir, to be sure, and a sad pity; and I am sure this is not the sort of sight you have come to see down in Meirion this beautiful summer. So don't you think, sir, that it would be more pleasant like, if you would leave us to this sad business of ours? I have heard many gentlemen staying in Porth say that there is nothing to beat the view from the hill over there, not in the whole of Wales."

Everyone is polite in Meirion, but somehow Merritt understood that, in English, this speech meant "move on."

Merritt moved back to Porth—he was not in the humour for any idle, pleasurable strolling after so dreadful a meeting with death. He made some inquiries in the town about the dead man, but nothing seemed known of him. It was said that he had been on his honeymoon, that he had been staying at the Porth Castle Hotel; but the people of the hotel declared that they had never heard of such a person. Merritt got the local paper at the end of the week; there was not a word in it of any fatal accident in the marsh. He met the sergeant of police in the street. That officer touched his helmet with the utmost politeness and a "hope you are enjoying yourself, sir; indeed you do look a lot better already"; but as to the poor man who was found drowned or stifled in the marsh, he knew nothing.

The next day Merritt made up his mind to go to the marsh to see whether he could find anything to account for so strange a death. What he found was a man with an armlet standing by the gate. The armlet had the letters "C.W." on it, which are understood to mean Coast Watcher. The Watcher said he had strict instructions to keep everybody away from the marsh. Why? He didn't know, but some said that the river was changing its course since the new railway embankment was built, and the marsh had become dangerous to people who didn't know it thoroughly.

"Indeed, sir," he added, "it is part of my orders not to set foot on the other side of that gate myself, not for one scrag-end of a minute."

Merritt glanced over the gate incredulously. The marsh looked as it had always looked; there was plenty of sound, hard ground to walk on; he could see the track that he used to follow as firm as ever. He did not believe in the story of the changing course of the river, and Lewis said he had never heard of anything of the kind. But Merritt had put the question in the middle of general conversation; he had not led up to it from any discussion of the death in the marsh, and so the doctor was taken unawares. If he had known of the connection in Merritt's mind between the alleged changing of the Afon's course and the tragical event in the marsh, no doubt he would have confirmed the official explanation. He was, above all things, anxious to prevent his sister and her husband from finding out that the invisible hand of terror that ruled at Midlingham was ruling also in Meirion.

Lewis himself had little doubt that the man who was found dead in the marsh had been struck down by the secret agency, whatever it was, that had already accomplished so much of evil; but it was a chief part of the terror that no one knew for certain that this or that particular event was to be ascribed to it. People do occasionally fall over cliffs through their own carelessness, and as the case of Garcia, the Spanish sailor, showed, cottagers and their wives and children are now and then the victims of savage and purposeless violence. Lewis had never wandered about the marsh himself; but Remnant had pottered round it and about it, and declared that the man who met his death there—his name was never known, in Porth at all events—must either have committed suicide by deliberately lying prone in the ooze and stifling himself, or else must have been held down in it. There were no details available, so it was clear that the authorities had classified this death with the others; still, the man might have committed suicide, or he might have had a sudden seizure and fallen in the slimy water face-downwards. And so on: it was possible to believe that case A *or* B *or* C was in the category of ordinary accidents or ordinary crimes. But it was not possible to believe that A *and* B *and* C were all in that category. And thus it was to the end, and thus it is now. We know that the terror reigned, and how it reigned, but there were many dreadful events ascribed to its rule about which there must always be room for doubt.

For example, there was the case of the *Mary Ann*, the rowing-boat which came to grief in so strange a manner, almost under Merritt's eyes. In my opinion he was quite wrong in associating the sorry fate of the boat and her occupants with a system of signaling by flashlights which he detected or thought that he detected, on the afternoon in which the *Mary Ann* was capsized. I believe his signaling theory to be all nonsense, in spite of the naturalized German governess who was lodging with her employers in the suspected house. But, on the other hand, there is no doubt in my own mind that the boat was overturned and those in it drowned by the work of the terror.

IX. THE LIGHT ON THE WATER

Let it be noted carefully that so far Merritt had not the slightest suspicion that the terror of Midlingham was quick over Meirion. Lewis had watched and shepherded him carefully. He had let out no suspicion of what had happened in Meirion, and before taking his brother-in-law to the club he had passed round a hint among the members. He did not tell the truth about Midlingham—and here again is a point of interest, that as the terror deepened the general public cooperated voluntarily, and, one would say, almost subconsciously, with the authorities in concealing what they knew from one another—but he gave out a desirable portion of the truth: that his brother-in-law was "nervy," not by any means up to the mark, and that it was therefore desirable that he should be spared the knowledge of the intolerable and tragic mysteries which were being enacted all about them.

"He knows about that poor fellow who was found in the marsh," said Lewis, "and he has a kind of vague suspicion that there is something out of the common about the case; but no more than that."

"A clear case of suggested, or rather commanded suicide," said Remnant. "I regard it as a strong confirmation of my theory."

"Perhaps so," said the doctor, dreading lest he might have to hear about the Z Ray all over again. "But please don't let anything out to him; I want him to get built up thoroughly before he goes back to Midlingham."

Then, on the other hand, Merritt was as still as death about the doings of the Midlands; he hated to think of them, much more to speak of them; and thus, as I say, he and the men at the Porth Club kept their secrets from one another; and thus, from the beginning to the end of the terror, the links were not drawn together. In many cases, no doubt, A and B met every day and talked familiarly, it may be confidentially, on other matters of all sorts, each having in his possession half of the truth, which he concealed from the other. So the two halves were never put together to make a whole.

Merritt, as the doctor guessed, had a kind of uneasy feeling—it scarcely amounted to a suspicion—as to the business of the marsh; chiefly because he thought the official talk about the railway embankment and the course of the river rank nonsense. But finding that nothing more happened, he let the matter drop from his mind, and settled himself down to enjoy his holiday.

He found to his delight that there were no sentries or watchers to hinder him from the approach to Larnac Bay, a delicious cove, a place where the ashgrove and the green meadow and the glistening bracken sloped gently down to red rocks and firm yellow sands. Merritt remembered a rock that formed a comfortable seat, and here he established himself of a golden afternoon, and gazed at the blue of the sea and the crimson bastions and bays of the coast as it bent inward to Sarnau and swept out again southward to the odd-shaped promontory called the Dragon's Head. Merritt gazed on, amused by the antics of the porpoises who were tumbling and splashing and gamboling a little way out at sea, charmed by the pure and radiant air that was so different from the oily smoke that often stood for heaven at Midlingham, and charmed, too, by the white farmhouses dotted here and there on the heights of the curving coast.

Then he noticed a little row-boat at about two hundred yards from the shore. There were two or three people aboard, he could not quite make out how many, and they seemed to be doing something with a line; they were no doubt fishing, and Merritt (who disliked fish) wondered how people could spoil such an afternoon, such a sea, such pellucid and radiant air by trying to catch white, flabby, offensive, evil-smelling creatures that would be excessively nasty when cooked. He puzzled over this problem and turned away from it to the contemplation of the crimson headlands. And then he says that he noticed that signaling was going on. Flashing lights of intense brilliance, he declares, were coming from one of those farms on the heights of the coast; it was as if white fire was spouting from it. Merritt was certain, as the light appeared and disappeared, that some message was being sent, and he regretted that he knew nothing of heliography. Three short flashes, a long and very brilliant flash, then two short flashes. Merritt fumbled in his pocket for pencil and paper so that he might record these signals, and, bringing his eyes down to the sea level, he became aware, with amazement and horror, that the boat had disappeared. All that he could see was some vague, dark object far to westward, running out with the tide.

Now it is certain, unfortunately, that the *Mary Ann* was capsized and that two schoolboys and the sailor in charge were drowned. The bones of the boat were found amongst the rocks far along the coast, and the three bodies were also washed ashore. The sailor could not swim at all, the boys only a little, and it needs an exceptionally fine swimmer to fight against the outward suck of the tide as it rushes past Pengareg Point.

But I have no belief whatever in Merritt's theory. He held (and still holds, for all I know), that the flashes of light which he saw coming from Penyrhaul, the farmhouse oh the height, had some connection with the disaster to the *Mary Ann*. When it was ascertained that a family were spending their summer at the farm, and that the governess was a German, though a long naturalized German, Merritt could not see that there was anything left to argue about, though there might be many details to discover. But, in my opinion, all this was a mere mare's nest; the flashes of brilliant light were caused, no doubt, by the sun lighting up one window of the farmhouse after the other.

Still, Merritt was convinced from the very first, even before the damning circumstance of the German governess was brought to light; and on the evening of the disaster, as Lewis and he sat together after dinner, he was endeavouring to put what he called the common sense of the matter to the doctor.

"If you hear a shot," said Merritt, "and you see a man fall, you know pretty well what killed him."

There was a flutter of wild wings in the room. A great moth beat to and fro and dashed itself madly against the ceiling, the walls, the glass bookcase. Then a sputtering sound, a momentary dimming of the lamp. The moth had succeeded in its mysterious quest.

"Can you tell me," said Lewis as if he were answering Merritt, "why moths rush into the flame?"

Lewis had put his question as to the strange habits of the common moth to Merritt with the deliberate intent of closing the debate on death by heliograph. The query was suggested, of course, by the incident of the moth in the lamp, and Lewis thought that he had said, "Oh, shut up!" in a somewhat elegant manner. And, in fact Merritt looked dignified, remained silent, and helped himself to port.

That was the end that the doctor had desired. He had no doubt in his own mind that the affair of the *Mary Ann* was but one more item in the long account of horrors that grew larger almost with every day; and he was in no humour to listen to wild and futile theories as to the manner in which the disaster had been accomplished. Here was a proof that the terror that was upon them was mighty not only on the land but on the waters; for Lewis could not see that the boat could have been attacked by any ordinary means of destruction. From Merritt's story, it must have been in shallow water. The shore of Larnac Bay shelves very gradually, and the Admiralty charts showed the depth of water two hundred yards out to be only two fathoms; this would be too shallow for a submarine. And it could not have been shelled, and it could not have been torpedoed; there was no explosion. The disaster might have been due to carelessness; boys, he considered, will play the fool anywhere, even in a boat; but he did not think so; the sailor would have stopped them. And, it may be mentioned, that the two boys were as a matter of fact extremely steady, sensible young fellows, not in the least likely to play foolish tricks of any kind.

Lewis was immersed in these reflections, having successfully silenced his brother-in-law; he was trying in vain to find some clue to the horrible enigma. The Midlingham theory of a concealed German force, hiding in places under the earth, was extravagant enough, and yet it seemed the only solution that approached plausibility; but then again even a subterranean German host would hardly account for this wreckage of a boat, floating on a calm sea. And then what of the tree with the burning in it that had appeared in the garden there a few weeks ago, and the cloud with a burning in it that had shown over the trees of the Midland village?

I think I have, already written something of the probable emotions of the mathematician confronted suddenly with an undoubted two-sided triangle. I said, if I remember, that he would be forced, in decency, to go mad; and I believe that Lewis was very near to this point. He felt himself confronted with an intolerable problem that most instantly demanded solution, and yet, with the same breath, as it were, denied the possibility of there being any solution. People were being killed in an inscrutable manner by some inscrutable means, day after day, and one asked "why" and "how"; and there seemed no answer. In the Midlands, where every kind of munitionment was manufactured, the explanation of German agency was plausible; and even if the subterranean notion was to be rejected as savoring altogether too much of the fairytale, or rather of the sensational romance, yet it was possible that the backbone of the theory was true; the Germans might have planted their agents in some way or another in the midst of our factories. But here in Meirion, what serious effect could be produced by the casual and indiscriminate slaughter of a couple of schoolboys in a boat, of a harmless holiday-maker in a marsh? The creation of an atmosphere of terror and dismay? It was possible, of course, but it hardly seemed tolerable, in spite of the enormities of Louvain and of the *Lusitania*.

Into these meditations, and into the still dignified silence of Merritt broke the rap on the door of Lewis's man, and those words which harass the ease of the country doctor when he tries to take any ease: "You're wanted in the surgery, if you please, sir." Lewis bustled out, and appeared no more that night.

The doctor had been summoned to a little hamlet on the outskirts of Porth, separated from it by half a mile or three-quarters of road. One dignifies, indeed, this settlement without a name in calling it a hamlet; it was a mere row of four cottages, built about a hundred years ago for the accommodation of the workers in a quarry long since disused. In one of these cottages the doctor found a father and mother weeping and crying out to "doctor bach, doctor bach," and two frightened children, and one little body, still and dead. It was the youngest of the three, little Johnnie, and he was dead.

The doctor found that the child had been asphyxiated. He felt the clothes; they were dry; it was not a case of drowning. He looked at the neck; there was no mark of strangling. He asked the father how it had happened, and father and mother, weeping most lamentably, declared they had no knowledge of how their child had been killed: "unless it was the People that had done it." The Celtic fairies are still malignant. Lewis asked what had happened that evening; where had the child been?

"Was he with his brother and sister? Don't they know anything about it?"

Reduced into some sort of order from its original piteous confusion, this is the story that the doctor gathered.

All three children had been well and happy through the day. They had walked in with the mother, Mrs. Roberts, to Porth on a marketing expedition in the afternoon; they had returned to the cottage, had had their tea, and afterwards played about on the road in front of the house. John Roberts had come home somewhat late from his work, and it was after dusk when the family sat down to supper. Supper over, the three children went out again to play with other children from the cottage next door, Mrs. Roberts telling them that they might have half an hour before going to bed.

The two mothers came to the cottage gates at the same moment and called out to their children to come along and be quick about it. The two small families had been playing on the strip of turf across the road, just by the stile into the fields. The children ran across the road; all of them except Johnnie Roberts. His brother Willie said that just as their mother called them he heard Johnnie cry out:

"Oh, what is that beautiful shiny thing over the stile?"

X. THE CHILD AND THE MOTH

The little Roberts's ran across the road, up the path, and into the lighted room. Then they noticed that Johnnie had not followed them. Mrs. Roberts was doing something in the back kitchen, and Mr Roberts had gone out to the shed to bring in some sticks for the next morning's fire. Mrs. Roberts heard the children run in and went on with her work. The children whispered to one another that Johnnie would "catch it" when their mother came out of the back room and found him missing; but they expected he would run in through the open door any minute. But six or seven, perhaps ten, minutes passed, and there was no Johnnie. Then the father and mother came into the kitchen together, and saw that their little boy was not there.

They thought it was some small piece of mischief—that the two other children had hidden the boy somewhere in the room: in the big cupboard perhaps.

"What have you done with him then?" said Mrs. Roberts. "Come out, you little rascal, directly in a minute."

There was no little rascal to come out, and Margaret Roberts, the girl, said that Johnnie had not come across the road with them: he must be still playing all by himself by the hedge.

"What did you let him stay like that for?" said Mrs. Roberts. "Can't I trust you for two minutes together? Indeed to goodness, you are all of you more trouble than you are worth." She went to the open door:

"Johnnie! Come you in directly, or you will be sorry for it. Johnnie!"

The poor woman called at the door. She went out to the gate and called there:

"Come you, little Johnnie. Come you, bachgen, there's a good boy. I do see you hiding there."

She thought he must be hiding in the shadow of the hedge, and that he would come running and laughing—"he was always such a happy little fellow"—to her across the road. But no little merry figure danced out of the gloom of the still, dark night; it was all silence.

It was then, as the mother's heart began to chill, though she still called cheerfully to the missing child, that the elder boy told how Johnnie had said there was something beautiful by the stile: "and perhaps he did climb over, and he is running now about the meadow, and has lost his way."

The father got his lantern then, and the whole family went crying and calling about the meadow, promising cakes and sweets and a fine toy to poor Johnnie if he would come to them.

They found the little body, under the ashgrove in the middle of the field. He was quite still and dead, so still that a great moth had settled on his forehead, fluttering away when they lifted him up.

Dr. Lewis heard this story. There was nothing to be done; little to be said to these most unhappy people.

"Take care of the two that you have left to you," said the doctor as he went away. "Don't let them out of your sight if you can help it. It is dreadful times that we are living in."

It is curious to record, that all through these dreadful times the simple little 'season' went through its accustomed course at Porth. The war and its consequences had somewhat thinned the numbers of the summer visitors; still a very fair contingent of them occupied the hotels and boarding-houses and lodging-houses and bathed from the old-fashioned machines on one beach, or from the new-fashioned tents on the other, and sauntered in the sun, or lay stretched out in the shade under the trees that grow down almost to the water's edge. Porth never tolerated Ethiopians or shows of any kind on its sands, but 'The Rockets"'did very well during that summer in their garden entertainment, given in the castle grounds, and the fit-up companies that came to the Assembly Rooms are said to have paid their bills to a woman and to a man.

Porth depends very largely on its midland and northern custom, custom of a prosperous, well-established sort. People who think Llandudno overcrowded and Colwyn Bay too raw and red and new, come year after year to the placid old town in the southwest and delight in its peace; and as I say, they enjoyed themselves much as usual there in the summer of 1915. Now and then they became conscious, as Mr Merritt became conscious, that they could not wander about quite in the old way; but they accepted sentries and coast-watchers and people who politely pointed out the advantages of seeing the view from this point rather than from that as very necessary consequences of the dreadful war that was being waged; nay, as a Manchester man said, after having been turned back from his favorite walk to Castell Coch, it was gratifying to think that they were so well looked after.

"So far as I can see," he added, "there's nothing to prevent a submarine from standing out there by Ynys Sant and landing half a dozen men in a collapsible boat in any of these little coves. And pretty fools we should look, shouldn't we, with our throats cut on the sands; or carried back to Germany in the submarine?" He tipped the coast-watcher half-a-crown.

"That's right, lad," he said, "you give us the tip."

Now here was a strange thing. The north-countryman had his thoughts on elusive submarines and German raiders; the watcher had simply received instructions to keep people off the Castell Coch fields, without reason assigned. And there can be no doubt that the authorities themselves, while they marked out the fields as in the 'terror zone,' gave their orders in the dark and were themselves profoundly in the dark as to the manner of the slaughter that had been done there; for if they had understood what had happened, they would have understood also that their restrictions were useless.

The Manchester man was warned off his walk about ten days after Johnnie Roberts's death. The Watcher had been placed at his post because, the night before, a young farmer had been found by his wife lying in the grass close to the Castle, with no scar on him, nor any mark of violence, but stone dead.

The wife of the dead man, Joseph Cradock, finding her husband lying motionless on the dewy turf, went white and stricken up the path to the village and got two men who bore the body to the farm. Lewis was sent for, and knew, at once when he saw the dead man that he had perished in the way that the little Roberts boy had perished—whatever that awful way might be. Cradock had been asphyxiated; and here again there was no mark of a grip on the throat. It might have been a piece of work by Burke and Hare, the doctor reflected; a pitch plaster might have been clapped over the man's mouth and nostrils and held there.

Then a thought struck him; his brother-in-law had talked of a new kind of poison gas that was said to be used against the munition workers in the Midlands: was it possible that the deaths of the man and the boy were due to some such instrument? He applied his tests but could find no trace of any gas having been employed. Carbonic acid gas? A man could not be killed with that in the open air; to be fatal that required a confined space, such a position as the bottom of a huge vat or of a well.

He did not know how Cradock had been killed; he confessed it to himself. He had been suffocated; that was all he could say.

It seemed that the man had gone out at about half-past nine to look after some beasts. The field in which they were was about five minutes' walk from the house. He told his wife he would be back in a quarter of an hour or twenty minutes. He did not return, and when he had been gone for three-quarters of an hour Mrs. Cradock went out to look for him. She went into the field where the beasts were, and everything seemed all right, but there was no trace of Cradock. She called out; there was no answer.

Now the meadow in which the cattle were pastured is high ground; a hedge divides it from the fields which fall gently down to the castle and the sea. Mrs. Cradock hardly seemed able to say why, having failed to find her husband among his beasts, she turned to the path which led to Castell Coch. She said at first that she had thought that one of the oxen might have broken through the hedge and strayed, and that Cradock had perhaps gone after it. And then, correcting herself, she said:

"There was that; and then there was something else that I could not make out at all. It seemed to me that the hedge did look different from usual. To be sure, things do look different at night, and there was a bit of sea mist about, but somehow it did look odd to me, and I said to myself, 'have I lost my way, then?'"

She declared that the shape of the trees in the hedge appeared to have changed, and besides, it had a look "as if it was lighted up, somehow," and so she went on towards the stile to see what all this could be, and when she came near everything was as usual. She looked over the stile and called and hoped to see her husband coming towards her or to hear his voice; but there was no answer, and glancing down the path she saw, or thought she saw, some sort of brightness on the ground, "a dim sort of light like a bunch of glow-worms in a hedge-bank.

"And so I climbed over the stile and went down the path, and the light seemed to melt away; and there was my poor husband lying on his back, saying not a word to me when I spoke to him and touched him."

So for Lewis the terror blackened and became altogether intolerable, and others, he perceived, felt as he did. He did not know, he never asked whether the men at the club had heard of these deaths of the child and the young farmer; but no one spoke of them. Indeed, the change was evident; at the beginning of the terror men spoke of nothing else; now it had become all too awful for ingenious chatter or labored and grotesque theories. And Lewis had received a letter from his brother-in-law at Midlingham; it contained the sentence, "I am afraid Fanny's health has not greatly benefited by her visit to Porth; there are still several symptoms I don't at all like." And this told him, in a phraseology that the doctor and Merritt had agreed upon, that the terror remained heavy in the Midland town.

It was soon after the death of Cradock that people began to tell strange tales of a sound that was to be heard of nights about the hills and valleys to the northward of Porth. A man who had missed the last train from Meiros and had been forced to tramp the ten miles between Meiros and Porth seems to have been the first to hear it. He said he had got to the top of the hill by Tredonoc, somewhere between half-past ten and eleven, when he first noticed an odd noise that he could not make out at all; it was like a shout, a long, drawn-out, dismal wail coming from a great way off, faint with distance. He stopped to listen, thinking at first that it might be owls hooting in the woods; but it was different, he said, from that: it was a long cry, and then there was silence and then it began over again. He could make nothing of it, and feeling frightened, he did not quite know of what, he walked on briskly and was glad to see the lights of Porth station.

He told his wife of this dismal sound that night, and she told the neighbours, and most of them thought that it was "all fancy"—or drink, or the owls after all. But the night after, two or three people, who had been to some small merry-making in a cottage just off the Meiros road, heard the sound as they were going home, soon after ten. They, too, described it as a long, wailing cry, indescribably dismal in the stillness of the autumn night; "like the ghost of a voice," said one; "as if it came up from the bottom of the earth," said another.

XI. AT TREFF LOYNE FARM

Let it be remembered, again and again, that, all the while that the terror lasted, there was no common stock of information as to the dreadful things that were being done. The press had not said one word upon it, there was no criterion by which the mass of the people could separate fact from mere vague rumour, no test by which ordinary misadventure or disaster could be distinguished from the achievements of the secret and awful force that was at work.

And so with every event of the passing day. A harmless commercial traveler might show himself in the course of his business in the tumbledown main street of Meiros and find himself regarded with looks of fear and suspicion as a possible worker of murder, while it is likely enough that the true agents of the terror went quite unnoticed. And since the real nature of all this mystery of death was unknown, it followed easily that the signs and warnings and omens of it were all the more unknown. Here was horror, there was horror; but there was no links to join one horror with another; no common basis of knowledge from which the connection between this horror and that horror might be inferred.

So there was no one who suspected at all that this dismal and hollow sound that was now heard of nights in the region to the north of Porth, had any relation at all to the case of the little girl who went out one afternoon to pick purple flowers and never returned, or to the case of the man whose body was taken out of the peaty slime of the marsh, or to the case of Cradock, dead in his fields, with a strange glimmering of light about his body, as his wife reported. And it is a question as to how far the rumour of this melancholy, nocturnal summons got abroad at all. Lewis heard of it, as a country doctor hears of most things, driving up and down the lanes, but he heard of it without much interest, with no sense that it was in any sort of relation to the terror. Remnant had been given the story of the hollow and echoing voice of the darkness in a coloured and picturesque form; he employed a Tredonoc man to work in his garden once a week. The gardener had not heard the summons himself, but he knew a man who had done so.

"Thomas Jenkins, Pentoppin, he did put his head out late last night to see what the weather was like, as he was cutting a field of corn the next day, and he did tell me that when he was with the Methodists in Cardigan he did never hear no singing eloquence in the chapels that was like to it. He did declare it was like a wailing of Judgment Day."

Remnant considered the matter, and was inclined to think that the sound must be caused by a subterranean inlet of the sea; there might be, he supposed, an imperfect or half-opened or tortuous blow-hole in the Tredonoc woods, and the noise of the tide, surging up below, might very well produce that effect of a hollow wailing, far away. But neither he nor any one else paid much attention to the matter; save the few who heard the call at dead of night, as it echoed awfully over the black hills.

The sound had been heard for three or perhaps four nights, when the people coming out of Tredonoc church after morning service on Sunday noticed that there was a big yellow sheepdog in the churchyard. The dog, it appeared, had been waiting for the congregation; for it at once attached itself to them, at first to the whole body, and then to a group of half a dozen who took the turning to the right. Two of these presently went off over the fields to their respective houses, and four strolled on in the leisurely Sunday-morning manner of the country, and these the dog followed, keeping to heel all the time. The men were talking hay, corn and markets and paid no attention to the animal, and so they strolled along the autumn lane till they came to a gate in the hedge, whence a roughly made farm road went through the fields, and dipped down into the woods and to Treff Loyne farm.

Then the dog became like a possessed creature. He barked furiously. He ran up to one of the men and looked up at him, "as if he were begging for his life," as the man said, and then rushed to the gate and stood by it, wagging his tail and barking at intervals. The men stared and laughed.

"Whose dog will that be?" said one of them.

"It will be Thomas Griffith's, Treff Loyne," said another.

"Well, then, why doesn't he go home? Go home then!" He went through the gesture of picking up a stone from the road and throwing it at the dog. "Go home, then! Over the gate with you."

But the dog never stirred. He barked and whined and ran up to the men and then back to the gate. At last he came to one of them, and crawled and abased himself on the ground and then took hold of the man's coat and tried to pull him in the direction of the gate. The farmer shook the dog off, and the four went on their way; and the dog stood in the road and watched them and then put up its head and uttered a long and dismal howl that was despair.

The four farmers thought nothing of it; sheepdogs in the country are dogs to look after sheep, and their whims and fancies are not studied. But the yellow dog—he was a kind of degenerate collie—haunted the Tredonoc lanes from that day. He came to a cottage door one night and scratched at it, and when it was opened lay down, and then, barking, ran to the garden gate and waited, entreating, as it seemed, the cottager to follow him. They drove him away and again he gave that long howl of anguish. It was almost as bad, they said, as the noise that they had heard a few nights before. And then it occurred to somebody, so far as I can make out with no particular reference to the odd conduct of the Treff Loyne sheepdog, that Thomas Griffith had not been seen for some time past. He had missed market day at Porth, he had not been at Tredonoc church, where he was a pretty regular attendant on Sunday; and then, as heads were put together, it appeared that nobody had seen any of the Griffith family for days and days.

Now in a town, even in a small town, this process of putting heads together is a pretty quick business. In the country, especially in a countryside of wild lands and scattered and lonely farms and cottages, the affair takes time. Harvest was going on, everybody was busy in his own fields, and after the long day's hard work neither the farmer nor his men felt inclined to stroll about in search of news or gossip. A harvester at the day's end is ready for supper and sleep and for nothing else.

And so it was late in that week when it was discovered that Thomas Griffith and all his house had vanished from this world.

I have often been reproached for my curiosity over questions which are apparently of slight importance, or of no importance at all. I love to inquire, for instance, into the question of the visibility of a lighted candle at a distance. Suppose, that is, a candle lighted on a still, dark night in the country; what is the greatest distance at which you can see that there is a light at all? And then as to the human voice; what is its carrying distance, under good conditions, as a mere sound, apart from any matter of making out words that may be uttered?

They are trivial questions, no doubt, but they have always interested me, and the latter point has its application to the strange business of Treff Loyne. That melancholy and hollow sound, that wailing summons that appalled the hearts of those who heard it was, indeed, a human voice, produced in a very exceptional manner; and it seems to have been heard at points varying from a mile and a half to two miles from the farm. I do not know whether this is anything extraordinary; I do not know whether the peculiar method of production was calculated to increase or to diminish the carrying power of the sound.

Again and again I have laid emphasis in this story of the terror on the strange isolation of many of the farms and cottages in Meirion. I have done so in the effort to convince the townsman of something that he has never known. To the Londoner a house a quarter of a mile from the outlying suburban lamp, with no other dwelling within two hundred yards, is a lonely house, a place to fit with ghosts and mysteries and terrors. How can he understand then, the true loneliness of the white farmhouses of Meirion, dotted here and there, for the most part not even on the little lanes and deep winding byways, but set in the very heart of the fields, or alone on huge bastioned headlands facing the sea, and whether on the high verge of the sea or on the hills or in the hollows of the inner country, hidden from the sight of men, far from the sound of any common call. There is Penyrhaul, for example, the farm from which the foolish Merritt thought he saw signals of light being made: from seaward it is of course, widely visible; but from landward, owing partly to the curving and indented configuration of the bay, I doubt whether any other habitation views it from a nearer distance than three miles.

And of all these hidden and remote places, I doubt if any is so deeply buried as Treff Loyne. I have little or no Welsh, I am sorry to say, but I suppose that the name is corrupted from Trellwyn, or Tref-y-llwyn, "the place in the grove," and, indeed, it lies in the very heart of dark, overhanging woods. A deep, narrow valley runs down from the high lands of the Allt, through these woods, through steep hillsides of bracken and gorse, right down to the great marsh, whence Merritt saw the dead man being carried. The valley lies away from any road, even from that by-road, little better than a bridlepath, where the four farmers, returning from church were perplexed by the strange antics of the sheepdog. One cannot say that the valley is overlooked, even from a distance, for so narrow is it that the ashgroves that rim it on either side seem to meet and shut it in. I, at all events, have never found any high place from which Treff Loyne is visible; though, looking down from the Allt, I have seen blue wood-smoke rising from its hidden chimneys.

Such was the place, then, to which one September afternoon a party went up to discover what had happened to Griffith and his family. There were half a dozen farmers, a couple of policemen, and four soldiers, carrying their arms; those last had been lent by the officer commanding at the camp. Lewis, too, was of the party; he had heard by chance that no one knew what had become of Griffith and his family; and he was anxious about a young fellow, a painter, of his acquaintance, who had been lodging at Treff Loyne all the summer.

They all met by the gate of Tredonoc churchyard, and tramped solemnly along the narrow lane; all of them, I think, with some vague discomfort of mind, with a certain shadowy fear, as of men who do not quite know what they may encounter. Lewis heard the corporal and the three soldiers arguing over their orders.

"The Captain says to me," muttered the corporal, "'Don't hesitate to shoot if there's any trouble.' 'Shoot what, sir,' I says. 'The trouble,' says he, and that's all I could get out of him."

The men grumbled in reply; Lewis thought he heard some obscure reference to rat poison, and wondered what they were talking about.

They came to the gate in the hedge, where the farm road led down to Treff Loyne. They followed this track, roughly made, with grass growing up between its loosely laid stones, down by the hedge from field to wood, till at last they came to the sudden walls of the valley, and the sheltering groves of the ash trees.

Here the way curved down the steep hillside, and bent southward, and followed henceforward the hidden hollow of the valley, under the shadow of the trees.

Here was the farm enclosure; the outlying walls of the yard and the barns and sheds and outhouses. One of the farmers threw open the gate and walked into the yard, and forthwith began bellowing at the top of his voice:

"Thomas Griffith! Thomas Griffith! Where be you, Thomas Griffith?"

The rest followed him. The corporal snapped out an order over his shoulder, and there was a rattling metallic noise as the men fixed their bayonets and became in an instant dreadful dealers out of death, in place of harmless fellows with a feeling for beer.

"Thomas Griffith!" again bellowed the farmer.

There was no answer to this summons. But they found poor Griffith lying on his face at the edge of the pond in the middle of the yard. There was a ghastly wound in his side, as if a sharp stake had been driven into his body.

XII. THE LETTER OF WRATH

It was a still September afternoon. No wind stirred in the hanging woods that were dark all about the ancient house of Treff Loyne; the only sound in the dim air was the lowing of the cattle; they had wandered, it seemed, from the fields and had come in by the gate of the farmyard and stood there melancholy, as if they mourned for their dead master. And the horses; four great, heavy, patient-looking beasts they were there too, and in the lower field the sheep were standing, as if they waited to be fed.

"You would think they all knew there was something wrong," one of the soldiers muttered to another. A pale sun showed for a moment and glittered on their bayonets. They were standing about the body of poor, dead Griffith, with a certain grimness growing on their faces and hardening there. Their corporal snapped something at them again; they were quite ready. Lewis knelt down by the dead man and looked closely at the great gaping wound in his side.

"He's been dead a long time," he said. "A week, two weeks, perhaps. He was killed by some sharp pointed weapon. How about the family? How many are there of them? I never attended them."

"There was Griffith, and his wife, and his son Thomas and Mary Griffith, his daughter. And I do think there was a gentleman lodging with them this summer."

That was from one of the farmers. They all looked at one another, this party of rescue, who knew nothing of the danger that had smitten this house of quiet people, nothing of the peril which had brought them to this pass of a farmyard with a dead man in it, and his beasts standing patiently about him, as if they waited for the farmer to rise up and give them their food. Then the party turned to the house. It was an old, sixteenth century building, with the singular round, 'Flemish' chimney that is characteristic of Meirion. The walls were snowy with whitewash, the windows were deeply set and stone mullioned, and a solid, stone-tiled porch sheltered the doorway from any winds that might penetrate to the hollow of that hidden valley. The windows were shut tight. There was no sign of any life or movement about the place. The party of men looked at one another, and the churchwarden amongst the farmers, the sergeant of police, Lewis, and the corporal drew together.

"What is it to goodness, doctor?" said the churchwarden.

"I can tell you nothing at all—except that that poor man there has been pierced to the heart," said Lewis.

"Do you think they are inside and they will shoot us?" said another farmer. He had no notion of what he meant by "they," and no one of them knew better than he. They did not know what the danger was, or where it might strike them, or whether it was from without or from within. They stared at the murdered man, and gazed dismally at one another.

"Come!" said Lewis, "we must do something. We must get into the house and see what is wrong."

"Yes, but suppose they are at us while we are getting in," said the sergeant. "Where shall we be then, Doctor Lewis?"

The corporal put one of his men by the gate at the top of the farmyard, another at the gate by the bottom of the farmyard, and told them to challenge and shoot. The doctor and the rest opened the little gate of the front garden and went up to the porch and stood listening by the door. It was all dead silence. Lewis took an ash stick from one of the farmers and beat heavily three times on the old, black, oaken door studded with antique nails.

He struck three thundering blows, and then they all waited. There was no answer from within. He beat again, and still silence. He shouted to the people within, but there was no answer. They all turned and looked at one another, that party of quest and rescue who knew not what they sought, what enemy they were to encounter. There was an iron ring on the door. Lewis turned it but the door stood fast; it was evidently barred and bolted. The sergeant of police called out to open, but again there was no answer.

They consulted together. There was nothing for it but to blow the door open, and some one of them called in a loud voice to anybody that might be within to stand away from the door, or they would be killed. And at this very moment the yellow sheepdog came bounding up the yard from the woods and licked their hands and fawned on them and barked joyfully.

"Indeed now," said one of the farmers; "he did know that there was something amiss. A pity it was, Thomas Williams, that we did not follow him when he implored us last Sunday."

The corporal motioned the rest of the party back, and they stood looking fearfully about them at the entrance to the porch. The corporal disengaged his bayonet and shot into the keyhole, calling out once more before he fired. He shot and shot again; so heavy and firm was the ancient door, so stout its bolts and fastenings. At last he had to fire at the massive hinges, and then they all pushed together and the door lurched open and fell forward. The corporal raised his left hand and stepped back a few paces. He hailed his two men at the top and bottom of the farmyard. They were all right, they said. And so the party climbed and struggled over the fallen door into the passage, and into the kitchen of the farmhouse.

Young Griffith was lying dead before the hearth, before a dead fire of white wood ashes. They went on towards the 'parlour,' and in the doorway of the room was the body of the artist, Secretan, as if he had fallen in trying to get to the kitchen. Upstairs the two women, Mrs. Griffith and her daughter, a girl of eighteen, were lying together on the bed in the big bedroom, clasped in each others' arms.

They went about the house, searched the pantries, the back kitchen and the cellars; there was no life in it.

"Look!" said Dr. Lewis, when they came back to the big kitchen, "look! It is as if they had been besieged. Do you see that piece of bacon, half gnawed through?"

Then they found these pieces of bacon, cut from the sides on the kitchen wall, here and there about the house. There was no bread in the place, no milk, no water.

"And," said one of the farmers, "they had the best water here in all Meirion. The well is down there in the wood; it is most famous water. The old people did use to call it Ffynnon Teilo; it was Saint Teilo's Well, they did say."

"They must have died of thirst," said Lewis. "They have been dead for days and days."

The group of men stood in the big kitchen and stared at one another, a dreadful perplexity in their eyes. The dead were all about them, within the house and without it; and it was in vain to ask why they had died thus. The old man had been killed with the piercing thrust of some sharp weapon; the rest had perished, it seemed probable, of thirst; but what possible enemy was this that besieged the farm and shut in its inhabitants? There was no answer.

The sergeant of police spoke of getting a cart and taking the bodies into Porth, and Dr. Lewis went into the parlour that Secretan had used as a sitting-room, intending to gather any possessions or effects of the dead artist that he might find there. Half a dozen portfolios were piled up in one corner, there were some books on a side table, a fishing-rod and basket behind the door—that seemed all. No doubt there would be clothes and such matters upstairs, and Lewis was about to rejoin the rest of the party in the kitchen, when he looked down at some scattered papers lying with the books on the side table. On one of the sheets he read to his astonishment the words: 'Dr. James Lewis, Porth.' This was written in a staggering trembling scrawl, and examining the other leaves he saw that they were covered with writing.

The table stood in a dark corner of the room, and Lewis gathered up the sheets of paper and took them to the window-ledge and began to read, amazed at certain phrases that had caught his eye. But the manuscript was in disorder; as if the dead man who had written it had not been equal to the task of gathering the leaves into their proper sequence; it was some time before the doctor had each page in its place. This was the statement that he read, with ever-growing wonder, while a couple of the farmers were harnessing one of the horses in the yard to a cart, and the others were bringing down the dead women.

"I do not think that I can last much longer. We shared out the last drops of water a long time ago. I do not know how many days ago. We fall asleep and dream and walk about the house in our dreams, and I am often not sure whether I am awake or still dreaming, and so the days and nights are confused in my mind. I awoke not long ago, at least I suppose I awoke and found I was lying in the passage. I had a confused feeling that I had had an awful dream which seemed horribly real, and I thought for a moment what a relief it was to know that it wasn't true, whatever it might have been. I made up my mind to have a good long walk to freshen myself up, and then I looked round and found that I had been lying on the stones of the passage; and it all came back to me. There was no walk for me.

"I have not seen Mrs. Griffith or her daughter for a long while. They said they were going upstairs to have a rest. I heard them moving about the room at first, now I can hear nothing. Young Griffith is lying in the kitchen, before the hearth. He was talking to himself about the harvest and the weather when I last went into the kitchen. He didn't seem to know I was there, as he went gabbling on in a low voice very fast, and then he began to call the dog, Tiger.

"There seems no hope for any of us. We are in the dream of death...."

Here the manuscript became unintelligible for half a dozen lines. Secretan had written the words 'dream of death' three or four times over. He had begun a fresh word and had scratched it out and then followed strange, unmeaning characters, the script, as Lewis thought, of a terrible language. And then the writing became clear, clearer than it was at the beginning of the manuscript, and the sentences flowed more easily, as if the cloud on Secretan's mind had lifted for a while. There was a fresh start, as it were, and the writer began again, in ordinary letter-form:

"DEAR LEWIS,

"I hope you will excuse all this confusion and wandering. I intended to begin a proper letter to you, and now I find all that stuff that you have been reading—if this ever gets into your hands. I have not the energy even to tear it up. If you read it you will know to what a sad pass I had come when it was written. It looks like delirium or a bad dream, and even now, though my mind seems to have cleared up a good deal, I have to hold myself in tightly to be sure that the experiences of the last days in this awful place are true, real things, not a long night-mare from which I shall wake up presently and find myself in my rooms at Chelsea.

"I have said of what I am writing, 'if it ever gets into your hands,' and I am not at all sure that it ever will. If what is happening here is happening everywhere else, then I suppose, the world is coming to an end. I cannot understand it, even now I can hardly believe it. I know that I dream such wild dreams and walk in such mad fancies that I have to look out and look about me to make sure that I am not still dreaming.

"Do you remember that talk we had about two months ago when I dined with you? We got on, somehow or other, to space and time, and I think we agreed that as soon as one tried to reason about space and time one was landed in a maze of contradictions. You said something to the effect that it was very curious but this was

just like a dream. 'A man will sometimes wake himself from his crazy dream,' you said, 'by realizing that he is thinking nonsense.' And we both wondered whether these contradictions that one can't avoid if one begins to think of time and space may not really be proofs that the whole of life is a dream, and the moon and the stars bits of nightmare. I have often thought over that lately. I kick at the walls as Dr. Johnson kicked at the stone, to make sure that the things about me are there. And then that other question gets into my mind—is the world really coming to an end, the world as we have always known it; and what on earth will this new world be like? I can't imagine it; it's a story like Noah's Ark and the Flood. People used to talk about the end of the world and fire, but no one ever thought of anything like this.

"And then there's another thing that bothers me. Now and then I wonder whether we are not all mad together in this house. In spite of what I see and know, or, perhaps, I should say, because what I see and know is so impossible, I wonder whether we are not all suffering from a delusion. Perhaps we are our own gaolers, and we are really free to go out and live. Perhaps what we think we see is not there at all. I believe I have heard of whole families going mad together, and I may have come under the influence of the house, having lived in it for the last four months. I know there have been people who have been kept alive by their keepers forcing food down their throats, because they are quite sure that their throats are closed, so that they feel they are unable to swallow a morsel. I wonder now and then whether we are all like this in Treff Loyne; yet in my heart I feel sure that it is not so.

"Still, I do not want to leave a madman's letter behind me, and so I will not tell you the full story of what I have seen, or believe I have seen. If I am a sane man you will be able to fill in the blanks for yourself from your own knowledge. If I am mad, burn the letter and say nothing about it. Or perhaps—and indeed, I am not quite sure—I may wake up and hear Mary Griffith calling to me in her cheerful sing-song that breakfast will be ready 'directly, in a minute,' and I shall enjoy it and walk over to Porth and tell you the queerest, most horrible dream that a man ever had, and ask what I had better take.

"I think that it was on a Tuesday that we first noticed that there was something queer about, only at the time we didn't know that there was anything really queer in what we noticed. I had been out since nine o'clock in the morning trying to paint the marsh, and I found it a very tough job. I came home about five or six o'clock and found the family at Treff Loyne laughing at

old Tiger, the sheepdog. He was making short runs from the farmyard to the door of the house, barking, with quick, short yelps. Mrs. Griffith and Miss Griffith were standing by the porch, and the dog would go to them, look in their faces, and then run up the farmyard to the gate, and then look back with that eager yelping bark, as if he were waiting for the women to follow him. Then, again and again, he ran up to them and tugged at their skirts as if he would pull them by main force away from the house.

"Then the men came home from the fields and he repeated this perfor-mance. The dog was running all up and down the farmyard, in and out of the barn and sheds yelping, barking; and always with that eager run to the person he addressed, and running away directly, and looking back as, if to see whether we were following him. When the house door was shut and they all sat down to supper, he would give them no peace, till at last they turned him out of doors. And then he sat in the porch and scratched at the door with his claws, barking all the while. When the daughter brought in my meal, she said: 'We can't think what is come to old Tiger, and indeed, he has always been a good dog, too.'

"The dog barked and yelped and whined and scratched at the door all through the evening. They let him in once, but he seemed to have become quite frantic. He ran up to one member of the family after another; his eyes were bloodshot and his mouth was foaming, and he tore at their clothes till they drove him out again into the darkness. Then he broke into a long, lamentable howl of anguish, and we heard no more of him."

XIII. THE LAST WORDS OF MR SECRETAN

"I slept ill that night I awoke again and again from uneasy M dreams, and I seemed in my sleep to hear strange calls and noises and a sound of murmurs and beatings on the door. There were deep, hollow voices, too, that echoed in my sleep, and when I woke I could hear the autumn wind, mournful, on the hills above us. I started up once with a dreadful scream in my ears; but then the house was all still, and I fell again into uneasy sleep.

"It was soon after dawn when I finally roused myself. The people in the house were talking to each other in high voices, arguing about something that I did not understand.

"'It is those damned gipsies, I tell you,' said old Griffith.

"'What would they do a thing like that for?' asked Mrs. Griffith. 'If it was stealing now—'"

"'It is more likely that John Jenkins has done it out of spite,' said the son. He said that he would remember you when we did catch him poaching.'

"They seemed puzzled and angry, so far as I could make out, but not at all frightened. I got up and began to dress. I don't think I looked out of the window. The glass on my dressing-table is high and broad, and the window is small; one would have to poke one's head round the glass to see anything.

"The voices were still arguing downstairs. I heard the old man say, 'Well, here's for a beginning anyhow,' and then the door slammed.

"A minute later the old man shouted, I think, to his son. Then there was a great noise which I will not describe more particularly, and a dreadful screaming and crying inside the house and a sound of rushing feet. They all cried out at once to each other. I heard the daughter crying, 'it is no good, mother, he is dead, indeed they have killed him,' and Mrs. Griffith screaming to the girl to let her go. And then one of them rushed out of the kitchen and shot the great bolts of oak across the door, just as something beat against it with a thundering crash.

"I ran downstairs. I found them all in wild confusion, in an agony of grief and horror and amazement. They were like people who had seen something so awful that they had gone mad.

"I went to the window looking out on the farmyard. I won't tell you all that I saw. But I saw poor old Griffith lying by the pond, with the blood pouring out of his side.

"I wanted to go out to him and bring him in. But they told me that he must be stone dead, and such things also that it was quite plain that any one who went out of the house would not live more than a moment. We could not believe it, even as we gazed at the body of the dead man; but it was there. I used to wonder sometimes what one would feel like if one saw an apple drop from the tree and shoot up into the air and disappear. I think I know now how one would feel.

"Even then we couldn't believe that it would last. We were not seriously afraid for ourselves. We spoke of getting out in an hour or two, before dinner anyhow. It couldn't last, because it was impossible. Indeed, at twelve o'clock young Griffith said he would go down to the well by the back way and draw another pail of water. I went to the door and stood by it. He had not gone a dozen yards before they were on him. He ran for his life, and we had all we could do to bar the door in time. And then I began to get frightened.

"Still we could not believe in it. Somebody would come along shouting in an hour or two and it would all melt away and vanish. There could not be any real danger. There was plenty of bacon in the house, and half the weekly baking of loaves and some beer in the cellar and a pound or so of tea, and a whole pitcher of water that had been drawn from the well the night before. We could do all right for the day and in the morning it would have all gone away.

"But day followed day and it was still there. I knew Treff Loyne was a lonely place—that was why I had gone there, to have a long rest from all the jangle and rattle and turmoil of London, that makes a man alive and kills him too. I went to Treff Loyne because it was buried in the narrow valley under the ash trees, far away from any track. There was not so much as a footpath that was near it; no one ever came that way. Young Griffith had told me that it was a mile and a half to the nearest house, and the thought of the silent peace and retirement of the farm used to be a delight to me.

"And now this thought came back without delight, with terror. Griffith thought that a shout might be heard on a still night up away on the Allt, 'if a man was listening for it,' he added, doubtfully. My voice was clearer and stronger than his, and on the second night I said I would go up to my bedroom and call for help through the open window. I waited till it was all dark and still, and looked out through the window before opening it. And then I saw over the ridge of the long barn across the yard what looked like a tree, though I knew there was no tree there. It was a dark mass against the sky, with wide-spread boughs, a tree of thick, dense growth. I wondered what this could be, and I threw open the window, not only because I was going to call for help, but because I wanted to see more clearly what the dark growth over the barn really was.

"I saw in the depth of the dark of it points of fire, and colours in light, all glowing and moving, and the air trembled. I stared out into the night, and the dark tree lifted over the roof of the barn and rose up in the air and floated towards me. I did not move till at the last moment when it was close to the house; and then I saw what it was and banged the window down only just in time. I had to fight, and I saw the tree that was like a burning cloud rise up in the night and sink again and settle over the barn.

"I told them downstairs of this. They sat with white faces, and Mrs. Griffith said that ancient devils were let loose and had come out of the trees and out of the old hills because of the wickedness that was on the earth. She began to, murmur something to herself, something that sounded to me like broken-down Latin.

"I went up to my room again an hour later, but the dark tree swelled over the barn. Another day went by, and at dusk I looked out, but the eyes of fire were watching me. I dared not open the window.

"And then I thought of another plan. There was the great old fireplace, with the round Flemish chimney going high above the house. If I stood beneath it and shouted I thought perhaps the sound might be carried better than if I called out of the window; for all I knew the round chimney might act as a sort of megaphone. Night after night, then, I stood in the hearth and called for help from nine o'clock to eleven. I thought of the lonely place, deep in the valley of the ashtrees, of the lonely hills and lands about it. I thought of the little cottages far away and hoped that my voice might reach to those within them. I thought of the winding lane high on the Allt, and of the few men that came there of nights; but I hoped that my cry might come to one of them.

"But we had drunk up the beer, and we would only let ourselves have water by little drops, and on the fourth night my throat was dry, and I began to feel strange and weak; I knew that all the voice I had in my lungs would hardly reach the length of the field by the farm.

"It was then we began to dream of wells and fountains, and water coming very cold, in little drops, out of rocky places in the middle of a cool wood. We had given up all meals; now and then one would cut a lump from the sides of bacon on the kitchen wall and chew a bit of it, but the saltness was like fire.

"There was a great shower of rain one night. The girl said we might open a window and hold out bowls and basins and catch the rain. I spoke of the cloud with burning eyes. She said 'we will go to the window in the dairy at the back, and one of us can get some water at all events,' She stood up with her basin on the stone slab in the dairy and looked out and heard the plashing of the rain, falling very fast. And she unfastened the catch of the window and had just opened it gently with one hand, for about an inch, and had her basin in the other hand. 'And then,' said she, 'there was something that began to tremble and shudder and shake as it did when we went to the Choral Festival at St. Teilo's, and the organ played, and there was the cloud and the burning close before me.'

"And then we began to dream, as I say. I woke up in my sitting-room one hot afternoon when the sun was shining, and I had been looking and searching in my dream all through the house, and I had gone down to the old cellar that wasn't used, the cellar with the pillars and the vaulted room, with an iron pike in my hand. Something said to me that there was water there, and in my dream I went to a heavy stone by the middle pillar and raised it up, and there beneath was a bubbling well of cold, clear water, and I had just hollowed my hand to drink it when I woke. I went into the kitchen and told young Griffith. I said I was sure there was water there. He shook his head, but he took up the great kitchen poker and we went down to the old cellar. I showed him the stone by the pillar, and he raised it up. But there was no well.

"Do you know, I reminded myself of many people whom I have met in life? I would not be convinced. I was sure that, after all, there was a well there. They had a butcher's cleaver in the kitchen and I took it down to the old cellar and hacked at the ground with it. The others didn't interfere with me. We were getting past that. We hardly ever spoke to one another. Each one would be wandering about the house, upstairs and downstairs, each one of us, I suppose, bent on his own foolish plan and mad design, but we hardly ever spoke. Years ago, I was an actor for a bit, and I remember how it was on first nights; the actors treading softly up and down the wings, by their entrance, their lips moving and muttering over the words of their parts, but without a word for one another. So it was with us. I came upon young Griffith one evening evidently trying to make a subterranean passage under one of the walls of the house. I knew he was mad, as he knew I was mad when he saw me digging for a well in the cellar; but neither said anything to the other.

"Now we are past all this. We are too weak. We dream when we are awake and when we dream we think we wake. Night and day come and go and we mistake one for another; I hear Griffith murmuring to himself about the stars when the sun is high at noonday, and at midnight I have found myself thinking that I walked in bright sunlit meadows beside cold, rushing streams that flowed from high rocks.

"Then at the dawn figures in black robes, carrying lighted tapers in their hands pass slowly about and about; and I hear great rolling organ music that sounds as if some tremendous rite were to begin, and voices crying in an ancient song shrill from the depths of the earth.

"Only a little while ago I heard a voice which sounded as if it were at my very ears, but rang and echoed and resounded as if it were rolling and reverberated from the vault of some cathedral, chanting in terrible modulations. I heard the words quite clearly.

"*Incipit liber irae Domini Dei nostri. (Here beginneth The Book of the Wrath of the Lord our God.)*

"*And then the voice sang the word Aleph, prolonging it, it seemed through ages, and a light was extinguished as it began the chapter:*

"*In that day, saith the Lord, there shall be a cloud over the land, and in the cloud a burning and a shape of fire, and out of the cloud shall issue forth my messengers; they shall run all together, they shall not turn aside; this shall be a day of exceeding bitterness, without salvation. And on every high hill, saith the Lord of Hosts, I will set my sentinels, and my armies shall encamp in the place of every valley; in the house that is amongst rushes I will execute judgment, and in vain shall they fly for refuge to the munitions of the rocks. In the groves of the woods, in the places where the leaves are as a tent above them, they shall find the sword of the slayer; and they that put their trust in walled cities shall be confounded. Woe unto the armed man, woe unto him that taketh pleasure in the strength of his artillery, for a little thing shall smite him, and by one that hath no might shall he be brought down into the dust. That which is low shall be set on high; I will make the lamb and the young sheep to be as the lion from the swellings of Jordan; they shall not spare, saith the Lord, and the doves shall be as eagles on the hill Engedi; none shall be found that may abide the onset of their battle.*

"Even now I can hear the voice rolling far away, as if it came from the altar of a great church and I stood at the door. There are lights very far away in the hollow of a vast darkness, and one by one they are put out. I hear a voice chanting again with that endless modulation that climbs and aspires to the stars, and shines there, and rushes down to the dark depths of the earth, again to ascend; the word is *Zain.*"

Here the manuscript lapsed again, and finally into utter, lamentable confusion. There were scrawled lines wavering across the page on which Secretan seemed to have been trying to note the unearthly music that swelled in his dying ears. As the scrapes and scratches of ink showed, he had tried hard to begin a new sentence. The pen had dropped at last out of his hand upon the paper, leaving a blot and a smear upon it.

Lewis heard the tramp of feet along the passage; they were carrying out the dead to the cart.

XIV. THE END OF THE TERROR

Dr. Lewis maintained that we should never begin to understand the real significance of life until we began to study just those aspects of it which we now dismiss and overlook as utterly inexplicable, and therefore, unimportant.

We were discussing a few months ago the awful shadow of the terror which at length had passed away from the land. I had formed my opinion, partly from observation, partly from certain facts which had been communicated to me, and the pass-words having been exchanged, I found that Lewis had come by very different ways to the same end.

"And yet," he said, "it is not a true end, or rather, it is like all the ends of human inquiry, it leads one to a great mystery. We must confess that what has happened might have happened at any time in the history of the world. It did not happen till a year ago as a matter of fact, and therefore we made up our minds that it never could happen; or, one would better say, it was outside the range even of imagination. But this is our way. Most people are quite sure that the Black Death—otherwise the Plague—will never invade Europe again. They have made up their complacent minds that it was due to dirt and bad drainage. As a matter of fact the Plague had nothing to do with dirt or with drains; and there is nothing to prevent its ravaging England tomorrow. But if you tell people so, they won't believe you. They won't believe in anything that isn't there at the particular moment when you are talking to them. As with the Plague, so with the Terror. We could not believe that such a thing could ever happen. Remnant said, truly enough, that whatever it was, it was outside theory, outside our theory. Flatland cannot believe in the cube or the sphere."

I agreed with all this. I added that sometimes the world was incapable of seeing, much less believing, that which was before its own eyes.

"Look," I said, "at any eighteenth century print of a Gothic cathedral. You will find that the trained artistic eye even could not behold in any true sense the building that was before it. I have seen an old print of Peterborough Cathedral that looks as if the artist had drawn it from a clumsy model, constructed of bent wire and children's bricks.

"Exactly; because Gothic was outside the aesthetic theory (and therefore vision) of the time. You can't believe what you don't see: rather, you can't see what you don't believe. It was so during the time of the Terror. All this bears out what Coleridge said as to the necessity of having the idea before the facts could be of any service to one. Of course, he was right; mere facts, without the correlating idea, are nothing and lead to no conclusion. We had plenty of facts, but we could make nothing of them. I went home at the tail of that dreadful procession from Treff Loyne in a state of mind very near to madness. I heard one of the soldiers saying to the other: "There's no rat that'll spike a man to the heart, Bill." I don't know why, but I felt that if I heard any more of such talk as that I should go crazy; it seemed to me that the anchors of reason were parting. I left the party and took the short cut across the fields into Porth. I looked up Davies in the High Street and arranged with him that he should take on any cases I might have that evening, and then I went home and gave my man his instructions to send people on. And then I shut myself up to think it all out—if I could.

"You must not suppose that my experiences of that afternoon had afforded me the slightest illumination. Indeed, if it had not been that I had seen poor old Griffith's body lying pierced in his own farmyard, I think I should have been inclined to accept one of Secretan's hints, and to believe that the whole family had fallen a victim to a collective delusion or hallucination, and had shut themselves up and died of thirst through sheer madness. I think there have been such cases. It's the insanity of inhibition, the belief that you can't do something which you are really perfectly capable of doing. But; I had seen the body of the murdered man and the wound that had killed him.

"Did the manuscript left by Secretan give me no hint? Well, it seemed to me to make confusion worse confounded. You have seen it; you know that in certain places it is evidently mere delirium, the wanderings of a dying mind. How was I to separate the facts from the phantasms—lacking the key to the whole enigma. Delirium is often a sort of cloud-castle, a sort of magnified and distorted shadow of actualities, but it is a very difficult thing, almost an impossible thing, to reconstruct the real house from the distortion of it, thrown on the clouds of the patient's brain. You see, Secretan in writing that extraordinary document almost insisted on the fact that he was not in his proper sense; that for days he had been part asleep, part awake, part delirious. How was one to judge his statement, to separate delirium from fact? In one thing he stood confirmed; you remember he speaks of calling for help up the old chimney of Treff Loyne; that did seem to fit in with the tales of a hollow, moaning cry that had been heard upon the Allt: so far one could take him as a recorder of actual experiences. And I looked in the old cellars of the farm and found a frantic sort of rabbit-hole dug by one of the pillars; again he was confirmed. But what was one to make of that story of the chanting voice, and the letters of the Hebrew alphabet, and the chapter out of some unknown Minor Prophet? When one has the key it is easy enough to sort out the facts, or the hints of facts from the delusions; but I hadn't the key on that September evening. I was forgetting the 'tree' with lights and fires in it; that, I think, impressed me more than anything with the feeling that Secretan's story was, in the main, a true story. I had seen a like appearance down there in my own garden; but what was it?

"Now, I was saying that, paradoxically, it is only by the inexplicable things that life can be explained. We are apt to say, you know, 'a very odd coincidence' and pass the matter by, as if there were no more to be said, or as if that were the end of it. Well, I believe that the only real path lies through the blind alleys."

"How do you mean?"

"Well, this is an instance of what I mean. I told you about Merritt, my brother-in-law, and the capsizing of that boat, the *Mary Ann*. He had seen, he said, signal lights flashing from one of the farms on the coast, and he was quite certain that the two things were intimately connected as cause and effect. I thought it all nonsense, and I was wondering how I was going to shut him up when a big moth flew into the room through that window, fluttered about, and succeeded in burning itself alive in the lamp. That gave me my cue; I asked Merritt if he knew why moths made for lamps or something of the kind; I thought it would be a hint to him that I was sick of his flashlights and his half-baked theories. So it was—he looked sulky and held his tongue.

"But a few minutes later I was called out by a man who had found his little boy dead in a field near his cottage about an hour before. The child was so still, they said, that a great moth had settled on his forehead and only fluttered away when they lifted up the body. It was absolutely illogical; but it was this odd 'coincidence' of the moth in my lamp and the moth on the dead boy's forehead that first set me on the track. I can't say that it guided me in any real sense; it was more like a great flare of red paint on a wall; it rang up my attention, if I may say so; it was a sort of shock like a bang on the big drum. No doubt Merritt was talking great nonsense that evening so far as his particular instance went; the flashes of light from the farm had nothing to do with the wreck of the boat. But his general principle was sound; when you hear a gun go off and see a man fall it is idle to talk of 'a mere coincidence.' I think a very interesting book might be written on this question: I would call it 'A Grammar of Coincidence.'

"But as you will remember, from having read my notes on the matter, I was called in about ten days later to see a man named Cradock, who had been found in a field near his farm quite dead. This also was at night. His wife found him, and there were some very queer things in her story. She said that the hedge of the field looked as if it were changed; she began to be afraid that she had lost her way and got into the wrong field. Then she said the hedge was lighted up as if there were a lot of glow-worms in it, and when she peered over the stile there seemed to be some kind of glimmering upon the ground, and then the glimmering melted away, and she found her husband's body near where this light had been. Now this man Cradock had been suffocated just as the little boy Roberts had been suffocated, and as that man in the Midlands who took a short cut one night had been suffocated. Then I remembered that poor Johnnie Roberts had called out about 'something shiny' over the stile just before he played truant. Then, on my part, I had to contribute the very remarkable sight I witnessed here, as I looked down over the garden; the appearance as of a spreading tree where I knew there was no such tree, and then the shining and burning of lights and moving colours. Like the poor child and Mrs. Cradock, I had seen something shiny, just as some man in Stratfordshire had seen a dark cloud with points of fire in it floating over the trees. And Mrs. Cradock thought that the shape of the trees in the hedge had changed.

"My mind almost uttered the word that was wanted; but you see the difficulties. This set of circumstances could not, so far as I could see, have any relation with the other circumstances of the Terror. How could I connect all this with the bombs and machine-guns of the Midlands, with the armed men who kept watch about the munition shops by day and night. Then there was the long list of people here who had fallen over the cliffs or into the quarry; there were the cases of the men stifled in the slime of the marshes; there was the affair of the family murdered in front of their cottage on the Highway; there was the capsized

Mary Ann. I could not see any thread that could bring all these incidents together; they seemed to me to be hopelessly disconnected. I could not make out any relation between the agency that beat out the brains of the Williams's and the agency, that overturned the boat. I don't know, but I think it's very likely if nothing more had happened that I should have put the whole thing down as an unaccountable series of crimes and accidents which chanced to occur in Meirion in the summer of 1915. Well, of course, that would have been an impossible standpoint in view of certain incidents in Merritt's story. Still, if one is confronted by the insoluble, one lets it go at last. If the mystery is inexplicable, one pretends that there isn't any mystery. That is the justification for what is called free thinking.

"Then came that extraordinary business of Treff Loyne. I couldn't put that on one side. I couldn't pretend that nothing strange or out of the way had happened. There was no getting over it or getting round it. I had seen with my eyes that there was a mystery, and a most horrible mystery. I have forgotten my logic, but one might say that Treff Loyne demonstrated the existence of a mystery in the figure of Death.

"I took it all home, as I have told you, and sat down for the evening before it. It appalled me, not only by its horror, but here again by the discrepancy between its terms. Old Griffith, so far as I could judge, had been killed by the thrust of a pike or perhaps of a sharpened stake: how could one relate this to the burning tree that had floated over the ridge of the barn. It was as if I said to you: 'here is a man drowned, and here is a man burned alive: show that each death was caused by the same agency!' And the moment that I left this particular case of Treff Loyne, and tried to get some light on it from other instances of the Terror, I would think of the man in the midlands who heard the feet of a thousand men rustling in the wood, and their voices as if dead men sat up in their bones and talked. And then I would say to myself, 'and how about that boat overturned in a calm sea?' There seemed no end to it, no hope of any solution.

"It was, I believe, a sudden leap of the mind that liberated me from the tangle. It was quite beyond logic. I went back to that evening when Merritt was boring me with his flashlights, to the moth in the candle, and to the moth on the forehead of poor Johnnie Roberts. There was no sense in it; but I suddenly determined that the child and Joseph Cradock the farmer, and that unnamed Stratfordshire man, all found at night, all asphyxiated, had been choked by vast swarms of moths. I don't pretend even now that this is demonstrated, but I'm sure it's true.

"Now suppose you encounter a swarm of these creatures in the dark. Suppose the smaller ones fly up your nostrils. You will gasp for breath and open your mouth. Then, suppose some hundreds of them fly into your mouth, into your gullet, into your windpipe, what will happen to you? You will be dead in a very short time, choked, asphyxiated."

"But the moths would be dead too. They would be found in the bodies."

"The moths? Do you know that it is extremely difficult to kill a moth with cyanide of potassium? Take a frog, kill it, open its stomach. There you will find its dinner of moths and small beetles, and the 'dinner' will shake itself and walk off cheerily, to resume an entirely active existence. No; that is no difficulty.

"Well, now I came to this. I was shutting out all the other cases. I was confining myself to those that came under the one formula. I got to the assumption or conclusion, whichever you like, that certain people had been asphyxiated by the action of moths. I had accounted for that extraordinary appearance of burning or coloured lights that I had witnessed myself, when I saw the growth of that strange tree in my garden. That was clearly the cloud with points of fire in it that the Stratfordshire man took for a new and terrible kind of poison gas, that was the shiny something that poor little Johnnie Roberts had seen over the stile, that was the glimmering light that had led Mrs. Cradock to her husband's dead body, that was the assemblage of terrible eyes that had watched over Treff Loyne by night. Once on the right track I understood all this, for coming into this room in the dark, I have been amazed by the wonderful burning and the strange fiery colours of the eyes of a single moth, as it crept up the pane of glass, outside. Imagine the effect of myriads of such eyes, of the movement of these lights and fires in a vast swarm of moths, each insect being in constant motion while it kept its place in the mass: I felt that all this was clear and certain.

"Then the next step. Of course, we know nothing really about moths; rather, we know nothing of moth reality. For all I know there may be hundreds of books which treat of moth and nothing but moth. But these are scientific books, and science only deals with surfaces; it has nothing to do with realities—it is impertinent if it attempts to do with realities. To take a very minor matter; we don't even know why the moth desires the flame. But we do know what the moth does not do; it does not gather itself into swarms with the object of destroying human life. But here, by the hypothesis, were cases in which the moth had done this very thing; the moth race had entered, it seemed, into a malignant conspiracy against the human race. It was quite impossible, no doubt—that is to say, it had never happened before—but I could see no escape from this conclusion.

"These insects, then, were definitely hostile to man; and then I stopped, for I could not see the next step, obvious though it seems to me now. I believe that the soldiers' scraps of talk on the way to Treff Loyne and back flung the next plank over the gulf. They had spoken of 'rat poison,' of no rat being able to spike a man through the heart; and then, suddenly, I saw my way clear. If the moths were infected with hatred of men, and possessed the design and the power of combining against him; why not suppose this hatred, this design, this power shared by other non-human creatures.

"The secret of the Terror might be condensed into a sentence: the animals had revolted against men.

"Now, the puzzle became easy enough; one had only to classify. Take the cases of the people who met their deaths by falling over cliffs or over the edge of quarries. We think of sheep as timid creatures, who always ran away. But suppose sheep that don't run away; and, after all, in reason why should they run away? Quarry or no quarry, cliff or no cliff; what would happen to you if a hundred sheep ran after you instead of running from you? There would be no help for it; they would have you down and beat you to death or stifle you. Then suppose man, woman, or child near a cliff's edge or a quarry-side, and a sudden rush of sheep. Clearly there is no help; there is nothing for it but to go over. There can be no doubt that that, is what happened in all these cases.

"And again; you know the country and you know how a herd of cattle will sometimes pursue people through the fields in a solemn, stolid sort of way. They behave as if they wanted to close in on you. Townspeople sometimes get frightened and scream and run; you or I would take no notice, or at the utmost, wave our sticks at the herd, which will stop dead or lumber off. But suppose they don't lumber off. The mildest old cow, remember, is stronger than any man. What can one man or half a dozen men do against half a hundred of these beasts no longer restrained by that mysterious inhibition, which has made for ages the strong the humble slaves of the weak? But if you are botanizing in the marsh, like that poor fellow who was staying at Porth, and forty or fifty young cattle gradually close round you, and refuse to move when you shout and wave your stick, but get closer and closer instead, and get you into the slime. Again, where is your help? If you haven't got an automatic pistol, you must go down and stay down, while the beasts lie quietly on you for five minutes. It was a quicker death for poor Griffith of Treff Loyne—one of his own beasts gored him to death with one sharp thrust of its horn into his heart. And from that morning those within the house were closely besieged by their own cattle and horses and sheep; and when those unhappy people within opened a window to call for help or to catch a few drops of rain water to relieve their burning thirst, the cloud waited for them with its myriad eyes of fire. Can you wonder that Secretan's statement reads in places like mania? You perceive the horrible position of those people in Treff Loyne; not only did they see death advancing on them, but advancing with incredible steps, as if one were to die not only in nightmare but by nightmare. But no one in his wildest, most fiery dreams had ever imagined such a fate. I am not astonished that Secretan at one moment suspected the evidence of his own senses, at another surmised that the world's end had come."

"And how about the Williams's who were murdered on the Highway near here?"

"The horses were the murderers; the horses that afterwards stampeded the camp below. By some means which is still obscure to me they lured that family into the road and beat their brains out; their shod hoofs were the instruments of execution. And, as for the *Mary Ann*, the boat that was capsized, I have no doubt that it was overturned by a sudden rush of the porpoises that were gamboling about in the water of Larnac Bay. A porpoise is a heavy beast—half a dozen of them could easily upset a light rowing-boat. The munition works? Their enemy was rats. I believe that it has been calculated that in 'greater London' the number of rats is about equal to the number of human beings, that is, there are about seven millions of them. The proportion would be about the same in all the great centers of population; and the rat, moreover, is, on occasion, migratory in its habits. You can understand now that story of the *Semiramis*, beating about the mouth of the Thames, and at last cast away by Arcachon, her only crew dry heaps of bones. The rat is an expert boarder of ships. And so one can understand the tale told by the frightened man who took the path by the wood that led up from the new munition works. He thought he heard a thousand men treading softly through the wood and chattering to one another in some horrible tongue; what he did hear was the marshaling of an army of rats—their array before the battle.

"And conceive the terror of such an attack. Even one rat in a fury is said to be an ugly customer to meet; conceive then, the irruption of these terrible, swarming myriads, rushing upon the helpless, unprepared, astonished workers in the munition shops."

There can be no doubt, I think, that Dr. Lewis was entirely justified in these extraordinary conclusions. As I say, I had arrived at pretty much the same end, by different ways; but this rather as to the general situation, while Lewis had made his own particular study of those circumstances of the Terror that were within his immediate purview, as a physician in large practice in the southern part of Meirion. Of some of the cases which he reviewed he had, no doubt, no immediate or first-hand knowledge; but he judged these instances by their similarity to the facts which had come under his personal notice. He spoke of the affairs of the quarry at Llanfihangel on the analogy of the people who were found dead at the bottom of the cliffs near Porth, and he was no doubt justified in doing so. He told me that, thinking the whole matter over, he was hardly more astonished by the Terror in itself than by the strange way in which he had arrived at his conclusions.

"You know," he said, "those certain evidences of animal malevolence which we knew of, the bees that stung the child to death, the trusted sheepdog's turning savage, and so forth. Well, I got no light whatever from all this; it suggested nothing to me—simply because I had not got that 'idea' which Coleridge rightly holds necessary in all inquiry; facts *qua* facts, as we said, mean nothing and, come to nothing. You do not believe, therefore you cannot see.

"And then, when the truth at last appeared it was through the whimsical 'coincidence' as we call such signs, of the moth in my lamp and the moth on the dead child's forehead. This, I think, is very extraordinary."

"And there seems to have been one beast that remained faithful; the dog at Treff Loyne. That is strange."

"That remains a mystery."

It would not be wise, even now, to describe too closely the terrible scenes that were to be seen in the munition areas of the north and the midlands during the black months of the Terror. Out of the factories issued at black midnight the shrouded dead in their coffins, and their very kinsfolk did not know how they had come by their deaths. All the towns were full of houses of mourning, were full of dark and terrible rumors; incredible, as the incredible reality. There were things done and suffered that perhaps never will be brought to light, memories and secret traditions of these things will be whispered in families, delivered from father to son, growing wilder with the passage of the years, but never growing wilder than the truth.

It is enough to say that the cause of the Allies was for awhile in deadly peril.

The men at the front called in their extremity for guns and shells. No one told them what was happening in the places where these munitions were made.

At first the position was nothing less than desperate; men in high places were almost ready to cry "mercy" to the enemy. But, after the first panic, measures were taken such as those described by Merritt in his account of the matter. The workers were armed with special weapons, guards were mounted, machine-guns were placed in position, bombs and liquid flame were ready against the obscene hordes of the enemy, and the "burning clouds" found a fire fiercer than their own. Many deaths occurred amongst the airmen; but they, too, were given special guns, arms that scattered shot broadcast, and so drove away the dark flights that threatened the airplanes.

And, then, in the winter of 1915-16, the Terror ended suddenly as it had begun. Once more a sheep was a frightened beast that ran instinctively from a little child; the cattle were again solemn, stupid creatures, void of harm; the spirit and the convention of malignant design passed out of the hearts of all the animals. The chains that they had cast off for awhile were thrown again about them.

And, finally, there comes the inevitable "why?" Why did the beasts who had been humbly and patiently subject to man, or affrighted by his presence, suddenly know their strength and learn how to league together, and declare bitter war against their ancient master?

It is a most difficult and obscure question. I give what explanation I have to give with very great diffidence, and an eminent disposition to be corrected, if a clearer light can be found.

Some friends of mine, for whose judgment I have very great respect, are inclined to think that there was a certain contagion of hate. They hold that the fury of the whole world at war, the great passion of death that seems driving all humanity to destruction, infected at last these lower creatures, and in place of their native instinct of submission, gave them rage and wrath and ravening.

This may be the explanation. I cannot say that it is not so, because I do not profess to understand the working of the universe. But I confess that the theory strikes me as fanciful. There may be a contagion of hate as there is a contagion of smallpox; I do not know, but I hardly believe it.

In my opinion, and it is only an opinion, the source of the great revolt of the beasts is to be sought in a much subtler region of inquiry. I believe that the subjects revolted because the king abdicated. Man has dominated the beasts throughout the ages, the spiritual has reigned over the rational through the peculiar quality and grace of spirituality that men possess, that makes a man to be that which he is. And when he maintained this power and grace, I think it is pretty clear that between him and the animals there was a certain treaty and alliance. There was supremacy on the one hand, and submission on the other; but at the same time there was between the two that cordiality which exists between lords and subjects in a well-organized state. I know a socialist who maintains that Chaucer's *Canterbury Tales* give a picture of true democracy. I do not know about that, but I see that knight and miller were able to get on quite pleasantly together, just because the knight knew that he was a knight and the miller knew that he was a miller. If the knight had had conscientious objections to his knightly grade, while the miller saw no reason why he should not be a knight, I am sure that their intercourse would have been difficult, unpleasant, and perhaps murderous.

So with man. I believe in the strength and truth of tradition. A learned man said to me a few weeks ago: "When I have to choose between the evidence of tradition and the evidence of a document, I always believe the evidence of tradition. Documents may be falsified, and often are falsified; tradition is never falsified." This is true; and, therefore, I think, one may put trust in the vast body of folklore which asserts that there was once a worthy and friendly alliance between man and the beasts. Our popular tale of Dick Whittington and his Cat no doubt represents the adaptation of a very ancient legend to a comparatively modern personage, but we may go back into the ages and find the popular tradition asserting that not only are the animals the subjects, but also the friends of man.

All that was in virtue of that singular spiritual element in man which the rational animals do not possess. Spiritual does not mean respectable, it does not even mean moral, it does not mean "good" in the ordinary acceptation of the word. It signifies the royal prerogative of man, differentiating him from the beasts.

For long ages he has been putting off this royal robe, he has been wiping the balm of consecration from his own breast. He has declared, again and again, that he is not spiritual, but rational, that is, the equal of the beasts over whom he was once sovereign. He has vowed that he is not Orpheus but Caliban.

But the beasts also have within them something which corresponds to the spiritual quality in men—we are content to call it instinct. They perceived that the throne was vacant—not even friendship was possible between them and the self-deposed monarch. If he were not king he was a sham, an imposter, a thing to be destroyed.

Hence, I think, the Terror. They have risen once—they may rise again.

Dracula's Guest

by Bram Stoker

When we started for our drive the sun was shining brightly on Munich, and the air was full of the joyousness of early summer. Just as we were about to depart, Herr Delbrück (the maître d'hôtel of the Quatre Saisons, where I was staying) came down, bareheaded, to the carriage and, after wishing me a pleasant drive, said to the coachman, still holding his hand on the handle of the carriage door:

"Remember you are back by nightfall. The sky looks bright but there is a shiver in the north wind that says there may be a sudden storm. But I am sure you will not be late." Here he smiled, and added, "for you know what night it is."

Johann answered with an emphatic, "Ja, mein Herr," and, touching his hat, drove off quickly. When we had cleared the town, I said, after signalling to him to stop:

"Tell me, Johann, what is tonight?"

He crossed himself, as he answered laconically: "Walpurgis nacht." Then he took out his watch, a great, old-fashioned German silver thing as big as a turnip, and looked at it, with his eyebrows gathered together and a little impatient shrug of his shoulders. I realised that this was his way of respectfully protesting against the unnecessary delay, and sank back in the carriage, merely motioning him to proceed. He started off rapidly, as if to make up for lost time. Every now and then the horses seemed to throw up their heads and sniffed the air suspiciously. On such occasions I often looked round in alarm. The road was pretty bleak, for we were traversing a sort of high, wind-swept plateau. As we drove, I saw a road that looked but little used, and which seemed to dip through a little, winding valley. It looked so inviting that, even at the risk of offending him, I called Johann to stop—and when he had pulled up, I told him I would like to drive down that road. He made all sorts of excuses, and frequently crossed himself as he spoke. This somewhat piqued my curiosity, so I asked him various questions. He answered fencingly, and repeatedly looked at his watch in protest. Finally I said:

"Well, Johann, I want to go down this road. I shall not ask you to come unless you like; but tell me why you do not like to go, that is all I ask." For answer he seemed to throw himself off the box, so quickly did he reach the ground. Then he stretched out his hands appealingly to me, and implored me not to go. There was just enough of English mixed with the German for me to understand the drift of his talk. He seemed always just about to tell me something—the very idea of which evidently frightened him; but each time he pulled himself up, saying, as he crossed himself: "Walpurgis Nacht!"

I tried to argue with him, but it was difficult to argue with a man when I did not know his language. The advantage certainly rested with him, for although he began to speak in English, of a very crude and broken kind, he always got excited and broke into his native tongue—and every time he did so, he looked at his watch. Then the horses became restless and sniffed the air. At this he grew very pale, and, looking around in a frightened way, he suddenly jumped forward, took them by the bridles and led them on some twenty feet. I followed, and asked why he had done this. For answer he crossed himself, pointed to the spot we had left and drew his carriage in the direction of the other road, indicating a cross, and said, first in German, then in English: "Buried him—him what killed themselves."

I remembered the old custom of burying suicides at cross-roads: "Ah! I see, a suicide. How interesting!" But for the life of me I could not make out why the horses were frightened.

Whilst we were talking, we heard a sort of sound between a yelp and a bark. It was far away; but the horses got very restless, and it took Johann all his time to quiet them. He was pale, and said, "It sounds like a wolf—but yet there are no wolves here now."

"No?" I said, questioning him; "isn't it long since the wolves were so near the city?"

"Long, long," he answered, "in the spring and summer; but with the snow the wolves have been here not so long."

Whilst he was petting the horses and trying to quiet them, dark clouds drifted rapidly across the sky. The sunshine passed away, and a breath of cold wind seemed to drift past us. It was only a breath, however, and more in the nature of a warning than a fact, for the sun came out brightly again. Johann looked under his lifted hand at the horizon and said:

"The storm of snow, he comes before long time." Then he looked at his watch again, and, straightway holding his reins firmly—for the horses were still pawing the ground restlessly and shaking their heads—he climbed to his box as though the time had come for proceeding on our journey.

I felt a little obstinate and did not at once get into the carriage.

"Tell me," I said, "about this place where the road leads," and I pointed down.

Again he crossed himself and mumbled a prayer, before he answered, "It is unholy."

"What is unholy?" I enquired.

"The village."

"Then there is a village?"

"No, no. No one lives there hundreds of years." My curiosity was piqued, "But you said there was a village."

"There was."

"Where is it now?"

Whereupon he burst out into a long story in German and English, so mixed up that I could not quite understand exactly what he said, but roughly I gathered that long ago, hundreds of years, men had died there and been buried in their graves; and sounds were heard under the clay, and when the graves were opened, men and women were found rosy with life, and their mouths red with blood. And so, in haste to save their lives (aye, and their souls!—and here he crossed himself) those who were left fled away to other places, where the living lived, and the dead were dead and not—not something. He was evidently afraid to speak the last words. As he proceeded with his narration, he grew more and more excited. It seemed as if his imagination had got hold of him, and he ended in a perfect paroxysm of fear—white-faced, perspiring, trembling and looking round him, as if expecting that some dreadful presence would manifest itself there in the bright sunshine on the open plain. Finally, in an agony of desperation, he cried:

"Walpurgis nacht!" and pointed to the carriage for me to get in. All my English blood rose at this, and, standing back, I said:

"You are afraid, Johann—you are afraid. Go home; I shall return alone; the walk will do me good.' The carriage door was open. I took from the seat my oak walking-stick—which I always carry on my holiday excursions—and closed the door, pointing back to Munich, and said, 'Go home, Johann—Walpurgis nacht doesn't concern Englishmen."

The horses were now more restive than ever, and Johann was trying to hold them in, while excitedly imploring me not to do anything so foolish. I pitied the poor fellow, he was deeply in earnest; but all the same I could not help laughing. His English was quite gone now. In his anxiety he had forgotten that his only means of making me understand was to talk my language, so he jabbered away in his native German. It began to be a little tedious. After giving the direction, "Home!" I turned to go down the cross-road into the valley.

With a despairing gesture, Johann turned his horses towards Munich. I leaned on my stick and looked after him. He went slowly along the road for a while: then there came over the crest of the hill a man tall and thin. I could see so much in the distance. When he drew near the horses, they began to jump and kick about, then to scream with terror. Johann could not hold them in; they bolted down the road, running away madly. I watched them out of sight, then looked for the stranger, but I found that he, too, was gone.

With a light heart I turned down the side road through the deepening valley to which Johann had objected. There was not the slightest reason, that I could see, for his objection; and I daresay I tramped for a couple of hours without thinking of time or distance, and certainly without seeing a person or a house. So far as the place was concerned, it was desolation itself. But I did not notice this particularly till, on turning a bend in the road, I came upon a scattered fringe of wood; then I recognised that I had been impressed unconsciously by the desolation of the region through which I had passed.

I sat down to rest myself, and began to look around. It struck me that it was considerably colder than it had been at the commencement of my walk—a sort of sighing sound seemed to be around me, with, now and then, high overhead, a sort of muffled roar. Looking upwards I noticed that great thick clouds were drifting rapidly across the sky from north to south at a great height. There were signs of coming storm in some lofty stratum of the air. I was a little chilly, and, thinking that it was the sitting still after the exercise of walking, I resumed my journey.

The ground I passed over was now much more picturesque. There were no striking objects that the eye might single out; but in all there was a charm of beauty. I took little heed of time and it was only when the deepening twilight forced itself upon me that I began to think of how I should find my way home. The brightness of the day had gone. The air was cold, and the drifting of clouds high overhead was more marked. They were accompanied by a sort of far-away rushing sound, through which seemed to come at intervals that mysterious cry which the driver had said came from a wolf. For a while I hesitated. I had said I would see the deserted village, so on I went, and presently came on a wide stretch of open country, shut in by hills all around. Their sides were covered with trees which spread down to the plain, dotting, in clumps, the gentler slopes and hollows which showed here and there. I followed with my eye the winding of the road, and saw that it curved close to one of the densest of these clumps and was lost behind it.

As I looked there came a cold shiver in the air, and the snow began to fall. I thought of the miles and miles of bleak country I had passed, and then hurried on to seek the shelter of the wood in front. Darker and darker grew the sky, and faster and heavier fell the snow, till the earth before and around me was a glistening white carpet the further edge of which was lost in misty vagueness. The road was here but crude, and when on the level its boundaries were not so marked, as when it passed through the cuttings; and in a little while I found that I must have strayed from it, for I missed underfoot the hard surface, and my feet sank deeper in the grass and moss. Then the wind grew stronger and blew with ever increasing force, till I was fain to run before it. The air became icy-cold, and in spite of my exercise I began to suffer. The snow was now falling so thickly and whirling around me in such rapid eddies that I could hardly keep my eyes open. Every now and then the heavens were torn asunder by vivid lightning, and in the flashes I could see ahead of me a great mass of trees, chiefly yew and cypress all heavily coated with snow.

I was soon amongst the shelter of the trees, and there, in comparative silence, I could hear the rush of the wind high overhead. Presently the blackness of the storm had become merged in the darkness of the night. By-and-by the storm seemed to be passing away: it now only came in fierce puffs or blasts. At such moments the weird sound of the wolf appeared to be echoed by many similar sounds around me.

Now and again, through the black mass of drifting cloud, came a straggling ray of moonlight, which lit up the expanse, and showed me that I was at the edge of a dense mass of cypress and yew trees. As the snow had ceased to fall, I walked out from the shelter and began to investigate more closely. It appeared to me that, amongst so many old foundations as I had passed, there might be still standing a house in which, though in ruins, I could find some sort of shelter for a while. As I skirted the edge of the copse, I found that a low wall encircled it, and following this I presently found an opening. Here the cypresses formed an alley leading up to a square mass of some kind of building. Just as I caught sight of this, however, the drifting clouds obscured the moon, and I passed up the path in darkness. The wind must have grown colder, for I felt myself shiver as I walked; but there was hope of shelter, and I groped my way blindly on.

I stopped, for there was a sudden stillness. The storm had passed; and, perhaps in sympathy with nature's silence, my heart seemed to cease to beat. But this was only momentarily; for suddenly the moonlight broke through the clouds, showing me that I was in a graveyard, and that the square object before me was a great massive tomb of marble, as white as the snow that lay on and all around it. With the moonlight there came a fierce sigh of the storm, which appeared to resume its course with a long, low howl, as of many dogs or wolves. I was awed and shocked, and felt the cold perceptibly grow upon me till it seemed to grip me by the heart. Then while the flood of moonlight still fell on the marble tomb, the storm gave further evidence of renewing, as though it was returning on its track. Impelled by some sort of fascination, I approached the sepulchre to see what it was, and why such a thing stood alone in such a place. I walked around it, and read, over the Doric door, in German:

COUNTESS DOLINGEN OF GRATZ
IN STYRIA
SOUGHT AND FOUND DEATH
1801

On the top of the tomb, seemingly driven through the solid marble—for the structure was composed of a few vast blocks of stone—was a great iron spike or stake. On going to the back I saw, graven in great Russian letters:

'The dead travel fast.'

There was something so weird and uncanny about the whole thing that it gave me a turn and made me feel quite faint. I began to wish, for the first time, that I had taken Johann's advice. Here a thought struck me, which came under almost mysterious circumstances and with a terrible shock. This was Walpurgis Night!

Walpurgis Night, when, according to the belief of millions of people, the devil was abroad—when the graves were opened and the dead came forth and walked. When all evil things of earth and air and water held revel. This very place the driver had specially shunned. This was the depopulated village of centuries ago. This was where the suicide lay; and this was the place where I was alone—unmanned, shivering with cold in a shroud of snow with a wild storm gathering again upon me! It took all my philosophy, all the religion I had been taught, all my courage, not to collapse in a paroxysm of fright.

And now a perfect tornado burst upon me. The ground shook as though thousands of horses thundered across it; and this time the storm bore on its icy wings, not snow, but great hailstones which drove with such violence that they might have come from the thongs of Balearic slingers—hailstones that beat down leaf and branch and made the shelter of the cypresses of no more avail than though their stems were standing-corn. At the first I had rushed to the nearest tree; but I was soon fain to leave it and seek the only spot that seemed to afford refuge, the deep Doric doorway of the marble tomb. There, crouching against the massive bronze door, I gained a certain amount of protection from the beating of the hailstones, for now they only drove against me as they ricocheted from the ground and the side of the marble.

As I leaned against the door, it moved slightly and opened inwards. The shelter of even a tomb was welcome in that pitiless tempest, and I was about to enter it when there came a flash of forked-lightning that lit up the whole expanse of the heavens. In the instant, as I am a living man, I saw, as my eyes were turned into the darkness of the tomb, a beautiful woman, with rounded cheeks and red lips, seemingly sleeping on a bier. As the thunder broke overhead, I was grasped as by the hand of a giant and hurled out into the storm. The whole thing was so sudden that, before I could realise the shock, moral as well as physical, I found the hailstones beating me down. At the same time I had a strange, dominating feeling that I was not alone. I looked towards the tomb. Just then there came another blinding flash, which seemed to strike the iron stake that surmounted the tomb and to pour through to the earth, blasting and crumbling the marble, as in a burst of flame. The dead woman rose for a moment of agony, while she was lapped in the flame, and her bitter scream of pain was drowned in the thundercrash. The last thing I heard was this mingling of dreadful sound, as again I was seized in the giant-grasp and dragged away, while the hailstones beat on me, and the air around seemed reverberant with the howling of wolves. The last sight that I remembered was a vague, white, moving mass, as if all the graves around me had sent out the phantoms of their sheeted-dead, and that they were closing in on me through the white cloudiness of the driving hail.

Gradually there came a sort of vague beginning of consciousness; then a sense of weariness that was dreadful. For a time I remembered nothing; but slowly my senses returned. My feet seemed positively racked with pain, yet I could not move them. They seemed to be numbed. There was an icy feeling at the back of my neck and all down my spine, and my ears, like my feet, were dead, yet in torment; but there was in my breast a sense of warmth which was, by comparison, delicious. It was as a nightmare—a physical nightmare, if one may use such an expression; for some heavy weight on my chest made it difficult for me to breathe.

This period of semi-lethargy seemed to remain a long time, and as it faded away I must have slept or swooned. Then came a sort of loathing, like the first stage of sea-sickness, and a wild desire to be free from something—I knew not what. A vast stillness enveloped me, as though all the world were asleep or dead—only broken by the low panting as of some animal close to me. I felt a warm rasping at my throat, then came a consciousness of the awful truth, which chilled me to the heart and sent the blood surging up through my brain. Some great animal was lying on me and now licking my throat. I feared to stir, for some instinct of prudence bade me lie still; but the brute seemed to realise that there was now some change in me, for it raised its head. Through my eyelashes I saw above me the two great flaming eyes of a gigantic wolf. Its sharp white teeth gleamed in the gaping red mouth, and I could feel its hot breath fierce and acrid upon me.

For another spell of time I remembered no more. Then I became conscious of a low growl, followed by a yelp, renewed again and again. Then, seemingly very far away, I heard a 'Holloa! holloa!' as of many voices calling in unison. Cautiously I raised my head and looked in the direction whence the sound came; but the cemetery blocked my view. The wolf still continued to yelp in a strange way, and a red glare began to move round the grove of cypresses, as though following the sound. As the voices drew closer, the wolf yelped faster and louder. I feared to make either sound or motion. Nearer came the red glow, over the white pall which stretched into the darkness around me. Then all at once from beyond the trees there came at a trot a troop of horsemen bearing torches. The wolf rose from my breast and made for the cemetery. I saw one of the horsemen (soldiers by their caps and their long military cloaks) raise his carbine and take aim. A companion knocked up his arm, and I heard the ball whizz over my head. He had evidently taken my body for that of the wolf. Another sighted the animal as it slunk away, and a shot followed. Then, at a gallop, the troop rode forward—some towards me, others following the wolf as it disappeared amongst the snow-clad cypresses.

As they drew nearer I tried to move, but was powerless, although I could see and hear all that went on around me. Two or three of the soldiers jumped from their horses and knelt beside me. One of them raised my head, and placed his hand over my heart.

"Good news, comrades!" he cried. "His heart still beats!"

Then some brandy was poured down my throat; it put vigour into me, and I was able to open my eyes fully and look around. Lights and shadows were moving among the trees, and I heard men call to one another. They drew together, uttering frightened exclamations; and the lights flashed as the others came pouring out of the cemetery pell-mell, like men possessed. When the further ones came close to us, those who were around me asked them eagerly:

"Well, have you found him?"

The reply rang out hurriedly:

"No! no! Come away quick—quick! This is no place to stay, and on this of all nights!"

"What was it?" was the question, asked in all manner of keys. The answer came variously and all indefinitely as though the men were moved by some common impulse to speak, yet were restrained by some common fear from giving their thoughts.

"It—it—indeed!" gibbered one, whose wits had plainly given out for the moment.

"A wolf—and yet not a wolf!" another put in shudderingly.

"No use trying for him without the sacred bullet," a third remarked in a more ordinary manner.

"Serve us right for coming out on this night! Truly we have earned our thousand marks!" were the ejaculations of a fourth.

"There was blood on the broken marble,' another said after a pause—"the lightning never brought that there. And for him—is he safe? Look at his throat! See, comrades, the wolf has been lying on him and keeping his blood warm."

The officer looked at my throat and replied:

"He is all right; the skin is not pierced. What does it all mean? We should never have found him but for the yelping of the wolf."

"What became of it?" asked the man who was holding up my head, and who seemed the least panic-stricken of the party, for his hands were steady and without tremor. On his sleeve was the chevron of a petty officer.

"It went to its home," answered the man, whose long face was pallid, and who actually shook with terror as he glanced around him fearfully. "There are graves enough there in which it may lie. Come, comrades—come quickly! Let us leave this cursed spot."

The officer raised me to a sitting posture, as he uttered a word of command; then several men placed me upon a horse. He sprang to the saddle behind me, took me in his arms, gave the word to advance; and, turning our faces away from the cypresses, we rode away in swift, military order.

As yet my tongue refused its office, and I was perforce silent. I must have fallen asleep; for the next thing I remembered was finding myself standing up, supported by a soldier on each side of me. It was almost broad daylight, and to the north a red streak of sunlight was reflected, like a path of blood, over the waste of snow. The officer was telling the men to say nothing of what they had seen, except that they found an English stranger, guarded by a large dog.

"Dog! that was no dog," cut in the man who had exhibited such fear. "I think I know a wolf when I see one."

The young officer answered calmly: "I said a dog."

"Dog!" reiterated the other ironically. It was evident that his courage was rising with the sun; and, pointing to me, he said, "Look at his throat. Is that the work of a dog, master?"

Instinctively I raised my hand to my throat, and as I touched it I cried out in pain. The men crowded round to look, some stooping down from their saddles; and again there came the calm voice of the young officer:

"A dog, as I said. If aught else were said we should only be laughed at."

I was then mounted behind a trooper, and we rode on into the suburbs of Munich. Here we came across a stray carriage, into which I was lifted, and it was driven off to the Quatre Saisons—the young officer accompanying me, whilst a trooper followed with his horse, and the others rode off to their barracks.

When we arrived, Herr Delbrück rushed so quickly down the steps to meet me, that it was apparent he had been watching within. Taking me by both hands he solicitously led me in. The officer saluted me and was turning to withdraw, when I recognised his purpose, and insisted that he should come to my rooms. Over a glass of wine I warmly thanked him and his brave comrades for saving me. He replied simply that he was more than glad, and that Herr Delbrück had at the first taken steps to make all the searching party pleased; at which ambiguous utterance the maître d'hôtel smiled, while the officer pleaded duty and withdrew.

"But Herr Delbrück," I enquired, "how and why was it that the soldiers searched for me?"

He shrugged his shoulders, as if in depreciation of his own deed, as he replied:

"I was so fortunate as to obtain leave from the commander of the regiment in which I served, to ask for volunteers."

"But how did you know I was lost?" I asked.

"The driver came hither with the remains of his carriage, which had been upset when the horses ran away."

"But surely you would not send a search-party of soldiers merely on this account?'

"Oh, no!" he answered; "but even before the coachman arrived, I had this telegram from the Boyar whose guest you are," and he took from his pocket a telegram which he handed to me, and I read:

Bistritz.

Be careful of my guest—his safety is most precious to me. Should aught happen to him, or if he be missed, spare nothing to find him and ensure his safety. He is English and therefore adventurous. There are often dangers from snow and wolves and night. Lose not a moment if you suspect harm to him. I answer your zeal with my fortune.

—Dracula.

As I held the telegram in my hand, the room seemed to whirl around me; and, if the attentive maître d'hôtel had not caught me, I think I should have fallen.

There was something so strange in all this, something so weird and impossible to imagine, that there grew on me a sense of my being in some way the sport of opposite forces—the mere vague idea of which seemed in a way to paralyse me. I was certainly under some form of mysterious protection. From a distant country had come, in the very nick of time, a message that took me out of the danger of the snow-sleep and the jaws of the wolf.

The Judge's House

by Bram Stoker

When the time for his examination drew near Malcolm Malcolmson made up his mind to go somewhere to read by himself. He feared the attractions of the seaside, and also he feared completely rural isolation, for of old he knew it charms, and so he determined to find some unpretentious little town where there would be nothing to distract him. He refrained from asking suggestions from any of his friends, for he argued that each would recommend some place of which he had knowledge, and where he had already acquaintances. As Malcolmson wished to avoid friends he had no wish to encumber himself with the attention of friends' friends, and so he determined to look out for a place for himself. He packed a portmanteau with some clothes and all the books he required, and then took ticket for the first name on the local time-table which he did not know.

When at the end of three hours' journey he alighted at Benchurch, he felt satisfied that he had so far obliterated his tracks as to be sure of having a peaceful opportunity of pursuing his studies. He went straight to the one inn which the sleepy little place contained, and put up for the night. Benchurch was a market town, and once in three weeks was crowded to excess, but for the remainder of the twenty-one days it was as attractive as a desert. Malcolmson looked around the day after his arrival to try to find quarters more isolated than even so quiet an inn as 'The Good Traveller' afforded. There was only one place which took his fancy, and it certainly satisfied his wildest ideas regarding quiet; in fact, quiet was not the proper word to apply to it—desolation was the only term conveying any suitable idea of its isolation. It was an old rambling, heavy-built house of the Jacobean style, with heavy gables and windows, unusually small, and set higher than was customary in such houses, and was surrounded with a high brick wall massively built. Indeed, on examination, it looked more like a fortified house than an ordinary dwelling. But all these things pleased Malcolmson. "Here," he thought, "is the very spot I have been looking for, and if I can get opportunity of using it I shall be happy." His joy was increased when he realised beyond doubt that it was not at present inhabited.

From the post-office he got the name of the agent, who was rarely surprised at the application to rent a part of the old house. Mr Carnford, the local lawyer and agent, was a genial old gentleman, and frankly confessed his delight at anyone being willing to live in the house.

"To tell you the truth," said he, "I should be only too happy, on behalf of the owners, to let anyone have the house rent free for a term of years if only to accustom the people here to see it inhabited. It has been so long empty that some kind of absurd prejudice has grown up about it, and this can be best put down by its occupation—if only," he added with a sly glance at Malcolmson, "by a scholar like yourself, who wants its quiet for a time."

Malcolmson thought it needless to ask the agent about the 'absurd prejudice'; he knew he would get more information, if he should require it, on that subject from other quarters. He paid his three months' rent, got a receipt, and the name of an old woman who would probably undertake to 'do' for him, and came away with the keys in his pocket. He then went to the landlady of the inn, who was a cheerful and most kindly person, and asked her advice as to such stores and provisions as he would be likely to require. She threw up her hands in amazement when he told her where he was going to settle himself.

"Not in the Judge's House!" she said, and grew pale as she spoke. He explained the locality of the house, saying that he did not know its name. When he had finished she answered:

"Aye, sure enough—sure enough the very place! It is the Judge's House sure enough.' He asked her to tell him about the place, why so called, and what there was against it. She told him that it was so called locally because it had been many years before—how long she could not say, as she was herself from another part of the country, but she thought it must have been a hundred years or more—the abode of a judge who was held in great terror on account of his harsh sentences and his hostility to prisoners at Assizes. As to what there was against the house itself she could not tell. She had often asked, but no one could inform her; but there was a general feeling that there was *something*, and for her own part she would not take all the money in Drinkwater's Bank and stay in the house an hour by herself. Then she apologised to Malcolmson for her disturbing talk.

"It is too bad of me, sir, and you—and a young gentlemen, too—if you will pardon me saying it, going to live there all alone. If you were my boy—and you'll excuse me for saying it—you wouldn't sleep there a night, not if I had to go there myself and pull the big alarm bell that's on the roof!" The good creature was so manifestly in earnest, and was so kindly in her intentions, that Malcolmson, although amused, was touched. He told her kindly how much he appreciated her interest in him, and added:

"But, my dear Mrs. Witham, indeed you need not be concerned about me! A man who is reading for the Mathematical Tripos has too much to think of to be disturbed by any of these mysterious 'somethings', and his work is of too exact and prosaic a kind to allow of his having any corner in his mind for mysteries of any kind. Harmonical Progression, Permutations and Combinations, and Elliptic Functions have sufficient mysteries for me!" Mrs. Witham kindly undertook to see after his commissions, and he went himself to look for the old woman who had been recommended to him. When he returned to the Judge's House with her, after an interval of a couple of hours, he found Mrs. Witham herself waiting with several men and boys carrying parcels, and an upholsterer's man with a bed in a car, for she said, though tables and chairs might be all very well, a bed that hadn't been aired for mayhap fifty years was not proper for young bones to lie on. She was evidently curious to see the inside of the house; and though manifestly so afraid of the 'somethings' that at the slightest sound she clutched on to Malcolmson, whom she never left for a moment, went over the whole place.

After his examination of the house, Malcolmson decided to take up his abode in the great dining-room, which was big enough to serve for all his requirements; and Mrs. Witham, with the aid of the charwoman, Mrs. Dempster, proceeded to arrange matters. When the hampers were brought in and unpacked, Malcolmson saw that with much kind forethought she had sent from her own kitchen sufficient provisions to last for a few days. Before going she expressed all sorts of kind wishes; and at the door turned and said:

"And perhaps, sir, as the room is big and draughty it might be well to have one of those big screens put round your bed at night—though, truth to tell, I would die myself if I were to be so shut in with all kinds of—of 'things', that put their heads round the sides, or over the top, and look on me!" The image which she had called up was too much for her nerves, and she fled incontinently.

Mrs. Dempster sniffed in a superior manner as the landlady disappeared, and remarked that for her own part she wasn't afraid of all the bogies in the kingdom.

"I'll tell you what it is, sir," she said; "bogies is all kinds and sorts of things—except bogies! Rats and mice, and beetles; and creaky doors, and loose slates, and broken panes, and stiff drawer handles, that stay out when you pull them and then fall down in the middle of the night. Look at the wainscot of the room! It is old—hundreds of years old! Do you think there's no rats and beetles there! And do you imagine, sir, that you won't see none of them? Rats is bogies, I tell you, and bogies is rats; and don't you get to think anything else!"

"Mrs. Dempster," said Malcolmson gravely, making her a polite bow, "you know more than a Senior Wrangler! And let me say, that, as a mark of esteem for your indubitable soundness of head and heart, I shall, when I go, give you possession of this house, and let you stay here by yourself for the last two months of my tenancy, for four weeks will serve my purpose."

"Thank you kindly, sir!" she answered, "but I couldn't sleep away from home a night. I am in Greenhow's Charity, and if I slept a night away from my rooms I should lose all I have got to live on. The rules is very strict; and there's too many watching for a vacancy for me to run any risks in the matter. Only for that, sir, I'd gladly come here and attend on you altogether during your stay."

"My good woman," said Malcolmson hastily, "I have come here on purpose to obtain solitude; and believe me that I am grateful to the late Greenhow for having so organised his admirable charity—whatever it is—that I am perforce denied the opportunity of suffering from such a form of temptation! Saint Anthony himself could not be more rigid on the point!"

The old woman laughed harshly. "Ah, you young gentlemen," she said, "you don't fear for naught; and belike you'll get all the solitude you want here." She set to work with her cleaning; and by nightfall, when Malcolmson returned from his walk—he always had one of his books to study as he walked—he found the room swept and tidied, a fire burning in the old hearth, the lamp lit, and the table spread for supper with Mrs. Witham's excellent fare. "This is comfort, indeed," he said, as he rubbed his hands.

When he had finished his supper, and lifted the tray to the other end of the great oak dining-table, he got out his books again, put fresh wood on the fire, trimmed his lamp, and set himself down to a spell of real hard work. He went on without pause till about eleven o'clock, when he knocked off for a bit to fix his fire and lamp, and to make himself a cup of tea. He had always been a tea-drinker, and during his college life had sat late at work and had taken tea late. The rest was a great luxury to him, and he enjoyed it with a sense of delicious, voluptuous ease. The renewed fire leaped and sparkled, and threw quaint shadows through the great old room; and as he sipped his hot tea he revelled in the sense of isolation from his kind. Then it was that he began to notice for the first time what a noise the rats were making.

"Surely," he thought, "they cannot have been at it all the time I was reading. Had they been, I must have noticed it!" Presently, when the noise increased, he satisfied himself that it was really new. It was evident that at first the rats had been frightened at the presence of a stranger, and the light of fire and lamp; but that as the time went on they had grown bolder and were now disporting themselves as was their wont.

How busy they were! and hark to the strange noises! Up and down behind the old wainscot, over the ceiling and under the floor they raced, and gnawed, and scratched! Malcolmson smiled to himself as he recalled to mind the saying of Mrs. Dempster, "Bogies is rats, and rats is bogies!" The tea began to have its effect of intellectual and nervous stimulus, he saw with joy another long spell of work to be done before the night was past, and in the sense of security which it gave him, he allowed himself the luxury of a good look round the room. He took his lamp in one hand, and went all around, wondering that so quaint and beautiful an old house had been so long neglected. The carving of the oak on the panels of the wainscot was fine, and on and round the doors and windows it was beautiful and of rare merit. There were some old pictures on the walls, but they were coated so thick with dust and dirt that he could not distinguish any detail of them, though he held his lamp as high as he could over his head. Here and there as he went round he saw some crack or hole blocked for a moment by the face of a rat with its bright eyes glittering in the light, but in an instant it was gone, and a squeak and a scamper followed. The thing that most struck him, however, was the rope of the great alarm bell on the roof, which hung down in a corner of the room on the right-hand side of the fireplace. He pulled up close to the hearth a great high-backed carved oak chair, and sat down to his last cup of tea. When this was done he made up the fire, and went back to his work, sitting at the corner of the table, having the fire to his left. For a little while the rats disturbed him somewhat with their perpetual scampering, but he got accustomed to the noise as one does to the ticking of a clock or to the roar of moving water; and he became so immersed in his work that everything in the world, except the problem which he was trying to solve, passed away from him.

He suddenly looked up, his problem was still unsolved, and there was in the air that sense of the hour before the dawn, which is so dread to doubtful life. The noise of the rats had ceased. Indeed it seemed to him that it must have ceased but lately and that it was the sudden cessation which had disturbed him. The fire had fallen low, but still it threw out a deep red glow. As he looked he started in spite of his *sang froid.*

There on the great high-backed carved oak chair by the right side of the fireplace sat an enormous rat, steadily glaring at him with baleful eyes. He made a motion to it as though to hunt it away, but it did not stir. Then he made the motion of throwing something. Still it did not stir, but showed its great white teeth angrily, and its cruel eyes shone in the lamplight with an added vindictiveness.

Malcolmson felt amazed, and seizing the poker from the hearth ran at it to kill it. Before, however, he could strike it, the rat, with a squeak that sounded like the concentration of hate, jumped upon the floor, and, running up the rope of the alarm bell, disappeared in the darkness beyond the range of the green-shaded lamp. Instantly, strange to say, the noisy scampering of the rats in the wainscot began again.

By this time Malcolmson's mind was quite off the problem; and as a shrill cock-crow outside told him of the approach of morning, he went to bed and to sleep.

He slept so sound that he was not even waked by Mrs. Dempster coming in to make up his room. It was only when she had tidied up the place and got his breakfast ready and tapped on the screen which closed in his bed that he woke. He was a little tired still after his night's hard work, but a strong cup of tea soon freshened him up and, taking his book, he went out for his morning walk, bringing with him a few sandwiches lest he should not care to return till dinner time. He found a quiet walk between high elms some way outside the town, and here he spent the greater part of the day studying his Laplace. On his return he looked in to see Mrs. Witham and to thank her for her kindness. When she saw him coming through the diamond-paned bay window of her sanctum she came out to meet him and asked him in. She looked at him searchingly and shook her head as she said:

"You must not overdo it, sir. You are paler this morning than you should be. Too late hours and too hard work on the brain isn't good for any man! But tell me, sir, how did you pass the night? Well, I hope? But my heart! sir, I was glad when Mrs. Dempster told me this morning that you were all right and sleeping sound when she went in."

"Oh, I was all right," he answered smiling, "the 'somethings' didn't worry me, as yet. Only the rats; and they had a circus, I tell you, all over the place. There was one wicked looking old devil that sat up on my own chair by the fire, and wouldn't go till I took the poker to him, and then he ran up the rope of the alarm bell and got to somewhere up the wall or the ceiling—I couldn't see where, it was so dark."

"Mercy on us," said Mrs. Witham, "an old devil, and sitting on a chair by the fireside! Take care, sir! take care! There's many a true word spoken in jest."

"How do you mean? Pon my word I don't understand."

"An old devil! The old devil, perhaps. There! sir, you needn't laugh," for Malcolmson had broken into a hearty peal. 'You young folks thinks it easy to laugh at things that makes older ones shudder. Never mind, sir! never mind! Please God, you'll laugh all the time. It's what I wish you myself!" and the good lady beamed all over in sympathy with his enjoyment, her fears gone for a moment.

"Oh, forgive me!" said Malcolmson presently. "Don't think me rude; but the idea was too much for me—that the old devil himself was on the chair last night!" And at the thought he laughed again. Then he went home to dinner.

This evening the scampering of the rats began earlier; indeed it had been going on before his arrival, and only ceased whilst his presence by its freshness disturbed them. After dinner he sat by the fire for a while and had a smoke; and then, having cleared his table, began to work as before. Tonight the rats disturbed him more than they had done on the previous night. How they scampered up and down and under and over! How they squeaked, and scratched, and gnawed! How they, getting bolder by degrees, came to the mouths of their holes and to the chinks and cracks and crannies in the wainscoting till their eyes shone like tiny lamps as the firelight rose and fell. But to him, now doubtless accustomed to them, their eyes were not wicked; only their playfulness touched him. Sometimes the boldest of them made sallies out on the floor or along the mouldings of the wainscot. Now and again as they disturbed him Malcolmson made a sound to frighten them, smiting the table with his hand or giving a fierce 'Hsh, hsh,' so that they fled straightway to their holes.

And so the early part of the night wore on; and despite the noise Malcolmson got more and more immersed in his work.

All at once he stopped, as on the previous night, being overcome by a sudden sense of silence. There was not the faintest sound of gnaw, or scratch, or squeak. The silence was as of the grave. He remembered the odd occurrence of the previous night, and instinctively he looked at the chair standing close by the fireside. And then a very odd sensation thrilled through him.

There, on the great old high-backed carved oak chair beside the fireplace sat the same enormous rat, steadily glaring at him with baleful eyes.

Instinctively he took the nearest thing to his hand, a book of logarithms, and flung it at it. The book was badly aimed and the rat did not stir, so again the poker performance of the previous night was repeated; and again the rat, being closely pursued, fled up the rope of the alarm bell. Strangely too, the departure of this rat was instantly followed by the renewal of the noise made by the general rat community. On this occasion, as on the previous one, Malcolmson could not see at what part of the room the rat disappeared, for the green shade of his lamp left the upper part of the room in darkness, and the fire had burned low.

On looking at his watch he found it was close on midnight; and, not sorry for the *divertissement*, he made up his fire and made himself his nightly pot of tea. He had got through a good spell of work, and thought himself entitled to a cigarette; and so he sat on the great oak chair before the fire and enjoyed it. Whilst smoking he began to think that he would like to know where the rat disappeared to, for he had certain ideas for the morrow not entirely disconnected with a rat-trap. Accordingly he lit another lamp and placed it so that it would shine well into the right-hand corner of the wall by the fireplace. Then he got all the books he had with him, and placed them handy to throw at the vermin. Finally he lifted the rope of the alarm bell and placed the end of it on the table, fixing the extreme end under the lamp. As he handled it he could not help noticing how pliable it was, especially for so strong a rope, and one not in use. "You could hang a man with it," he thought to himself. When his preparations were made he looked around, and said complacently:

"There now, my friend, I think we shall learn something of you this time!" He began his work again, and though as before somewhat disturbed at first by the noise of the rats, soon lost himself in his propositions and problems.

Again he was called to his immediate surroundings suddenly. This time it might not have been the sudden silence only which took his attention; there was a slight movement of the rope, and the lamp moved. Without stirring, he looked to see if his pile of books was within range, and then cast his eye along the rope. As he looked he saw the great rat drop from the rope on the oak arm-chair and sit there glaring at him. He raised a book in his right hand, and taking careful aim, flung it at the rat. The latter, with a quick movement, sprang aside and dodged the missile. He then took another book, and a third, and flung them one after another at the rat, but each time unsuccessfully. At last, as he stood with a book poised in his hand to throw, the rat squeaked and seemed afraid. This made Malcolmson more than ever eager to strike, and the book flew and struck the rat a resounding blow. It gave a terrified squeak, and turning on his pursuer a look of terrible malevolence, ran up the chair-back and made a great jump to the rope of the alarm bell and ran up it like lightning. The lamp rocked under the sudden strain, but it was a heavy one and did not topple over. Malcolmson kept his eyes on the rat, and saw it by the light of the second lamp leap to a moulding of the wainscot and disappear through a hole in one of the great pictures which hung on the wall, obscured and invisible through its coating of dirt and dust.

"I shall look up my friend's habitation in the morning," said the student, as he went over to collect his books. "The third picture from the fireplace; I shall not forget." He picked up the books one by one, commenting on them as he lifted them. "*Conic Sections* he does not mind, nor *Cycloidal Oscillations*, nor the *Principia*, nor *Quaternions*, nor *Thermodynamics*. Now for the book that fetched him!" Malcolmson took it up and looked at it. As he did so he started, and a sudden pallor overspread his face. He looked round uneasily and shivered slightly, as he murmured to himself:

"The Bible my mother gave me! What an odd coincidence." He sat down to work again, and the rats in the wainscot renewed their gambols. They did not disturb him, however; somehow their presence gave him a sense of companionship. But he could not attend to his work, and after striving to master the subject on which he was engaged gave it up in despair, and went to bed as the first streak of dawn stole in through the eastern window.

He slept heavily but uneasily, and dreamed much; and when Mrs. Dempster woke him late in the morning he seemed ill at ease, and for a few minutes did not seem to realise exactly where he was. His first request rather surprised the servant.

"Mrs. Dempster, when I am out today I wish you would get the steps and dust or wash those pictures—specially that one the third from the fireplace—I want to see what they are."

Late in the afternoon Malcolmson worked at his books in the shaded walk, and the cheerfulness of the previous day came back to him as the day wore on, and he found that his reading was progressing well. He had worked out to a satisfactory conclusion all the problems which had as yet baffled him, and it was in a state of jubilation that he paid a visit to Mrs. Witham at 'The Good Traveller'. He found a stranger in the cosy sitting-room with the landlady, who was introduced to him as Dr. Thornhill. She was not quite at ease, and this, combined with the doctor's plunging at once into a series of questions, made Malcolmson come to the conclusion that his presence was not an accident, so without preliminary he said:

"Dr. Thornhill, I shall with pleasure answer you any question you may choose to ask me if you will answer me one question first."

The doctor seemed surprised, but he smiled and answered at once, "Done! What is it?"

"Did Mrs. Witham ask you to come here and see me and advise me?"

Dr. Thornhill for a moment was taken aback, and Mrs. Witham got fiery red and turned away; but the doctor was a frank and ready man, and he answered at once and openly.

"She did: but she didn't intend you to know it. I suppose it was my clumsy haste that made you suspect. She told me that she did not like the idea of your being in that house all by yourself, and that she thought you took too much strong tea. In fact, she wants me to advise you if possible to give up the tea and the very late hours. I was a keen student in my time, so I suppose I may take the liberty of a college man, and without offence, advise you not quite as a stranger.'

Malcolmson with a bright smile held out his hand. "Shake! as they say in America," he said. "I must thank you for your kindness and Mrs. Witham too, and your kindness deserves a return on my part. I promise to take no more strong tea—no tea at all till you let me—and I shall go to bed tonight at one o'clock at latest. Will that do?"

"Capital," said the doctor. "Now tell us all that you noticed in the old house,'"and so Malcolmson then and there told in minute detail all that had happened in the last two nights. He was interrupted every now and then by some exclamation from Mrs. Witham, till finally when he told of the episode of the Bible the landlady's pent-up emotions found vent in a shriek; and it was not till a stiff glass of brandy and water had been administered that she grew composed again. Dr. Thornhill listened with a face of growing gravity, and when the narrative was complete and Mrs. Witham had been restored he asked:

"The rat always went up the rope of the alarm bell?"

"Always."

"I suppose you know,' said the Doctor after a pause, "what the rope is?"

"No!"

"It is," said the Doctor slowly, 'the very rope which the hangman used for all the victims of the Judge's judicial rancour!' Here he was interrupted by another scream from Mrs. Witham, and steps had to be taken for her recovery. Malcolmson having looked at his watch, and found that it was close to his dinner hour, had gone home before her complete recovery.

When Mrs. Witham was herself again she almost assailed the Doctor with angry questions as to what he meant by putting such horrible ideas into the poor young man's mind. "He has quite enough there already to upset him," she added. Dr. Thornhill replied:

"My dear madam, I had a distinct purpose in it! I wanted to draw his attention to the bell rope, and to fix it there. It may be that he is in a highly overwrought state, and has been studying too much, although I am bound to say that he seems as sound and healthy a young man, mentally and bodily, as ever I saw—but then the rats—and that suggestion of the devil." The doctor shook his head and went on. "I would have offered to go and stay the first night with him but that I felt sure it would have been a cause of offence. He may get in the night some strange fright or hallucination, and if he does I want him to pull that rope. All alone as he is it will give us warning, and we may reach him in time to be of service. I shall be sitting up pretty late tonight and shall keep my ears open. Do not be alarmed if Benchurch gets a surprise before morning."

"Oh, Doctor, what do you mean? What do you mean?"

"I mean this; that possibly—nay, more probably—we shall hear the great alarm bell from the Judge's House tonight," and the Doctor made about as effective an exit as could be thought of.

When Malcolmson arrived home he found that it was a little after his usual time, and Mrs. Dempster had gone away—the rules of Greenhow's Charity were not to be neglected. He was glad to see that the place was bright and tidy with a cheerful fire and a well-trimmed lamp. The evening was colder than might have been expected in April, and a heavy wind was blowing with such rapidly-increasing strength that there was every promise of a storm during the night. For a few minutes after his entrance the noise of the rats ceased; but so soon as they became accustomed to his presence they began again. He was glad to hear them, for he felt once more the feeling of companionship in their noise, and his mind ran back to the strange fact that they only ceased to manifest themselves when that other—the great rat with the baleful eyes—came upon the scene. The reading-lamp only was lit and its green shade kept the ceiling and the upper part of the room in darkness, so that the cheerful light from the hearth spreading over the floor and shining on the white cloth laid over the end of the table was warm and cheery. Malcolmson sat down to his dinner with a good appetite and a buoyant spirit. After his dinner and a cigarette he sat steadily down to work, determined not to let anything disturb him, for he remembered his promise to the doctor, and made up his mind to make the best of the time at his disposal.

For an hour or so he worked all right, and then his thoughts began to wander from his books. The actual circumstances around him, the calls on his physical attention, and his nervous susceptibility were not to be denied. By this time the wind had become a gale, and the gale a storm. The old house, solid though it was, seemed to shake to its foundations, and the storm roared and raged through its many chimneys and its queer old gables, producing strange, unearthly sounds in the empty rooms and corridors. Even the great alarm bell on the roof must have felt the force of the wind, for the rope rose and fell slightly, as though the bell were moved a little from time to time and the limber rope fell on the oak floor with a hard and hollow sound.

As Malcolmson listened to it he bethought himself of the doctor's words, "It is the rope which the hangman used for the victims of the Judge's judicial rancour," and he went over to the corner of the fireplace and took it in his hand to look at it. There seemed a sort of deadly interest in it, and as he stood there he lost himself for a moment in speculation as to who these victims were, and the grim wish of the Judge to have such a ghastly relic ever under his eyes. As he stood there the swaying of the bell on the roof still lifted the rope now and again; but presently there came a new sensation—a sort of tremor in the rope, as though something was moving along it.

Looking up instinctively Malcolmson saw the great rat coming slowly down towards him, glaring at him steadily. He dropped the rope and started back with a muttered curse, and the rat turning ran up the rope again and disappeared, and at the same instant Malcolmson became conscious that the noise of the rats, which had ceased for a while, began again.

All this set him thinking, and it occurred to him that he had not investigated the lair of the rat or looked at the pictures, as he had intended. He lit the other lamp without the shade, and, holding it up went and stood opposite the third picture from the fireplace on the right-hand side where he had seen the rat disappear on the previous night.

At the first glance he started back so suddenly that he almost dropped the lamp, and a deadly pallor overspread his face. His knees shook, and heavy drops of sweat came on his forehead, and he trembled like an aspen. But he was young and plucky, and pulled himself together, and after the pause of a few seconds stepped forward again, raised the lamp, and examined the picture which had been dusted and washed, and now stood out clearly.

It was of a judge dressed in his robes of scarlet and ermine. His face was strong and merciless, evil, crafty, and vindictive, with a sensual mouth, hooked nose of ruddy colour, and shaped like the beak of a bird of prey. The rest of the face was of a cadaverous colour. The eyes were of peculiar brilliance and with a terribly malignant expression. As he looked at them, Malcolmson grew cold, for he saw there the very counterpart of the eyes of the great rat. The lamp almost fell from his hand, he saw the rat with its baleful eyes peering out through the hole in the corner of the picture, and noted the sudden cessation of the noise of the other rats. However, he pulled himself together, and went on with his examination of the picture.

The Judge was seated in a great high-backed carved oak chair, on the right-hand side of a great stone fireplace where, in the corner, a rope hung down from the ceiling, its end lying coiled on the floor. With a feeling of something like horror, Malcolmson recognised the scene of the room as it stood, and gazed around him in an awestruck manner as though he expected to find some strange presence behind him. Then he looked over to the corner of the fireplace—and with a loud cry he let the lamp fall from his hand.

There, in the Judge's arm-chair, with the rope hanging behind, sat the rat with the Judge's baleful eyes, now intensified and with a fiendish leer. Save for the howling of the storm without there was silence.

The fallen lamp recalled Malcolmson to himself. Fortunately it was of metal, and so the oil was not spilt. However, the practical need of attending to it settled at once his nervous apprehensions. When he had turned it out, he wiped his brow and thought for a moment.

"This will not do," he said to himself. "If I go on like this I shall become a crazy fool. This must stop! I promised the doctor I would not take tea. Faith, he was pretty right! My nerves must have been getting into a queer state. Funny I did not notice it. I never felt better in my life. However, it is all right now, and I shall not be such a fool again."

Then he mixed himself a good stiff glass of brandy and water and resolutely sat down to his work.

It was nearly an hour when he looked up from his book, disturbed by the sudden stillness. Without, the wind howled and roared louder than ever, and the rain drove in sheets against the windows, beating like hail on the glass; but within there was no sound whatever save the echo of the wind as it roared in the great chimney, and now and then a hiss as a few raindrops found their way down the chimney in a lull of the storm. The fire had fallen low and had ceased to flame, though it threw out a red glow. Malcolmson listened attentively, and presently heard a thin, squeaking noise, very faint. It came from the corner of the room where the rope hung down, and he thought it was the creaking of the rope on the floor as the swaying of the bell raised and lowered it. Looking up, however, he saw in the dim light the great rat clinging to the rope and gnawing it. The rope was already nearly gnawed through—he could see the lighter colour where the strands were laid bare. As he looked the job was completed, and the severed end of the rope fell clattering on the oaken floor, whilst for an instant the great rat remained like a knob or tassel at the end of the rope, which now began to sway to and fro. Malcolmson felt for a moment another pang of terror as he thought that now the possibility of calling the outer world to his assistance was cut off, but an intense anger took its place, and seizing the book he was reading he hurled it at the rat. The blow was well aimed, but before the missile could reach him the rat dropped off and struck the floor with a soft thud. Malcolmson instantly rushed over towards him, but it darted away and disappeared in the darkness of the shadows of the room. Malcolmson felt that his work was over for the night, and determined then and there to vary the monotony of the proceedings by a hunt for the rat, and took off the green shade of the lamp so as to insure a wider spreading light. As he did so the gloom of the upper part of the room was relieved, and in the new flood of light, great by comparison with the previous darkness, the pictures on the wall stood out boldly. From where he stood, Malcolmson saw right opposite to him the third picture on the wall from the right of the fireplace. He rubbed his eyes in surprise, and then a great fear began to come upon him.

In the centre of the picture was a great irregular patch of brown canvas, as fresh as when it was stretched on the frame. The background was as before, with chair and chimney-corner and rope, but the figure of the Judge had disappeared.

Malcolmson, almost in a chill of horror, turned slowly round, and then he began to shake and tremble like a man in a palsy. His strength seemed to have left him, and he was incapable of action or movement, hardly even of thought. He could only see and hear.

There, on the great high-backed carved oak chair sat the Judge in his robes of scarlet and ermine, with his baleful eyes glaring vindictively, and a smile of triumph on the resolute, cruel mouth, as he lifted with his hands a *black cap*. Malcolmson felt as if the blood was running from his heart, as one does in moments of prolonged suspense. There was a singing in his ears. Without, he could hear the roar and howl of the tempest, and through it, swept on the storm, came the striking of midnight by the great chimes in the market place. He stood for a space of time that seemed to him endless still as a statue, and with wide-open, horror-struck eyes, breathless. As the clock struck, so the smile of triumph on the Judge's face intensified, and at the last stroke of midnight he placed the black cap on his head.

Slowly and deliberately the Judge rose from his chair and picked up the piece of the rope of the alarm bell which lay on the floor, drew it through his hands as if he enjoyed its touch, and then deliberately began to knot one end of it, fashioning it into a noose. This he tightened and tested with his foot, pulling hard at it till he was satisfied and then making a running noose of it, which he held in his hand. Then he began to move along the table on the opposite side to Malcolmson keeping his eyes on him until he had passed him, when with a quick movement he stood in front of the door. Malcolmson then began to feel that he was trapped, and tried to think of what he should do. There was some fascination in the Judge's eyes, which he never took off him, and he had, perforce, to look. He saw the Judge approach—still keeping between him and the door—and raise the noose and throw it towards him as if to entangle him. With a great effort he made a quick movement to one side, and saw the rope fall beside him, and heard it strike the oaken floor. Again the Judge raised the noose and tried to ensnare him, ever keeping his baleful eyes fixed on him, and each time by a mighty effort the student just managed to evade it. So this went on for many times, the Judge seeming never discouraged nor discomposed at failure, but playing as a cat does with a mouse. At last in despair, which had reached its climax, Malcolmson cast a quick glance round him. The lamp seemed to have blazed up, and there was a fairly good light in the room. At the many rat-holes and in the chinks and crannies of the wainscot he saw the rats' eyes; and this aspect, that was purely physical, gave him a gleam of comfort. He looked around and saw that the rope of the great alarm bell was laden with rats. Every inch of it was covered with them, and more and more were pouring through the small circular hole in the ceiling whence it emerged, so that with their weight the bell was beginning to sway.

Hark! it had swayed till the clapper had touched the bell. The sound was but a tiny one, but the bell was only beginning to sway, and it would increase.

At the sound the Judge, who had been keeping his eyes fixed on Malcolmson, looked up, and a scowl of diabolical anger overspread his face. His eyes fairly glowed like hot coals, and he stamped his foot with a sound that seemed to make the house shake. A dreadful peal of thunder broke overhead as he raised the rope again, whilst the rats kept running up and down the rope as though working against time. This time, instead of throwing it, he drew close to his victim, and held open the noose as he approached. As he came closer there seemed something paralysing in his very presence, and Malcolmson stood rigid as a corpse. He felt the Judge's icy fingers touch his throat as he adjusted the rope. The noose tightened—tightened. Then the Judge, taking the rigid form of the student in his arms, carried him over and placed him standing in the oak chair, and stepping up beside him, put his hand up and caught the end of the swaying rope of the alarm bell. As he raised his hand the rats fled squeaking, and disappeared through the hole in the ceiling. Taking the end of the noose which was round Malcolmson's neck he tied it to the hanging-bell rope, and then descending pulled away the chair.

When the alarm bell of the Judge's House began to sound a crowd soon assembled. Lights and torches of various kinds appeared, and soon a silent crowd was hurrying to the spot. They knocked loudly at the door, but there was no reply. Then they burst in the door, and poured into the great dining-room, the doctor at the head.

There at the end of the rope of the great alarm bell hung the body of the student, and on the face of the Judge in the picture was a malignant smile.

The Crystal Cup

by Bram Stoker

I. THE DREAM-BIRTH

The blue waters touch the walls of the palace; I can hear their soft, lapping wash against the marble whenever I listen. Far out at sea I can see the waves glancing in the sunlight, ever-smiling, ever-glancing, ever-sunny. Happy waves! Happy in your gladness, thrice happy that ye are free!

I rise from my work and spring up the wall till I reach the embrasure. I grasp the corner of the stonework and draw myself up till I crouch in the wide window. Sea, sea, out away as far as my vision extends. There I gaze till my eyes grow dim; and in the dimness of my eyes my spirit finds its sight. My soul flies on the wings of memory away beyond the blue, smiling sea-away beyond the glancing waves and the gleaming sails, to the land I call my home. As the minutes roll by, my actual eyesight seems to be restored, and I look round me in my old birth-house. The rude simplicity of the dwelling comes back to me as something new. There I see my old books and manuscripts and pictures, and there, away on their old shelves, high up above the door, I see my first rude efforts in art.

How poor they seem to me now! And yet, were I free, I would not give the smallest of them for all I now possess. Possess? How I dream.

The dream calls me back to waking life. I spring down from my window-seat and work away frantically, for every line I draw on paper, every new form that springs on the plaster, brings me nearer freedom. I will make a vase whose beauty will put to shame the glorious works of Greece in her golden prime! Surely a love like mine and a hope like mine must in time make some form of beauty spring to life! When He beholds it he will exclaim with rapture, and will order my instant freedom. I can forget my hate, and the deep debt of revenge which I owe him when I think of liberty—even from his hands. Ah! then on the wings of the morning shall I fly beyond the sea to my home-her home-and clasp her to my arms, never more to be separated!

But, oh Spirit of Day! if she should be—No, no, I cannot think of it, or I shall go mad. Oh Time, Time! maker and destroyer of men's fortunes, why hasten so fast for others whilst thou laggest so slowly for me? Even now my home may have become desolate, and she—my bride of an hour—may sleep calmly in the cold earth. Oh this suspense will drive me mad! Work, work! Freedom is before me; Aurora is the reward of my labour!

So I rush to my work; but to my brain and hand, heated alike, no fire or no strength descends. Half mad with despair, I beat myself against the walls of my prison, and then climb into the embrasure, and once more gaze upon the ocean, but find there no hope. And so I stay till night, casting its pall of blackness over nature, puts the possibility of effort away from me for yet another day.

So my days go on, and grow to weeks and months. So will they grow to years, should life so long remain an unwelcome guest within me; for what is man without hope? And is not hope nigh dead within this weary breast?

Last night, in my dreams, there came, like an inspiration from the Day-Spirit, a design for my vase.

All day my yearning for freedom—for Aurora, or news of her—had increased tenfold, and my heart and brain were on fire. Madly I beat myself, like a caged bird, against my prison-bars. Madly I leaped to my window-seat, and gazed with bursting eyeballs out on the free, open sea. And there I sat till my passion had worn itself out; and then I slept, and dreamed of thee, Aurora—of thee and freedom. In my ears I heard again the old song we used to sing together, when as children we wandered on the beach; when, as lovers, we saw the sun sink in the ocean, and I would see its glory doubled as it shone in thine eyes, and was mellowed against thy cheek; and when, as my bride, you clung to me as my arms went round you on that desert tongue of land whence rushed that band of sea-robbers that tore me away. Oh! how my heart curses those men-not men, but fiends! But one solitary gleam of joy remains from that dread encounter, that my struggle stayed those hell-hounds, and that, ere I was stricken down, this right hand sent one of them to his home. My spirit rises as I think of that blow that saved thee from a life worse than death. With the thought I feel my cheeks burning, and my forehead swelling with mighty veins. My eyes burn, and I rush wildly round my prison-house, "Oh! for one of my enemies, that I might dash out his brains against these marble walls, and trample his heart out as he lay before me!" These walls would spare him not. They are pitiless, alas! I know too well. "Oh, cruel mockery of kindness, to make a palace a prison, and to taunt a captive's aching heart with forms of beauty and sculptured marble!" Wondrous, indeed, are these sculptured walls! Men call them passing fair; but oh, Aurora! with thy beauty ever before my eyes, what form that men call lovely can be fair to me? Like him who gazes sun-wards, and then sees no light on earth, from the glory that dyeshis iris, so thy beauty or its memory has turned the fairest thingsof earth to blackness and deformity.

In my dream last night, when in my ears came softly, like music stealing across the waters from afar, the old song we used to sing together, then to my brain, like a ray of light, came an idea whose grandeur for a moment struck me dumb. Before my eyes grew a vase of such beauty that I knew my hope was born to life, and that the Great Spirit had placed my foot on the ladder that leads from this my palace-dungeon to freedom and to thee. Today I have got a block of crystal—for only in such pellucid substance can I body forth my dream—and have commenced my work.

I found at first that my hand had lost its cunning, and I was beginning to despair, when, like the memory of a dream, there came back in my ears the strains of the old song. I sang it softly to myself, and as I did so I grew calmer; but oh! how differently thesong sounded to me when thy voice, Aurora, rose not in unison with my own! But what avails pining? To work! To work! Every touch of my chisel will bring me nearer thee.

My vase is daily growing nearer to completion. I sing as I work, and my constant song is the one I love so well. I can hear the echo of my voice in the vase; and as I end, the wailing song note is prolonged in sweet, sad music in the crystal cup. I listen, ear down, and sometimes I weep as I listen, so sadly comes the echo to my song. Imperfect though it be, my voice makes sweet music, and its echo in the cup guides my hand towards perfection as I work. Would that thy voice rose and fell with mine, Aurora, and then the world would behold a vase of such beauty as never before woke up the slumbering fires of mans love for what is fair; for if I do such work in sadness, imperfect as I am in my solitude and sorrow, what would I do in joy, perfect when with thee? I know that my work is good as an artist, and I feel that it is as a man; and the cup itself, as it daily grows in beauty, gives back a clearer echo. Oh! if I worked in joy how gladly would it give back our voices! Then would we hear an echo and music such as mortals seldom hear; but now the echo, like my song, seems imperfect. I grow daily weaker; but still I work on—work with my whole soul—for am I not working for freedom and for thee?

My work is nearly done. Day by day, hour by hour, the vase grows more finished. Ever clearer comes the echo whilst I sing; ever softer, ever more sad and heart-rending comes the echo of the wail at the end of the song. Day by day I grow weaker and weaker; still I work on with all my soul. At night the thought comes to me, whilst I think of thee, that I will never see thee more—that I breathe out my life into the crystal cup, and that it will last there when I am gone.

So beautiful has it become, so much do I love it, that I could gladly die to be maker of such a work, were it not for thee—for my love for thee, and my hope of thee, and my fear for thee, and my anguish for thy grief when thou knowest I am gone.

My work requires but few more touches. My life is slowly ebbing away, and I feel that with my last touch my life will pass out for ever into the cup. Till that touch is given I must not die—I will not die. My hate has passed away. So great are my wrongs that revenge of mine would be too small a compensation for my woe. I leave revenge to a juster and a mightier than I. Thee, oh Aurora, I will await in the land of flowers, where thou and I will wander, never more to part, never more! Ah, never more! Farewell, Aurora-Aurora-Aurora!

II. THE FEAST OF BEAUTY

The Feast of Beauty approaches rapidly, yet hardly so fast as my royal master wishes. He seems to have no other thought than to have this feast greater and better than any ever held before. Five summers ago his Feast of Beauty was nobler than all held in his sires reign together; yet scarcely was it over, and the rewards given to the victors, when he conceived the giant project whose success is to be tested when the moon reaches her full. It was boldly chosen and boldly done; chosen and done as boldly as the project of a monarch should be. But still I cannot think that it will end well. This yearning after completeness must be unsatisfied in the end—this desire that makes a monarch fling his kingly justice to the winds, and strive to reach his Mecca over a desert of blighted hopes and lost lives. But hush! I must not dare to think ill of my master or his deeds; and besides, walls have ears. I must leave alone these dangerous topics, and confine my thoughts within proper bounds.

The moon is waxing quickly, and with its fulness comes the Feast of Beauty, whose success as a whole rests almost solely on my watchfulness and care; for if the ruler of the feast should fail in his duty, who could fill the void? Let me see what arts are represented, and what works compete. All the arts will have trophies: poetry in its various forms, and prose-writing; sculpture with carving in various metals, and glass, and wood, and ivory, and engraving gems, and setting jewels; painting on canvas, and glass, and wood, and stone and metal; music, vocal and instrumental; and dancing. If that woman will but sing, we will have a real triumph of music; but she appears sickly too. All our best artists either get ill or die, although we promise them freedom or rewards or both if they succeed.

Surely never yet was a Feast of Beauty so fair or so richly dowered as this which the full moon shall behold and hear; but ah! the crowning glory of the feast will be the crystal cup. Never yet have these eyes beheld such a form of beauty, such a wondrous mingling of substance and light. Surely some magic power must have helped to draw such loveliness from a cold block of crystal. I must be careful that no harm happens the vase. Today when I touched it, it gave forth such a ringing sound that my heart jumped with fear lest it should sustain any injury. Henceforth, till I deliver it up to my master, no hand but my own shall touch it lest any harm should happen to it.

Strange story has that cup. Born to life in the cell of a captive torn from his artist home beyond the sea, to enhance the splendour of a feast by his labour-seen at work by spies, and traced and followed till a chance-cruel chance for him-gave him into the hands of the emissaries of my master. He too, poor moth, fluttered about the flame: the name of freedom spurred him on to exertion till he wore away his life. The beauty of that cup was dearly bought for him. Many a man would forget his captivity whilst he worked at such a piece of loveliness;

but he appeared to have some sorrow at his heart, some sorrow so great that it quenched his pride.

How he used to rave at first! How he used to rush about his chamber, and then climb into the embrasure of his window, and gaze out away over the sea! Poor captive! perhaps over the sea some one waited for his coming who was dearer to him than many cups, even many cups as beautiful as this, if such could be on earth . . . Well, well, we must all die soon or late, and who dies first escapes the more sorrow, perhaps, who knows? How, when he had commenced the cup, he used to sing all day long, from the moment the sun shot its first fiery arrow into the retreating hosts of night-clouds, till the shades of evening advancing drove the lingering sunbeams into the west-and always the same song!

How he used to sing, all alone! Yet sometimes I could almost imagine I heard not one voice from his chamber, but two . . . No more will it echo again from the wall of a dungeon, or from a hillside in free air. No more will his eyes behold the beauty of his crystal cup.

It was well he lived to finish it. Often and often have I trembled to think of his death, as I saw him day by day grow weaker as he worked at the unfinished vase. Must his eyes never more behold the beauty that was born of his soul? Oh, never more! Oh Death, grim King of Terrors, how mighty is thy sceptre! All-powerful is the wave of thy hand that summons us in turn to thy kingdom away beyond the poles!

Would that thou, poor captive, hadst lived to behold thy triumph, for victory will be thine at the Feast of Beauty such as man never before achieved. Then thou mightst have heard the shout that hails the victor in the contest, and the plaudits that greet him as he passes out, a free man, through the palace gates. But now thy cup will come to light amid the smiles of beauty and rank and power, whilst thou liest there in thy lonely chamber, cold as the marble of its walls.

And, after all, the feast will be imperfect, since the victors cannot all be crowned. I must ask my master's direction as to how a blank place of a competitor, should he prove a victor, is to be filled up. So late? I must see him ere the noontide hour of rest be past.

Great Spirit! how I trembled as my master answered my question!

I found him in his chamber, as usual in the noontide. He was lying on his couch disrobed, half-sleeping; and the drowsy zephyr, scented with rich odours from the garden, wafted through the windows at either side by the fans, lulled him to complete repose. The darkened chamber was cool and silent. From the vestibule came the murmuring of many fountains, and the pleasant splash of falling waters. "Oh, happy," said I, in my heart, "oh, happy great King, that has such pleasures to enjoy!" The breeze from the fans swept over the strings of the Aeolian harps, and a sweet, confused, happy melody arose like the murmuring of children's voices singing afar off in the valleys, and floating on the wind.

As I entered the chamber softly, with muffled foot-fall and pent-in breath, I felt a kind of awe stealing over me. To me who was born and have dwelt all my life within the precincts of the court—to me who talk daily with my royal master, and take his minutest directions as to the coming feast—to me who had all my life looked up to my king as to a spirit, and had venerated him as more than mortal—came a feeling of almost horror; for my master looked then, in his quiet chamber, half-sleeping amid the drowsy music of the harps and fountains, more like a common man than a God. As the thought came to me I shuddered in affright, for it seemed to me that I had been guilty of sacrilege. So much had my veneration for my royal master become a part of my nature, that but to think of him as another man seemed like the anarchy of my own soul.

I came beside the couch, and watched him in silence. He seemed to be half-listening to the fitful music; and as the melody swelled and died away his chest rose and fell as he breathed in unison with the sound.

After a moment or two he appeared to become conscious of the presence of some one in the room, although by no motion of his face could I see that he heard any sound, and his eyes were shut. He opened his eyes, and, seeing me, asked, "Was all right about the Feast of Beauty?" for that is the subject ever nearest to his thoughts. I answered that all was well, but that I had come to ask his royal pleasure as to how a vacant place amongst the competitors was to be filled up. He asked, "How vacant?" and on my telling him, "from death," he asked again, quickly, "Was the work finished?" When I told him that it was, he lay back again on his couch with a sigh of relief, for he had half arisen in his anxiety as he asked the question. Then he said, after a minute, "All the competitors must be present at the feast." "All?" said I. "All," he answered again, "alive or dead; for the old custom must be preserved, and the victors crowned." He stayed still for a minute more, and then said, slowly, "Victors or martyrs." And I could see that the kingly spirit was coming back to him.

Again he went on. "This will be my last Feast of Beauty; and all the captives shall be set free. Too much sorrow has sprung already from my ambition. Too much injustice has soiled the name of king."

He said no more, but lay still and closed his eyes. I could see by the working of his hands and the heaving of his chest that some violent emotion troubled him, and the thought arose, "He is a man, but he is yet a king; and, though a king as he is, still happiness is not for him. Great Spirit of Justice! thou metest out his pleasures and his woes to man, to king and slave alike! Thou lovest best to whom thou givest peace!"

Gradually my master grew more calm, and at length sunk into a gentle slumber; but even in his sleep he breathed in unison with the swelling murmur of the harps.

"To each is given," said I gently, "something in common with the world of actual things. Thy life, oh King, is bound by chains of sympathy to the voice of Truth, which is Music! Tremble, lest in the presence of a master-strain thou shouldst feel thy littleness, and die!" and I softly left the room.

III. THE STORY OF THE MOONBEAM

Slowly I creep along the bosom of the waters.

Sometimes I look back as I rise upon a billow, and see behind me many of my kin sitting each upon a wave-summit as upon a throne. So I go on for long, a power that I wist not forcing me onward, without will or purpose of mine.

At length, as I rise upon a mimic wave, I see afar a hazy lightthat springs from a vast palace, through whose countless windowsflame lamps and torches. But at the first view, as if my coming had been the signal, the lights disappear in an instant.

Impatiently I await what may happen; and as I rise with each heart-beat of the sea, I look forward to where the torches had gleamed. Can it be a deed of darkness that shuns the light?

The time has come when I can behold the palace without waiting to mount upon the waves. It is built of white marble, and rises steep from the brine. Its sea-front is glorious with columns and statues; and from the portals the marble steps sweep down, broad and wide to the waters, and below them, down as deep as I can see.

No sound is heard, no light is seen. A solemn silence abounds, a perfect calm.

Slowly I climb the palace walls, my brethren following as soldiers up a breach. I slide along the roofs, and as I look behind me walls and roofs are glistening as with silver. At length I meet with something smooth and hard and translucent; but through it I pass and enter a vast hall, where for an instant I hang in mid-air and wonder.

My coming has been the signal for such a burst of harmony as brings back to my memory the music of the spheres as they rush through space; and in the full-swelling anthem of welcome I feel that I am indeed a sun-spirit, a child of light, and that this is homage to my master.

I look upon the face of a great monarch, who sits at the head of a banquet-table. He has turned his head upwards and backwards, and looks as if he had been awaiting my approach. He rises and fronts me with the ringing out of the welcome-song, and all the others in the great hall turn towards me as well. I can see their eyes gleaming. Down along the immense table, laden with plate and glass and flowers, they stand holding each a cup of ruby wine, with which they pledge the monarch when the song is ended, as they drink success to him and to the 'Feast of Beauty.'

I survey the hall. An immense chamber, with marble walls covered with bas-reliefs and frescoes and sculptured figures, and panelled by great columns that rise along the surface and support a dome-ceiling painted wondrously; in its centre the glass lantern by which I entered.

On the walls are hung pictures of various forms and sizes, and down the centre of the table stretches a raised platform on which are placed works of art of various kinds.

At one side of the hall is a dais on which sit persons of both sexes with noble faces and lordly brows, but all wearing the same expression—care tempered by hope. All these hold scrolls in their hands.

At the other side of the hall is a similar dais, on which sit others fairer to earthly view, less spiritual and more marked by surface-passion. They hold music-scores. All these look more joyous than those on the other platform, all save one, a woman, who sits with downcast face and dejected mien, as of one without hope. As my light falls at her feet she looks up, and I feel happy. The sympathy between us has called a faint gleam of hope to cheer that poor pale face.

Many are the forms of art that rise above the banquet-table, and all are lovely to behold. I look on all with pleasure one by one, till I see the last of them at the end of the table away from the monarch, and then all the others seem as nothing to me. What is this that makes other forms of beauty seem as nought when compared with it, when brought within the radius of its lustre? A crystal cup, wrought with such wondrous skill that light seems to lose its individual glory as it shines upon it and is merged in its beauty. "Oh Universal Mother, let me enter there. Let my life be merged in its beauty, and no more will I regret my sun-strength hidden deep in the chasms of my moon-mother. Let me live there and perish there, and I will be joyous whilst it lasts, and content to pass into the great vortex of nothingness to be born again when the glory of the cup has fled."

Can it be that my wish is granted, that I have entered the cup and become a part of its beauty? "Great Mother, I thank thee."

Has the cup life? or is it merely its wondrous perfectness that makes it tremble, like a beating heart, in unison with the ebb and flow, the great wave-pulse of nature? To me it feels as if it had life.

I look through the crystal walls and see at the end of the table, isolated from all others, the figure of a man seated. Are those cords that bind his limbs? How suits that crown of laurel those wide, dim eyes, and that pallid hue? It is passing strange. This Feast of Beauty holds some dread secrets, and sees some wondrous sights.

I hear a voice of strange, rich sweetness, yet wavering-the voice of one almost a king by nature. He is standing up; I see him through my palace-wall. He calls a name and sits down again.

Again I hear a voice from the platform of scrolls, the Throne of Brows; and again I look and behold a man who stands trembling yet flushed, as though the morning light shone bright upon his soul. He reads in cadenced measure a song in praise of my moon-mother, the Feast of Beauty, and the king. As he speaks, he trembles no more, but seems inspired, and his voice rises to a tone of power and grandeur, and rings back from walls and dome. I hear his words distinctly, though saddened in tone, in the echo from my crystal home. He concludes and sits down, half-fainting, amid a whirlwind of applause, every note, every beat of which is echoed as the words had been.

Again the monarch rises and calls "Aurora," that she may sing for freedom. The name echoes in the cup with a sweet, sad sound. So sad, so despairing seems the echo, that the hall seems to darken and the scene to grow dim.

"Can a sun-spirit mourn, or a crystal vessel weep?"

She, the dejected one, rises from her seat on the Throne of Sound, and all eyes turn upon her save those of the pale one, laurel-crowned. Thrice she essays to begin, and thrice noughtcomes from her lips but a dry, husky sigh, till an old man who has been moving round the hall settling all things, cries out, in fear lest she should fail, "Freedom!"

The word is re-echoed from the cup. She hears the sound, turns towards it and begins.

Oh, the melody of that voice! And yet it is not perfect alone; for after the first note comes an echo from the cup that swells in unison with the voice, and the two sounds together, seem as if one strain came ringing sweet from the lips of the All-Father himself. So sweet it is, that all throughout the hall sit spell-bound, and scarcely dare to breathe.

In the pause after the first verses of the song, I hear the voice of the old man speaking to a comrade, but his words are unheard by any other, "Look at the king. His spirit seems lost in a trance of melody. Ah! I fear me some evil: the nearer the music approaches to perfection the more rapt he becomes. I dread lest a perfect note shall prove his death-call." His voice dies away as the singer commences the last verse.

Sad and plaintive is the song; full of feeling and tender love, but love over-shadowed by grief and despair. As it goes on the voice of the singer grows sweeter and more thrilling, more real; and the cup, my crystal time-home, vibrates more and more as it gives back the echo. The monarch looks like one entranced, and no movement is within the hall . . . The song dies away in a wild wail that seems to tear the heart of the singer in twain; and the cup vibrates still more as it gives back the echo. As the note, long-swelling, reaches its highest, the cup, the Crystal Cup, my wondrous home, the gift of the All-Father, shivers into millions of atoms, and passes away.

Ere I am lost in the great vortex I see the singer throw up her arms and fall, freed at last, and the King sitting, glory-faced, but pallid with the hue of Death.

The Room in the Tower

by E. F. Benson

It is probable that everybody who is at all a constant dreamer has had at least one experience of an event or a sequence of circumstances which have come to his mind in sleep being subsequently realized in the material world. But, in my opinion, so far from this being a strange thing, it would be far odder if this fulfilment did not occasionally happen, since our dreams are, as a rule, concerned with people whom we know and places with which we are familiar, such as might very naturally occur in the awake and daylit world. True, these dreams are often broken into by some absurd and fantastic incident, which puts them out of court in regard to their subsequent fulfilment, but on the mere calculation of chances, it does not appear in the least unlikely that a dream imagined by anyone who dreams constantly should occasionally come true. Not long ago, for instance, I experienced such a fulfilment of a dream which seems to me in no way remarkable and to have no kind of psychical significance. The manner of it was as follows.

A certain friend of mine, living abroad, is amiable enough to write to me about once in a fortnight. Thus, when fourteen days or thereabouts have elapsed since I last heard from him, my mind, probably, either consciously or subconsciously, is expectant of a letter from him. One night last week I dreamed that as I was going upstairs to dress for dinner I heard, as I often heard, the sound of the postman's knock on my front door, and diverted my direction downstairs instead. There, among other correspondence, was a letter from him. Thereafter the fantastic entered, for on opening it I found inside the ace of diamonds, and scribbled across it in his well-known handwriting, "I am sending you this for safe custody, as you know it is running an unreasonable risk to keep aces in Italy." The next evening I was just preparing to go upstairs to dress when I heard the postman's knock, and did precisely as I had done in my dream. There, among other letters, was one from my friend. Only it did not contain the ace of diamonds. Had it done so, I should have attached more weight to the matter, which, as it stands, seems to me a perfectly ordinary coincidence. No doubt I consciously or subconsciously expected a letter from him, and this suggested to me my dream. Similarly, the fact that my friend had not written to me for a fortnight suggested to him that he should do so. But occasionally it is not so easy to find such an explanation, and for the following story I can find no explanation at all. It came out of the dark, and into the dark it has gone again.

All my life I have been a habitual dreamer: the nights are few, that is to say, when I do not find on awaking in the morning that some mental experience has been mine, and sometimes, all night long, apparently, a series of the most dazzling adventures befall me. Almost without exception these adventures are pleasant, though often merely trivial. It is of an exception that I am going to speak.

It was when I was about sixteen that a certain dream first came to me, and this is how it befell. It opened with my being set down at the door of a big red-brick house, where, I understood, I was going to stay. The servant who opened the door told me that tea was being served in the garden, and led me through a low dark-panelled hall, with a large open fireplace, on to a cheerful green lawn set round with flower beds. There were grouped about the tea-table a small party of people, but they were all strangers to me except one, who was a schoolfellow called Jack Stone, clearly the son of the house, and he introduced me to his mother and father and a couple of sisters. I was, I remember, somewhat astonished to find myself here, for the boy in question was scarcely known to me, and I rather disliked what I knew of him; moreover, he had left school nearly a year before. The afternoon was very hot, and an intolerable oppression reigned. On the far side of the lawn ran a red-brick wall, with an iron gate in its center, outside which stood a walnut tree. We sat in the shadow of the house opposite a row of long windows, inside which I could see a table with cloth laid, glimmering with glass and silver. This garden front of the house was very long, and at one end of it stood a tower of three stories, which looked to me much older than the rest of the building.

Before long, Mrs. Stone, who, like the rest of the party, had sat in absolute silence, said to me, "Jack will show you your room: I have given you the room in the tower."

Quite inexplicably my heart sank at her words. I felt as if I had known that I should have the room in the tower, and that it contained something dreadful and significant. Jack instantly got up, and I understood that I had to follow him. In silence we passed through the hall, and mounted a great oak staircase with many corners, and arrived at a small landing with two doors set in it. He pushed one of these open for me to enter, and without coming in himself, closed it after me. Then I knew that my conjecture had been right: there was something awful in the room, and with the terror of nightmare growing swiftly and enveloping me, I awoke in a spasm of terror.

Now that dream or variations on it occurred to me intermittently for fifteen years. Most often it came in exactly this form, the arrival, the tea laid out on the lawn, the deadly silence succeeded by that one deadly sentence, the mounting with Jack Stone up to the room in the tower where horror dwelt, and it always came to a close in the nightmare of terror at that which was in the room, though I never saw what it was. At other times I experienced variations on this same theme. Occasionally, for instance, we would be sitting at dinner in the dining-room, into the windows of which I had looked on the first night when the dream of this house visited me, but wherever we were, there was the same silence, the same sense of dreadful oppression and foreboding. And the silence I knew would always be broken by Mrs. Stone saying to me, "Jack will show you your room: I have given you the room in the tower." Upon which (this was invariable) I had to follow him up the oak staircase with many corners, and enter the place that I dreaded more and more each time that I visited it in sleep. Or, again, I would find myself playing cards still in silence in a drawing-room lit with immense chandeliers, that gave a blinding illumination. What the game was I have no idea; what I remember, with a sense of miserable anticipation, was that soon Mrs. Stone would get up and say to me, "Jack will show you your room: I have given you the room in the tower." This drawing-room where we played cards was next to the dining-room, and, as I have said, was always brilliantly illuminated, whereas the rest of the house was full of dusk and shadows. And yet, how often, in spite of those bouquets of lights, have I not pored over the cards that were dealt me, scarcely able for some reason to see them. Their designs, too, were strange: there were no red suits, but all were black, and among them there were certain cards which were black all over. I hated and dreaded those.

As this dream continued to recur, I got to know the greater part of the house. There was a smoking-room beyond the drawing-room, at the end of a passage with a green baize door. It was always very dark there, and as often as I went there I passed somebody whom I could not see in the doorway coming out. Curious developments, too, took place in the characters that peopled the dream as might happen to living persons. Mrs. Stone, for instance, who, when I first saw her, had been black-haired, became grey, and instead of rising briskly, as she had done at first when she said, "Jack will show you your room: I have given you the room in the tower," got up very feebly, as if the strength was leaving her limbs. Jack also grew up, and became a rather ill-looking young man, with a brown moustache, while one of the sisters ceased to appear, and I understood she was married.

Then it so happened that I was not visited by this dream for six months or more, and I began to hope, in such inexplicable dread did I hold it, that it had passed away for good. But one night after this interval I again found myself being shown out onto the lawn for tea, and Mrs. Stone was not there, while the others were all dressed in black. At once I guessed the reason, and my heart leaped at the thought that perhaps this time I should not have to sleep in the room in the tower, and though we usually all sat in silence, on this occasion the sense of relief made me talk and laugh as I had never yet done. But even then matters were not altogether comfortable, for no one else spoke, but they all looked secretly at each other. And soon the foolish stream of my talk ran dry, and gradually an apprehension worse than anything I had previously known gained on me as the light slowly faded.

Suddenly a voice which I knew well broke the stillness, the voice of Mrs. Stone, saying, "Jack will show you your room: I have given you the room in the tower." It seemed to come from near the gate in the red-brick wall that bounded the lawn, and looking up, I saw that the grass outside was sown thick with gravestones. A curious greyish light shone from them, and I could read the lettering on the grave nearest me, and it was, "In evil memory of Julia Stone." And as usual Jack got up, and again I followed him through the hall and up the staircase with many corners. On this occasion it was darker than usual, and when I passed into the room in the tower I could only just see the furniture, the position of which was already familiar to me. Also there was a dreadful odour of decay in the room, and I woke screaming.

The dream, with such variations and developments as I have mentioned, went on at intervals for fifteen years. Sometimes I would dream it two or three nights in succession; once, as I have said, there was an intermission of six months, but taking a reasonable average, I should say that I dreamed it quite as often as once in a month. It had, as is plain, something of nightmare about it, since it always ended in the same appalling terror, which so far from getting less, seemed to me to gather fresh fear every time that I experienced it. There was, too, a strange and dreadful consistency about it. The characters in it, as I have mentioned, got regularly older, death and marriage visited this silent family, and I never in the dream, after Mrs. Stone had died, set eyes on her again. But it was always her voice that told me that the room in the tower was prepared for me, and whether we had tea out on the lawn, or the scene was laid in one of the rooms overlooking it, I could always see her gravestone standing just outside the iron gate. It was the same, too, with the married daughter; usually she was not present, but once or twice she returned again, in company with a man, whom I took to be her husband. He, too, like the rest of them, was always silent. But, owing to the constant repetition of the dream, I had ceased to attach, in my waking hours, any significance to it. I never met Jack Stone again during all those years, nor did I ever see a house that resembled this dark house of my dream. And then something happened.

I had been in London in this year, up till the end of the July, and during the first week in August went down to stay with a friend in a house he had taken for the summer months, in the Ashdown Forest district of Sussex. I left London early, for John Clinton was to meet me at Forest Row Station, and we were going to spend the day golfing, and go to his house in the evening. He had his motor with him, and we set off, about five of the afternoon, after a thoroughly delightful day, for the drive, the distance being some ten miles. As it was still so early we did not have tea at the club house, but waited till we should get home. As we drove, the weather, which up till then had been, though hot, deliciously fresh, seemed to me to alter in quality, and become very stagnant and oppressive, and I felt that indefinable sense of ominous apprehension that I am accustomed to before thunder. John, however, did not share my views, attributing my loss of lightness to the fact that I had lost both my matches. Events proved, however, that I was right, though I do not think that the thunderstorm that broke that night was the sole cause of my depression.

Our way lay through deep high-banked lanes, and before we had gone very far I fell asleep, and was only awakened by the stopping of the motor. And with a sudden thrill, partly of fear but chiefly of curiosity, I found myself standing in the doorway of my house of dream. We went, I half wondering whether or not I was dreaming still, through a low oak-panelled hall, and out onto the lawn, where tea was laid in the shadow of the house. It was set in flower beds, a red-brick wall, with a gate in it, bounded one side, and out beyond that was a space of rough grass with a walnut tree. The facade of the house was very long, and at one end stood a three-storied tower, markedly older than the rest.

Here for the moment all resemblance to the repeated dream ceased. There was no silent and somehow terrible family, but a large assembly of exceedingly cheerful persons, all of whom were known to me. And in spite of the horror with which the dream itself had always filled me, I felt nothing of it now that the scene of it was thus reproduced before me. But I felt intensest curiosity as to what was going to happen.

Tea pursued its cheerful course, and before long Mrs. Clinton got up. And at that moment I think I knew what she was going to say. She spoke to me, and what she said was:

"Jack will show you your room: I have given you the room in the tower."

At that, for half a second, the horror of the dream took hold of me again. But it quickly passed, and again I felt nothing more than the most intense curiosity. It was not very long before it was amply satisfied.

John turned to me.

"Right up at the top of the house," he said, "but I think you'll be comfortable. We're absolutely full up. Would you like to go and see it now? By Jove, I believe that you are right, and that we are going to have a thunderstorm. How dark it has become."

I got up and followed him. We passed through the hall, and up the perfectly familiar staircase. Then he opened the door, and I went in. And at that moment sheer unreasoning terror again possessed me. I did not know what I feared: I simply feared. Then like a sudden recollection, when one remembers a name which has long escaped the memory, I knew what I feared. I feared Mrs. Stone, whose grave with the sinister inscription, "In evil memory," I had so often seen in my dream, just beyond the lawn which lay below my window. And then once more the fear passed so completely that I wondered what there was to fear, and I found myself, sober and quiet and sane, in the room in the tower, the name of which I had so often heard in my dream, and the scene of which was so familiar.

I looked around it with a certain sense of proprietorship, and found that nothing had been changed from the dreaming nights in which I knew it so well. Just to the left of the door was the bed, lengthways along the wall, with the head of it in the angle. In a line with it was the fireplace and a small bookcase; opposite the door the outer wall was pierced by two lattice-paned windows, between which stood the dressing-table, while ranged along the fourth wall was the washing-stand and a big cupboard. My luggage had already been unpacked, for the furniture of dressing and undressing lay orderly on the wash-stand and toilet-table, while my dinner clothes were spread out on the coverlet of the bed. And then, with a sudden start of unexplained dismay, I saw that there were two rather conspicuous objects which I had not seen before in my dreams: one a life-sized oil painting of Mrs. Stone, the other a black-and-white sketch of Jack Stone, representing him as he had appeared to me only a week before in the last of the series of these repeated dreams, a rather secret and evil-looking man of about thirty. His picture hung between the windows, looking straight across the room to the other portrait, which hung at the side of the bed. At that I looked next, and as I looked I felt once more the horror of nightmare seize me.

It represented Mrs. Stone as I had seen her last in my dreams: old and withered and white-haired. But in spite of the evident feebleness of body, a dreadful exuberance and vitality shone through the envelope of flesh, an exuberance wholly malign, a vitality that foamed and frothed with unimaginable evil. Evil beamed from the narrow, leering eyes; it laughed in the demon-like mouth. The whole face was instinct with some secret and appalling mirth; the hands, clasped together on the knee, seemed shaking with suppressed and nameless glee. Then I saw also that it was signed in the left-hand bottom corner, and wondering who the artist could be, I looked more closely, and read the inscription, 'Julia Stone by Julia Stone.'

There came a tap at the door, and John Clinton entered.

"Got everything you want?" he asked.

"Rather more than I want," said I, pointing to the picture.

He laughed.

"Hard-featured old lady," he said. "By herself, too, I remember. Anyhow she can't have flattered herself much."

"But don't you see?" said I. "It's scarcely a human face at all. It's the face of some witch, of some devil."

He looked at it more closely.

"Yes; it isn't very pleasant," he said. "Scarcely a bedside manner, eh? Yes; I can imagine getting the nightmare if I went to sleep with that close by my bed. I'll have it taken down if you like."

"I really wish you would," I said. He rang the bell, and with the help of a servant we detached the picture and carried it out onto the landing, and put it with its face to the wall.

"By Jove, the old lady is a weight," said John, mopping his forehead. "I wonder if she had something on her mind."

The extraordinary weight of the picture had struck me too. I was about to reply, when I caught sight of my own hand. There was blood on it, in considerable quantities, covering the whole palm.

"I've cut myself somehow," said I.

John gave a little startled exclamation.

"Why, I have too," he said.

Simultaneously the footman took out his handkerchief and wiped his hand with it. I saw that there was blood also on his handkerchief.

John and I went back into the tower room and washed the blood off; but neither on his hand nor on mine was there the slightest trace of a scratch or cut. It seemed to me that, having ascertained this, we both, by a sort of tacit consent, did not allude to it again. Something in my case had dimly occurred to me that I did not wish to think about. It was but a conjecture, but I fancied that I knew the same thing had occurred to him.

The heat and oppression of the air, for the storm we had expected was still undischarged, increased very much after dinner, and for some time most of the party, among whom were John Clinton and myself, sat outside on the path bounding the lawn, where we had had tea. The night was absolutely dark, and no twinkle of star or moon ray could penetrate the pall of cloud that overset the sky. By degrees our assembly thinned, the women went up to bed, men dispersed to the smoking or billiard room, and by eleven o'clock my host and I were the only two left. All the evening I thought that he had something on his mind, and as soon as we were alone he spoke.

"The man who helped us with the picture had blood on his hand, too, did you notice?" he said.

"I asked him just now if he had cut himself, and he said he supposed he had, but that he could find no mark of it. Now where did that blood come from?"

By dint of telling myself that I was not going to think about it, I had succeeded in not doing so, and I did not want, especially just at bedtime, to be reminded of it.

"I don't know," said I, "and I don't really care so long as the picture of Mrs. Stone is not by my bed."

He got up.

"But it's odd," he said. "Ha! Now you'll see another odd thing."

A dog of his, an Irish terrier by breed, had come out of the house as we talked. The door behind us into the hall was open, and a bright oblong of light shone across the lawn to the iron gate which led on to the rough grass outside, where the walnut tree stood. I saw that the dog had all his hackles up, bristling with rage and fright; his lips were curled back from his teeth, as if he was ready to spring at something, and he was growling to himself. He took not the slightest notice of his master or me, but stiffly and tensely walked across the grass to the iron gate. There he stood for a moment, looking through the bars and still growling. Then of a sudden his courage seemed to desert him: he gave one long howl, and scuttled back to the house with a curious crouching sort of movement.

"He does that half-a-dozen times a day." said John. "He sees something which he both hates and fears."

I walked to the gate and looked over it. Something was moving on the grass outside, and soon a sound which I could not instantly identify came to my ears. Then I remembered what it was: it was the purring of a cat. I lit a match, and saw the purrer, a big blue Persian, walking round and round in a little circle just outside the gate, stepping high and ecstatically, with tail carried aloft like a banner. Its eyes were bright and shining, and every now and then it put its head down and sniffed at the grass.

I laughed.

"The end of that mystery, I am afraid." I said. "Here's a large cat having Walpurgis night all alone."

"Yes, that's Darius," said John. "He spends half the day and all night there. But that's not the end of the dog mystery, for Toby and he are the best of friends, but the beginning of the cat mystery. What's the cat doing there? And why is Darius pleased, while Toby is terror-stricken?"

At that moment I remembered the rather horrible detail of my dreams when I saw through the gate, just where the cat was now, the white tombstone with the sinister inscription. But before I could answer the rain began, as suddenly and heavily as if a tap had been turned on, and simultaneously the big cat squeezed through the bars of the gate, and came leaping across the lawn to the house for shelter. Then it sat in the doorway, looking out eagerly into the dark. It spat and struck at John with its paw, as he pushed it in, in order to close the door.

Somehow, with the portrait of Julia Stone in the passage outside, the room in the tower had absolutely no alarm for me, and as I went to bed, feeling very sleepy and heavy, I had nothing more than interest for the curious incident about our bleeding hands, and the conduct of the cat and dog. The last thing I looked at before I put out my light was the square empty space by my bed where the portrait had been. Here the paper was of its original full tint of dark red: over the rest of the walls it had faded. Then I blew out my candle and instantly fell asleep.

My awaking was equally instantaneous, and I sat bolt upright in bed under the impression that some bright light had been flashed in my face, though it was now absolutely pitch dark. I knew exactly where I was, in the room which I had dreaded in dreams, but no horror that I ever felt when asleep approached the fear that now invaded and froze my brain. Immediately after a peal of thunder crackled just above the house, but the probability that it was only a flash of lightning which awoke me gave no reassurance to my galloping heart. Something I knew was in the room with me, and instinctively I put out my right hand, which was nearest the wall, to keep it away. And my hand touched the edge of a picture-frame hanging close to me.

I sprang out of bed, upsetting the small table that stood by it, and I heard my watch, candle, and matches clatter onto the floor. But for the moment there was no need of light, for a blinding flash leaped out of the clouds, and showed me that by my bed again hung the picture of Mrs. Stone. And instantly the room went into blackness again. But in that flash I saw another thing also, namely a figure that leaned over the end of my bed, watching me. It was dressed in some close-clinging white garment, spotted and stained with mold, and the face was that of the portrait.

Overhead the thunder cracked and roared, and when it ceased and the deathly stillness succeeded, I heard the rustle of movement coming nearer me, and, more horrible yet, perceived an odor of corruption and decay. And then a hand was laid on the side of my neck, and close beside my ear I heard quick-taken, eager breathing. Yet I knew that this thing, though it could be perceived by touch, by smell, by eye and by ear, was still not of this earth, but something that had passed out of the body and had power to make itself manifest. Then a voice, already familiar to me, spoke.

"I knew you would come to the room in the tower," it said. "I have been long waiting for you. At last you have come. Tonight I shall feast; before long we will feast together."

And the quick breathing came closer to me; I could feel it on my neck.

At that the terror, which I think had paralyzed me for the moment, gave way to the wild instinct of self-preservation. I hit wildly with both arms, kicking out at the same moment, and heard a little animal-squeal, and something soft dropped with a thud beside me. I took a couple of steps forward, nearly tripping up over whatever it was that lay there, and by the merest good-luck found the handle of the door. In another second I ran out on the landing, and had banged the door behind me. Almost at the same moment I heard a door open somewhere below, and John Clinton, candle in hand, came running upstairs.

"What is it?" he said. "I sleep just below you, and heard a noise as if—Good heavens, there's blood on your shoulder."

I stood there, so he told me afterwards, swaying from side to side, white as a sheet, with the mark on my shoulder as if a hand covered with blood had been laid there.

"It's in there," I said, pointing. "She, you know. The portrait is in there, too, hanging up on the place we took it from."

At that he laughed.

"My dear fellow, this is mere nightmare," he said.

He pushed by me, and opened the door, I standing there simply inert with terror, unable to stop him, unable to move.

"Phew! What an awful smell," he said.

Then there was silence; he had passed out of my sight behind the open door. Next moment he came out again, as white as myself, and instantly shut it.

"Yes, the portrait's there," he said, "and on the floor is a thing—a thing spotted with earth, like what they bury people in. Come away, quick, come away."

How I got downstairs I hardly know. An awful shuddering and nausea of the spirit rather than of the flesh had seized me, and more than once he had to place my feet upon the steps, while every now and then he cast glances of terror and apprehension up the stairs. But in time we came to his dressing-room on the floor below, and there I told him what I have here described.

The sequel can be made short; indeed, some of my readers have perhaps already guessed what it was, if they remember that inexplicable affair of the churchyard at West Fawley, some eight years ago, where an attempt was made three times to bury the body of a certain woman who had committed suicide. On each occasion the coffin was found in the course of a few days again protruding from the ground. After the third attempt, in order that the thing should not be talked about, the body was buried elsewhere in unconsecrated ground. Where it was buried was just outside the iron gate of the garden belonging to the house where this woman had lived. She had committed suicide in a room at the top of the tower in that house. Her name was Julia Stone.

Subsequently the body was again secretly dug up, and the coffin was found to be full of blood.

The Confession of Charles Linkworth

by E. F. Benson

Dr. Teesdale had occasion to attend the condemned man once or twice during the week before his execution, and found him, as is often the case, when his last hope of life has vanished, quiet and perfectly resigned to his fate, and not seeming to look forward with any dread to the morning that each hour that passed brought nearer and nearer. The bitterness of death appeared to be over for him: it was done with when he was told that his appeal was refused. But for those days while hope was not yet quite abandoned, the wretched man had drunk of death daily. In all his experience the doctor had never seen a man so wildly and passionately tenacious of life, nor one so strongly knit to this material world by the sheer animal lust of living. Then the news that hope could no longer be entertained was told him, and his spirit passed out of the grip of that agony of torture and suspense, and accepted the inevitable with indifference. Yet the change was so extraordinary that it seemed to the doctor rather that the news had completely stunned his powers of feeling, and he was below the numbed surface, still knit into material things as strongly as ever. He had fainted when the result was told him, and Dr. Teesdale had been called in to attend him. But the fit was but transient, and he came out of it into full consciousness of what had happened.

The murder had been a deed of peculiar horror, and there was nothing of sympathy in the mind of the public towards the perpetrator. Charles Linkworth, who now lay under capital sentence, was the keeper of a small stationery store in Sheffield, and there lived with him his wife and mother. The latter was the victim of his atrocious crime; the motive of it being to get possession of the sum of five hundred pounds, which was this woman's property. Linkworth, as came out at the trial, was in debt to the extent of a hundred pounds at the time, and during his wife's absence from home on a visit to relations, he strangled his mother, and during the night buried the body in the small back-garden of his house. On his wife's return, he had a sufficiently plausible tale to account for the elder Mrs. Linkworth's disappearance, for there had been constant jarrings and bickerings between him and his mother for the last year or two, and she had more than once threatened to withdraw herself and the eight shillings a week which she contributed to household expenses, and purchase an annuity with her money. It was true, also, that during the younger Mrs. Linkworth's absence from home, mother and son had had a violent quarrel arising originally from some trivial point in household management, and that in consequence of this, she had actually drawn her money out of the bank, intending to leave Sheffield next day and settle in London, where she had friends. That evening she told him this, and during the night he killed her.

His next step, before his wife's return, was logical and sound. He packed up all his mother's possessions and took them to the station, from which he saw them despatched to town by passenger train, and in the evening he asked several friends in to supper, and told them of his mother's departure. He did not (logically also, and in accordance with what they probably already knew) feign regret, but said that he and she had never got on well together, and that the cause of peace and quietness was furthered by her going. He told the same story to his wife on her return, identical in every detail, adding, however, that the quarrel had been a violent one, and that his mother had not even left him her address. This again was wisely thought of: it would prevent his wife from writing to her. She appeared to accept his story completely: indeed there was nothing strange or suspicious about it.

For a while he behaved with the composure and astuteness which most criminals possess up to a certain point, the lack of which, after that, is generally the cause of their detection. He did not, for instance, immediately pay off his debts, but took into his house a young man as lodger, who occupied his mother's room, and he dismissed the assistant in his shop, and did the entire serving himself. This gave the impression of economy, and at the same time he openly spoke of the great improvement in his trade, and not till a month had passed did he cash any of the bank-notes which he had found in a locked drawer in his mother's room. Then he changed two notes of fifty pounds and paid off his creditors.

At that point his astuteness and composure failed him. He opened a deposit account at a local bank with four more fifty-pound notes, instead of being patient, and increasing his balance at the savings bank pound by pound, and he got uneasy about that which he had buried deep enough for security in the back-garden. Thinking to render himself safer in this regard, he ordered a cartload of slag and stone fragments, and with the help of his lodger employed the summer evenings when work was over in building a sort of rockery over the spot. Then came the chance circumstance which really set match to this dangerous train. There was a fire in the lost luggage office at King's Cross Station (from which he ought to have claimed his mother's property) and one of the two boxes was partially burned. The company was liable for compensation, and his mother's name on her linen, and a letter with the Sheffield address on it, led to the arrival of a purely official and formal notice, stating that the company were prepared to consider claims. It was directed to Mrs. Linkworth's and Charles Linkworth's wife received and read it.

It seemed a sufficiently harmless document, but it was endorsed with his death-warrant. For he could give no explanation at all of the fact of the boxes still lying at King's Cross Station, beyond suggesting that some accident had happened to his mother. Clearly he had to put the matter in the hands of the police, with a view to tracing her movements, and if it proved that she was dead, claiming her property, which she had already drawn out of the bank. Such at least was the course urged on him by his wife and lodger, in whose presence the communication from the railway officials was read out, and it was impossible to refuse to take it. Then the silent, uncreaking machinery of justice, characteristic of England, began to move forward. Quiet men lounged about Smith Street, visited banks, observed the supposed increase in trade, and from a house near by looked into the garden where ferns were already flourishing on the rockery. Then came the arrest and the trial, which did not last very long, and on a certain Saturday night the verdict. Smart women in large hats had made the court bright with colour, and in all the crowd there was not one who felt any sympathy with the young athletic-looking man who was condemned. Many of the audience were elderly and respectable mothers, and the crime had been an outrage on motherhood, and they listened to the unfolding of the flawless evidence with strong approval. They thrilled a little when the judge put on the awful and ludicrous little black cap, and spoke the sentence appointed by God.

Linkworth went to pay the penalty for the atrocious deed, which no one who had heard the evidence could possibly doubt that he had done with the same indifference as had marked his entire demeanour since he knew his appeal had failed. The prison chaplain who had attended him had done his utmost to get him to confess, but his efforts had been quite ineffectual, and to the last he asserted, though without protestation, his innocence. On a bright September morning, when the sun shone warm on the terrible little procession that crossed the prison yard to the shed where was erected the apparatus of death, justice was done, and Dr. Teesdale was satisfied that life was immediately extinct. He had been present on the scaffold, had watched the bolt drawn, and the hooded and pinioned figure drop into the pit. He had heard the chunk and creak of the rope as the sudden weight came on to it, and looking down he had seen the queer twitchings of the hanged body. They had lasted but a second for the execution had been perfectly satisfactory.

An hour later he made the post-mortem examination and found that his view had been correct: the vertebrae of the spine had been broken at the neck, and death must have been absolutely instantaneous. It was hardly necessary even to make that little piece of dissection that proved this, but for the sake of form he did so. And at that moment he had a very curious and vivid mental impression that the spirit of the dead man was close beside him, as if it still dwelt in the broken habitation of its body. But there was no question at all that the body was dead: it had been dead an hour. Then followed another little circumstance that at the first seemed insignificant though curious also. One of the warders entered, and asked if the rope which had been used an hour ago, and was the hangman's perquisite, had by mistake been brought into the mortuary with the body. But there was no trace of it, and it seemed to have vanished altogether, though it a singular thing to be lost: it was not here; it was not on the scaffold. And though the disappearance was of no particular moment it was quite inexplicable.

Dr. Teesdale was a bachelor and a man of independent means, and lived in a tall-windowed and commodious house in Bedford Square, where a plain cook of surpassing excellence looked after his food, and her husband his person. There was no need for him to practise a profession at all, and he performed his work at the prison for the sake of the study of the minds of criminals.

Most crime—the transgression, that is, of the rule of conduct which the human race has framed for the sake of its own preservation—he held to be either the result of some abnormality, of the brain or of starvation. Crimes of theft, for instance, he would by no means refer to one head; often it is true they were the result of actual want, but more often dictated by some obscure disease of the brain. In marked cases it was labelled as kleptomania, but he was convinced there were many others which did not fall directly under the dictation of physical need. More especially was this the case where the crime in question involved also some deed of violence, and he mentally placed underneath this heading, as he went home that evening, the criminal at whose last moments he had been present that morning. The crime had been abominable, the need of money not so very pressing, and the very abomination and unnaturalness of the murder inclined him to consider the murderer as lunatic rather than criminal. He had been, as far as was known, a man of quiet and kindly disposition, a good husband, a sociable neighbour. And then he had committed a crime, just one, which put him outside all pales. So monstrous a deed, whether perpetrated by a sane man or a mad one, was intolerable; there was no use for the doer of it on this planet at all. But somehow the doctor felt that he would have been more at one with the execution of justice, if the dead man had confessed. It was morally certain that he was guilty, but he wished that when there was no longer any hope for him he had endorsed the verdict himself.

He dined alone that evening, and after dinner sat in his study which adjoined the dining-room, and feeling disinclined to read, sat in his great red chair opposite the fireplace, and let his mind graze where it would. At once almost, it went back to the curious sensation he had experienced that morning, of feeling that the spirit of Linkworth was present in the mortuary, though life had been extinct for an hour. It was not the first time, especially in cases of sudden death, that he had felt a similar conviction, though perhaps it had never been quite so unmistakable as it had been today. Yet the feeling, to his mind, was quite probably formed on a natural and psychical truth.

The spirit—it may be remarked that he was a believer in the doctrine of future life, and the non-extinction of the soul with the death of the body—was very likely unable or unwilling to quit at once and altogether the earthly habitation, very likely it lingered there, earth-bound, for a while.

In his leisure hours Dr. Teesdale was a considerable student of the occult, for like most advanced and proficient physicians, he clearly recognised how narrow was the boundary of separation between soul and body, how tremendous the influence of the intangible was over material things, and it presented no difficulty to his mind that a disembodied spirit should be able to communicate directly with those who still were bounded by the finite and material.

His meditations, which were beginning to group themselves into definite sequence, were interrupted at this moment. On his desk near at hand stood his telephone, and the bell rang, not with its usual metallic insistence, but very faintly, as if the current was weak, or the mechanism impaired. However, it certainly was ringing, and he got up and took the combined ear and mouth-piece off its hook.

"Yes, yes," he said, "who is it?"

There was a whisper in reply almost inaudible, and quite unintelligible.

"I can't hear you," he said.

Again the whisper sounded, but with no greater distinctness. Then it ceased altogether.

He stood there, for some half minute or so, waiting for it to be renewed, but beyond the usual chuckling and croaking, which showed, however, that he was in communication with some other instrument, there was silence. Then he replaced the receiver, rang up the Exchange, and gave his number.

"Can you tell me what number rang me up just now?" he asked.

There was a short pause, then it was given him. It was the number of the prison, where he was doctor.

"Put me on to it, please," he said.

This was done.

"You rang me up just now," he said down the tube. "Yes; I am Doctor Teesdale. What is it? I could not hear what you said."

The voice came back quite clear and intelligible.

"Some mistake, sir," it said. "We haven't rung you up."

"But the Exchange tells me you did, three minutes ago."

"Mistake at the Exchange, sir," said the voice.

"Very odd. Well, good-night. Warder Draycott, isn't it?"

"Yes, sir; good-night, sir."

Dr. Teesdale went back to his big arm-chair, still less inclined to read. He let his thoughts wander on for a while, without giving them definite direction, but ever and again his mind kept coming back to that strange little incident of the telephone. Often and often he had been rung up by some mistake, often and often he had been put on to the wrong number by the Exchange, but there was something in this very subdued ringing of the telephone bell, and the unintelligible whisperings at the other end that suggested a very curious train of reflection to his mind, and soon he found himself pacing up and down his room, with his thoughts eagerly feeding on a most unusual pasture.

"But it's impossible," he said, aloud.

He went down as usual to the prison next morning, and once again he was strangely beset with the feeling that there was some unseen presence there. He had before now had some odd psychical experiences, and knew that he was a 'sensitive' one, that is, who is capable, under certain circumstances, of receiving supernormal impressions, and of having glimpses of the unseen world that lies about us. And this morning the presence of which he was conscious was that of the man who had been executed yesterday morning. It was local, and he felt it most strongly in the little prison yard, and as he passed the door of the condemned cell. So strong was it there that he would not have been surprised if the figure of the man had been visible to him, and as he passed through the door at the end of the passage, he turned round, actually expecting to see it. All the time, too, he was aware of a profound horror at his heart; this unseen presence strangely disturbed him. And the poor soul, he felt, wanted something done for it. Not for a moment did he doubt that this impression of his was objective, it was no imaginative phantom of his own invention that made itself so real. The spirit of Linkworth was there.

He passed into the infirmary, and for a couple of hours busied himself with his work. But all the time he was aware that the same invisible presence was near him, though its force was manifestly less here than in those places which had been more intimately associated with the man. Finally, before he left, in order to test his theory he looked into the execution shed. But next moment with a face suddenly stricken pale, he came out again, closing the door hastily. At the top of the steps stood a figure hooded and pinioned, but hazy of outline and only faintly visible.

But it was visible, there was no mistake about it.

Dr. Teesdale was a man of good nerve, and he recovered himself almost immediately, ashamed of his temporary panic. The terror that had blanched his face was chiefly the effect of startled nerves, not of terrified heart, and yet deeply interested as he was in psychical phenomena, he could not command himself sufficiently to go back there. Or rather he commanded himself, but his muscles refused to act on the message. If this poor earth-bound spirit had any communication to make to him, he certainly much preferred that it should be made at a distance. As far as he could understand, its range was circumscribed. It haunted the prison yard, the condemned cell, the execution shed, it was more faintly felt in the infirmary. Then a further point suggested itself to his mind, and he went back to his room and sent for Warder Draycott, who had answered him on the telephone last night.

"You are quite sure," he asked, "that nobody rang me up last night, just before I rang you up?"

There was a certain hesitation in the man's manner which the doctor noticed.

"I don't see how it could be possible, sir," he said. "I had been sitting close by the telephone for half an hour before, and again before that. I must have seen him, if anyone had been to the instrument."

"And you saw no one?" said the doctor with a slight emphasis.

The man became more markedly ill at ease.

"No, sir, I saw no one," he said, with the same emphasis.

Dr. Teesdale looked away from him.

"But you had perhaps the impression that there was some one there?" he asked, carelessly, as if it was a point of no interest.

Clearly Warder Draycott had something on his mind, which he found it hard to speak of.

"Well, sir, if you put it like that," he began. "But you would tell me I was half asleep, or had eaten something that disagreed with me at my supper."

The doctor dropped his careless manner.

"I should do nothing of the kind," he said, "any more than you would tell me that I had dropped asleep last night, when I heard my telephone bell ring. Mind you, Draycott, it did not ring as usual, I could only just hear it ringing, though it was close to me. And I could only hear a whisper when I put my ear to it. But when you spoke I heard you quite distinctly. Now I believe there was something—somebody—at this end of the telephone. You were here, and though you saw no one, you, too, felt there was someone there."

The man nodded.

"I'm not a nervous man, sir," he said, "and I don't deal in fancies. But there was something there. It was hovering about the instrument, and it wasn't the wind, because there wasn't a breath of wind stirring, and the night was warm.

And I shut the window to make certain. But it went about the room, sir, for an hour or more. It rustled the leaves of the telephone book, and it ruffled my hair when it came close to me. And it was bitter cold, sir."

The doctor looked him straight in the face.

"Did it remind you of what had been done yesterday morning?" he asked suddenly.

Again the man hesitated.

"Yes, sir," he said at length. "Convict Charles Linkworth."

Dr. Teesdale nodded reassuringly.

"That's it," he said. "Now, are you on duty tonight?"

"Yes, sir, I wish I wasn't."

"I know how you feel, I have felt exactly the same myself. Now whatever this is, it seems to want to communicate with me. By the way, did you have any disturbance in the prison last night?"

"Yes, sir, there was half a dozen men who had the nightmare. Yelling and screaming they were, and quiet men too, usually. It happens sometimes the night after an execution. I've known it before, though nothing like what it was last night."

"I see. Now, if this—this thing you can't see wants to get at the telephone again tonight, give it every chance. It will probably come about the same time. I can't tell you why, but that usually happens. So unless you must, don't be in this room where the telephone is, just for an hour to give it plenty of time between half-past nine and half-past ten. I will be ready for it at the other end. Supposing I am rung up, I will, when it has finished, ring you up to make sure that I was not being called in—in the usual way."

"And there is nothing to be afraid of, sir?" asked the man.

Dr. Teesdale remembered his own moment of terror this morning, but he spoke quite sincerely.

"I am sure there is nothing to be afraid of," he said, reassuringly.

Dr. Teesdale had a dinner engagement that night, which he broke, and was sitting alone in his study by half past-nine. In the present state of human ignorance as to the law which governs the movements of spirits severed from the body, he could not tell the warder why it was that their visits are so often periodic, timed to punctuality according to our scheme of hours, but in scenes of tabulated instances of the appearance of revenants, especially if the soul was in sore need of help, as might be the case here, he found that they came at the same hour of day or night. As a rule, too, their power of making themselves seen or heard or felt grew greater for some little while after death, subsequently growing weaker as they became less earth-bound, or often after that ceasing altogether, and he was prepared tonight for a less indistinct impression. The spirit apparently for the early hours of its disembodiment is weak, like a moth newly broken out from its chrysalis—and then suddenly the telephone bell rang, not so faintly as the night before, but still not with its ordinary imperative tone.

Dr. Teesdale instantly got up, put the receiver to his ear. And what he heard was heartbroken sobbing, strong spasms that seemed to tear the weeper.

He waited for a little before speaking, himself cold with some nameless fear, and yet profoundly moved to help, if he was able.

"Yes, yes," he said at length, hearing his own voice tremble. "I am Dr. Teesdale. What can I do for you? And who are you?" he added, though he felt that it was a needless question.

Slowly the sobbing died down, the whispers took its place, still broken by crying.

"I want to tell, sir—I want to tell—I must tell."

"Yes, tell me, what is it?" said the doctor.

"No, not you—another gentleman, who used to come to see me. Will you speak to him what I say to you?—I can't make him hear me or see me."

"Who are you?" asked Dr. Teesdale suddenly.

"Charles Linkworth. I thought you knew. I am very miserable. I can't leave the prison—and it is cold. Will you send for the other gentleman?"

"Do you mean the chaplain?" asked Dr. Teesdale.

"Yes, the chaplain. He read the service when I went across the yard yesterday. I shan't be so miserable when I have told."

The doctor hesitated a moment. This was a strange story that he would have to tell Mr Dawkins, the prison chaplain, that at the other end of the telephone was the spirit of the man executed yesterday. And yet he soberly believed that it was so, that this unhappy spirit was in misery and wanted to "tell." There was no need to ask what he wanted to tell.

"Yes, I will ask him to come here," he said at length.

"Thank you, sir, a thousand times. You will make him come, won't you?"

The voice was growing fainter.

"It must be tomorrow night," it said. "I can't speak longer now. I have to go to see—oh, my God, my God."

The sobs broke out afresh, sounding fainter and fainter. But it was in a frenzy of terrified interest that Dr. Teesdale spoke.

"To see what?" he cried. "Tell me what you are doing, what is happening to you?"

"I can't tell you; I mayn't tell you," said the voice very faint. "That is part—" and it died away altogether.

Dr. Teesdale waited a little, but there was no further sound of any kind, except the chuckling and croaking of the instrument. He put the receiver on to its hook again, and then became aware for the first time that his forehead was streaming with some cold dew of horror. His ears sang; his heart beat very quick and faint, and he sat down to recover himself. Once or twice he asked himself if it was possible that some terrible joke was being played on him, but he knew that could not be so; he felt perfectly sure that he had been speaking with a soul in torment of contrition for the terrible and irremediable act it had committed. It was no delusion of his senses, either; here in this comfortable room of his in Bedford Square, with London cheerfully roaring round him, he had spoken with the spirit of Charles Linkworth.

But he had no time (nor indeed inclination, for somehow his soul sat shuddering within him) to indulge in meditation. First of all he rang up the prison.

"Warder Draycott?" he asked.

There was a perceptible tremor in the man's voice as he answered.

"Yes, sir. Is it Dr. Teesdale?"

"Yes. Has anything happened here with you?"

Twice it seemed that the man tried to speak and could not. At the third attempt the words came "Yes, sir. He has been here. I saw him go into the room where the telephone is."

"Ah! Did you speak to him?"

"No, sir: I sweated and prayed. And there's half a dozen men as have been screaming in their sleep tonight. But it's quiet again now. I think he has gone into the execution shed."

"Yes. Well, I think there will be no more disturbance now. By the way, please give me Mr Dawkins's home address."

This was given him, and Dr. Teesdale proceeded to write to the chaplain, asking him to dine with him on the following night. But suddenly he found that he could not write at his accustomed desk, with the telephone standing close to him, and he went upstairs to the drawing-room which he seldom used, except when he entertained his friends. There he recaptured the serenity of his nerves, and could control his hand. The note simply asked Mr Dawkins to dine with him next night, when he wished to tell him a very strange history and ask his help. "Even if you have any other engagement," he concluded, "I seriously request you to give it up. Tonight, I did the same.

"I should bitterly have regretted it if I had not."

Next night accordingly, the two sat at their dinner in the doctor's dining-room, and when they were left to their cigarettes and coffee the doctor spoke.

"You must not think me mad, my dear Dawkins," he said, "when you hear what I have got to tell you."

Mr Dawkins laughed.

"I will certainly promise not to do that," he said.

"Good. Last night and the night before, a little later in the evening than this, I spoke through the telephone with the spirit of the man we saw executed two days ago. Charles Linkworth."

The chaplain did not laugh. He pushed back his chair, looking annoyed.

"Teesdale," he said, "is it to tell me this—I don't want to be rude—but this bogey-tale that you have brought me here this evening?"

"Yes. You have not heard half of it. He asked me last night to get hold of you. He wants to tell you something. We can guess, I think, what it is."

Dawkins got up.

"Please let me hear no more of it," he said. "The dead do not return. In what state or under what condition they exist has not been revealed to us. But they have done with all material things."

"But I must tell you more," said the doctor. "Two nights ago I was rung up, but very faintly, and could only hear whispers. I instantly inquired where the call came from and was told it came from the prison. I rang up the prison, and Warder Draycott told me that nobody had rung me up. He, too, was conscious of a presence."

"I think that man drinks," said Dawkins, sharply.

The doctor paused a moment.

"My dear fellow, you should not say that sort of thing," he said. "He is one of the steadiest men we have got. And if he drinks, why not I also?"

The chaplain sat down again.

"You must forgive me," he said, "but I can't go into this. These are dangerous matters to meddle with. Besides, how do you know it is not a hoax?"

"Played by whom?" asked the doctor. "Hark!"

The telephone bell suddenly rang. It was clearly audible to the doctor.

"Don't you hear it?" he said.

"Hear what?"

"The telephone bell ringing."

"I hear no bell," said the chaplain, rather angrily. "There is no bell ringing."

The doctor did not answer, but went through into his study, and turned on the lights. Then he took the receiver and mouthpiece off its hook.

"Yes?" he said, in a voice that trembled. "Who is it? Yes: Mr Dawkins is here. I will try and get him to speak to you." He went back into the other room.

"Dawkins," he said, "there is a soul in agony. I pray you to listen. For God's sake come and listen."

The chaplain hesitated a moment.

"As you will," he said.

He took up the receiver and put it to his ear.

"I am Mr Dawkins," he said.

He waited.

"I can hear nothing whatever," he said at length. "Ah, there was something there. The faintest whisper."

"Ah, try to hear, try to hear!" said the doctor.

Again the chaplain listened. Suddenly he laid the instrument down, frowning.

"Something—somebody said, 'I killed her, I confess it. I want to be forgiven.' It's a hoax, my dear Teesdale. Somebody knowing your spiritualistic leanings is playing a very grim joke on you. I can't believe it."

Dr. Teesdale took up the receiver.

"I am Dr. Teesdale," he said. "Can you give Mr Dawkins some sign that it is you?"

Then he laid it down again.

"He says he thinks he can," he said. "We must wait."

The evening was again very warm, and the window into the paved yard at the back of the house was open. For five minutes or so the two men stood in silence, waiting, and nothing happened. Then the chaplain spoke.

"I think that is sufficiently conclusive," he said.

Even as he spoke a very cold draught of air suddenly blew into the room, making the papers on the desk rustle. Dr. Teesdale went to the window and closed it.

"Did you feel that?" he asked.

"Yes, a breath of air. Chilly."

Once again in the closed room it stirred again.

"And did you feel that?" asked the doctor.

The chaplain nodded. He felt his heart hammering in his throat suddenly.

"Defend us from all peril and danger of this coming night," he exclaimed.

"Something is coming!" said the doctor.

As he spoke it came. In the centre of the room not three yards away from them stood the figure of a man with his head bent over on to his shoulder, so that the face was not visible. Then he took his head in both his hands and raised it like a weight, and looked them in the face. The eyes and tongue protruded, a livid mark was round the neck. Then there came a sharp rattle on the boards of the floor, and the figure was no longer there. But on the floor there lay a new rope.

For a long while neither spoke. The sweat poured off the doctor's face, and the chaplain's white lips whispered prayers. Then by a huge effort the doctor pulled himself together. He pointed at the rope.

"It has been missing since the execution," he said.

Then again the telephone bell rang. This time the chaplain needed no prompting. He went to it at once and the ringing ceased. For a while he listened in silence.

"Charles Linkworth," he said at length, "in the sight of God, in whose presence you stand, are you truly sorry for your sin?"

Some answer inaudible to the doctor came, and the chaplain closed his eyes. And Dr. Teesdale knelt as he heard the words of the Absolution.

At the close there was silence again.

"I can hear nothing more," said the chaplain, replacing the receiver.

Presently the doctor's man-servant came in with the tray of spirits and syphon. Dr. Teesdale pointed without looking to where the apparition had been.

"Take the rope that is there and burn it, Parker," he said.

There was a moment's silence.

"There is no rope, sir," said Parker.

The Face

by E. S. Benson

Hester Ward, sitting by the open window on this hot afternoon in June, began seriously to argue with herself about the cloud of foreboding and depression which had encompassed her all day, and, very sensibly, she enumerated to herself the manifold causes for happiness in the fortunate circumstances of her life. She was young, she was extremely good-looking, she was well-off, she enjoyed excellent health, and above all, she had an adorable husband and two small, adorable children. There was no break, indeed, anywhere in the circle of prosperity which surrounded her, and had the wishing-cap been handed to her that moment by some beneficent fairy, she would have hesitated to put it on her head, for there was positively nothing that she could think of which would have been worthy of such solemnity. Moreover, she could not accuse herself of a want of appreciation of her blessings; she appreciated enormously, she enjoyed enormously, and she thoroughly wanted all those who so munificently contributed to her happiness to share in it.

She made a very deliberate review of these things, for she was really anxious, more anxious, indeed, than she admitted to herself, to find anything tangible which could possibly warrant this ominous feeling of approaching disaster. Then there was the weather to consider; for the last week London had been stiflingly hot, but if that was the cause, why had she not felt it before? Perhaps the effect of these broiling, airless days had been cumulative. That was an idea, but, frankly, it did not seem a very good one, for, as a matter of fact, she loved the heat; Dick, who hated it, said that it was odd he should have fallen in love with a salamander.

She shifted her position, sitting up straight in this low window-seat, for she was intending to make a call on her courage. She had known from the moment she awoke this morning what it was that lay so heavy on her, and now, having done her best to shift the reason of her depression on to anything else, and having completely failed, she meant to look the thing in the face. She was ashamed of doing so, for the cause of this leaden mood of fear which held her in its grip, was so trivial, so fantastic, so excessively silly.

"Yes, there never was anything so silly," she said to herself. "I must look at it straight, and convince myself how silly it is." She paused a moment, clenching her hands.

"Now for it," she said.

She had had a dream the previous night, which, years ago, used to be familiar to her, for again and again when she was a child she had dreamed it. In itself the dream was nothing, but in those childish days, whenever she had this dream which had visited her last night, it was followed on the next night by another, which contained the source and the core of the horror, and she would awake screaming and struggling in the grip of overwhelming nightmare. For some ten years now she had not experienced it, and would have said that, though she remembered it, it had become dim and distant to her. But last night she had had that warning dream, which used to herald the visitation of the nightmare, and now that whole store-house of memory crammed as it was with bright things and beautiful contained nothing so vivid.

The warning dream, the curtain that was drawn up on the succeeding night, and disclosed the vision she dreaded, was simple and harmless enough in itself. She seemed to be walking on a high sandy cliff covered with short down-grass; twenty yards to the left came the edge of this cliff, which sloped steeply down to the sea that lay at its foot. The path she followed led through fields bounded by low hedges, and mounted gradually upwards. She went through some half-dozen of these, climbing over the wooden stiles that gave communication; sheep grazed there, but she never saw another human being, and always it was dusk, as if evening was falling, and she had to hurry on, because someone (she knew not whom) was waiting for her, and had been waiting not a few minutes only, but for many years. Presently, as she mounted this slope, she saw in front of her a copse of stunted trees, growing crookedly under the continual pressure of the wind that blew from the sea, and when she saw those she knew her journey was nearly done, and that the nameless one, who had been waiting for her so long was somewhere close at hand. The path she followed was cut through this wood, and the slanting boughs of the trees on the sea-ward side almost roofed it in; it was like walking through a tunnel. Soon the trees in front began to grow thin, and she saw through them the grey tower of a lonely church. It stood in a grave-yard, apparently long disused, and the body of the church, which lay between the tower and the edge of the cliff, was in ruins, roofless, and with gaping windows, round which ivy grew thickly.

At that point this prefatory dream always stopped. It was a troubled, uneasy dream, for there was over it the sense of dusk and of the man who had been waiting for her so long, but it was not of the order of nightmare. Many times in childhood had she experienced it, and perhaps it was the subconscious knowledge of the night that so surely followed it, which gave it its disquiet. And now last night it had come again, identical in every particular but one. For last night it seemed to her that in the course of these ten years which had intervened since last it had visited her, the glimpse of the church and churchyard was changed. The edge of the cliff had come nearer to the tower, so that it now was within a yard or two of it, and the ruined body of the church, but for one broken arch that remained, had vanished. The sea had encroached, and for ten years had been busily eating at the cliff.

Hester knew well that it was this dream and this alone which had darkened the day for her, by reason of the nightmares that used to follow it, and, like a sensible woman, having looked it once in the face, she refused to admit into her mind any conscious calling-up of the sequel. If she let herself contemplate that, as likely or not the very thinking about it would be sufficient to ensure its return, and of one thing she was very certain, namely, that she didn't at all want it to do so. It was not like the confused jumble and jangle of ordinary nightmare, it was very simple, and she felt it concerned the nameless one who waited for her... But she must not think of it; her whole will and intention was set on not thinking of it, and to aid her resolution, there was the rattle of Dick's latch-key in the front-door, and his voice calling her.

She went out into the little square front hall; there he was, strong and large, and wonderfully undreamlike.

"This heat's a scandal, it's an outrage, it's an abomination of desolation," he cried, vigorously mopping. "What have we done that Providence should place us in this frying-pan? Let us thwart him, Hester! Let us drive out of this inferno and have our dinner at—I'll whisper it so that he shan't overhear—at Hampton Court!"

She laughed: this plan suited her excellently. They would return late, after the distraction of a fresh scene; and dining out at night was both delicious and stupefying.

"The very thing," she said, "and I'm sure Providence didn't hear. Let's start now!"

"Rather. Any letters for me?"

He walked to the table where there were a few rather uninteresting-looking envelopes with half penny stamps.

"Ah, receipted bill," he said. "Just a reminder of one's folly in paying it. Circular … unasked advice to invest in German marks… Circular begging letter, beginning 'Dear Sir or Madam.' Such impertinence to ask one to subscribe to something without ascertaining one's sex… Private view, portraits at the Walton Gallery… Can't go: business meetings all day. You might like to have a look in, Hester. Some one told me there were some fine Vandycks. That's all: let's be off."

Hester spent a thoroughly reassuring evening, and though she thought of telling Dick about the dream that had so deeply imprinted itself on her consciousness all day, in order to hear the great laugh he would have given her for being such a goose, she refrained from doing so, since nothing that he could say would be so tonic to these fantastic fears as his general robustness. Besides, she would have to account for its disturbing effect, tell him that it was once familiar to her, and recount the sequel of the nightmares that followed. She would neither think of them, nor mention them: it was wiser by far just to soak herself in his extraordinary sanity, and wrap herself in his affection… They dined out-of-doors at a river-side restaurant and strolled about afterwards, and it was very nearly midnight when, soothed with coolness and fresh air, and the vigour of his strong companionship, she let herself into the house, while he took the car back to the garage. And now she marvelled at the mood which had beset her all day, so distant and unreal had it become. She felt as if she had dreamed of shipwreck, and had awoke to find herself in some secure and sheltered garden where no tempest raged nor waves beat. But was there, ever so remotely, ever so dimly, the noise of far-off breakers somewhere?

He slept in the dressing-room which communicated with her bedroom, the door of which was left open for the sake of air and coolness, and she fell asleep almost as soon as her light was out, and while his was still burning. And immediately she began to dream.

She was standing on the sea-shore; the tide was out, for level sands strewn with stranded jetsam glimmered in a dusk that was deepening into night. Though she had never seen the place it was awfully familiar to her. At the head of the beach there was a steep cliff of sand, and perched on the edge of it was a grey church tower. The sea must have encroached and undermined the body of the church, for tumbled blocks of masonry lay close to her at the bottom of the cliff, and there were gravestones there, while others still in place were silhouetted whitely against the sky. To the right of the church tower there was a wood of stunted trees, combed sideways by the prevalent sea-wind, and she knew that along the top of the cliff a few yards inland there lay a path through fields, with wooden stiles to climb, which led through a tunnel of trees and so out into the churchyard. All this she saw in a glance, and waited, looking at the sand-cliff crowned by the church tower, for the terror that was going to reveal itself. Already she knew what it was, and, as so many times before, she tried to run away. But the catalepsy of nightmare was already on her; frantically she strove to move, but her utmost endeavour could not raise a foot from the sand. Frantically she tried to look away from the sand-cliffs close in front of her, where in a moment now the horror would be manifested…

It came. There formed a pale oval light, the size of a man's face, dimly luminous in front of her and a few inches above the level of her eyes. It outlined itself, short reddish hair grew low on the forehead, below were two grey eyes, set very close together, which steadily and fixedly regarded her. On each side the ears stood noticeably away from the head, and the lines of the jaw met in a short pointed chin. The nose was straight and rather long, below it came a hairless lip, and last of all the mouth took shape and colour, and there lay the crowning terror. One side of it, soft-curved and beautiful, trembled into a smile, the other side, thick and gathered together as by some physical deformity, sneered and lusted.

The whole face, dim at first, gradually focused itself into clear outline: it was pale and rather lean, the face of a young man. And then the lower lip dropped a little, showing the glint of teeth, and there was the sound of speech. "I shall soon come for you now," it said, and on the words it drew a little nearer to her, and the smile broadened. At that the full hot blast of nightmare poured in upon her. Again she tried to run, again she tried to scream, and now she could feel the breath of that terrible mouth upon her. Then with a crash and a rending like the tearing asunder of soul and body she broke the spell, and heard her own voice yelling, and felt with her fingers for the switch of her light. And then she saw that the room was not dark, for Dick's door was open, and the next moment, not yet undressed, he was with her.

"My darling, what is it?" he said. "What's the matter?"

She clung desperately to him, still distraught with terror.

"Ah, he has been here again," she cried. "He says he will soon come to me. Keep him away, Dick."

For one moment her fear infected him, and he found himself glancing round the room.

"But what do you mean?" he said. "No one has been here."

She raised her head from his shoulder.

"No, it was just a dream," she said. "But it was the old dream, and I was terrified. Why, you've not undressed yet. What time is it?"

"You haven't been in bed ten minutes, dear," he said. "You had hardly put out your light when I heard you screaming."

She shuddered.

"Ah, it's awful," she said. "And he will come again...."

He sat down by her.

"Now tell me all about it," he said.

She shook her head.

"No, it will never do to talk about it," she said, "it will only make it more real. I suppose the children are all right, are they?"

"Of course they are. I looked in on my way upstairs."

"That's good. But I'm better now, Dick. A dream hasn't anything real about it, has it? It doesn't mean anything?"

He was quite reassuring on this point, and soon she quieted down. Before he went to bed he looked in again on her, and she was asleep.

Hester had a stern interview with herself when Dick had gone down to his office next morning. She told herself that what she was afraid of was nothing more than her own fear. How many times had that ill-omened face come to her in dreams, and what significance had it ever proved to possess? Absolutely none at all, except to make her afraid. She was afraid where no fear was: she was guarded, sheltered, prosperous, and what if a nightmare of childhood returned? It had no more meaning now than it had then, and all those visitations of her childhood had passed away without trace... And then, despite herself, she began thinking over that vision again. It was grimly identical with all its previous occurrences, except... And then, with a sudden shrinking of the heart, she remembered that in earlier years those terrible lips had said: "I shall come for you when you are older," and last night they had said: "I shall soon come for you now." She remembered, too, that in the warning dream the sea had encroached, and it had now demolished the body of the church. There was an awful consistency about these two changes in the otherwise identical visions. The years had brought their change to them, for in the one the encroaching sea had brought down the body of the church, in the other the time was now near....

It was no use to scold or reprimand herself, for to bring her mind to the contemplation of the vision meant merely that the grip of terror closed on her again; it was far wiser to occupy herself, and starve her fear out by refusing to bring it the sustenance of thought. So she went about her household duties, she took the children out for their airing in the park, and then, determined to leave no moment unoccupied, set off with the card of invitation to see the pictures in the private view at the Walton Gallery. After that her day was full enough, she was lunching out, and going on to a matinée, and by the time she got home Dick would have returned, and they would drive down to his little house at Rye for the week-end. All Saturday and Sunday she would be playing golf, and she felt that fresh air and physical fatigue would exorcise the dread of these dreaming fantasies.

The gallery was crowded when she got there; there were friends among the sightseers, and the inspection of the pictures was diversified by cheerful conversation. There were two or three fine Raeburns, a couple of Sir Joshuas, but the gems, so she gathered, were three Vandycks that hung in a small room by themselves. Presently she strolled in there, looking at her catalogue. The first of them, she saw, was a portrait of Sir Roger Wyburn. Still chatting to her friend she raised her eye and saw it....

Her heart hammered in her throat, and then seemed to stand still altogether. A qualm, as of some mental sickness of the soul overcame her, for there in front of her was he who would soon come for her. There was the reddish hair, the projecting ears, the greedy eyes set close together, and the mouth smiling on one side, and on the other gathered up into the sneering menace that she knew so well. It might have been her own nightmare rather than a living model which had sat to the painter for that face.

"Ah, what a portrait, and what a brute!" said her companion. "Look, Hester, isn't that marvellous?"

She recovered herself with an effort. To give way to this ever-mastering dread would have been to allow nightmare to invade her waking life, and there, for sure, madness lay. She forced herself to look at it again, but there were the steady and eager eyes regarding her; she could almost fancy the mouth began to move. All round her the crowd bustled and chattered, but to her own sense she was alone there with Roger Wyburn.

And yet, so she reasoned with herself, this picture of him—for it was he and no other—should have reassured her. Roger Wyburn, to have been painted by Vandyck, must have been dead near on two hundred years; how could he be a menace to her? Had she seen that portrait by some chance as a child; had it made some dreadful impression on her, since overscored by other memories, but still alive in the mysterious subconsciousness, which flows eternally, like some dark underground river, beneath the surface of human life? Psychologists taught that these early impressions fester or poison the mind like some hidden abscess. That might account for this dread of one, nameless no longer, who waited for her.

That night down at Rye there came again to her the prefatory dream, followed by the nightmare, and clinging to her husband as the terror began to subside, she told him what she had resolved to keep to herself. Just to tell it brought a measure of comfort, for it was so outrageously fantastic, and his robust common sense upheld her. But when on their return to London there was a recurrence of these visions, he made short work of her demur and took her straight to her doctor.

"Tell him all, darling," he said. "Unless you promise to do that, I will. I can't have you worried like this. It's all nonsense, you know, and doctors are wonderful people for curing nonsense."

She turned to him.

"Dick, you're frightened," she said quietly.

He laughed.

"I'm nothing of the kind," he said, "but I don't like being awakened by your screaming. Not my idea of a peaceful night. Here we are."

The medical report was decisive and peremptory. There was nothing whatever to be alarmed about; in brain and body she was perfectly healthy, but she was run down. These disturbing dreams were, as likely as not, an effect, a symptom of her condition, rather than the cause of it, and Dr. Baring unhesitatingly recommended a complete change to some bracing place. The wise thing would be to send her out of this stuffy furnace to some quiet place to where she had never been. Complete change; quite so. For the same reason her husband had better not go with her; he must pack her off to, let us say, the East coast. Sea-air and coolness and complete idleness. No long walks; no long bathings; a dip, and a deck-chair on the sands. A lazy, soporific life. How about Rushton? He had no doubt that Rushton would set her up again. After a week or so, perhaps, her husband might go down and see her. Plenty of sleep—never mind the night-mares—plenty of fresh air.

Hester, rather to her husband's surprise, fell in with this suggestion at once, and the following evening saw her installed in solitude and tranquillity. The little hotel was still almost empty, for the rush of summer tourists had not yet begun, and all day she sat out on the beach with the sense of a struggle over. She need not fight the terror any more; dimly it seemed to her that its malignancy had been relaxed. Had she in some way yielded to it and done its secret bidding? At any rate no return of its nightly visitations had occurred, and she slept long and dreamlessly, and woke to another day of quiet. Every morning there was a line for her from Dick, with good news of himself and the children, but he and they alike seemed somehow remote, like memories of a very distant time. Something had driven in between her and them, and she saw them as if through glass. But equally did the memory of the face of Roger Wyburn, as seen on the master's canvas or hanging close in front of her against the crumbling sand-cliff, become blurred and indistinct, and no return of her nightly terrors visited her. This truce from all emotion reacted not on her mind alone, lulling her with a sense of soothed security, but on her body also, and she began to weary of this day-long inactivity.

The village lay on the lip of a stretch of land reclaimed from the sea. To the north the level marsh, now beginning to glow with the pale bloom of the sea-lavender, stretched away featureless till it lost itself in distance, but to the south a spur of hill came down to the shore ending in a wooded promontory. Gradually, as her physical health increased, she began to wonder what lay beyond this ridge which cut short the view, and one afternoon she walked across the intervening level and strolled up its wooded slopes. The day was close and windless, the invigorating sea-breeze which till now had spiced the heat with freshness had died, and she looked forward to finding a current of air stirring when she had topped the hill. To the south a mass of dark cloud lay along the horizon, but there was no imminent threat of storm. The slope was easily surmounted, and presently she stood at the top and found herself on the edge of a tableland of wooded pasture, and following the path, which ran not far from the edge of the cliff, she came out into more open country. Empty fields, where a few sheep were grazing, mounted gradually upwards. Wooden stiles made a communication in the hedges that bounded them. And there, not a mile in front of her, she saw a wood, with trees growing slantingly away from the push of the prevalent sea winds, crowning the upward slope, and over the top of it peered a grey church tower.

For the moment, as the awful and familiar scene identified itself, Hester's heart stood still: the next a wave of courage and resolution poured in upon her. Here, at last was the scene of that prefatory dream, and here was she presented with the opportunity of fathoming and dispelling it. Instantly her mind was made up, and under the strange twilight of the shrouded sky, she walked swiftly on through the fields she had so often traversed in sleep, and up to the wood, beyond which he was waiting for her. She closed her ears against the clanging bell of terror, which now she could silence for ever, and unfalteringly entered that dark tunnel of wood. Soon in front of her the trees began to thin, and through them, now close at hand, she saw the church tower. In a few yards farther she came out of the belt of trees, and round her were the monuments of a graveyard long disused. The cliff was broken off close to the church tower: between it and the edge there was no more of the body of the church than a broken arch, thick hung with ivy. Round this she passed and saw below the ruin of fallen masonry, and the level sands strewn with headstones and disjected rubble, and at the edge of the cliff were graves already cracked and toppling. But there was no one here, none waited for her, and the churchyard where she had so often pictured him was as empty as the fields she had just traversed.

A huge elation filled her; her courage had been rewarded, and all the terrors of the past became to her meaningless phantoms. But there was no time to linger, for now the storm threatened, and on the horizon a blink of lightning was followed by a crackling peal. Just as she turned to go her eye fell on a tombstone that was balanced on the very edge of the cliff, and she read on it that here lay the body of Roger Wyburn.

Fear, the catalepsy of nightmare, rooted her for the moment to the spot; she stared in stricken amazement at the moss-grown letters; almost she expected to see that fell terror of a face rise and hover over his resting-place. Then the fear which had frozen her lent her wings, and with hurrying feet she sped through the arched pathway in the wood and out into the fields. Not one backward glance did she give till she had come to the edge of the ridge above the village, and, turning, saw the pastures she had traversed empty of any living presence. None had followed; but the sheep, apprehensive of the coming storm, had ceased to feed, and were huddling under shelter of the stunted hedges.

Her first idea, in the panic of her mind, was to leave the place at once, but the last train for London had left an hour before, and besides, where was the use of flight if it was the spirit of a man long dead from which she fled? The distance from the place where his bones lay did not afford her safety; that must be sought for within. But she longed for Dick's sheltering and confident presence; he was arriving in any case tomorrow, but there were long dark hours before tomorrow, and who could say what the perils and dangers of the coming night might be? If he started this evening instead of tomorrow morning, he could motor down here in four hours, and would be with her by ten o'clock or eleven. She wrote an urgent telegram: "Come at once," she said. "Don't delay."

The storm which had flickered on the south now came quickly up, and soon after it burst in appalling violence. For preface there were but a few large drops that splashed and dried on the roadway as she came back from the post-office, and just as she reached the hotel again the roar of the approaching rain sounded, and the sluices of heaven were opened. Through the deluge flared the fire of the lightning, the thunder crashed and echoed overhead, and presently the street of the village was a torrent of sandy turbulent water, and sitting there in the dark one picture leapt floating before her eyes, that of the tombstone of Roger Wyburn, already tottering to its fall at the edge of the cliff of the church tower. In such rains as these, acres of the cliffs were loosened; she seemed to hear the whisper of the sliding sand that would precipitate those perished sepulchres and what lay within to the beach below.

By eight o'clock the storm was subsiding, and as she dined she was handed a telegram from Dick, saying that he had already started and sent this off en route. By half-past ten, therefore, if all was well, he would be here, and somehow he would stand between her and her fear. Strange how a few days ago both it and the thought of him had become distant and dim to her; now the one was as vivid as the other, and she counted the minutes to his arrival. Soon the rain ceased altogether, and looking out of the curtained window of her sitting-room where she sat watching the slow circle of the hands of the clock, she saw a tawny moon rising over the sea. Before it had climbed to the zenith, before her clock had twice told the hour again, Dick would be with her.

It had just struck ten when there came a knock at her door, and the page-boy entered with the message that a gentleman had come for her. Her heart leaped at the news; she had not expected Dick for half an hour yet, and now the lonely vigil was over. She ran downstairs, and there was the figure standing on the step outside. His face was turned away from her; no doubt he was giving some order to his chauffeur. He was outlined against the white moonlight, and in contrast with that, the gas-jet in the entrance just above his head gave his hair a warm, reddish tinge.

She ran across the hall to him.

"Ah, my darling, you've come," she said. "It was good of you. How quick you've been!" Just as she laid her hand on his shoulder he turned. His arm was thrown out round her, and she looked into a face with eyes close set, and a mouth smiling on one side, the other, thick and gathered together as by some physical deformity, sneered and lusted.

The nightmare was on her; she could neither run nor scream, and supporting her dragging steps, he went forth with her into the night.

Half an hour later Dick arrived. To his amazement he heard that a man had called for his wife not long before, and that she had gone out with him. He seemed to be a stranger here, for the boy who had taken his message to her had never seen him before, and presently surprise began to deepen into alarm; enquiries were made outside the hotel, and it appeared that a witness or two had seen the lady whom they knew to be staying there walking, hatless, along the top of the beach with a man whose arm was linked in hers. Neither of them knew him, but one had seen his face and could describe it.

The direction of the search thus became narrowed down, and though with a lantern to supplement the moonlight they came upon footprints which might have been hers, there were no marks of any who walked beside her. But they followed these until they came to an end, a mile away, in a great landslide of sand, which had fallen from the old churchyard on the cliff, and had brought down with it half the tower and a gravestone, with the body that had lain below.

The gravestone was that of Roger Wyburn, and his body lay by it, untouched by corruption or decay, though two hundred years had elapsed since it was interred there. For a week afterwards the work of searching the landslide went on, assisted by the high tides that gradually washed it away. But no further discovery was made.

Caterpillars

by E. F. Benson

I saw a month or two ago in an Italian paper that the Villa Cascana, in which I once stayed, had been pulled down, and that a manufactory of some sort was in process of erection on its site.

There is therefore no longer any reason for refraining from writing of those things which I myself saw (or imagined I saw) in a certain room and on a certain landing of the villa in question, nor from mentioning the circumstances which followed, which may or may not (according to the opinion of the reader) throw some light on or be somehow connected with this experience.

The Villa Cascana was in all ways but one a perfectly delightful house, yet, if it were standing now, nothing in the world—I use the phrase in its literal sense—would induce me to set foot in it again, for I believe it to have been haunted in a very terrible and practical manner.

Most ghosts, when all is said and done, do not do much harm; they may perhaps terrify, but the person whom they visit usually gets over their visitation. They may on the other hand be entirely friendly and beneficent. But the appearances in the Villa Cascana were not beneficent, and had they made their "visit" in a very slightly different manner, I do not suppose I should have got over it any more than Arthur Inglis did.

The house stood on an ilex-clad hill not far from Sestri di Levante on the

Italian Riviera, looking out over the iridescent blues of that enchanted sea, while behind it rose the pale green chestnut woods that climb up the hillsides till they give place to the pines that, black in contrast with them, crown the slopes. All round it the garden in the luxuriance of mid-spring bloomed and was fragrant, and the scent of magnolia and rose, borne on the salt freshness of the winds from the sea, flowed like a stream through the cool vaulted rooms.

On the ground floor a broad pillared loggia ran round three sides of the house, the top of which formed a balcony for certain rooms of the first floor. The main staircase, broad and of grey marble steps, led up from the hall to the landing outside these rooms, which were three in number, namely, two big sitting-rooms and a bedroom arranged en suite. The latter was unoccupied, the sitting-rooms were in use. From these the main staircase was continued to the second floor, where were situated certain bedrooms, one of which I occupied, while from the other side of the first-floor landing some half-dozen steps led to another suite of rooms, where, at the time I am speaking of, Arthur Inglis, the artist, had his bedroom and studio. Thus the landing outside my bedroom at the top of the house commanded both the landing of the first floor and also the steps that led to Inglis' rooms. Jim Stanley and his wife, finally (whose guest I was), occupied rooms in another wing of the house, where also were the servants' quarters.

I arrived just in time for lunch on a brilliant noon of mid-May. The garden was shouting with colour and fragrance, and not less delightful after my broiling walk up from the marina, should have been the coming from the reverberating heat and blaze of the day into the marble coolness of the villa. Only (the reader has my bare word for this, and nothing more), the moment I set foot in the house I felt that something was wrong. This feeling, I may say, was quite vague, though very strong, and I remember that when I saw letters waiting for me on the table in the hall I felt certain that the explanation was here: I was convinced that there was bad news of some sort for me. Yet when I opened them I found no such explanation of my premonition: my correspondents all reeked of prosperity. Yet this clear miscarriage of a presentiment did not dissipate my uneasiness. In that cool fragrant house there was something wrong.

I am at pains to mention this because to the general view it may explain that though I am as a rule so excellent a sleeper that the extinction of my light on getting into bed is apparently contemporaneous with being called on the following morning, I slept very badly on my first night in the Villa Cascana. It may also explain the fact that when I did sleep (if it was indeed in sleep that I saw what

I thought I saw) I dreamed in a very vivid and original manner, original, that is to say, in the sense that something that, as far as I knew, had never previously entered into my consciousness, usurped it then. But since, in addition to this evil premonition, certain words and events occurring during the rest of the day might have suggested something of what I thought happened that night, it will be well to relate them.

After lunch, then, I went round the house with Mrs. Stanley, and during our tour she referred, it is true, to the unoccupied bedroom on the first floor, which opened out of the room where we had lunched.

"We left that unoccupied," she said, "because Jim and I have a charming bedroom and dressing-room, as you saw, in the wing, and if we used it ourselves we should have to turn the dining-room into a dressing-room and have our meals downstairs. As it is, however, we have our little flat there, Arthur Inglis has his little flat in the other passage; and I remembered (aren't I extraordinary?) that you once said that the higher up you were in a house the better you were pleased. So I put you at the top of the house, instead of giving you that room."

It is true, that a doubt, vague as my uneasy premonition, crossed my mind at this. I did not see why Mrs. Stanley should have explained all this, if there had not been more to explain. I allow, therefore, that the thought that there was something to explain about the unoccupied bedroom was momentarily present to my mind.

The second thing that may have borne on my dream was this.

At dinner the conversation turned for a moment on ghosts. Inglis, with the certainty of conviction, expressed his belief that anybody who could possibly believe in the existence of supernatural phenomena was unworthy of the name of an ass. The subject instantly dropped. As far as I can recollect, nothing else occurred or was said that could bear on what follows.

We all went to bed rather early, and personally I yawned my way upstairs, feeling hideously sleepy. My room was rather hot, and I threw all the windows wide, and from without poured in the white light of the moon, and the love-song of many nightingales. I undressed quickly, and got into bed, but though I had felt so sleepy before, I now felt extremely wide-awake. But I was quite content to be awake: I did not toss or turn, I felt perfectly happy listening to the song and seeing the light. Then, it is possible, I may have gone to sleep, and what follows may have been a dream. I thought, anyhow, that after a time the nightingales ceased singing and the moon sank. I thought also that if, for some unexplained reason, I was going to lie awake all night, I might as well read, and

I remembered that I had left a book in which I was interested in the dining-room on the first floor. So I got out of bed, lit a candle, and went downstairs. I went into the room, saw on a side-table the book I had come to look for, and then, simultaneously, saw that the door into the unoccupied bedroom was open. A curious grey light, not of dawn nor of moonshine, came out of it, and I looked in. The bed stood just opposite the door, a big four-poster, hung with tapestry at the head. Then I saw that the greyish light of the bedroom came from the bed, or rather from what was on the bed. For it was covered with great caterpillars, a foot or more in length, which crawled over it. They were faintly luminous, and it was the light from them that showed me the room. Instead of the sucker-feet of ordinary caterpillars they had rows of pincers like crabs, and they moved by grasping what they lay on with their pincers, and then sliding their bodies forward. In colour these dreadful insects were yellowish-grey, and they were covered with irregular lumps and swellings. There must have been hundreds of them, for they formed a sort of writhing, crawling pyramid on the bed. Occasionally one fell off on to the floor, with a soft fleshy thud, and though the floor was of hard concrete, it yielded to the pincerfeet as if it had been putty, and, crawling back, the caterpillar would mount on to the bed again, to rejoin its fearful companions. They appeared to have no faces, so to speak, but at one end of them there was a mouth that opened sideways in respiration.

Then, as I looked, it seemed to me as if they all suddenly became conscious of my presence.

All the mouths, at any rate, were turned in my direction, and next moment they began dropping off the bed with those soft fleshy thuds on to the floor, and wriggling towards me. For one second a paralysis as of a dream was on me, but the next I was running upstairs again to my room, and I remember feeling the cold of the marble steps on my bare feet. I rushed into my bedroom, and slammed the door behind me, and then—I was certainly wide-awake now—I found myself standing by my bed with the sweat of terror pouring from me. The noise of the banged door still rang in my ears. But, as would have been more usual, if this had been mere nightmare, the terror that had been mine when I saw those foul beasts crawling about the bed or dropping softly on to the floor did not cease then. Awake, now, if dreaming before, I did not at all recover from the horror of dream: it did not seem to me that I had dreamed. And until dawn, I sat or stood, not daring to lie down, thinking that every rustle or movement that I heard was the approach of the caterpillars. To them and the claws that bit into the cement the wood of the door was child's play: steel would not keep them out.

But with the sweet and noble return of day the horror vanished: the whisper of wind became benignant again: the nameless fear, whatever it was, was smoothed out and terrified me no longer. Dawn broke, hueless at first; then it grew dove-coloured, then the flaming pageant of light spread over the sky.

The admirable rule of the house was that everybody had breakfast where and when he pleased, and in consequence it was not till lunch-time that I met any of the other members of our party, since I had breakfast on my balcony, and wrote letters and other things till lunch. In fact, I got down to that meal rather late, after the other three had begun. Between my knife and fork there was a small pill-box of cardboard, and as I sat down Inglis spoke.

"Do look at that," he said, "since you are interested in natural history. I found it crawling on my counterpane last night, and I don't know what it is."

I think that before I opened the pill-box I expected something of the sort which I found in it.

Inside it, anyhow, was a small caterpillar, greyish-yellow in colour, with curious bumps and excrescences on its rings. It was extremely active, and hurried round the box, this way and that.

Its feet were unlike the feet of any caterpillar I ever saw: they were like the pincers of a crab. I looked, and shut the lid down again.

"No, I don't know it," I said, "but it looks rather unwholesome. What are you going to do with it?"

"Oh, I shall keep it," said Inglis. "It has begun to spin: I want to see what sort of a moth it turns into."

I opened the box again, and saw that these hurrying movements were indeed the beginning of the spinning of the web of its cocoon. Then Inglis spoke again.

"It has got funny feet, too," he said. "They are like crabs' pincers. What's the Latin for crab?"

"Oh, yes, Cancer. So in case it is unique, let's christen it: 'Cancer Inglisensis.'" Then something happened in my brain, some momentary piecing together of all that I had seen or dreamed. Something in his words seemed to me to throw light on it all, and my own intense horror at the experience of the night before linked itself on to what he had just said. In effect, I took the box and threw it, caterpillar and all, out of the window. There was a gravel path just outside, and beyond it, a fountain playing into a basin. The box fell on to the middle of this.

Inglis laughed.

"So the students of the occult don't like solid facts," he said. "My poor caterpillar!"

The talk went off again at once on to other subjects, and I have only given in detail, as they happened, these trivialities in order to be sure myself that I have recorded everything that could have borne on occult subjects or on the subject of caterpillars. But at the moment when I threw the pill-box into the fountain, I lost my head: my only excuse is that, as is probably plain, the tenant of it was, in miniature, exactly what I had seen crowded on to the bed in the unoccupied room. And though this translation of those phantoms into flesh and blood—or whatever it is that caterpillars are made of—ought perhaps to have relieved the horror of the night, as a matter of fact it did nothing of the kind. It only made the crawling pyramid that covered the bed in the unoccupied room more hideously real.

After lunch we spent a lazy hour or two strolling about the garden or sitting in the loggia, and it must have been about four o'clock when Stanley and I started off to bathe, down the path that led by the fountain into which I had thrown the pill-box. The water was shallow and clear, and at the bottom of it I saw its white remains. The water had disintegrated the cardboard, and it had become no more than a few strips and shreds of sodden paper. The centre of the fountain was a marble Italian Cupid which squirted the water out of a wine-skin held under its arm. And crawling up its leg was the caterpillar. Strange and scarcely credible as it seemed, it must have survived the falling-to-bits of its prison, and made its way to shore, and there it was, out of arm's reach, weaving and waving this way and that as it evolved its cocoon.

Then, as I looked at it, it seemed to me again that, like the caterpillar I had seen last night, it saw me, and breaking out of the threads that surrounded it, it crawled down the marble leg of the Cupid and began swimming like a snake across the water of the fountain towards me. It came with extraordinary speed (the fact of a caterpillar being able to swim was new to me), and in another moment was crawling up the marble lip of the basin. Just then Inglis joined us.

"Why, if it isn't old 'Cancer Inglisensis' again," he said, catching sight of the beast. "What a tearing hurry it is in!"

We were standing side by side on the path, and when the caterpillar had advanced to within about a yard of us, it stopped, and began waving again as if in doubt as to the direction in which it should go. Then it appeared to make up its mind, and crawled on to Inglis' shoe.

"It likes me best," he said, "but I don't really know that I like it. And as it won't drown I think perhaps—"

He shook it off his shoe on to the gravel path and trod on it.

All afternoon the air got heavier and heavier with the Sirocco that was without doubt coming up from the south, and that night again I went up to bed feeling very sleepy; but below my drowsiness, so to speak, there was the consciousness, stronger than before, that there was something wrong in the house, that something dangerous was close at hand. But I fell asleep at once, and—how long after I do not know—either woke or dreamed I awoke, feeling that I must get up at once, or I should be too late. Then (dreaming or awake) I lay and fought this fear, telling myself that I was but the prey of my own nerves disordered by Sirocco or what not, and at the same time quite clearly knowing in another part of my mind, so to speak, that every moment's delay added to the danger. At last this second feeling became irresistible, and I put on coat and trousers and went out of my room on to the landing. And then I saw that I had already delayed too long, and that I was now too late.

The whole of the landing of the first floor below was invisible under the swarm of caterpillars that crawled there. The folding doors into the sitting-room from which opened the bedroom where I had seen them last night were shut, but they were squeezing through the cracks of it and dropping one by one through the keyhole, elongating themselves into mere string as they passed, and growing fat and lumpy again on emerging. Some, as if exploring, were nosing about the steps into the passage at the end of which were Inglis' rooms, others were crawling on the lowest steps of the staircase that led up to where I stood. The landing, however, was completely covered with them: I was cut off. And of the frozen horror that seized me when I saw that I can give no idea in words.

Then at last a general movement began to take place, and they grew thicker on the steps that led to Inglis' room. Gradually, like some hideous tide of flesh, they advanced along the passage, and I saw the foremost, visible by the pale grey luminousness that came from them, reach his door. Again and again I tried to shout and warn him, in terror all the time that they would turn at the sound of my voice and mount my stair instead, but for all my efforts I felt that no sound came from my throat. They crawled along the hinge-crack of his door, passing through as they had done before, and still I stood there, making impotent efforts to shout to him, to bid him escape while there was time.

At last the passage was completely empty: they had all gone, and at that moment I was conscious for the first time of the cold of the marble landing on which I stood barefooted. The dawn was just beginning to break in the Eastern sky.

Six months after I met Mrs. Stanley in a country house in England. We talked on many subjects and at last she said:

"I don't think I have seen you since I got that dreadful news about Arthur Inglis a month ago."

"I haven't heard," said I.

"No? He has got cancer. They don't even advise an operation, for there is no hope of a cure: he is riddled with it, the doctors say."

Now during all these six months I do not think a day had passed on which I had not had in my mind the dreams (or whatever you like to call them) which I had seen in the Villa Cascana.

"It is awful, is it not?" she continued, "and I feel I can't help feeling, that he may have—"

"Caught it at the villa?" I asked.

She looked at me in blank surprise.

"Why did you say that?" she asked. "How did you know?"

Then she told me. In the unoccupied bedroom a year before there had been a fatal case of cancer. She had, of course, taken the best advice and had been told that the utmost dictates of prudence would be obeyed so long as she did not put anybody to sleep in the room, which had also been thoroughly disinfected and newly white-washed and painted. But—

The Haunted Doll's House

by M. R. James

"I suppose you get stuff of that kind through your hands pretty often?" said Mr Dillet, as he pointed with his stick to an object which shall be described when the time comes: and when he said it, he lied in his throat, and knew that he lied. Not once in twenty years—perhaps not once in a lifetime—could Mr Chittenden, skilled as he was in ferreting out the forgotten treasures of half a dozen counties, expect to handle such a specimen. It was collectors' palaver, and Mr Chittenden recognized it as such.

"Stuff of that kind, Mr Dillet! It's a museum piece, that is."

"Well, I suppose there are museums that'll take anything."

"I've seen one, not as good as that, years back," said Mr Chittenden thoughtfully. "But that's not likely to come into the market: and I'm told they 'ave some fine ones of the period over the water. No: I'm only telling you the truth, Mr Dillet, when I was to say that if you was to place an unlimited order with me for the very best that could be got—and you know I 'ave facilities for getting to know of such things, and a reputation to maintain—well, all I can say is, I should lead you straight up to that one and say, 'I can't do no better for you than that, sir.'"

"Hear, hear!" said Mr Dillet, applauding ironically with the end of his stick on the floor of the shop. "How much are you sticking the innocent American buyer for it, eh?"

"Oh, I shan't be over hard on the buyer, American or otherwise. You see, it stands this way, Mr Dillet—if I knew just a bit more about the pedigree—"

"Or just a bit less," Mr Dillet put in.

"Ha, ha! you will have your joke, sir. No, but as I was saying, if I knew just a little more than what I do about the piece—though anyone can see for themselves it's a genuine thing, every last corner of it, and there's not been one of my men allowed to so much as touch it since it came into the shop—there'd be another figure in the price I'm asking."

"And what's that: five and twenty?"

"Multiply that by three and you've got it, sir. Seventy-five's my price."

"And fifty's mine," said Mr Dillet. The point of agreement was, of course, somewhere between the two, it does not matter exactly where—I think sixty guineas. But half an hour later the object was being packed, and within an hour Mr Dillet had called for it in his car and driven away. Mr Chittenden, holding the cheque in his hand, saw him off from the door with smiles, and returned, still smiling, into the parlour where his wife was making the tea. He stopped at the door.

"It's gone," he said. "Thank God for that!" said Mrs. Chittenden, putting down the teapot. "Mr Dillet, was it?"

"Yes, it was."

"Well, I'd sooner it was him than another."

"Oh, I don't know; he ain't a bad feller, my dear."

"Maybe not, but in my opinion he'd be none the worse for a bit of a shake up."

"Well, if that's your opinion, it's my opinion he's put himself into the way of getting one. Anyhow, we shan't have no more of it, and that's something to be thankful for." And so Mr and Mrs. Chittenden sat down to tea.

And what of Mr Dillet and his new acquisition? What it was, the title of this story will have told you. What it was like, I shall have to indicate as well as I can.

There was only just enough room for it in the car, and Mr Dillet had to sit with the driver: he had also to go slow, for though the rooms of the Dolls' House had all been stuffed carefully with soft cottonwool, jolting was to be avoided, in view of the immense number of small objects which thronged them; and the ten-mile drive was an anxious time for him, in spite of all the precautions he insisted upon. At last his front door was reached, and Collins, the butler, came out.

"Look here, Collins, you must help me with this thing – it's a delicate job. We must get it out upright, see? It's full of little things that mustn't be displaced more than we can help. Let's see, where shall we have it? (After a pause for consideration.) Really, I think I shall have to put it in my own room, to begin with at any rate. On the big table—that's it."

It was conveyed—with much talking—to Mr Dillet's spacious room on the first floor, looking out on the drive. The sheeting was unwound from it, and the front thrown open, and for the next hour or two Mr Dillet was fully occupied in extracting the padding and setting in order the contents of the rooms.

When this thoroughly congenial task was finished, I must say that it would have been difficult to find a more perfect and attractive specimen of a Dolls' House in Strawberry Hill Gothic than that which now stood on Mr Dillet's large kneehole table, lighted up by the evening sun which came slanting through three tall slash-windows.

It was quite six feet long, including the Chapel or Oratory which flanked the front on the left as you faced it, and the stable on the right. The main block of the house was, as I have said, in the Gothic manner: that is to say, the windows had pointed arches and were surmounted by what are called ogival hoods, with crockets and finials such as we see on the canopies of tombs built into church walls. At the angles were absurd turrets covered with arched panels. The Chapel had pinnacles and buttresses, and a bell in the turret and coloured glass in the windows. When the front of the house was open you saw four large rooms, bedroom, dining-room, drawing-room, and kitchen, each with its appropriate furniture in a very complete state.

The stable on the right was in two storeys, with its proper complement of horses, coaches and grooms, and with its clock and Gothic cupola for the clock bell.

Pages, of course, might be written on the outfit of the mansion—how many frying-pans, how many gilt chairs, what pictures, carpets, chandeliers, four-posters, table linen, glass, crockery and plate it possessed; but all this must be left to the imagination. I will only say that the base or plinth on which the house stood (for it was fitted with one of some depth which allowed of a flight of steps to the front door and a terrace, partly balustraded) contained a shallow drawer or drawers in which were neatly stored sets of embroidered curtains, changes of raiment for the inmates, and, in short, all the materials for an infinite series of variations and refittings of the most absorbing and delightful kind.

"Quintessence of Horace Walpole, that's what it is: he must have had something to do with the making of it." Such was Mr Dillet's murmured reflection as he knelt before it in a reverent ecstasy. "Simply wonderful! this is my day and no mistake. Five hundred pounds coming in this morning for that cabinet which I never cared about, and now this tumbling into my hands for a tenth, at the very most, of what it would fetch in town. Well, well! It almost makes one afraid something'll happen to counter it. Let's have a look at the population, anyhow."

Accordingly, he set them before him in a row. Again, here is an opportunity, which some would snatch at, of making an inventory of costume: I am incapable of it.

There were a gentleman and lady, in blue satin and brocade respectively. There were two children, a boy and a girl. There was a cook, a nurse, a footman, and there were the stable servants, two postilions, a coachman, two grooms.

"Anyone else? Yes, possibly."

The curtains of the four-poster in the bedroom were closely drawn round all four sides of it, and he put his finger in between them and felt in the bed. He drew the finger back hastily, for it almost seemed to him as if something had – not stirred, perhaps, but yielded – in an odd live way as he pressed it. Then he put back the curtains, which ran on rods in the proper manner, and extracted from the bed a white-haired old gentleman in a long linen night-dress and cap, and laid him down by the rest. The tale was complete.

Dinner-time was now near, so Mr Dillet spent but five minutes in putting the lady and children into the drawing-room, the gentleman into the dining-room, the servants into the kitchen and stables, and the old man back into his bed. He retired into his dressing-room next door, and we see and hear no more of him until something like eleven o'clock at night.

His whim was to sleep surrounded by some of the gems of his collection. The big room in which we have seen him contained his bed: bath, wardrobe, and all the appliances of dressing were in a commodious room adjoining: but his four-poster, which itself was a valued treasure, stood in the large room where he sometimes wrote, and often sat, and even received visitors. Tonight he repaired to it in a highly complacent frame of mind.

There was no striking clock within earshot—none on the staircase, none in the stable, none in the distant church tower. Yet it is indubitable that Mr Dillet was started out of a very pleasant slumber by a bell tolling One.

He was so much startled that he did not merely lie breathless with wide-open eyes, but actually sat up in his bed.

He never asked himself, till the morning hours, how it was that, though there was no light at all in the room, the Dolls' House on the kneehole table stood out with complete clearness. But it was so. The effect was that of a bright harvest moon shining full on the front of a big white stone mansion—a quarter of a mile away it might be, and yet every detail was photographically sharp. There were trees about it, too—trees rising behind the chapel and the house. He seemed to be conscious of the scent of a cool still September night. He thought he could hear an occasional stamp and clink from the stables, as of horses stirring. And with another shock he realized that, above the house, he was looking, not at the wall of his room with its pictures, but into the profound blue of a night sky.

There were lights, more than one, in the windows, and he quickly saw that this was no four-roomed house with a movable front, but one of many rooms and staircases—a real house, but seen as if through the wrong end of a telescope.

"You mean to show me something," he muttered to himself, and he gazed earnestly on the lighted windows. They would in real life have been shuttered or curtained, no doubt, he thought; but, as it was, there was nothing to intercept his view of what was being transacted inside the rooms.

Two rooms were lighted—one on the ground floor to the right of the door, one upstairs, on the left—the first brightly enough, the other rather dimly. The lower room was the dining-room: a table was laid, but the meal was over, and only wine and glasses were left on the table. The man of the blue satin and the woman of the brocade were alone in the room, and they were talking very earnestly, seated close together at the table, their elbows on it: every now and again stopping to listen, as it seemed. Once he rose, came to the window and opened it and put his head out and his hand to his ear. There was a lighted taper in a silver candlestick on a sideboard. When the man left the window he seemed to leave the room also; and the lady, taper in hand, remained standing and listening. The expression on her face was that of one striving her utmost to keep down a fear that threatened to master her—and succeeding. It was a hateful face, too; broad, flat and sly. Now the man came back and she took some small thing from him and hurried out of the room. He, too, disappeared, but only for a moment or two. The front door slowly opened and he stepped out and stood on the top of the perron, looking this way and that; then turned towards the upper window that was lighted, and shook his fist.

It was time to look at that upper window. Through it was seen a four-post bed: a nurse or other servant in an arm-chair, evidently sound asleep; in the bed an old man lying: awake, and, one would say, anxious, from the way in which he shifted about and moved his fingers, beating tunes on the coverlet. Beyond the bed a door opened. Light was seen on the ceiling, and the lady came in: she set down her candle on a table, came to the fireside and roused the nurse. In her hand she had an old-fashioned wine bottle, ready uncorked. The nurse took it, poured some of the contents into a little silver saucepan, added some spice and sugar from casters on the table, and set it to warm on the fire. Meanwhile the old man in the bed beckoned feebly to the lady, who came to him, smiling, took his wrist as if to feel his pulse, and bit her lip as if in consternation. He looked at her anxiously, and then pointed to the window, and spoke. She nodded, and did as the man below had done; opened the casement and listened—perhaps rather ostentatiously: then drew in her head and shook it, looking at the old man, who seemed to sigh.

By this time the posset on the fire was steaming, and the nurse poured it into a small two-handled silver bowl and brought it to the bedside. The old man seemed disinclined for it and was waving it away, but the lady and the nurse together bent over him and evidently pressed it upon him. He must have yielded, for they supported him into a sitting position, and put it to his lips. He drank most of it, in several draughts, and they laid him down. The lady left the room, smiling good night to him, and took the bowl, the bottle and the silver saucepan with her. The nurse returned to the chair, and there was an interval of complete quiet.

Suddenly the old man started up in his bed—and he must have uttered some cry, for the nurse started out of her chair and made but one step of it to the bedside. He was a sad and terrible sight—flushed in the face, almost to blackness, the eyes glaring whitely, both hands clutching at his heart, foam at his lips. For a moment the nurse left him, ran to the door, flung it wide open, and, one supposes, screamed aloud for help, then darted back to the bed and seemed to try feverishly to soothe him—to lay him down—anything. But as the lady, her husband, and several servants, rushed into the room with horrified faces, the old man collapsed under the nurse's hands and lay back, and his features, contorted with agony and rage, relaxed slowly into calm.

A few moments later, lights showed out to the left of the house, and a coach with flambeaux drove up to the door. A white-wigged man in black got nimbly out and ran up the steps, carrying a small leather trunk-shaped box. He was met in the doorway by the man and his wife, she with her handkerchief clutched between her hands, he with a tragic face, but retaining his self-control. They led the new-comer into the dining-room, where he set his box of papers on the table, and, turning to them, listened with a face of consternation at what they had to tell. He nodded his head again and again, threw out his hands slightly, declined, it seemed, offers of refreshment and lodging for the night, and within a few minutes came slowly down the steps, entering the coach and driving off the way he had come. As the man in blue watched him from the top of the steps, a smile not pleasant to see stole slowly over his fat white face. Darkness fell over the whole scene as the lights of the coach disappeared.

But Mr Dillet remained sitting up in the bed: he had rightly guessed that there would be a sequel. The house front glimmered out again before long. But now there was a difference. The lights were in other windows, one at the top of the house, the other illuminating the range of coloured windows of the chapel. How he saw through these is not quite obvious, but he did. The interior was as carefully furnished as the rest of the establishment, with its minute red cushions on the desks, its Gothic stall-canopies, and its western gallery and pinnacled organ with gold pipes. On the centre of the black and white pavement was a bier: four tall candles burned at the corners. On the bier was a coffin covered with a pall of black velvet.

As he looked the folds of the pall stirred. It seemed to rise at one end: it slid downwards: it fell away, exposing the black coffin with its silver handles and name-plate. One of the tall candlesticks swayed and toppled over. Ask no more, but turn, as Mr Dillet hastily did, and look in at the lighted window at the top of the house, where a boy and girl lay in two truckle-beds, and a four-poster for the nurse rose above them. The nurse was not visible for the moment; but the father and mother were there, dressed now in mourning, but with very little sign of mourning in their demeanour. Indeed, they were laughing and talking with a good deal of animation, sometimes to each other, and sometimes throwing a remark to one or other of the children, and again laughing at the answers. Then the father was seen to go on tiptoe out of the room, taking with him as he went a white garment that hung on a peg near the door. He shut the door after him. A minute or two later it was slowly opened again, and a muffled head poked round it. A bent form of sinister shape stepped across to the truckle-beds, and suddenly stopped, threw up its arms and revealed, of course, the father, laughing. The children were in agonies of terror, the boy with the bedclothes over his head, the girl throwing herself out of bed into her mother's arms. Attempts at consolation followed—the parents took the children on their laps, patted them, picked up the white gown and showed there was no harm in it, and so forth; and at last putting the children back into bed, left the room with encouraging waves of the hand. As they left it, the nurse came in, and soon the light died down.

Still Mr Dillet watched immovable.

A new sort of light—not of lamp or candle—a pale ugly light, began to dawn around the door-case at the back of the room. The door was opening again. The seer does not like to dwell upon what he saw entering the room: he says it might be described as a frog—the size of a man—but it had scanty white hair about its head. It was busy about the truckle-beds, but not for long. The sound of cries—faint, as if coming out of a vast distance—but, even so, infinitely appalling, reached the ear.

There were signs of a hideous commotion all over the house: lights moved along and up, and doors opened and shut, and running figures passed within the windows. The clock in the stable turret tolled one, and darkness fell again.

It was only dispelled once more, to show the house front. At the bottom of the steps dark figures were drawn up in two lines, holding flaming torches. More dark figures came down the steps, bearing, first one, then another small coffin. And the lines of torch-bearers with the coffins between them moved silently onward to the left.

The hours of night passed on—never so slowly, Mr Dillet thought. Gradually he sank down from sitting to lying in his bed—but he did not close an eye: and early next morning he sent for the doctor.

The doctor found him in a disquieting state of nerves, and recommended sea-air. To a quiet place on the East Coast he accordingly repaired by easy stages in his car.

One of the first people he met on the sea front was Mr Chittenden, who, it appeared, had likewise been advised to take his wife away for a bit of a change.

Mr Chittenden looked somewhat askance upon him when they met: and not without cause.

"Well, I don't wonder at you being a bit upset, Mr Dillet. What? yes, well, I might say 'orrible upset, to be sure, seeing what me and my poor wife went through ourselves. But I put it to you, Mr Dillet, one of two things: was I going to scrap a lovely piece like that on the one 'and, or was I going to tell customers: 'I'm selling you a regular picture-palace-dramar in reel life of the olden time, billed to perform regular at one o'clock A.M.'? Why, what would you 'ave said yourself? And next thing you know, two Justices of the Peace in the back parlour, and pore Mr and Mrs. Chittenden off in a spring cart to the County Asylum and everyone in the street saying, 'Ah, I thought it 'ud come to that. Look at the way the man drank!'—and me next door, or next door but one, to a total abstainer, as you know. Well, there was my position. What? Me 'ave it back in the shop? Well, what do you think? No, but I'll tell you what I will do. You shall have your money back, bar the ten pound I paid for it, and you make what you can."

Later in the day, in what is offensively called the "smoke-room" of the hotel, a murmured conversation between the two went on for some time.

"How much do you really know about that thing, and where it came from?"

"Honest, Mr Dillet, I don't know the 'ouse. Of course, it came out of the lumber room of a country 'ouse—that anyone could guess. But I'll go as far as say this, that I believe it's not a hundred miles from this place. Which direction and how far I've no notion. I'm only judging by guess-work. The man as I actually paid the cheque to ain't one of my regular men, and I've lost sight of him; but I 'ave the idea that this part of the country was his beat, and that's every word I can tell you. But now, Mr Dillet, there's one thing that rather physicks me. That old chap,—I suppose you saw him drive up to the door—I thought so: now, would he have been the medical man, do you take it? My wife would have it so, but I stuck to it that was the lawyer, because he had papers with him, and one he took out was folded up."

"I agree," said Mr Dillet. "Thinking it over, I came to the conclusion that was the old man's will, ready to be signed."

"Just what I thought," said Mr Chittenden, "and I took it that will would have cut out the young people, eh? Well, well! It's been a lesson to me, I know that. I shan't buy no more dolls' houses, nor waste no more money on the pictures—and as to this business of poisonin' grandpa, well, if I know myself, I never 'ad much of a turn for that. Live and let live: that's bin my motto throughout life, and I ain't found it a bad one."

Filled with these elevated sentiments, Mr Chittenden retired to his lodgings. Mr Dillet next day repaired to the local Institute, where he hoped to find some clue to the riddle that absorbed him. He gazed in despair at a long file of the Canterbury and York Society's publications of the Parish Registers of the District. No print resembling the house of his nightmare was among those that hung on the staircase and in the passages. Disconsolate, he found himself at last in a derelict room, staring at a dusty model of a church in a dusty glass case: Model of St. Stephen's Church, Coxham. Presented by J. Merewether, Esq., of Ilbridge House, 1877. The work of his ancestor James Merewether, d. 1786. There was something in the fashion of it that reminded him dimly of his horror. He retraced his steps to a wall map he had noticed, and made out that Ilbridge House was in Coxham Parish. Coxham was, as it happened, one of the parishes of which he had retained the name when he glanced over the file of printed registers, and it was not long before he found in them the record of the burial of Roger Milford, aged 76, on the 11th of September, 1757, and of Roger and Elizabeth Merewether, aged 9 and 7, on the 19th of the same month. It seemed worth while to follow up this clue, frail as it was; and in the afternoon he drove out to Coxham. The east end of the north aisle of the church is a Milford chapel, and on its north wall are tablets to the same persons; Roger, the elder, it seems, was distinguished by all the qualities which adorn 'the Father, the Magistrate and the Man': the memorial was erected by his attached daughter Elizabeth, 'who did not long survive the loss of a parent ever solicitous for her welfare, and of two amiable children.' The last sentence was plainly an addition to the original inscription.

A yet later slab told of James Merewether, husband of Elizabeth, 'who in the dawn of life practised, not without success, those arts which, had he continued their exercise, might in the opinion of the most competent judges have earned for him the name of the British Vitruvius: but who, overwhelmed by the visitation which deprived him of an affectionate partner and a blooming offspring, passed his Prime and Age in a secluded yet elegant Retirement: his grateful Nephew and Heir indulges a pious sorrow by this too brief recital of his excellences.'

The children were more simply commemorated. Both died on the night of the 12th of September.

Mr Dillet felt sure that in Ilbridge House he had found the scene of his drama. In some old sketchbook, possibly in some old print, he may yet find convincing evidence that he is right. But the Ilbridge House of today is not that which he sought; it is an Elizabethan erection of the forties, in red brick with stone quoins and dressings. A quarter of a mile from it, in a low part of the park, backed by ancient, staghorned, ivy-strangled trees and thick undergrowth, are marks of a terraced platform overgrown with rough grass. A few stone balusters lie here and there, and a heap or two, covered with nettles and ivy, of wrought stones with badly-carved crockets. This, someone told Mr Dillet, was the site of an older house.

As he drove out of the village, the hall clock struck four, and Mr Dillet started up and clapped his hands to his ears. It was not the first time he had heard that bell.

Awaiting an offer from the other side of the Atlantic, the dolls' house still reposes, carefully sheeted, in a loft over Mr Dillet's stables, whither Collins conveyed it on the day when Mr Dillet started for the sea coast.

* * * * *

[It will be said, perhaps, and not unjustly, that this is no more than a variation on a former story of mine called The Mezzotint. I can only hope that there is enough of variation in the setting to make the repetition of the motif tolerable.]

Lost Hearts

by M. R. James

It was, as far as I can ascertain, in September of the year 1811 that a post-chaise drew up before the door of Aswarby Hall, in the heart of Lincolnshire. The little boy who was the only passenger in the chaise, and who jumped out as soon as it had stopped, looked about him with the keenest curiosity during the short interval that elapsed between the ringing of the bell and the opening of the hall door. He saw a tall, square, red-brick house, built in the reign of Anne; a stone-pillared porch had been added in the purer classical style of 1790; the windows of the house were many, tall and narrow, with small panes and thick white woodwork. A pediment, pierced with a round window, crowned the front. There were wings to right and left, connected by curious glazed galleries, supported by colonnades, with the central block. These wings plainly contained the stables and offices of the house. Each was surmounted by an ornamental cupola with a gilded vane.

An evening light shone on the building, making the window-panes glow like so many fires. Away from the Hall in front stretched a flat park studded with oaks and fringed with firs, which stood out against the sky. The clock in the church-tower, buried in trees on the edge of the park, only its golden weather-cock catching the light, was striking six, and the sound came gently beating down the wind. It was altogether a pleasant impression, though tinged with the sort of melancholy appropriate to an evening in early autumn, that was conveyed to the mind of the boy who was standing in the porch waiting for the door to open to him.

The post-chaise had brought him from Warwickshire, where, some six months before, he had been left an orphan. Now, owing to the generous offer of his elderly cousin, Mr Abney, he had come to live at Aswarby. The offer was unexpected, because all who knew anything of Mr Abney looked upon him as a somewhat austere recluse, into whose steady-going household the advent of a small boy would import a new and, it seemed, incongruous element. The truth is that very little was known of Mr Abney's pursuits or temper. The Professor of Greek at Cambridge had been heard to say that no one knew more of the religious beliefs of the later pagans than did the owner of Aswarby. Certainly his library contained all the then available books bearing on the Mysteries, the Orphic poems, the worship of Mithras, and the Neo–Platonists. In the marble-paved hall stood a fine group of Mithras slaying a bull, which had been imported from the Levant at great expense by the owner. He had contributed a description of it to the Gentleman's Magazine, and he had written a remarkable series of articles in the Critical Museum on the superstitions of the Romans of the Lower Empire. He was looked upon, in fine, as a man wrapped up in his books, and it was a matter of great surprise among his neighbours that he should ever have heard of his orphan cousin, Stephen Elliott, much more that he should have volunteered to make him an inmate of Aswarby Hall.

Whatever may have been expected by his neighbours, it is certain that Mr Abney—the tall, the thin, the austere—seemed inclined to give his young cousin a kindly reception. The moment the front-door was opened he darted out of his study, rubbing his hands with delight.

"How are you, my boy?—how are you? How old are you?" said he—"that is, you are not too much tired, I hope, by your journey to eat your supper?"

"No, thank you, sir," said Master Elliott; 'I am pretty well."

"That's a good lad," said Mr Abney. "And how old are you, my boy?"

It seemed a little odd that he should have asked the question twice in the first two minutes of their acquaintance.

"I'm twelve years old next birthday, sir," said Stephen.

"And when is your birthday, my dear boy? Eleventh of September, eh? That's well—that's very well. Nearly a year hence, isn't it? I like—ha, ha!— I like to get these things down in my book. Sure it's twelve? Certain?"

"Yes, quite sure, sir."

"Well, well! Take him to Mrs Bunch's room, Parkes, and let him have his tea—supper—whatever it is."

"Yes, sir," answered the staid Mr Parkes; and conducted Stephen to the lower regions.

Mrs Bunch was the most comfortable and human person whom Stephen had as yet met at Aswarby. She made him completely at home; they were great friends in a quarter of an hour: and great friends they remained. Mrs Bunch had been born in the neighbourhood some fifty-five years before the date of Stephen's arrival, and her residence at the Hall was of twenty years' standing. Consequently, if anyone knew the ins and outs of the house and the district, Mrs Bunch knew them; and she was by no means disinclined to communicate her information.

Certainly there were plenty of things about the Hall and the Hall gardens which Stephen, who was of an adventurous and inquiring turn, was anxious to have explained to him. "Who built the temple at the end of the laurel walk? Who was the old man whose picture hung on the staircase, sitting at a table, with a skull under his hand?" These and many similar points were cleared up by the resources of Mrs Bunch's powerful intellect. There were others, however, of which the explanations furnished were less satisfactory.

One November evening Stephen was sitting by the fire in the housekeeper's room reflecting on his surroundings.

"Is Mr Abney a good man, and will he go to heaven?" he suddenly asked, with the peculiar confidence which children possess in the ability of their elders to settle these questions, the decision of which is believed to be reserved for other tribunals.

"Good?—bless the child!" said Mrs Bunch. "Master's as kind a soul as ever I see! Didn't I never tell you of the little boy as he took in out of the street, as you may say, this seven years back? and the little girl, two years after I first come here?"

"No. Do tell me all about them, Mrs Bunch—now, this minute!"

"Well," said Mrs Bunch, "the little girl I don't seem to recollect so much about. I know master brought her back with him from his walk one day, and give orders to Mrs Ellis, as was housekeeper then, as she should be took every care with. And the pore child hadn't no one belonging to her—she telled me so her own self—and here she lived with us a matter of three weeks it might be; and then, whether she were somethink of a gipsy in her blood or what not, but one morning she out of her bed afore any of us had opened a eye, and neither track nor yet trace of her have I set eyes on since. Master was wonderful put about, and had all the ponds dragged; but it's my belief she was had away by them gipsies, for there was singing round the house for as much as an hour the night she went, and Parkes, he declare as he heard them a-calling in the woods all that afternoon. Dear, dear! a hodd child she was, so silent in her ways and all, but I was wonderful taken up with her, so domesticated she was—surprising.'

"And what about the little boy?" said Stephen.

"Ah, that pore boy!" sighed Mrs Bunch. 'He were a foreigner—Jevanny he called hisself—and he come a-tweaking his 'urdy-gurdy round and about the drive one winter day, and master 'ad him in that minute, and ast all about where he came from, and how old he was, and how he made his way, and where was his relatives, and all as kind as heart could wish. But it went the same way with him. They're a hunruly lot, them foreign nations, I do suppose, and he was off one fine morning just the same as the girl. Why he went and what he done was our question for as much as a year after; for he never took his 'urdy-gurdy, and there it lays on the shelf."

The remainder of the evening was spent by Stephen in miscellaneous cross-examination of Mrs Bunch and in efforts to extract a tune from the hurdy-gurdy.

That night he had a curious dream. At the end of the passage at the top of the house, in which his bedroom was situated, there was an old disused bathroom. It was kept locked, but the upper half of the door was glazed, and, since the muslin curtains which used to hang there had long been gone, you could look in and see the lead-lined bath affixed to the wall on the right hand, with its head towards the window.

On the night of which I am speaking, Stephen Elliott found himself, as he thought, looking through the glazed door. The moon was shining through the window, and he was gazing at a figure which lay in the bath.

His description of what he saw reminds me of what I once beheld myself in the famous vaults of St Michan's Church in Dublin, which possesses the horrid property of preserving corpses from decay for centuries. A figure inexpressibly thin and pathetic, of a dusty leaden colour, enveloped in a shroud-like garment, the thin lips crooked into a faint and dreadful smile, the hands pressed tightly over the region of the heart.

As he looked upon it, a distant, almost inaudible moan seemed to issue from its lips, and the arms began to stir. The terror of the sight forced Stephen backwards and he awoke to the fact that he was indeed standing on the cold boarded floor of the passage in the full light of the moon. With a courage which I do not think can be common among boys of his age, he went to the door of the bathroom to ascertain if the figure of his dreams were really there. It was not, and he went back to bed.

Mrs Bunch was much impressed next morning by his story, and went so far as to replace the muslin curtain over the glazed door of the bathroom. Mr Abney, moreover, to whom he confided his experiences at breakfast, was greatly interested and made notes of the matter in what he called 'his book'.

The spring equinox was approaching, as Mr Abney frequently reminded his cousin, adding that this had been always considered by the ancients to be a critical time for the young: that Stephen would do well to take care of himself, and to shut his bedroom window at night; and that Censorinus had some valuable remarks on the subject. Two incidents that occurred about this time made an impression upon Stephen's mind.

The first was after an unusually uneasy and oppressed night that he had passed—though he could not recall any particular dream that he had had.

The following evening Mrs Bunch was occupying herself in mending his nightgown.

"Gracious me, Master Stephen!" she broke forth rather irritably, "how do you manage to tear your nightdress all to flinders this way? Look here, sir, what trouble you do give to poor servants that have to darn and mend after you!"

There was indeed a most destructive and apparently wanton series of slits or scorings in the garment, which would undoubtedly require a skilful needle to make good. They were confined to the left side of the chest—long, parallel slits about six inches in length, some of them not quite piercing the texture of the linen. Stephen could only express his entire ignorance of their origin: he was sure they were not there the night before.

"But," he said, "Mrs Bunch, they are just the same as the scratches on the outside of my bedroom door: and I'm sure I never had anything to do with making them."

Mrs Bunch gazed at him open-mouthed, then snatched up a candle, departed hastily from the room, and was heard making her way upstairs. In a few minutes she came down.

"Well," she said, "Master Stephen, it's a funny thing to me how them marks and scratches can 'a' come there—too high up for any cat or dog to 'ave made 'em, much less a rat: for all the world like a Chinaman's finger-nails, as my uncle in the tea-trade used to tell us of when we was girls together. I wouldn't say nothing to master, not if I was you, Master Stephen, my dear; and just turn the key of the door when you go to your bed."

"I always do, Mrs Bunch, as soon as I've said my prayers."

"Ah, that's a good child: always say your prayers, and then no one can't hurt you."

Herewith Mrs Bunch addressed herself to mending the injured nightgown, with intervals of meditation, until bed-time. This was on a Friday night in March, 1812.

On the following evening the usual duet of Stephen and Mrs Bunch was augmented by the sudden arrival of Mr Parkes, the butler, who as a rule kept himself rather to himself in his own pantry. He did not see that Stephen was there: he was, moreover, flustered and less slow of speech than was his wont.

"Master may get up his own wine, if he likes, of an evening," was his first remark. "Either I do it in the daytime or not at all, Mrs Bunch. I don't know what it may be: very like it's the rats, or the wind got into the cellars; but I'm not so young as I was, and I can't go through with it as I have done."

"Well, Mr Parkes, you know it is a surprising place for the rats, is the Hall."

"I'm not denying that, Mrs Bunch; and, to be sure, many a time I've heard the tale from the men in the shipyards about the rat that could speak. I never laid no confidence in that before; but tonight, if I'd demeaned myself to lay my ear to the door of the further bin, I could pretty much have heard what they was saying."

"Oh, there, Mr Parkes, I've no patience with your fancies! Rats talking in the wine-cellar indeed!"

"Well, Mrs Bunch, I've no wish to argue with you: all I say is, if you choose to go to the far bin, and lay your ear to the door, you may prove my words this minute."

"What nonsense you do talk, Mr Parkes—not fit for children to listen to! Why, you'll be frightening Master Stephen there out of his wits."

"What! Master Stephen?" said Parkes, awaking to the consciousness of the boy's presence. "Master Stephen knows well enough when I'm a-playing a joke with you, Mrs Bunch."

In fact, Master Stephen knew much too well to suppose that Mr Parkes had in the first instance intended a joke. He was interested, not altogether pleasantly, in the situation; but all his questions were unsuccessful in inducing the butler to give any more detailed account of his experiences in the wine-cellar.

We have now arrived at March 24, 1812. It was a day of curious experiences for Stephen: a windy, noisy day, which filled the house and the gardens with a restless impression. As Stephen stood by the fence of the grounds, and looked out into the park, he felt as if an endless procession of unseen people were sweeping past him on the wind, borne on resistlessly and aimlessly, vainly striving to stop themselves, to catch at something that might arrest their flight and bring them once again into contact with the living world of which they had formed a part. After luncheon that day Mr Abney said:

"Stephen, my boy, do you think you could manage to come to me tonight as late as eleven o'clock in my study? I shall be busy until that time, and I wish to show you something connected with your future life which it is most important that you should know. You are not to mention this matter to Mrs Bunch nor to anyone else in the house; and you had better go to your room at the usual time."

Here was a new excitement added to life: Stephen eagerly grasped at the opportunity of sitting up till eleven o'clock. He looked in at the library door on his way upstairs that evening, and saw a brazier, which he had often noticed in the corner of the room, moved out before the fire; an old silver-gilt cup stood on the table, filled with red wine, and some written sheets of paper lay near it. Mr Abney was sprinkling some incense on the brazier from a round silver box as Stephen passed, but did not seem to notice his step.

The wind had fallen, and there was a still night and a full moon. At about ten o'clock Stephen was standing at the open window of his bedroom, looking out over the country. Still as the night was, the mysterious population of the distant moon-lit woods was not yet lulled to rest. From time to time strange cries as of lost and despairing wanderers sounded from across the mere. They might be the notes of owls or water-birds, yet they did not quite resemble either sound. Were not they coming nearer? Now they sounded from the nearer side of the water, and in a few moments they seemed to be floating about among the shrubberies. Then they ceased; but just as Stephen was thinking of shutting the window and resuming his reading of Robinson Crusoe , he caught sight of two figures standing on the gravelled terrace that ran along the garden side of the Hall—the figures of a boy and girl, as it seemed; they stood side by side, looking up at the windows. Something in the form of the girl recalled irresistibly his dream of the figure in the bath. The boy inspired him with more acute fear.

Whilst the girl stood still, half smiling, with her hands clasped over her heart, the boy, a thin shape, with black hair and ragged clothing, raised his arms in the air with an appearance of menace and of unappeasable hunger and longing. The moon shone upon his almost transparent hands, and Stephen saw that the nails were fearfully long and that the light shone through them. As he stood with his arms thus raised, he disclosed a terrifying spectacle. On the left side of his chest there opened a black and gaping rent; and there fell upon Stephen's brain, rather than upon his ear, the impression of one of those hungry and desolate cries that he had heard resounding over the woods of Aswarby all that evening. In another moment this dreadful pair had moved swiftly and noiselessly over the dry gravel, and he saw them no more.

Inexpressibly frightened as he was, he determined to take his candle and go down to Mr Abney's study, for the hour appointed for their meeting was near at hand. The study or library opened out of the front-hall on one side, and Stephen, urged on by his terrors, did not take long in getting there. To effect an entrance was not so easy. It was not locked, he felt sure, for the key was on the outside of the door as usual. His repeated knocks produced no answer. Mr Abney was engaged: he was speaking. What! Why did he try to cry out? and why was the cry choked in his throat? Had he, too, seen the mysterious children? But now everything was quiet, and the door yielded to Stephen's terrified and frantic pushing.

On the table in Mr Abney's study certain papers were found which explained the situation to Stephen Elliott when he was of an age to understand them. The most important sentences were as follows:

"It was a belief very strongly and generally held by the ancients—of whose wisdom in these matters I have had such experience as induces me to place confidence in their assertions—that by enacting certain processes, which to us moderns have something of a barbaric complexion, a very remarkable enlightenment of the spiritual faculties in man may be attained: that, for example, by absorbing the personalities of a certain number of his fellow-creatures, an individual may gain a complete ascendancy over those orders of spiritual beings which control the elemental forces of our universe.

"It is recorded of Simon Magus that he was able to fly in the air, to become invisible, or to assume any form he pleased, by the agency of the soul of a boy whom, to use the libellous phrase employed by the author of the Clementine Recognitions, he had 'murdered'. I find it set down, moreover, with considerable detail in the writings of Hermes Trismegistus, that similar happy results may be produced by the absorption of the hearts of not less than three human beings below the age of twenty-one years. To the testing of the truth of this receipt I have devoted the greater part of the last twenty years, selecting as the corpora vilia of my experiment such persons as could conveniently be removed without occasioning a sensible gap in society. The first step I effected by the removal of one Phoebe Stanley, a girl of gipsy extraction, on March 24, 1792. The second, by the removal of a wandering Italian lad, named Giovanni Paoli, on the night of March 23, 1805. The final 'victim'— to employ a word repugnant in the highest degree to my feelings—must be my cousin, Stephen Elliott. His day must be this March 24, 1812.

"The best means of effecting the required absorption is to remove the heart from the living subject, to reduce it to ashes, and to mingle them with about a pint of some red wine, preferably port. The remains of the first two subjects, at least, it will be well to conceal: a disused bathroom or wine-cellar will be found convenient for such a purpose. Some annoyance may be experienced from the psychic portion of the subjects, which popular language dignifies with the name of ghosts. But the man of philosophic temperament—to whom alone the experiment is appropriate—will be little prone to attach importance to the feeble efforts of these beings to wreak their vengeance on him. I contemplate with the liveliest satisfaction the enlarged and emancipated existence which the experiment, if successful, will confer on me; not only placing me beyond the reach of human justice (so-called), but eliminating to a great extent the prospect of death itself."

Mr Abney was found in his chair, his head thrown back, his face stamped with an expression of rage, fright, and mortal pain. In his left side was a terrible lacerated wound, exposing the heart. There was no blood on his hands, and a long knife that lay on the table was perfectly clean. A savage wild-cat might have inflicted the injuries. The window of the study was open, and it was the opinion of the coroner that Mr Abney had met his death by the agency of some wild creature. But Stephen Elliott's study of the papers I have quoted led him to a very different conclusion.

Number 13

by M. R. James

Among the towns of Jutland, Viborg justly holds a high place. It is the seat of a bishopric; it has a handsome but almost entirely new cathedral, a charming garden, a lake of great beauty, and many storks. Near it is Hald, accounted one of the prettiest things in Denmark; and hard by is Finderup, where Marsk Stig murdered King Erik Clipping on St. Cecilia's Day, in the year 1286. Fifty-six blows of square-headed iron maces were traced on Erik's skull when his tomb was opened in the seventeenth century. But I am not writing a guide-book.

There are good hotels in Viborg—Preisler's and the Phœnix are all that can be desired. But my cousin, whose experiences I have to tell you now, went to the Golden Lion the first time that he visited Viborg. He has not been there since, and the following pages will perhaps explain the reason of his abstention.

The Golden Lion is one of the very few houses in the town that were not destroyed in the great fire of 1726, which practically demolished the cathedral, the Sognekirke, the Raadhuus, and so much else that was old and interesting. It is a great red-brick house—that is, the front is of brick, with corbie steps on the gables and a text over the door; but the courtyard into which the omnibus drives is of black and white wood and plaster.

The sun was declining in the heavens when my cousin walked up to the door, and the light smote full upon the imposing façade of the house. He was delighted with the old-fashioned aspect of the place, and promised himself a thoroughly satisfactory and amusing stay in an inn so typical of old Jutland.

It was not business in the ordinary sense of the word that had brought Mr Anderson to Viborg. He was engaged upon some researches into the Church history of Denmark, and it had come to his knowledge that in the Kigsarkiv of Viborg there were papers, saved from the fire, relating to the last days of Roman Catholicism in the country. He proposed, therefore, to spend a considerable time—perhaps as much as a fortnight or three weeks—in examining and copying these, and he hoped that the Golden Lion would be able to give him a room of sufficient size to serve alike as a bedroom and a study. His wishes were explained to the landlord, and, after a certain amount of thought, the latter suggested that perhaps it might be the best way for the gentleman to look at one or two of the larger rooms and pick one for himself. It seemed a good idea.

The top floor was soon rejected as entailing too much getting upstairs after the day's work; the second floor contained no room of exactly the dimensions required; but on the first floor there was a choice of two or three rooms which would, so far as size went, suit admirably.

The landlord was strongly in favour of Number 17, but Mr Anderson pointed out that its windows commanded only the blank wall of the next house, and that it would be very dark in the afternoon. Either Number 12 or Number 14 would be better, for both of them looked on the street, and the bright evening light and the pretty view would more than compensate him for the additional amount of noise.

Eventually Number 12 was selected. Like its neighbours, it had three windows, all on one side of the room; it was fairly high and unusually long. There was, of course, no fireplace, but the stove was handsome and rather old—a cast-iron erection, on the side of which was a representation of Abraham sacrificing Isaac, and the inscription, '1 Bog Mose, Cap. 22,' above. Nothing else in the room was remarkable; the only interesting picture was an old coloured print of the town, date about 1820.

Supper-time was approaching, but when Anderson, refreshed by the ordinary ablutions, descended the staircase, there were still a few minutes before the bell rang. He devoted them to examining the list of his fellow-lodgers. As is usual in Denmark, their names were displayed on a large blackboard, divided into columns and lines, the numbers of the rooms being painted in at the beginning of each line. The list was not exciting. There was an advocate, or Sagförer, a German, and some bagmen from Copenhagen. The one and only point which suggested any food for thought was the absence of any Number 13 from the tale of the rooms, and even this was a thing which Anderson had already noticed half a dozen times in his experience of Danish hotels. He could not help wondering whether the objection to that particular number, common as it is, was so widespread and so strong as to make it difficult to let a room so ticketed, and he resolved to ask the landlord if he and his colleagues in the profession had actually met with many clients who refused to be accommodated in the thirteenth room.

He had nothing to tell me (I am giving the story as I heard it from him) about what passed at supper, and the evening, which was spent in unpacking and arranging his clothes, books, and papers, was not more eventful. Towards eleven o'clock he resolved to go to bed, but with him, as with a good many other people nowadays, an almost necessary preliminary to bed, if he meant to sleep, was the reading of a few pages of print, and he now remembered that the particular book which he had been reading in the train, and which alone would satisfy him at that present moment, was in the pocket of his great-coat, then hanging on a peg outside the dining-room.

To run down and secure it was the work of a moment, and, as the passages were by no means dark, it was not difficult for him to find his way back to his own door. So, at least, he thought; but when he arrived there, and turned the handle, the door entirely refused to open, and he caught the sound of a hasty movement towards it from within. He had tried the wrong door, of course. Was his own room to the right or to the left? He glanced at the number: it was 13. His room would be on the left; and so it was. And not before he had been in bed for some minutes, had read his wonted three or four pages of his book, blown out his light, and turned over to go to sleep, did it occur to him that, whereas on the blackboard of the hotel there had been no Number 13, there was undoubtedly a room numbered 13 in the hotel. He felt rather sorry he had not chosen it for his own. Perhaps he might have done the landlord a little service by occupying it, and given him the chance of saying that a well-born English gentleman had lived in it for three weeks and liked it very much. But probably it was used as a servant's room or something of the kind. After all, it was most likely not so large or good a room as his own. And he looked drowsily about the room, which was fairly perceptible in the half-light from the street-lamp. It was a curious effect, he thought. Rooms usually look larger in a dim light than a full one, but this seemed to have contracted in length and grown proportionately higher. Well, well! sleep was more important than these vague ruminations—and to sleep he went.

On the day after his arrival Anderson attacked the Rigsarkiv of Viborg. He was, as one might expect in Denmark, kindly received, and access to all that he wished to see was made as easy for him as possible. The documents laid before him were far more numerous and interesting than he had at all anticipated. Besides official papers, there was a large bundle of correspondence relating to Bishop Jörgen Friis, the last Roman Catholic who held the see, and in these there cropped up many amusing and what are called 'intimate' details of private life and individual character. There was much talk of a house owned by the Bishop, but not inhabited by him, in the town. Its tenant was apparently somewhat of a scandal and a stumbling-block to the reforming party. He was a disgrace, they wrote, to the city; he practised secret and wicked arts, and had sold his soul to the enemy. It was of a piece with the gross corruption and superstition of the Babylonish Church that such a viper and blood-sucking *Troldmand* should be patronized and harboured by the Bishop. The Bishop met these reproaches boldly; he protested his own abhorrence of all such things as secret arts, and required his antagonists to bring the matter before the proper court—of course, the spiritual court—and sift it to the bottom. No one could be more ready and willing than himself to condemn Mag. Nicolas Francken if the evidence showed him to have been guilty of any of the crimes informally alleged against him.

Anderson had not time to do more than glance at the next letter of the Protestant leader, Rasmus Nielsen, before the record office was closed for the day, but he gathered its general tenor, which was to the effect that Christian men were now no longer bound by the decisions of Bishops of Rome, and that the Bishop's Court was not, and could not be, a fit or competent tribunal to judge so grave and weighty a cause.

On leaving the office, Mr Anderson was accompanied by the old gentleman who presided over it, and, as they walked, theconversation very naturally turned to the papers of which I have just been speaking.

Herr Scavenius, the Archivist of Viborg, though very well informed as to the general run of the documents under his charge, was not a specialist in those of the Reformation period. He was much interested in what Anderson had to tell him about them. He looked forward with great pleasure, he said, to seeing the publication in which Mr Anderson spoke of embodying their contents. "This house of the Bishop Friis," he added, "it is a great puzzle to me where it can have stood. I have studied carefully the topography of old Viborg, but it is most unlucky—of the old terrier of, the Bishop's property which was made in 1560, and of which we have the greater part in the Arkiv, just the piece which had the list of the town property is missing. Never mind. Perhaps I shall some day succeed to find him."

After taking some exercise—I forget exactly how or where—Anderson went back to the Golden Lion, his supper, his game of patience, and his bed. On the way to his room it occurred to him that he had forgotten to talk to the landlord about the omission of Number 13 from the hotel board, and also that he might as well make sure that Number 13 did actually exist before he made any reference to the matter.

The decision was not difficult to arrive at. There was the door with its number as plain as could be, and work of some kind was evidently going on inside it, for as he neared the door he could hear footsteps and voices, or a voice, within. During the few seconds in which he halted to make sure of the number, the footsteps ceased, seemingly very near the door, and he was a little startled at hearing a quick hissing breathing as of a person in strong excitement. He went on to his own room, and again he was surprised to find how much smaller it seemed now than it had when he selected it. It was a slight disappointment, but only slight. If he found it really not large enough, he could very easily shift to another. In the meantime he wanted something—as far as I remember it was a pocket handkerchief—out of his portmanteau, which had been placed by the porter on a very inadequate trestle or stool against the wall at the furthest end of the room from his bed. Here was a very curious thing: the portmanteau was not to be seen. It had been moved by officious servants; doubtless the contents had been put in the wardrobe. No, none of them were there. This was vexatious. The idea of a theft he dismissed at once. Such things rarely happen in Denmark, but some piece of stupidity had certainly been performed (which is not so uncommon), and the *stuepige* must be severely spoken to. Whatever it was that he wanted, it was not so necessary to his comfort that he could not wait till the morning for it, and he therefore settled not to ring the bell and disturb the servants. He went to the window—the right-hand window it was—and looked out on the quiet street. There was a tall building opposite, with large spaces of dead wall; no passers by; a dark night; and very little to be seen of any kind.

The light was behind him, and he could see his own shadow clearly cast on the wall opposite. Also the shadow of the bearded man in Number 11 on the left, who passed to and fro in shirtsleeves once or twice, and was seen first brushing his hair, and later on in a nightgown. Also the shadow of the occupant of Number 13 on the right. This might be more interesting. Number 13 was, like himself, leaning on his elbows on the window-sill looking out into the street. He seemed to be a tall thin man—or was it by any chance a woman?—at least, it was someone who covered his or her head with some kind of drapery before going to bed, and, he thought, must be possessed of a red lamp-shade—and the lamp must be flickering very much. There was a distinct playing up and down of a dull red light on the opposite wall. He craned out a little to see if he could make any more of the figure, but beyond a fold of some light, perhaps white, material on the window-sill he could see nothing.

Now came a distant step in the street, and its approach seemed to recall Number 13 to a sense of his exposed position, for very swiftly and suddenly he swept aside from the window, and his red light went out. Anderson, who had been smoking a cigarette, laid the end of it on the window-sill and went to bed.

Next morning he was woke by the *stuepige* with hot water, etc. He roused himself, and after thinking out the correct Danish words, said as distinctly as he could:

"You must not move my portmanteau. Where is it?"

As is not uncommon, the maid laughed, and went away without making any distinct answer.

Anderson, rather irritated, sat up in bed, intending to call her back, but he remained sitting up, staring straight in front of him. There was his portmanteau on its trestle, exactly where he had seen the porter put it when he first arrived. This was a rude shock for a man who prided himself on his accuracy of observation. How it could possibly have escaped him the night before he did, not pretend to understand; at any rate, there it was now.

The daylight showed more than the portmanteau; it let the true proportions of the room with its three windows appear, and satisfied its tenant that his choice after all had not been a bad one. When he was almost dressed he walked to the middle one of the three windows to look out at the weather. Another shock awaited him. Strangely unobservant he must have been last night. He could have sworn ten times over that he had been smoking at the right-hand window the last thing before he went to bed, and here was his cigarette-end on the sill of the middle window.

He started to go down to breakfast. Rather late, but Number 13 was later: here were his boots still outside his door—a gentleman's boots. So then Number

13 was a man, not a woman. Just then he caught sight of the number on the door. It was 14. He thought he must have passed Number 13 without noticing it. Three stupid mistakes in twelve hours were too much for a methodical, accurate-minded man, so he turned back to make sure. The next number to 14 was number 12, his own room. There was no Number 13 at all.

After some minutes devoted to a careful consideration of everything he had had to eat and drink during the last twenty-four hours, Anderson decided to give the question up. If his eyes or his brain were giving way he would have plenty of opportunities for ascertaining that fact; if not, then he was evidently being treated to a very interesting experience. In either case the development of events would certainly be worth watching.

During the day he continued his examination of the episcopal correspondence which I have already summarized. To his disappointment, it was incomplete. Only one other letter could be found which referred to the affair of Mag. Nicolas Francken. It was from the Bishop Jörgen Friis to Rasmus Nielsen. He said:

> *"Although we are not in the least degree inclined to assent to your judgment concerning our court, and shall be prepared if need be to withstand you to the uttermost in that behalf, yet forasmuch as our trusty and well-beloved Mag. Nicolas Francken, against whom you have dared to allege certain false and malicious charges, hath been suddenly removed from among us, it is apparent that the question for this term falls. But forasmuch as you further allege that the Apostle and Evangelist St. John in his heavenly Apocalypse describes the Holy Roman Church under the guise and symbol of the Scarlet Woman, be it known to you," etc.*

Search as he would, Anderson could find no sequel to this letter nor any clue to the cause or manner of the 'removal' of the *casus belli.* He could only suppose that Francken had died suddenly; and as there were only two days between the date of Nielsen's last letter—when Francken was evidently still in being—and that of the Bishop's letter, the death must have been completely unexpected.

In the afternoon he paid a short visit to Hald, and took his tea at Baekkelund; nor could he notice, though he was in a somewhat nervous frame of mind, that there was any indication of such a failure of eye or brain as his experiences of the morning had led him to fear.

At supper he found himself next to the landlord.

"What," he asked him, after some indifferent conversation, "is the reason why in most of the hotels one visits in this country the number thirteen is left out of the list of rooms? I see you have none here."

The landlord seemed amused.

"To think that you should have noticed a thing like that! I've thought about it once or twice myself, to tell the truth. An educated man, I've said, has no business with these superstitious notions. I was brought up myself here in the high school of Viborg, and our old master was always a man to set his face against anything of that kind. He's been dead now this many years—a fine upstanding man he was, and ready with his hands as well as his head. I recollect us boys, one snowy day—"

Here he plunged into reminiscence.

"Then you don't think there is any particular objection to having a Number 13?" said Anderson.

"Ah! to be sure. Well, you understand, I was brought up to the business by my poor old father. He kept an hotel in Aarhuus first, and then, when we were born, he moved to Viborg here, which was his native place, and had the Phœnix here until he died. That was in 1876. Then I started business in Silkeborg, and only the year before last I moved into this house."

Then followed more details as to the state of the house and business when first taken over.

"And when you came here, was there a Number 13?"

"No, no. I was going to tell you about that. You see, in a place like this, the commercial class—the travellers—are what we have to provide for in general. And put them in Number 13? Why, they'd as soon sleep in the street, or sooner. As far as I'm concerned myself, it wouldn't make a penny difference to me what the number of my room was, and so I've often said to them; but they stick to it that it brings them bad luck. Quantities of stories they have among them of men that have slept in a Number 13 and never been the same again, or lost their best customers, or—one thing and another," said the landlord, after searching for a more graphic phrase.

"Then, what do you use your Number 13 for?" said Anderson, conscious as he said the words of a curious anxiety quite disproportionate to the importance of the question.

"My Number 13? Why, don't I tell you that there isn't such a thing in the house? I thought you might have noticed that. If there was it would be next door to your own room."

"Well, yes; only I happened to think—that is, I fancied last night that I had seen a door numbered thirteen in that passage; and, really, I am almost certain I must have been right, for I saw it the night before as well."

Of course, Herr Kristensen laughed this notion to scorn, as Anderson had expected, and emphasized with much iteration the fact that no Number 13 existed or had existed before him in that hotel.

Anderson was in some ways relieved by his certainty, but still puzzled, and he began to think that the best way to make sure whether he had indeed been subject to an illusion or not was to invite the landlord to his room to smoke a cigar later on in the evening. Some photographs of English towns which he had with him formed a sufficiently good excuse.

Herr Kristensen was flattered by the invitation, and most willingly accepted it. At about ten o'clock he was to make his appearance, but before that Anderson had some letters to write, and retired for the purpose of writing them. He almost blushed to himself at confessing it, but he could not deny that it was the fact that he was becoming quite nervous about the question of the existence of Number 13; so much so that he approached his room by way of Number 11, in order that he might not be obliged to pass the door, or the place where the door ought to be. He looked quickly and suspiciously about the room when entered it, but there was nothing, beyond that indefinable air of being smaller than usual, to warrant any misgivings. There was no question of the presence or absence of his portmanteau tonight. He had himself emptied it of its contents and lodged it under his bed. With a certain effort he dismissed the thought of Number 13 from his mind, and sat down to his writing.

His neighbours were quiet enough. Occasionally a door opened in the passage and pair of boots was thrown out, or a bagman walked past humming to himself, and outside, from time to time a cart thundered over the atrocious cobble-stones, or a quick step hurried along the flags.

Anderson finished his letters, ordered whisky and soda, and then went to the window and studied the dead wall opposite and and the shadows upon it.

As far as he could remember, Number 14 had been occupied by the lawyer, a staid man, who said little at meals, being generally engaged in studying a small bundle of papers beside his plate. Apparently, however, he was in the habit of giving vent to his animal spirits when alone. Why else should he be dancing? The shadow from the next room evidently showed that he was. Again and again his thin form crossed the window, his arms waved, and a gaunt leg was kicked up with surprising agility. He seemed to be barefooted, and the floor must be well laid, for no sound betrayed his movements. Sagförer Herr Anders Jensen, dancing at ten o'clock at night in a hotel bedroom, seemed a fitting subject for a historical painting in the grand style; and Anderson's thoughts, like those of Emily in the *Mysteries of Udolpho*, began to arrange themselves in the following lines:

When I return to my hotel.
  At ten o'clock p.m.,
The waiters think I am unwell;
  I do not care for them.
But when I've locked my chamber door,
  And put my boots outside.

I dance all night upon the floor.
  And even if my neighbours swore,
I' go on dancing all the more.
  For I'm acquainted with the law.
And in despite of all their jaw.
  Their protests I deride.

Had not the landlord at this moment knocked at the door, it is probable that quite a long poem might have been laid before the reader. To judge from his look of surprise when he found himself in the room, Herr Kristensen was struck, as Anderson had been, by something unusual in its aspect. But he made no remark. Anderson's photographs interested him mightily, and formed the text of many autobiographical discourses. Nor is it quite clear how the conversation could have been diverted into the desired channel of Number 13, had not the lawyer at this moment begun to sing, and to sing in a manner which could leave no doubt in anyone's mind that he was either exceedingly drunk or raving mad. It was a high, thin voice that they heard, and it seemed dry, as if from long disuse. Of words or tune there was no question. It went sailing up to a surprising height, and was carried down with a despairing moan as of a winter wind in a hollow chimney, or an organ whose wind fails suddenly. It was a really horrible sound, and Anderson felt that if he had been alone he must have fled for refuge and society to some neighbour bagman's room.

The landlord sat open-mouthed.

"I don't understand it" he said at last, wiping his forehead. "It is dreadful. I have heard it once before, but I made sure it was a cat."

"Is he mad?" said Anderson.

"He must be; and what a sad thing! Such a good customer, too, and so successful in his business, by what I hear, and a young family to bring up."

Just then came an impatient knock at the door, and the knocker entered, without waiting to be asked. It was the lawyer, in deshabille and very rough-haired; and very angry he looked.

"I beg pardon, sir," he said, "but I should be much obliged if you would kindly desist—"

Here he stopped, for it was evident that neither of the persons before him was responsible for the disturbance; and after a moment's lull it swelled forth again more wildly than before.

"But what in the name of Heaven does it mean?" broke out the lawyer. "Where is it? Who is it? Am I going out of my mind?"

"Surely, Herr Jensen, it comes from your room next door? Isn't there a cat or something stuck in the chimney?"

This was the best that occurred to Anderson to say, and he realized its futility as he spoke; but anything was better than to stand and listen to that horrible voice, and look at the broad, white face of the landlord, all perspiring and quivering as he clutched the arms of his chair.

"Impossible," said the lawyer, "impossible. There is no chimney. I came here because I was convinced the noise was going on here. It was certainly in the next room to mine."

"Was there no door between yours and mine?" said Anderson eagerly.

"No, sir," said Herr Jensen, rather sharply. "At least, not this morning."

"Ah!" said Anderson. "Nor tonight?"

"I am not sure," said the lawyer with some hesitation.

Suddenly the crying or singing voice in the next room died away, and the singer was heard seemingly to laugh to himself in a crooning manner. The three men actually shivered at the sound. Then there was a silence.

"Come," said the lawyer, "what have you to say, Herr Kristensen? What does this mean?"

"Good Heaven!' said Kristensen. "How should I tell! I know no more than you, gentlemen. I pray I may never hear such a noise again."

"So do I," said Herr Jensen, and he added something under his breath. Anderson thought it sounded like the last words of the Psalter, "*omnis spirittis laudet Dominum*" but he could not be sure.

"But we must do something," said Anderson—"the three of us. Shall we go and investigate in the next room?'

"But that is Herr Jensen's room," wailed the landlord. "It is no use; he has come from there himself.'

"I am not so sure" said Jensen. "I think this gentleman is right: we must go and see."

The only weapons of defence that could be mustered on the spot were a stick and umbrella. The expedition went out into the passage, not without quakings. There was a deadly quiet outside, but a light shone from under the next door. Anderson and Jensen approached it. The latter turned the handle, and gave a sudden vigorous push. No use. The door stood fast.

"Herr Kristensen," said Jensen, "will you go and fetch the strongest servant you have in the place? We must see this through."

The landlord nodded, and hurried off, glad to be away from the scene of action. Jensen and Anderson remained outside looking at the door.

"It *is* Number 13, you see," said the latter.

"Yes; there is your door, and there is mine," said Jensen.

"My room has three windows in the daytime," said Anderson, with difficulty suppressing a nervous laugh.

"By George, so has mine!" said the lawyer, turning and looking at Anderson. His back was now to the door. In that moment the door opened, and an arm came out and clawed at his shoulder. It was clad in ragged, yellowish linen, and the bare skin, where it could be seen, had long gray hair upon it.

Anderson was just in time to pull Jensen out of its reach with a cry of disgust and fright, when the door shut again, and a low laugh was heard.

Jensen had seen nothing, but when Anderson hurriedly told him what a risk he had run, he fell into a great state of agitation, and suggested that they should retire from the enterprise and lock themselves up in one or other of their rooms.

However, while he was developing this plan, the landlord and two able-bodied men arrived on the scene, all looking rather serious and alarmed. Jensen met them with a torrent of description and explanation, which did not at all tend to encourage them for the fray.

The men dropped the crowbars they brought, and said flatly that they were going to risk their throats in that devil's den. The landlord was miserably nervous and decided, conscious that if the danger were faced his hotel was ruined, and very loath to face it himself. Luckily Anderson hit upon; way of rallying the demoralized force.

"Is this," he said, "the Danish courage I heard so much of? It isn't a German in the and if it was, we are five to one."

The two servants and Jensen were stung action by this, and made a dash at the door.

"Stop!" said Anderson. "Don't lose your heads. You stay out here with the light, landlord, and one of you two men break the door, and don't go in when it gives way."

The men nodded, and the younger stepped forward, raised his crowbar, and dealt tremendous blow on the upper panel. The result was not in the least what any of them anticipated. There was no cracking or rending of wood—only a dull sound, as if the solid wall had been struck. The man dropped his tool with a shout, and began rubbing his elbow. His cry drew their eyes upon him for a moment; then Anderson looked at the door again. It was gone; the plaster wall of the passage stared him in the face, with a considerable gash in it where the crowbar had struck it. Number 13 had passed out of existence.

For a brief space they stood perfectly still, gazing at the blank wall. An early cock in the yard beneath was heard to crow; and as Anderson glanced in the direction of the sound, he saw through the window at the end of the long passage that the eastern sky was paling to the dawn.

"Perhaps," said the landlord, with hesitation, "you gentlemen would like another room for tonight—a double-bedded one?"

Neither Jensen nor Anderson was averse to the suggestion. They felt inclined to hunt in couples after their late experience. It was found convenient, when each of them went to his room to collect the articles he wanted for the night, that the other should go with him and hold the candle. They noticed that both Number 12 and Number 14 had *three* windows.

Next morning the same party re-assembled in Number 12. The landlord was naturally anxious to avoid engaging outside help, and yet it was imperative that the mystery attaching to that part of the house should be cleared up. Accordingly the two servants had been induced to take upon them the function of carpenters. The furniture was cleared away, and, at the cost of a good many irretrievably damaged planks, that portion of the floor was taken up which lay nearest to Number 14.

You will naturally suppose that a skeleton—say that of Mag. Nicolas Francken—was discovered. That was not so. What they did find lying between the beams which supported the flooring was a small copper box. In it was a neatly-folded vellum document, with about twenty lines of writing. Both Anderson and Jensen (who proved to be something of apalæographer) were much excited by this discovery, which promised to afford the key to these extraordinary phenomena.

I possess a copy of an astrological work which I have never read. It has, by way of frontispiece, a woodcut by Hans Sebald Beham, representing a number of sages seated round a table. This detail may enable connoisseurs to identify the book. I cannot myself recollect its title, and it is not at this moment within reach; but the fly-leaves of it are covered with writing, and, during the ten years in which I have owned the volume, I have not been able to determine which way up this writing ought to be read, much less in what language it is. Not dissimilar was the position of Anderson and Jensen after the protracted examination to which they submitted the document in the copper box.

After two days' contemplation of it, Jensen, who was the bolder spirit of the two, hazarded the conjecture that the language was either Latin or Old Danish.

Anderson ventured upon no surmises, and was very willing to surrender the box and the parchment to the Historical Society of Viborg to be placed in their museum.

I had the whole story from him a few months later, as we sat in a wood near Upsala, after a visit to the library there, where we—or, rather, I—had laughed over the contract by which Daniel Salthenius (in later life Professor of Hebrew at Königsberg) sold himself to Satan. Anderson was not really amused.

"Young idiot!" he said, meaning Salthenius, who was only an undergraduate when he committed that indiscretion, "how did he know what company he was courting?"

And when I suggested the usual considerations he only grunted. That same afternoon he told me what you have read; but he refused to draw any inferences from it, and to assent to any that I drew for him.

The Wailing Well

by M. R. James

In the year 19— there were two members of the Troop of Scouts attached to a famous school, named respectively Arthur Wilcox and Stanley Judkins. They were the same age, boarded in the same house, were in the same division, and naturally were members of the same patrol. They were so much alike in appearance as to cause anxiety and trouble, and even irritation, to the masters who came in contact with them. But oh how different were they in their inward man, or boy!

It was to Arthur Wilcox that the Head Master said, looking up with a smile as the boy entered chambers, "Why, Wilcox, there will be a deficit in the prize fund if you stay here much longer! Here, take this handsomely bound copy of the *Life and Works of Bishop Ken*, and with it my hearty congratulations to yourself and your excellent parents." It was Wilcox again, whom the Provost noticed as he passed through the playing fields, and, pausing for a moment, observed to the Vice-Provost, "That lad has a remarkable brow!" "Indeed, yes," said the Vice-Provost. "It denotes either genius or water on the brain."

As a Scout, Wilcox secured every badge and distinction for which he competed. The Cookery Badge, the Map-making Badge, the Life-saving Badge, the Badge for picking up bits of newspaper, the Badge for not slamming the door when leaving pupil-room, and many others. Of the Life-saving Badge I may have a word to say when we come to treat of Stanley Judkins.

You cannot be surprised to hear that Mr Hope Jones added a special verse to each of his songs, in commendation of Arthur Wilcox, or that the Lower Master burst into tears when handing him the Good Conduct Medal in its handsome claret-coloured case: the medal which had been unanimously voted to him by the whole of Third Form. Unanimously, did I say? I am wrong. There was one dissentient, Judkins mi., who said that he had excellent reasons for acting as he did. He shared, it seems, a room with his major. You cannot, again, wonder that in after years Arthur Wilcox was the first, and so far the only boy, to become Captain of both the School and of the Oppidans, or that the strain of carrying out the duties of both positions, coupled with the ordinary work of the school, was so severe that a complete rest for six months, followed by a voyage round the world, was pronounced an absolute necessity by the family doctor.

It would be a pleasant task to trace the steps by which he attained the giddy eminence he now occupies; but for the moment enough of Arthur Wilcox. Time presses, and we must turn to a very different matter: the career of Stanley Judkins—Judkins ma.

Stanley Judkins, like Arthur Wilcox, attracted the attention of the authorities; but in quite another fashion. It was to him that the Lower Master said, with no cheerful smile, "What, again, Judkins? A very little persistence in this course of conduct, my boy, and you will have cause to regret that you ever entered this academy. There, take that, and that, and think yourself very lucky you don't get that and that!" It was Judkins, again, whom the Provost had cause to notice as he passed through the playing fields, when a cricket ball struck him with considerable force on the ankle, and a voice from a short way off cried, "Thank you, cut-over!" "I think," said the Provost, pausing for a moment to rub his ankle, "that that boy had better fetch his cricket ball for himself!" "Indeed, yes," said the Vice-Provost, "and if he comes within reach, I will do my best to fetch him something else."

As a Scout, Stanley Judkins secured no badge save those which he was able to abstract from members of other patrols. In the cookery competition he was detected trying to introduce squibs into the Dutch oven of the next-door competitors. In the tailoring competition he succeeded in sewing two boys together very firmly, with disastrous effect when they tried to get up. For the Tidiness Badge he was disqualified, because, in the Midsummer schooltime, which chanced to be hot, he could not be dissuaded from sitting with his fingers in the ink: as he said, for coolness' sake. For one piece of paper which he picked up, he must have dropped at least six banana skins or orange peels. Aged women seeing him approaching would beg him with tears in their eyes not to carry their pails of water across the road. They knew too well what the result would inevitably be. But it was in the life-saving competition that Stanley Judkins's conduct was most blameable and had the most far-reaching effects. The practice, as you know, was to throw a selected lower boy, of suitable dimensions, fully dressed, with his hands and feet tied together, into the deepest part of Cuckoo Weir, and to time the Scout whose turn it was to rescue him. On every occasion when he was entered for this competition Stanley Judkins was seized, at the critical moment, with a severe fit of cramp, which caused him to roll on the ground and utter alarming cries. This naturally distracted the attention of those present from the boy in the water, and had it not been for the presence of Arthur Wilcox the death-roll would have been a heavy one. As it was, the Lower Master found it necessary to take a firm line and say that the competition must be discontinued. It was in vain that Mr Beasley Robinson represented to him that in five competitions only four lower boys had actually succumbed. The Lower Master said that he would be the last to interfere in any way with the work of the Scouts; but that three of these boys had been valued members of his choir, and both he and Dr. Ley felt that the inconvenience caused by the losses outweighed the advantages of the competitions. Besides, the correspondence with the parents of these boys had become annoying, and even distressing: they were no longer satisfied with the printed form which he was in the habit of sending out, and more than one of them had actually visited Eton and taken up much of his valuable time with complaints. So the life-saving competition is now a thing of the past.

In short, Stanley Judkins was no credit to the Scouts, and, there was talk on more than one occasion of informing him that his services were no longer required. This course was strongly advocated by Mr Lambart: but in the end milder counsels prevailed, and it was decided to give him another chance.

So it is that we find him at the beginning of the Midsummer Holidays of 19— at the Scouts' camp in the beautiful district of W (or X) in the county of D (or Y).

It was a lovely morning, and Stanley Judkins and one or two of his friends—for he still had friends—lay basking on the top of the down. Stanley was lying on his stomach with his chin propped on his hands, staring into the distance.

"I wonder what that place is," he said.

"Which place?" said one of the others.

"That sort of clump in the middle of the field down there."

"Oh, ah! How should I know what it is?"

"What do you want to know for?" said another.

"I don't know: I like the look of it. What's it called? Nobody got a map?" said Stanley. "Call yourselves Scouts!"

"Here's a map all right," said Wilfred Pipsqueak, ever resourceful, "and there's the place marked on it. But it's inside the red ring. We can't go there."

"Who cares about a red ring?" said Stanley. "But it's got no name on your silly map."

"Well, you can ask this old chap what it's called if you're so keen to find out." "This old chap" was an old shepherd who had come up and was standing behind them.

"Good morning, young gents," he said, "you've got a fine day for your doin's, ain't you?"

"Yes, thank you," said Algernon de Montmorency, with native politeness. "Can you tell us what that clump over there's called? And what's that thing inside it?"

"Course I can tell you," said the shepherd. "That's Wailin' Well, that is. But you ain't got no call to worry about that."

"Is it a well in there?" said Algernon. "Who uses it?"

The shepherd laughed. "Bless you," he said, "there ain't from a man to a sheep in these parts uses Wailin' Well, nor haven't done all the years I've lived here."

"Well, there'll be a record broken today, then," said Stanley Judkins, "because I shall go and get some water out of it for tea!"

"Sakes alive, young gentleman!" said the shepherd in a startled voice, "don't you get to talkin' that way! Why, ain't your masters give you notice not to go by there? They'd ought to have done."

"Yes, they have," said Wilfred Pipsqueak

"Shut up, you ass!" said Stanley Judkins. "What's the matter with it? Isn't the water good? Anyhow, if it was boiled, it would be all right."

"I don't know as there's anything much wrong with the water," said the shepherd. "All I know is, my old dog wouldn't go through that field, let alone me or anyone else that's got a morsel of brains in their heads."

"More fool them," said Stanley Judkins, at once rudely and ungrammatically. "Who ever took any harm going there?" he added.

"Three women and a man," said the shepherd gravely. "Now just you listen to me. I know these 'ere parts and you don't, and I can tell you this much: for these ten years last past there ain't been a sheep fed in that field, nor a crop raised off of it—and it's good land, too. You can pretty well see from here what a state it's got into with brambles and suckers and trash of all kinds. You've got a glass, young gentleman," he said to Wilfred Pipsqueak, "you can tell with that anyway."

"Yes," said Wilfred, "but I see there's tracks in it. Someone must go through it sometimes."

"Tracks!" said the shepherd. "I believe you! Four tracks: three women and a man."

"What d'you mean, three women and a man?" said Stanley, turning over for the first time and looking at the shepherd (he had been talking with his back to him till this moment: he was an ill-mannered boy).

"Mean? Why, what I says: three women and a man."

"Who are they?" asked Algernon. "Why do they go there?"

"There's some p'r'aps could tell you who they was," said the shepherd, "but it was afore my time they come by their end. And why they goes there still is more than the children of men can tell: except I've heard they was all bad 'uns when they was alive."

"By George, what a rum thing!" Algernon and Wilfred muttered: but Stanley was scornful and bitter.

"Why, you don't mean they're deaders? What rot! You must be a lot of fools to believe that. Who's ever seen them, I'd like to know?"

"I've seen 'em, young gentleman!" said the shepherd, "seen 'em from near by on that bit of down: and my old dog, if he could speak, he'd tell you he've seen 'em, same time. About four o'clock of the day it was, much such a day as this. I see 'em, each one of 'em, come peerin' out of the bushes and stand up, and work their way slow by them tracks towards the trees in the middle where the well is."

"And what were they like? Do tell us!" said Algernon and Wilfred eagerly.

"Rags and bones, young gentlemen: all four of 'em: flutterin' rags and whity bones. It seemed to me as if I could hear 'em clackin' as they got along. Very slow they went, and lookin' from side to side."

"What were their faces like? Could you see?"

"They hadn't much to call faces," said the shepherd, "but I could seem to see as they had teeth."

"Lor'!" said Wilfred, "and what did they do when they got to the trees?"

"I can't tell you that, sir," said the shepherd. "I wasn't for stayin' in that place, and if I had been, I was bound to look to my old dog: he'd gone! Such a thing he never done before as leave me; but gone he had, and when I came up with him in the end, he was in that state he didn't know me, and was fit to fly at my throat. But I kep' talkin' to him, and after a bit he remembered my voice and came creepin' up like a child askin' pardon. I never want to see him like that again, nor yet no other dog."

The dog, who had come up and was making friends all round, looked up at his master, and expressed agreement with what he was saying very fully.

The boys pondered for some moments on what they had heard: after which Wilfred said: "And why's it called Wailing Well?"

"If you was round here at dusk of a winter's evening, you wouldn't want to ask why," was all the shepherd said.

"Well, I don't believe a word of it," said Stanley Judkins, "and I'll go there next chance I get: blowed if I don't!"

"Then you won't be ruled by me?" said the shepherd. "Nor yet by your masters as warned you off? Come now, young gentleman, you don't want for sense, I should say. What should I want tellin' you a pack of lies? It ain't sixpence to me anyone goin' in that field: but I wouldn't like to see a young chap snuffed out like in his prime."

"I expect it's a lot more than sixpence to you," said Stanley. "I expect you've got a whisky still or something in there, and want to keep other people away. Rot I call it. Come on back, you boys."

So they turned away. The two others said, "Good evening" and "Thank you" to the shepherd, but Stanley said nothing. The shepherd shrugged his shoulders and stood where he was, looking after them rather sadly.

On the way back to the camp there was great argument about it all, and Stanley was told as plainly as he could be told all the sorts of fools he would be if he went to the Wailing Well.

That evening, among other notices, Mr Beasley Robinson asked if all maps had got the red ring marked on them. "Be particular," he said, "not to trespass inside it."

Several voices—among them the sulky one of Stanley Judkins—said, "Why not, sir?"

"Because not," said Mr Beasley Robinson, "and if that isn't enough for you, I can't help it." He turned and spoke to Mr Lambart in a low voice, and then said, "I'll tell you this much: we've been asked to warn Scouts off that field. It's very good of the people to let us camp here at all, and the least we can do is to oblige them—I'm sure you'll agree to that."

Everybody said, "Yes, sir!" except Stanley Judkins, who was heard to mutter, "Oblige them be blowed!"

Early in the afternoon of the next day, the following dialogue was heard. "Wilcox, is all your tent there?"

"No, sir, Judkins isn't!"

"That boy is the most infernal nuisance ever invented! Where do you suppose he is?"

"I haven't an idea, sir."

"Does anybody else know?"

"Sir, I shouldn't wonder if he'd gone to the Wailing Well."

"Who's that? Pipsqueak? What's the Wailing Well?"

"Sir, it's that place in the field by—well, sir, it's in a clump of trees in a rough field."

"D'you mean inside the red ring? Good heavens! What makes you think he's gone there?"

"Why, he was terribly keen to know about it yesterday, and we were talking to a shepherd man, and he told us a lot about it and advised us not to go there: but Judkins didn't believe him, and said he meant to go."

"Young ass!" said Mr Hope Jones, "did he take anything with him?"

"Yes, I think he took some rope and a can. We did tell him he'd be a fool to go."

"Little brute! What the deuce does he mean by pinching stores like that! Well, come along, you three, we must see after him. Why can't people keep the simplest orders? What was it the man told you? No, don't wait, let's have it as we go along."

And off they started—Algernon and Wilfred talking rapidly and the other two listening with growing concern. At last they reached that spur of down overlooking the field of which the shepherd had spoken the day before. It commanded the place completely; the well inside the dump of bent and gnarled Scotch firs was plainly visible, and so were the four tracks winding about among the thorns and rough growth.

It was a wonderful day of shimmering heat. The sea looked like a floor of metal. There was no breath of wind. They were all exhausted when they got to the top, and flung themselves down on the hot grass.

"Nothing to be seen of him yet," said Mr Hope Jones, "but we must stop here a bit. You're done up—not to speak of me. Keep a sharp look-out," he went on after a moment, "I thought I saw the bushes stir."

"Yes," said Wilcox, "so did I. Look … no, that can't be him. It's somebody though, putting their head up, isn't it?"

"I thought it was, but I'm not sure."

Silence for a moment. Then:

"That's him, sure enough," said Wilcox, "getting over the hedge on the far side. Don't you see? With a shiny thing. That's the can you said he had."

"Yes, it's him, and he's making straight for the trees," said Wilfred.

At this moment Algernon, who had been staring with all his might, broke into a scream.

"What's that on the track? On all fours—O, it's the woman. O, don't let me look at her! Don't let it happen!" And he rolled over, clutching at the grass and trying to bury his head in it.

"Stop that!" said Mr Hope Jones loudly—but it was no use. "Look here," he said, "I must go down there. You stop here, Wilfred, and look after that boy. Wilcox, you run as hard as you can to the camp and get some help."

They ran off, both of them. Wilfred was left alone with Algernon, and did his best to calm him, but indeed he was not much happier himself. From time to time he glanced down the hill and into the held. He saw Mr Hope Jones drawing nearer at a swift pace, and then, to his great surprise, he saw him stop, look up and round about him, and turn quickly off at an angle! What could be the reason? He looked at the field, and there he saw a terrible figure—something in ragged black—with whitish patches breaking out of it: the head, perched on a long thin neck, half hidden by a shapeless sort of blackened sun-bonnet. The creature was waving thin arms in the direction of the rescuer who was approaching, as if to ward him off: and between the two figures the air seemed to shake and shimmer as he had never seen it: and as he looked, he began himself to feel something of a waviness and confusion in his brain, which made him guess what might be the effect on someone within closer range of the influence. He looked away hastily, to see Stanley Judkins making his way pretty quickly towards the clump, and in proper Scout fashion; evidently picking his steps with care to avoid treading on snapping sticks or being caught by arms of brambles. Evidently, though he saw nothing, he suspected some sort of ambush, and was trying to go noiselessly. Wilfred saw all that, and he saw more, too. With a sudden and dreadful sinking at the heart, he caught sight of someone among the trees, waiting: and again of someone—another of the hideous black figures—working slowly along the track from another side of the held, looking from side to side, as the shepherd had described it. Worst of all, he saw a fourth—unmistakably a man this time—rising out of the bushes a few yards behind the wretched Stanley, and painfully, as it seemed, crawling into the track. On all sides the miserable victim was cut off.

Wilfred was at his wits' end. He rushed at Algernon and shook him. "Get up," he said. "Yell! Yell as loud as you can. Oh, if we'd got a whistle!"

Algernon pulled himself together. "There's one," he said, "Wilcox's: he must have dropped it."

So one whistled, the other screamed. In the still air the sound carried. Stanley heard: he stopped: he turned round: and then indeed a cry was heard more piercing and dreadful than any that the boys on the hill could raise. It was too late. The crouched figure behind Stanley sprang at him and caught him about the waist. The dreadful one that was standing waving her arms waved them again, but in exultation. The one that was lurking among the trees shuffled forward, and she too stretched out her arms as if to clutch at something coming her way; and the other, farthest off, quickened her pace and came on, nodding gleefully. The boys took it all in in an instant of terrible silence, and hardly could they breathe as they watched the horrid struggle between the man and his victim. Stanley struck with his can, the only weapon he had. The rim of a broken black hat fell off the creature's head and showed a white skull with stains that might be wisps of hair. By this time one of the women had reached the pair, and was pulling at the rope that was coiled about Stanley's neck. Between them they overpowered him in a moment: the awful screaming ceased, and then the three passed within the circle of the clump of firs.

Yet for a moment it seemed as if rescue might come. Mr Hope Jones, striding quickly along, suddenly stopped, turned, seemed to rub his eyes, and then started running towards the field. More: the boys glanced behind them, and saw not only a troop of figures from the camp coming over the top of the next down, but the shepherd running up the slope of their own hill. They beckoned, they shouted, they ran a few yards towards him and then back again. He mended his pace.

Once more the boys looked towards the field. There was nothing. Or, was there something among the trees? Why was there a mist about the trees? Mr

Hope Jones had scrambled over the hedge, and was plunging through the bushes.

The shepherd stood beside them, panting. They ran to him and clung to his arms. "They've got him! In the trees!" was as much as they could say, over and over again.

"What? Do you tell me he've gone in there after all I said to him yesterday? Poor young thing! Poor young thing!" He would have said more, but other voices broke in. The rescuers from the camp had arrived. A few hasty words, and all were dashing down the hill.

They had just entered the field when they met Mr Hope Jones. Over his shoulder hung the corpse of Stanley Judkins. He had cut it from the branch to which he found it hanging, waving to and fro. There was not a drop of blood in the body.

On the following day Mr Hope Jones sallied forth with an axe and with the expressed intention of cutting down every tree in the clump, and of burning every bush in the field. He returned with a nasty cut in his leg and a broken axe-helve. Not a spark of fire could he light, and on no single tree could he make the least impression.

I have heard that the present population of the Wailing Well field consists of three women, a man, and a boy.

The shock experienced by Algernon de Montmorency and Wilfred Pipsqueak was severe. Both of them left the camp at once; and the occurrence undoubtedly cast a gloom—if but a passing one—on those who remained. One of the first to recover his spirits was Judkins mi.

Such, gentlemen, is the story of the career of Stanley Judkins, and of a portion of the career of Arthur Wilcox. It has, I believe, never been told before. If it has a moral, that moral is, I trust, obvious: if it has none, I do not well know how to help it.

The Voice in the Night

by William Hope Hodgson

It was a dark, starless night. We were becalmed in the northern Pacific. Our exact position I do not know; for the sun had been hidden during the course of a weary, breathless week by a thin haze which had seemed to float above us, about the height of our mastheads, at whiles descending and shrouding the surrounding sea.

With there being no wind, we had steadied the tiller, and I was the only man on deck. The crew, consisting of two men and a boy, were sleeping forward in their den, while Will—my friend, and the master of our little craft—was aft in his bunk on the port side of the little cabin.

Suddenly, from out of the surrounding darkness, there came a hail:

"Schooner, ahoy!"

The cry was so unexpected that I gave no immediate answer, because of my surprise.

It came again—a voice curiously throaty and inhuman, calling from somewhere upon the dark sea away on our port broadside:

"Schooner, ahoy!"

"Hullo!" I sang out, having gathered my wits somewhat. "What are you? What do you want?"

"You need not be afraid," answered the queer voice, having probably noticed some trace of confusion in my tone. "I am only an old—man."

The pause sounded odd, but it was only afterward that it came back to me with any significance.

"Why don't you come alongside, then?" I queried somewhat snappishly, for I liked not his hinting at my having been a trifle shaken.

"I—I—can't. It wouldn't be safe. I—" The voice broke off, and there was silence.

"What do you mean?" I asked, growing more and more astonished. "What's not safe? Where are you?"

I listened for a moment, but there came no answer. And then, a sudden indefinite suspicion, of I knew not what, coming to me, I stepped swiftly to the binnacle and took out the lighted lamp. At the same time, I knocked on the deck with my heel to waken Will. Then I was back at the side, throwing the yellow funnel of light out into the silent immensity beyond our rail. As I did so, I heard a slight muffled cry, and then the sound of a splash, as though someone had dipped oars abruptly. Yet I cannot say with certainty that I saw anything; save, it seemed to me, that with the first flash of the light there had been something upon the waters, where now there was nothing.

"Hullo, there!" I called. "What foolery is this?"

But there came only the indistinct sounds of a boat being pulled away into the night.

Then I heard Will's voice from the direction of the after scuttle:

"What's up, George?"

"Come here, Will!" I said.

"What is it?" he asked, coming across the deck.

I told him the queer thing that had happened. He put several questions; then, after a moment's silence, he raised his hands to his lips and hailed:

"Boat, ahoy!"

From a long distance away there came back to us a faint reply, and my companion repeated his call. Presently, after a short period of silence, there grew on our hearing the muffled sound of oars, at which Will hailed again.

This time there was a reply: "Put away the light."

"I'm damned if I will," I muttered; but Will told me to do as the voice bade, and I shoved it down under the bulwarks.

"Come nearer," he said, and the oar strokes continued. Then, when apparently some half dozen fathoms distant, they again ceased.

"Come alongside!" exclaimed Will. "There's nothing to be frightened of aboard here."

"Promise that you will not show the light?"

"What's to do with you," I burst out, "that you're so infernally afraid of the light?"

"Because—" began the voice, and stopped short.

"Because what?" I asked quickly.

Will put his hand on my shoulder. "Shut up a minute, old man," he said in a low voice. "Let me tackle him."

He leaned more over the rail. "See here, mister," he said, "this is a pretty queer business, you coming upon us like this, right out in the middle of the blessed Pacific. How are we to know what sort of a hanky-panky trick you're up to? You say there's only one of you. How are we to know, unless we get a squint at you—eh? What's your objection to the light, anyway?"

As he finished, I heard the noise of the oars again, and then the voice came; but now from a greater distance, and sounding extremely hopeless and pathetic.

"I am sorry—sorry! I would not have troubled you, only I am hungry, and—so is she."

The voice died away, and the sound of the oars, dipping irregularly, was borne to us.

"Stop!" sang out Will. "I don't want to drive you away. Come back! We'll keep the light hidden if you don't like it."

He turned to me. "It's a damned queer rig, this; but I think there's nothing to be afraid of?"

There was a question in his tone, and I replied, "No, I think the poor devil's been wrecked around here, and gone crazy."

The sound of the oars drew nearer.

"Shove that lamp back in the binnacle," said Will; then he leaned over the rail and listened. I replaced the lamp and came back to his side. The dipping of the oars ceased some dozen yards distant.

"Won't you come alongside now?" asked Will in an even voice. "I have had the lamp put back in the binnacle."

"I—I cannot," replied the voice. "I dare not come nearer. I dare not even pay you for the—the provisions."

"That's all right," said Will, and hesitated. "You're welcome to as much grub as you can take—" Again he hesitated.

"You are very good!" exclaimed the voice. "May God, who understands everything, reward you—" It broke off huskily.

"The—the lady?" said Will abruptly. "Is she—"

"I have left her behind upon the island," came the voice.

"What island?" I cut in.

"I know not its name," returned the voice. "I would to God—" it began, and checked itself as suddenly.

"Could we not send a boat for her?" asked Will at this point.

"No!" said the voice, with extraordinary emphasis. "My God! No!" There was a moment's pause; then it added, in a tone which seemed a merited reproach, "It was because of our want I ventured—because her agony tortured me."

"I am a forgetful brute!" exclaimed Will. "Just wait a minute, whoever you are, and I will bring you up something at once."

In a couple of minutes he was back again, and his arms were full of various edibles. He paused at the rail.

"Can't you come alongside for them?" he asked.

"No—I dare not," replied the voice, and it seemed to me that in its tones I detected a note of stifled craving, as though the owner hushed a mortal desire. It came to me then in a flash that the poor old creature out there in the darkness was suffering for actual need for that which Will held in his arms; and yet, because of some unintelligible dread, refraining from dashing to the side of our schooner and receiving it. And with the lightninglike conviction there came the knowledge that the Invisible was not mad, but sanely facing some intolerable horror.

"Damn it, Will!" I said, full of many feelings, over which predominated a vast sympathy. "Get a box. We must float off the stuff to him in it."

This we did, propelling it away from the vessel, out into the darkness, by means of a boat hook.

In a minute a slight cry from the Invisible came to us, and we knew that he had secured the box.

A little later he called out a farewell to us, and so heartful a blessing that I am sure we were the better for it. Then, without more ado, we heard the ply of oars across the darkness.

"Pretty soon off," remarked Will, with perhaps just a little sense of injury.

"Wait," I replied. "I think somehow he'll come back. He must have been badly needing that food."

"And the lady," said Will. For a moment he was silent; then he continued, "It's the queerest thing ever I've tumbled across since I've been fishing."

"Yes," I said, and fell to pondering.

And so the time slipped away—an hour, another, and still Will stayed with me; for the queer adventure had knocked all desire for sleep out of him.

The third hour was three parts through when we heard again the sound of oars across the silent ocean.

"Listen!" said Will, a low note of excitement in his voice.

"He's coming, just as I thought," I muttered.

The dipping of the oars grew nearer, and I noted that the strokes were firmer and longer. The food had been needed.

They came to a stop a little distance off the broadside, and the queer voice came again to us through the darkness:

"Schooner, ahoy!"

"That you?" asked Will.

"Yes," replied the voice. "I left you suddenly, but—but there was great need."

"The lady?" questioned Will.

"The—lady is grateful now on earth. She will be more grateful soon in—in heaven."

Will began to make some reply, in a puzzled voice, but became confused and broke off. I said nothing. I was wondering at the curious pauses, and apart from my wonder, I was full of a great sympathy.

The voice continued, "We—she and I, have talked, as we shared the result of God's tenderness and yours—"

Will interposed, but without coherence

"I beg of you not to—to belittle your deed of Christian charity this night," said the voice. "Be sure that it has not escaped His notice."

It stopped, and there was a full minute's silence. Then it came again. "We have spoken together upon that which—which has befallen us. We had thought to go out, without telling anyone of the terror which has come into our—lives. She is with me in believing that tonight's happenings are under a special ruling, and that it is God's wish that we should tell to you all that we have suffered since—since—"

"Yes?" said Will softly.

"Since the sinking of the Albatross."

"Ah!" I exclaimed involuntarily. "She left Newcastle for 'Frisco some six months ago, and hasn't been heard of since."

"Yes" answered the voice. "But some few degrees to the north of the line, she was caught in a terrible storm and dismasted. When the calm came, it was found that she was leaking badly, and presently, it falling to a calm, the sailors took to the boats, leaving—leaving a young lady—my fiancée—and myself upon the wreck.

"We were below, gathering together a few of our belongings, when they left. They were entirely callous, through fear, and when we came up upon the decks, we saw them only as small shapes afar off upon the horizon. Yet we did not despair, but set to work and constructed a small raft. Upon this we put such few matters as it would hold, including a quantity of water and some ship's biscuit. Then, the vessel being very deep in the water, we got ourselves onto the raft and pushed off.

"It was later that I observed we seemed to be in the way of some tide or current, which bore us from the ship at an angle, so that in the course of three hours, by my watch, her hull became invisible to our sight, her broken masts remaining in view for a somewhat longer period. Then, toward evening, it grew misty, and so through the night. The next day we were still encompassed by the mist, the weather remaining quiet.

"For four days we drifted through this strange haze, until, on the evening of the fourth day, there grew upon our ears the murmur of breakers at a distance. Gradually it became plainer, and somewhat after midnight, it appeared to sound upon either hand at no very great space. The raft was raised upon a swell several times, and then we were in smooth water, and the noise of the breakers was behind.

"When the morning came, we found that we were in a sort of great lagoon, but of this we noticed little at the time; for close before us, through the enshrouding mist, loomed the hull of a large sailing vessel. With one accord we fell upon our knees and thanked God, for we thought that here was an end to our perils. We had much to learn.

"The raft drew near to the ship, and we shouted on them to take us aboard; but none answered. Presently the raft touched against the side of the vessel, and seeing a rope hanging downward, I seized it and began to climb. Yet I had much ado to make my way up, because of a kind of grey, lichenous fungus that had seized upon the rope and blotched the side of the ship lividly.

"I reached the rail and clambered over it, onto the deck. Here I saw that the decks were covered in great patches with the grey masses, some of them rising into nodules several feet in height; but at the time I thought less of this matter than of the possibility of there being people aboard the ship. I shouted, but none answered. Then I went to the door below the poop deck. I opened it and peered in. There was a great smell of staleness, so that I knew in a moment that nothing living was within, and with the knowledge, I shut the door quickly, for I felt suddenly lonely.

"I went back to the side where I had scrambled up. My—my sweetheart was still sitting quietly upon the raft. Seeing me look down, she called up to know whether there were any aboard the ship. I replied that the vessel had the appearance of having been long deserted, but that if she would wait a little, I would see whether there was anything in the shape of a ladder by which she could ascend to the deck. Then we would make a search through the vessel together. A little later, on the opposite side of the decks, I found a rope side ladder. This I carried across, and a minute afterward she was beside me.

"Together we explored the cabins and apartments in the afterpart of the ship, but nowhere was there any sign of life. Here and there, within the cabins themselves, we came across odd patches of that queer fungus; but this, as my sweetheart said, could be cleansed away.

"In the end, having assured ourselves that the after portion of the vessel was empty, we picked our ways to the bows, between the ugly grey nodules of that strange growth; and here we made a further search, which told us that there was indeed none aboard but ourselves.

"This being now beyond any doubt, we returned to the stern of the ship and proceeded to make ourselves as comfortable as possible. Together we cleared out and cleaned two of the cabins, and after that I made examination whether there was anything eatable in the ship. This I soon found was so, and thanked God for His goodness. In addition to this I discovered a fresh-water pump, and having fixed it, I found the water drinkable, though somewhat unpleasant to the taste.

"For several days we stayed aboard the ship without attempting to get to the shore. We were busily engaged in making the place habitable. Yet even thus early we became aware that our lot was even less to be desired than might have been imagined; for though, as a first step, we scraped away the odd patches of growth that studded the floors and walls of the cabins and saloon, yet they returned almost to their original size within the space of twenty-four hours, which not only discouraged us but gave us a feeling of vague unease.

"Still we would nor admit ourselves beaten, so set to work afresh, and not only scraped away the fungus but soaked the places where it had been with carbolic, a canful of which I had found in the pantry. Yet by the end of the week the growth had returned in full strength, and in addition it had spread to other places, as though our touching it had allowed germs from it to travel elsewhere.

"On the seventh morning, my sweetheart woke to find a small patch of it growing on her pillow, close to her face. At that, she came to me, as soon as she could get her garments upon her. I was in the galley at the time, lighting the fire for breakfast."

'Come here, John,' she said, and led me aft. When I saw the thing upon her pillow I shuddered, and then and there we agreed to go right out of the ship and see whether we could not fare to make ourselves more comfortable ashore.

"Hurriedly we gathered together our few belongings, and even among these I found that the fungus had been at work, for one of her shawls had a little lump of it growing near one edge. I threw the whole thing over the side without saying anything to her.

"The raft was still alongside, but it was too clumsy to guide, and I lowered down a small boat that hung across the stern, and in this we made our way to the shore. Yet as we drew near to it, I became gradually aware that here the vile fungus, which had driven us from the ship, was growing riot. In places it rose into horrible, fantastic mounds, which seemed almost to quiver, as with a quiet life, when the wind blew across them. Here and there it took on the forms of vast fingers, and in others it just spread out flat and smooth and treacherous. Odd places, it appeared as grotesque stunted trees, extraordinarily kinked and gnarled—the whole quaking vilely at times.

"At first it seemed to us that there was no single portion of the surrounding shore which was not hidden beneath the masses of the hideous lichen; yet in this I found we were mistaken, for somewhat later, coasting along the shore at a little distance, we descried a smooth white patch of what appeared to be fine sand, and there we landed. It was not sand. What it was I do not know.

All that I have observed is that upon it the fungus will not grow; while everywhere else, save where the sandlike earth wanders oddly, pathwise, amid the gray desolation of the lichen, there is nothing but that loathsome grayness.

"It is difficult to make you understand how cheered we were to find one place that was absolutely free from the growth, and here we deposited our belongings. Then we went back to the ship for such things as it seemed to us we should need. Among other matters, I managed to bring ashore with me one of the ship's sails. With it I constructed two small tents, which, though exceedingly rough-shaped, served the purposes for which they were intended. In these we lived and stored our various necessities, and thus for a matter of some four weeks all went smoothly and without particular unhappiness. Indeed, I may say with much happiness—for—we were together.

"It was on the thumb of her right hand that the growth first showed. It was only a small circular spot, much like a little grey mole. My God! How the fear leaped to my heart when she showed me the place. We cleansed it, between us, washing it with carbolic and water. In the morning of the following day she showed her hand to me again. The grey warty thing had returned. For a little while we looked at one another in silence. Then, still wordless, we started again to remove it. In the midst of the operation she spoke suddenly."

'What's that on the side of your face, dear?' Her voice was sharp with anxiety. I put my hand up to feel."

'There! Under the hair by your ear. A little to the front a bit.' My finger rested upon the place, and then I knew."

'Let us get your thumb done first,' I said. And she submitted, only because she was afraid to touch me until it was cleansed. I finished washing and disinfecting her thumb, and then she turned to my face. After it was finished we sat together and talked awhile of many things; for there had come into our lives sudden, very terrible thoughts. We were, all at once, afraid of something worse than death. We spoke of loading the boat with provisions and water and making our way out onto the sea; yet we were helpless, for many causes, and—and the growth had attacked us already. We decided to stay. God would do with us what was His will. We would wait.

"A month, two months, three months passed and the places grew somewhat, and there had come others. Yet we fought so strenuously with the fear that its headway was but slow, comparatively speaking.

"Occasionally we ventured off to the ship for such stores as we needed. There we found that the fungus grew persistently. One of the nodules on the main deck soon became as high as my head.

"We had now given up all thought or hope of leaving the island. We had realized that it would be unallowable to go among healthy humans with the thing from which we were suffering.

"With this determination and knowledge in our minds we knew that we should have to husband our food and water; for we did not know, at that time, but that we should possibly live for many years.

"This reminds me that I have told you that I am an old man. Judged by years this is not so. But—but—"

He broke off, then continued somewhat abruptly, "As I was saying, we knew that we should have to use care in the matter of food. But we had no idea then how little food there was left of which to take care. It was a week later that I made the discovery that all the other bread tanks—which I had supposed full—were empty, and that (beyond odd tins of vegetables and meat, and some other matters) we had nothing on which to depend but the bread in the tank which I had already opened.

"After learning this I bestirred myself to do what I could, and set to work at fishing in the lagoon; but with no success. At this I was somewhat inclined to feel desperate, until the thought came to me to try outside the lagoon, in the open sea.

"Here, at times, I caught odd fish, but so infrequently that they proved of but little help in keeping us from the hunger which threatened. It seemed to me that our deaths were likely to come by hunger, and not by the growth of the thing which had seized upon our bodies.

"We were in this state of mind when the fourth month wore out. Then I made a very horrible discovery. One morning, a little before midday, I came off from the ship with a portion of the biscuits which were left. In the mouth of her tent I saw my sweetheart sitting, eating something." 'What is it, my dear?' I called out as I leaped ashore. Yet, on hearing my voice, she seemed confused, and turning, slyly threw something toward the edge of the little clearing. It fell short, and a vague suspicion having arisen within me, I walked across and picked it up. It was a piece of the grey fungus.

"As I went to her with it in my hand, she turned deadly pale; then a rose red.

"I felt strangely dazed and frightened.

" 'My dear! My dear!' I said, and could say no more. Yet at my words she broke down and cried bitterly. Gradually, as she calmed, I got from her the news that she had tried it the preceding day, and—and liked it. I got her to promise on her knees not to touch it again, however great our hunger. After she had promised, she told me that the desire for it had come suddenly, and that until the moment of desire, she had experienced nothing toward it but the most extreme repulsion.

"Later in the day, feeling strangely restless and much shaken with the thing which I had discovered, I made my way along one of the twisted paths—formed by the white, sandlike substance—which led among the fungoid growth. I had, once before, ventured along there, but not to any great distance. This time, being involved in perplexing thought, I went much farther than hitherto.

"Suddenly I was called to myself by a queer hoarse sound on my left. Turning quickly, I saw that there was movement among an extraordinarily shaped mass of fungus close to my elbow. It was swaying uneasily, as though it possessed life of its own. Abruptly, as I stared, the thought came to me that the thing had a grotesque resemblance to the figure of a distorted human creature. Even as the fancy flashed into my brain, there was a slight, sickening noise of tearing, and I saw that one of the branchlike arms was detaching itself from the surrounding masses, and coming toward me. The head of the thing, a shapeless grey ball, inclined in my direction. I stood stupidly, and the vile arm brushed across my face. I gave out a frightened cry and ran back a few paces. There was a sweetish taste upon my lips where the thing had touched me. I licked them, and was immediately filled with an inhuman desire. I turned and seized a mass of the fungus.

Then more, and—more. I was insatiable. In the midst of devouring, the remembrance of the morning's discovery swept into my amazed brain. It was sent by God. I dashed the fragment I held to the ground. Then, utterly wretched and feeling a dreadful guiltiness, I made my way back to the encampment.

"I think she knew, by some marvelous intuition which love must have given, so soon as she set eyes on me. Her quiet sympathy made it easier for me, and I told her of my sudden weakness, yet omitted to mention the extraordinary thing which had gone before. I desired to spare her all unnecessary terror.

"But for myself I had added an intolerable knowledge, to breed an incessant terror in my brain; for I doubted not that I had seen the end of one of these men who had come to the island in the ship in the lagoon; and in that monstrous ending I had seen our own.

"Thereafter we kept from the abominable food, though the desire for it had entered into our blood. Yet our dreary punishment was upon us; for day by day, with monstrous rapidity, the fungoid growth took hold of our poor bodies. Nothing we could do would check it materially, and so—and so—we who had been human became—Well, it matters less each day. Only—only we had been man and maid!

"And day by day the fight is more dreadful to withstand the hunger-lust for the terrible lichen.

"A week ago we ate the last of the biscuit, and since that time I have caught three fish. I was out here fishing tonight when your schooner drifted upon me out of the mist. I hailed you. You know the rest, and may God, out of His great heart, bless you for your goodness to a—a couple of poor outcast souls."

There was the dip of an oar—another. Then the voice came again, and for the last time, sounding through the slight surrounding mist, ghostly and mournful.

"God bless you! Good-by!"

"Good-by," we shouted together hoarsely, our hearts full of many emotions I glanced about me. I became aware that the dawn was upon us.

The sun flung a stray beam across the hidden sea, pierced the mist dully, and lit up the receding boat with a gloomy fire. Indistinctly I saw something nodding between the oars. I thought of a sponge—a great, grey nodding sponge. The oars continued to ply. They were grey—as was the boat—and my eyes searched a moment vainly for the conjunction of hand and oar. My gaze flashed back to the—head. It nodded forward as the oars went backward for the stroke. Then the oars were dipped, the boat shot out of the patch of light, and the—the thing went nodding into the mist.

The Derelict

by William Hope Hodgson

"It's the material," said the old ship's doctor—"the material plus the conditions—and, maybe," he added slowly, "a third factor—yes, a third factor; but there, there—" He broke off his half-meditative sentence and began to charge his pipe.

"Go on, doctor," we said encouragingly, and with more than a little expectancy. We were in the smoke-room of the Sand-a-lea, running across the North Atlantic; and the doctor was a character. He concluded the charging of his pipe, and lit it; then settled himself, and began to express himself more fully.

"The material," he said with conviction, "is inevitably the medium of expression of the life-force—the fulcrum, as it were; lacking which it is unable to exert itself, or, indeed, to express itself in any form or fashion that would be intelligible or evident to us. So potent is the share of the material in the production of that thing which we name life, and so eager the life-force to express itself, that I am convinced it would, if given the right conditions, make itself manifest even through so hopeless seeming a medium as a simple block of sawn wood; for I tell you, gentlemen, the life-force is both as fiercely urgent and as indiscriminate as fire—the destructor; yet which some are now growing to consider the very essence of life rampant. There is a quaint seeming paradox there," he concluded, nodding his old grey head.

"Yes, doctor," I said. "In brief, your argument is that life is a thing, state, fact, or element, call it what you like, which requires the material through which to manifest itself, and that given the material, plus the conditions, the result is life. In other words, that life is an evolved product, manifested through matter and bred of conditions—eh?"

"As we understand the word," said the old doctor. "Though, mind you, there may be a third factor. But, in my heart, I believe that it is a matter of chemistry—conditions and a suitable medium; but given the conditions, the brute is so almighty that it will seize upon anything through which to manifest itself. It is a force generated by conditions; but, nevertheless, this does not bring us one iota nearer to its explanation, any more than to the explanation of electricity or fire. They are, all three, of the outer forces—monsters of the void. Nothing we can do will create any one of them, our power is merely to be able, by providing the conditions, to make each one of them manifest to our physical senses. Am I clear?"

"Yes, doctor, in a way, you are," I said. "But I don't agree with you, though I think I understand you. Electricity and fire are both what I might call natural things, but life is an abstract something—a kind of all-permeating wakefulness. Oh, I can't explain it! Who could? But it's spiritual, not just a thing bred out of a condition, like fire, as you say, or electricity. It's a horrible thought of yours. Life's a kind of spiritual mystery—"

"Easy, my boy!" said the old doctor, laughing gently to himself. "Or else I may be asking you to demonstrate the spiritual mystery of life of the limpet, or the crab, shall we say." He grinned at me with ineffable perverseness. "Anyway," he continued, "as I suppose you've all guessed, I've a yarn to tell you in support of my impression that life is no more a mystery or a miracle than fire or electricity. But, please to remember, gentlemen, that because we've succeeded in naming and making good use of these two forces, they're just as much mysteries, fundamentally as ever. And, anyway, the thing I'm going to tell you won't explain the mystery of life, but only give you one of my pegs on which I hang my feeling that life is as I have said, a force made manifest through conditions—that is to say, natural chemistry—and that it can take for its purpose and need, the most incredible and unlikely matter; for without matter it cannot come into existence—it cannot become manifest—"

"I don't agree with you, doctor," I interrupted. "Your theory would destroy all belief in life after death. It would—"

"Hush, sonny," said the old man, with a quiet little smile of comprehension. "Hark to what I've to say first; and, anyway, what objection have you to material life after death? And if you object to a material framework, I would still have you remember that I am speaking of life, as we understand the word in this our life. Now do be a quiet lad, or I'll never be done:

"It was when I was a young man, and that is a good many years ago, gentlemen. I had passed my examinations, but was so run down with overwork that it was decided that I had better take a trip to sea. I was by no means well off, and very glad in the end to secure a nominal post as doctor in the sailing passenger clipper running out to China.

"The name of the ship was the *Bheospse*, and soon after I had got all my gear aboard she cast off, and we dropped down the Thames, and next day were well away out in the Channel.

"The captain's name was Gannington, a very decent man, though quite illiterate. The first mate, Mr Berlies, was a quiet, sternish, reserved man, very well-read. The second mate, Mr Selvern, was, perhaps, by birth and upbringing, the most socially cultured of the three, but he lacked the stamina and indomitable pluck of the two others. He was more of a sensitive, and emotionally and even mentally, the most alert man of the three.

"On our way out, we called at Madagascar, where we landed some of our passengers; then we ran eastward, meaning to call at North-West Cape; but about a hundred degrees east we encountered very dreadful weather, which carried away all our sails, and sprung the jibboom and foret'gallantmast.

"The storm carried us northward for several hundred miles, and when it dropped us finally, we found ourselves in a very bad state. The ship had been strained, and had taken some three feet of water through her seams; the maintopmast had been sprung, in addition to the jibboom and foret'gallantmast, two of our boats had gone, as also one of the pigstys, with three fine pigs, these latter having been washed overboard but some half-hour before the wind began to ease, which it did very quickly, though a very ugly sea ran for some hours after.

"The wind left us just before dark, and when morning came it brought splendid weather—a calm, mildly undulating sea, and a brilliant sun, with no wind. It showed us also that we were not alone, for about two miles away to the westward was another vessel, which Mr Selvern, the second mate, pointed out to me.

"'That's a pretty rum-looking, packet, doctor,' he said, and handed me his glass.

"I looked through it at the other vessel, and saw what he meant; at least, I thought I did.

"'Yes, Mr Selvern,' I said. 'She's got a pretty old-fashioned look about her.'

"He laughed at me in his pleasant way.

"'It's easy to see you're not a sailor, doctor,' he remarked. 'There's a dozen rum things about her. She's a derelict, and has been floating round, by the look of her, for many a score of years. Look at the shape of her counter, and the bows and cutwater. She's as old as the hills, as you might say, and ought to have gone down to Davy Jones a good while ago. Look at the growths on her, and the thickness of her standing rigging; that's all salt encrustations, I fancy, if you notice the white colour. She's been a small barque; but, don't you see, she's not a yard left aloft. They've all dropped out of the slings; everything rotted away; wonder the standing rigging hasn't gone, too. I wish the old man would let us take the boat and have a look at her. She'd be well worth it.'

"'There seemed little chance, however, of this, for all hands were turned to and kept hard at it all day long repairing the damage to the masts and gear; and this took a long while, as you may think. Part of the time I gave a hand heaving on one of the deck capstans, for the exercise was good for my liver. Old Captain Gannington approved, and I persuaded him to come along and try some of the same medicine, which he did; and we got very chummy over the job.

"We got talking about the derelict, and he remarked how lucky we were not to have run full tilt on to her in the darkness, for she lay right away to leeward of us, according, to the way that we had been drifting in the storm. He also was of the opinion that she had a strange look about her, and that she was pretty old; but on this latter point he plainly had far less knowledge than the second mate, for he was, as I have said, an illiterate man, and knew nothing of seacraft beyond what experience had taught him. He lacked the book knowledge which the second mate had of vessels previous to his day, which it appeared the derelict was.

"'She's an old 'un, doctor,' was the extent of observations in this direction.

"Yet, when I mentioned to him that it would be interesting to go aboard and give her a bit of an overhaul, he nodded his head as if the idea had been already in his mind and accorded with his own inclinations.

"'When the work's over, doctor,' he said. 'Can't spare the men now, ye know. Got to get all shipshape an' ready as smart as we can. But, we'll take my gig, an' go off in the second dog-watch. The glass is steady, an' it'll be a bit of gam for us.'

"That evening, after tea, the captain gave orders to clear the gig and get her overboard. The second mate was to come with us, and the skipper gave him word to see that two or three lamps were put into the boat, as it would soon fall dark. A little later we were pulling across the calmness of the sea with a crew of six at the oars, and making very good speed of it.

"Now, gentlemen, I have detailed to you with great exactness all the facts, both big and little, so that you can follow step by step each incident in this extraordinary affair, and I want you now to pay the closest attention. I was sitting in the stern-sheets with the second mate and the captain, who was steering, and as we drew nearer and nearer to the stranger I studied her with an ever-growing attention, as, indeed, did Captain Gannington and the second mate. She was, as you know, to the west-ward of us, and the sunset was making a great flame of red light to the back of her, so that she showed a little blurred and indistinct by reason of the halation of the light, which almost defeated the eye in any attempt to see her rotting spars and standing rigging, submerged, as they were, in the fiery glory of the sunset.

"It was because of this effect of the sunset that we had come quite close, comparatively, to the derelict before we saw that she was all surrounded by a sort of curious scum, the colour of which was difficult to decide upon by reason of the red light that was in the atmosphere, but which afterwards we discovered to be brown. This scum spread all about the old vessel for many hundreds of yards in a huge, irregular patch, a great stretch of which reached out to the eastward, upon the starboard side of the boat some score or so fathoms away.

"'Queer stuff,' said Captain Gannington, leaning to the side and looking over. 'Something in the cargo as 'as gone rotten, and worked out through 'er seams.'

"'Look at her bows and stern,' said the second mate. 'Just look at the growth on her!'

"There were, as he said, great clumpings of strange-looking sea-fungi under the bows and the short counter astern. From the stump of her jibboom and her cutwater great beards of rime and marine growths hung downward into the scum that held her in. Her blank starboard side was presented to us—all a dead, dirtyish white, streaked and mottled vaguely with dull masses of heavier colour.

"'There's a steam or haze rising off her,' said the second mate, speaking again. 'You can see it against the light. It keeps coming and going. Look!'

"I saw then what he meant—a faint haze or steam, either suspended above the old vessel or rising from her. And Captain Gannington saw it also.

"'Spontaneous combustion!' he exclaimed. 'We'll 'ave to watch when we lift the 'atches, 'nless it's some poor devil that's got aboard of 'er. But that ain't likely.'

"We were now within a couple of hundred yards of the old derelict, and had entered into the brown scum. As it poured off the lifted oars I heard one of the men mutter to himself, 'Dam' treacle!' And, indeed, it was not something unlike it. As the boat continued to forge nearer and nearer to the old ship the scum grew thicker and thicker, so that, at last, it perceptibly slowed us.

"'Give way, lads! Put some beef to it!' sang out Captain Gannington. And thereafter there was no sound except the panting of the men and the faint, reiterated suck, suck of the sullen brown scum upon the oars as the boat was forced ahead. As we went, I was conscious of a peculiar smell in the evening air, and whilst I had no doubt that the puddling of the scum by the oars made it rise, I could give no name to it; yet, in a way, it was vaguely familiar.

"We were now very close to the old vessel, and presently she was high about us against the dying light. The captain called out then to 'in with the bow oars and stand by with the boat-hook,' which was done.

"'Aboard there! Ahoy! Aboard there! Ahoy!' shouted Captain Gannington; but there came no answer, only the dull sound his voice going lost into the open sea, each time he sung out.

"'Ahoy! Aboard there! Ahoy!' he shouted time after time, but there was only the weary silence of the old hulk that answered us; and, somehow as he shouted, the while that I stared up half expectantly at her, a queer little sense of oppression, that amounted almost to nervousness, came upon me. It passed, but I remember how I was suddenly aware that it was growing dark. Darkness comes fairly rapidly in the tropics, though not so quickly as many fiction writers seem to think; but it was not that the coming dusk had perceptibly deepened in that brief time of only a few moments, but rather that my nerves had made me suddenly a little hypersensitive. I mention my state particularly, for I am not a nervy man normally, and my abrupt touch of nerves is significant, in the light of what happened.

"'There's no one on board there!' said Captain Gannington. 'Give way, men!' For the boat's crew had instinctively rested on their oars, as the captain hailed the old craft. The men gave way again; and then the second mate called out excitedly, 'Why, look there, there's our pigsty! See, it's got *Bheospse* painted on the end. It's drifted down here and the scum's caught it. What a blessed wonder!'

"It was, as he had said, our pigsty that had been washed overboard in the storm; and most extraordinary to come across it there.

"'We'll tow it off with us, when we go,' said the captain, and shouted to the crew to get down to their oars; for they were hardly moving the boat, because the scum was so thick, close in around the old ship, that it literally clogged the boat from moving. I remember that it struck me, in a half-conscious sort of way, as curious that the pigsty, containing our three dead pigs, had managed to drift in so far unaided, whilst we could scarcely manage to force the boat in, now that we had come right into the scum. But the thought passed from my mind, for so many things happened within the next few minutes.

"The men managed to bring the boat in alongside, within a couple of feet of the derelict, and the man with the boat-hook hooked on.

"Ave ye got 'old there, forrard?' asked Captain Gannington.

"'Yessir!' said the bowman; and as he spoke there came a queer noise of tearing.

"'What's that?' asked the Captain.

"'It's tore, sir. Tore clean away!' said the man, and his tone showed that he had received something of a shock.

"'Get a hold again, then!' said Captain Gannington irritably. 'You don't s'pose this packet was built yesterday! Shove the hook into the main chains' The man did so gingerly, as you might say, for it seemed to me, in the growing dusk, that he put no strain on to the hook, though, of course there was no need—you see the boat could not go very far of herself, in the stuff in which she was imbedded. I remember thinking this, also as I looked up at the bulging side of the old vessel. Then I heard Captain Gannington's voice:

"'Lord, but she s old! An' what a colour, doctor! She don't half want paint, do she? Now then, somebody, one of them oars.' An oar was passed to him, and he leant it up against the ancient, bulging side; then he paused, and called to the second mate to light a couple of the lamps, and stand by to pass them up, for darkness had settled down now upon the sea.

"The second mate lit two of the lamps, and told one of the men to light a third, and keep it handy in the boat; then he stepped across, with a lamp in each hand, to where Captain Gannington stood by the oar against the side of the ship.

"'Now, my lad,' said the captain to the man who had pulled stroke, 'up with you, an' we'll pass ye up the lamps.'

"The man jumped to obey, caught the oar, and put his weight upon it; and as he did so, something seemed to give way a little.

"'Look!' cried out the second mate, and pointed, lamp in hand. 'It's sunk in!'

"This was true. The oar had made quite an indentation into the bulging, somewhat slimy side of the old vessel.

"'Mould, I reckon,' said Captain Gannington, bending towards the derelict to look. Then to the man:

"'Up you go, my lad, and be smart! Don't stand there waitin'!'

"At that the man, who had paused a moment as he felt the oar give beneath his weight began to shin' up, and in a few seconds he was aboard, and leant out over the rail for the lamps. These were passed up to him, and the captain called to him to steady the oar. Then Captain Gannington went, calling to me to follow, and after me the second mate.

"As the captain put his face over the rail, he gave a cry of astonishment.

"'Mould, by gum! Mould—tons of it. Good lord!'

"As I heard him shout that I scrambled the more eagerly after him, and in a moment or two I was able to see what he meant—everywhere that the light from the two lamps struck there was nothing but smooth great masses and surfaces of a dirty white coloured mould. I climbed over the rail, with the second mate close behind, and stood upon the mould covered decks. There might have been no planking beneath the mould, for all that our feet could feel. It gave under our tread with a spongy, puddingy feel. It covered the deck furniture of the old ship, so that the shape of each article and fitment was often no more than suggested through it.

"Captain Gannington snatched a lamp from the man and the second mate reached for the other. They held the lamps high, and we all stared. It was most extraordinary, and somehow most abominable. I can think of no other word, gentlemen, that so much describes the predominant feeling that affected me at the moment.

"'Good lord!' said Captain Gannington several times. 'Good lord!' But neither the second mate nor the man said anything, and, for my part I just stared, and at the same time began to smell a little at the air, for there was a vague odour of something half familiar, that somehow brought to me a sense of half-known fright.

"I turned this way and that, staring, as I have said. Here and there the mould was so heavy as to entirely disguise what lay beneath, converting the deck-fittings into indistinguishable mounds of mould all dirty-white and blotched and veined with irregular, dull, purplish markings.

"There was a strange thing about the mould which Captain Gannington drew attention to—it was that our feet did not crush into it and break the surface, as might have been expected, but merely indented it.

"'Never seen nothin' like it before! Never!' said the captain after having stooped with his lamp to examine the mould under our feet. He stamped with his heel, and the mould gave out a dull, puddingy sound. He stooped again, with a quick movement, and stared, holding the lamp close to the deck. 'Blest if it ain't a reg'lar skin to it!'

"The second mate and the man and I all stooped and looked at it. The second mate progged it with his forefinger, and I remember I rapped it several times with my knuckles, listening to the dead sound it gave out, and noticing the close, firm texture of the mould.

"'Dough!' the second mate. 'It's just like blessed dough! Pouf!' He stood up with a quick movement. 'I could fancy it stinks a bit,' he said.

"As he said this I knew, suddenly, what the familiar thing was in the vague odour that hung about us—it was that the smell had something animal-like in it; something of the same smell, only heavier, that you would smell in any place that is infested with mice. I began to look about with a sudden very real uneasiness. There might be vast numbers of hungry rats aboard. They might prove exceedingly dangerous, if in a starving condition; yet, as you will understand, somehow I hesitated to put forward my idea as a reason for caution, it was too fanciful.

"Captain Gannington had begun to go aft along the mould-covered main-deck with the second mate, each of them holding their lamps high up, so as to cast a good light about the vessel. I turned quickly and followed them, the man with me keeping close to my heels, and plainly uneasy. As we went, I became aware that there was a feeling of moisture in the air, and I remembered the slight mist, or smoke, above the hulk, which had made Captain Gannington suggest spontaneous combustion in explanation.

"And always, as we went, there was that vague, animal smell; suddenly I found myself wishing we were well away from the old vessel.

"Abruptly, after a few paces, the captain stopped and pointed at a row of mould-hidden shapes on each side of the maindeck. 'Guns,' he said. 'Been a privateer in the old days, I guess—maybe worse! We'll 'ave a look below, doctor; there may be something worth touchin'. She's older than I thought. Mr Selvern thinks she's about two hundred years old; but I scarce think it.'

"We continued our way aft, and I remember that I found myself walking as lightly and gingerly as possible, as if I were subconsciously afraid of treading through the rotten, mould-hid decks. I think the others had a touch of the same feeling, from the way that they walked. Occasionally the soft stuff would grip our heels, releasing them with a little sullen suck.

"The captain forged somewhat ahead of the second mate; and I know that the suggestion he had made himself, that perhaps there might be something below worth carrying away, had stimulated his imagination. The second mate was, however, beginning to feel somewhat the same way that I did; at least I have that impression. I think, if it had not been for what I might truly describe as Captain Gannington's sturdy courage, we should all of us have just gone back over the side very soon, for there was most certainly an unwholesome feeling abroad that made one feel queerly lacking in pluck; and you will soon see that this feeling was justified.

"Just as the captain reached the few mould-covered steps leading up on to the short half-poop, I was suddenly aware that the feeling of moisture in the air had grown very much more definite. It was perceptible now, intermittently, as a sort of thin, moist, fog-like vapour, that came and went oddly, and seemed to make the decks a little indistinct to the view, this time and that. Once an odd puff of it beat up suddenly from somewhere, and caught me in the face, carrying a queer, sickly, heavy odour with it that somehow frightened me strangely with a suggestion of a waiting and half-comprehended danger.

"We had followed Captain Gannington up the three mould covered steps, and now went slowly along the raised after-deck. By the mizzenmast Captain Gannington paused, and held his lantern near to it. 'My word, mister,' he said to the second mate, 'it's fair thickened up with mould! Why, I'll g'antee it's close on four foot thick.' He shone the light down to where it met the deck. 'Good lord!' he said. 'Look at the sea-lice on it!' I stepped up, and it was as he had said; the sea-lice were thick upon it, some of them huge, not less than the size of large beetles, and all a clear, colourless shade, like water, except where there were little spots of grey on them.

"'I've never seen the like of them, 'cept on a live cod,' said Captain Gannington, in an extremely puzzled voice. 'My word! But they're whoppers!' Then he passed on; but a few paces farther aft he stopped again, and held his lamp near to the mould-hidden deck.

"'Lord bless me, doctor,' he called out, in a low voice, 'did ye ever see the like of that? Why, it's a foot long, if it's a hinch!'

"I stooped over his shoulder, and saw what he meant; it was a clear, colourless creature about a foot long, and about eight inches high, with a curved back that was extraordinarily narrow. As we stared, all in a group, it gave a queer little flick, and was gone.

"'Jumped!' said the captain. 'Well, if that ain't a giant of all the sea-lice that ever I've seen. I guess it's jumped twenty foot clear.' He straightened his back, and scratched his head a moment, swinging the lantern this way and that with the other hand, and staring about us. 'Wot are they doin' aboard 'ere?' he said. 'You'll see 'em—little things—on fat cod an' such-like. I'm blowed, doctor, if I understand.'

"He held his lamp towards a big mound of the mould that occupied part of the after portion of the low poop-deck, a little foreside of where there came a two-foot high 'break' to a kind of second and loftier poop, that ran away aft to the taffrail. The mound was pretty big, several feet across, and more than a yard high. Captain Gannington walked up to it.

"'I reck'n this's the scuttle,' he remarked, and gave it a heavy kick. The only result was a deep indentation into the huge, whiteish hump of mould, as if he had driven his foot into a mass of some doughy substance. Yet I am not altogether correct in saying that this was the only result, for a certain other thing happened. From the place made by the captain's foot there came a sudden gush of a purplish fluid, accompanied by a peculiar smell, that was, and was not, half familiar. Some of the mould-like substance had stuck to the toe of the captain's boot, and from this likewise there issued a sweat, as it were, of the same colour.

"'Well?' said Captain Gannington, in surprise, and drew back his foot to make another kick at the hump of mould. But he paused at an exclamation from the second mate:

"'Don't sir,' said the second mate.

"I glanced at him, and the light from Captain Gannington's lamp showed me that his face had a bewildered, half-frightened look, as if he were suddenly and unexpectedly half afraid of something, and as if his tongue had given away his sudden fright, without any intention on his part to speak. The captain also turned and stared at him.

"'Why, mister?' he asked, in a somewhat puzzled voice, through which there sounded just the vaguest hint of annoyance. 'We've got to shift this muck, if we're to get below.'

"I looked at the second mate, and it seemed to me that, curiously enough he was listening less to the captain than to some other sound. Suddenly he said, in a queer voice, 'Listen, everybody!'

"Yet we heard nothing, beyond the faint murmur of the men talking together in the boat alongside.

"'I don't, hear nothing,' said Captain Gannington, after a short pause. 'Do you, doctor?'

"'No,' I said.

"'Wot was it you thought you heard?' the captain, turning again to the second mate. But the second mate shook his head in a curious, almost irritable way, as if the captain's question interrupted his listening. Captain Gannington stared a moment at him, then held his lantern up and glanced about him almost uneasily. I know I felt a queer sense of strain. But the light showed nothing beyond the greyish dirty-white of the mould in all directions.

"'Mister Selvern,' said the captain, at last, looking at him, 'don't get fancying, things. Get hold of your bloomin' self. Ye know ye heard nothin'?'

"'I'm quite sure I heard something, sir,' said the second mate. 'I seemed to hear—' He broke off sharply, and appeared to listen with an almost painful intensity.

"'What did it sound like?' I asked.

"'It's all right, doctor,' said Captain Gannington, laughing gently. 'Ye can give him a tonic when we get back. I'm goin' to shift this stuff.' He drew back, and kicked for the second time at the ugly mass which he took to hide the companionway. The result of his kick was startling, for the whole thing wobbled sloppily, like a mound of unhealthy-looking jelly.

"He drew his foot out of it quickly, and took a step backward, staring, and holding his lamp towards it. 'By gum,' he said, and it was plain that he was generally startled, 'the blessed thing's gone soft!'

"The man had run back several steps from the suddenly flaccid mound, and looking horribly frightened. Though of what, I am sure he had not the least idea. The second mate stood where he was, and stared. For my part, I know I had a most hideous uneasiness upon me. The captain continued to hold his light towards the wobbling mound and stare.

"'It's gone squashy all through,' he said. 'There's no scuttle there. There's no bally woodwork inside that lot! Phoo! What a rum smell!'

"He walked round to the after side of the strange mound, to see whether there might be some signs of an opening, into the hull at the back of the great heap of mould-stuff. And then:

"'Listen!' said the second mate again, in the strangest sort of voice.

"Captain Gannington straightened himself upright, and there succeeded a pause of the most intense quietness, in which there was not even the hum of talk from the men alongside in the boat. We all heard it—a kind of dull, soft thud, thud, thud, thud, somewhere in the hull under us, yet so vague as to make me half doubtful I heard it, only that the others did so, too.

"Captain Gannington turned suddenly to where the man stood.

"'Tell them—' he began. But the fellow cried out something, and pointed. There had come a strange intensity into his somewhat unemotional face, so that the captain's glance followed his action instantly. I stared also as you may think. It was the great mound at which the man was pointing. I saw what he meant. From the two gapes made in the mould-like stuff by Captain Gannington's boot, the purple fluid was jetting out in a queerly regular fashion, almost as if it were being forced out by a pump. My word! But I stared! And even as I stared a larger jet squirted out, and splashed as far as the man, spattering his boots and trouser legs.

"The fellow had been pretty nervous before, in a stolid, ignorant sort of way, and his funk had been growing steadily; but at this he simply let out a yell, and turned about to run. He paused an instant, as if a sudden fear of the darkness that held the decks, between him and the boat, had taken him. He snatched at the second mate's lantern, tore it out of his hand, and plunged heavily away over the vile stretch of mould.

"Mr Selvern, the second mate, said not a word; he was just staring, staring at the strange-smelling twin-streams of dull purple that were jetting out from the wobbling mound. Captain Gannington, however, roared an order to the man to come back, but the man plunged on and on across the mould, his feet seeming to be clogged by the stuff, as if it had grown suddenly soft. He zigzagged as he ran, the lantern swaying, in wild circles as he wrenched his feet free with a constant plop, plop; and I could hear his frightened gasps even from where I stood.

"'Come back with that lamp!' roared the captain again; but still the man took no notice.

"And Captain Gannington was silent an instant, his lips working in a queer, inarticulate fashion, as if he were stunned momentarily by the very violence of his anger at the man's insubordination. And in the silence I heard the sounds again—thud, thud, thud, thud! Quite distinctly now, beating, it seemed suddenly to me, right down under my feet, but deep.

"I stared down at the mould on which I was standing, with a quick, disgusting sense of the terrible all about me; then I looked at the captain, and tried to say something, without appearing frightened. I saw that he had turned again to the mound, and all the anger had gone out of his face. He had his lamp out towards the mound, and was listening. There was another moment of absolute silence, at least, I knew that I was not conscious of any sound at all in all the world, except that extraordinary thud, thud, thud, thud, down somewhere in the huge bulk under us.

"The captain shifted his feet with a sudden, nervous movement, and as he lifted them the mould went plop, plop! He looked quickly at me, trying to smile, as if he were not thinking anything very much about it.

"'What do you make of it, doctor?' he said.

"'I think—' I began. But the second mate interrupted with a single word, his voice pitched a little high, in a tone that made us both stare instantly at him.

"'Look!' he said, and pointed at the mound. The thing was all of a slow quiver. A strange ripple ran outward from it, along the deck, like you will see a ripple run inshore out of a calm sea. It reached a mound a little foreside of us, which I had supposed to be the cabin skylight, and in a moment the second mound sank nearly level with the surrounding decks, quivering floppily in a most extraordinary fashion. A sudden quick tremor took the mould right under the second mate, and he gave out a hoarse little cry, and held his arms out on each side of him, to keep his balance. The tremor in the mould spread, and Captain Gannington swayed, and spread out his feet with a sudden curse of fright. The second mate jumped across to him, and caught him by the wrist.

"'The boat, sir!' he said, saying the very thing that I had lacked the pluck to say. 'For God's sake—'

"But he never finished, for a tremendous hoarse scream cut off his words. They hove themselves round and looked. I could see without turning. The man who had run from us was standing in the waist of the ship, about a fathom from the starboard bulwarks. He was swaying from side to side, and screaming, in a dreadful fashion. He appeared to be trying to lift his feet, and the light from his swaying lantern showed an almost incredible sight. All about him the mould was in active movement. His feet had sunk out of sight. The stuff appeared to be lapping at his legs and abruptly his bare flesh showed. The hideous stuff had rent his trouser-leg away as if it were paper. He gave out a simply sickening scream, and, with a vast effort, wrenched one leg free. It was partly destroyed. The next instant he pitched face downward, and the stuff heaped itself upon him, as if it were actually alive, with a dreadful, severe life. It was simply infernal. The man had gone from sight. Where he had fallen was now a writhing, elongated mound, in constant and horrible increase, as the mould appeared to move towards it in strange ripples from all sides.

"Captain Gannington and the second mate were stone silent, in amazed and incredulous horror, but I had begun to reach towards a grotesque and terrific conclusion, both helped and hindered by my professional training.

"From the men in the boat alongside there was a loud shouting. and I saw two of their faces appear suddenly above the rail. They showed clearly a moment in the light from the lamp which the man had snatched from Mr Selvern; for, strangely enough, this lamp was standing upright and unharmed on the deck, a little way foreside of that dreadful, elongated, growing mound, that still swayed and writhed with an incredible horror. The lamp rose and fell on the passing ripples of the mould, just—for all the world—as you will see a boat rise and fall on little swells. It is of some interest to me now, psychologically, to remember how that rising and falling lantern brought home to me more than anything the incomprehensible dreadful strangeness of it all.

"The men's faces disappeared with sudden yells, as if they had slipped, or been suddenly hurt; and there was a fresh uproar of shouting from the boat. The men were calling to us to come away—to come away. In the same instant I felt my left boot drawn suddenly and forcibly downward, with a horrible, painful grip. I wrenched it free, with a yell of angry fear. Forrard of us, I saw that the vile surface was all amove, and abruptly I found myself shouting in a queer, frightened voice, 'The boat, captain! The boat, captain!'

"Captain Gannington stared round at me, over his right shoulder, in a peculiar, dull way, that told me he was utterly dazed with bewilderment and the incomprehensibleness of it all. I took a quick, clogged, nervous step towards him, and gripped his arm, and shook it fiercely. 'The boat!' I shouted at him. 'The boat! For God's sake, tell the men to bring the boat aft!'

"Then the mound must have drawn his feet down, for abruptly he bellowed fiercely with terror, his momentary apathy giving place to furious energy. His thickset, vastly muscular body doubled and writhed with his enormous effort, and he struck out madly dropping the lantern. He tore his feet free, something ripping as he did so. The reality and necessity of the situation had come upon him brutishly real, and he was roaring to the men in the boat, 'Bring the boat aft! Bring 'er aft! Bring 'er aft!' The second mate and I were shouting the same thing madly.

"'For God's sake, be smart, lads!' roared the captain, and stooped quickly for his lamp, which still burned. His feet were gripped again, and he hove them out, blaspheming breathlessly, aud leaping a yard high with his effort. Then he made a run for the side, wrenching his feet free at each step. In the same instant the second mate cried out something, and grabbed at the captain.

"'It's got hold of my feet! It's got hold of my feet!' he screamed. His feet, had disappeared up to his boot-tops, and Captain Gannington caught him round the waist with his powerful left arm, gave a mighty heave, and the next instant had him free; but both his boot-soles had gone. For my part, I jumped madly from foot to foot, to avoid the plucking of the mould; and suddenly I made a run for the ship's side. But before I could get there, a queer gape came in the mould between us and the side, at least a couple of feet wide, and how deep I don't know. It closed up in an instant, and all the mould where the cape had been vent into a sort of flurry of horrible ripplings, so that I ran back from it; for I did not dare to put my foot upon it. Then the captain was shouting to me:

"'Aft, doctor! Aft, doctor! This way, doctor! Run!' I saw then that he had passed me, and was up on the after raised portion of the poop. He had the second mate, thrown like a sack, all loose and quiet, over his left shoulder; for Mr Selvern had fainted, and his long legs flogged limp and helpless against the captain's massive knees as he ran. I saw, with a queer, unconscious noting of minor details, how the torn soles of the second mate's boots flapped and jigged as the captain staggered aft.

"'Boat ahoy! Boat ahoy! Boat ahoy!' shouted the captain; and then I was beside him, shouting also. The men were answering with loud yells of encouragement, and it was plain they were working desperately to force the boat aft through the thick scum about the ship.

"We reached the ancient, mould-hid taffrail, and slewed about breathlessly in the half-darkness to see what was happening. Captain Gannington had left his lantern by the big mound when he picked up the second mate; and as we stood, gasping we discovered suddenly that all the mould between us and the light was full of movement. Yet, the part on which we stood, for about six or eight feet forrard of us, was still firm.

"Every couple of seconds we shouted to the men to hasten, and they kept on calling to us that they would be with us in an instant. And all the time we watched the deck of that dreadful hulk, feeling, for my part, literally sick with mad suspense, and ready to jump overboard into that filthy scum all about us.

"Down somewhere in the huge bulk of the ship there was all the time that extraordinary dull, ponderous thud, thud, thud, thud growing ever louder. I seemed to feel the whole hull of the derelict, beginning to quiver and thrill with each dull beat. And to me, with the grotesque and hideous suspicion of what made that noise, it was at once the most dreadful and incredible sound I have ever heard.

"As we waited desperately for the boat, I scanned incessantly so much of the grey white bulk as the lamp showed. The whole of the decks seemed to be in strange movement. Forrard of the lamp, I could see indistinctly the moundings of the mould swaying and nodding hideously beyond the circle of the brightest rays. Nearer, and full in the glow of the lamp, the mound which should have indicated the skylight, was swelling steadily. There were ugly, purple veinings on it, and as it swelled, it seemed to me that the veinings and mottlings on it were becoming plainer, rising as though embossed upon it, like you will see the veins stand out on the body of a powerful, full-blooded horse. It was most extraordinary. The mound that we had supposed to cover the companionway had sunk flat with the surrounding mould, and I could not see that it jetted out any more of the purplish fluid.

"A quaking movement of the mound began away forrard of the lamp, and came flurrying away aft towards us, and at the sight of that I climbed up on to the spongy-feeling taffrail, and yelled afresh for the boat. The men answered with a shout, which told me they were nearer, but the beastly scum was so thick that it was evidently a fight to move the boat at all. Beside me, Captain Gannington was shaking the second mate furiously, and the man stirred and began to moan. The captain shook him again, 'Wake up! Wake up, mister!' he shouted.

"The second mate staggered out of the captain's arms, and collapsed suddenly, shrieking: 'My feet! Oh, God! My feet!' The captain and I lugged him off the mound, and got him into a sitting position upon the taffrail, where he kept up a continual moaning.

"'Hold 'im, doctor,' said the captain. And whilst I did so, he ran forrard a few yards, and peered down over the starboard quarter rail. 'For God's sake, be smart, lads! Be smart! Be smart!' he shouted down to the men, and they answered him, breathless, from close at hand, yet still too far away for the boat to be any use to us on the instant.

"I was holding the moaning, half-unconscious officer, and staring forrard along the poop decks. The flurrying of the mould was coming aft, slowly and noiselessly. And then, suddenly, I saw something closer:

"'Look out, captain!' I shouted. And even as I shouted, the mould near to him gave a sudden, peculiar slobber. I had seen a ripple stealing towards him through the mould. He gave an enormous, clumsy leap, and landed near to us on the sound part of the mould, but the movement followed him. He turned and faced it, swearing fiercely. All about his feet there came abruptly little gapings, which made horrid sucking noises. 'Come back, captain!' I yelled. 'Come back, quick!' As I shouted, a ripple came at his feet—lipping at them; and he stamped insanely at it, and leaped back, his boot torn half off his foot. He swore madly with pain and anger, and jumped swiftly for the taffrail.

"'Come on, doctor! Over we go!' he called. Then he remembered the filthy scum, and hesitated, and roared out desperately to the men to hurry. I stared down, also.

"'The second mate?' I said.

"'I'll take charge doctor,' said Captain Gannington, and caught hold of Mr Selvern. As he spoke, I thought I saw something beneath us, outlined against the scum. I leaned out over the stern, and peered. There was something under the port-quarter.

"'There's something down there, captain!' I called, and pointed in the darkness. He stooped far over, and stared.

"'A boat, by gum! A boat!' he yelled, and began to wriggle swiftly along the taffrail, dragging the second mate after him. I followed. 'A boat it is, sure!' he exclaimed a few moments later, and, picking up the second mate clear of the rail, he hove him down into the boat, where he fell with a crash into the bottom.

"'Over ye go, doctor!' he yelled at me, and pulled me bodily off the rail and dropped me after the officer. As he did so, I felt the whole of the ancient, spongy rail give a peculiar, sickening quiver, and begin to wobble. I fell on to the second mate, and the captain came after, almost in the same instant, but, fortunately, he landed clear of us, on to the fore thwart, which broke under his weight, with a loud crack and splintering of wood.

"'Thank God!' I heard him mutter. 'Thank God! I guess that was a mighty near thing to going to Hades.'

"He struck a match, just as I got to my feet, and between us we got the second mate straightened out on one of the after fore-and-aft thwarts. We shouted to the men in the boat, telling them where we were, and saw the light of their lantern shining round the starboard counter of the derelict. They called back to us to tell us they were doing their best, and then, whilst we waited, Captain Gannington struck another match, and began to overhaul the boat we had dropped into. She was a modern, two-bowed boat, and on the stern there was painted '*Cyclone*, Glasgow.' She was in pretty fair condition, and had evidently drifted into the scum and been held by it.

"Captain Gannington struck several matches, and went forrard towards the derelict. Suddenly he called to me, and I jumped over the thwarts to him. 'Look, doctor,' he said, and I saw what he meant—a mass of bones up in the bows of the boat. I stooped over them, and looked; there were the bones of at least three people, all mixed together in an extraordinary fashion, and quite clean and dry. I had a sudden thought concerning the bones, but I said nothing, for my thought was vague in some ways, and concerned the grotesque and incredible suggestion that had come to me as to the cause of that ponderous, dull thud, thud, thud thud, that beat on so infernally within the hull, and was plain to hear even now that we had got off the vessel herself. And all the while, you know, I had a sick, horrible mental picture of that frightful, wriggling mound aboard the hulk.

"As Captain Gannington struck a final match, I saw something that sickened me and the captain saw it in the same instant. The match went out, and he fumbled clumsily for another, and struck it. We saw the thing again. We had not been mistaken. A great lip of grey-white was protruding in over the edge of the boat—a great lappet of the mould was coming stealthily towards us—a live mass of the very hull itself! And suddenly Captain Gannington yelled out in so many words the grotesque and incredible thing I was thinking: 'She's alive!'

"I never heard such a sound of comprehension and terror in a man's voice. The very horrified assurance of it made actual to me the thing that before had only lurked in my subconscious mind. I knew he was right; I knew that the explanation my reason and my training both repelled and reached towards was the true one. Oh, I wonder whether anyone can possibly understand our feelings in that moment? The unmitigated horror of it and the incredibleness!

"As the light of the match burned up fully, I saw that the mass of living matter coming towards us was streaked and veined with purple, the veins standing out, enormously distended. The whole thing quivered continuously to each ponderous thud, thud, thud, thud, of that gargantuan organ that pulsed within the huge grey-white bulk. The flame of the match reached the captain's fingers, and there came to me a little sickly whiff of burned flesh, but he seemed unconscious of any pain. Then the flame went out in a brief sizzle, yet at the last moment I had seen an extraordinary raw look become visible upon the end of that monstrous, protruding lappet. It had become dewed with a hideous, purplish sweat. And with the darkness there came a sudden charnel-like stench.

"I heard the matchbox split in Captain Gannington's hands as he wrenched it open. Then he swore, in a queer frightened voice, for he had come to the end of his matches. He turned clumsily in the darkness, and tumbled over the nearest thwart, in his eagerness to get to the stern of the boat; and I after him. For we knew that thing was coming towards us through the darkness, reaching over that piteous mingled heap of human bones all jumbled together in the bows. We shouted madly to the men, and for answer saw the bows of the boat emerge dimly into view round the starboard counter of the derelict.

"'Thank God!' I gasped out. But Captain Gannington roared to them to show a light. Yet this they could not do, for the lamp had just been stepped on in their desperate efforts to force the boat round to us.

"'Quick! Quick!' I shouted.

"'For God's sake, be smart, men!' roared the captain.

"And both of us faced the darkness under the port-counter, out of which we knew—but could not see—the thing was coming to us.

"'An oar! Smart, now—pass me an oar!' shouted the captain; and reached out his hands through the gloom towards the on-coming boat. I saw a figure stand up in the bows, and hold something out to us across the intervening yards of scum. Captain Gannington swept his hands through the darkness, and encountered it.

"'I've got it! Let go there!' he said, in a quick, tense voice.

"In the same instant the boat we were in was pressed over suddenly to starboard by some tremendous weight. Then I heard the captain shout, 'Duck y'r head, doctor!' And directly afterwards he swung the heavy, fourteen-foot oar round his head, and struck into the darkness. There came a sudden squelch, and he struck again, with a savage grunt of fierce energy. At the second blow the boat righted with a slow movement, and directly afterwards the other boat bumped gently into ours.

"Captain Gannington dropped the oar, and, springing across to the second mate, hove him up off the thwart, and pitched him with knee and arms clear in over the bows among the men; then he shouted to me to follow, which I did, and he came after me, bringing the oar with him. We carried the second mate aft, and the captain shouted to the men to back the boat a little; then they got her bows clear of the boat we had just left, and so headed out through the scum for the open sea.

"'Where's Tom 'Arrison?" gasped one of the men, in the midst of his exertions. He happened to be Tom Harrison's particular chum, and Captain Gannington answered him briefly enough:

"'Dead! Pull! Don't talk!"

"Now, difficult as it had been to force the boat through the scum to our rescue, the difficulty to get clear seemed tenfold. After some five minutes pulling, the boat seemed hardly to have moved a fathom, if so much, and a quite dreadful fear took me afresh, which one of the panting men put suddenly into words, 'It's got us!' he gasped out. 'Same as poor Tom!' It was the man who had inquired where Harrison was.

"'Shut y'r mouth an' pull!' roared the captain. And so another few minutes passed. Abruptly, it seemed to me that the dull, ponderous thud, thud, thud, thud came more plainly through the dark, and I stared intently over the stern. I sickened a little, for I could almost swear that the dark mass of the monster was actually nearer—that it was coming nearer to us through the darkness. Captain Gannington must have had the same thought, for, after a brief look into the darkness, he jumped forrard, and began to double-bank the stroke-oar.

"'Get forrid under the oars, doctor,' he said to me rather breathlessly. 'Get in the bows, an' see if you can't free the stuff a bit round the bows.'

"I did as he told me, and a minute later I was in the bows of the boat, puddling the scum from side to side, and trying to break up the viscid, clinging muck. A heavy almost animal-like smell rose off it, and all the air seemed full of the deadening, heavy smell. I shall never find words to tell anyone on earth the whole horror of it all—the threat that seemed to hang in the very air around us, and but a little astern that incredible thing, coming, as I firmly believed, nearer, and scum holding us, like half-melted glue.

"The minutes passed in a deadly, eternal fashion, and I kept staring back astern into the darkness but never ceasing to puddle that filthy scum, striking at it and switching it from side to side until I sweated.

"Abruptly Captain Gannington sang out: 'We're gaining, lads. Pull!' And I felt the boat forge ahead perceptibly, as they gave way with renewed hope and energy. There was soon no doubt of it, for presently that hideous thud, thud, thud, thud had grown quite dim and vague somewhere astern and I could no longer see the derelict, for the night had come down tremendously dark and all the sky was thick, overset with heavy clouds. As we drew nearer and nearer to the edge of the scum, the boat moved more and more perceptibly, until suddenly we emerged with a clean, sweet, fresh sound into the open sea.

"'Thank God!' I said aloud, and drew in the boathook, and made my way aft again to where Captain Gannington now sat once more at the tiller. I saw him looking anxiously up at the sky and across to where the lights of our vessel burned, and again he would seem to listen intently, so that I found myself listening also.

"'What's that, Captain?' I said sharply; for it seemed to me that I heard a sound far astern, something, between a queer whine and a low whistling. 'What's that?'

"'It's wind, doctor.' he said in a low voice. 'I wish to God we were aboard.' Then to the men: 'Pull! Put y'r backs into it, or ye'll never put y'r teeth through good bread again!' The men obeyed nobly, and we reached the vessel safely, and had the boat safely stowed before the storm came, which it did in a furious white smother out of the west. I could see it for some minutes beforehand, tearing the sea in the gloom into a wall of phosphorescent foam; and as it came nearer, that peculiar whining, piping sound grew louder and louder, until it was like a vast steam whistle rushing towards us. And when it did come, we got it very heavy indeed, so that the morning showed us nothing but a welter of white seas, with that grim derelict many a score of miles away in the smother, lost as utterly as our hearts could wish to lose her.

"When I came to examine the second mate's feet, I found them in a very extraordinary condition. The soles of them had the appearance of having been partly digested. I know of no other word that so exactly describes their condition, and the agony the man suffered must have been dreadful.

"Now," concluded the doctor, "that is what I call a case in point. If we could know exactly what the old vessel had originally been loaded with, and the juxtaposition of the various articles of her cargo, plus the heat and time she had endured, plus one or two other only guessable quantities, we should have solved the chemistry of the life-force, gentlemen. Not necessarily the origin, mind you; but, at least, we should have taken a big step on the way. I've often regretted that gale, you know—in a way, that is, in a way. It was a most amazing discovery, but at the same time I had nothing but thankfulness to be rid of it. A most amazing chance. I often think of the way the monster woke out of its torpor. And that scum! The dead pigs caught in i! I fancy that was a grim kind of a net, gentlemen. It caught many things. It—"

The old doctor sighed and nodded.

"If I could have had her bill of lading," he said, his eyes full of regret. "If—It might have told me something to help. But, anyway—" He began to fill his pipe again. "I suppose," he ended, looking round at us gravely, "I s'pose we humans are an ungrateful lot of beggars at the best! But—but, what a chance? What a chance, eh?"

The Thing Invisible

by William Hope Hodgson

THE WEIRD STORY OF THE
WAEFUL DAGGER OF THE JARNOCK FAMILY

Carnacki had just returned to Cheyne Walk, Chelsea. I was aware of this interesting fact by reason of the curtly worded postcard which I was re-reading, and by which I was requested to present myself at No. 472, not later than seven o'clock on that same evening.

Mr Carnacki had, as I and the others of his strictly limited circle of friends knew, been away in Kent for the past three weeks; but, beyond that, we had no knowledge. Carnacki was always secretive, and generally curt, and spoke only when he was ready to speak. When this stage arrived, I and his three other friends, Jessop, Arkright, and Taylor, would receive a card or a wire, asking us to call. Not one of us ever willingly missed; for after a thoroughly sensible little dinner, Carnacki would snuggle down into his big armchair, and begin to talk. And what talks they were! Stories, true in every word; yet full of weird and extraordinary incidents that held one silent and awed until had made an end of speaking. And afterwards, we four would shake him silently by the hand and stumble out into the dark streets, fearful even of our own shadows, and so with haste to our homes.

Upon this particular night I was the first to arrive, and found Carnacki sitting, quietly smoking over a paper. He stood up; shook me firmly by the hand; pointed to a chair and sat down again, never having uttered a word. A man such a mixture of curtness and courtesy I never met.

For my part I said nothing. I knew the man too well to bother him with questions or the weather, and so took a seat and a cigarette. Presently the three others turned up, and after that we spent a comfortable and busy hour at dinner.

Dinner over, Carnacki snugged himself down luxuriously into his great chair, filled his pipe, and puffed for awhile, his gaze directed on the fire. The rest of us made ourselves comfortable, each after his own particular manner. A minute later Carnacki began to speak, ignoring any preliminary remarks, and going straight to the subject of the story we knew he had to tell.

"I've just come back from Sir Alfred Jarnock's place at Burtontree, in South Kent," he began, without removing his gaze from the fire. "Most extraordinary things have been happening there lately, and Mr George Jarnock, the eldest son, wired me to come over and see if I could help to clear things up a bit. I went. When I got there I found that they've an old chapel with a fine reputation for being haunted. They've been rather proud of this, I could see, until, suddenly, quite lately, the ghost has started being dangerous—deadly dangerous, too—the butler being nearly stabbed to death in the chapel with a queer old dagger. It's this dagger that's supposed to haunt the chapel. At least, there has always been an old yarn in the family that this dagger would attack any enemy who should dare to venture into the chapel after night-fall. But, of course, it's all been taken as most ghost-tales are. Yet, now, it would seem that there must be something in the old story about it being able to act on its own, or in the hand of some invisible thing. At least, that's how it seemed to everyone when I arrived and began to look into things a bit.

"Of course, the first thing I did was to make sure that there was no obvious human agency in the matter, and this I found to be a simpler thing than I had anticipated; for the butler was stabbed when there were other people in the chapel and the place lighted up. Stabbed there right before the onlookers, and no one could tell how it had been done, not even the man himself. And the force used must have been prodigious, for he was driven back into the body of the chapel as though he had been kicked by a horse. Fortunately, his injury was not mortal, and when I got there he was sufficiently recovered to be able to talk to me. Yet I got little from him to help me to any sane conclusion. He had just gone up the chancel to extinguish the candles on the altar when he was attacked. He had seen nothing, heard nothing—just been stricken down with tremendous power and hurled down the aisle.

"I felt very much mystified, but kept my mind open until I had examined the chapel. This I found to be small and extremely old. It is very massively built, and entered through only one door, which leads out of the castle itself; and the key of which is kept by Sir Jarnock himself, the butler having no duplicate. The shape of the chapel is oblong, and the altar is railed off after the usual fashion. There are two tombs in the body of the place; but none in the chancel, which is bare, except for the tall candlesticks, and the chancel rail, beyond which is the undraped altar of solid marble, upon which stand two candlesticks, one at each end. Above the altar hangs the 'waeful dagger,' as it has been called through the past five hundred years. I reached up and took it down to examine it. The blade is ten inches long, two inches broad at the base, and tapering to a sharp point. It is double-edged. The sheath is rather curious for having a cross-piece, which, taken in conjunction with the fact that the sheath itself is continued three parts the way up the hilt of the dagger, gives it the appearance of a cross. That this is not unintentional is shown by an engraving of the Christ crucified upon one side. Upon the other, in Latin, is the inscription: 'Vengeance is Mine, I will Repay.' A quaint and rather terrible conjunction of ideas. Upon the blade of the dagger itself is graven in old English capitals: 'I Watch. I Strike.' On the butt of the hilt there is carved deeply a Pentacle.

"There; you have a pretty accurate description of the weapon that for five hundred years or more has had the reputation of being able, either of its own accord, or in the hand of some thing invisible, to strike murderously any enemy of the Jarnock family who may chance to enter the old chapel after dark. And what is to the point, I can tell you that before I left I had pretty good reason to think that there was more in the old story than any sane man would care to credit.

"However, as is my way, I was treating everything with an open mind, and I continued my investigation of the chapel, sounding and examining walls and floor, not omitting the two ancient tombs, and by evening had come to the conclusion that the only means of ingress and egress was through the doorway into the castle, the door of which is kept always locked. That is, I mean to say, that this was the only entrance practicable for material beings. Although, even had I discovered some other opening, secret or otherwise, it would have helped but little to solve the mystery; for the butler, you must remember, had been struck down before the eyes of most of the family and many of the servants, and a short questioning of each of these showed me that no visible thing could have come near to the man without having been seen by one or more of those present.

"And this was the mystery to which I had been called in to find a sane and normal solution!

"From Tommie, the second son, a bright boy of about fifteen, I got some further details. He had seen the butler struck, or, to be more correct, had seen the butler at the moment he was struck. He told me that if a horse had kicked the man he couldn't have been thrown further, or with more force. It was just as he was going in to put out the candles on the altar. The dagger had been driven right through him, the point appearing behind the left shoulder; and the doctor who had been called immediately had been put to it to remove the weapon, so forcibly had it penetrated the scapula. This latter information I got from the doctor himself, who, along with the rest, was completely and absolutely mystified; as indeed I was myself, for it seemed that there was nothing for it but to accept the fact that some unseen thing—some creature of the invisible world—had actually done a human being nearly to death. And more was to follow. I was, with my own eyes, to see a miracle happen in this so-called prosaic century of ours. Yes, with my own eyes! I was, as it were, to have proof of the supernatural forced upon me!

"That night I proposed to Sir Jarnock (a little, wizened, nervous old man) that I should spend the night in the chapel and keep a constant watch upon the dagger, but to this he would not listen for a moment, informing me that it had been his habit each night, since he inherited the place, to lock up the chapel door so that none might foolishly or heedlessly run the risk of the peril of the dagger. At that, I must say, I stared at him moment, thinking him a bit of an old woman; but when he went on to point out how too well his precautions had been justified by the attack upon the butler I had nothing to say. Yet it seemed a strange thing for a man in this twentieth century to be listening seriously to such talk.

"One thing there was, however, that I pointed out to Sir Jarnock, in reply to his story of the care he had used through all these years to lock the ghost in by itself at nights, so that it could have no chance to work hurt on any, and that was that the dagger had not been used upon an enemy of the family, but upon an old and tried servant. Moreover, that the attack had not been made in the dark, but when the chapel was lighted up.

"To my remarks upon this point the old gentleman replied, in a somewhat troubled voice, that I was certainly right about the latter, but who could we say for certain was trustworthy in this world.

"'Well anyway, Sir Jarnock,' I replied, 'you've no reason for suspecting your butler of being an enemy of the family?' I spoke half-jestingly; but the old man answered me seriously enough that he had never found reason to mistrust Parker in any way. And then, with a little courteous movement, and pleading the fatigue of his years, he said good-night, and left me, having given me the impression of being a polite but rather superstitious old gentleman.

"That night, whilst I was undressing, an idea came to me. I had a feeling that if ever I were to make any progress in the case before me I should have to find some way of getting in and out of the chapel at any hour of the day or night that suited me. The idea that struck me was, on the morrow when the key should be handed to me, to take an impression, and have a duplicate made of it. This I could manage, and no one need ever be the wiser. I should be able then to enter the chapel after dark, and keep a watch over the 'waeful dagger' without affronting old Sir Jarnock by appearing to laugh at his long-continued precautions.

"On the morrow I got the key from the old gentleman and opened the chapel, he accompanying me. Then I went up to my room for my stand camera, and whilst I was up there I took the impression, returning the key to its owner when I came back with the camera. I fixed my camera up in the aisle, and took a photograph of the chancel; then, saying I would leave my camera where it was, Sir Jarnock accompanying me and locking the door after us. He told me that any time I wanted to enter the chapel he would be pleased to let me have the key, but not after dark, for he was resolved that no other person should run the risk of the stroke of the enchanted dagger.

"I took my dark-slide into Burtontree, and left it with the local photographer, telling him to develop the one plate it contained, but take no print off it until he should hear from me. Then I enquired for a locksmith, and when I found one I gave him an order to get me a key made from the impression as quickly as the thing could be done, insisting that I would call for it that evening. This I did, and found it finished, much to my satisfaction.

"I returned to the castle in time for dinner, after which, making my excuses, I retired to my room. Here, from beneath my bed, where I had hidden them earlier in the evening, I drew out several fine pieces of plate armour that I had removed from the armoury. There was also a shirt of chain-mail, with a sort of quilted hood to go over the head. I buckled on the plate armour, and after that I drew on the chain-mail. I don't know much about armour; but from what I've learned since, I must have put on parts of two suits. Anyway, I felt beastly. But I knew that the thing I was thinking of doing called for some sort of protection for my body, so I made the best of matters. Then I pulled on my dressing gown over the armour, and shoved my revolver into one of the side pockets, and my repeating flashlight into the other. My dark lantern I carried in my hand.

"I went out into the passage and closed and locked my bedroom door. Then I descended quietly to the chapel, praying no one would see me as I went. I reached the door, and tried my key. It fitted perfectly, and the next minute I was in the dark, silent chapel, and the door locked behind me.

"I don't mind saying that I felt a bit queer. To stand there in the utter darkness, and not know but some invisible thing was coming for you, isn't as nice as some of you might think. Yet it was no use funking, so I switched on the light of my lantern and made the tour of the place.

"I found nothing unusual. The dagger hung demurely in its place above the altar, and for the rest, all was still and cold and very quiet. Then I wend down to where my camera stood, as I had left it. From the satchel that I had put beneath the tripod I took out a dark-slide, and inserted it in the camera, drawing the shutter. After that I uncapped the lens, pulled out my flashlight apparatus, and pressed the trigger. There was an intense, brilliant flash of light that made the whole of the interior of the chapel jump into sight and disappear as quickly. Then, in the light from my lantern, I inserted the shutter into the slide, and reversed it, so as to have a fresh plate ready to expose at any time.

"I shut off the light of my lantern then, and sat down in one of the pews beside my camera. I don't know what I expected to happen, but I had an extraordinary feeling that something would. It was as though I knew.

"An hour passed—an hour of absolute silence. I was beastly cold, for the whole place was without any kind of heating pipes or furnace, as I'd noticed during my search; so that the inside of the chapel was about as cold as a blessed tomb. Also, in addition to the coldness about me, my feelings were not of the kind to warm one, as you can imagine. All at once I had a horrible feeling that something was a-move in the place. It wasn't that I could hear anything; but I had a sort of intuitive knowledge that something was stirring in the darkness. And I tell you, for a few moments I just sweated—cold sweat. Not a pleasant feeling, either.

"Suddenly I put my mailed arms up over my face. I wanted to hide it—I mean, to protect it. I had had a sudden horrible feeling that something was hovering over me in the dark—waiting. Talk about a man's heart melting in his breast! Mine seemed to have gone to a puddle. I could have shouted, if I'd not been afraid of the noise. And then, abruptly, I heard something. Away up the aisle there sounded a dull clang of metal, as it might be the tread of a mailed heel upon the stone of the aisle. I sat, immovable, fighting with myself to keep from being a putrid coward. I still kept my face covered, but I was getting hold of the man part of me again. I made a mighty effort, and took my arms down from my face, holding it up in the darkness. I tell you, I realised then that the Thing, whatever it was, had better strike me dead than that I should let all my courage rot like that. But nothing touched me, and I got a bit calmer.

"I dare say a couple of minutes passed, and then, away up near the chancel, there came again that clang, as though of an armoured foot stepping cautiously. By Jove! but I can tell you, I felt myself stiffen all over. And then, suddenly, came the thought that the sound I had heard might be the rattle of the dagger above the altar. The idea of that insensate thing becoming animate, and attacking me, did not occur to me with any sense of reality. I thought rather of some invisible monster of the other world fumbling at it. I remembered the butler's remark that it was like the kick of a horse, and with that I felt swiftly for my lantern. I found it on the seat beside me, and switched on the light. Then I flashed it up the aisle. I could see nothing to frighten me. To and fro I sent the jet of light darting, and saw nothing to fear. Before and behind me, up at the roof, and down at the floor, I shone the light. There was nothing visible that need have set my flesh thrilling as it did. I had been standing whilst I sent the light about the chapel, but now I pulled out my revolver, and then, with a tremendous effort of will, I switched off the light and sat down again in the darkness, once more to watch.

"It seemed to me that some half-hour or so must have passed like this, and no sound had broken the intense stillness of the chapel. As for my own feelings, they were much easier, which was foolish, for the thing that made the chapel dangerous couldn't be seen, however much the light. And then, after I'd sat there, as I've said, waiting, with my revolver in my fist, and feeling more like myself, I thought I heard something. I listened extra hard, if that were possible, and presently I could almost swear I heard something move up near the top of the aisle, but so quiet that I couldn't be sure. And then I thought I heard it again, and afterwards there was a horrible time of silence, and then it seemed to come again, nearer to me, as though a vast, soft tread was coming slowly down the aisle.

"I didn't move, but just sat and stiffened, and listened, so that I fancied I heard the tread all about the chapel; and then I was just as sure I couldn't hear it. And so some precious long minutes passed.

"After a little, though, I fancy I must have quietened down a bit, for I remember knowing that my shoulders just ached with the way they'd contracted with my hunching them rigid. Mind you, I was still in a pretty awful funk, but not with the feeling that any moment I might have to fight for my blessed soul. The worst of it was, though, I couldn't hear very plainly for quite a time, with the blood beating in my ears; and this is a simply beastly feeling.

"I was sitting like this, and listening, body and soul, when suddenly I got that awful feeling again that something was moving the air of the place. The feeling got so awful that it made my head go tight all over, so that it actually pained. And I can tell you that's a pretty rotten sensation, when it's caused the way it was. But I kept my arms off my face, I'm glad to say. If I'd done that again I should simply have bunked out of the place; so I just sat and sweated, cold, and the 'creep' busy with my head and spine. And then, suddenly, once more I thought I heard the sound of that queer, soft tread—huge, somehow I thought of it—on the aisle; and this time it seemed a heap closer to me. Then there was an awful little time of quietness, with the feeling in it that something was hovering or bending over towards me from the aisle; and then, through the booming of the blood in my ears, there came a slight sound from the place where my camera stood—a disagreeable sort of slithering sound, and then a sharp tap. I'd had the lantern ready in my left hand, and now I snapped it on, desperately, and shone it straight above my head; for I'd a conviction that there was something there; but I saw nothing, and then I flashed the light at the camera, and along the aisle; but again there was nothing, and after that I sent it to and fro, all about the place, jerking it here and there, but there was nothing anywhere visible.

"I had stood up, the instant that I had seen that there was nothing in sight over me, and now forced myself to go up the aisle towards the altar. I would see, I thought, whether the dagger had been touched. As I went, I kept glancing round and about me, flashing the light to and fro all the time. But there was never for an instant anything unusual to be seen. Then I had reached the step that led up to the chancel rail, and the little gate. I threw the beam from the lantern upon the dagger. Yes, I thought, it's all right. Abruptly, it seemed to me that there was something wanting, and I leaned forward over the little chancel gate, to peer, holding the light high. I was only too correct in my thought. The dagger had gone. Only the sheath hung there above the altar. In a sudden, frightened flash of imagination, I pictured the thing adrift in the chapel, moving here and there, as though of its own volition, for the Thing that wielded would be invisible to mortal eyes. I turned my head swiftly over to the left, glancing frightenedly behind me, and flashing the light to help my eyes. In the same instant I was struck a tremendous blow over the left breast and hurled backward from the chancel rail, down the aisle, my armour clanging loudly. I landed on my back, but scrambled up quickly, though half stunned, and began to run blindly down the aisle towards the door. I bowed my head as I ran, putting my mailed arms over my face. I plunged into my camera, hurling it among the pews. I crashed into the font and staggered back. Then I was at the exit. I fumbled madly for the key in the pocket of my dressing-gown. I found it, and scraped at the door feverishly for the keyhole. Behind me, for all I knew, threatened that incredible thing. I found the keyhole, turned the key, burst the door open, and was in the passage. I slammed the door and leant hard against it whilst I fumbled again with the key, this time to lock it. I succeeded, and reeled more than walked to my room.

"There I sat for a while, until my nerves had steadied somewhat. Then I commenced to strip off the armour. I saw then that both the chain mail and the plate had been pierced over the breast; And suddenly, it came home to me that the Thing had struck for my heart.

"Stripping rapidly, I found that the skin over the heart had just been pierced sufficiently to allow a few drops of blood to stain my shirt - nothing more. I thought of what would have happened if I had not worn the armour!

"I did not go to sleep that night at all, but sat upon the edge of my bed, thinking and thinking. In the morning, so soon as it was light, I made my way quietly down to the chapel. I opened the door, and peered in; but though the whole place was now flooded with the rays of the rising sun it took a tremendous effort of will before I could force myself to enter.

"After a minute's hesitation, however, I plucked up sufficient courage. I went over to where I had overthrown my camera. The ground glass was smashed, but otherwise it did not seem to have suffered. I replaced it in the position in which it had been overnight; but the slide containing the flashlight photograph I removed and put in one of my side pockets, regretting that I had not taken a second one at the instant when I heard those strange sounds up near the chancel.

"Having tidied my photographic apparatus, I went up the aisle to recover my lantern and revolver, which had both been knocked from my hands when I was stabbed. The lantern was hopelessly bent, but the pistol seemed all right. These secured, I made considerable haste to get out of the place and lock the door. I can tell you that I felt less inclined than the night before to call Sir Alfred an old woman for his precautions regarding the chapel, and a sudden thought flashed into my mind whether he might not have knowledge of some previous tragedy concerned with the dagger that made his so particular to see that the chapel should not be entered at night.

"I returned to my room, washed, shaved, and dressed; then went downstairs and got the acting butler to give me some sandwiches and a cup of coffee.

"A little later I was heading for Burtontree as hard as I could walk, for a sudden idea had come to me, which I was anxious to test. I reached the place a little before eight-thirty, and found the local photographer with his shutters still up. But I did not wait. I just knocked until he appeared with his coat off, evidently in the act of dealing with his breakfast. In a few words I made clear that I wanted the use of his dark room immediately, and this he placed at once at my disposal.

"I set to work immediately to develop, not the plate I had exposed, but the one that had been in the camera during all the time of waiting in the darkness. You see, the lens had been uncapped all that while, so that the whole chancel had been, as it were, under observation. You all know something of my experiments in lightless photography, that is "lightless" so far as our human eyes are capable of appreciating light? It was X-ray work that started me in that direction, and now I had vague and indefinite hopes that, if anything immaterial had been moving in the chapel the camera might have recorded it.

"And so it was with the most intense and absorbing interest that I watched that plate under the action of the developer. Presently I saw a faint smudge of black appear, and after that others, vague and wavering in outline. I held the negative up to the red light. The marks appeared all over the plate, but had no definiteness, yet they were sufficient to make me very excited, and I put the thing back into the solution. For some minutes further I watched it, lifting it out once or twice to make a more careful scrutiny, but could not discover what the markings might represent, until, suddenly, it occurred to me that in one of two places they appeared to have the shape of a dagger, but so indefinite that I could not be sure. Yet the very idea made me, as you may imagine, feel thrilly. I carried development a little further, then put the negative into the hypo, and commenced work upon the other plate. It came up nicely, and very soon I had a decent negative that appeared similar in every respect—except for the difference of lighting—to the negative I had taken the previous day. This plate I also fixed; then I washed the two quickly, and put them in methylated spirits for ten or fifteen minutes; after which I took them into the man's kitchen and dried them in the oven.

"Whilst the two plates were drying, the photographer and I made an enlargement from the negative I had taken by daylight. Then we did the same with the two that I had just developed, washing and mounting them as quickly as possible, for I was not troubling about the permanency of the prints. When this was done I took them out into the daylight and made a thorough examination of them, commencing with the one that seemed to show shadowy daggers in several places; but now that it was enlarged I could not be certain that I was not letting my imagination play too large a part in constructing weapons out of the indefinite outlines. And it was with a certain queer disappointment that I put the photograph down and took up the other two to compare.

"For a minute I looked from one to the other, but could distinguish no difference in the scene they portrayed. Then, abruptly, my interest was gripped, for there was a difference. In the second one the dagger was not in its sheath, though I had felt sure it was.

"After that I commenced to compare the two enlargements in a very different manner, using a pair of calipers and the most exacting scrutiny, and so, at last, came upon something that set me all tingling with excitement.

"I paid the photographer, put the three enlargements under my arm without waiting to have them wrapped up, and hurried back to the castle.

"I put the photographs in my room, then went down to see if I could find Sir Alfred, but Mr George Jarnock, who met me, told me his father was too unwell to rise, and would prefer that no one entered the chapel unless he was about. He made an apologetic excuse that his father was inclined to be, perhaps, a little over-careful; but that, even before the 'thing' happened, his father had been just as particular, always keeping the key, and never allowing the door to be unlocked, except when the place was in use. And, as the young fellow told me, with something of a troubled smile, this attack upon the butler seemed to have justified his father's superstitious attitude towards the place.

"When the young man had left me I took my duplicate key and made for the door of the chapel, and presently had it locked behind me, whilst I carried out some intensely interesting and rather weird experiments. These proved successful to such an extent that I came out of the place in a perfect little fever of excitement. I inquired for Mr George Jarnock, and was told that he was in the morning room.

"'Come along,' I said, when I had rooted him out. 'I want you to give me a lift.'

"He was palpably very much puzzled, but came quickly and asking questions, to which, however, I shook my head, telling him to wait a few minutes.

"I led the way to the armoury. Here I directed him to take one side of a dummy dressed in full armour, whilst I took the other. He obeyed, though evidently vastly bewildered; and I led the way to the chapel door. When he saw that this was open he seemed even more astonished, but held himself in, waiting for me to explain. I locked the door of the chapel behind us, and then we carried the armoured dummy up the aisle to the gate of the chancel.

"'Stand back!' I shouted, as he made a sudden movement to open the gate. "Heavens, man! you mustn't do that!"

"'Do what?' he asked, half frightened and half irritated by my manner and words.

"'Stand to one side a moment, and watch!' I said, and he obeyed. I took the dummy in my arms and turned it to face the altar so that it stood close to the gate. Then, standing well to one side, I pressed its back so that it leant forward a little upon the gate, which flew open. In the same instant it was struck a tremendous blow that hurled it into the aisle, rattling and clanging upon the stone floor.

"'Good lord!' said Jarnock in a frightened voice. 'It's the dagger! The thing's been stabbed, same as Parker!"

"'Yes,' I replied, and saw him glance swiftly towards the doorway; but I'll do him the justice to say he never budged an inch.

"'Come and see how it was done,' I said, and led the way back to the chancel rail. From the wall to the left of the altar I took down a long, curiously ornamented iron instrument, not unlike a short spear. The sharp end of this I inserted in a hole in the left-hand gate-post. I lifted hard, and a section of the post, from the floor upwards, bent inwards towards the chancel as though hinged at the bottom. Down it went, leaving the remaining part of the post standing. As the movable portion was bent lower, a section of the floor slid to one side, showing a long, shallow cavity, sufficient to enclose the post. I hove it down into the niche, and there was a sharp clang as some catch caught and held it. Then I went and wrenched the dagger from the dummy. I brought the old weapon and placed its hilt in a hole near the top of the post, where it fitted loosely, the point upwards. After that I went to the lever and gave another heave, and the post descended about a foot to the bottom of the cavity, catching there with another clang. I withdrew the lever, and the floor slid back covering post and dagger, and looking no different from the surrounding surface.

"Then I shut the gate, and we both stood well to one side. I took the spear-like lever and gave the gate a little push so that it opened. Instantly there was a loud thud, and something sang through the air, striking the bottom wall of the chapel. It was the dagger. I showed Jarnock then that the portion of the post had sprung back into its place, making the whole as thick as the one upon the right-hand side of the gate.

"'There!' I said, turning to the young man, and tapping the post. 'There's the invisible thing that uses the dagger, but who the deuce is the person who sets the trap?' I looked at him keenly as I spoke.

"'My father is the only one who has a key,' he said. 'So that I don't see who could get in to meddle.'

"I looked at him again.

"'Look here, Mr Jarnock," I said, perhaps a bit curter than I should, considering what I said. "Are you quite sure that Sir Alfred is quite balanced—mentally?"

"He looked at me, half frightenedly and flushing a little. 'I—I don't know,' he said, after a slight pause.

"'Tell the truth,' I replied. 'Haven't you suspected his balance a bit at times? You needn't be afraid to tell me.'

"'Well, I'll admit I've thought him a bit - a bit strange at times.' he admitted: 'but I've always tried to blind myself and others to it. You see, he's my dad.

"I nodded. 'Quite right, too; and there's no need, now, to make any scandal about this, but something must be done - in a quiet sort of way, you know. I should go and have a chat with your father, and tell him you've found out about this thing.' and I touched the divided post.

"He seemed very grateful for my advice; and after shaking my hand very hard, took my key and let himself out of the chapel. He came back in about an hour rather pale, but otherwise quite collected. I was quite right in my surmise. It was old Sir Alfred who set the trap every night, having learnt from an old M.S. of its existence and how it was worked, it having been used in the old days as a protection for the golden vessels of the altar, which were kept in a secret recess at the back. This recess Sir Alfred had utilised to store his wife's jewellery. She had died some twelve years back, and young Jarnock averred that his father had never been the same since.

"I mentioned to him about my puzzlement regarding the trap having been set before the service, when the butler was struck; for, if I understood him aright, his father had been in the habit of setting the trap last thing every night and unsetting it each morning before anyone entered the chapel. He replied that his father, in a fit of temporary forgetfulness, must have set it too early, and hence the almost fatal tragedy.

"That is about all. I don't think the old man is really insane. I believe it's more a case of hypochondria through dwelling too much upon his wife's death and being too much alone. Young Jarnock told me that his father would sometimes pray for hours at a time in the chapel."

"But you've never told us just how you discovered the secret," I said, speaking for the four of us.

"Oh, that!" replied Carnacki. "I found, on comparing the photos, that the photo taken in the daytime showed a thicker left-hand gate-post than the one taken by flashlight. That put me on to the track that there might be some mechanical dodge in the business and no ghost at all. I examined the post, and I soon found out the business then. It was simple enough, you know, once I hit the right track.

"By the way," he continued, rising and going to the mantelpiece, "you may be interested to have a look at the 'waeful dagger.' Young Jarnock was kind enough to present it to me as a little memento of my adventure. He handed it round to us; and whilst we examined it, filled and lit his pipe, warning us, between puffs, not to make the story he had told us public. "You see," he said "young Jarnock and I made the trap so that it couldn't work, and I've got the dagger; so the whole thing can be hushed up, especially as the butler is on his feet again. But, all the same," he concluded, with a grim little smile, "I fancy the chapel'll never lose its reputation as a dangerous place—eh? Should be pretty safe not, I should think, to keep valuables in. As for the old man, I recommended that he should have a decent male attendant. Best thing in such cases, you know."

"There's two things, Carnacki, you haven't explained yet," I remarked. "What do you think caused the two clangey sounds when you were in the chapel in the dark? And do you think the soft tready sounds were real, or only a fancy, with your being so tense?"

"Don't just know, for certain, about the clangs," he replied. "I've puzzled a bit about them. I can only think that the spring which worked the post must have 'given' a trifle. If it did, under such a tension, it would make a bit of a ringing noise. And a little sound goes a long way in the middle of the night when you're thinking of 'ghosteses.' You can understand that—eh?"

"Yes," I assented. "And the other sounds?"

"Well, the same thing—I mean the extraordinary quietness—may help to explain these a bit. They may have been some usual enough sound that would never have been noticed under ordinary circumstances, or they may have been only fancy. It's just impossible to say. As for the slithery noise, I'm pretty sure, now, that the tripod leg of my camera must have slipped a little, and if it did, it may have jolted the cap off the base board, which would make a little tap when it struck the floor of the aisle. At least, that's how I've tried to explain it to myself."

"And the dagger being there in its place that night when first you entered the chapel?" I queried.

"It wasn't; I mistook the cross-hilted sheath for the complete weapon, you see."

I nodded.

"Now, you chaps," he said "clear out, I want to get a sleep."

We rose, shook him by the hand, and passed out into the night, each to his separate home; and as we went, I doubt not that each pondered upon the strange story he had heard; for, truly, it is the true things that are strange. Very much so!

The Gateway of the Monster

by William Hope Hodgson

(THOMAS CARNACKI, THE FAMOUS INVESTIGATOR OF REAL GHOST STORIES, TELLS HERE HIS INCREDIBLY WEIRD EXPERIENCE IN THE ELECTRIC PENTACLE)

In response to Carnacki's usual card of invitation to have dinner and listen to a story, I arrived promptly at 427, Cheyne Walk, to find the three others who were always invited to these happy little times, there before me. Five minutes later, Carnacki, Arkright, Jessop, Taylor and I were all engaged in the 'pleasant occupation' of dining.

"You've not been long away, this time," I remarked, as I finished my soup; forgetting momentarily, Carnacki's dislike of being asked even to skirt the borders of his story until such time as he was ready. Then he would not stint words.

"That's all," he replied, with brevity; and I changed the subject, remarking that I had been buying a new gun, to which piece of news he gave an intelligent nod, and a smile which I think showed a genuinely good-humoured appreciation of my intentional changing of the conversation.

Later, when dinner was finished, Carnacki snugged himself comfortably down in his big chair, along with his pipe, and began his story, with very little circumlocution:—

"As Dodgson was remarking just now, I've only been away a short time, and for a very good reason too—I've only been away a short distance. The exact locality I am afraid I must not tell you; but it is less than twenty miles from here; though, except for changing a name, that won't spoil the story. And it is a story too! One of the most extraordinary things ever I have run against.

"I received a letter a fortnight ago from a man I must call Anderson, asking for an appointment. I arranged a time, and when he came, I found that he wished me to investigate, and see whether I could not clear up a long-standing and well—too well—authenticated case of what he termed 'haunting.' He gave me very full particulars, and, finally, as the came seemed to present something unique, I decided to take it up.

"Two days later, I drove to the house, late in the afternoon. I found it a very old place, standing quite alone in its own grounds. Anderson had left a letter with the butler, I found, pleading excuses for his absence, and leaving the whole house at my disposal for my investigations. The butler evidently knew the object of my visit, and I questioned him pretty thoroughly during dinner, which I had in rather lonely state. He is an old and privileged servant, and had the history of the Grey Room exact in detail. From him I learned more particulars regarding two things that Anderson had mentioned in but a casual manner. The first was that the door of the Grey Room would be heard in the dead of night to open, and slam heavily, and this even though the butler knew it was locked, and the key on the bunch in his pantry. The second was that the bedclothes would always be found torn off the bed, and hurled in a heap into a corner.

"But it was the door slamming that chiefly bothered the old butler. Many and many a time, he told me, had he lain awake and just got shivering with fright, listening; for sometimes the door would be slammed time after time—thud! thud! thud!—so that sleep was impossible.

"From Anderson, I knew already that the room had a history extending back over a hundred and fifty years. Three people had been strangled in it—an ancestor of his and his wife and child. This is authentic, as I had taken very great pains to discover; so that you can imagine it was with a feeling I had a striking case to investigate, that I went upstairs after dinner to have a look at the Grey Room.

"Peter, the old butler, was in rather a state about my going, and assured me with much solemnity that in all the twenty years of his service, no one had ever entered that room after nightfall. He begged me, in quite a fatherly way, to wait till the morning, when there would be no danger, and then he could accompany me himself.

"Of course, I smiled a little at him, and told him not to bother. I explained that I should do no more than look round a bit, and, perhaps, affix a few seals. He need not fear; I was used to that sort of thing. But he shook his head, when I said that.

"'There isn't many ghosts like ours, sir,' he assured me, with mournful pride. And, by Jove! he was right, as you will see.

"I took a couple of candles, and Peter followed, with his bunch of keys. He unlocked the door; but would not come inside with me. He was evidently in a fright, and he renewed his request, that I would put off my examination, until daylight. Of course, I laughed at him again, and told him he could stand sentry at the door, and catch anything that came out.

"'It never comes outside, sir,' he said, in his funny, old, solemn manner. Somehow, he managed to make me feel as if I were going to have the 'creeps' right away. Anyway, it was one to him, you know.

"I left him there, and examined the room. It is a big apartment, and well furnished in the grand style, with a huge four-poster, which stands with its head to the end wall. There were two candles on the mantelpiece, and two on each of the three tables that were in the room. I lit the lot, and after that, the room felt a little less inhumanly dreary; though, mind you, it was quite fresh, and well kept in every way.

"After I had taken a good look round, I sealed lengths of baby ribbon across the windows, along the walls, over the pictures, and over the fireplace and the wall-closets. All the time, as I worked, the butler stood just without the door, and I could not persuade him to enter; though I jested him a little, as I stretched the ribbons, and went here and there about my work. Every now and again, he would say:—'You'll excuse me, I'm sure, sir; but I do wish you would come out, sir. I'm fair in a quake for you.'

"I told him he need not wait; but he was loyal enough in his way to what he considered his duty. He said he could not go away and leave me all alone there. He apologised; but made it very clear that I did not realise the danger of the room; and I could see, generally, that he was in a pretty frightened state. All the same, I had to make the room so that I should know if anything material entered it; so I asked him not to bother me, unless he really heard or saw something. He was beginning to get on my nerves, and the 'feel' of the room was bad enough, without making it any nastier.

"For a time further, I worked, stretching ribbons across the floor, and sealing them, so that the merest touch would have broken them, were anyone to venture into the room in the dark with the intention of playing the fool. All this had taken me far longer than I had anticipated; and, suddenly, I heard a clock strike eleven. I had taken off my coat soon after commencing work; now, however, as I had practically made an end of all that I intended to do, I walked across to the settee, and picked it up. I was in the act of getting into it, when the old butler's voice (he had not said a word for the last hour) came sharp and frightened:—'Come out, sir, quick! There's something going to happen!' Jove! but I jumped, and then, in the same moment, one of the candles on the table to the left went out. Now whether it was the wind, or what, I do not know; but, just for a moment, I was enough startled to make a run for the door; though I am glad to say that I pulled up, before I reached it. I simply could not bunk out, with the butler standing there, after having, as it were, read him a sort of lesson on 'bein' brave, y'know.' So I just turned right round, picked up the two candles off the mantelpiece, and walked across to the table near the bed. Well, I saw nothing. I blew out the candle that was still alight; then I went to those on the two tables, and blew them out. Then, outside of the door, the old man called again:—'Oh! sir, do be told! Do be told!'

"'All right, Peter,' I said, and by Jove, my voice was not as steady as I should have liked! I made for the door, and had a bit of work, not to start running. I took some thundering long strides, as you can imagine. Near the door, I had a sudden feeling that there was a cold wind in the room. It was almost as if the window had been suddenly opened a little. I got to the door, and the old butler gave back a step, in a sort of instinctive way. 'Collar the candles, Peter!' I said, pretty sharply, and shoved them into his hands. I turned, and caught the handle, and slammed the door shut, with a crash. Somehow, do you know, as I did so, I thought I felt something pull back on it; but it must have been only fancy. I turned the key in the lock, and then again, double-locking the door. I felt easier then, and set-to and sealed the door. In addition, I put my card over the keyhole, and sealed it there; after which I pocketed the key, and went downstairs—with Peter; who was nervous and silent, leading the way. Poor old beggar! It had not struck me until that moment that he had been enduring a considerable strain during the last two or three hours.

"About midnight, I went to bed. My room lay at the end of the corridor upon which opens the door of the Grey Room. I counted the doors between it and mine, and found that five rooms lay between. And I am sure you can understand that I was not sorry. Then, just as I was beginning to undress, an idea came to me, and I took my candle and sealing wax, and sealed the doors of all five rooms. If any door slammed in the night, I should know just which one.

"I returned to my room, locked the door, and went to bed. I was waked suddenly from a deep sleep by a loud crash somewhere out in the passage. I sat up in bed, and listened, but heard nothing. Then I lit my candle. I was in the very act of lighting it when there came the bang of a door being violently slammed, along the corridor. I jumped out of bed, and got my revolver. I unlocked the door, and went out into the passage, holding my candle high, and keeping the pistol ready. Then a queer thing happened. I could not go a step towards the Grey Room. You all know I am not really a cowardly chap. I've gone into too many cases connected with ghostly things, to be accused of that; but I tell you I funked it; simply funked it, just like any blessed kid. There was something precious unholy in the air that night. I ran back into my bedroom, and shut and locked the door. Then I sat on the bed all night, and listened to the dismal thudding of a door up the corridor. The sound seemed to echo through all the house.

"Daylight came at last, and I washed and dressed. The door had not slammed for about an hour, and I was getting back my nerve again. I felt ashamed of myself; though, in some ways it was silly; for when you're meddling with that sort of thing, your nerve is bound to go, sometimes. And you just have to sit quiet and call yourself a coward until daylight. Sometimes it is more than just cowardice, I fancy. I believe at times it is something warning you, and fighting for you. But, all the same, I always feel mean and miserable, after a time like that.

"When the day came properly, I opened my door, and, keeping my revolver handy, went quietly along the passage. I had to pass the head of the stairs, along the way, and who should I see coming up, but the old butler, carrying a cup of coffee. He had merely tucked his nightshirt into his trousers, and he had an old pair of carpet slippers on.

"'Hullo, Peter!' I said, feeling suddenly cheerful; for I was as glad as any lost child to have a live human being close to me. 'Where are you off to with the refreshments?'

"The old man gave a start, and slopped some of the coffee. He stared up at me, and I could see that he looked white and done-up. He came on up the stairs, and held out the little tray to me. 'I'm very thankful indeed, sir, to see you safe and well,' he said. 'I feared, one time, you might risk going into the Grey Room, sir. I've lain awake all night, with the sound of the Door. And when it came light, I thought I'd make you a cup of coffee. I knew you would want to look at the seals, and somehow it seems safer if there's two, sir.'

"'Peter,' I said, 'you're a brick. This is very thoughtful of you.' And I drank the coffee. 'Come along,' I told him, and handed him back the tray. 'I'm going to have a look at what the Brutes have been up to. I simply hadn't the pluck to in the night.'

"'I'm very thankful, sir,' he replied. 'Flesh and blood can do nothing, sir, against devils; and that's what's in the Grey Room after dark.'

"I examined the seals on all the doors, as I went along, and found them right; but when I got to the Grey Room, the seal was broken; though the card, over the keyhole, was untouched. I ripped it off, and unlocked the door, and went in, rather cautiously, as you can imagine; but the whole room was empty of anything to frighten one, and there was heaps of light. I examined all my seals, and not a single one was disturbed. The old butler had followed me in, and, suddenly, he called out:— 'The bedclothes, sir!'

"I ran up to the bed, and looked over; and, surely, they were lying in the corner to the left of the bed. Jove! you can imagine how queer I felt. Something had been in the room. I stared for a while, from the bed, to the clothes on the floor. I had a feeling that I did not want to touch either. Old Peter, though, did not seem to be affected that way. He went over to the bed-coverings, and was going to pick them up, as, doubtless, he had done every day these twenty years back; but I stopped him. I wanted nothing touched, until I had finished my examination. This, I must have spent a full hour over, and then I let Peter straighten up the bed; after which we went out, and I locked the door; for the room was getting on my nerves.

"I had a short walk, and then breakfast; after which I felt more my own man, and so returned to the Grey Room, and, with Peter's help, and one of the maids, I had everything taken out of the room, except the bed—even the very pictures. I examined the walls, floor and ceiling then, with probe, hammer and magnifying glass; but found nothing suspicious. And I can assure you, I began to realise, in very truth, that some incredible thing had been loose in the room during the past night. I sealed up everything again, and went out, locking and sealing the door, as before.

"After dinner, Peter and I unpacked some of my stuff, and I fixed up my camera and flashlight opposite to the door of the Grey Room, with a string from the trigger of the flashlight to the door. Then, you see, if the door were really opened, the flashlight would blare out, and there would be, possibly, a very queer picture to examine in the morning. The last thing I did, before leaving, was to uncap the lens; and after that I went off to my bedroom, and to bed; for I intended to be up at midnight; and to ensure this, I set my little alarm to call me; also I left my candle burning.

"The clock woke me at twelve, and I got up and into my dressing-gown and slippers. I shoved my revolver into my right side-pocket, and opened my door. Then, I lit my dark-room lamp, and withdrew the slide, so that it would give a clear light. I carried it up the corridor, about thirty feet, and put it down on the floor, with the open side away from me, so that it would show me anything that might approach along the dark passage. Then I went back, and sat in the doorway of my room, with my revolver handy, staring up the passage towards the place where I knew my camera stood outside the door of the Grey Room.

"I should think I had watched for about an hour and a half, when, suddenly, I heard a faint noise, away up the corridor. I was immediately conscious of a queer prickling sensation about the back of my head, and my hands began to sweat a little. The following instant, the whole end of the passage flicked into sight in the abrupt glare of the flashlight. There came the succeeding darkness, and I peered nervously up the corridor, listening tensely, and trying to find what lay beyond the faint glow of my dark-lamp, which now seemed ridiculously dim by contrast with the tremendous blaze of the flash-power … And then, as I stooped forward, staring and listening, there came the crashing thud of the door of the Grey Room. The sound seemed to fill the whole of the large corridor, and go echoing hollowly through the house. I tell you, I felt horrible—as if my bones were water. Simply beastly. Jove! how I did stare, and how I listened. And then it came again—thud, thud, thud, and then a silence that was almost worse than the noise of the door; for I kept fancying that some awful thing was stealing upon me along the corridor. And then, suddenly, my lamp was put out, and I could not see a yard before me. I realised all at once that I was doing a very silly thing, sitting there, and I jumped up. Even as I did so, I thought I heard a sound in the passage, and quite near me. I made one backward spring into my room, and slammed and locked the door. I sat on my bed, and stared at the door. I had my revolver in my hand; but it seemed an abominably useless thing. I felt that there was something the other side of that door. For some unknown reason I knew it was pressed up against the door, and it was soft. That was just what I thought. Most extraordinary thing to think.

"Presently I got hold of myself a bit, and marked out a pentacle hurriedly with chalk on the polished floor; and there I sat in it almost until dawn. And all the time, away up the corridor, the door of the Grey Room thudded at solemn and horrid intervals. It was a miserable, brutal night.

"When the day began to break, the thudding of the door came gradually to an end, and, at last, I got hold of my courage, and went along the corridor, and went along the corridor, in the half light, to cap the lense of my camera. I can tell you, it took some doing; but if I had not done so my photograph would have been spoilt, and I was tremendously keen to save it. I got back to my room, and then set-to and rubbed out the five-pointed star in which I had been sitting.

"Half an hour later there was a tap at my door. It was Peter with my coffee. When I had drunk it, we both went along to the Grey Room. As we went, I had a look at the seals on the other doors; but they were untouched. The seal on the door of the Grey Room was broken, as also was the string from the trigger of the flashlight; but the card over the keyhole was still there. I ripped it off, and opened the door. Nothing unusual was to be seen until we came to the bed; then I saw that, as on the previous day, the bedclothes had been torn off, and hurled into the left-hand corner, exactly where I had seen them before. I felt very queer; but I did not forget to look at all the seals, only to find that not one had been broken.

"Then I turned and looked at old Peter, and he looked at me, nodding his head.

"'Let's get out of here!' I said. 'It's no place for any living human to enter, without proper protection.'

"We went out then, and I locked and sealed the door, again.

"After breakfast, I developed the negative; but it showed only the door of the Grey Room, half opened. Then I left the house, as I wanted to get certain matters and implements that might be necessary to life; perhaps to the spirit; for I intended to spend the coming night in the Grey Room.

"I go back in a cab, about half-past five, with my apparatus, and this, Peter and I carried up to the Grey Room, where I piled it carefully in the centre of the floor. When everything was in the room, including a cat which I had brought, I locked and sealed the door, and went towards the bedroom, telling Peter I should not be down for dinner. He said, 'Yes, sir,' and went downstairs, thinking that I was going to turn in, which was what I wanted him to believe, as I knew he would have worried both me and himself, if he had known what I intended.

"But I merely got my camera and flashlight from my bedroom, and hurried back to the Grey Room. I locked and sealed myself in, and set to work, for I had a lot to do before it got dark.

"First, I cleared away all the ribbons across the floor; then I carried the cat—still fastened in its basket—over towards the far wall, and left it. I returned then to the centre of the room, and measured out a space twenty-one feet in diameter, which I swept with a 'broom of hyssop.' About this, I drew a circle of chalk, taking care never to step over the circle. Beyond this I smudged, with a bunch of garlic, a broad belt right around the chalked circle, and when this was complete, I took from among my stores in the centre a small jar of a certain water. I broke away the parchment, and withdrew the stopper. Then, dipping my left forefinger in the little jar, I went round the circle again, making upon the floor, just within the line of chalk, the Second Sign of the Saaamaaa Ritual, and joining each Sign most carefully with the left-handed crescent. I can tell you, I felt easier when this was done, and the 'water circle' complete. Then, I unpacked some more of the stuff that I had brought, and placed a lighted candle in the 'valley' of each Crescent. After that, I drew a Pentacle, so that each of the five points of the defensive star touched the chalk circle. In the five points of the star I placed five portions of the bread, each wrapped in linen, and in the five 'vales,' five opened jars of the water I had used to make the 'water circle.' And now I had my first protective barrier complete.

"Now, anyone, except you who know something of my methods of investigation, might consider all this a piece of useless and foolish superstition; but you all remember the Black Veil case, in which I believe my life was saved by a very similar form of protection, whilst Aster, who sneered at it, and would not come inside, died. I got the idea from the Sigsand M.S., written, so far as I can make out, in the 14th century. At first, naturally, I imagined it was just an expression of the superstition of his time; and it was not until a year later that it occurred to me to test his 'Defence,' which I did, as I've just said, in that horrible Black

Veil business. You know how that turned out. Later, I used it several times, and always I came through safe, until that Moving Fur case. It was only a partial 'defence' therefore, and I nearly died in the pentacle. After that I came across Professor Garder's *Experiments with a Medium*. When they surrounded the Medium with a current, in vacuum, he lost his power—almost as if it cut him off from the Immaterial. That made me think a lot; and that is how I came to make the Electric Pentacle, which is a most marvellous 'Defence' against certain manifestations. I used the shape of the defensive star for this protection, because I have, personally, no doubt at all but that there is some extraordinary virtue in the old magic figure. Curious thing for a Twentieth Century man to admit, is it not? But, then, as you all know, I never did, and never will, allow myself to be blinded by the little cheap laughter. I ask questions, and keep my eyes open.

"In this last case I had little doubt that I had run up against a supernatural monster, and I meant to take every possible care; for the danger is abominable.

"I turned-to now to fit the Electric Pentacle, setting it so that each of its 'points' and 'vales' coincided exactly with the 'points' and 'vales' of the drawn pentagram upon the floor. Then I connected up the battery, and the next instant the pale blue glare from the intertwining vacuum tubes shone out.

"I glanced about me then, with something of a sigh of relief, and realised suddenly that the dusk was upon me, for the window was grey and unfriendly. Then round at the big, empty room, over the double barrier of electric and candle light. I had an abrupt, extraordinary sense of weirdness thrust upon me—in the air, you know; as it were, a sense of something inhuman impending. The room was full of the stench of bruised garlic, a smell I hate.

"I turned now to the camera, and saw that it and the flashlight were in order. Then I tested my revolver, carefully; though I had little thought that it would be needed. Yet, to what extent materialisation of an ab-natural creature is possible, given favourable conditions, no one can say; and I had no idea what horrible thing I was going to see, or feel the presence of. I might, in the end, have to fight with a materialised monster. I did not know, and could only be prepared. You see, I never forgot that three other people had been strangled in the bed close to me, and the fierce slamming of the door I had heard myself. I had no doubt that I was investigating a dangerous and ugly case.

"By this time, the night had come; though the room was very light with the burning candles; and I found myself glancing behind me, constantly, and then all round the room. It was nervy work waiting for that thing to come. Then, suddenly, I was aware of a little, cold wind sweeping over me, coming from behind. I gave one great nerve-thrill, and a prickly feeling went all over the back of my head. Then I hove myself round with a sort of stiff jerk, and stared straight against that queer wind. It seemed to come from the corner of the room to the left of the bed—the place where both times I had found the heap of tossed bedclothes. Yet, I could see nothing unusual; no opening—nothing!...

"Abruptly, I was aware that the candles were all a-flicker in that unnatural wind.... I believe I just squatted there and stared in a horribly frightened, wooden way for some minutes. I shall never be able to let you know how disgustingly horrible it was sitting in that vile, cold wind! And then, flick! flick! flick! all the candles round the outer barrier went out; and there was I, locked and sealed in that room, and with no light beyond the weakish blue glare of the Electric Pentacle.

"A time of abominable tenseness passed, and still that wind blew upon me; and then, suddenly, I knew that something stirred in the corner to the left of the bed. I was made conscious of it, rather by some inward, unused sense than by either sight or sound; for the pale, short-radius glare of the Pentacle gave but a very poor light for seeing by. Yet, as I stared, something began slowly to grow upon my sight—a moving shadow, a little darker than the surrounding shadows. I lost the thing amid the vagueness, and for a moment or two I glanced swiftly from side to side, with a fresh, new sense of impending danger. Then my attention was directed to the bed. All the coverings were being drawn steadily off, with a hateful, stealthy sort of motion. I heard the slow, dragging slither of the clothes; but I could see nothing of the thing that pulled. I was aware in a funny, subconscious, introspective fashion that the 'creep' had come upon me; yet that I was cooler mentally than I had been for some minutes; sufficiently so to feel that my hands were sweating coldly, and to shift my revolver, half-consciously, whilst I rubbed my right hand dry upon my knee; though never, for an instant, taking my gaze or my attention from those moving clothes.

"The faint noises from the bed ceased once, and there was a most intense silence, with only the sound of the blood beating in my head. Yet, immediately afterwards, I heard again the slurring of the bedclothes being dragged off the bed. In the midst of my nervous tension I remembered the camera, and reached round for it; but without looking away from the bed. And then, you know, all in a moment, the whole of the bed coverings were torn off with extraordinary violence, and I heard the flump they made as they were hurled into the corner.

"There was a time of absolute quietness then for perhaps a couple of minutes; and you can imagine how horrible I felt. The bedclothes had been thrown with such savageness! And, then again, the brutal unnaturalness of the thing that had just been done before me!

"Abruptly, over by the door, I heard a faint noise—a sort of crickling sound, and then a pitter or two upon the floor. A great nervous thrill swept over me, seeming to run up my spine and over the back of my head; for the seal that secured the door had just been broken. Something was there. I could not see the door; at least, I mean to say that it was impossible to say how much I actually saw, and how much my imagination supplied. I made it out, only as a continuation of the grey walls… And then it seemed to me that something dark and indistinct moved and wavered there among the shadows.

"Abruptly, I was aware that the door was opening, and with an effort I reached again for my camera; but before I could aim it the door was slammed with a terrific crash that filled the whole room with a sort of hollow thunder. I jumped, like a frightened child. There seemed such a power behind the noise; as though a vast, wanton Force were 'out.' Can you understand?

"The door was not touched again; but, directly afterwards, I heard the basket, in which the cat lay, creak. I tell you, I fairly pringled all along my back. I knew that I was going to learn definitely whether whatever was abroad was dangerous to Life. From the cat there rose suddenly a hideous catterwaul, that ceased abruptly; and then—too late—I snapped off the flashlight. In the great glare, I saw that the basket had been overturned, and the lid was wrenched open, with the cat lying half in, and half out upon the floor. I saw nothing else, but I was full of the knowledge that I was in the presence of some Being or Thing that had power to destroy.

"During the next two or three minutes, there was an odd, noticeable quietness in the room, and you much remember I was half-blinded, for the time, because of the flashlight; so that the whole place seemed to be pitchy dark just beyond the shine of the Pentacle. I tell you it was most horrible. I just knelt there in the star, and whirled round, trying to see whether anything was coming at me.

"My power of sight came gradually, and I got a little hold of myself; and abruptly I saw the thing I was looking for, close to the 'water circle.' It was big and indistinct, and wavered curiously, as though the shadow of a vast spider hung suspended in the air, just beyond the barrier. It passed swiftly round the circle, and seemed to probe ever towards me; but only to draw back with extraordinary jerky movements, as might a living person if they touched the hot bar of a grate.

"Round and round it moved, and round and round I turned. Then, just opposite to one of the 'vales' in the pentacles, it seemed to pause, as though preliminary to a tremendous effort. It retired almost beyond the glow of the vacuum light, and then came straight towards me, appearing to gather form and solidity as it came. There seemed a vast, malign determination behind the movement, that must succeed. I was on my knees, and I jerked back, falling on to my left hand and hip, in a wild endeavour to get back from the advancing thing. With my right hand I was grabbing madly for my revolver, which I had let slip. The brutal thing came with one great sweep straight over the garlic and the 'water circle,' almost to the vale of the pentacle. I believe I yelled. Then, just as suddenly as it had swept over, it seemed to be hurled back by some mighty, invisible force.

"It must have been some moments before I realised that I was safe; and then I got myself together in the middle of the pentacles, feeling horribly gone and shaken, and glancing round and round the barrier; but the thing had vanished. Yet, I had learnt something, for I knew now that the Grey Room was haunted by a monstrous hand.

"Suddenly, as I crouched there, I saw what had so nearly given the monster an opening through the barrier. In my movements within the pentacle I must have touched one of the jars of water; for just where the thing had made its attack the jar that guarded the 'deep' of the 'vale' had been moved to one side, and this had left one of the 'five doorways' unguarded. I put it back, quickly, and felt almost safe again, for I had found the cause, and the 'defence' was still good. And I began to hope again that I should see the morning come in. When I saw that thing so nearly succeed, I had an awful, weak, overwhelming feeling that the 'barriers' could never bring me safe through the night against such a Force. You can understand?

"For a long time I could not see the hand; but, presently, I thought I saw, once or twice, an odd wavering, over among the shadows near the door. A little later, as though in a sudden fit of malignant rage, the dead body of the cat was picked up, and beaten with dull, sickening blows against the solid floor. That made me feel rather queer.

"A minute afterwards, the door was opened and slammed twice with tremendous force. The next instant the thing made one swift, vicious dart at me, from out of the shadows. Instinctively, I started sideways from it, and so plucked my hand from upon the Electric Pentacle, where—for a wickedly careless moment—I had placed it. The monster was hurled off from the neighbourhood of the pentacles; though—owing to my inconceivable foolishness—it had been enabled for a second time to pass the outer barriers. I can tell you, I shook for a time, with sheer funk. I moved right to the centre of the pentacles again, and knelt there, making myself as small and compact as possible.

"As I knelt, there came to me presently, a vague wonder at the two 'accidents' which had so nearly allowed the brute to get at me. Was I being influenced to unconscious voluntary actions that endangered me? The thought took hold of me, and I watched my every movement. Abruptly, I stretched a tired leg, and knocked over one of the jars of water. Some was spilled; but, because of my suspicious watchfulness, I had it upright and back within the vale while yet some of the water remained. Even as I did so, the vast, black, half-materialised hand beat up at me out of the shadows, and seemed to leap almost into my face; so nearly did it approach; but for the third time it was thrown back by some altogether enormous, over-mastering force. Yet, apart from the dazed fright in which it left me, I had for a moment that feeling of spiritual sickness, as if some delicate, beautiful, inward grace had suffered, which is felt only upon the too near approach of the ab-human, and is more dreadful, in a strange way, than any physical pain that can be suffered. I knew by this more of the extent and closeness of the danger; and for a long time I was simply cowed by the butt-headed brutality of that Force upon my spirit. I can put it no other way.

"I knelt again in the centre of the pentacles, watching myself with more fear, almost, than the monster; for I knew now that, unless I guarded myself from every sudden impulse that came to me, I might simply work my own destruction. Do you see how horrible it all was?

"I spent the rest of the night in a haze of sick fright, and so tense that I could not make a single movement naturally. I was in such fear that any desire for action that came to me might be prompted by the Influence that I knew was at work on me. And outside of the barrier that ghastly thing went round and round, grabbing and grabbing in the air at me. Twice more was the body of the dead cat molested. The second time, I heard every bone in its body scrunch and crack. And all the time the horrible wind was blowing upon me from the corner of the room to the left of the bed.

"Then, just as the first touch of dawn came into the sky, that unnatural wind ceased, in a single moment; and I could see no sign of the hand. The dawn came slowly, and presently the wan light filled all the room, and made the pale glare of the Electric Pentacle look more unearthly. Yet, it was not until the day had fully come, that I made any attempt to leave the barrier, for I did not know but that there was some method abroad, in the sudden stopping of that wind, to entice me from the pentacles.

"At last, when the dawn was strong and bright, I took one last look round, and ran for the door. I got it unlocked, in a nervous and clumsy fashion, then locked it hurriedly, and went to my bedroom, where I lay on the bed, and tried to steady my nerves. Peter came, presently, with the coffee, and when I had drunk it, I told him I meant to have a sleep, as I had been up all night. He took the tray, and went out quietly; and after I had locked my door I turned in properly, and at last got to sleep.

"I woke about midday, and after some lunch, went up to the Grey Room. I switched off the current from the Pentacle, which I had left on in my hurry; also, I removed the body of the cat. You can understand I did not want anyone to see the poor brute. After that, I made a very careful search of the corner where the bedclothes had been thrown. I made several holes, and probed, and found nothing. Then it occurred to me to try with my instrument under the skirting. I did so, and heard my wire ring on metal. I turned the hook end that way, and fished for the thing. At the second go, I got it. It was a small object, and I took it to the window. I found it to be a curious ring, made of some greying material. The curious thing about it was that it was made in the form of a pentagon; that is, the same shape as the inside of the magic pentacle, but without the 'mounts,' which form the points of the defensive star. It was free from all chasing or engraving.

"You will understand that I was excited, when I tell you that I felt sure I held in my hand the famous Luck Ring of the Anderson family; which, indeed, was of all things the one most intimately connected with the history of the haunting. This ring was handed on from father to son through generations, and always—in obedience to some ancient family tradition—each son had to promise never to wear the ring. The ring, I may say, was brought home by one of the Crusaders, under very peculiar circumstances; but the story is too long to go into here.

"It appears that young Sir Hulbert, an ancestor of Anderson's, made a bet, in drink, you know, that he would wear the ring that night. He did so, and in the morning his wife and child were found strangled in the bed, in the very room in which I stood. Many people, it would seem, thought young Sir Hulbert was guilty of having done the thing in drunken anger; and he, in an attempt to prove his innocence, slept a second night in the room. He also was strangled. Since then, as you may imagine, no one has ever spent a night in the Grey Room, until I did so. The ring had been lost so long, that it had become almost a myth; and it was most extraordinary to stand there, with the actual thing in my hand, as you can understand.

"It was whilst I stood there, looking at the ring, that I got an idea. Supposing that it were, in a way, a doorway—you see what I mean? A sort of gap in the world-hedge. It was a queer idea, I know, and probably was not my own, but came to me from the Outside. You see, the wind had come from that part of the room where the ring lay. I thought a lot about it. Then the shape—the inside of a pentacle. It had no 'mounts,' and without mounts, as the Sigsand M.S. has it:—'Thee mownts wych are thee Five Hills of safetie. To lack is to gyve pow'r to thee daemon; and surelie to fayvor the Evill Thynge.' You see, the very shape of the ring was significant; and I determined to test it.

"I unmade the pentacle, for it must be made afresh and around the one to be protected. Then I went out and locked the door; after which I left the house, to get certain matters, for neither 'yarbs nor fyre nor waier' must be used a second time. I returned about seven-thirty, and as soon as the things I had brought had been carried up to the Grey Room, I dismissed Peter for the night, just as I had done the evening before. When he had gone downstairs, I let myself into the room, and locked and sealed the door. I went to the place in the centre of the room where all the stuff had been packed, and set to work with all my speed to construct a barrier about me and the ring.

"I do not remember whether I explained it to you. But I had reasoned that, if the ring were in any way a 'medium of admission,' and it were enclosed with me in the Electric Pentacle, it would be, to express it loosely, insulated. Do you see? The Force, which had visible expression as a Hand, would have to stay beyond the Barrier which separates the Ab from the Normal; for the 'gateway' would be removed from accessibility.

"As I was saying, I worked with all my speed to get the barrier completed about me and the ring, for it was already later than I cared to be in that room 'unprotected.' Also, I had a feeling that there would be a vast effort made that night to regain the use of the ring. For I had the strongest conviction that the ring was a necessity to materialisation. You will see whether I was right.

"I completed the barriers in about an hour, and you can imagine something of the relief I felt when I felt the pale glare of the Electric Pentacle once more all about me. From then, onwards, for about two hours, I sat quietly, facing the corner from which the wind came. About eleven o'clock a queer knowledge came that something was near to me; yet nothing happened for a whole hour after that. Then, suddenly, I felt the cold, queer wind begin to blow upon me. To my astonishment, it seemed now to come from behind me, and I whipped round, with a hideous quake of fear. The wind met me in the face. It was blowing up from the floor close to me. I stared down, in a sickening maze of new frights. What on earth had I done now! The ring was there, close beside me, where I had put it. Suddenly, as I stared, bewildered, I was aware that there was something queer about the ring—funny shadowy movements and convolutions. I looked at them, stupidly. And then, abruptly, I knew that the wind was blowing up at me from the ring. A queer indistinct smoke became visible to me, seeming to pour upwards through the ring, and mix with the moving shadows. Suddenly, I realised that I was in more than any mortal danger; for the convoluting shadows about the ring were taking shape, and the death-hand was forming within the Pentacle. My Goodness! do you realise it! I had brought the 'gateway' into the pentacles, and the brute was coming through—pouring into the material world, as gas might pour out from the mouth of a pipe.

"I should think that I knelt for a moment in a sort of stunned fright. Then, with a mad, awkward movement, I snatched at the ring, intending to hurl it out of the Pentacle. Yet it eluded me, as though some invisible, living thing jerked it hither and thither. At last, I gripped it; yet, in the same instant, it was torn from my grasp with incredible and brutal force. A great, black shadow covered it, and rose into the air, and came at me. I saw that it was the Hand, vast and nearly perfect in form. I gave one crazy yell, and jumped over the Pentacle and the ring of burning candles, and ran despairingly for the door. I fumbled idiotically and ineffectually with the key, and all the time I stared, with a fear that was like insanity, towards the Barriers. The hand was plunging towards me; yet, even as it had been unable to pass into the Pentacle when the ring was without, so, now that the ring was within, it had no power to pass out. The monster was chained, as surely as any beast would be, were chains riveted upon it.

"Even then, I got a flash of this knowledge; but I was too utterly shaken with fright, to reason; and the instant I managed to get the key turned, I sprang into the passage, and slammed the door with a crash. I locked it, and got to my room somehow; for I was trembling so that I could hardly stand, as you can imagine.

I locked myself in, and managed to get the candle lit; then I lay down on my bed, and kept quiet for an hour or two, and so I got steadied.

"I got a little sleep, later; but woke when Peter brought my coffee. When I had drunk it I felt altogether better, and took the old man along with me whilst I had a look into the Grey Room. I opened the door, and peeped in. The candles were still burning, wan against the daylight; and behind them was the pale, glowing star of the Electric Pentacle. And there, in the middle, was the ring ... the gateway of the monster, lying demure and ordinary.

"Nothing in the room was touched, and I knew that the brute had never managed to cross the Pentacles. Then I went out, and locked the door.

"After a sleep of some hours, I left the house. I returned in the afternoon in a cab. I had with me an oxy-hydrogen jet, and two cylinders, containing the gases. I carried the things into the Grey Room, and there, in the centre of the Electric Pentacle, I erected the little furnace. Five minutes later the Luck Ring, once the 'luck,' but now the 'bane,' of the Anderson family, was no more than a little solid splash of hot metal."

Carnacki felt in his pocket, and pulled out something wrapped in tissue paper. He passed it to me. I opened it, and found a small circle of greyish metal, something like lead, only harder and rather brighter.

"Well?" I asked, at length, after examining it and handing it round to the others. "Did that stop the haunting?"

Carnacki nodded. "Yes," he said. "I slept three nights in the Grey Room, before I left. Old Peter nearly fainted when he knew that I meant to; but by the third night he seemed to realise that the house was just safe and ordinary. And, you know, I believe, in his heart, he hardly approved."

Carnacki stood up and began to shake hands. "Out you go!" he said, genially. And, presently, we went, pondering, to our various homes.

Amour Dure

by Vernon Lee

PASSAGES FROM THE DIARY OF SPIRIDION TREPKA

PART I

Urbania, August 20th, 1885.—

I had longed, these years and years, to be in Italy, to come face to face with the Past; and was this Italy, was this the Past? I could have cried, yes cried, for disappointment when I first wandered about Rome, with an invitation to dine at the German Embassy in my pocket, and three or four Berlin and Munich Vandals at my heels, telling me where the best beer and sauerkraut could be had, and what the last article by Grimm or Mommsen was about.

Is this folly? Is it falsehood? Am I not myself a product of modern, northern civilization; is not my coming to Italy due to this very modern scientific vandalism, which has given me a traveling scholarship because I have written a book like all those other atrocious books of erudition and art-criticism? Nay, am I not here at Urbania on the express understanding that, in a certain number of months, I shall produce just another such book? Dost thou imagine, thou miserable Spiridion, thou Pole grown into the semblance of a German pedant, doctor of philosophy, professor even, author of a prize essay on the despots of the fifteenth century, dost thou imagine that thou, with thy ministerial letters and proof-sheets in thy black professorial coat-pocket, canst ever come in spirit into the presence of the Past?

Too true, alas! But let me forget it, at least, every now and then; as I forgot it this afternoon, while the white bullocks dragged my gig slowly winding along interminable valleys, crawling along interminable hill-sides, with the invisible droning torrent far below, and only the bare grey and reddish peaks all around, up to this town of Urbania, forgotten of mankind, towered and battlemented on the high Apennine ridge. Sigillo, Penna, Fossombrone, Mercatello, Montemurlo—each single village name, as the driver pointed it out, brought to my mind the recollection of some battle or some great act of treachery of former days. And as the huge mountains shut out the setting sun, and the valleys filled with bluish shadow and mist, only a band of threatening smoke-red remaining behind the towers and cupolas of the city on its mountain-top, and the sound of church bells floated across the precipice from Urbania, I almost expected, at every turning of the road, that a troop of horsemen, with beaked helmets and clawed shoes, would emerge, with armor glittering and pennons waving in the sunset. And then, not two hours ago, entering the town at dusk, passing along the deserted streets, with only a smoky light here and there under a shrine or in front of a fruit-stall, or a fire reddening the blackness of a smithy; passing beneath the battlements and turrets of the palace… Ah, that was Italy, it was the Past!

August 21st.—
And this is the Present! Four letters of introduction to deliver, and an hour's polite conversation to endure with the Vice-Prefect, the Syndic, the Director of the Archives, and the good man to whom my friend Max had sent me for lodgings….

August 22nd-27th.—
Spent the greater part of the day in the Archives, and the greater part of my time there in being bored to extinction by the Director thereof, who today spouted Aeneas Sylvius' Commentaries for three-quarters of an hour without taking breath. From this sort of martyrdom (what are the sensations

of a former racehorse being driven in a cab? If you can conceive them, they are those of a Pole turned Prussian professor) I take refuge in long rambles through the town. This town is a handful of tall black houses huddled on to the top of an Alp, long narrow lanes trickling down its sides, like the slides we made on hillocks in our boyhood, and in the middle the superb red brick structure, turreted and battlemented, of Duke Ottobuono's palace, from whose windows you look down upon a sea, a kind of whirlpool, of melancholy grey mountains. Then there are the people, dark, bushy-bearded men, riding about like brigands, wrapped in green-lined cloaks upon their shaggy pack-mules; or loitering about, great, brawny, low-headed youngsters, like the parti-colored bravos in Signorelli's frescoes; the beautiful boys, like so many young Raphaels, with eyes like the eyes of bullocks, and the huge women, Madonnas or St. Elizabeths, as the case may be, with their clogs firmly poised on their toes and their brass pitchers on their heads, as they go up and down the steep black alleys. I do not talk much to these people; I fear my illusions being dispelled. At the corner of a street, opposite Francesco di Giorgio's beautiful little portico, is a great blue and red advertisement, representing an angel descending to crown Elias Howe, on account of his sewing-machines; and the clerks of the Vice-Prefecture, who dine at the place where I get my dinner, yell politics, Minghetti, Cairoli, Tunis, ironclads, &c., at each other, and sing snatches of *La Fille de Mme. Angot,* which I imagine they have been performing here recently.

No; talking to the natives is evidently a dangerous experiment. Except indeed, perhaps, to my good landlord, Signor Notaro Porri, who is just as learned, and takes considerably less snuff (or rather brushes it off his coat more often) than the Director of the Archives. I forgot to jot down (and I feel I must jot down, in the vain belief that some day these scraps will help, like a withered twig of olive or a three-wicked Tuscan lamp on my table, to bring to my mind, in that hateful Babylon of Berlin, these happy Italian days)—I forgot to record that I am lodging in the house of a dealer in antiquities. My window looks up the principal street to where the little column with Mercury on the top rises in the midst of the awnings and porticoes of the market-place. Bending over the chipped ewers and tubs full of sweet basil, clove pinks, and marigolds, I can just see a corner of the palace turret, and the vague ultramarine of the hills beyond. The house, whose back goes sharp down into the ravine, is a queer up-and-down black place, whitewashed rooms, hung with the Raphaels and Francias and Peruginos, whom mine host regularly carries to the chief inn whenever a stranger is expected; and surrounded by old carved chairs, sofas of the Empire, embossed and gilded wedding-chests, and the cupboards which contain bits of old damask and embroidered altar-cloths scenting the place with the smell of old incense and mustiness; all of which are presided over by Signor Porri's three maiden sisters—Sora Serafina, Sora Lodovica, and Sora Adalgisa—the three Fates in person, even to the distaffs and their black cats.

Sor Asdrubale, as they call my landlord, is also a notary. He regrets the Pontifical Government, having had a cousin who was a Cardinal's train-bearer, and believes that if only you lay a table for two, light four candles made of dead men's fat, and perform certain rites about which he is not very precise, you can, on Christmas Eve and similar nights, summon up San Pasquale Baylon, who will write you the winning numbers of the lottery upon the smoked back of a plate, if you have previously slapped him on both cheeks and repeated three Ave Marias. The difficulty consists in obtaining the dead men's fat for the candles, and also in slapping the saint before he has time to vanish.

"If it were not for that," says Sor Asdrubale, "the Government would have had to suppress the lottery ages ago—eh!"

Sept. 9th.—

This history of Urbania is not without its romance, although that romance (as usual) has been overlooked by our Dryasdusts. Even before coming here I felt attracted by the strange figure of a woman, which appeared from out of the dry pages of Gualterio's and Padre de Sanctis' histories of this place. This woman is Medea, daughter of Galeazzo IV. Malatesta, Lord of Carpi, wife first of Pierluigi Orsini, Duke of Stimigliano, and subsequently of Guidalfonso II., Duke of Urbania, predecessor of the great Duke Robert II.

This woman's history and character remind one of that of Bianca Cappello, and at the same time of Lucrezia Borgia. Born in 1556, she was affianced at the age of twelve to a cousin, a Malatesta of the Rimini family. This family having greatly gone down in the world, her engagement was broken, and she was betrothed a year later to a member of the Pico family, and married to him by proxy at the age of fourteen. But this match not satisfying her own or her father's ambition, the marriage by proxy was, upon some pretext, declared null, and the suit encouraged of the Duke of Stimigliano, a great Umbrian feudatory of the Orsini family. But the bridegroom, Giovanfrancesco Pico, refused to submit, pleaded his case before the Pope, and tried to carry off by force his bride, with whom he was madly in love, as the lady was most lovely and of most cheerful and amiable manner, says an old anonymous chronicle. Pico waylaid her litter as she was going to a villa of her father's, and carried her to his castle near Mirandola, where he respectfully pressed his suit; insisting that he had a right to consider her as his wife. But the lady escaped by letting herself into the moat by a rope of sheets, and Giovanfrancesco Pico was discovered stabbed in the chest, by the hand of Madonna Medea da Carpi. He was a handsome youth only eighteen years old.

The Pico having been settled, and the marriage with him declared null by the Pope, Medea da Carpi was solemnly married to the Duke of Stimigliano, and went to live upon his domains near Rome.

Two years later, Pierluigi Orsini was stabbed by one of his grooms at his castle of Stimigliano, near Orvieto; and suspicion fell upon his widow, more especially as, immediately after the event, she caused the murderer to be cut down by two servants in her own chamber; but not before he had declared that she had induced him to assassinate his master by a promise of her love. Things became so hot for Medea da Carpi that she fled to Urbania and threw herself at the feet of Duke Guidalfonso II., declaring that she had caused the groom to be killed merely to avenge her good fame, which he had slandered, and that she was absolutely guiltless of the death of her husband. The marvelous beauty of the widowed Duchess of Stimigliano, who was only nineteen, entirely turned the head of the Duke of Urbania. He affected implicit belief in her innocence, refused to give her up to the Orsinis, kinsmen of her late husband, and assigned to her magnificent apartments in the left wing of the palace, among which the room containing the famous fireplace ornamented with marble Cupids on a blue ground. Guidalfonso fell madly in love with his beautiful guest. Hitherto timid and domestic in character, he began publicly to neglect his wife, Maddalena Varano of Camerino, with whom, although childless, he had hitherto lived on excellent terms; he not only treated with contempt the admonitions of his advisers and of his suzerain the Pope, but went so far as to take measures to repudiate his wife, on the score of quite imaginary ill-conduct. The Duchess Maddalena, unable to bear this treatment, fled to the convent of the barefooted sisters at Pesaro, where she pined away, while Medea da Carpi reigned in her place at Urbania, embroiling Duke Guidalfonso in quarrels both with the powerful Orsinis, who continued to accuse her of Stimigliano's murder, and with the Varanos, kinsmen of the injured Duchess Maddalena; until at length, in the year 1576, the Duke of Urbania, having become suddenly, and not without suspicious circumstances, a widower, publicly married Medea da Carpi two days after the decease of his unhappy wife. No child was born of this marriage; but such was the infatuation of Duke Guidalfonso, that the new Duchess induced him to settle the inheritance of the Duchy (having, with great difficulty, obtained the consent of the Pope) on the boy Bartolommeo, her son by Stimigliano, but whom the Orsinis refused to acknowledge as such, declaring him to be the child of that Giovanfrancesco Pico to whom Medea had been married by proxy, and whom, in defense, as she had said, of her honor, she had assassinated; and this investiture of the Duchy of Urbania on to a stranger and a bastard was at the expense of the obvious rights of the Cardinal Robert, Guidalfonso's younger brother.

In May 1579 Duke Guidalfonso died suddenly and mysteriously, Medea having forbidden all access to his chamber, lest, on his deathbed, he might repent and reinstate his brother in his rights. The Duchess immediately caused her son, Bartolommeo Orsini, to be proclaimed Duke of Urbania, and herself regent; and, with the help of two or three unscrupulous young men, particularly a certain Captain Oliverotto da Narni, who was rumoured to be her lover, seized the reins of government with extraordinary and terrible vigor, marching an army against the Varanos and Orsinis, who were defeated at Sigillo, and ruthlessly exterminating every person who dared question the lawfulness of the succession; while, all the time, Cardinal Robert, who had flung aside his priest's garb and vows, went about in Rome, Tuscany, Venice—nay, even to the Emperor and the King of Spain, imploring help against the usurper. In a few months he had turned the tide of sympathy against the Duchess-Regent; the Pope solemnly declared the investiture of Bartolommeo Orsini worthless, and published the accession of Robert II., Duke of Urbania and Count of Montemurlo; the Grand Duke of Tuscany and the Venetians secretly promised assistance, but only if Robert were able to assert his rights by main force. Little by little, one town after the other of the Duchy went over to Robert, and Medea da Carpi found herself surrounded in the mountain citadel of Urbania like a scorpion surrounded by flames. (This simile is not mine, but belongs to Raffaello Gualterio, historiographer to Robert II.) But, unlike the scorpion, Medea refused to commit suicide. It is perfectly marvelous how, without money or allies, she could so long keep her enemies at bay; and Gualterio attributes this to those fatal fascinations which had brought Pico and Stimigliano to their deaths, which had turned the once honest Guidalfonso into a villain, and which were such that, of all her lovers, not one but preferred dying for her, even after he had been treated with ingratitude and ousted by a rival; a faculty which Messer Raffaello Gualterio clearly attributed to hellish connivance.

At last the ex-Cardinal Robert succeeded, and triumphantly entered Urbania in November 1579. His accession was marked by moderation and clemency. Not a man was put to death, save Oliverotto da Narni, who threw himself on the new Duke, tried to stab him as he alighted at the palace, and who was cut down by the Duke's men, crying, "Orsini, Orsini! Medea, Medea! Long live Duke Bartolommeo!" with his dying breath, although it is said that the Duchess had treated him with ignominy. The little Bartolommeo was sent to Rome to the Orsinis; the Duchess, respectfully confined in the left wing of the palace.

It is said that she haughtily requested to see the new Duke, but that he shook his head, and, in his priest's fashion, quoted a verse about Ulysses and the Sirens; and it is remarkable that he persistently refused to see her, abruptly leaving his chamber one day that she had entered it by stealth. After a few months a conspiracy was discovered to murder Duke Robert, which had obviously been set on foot by Medea. But the young man, one Marcantonio Frangipani of Rome, denied, even under the severest torture, any complicity of hers; so that Duke Robert, who wished to do nothing violent, merely transferred the Duchess from his villa at Sant' Elmo to the convent of the Clarisse in town, where she was guarded and watched in the closest manner. It seemed impossible that Medea should intrigue any further, for she certainly saw and could be seen by no one. Yet she contrived to send a letter and her portrait to one Prinzivalle degli Ordelaffi, a youth, only nineteen years old, of noble Romagnole family, and who was betrothed to one of the most beautiful girls of Urbania. He immediately broke off his engagement, and, shortly afterwards, attempted to shoot Duke Robert with a holster-pistol as he knelt at mass on the festival of Easter Day. This time Duke Robert was determined to obtain proofs against Medea. Prinzivalle degli Ordelaffi was kept some days without food, then submitted to the most violent tortures, and finally condemned. When he was going to be flayed with red-hot pincers and quartered by horses, he was told that he might obtain the grace of immediate death by confessing the complicity of the Duchess; and the confessor and nuns of the convent, which stood in the place of execution outside Porta San Romano, pressed Medea to save the wretch, whose screams reached her, by confessing her own guilt. Medea asked permission to go to a balcony, where she could see Prinzivalle and be seen by him. She looked on coldly, then threw down her embroidered kerchief to the poor mangled creature. He asked the executioner to wipe his mouth with it, kissed it, and cried out that Medea was innocent. Then, after several hours of torments, he died. This was too much for the patience even of Duke Robert. Seeing that as long as Medea lived his life would be in perpetual danger, but unwilling to cause a scandal (somewhat of the priest-nature remaining), he had Medea strangled in the convent, and, what is remarkable, insisted that only women—two infanticides to whom he remitted their sentence—should be employed for the deed.

"This clement prince," writes Don Arcangelo Zappi in his life of him, published in 1725, "can be blamed only for one act of cruelty, the more odious as he had himself, until released from his vows by the Pope, been in holy orders. It is said that when he caused the death of the infamous Medea da Carpi, his fear lest her extraordinary charms should seduce any man was such, that he not only employed women as executioners, but refused to permit her a priest or monk, thus forcing her to die unshriven, and refusing her the benefit of any penitence that may have lurked in her adamantine heart."

Such is the story of Medea da Carpi, Duchess of Stimigliano Orsini, and then wife of Duke Guidalfonso II. of Urbania. She was put to death just two hundred and ninety-seven years ago, December 1582, at the age of barely seven-and twenty, and having, in the course of her short life, brought to a violent end five of her lovers, from Giovanfrancesco Pico to Prinzivalle degli Ordelaffi.

Sept. 20th.—

A grand illumination of the town in honour of the taking of Rome fifteen years ago. Except Sor Asdrubale, my landlord, who shakes his head at the

Piedmontese, as he calls them, the people here are all Italianissimi. The Popes kept them very much down since Urbania lapsed to the Holy See in 1645.

Sept. 28th.—

I have for some time been hunting for portraits of the Duchess Medea. Most of them, I imagine, must have been destroyed, perhaps by Duke Robert II.'s fear lest even after her death this terrible beauty should play him a trick. Three or four I have, however, been able to find—one a miniature in the Archives, said to be that which she sent to poor Prinzivalle degli Ordelaffi in order to turn his head; one a marble bust in the palace lumber-room; one in a large composition, possibly by Baroccio, representing Cleopatra at the feet of Augustus. Augustus is the idealized portrait of Robert II., round cropped head, nose a little awry, clipped beard and scar as usual, but in Roman dress. Cleopatra seems to me, for all her Oriental dress, and although she wears a black wig, to be meant for Medea da Carpi; she is kneeling, baring her breast for the victor to strike, but in reality to captivate him, and he turns away with an awkward gesture of loathing. None of these portraits seem very good, save the miniature, but that is an exquisite work, and with it, and the suggestions of the bust, it is easy to reconstruct the beauty of this terrible being. The type is that most admired by the late Renaissance, and, in some measure, immortalized by Jean Goujon and the French. The face is a perfect oval, the forehead somewhat over-round, with minute curls, like a fleece, of bright auburn hair; the nose a trifle over-aquiline, and the cheek-bones a trifle too low; the eyes grey, large, prominent, beneath exquisitely curved brows and lids just a little too tight at the corners; the mouth also, brilliantly red and most delicately designed, is a little too tight, the lips strained a trifle over the teeth. Tight eyelids and tight lips give a strange refinement, and, at the same time, an air of mystery, a somewhat sinister seductiveness; they seem to take, but not to give. The mouth with a kind of childish pout, looks as if it could bite or suck like a leech. The complexion is dazzlingly fair, the perfect transparent rosette lily of a red-haired beauty; the head, with hair elaborately curled and plaited close to it, and adorned with pearls, sits like that of the antique Arethusa on a long, supple, swan-like neck. A curious, at first rather conventional, artificial-looking sort of beauty, voluptuous yet cold, which, the more it is contemplated, the more it troubles and haunts the mind. Round the lady's neck is a gold chain with little gold lozenges at intervals, on which is engraved the posy or pun (the fashion of French devices is common in those days), 'Amour Dure—Dure Amour.' The same posy is inscribed in the hollow of the bust, and, thanks to it, I have been able to identify the latter as Medea's portrait. I often examine these tragic portraits, wondering what this face, which led so many men to their death, may have been like when it spoke or smiled, what at the moment when Medea da Carpi fascinated her victims into love unto death—'Amour Dure—Dure Amour,' as runs her device—love that lasts, cruel love—yes indeed, when one thinks of the fidelity and fate of her lovers.

Oct. 13th.—

I have literally not had time to write a line of my diary all these days. My whole mornings have gone in those Archives, my afternoons taking long walks in this lovely autumn weather (the highest hills are just tipped with snow). My evenings go in writing that confounded account of the Palace of Urbania which Government requires, merely to keep me at work at something useless. Of my history I have not yet been able to write a word… By the way, I must note down a curious circumstance mentioned in an anonymous M.S. life of Duke Robert, which I fell upon today. When this prince had the equestrian statue of himself by Antonio Tassi, Gianbologna's pupil, erected in the square of the *Corte*, he secretly caused to be made, says my anonymous M.S., a silver statuette of his familiar genius or angel—'*familiaris ejus angelus seu genius, quod a vulgo dicitur idolino*'—which statuette or idol, after having been consecrated by the astrologers—'*ab astrologis quibusdam ritibus sacrato*'—was placed in the cavity of the chest of the effigy by Tassi, in order, says the M.S., that his soul might rest until the general Resurrection. This passage is curious, and to me somewhat puzzling; how could the soul of Duke Robert await the general Resurrection, when, as a Catholic, he ought to have believed that it must, as soon as separated from his body, go to Purgatory? Or is there some semi-pagan superstition of the Renaissance (most strange, certainly, in a man who had been a Cardinal) connecting the soul with a guardian genius, who could be compelled, by magic rites ('*ab astrologis sacrato*,' the M.S. says of the little idol), to remain fixed to earth, so that the soul should sleep in the body until the Day of Judgment? I confess this story baffles me. I wonder whether such an idol ever existed, or exists nowadays, in the body of Tassi's bronze effigy?

Oct. 20th.—

I have been seeing a good deal of late of the Vice-Prefect's son: an amiable young man with a love-sick face and a languid interest in Urbanian history and archaeology, of which he is profoundly ignorant. This young man, who has lived at Siena and Lucca before his father was promoted here, wears extremely long and tight trousers, which almost preclude his bending his knees, a stick-up collar and an eyeglass, and a pair of fresh kid gloves stuck in the breast of his coat, speaks of Urbania as Ovid might have spoken of Pontus, and complains (as well he may) of the barbarism of the young men, the officials who dine at my inn and howl and sing like madmen, and the nobles who drive gigs, showing almost as much throat as a lady at a ball. This person frequently entertains me with his *amori*, past, present, and future; he evidently thinks me very odd for having none to entertain him with in return; he points out to me the pretty (or ugly) servant-girls and dressmakers as we walk in the street, sighs deeply or sings in falsetto behind every tolerably young-looking woman, and has finally taken me to the house of the lady of his heart, a great black-mustachioed countess, with a voice like a fish-crier; here, he says, I shall meet all the best company in Urbania and some beautiful women—ah, too beautiful, alas! I find three huge half-furnished rooms, with bare brick floors, petroleum lamps, and horribly bad pictures on bright washball-blue and gamboge walls, and in the midst of it all, every evening, a dozen ladies and gentlemen seated in a circle, vociferating at each other the same news a year old; the younger ladies in bright yellows and greens, fanning themselves while my teeth chatter, and having sweet things whispered behind their fans by officers with hair brushed up like a hedgehog. And these are the women my friend expects me to fall in love with! I vainly wait for tea or supper which does not come, and rush home, determined to leave alone the Urbanian *beau monde*.

It is quite true that I have no *amori*, although my friend does not believe it. When I came to Italy first, I looked out for romance; I sighed, like Goethe in Rome, for a window to open and a wondrous creature to appear, '*welch mich versengend erquickt*.' Perhaps it is because Goethe was a German, accustomed to German *Fraus*, and I am, after all, a Pole, accustomed to something very different from *Fraus*; but anyhow, for all my efforts, in Rome, Florence, and Siena, I never could find a woman to go mad about, either among the ladies, chattering bad French, or among the lower classes, as 'cute and cold as money-lenders; so I steer clear of Italian womankind, its shrill voice and gaudy toilettes. I am wedded to history, to the Past, to women like Lucrezia Borgia, Vittoria Accoramboni, or that Medea da Carpi, for the present; some day I shall perhaps find a grand passion, a woman to play the Don Quixote about, like the Pole that I am; a woman out of whose slipper to drink, and for whose pleasure to die; but not here! Few things strike me so much as the degeneracy of Italian women. What has become of the race of Faustinas, Marozias, Bianca Cappellos? Where discover nowadays (I confess she haunts me) another Medea da Carpi? Were it only possible to meet a woman of that extreme distinction of beauty, of that terribleness of nature, even if only potential, I do believe I could love her, even to the Day of Judgment, like any Oliverotto da Narni, or Frangipani or Prinzivalle.

Oct. 27th.—
Fine sentiments the above are for a professor, a learned man! I thought the young artists of Rome childish because they played practical jokes and yelled at night in the streets, returning from the Caffè Greco or the cellar in the Via Palombella; but am I not as childish to the full—I, melancholy wretch, whom they called Hamlet and the Knight of the Doleful Countenance?

Nov. 5th.—
I can't free myself from the thought of this Medea da Carpi. In my walks, my mornings in the Archives, my solitary evenings, I catch myself thinking over the woman. Am I turning novelist instead of historian? And still it seems to me that I understand her so well; so much better than my facts warrant. First, we must put aside all pedantic modern ideas of right and wrong. Right and wrong in a century of violence and treachery does not exist, least of all for creatures like Medea. Go preach right and wrong to a tigress, my dear sir! Yet is there in the world anything nobler than the huge creature, steel when she springs, velvet when she treads, as she stretches her supple body, or smooths her beautiful skin, or fastens her strong claws into her victim?

Yes; I can understand Medea. Fancy a woman of superlative beauty, of the highest courage and calmness, a woman of many resources, of genius, brought up by a petty princelet of a father, upon Tacitus and Sallust, and the tales of the great Malatestas, of Caesar Borgia and such-like!—a woman whose one passion is conquest and empire—fancy her, on the eve of being wedded to a man of the power of the Duke of Stimigliano, claimed, carried off by a small fry of a Pico, locked up in his hereditary brigand's castle, and having to receive the young fool's red-hot love as an honour and a necessity! The mere thought of any violence to such a nature is an abominable outrage; and if Pico chooses to embrace such a woman at the risk of meeting a sharp piece of steel in her arms, why, it is a fair bargain. Young hound—or, if you prefer, young hero—to think to treat a woman like this as if she were any village wench! Medea marries her Orsini. A marriage, let it be noted, between an old soldier of fifty and a girl of sixteen. Reflect what that means: it means that this imperious woman is soon treated like a chattel, made roughly to understand that her business is to give the Duke an heir, not advice; that she must never ask "wherefore this or that?" that she must courtesy before the Duke's counselors, his captains, his mistresses; that, at the least suspicion of rebelliousness, she is subject to his foul words and blows; at the least suspicion of infidelity, to be strangled or starved to death, or thrown down an oubliette. Suppose that she knew that her husband has taken it into his head that she has looked too hard at this man or that, that one of his lieutenants or one of his women have whispered that, after all, the boy Bartolommeo might as soon be a Pico as an Orsini. Suppose she knew that she must strike or be struck? Why, she strikes, or gets some one to strike for her. At what price? A promise of love, of love to a groom, the son of a serf! Why, the dog must be mad or drunk to believe such a thing possible; his very belief in anything so monstrous makes him worthy of death. And then he dares to blab! This is much worse than Pico. Medea is bound to defend her honor a second time; if she could stab Pico, she can certainly stab this fellow, or have him stabbed.

Hounded by her husband's kinsmen, she takes refuge at Urbania. The Duke, like every other man, falls wildly in love with Medea, and neglects his wife; let us even go so far as to say, breaks his wife's heart. Is this Medea's fault? Is it her fault that every stone that comes beneath her chariot-wheels is crushed? Certainly not. Do you suppose that a woman like Medea feels the smallest ill-will against a poor, craven Duchess Maddalena? Why, she ignores her very existence. To suppose Medea a cruel woman is as grotesque as to call her an immoral woman. Her fate is, sooner or later, to triumph over her enemies, at all events to make their victory almost a defeat; her magic faculty is to enslave all the men who come across her path; all those who see her, love her, become her slaves; and it is the destiny of all her slaves to perish. Her lovers, with the exception of Duke Guidalfonso, all come to an untimely end; and in this there is nothing unjust. The possession of a woman like Medea is a happiness too great for a mortal man; it would turn his head, make him forget even what he owed her; no man must survive long who conceives himself to have a right over her; it is a kind of sacrilege. And only death, the willingness to pay for such happiness by death, can at all make a man worthy of being her lover; he must be willing to love and suffer and die. This is the meaning of her device—'Amour Dure—Dure Amour.' The love of Medea da Carpi cannot fade, but the lover can die; it is a constant and a cruel love.

Nov. 11th.—

I was right, quite right in my idea. I have found—Oh, joy! I treated the Vice-Prefect's son to a dinner of five courses at the Trattoria La Stella d'Italia out of sheer jubilation—I have found in the Archives, unknown, of course, to the Director, a heap of letters—letters of Duke Robert about Medea da Carpi, letters of Medea herself! Yes, Medea's own handwriting—a round, scholarly character, full of abbreviations, with a Greek look about it, as befits a learned princess who could read Plato as well as Petrarch. The letters are of little importance, mere drafts of business letters for her secretary to copy, during the time that she governed the poor weak Guidalfonso. But they are her letters, and I can imagine almost that there hangs about these moldering pieces of paper a scent as of a woman's hair.

The few letters of Duke Robert show him in a new light. A cunning, cold, but craven priest. He trembles at the bare thought of Medea—'*la pessima Medea*'—worse than her namesake of Colchis, as he calls her. His long clemency is a result of mere fear of laying violent hands upon her. He fears her as something almost supernatural; he would have enjoyed having had her burnt as a witch. After letter on letter, telling his crony, Cardinal Sanseverino, at Rome his various precautions during her lifetime—how he wears a jacket of mail under his coat; how he drinks only milk from a cow which he has milked in his presence; how he tries his dog with morsels of his food, lest it be poisoned; how he suspects the wax-candles because of their peculiar smell; how he fears riding out lest some one should frighten his horse and cause him to break his neck—after all this, and when Medea has been in her grave two years, he tells his correspondent of his fear of meeting the soul of Medea after his own death, and chuckles over the ingenious device (concocted by his astrologer and a certain Fra Gaudenzio, a Capuchin) by which he shall secure the absolute peace of his soul until that of the wicked Medea be finally 'chained up in hell among the lakes of boiling pitch and the ice of Caina described by the immortal bard'—old pedant! Here, then, is the explanation of that silver image—*quod vulgo dicitur idolino*—which he caused to be soldered into his effigy by Tassi. As long as the image of his soul was attached to the image of his body, he should sleep awaiting the Day of Judgment, fully convinced that Medea's soul will then be properly tarred and feathered, while his—honest man!—will fly straight to Paradise. And to think that, two weeks ago, I believed this man to be a hero! Aha! my good Duke Robert, you shall be shown up in my history; and no amount of silver idolinos shall save you from being heartily laughed at!

Nov. 15th.—

Strange! That idiot of a Prefect's son, who has heard me talk a hundred times of Medea da Carpi, suddenly recollects that, when he was a child at Urbania, his nurse used to threaten him with a visit from Madonna Medea, who rode in the sky on a black he-goat. My Duchess Medea turned into a bogey for naughty little boys!

Nov. 20th.—

I have been going about with a Bavarian Professor of mediaeval history, showing him all over the country. Among other places we went to Rocca Sant'Elmo, to see the former villa of the Dukes of Urbania, the villa where Medea was confined between the accession of Duke Robert and the conspiracy of Marcantonio Frangipani, which caused her removal to the nunnery immediately outside the town. A long ride up the desolate Apennine valleys, bleak beyond words just now with their thin fringe of oak scrub turned russet, thin patches of grass seared by the frost, the last few yellow leaves of the poplars by the torrents shaking and fluttering about in the chill Tramontana; the mountaintops are wrapped in thick grey cloud; tomorrow, if the wind continues, we shall see them round masses of snow against the cold blue sky. Sant' Elmo is a wretched hamlet high on the

Apennine ridge, where the Italian vegetation is already replaced by that of the North. You ride for miles through leafless chestnut woods, the scent of the soaking brown leaves filling the air, the roar of the torrent, turbid with autumn rains, rising from the precipice below; then suddenly the leafless chestnut woods are replaced, as at Vallombrosa, by a belt of black, dense fir plantations. Emerging from these, you come to an open space, frozen blasted meadows, the rocks of snow clad peak, the newly fallen snow, close above you; and in the midst, on a knoll, with a gnarled larch on either side, the ducal villa of Sant' Elmo, a big black stone box with a stone escutcheon, grated windows, and a double flight of steps in front. It is now let out to the proprietor of the neighbouring woods, who uses it for the storage of chestnuts, faggots, and charcoal from the neighbouring ovens. We tied our horses to the iron rings and entered: an old woman, with disheveled hair, was alone in the house. The villa is a mere hunting-lodge, built by Ottobuono IV., the father of Dukes Guidalfonso and Robert, about 1530. Some of the rooms have at one time been frescoed and paneled with oak carvings, but all this has disappeared. Only, in one of the big rooms, there remains a large marble fireplace, similar to those in the palace at Urbania, beautifully carved with Cupids on a blue ground; a charming naked boy sustains a jar on either side, one containing clove pinks, the other roses. The room was filled with stacks of faggots.

We returned home late, my companion in excessively bad humour at the fruitlessness of the expedition. We were caught in the skirt of a snow-storm as we got into the chestnut woods. The sight of the snow falling gently, of the earth and bushes whitened all round, made me feel back at Posen, once more a child. I sang and shouted, to my companion's horror. This will be a bad point against me if reported at Berlin. A historian of twenty-four who shouts and sings, and that when another historian is cursing at the snow and the bad roads! All night I lay awake watching the embers of my wood fire, and thinking of Medea da Carpi mewed up, in winter, in that solitude of Sant' Elmo, the firs groaning, the torrent roaring, the snow falling all round; miles and miles away from human creatures. I fancied I saw it all, and that I, somehow, was Marcantonio Frangipani come to liberate her—or was it Prinzivalle degli Ordelaffi? I suppose it was because of the long ride, the unaccustomed pricking feeling of the snow in the air; or perhaps the punch which my professor insisted on drinking after dinner.

Nov. 23rd.—

Thank goodness, that Bavarian professor has finally departed! Those days he spent here drove me nearly crazy. Talking over my work, I told him one day my views on Medea da Carpi; whereupon he condescended to answer that those were the usual tales due to the mythopoeic (old idiot!) tendency of the Renaissance; that research would disprove the greater part of them, as it had disproved the stories current about the Borgias, &c.; that, moreover, such a woman as I made out was psychologically and physiologically impossible. Would that one could say as much of such professors as he and his fellows!

Nov. 24th.—

I cannot get over my pleasure in being rid of that imbecile; I felt as if I could have throttled him every time he spoke of the Lady of my thoughts—for such she has become—*Metea*, as the animal called her!

Nov. 30th.—

I feel quite shaken at what has just happened; I am beginning to fear that that old pedant was right in saying that it was bad for me to live all alone in a strange country, that it would make me morbid. It is ridiculous that I should be put into such a state of excitement merely by the chance discovery of a portrait of a woman dead these three hundred years. With the case of my uncle Ladislas, and other suspicions of insanity in my family, I ought really to guard against such foolish excitement.

Yet the incident was really dramatic, uncanny. I could have sworn that I knew every picture in the palace here; and particularly every picture of Her. Anyhow, this morning, as I was leaving the Archives, I passed through one of the many small rooms—irregular-shaped closets—which fill up the ins and outs of this curious palace, turreted like a French château. I must have passed through that closet before, for the view was so familiar out of its window; just the particular bit of round tower in front, the cypress on the other side of the ravine, the belfry beyond, and the piece of the line of Monte Sant' Agata and the Leonessa, covered with snow, against the sky. I suppose there must be twin rooms, and that I had got into the wrong one; or rather, perhaps some shutter had been opened or curtain withdrawn. As I was passing, my eye was caught by a very beautiful old mirror-frame let into the brown and yellow inlaid wall. I approached, and looking at the frame, looked also, mechanically, into the glass. I gave a great start, and almost shrieked, I do believe—(it's lucky the Munich professor is safe out of Urbania!). Behind my own image stood another, a figure close to my shoulder, a face close to mine; and that figure, that face, hers! Medea da Carpi's! I turned sharp round, as white, I think, as the ghost I expected to see. On the wall opposite the mirror, just a pace or two behind where I had been standing, hung a portrait. And such a portrait!—Bronzino never painted a grander one. Against a background of harsh, dark blue, there stands out the figure of the Duchess (for it is Medea, the real Medea, a thousand times more real, individual, and powerful than in the other portraits), seated stiffly in a high-backed chair, sustained, as it were, almost rigid, by the stiff brocade of skirts and stomacher, stiffer for plaques of embroidered silver flowers and rows of seed pearl. The dress is, with its mixture of silver and pearl, of a strange dull red, a wicked poppy-juice colour, against which the flesh of the long, narrow hands with fringe-like fingers; of the long slender neck, and the face with bared forehead, looks white and hard, like alabaster. The face is the same as in the other portraits: the same rounded forehead, with the short fleece-like, yellowish-red curls; the same beautifully curved eyebrows, just barely marked; the same eyelids, a little tight across the eyes; the same lips, a little tight across the mouth; but with a purity of line, a dazzling splendour of skin, and intensity of look immeasurably superior to all the other portraits.

She looks out of the frame with a cold, level glance; yet the lips smile. One hand holds a dull-red rose; the other, long, narrow, tapering, plays with a thick rope of silk and gold and jewels hanging from the waist; round the throat, white as marble, partially confined in the tight dull-red bodice, hangs a gold collar, with the device on alternate enameled medallions, 'AMOUR DURE—DURE AMOUR.'

On reflection, I see that I simply could never have been in that room or closet before; I must have mistaken the door. But, although the explanation is so simple, I still, after several hours, feel terribly shaken in all my being. If I grow so excitable I shall have to go to Rome at Christmas for a holiday. I feel as if some danger pursued me here (can it be fever?); and yet, and yet, I don't see how I shall ever tear myself away.

Dec. 10th.—

I have made an effort, and accepted the Vice-Prefect's son's invitation to see the oil-making at a villa of theirs near the coast. The villa, or farm, is an old fortified, towered place, standing on a hillside among olive-trees and little osier-bushes, which look like a bright orange flame. The olives are squeezed in a tremendous black cellar, like a prison: you see, by the faint white daylight, and the smoky yellow flare of resin burning in pans, great white bullocks moving round a huge millstone; vague figures working at pulleys and handles: it looks, to my fancy, like some scene of the Inquisition. The Cavaliere regaled me with his best wine and rusks. I took some long walks by the seaside; I had left Urbania wrapped in snow-clouds; down on the coast there was a bright sun; the sunshine, the sea, the bustle of the little port on the Adriatic seemed to do me good. I came back to Urbania another man. Sor Asdrubale, my landlord, poking about in slippers among the gilded chests, the Empire sofas, the old cups and saucers and pictures which no one will buy, congratulated me upon the improvement in my looks. "You work too much," he says; "youth requires amusement, theatres, promenades, *amori*—it is time enough to be serious when one is bald"—and he took off his greasy red cap. Yes, I am better! and, as a result, I take to my work with delight again. I will cut them out still, those wiseacres at Berlin!

Dec. 14th.—

I don't think I have ever felt so happy about my work. I see it all so well—that crafty, cowardly Duke Robert; that melancholy Duchess Maddalena; that weak, showy, would-be chivalrous Duke Guidalfonso; and above all, the splendid figure of Medea. I feel as if I were the greatest historian of the age; and, at the same time, as if I were a boy of twelve. It snowed yesterday for the first time in the city, for two good hours. When it had done, I actually went into the square and taught the ragamuffins to make a snowman; no, a snow-woman; and I had the fancy to call her Medea. "La pessima Medea!" cried one of the boys—"the one who used to ride through the air on a goat?" "No, no," I said; "she was a beautiful lady, the Duchess of Urbania, the most beautiful woman that ever lived." I made her a crown of tinsel, and taught the boys to cry "Evviva, Medea!" But one of them said, "She is a witch! She must be burnt!" At which they all rushed to fetch burning faggots and tow; in a minute the yelling demons had melted her down.

Dec. 15th.—

What a goose I am, and to think I am twenty-four, and known in literature! In my long walks I have composed to a tune (I don't know what it is) which all the people are singing and whistling in the street at present, a poem in frightful Italian, beginning 'Medea, mia dea,' calling on her in the name of her various lovers. I go about humming between my teeth, "Why am I not Marcantonio? or Prinzivalle? or he of Narni? or the good Duke Alfonso? that I might be beloved by thee, Medea, mia dea," &c. &c. Awful rubbish! My landlord, I think, suspects that Medea must be some lady I met while I was staying by the seaside. I am sure Sora Serafina, Sora Lodovica, and Sora Adalgisa—the three Parcae or *Norns*, as I call them—have some such notion. This afternoon, at dusk, while tidying my room, Sora Lodovica said to me, "How beautifully the Signorino has taken to singing!" I was scarcely aware that I had been vociferating, "Vieni, Medea, mia dea," while the old lady bobbed about making up my fire. I stopped; a nice reputation I shall get! I thought, and all this will somehow get to Rome, and thence to Berlin. Sora Lodovica was leaning out of the window, pulling in the iron hook of the shrine-lamp which marks Sor Asdrubale's house. As she was trimming the lamp previous to swinging it out again, she said in her odd, prudish little way, "You are wrong to stop singing, my son" (she varies between calling me Signor Professore and such terms of affection as "Nino," "Viscere mie," &c.); "you are wrong to stop singing, for there is a young lady there in the street who has actually stopped to listen to you."

I ran to the window. A woman, wrapped in a black shawl, was standing in an archway, looking up to the window.

"Eh, eh! the Signor Professore has admirers," said Sora Lodovica.

"Medea, mia dea!" I burst out as loud as I could, with a boy's pleasure in disconcerting the inquisitive passer-by. She turned suddenly round to go away, waving her hand at me; at that moment Sora Lodovica swung the shrine-lamp back into its place. A stream of light fell across the street. I felt myself grow quite cold; the face of the woman outside was that of Medea da Carpi!

What a fool I am, to be sure!

PART II

Dec. 17th.—

I fear that my craze about Medea da Carpi has become well known, thanks to my silly talk and idiotic songs. That Vice-Prefect's son—or the assistant at the Archives, or perhaps some of the company at the Contessa's, is trying to play me a trick! But take care, my good ladies and gentlemen, I shall pay you out in your own coin! Imagine my feelings when, this morning, I found on my desk a folded letter addressed to me in a curious handwriting which seemed strangely familiar to me, and which, after a moment, I recognized as that of the letters of Medea da Carpi at the Archives. It gave me a horrible shock. My next idea was that it must be a present from some one who knew my interest in Medea—a genuine letter of hers on which some idiot had written my address instead of putting it into an envelope. But it was addressed to me, written to me, no old letter; merely four lines, which ran as follows:—

"To Spiridion.—

"A person who knows the interest you bear her will be at the Church of San Giovanni Decollato this evening at nine. Look out, in the left aisle, for a lady wearing a black mantle, and holding a rose."

By this time I understood that I was the object of a conspiracy, the victim of a hoax. I turned the letter round and round. It was written on paper such as was made in the sixteenth century, and in an extraordinarily precise imitation of Medea da Carpi's characters. Who had written it? I thought over all the possible people. On the whole, it must be the Vice-Prefect's son, perhaps in combination with his lady-love, the Countess. They must have torn a blank page off some old letter; but that either of them should have had the ingenuity of inventing such a hoax, or the power of committing such a forgery, astounds me beyond measure. There is more in these people than I should have guessed. How pay them off? By taking no notice of the letter? Dignified, but dull. No, I will go; perhaps some one will be there, and I will mystify them in their turn. Or, if no one is there, how I shall crow over them for their imperfectly carried out plot! Perhaps this is some folly of the Cavalier Muzio's to bring me into the presence of some lady whom he destines to be the flame of my future *amori*. That is likely enough. And it would be too idiotic and professorial to refuse such an invitation; the lady must be worth knowing who can forge sixteenth-century letters like this, for I am sure that languid swell Muzio never could. I will go! By Heaven! I'll pay them back in their own coin! It is now five—how long these days are!

Dec. 18th.—

Am I mad? Or are there really ghosts? That adventure of last night has shaken me to the very depth of my soul.

I went at nine, as the mysterious letter had bid me. It was bitterly cold, and the air full of fog and sleet; not a shop open, not a window unshuttered, not a creature visible; the narrow black streets, precipitous between their, high walls and under their lofty archways, were only the blacker for the dull light of an oil-lamp here and there, with its flickering yellow reflection on the wet flags. San Giovanni Decollato is a little church, or rather oratory, which I have always hitherto seen shut up (as so many churches here are shut up except on great festivals); and situate behind the ducal palace, on a sharp ascent, and forming the bifurcation of two steep paved lanes. I have passed by the place a hundred times, and scarcely noticed the little church, except for the marble high relief over the door, showing the grizzly head of the Baptist in the charger, and for the iron cage close by, in which were formerly exposed the heads of criminals; the decapitated, or, as they call him here, decollated, John the Baptist, being apparently the patron of axe and block.

A few strides took me from my lodgings to San Giovanni Decollato. I confess I was excited; one is not twenty-four and a Pole for nothing. On getting to the kind of little platform at the bifurcation of the two precipitous streets, I found, to my surprise, that the windows of the church or oratory were not lighted, and that the door was locked! So this was the precious joke that had been played upon me; to send me on a bitter cold, sleety night, to a church which was shut up and had perhaps been shut up for years! I don't know what I couldn't have done in that moment of rage; I felt inclined to break open the church door, or to go and pull the Vice-Prefect's son out of bed (for I felt sure that the joke was his). I determined upon the latter course; and was walking towards his door, along the black alley to the left of the church, when I was suddenly stopped by the sound as of an organ close by, an organ, yes, quite plainly, and the voice of choristers and the drone of a litany. So the church was not shut, after all! I retraced my steps to the top of the lane. All was dark and in complete silence. Suddenly there came again a faint gust of organ and voices. I listened; it clearly came from the other lane, the one on the right-hand side. Was there, perhaps, another door there? I passed beneath the archway, and descended a little way in the direction whence the sounds seemed to come. But no door, no light, only the black walls, the black wet flags, with their faint yellow reflections of flickering oil-lamps; moreover, complete silence. I stopped a minute, and then the chant rose again; this time it seemed to me most certainly from the lane I had just left. I went back—nothing. Thus backwards and forwards, the sounds always beckoning, as it were, one way, only to beckon me back, vainly, to the other.

At last I lost patience; and I felt a sort of creeping terror, which only a violent action could dispel. If the mysterious sounds came neither from the street to the right, nor from the street to the left, they could come only from the church. Half-maddened, I rushed up the two or three steps, and prepared to wrench the door open with a tremendous effort. To my amazement, it opened with the greatest ease. I entered, and the sounds of the litany met me louder than before, as I paused a moment between the outer door and the heavy leathern curtain. I raised the latter and crept in. The altar was brilliantly illuminated with tapers and garlands of chandeliers; this was evidently some evening service connected with Christmas. The nave and aisles were comparatively dark, and about half-full. I elbowed my way along the right aisle towards the altar. When my eyes had got accustomed to the unexpected light, I began to look round me, and with a beating heart. The idea that all this was a hoax, that I should meet merely some acquaintance of my friend the Cavaliere's, had somehow departed: I looked about. The people were all wrapped up, the men in big cloaks, the women in woolen veils and mantles. The body of the church was comparatively dark, and I could not make out anything very clearly, but it seemed to me, somehow, as if, under the cloaks and veils, these people were dressed in a rather extraordinary fashion. The man in front of me, I remarked, showed yellow stockings beneath his cloak; a woman, hard by, a red bodice, laced behind with gold tags. Could these be peasants from some remote part come for the Christmas festivities, or did the inhabitants of Urbania don some old-fashioned garb in honour of Christmas?

As I was wondering, my eye suddenly caught that of a woman standing in the opposite aisle, close to the altar, and in the full blaze of its lights. She was wrapped in black, but held, in a very conspicuous way, a red rose, an unknown luxury at this time of the year in a place like Urbania. She evidently saw me, and turning even more fully into the light, she loosened her heavy black cloak, displaying a dress of deep red, with gleams of silver and gold embroideries; she turned her face towards me; the full blaze of the chandeliers and tapers fell upon it. It was the face of Medea da Carpi! I dashed across the nave, pushing people roughly aside, or rather, it seemed to me, passing through impalpable bodies. But the lady turned and walked rapidly down the aisle towards the door. I followed close upon her, but somehow I could not get up with her. Once, at the curtain, she turned round again. She was within a few paces of me. Yes, it was Medea. Medea herself, no mistake, no delusion, no sham; the oval face, the lips tightened over the mouth, the eyelids tight over the corner of the eyes, the exquisite alabaster complexion! She raised the curtain and glided out. I followed; the curtain alone separated me from her. I saw the wooden door swing to behind her. One step ahead of me! I tore open the door; she must be on the steps, within reach of my arm!

I stood outside the church. All was empty, merely the wet pavement and the yellow reflections in the pools: a sudden cold seized me; I could not go on. I tried to re-enter the church; it was shut. I rushed home, my hair standing on end, and trembling in all my limbs, and remained for an hour like a maniac. Is it a delusion? Am I too going mad? O God, God! am I going mad?

Dec. 19th.—

A brilliant, sunny day; all the black snow-slush has disappeared out of the town, off the bushes and trees. The snow-clad mountains sparkle against the bright blue sky. A Sunday, and Sunday weather; all the bells are ringing for the approach of Christmas. They are preparing for a kind of fair in the square with the colonnade, putting up booths filled with colored cotton and woolen ware, bright shawls and kerchiefs, mirrors, ribbons, brilliant pewter lamps; the whole turn-out of the peddler in *Winter's Tale*. The pork-shops are all garlanded with green and with paper flowers, the hams and cheeses stuck full of little flags and green twigs. I strolled out to see the cattle-fair outside the gate; a forest of interlacing horns, an ocean of lowing and stamping: hundreds of immense white bullocks, with horns a yard long and red tassels, packed close together on the little piazza d'armi under the city walls. Bah! Why do I write this trash? What's the use of it all? While I am forcing myself to write about bells, and Christmas festivities, and cattle-fairs, one idea goes on like a bell within me: Medea, Medea! Have I really seen her, or am I mad?

Two hours later.—That Church of San Giovanni Decollato—so my landlord informs me—has not been made use of within the memory of man. Could it have been all a hallucination or a dream—perhaps a dream dreamed that night? I have been out again to look at that church. There it is, at the bifurcation of the two steep lanes, with its bas-relief of the Baptist's head over the door. The door does look as if it had not been opened for years. I can see the cobwebs in the windowpanes; it does look as if, as Sor Asdrubale says, only rats and spiders congregated within it. And yet—and yet; I have so clear a remembrance, so distinct a consciousness of it all. There was a picture of the daughter of Herodias dancing, upon the altar; I remember her white turban with a scarlet tuft of feathers, and Herod's blue caftan; I remember the shape of the central chandelier; it swung round slowly, and one of the wax lights had got bent almost in two by the heat and draught.

Things, all these, which I may have seen elsewhere, stored unawares in my brain, and which may have come out, somehow, in a dream; I have heard physiologists allude to such things. I will go again: if the church be shut, why then it must have been a dream, a vision, the result of over-excitement. I must leave at once for Rome and see doctors, for I am afraid of going mad. If, on the other hand—pshaw! there *is no other hand* in such a case. Yet if there were—why then, I should really have seen Medea; I might see her again; speak to her. The mere thought sets my blood in a whirl, not with horror, but with… I know not what to call it. The feeling terrifies me, but it is delicious. Idiot! There is some little coil of my brain, the twentieth of a hair's-breadth out of order—that's all!

Dec. 20th.—

I have been again; I have heard the music; I have been inside the church; I have seen Her! I can no longer doubt my senses. Why should I? Those pedants say that the dead are dead, the past is past. For them, yes; but why for me?—

why for a man who loves, who is consumed with the love of a woman?—a woman who, indeed—yes, let me finish the sentence. Why should there not be ghosts to such as can see them? Why should she not return to the earth, if she knows that it contains a man who thinks of, desires, only her?

A hallucination? Why, I saw her, as I see this paper that I write upon; standing there, in the full blaze of the altar. Why, I heard the rustle of her skirts, I smelt the scent of her hair, I raised the curtain which was shaking from her touch. Again I missed her. But this time, as I rushed out into the empty moonlit street, I found upon the church steps a rose—the rose which I had seen in her hand the moment before—I felt it, smelt it; a rose, a real, living rose, dark red and only just plucked. I put it into water when I returned, after having kissed it, who knows how many times? I placed it on the top of the cupboard; I determined not to look at it for twenty-four hours lest it should be a delusion. But I must see it again; I must... Good Heavens! this is horrible, horrible; if I had found a skeleton it could not have been worse! The rose, which last night seemed freshly plucked, full of colour and perfume, is brown, dry—a thing kept for centuries between the leaves of a book—it has crumbled into dust between my fingers. Horrible, horrible! But why so, pray? Did I not know that I was in love with a woman dead three hundred years? If I wanted fresh roses which bloomed yesterday, the Countess Fiammetta or any little sempstress in Urbania might have given them me. What if the rose has fallen to dust? If only I could hold Medea in my arms as I held it in my fingers, kiss her lips as I kissed its petals, should I not be satisfied if she too were to fall to dust the next moment, if I were to fall to dust myself?

Dec. 22nd— Eleven at night.—

I have seen her once more!—almost spoken to her. I have been promised her love! Ah, Spiridion! you were right when you felt that you were not made for any earthly *amori*. At the usual hour I betook myself this evening to San Giovanni Decollato. A bright winter night; the high houses and belfries standing out against a deep blue heaven luminous, shimmering like steel with myriads of stars; the moon has not yet risen. There was no light in the windows; but, after a little effort, the door opened and I entered the church, the altar, as usual, brilliantly illuminated. It struck me suddenly that all this crowd of men and women standing all round, these priests chanting and moving about the altar, were dead—that they did not exist for any man save me. I touched, as if by accident, the hand of my neighbor; it was cold, like wet clay. He turned round, but did not seem to see me: his face was ashy, and his eyes staring, fixed, like those of a blind man or a corpse. I felt as if I must rush out. But at that moment my eye fell upon Her, standing as usual by the altar steps, wrapped in a black mantle, in the full blaze of the lights. She turned round; the light fell straight upon her face, the face with the delicate features, the eyelids and lips a little tight, the alabaster skin faintly tinged with pale pink. Our eyes met.

I pushed my way across the nave towards where she stood by the altar steps; she turned quickly down the aisle, and I after her. Once or twice she lingered, and I thought I should overtake her; but again, when, not a second after the door had closed upon her, I stepped out into the street, she had vanished. On the church step lay something white. It was not a flower this time, but a letter. I rushed back to the church to read it; but the church was fast shut, as if it had not been opened for years. I could not see by the flickering shrine-lamps—I rushed home, lit my lamp, pulled the letter from my breast. I have it before me. The handwriting is hers; the same as in the Archives, the same as in that first letter:—

"To Spiridion.—
"Let thy courage be equal to thy love, and thy love shall be rewarded. On the night preceding Christmas, take a hatchet and saw; cut boldly into the body of the bronze rider who stands in the Corte, on the left side, near the waist. Saw open the body, and within it thou wilt find the silver effigy of a winged genius. Take it out, hack it into a hundred pieces, and fling them in all directions, so that the winds may sweep them away. That night she whom thou lovest will come to reward thy fidelity."

On the brownish wax is the device—'AMOUR DURE—DURE AMOUR.'

Dec. 23rd.—
So it is true! I was reserved for something wonderful in this world. I have at last found that after which my soul has been straining. Ambition, love of art, love of Italy, these things which have occupied my spirit, and have

yet left me continually unsatisfied, these were none of them my real destiny. I have sought for life, thirsting for it as a man in the desert thirsts for a well; but the life of the senses of other youths, the life of the intellect of other men, have never slaked that thirst. Shall life for me mean the love of a dead woman? We smile at what we choose to call the superstition of the past, forgetting that all our vaunted science of today may seem just such another superstition to the men of the future; but why should the present be right and the past wrong? The men who painted the pictures and built the palaces of three hundred years ago were certainly of as delicate fibre, of as keen reason, as ourselves, who merely print calico and build locomotives. What makes me think this, is that I have been calculating my nativity by help of an old book belonging to Sor Asdrubale—and see, my horoscope tallies almost exactly with that of Medea da Carpi, as given by a chronicler. May this explain? No, no; all is explained by the fact that the first time I read of this woman's career, the first time I saw her portrait, I loved her, though I hid my love to myself in the garb of historical interest. Historical interest indeed!

I have got the hatchet and the saw. I bought the saw of a poor joiner, in a village some miles off; he did not understand at first what I meant, and I think he thought me mad; perhaps I am. But if madness means the happiness of one's life, what of it? The hatchet I saw lying in a timber-yard, where they prepare the great trunks of the fir-trees which grow high on the Apennines of Sant' Elmo. There was no one in the yard, and I could not resist the temptation; I handled the thing, tried its edge, and stole it. This is the first time in my life that I have been a thief; why did I not go into a shop and buy a hatchet? I don't know; I seemed unable to resist the sight of the shining blade. What I am going to do is, I suppose, an act of vandalism; and certainly I have no right to spoil the property of this city of Urbania. But I wish no harm either to the statue or the city, if I could plaster up the bronze, I would do so willingly. But I must obey Her; I must avenge Her; I must get at that silver image which Robert of Montemurlo had made and consecrated in order that his cowardly soul might sleep in peace, and not encounter that of the being whom he dreaded most in the world. Aha! Duke Robert, you forced her to die unshriven, and you stuck the image of your soul into the image of your body, thinking thereby that, while she suffered the tortures of Hell, you would rest in peace, until your well-scoured little soul might fly straight up to Paradise;—you were afraid of Her when both of you should be dead, and thought yourself very clever to have prepared for all emergencies! Not so, Serene Highness. You too shall taste what it is to wander after death, and to meet the dead whom one has injured.

What an interminable day! But I shall see her again tonight.

Eleven o'clock.—No; the church was fast closed; the spell had ceased. Until tomorrow I shall not see her. But tomorrow! Ah, Medea! did any of thy lovers love thee as I do?

Twenty-four hours more till the moment of happiness—the moment for which I seem to have been waiting all my life. And after that, what next? Yes, I see it plainer every minute; after that, nothing more. All those who loved Medea da Carpi, who loved and who served her, died: Giovanfrancesco Pico, her first husband, whom she left stabbed in the castle from which she fled; Stimigliano, who died of poison; the groom who gave him the poison, cut down by her orders; Oliverotto da Narni, Marcantonio Frangipani, and that poor boy of the Ordelaffi, who had never even looked upon her face, and whose only reward was that handkerchief with which the hangman wiped the sweat off his face, when he was one mass of broken limbs and torn flesh: all had to die, and I shall die also.

The love of such a woman is enough, and is fatal—'Amour Dure,' as her device says. I shall die also. But why not? Would it be possible to live in order to love another woman? Nay, would it be possible to drag on a life like this one after the happiness of tomorrow? Impossible; the others died, and I must die. I always felt that I should not live long; a gipsy in Poland told me once that I had in my hand the cut-line which signifies a violent death. I might have ended in a duel with some brother-student, or in a railway accident. No, no; my death will not be of that sort! Death—and is not she also dead? What strange vistas does such a thought not open! Then the others—Pico, the Groom, Stimigliano, Oliverotto, Frangipani, Prinzivalle degli Ordelaffi—will they all be *there?* But she shall love me best—me by whom she has been loved after she has been three hundred years in the grave!

Dec. 24th.—

I have made all my arrangements. Tonight at eleven I slip out; Sor Asdrubale and his sisters will be sound asleep. I have questioned them; their fear of rheumatism prevents their attending midnight mass. Luckily there are no churches between this and the Corte; whatever movement Christmas night may entail will be a good way off. The Vice-Prefect's rooms are on the other side of the palace; the rest of the square is taken up with state-rooms, archives, and empty stables and coach-houses of the palace. Besides, I shall be quick at my work.

I have tried my saw on a stout bronze vase I bought of Sor Asdrubale; and the bronze of the statue, hollow and worn away by rust (I have even noticed holes), cannot resist very much, especially after a blow with the sharp hatchet. I have put my papers in order, for the benefit of the Government which has sent me hither. I am sorry to have defrauded them of their *History of Urbania*. To pass the endless day and calm the fever of impatience, I have just taken a long walk. This is the coldest day we have had. The bright sun does not warm in the least, but seems only to increase the impression of cold, to make the snow on the mountains glitter, the blue air to sparkle like steel. The few people who are out are muffled to the nose, and carry earthenware braziers beneath their cloaks; long icicles hang from the fountain with the figure of Mercury upon it; one can imagine the wolves trooping down through the dry scrub and beleaguering this town. Somehow this cold makes me feel wonderfully calm—it seems to bring back to me my boyhood.

As I walked up the rough, steep, paved alleys, slippery with frost, and with their vista of snow mountains against the sky, and passed by the church steps strewn with box and laurel, with the faint smell of incense coming out, there returned to me—I know not why—the recollection, almost the sensation, of those Christmas Eves long ago at Posen and Breslau, when I walked as a child along the wide streets, peeping into the windows where they were beginning to light the tapers of the Christmas-trees, and wondering whether I too, on returning home, should be let into a wonderful room all blazing with lights and gilded nuts and glass beads. They are hanging the last strings of those blue and red metallic beads, fastening on the last gilded and silvered walnuts on the trees out there at home in the North; they are lighting the blue and red tapers; the wax is beginning to run on to the beautiful spruce green branches; the children are waiting with beating hearts behind the door, to be told that the Christ-Child has been. And I, for what am I waiting? I don't know; all seems a dream; everything vague and unsubstantial about me, as if time had ceased, nothing could happen, my own desires and hopes were all dead, myself absorbed into I know not what passive dreamland. Do I long for tonight? Do I dread it? Will tonight ever come? Do I feel anything, does anything exist all round me?

I sit and seem to see that street at Posen, the wide street with the windows illuminated by the Christmas lights, the green fir-branches grazing the window-panes.

Christmas Eve, Midnight.—

I have done it. I slipped out noiselessly. Sor Asdrubale and his sisters were fast asleep. I feared I had waked them, for my hatchet fell as I was passing through the principal room where my landlord keeps his curiosities for sale; it struck against some old armour which he has been piecing. I heard him exclaim, half in his sleep; and blew out my light and hid in the stairs. He came out in his dressing-gown, but finding no one, went back to bed again. "Some cat, no doubt!" he said. I closed the house door softly behind me. The sky had become stormy since the afternoon, luminous with the full moon, but strewn with grey and buff-colored vapours; every now and then the moon disappeared entirely. Not a creature abroad; the tall gaunt houses staring in the moonlight.

I know not why, I took a roundabout way to the Corte, past one or two church doors, whence issued the faint flicker of midnight mass. For a moment I felt a temptation to enter one of them; but something seemed to restrain me. I caught snatches of the Christmas hymn. I felt myself beginning to be unnerved, and hastened towards the Corte. As I passed under the portico at San Francesco I heard steps behind me; it seemed to me that I was followed. I stopped to let the other pass. As he approached his pace flagged; he passed close by me and murmured, "Do not go: I am Giovanfrancesco Pico." I turned round; he was gone. A coldness numbed me; but I hastened on.

Behind the cathedral apse, in a narrow lane, I saw a man leaning against a wall. The moonlight was full upon him; it seemed to me that his face, with a thin pointed beard, was streaming with blood. I quickened my pace; but as I grazed by him he whispered, "Do not obey her; return home: I am Marcantonio Frangipani." My teeth chattered, but I hurried along the narrow lane, with the moonlight blue upon the white walls. At last I saw the Corte before me: the square was flooded with moonlight, the windows of the palace seemed brightly illuminated, and the statue of Duke Robert, shimmering green, seemed advancing towards me on its horse. I came into the shadow. I had to pass beneath an archway. There started a figure as if out of the wall, and barred my passage with his outstretched cloaked arm. I tried to pass. He seized me by the arm, and his grasp was like a weight of ice. "You shall not pass!" he cried, and, as the moon came out once more, I saw his face, ghastly white and bound with an embroidered kerchief; he seemed almost a child. "You shall not pass!" he cried; "you shall not have her! She is mine, and mine alone! I am Prinzivalle degli Ordelaffi." I felt his ice-cold clutch, but with my other arm I laid about me wildly with the hatchet which I carried beneath my cloak. The hatchet struck the wall and rang upon the stone. He had vanished.

I hurried on. I did it. I cut open the bronze; I sawed it into a wider gash. I tore out the silver image, and hacked it into innumerable pieces. As I scattered the last fragments about, the moon was suddenly veiled; a great wind arose, howling down the square; it seemed to me that the earth shook. I threw down the hatchet and the saw, and fled home. I felt pursued, as if by the tramp of hundreds of invisible horsemen.

Now I am calm. It is midnight; another moment and she will be here! Patience, my heart! I hear it beating loud. I trust that no one will accuse poor Sor Asdrubale. I will write a letter to the authorities to declare his innocence should anything happen… One! the clock in the palace tower has just struck… "I hereby certify that, should anything happen this night to me, Spiridion Trepka, no one but myself is to be held…" A step on the staircase! It is she! it is she! At last, Medea, Medea! Ah! AMOUR DURE—DURE AMOUR!

* * * * *

NOTE.—Here ends the diary of the late Spiridion Trepka. The chief newspapers of the province of Umbria informed the public that, on Christmas morning of the year 1885, the bronze equestrian statue of Robert II. had been found grievously mutilated; and that Professor Spiridion Trepka of Posen, in the German Empire, had been discovered dead of a stab in the region of the heart, given by an unknown hand.

Dionea

by Vernon Lee

FROM THE LETTERS OF DOCTOR ALESSANDRO DE ROSIS TO THE LADY EVELYN SAVELLI, PRINCESS OF SABINA

Montemiro Ligure, June 29, 1873.

I take immediate advantage of the generous offer of your Excellency (allow an old Republican who has held you on his knees to address you by that title sometimes, 'tis so appropriate) to help our poor people. I never expected to come a-begging so soon. For the olive crop has been unusually plenteous. We semi-Genoese don't pick the olives unripe, like our Tuscan neighbours, but let them grow big and black, when the young fellows go into the trees with long reeds and shake them down on the grass for the women to collect—a pretty sight which your Excellency must see some day: the grey trees with the brown, barefoot lads craning, balanced in the branches, and the turquoise sea as background just beneath… That sea of ours—it is all along of it that I wish to ask for money. Looking up from my desk, I see the sea through the window, deep below and beyond the olive woods, bluish-green in the sunshine and veined with violet under the cloud-bars, like one of your Ravenna mosaics spread out as pavement for the world: a wicked sea, wicked in its loveliness, wickeder than your grey northern ones, and from which must have arisen in times gone by (when Phoenicians or Greeks built the temples at Lerici and Porto Venere) a baleful goddess of beauty, a Venus Verticordia, but in the bad sense of the word, overwhelming men's lives in sudden darkness like that squall of last week.

To come to the point. I want you, dear Lady Evelyn, to promise me some money, a great deal of money, as much as would buy you a little mannish cloth frock—for the complete bringing-up, until years of discretion, of a young stranger whom the sea has laid upon our shore. Our people, kind as they are, are very poor, and overburdened with children; besides, they have got a certain repugnance for this poor little waif, cast up by that dreadful storm, and who is doubtless a heathen, for she had no little crosses or scapulars on, like proper Christian children. So, being unable to get any of our women to adopt the child, and having an old bachelor's terror of my housekeeper, I have bethought me of certain nuns, holy women, who teach little girls to say their prayers and make lace close by here; and of your dear Excellency to pay for the whole business.

Poor little brown mite! She was picked up after the storm (such a set-out of ship-models and votive candles as that storm must have brought the Madonna at Porto Venere!) on a strip of sand between the rocks of our castle: the thing was really miraculous, for this coast is like a shark's jaw, and the bits of sand are tiny and far between. She was lashed to a plank, swaddled up close in outlandish garments; and when they brought her to me they thought she must certainly be dead: a little girl of four or five, decidedly pretty, and as brown as a berry, who, when she came to, shook her head to show she understood no kind of Italian, and jabbered some half-intelligible Eastern jabber, a few Greek words embedded in I know not what; the Superior of the College De Propagandâ Fide would be puzzled to know. The child appears to be the only survivor from a ship which must have gone down in the great squall, and whose timbers have been strewing the bay for some days past; no one at Spezia or in any of our ports knows anything about her, but she was seen, apparently making for Porto Venere, by some of our sardine-fishers: a big, lumbering craft, with eyes painted on each side of the prow, which, as you know, is a peculiarity of Greek boats. She was sighted for the last time off the island of Palmaria, entering, with all sails spread, right into the thick of the storm-darkness. No bodies, strangely enough, have been washed ashore.

July 10.
I have received the money, dear Donna Evelina. There was tremendous excitement down at San Massimo when the carrier came in with a registered letter, and I was sent for, in presence of all the village authorities, to sign my name on the postal register.

The child has already been settled some days with the nuns; such dear little nuns (nuns always go straight to the heart of an old priest-hater and conspirator against the Pope, you know), dressed in brown robes and close, white caps, with an immense round straw-hat flapping behind their heads like a nimbus: they are called Sisters of the Stigmata, and have a convent and school at San Massimo, a little way inland, with an untidy garden full of lavender and cherry-trees. Your *protégée* has already half set the convent, the village, the Episcopal See, the Order of St. Francis, by the ears. First, because nobody could make out whether or not she had been christened. The question was a grave one, for it appears (as your uncle-in-law, the Cardinal, will tell you) that it is almost equally undesirable to be christened twice over as not to be christened at all. The first danger was finally decided upon as the less terrible; but the child, they say, had evidently been baptized before, and knew that the operation ought not to be repeated, for she kicked and plunged and yelled like twenty little devils, and positively would not let the holy water touch her. The Mother Superior, who always took for granted that the baptism had taken place before, says that the child was quite right, and that Heaven was trying to prevent a sacrilege; but the priest and the barber's wife, who had to hold her, think the occurrence fearful, and suspect the little girl of being a Protestant. Then the question of the name. Pinned to her clothes—striped Eastern things, and that kind of crinkled silk stuff they weave in Crete and Cyprus—was a piece of parchment, a scapular we thought at first, but which was found to contain only the name *Dionea*—Dionea, as they pronounce it here. The question was, Could such a name be fitly borne by a young lady at the Convent of the Stigmata? Half the population here have names as unchristian quite—Norma, Odoacer, Archimedes—my housemaid is called Themis—but Dionea seemed to scandalize every one, perhaps because these good folk had a mysterious instinct that the name is derived from Dione, one of the loves of Father Zeus, and mother of no less a lady than the goddess Venus. The child was very near being called Maria, although there are already twenty-three other Marias, Mariettas, Mariuccias, and so forth at the convent. But the sister-bookkeeper, who apparently detests monotony, bethought her to look out Dionea first in the Calendar, which proved useless; and then in a big vellum-bound book, printed at Venice in 1625, called '*Flos Sanctorum, or Lives of the Saints, by Father Ribadeneira, S.J., with the addition of such Saints as have no assigned place in the Almanack, otherwise called the Movable or Extravagant Saints.*' The zeal of Sister Anna Maddalena has been rewarded, for there, among the Extravagant Saints, sure enough, with a border of palm-branches and hour-glasses, stands the name of Saint Dionea, Virgin and Martyr, a lady of Antioch, put to death by the Emperor Decius. I know your Excellency's taste for historical information, so I forward this item. But I fear, dear Lady Evelyn, I fear that the heavenly patroness of your little sea-waif was a much more extravagant saint than that.

December 21, 1879.

Many thanks, dear Donna Evelina, for the money for Dionea's schooling. Indeed, it was not wanted yet: the accomplishments of young ladies are taught at a very moderate rate at Montemirto: and as to clothes, which you mention, a pair of wooden clogs, with pretty red tips, costs sixty-five centimes, and ought to last three years, if the owner is careful to carry them on her head in a neat parcel when out walking, and to put them on again only on entering the village. The Mother Superior is greatly overcome by your Excellency's munificence towards the convent, and much perturbed at being unable to send you a specimen of your *protégée's* skill, exemplified in an embroidered pocket-handkerchief or a pair of mittens; but the fact is that poor Dionea *has* no skill. "We will pray to the Madonna and St. Francis to make her more worthy," remarked the Superior. Perhaps, however, your Excellency, who is, I fear but a Pagan woman (for all the Savelli Popes and St. Andrew Savelli's miracles), and insufficiently appreciative of embroidered pocket-handkerchiefs, will be quite as satisfied to hear that Dionea, instead of skill, has got the prettiest face of any little girl in Montemirto. She is tall, for her age (she is eleven) quite wonderfully well proportioned and extremely strong: of all the convent-full, she is the only one for whom I have never been called in. The features are very regular, the hair black, and despite all the good Sisters' efforts to keep it smooth like a Chinaman's, beautifully curly. I am glad she should be pretty, for she will more easily find a husband; and also because it seems fitting that your*protégée* should be beautiful. Unfortunately her character is not so satisfactory: she hates learning, sewing, washing up the dishes, all equally. I am sorry to say she shows no natural piety. Her companions detest her, and the nuns, although they admit that she is not exactly naughty, seem to feel her as a dreadful thorn in the flesh. She spends hours and hours on the terrace overlooking the sea (her great desire, she confided to me, is to get to the sea—to get *back to the sea*, as she expressed it), and lying in the garden, under the big myrtle-bushes, and, in spring and summer, under the rose-hedge. The nuns say that rose-hedge and that myrtle-bush are growing a great deal too big, one would think from Dionea's lying under them; the fact, I suppose, has drawn attention to them. "That child makes all the useless weeds grow," remarked Sister Reparata. Another of Dionea's amusements is playing with pigeons. The number of pigeons she collects about her is quite amazing; you would never have thought that San Massimo or the neighbouring hills contained as many. They flutter down like snowflakes, and strut and swell themselves out, and furl and unfurl their tails, and peck with little sharp movements of their silly, sensual heads and a little throb and gurgle in their throats, while Dionea lies stretched out full length in the sun, putting out her lips, which they come to kiss, and uttering strange, cooing sounds; or hopping about, flapping her arms slowly like wings, and raising her little head with much the same odd gesture as they;—'tis a lovely sight, a thing fit for one of your painters, Burne Jones or Tadema, with the myrtle-bushes all round, the bright, white-washed convent walls behind, the white marble chapel steps (all steps are marble in this Carrara country) and the enamel blue sea through the ilex-branches beyond. But the good Sisters abominate these pigeons, who, it appears, are messy little creatures, and they complain that, were it not that the Reverend Director likes a pigeon in his pot on a holiday, they could not stand the bother of perpetually sweeping the chapel steps and the kitchen threshold all along of those dirty birds....

August 6, 1882.

Do not tempt me, dearest Excellency, with your invitations to Rome. I should not be happy there, and do but little honour to your friendship. My many years of exile, of wanderings in northern countries, have made me a little bit into a northern man: I cannot quite get on with my own fellow-countrymen, except with the good peasants and fishermen all round. Besides—forgive the vanity of an old man, who has learned to make triple acrostic sonnets to cheat the days and months at Theresienstadt and Spielberg—I have suffered too much for Italy to endure patiently the sight of little parliamentary cabals and municipal wranglings, although they also are necessary in this day as conspiracies and battles were in mine. I am not fit for your roomful of ministers and learned men and pretty women: the former would think me an ignoramus, and the latter—what would afflict me much more—a pedant… Rather, if your Excellency really wants to show yourself and your children to your father's old *protégé* of Mazzinian times, find a few days to come here next spring. You shall have some very bare rooms with brick floors and white curtains opening out on my terrace; and a dinner of all manner of fish and milk (the white garlic flowers shall be mown away from under the olives lest my cow should eat it) and eggs cooked in herbs plucked in the hedges. Your boys can go and see the big ironclads at Spezia; and you shall come with me up our lanes fringed with delicate ferns and overhung by big olives, and into the fields where the cherry-trees shed their blossoms on to the budding vines, the fig-trees stretching out their little green gloves, where the goats nibble perched on their hind legs, and the cows low in the huts of reeds; and there rise from the ravines, with the gurgle of the brooks, from the cliffs with the boom of the surf, the voices of unseen boys and girls, singing about love and flowers and death, just as in the days of Theocritus, whom your learned Excellency does well to read. Has your Excellency ever read Longus, a Greek pastoral novelist? He is a trifle free, a trifle nude for us readers of Zola; but the old French of Amyot has a wonderful charm, and he gives one an idea, as no one else does, how folk lived in such valleys, by such sea-boards, as these in the days when daisy-chains and garlands of roses were still hung on the olive-trees for the nymphs of the grove; when across the bay, at the end of the narrow neck of blue sea, there clung to the marble rocks not a church of Saint Laurence, with the sculptured martyr on his gridiron, but the temple of Venus, protecting her harbour… Yes, dear Lady Evelyn, you have guessed aright. Your old friend has returned to his sins, and is scribbling once more. But no longer at verses or political pamphlets. I am enthralled by a tragic history, the history of the fall of the Pagan Gods… Have you ever read of their wanderings and disguises, in my friend Heine's little book?

And if you come to Montemirto, you shall see also your *protégée*, of whom you ask for news. It has just missed being disastrous. Poor Dionea! I fear that early voyage tied to the spar did no good to her wits, poor little waif! There has been a fearful row; and it has required all my influence, and all the awfulness of your Excellency's name, and the Papacy, and the Holy Roman Empire, to prevent her expulsion by the Sisters of the Stigmata. It appears that this mad creature very nearly committed a sacrilege: she was discovered handling in a suspicious manner the Madonna's gala frock and her best veil of *pizzo di Cantù*, a gift of the late Marchioness Violante Vigalcila of Fornovo. One of the orphans, Zaira Barsanti, whom they call the Rossaccia, even pretends to have surprised Dionea as she was about to adorn her wicked little person with these sacred garments; and, on another occasion, when Dionea had been sent to pass some oil and sawdust over the chapel floor (it was the eve of Easter of the Roses), to have discovered her seated on the edge of the altar, in the very place of the Most Holy Sacrament. I was sent for in hot haste, and had to assist at an ecclesiastical council in the convent parlour, where Dionea appeared, rather out of place, an amazing little beauty, dark, lithe, with an odd, ferocious gleam in her eyes, and a still odder smile, tortuous, serpentine, like that of Leonardo da Vinci's women, among the plaster images of St. Francis, and the glazed and framed samplers before the little statue of the Virgin, which wears in summer a kind of mosquito-curtain to guard it from the flies, who, as you know, are creatures of Satan.

Speaking of Satan, does your Excellency know that on the inside of our little convent door, just above the little perforated plate of metal (like the rose of a watering-pot) through which the Sister-portress peeps and talks, is pasted a printed form, an arrangement of holy names and texts in triangles, and the stigmatized hands of St. Francis, and a variety of other devices, for the purpose, as is explained in a special notice, of baffling the Evil One, and preventing his entrance into that building? Had you seen Dionea, and the stolid, contemptuous way in which she took, without attempting to refute, the various shocking allegations against her, your Excellency would have reflected, as I did, that the door in question must have been accidentally absent from the premises, perhaps at the joiner's for repair, the day that your *protégée* first penetrated into the convent. The ecclesiastical tribunal, consisting of the Mother Superior, three Sisters, the Capuchin Director, and your humble servant (who vainly attempted to be Devil's advocate), sentenced Dionea, among other things, to make the sign of the cross twenty-six times on the bare floor with her tongue. Poor little child! One might almost expect that, as happened when Dame Venus scratched her hand on the thorn-bush, red roses should sprout up between the fissures of the dirty old bricks.

October 14, 1883.

You ask whether, now that the Sisters let Dionea go and do half a day's service now and then in the village, and that Dionea is a grown-up creature, she does not set the place by the ears with her beauty. The people here are quite aware of its existence. She is already dubbed *La bella Dionea*; but that does not bring her any nearer getting a husband, although your Excellency's generous offer of a wedding-portion is well known throughout the district of San Massimo and Montemirto. None of our boys, peasants or fishermen, seem to hang on her steps; and if they turn round to stare and whisper as she goes by straight and dainty in her wooden clogs, with the pitcher of water or the basket of linen on her beautiful crisp dark head, it is, I remark, with an expression rather of fear than of love. The women, on their side, make horns with their fingers as she passes, and as they sit by her side in the convent chapel; but that seems natural. My housekeeper tells me that down in the village she is regarded as possessing the evil eye and bringing love misery. "You mean," I said, "that a glance from her is too much for our lads' peace of mind." Veneranda shook her head, and explained, with the deference and contempt with which she always mentions any of her country-folk's superstitions to me, that the matter is different: it's not with her they are in love (they would be afraid of her eye), but wherever she goes the young people must needs fall in love with each other, and usually where it is far from desirable. "You know Sora Luisa, the blacksmith's widow? Well, Dionea did a *half-service* for her last month, to prepare for the wedding of Luisa's daughter. Well, now, the girl must say, forsooth! that she won't have Pieriho of Lerici any longer, but will have that raggamuffin Wooden Pipe from Solaro, or go into a convent. And the girl changed her mind the very day that Dionea had come into the house. Then there is the wife of Pippo, the coffee-house keeper; they say she is carrying on with one of the coastguards, and Dionea helped her to do her washing six weeks ago. The son of Sor Temistocle has just cut off a finger to avoid the conscription, because he is mad about his cousin and afraid of being taken for a soldier; and it is a fact that some of the shirts which were made for him at the Stigmata had been sewn by Dionea;" ... and thus a perfect string of love misfortunes, enough to make a little 'Decameron,' I assure you, and all laid to Dionea's account. Certain it is that the people of San Massimo are terribly afraid of Dionea....

July 17, 1884.

Dionea's strange influence seems to be extending in a terrible way. I am almost beginning to think that our folk are correct in their fear of the young witch. I used to think, as physician to a convent, that nothing was more erroneous than all the romancings of Diderot and Schubert (your Excellency sang me his 'Young Nun' once: do you recollect, just before your marriage?), and that no more humdrum creature existed than one of our little nuns, with their pink baby faces under their tight white caps. It appeared the romancing was more correct than the prose. Unknown things have sprung up in these good Sisters' hearts, as unknown flowers have sprung up among the myrtle-bushes and the rose-hedge which Dionea lies under. Did I ever mention to you a certain little Sister Giuliana, who professed only two years ago?—a funny rose and white little creature presiding over the infirmary, as prosaic a little saint as ever kissed a crucifix or scoured a saucepan. Well, Sister Giuliana has disappeared, and the same day has disappeared also a sailor-boy from the port.

August 20, 1884.

The case of Sister Giuliana seems to have been but the beginning of an extraordinary love epidemic at the Convent of the Stigmata: the elder schoolgirls have to be kept under lock and key lest they should talk over the wall in the moonlight, or steal out to the little hunchback who writes love-letters at a penny a-piece, beautiful flourishes and all, under the portico by the Fishmarket. I wonder does that wicked little Dionea, whom no one pays court to, smile (her lips like a Cupid's bow or a tiny snake's curves) as she calls the pigeons down around her, or lies fondling the cats under the myrtle-bush, when she sees the pupils going about with swollen, red eyes; the poor little nuns taking fresh penances on the cold chapel flags;

and hears the long-drawn guttural vowels, *amore* and *morte* and *mio bene*, which rise up of an evening, with the boom of the surf and the scent of the lemon-flowers, as the young men wander up and down, arm-in-arm, twanging their guitars along the moonlit lanes under the olives?

October 20, 1885.

A terrible, terrible thing has happened! I write to your Excellency with hands all a-tremble; and yet I *must* write, I must speak, or else I shall cry out. Did I ever mention to you Father Domenico of Casoria, the confessor of our Convent of the Stigmata? A young man, tall, emaciated with fasts and vigils, but handsome like the monk playing the virginal in Giorgione's 'Concert,' and under his brown serge still the most stalwart fellow of the country all round? One has heard of men struggling with the tempter. Well, well, Father Domenico had struggled as hard as any of the Anchorites recorded by St. Jerome, and he had conquered. I never knew anything comparable to the angelic serenity of gentleness of this victorious soul. I don't like monks, but I loved Father Domenico. I might have been his father, easily, yet I always felt a certain shyness and awe of him; and yet men have accounted me a clean-lived man in my generation; but I felt, whenever I approached him, a poor worldly creature, debased by the knowledge of so many mean and ugly things. Of late Father Domenico had seemed to me less calm than usual: his eyes had grown strangely bright, and red spots had formed on his salient cheekbones. One day last week, taking his hand, I felt his pulse flutter, and all his strength as it were, liquefy under my touch. "You are ill," I said. "You have fever, Father Domenico. You have been overdoing yourself—some new privation, some new penance. Take care and do not tempt Heaven; remember the flesh is weak." Father Domenico withdrew his hand quickly. "Do not say that," he cried; "the flesh is strong!" and turned away his face. His eyes were glistening and he shook all over. "Some quinine," I ordered. But I felt it was no case for quinine. Prayers might be more useful, and could I have given them he should not have wanted. Last night I was suddenly sent for to Father Domenico's monastery above Montemirto: they told me he was ill. I ran up through the dim twilight of moonbeams and olives with a sinking heart. Something told me my monk was dead. He was lying in a little low white-washed room; they had carried him there from his own cell in hopes he might still be alive. The windows were wide open; they framed some olive-branches, glistening in the moonlight, and far below, a strip of moonlit sea. When I told them that he was really dead, they brought some tapers and lit them at his head and feet, and placed a crucifix between his hands. "The Lord has been pleased to call our poor brother to Him," said the Superior. "A case of apoplexy, my dear Doctor—a case of apoplexy. You will make out the certificate for the authorities." I made out the certificate. It was weak of me. But, after all, why make a scandal? He certainly had no wish to injure the poor monks.

Next day I found the little nuns all in tears. They were gathering flowers to send as a last gift to their confessor. In the convent garden I found Dionea, standing by the side of a big basket of roses, one of the white pigeons perched on her shoulder.

"So," she said, "he has killed himself with charcoal, poor Padre Domenico!"

Something in her tone, her eyes, shocked me.

"God has called to Himself one of His most faithful servants," I said gravely.

Standing opposite this girl, magnificent, radiant in her beauty, before the rose-hedge, with the white pigeons furling and unfurling, strutting and pecking all round, I seemed to see suddenly the whitewashed room of last night, the big crucifix, that poor thin face under the yellow waxlight. I felt glad for Father Domenico; his battle was over.

"Take this to Father Domenico from me," said Dionea, breaking off a twig of myrtle starred over with white blossom; and raising her head with that smile like the twist of a young snake, she sang out in a high guttural voice a strange chant, consisting of the word *Amor—amor—amor*. I took the branch of myrtle and threw it in her face.

January 3, 1886

It will be difficult to find a place for Dionea, and in this neighborhood well-nigh impossible. The people associate her somehow with the death of Father Domenico, which has confirmed her reputation of having the evil eye. She left the convent (being now seventeen) some two months back, and is at present gaining her bread working with the masons at our notary's new house at Lerici: the work is hard, but our women often do it, and it is magnificent to see Dionea, in her short white skirt and tight white bodice, mixing the smoking lime with her beautiful strong arms; or, an empty sack drawn over her head and shoulders, walking majestically up the cliff, up the scaffoldings with her load of bricks… I am, however, very anxious to get Dionea out of the neighbourhood, because I cannot help dreading the annoyances to which her reputation for the evil eye exposes her, and even some explosion of rage if ever she should lose the indifferent contempt with which she treats them. I hear that one of the rich men of our part of the world, a certain Sor Agostino of Sarzana, who owns a whole flank of marble mountain, is looking out for a maid for his daughter, who is about to be married; kind people and patriarchal in their riches, the old man still sitting down to table with all his servants; and his nephew, who is going to be his son-in-law, a splendid young fellow, who has worked like Jacob, in the quarry and at the saw-mill, for love of his pretty cousin. That whole house is so good, simple, and peaceful, that I hope it may tame down even Dionea. If I do not succeed in getting Dionea this place (and all your Excellency's illustriousness and all my poor eloquence will be needed to counteract the sinister reports attaching to our poor little waif), it will be best to accept your suggestion of taking the girl into your household at Rome, since you are curious to see what you call our baleful beauty. I am amused, and a little indignant at what you say about your footmen being handsome: Don Juan himself, my dear Lady Evelyn, would be cowed by Dionea….

May 29, 1886.

Here is Dionea back upon our hands once more! but I cannot send her to your Excellency. Is it from living among these peasants and fishing-folk, or is it because, as people pretend, a skeptic is always superstitious? I could not muster courage to send you Dionea, although your boys are still in sailor-clothes and your uncle, the Cardinal, is eighty-four; and as to the Prince, why, he bears the most potent amulet against Dionea's terrible powers in your own dear capricious person. Seriously, there is something eerie in this coincidence. Poor Dionea! I feel sorry for her, exposed to the passion of a once patriarchally respectable old man. I feel even more abashed at the incredible audacity, I should almost say sacrilegious madness, of the vile old creature. But still the coincidence is strange and uncomfortable. Last week the lightning struck a huge olive in the orchard of Sor Agostino's house above Sarzana. Under the olive was Sor Agostino himself, who was killed on the spot; and opposite, not twenty paces off, drawing water from the well, unhurt and calm, was Dionea. It was the end of a sultry afternoon: I was on a terrace in one of those villages of ours, jammed, like some hardy bush, in the gash of a hill-side. I saw the storm rush down the valley, a sudden blackness, and then, like a curse, a flash, a tremendous crash, re-echoed by a dozen hills. "I told him," Dionea said very quietly, when she came to stay with me the next day (for Sor Agostino's family would not have her for another half-minute), "that if he did not leave me alone Heaven would send him an accident."

July 15, 1886.

My book? Oh, dear Donna Evelina, do not make me blush by talking of my book! Do not make an old man, respectable, a Government functionary (communal physician of the district of San Massimo and Montemirto Ligure), confess that he is but a lazy unprofitable dreamer, collecting materials as a child picks hips out of a hedge, only to throw them away, liking them merely for the little occupation of scratching his hands and standing on tiptoe, for their pretty redness... You remember what Balzac says about projecting any piece of work?—"*C'est fumier des cigarettes enchantées...*" Well, well! The data obtainable about the ancient gods in their days of adversity are few and far between: a quotation here and there from the Fathers; two or three legends; Venus reappearing; the persecutions of Apollo in Styria; Proserpina going, in Chaucer, to reign over the fairies; a few obscure religious persecutions in the Middle Ages on the score of Paganism; some strange rites practiced till lately in the depths of a Breton forest near Lannion... As to Tannhäuser, he was a real knight, and a sorry one, and a real Minnesinger not of the best. Your Excellency will find some of his poems in Von der Hagen's four immense volumes, but I recommend you to take your notions of Ritter Tannhäuser's poetry rather from Wagner. Certain it is that the Pagan divinities lasted much longer than we suspect, sometimes in their own nakedness, sometimes in the stolen garb of the Madonna or the saints. Who knows whether they do not exist to this day? And, indeed, is it possible they should not? For the awfulness of the deep woods, with their filtered green light, the creak of the swaying, solitary reeds, exists, and is Pan; and the blue, starry May night exists, the sough of the waves, the warm wind carrying the sweetness of the lemon-blossoms, the bitterness of the myrtle on our rocks, the distant chant of the boys cleaning out their nets, of the girls sickling the grass under the olives, *Amor—amor—amor,* and all this is the great goddess Venus. And opposite to me, as I write, between the branches of the ilexes, across the blue sea, streaked like a Ravenna mosaic with purple and green, shimmer the white houses and walls, the steeple and towers, an enchanted Fata Morgana city, of dim Porto Venere; … and I mumble to myself the verse of Catullus, but addressing a greater and more terrible goddess than he did:—

"*Procul a mea sit furor omnis, Hera, domo; alios; age incitatos, alios age rabidos.*"

March 25, 1887.

Yes; I will do everything in my power for your friends. Are you well-bred folk as well bred as we, Republican *bourgeois,* with the coarse hands (though you once told me mine were psychic hands when the mania of palmistry had not yet been succeeded by that of the Reconciliation between Church and State), I wonder, that you should apologize, you whose father fed me and housed me and clothed me in my exile, for giving me the horrid trouble of hunting for lodgings? It is like you, dear Donna Evelina, to have sent me photographs of my future friend Waldemar's statue… I have no love for modern sculpture, for all the hours I have spent in Gibson's and Dupré's studio: 'tis a dead art we should do better to bury. But your Waldemar has something of the old spirit: he seems to feel the divineness of the mere body, the spirituality of a limpid stream of mere physical life. But why among these statues only men and boys, athletes and fauns? Why only the bust of that thin, delicate-lipped little Madonna wife of his? Why no wide-shouldered Amazon or broad-flanked Aphrodite?

April 10, 1887.

You ask me how poor Dionea is getting on. Not as your Excellency and I ought to have expected when we placed her with the good Sisters of the Stigmata: although I wager that, fantastic and capricious as you are, you would be better pleased (hiding it carefully from that grave side of you which bestows devout little books and carbolic acid upon the indigent) that your *protégée* should be a witch than a serving-maid, a maker of philters rather than a knitter of stockings and sewer of shirts.

A maker of philters. Roughly speaking, that is Dionea's profession. She lives upon the money which I dole out to her (with many useless objurgations) on behalf of your Excellency, and her ostensible employment is mending nets, collecting olives, carrying bricks, and other miscellaneous jobs; but her real status is that of village sorceress. You think our peasants are skeptical? Perhaps they do not believe in thought-reading, mesmerism, and ghosts, like you, dear Lady Evelyn. But they believe very firmly in the evil eye, in magic, and in love-potions. Every one has his little story of this or that which happened to his brother or cousin or neighbour. My stable-boy and male factotum's brother-in-law, living some years ago in Corsica, was seized with a longing for a dance with his beloved at one of those balls which our peasants give in the winter, when the snow makes leisure in the mountains. A wizard anointed him for money, and straightway he turned into a black cat, and in three bounds was over the seas, at the door of his uncle's cottage, and among the dancers. He caught his beloved by the skirt to draw her attention; but she replied with a kick which sent him squealing back to Corsica. When he returned in summer he refused to marry the lady, and carried his left arm in a sling. "You broke it when I came to the Veglia!" he said, and all seemed explained. Another lad, returning from working in the vineyards near Marseilles, was walking up to his native village, high in our hills, one moonlight night. He heard sounds of fiddle and fife from a roadside barn, and saw yellow light from its chinks; and then entering, he found many women dancing, old and young, and among them his affianced. He tried to snatch her round the waist for a waltz (they play *Mme. Angot* at our rustic balls), but the girl was unclutchable, and whispered, "Go; for these are witches, who will kill thee; and I am a witch also. Alas! I shall go to hell when I die."

I could tell your Excellency dozens of such stories. But love-philters are among the commonest things to sell and buy. Do you remember the sad little story of Cervantes' Licentiate, who, instead of a love-potion, drank a philter which made him think he was made of glass, fit emblem of a poor mad poet? … It is love-philters that Dionea prepares. No; do not misunderstand; they do not give love of her, still less her love.

Your seller of love-charms is as cold as ice, as pure as snow. The priest has crusaded against her, and stones have flown at her as she went by from dissatisfied lovers; and the very children, paddling in the sea and making mud-pies in the sand, have put out forefinger and little finger and screamed, "Witch, witch! ugly witch!" as she passed with basket or brick load; but Dionea has only smiled, that snake-like, amused smile, but more ominous than of yore. The other day I determined to seek her and argue with her on the subject of her evil trade. Dionea has a certain regard for me; not, I fancy, a result of gratitude, but rather the recognition of a certain admiration and awe which she inspires in your Excellency's foolish old servant. She has taken up her abode in a deserted hut, built of dried reeds and thatch, such as they keep cows in, among the olives on the cliffs. She was not there, but about the hut pecked some white pigeons, and from it, startling me foolishly with its unexpected sound, came the eerie bleat of her pet goat… Among the olives it was twilight already, with streakings of faded rose in the sky, and faded rose, like long trails of petals, on the distant sea. I clambered down among the myrtle-bushes and came to a little semicircle of yellow sand, between two high and jagged rocks, the place where the sea had deposited Dionea after the wreck. She was seated there on the sand, her bare foot dabbling in the waves; she had twisted a wreath of myrtle and wild roses on her black, crisp hair. Near her was one of our prettiest girls, the Lena of Sor Tullio the blacksmith, with ashy, terrified face under her flowered kerchief. I determined to speak to the child, but without startling her now, for she is a nervous, hysteric little thing. So I sat on the rocks, screened by the myrtle-bushes, waiting till the girl had gone. Dionea, seated listless on the sands, leaned over the sea and took some of its water in the hollow of her hand. "Here," she said to the Lena of Sor Tullio, "fill your bottle with this and give it to drink to Tommasino the Rosebud." Then she set to singing:—

"Love is salt, like sea-water—I drink and I die of thirst… Water! water! Yet the more I drink, the more I burn. Love! thou art bitter as the seaweed."

April 20, 1887.

Your friends are settled here, dear Lady Evelyn. The house is built in what was once a Genoese fort, growing like a grey spiked aloes out of the marble rocks of our bay; rock and wall (the walls existed long before Genoa was ever heard of) grown almost into a homogeneous mass, delicate grey, stained with black and yellow lichen, and dotted here and there with myrtle-shoots and crimson snapdragon. In what was once the highest enclosure of the fort, where your friend Gertrude watches the maids hanging out the fine white sheets and pillow-cases to dry (a bit of the North, of Hermann and Dorothea transferred to the South), a great twisted fig-tree juts out like an eccentric gargoyle over the sea, and drops its ripe fruit into the deep blue pools. There is but scant furniture in the house, but a great oleander overhangs it, presently to burst into pink splendour; and on all the window-sills, even that of the kitchen (such a background of shining brass saucepans Waldemar's wife has made of it!) are pipkins and tubs full of trailing carnations, and tufts of sweet basil and thyme and mignonette. She pleases me most, your Gertrude, although you foretold I should prefer the husband; with her thin white face, a Memling Madonna finished by some Tuscan sculptor, and her long, delicate white hands ever busy, like those of a mediaeval lady, with some delicate piece of work; and the strange blue, more limpid than the sky and deeper than the sea, of her rarely lifted glance.

It is in her company that I like Waldemar best; I prefer to the genius that infinitely tender and respectful, I would not say *lover* —yet I have no other word—of his pale wife. He seems to me, when with her, like some fierce, generous, wild thing from the woods, like the lion of Una, tame and submissive to this saint... This tenderness is really very beautiful on the part of that big lion Waldemar, with his odd eyes, as of some wild animal—odd, and, your Excellency remarks, not without a gleam of latent ferocity. I think that hereby hangs the explanation of his never doing any but male figures: the female figure, he says (and your Excellency must hold him responsible, not me, for such profanity), is almost inevitably inferior in strength and beauty; woman is not form, but expression, and therefore suits painting, but not sculpture. The point of a woman is not her body, but (and here his eyes rested very tenderly upon the thin white profile of his wife) her soul. "Still," I answered, "the ancients, who understood such matters, did manufacture some tolerable female statues: the Fates of the Parthenon, the Phidian Pallas, the Venus of Milo...."

"Ah! yes," exclaimed Waldemar, smiling, with that savage gleam of his eyes; "but those are not women, and the people who made them have left as the tales of Endymion, Adonis, Anchises: a goddess might sit for them...."

May 5, 1887.

Has it ever struck your Excellency in one of your La Rochefoucauld fits (in Lent say, after too many balls) that not merely maternal but conjugal unselfishness may be a very selfish thing? There! You toss your little head at my words; yet I wager I have heard you say that *other* women may think it right to humour their husbands, but as to you, the Prince must learn that a wife's duty is as much to chasten her husband's whims as to satisfy them. I really do feel indignant that such a snow-white saint should wish another woman to part with all instincts of modesty merely because that other woman would be a good model for her husband; really it is intolerable. "Leave the girl alone," Waldemar said, laughing. "What do I want with the unaesthetic sex, as Schopenhauer calls it?" But Gertrude has set her heart on his doing a female figure; it seems that folk have twitted him with never having produced one. She has long been on the look-out for a model for him. It is odd to see this pale, demure, diaphanous creature, not the more earthly for approaching motherhood, scanning the girls of our village with the eyes of a slave-dealer.

"If you insist on speaking to Dionea," I said, "I shall insist on speaking to her at the same time, to urge her to refuse your proposal." But Waldemar's pale wife was indifferent to all my speeches about modesty being a poor girl's only dowry. "She will do for a Venus," she merely answered.

We went up to the cliffs together, after some sharp words, Waldemar's wife hanging on my arm as we slowly clambered up the stony path among the olives. We found Dionea at the door of her hut, making faggots of myrtle-branches. She listened sullenly to Gertrude's offer and explanations; indifferently to my admonitions not to accept. The thought of stripping for the view of a man, which would send a shudder through our most brazen village girls, seemed not to startle her, immaculate and savage as she is accounted. She did not answer, but sat under the olives, looking vaguely across the sea. At that moment Waldemar came up to us; he had followed with the intention of putting an end to these wranglings.

"Gertrude," he said, "do leave her alone. I have found a model—a fisher-boy, whom I much prefer to any woman."

Dionea raised her head with that serpentine smile. "I will come," she said.

Waldemar stood silent; his eyes were fixed on her, where she stood under the olives, her white shift loose about her splendid throat, her shining feet bare in the grass. Vaguely, as if not knowing what he said, he asked her name. She answered that her name was Dionea; for the rest, she was an Innocentina, that is to say, a foundling; then she began to sing:—

"Flower of the myrtle!
My father is the starry sky,
The mother that made me is the sea."

June 22, 1887.

I confess I was an old fool to have grudged Waldemar his model. As I watch him gradually building up his statue, watch the goddess gradually emerging from the clay heap, I ask myself—and the case might trouble a more subtle moralist than me—whether a village girl, an obscure, useless life within the bounds of what we choose to call right and wrong, can be weighed against the possession by mankind of a great work of art, a Venus immortally beautiful? Still, I am glad that the two alternatives need not be weighed against each other. Nothing can equal the kindness of Gertrude, now that Dionea has consented to sit to her husband; the girl is ostensibly merely a servant like any other; and, lest any report of her real functions should get abroad and discredit her at San Massimo or Montemirto, she is to be taken to Rome, where no one will be the wiser, and where, by the way, your Excellency will have an opportunity of comparing Waldemar's goddess of love with our little orphan of the Convent of the Stigmata. What reassures me still more is the curious attitude of Waldemar towards the girl. I could never have believed that an artist could regard a woman so utterly as a mere inanimate thing, a form to copy, like a tree or flower. Truly he carries out his theory that sculpture knows only the body, and the body scarcely considered as human. The way in which he speaks to Dionea after hours of the most rapt contemplation of her is almost brutal in its coldness. And yet to hear him exclaim, "How beautiful she is! Good God, how beautiful!" No love of mere woman was ever so violent as this love of woman's mere shape.

June 27, 1887.

You asked me once, dearest Excellency, whether there survived among our people (you had evidently added a volume on folk-lore to that heap of half-cut, dog's-eared books that litter about among the Chineseries and mediaeval brocades of your rooms) any trace of Pagan myths. I explained to you then that all our fairy mythology, classic gods, and demons and heroes, teemed with fairies, ogres, and princes. Last night I had a curious proof of this. Going to see the Waldemar, I found Dionea seated under the oleander at the top of the old Genoese fort, telling stories to the two little blonde children who were making the falling pink blossoms into necklaces at her feet; the pigeons, Dionea's white pigeons, which never leave her, strutting and pecking among the basil pots, and the white gulls flying round the rocks overhead. This is what I heard... "And the three fairies said to the youngest son of the King, to the one who had been brought up as a shepherd, 'Take this apple, and give it to her among us who is most beautiful.' And the first fairy said, 'If thou give it to me thou shalt be Emperor of Rome, and have purple clothes, and have a gold crown and gold armour, and horses and courtiers;' and the second said, 'If thou give it to me thou shalt be Pope, and wear a mitre, and have the keys of heaven and hell;' and the third fairy said, 'Give the apple to me, for I will give thee the most beautiful lady to wife.' And the youngest son of the King sat in the green meadow and thought about it a little, and then said, 'What use is there in being Emperor or Pope? Give me the beautiful lady to wife, since I am young myself.' And he gave the apple to the third of the three fairies."...

Dionea droned out the story in her half-Genoese dialect, her eyes looking far away across the blue sea, dotted with sails like white sea-gulls, that strange serpentine smile on her lips.

"Who told thee that fable?" I asked.

She took a handful of oleander-blossoms from the ground, and throwing them in the air, answered listlessly, as she watched the little shower of rosy petals descend on her black hair and pale breast—

"Who knows?"

July 6, 1887.

How strange is the power of art! Has Waldemar's statue shown me the real Dionea, or has Dionea really grown more strangely beautiful than before? Your Excellency will laugh; but when I meet her I cast down my eyes after the first glimpse of her loveliness; not with the shyness of a ridiculous old pursuer of the Eternal Feminine, but with a sort of religious awe—the feeling with which, as a child kneeling by my mother's side, I looked down on the church flags when the Mass bell told the elevation of the Host... Do you remember the story of Zeuxis and the ladies of Crotona, five of the fairest not being too much for his Juno? Do you remember—you, who have read everything—all the bosh of our writers about the Ideal in Art? Why, here is a girl who disproves all this nonsense in a minute; she is far, far more beautiful than Waldemar's statue of her. He said so angrily, only yesterday, when his wife took me into his studio (he has made a studio of the long-desecrated chapel of the old Genoese fort, itself, they say, occupying the site of the temple of Venus).

As he spoke that odd spark of ferocity dilated in his eyes, and seizing the largest of his modeling tools, he obliterated at one swoop the whole exquisite face. Poor Gertrude turned ashy white, and a convulsion passed over her face....

July 15.

I wish I could make Gertrude understand, and yet I could never, never bring myself to say a word. As a matter of fact, what is there to be said? Surely she knows best that her husband will never love any woman but herself. Yet ill, nervous as she is, I quite understand that she must loathe this unceasing talk of Dionea, of the superiority of the model over the statue. Cursed statue! I wish it were finished, or else that it had never been begun.

July 20.

This morning Waldemar came to me. He seemed strangely agitated: I guessed he had something to tell me, and yet I could never ask. Was it cowardice on my part? He sat in my shuttered room, the sunshine making pools on the red bricks and tremulous stars on the ceiling, talking of many things at random, and mechanically turning over the manuscript, the heap of notes of my poor, never-finished book on the Exiled Gods. Then he rose, and walking nervously round my study, talking disconnectedly about his work, his eye suddenly fell upon a little altar, one of my few antiquities, a little block of marble with a carved garland and rams' heads, and a half-effaced inscription dedicating it to Venus, the mother of Love.

"It was found," I explained, "in the ruins of the temple, somewhere on the site of your studio: so, at least, the man said from whom I bought it."

Waldemar looked at it long. "So," he said, "this little cavity was to burn the incense in; or rather, I suppose, since it has two little gutters running into it, for collecting the blood of the victim? Well, well! they were wiser in that day, to wring the neck of a pigeon or burn a pinch of incense than to eat their own hearts out, as we do, all along of Dame Venus;" and he laughed, and left me with that odd ferocious lighting-up of his face. Presently there came a knock at my door. It was Waldemar. "Doctor," he said very quietly, "will you do me a favour? Lend me your little Venus altar—only for a few days, only till the day after tomorrow. I want to copy the design of it for the pedestal of my statue: it is appropriate." I sent the altar to him: the lad who carried it told me that Waldemar had set it up in the studio, and calling for a flask of wine, poured out two glasses. One he had given to my messenger for his pains; of the other he had drunk a mouthful, and thrown the rest over the altar, saying some unknown words. "It must be some German habit," said my servant. What odd fancies this man has!

July 25.

You ask me, dearest Excellency, to send you some sheets of my book: you want to know what I have discovered. Alas! dear Donna Evelina, I have discovered, I fear, that there is nothing to discover; that Apollo was never in Styria; that Chaucer, when he called the Queen of the Fairies Proserpine, meant nothing more than an eighteenth century poet when he called Dolly or Betty Cynthia or Amaryllis; that the lady who damned poor Tannhäuser was not Venus, but a mere little Suabian mountain sprite; in fact, that poetry is only the invention of poets, and that that rogue, Heinrich Heine, is entirely responsible for the existence of *Dieux en Exil*… My poor manuscript can only tell you what St. Augustine, Tertullian, and sundry morose old Bishops thought about the loves of Father Zeus and the miracles of the Lady Isis, none of which is much worth your attention… Reality, my dear Lady Evelyn, is always prosaic: at least when investigated into by bald old gentlemen like me.

And yet, it does not look so. The world, at times, seems to be playing at being poetic, mysterious, full of wonder and romance. I am writing, as usual, by my window, the moonlight brighter in its whiteness than my mean little yellow-shining lamp. From the mysterious greyness, the olive groves and lanes beneath my terrace, rises a confused quaver of frogs, and buzz and whirr of insects: something, in sound, like the vague trails of countless stars, the galaxies on galaxies blurred into mere blue shimmer by the moon, which rides slowly across the highest heaven. The olive twigs glisten in the rays: the flowers of the pomegranate and oleander are only veiled as with bluish mist in their scarlet and rose. In the sea is another sea, of molten, rippled silver, or a magic causeway leading to the shining vague offing, the luminous pale sky-line, where the islands of Palmaria and Tino float like unsubstantial, shadowy dolphins. The roofs of Montemirto glimmer among the black, pointing cypresses: farther below, at the end of that half-moon of land, is San Massimo: the Genoese fort inhabited by our friends is profiled black against the sky. All is dark: our fisher-folk go to bed early; Gertrude and the little ones are asleep: they at least are, for I can imagine Gertrude lying awake, the moonbeams on her thin Madonna face, smiling as she thinks of the little ones around her, of the other tiny thing that will soon lie on her breast… There is a light in the old desecrated chapel, the thing that was once the temple of Venus, they say, and is now Waldemar's workshop, its broken roof mended with reeds and thatch. Waldemar has stolen in, no doubt to see his statue again. But he will return, more peaceful for the peacefulness of the night, to his sleeping wife and children. God bless and watch over them! Good-night, dearest Excellency.

July 26.

I have your Excellency's telegram in answer to mine. Many thanks for sending the Prince. I await his coming with feverish longing; it is still something to look forward to. All does not seem over. And yet what can he do?

The children are safe: we fetched them out of their bed and brought them up here. They are still a little shaken by the fire, the bustle, and by finding themselves in a strange house; also, they want to know where their mother is; but they have found a tame cat, and I hear them chirping on the stairs.

It was only the roof of the studio, the reeds and thatch, that burned, and a few old pieces of timber. Waldemar must have set fire to it with great care; he had brought armfuls of faggots of dry myrtle and heather from the bakehouse close by, and thrown into the blaze quantities of pine-cones, and of some resin, I know not what, that smelt like incense. When we made our way, early this morning, through the smoldering studio, we were stifled with a hot church-like perfume: my brain swam, and I suddenly remembered going into St. Peter's on Easter Day as a child.

It happened last night, while I was writing to you. Gertrude had gone to bed, leaving her husband in the studio. About eleven the maids heard him come out and call to Dionea to get up and come and sit to him. He had had this craze once before, of seeing her and his statue by an artificial light: you remember he had theories about the way in which the ancients lit up the statues in their temples. Gertrude, the servants say, was heard creeping downstairs a little later.

Do you see it? I have seen nothing else these hours, which have seemed weeks and months. He had placed Dionea on the big marble block behind the altar, a great curtain of dull red brocade—you know that Venetian brocade with the gold pomegranate pattern—behind her, like a Madonna of Van Eyck's. He showed her to me once before like this, the whiteness of her neck and breast, the whiteness of the drapery round her flanks, toned to the colour of old marble by the light of the resin burning in pans all round… Before Dionea was the altar—the altar of Venus which he had borrowed from me. He must have collected all the roses about it, and thrown the incense upon the embers when Gertrude suddenly entered. And then, and then…

We found her lying across the altar, her pale hair among the ashes of the incense, her blood—she had but little to give, poor white ghost!—trickling among the carved garlands and rams' heads, blackening the heaped-up roses. The body of Waldemar was found at the foot of the castle cliff. Had he hoped, by setting the place on fire, to bury himself among its ruins, or had he not rather wished to complete in this way the sacrifice, to make the whole temple an immense votive pyre? It looked like one, as we hurried down the hills to San Massimo: the whole hillside, dry grass, myrtle, and heather, all burning, the pale short flames waving against the blue moonlit sky, and the old fortress outlined black against the blaze.

August 30.

Of Dionea I can tell you nothing certain. We speak of her as little as we can. Some say they have seen her, on stormy nights, wandering among the cliffs: but a sailor-boy assures me, by all the holy things, that the day after the burning of the Castle Chapel—we never call it anything else—he met at dawn, off the island of Palmaria, beyond the Strait of Porto Venere, a Greek boat, with eyes painted on the prow, going full sail to sea, the men singing as she went. And against the mast, a robe of purple and gold about her, and a myrtle-wreath on her head, leaned Dionea, singing words in an unknown tongue, the white pigeons circling around her.

Oke of Okehurst

by Vernon Lee

To Count Peter Boutourline, at Tagantcha, Government of Kiew, Russia.

MY DEAR BOUTOURLINE,

Do you remember my telling you, one afternoon that you sat upon the hearth-stool at Florence, the story of Mrs Oke of Okehurst?

You thought it a fantastic tale, you lover of fantastic things, and urged me to write it out at once, although I protested that, in such matters, to write is to exorcise, to dispel the charm; and that printers' ink chases away the ghosts that may pleasantly haunt us, as efficaciously as gallons of holy water.

But if, as I suspect, you will now put down any charm that story may have possessed to the way in which we had been working ourselves up, that firelight evening, with all manner of fantastic stuff—if, as I fear, the story of Mrs Oke of Okehurst will strike you as stale and unprofitable—the sight of this little book will serve at least to remind you, in the middle of your Russian summer, that there is such a season as winter, such a place as Florence, and such a person as your friend,

VERNON LEE

Kensington, *July* 1886.

I.

That sketch up there with the boy's cap? Yes; that's the same woman. I wonder whether you could guess who she was. A singular being, is she not? The most marvellous creature, quite, that I have ever met: a wonderful elegance, exotic, far-fetched, poignant; an artificial perverse sort of grace and research in every outline and movement and arrangement of head and neck, and hands and fingers. Here are a lot of pencil sketches I made while I was preparing to paint her portrait. Yes; there's nothing but her in the whole sketchbook. Mere scratches, but they may give some idea of her marvellous, fantastic kind of grace. Here she is leaning over the staircase, and here sitting in the swing. Here she is walking quickly out of the room. That's her head. You see she isn't really handsome; her forehead is too big, and her nose too short. This gives no idea of her. It was altogether a question of movement. Look at the strange cheeks, hollow and rather flat; well, when she smiled she had the most marvellous dimples here. There was something exquisite and uncanny about it. Yes; I began the picture, but it was never finished. I did the husband first. I wonder who has his likeness now? Help me to move these pictures away from the wall. Thanks. This is her portrait; a huge wreck. I don't suppose you can make much of it; it is merely blocked in, and seems quite mad. You see my idea was to make her leaning against a wall—there was one hung with yellow that seemed almost brown—so as to bring out the silhouette.

It was very singular I should have chosen that particular wall. It does look rather insane in this condition, but I like it; it has something of her. I would frame it and hang it up, only people would ask questions. Yes; you have guessed quite right—it is Mrs Oke of Okehurst. I forgot you had relations in that part of the country; besides, I suppose the newspapers were full of it at the time. You didn't know that it all took place under my eyes? I can scarcely believe now that it did: it all seems so distant, vivid but unreal, like a thing of my own invention. It really was much stranger than any one guessed. People could no more understand it than they could understand her. I doubt whether any one ever understood Alice Oke besides myself. You mustn't think me unfeeling. She was a marvellous, weird, exquisite creature, but one couldn't feel sorry for her. I felt much sorrier for the wretched creature of a husband. It seemed such an appropriate end for her; I fancy she would have liked it could she have known. Ah! I shall never have another chance of painting such a portrait as I wanted. She seemed sent me from heaven or the other place. You have never heard the story in detail? Well, I don't usually mention it, because people are so brutally stupid or sentimental; but I'll tell it you. Let me see. It's too dark to paint any more today, so I can tell it you now. Wait; I must turn her face to the wall. Ah, she was a marvellous creature!

II.

You remember, three years ago, my telling you I had let myself in for painting a couple of Kentish squireen? I really could not understand what had possessed me to say yes to that man. A friend of mine had brought him one day to my studio—Mr Oke of Okehurst, that was the name on his card. He was a very tall, very well-made, very good-looking young man, with a beautiful fair complexion, beautiful fair moustache, and beautifully fitting clothes; absolutely like a hundred other young men you can see any day in the Park, and absolutely uninteresting from the crown of his head to the tip of his boots. Mr Oke, who had been a lieutenant in the Blues before his marriage, was evidently extremely uncomfortable on finding himself in a studio. He felt misgivings about a man who could wear a velvet coat in town, but at the same time he was nervously anxious not to treat me in the very least like a tradesman. He walked round my place, looked at everything with the most scrupulous attention, stammered out a few complimentary phrases, and then, looking at his friend for assistance, tried to come to the point, but failed. The point, which the friend kindly explained, was that Mr Oke was desirous to know whether my engagements would allow of my painting him and his wife, and what my terms would be. The poor man blushed perfectly crimson during this explanation, as if he had come with the most improper proposal; and I noticed—the only interesting thing about him—a very odd nervous frown between his eyebrows, a perfect double gash,—a thing which usually means something abnormal: a mad-doctor of my acquaintance calls it the maniac-frown. When I had answered, he suddenly burst out into rather confused explanations: his wife—Mrs Oke—had seen some of my—pictures—paintings—portraits—at the—the—what d'you call it?—Academy. She had—in short, they had made a very great impression upon her. Mrs Oke had a great taste for art; she was, in short, extremely desirous of having her portrait and his painted by me, *etcetera*.

"My wife," he suddenly added, "is a remarkable woman. I don't know whether you will think her handsome,—she isn't exactly, you know. But she's awfully strange," and Mr Oke of Okehurst gave a little sigh and frowned that curious frown, as if so long a speech and so decided an expression of opinion had cost him a great deal.

It was a rather unfortunate moment in my career. A very influential sitter of mine—you remember the fat lady with the crimson curtain behind her?—had come to the conclusion or been persuaded that I had painted her old and vulgar, which, in fact, she was. Her whole clique had turned against me, the newspapers had taken up the matter, and for the moment I was considered as a painter to whose brushes no woman would trust her reputation. Things were going badly. So I snapped but too gladly at Mr Oke's offer, and settled to go down to Okehurst at the end of a fortnight. But the door had scarcely closed upon my future sitter when I began to regret my rashness; and my disgust at the thought of wasting a whole summer upon the portrait of a totally uninteresting Kentish squire, and his doubtless equally uninteresting wife, grew greater and greater as the time for execution approached. I remember so well the frightful temper in which I got into the train for Kent, and the even more frightful temper in which I got out of it at the little station nearest to Okehurst. It was pouring floods. I felt a comfortable fury at the thought that my canvases would get nicely wetted before Mr Oke's coachman had packed them on the top of the waggonette. It was just what served me right for coming to this confounded place to paint these confounded people. We drove off in the steady downpour. The roads were a mass of yellow mud; the endless flat grazing-grounds under the oak-trees, after having been burnt to cinders in a long drought, were turned into a hideous brown sop; the country seemed intolerably monotonous.

My spirits sank lower and lower. I began to meditate upon the modern Gothic country-house, with the usual amount of Morris furniture, Liberty rugs, and Mudie novels, to which I was doubtless being taken. My fancy pictured very vividly the five or six little Okes—that man certainly must have at least five children—the aunts, and sisters-in-law, and cousins; the eternal routine of afternoon tea and lawn-tennis; above all, it pictured Mrs Oke, the bouncing, well-informed, model housekeeper, electioneering, charity-organising young lady, whom such an individual as Mr Oke would regard in the light of a remarkable woman. And my spirit sank within me, and I cursed my avarice in accepting the commission, my spiritlessness in not throwing it over while yet there was time. We had meanwhile driven into a large park, or rather a long succession of grazing-grounds, dotted about with large oaks, under which the sheep were huddled together for shelter from the rain. In the distance, blurred by the sheets of rain, was a line of low hills, with a jagged fringe of bluish firs and a solitary windmill. It must be a good mile and a half since we had passed a house, and there was none to be seen in the distance—nothing but the undulation of sere grass, sopped brown beneath the huge blackish oak-trees, and whence arose, from all sides, a vague disconsolate bleating. At last the road made a sudden bend, and disclosed what was evidently the home of my sitter. It was not what I had expected. In a dip in the ground a large red-brick house, with the rounded gables and high chimney-stacks of the time of James I.,—a forlorn, vast place, set in the midst of the pasture-land, with no trace of garden before it, and only a few large trees indicating the possibility of one to the back; no lawn either, but on the other side of the sandy dip, which suggested a filled-up moat, a huge oak, short, hollow, with wreathing, blasted, black branches, upon which only a handful of leaves shook in the rain. It was not at all what I had pictured to myself the home of Mr Oke of Okehurst.

My host received me in the hall, a large place, panelled and carved, hung round with portraits up to its curious ceiling—vaulted and ribbed like the inside of a ship's hull. He looked even more blond and pink and white, more absolutely mediocre in his tweed suit; and also, I thought, even more good-natured and duller. He took me into his study, a room hung round with whips and fishing-tackle in place of books, while my things were being carried upstairs. It was very damp, and a fire was smouldering. He gave the embers a nervous kick with his foot, and said, as he offered me a cigar—

"You must excuse my not introducing you at once to Mrs Oke. My wife—in short, I believe my wife is asleep."

"Is Mrs Oke unwell?" I asked, a sudden hope flashing across me that I might be off the whole matter.

"Oh no! Alice is quite well; at least, quite as well as she usually is. My wife," he added, after a minute, and in a very decided tone, "does not enjoy very good health—a nervous constitution. Oh no! Not at all ill, nothing at all serious, you know. Only nervous, the doctors say; mustn't be worried or excited, the doctors say; requires lots of repose,—that sort of thing."

There was a dead pause. This man depressed me, I knew not why. He had a listless, puzzled look, very much out of keeping with his evident admirable health and strength.

"I suppose you are a great sportsman?" I asked from sheer despair, nodding in the direction of the whips and guns and fishing-rods.

"Oh no! Not now. I was once. I have given up all that," he answered, standing with his back to the fire, and staring at the polar bear beneath his feet. "I—I have no time for all that now," he added, as if an explanation were due. "A married man—you know. Would you like to come up to your rooms?" he suddenly interrupted himself. "I have had one arranged for you to paint in. My wife said you would prefer a north light. If that one doesn't suit, you can have your choice of any other."

I followed him out of the study, through the vast entrance-hall. In less than a minute I was no longer thinking of Mr and Mrs Oke and the boredom of doing their likeness; I was simply overcome by the beauty of this house, which I had pictured modern and philistine. It was, without exception, the most perfect example of an old English manor-house that I had ever seen; the most magnificent intrinsically, and the most admirably preserved. Out of the huge hall, with its immense fireplace of delicately carved and inlaid grey and black stone, and its rows of family portraits, reaching from the wainscoting to the oaken ceiling, vaulted and ribbed like a ship's hull, opened the wide, flat-stepped staircase, the parapet surmounted at intervals by heraldic monsters, the wall covered with oak carvings of coats-of-arms, leafage, and little mythological scenes, painted a faded red and blue, and picked out with tarnished gold, which harmonised with the tarnished blue and gold of the stamped leather that reached to the oak cornice, again delicately tinted and gilded. The beautifully damascened suits of court armour looked, without being at all rusty, as if no modern hand had ever touched them; the very rugs under foot were of sixteenth-century Persian make; the only things of today were the big bunches of flowers and ferns, arranged in majolica dishes upon the landings. Everything was perfectly silent; only from below came the chimes, silvery like an Italian palace fountain, of an old-fashioned clock.

It seemed to me that I was being led through the palace of the Sleeping Beauty.

"What a magnificent house!" I exclaimed as I followed my host through a long corridor, also hung with leather, wainscoted with carvings, and furnished with big wedding coffers, and chairs that looked as if they came out of some Vandyck portrait. In my mind was the strong impression that all this was natural, spontaneous—that it had about it nothing of the picturesqueness which swell studios have taught to rich and aesthetic houses. Mr Oke misunderstood me.

"It is a nice old place," he said, "but it's too large for us. You see, my wife's health does not allow of our having many guests; and there are no children."

I thought I noticed a vague complaint in his voice; and he evidently was afraid there might have seemed something of the kind, for he added immediately—

"I don't care for children one jackstraw, you know, myself; can't understand how any one can, for my part."

If ever a man went out of his way to tell a lie, I said to myself, Mr Oke of Okehurst was doing so at the present moment.

When he had left me in one of the two enormous rooms that were allotted to me, I threw myself into an arm-chair and tried to focus the extraordinary imaginative impression which this house had given me.

I am very susceptible to such impressions; and besides the sort of spasm of imaginative interest sometimes given to me by certain rare and eccentric personalities, I know nothing more subduing than the charm, quieter and less analytic, of any sort of complete and out-of-the-common-run sort of house. To sit in a room like the one I was sitting in, with the figures of the tapestry glimmering grey and lilac and purple in the twilight, the great bed, columned and curtained, looming in the middle, and the embers reddening beneath the overhanging mantelpiece of inlaid Italian stonework, a vague scent of rose-leaves and spices, put into the china bowls by the hands of ladies long since dead, while the clock downstairs sent up, every now and then, its faint silvery tune of forgotten days, filled the room;—to do this is a special kind of voluptuousness, peculiar and complex and indescribable, like the half-drunkenness of opium or haschisch, and which, to be conveyed to others in any sense as I feel it, would require a genius, subtle and heady, like that of Baudelaire.

After I had dressed for dinner I resumed my place in the arm-chair, and resumed also my reverie, letting all these impressions of the past—which seemed faded like the figures in the arras, but still warm like the embers in the fireplace, still sweet and subtle like the perfume of the dead rose-leaves and broken spices in the china bowls—permeate me and go to my head. Of Oke and Oke's wife I did not think; I seemed quite alone, isolated from the world, separated from it in this exotic enjoyment.

Gradually the embers grew paler; the figures in the tapestry more shadowy; the columned and curtained bed loomed out vaguer; the room seemed to fill with greyness; and my eyes wandered to the mullioned bow-window, beyond whose panes, between whose heavy stonework, stretched a greyish-brown expanse of sore and sodden park grass, dotted with big oaks; while far off, behind a jagged fringe of dark Scotch firs, the wet sky was suffused with the blood-red of the sunset. Between the falling of the raindrops from the ivy outside, there came, fainter or sharper, the recurring bleating of the lambs separated from their mothers, a forlorn, quavering, eerie little cry.

I started up at a sudden rap at my door.

"Haven't you heard the gong for dinner?" asked Mr Oke's voice.

I had completely forgotten his existence.

III.

I feel that I cannot possibly reconstruct my earliest impressions of Mrs Oke. My recollection of them would be entirely coloured by my subsequent knowledge of her; whence I conclude that I could not at first have experienced the strange interest and admiration which that extraordinary woman very soon excited in me. Interest and admiration, be it well understood, of a very unusual kind, as she was herself a very unusual kind of woman; and I, if you choose, am a rather unusual kind of man. But I can explain that better anon.

This much is certain, that I must have been immeasurably surprised at finding my hostess and future sitter so completely unlike everything I had anticipated. Or no—now I come to think of it, I scarcely felt surprised at all; or if I did, that shock of surprise could have lasted but an infinitesimal part of a minute. The fact is, that, having once seen Alice Oke in the reality, it was quite impossible to remember that one could have fancied her at all different: there was something so complete, so completely unlike every one else, in her personality, that she seemed always to have been present in one's consciousness, although present, perhaps, as an enigma.

Let me try and give you some notion of her: not that first impression, whatever it may have been, but the absolute reality of her as I gradually learned to see it. To begin with, I must repeat and reiterate over and over again, that she was, beyond all comparison, the most graceful and exquisite woman I have ever seen, but with a grace and an exquisiteness that had nothing to do with any preconceived notion or previous experience of what goes by these names: grace and exquisiteness recognised at once as perfect, but which were seen in her for the first, and probably, I do believe, for the last time. It is conceivable, is it not, that once in a thousand years there may arise a combination of lines, a system of movements, an outline, a gesture, which is new, unprecedented, and yet hits off exactly our desires for beauty and rareness? She was very tall; and I suppose people would have called her thin. I don't know, for I never thought about her as a body—bones, flesh, that sort of thing; but merely as a wonderful series of lines, and a wonderful strangeness of personality. Tall and slender, certainly, and with not one item of what makes up our notion of a well-built woman. She was as straight—I mean she had as little of what people call figure—as a bamboo; her shoulders were a trifle high, and she had a decided stoop; her arms and her shoulders she never once wore uncovered. But this bamboo figure of hers had a suppleness and a stateliness, a play of outline with every step she took, that I can't compare to anything else; there was in it something of the peacock and something also of the stag; but, above all, it was her own. I wish I could describe her. I wish, alas!—I wish, I wish, I have wished a hundred thousand times—I could paint her, as I see her now, if I shut my eyes—even if it were only a silhouette. There! I see her so plainly, walking slowly up and down a room, the slight highness of her shoulders; just completing the exquisite arrangement of lines made by the straight supple back, the long exquisite neck, the head, with the hair cropped in short pale curls, always drooping a little, except when she would suddenly throw it back, and smile, not at me, nor at any one, nor at anything that had been said, but as if she alone had suddenly seen or heard something, with the strange dimple in her thin, pale cheeks, and the strange whiteness in her full, wide-opened eyes: the moment when she had something of the stag in her movement. But where is the use of talking about her? I don't believe, you know, that even the greatest painter can show what is the real beauty of a very beautiful woman in the ordinary sense: Titian's and Tintoretto's women must have been miles handsomer than they have made them. Something—and that the very essence—always escapes, perhaps because real beauty is as much a thing in time—a thing like music, a succession, a series—as in space. Mind you, I am speaking of a woman beautiful in the conventional sense. Imagine, then, how much more so in the case of a woman like Alice Oke; and if the pencil and brush, imitating each line and tint, can't succeed, how is it possible to give even the vaguest notion with mere wretched words—words possessing only a wretched abstract meaning, an impotent conventional association? To make a long story short, Mrs Oke of Okehurst was, in my opinion, to the highest degree exquisite and strange,—an exotic creature, whose charm you can no more describe than you could bring home the perfume of some newly discovered tropical flower by comparing it with the scent of a cabbage-rose or a lily.

That first dinner was gloomy enough. Mr Oke—Oke of Okehurst, as the people down there called him—was horribly shy, consumed with a fear of making a fool of himself before me and his wife, I then thought. But that sort of shyness did not wear off; and I soon discovered that, although it was doubtless increased by the presence of a total stranger, it was inspired in Oke, not by me, but by his wife. He would look every now and then as if he were going to make a remark, and then evidently restrain himself, and remain silent. It was very curious to see this big, handsome, manly young fellow, who ought to have had any amount of success with women, suddenly stammer and grow crimson in the presence of his own wife. Nor was it the consciousness of stupidity; for when you got him alone, Oke, although always slow and timid, had a certain amount of ideas, and very defined political and social views, and a certain childlike earnestness and desire to attain certainty and truth which was rather touching. On the other hand, Oke's singular shyness was not, so far as I could see, the result of any kind of bullying on his wife's part. You can always detect, if you have any observation, the husband or the wife who is accustomed to be snubbed, to be corrected, by his or her better-half: there is a self-consciousness in both parties, a habit of watching and fault-finding, of being watched and found fault with. This was clearly not the case at Okehurst. Mrs Oke evidently did not trouble herself about her husband in the very least; he might say or do any amount of silly things without rebuke or even notice; and he might have done so, had he chosen, ever since his wedding-day. You felt that at once. Mrs Oke simply passed over his existence. I cannot say she paid much attention to any one's, even to mine. At first I thought it an affectation on her part—for there was something far-fetched in her whole appearance, something suggesting study, which might lead one to tax her with affectation at first; she was dressed in a strange way, not according to any established aesthetic eccentricity, but individually, strangely, as if in the clothes of an ancestress of the seventeenth century. Well, at first I thought it a kind of pose on her part, this mixture of extreme graciousness and utter indifference which she manifested towards me. She always seemed to be thinking of something else; and although she talked quite sufficiently, and with every sign of superior intelligence, she left the impression of having been as taciturn as her husband.

In the beginning, in the first few days of my stay at Okehurst, I imagined that Mrs Oke was a highly superior sort of flirt; and that her absent manner, her look, while speaking to you, into an invisible distance, her curious irrelevant smile, were so many means of attracting and baffling adoration. I mistook it for the somewhat similar manners of certain foreign women—it is beyond English ones—which mean, to those who can understand, "pay court to me." But I soon found I was mistaken. Mrs Oke had not the faintest desire that I should pay court to her; indeed she did not honour me with sufficient thought for that; and I, on my part, began to be too much interested in her from another point of view to dream of such a thing. I became aware, not merely that I had before me the most marvellously rare and exquisite and baffling subject for a portrait, but also one of the most peculiar and enigmatic of characters. Now that I look back upon it, I am tempted to think that the psychological peculiarity of that woman might be summed up in an exorbitant and absorbing interest in herself—a Narcissus attitude—curiously complicated with a fantastic imagination, a sort of morbid day-dreaming, all turned inwards, and with no outer characteristic save a certain restlessness, a perverse desire to surprise and shock, to surprise and shock more particularly her husband, and thus be revenged for the intense boredom which his want of appreciation inflicted upon her.

I got to understand this much little by little, yet I did not seem to have really penetrated the something mysterious about Mrs Oke. There was a waywardness, a strangeness, which I felt but could not explain—a something as difficult to define as the peculiarity of her outward appearance, and perhaps very closely connected therewith. I became interested in Mrs Oke as if I had been in love with her; and I was not in the least in love. I neither dreaded parting from her, nor felt any pleasure in her presence. I had not the smallest wish to please or to gain her notice. But I had her on the brain. I pursued her, her physical image, her psychological explanation, with a kind of passion which filled my days, and prevented my ever feeling dull. The Okes lived a remarkably solitary life. There were but few neighbours, of whom they saw but little; and they rarely had a guest in the house. Oke himself seemed every now and then seized with a sense of responsibility towards me. He would remark vaguely, during our walks and after-dinner chats, that I must find life at Okehurst horribly dull; his wife's health had accustomed him to solitude, and then also his wife thought the neighbours a bore. He never questioned his wife's judgment in these matters. He merely stated the case as if resignation were quite simple and inevitable; yet it seemed to me, sometimes, that this monotonous life of solitude, by the side of a woman who took no more heed of him than of a table or chair, was producing a vague depression and irritation in this young man, so evidently cut out for a cheerful, commonplace life. I often wondered how he could endure it at all, not having, as I had, the interest of a strange psychological riddle to solve, and of a great portrait to paint. He was, I found, extremely good,—the type of the perfectly conscientious young Englishman, the sort of man who ought to have been the Christian soldier kind of thing; devout, pure-minded, brave, incapable of any baseness, a little intellectually dense, and puzzled by all manner of moral scruples. The condition of his tenants and of his political party—he was a regular Kentish Tory—lay heavy on his mind. He spent hours every day in his study, doing the work of a land agent and a political whip, reading piles of reports and newspapers and agricultural treatises; and emerging for lunch with piles of letters in his hand, and that odd puzzled look in his good healthy face, that deep gash between his eyebrows, which my friend the mad-doctor calls the *maniac-frown*. It was with this expression of face that I should have liked to paint him; but I felt that he would not have liked it, that it was more fair to him to represent him in his mere wholesome pink and white and blond conventionality. I was perhaps rather unconscientious about the likeness of Mr Oke; I felt satisfied to paint it no matter how, I mean as regards character, for my whole mind was swallowed up in thinking how I should paint Mrs Oke, how I could best transport on to canvas that singular and enigmatic personality. I began with her husband, and told her frankly that I must have much longer to study her. Mr Oke couldn't understand why it should be necessary to make a hundred and one pencil-sketches of his wife before even determining in what attitude to paint her; but I think he was rather pleased to have an opportunity of keeping me at Okehurst; my presence evidently broke the monotony of his life. Mrs Oke seemed perfectly indifferent to my staying, as she was perfectly indifferent to my presence. Without being rude, I never saw a woman pay so little attention to a guest; she would talk with me sometimes by the hour, or rather let me talk to her, but she never seemed to be listening. She would lie back in a big seventeenth-century armchair while I played the piano, with that strange smile every now and then in her thin cheeks, that strange whiteness in her eyes; but it seemed a matter of indifference whether my music stopped or went on. In my portrait of her husband she did not take, or pretend to take, the very faintest interest; but that was nothing to me. I did not want Mrs Oke to think me interesting; I merely wished to go on studying her.

The first time that Mrs Oke seemed to become at all aware of my presence as distinguished from that of the chairs and tables, the dogs that lay in the porch, or the clergyman or lawyer or stray neighbour who was occasionally asked to dinner, was one day—I might have been there a week—when I chanced to remark to her upon the very singular resemblance that existed between herself and the portrait of a lady that hung in the hall with the ceiling like a ship's hull. The picture in question was a full length, neither very good nor very bad, probably done by some stray Italian of the early seventeenth century. It hung in a rather dark corner, facing the portrait, evidently painted to be its companion, of a dark man, with a somewhat unpleasant expression of resolution and efficiency, in a black Vandyck dress. The two were evidently man and wife; and in the corner of the woman's portrait were the words, 'Alice Oke, daughter of Virgil Pomfret, Esq., and wife to Nicholas Oke of Okehurst,' and the date 1626—'Nicholas Oke' being the name painted in the corner of the small portrait. The lady was really wonderfully like the present Mrs Oke, at least so far as an indifferently painted portrait of the early days of Charles I, can be like a living woman of the nineteenth century. There were the same strange lines of figure and face, the same dimples in the thin cheeks, the same wide-opened eyes, the same vague eccentricity of expression, not destroyed even by the feeble painting and conventional manner of the time. One could fancy that this woman had the same walk, the same beautiful line of nape of the neck and stooping head as her descendant; for I found that Mr and Mrs Oke, who were first cousins, were both descended from that Nicholas Oke and that Alice, daughter of Virgil Pomfret. But the resemblance was heightened by the fact that, as I soon saw, the present Mrs Oke distinctly made herself up to look like her ancestress, dressing in garments that had a seventeenth-century look; nay, that were sometimes absolutely copied from this portrait.

"You think I am like her," answered Mrs Oke dreamily to my remark, and her eyes wandered off to that unseen something, and the faint smile dimpled her thin cheeks.

"You are like her, and you know it. I may even say you wish to be like her, Mrs Oke," I answered, laughing.

"Perhaps I do."

And she looked in the direction of her husband. I noticed that he had an expression of distinct annoyance besides that frown of his.

"Isn't it true that Mrs Oke tries to look like that portrait?" I asked, with a perverse curiosity.

"Oh, fudge!" he exclaimed, rising from his chair and walking nervously to the window. "It's all nonsense, mere nonsense. I wish you wouldn't, Alice."

"Wouldn't what?" asked Mrs Oke, with a sort of contemptuous indifference.

"If I am like that Alice Oke, why I am; and I am very pleased any one should think so. She and her husband are just about the only two members of our family—our most flat, stale, and unprofitable family—that ever were in the least degree interesting."

Oke grew crimson, and frowned as if in pain.

"I don't see why you should abuse our family, Alice," he said. "Thank God, our people have always been honourable and upright men and women!"

"Excepting always Nicholas Oke and Alice his wife, daughter of Virgil Pomfret, Esq.," she answered, laughing, as he strode out into the park.

"How childish he is!" she exclaimed when we were alone. "He really minds, really feels disgraced by what our ancestors did two centuries and a half ago. I do believe William would have those two portraits taken down and burned if he weren't afraid of me and ashamed of the neighbours. And as it is, these two people really are the only two members of our family that ever were in the least interesting. I will tell you the story some day."

As it was, the story was told to me by Oke himself. The next day, as we were taking our morning walk, he suddenly broke a long silence, laying about him all the time at the sere grasses with the hooked stick that he carried, like the conscientious Kentishman he was, for the purpose of cutting down his and other folk's thistles.

"I fear you must have thought me very ill-mannered towards my wife yesterday," he said shyly; "and indeed I know I was."

Oke was one of those chivalrous beings to whom every woman, every wife—and his own most of all—appeared in the light of something holy. "But—but—I have a prejudice which my wife does not enter into, about raking up ugly things in one's own family. I suppose Alice thinks that it is so long ago that it has really got no connection with us; she thinks of it merely as a picturesque story. I daresay many people feel like that; in short, I am sure they do, otherwise there wouldn't be such lots of discreditable family traditions afloat. But I feel as if it were all one whether it was long ago or not; when it's a question of one's own people, I would rather have it forgotten. I can't understand how people can talk about murders in their families, and ghosts, and so forth."

"Have you any ghosts at Okehurst, by the way?" I asked. The place seemed as if it required some to complete it.

"I hope not," answered Oke gravely.

His gravity made me smile.

"Why, would you dislike it if there were?" I asked.

"If there are such things as ghosts," he replied, "I don't think they should be taken lightly. God would not permit them to be, except as a warning or a punishment."

We walked on some time in silence, I wondering at the strange type of this commonplace young man, and half wishing I could put something into my portrait that should be the equivalent of this curious unimaginative earnestness. Then Oke told me the story of those two pictures—told it me about as badly and hesitatingly as was possible for mortal man.

He and his wife were, as I have said, cousins, and therefore descended from the same old Kentish stock. The Okes of Okehurst could trace back to Norman, almost to Saxon times, far longer than any of the titled or better-known families of the neighbourhood. I saw that William Oke, in his heart, thoroughly looked down upon all his neighbours. "We have never done anything particular, or been anything particular—never held any office," he said; "but we have always been here, and apparently always done our duty. An ancestor of ours was killed in the Scotch wars, another at Agincourt—mere honest captains." Well, early in the seventeenth century, the family had dwindled to a single member, Nicholas Oke, the same who had rebuilt Okehurst in its present shape. This Nicholas appears to have been somewhat different from the usual run of the family. He had, in his youth, sought adventures in America, and seems, generally speaking, to have been less of a nonentity than his ancestors. He married, when no longer very young, Alice, daughter of Virgil Pomfret, a beautiful young heiress from a neighbouring county. "It was the first time an Oke married a Pomfret," my host informed me, "and the last time. The Pomfrets were quite different sort of people—restless, self-seeking; one of them had been a favourite of Henry VIII." It was clear that William Oke had no feeling of having any Pomfret blood in his veins; he spoke of these people with an evident family dislike—the dislike of an Oke, one of the old, honourable, modest stock, which had quietly done its duty, for a family of fortune-seekers and Court minions. Well, there had come to live near Okehurst, in a little house recently inherited from an uncle, a certain Christopher Lovelock, a young gallant and poet, who was in momentary disgrace at Court for some love affair. This Lovelock had struck up a great friendship with his neighbours of Okehurst—too great a friendship, apparently, with the wife, either for her husband's taste or her own. Anyhow, one evening as he was riding home alone, Lovelock had been attacked and murdered, ostensibly by highwaymen, but as was afterwards rumoured, by Nicholas Oke, accompanied by his wife dressed as a groom. No legal evidence had been got, but the tradition had remained. "They used to tell it us when we were children," said my host, in a hoarse voice, "and to frighten my cousin—I mean my wife—and me with stories about Lovelock. It is merely a tradition, which I hope may die out, as I sincerely pray to heaven that it may be false." "Alice—Mrs Oke—you see," he went on after some time, "doesn't feel about it as I do. Perhaps I am morbid. But I do dislike having the old story raked up."

And we said no more on the subject.

IV.

From that moment I began to assume a certain interest in the eyes of Mrs Oke; or rather, I began to perceive that I had a means of securing her attention. Perhaps it was wrong of me to do so; and I have often reproached myself very seriously later on. But after all, how was I to guess that I was making mischief merely by chiming in, for the sake of the portrait I had undertaken, and of a very harmless psychological mania, with what was merely the fad, the little romantic affectation or eccentricity, of a scatter-brained and eccentric young woman? How in the world should I have dreamed that I was handling explosive substances? A man is surely not responsible if the people with whom he is forced to deal, and whom he deals with as with all the rest of the world, are quite different from all other human creatures.

So, if indeed I did at all conduce to mischief, I really cannot blame myself. I had met in Mrs Oke an almost unique subject for a portrait-painter of my particular sort, and a most singular, *bizarre* personality. I could not possibly do my subject justice so long as I was kept at a distance, prevented from studying the real character of the woman. I required to put her into play. And I ask you whether any more innocent way of doing so could be found than talking to a woman, and letting her talk, about an absurd fancy she had for a couple of ancestors of hers of the time of Charles I., and a poet whom they had murdered?—particularly as I studiously respected the prejudices of my host, and refrained from mentioning the matter, and tried to restrain Mrs Oke from doing so, in the presence of William Oke himself.

I had certainly guessed correctly. To resemble the Alice Oke of the year 1626 was the caprice, the mania, the pose, the whatever you may call it, of the Alice

Oke of 1880; and to perceive this resemblance was the sure way of gaining her good graces. It was the most extraordinary craze, of all the extraordinary crazes of childless and idle women, that I had ever met; but it was more than that, it was admirably characteristic. It finished off the strange figure of Mrs Oke, as I saw it in my imagination—this *bizarre* creature of enigmatic, far-fetched exquisiteness—that she should have no interest in the present, but only an eccentric passion in the past. It seemed to give the meaning to the absent look in her eyes, to her irrelevant and far-off smile. It was like the words to a weird piece of gipsy music, this that she, who was so different, so distant from all women of her own time, should try and identify herself with a woman of the past—that she should have a kind of flirtation—But of this anon.

I told Mrs Oke that I had learnt from her husband the outline of the tragedy, or mystery, whichever it was, of Alice Oke, daughter of Virgil Pomfret, and the poet Christopher Lovelock. That look of vague contempt, of a desire to shock, which I had noticed before, came into her beautiful, pale, diaphanous face.

"I suppose my husband was very shocked at the whole matter," she said—"told it you with as little detail as possible, and assured you very solemnly that he hoped the whole story might be a mere dreadful calumny? Poor Willie! I remember already when we were children, and I used to come with my mother to spend Christmas at Okehurst, and my cousin was down here for his holidays, how I used to horrify him by insisting upon dressing up in shawls and waterproofs, and playing the story of the wicked Mrs Oke; and he always piously refused to do the part of Nicholas, when I wanted to have the scene on Cotes Common. I didn't know then that I was like the original Alice Oke; I found it out only after our marriage. You really think that I am?"

She certainly was, particularly at that moment, as she stood in a white Vandyck dress, with the green of the park-land rising up behind her, and the low sun catching her short locks and surrounding her head, her exquisitely bowed head, with a pale-yellow halo. But I confess I thought the original Alice Oke, siren and murderess though she might be, very uninteresting compared with this wayward and exquisite creature whom I had rashly promised myself to send down to posterity in all her unlikely wayward exquisiteness.

One morning while Mr Oke was despatching his Saturday heap of Conservative manifestoes and rural decisions—he was justice of the peace in a most literal sense, penetrating into cottages and huts, defending the weak and admonishing the ill-conducted—one morning while I was making one of my many pencil-sketches (alas, they are all that remain to me now!) of my future sitter, Mrs Oke gave me her version of the story of Alice Oke and Christopher Lovelock.

"Do you suppose there was anything between them?" I asked—"that she was ever in love with him? How do you explain the part which tradition ascribes to her in the supposed murder? One has heard of women and their lovers who have killed the husband; but a woman who combines with her husband to kill her lover, or at least the man who is in love with her—that is surely very singular." I was absorbed in my drawing, and really thinking very little of what I was saying.

"I don't know," she answered pensively, with that distant look in her eyes. "Alice Oke was very proud, I am sure. She may have loved the poet very much, and yet been indignant with him, hated having to love him. She may have felt that she had a right to rid herself of him, and to call upon her husband to help her to do so."

"Good heavens! what a fearful idea!" I exclaimed, half laughing. "Don't you think, after all, that Mr Oke may be right in saying that it is easier and more comfortable to take the whole story as a pure invention?"

"I cannot take it as an invention," answered Mrs Oke contemptuously, "because I happen to know that it is true."

"Indeed!" I answered, working away at my sketch, and enjoying putting this strange creature, as I said to myself, through her paces; "how is that?"

"How does one know that anything is true in this world?" she replied evasively; "because one does, because one feels it to be true, I suppose."

And, with that far-off look in her light eyes, she relapsed into silence.

"Have you ever read any of Lovelock's poetry?" she asked me suddenly the next day.

"Lovelock?" I answered, for I had forgotten the name. "Lovelock, who"—But I stopped, remembering the prejudices of my host, who was seated next to me at table.

"Lovelock who was killed by Mr Oke's and my ancestors."

And she looked full at her husband, as if in perverse enjoyment of the evident annoyance which it caused him.

"Alice," he entreated in a low voice, his whole face crimson, "for mercy's sake, don't talk about such things before the servants."

Mrs Oke burst into a high, light, rather hysterical laugh, the laugh of a naughty child.

"The servants! Gracious heavens! do you suppose they haven't heard the story? Why, it's as well known as Okehurst itself in the neighbourhood. Don't they believe that Lovelock has been seen about the house? Haven't they all heard his footsteps in the big corridor? Haven't they, my dear Willie, noticed a thousand times that you never will stay a minute alone in the yellow drawing-room—that you run out of it, like a child, if I happen to leave you there for a minute?"

True! How was it I had not noticed that? Or rather, that I only now remembered having noticed it? The yellow drawing-room was one of the most charming rooms in the house: a large, bright room, hung with yellow damask and panelled with carvings, that opened straight out on to the lawn, far superior to the room in which we habitually sat, which was comparatively gloomy. This time Mr Oke struck me as really too childish. I felt an intense desire to badger him.

"The yellow drawing-room!" I exclaimed. "Does this interesting literary character haunt the yellow drawing-room? Do tell me about it. What happened there?"

Mr Oke made a painful effort to laugh.

"Nothing ever happened there, so far as I know," he said, and rose from the table.

"Really?" I asked incredulously.

"Nothing did happen there," answered Mrs Oke slowly, playing mechanically with a fork, and picking out the pattern of the tablecloth. "That is just the extraordinary circumstance, that, so far as any one knows, nothing ever did happen there; and yet that room has an evil reputation. No member of our family, they say, can bear to sit there alone for more than a minute. You see, William evidently cannot."

"Have you ever seen or heard anything strange there?" I asked of my host.

He shook his head. "Nothing," he answered curtly, and lit his cigar.

"I presume you have not," I asked, half laughing, of Mrs Oke, "since you don't mind sitting in that room for hours alone? How do you explain this uncanny reputation, since nothing ever happened there?"

"Perhaps something is destined to happen there in the future," she answered, in her absent voice. And then she suddenly added, "Suppose you paint my portrait in that room?"

Mr Oke suddenly turned round. He was very white, and looked as if he were going to say something, but desisted.

"Why do you worry Mr Oke like that?" I asked, when he had gone into his smoking-room with his usual bundle of papers. "It is very cruel of you, Mrs Oke.

You ought to have more consideration for people who believe in such things, although you may not be able to put yourself in their frame of mind."

"Who tells you that I don't believe in *such things*, as you call them?" she answered abruptly.

"Come," she said, after a minute, "I want to show you why I believe in Christopher Lovelock. Come with me into the yellow room."

V.

What Mrs Oke showed me in the yellow room was a large bundle of papers, some printed and some manuscript, but all of them brown with age, which she took out of an old Italian ebony inlaid cabinet. It took her some time to get them, as a complicated arrangement of double locks and false drawers had to be put in play; and while she was doing so, I looked round the room, in which I had been only three or four times before. It was certainly the most beautiful room in this beautiful house, and, as it seemed to me now, the most strange. It was long and low, with something that made you think of the cabin of a ship, with a great mullioned window that let in, as it were, a perspective of the brownish green park-land, dotted with oaks, and sloping upwards to the distant line of bluish firs against the horizon. The walls were hung with flowered damask, whose yellow, faded to brown, united with the reddish colour of the carved wainscoting and the carved oaken beams. For the rest, it reminded me more of an Italian room than an English one. The furniture was Tuscan of the early seventeenth century, inlaid and carved; there were a couple of faded allegorical pictures, by some Bolognese master, on the walls; and in a corner, among a stack of dwarf orange-trees, a little Italian harpsichord of exquisite curve and slenderness, with flowers and landscapes painted upon its cover. In a recess was a shelf of old books, mainly English and Italian poets of the Elizabethan time; and close by it, placed upon a carved wedding-chest, a large and beautiful melon-shaped lute. The panes of the mullioned window were open, and yet the air seemed heavy, with an indescribable heady perfume, not that of any growing flower, but like that of old stuff that should have lain for years among spices.

"It is a beautiful room!" I exclaimed. "I should awfully like to paint you in it"; but I had scarcely spoken the words when I felt I had done wrong. This woman's husband could not bear the room, and it seemed to me vaguely as if he were right in detesting it.

Mrs Oke took no notice of my exclamation, but beckoned me to the table where she was standing sorting the papers.

"Look!" she said, "these are all poems by Christopher Lovelock"; and touching the yellow papers with delicate and reverent fingers, she commenced reading some of them out loud in a slow, half-audible voice. They were songs in the style of those of Herrick, Waller, and Drayton, complaining for the most part of the cruelty of a lady called Dryope, in whose name was evidently concealed a reference to that of the mistress of Okehurst. The songs were graceful, and not without a certain faded passion: but I was thinking not of them, but of the woman who was reading them to me.

Mrs Oke was standing with the brownish yellow wall as a background to her white brocade dress, which, in its stiff seventeenth-century make, seemed but to bring out more clearly the slightness, the exquisite suppleness, of her tall figure. She held the papers in one hand, and leaned the other, as if for support, on the inlaid cabinet by her side. Her voice, which was delicate, shadowy, like her person, had a curious throbbing cadence, as if she were reading the words of a melody, and restraining herself with difficulty from singing it; and as she read, her long slender throat throbbed slightly, and a faint redness came into her thin face. She evidently knew the verses by heart, and her eyes were mostly fixed with that distant smile in them, with which harmonised a constant tremulous little smile in her lips.

"That is how I would wish to paint her!" I exclaimed within myself; and scarcely noticed, what struck me on thinking over the scene, that this strange being read these verses as one might fancy a woman would read love-verses addressed to herself.

"Those are all written for Alice Oke—Alice the daughter of Virgil Pomfret," she said slowly, folding up the papers. "I found them at the bottom of this cabinet. Can you doubt of the reality of Christopher Lovelock now?"

The question was an illogical one, for to doubt of the existence of Christopher Lovelock was one thing, and to doubt of the mode of his death was another; but somehow I did feel convinced.

"Look!" she said, when she had replaced the poems, "I will show you something else." Among the flowers that stood on the upper storey of her writing-table—for I found that Mrs Oke had a writing-table in the yellow room—stood, as on an altar, a small black carved frame, with a silk curtain drawn over it: the sort of thing behind which you would have expected to find a head of Christ or of the Virgin Mary. She drew the curtain and displayed a large-sized miniature, representing a young man, with auburn curls and a peaked auburn beard, dressed in black, but with lace about his neck, and large pear-shaped pearls in his ears: a wistful, melancholy face. Mrs Oke took the miniature religiously off its stand, and showed me, written in faded characters upon the back, the name "Christopher Lovelock," and the date 1626.

"I found this in the secret drawer of that cabinet, together with the heap of poems," she said, taking the miniature out of my hand.

I was silent for a minute.

"Does—does Mr Oke know that you have got it here?" I asked; and then wondered what in the world had impelled me to put such a question.

Mrs Oke smiled that smile of contemptuous indifference. "I have never hidden it from any one. If my husband disliked my having it, he might have taken it away, I suppose. It belongs to him, since it was found in his house."

I did not answer, but walked mechanically towards the door. There was something heady and oppressive in this beautiful room; something, I thought, almost repulsive in this exquisite woman. She seemed to me, suddenly, perverse and dangerous.

I scarcely know why, but I neglected Mrs Oke that afternoon. I went to Mr Oke's study, and sat opposite to him smoking while he was engrossed in his accounts, his reports, and electioneering papers. On the table, above the heap of paper-bound volumes and pigeon-holed documents, was, as sole ornament of his den, a little photograph of his wife, done some years before. I don't know why, but as I sat and watched him, with his florid, honest, manly beauty, working away conscientiously, with that little perplexed frown of his, I felt intensely sorry for this man.

But this feeling did not last. There was no help for it: Oke was not as interesting as Mrs Oke; and it required too great an effort to pump up sympathy for this normal, excellent, exemplary young squire, in the presence of so wonderful a creature as his wife. So I let myself go to the habit of allowing Mrs Oke daily to talk over her strange craze, or rather of drawing her out about it. I confess that I derived a morbid and exquisite pleasure in doing so: it was so characteristic in her, so appropriate to the house! It completed her personality so perfectly, and made it so much easier to conceive a way of painting her. I made up my mind little by little, while working at William Oke's portrait (he proved a less easy subject than I had anticipated, and, despite his conscientious efforts, was a nervous, uncomfortable sitter, silent and brooding)—I made up my mind that I would paint Mrs Oke standing by the cabinet in the yellow room, in the white Vandyck dress copied from the portrait of her ancestress. Mr Oke might resent it, Mrs Oke even might resent it; they might refuse to take the picture, to pay for it, to allow me to exhibit; they might force me to run my umbrella through the picture. No matter. That picture should be painted, if merely for the sake of having painted it; for I felt it was the only thing I could do, and that it would be far away my best work. I told neither of my resolution, but prepared sketch after sketch of Mrs Oke, while continuing to paint her husband.

Mrs Oke was a silent person, more silent even than her husband, for she did not feel bound, as he did, to attempt to entertain a guest or to show any interest in him. She seemed to spend her life—a curious, inactive, half-invalidish life, broken by sudden fits of childish cheerfulness—in an eternal daydream, strolling about the house and grounds, arranging the quantities of flowers that always filled all the rooms, beginning to read and then throwing aside novels and books of poetry, of which she always had a large number; and, I believe, lying for hours, doing nothing, on a couch in that yellow drawing-room, which, with her sole exception, no member of the Oke family had ever been known to stay in alone. Little by little I began to suspect and to verify another eccentricity of this eccentric being, and to understand why there were stringent orders never to disturb her in that yellow room.

It had been a habit at Okehurst, as at one or two other English manor-houses, to keep a certain amount of the clothes of each generation, more particularly wedding dresses. A certain carved oaken press, of which Mr Oke once displayed the contents to me, was a perfect museum of costumes, male and female, from the early years of the seventeenth to the end of the eighteenth century—a thing to take away the breath of a *bric-a-brac* collector, an antiquary, or a *genre* painter. Mr Oke was none of these, and therefore took but little interest in the collection, save in so far as it interested his family feeling. Still he seemed well acquainted with the contents of that press.

He was turning over the clothes for my benefit, when suddenly I noticed that he frowned. I know not what impelled me to say, "By the way, have you any dresses of that Mrs Oke whom your wife resembles so much? Have you got that particular white dress she was painted in, perhaps?"

Oke of Okehurst flushed very red.

"We have it," he answered hesitatingly, "but—it isn't here at present—I can't find it. I suppose," he blurted out with an effort, "that Alice has got it. Mrs Oke sometimes has the fancy of having some of these old things down. I suppose she takes ideas from them."

A sudden light dawned in my mind. The white dress in which I had seen Mrs Oke in the yellow room, the day that she showed me Lovelock's verses, was not, as I had thought, a modern copy; it was the original dress of Alice Oke, the daughter of Virgil Pomfret—the dress in which, perhaps, Christopher Lovelock had seen her in that very room.

The idea gave me a delightful picturesque shudder. I said nothing. But I pictured to myself Mrs Oke sitting in that yellow room—that room which no Oke of Okehurst save herself ventured to remain in alone, in the dress of her ancestress, confronting, as it were, that vague, haunting something that seemed to fill the place—that vague presence, it seemed to me, of the murdered cavalier poet.

Mrs Oke, as I have said, was extremely silent, as a result of being extremely indifferent. She really did not care in the least about anything except her own ideas and day-dreams, except when, every now and then, she was seized with a sudden desire to shock the prejudices or superstitions of her husband. Very soon she got into the way of never talking to me at all, save about Alice and Nicholas Oke and Christopher Lovelock; and then, when the fit seized her, she would go on by the hour, never asking herself whether I was or was not equally interested in the strange craze that fascinated her. It so happened that I was. I loved to listen to her, going on discussing by the hour the merits of Lovelock's poems, and analysing her feelings and those of her two ancestors. It was quite wonderful to watch the exquisite, exotic creature in one of these moods, with the distant look in her grey eyes and the absent-looking smile in her thin cheeks, talking as if she had intimately known these people of the seventeenth century, discussing every minute mood of theirs, detailing every scene between them and their victim, talking of Alice, and Nicholas, and Lovelock as she might of her most intimate friends. Of Alice particularly, and of Lovelock. She seemed to know every word that Alice had spoken, every idea that had crossed her mind. It sometimes struck me as if she were telling me, speaking of herself in the third person, of her own feelings—as if I were listening to a woman's confidences, the recital of her doubts, scruples, and agonies about a living lover. For Mrs Oke, who seemed the most self-absorbed of creatures in all other matters, and utterly incapable of understanding or sympathising with the feelings of other persons, entered completely and passionately into the feelings of this woman, this Alice, who, at some moments, seemed to be not another woman, but herself.

"But how could she do it—how could she kill the man she cared for?" I once asked her.

"Because she loved him more than the whole world!" she exclaimed, and rising suddenly from her chair, walked towards the window, covering her face with her hands.

I could see, from the movement of her neck, that she was sobbing. She did not turn round, but motioned me to go away.

"Don't let us talk any more about it," she said. "I am ill today, and silly."

I closed the door gently behind me. What mystery was there in this woman's life? This listlessness, this strange self-engrossment and stranger mania about people long dead, this indifference and desire to annoy towards her husband—did it all mean that Alice Oke had loved or still loved some one who was not the master of Okehurst? And his melancholy, his preoccupation, the something about him that told of a broken youth—did it mean that he knew it?

VI.

The following days Mrs Oke was in a condition of quite unusual good spirits. Some visitors—distant relatives—were expected, and although she had expressed the utmost annoyance at the idea of their coming, she was now seized with a fit of housekeeping activity, and was perpetually about arranging things and giving orders, although all arrangements, as usual, had been made, and all orders given, by her husband.

William Oke was quite radiant.

"If only Alice were always well like this!" he exclaimed; "if only she would take, or could take, an interest in life, how different things would be! But," he added, as if fearful lest he should be supposed to accuse her in any way, "how can she, usually, with her wretched health? Still, it does make me awfully happy to see her like this."

I nodded. But I cannot say that I really acquiesced in his views. It seemed to me, particularly with the recollection of yesterday's extraordinary scene, that Mrs Oke's high spirits were anything but normal. There was something in her unusual activity and still more unusual cheerfulness that was merely nervous and feverish; and I had, the whole day, the impression of dealing with a woman who was ill and who would very speedily collapse.

Mrs Oke spent her day wandering from one room to another, and from the garden to the greenhouse, seeing whether all was in order, when, as a matter of fact, all was always in order at Okehurst. She did not give me any sitting, and not a word was spoken about Alice Oke or Christopher Lovelock. Indeed, to a casual observer, it might have seemed as if all that craze about Lovelock had completely departed, or never existed. About five o'clock, as I was strolling among the red-brick round-gabled outhouses—each with its armorial oak—and the old-fashioned spalliered kitchen and fruit garden, I saw Mrs Oke standing, her hands full of York and Lancaster roses, upon the steps facing the stables. A groom was currycombing a horse, and outside the coach-house was Mr Oke's little high-wheeled cart.

"Let us have a drive!" suddenly exclaimed Mrs Oke, on seeing me. "Look what a beautiful evening—and look at that dear little cart! It is so long since I have driven, and I feel as if I must drive again. Come with me. And you, harness Jim at once and come round to the door."

I was quite amazed; and still more so when the cart drove up before the door, and Mrs Oke called to me to accompany her. She sent away the groom, and in a minute we were rolling along, at a tremendous pace, along the yellow-sand road, with the sere pasture-lands, the big oaks, on either side.

I could scarcely believe my senses. This woman, in her mannish little coat and hat, driving a powerful young horse with the utmost skill, and chattering like a school-girl of sixteen, could not be the delicate, morbid, exotic, hot-house creature, unable to walk or to do anything, who spent her days lying about on couches in the heavy atmosphere, redolent with strange scents and associations, of the yellow drawing-room. The movement of the light carriage, the cool draught, the very grind of the wheels upon the gravel, seemed to go to her head like wine.

"It is so long since I have done this sort of thing," she kept repeating; "so long, so long. Oh, don't you think it delightful, going at this pace, with the idea that any moment the horse may come down and we two be killed?" and she laughed her childish laugh, and turned her face, no longer pale, but flushed with the movement and the excitement, towards me.

The cart rolled on quicker and quicker, one gate after another swinging to behind us, as we flew up and down the little hills, across the pasture lands, through the little red-brick gabled villages, where the people came out to see us pass, past the rows of willows along the streams, and the dark-green compact hop-fields, with the blue and hazy tree-tops of the horizon getting bluer and more hazy as the yellow light began to graze the ground. At last we got to an open space, a high-lying piece of common-land, such as is rare in that ruthlessly utilised country of grazing-grounds and hop-gardens. Among the low hills of the Weald, it seemed quite preternaturally high up, giving a sense that its extent of flat heather and gorse, bound by distant firs, was really on the top of the world. The sun was setting just opposite, and its lights lay flat on the ground, staining it with the red and black of the heather, or rather turning it into the surface of a purple sea, canopied over by a bank of dark-purple clouds—the jet-like sparkle of the dry ling and gorse tipping the purple like sunlit wavelets. A cold wind swept in our faces.

"What is the name of this place?" I asked. It was the only bit of impressive scenery that I had met in the neighbourhood of Okehurst.

"It is called Cotes Common," answered Mrs Oke, who had slackened the pace of the horse, and let the reins hang loose about his neck. "It was here that Christopher Lovelock was killed."

There was a moment's pause; and then she proceeded, tickling the flies from the horse's ears with the end of her whip, and looking straight into the sunset, which now rolled, a deep purple stream, across the heath to our feet—

"Lovelock was riding home one summer evening from Appledore, when, as he had got half-way across Cotes Common, somewhere about here—for I have always heard them mention the pond in the old gravel-pits as about the place—he saw two men riding towards him, in whom he presently recognised Nicholas Oke of Okehurst accompanied by a groom. Oke of Okehurst hailed him; and Lovelock rode up to meet him. 'I am glad to have met you, Mr Lovelock,' said Nicholas, 'because I have some important news for you'; and so saying, he brought his horse close to the one that Lovelock was riding, and suddenly turning round, fired off a pistol at his head. Lovelock had time to move, and the bullet, instead of striking him, went straight into the head of his horse, which fell beneath him. Lovelock, however, had fallen in such a way as to be able to extricate himself easily from his horse; and drawing his sword, he rushed upon Oke, and seized his horse by the bridle. Oke quickly jumped off and drew his sword; and in a minute, Lovelock, who was much the better swordsman of the two, was having the better of him. Lovelock had completely disarmed him, and got his sword at Oke's throat, crying out to him that if he would ask forgiveness he should be spared for the sake of their old friendship, when the groom suddenly rode up from behind and shot Lovelock through the back. Lovelock fell, and Oke immediately tried to finish him with his sword, while the groom drew up and held the bridle of Oke's horse. At that moment the sunlight fell upon the groom's face, and Lovelock recognised Mrs Oke. He cried out, 'Alice, Alice! it is you who have murdered me!' and died. Then Nicholas Oke sprang into his saddle and rode off with his wife, leaving Lovelock dead by the side of his fallen horse. Nicholas Oke had taken the precaution of removing Lovelock's purse and throwing it into the pond, so the murder was put down to certain highwaymen who were about in that part of the country. Alice Oke died many years afterwards, quite an old woman, in the reign of Charles II.; but Nicholas did not live very long, and shortly before his death got into a very strange condition, always brooding, and sometimes threatening to kill his wife. They say that in one of these fits, just shortly before his death, he told the whole story of the murder, and made a prophecy that when the head of his house and master of Okehurst should marry another Alice Oke descended from himself and his wife, there should be an end of the Okes of Okehurst. You see, it seems to be coming true. We have no children, and I don't suppose we shall ever have any. I, at least, have never wished for them."

Mrs Oke paused, and turned her face towards me with the absent smile in her thin cheeks: her eyes no longer had that distant look; they were strangely eager and fixed. I did not know what to answer; this woman positively frightened me. We remained for a moment in that same place, with the sunlight dying away in crimson ripples on the heather, gilding the yellow banks, the black waters of the pond, surrounded by thin rushes, and the yellow gravel-pits; while the wind blew in our faces and bent the ragged warped bluish tops of the firs. Then Mrs Oke touched the horse, and off we went at a furious pace. We did not exchange a single word, I think, on the way home. Mrs Oke sat with her eyes fixed on the reins, breaking the silence now and then only by a word to the horse, urging him to an even more furious pace. The people we met along the roads must have thought that the horse was running away, unless they noticed Mrs Oke's calm manner and the look of excited enjoyment in her face. To me it seemed that I was in the hands of a madwoman, and I quietly prepared myself for being upset or dashed against a cart. It had turned cold, and the draught was icy in our faces when we got within sight of the red gables and high chimney-stacks of Okehurst. Mr Oke was standing before the door. On our approach I saw a look of relieved suspense, of keen pleasure come into his face.

He lifted his wife out of the cart in his strong arms with a kind of chivalrous tenderness.

"I am so glad to have you back, darling," he exclaimed—"so glad! I was delighted to hear you had gone out with the cart, but as you have not driven for so long, I was beginning to be frightfully anxious, dearest. Where have you been all this time?"

Mrs Oke had quickly extricated herself from her husband, who had remained holding her, as one might hold a delicate child who has been causing anxiety. The gentleness and affection of the poor fellow had evidently not touched her—she seemed almost to recoil from it.

"I have taken him to Cotes Common," she said, with that perverse look which I had noticed before, as she pulled off her driving-gloves. "It is such a splendid old place."

Mr Oke flushed as if he had bitten upon a sore tooth, and the double gash painted itself scarlet between his eyebrows.

Outside, the mists were beginning to rise, veiling the park-land dotted with big black oaks, and from which, in the watery moonlight, rose on all sides the eerie little cry of the lambs separated from their mothers. It was damp and cold, and I shivered.

VII.

The next day Okehurst was full of people, and Mrs Oke, to my amazement, was doing the honours of it as if a house full of commonplace, noisy young creatures, bent upon flirting and tennis, were her usual idea of felicity.

The afternoon of the third day—they had come for an electioneering ball, and stayed three nights—the weather changed; it turned suddenly very cold and began to pour. Every one was sent indoors, and there was a general gloom suddenly over the company. Mrs Oke seemed to have got sick of her guests, and was listlessly lying back on a couch, paying not the slightest attention to the chattering and piano-strumming in the room, when one of the guests suddenly proposed that they should play charades. He was a distant cousin of the Okes, a sort of fashionable artistic Bohemian, swelled out to intolerable conceit by the amateur-actor vogue of a season.

"It would be lovely in this marvellous old place," he cried, "just to dress up, and parade about, and feel as if we belonged to the past. I have heard you have a marvellous collection of old costumes, more or less ever since the days of Noah, somewhere, Cousin Bill."

The whole party exclaimed in joy at this proposal. William Oke looked puzzled for a moment, and glanced at his wife, who continued to lie listless on her sofa.

"There is a press full of clothes belonging to the family," he answered dubiously, apparently overwhelmed by the desire to please his guests; "but—but—I don't know whether it's quite respectful to dress up in the clothes of dead people."

"Oh, fiddlestick!" cried the cousin. "What do the dead people know about it? Besides," he added, with mock seriousness, "I assure you we shall behave in the most reverent way and feel quite solemn about it all, if only you will give us the key, old man."

Again Mr Oke looked towards his wife, and again met only her vague, absent glance.

"Very well," he said, and led his guests upstairs.

An hour later the house was filled with the strangest crew and the strangest noises. I had entered, to a certain extent, into William Oke's feeling of unwillingness to let his ancestors' clothes and personality be taken in vain; but when the masquerade was complete, I must say that the effect was quite magnificent. A dozen youngish men and women—those who were staying in the house and some neighbours who had come for lawn-tennis and dinner—were rigged out, under the direction of the theatrical cousin, in the contents of that oaken press: and I have never seen a more beautiful sight than the panelled corridors, the carved and escutcheoned staircase, the dim drawing-rooms with their faded tapestries, the great hall with its vaulted and ribbed ceiling, dotted about with groups or single figures that seemed to have come straight from the past. Even William Oke, who, besides myself and a few elderly people, was the only man not masqueraded, seemed delighted and fired by the sight. A certain schoolboy character suddenly came out in him; and finding that there was no costume left for him, he rushed upstairs and presently returned in the uniform he had worn before his marriage. I thought I had really never seen so magnificent a specimen of the handsome Englishman; he looked, despite all the modern associations of his costume, more genuinely old-world than all the rest, a knight for the Black Prince or Sidney, with his admirably regular features and beautiful fair hair and complexion. After a minute, even the elderly people had got costumes of some sort—dominoes arranged at the moment, and hoods and all manner of disguises made out of pieces of old embroidery and Oriental stuffs and furs; and very soon this rabble of masquers had become, so to speak, completely drunk with its own amusement—with the childishness, and, if I may say so, the barbarism, the vulgarity underlying the majority even of well-bred English men and women—Mr Oke himself doing the mountebank like a schoolboy at Christmas.

"Where is Mrs Oke? Where is Alice?" some one suddenly asked.

Mrs Oke had vanished. I could fully understand that to this eccentric being, with her fantastic, imaginative, morbid passion for the past, such a carnival as this must be positively revolting; and, absolutely indifferent as she was to giving offence, I could imagine how she would have retired, disgusted and outraged, to dream her strange day-dreams in the yellow room.

But a moment later, as we were all noisily preparing to go in to dinner, the door opened and a strange figure entered, stranger than any of these others who were profaning the clothes of the dead: a boy, slight and tall, in a brown riding-coat, leathern belt, and big buff boots, a little grey cloak over one shoulder, a large grey hat slouched over the eyes, a dagger and pistol at the waist. It was Mrs Oke, her eyes preternaturally bright, and her whole face lit up with a bold, perverse smile.

Every one exclaimed, and stood aside. Then there was a moment's silence, broken by faint applause. Even to a crew of noisy boys and girls playing the fool in the garments of men and women long dead and buried, there is something questionable in the sudden appearance of a young married woman, the mistress of the house, in a riding-coat and jackboots; and Mrs Oke's expression did not make the jest seem any the less questionable.

"What is that costume?" asked the theatrical cousin, who, after a second, had come to the conclusion that Mrs Oke was merely a woman of marvellous talent whom he must try and secure for his amateur troop next season.

"It is the dress in which an ancestress of ours, my namesake Alice Oke, used to go out riding with her husband in the days of Charles I.," she answered, and took her seat at the head of the table. Involuntarily my eyes sought those of Oke of Okehurst. He, who blushed as easily as a girl of sixteen, was now as white as ashes, and I noticed that he pressed his hand almost convulsively to his mouth.

"Don't you recognise my dress, William?" asked Mrs Oke, fixing her eyes upon him with a cruel smile.

He did not answer, and there was a moment's silence, which the theatrical cousin had the happy thought of breaking by jumping upon his seat and emptying off his glass with the exclamation—

"To the health of the two Alice Okes, of the past and the present!"

Mrs Oke nodded, and with an expression I had never seen in her face before, answered in a loud and aggressive tone—

"To the health of the poet, Mr Christopher Lovelock, if his ghost be honouring this house with its presence!"

I felt suddenly as if I were in a madhouse. Across the table, in the midst of this room full of noisy wretches, tricked out red, blue, purple, and parti-coloured, as men and women of the sixteenth, seventeenth, and eighteenth centuries, as improvised Turks and Eskimos, and dominoes, and clowns, with faces painted and corked and floured over, I seemed to see that sanguine sunset, washing like a sea of blood over the heather, to where, by the black pond and the wind-warped firs, there lay the body of Christopher Lovelock, with his dead horse near him, the yellow gravel and lilac ling soaked crimson all around; and above emerged, as out of the redness, the pale blond head covered with the grey hat, the absent eyes, and strange smile of Mrs Oke. It seemed to me horrible, vulgar, abominable, as if I had got inside a madhouse.

VIII.

From that moment I noticed a change in William Oke; or rather, a change that had probably been coming on for some time got to the stage of being noticeable.

I don't know whether he had any words with his wife about her masquerade of that unlucky evening. On the whole I decidedly think not. Oke was with every one a diffident and reserved man, and most of all so with his wife; besides, I can fancy that he would experience a positive impossibility of putting into words any strong feeling of disapprobation towards her, that his disgust would necessarily be silent. But be this as it may, I perceived very soon that the relations between my host and hostess had become exceedingly strained. Mrs Oke, indeed, had never paid much attention to her husband, and seemed merely a trifle more indifferent to his presence than she had been before. But Oke himself, although he affected to address her at meals from a desire to conceal his feeling, and a fear of making the position disagreeable to me, very clearly could scarcely bear to speak to or even see his wife. The poor fellow's honest soul was quite brimful of pain, which he was determined not to allow to overflow, and which seemed to filter into his whole nature and poison it. This woman had shocked and pained him more than was possible to say, and yet it was evident that he could neither cease loving her nor commence comprehending her real nature. I sometimes felt, as we took our long walks through the monotonous country, across the oak-dotted grazing-grounds, and by the brink of the dull-green, serried hop-rows, talking at rare intervals about the value of the crops, the drainage of the estate, the village schools, the Primrose League, and the iniquities of Mr Gladstone, while Oke of Okehurst carefully cut down every tall thistle that caught his eye—I sometimes felt, I say, an intense and impotent desire to enlighten this man about his wife's character. I seemed to understand it so well, and to understand it well seemed to imply such a comfortable acquiescence; and it seemed so unfair that just he should be condemned to puzzle for ever over this enigma, and wear out his soul trying to comprehend what now seemed so plain to me. But how would it ever be possible to get this serious, conscientious, slow-brained representative of English simplicity and honesty and thoroughness to understand the mixture of self-engrossed vanity, of shallowness, of poetic vision, of love of morbid excitement, that walked this earth under the name of Alice Oke?

So Oke of Okehurst was condemned never to understand; but he was condemned also to suffer from his inability to do so. The poor fellow was constantly straining after an explanation of his wife's peculiarities; and although the effort was probably unconscious, it caused him a great deal of pain. The gash—the maniac-frown, as my friend calls it—between his eyebrows, seemed to have grown a permanent feature of his face.

Mrs Oke, on her side, was making the very worst of the situation. Perhaps she resented her husband's tacit reproval of that masquerade night's freak, and determined to make him swallow more of the same stuff, for she clearly thought that one of William's peculiarities, and one for which she despised him, was that he could never be goaded into an outspoken expression of disapprobation; that from her he would swallow any amount of bitterness without complaining. At any rate she now adopted a perfect policy of teasing and shocking her husband about the murder of Lovelock. She was perpetually alluding to it in her conversation, discussing in his presence what had or had not been the feelings of the various actors in the tragedy of 1626, and insisting upon her resemblance and almost identity with the original Alice Oke. Something had suggested to her eccentric mind that it would be delightful to perform in the garden at Okehurst, under the huge ilexes and elms, a little masque which she had discovered among Christopher Lovelock's works; and she began to scour the country and enter into vast correspondence for the purpose of effectuating this scheme. Letters arrived every other day from the theatrical cousin, whose only objection was that Okehurst was too remote a locality for an entertainment in which he foresaw great glory to himself. And every now and then there would arrive some young gentleman or lady, whom Alice Oke had sent for to see whether they would do.

I saw very plainly that the performance would never take place, and that Mrs Oke herself had no intention that it ever should. She was one of those creatures to whom realisation of a project is nothing, and who enjoy plan-making almost the more for knowing that all will stop short at the plan. Meanwhile, this perpetual talk about the pastoral, about Lovelock, this continual attitudinising as the wife of Nicholas Oke, had the further attraction to Mrs Oke of putting her husband into a condition of frightful though suppressed irritation, which she enjoyed with the enjoyment of a perverse child. You must not think that I looked on indifferent, although I admit that this was a perfect treat to an amateur student of character like myself. I really did feel most sorry for poor Oke, and frequently quite indignant with his wife. I was several times on the point of begging her to have more consideration for him, even of suggesting that this kind of behavior, particularly before a comparative stranger like me, was very poor taste. But there was something elusive about Mrs Oke, which made it next to impossible to speak seriously with her; and besides, I was by no means sure that any interference on my part would not merely animate her perversity.

One evening a curious incident took place. We had just sat down to dinner, the Okes, the theatrical cousin, who was down for a couple of days, and three or four neighbours. It was dusk, and the yellow light of the candles mingled charmingly with the greyness of the evening. Mrs Oke was not well, and had been remarkably quiet all day, more diaphanous, strange, and far-away than ever; and her husband seemed to have felt a sudden return of tenderness, almost of compassion, for this delicate, fragile creature. We had been talking of quite indifferent matters, when I saw Mr Oke suddenly turn very white, and look fixedly for a moment at the window opposite to his seat.

"Who's that fellow looking in at the window, and making signs to you, Alice? Damn his impudence!" he cried, and jumping up, ran to the window, opened it, and passed out into the twilight. We all looked at each other in surprise; some of the party remarked upon the carelessness of servants in letting nasty-looking fellows hang about the kitchen, others told stories of tramps and burglars. Mrs Oke did not speak; but I noticed the curious, distant-looking smile in her thin cheeks.

After a minute William Oke came in, his napkin in his hand. He shut the window behind him and silently resumed his place.

"Well, who was it?" we all asked.

"Nobody. I—I must have made a mistake," he answered, and turned crimson, while he busily peeled a pear.

"It was probably Lovelock," remarked Mrs Oke, just as she might have said, "It was probably the gardener," but with that faint smile of pleasure still in her face. Except the theatrical cousin, who burst into a loud laugh, none of the company had ever heard Lovelock's name, and, doubtless imagining him to be some natural appanage of the Oke family, groom or farmer, said nothing, so the subject dropped.

From that evening onwards things began to assume a different aspect. That incident was the beginning of a perfect system—a system of what? I scarcely know how to call it. A system of grim jokes on the part of Mrs Oke, of superstitious fancies on the part of her husband—a system of mysterious persecutions on the part of some less earthly tenant of Okehurst. Well, yes, after all, why not? We have all heard of ghosts, had uncles, cousins, grandmothers, nurses, who have seen them; we are all a bit afraid of them at the bottom of our soul; so why shouldn't they be? I am too sceptical to believe in the impossibility of anything, for my part!

Besides, when a man has lived throughout a summer in the same house with a woman like Mrs Oke of Okehurst, he gets to believe in the possibility of a great many improbable things, I assure you, as a mere result of believing in her. And when you come to think of it, why not? That a weird creature, visibly not of this earth, a reincarnation of a woman who murdered her lover two centuries and a half ago, that such a creature should have the power of attracting about her (being altogether superior to earthly lovers) the man who loved her in that previous existence, whose love for her was his death—what is there astonishing in that? Mrs Oke herself, I feel quite persuaded, believed or half believed it; indeed she very seriously admitted the possibility thereof, one day that I made the suggestion half in jest. At all events, it rather pleased me to think so; it fitted in so well with the woman's whole personality; it explained those hours and hours spent all alone in the yellow room, where the very air, with its scent of heady flowers and old perfumed stuffs, seemed redolent of ghosts. It explained that strange smile which was not for any of us, and yet was not merely for herself—that strange, far-off look in the wide pale eyes. I liked the idea, and I liked to tease, or rather to delight her with it. How should I know that the wretched husband would take such matters seriously?

He became day by day more silent and perplexed-looking; and, as a result, worked harder, and probably with less effect, at his land-improving schemes and political canvassing. It seemed to me that he was perpetually listening, watching, waiting for something to happen: a word spoken suddenly, the sharp opening of a door, would make him start, turn crimson, and almost tremble; the mention of Lovelock brought a helpless look, half a convulsion, like that of a man overcome by great heat, into his face. And his wife, so far from taking any interest in his altered looks, went on irritating him more and more. Every time that the poor fellow gave one of those starts of his, or turned crimson at the sudden sound of a footstep, Mrs Oke would ask him, with her contemptuous indifference, whether he had seen Lovelock. I soon began to perceive that my host was getting perfectly ill. He would sit at meals never saying a word, with his eyes fixed scrutinisingly on his wife, as if vainly trying to solve some dreadful mystery; while his wife, ethereal, exquisite, went on talking in her listless way about the masque, about Lovelock, always about Lovelock. During our walks and rides, which we continued pretty regularly, he would start whenever in the roads or lanes surrounding Okehurst, or in its grounds, we perceived a figure in the distance. I have seen him tremble at what, on nearer approach, I could scarcely restrain my laughter on discovering to be some well-known farmer or neighbour or servant. Once, as we were returning home at dusk, he suddenly caught my arm and pointed across the oak-dotted pastures in the direction of the garden, then started off almost at a run, with his dog behind him, as if in pursuit of some intruder.

"Who was it?" I asked. And Mr Oke merely shook his head mournfully. Sometimes in the early autumn twilights, when the white mists rose from the park-land, and the rooks formed long black lines on the palings, I almost fancied I saw him start at the very trees and bushes, the outlines of the distant oast-houses, with their conical roofs and projecting vanes, like gibing fingers in the half light.

"Your husband is ill," I once ventured to remark to Mrs Oke, as she sat for the hundred-and-thirtieth of my preparatory sketches (I somehow could never get beyond preparatory sketches with her). She raised her beautiful, wide, pale eyes, making as she did so that exquisite curve of shoulders and neck and delicate pale head that I so vainly longed to reproduce.

"I don't see it," she answered quietly. "If he is, why doesn't he go up to town and see the doctor? It's merely one of his glum fits."

"You should not tease him about Lovelock," I added, very seriously. "He will get to believe in him."

"Why not? If he sees him, why he sees him. He would not be the only person that has done so"; and she smiled faintly and half perversely, as her eyes sought that usual distant indefinable something.

But Oke got worse. He was growing perfectly unstrung, like a hysterical woman. One evening that we were sitting alone in the smoking-room, he began unexpectedly a rambling discourse about his wife; how he had first known her when they were children, and they had gone to the same dancing-school near Portland Place; how her mother, his aunt-in-law, had brought her for Christmas to Okehurst while he was on his holidays; how finally, thirteen years ago, when he was twenty-three and she was eighteen, they had been married; how terribly he had suffered when they had been disappointed of their baby, and she had nearly died of the illness.

"I did not mind about the child, you know," he said in an excited voice; "although there will be an end of us now, and Okehurst will go to the Curtises. I minded only about Alice." It was next to inconceivable that this poor excited creature, speaking almost with tears in his voice and in his eyes, was the quiet, well-got-up, irreproachable young ex-Guardsman who had walked into my studio a couple of months before.

Oke was silent for a moment, looking fixedly at the rug at his feet, when he suddenly burst out in a scarce audible voice—

"If you knew how I cared for Alice—how I still care for her. I could kiss the ground she walks upon. I would give anything—my life any day—if only she would look for two minutes as if she liked me a little—as if she didn't utterly despise me"; and the poor fellow burst into a hysterical laugh, which was almost a sob. Then he suddenly began to laugh outright, exclaiming, with a sort of vulgarity of intonation which was extremely foreign to him—

"Damn it, old fellow, this is a queer world we live in!" and rang for more brandy and soda, which he was beginning, I noticed, to take pretty freely now, although he had been almost a blue-ribbon man—as much so as is possible for a hospitable country gentleman—when I first arrived.

IX.

It became clear to me now that, incredible as it might seem, the thing that ailed William Oke was jealousy. He was simply madly in love with his wife, and madly jealous of her. Jealous—but of whom? He himself would probably have been quite unable to say. In the first place—to clear off any possible suspicion—certainly not of me. Besides the fact that Mrs Oke took only just a very little more interest in me than in the butler or the upper-housemaid, I think that Oke himself was the sort of man whose imagination would recoil from realising any definite object of jealousy, even though jealously might be killing him inch by inch. It remained a vague, permeating, continuous feeling—the feeling that he loved her, and she did not care a jackstraw about him, and that everything with which she came into contact was receiving some of that notice which was refused to him—every person, or thing, or tree, or stone: it was the recognition of that strange far-off look in Mrs Oke's eyes, of that strange absent smile on Mrs Oke's lips—eyes and lips that had no look and no smile for him.

Gradually his nervousness, his watchfulness, suspiciousness, tendency to start, took a definite shape. Mr Oke was for ever alluding to steps or voices he had heard, to figures he had seen sneaking round the house. The sudden bark of one of the dogs would make him jump up. He cleaned and loaded very carefully all the guns and revolvers in his study, and even some of the old fowling-pieces and holster-pistols in the hall. The servants and tenants thought that Oke of Okehurst had been seized with a terror of tramps and burglars. Mrs Oke smiled contemptuously at all these doings.

"My dear William," she said one day, "the persons who worry you have just as good a right to walk up and down the passages and staircase, and to hang about the house, as you or I. They were there, in all probability, long before either of us was born, and are greatly amused by your preposterous notions of privacy."

Mr Oke laughed angrily. "I suppose you will tell me it is Lovelock—your eternal Lovelock—whose steps I hear on the gravel every night. I suppose he has as good a right to be here as you or I." And he strode out of the room.

"Lovelock—Lovelock! Why will she always go on like that about Lovelock?" Mr Oke asked me that evening, suddenly staring me in the face.

I merely laughed.

"It's only because she has that play of his on the brain," I answered; "and because she thinks you superstitious, and likes to tease you."

"I don't understand," sighed Oke.

How could he? And if I had tried to make him do so, he would merely have thought I was insulting his wife, and have perhaps kicked me out of the room. So I made no attempt to explain psychological problems to him, and he asked me no more questions until once.—But I must first mention a curious incident that happened.

The incident was simply this. Returning one afternoon from our usual walk, Mr Oke suddenly asked the servant whether any one had come. The answer was in the negative; but Oke did not seem satisfied. We had hardly sat down to dinner when he turned to his wife and asked, in a strange voice which I scarcely recognised as his own, who had called that afternoon.

"No one," answered Mrs Oke; "at least to the best of my knowledge."

William Oke looked at her fixedly.

"No one?" he repeated, in a scrutinising tone; "no one, Alice?"

Mrs Oke shook her head. "No one," she replied.

There was a pause.

"Who was it, then, that was walking with you near the pond, about five o'clock?" asked Oke slowly.

His wife lifted her eyes straight to his and answered contemptuously—

"No one was walking with me near the pond, at five o'clock or any other hour."

Mr Oke turned purple, and made a curious hoarse noise like a man choking.

"I—I thought I saw you walking with a man this afternoon, Alice," he brought out with an effort; adding, for the sake of appearances before me, "I thought it might have been the curate come with that report for me."

Mrs Oke smiled.

"I can only repeat that no living creature has been near me this afternoon," she said slowly. "If you saw any one with me, it must have been Lovelock, for there certainly was no one else."

And she gave a little sigh, like a person trying to reproduce in her mind some delightful but too evanescent impression.

I looked at my host; from crimson his face had turned perfectly livid, and he breathed as if some one were squeezing his windpipe.

No more was said about the matter. I vaguely felt that a great danger was threatening. To Oke or to Mrs Oke? I could not tell which; but I was aware of an imperious inner call to avert some dreadful evil, to exert myself, to explain, to interpose. I determined to speak to Oke the following day, for I trusted him to give me a quiet hearing, and I did not trust Mrs Oke. That woman would slip through my fingers like a snake if I attempted to grasp her elusive character.

I asked Oke whether he would take a walk with me the next afternoon, and he accepted to do so with a curious eagerness. We started about three o'clock. It was a stormy, chilly afternoon, with great balls of white clouds rolling rapidly in the cold blue sky, and occasional lurid gleams of sunlight, broad and yellow, which made the black ridge of the storm, gathered on the horizon, look blue-black like ink.

We walked quickly across the sere and sodden grass of the park, and on to the highroad that led over the low hills, I don't know why, in the direction of Cotes Common. Both of us were silent, for both of us had something to say, and did not know how to begin. For my part, I recognised the impossibility of starting the subject: an uncalled-for interference from me would merely indispose Mr Oke, and make him doubly dense of comprehension. So, if Oke had something to say, which he evidently had, it was better to wait for him.

Oke, however, broke the silence only by pointing out to me the condition of the hops, as we passed one of his many hop-gardens. "It will be a poor year," he said, stopping short and looking intently before him—"no hops at all. No hops this autumn."

I looked at him. It was clear that he had no notion what he was saying. The dark-green bines were covered with fruit; and only yesterday he himself had informed me that he had not seen such a profusion of hops for many years.

I did not answer, and we walked on. A cart met us in a dip of the road, and the carter touched his hat and greeted Mr Oke. But Oke took no heed; he did not seem to be aware of the man's presence.

The clouds were collecting all round; black domes, among which coursed the round grey masses of fleecy stuff.

"I think we shall be caught in a tremendous storm," I said; "hadn't we better be turning?" He nodded, and turned sharp round.

The sunlight lay in yellow patches under the oaks of the pasture-lands, and burnished the green hedges. The air was heavy and yet cold, and everything seemed preparing for a great storm. The rooks whirled in black clouds round the trees and the conical red caps of the oast-houses which give that country the look of being studded with turreted castles; then they descended—a black line—upon the fields, with what seemed an unearthly loudness of caw. And all round there arose a shrill quavering bleating of lambs and calling of sheep, while the wind began to catch the topmost branches of the trees.

Suddenly Mr Oke broke the silence.

"I don't know you very well," he began hurriedly, and without turning his face towards me; "but I think you are honest, and you have seen a good deal of the world—much more than I. I want you to tell me—but truly, please—what do you think a man should do if"—and he stopped for some minutes.

"Imagine," he went on quickly, "that a man cares a great deal—a very great deal for his wife, and that he finds out that she—well, that—that she is deceiving him. No—don't misunderstand me; I mean—that she is constantly surrounded by some one else and will not admit it—some one whom she hides away. Do you understand? Perhaps she does not know all the risk she is running, you know, but she will not draw back—she will not avow it to her husband"—

"My dear Oke," I interrupted, attempting to take the matter lightly, "these are questions that can't be solved in the abstract, or by people to whom the thing has not happened. And it certainly has not happened to you or me."

Oke took no notice of my interruption. "You see," he went on, "the man doesn't expect his wife to care much about him. It's not that; he isn't merely jealous, you know. But he feels that she is on the brink of dishonouring herself—because I don't think a woman can really dishonour her husband; dishonour is in our own hands, and depends only on our own acts. He ought to save her, do you see? He must, must save her, in one way or another. But if she will not listen to him, what can he do? Must he seek out the other one, and try and get him out of the way? You see it's all the fault of the other—not hers, not hers. If only she would trust in her husband, she would be safe. But that other one won't let her."

"Look here, Oke," I said boldly, but feeling rather frightened; "I know quite well what you are talking about. And I see you don't understand the matter in the very least. I do. I have watched you and watched Mrs Oke these six weeks, and I see what is the matter. Will you listen to me?"

And taking his arm, I tried to explain to him my view of the situation—that his wife was merely eccentric, and a little theatrical and imaginative, and that she took a pleasure in teasing him. That he, on the other hand, was letting himself get into a morbid state; that he was ill, and ought to see a good doctor. I even offered to take him to town with me.

I poured out volumes of psychological explanations. I dissected Mrs Oke's character twenty times over, and tried to show him that there was absolutely nothing at the bottom of his suspicions beyond an imaginative *pose* and a garden-play on the brain. I adduced twenty instances, mostly invented for the nonce, of ladies of my acquaintance who had suffered from similar fads. I pointed out to him that his wife ought to have an outlet for her imaginative and theatrical over-energy. I advised him to take her to London and plunge her into some set where every one should be more or less in a similar condition. I laughed at the notion of there being any hidden individual about the house. I explained to Oke that he was suffering from delusions, and called upon so conscientious and religious a man to take every step to rid himself of them, adding innumerable examples of people who had cured themselves of seeing visions and of brooding over morbid fancies. I struggled and wrestled, like Jacob with the angel, and I really hoped I had made some impression. At first, indeed, I felt that not one of my words went into the man's brain—that, though silent, he was not listening. It seemed almost hopeless to present my views in such a light that he could grasp them. I felt as if I were expounding and arguing at a rock. But when I got on to the tack of his duty towards his wife and himself, and appealed to his moral and religious notions, I felt that I was making an impression.

"I daresay you are right," he said, taking my hand as we came in sight of the red gables of Okehurst, and speaking in a weak, tired, humble voice. "I don't understand you quite, but I am sure what you say is true. I daresay it is all that I'm seedy. I feel sometimes as if I were mad, and just fit to be locked up. But don't think I don't struggle against it. I do, I do continually, only sometimes it seems too strong for me. I pray God night and morning to give me the strength to overcome my suspicions, or to remove these dreadful thoughts from me. God knows, I know what a wretched creature I am, and how unfit to take care of that poor girl."

And Oke again pressed my hand. As we entered the garden, he turned to me once more.

"I am very, very grateful to you," he said, "and, indeed, I will do my best to try and be stronger. If only," he added, with a sigh, "if only Alice would give me a moment's breathing-time, and not go on day after day mocking me with her Lovelock."

X.

I had begun Mrs Oke's portrait, and she was giving me a sitting. She was unusually quiet that morning; but, it seemed to me, with the quietness of a woman who is expecting something, and she gave me the impression of being extremely happy. She had been reading, at my suggestion, the *Vita Nuova*, which she did not know before, and the conversation came to roll upon that, and upon the question whether love so abstract and so enduring was a possibility. Such a discussion, which might have savoured of flirtation in the case of almost any other young and beautiful woman, became in the case of Mrs Oke something quite different; it seemed distant, intangible, not of this earth, like her smile and the look in her eyes.

"Such love as that," she said, looking into the far distance of the oak-dotted park-land, "is very rare, but it can exist. It becomes a person's whole existence, his whole soul; and it can survive the death, not merely of the beloved, but of the lover. It is unextinguishable, and goes on in the spiritual world until it meet a reincarnation of the beloved; and when this happens, it jets out and draws to it all that may remain of that lover's soul, and takes shape and surrounds the beloved one once more."

Mrs Oke was speaking slowly, almost to herself, and I had never, I think, seen her look so strange and so beautiful, the stiff white dress bringing out but the more the exotic exquisiteness and incorporealness of her person.

I did not know what to answer, so I said half in jest—

"I fear you have been reading too much Buddhist literature, Mrs Oke. There is something dreadfully esoteric in all you say."

She smiled contemptuously.

"I know people can't understand such matters," she replied, and was silent for some time. But, through her quietness and silence, I felt, as it were, the throb of a strange excitement in this woman, almost as if I had been holding her pulse.

Still, I was in hopes that things might be beginning to go better in consequence of my interference. Mrs Oke had scarcely once alluded to Lovelock in the last two or three days; and Oke had been much more cheerful and natural since our conversation. He no longer seemed so worried; and once or twice I had caught in him a look of great gentleness and loving-kindness, almost of pity, as towards some young and very frail thing, as he sat opposite his wife.

But the end had come. After that sitting Mrs Oke had complained of fatigue and retired to her room, and Oke had driven off on some business to the nearest town. I felt all alone in the big house, and after having worked a little at a sketch I was making in the park, I amused myself rambling about the house.

It was a warm, enervating, autumn afternoon: the kind of weather that brings the perfume out of everything, the damp ground and fallen leaves, the flowers in the jars, the old woodwork and stuffs; that seems to bring on to the surface of one's consciousness all manner of vague recollections and expectations, a something half pleasurable, half painful, that makes it impossible to do or to think. I was the prey of this particular, not at all unpleasurable, restlessness. I wandered up and down the corridors, stopping to look at the pictures, which I knew already in every detail, to follow the pattern of the carvings and old stuffs, to stare at the autumn flowers, arranged in magnificent masses of colour in the big china bowls and jars. I took up one book after another and threw it aside; then I sat down to the piano and began to play irrelevant fragments. I felt quite alone, although I had heard the grind of the wheels on the gravel, which meant that my host had returned. I was lazily turning over a book of verses—I remember it perfectly well, it was Morris's '*Love is Enough*'—in a corner of the drawing-room, when the door suddenly opened and William Oke showed himself. He did not enter, but beckoned to me to come out to him. There was something in his face that made me start up and follow him at once. He was extremely quiet, even stiff, not a muscle of his face moving, but very pale.

"I have something to show you," he said, leading me through the vaulted hall, hung round with ancestral pictures, into the gravelled space that looked like a filled-up moat, where stood the big blasted oak, with its twisted, pointing branches. I followed him on to the lawn, or rather the piece of park-land that ran up to the house. We walked quickly, he in front, without exchanging a word. Suddenly he stopped, just where there jutted out the bow-window of the yellow drawing-room, and I felt Oke's hand tight upon my arm.

"I have brought you here to see something," he whispered hoarsely; and he led me to the window.

I looked in. The room, compared with the out door, was rather dark; but against the yellow wall I saw Mrs Oke sitting alone on a couch in her white dress, her head slightly thrown back, a large red rose in her hand.

"Do you believe now?" whispered Oke's voice hot at my ear. "Do you believe now? Was it all my fancy? But I will have him this time. I have locked the door inside, and, by God! he shan't escape."

The words were not out of Oke's mouth. I felt myself struggling with him silently outside that window. But he broke loose, pulled open the window, and leapt into the room, and I after him. As I crossed the threshold, something flashed in my eyes; there was a loud report, a sharp cry, and the thud of a body on the ground.

Oke was standing in the middle of the room, with a faint smoke about him; and at his feet, sunk down from the sofa, with her blond head resting on its seat, lay Mrs Oke, a pool of red forming in her white dress. Her mouth was convulsed, as if in that automatic shriek, but her wide-open white eyes seemed to smile vaguely and distantly.

I know nothing of time. It all seemed to be one second, but a second that lasted hours. Oke stared, then turned round and laughed.

"The damned rascal has given me the slip again!" he cried; and quickly unlocking the door, rushed out of the house with dreadful cries.

That is the end of the story. Oke tried to shoot himself that evening, but merely fractured his jaw, and died a few days later, raving. There were all sorts of legal inquiries, through which I went as through a dream; and whence it resulted that Mr Oke had killed his wife in a fit of momentary madness. That was the end of Alice Oke. By the way, her maid brought me a locket which was found round her neck, all stained with blood. It contained some very dark auburn hair, not at all the colour of William Oke's. I am quite sure it was Lovelock's.

A Wicked Voice

by Vernon Lee

To M.W.,
IN REMEMBRANCE OF THE LAST SONG
AT PALAZZO BARBARO,
Chi ha inteso, intenda.

They have been congratulating me again today upon being the only composer of our days—of these days of deafening orchestral effects and poetical quackery—who has despised the new-fangled nonsense of Wagner, and returned boldly to the traditions of Handel and Gluck and the divine Mozart, to the supremacy of melody and the respect of the human voice.

O cursed human voice, violin of flesh and blood, fashioned with the subtle tools, the cunning hands, of Satan! O execrable art of singing, have you not wrought mischief enough in the past, degrading so much noble genius, corrupting the purity of Mozart, reducing Handel to a writer of high-class singing-exercises, and defrauding the world of the only inspiration worthy of Sophocles and Euripides, the poetry of the great poet Gluck? Is it not enough to have dishonored a whole century in idolatry of that wicked and contemptible wretch the singer, without persecuting an obscure young composer of our days, whose only wealth is his love of nobility in art, and perhaps some few grains of genius?

And then they compliment me upon the perfection with which I imitate the style of the great dead masters; or ask me very seriously whether, even if I could gain over the modern public to this bygone style of music, I could hope to find singers to perform it. Sometimes, when people talk as they have been talking today, and laugh when I declare myself a follower of Wagner, I burst into a paroxysm of unintelligible, childish rage, and exclaim, "We shall see that some day!"

Yes; some day we shall see! For, after all, may I not recover from this strangest of maladies? It is still possible that the day may come when all these things shall seem but an incredible nightmare; the day when *Ogier the Dane* shall be completed, and men shall know whether I am a follower of the great master of the Future or the miserable singing-masters of the Past. I am but half-bewitched, since I am conscious of the spell that binds me. My old nurse, far off in Norway, used to tell me that were-wolves are ordinary men and women half their days, and that if, during that period, they become aware of their horrid transformation they may find the means to forestall it. May this not be the case with me? My reason, after all, is free, although my artistic inspiration be enslaved; and I can despise and loathe the music I am forced to compose, and the execrable power that forces me.

Nay, is it not because I have studied with the doggedness of hatred this corrupt and corrupting music of the Past, seeking for every little peculiarity of style and every biographical trifle merely to display its vileness, is it not for this presumptuous courage that I have been overtaken by such mysterious, incredible vengeance?

And meanwhile, my only relief consists in going over and over again in my mind the tale of my miseries. This time I will write it, writing only to tear up, to throw the manuscript unread into the fire. And yet, who knows? As the last charred pages shall crackle and slowly sink into the red embers, perhaps the spell may be broken, and I may possess once more my long-lost liberty, my vanished genius.

It was a breathless evening under the full moon, that implacable full moon beneath which, even more than beneath the dreamy splendor of noon-tide, Venice seemed to swelter in the midst of the waters, exhaling, like some great lily, mysterious influences, which make the brain swim and the heart faint—a moral malaria, distilled, as I thought, from those languishing melodies, those cooing vocalizations which I had found in the musty music-books of a century ago. I see that moonlight evening as if it were present. I see my fellow-lodgers of that little artists' boarding-house. The table on which they lean after supper is strewn with bits of bread, with napkins rolled in tapestry rollers, spots of wine here and there, and at regular intervals chipped pepper-pots, stands of toothpicks, and heaps of those huge hard peaches which nature imitates from the marble-shops of Pisa. The whole pension-full is assembled, and examining stupidly the engraving which the American etcher has just brought for me, knowing me to be mad about eighteenth century music and musicians, and having noticed, as he turned over the heaps of penny prints in the square of San Polo, that the portrait is that of a singer of those days.

Singer, thing of evil, stupid and wicked slave of the voice, of that instrument which was not invented by the human intellect, but begotten of the body, and which, instead of moving the soul, merely stirs up the dregs of our nature! For what is the voice but the Beast calling, awakening that other Beast sleeping in the depths of mankind, the Beast which all great art has ever sought to chain up, as the archangel chains up, in old pictures, the demon with his woman's face? How could the creature attached to this voice, its owner and its victim, the singer, the great, the real singer who once ruled over every heart, be otherwise than wicked and contemptible? But let me try and get on with my story.

I can see all my fellow-boarders, leaning on the table, contemplating the print, this effeminate beau, his hair curled into *ailes de pigeon*, his sword passed through his embroidered pocket, seated under a triumphal arch somewhere among the clouds, surrounded by puffy Cupids and crowned with laurels by a bouncing goddess of fame. I hear again all the insipid exclamations, the insipid questions about this singer:—"When did he live? Was he very famous? Are you sure, Magnus, that this is really a portrait," &c. &c. And I hear my own voice, as if in the far distance, giving them all sorts of information, biographical and critical, out of a battered little volume called *The Theatre of Musical Glory; or, Opinions upon the most Famous Chapel-masters and Virtuosi of this Century*, by Father Prosdocimo Sabatelli, Barnalite, Professor of Eloquence at the College of Modena, and Member of the Arcadian Academy, under the pastoral name of Evander Lilybaean, Venice, 1785, with the approbation of the Superiors. I tell them all how this singer, this Balthasar Cesari, was nick-named Zaffirino because of a sapphire engraved with cabalistic signs presented to him one evening by a masked stranger, in whom wise folk recognized that great cultivator of the human voice, the devil; how much more wonderful had been this Zaffirino's vocal gifts than those of any singer of ancient or modern times; how his brief life had been but a series of triumphs, petted by the greatest kings, sung by the most famous poets, and finally, adds Father Prosdocimo, "courted (if the grave Muse of history may incline her ear to the gossip of gallantry) by the most charming nymphs, even of the very highest quality."

My friends glance once more at the engraving; more insipid remarks are made; I am requested—especially by the American young ladies—to play or sing one of this Zaffirino's favorite songs—"For of course you know them, dear Maestro Magnus, you who have such a passion for all old music. Do be good, and sit down to the piano." I refuse, rudely enough, rolling the print in my fingers. How fearfully this cursed heat, these cursed moonlight nights, must have unstrung me! This Venice would certainly kill me in the long-run! Why, the sight of this idiotic engraving, the mere name of that coxcomb of a singer, have made my heart beat and my limbs turn to water like a love-sick hobbledehoy.

After my gruff refusal, the company begins to disperse; they prepare to go out, some to have a row on the lagoon, others to saunter before the cafés at St. Mark's; family discussions arise, gruntings of fathers, murmurs of mothers, peals of laughing from young girls and young men. And the moon, pouring in by the wide-open windows, turns this old palace ballroom, nowadays an inn dining-room, into a lagoon, scintillating, undulating like the other lagoon, the real one, which stretches out yonder furrowed by invisible gondolas betrayed by the red prow-lights. At last the whole lot of them are on the move. I shall be able to get some quiet in my room, and to work a little at my opera of *Ogier the Dane*. But no! Conversation revives, and, of all things, about that singer, that Zaffirino, whose absurd portrait I am crunching in my fingers.

The principal speaker is Count Alvise, an old Venetian with dyed whiskers, a great check tie fastened with two pins and a chain; a threadbare patrician who is dying to secure for his lanky son that pretty American girl, whose mother is intoxicated by all his mooning anecdotes about the past glories of Venice in general, and of his illustrious family in particular. Why, in Heaven's name, must he pitch upon Zaffirino for his mooning, this old duffer of a patrician?

"Zaffirino,—ah yes, to be sure! Balthasar Cesari, called Zaffirino," snuffles the voice of Count Alvise, who always repeats the last word of every sentence at least three times. "Yes, Zaffirino, to be sure! A famous singer of the days of my forefathers; yes, of my forefathers, dear lady!" Then a lot of rubbish about the former greatness of Venice, the glories of old music, the former Conservatoires, all mixed up with anecdotes of Rossini and Donizetti, whom he pretends to have known intimately. Finally, a story, of course containing plenty about his illustrious family:—"My great grand-aunt, the Procuratessa Vendramin, from whom we have inherited our estate of Mistrà, on the Brenta"—a hopelessly muddled story, apparently, fully of digressions, but of which that singer Zaffirino is the hero. The narrative, little by little, becomes more intelligible, or perhaps it is I who am giving it more attention.

"It seems," says the Count, "that there was one of his songs in particular which was called the 'Husbands' Air'—*L'Aria dei Marit*—because they didn't enjoy it quite as much as their better-halves... My grand-aunt, Pisana Renier, married to the Procuratore Vendramin, was a patrician of the old school, of the style that was getting rare a hundred years ago. Her virtue and her pride rendered her unapproachable. Zaffirino, on his part, was in the habit of boasting that no woman had ever been able to resist his singing, which, it appears, had its foundation in fact—the ideal changes, my dear lady, the ideal changes a good deal from one century to another!—and that his first song could make any woman turn pale and lower her eyes, the second make her madly in love, while the third song could kill her off on the spot, kill her for love, there under his very eyes, if he only felt inclined. My grand-aunt Vendramin laughed when this story was told her, refused to go to hear this insolent dog, and added that it might be quite possible by the aid of spells and infernal pacts to kill a *gentildonna*, but as to making her fall in love with a lackey—never! This answer was naturally reported to Zaffirino, who piqued himself upon always getting the better of any one who was wanting in deference to his voice. Like the ancient Romans, *parcere subjectis et debellare superbos*. You American ladies, who are so learned, will appreciate this little quotation from the divine Virgil. While seeming to avoid the Procuratessa Vendramin, Zaffirino took the opportunity, one evening at a large assembly, to sing in her presence. He sang and sang and sang until the poor grand-aunt Pisana fell ill for love. The most skilful physicians were kept unable to explain the mysterious malady which was visibly killing the poor young lady; and the Procuratore Vendramin applied in vain to the most venerated Madonnas, and vainly promised an altar of silver, with massive gold candlesticks, to Saints Cosmas and Damian, patrons of the art of healing. At last the brother-in-law of the Procuratessa, Monsignor Almorò Vendramin, Patriarch of Aquileia, a prelate famous for the sanctity of his life, obtained in a vision of Saint Justina, for whom he entertained a particular devotion, the information that the only thing which could benefit the strange illness of his sister-in-law was the voice of Zaffirino. Take notice that my poor grand-aunt had never condescended to such a revelation.

"The Procuratore was enchanted at this happy solution; and his lordship the

Patriarch went to seek Zaffirino in person, and carried him in his own coach to the Villa of Mistrà, where the Procuratessa was residing.

"On being told what was about to happen, my poor grand-aunt went into fits of rage, which were succeeded immediately by equally violent fits of joy. However, she never forgot what was due to her great position. Although sick almost unto death, she had herself arrayed with the greatest pomp, caused her face to be painted, and put on all her diamonds: it would seem as if she were anxious to affirm her full dignity before this singer. Accordingly she received Zaffirino reclining on a sofa which had been placed in the great ballroom of the Villa of Mistrà, and beneath the princely canopy; for the Vendramins, who had intermarried with the house of Mantua, possessed imperial fiefs and were princes of the Holy Roman Empire. Zaffirino saluted her with the most profound respect, but not a word passed between them. Only, the singer inquired from the Procuratore whether the illustrious lady had received the Sacraments of the Church. Being told that the Procuratessa had herself asked to be given extreme unction from the hands of her brother-in-law, he declared his readiness to obey the orders of His Excellency, and sat down at once to the harpsichord.

"Never had he sung so divinely. At the end of the first song the Procuratessa Vendramin had already revived most extraordinarily; by the end of the second she appeared entirely cured and beaming with beauty and happiness; but at the third air—the *Aria dei Mariti*, no doubt—she began to change frightfully; she gave a dreadful cry, and fell into the convulsions of death. In a quarter of an hour she was dead! Zaffirino did not wait to see her die. Having finished his song, he withdrew instantly, took post-horses, and traveled day and night as far as Munich. People remarked that he had presented himself at Mistrà dressed in mourning, although he had mentioned no death among his relatives; also that he had prepared everything for his departure, as if fearing the wrath of so powerful a family. Then there was also the extraordinary question he had asked before beginning to sing, about the Procuratessa having confessed and received extreme unction… No, thanks, my dear lady, no cigarettes for me. But if it does not distress you or your charming daughter, may I humbly beg permission to smoke a cigar?"

And Count Alvise, enchanted with his talent for narrative, and sure of having secured for his son the heart and the dollars of his fair audience, proceeds to light a candle, and at the candle one of those long black Italian cigars which require preliminary disinfection before smoking.

… If this state of things goes on I shall just have to ask the doctor for a bottle; this ridiculous beating of my heart and disgusting cold perspiration have increased steadily during Count Alvise's narrative. To keep myself in countenance among the various idiotic commentaries on this cock-and-bull story of a vocal coxcomb and a vaporing great lady, I begin to unroll the engraving, and to examine stupidly the portrait of Zaffirino, once so renowned, now so forgotten. A ridiculous ass, this singer, under his triumphal arch, with his stuffed Cupids and the great fat winged kitchenmaid crowning him with laurels. How flat and vapid and vulgar it is, to be sure, all this odious eighteenth century!

But he, personally, is not so utterly vapid as I had thought. That effeminate, fat face of his is almost beautiful, with an odd smile, brazen and cruel. I have seen faces like this, if not in real life, at least in my boyish romantic dreams, when I read Swinburne and Baudelaire, the faces of wicked, vindictive women. Oh yes! he is decidedly a beautiful creature, this Zaffirino, and his voice must have had the same sort of beauty and the same expression of wickedness....

"Come on, Magnus," sound the voices of my fellow-boarders, "be a good fellow and sing us one of the old chap's songs; or at least something or other of that day, and we'll make believe it was the air with which he killed that poor lady."

"Oh yes! the *Aria dei Mariti*, the 'Husbands' Air,'" mumbles old Alvise, between the puffs at his impossible black cigar. "My poor grand-aunt, Pisana Vendramin; he went and killed her with those songs of his, with that *Aria dei Mariti*."

I feel senseless rage overcoming me. Is it that horrible palpitation (by the way, there is a Norwegian doctor, my fellow-countryman, at Venice just now) which is sending the blood to my brain and making me mad? The people round the piano, the furniture, everything together seems to get mixed and to turn into moving blobs of colour. I set to singing; the only thing which remains distinct before my eyes being the portrait of Zaffirino, on the edge of that boarding-house piano; the sensual, effeminate face, with its wicked, cynical smile, keeps appearing and disappearing as the print wavers about in the draught that makes the candles smoke and gutter. And I set to singing madly, singing I don't know what. Yes; I begin to identify it: 'tis the *Biondina in Gondoleta*, the only song of the eighteenth century which is still remembered by the Venetian people. I sing it, mimicking every old-school grace; shakes, cadences, languishingly swelled and diminished notes, and adding all manner of buffooneries, until the audience, recovering from its surprise, begins to shake with laughing; until I begin to laugh myself, madly, frantically, between the phrases of the melody, my voice finally smothered in this dull, brutal laughter… And then, to crown it all, I shake my fist at this long-dead singer, looking at me with his wicked woman's face, with his mocking, fatuous smile.

"Ah! you would like to be revenged on me also!" I exclaim. "You would like me to write you nice roulades and flourishes, another nice *Aria dei Mariti*, my fine Zaffirino!"

That night I dreamed a very strange dream. Even in the big half-furnished room the heat and closeness were stifling. The air seemed laden with the scent of all manner of white flowers, faint and heavy in their intolerable sweetness: tuberoses, gardenias, and jasmines drooping I know not where in neglected vases. The moonlight had transformed the marble floor around me into a shallow, shining, pool. On account of the heat I had exchanged my bed for a big old-fashioned sofa of light wood, painted with little nosegays and sprigs, like an old silk; and I lay there, not attempting to sleep, and letting my thoughts go vaguely to my opera of*Ogier the Dane*, of which I had long finished writing the words, and for whose music I had hoped to find some inspiration in this strange Venice, floating, as it were, in the stagnant lagoon of the past. But Venice had merely put all my ideas into hopeless confusion; it was as if there arose out of its shallow waters a miasma of long-dead melodies, which sickened but intoxicated my soul. I lay on my sofa watching that pool of whitish light, which rose higher and higher, little trickles of light meeting it here and there, wherever the moon's rays struck upon some polished surface; while huge shadows waved to and fro in the draught of the open balcony.

I went over and over that old Norse story: how the Paladin, Ogier, one of the knights of Charlemagne, was decoyed during his homeward wanderings from the Holy Land by the arts of an enchantress, the same who had once held in bondage the great Emperor Caesar and given him King Oberon for a son; how Ogier had tarried in that island only one day and one night, and yet, when he came home to his kingdom, he found all changed, his friends dead, his family dethroned, and not a man who knew his face; until at last, driven hither and thither like a beggar, a poor minstrel had taken compassion of his sufferings and given him all he could give—a song, the song of the prowess of a hero dead for hundreds of years, the Paladin Ogier the Dane.

The story of Ogier ran into a dream, as vivid as my waking thoughts had been vague. I was looking no longer at the pool of moonlight spreading round my couch, with its trickles of light and looming, waving shadows, but the frescoed walls of a great saloon. It was not, as I recognized in a second, the dining-room of that Venetian palace now turned into a boarding-house. It was a far larger room, a real ballroom, almost circular in its octagon shape, with eight huge white doors surrounded by stucco moldings, and, high on the vault of the ceiling, eight little galleries or recesses like boxes at a theatre, intended no doubt for musicians and spectators. The place was imperfectly lighted by only one of the eight chandeliers, which revolved slowly, like huge spiders, each on its long cord. But the light struck upon the gilt stuccoes opposite me, and on a large expanse of fresco, the sacrifice of Iphigenia, with Agamemnon and Achilles in Roman helmets, lappets, and knee-breeches. It discovered also one of the oil panels let into the moldings of the roof, a goddess in lemon and lilac draperies, foreshortened over a great green peacock. Round the room, where the light reached, I could make out big yellow satin sofas and heavy gilded consoles; in the shadow of a corner was what looked like a piano, and farther in the shade one of those big canopies which decorate the anterooms of Roman palaces. I looked about me, wondering where I was: a heavy, sweet smell, reminding me of the flavour of a peach, filled the place.

Little by little I began to perceive sounds; little, sharp, metallic, detached notes, like those of a mandolin; and there was united to them a voice, very low and sweet, almost a whisper, which grew and grew and grew, until the whole place was filled with that exquisite vibrating note, of a strange, exotic, unique quality. The note went on, swelling and swelling. Suddenly there was a horrible piercing shriek, and the thud of a body on the floor, and all manner of smothered exclamations. There, close by the canopy, a light suddenly appeared; and I could see, among the dark figures moving to and fro in the room, a woman lying on the ground, surrounded by other women. Her blond hair, tangled, full of diamond-sparkles which cut through the half-darkness, was hanging disheveled; the laces of her bodice had been cut, and her white breast shone among the sheen of jeweled brocade; her face was bent forwards, and a thin white arm trailed, like a broken limb, across the knees of one of the women who were endeavouring to lift her. There was a sudden splash of water against the floor, more confused exclamations, a hoarse, broken moan, and a gurgling, dreadful sound… I awoke with a start and rushed to the window.

Outside, in the blue haze of the moon, the church and belfry of St. George loomed blue and hazy, with the black hull and rigging, the red lights, of a large steamer moored before them. From the lagoon rose a damp sea-breeze. What was it all? Ah! I began to understand: that story of old Count Alvise's, the death of his grand-aunt, Pisana Vendramin. Yes, it was about that I had been dreaming.

I returned to my room; I struck a light, and sat down to my writing-table. Sleep had become impossible. I tried to work at my opera. Once or twice I thought I had got hold of what I had looked for so long… But as soon as I tried to lay hold of my theme, there arose in my mind the distant echo of that voice, of that long note swelled slowly by insensible degrees, that long note whose tone was so strong and so subtle.

There are in the life of an artist moments when, still unable to seize his own inspiration, or even clearly to discern it, he becomes aware of the approach of that long-invoked idea. A mingled joy and terror warn him that before another day, another hour have passed, the inspiration shall have crossed the threshold of his soul and flooded it with its rapture. All day I had felt the need of isolation and quiet, and at nightfall I went for a row on the most solitary part of the lagoon. All things seemed to tell that I was going to meet my inspiration, and I awaited its coming as a lover awaits his beloved.

I had stopped my gondola for a moment, and as I gently swayed to and fro on the water, all paved with moonbeams, it seemed to me that I was on the confines of an imaginary world. It lay close at hand, enveloped in luminous, pale blue mist, through which the moon had cut a wide and glistening path; out to sea, the little islands, like moored black boats, only accentuated the solitude of this region of moonbeams and wavelets; while the hum of the insects in orchards hard by merely added to the impression of untroubled silence. On some such seas, I thought, must the Paladin Ogier, have sailed when about to discover that during that sleep at the enchantress's knees centuries had elapsed and the heroic world had set, and the kingdom of prose had come.

While my gondola rocked stationary on that sea of moonbeams, I pondered over that twilight of the heroic world. In the soft rattle of the water on the hull I seemed to hear the rattle of all that armor, of all those swords swinging rusty on the walls, neglected by the degenerate sons of the great champions of old. I had long been in search of a theme which I called the theme of the 'Prowess of Ogier;' it was to appear from time to time in the course of my opera, to develop at last into that song of the Minstrel, which reveals to the hero that he is one of a long-dead world. And at this moment I seemed to feel the presence of that theme. Yet an instant, and my mind would be overwhelmed by that savage music, heroic, funereal.

Suddenly there came across the lagoon, cleaving, checkering, and fretting the silence with a lacework of sound even as the moon was fretting and cleaving the water, a ripple of music, a voice breaking itself in a shower of little scales and cadences and trills.

I sank back upon my cushions. The vision of heroic days had vanished, and before my closed eyes there seemed to dance multitudes of little stars of light, chasing and interlacing like those sudden vocalizations.

"To shore! Quick!" I cried to the gondolier.

But the sounds had ceased; and there came from the orchards, with their mulberry-trees glistening in the moonlight, and their black swaying cypress-plumes, nothing save the confused hum, the monotonous chirp, of the crickets.

I looked around me: on one side empty dunes, orchards, and meadows, without house or steeple; on the other, the blue and misty sea, empty to where distant islets were profiled black on the horizon.

A faintness overcame me, and I felt myself dissolve. For all of a sudden a second ripple of voice swept over the lagoon, a shower of little notes, which seemed to form a little mocking laugh.

Then again all was still. This silence lasted so long that I fell once more to meditating on my opera. I lay in wait once more for the half-caught theme. But no. It was not that theme for which I was waiting and watching with baited breath. I realized my delusion when, on rounding the point of the Giudecca, the murmur of a voice arose from the midst of the waters, a thread of sound slender as a moonbeam, scarce audible, but exquisite, which expanded slowly, insensibly, taking volume and body, taking flesh almost and fire, an ineffable quality, full, passionate, but veiled, as it were, in a subtle, downy wrapper. The note grew stronger and stronger, and warmer and more passionate, until it burst through that strange and charming veil, and emerged beaming, to break itself in the luminous facets of a wonderful shake, long, superb, triumphant.

There was a dead silence.

"Row to St. Mark's!" I exclaimed. "Quick!"

The gondola glided through the long, glittering track of moonbeams, and rent the great band of yellow, reflected light, mirroring the cupolas of St. Mark's, the lace-like pinnacles of the palace, and the slender pink belfry, which rose from the lit-up water to the pale and bluish evening sky.

In the larger of the two squares the military band was blaring through the last spirals of a *crescendo* of Rossini. The crowd was dispersing in this great open-air ballroom, and the sounds arose which invariably follow upon out-of-door music. A clatter of spoons and glasses, a rustle and grating of frocks and of chairs, and the click of scabbards on the pavement. I pushed my way among the fashionable youths contemplating the ladies while sucking the knob of their sticks; through the serried ranks of respectable families, marching arm in arm with their white frocked young ladies close in front. I took a seat before Florian's, among the customers stretching themselves before departing, and the waiters hurrying to and fro, clattering their empty cups and trays. Two imitation Neapolitans were slipping their guitar and violin under their arm, ready to leave the place.

"Stop!" I cried to them; "don't go yet. Sing me something—sing *La Camesella* or *Funiculì, funiculà*—no matter what, provided you make a row;" and as they screamed and scraped their utmost, I added, "But can't you sing louder, d—n you!—sing louder, do you understand?"

I felt the need of noise, of yells and false notes, of something vulgar and hideous to drive away that ghost-voice which was haunting me.

Again and again I told myself that it had been some silly prank of a romantic amateur, hidden in the gardens of the shore or gliding unperceived on the lagoon; and that the sorcery of moonlight and sea-mist had transfigured for my excited brain mere humdrum roulades out of exercises of Bordogni or Crescentini.

But all the same I continued to be haunted by that voice. My work was interrupted ever and anon by the attempt to catch its imaginary echo; and the heroic harmonies of my Scandinavian legend were strangely interwoven with voluptuous phrases and florid cadences in which I seemed to hear again that same accursed voice.

To be haunted by singing-exercises! It seemed too ridiculous for a man who professedly despised the art of singing. And still, I preferred to believe in that childish amateur, amusing himself with warbling to the moon.

One day, while making these reflections the hundredth time over, my eyes chanced to light upon the portrait of Zaffirino, which my friend had pinned against the wall. I pulled it down and tore it into half a dozen shreds. Then, already ashamed of my folly, I watched the torn pieces float down from the window, wafted hither and thither by the sea-breeze. One scrap got caught in a yellow blind below me; the others fell into the canal, and were speedily lost to sight in the dark water. I was overcome with shame. My heart beat like bursting. What a miserable, unnerved worm I had become in this cursed Venice, with its languishing moonlights, its atmosphere as of some stuffy boudoir, long unused, full of old stuffs and potpourri!

That night, however, things seemed to be going better. I was able to settle down to my opera, and even to work at it. In the intervals my thoughts returned, not without a certain pleasure, to those scattered fragments of the torn engraving fluttering down to the water. I was disturbed at my piano by the hoarse voices and the scraping of violins which rose from one of those music-boats that station at night under the hotels of the Grand Canal. The moon had set. Under my balcony the water stretched black into the distance, its darkness cut by the still darker outlines of the flotilla of gondolas in attendance on the music-boat, where the faces of the singers, and the guitars and violins, gleamed reddish under the unsteady light of the Chinese-lanterns.

"*Jammo, jammo; jammo, jammo jà*," sang the loud, hoarse voices; then a tremendous scrape and twang, and the yelled-out burden, "*Funiculi, funiculà; funiculi, funiculà; jammo, jammo, jammo, jammo, jammo jà.*"

Then came a few cries of "*Bis, Bis!*" from a neighbouring hotel, a brief clapping of hands, the sound of a handful of coppers rattling into the boat, and the oar-stroke of some gondolier making ready to turn away.

"Sing the *Camesella*," ordered some voice with a foreign accent.

"No, no! *Santa Lucia*."

"I want the *Camesella*."

"No! *Santa Lucia*. Hi! Sing *Santa Lucia*—d'you hear?"

The musicians, under their green and yellow and red lamps, held a whispered consultation on the manner of conciliating these contradictory demands. Then, after a minute's hesitation, the violins began the prelude of that once famous air, which has remained popular in Venice—the words written, some hundred years ago, by the patrician Gritti, the music by an unknown composer—*La Biondina in Gondoleta*.

That cursed eighteenth century! It seemed a malignant fatality that made these brutes choose just this piece to interrupt me.

At last the long prelude came to an end; and above the cracked guitars and squeaking fiddles there arose, not the expected nasal chorus, but a single voice singing below its breath.

My arteries throbbed. How well I knew that voice! It was singing, as I have said, below its breath, yet none the less it sufficed to fill all that reach of the canal with its strange quality of tone, exquisite, far-fetched.

They were long-drawn-out notes, of intense but peculiar sweetness, a man's voice which had much of a woman's, but more even of a chorister's, but a chorister's voice without its limpidity and innocence; its youthfulness was veiled, muffled, as it were, in a sort of downy vagueness, as if a passion of tears withheld.

There was a burst of applause, and the old palaces re-echoed with the clapping. "Bravo, bravo! Thank you, thank you! Sing again—please, sing again. Who can it be?"

And then a bumping of hulls, a splashing of oars, and the oaths of gondoliers trying to push each other away, as the red prow-lamps of the gondolas pressed round the gaily lit singing-boat.

But no one stirred on board. It was to none of them that this applause was due. And while every one pressed on, and clapped and vociferated, one little red prow-lamp dropped away from the fleet; for a moment a single gondola stood forth black upon the black water, and then was lost in the night.

For several days the mysterious singer was the universal topic. The people of the music-boat swore that no one besides themselves had been on board, and that they knew as little as ourselves about the owner of that voice. The gondoliers, despite their descent from the spies of the old Republic, were equally unable to furnish any clue. No musical celebrity was known or suspected to be at Venice; and every one agreed that such a singer must be a European celebrity. The strangest thing in this strange business was, that even among those learned in music there was no agreement on the subject of this voice: it was called by all sorts of names and described by all manner of incongruous adjectives; people went so far as to dispute whether the voice belonged to a man or to a woman: every one had some new definition.

In all these musical discussions I, alone, brought forward no opinion. I felt a repugnance, an impossibility almost, of speaking about that voice; and the more or less commonplace conjectures of my friend had the invariable effect of sending me out of the room.

Meanwhile my work was becoming daily more difficult, and I soon passed from utter impotence to a state of inexplicable agitation. Every morning I arose with fine resolutions and grand projects of work; only to go to bed that night without having accomplished anything. I spent hours leaning on my balcony, or wandering through the network of lanes with their ribbon of blue sky, endeavoring vainly to expel the thought of that voice, or endeavouring in reality to reproduce it in my memory; for the more I tried to banish it from my thoughts, the more I grew to thirst for that extraordinary tone, for those mysteriously downy, veiled notes; and no sooner did I make an effort to work at my opera than my head was full of scraps of forgotten eighteenth century airs, of frivolous or languishing little phrases; and I fell to wondering with a bitter-sweet longing how those songs would have sounded if sung by that voice.

At length it became necessary to see a doctor, from whom, however, I carefully hid away all the stranger symptoms of my malady. The air of the lagoons, the great heat, he answered cheerfully, had pulled me down a little; a tonic and a month in the country, with plenty of riding and no work, would make me myself again. That old idler, Count Alvise, who had insisted on accompanying me to the physician's, immediately suggested that I should go and stay with his son, who was boring himself to death superintending the maize harvest on the mainland: he could promise me excellent air, plenty of horses, and all the peaceful surroundings and the delightful occupations of a rural life—"Be sensible, my dear Magnus, and just go quietly to Mistrà."

Mistrà—the name sent a shiver all down me. I was about to decline the invitation, when a thought suddenly loomed vaguely in my mind.

"Yes, dear Count," I answered; "I accept your invitation with gratitude and pleasure. I will start tomorrow for Mistrà."

The next day found me at Padua, on my way to the Villa of Mistrà. It seemed as if I had left an intolerable burden behind me. I was, for the first time since how long, quite light of heart. The tortuous, rough-paved streets, with their empty, gloomy porticoes; the ill-plastered palaces, with closed, discoloured shutters; the little rambling square, with meager trees and stubborn grass; the Venetian garden-houses reflecting their crumbling graces in the muddy canal; the gardens without gates and the gates without gardens, the avenues leading nowhere; and the population of blind and legless beggars, of whining sacristans, which issued as by magic from between the flag-stones and dust-heaps and weeds under the fierce August sun, all this dreariness merely amused and pleased me. My good spirits were heightened by a musical mass which I had the good fortune to hear at St. Anthony's.

Never in all my days had I heard anything comparable, although Italy affords many strange things in the way of sacred music. Into the deep nasal chanting of the priests there had suddenly burst a chorus of children, singing absolutely independent of all time and tune; grunting of priests answered by squealing of boys, slow Gregorian modulation interrupted by jaunty barrel-organ pipings, an insane, insanely merry jumble of bellowing and barking, mewing and cackling and braying, such as would have enlivened a witches' meeting, or rather some mediaeval Feast of Fools. And, to make the grotesqueness of such music still more fantastic and Hoffmannlike, there was, besides, the magnificence of the piles of sculptured marbles and gilded bronzes, the tradition of the musical splendor for which St. Anthony's had been famous in days gone by. I had read in old travelers, Lalande and Burney, that the Republic of St. Mark had squandered immense sums not merely on the monuments and decoration, but on the musical establishment of its great cathedral of Terra Firma. In the midst of this ineffable concert of impossible voices and instruments, I tried to imagine the voice of Guadagni, the soprano for whom Gluck had written *Che faru senza Euridice*, and the fiddle of Tartini, that Tartini with whom the devil had once come and made music. And the delight in anything so absolutely, barbarously, grotesquely, fantastically incongruous as such a performance in such a place was heightened by a sense of profanation: such were the successors of those wonderful musicians of that hated eighteenth century!

The whole thing had delighted me so much, so very much more than the most faultless performance could have done, that I determined to enjoy it once more; and towards vesper-time, after a cheerful dinner with two bagmen at the inn of the Golden Star, and a pipe over the rough sketch of a possible cantata upon the music which the devil made for Tartini, I turned my steps once more towards St. Anthony's.

The bells were ringing for sunset, and a muffled sound of organs seemed to issue from the huge, solitary church; I pushed my way under the heavy leathern curtain, expecting to be greeted by the grotesque performance of that morning.

I proved mistaken. Vespers must long have been over. A smell of stale incense, a crypt-like damp filled my mouth; it was already night in that vast cathedral. Out of the darkness glimmered the votive-lamps of the chapels, throwing wavering lights upon the red polished marble, the gilded railing, and chandeliers, and plaqueing with yellow the muscles of some sculptured figure. In a corner a burning taper put a halo about the head of a priest, burnishing his shining bald skull, his white surplice, and the open book before him. "Amen" he chanted; the book was closed with a snap, the light moved up the apse, some dark figures of women rose from their knees and passed quickly towards the door; a man saying his prayers before a chapel also got up, making a great clatter in dropping his stick.

The church was empty, and I expected every minute to be turned out by the sacristan making his evening round to close the doors. I was leaning against a pillar, looking into the greyness of the great arches, when the organ suddenly burst out into a series of chords, rolling through the echoes of the church: it seemed to be the conclusion of some service. And above the organ rose the notes of a voice; high, soft, enveloped in a kind of downiness, like a cloud of incense, and which ran through the mazes of a long cadence. The voice dropped into silence; with two thundering chords the organ closed in. All was silent. For a moment I stood leaning against one of the pillars of the nave: my hair was clammy, my knees sank beneath me, an enervating heat spread through my body; I tried to breathe more largely, to suck in the sounds with the incense-laden air. I was supremely happy, and yet as if I were dying; then suddenly a chill ran through me, and with it a vague panic. I turned away and hurried out into the open.

The evening sky lay pure and blue along the jagged line of roofs; the bats and swallows were wheeling about; and from the belfries all around, half-drowned by the deep bell of St. Anthony's, jangled the peel of the *Ave Maria*.

"You really don't seem well," young Count Alvise had said the previous evening, as he welcomed me, in the light of a lantern held up by a peasant, in the weedy back-garden of the Villa of Mistrà. Everything had seemed to me like a dream: the jingle of the horse's bells driving in the dark from Padua, as the lantern swept the acacia-hedges with their wide yellow light; the grating of the wheels on the gravel; the supper-table, illumined by a single petroleum lamp for fear of attracting mosquitoes, where a broken old lackey, in an old stable jacket, handed round the dishes among the fumes of onion; Alvise's fat mother gabbling dialect in a shrill, benevolent voice behind the bullfights on her fan; the unshaven village priest, perpetually fidgeting with his glass and foot, and sticking one shoulder up above the other. And now, in the afternoon, I felt as if I had been in this long, rambling, tumble-down Villa of Mistrà—a villa three-quarters of which was given up to the storage of grain and garden tools, or to the exercise of rats, mice, scorpions, and centipedes—all my life; as if I had always sat there, in Count Alvise's study, among the pile of undusted books on agriculture, the sheaves of accounts, the samples of grain and silkworm seed, the ink-stains and the cigar-ends; as if I had never heard of anything save the cereal basis of Italian agriculture, the diseases of maize, the peronospora of the vine, the breeds of bullocks, and the iniquities of farm labourers; with the blue cones of the Euganean hills closing in the green shimmer of plain outside the window.

After an early dinner, again with the screaming gabble of the fat old Countess, the fidgeting and shoulder-raising of the unshaven priest, the smell of fried oil and stewed onions, Count Alvise made me get into the cart beside him, and whirled me along among clouds of dust, between the endless glister of poplars, acacias, and maples, to one of his farms.

In the burning sun some twenty or thirty girls, in coloured skirts, laced bodices, and big straw-hats, were threshing the maize on the big red brick threshing-floor, while others were winnowing the grain in great sieves. Young Alvise III. (the old one was Alvise II.: every one is Alvise, that is to say, Lewis, in that family; the name is on the house, the carts, the barrows, the very pails) picked up the maize, touched it, tasted it, said something to the girls that made them laugh, and something to the head farmer that made him look very glum; and then led me into a huge stable, where some twenty or thirty white bullocks were stamping, switching their tails, hitting their horns against the mangers in the dark. Alvise III. patted each, called him by his name, gave him some salt or a turnip, and explained which was the Mantuan breed, which the Apulian, which the Romagnolo, and so on. Then he bade me jump into the trap, and off we went again through the dust, among the hedges and ditches, till we came to some more brick farm buildings with pinkish roofs smoking against the blue sky. Here there were more young women threshing and winnowing the maize, which made a great golden Danaë cloud; more bullocks stamping and lowing in the cool darkness; more joking, fault-finding, explaining; and thus through five farms, until I seemed to see the rhythmical rising and falling of the flails against the hot sky, the shower of golden grains, the yellow dust from the winnowing-sieves on to the bricks, the switching of innumerable tails and plunging of innumerable horns, the glistening of huge white flanks and foreheads, whenever I closed my eyes.

"A good day's work!" cried Count Alvise, stretching out his long legs with the tight trousers riding up over the Wellington boots. "Mamma, give us some aniseed-syrup after dinner; it is an excellent restorative and precaution against the fevers of this country."

"Oh! you've got fever in this part of the world, have you? Why, your father said the air was so good!"

"Nothing, nothing," soothed the old Countess. "The only thing to be dreaded are mosquitoes; take care to fasten your shutters before lighting the candle."

"Well," rejoined young Alvise, with an effort of conscience, "of course there *are* fevers. But they needn't hurt you. Only, don' go out into the garden at night, if you don't want to catch them. Papa told me that you have fancies for moonlight rambles. It won't do in this climate, my dear fellow; it won't do. If you must stalk about at night, being a genius, take a turn inside the house; you can get quite exercise enough."

After dinner the aniseed-syrup was produced, together with brandy and cigars, and they all sat in the long, narrow, half-furnished room on the first floor; the old Countess knitting a garment of uncertain shape and destination, the priest reading out the newspaper; Count Alvise puffing at his long, crooked cigar, and pulling the ears of a long, lean dog with a suspicion of mange and a stiff eye. From the dark garden outside rose the hum and whirr of countless insects, and the smell of the grapes which hung black against the starlit, blue sky, on the trellis. I went to the balcony. The garden lay dark beneath; against the twinkling horizon stood out the tall poplars. There was the sharp cry of an owl; the barking of a dog; a sudden whiff of warm, enervating perfume, a perfume that made me think of the taste of certain peaches, and suggested white, thick, wax-like petals. I seemed to have smelt that flower once before: it made me feel languid, almost faint.

"I am very tired," I said to Count Alvise. "See how feeble we city folk become!"

But, despite my fatigue, I found it quite impossible to sleep. The night seemed perfectly stifling. I had felt nothing like it at Venice. Despite the injunctions of the Countess I opened the solid wooden shutters, hermetically closed against mosquitoes, and looked out.

The moon had risen; and beneath it lay the big lawns, the rounded tree-tops, bathed in a blue, luminous mist, every leaf glistening and trembling in what seemed a heaving sea of light. Beneath the window was the long trellis, with the white shining piece of pavement under it. It was so bright that I could distinguish the green of the vine-leaves, the dull red of the catalpa-flowers. There was in the air a vague scent of cut grass, of ripe American grapes, of that white flower (it must be white) which made me think of the taste of peaches all melting into the delicious freshness of falling dew. From the village church came the stroke of one: Heaven knows how long I had been vainly attempting to sleep. A shiver ran through me, and my head suddenly filled as with the fumes of some subtle wine; I remembered all those weedy embankments, those canals full of stagnant water, the yellow faces of the peasants; the word malaria returned to my mind. No matter! I remained leaning on the window, with a thirsty longing to plunge myself into this blue moonmist, this dew and perfume and silence, which seemed to vibrate and quiver like the stars that strewed the depths of heaven… What music, even Wagner's, or of that great singer of starry nights, the divine Schumann, what music could ever compare with this great silence, with this great concert of voiceless things that sing within one's soul?

As I made this reflection, a note, high, vibrating, and sweet, rent the silence, which immediately closed around it. I leaned out of the window, my heart beating as though it must burst. After a brief space the silence was cloven once more by that note, as the darkness is cloven by a falling star or a firefly rising slowly like a rocket. But this time it was plain that the voice did not come, as I had imagined, from the garden, but from the house itself, from some corner of this rambling old villa of Mistrà.

Mistrà—Mistrà! The name rang in my ears, and I began at length to grasp its significance, which seems to have escaped me till then. "Yes," I said to myself, "it is quite natural." And with this odd impression of naturalness was mixed a feverish, impatient pleasure. It was as if I had come to Mistrà on purpose, and that I was about to meet the object of my long and weary hopes.

Grasping the lamp with its singed green shade, I gently opened the door and made my way through a series of long passages and of big, empty rooms, in which my steps re-echoed as in a church, and my light disturbed whole swarms of bats. I wandered at random, farther and farther from the inhabited part of the buildings.

This silence made me feel sick; I gasped as under a sudden disappointment.

All of a sudden there came a sound—chords, metallic, sharp, rather like the tone of a mandolin—close to my ear. Yes, quite close: I was separated from the sounds only by a partition. I fumbled for a door; the unsteady light of my lamp was insufficient for my eyes, which were swimming like those of a drunkard. At last I found a latch, and, after a moment's hesitation, I lifted it and gently pushed open the door. At first I could not understand what manner of place I was in. It was dark all round me, but a brilliant light blinded me, a light coming from below and striking the opposite wall. It was as if I had entered a dark box in a half-lighted theatre. I was, in fact, in something of the kind, a sort of dark hole with a high balustrade, half-hidden by an up-drawn curtain. I remembered those little galleries or recesses for the use of musicians or lookers-on—which exist under the ceiling of the ballrooms in certain old Italian palaces. Yes; it must have been one like that. Opposite me was a vaulted ceiling covered with gilt moldings, which framed great time-blackened canvases; and lower down, in the light thrown up from below, stretched a wall covered with faded frescoes. Where had I seen that goddess in lilac and lemon draperies foreshortened over a big, green peacock? For she was familiar to me, and the stucco Tritons also who twisted their tails round her gilded frame. And that fresco, with warriors in Roman cuirasses and green and blue lappets, and knee-breeches—where could I have seen them before? I asked myself these questions without experiencing any surprise. Moreover, I was very calm, as one is calm sometimes in extraordinary dreams—could I be dreaming?

I advanced gently and leaned over the balustrade. My eyes were met at first by the darkness above me, where, like gigantic spiders, the big chandeliers rotated slowly, hanging from the ceiling. Only one of them was lit, and its Murano-glass pendants, its carnations and roses, shone opalescent in the light of the guttering wax. This chandelier lighted up the opposite wall and that piece of ceiling with the goddess and the green peacock; it illumined, but far less well, a corner of the huge room, where, in the shadow of a kind of canopy, a little group of people were crowding round a yellow satin sofa, of the same kind as those that lined the walls. On the sofa, half-screened from me by the surrounding persons, a woman was stretched out: the silver of her embroidered dress and the rays of her diamonds gleamed and shot forth as she moved uneasily. And immediately under the chandelier, in the full light, a man stooped over a harpsichord, his head bent slightly, as if collecting his thoughts before singing.

He struck a few chords and sang. Yes, sure enough, it was the voice, the voice that had so long been persecuting me! I recognized at once that delicate, voluptuous quality, strange, exquisite, sweet beyond words, but lacking all youth and clearness. That passion veiled in tears which had troubled my brain that night on the lagoon, and again on the Grand Canal singing the *Biondina*, and yet again, only two days since, in the deserted cathedral of Padua. But I recognized now what seemed to have been hidden from me till then, that this voice was what I cared most for in all the wide world.

The voice wound and unwound itself in long, languishing phrases, in rich, voluptuous *rifiorituras*, all fretted with tiny scales and exquisite, crisp shakes; it stopped ever and anon, swaying as if panting in languid delight. And I felt my body melt even as wax in the sunshine, and it seemed to me that I too was turning fluid and vaporous, in order to mingle with these sounds as the moonbeams mingle with the dew.

Suddenly, from the dimly lighted corner by the canopy, came a little piteous wail; then another followed, and was lost in the singer's voice. During a long phrase on the harpsichord, sharp and tinkling, the singer turned his head towards the dais, and there came a plaintive little sob. But he, instead of stopping, struck a sharp chord; and with a thread of voice so hushed as to be scarcely audible, slid softly into a long *cadenza*. At the same moment he threw his head backwards, and the light fell full upon the handsome, effeminate face, with its ashy pallor and big, black brows, of the singer Zaffirino. At the sight of that face, sensual and sullen, of that smile which was cruel and mocking like a bad woman's, I understood—I knew not why, by what process—that his singing *must* be cut short, that the accursed phrase *must* never be finished. I understood that I was before an assassin, that he was killing this woman, and killing me also, with his wicked voice.

I rushed down the narrow stair which led down from the box, pursued, as it were, by that exquisite voice, swelling, swelling by insensible degrees. I flung myself on the door which must be that of the big saloon. I could see its light between the panels. I bruised my hands in trying to wrench the latch. The door was fastened tight, and while I was struggling with that locked door I heard the voice swelling, swelling, rending asunder that downy veil which wrapped it, leaping forth clear, resplendent, like the sharp and glittering blade of a knife that seemed to enter deep into my breast. Then, once more, a wail, a death-groan, and that dreadful noise, that hideous gurgle of breath strangled by a rush of blood. And then a long shake, acute, brilliant, triumphant.

The door gave way beneath my weight, one half crashed in. I entered. I was blinded by a flood of blue moonlight. It poured in through four great windows, peaceful and diaphanous, a pale blue mist of moonlight, and turned the huge room into a kind of submarine cave, paved with moonbeams, full of shimmers, of pools of moonlight. It was as bright as at midday, but the brightness was cold, blue, vaporous, supernatural. The room was completely empty, like a great hayloft. Only, there hung from the ceiling the ropes which had once supported a chandelier; and in a corner, among stacks of wood and heaps of Indian-corn, whence spread a sickly smell of damp and mildew, there stood a long, thin harpsichord, with spindle-legs, and its cover cracked from end to end.

I felt, all of a sudden, very calm. The one thing that mattered was the phrase that kept moving in my head, the phrase of that unfinished cadence which I had heard but an instant before. I opened the harpsichord, and my fingers came down boldly upon its keys. A jingle-jangle of broken strings, laughable and dreadful, was the only answer.

Then an extraordinary fear overtook me. I clambered out of one of the windows; I rushed up the garden and wandered through the fields, among the canals and the embankments, until the moon had set and the dawn began to shiver, followed, pursued for ever by that jangle of broken strings.

People expressed much satisfaction at my recovery.

It seems that one dies of those fevers.

Recovery? But have I recovered? I walk, and eat and drink and talk; I can even sleep. I live the life of other living creatures. But I am wasted by a strange and deadly disease. I can never lay hold of my own inspiration. My head is filled with music which is certainly by me, since I have never heard it before, but which still is not my own, which I despise and abhor: little, tripping flourishes and languishing phrases, and long-drawn, echoing cadences.

O wicked, wicked voice, violin of flesh and blood made by the Evil One's hand, may I not even execrate thee in peace; but is it necessary that, at the moment when I curse, the longing to hear thee again should parch my soul like hell-thirst? And since I have satiated thy lust for revenge, since thou hast withered my life and withered my genius, is it not time for pity? May I not hear one note, only one note of thine, O singer, O wicked and contemptible wretch?

The Open Door

by Charlotte Riddell

Some people do not believe in ghosts. For that matter, some people do not believe in anything.

There are persons who even affect incredulity concerning that open door at Ladlow Hall. They say it did not stand wide open—that they could have shut it; that the whole affair was a delusion; that they are sure it must have been a conspiracy; that they are doubtful whether there is such a place as Ladlow on the face of the earth; that the first time they are in Meadowshire they will look it up.

That is the manner in which this story, hitherto unpublished, has been greeted by my acquaintances. How it will be received by strangers is quite another matter. I am going to tell what happened to me exactly as it happened, and readers can credit or scoff at the tale as it pleases them. It is not necessary for me to find faith and comprehension in addition to a ghost story, for the world at large. If such were the case, I should lay down my pen.

Perhaps, before going further, I ought to premise there was a time when I did not believe in ghosts either. If you had asked me one summer's morning years ago when you met me on London Bridge if I held such appearances to be probable or possible, you would have received an emphatic "No" for answer.

But, at this rate, the story of the Open Door will never be told; so we will, with your permission, plunge into it immediately.

"Sandy!"

"What do you want?"

"Should you like to earn a sovereign?"

"Of course I should."

A somewhat curt dialogue, but we were given to curtness in the office of Messrs Frimpton, Frampton, and Fryer, auctioneers and estate agents, St Benet's Hill, City.

(My name is not Sandy or anything like it, but the other clerks so styled me because of a real or fancied likeness to some character, an ill-looking Scotchman, they had seen at the theatre. From this it may be inferred I was not handsome. Far from it. The only ugly specimen in my family, I knew I was very plain; and it chanced to be no secret to me either that I felt grievously discontented with my lot. I did not like the occupation of clerk in an auctioneer's office, and I did not like my employers.

We are all of us inconsistent, I suppose, for it was a shock to me to find they entertained a most cordial antipathy to me.)

"Because," went on Parton, a fellow, my senior by many years—a fellow who delighted in chaffing me, "I can tell you how to lay hands on one."

"How?" I asked, sulkily enough, for I felt he was having what he called his fun.

"You know that place we let to Carrison, the tea-dealer?" Carrison was a merchant in the China trade, possessed of fleets of vessels and towns of warehouses; but I did not correct Parton's expression, I simply nodded.

"He took it on a long lease, and he can't live in it; and our governor said this morning he wouldn't mind giving anybody who could find out what the deuce is the matter, a couple of sovereigns and his travelling expenses."

"Where is the place?" I asked, without turning my head; for the convenience of listening I had put my elbows on the desk and propped up my face with both hands.

"Away down in Meadowshire, in the heart of the grazing country."

"And what is the matter?" I further enquired.

"A door that won't keep shut."

"What?"

"A door that will keep open, if you prefer that way of putting it," said Parton.

"You are jesting."

"If I am, Carrison is not, or Fryer either. Carrison came here in a nice passion, and Fryer was in a fine rage; I could see he was, though he kept his temper outwardly. They have had an active correspondence it appears, and Carrison went away to talk to his lawyer. Won't make much by that move, I fancy."

"But tell me," I entreated, "why the door won't keep shut?"

"They say the place is haunted."

"What nonsense!" I exclaimed.

"Then you are just the person to take the ghost in hand. I thought so while old Fryer was speaking."

"If the door won't keep shut," I remarked, pursuing my own train of thought, "why can't they let it stay open?"

"I have not the slightest idea. I only know there are two sovereigns to be made, and that I give you a present of the information."

And having thus spoken, Parton took down his hat and went out, either upon his own business or that of his employers.

There was one thing I can truly say about our office, we were never serious in it. I fancy that is the case in most offices nowadays; at all events, it was the case in ours. We were always chaffing each other, playing practical jokes, telling stupid stories, scamping our work, looking at the clock, counting the weeks to next St Lubbock's Day, counting the hours to Saturday.

For all that we were all very earnest in our desire to have our salaries raised, and unanimous in the opinion no fellows ever before received such wretched pay. I had twenty pounds a year, which I was aware did not half provide for what I ate at home. My mother and sisters left me in no doubt on the point, and when new clothes were wanted I always hated to mention the fact to my poor worried father.

We had been better off once, I believe, though I never remember the time. My father owned a small property in the country, but owing to the failure of some bank, I never could understand what bank, it had to be mortgaged; then the interest was not paid, and the mortgages foreclosed, and we had nothing left save the half-pay of a major, and about a hundred a year which my mother brought to the common fund.

We might have managed on our income, I think, if we had not been so painfully genteel; but we were always trying to do something quite beyond our means, and consequently debts accumulated, and creditors ruled us with rods of iron.

Before the final smash came, one of my sisters married the younger son of a distinguished family, and even if they had been disposed to live comfortably and sensibly she would have kept her sisters up to the mark. My only brother, too, was an officer, and of course the family thought it necessary he should see we preserved appearances.

It was all a great trial to my father, I think, who had to bear the brunt of the dunning and harass, and eternal shortness of money; and it would have driven me crazy if I had not found a happy refuge when matters were going wrong at home at my aunt's. She was my father's sister, and had married so "dreadfully below her" that my mother refused to acknowledge the relationship at all.

For these reasons and others, Parton's careless words about the two sovereigns stayed in my memory.

I wanted money badly—I may say I never had sixpence in the world of my own—and I thought if I could earn two sovereigns I might buy some trifles I needed for myself, and present my father with a new umbrella. Fancy is a dangerous little jade to flirt with, as I soon discovered.

She led me on and on. First I thought of the two sovereigns; then I recalled the amount of the rent Mr Carrison agreed to pay for Ladlow Hall; then I decided he would gladly give more than two sovereigns if he could only have the ghost turned out of possession. I fancied I might get ten pounds—twenty pounds. I considered the matter all day, and I dreamed of it all night, and when I dressed myself next morning I was determined to speak to Mr Fryer on the subject.

I did so—I told that gentleman Parton had mentioned the matter to me, and that if Mr Fryer had no objection, I should like to try whether I could not solve the mystery. I told him I had been accustomed to lonely houses, and that I should not feel at all nervous; that I did not believe in ghosts, and as for burglars, I was not afraid of them.

"I don't mind your trying," he said at last. "Of course you understand it is no cure, no pay. Stay in the house for a week; if at the end of that time you can keep the door shut, locked, bolted, or nailed up, telegraph for me, and I will go down—if not, come back. If you like to take a companion there is no objection."

I thanked him, but said I would rather not have a companion.

"There is only one thing, sir, I should like," I ventured.

"And that—?" he interrupted.

"Is a little more money. If I lay the ghost, or find out the ghost, I think I ought to have more than two sovereigns."

"How much more do you think you ought to have?" he asked.

His tone quite threw me off my guard, it was so civil and conciliatory, and I answered boldly:

"Well, if Mr Carrison cannot now live in the place perhaps he wouldn't mind giving me a ten-pound note."

Mr Fryer turned, and opened one of the books lying on his desk. He did not look at or refer to it in any war—I saw that.

"You have been with us how long, Edlyd?" he said.

"Eleven months tomorrow," I replied.

"And our arrangement was, I think, quarterly payments, and one month's notice on either side?"

"Yes, sir." I heard my voice tremble, though I could not have said what frightened me.

"Then you will please to take your notice now. Come in before you leave this evening, and I'll pay you three months' salary, and then we shall be quits."

"I don't think I quite understand," I was beginning, when he broke in:

"But I understand, and that's enough. I have had enough of you and your airs, and your indifference, and your insolence here. I never had a clerk I disliked as I do you. Coming and dictating terms, forsooth! No, you shan't go to Ladlow. Many a poor chap"—(he said 'devil')—"would have been glad to earn half a guinea, let alone two sovereigns; and perhaps you may be before you are much older."

"Do you mean that you won't keep me here any longer, sir?" I asked in despair. "I had no intention of offending you. I—"

"Now you need not say another word," he interrupted, "for I won't bandy words with you."

"Since you have been in this place you have never known your position, and you don't seem able to realize it. When I was foolish enough to take you, I did it on the strength of your connections, but your connections have done nothing for me. I have never had a penny out of any one of your friends—if you have any. You'll not do any good in business for yourself or anybody else, and the sooner you go to Australia"—(here he was very emphatic)—and get off these premises, the better I shall be pleased."

I did not answer him—I could not. He had worked himself to a white heat by this time, and evidently intended I should leave his premises then and there. He counted five pounds out of his cash-box, and, writing a receipt, pushed it and the money across the table, and bade me sign and be off at once.

My hand trembled so I could scarcely hold the pen, but I had presence of mind enough left to return one pound ten in gold, and three shillings and fourpence I had, quite by the merest good fortune, in my waistcoat pocket.

"I can't take wages for work I haven't done," I said, as well as sorrow and passion would let me. "Good-morning," and I left his office and passed out among the clerks.

I took from my desk the few articles belonging to me, left the papers it contained in order, and then, locking it, asked Parton if he would be so good as to give the key to Mr Fryer.

"What's up?" he asked "Are you going?"

I said, "Yes, I am going."

"Got the sack?"

"That is exactly what has happened."

"Well, I'm—!" exclaimed Mr Parton.

I did not stop to hear any further commentary on the matter, but bidding my fellow-clerks goodbye, shook the dust of Frimpton's Estate and Agency Office from off my feet.

I did not like to go home and say I was discharged, so I walked about aimlessly, and at length found myself in Regent Street. There I met my father, looking more worried than usual.

"Do you think, Phil," he said (my name is Theophilus), "you could get two or three pounds from your employers?"

Maintaining a discreet silence regarding what had passed, I answered:

"No doubt I could."

"I shall be glad if you will then, my boy," he went on, "for we are badly in want of it."

I did not ask him what was the special trouble. Where would have been the use? There was always something—gas, or water, or poor-rates, or the butcher, or the baker, or the bootmaker.

Well, it did not much matter, for we were well accustomed to the life; but, I thought, "if ever I marry, we will keep within our means." And then there rose up before me a vision of Patty, my cousin—the blithest, prettiest, most useful, most sensible girl that ever made sunshine in poor man's house.

My father and I had parted by this time, and I was still walking aimlessly on, when all at once an idea occurred to me. Mr Fryer had not treated me well or fairly. I would hoist him on his own petard. I would go to headquarters, and try to make terms with Mr Carrison direct.

No sooner thought than done. I hailed a passing omnibus, and was ere long in the heart of the city. Like other great men, Mr Carrison was difficult of access—indeed, so difficult of access, that the clerk to whom I applied for an audience told me plainly I could not see him at all. I might send in my message if I liked, he was good enough to add, and no doubt it would be attended to. I said I should not send in a message, and was then asked what I would do. My answer was simple. I meant to wait till I did see him. I was told they could not have people waiting about the office in this way.

I said I supposed I might stay in the street. "Carrison didn't own that," I suggested.

The clerk advised me not to try that game, or I might get locked up.

I said I would take my chance of it.

After that we went on arguing the question at some length, and we were in the middle of a heated argument, in which several of Carrison's 'young gentlemen', as they called themselves, were good enough to join, when we were all suddenly silenced by a grave-looking individual, who authoritatively enquired:

"What is all this noise about?"

Before anyone could answer I spoke up:

"I want to see Mr Carrison, and they won't let me."

"What do you want with Mr Carrison?"

"I will tell that to himself only."

"Very well, say on—I am Mr Carrison."

For a moment I felt abashed and almost ashamed of my persistency; next instant, however, what Mr Fryer would have called my 'native audacity' came to the rescue, and I said, drawing a step or two nearer to him, and taking off my hat:

"I wanted to speak to you about Ladlow Hall, if you please, sir."

In an instant the fashion of his face changed, a look of irritation succeeded to that of immobility; an angry contraction of the eyebrows disfigured the expression of his countenance.

"Ladlow Hall!" he repeated; "and what have you got to say about Ladlow Hall?"

"That is what I wanted to tell you, sir," I answered, and a dead hush seemed to fall on the office as I spoke.

The silence seemed to attract his attention, for he looked sternly at the clerks, who were not using a pen or moving a finger.

"Come this way, then," he said abruptly; and next minute I was in his private office.

"Now, what is it?" he asked, flinging himself into a chair, and addressing me, who stood hat in hand beside the great table in the middle of the room.

I began—I will say he was a patient listener—at the very beginning, and told my story straight through. I concealed nothing. I enlarged on nothing. A discharged clerk I stood before him, and in the capacity of a discharged clerk I said what I had to say. He heard me to the end, then he sat silent, thinking.

At last he spoke.

"You have heard a great deal of conversation about Ladlow, I suppose?" he remarked.

"No sir; I have heard nothing except what I have told you."

"And why do you desire to strive to solve such a mystery?"

"If there is any money to be made, I should like to make it, sir."

"How old are you?"

"Two-and-twenty last January."

"And how much salary had you at Frimpton's?"

"Twenty pounds a year."

"Humph! More than you are worth, I should say."

"Mr Fryer seemed to imagine so, sir, at any rate," I agreed, sorrowfully.

"But what do you think?" he asked, smiling in spite of himself.

"I think I did quite as much work as the other clerks," I answered.

"That is not saying much, perhaps," he observed. I was of his opinion, but I held my peace.

"You will never make much of a clerk, I am afraid," Mr Garrison proceeded, fitting his disparaging remarks upon me as he might on a lay figure. "You don't like desk work?"

"Not much, sir."

"I should judge the best thing you could do would be to emigrate," he went on, eyeing me critically.

"Mr Fryer said I had better go to Australia or—" I stopped, remembering the alternative that gentleman had presented.

"Or where?" asked Mr Carrison.

"The—, sir" I explained, softly and apologetically.

He laughed—he lay back in his chair and laughed—and I laughed myself, though ruefully.

After all, twenty pounds was twenty pounds, though I had not thought much of the salary till I lost it.

We went on talking for a long time after that; he asked me all about my father and my early life, and how we lived, and where we lived, and the people we knew; and, in fact, put more questions than I can well remember.

"It seems a crazy thing to do," he said at last; "and yet I feel disposed to trust you. The house is standing perfectly empty. I can't live in it, and I can't get rid of it; all my own furniture I have removed, and there is nothing in the place except a few old-fashioned articles belonging to Lord Ladlow. The place is a loss to me. It is of no use trying to let it, and thus, in fact, matters are at a deadlock. You won't be able to find out anything, I know, because, of course, others have tried to solve the mystery ere now; still, if you like to try you may. I will make this bargain with you.

"If you like to go down, I will pay your reasonable expenses for a fortnight; and if you do any good for me, I will give you a ten-pound note for yourself. Of course I must be satisfied that what you have told me is true and that you are what you represent. Do you know anybody in the city who would speak for you?"

I could think of no one but my uncle. I hinted to Mr Carrison he was not grand enough or rich enough, perhaps, but I knew nobody else to whom I could refer him.

"What!" he said, "Robert Dorland, of Cullum Street. He does business with us. If he will go bail for your good behaviour I shan't want any further guarantee. Come along." And to my intense amazement, he rose, put on his hat, walked me across the outer office and along the pavements till we came to Cullum Street.

"Do you know this youth, Mr Dorland?" he said, standing in front of my uncle's desk, and laying a hand on my shoulder.

"Of course I do, Mr Carrison," answered my uncle, a little apprehensively; for, as he told me afterwards, he could not imagine what mischief I had been up to. "He is my nephew."

"And what is your opinion of him—do you think he is a young fellow I may safely trust?"

My uncle smiled, and answered, 'That depends on what you wish to trust him with."

"A long column of addition, for instance."

"It would be safer to give that task to somebody else."

"Oh, uncle!" I remonstrated; for I had really striven to conquer my natural antipathy to figures—worked hard, and every bit of it against the collar.

My uncle got off his stool, and said, standing with his back to the empty fire-grate: "Tell me what you wish the boy to do, Mr Carrison, and I will tell you whether he will suit your purpose or not. I know him, I believe, better than he knows himself."

In an easy, affable way, for so rich a man, Mr Carrison took possession of the vacant stool, and nursing his right leg over his left knee, answered:

"He wants to go and shut the open door at Ladlow for me. Do you think he can do that?"

My uncle looked steadily back at the speaker, and said, "I thought, Mr Carrison, it was quite settled no one could shut it?"

Mr Carrison shifted a little uneasily on his scat, and replied: "I did not set your nephew the task he fancies he would like to undertake."

"Have nothing to do with it, Phil," advised my uncle, shortly.

"You don't believe in ghosts, do you, Mr Dorland?" asked Mr Carrison, with a slight sneer.

"Don't you, Mr Carrison?" retorted my uncle.

There was a pause—an uncomfortable pause—during the course of which I felt the ten pounds, which, in imagination, I had really spent, trembling in the scale. I was not afraid. For ten pounds, or half the money, I would have faced all the inhabitants of spirit land. I longed to tell them so; but something in the way those two men looked at each other stayed my tongue.

"If you ask me the question here in the heart of the city, Mr Dorland," said Mr Carrison, at length, slowly and carefully, "I answer 'No'; but it you were to put it to me on a dark night at Ladlow, I should beg time to consider. I do not believe in supernatural phenomena myself, and yet—the door at Ladlow is as much beyond my comprehension as the ebbing and flowing of the sea."

"And you can't Live at Ladlow?" remarked my uncle.

"I can't live at Ladlow, and what is more, I can't get anyone else to live at Ladlow."

"And you want to get rid of your lease?"

"I want so much to get rid of my lease that I told Fryer I would give him a handsome sum if he could induce anyone to solve the mystery. Is there any other information you desire, Mr Dorland? Because if here is, you have only to ask and have. I feel I am not here in a prosaic office in the city of London, but in the Palace of Truth."

My uncle took no notice of the implied compliment. When wine is good it needs no bush. If a man is habitually honest in his speech and in his thoughts, he desires no recognition of the fact.

"I don't think so," he answered; "it is for the boy to say what he will do. If he be advised by me he will stick to his ordinary work in his employers' office, and leave ghost-hunting and spirit-laying alone."

Mr Carrison shot a rapid glance in my direction, a glance which, implying a secret understanding, might have influenced my uncle could I have stooped to deceive my uncle.

"I can't stick to my work there any longer," I said. "I got my marching orders today."

"What had you been doing, Phil?" asked my uncle.

"I wanted ten pounds to go and lay the ghost!" I answered, so dejectedly, that both Mr Carrison and my uncle broke out laughing.

"Ten pounds!" cried my uncle, almost between laughing and crying. "Why, Phil boy, I had rather, poor man though I am, have given thee ten pounds than that thou should'st go ghost-hunting or ghostlaying."

When he was very much in earnest my uncle went back to thee and thou of his native dialect. I liked the vulgarism, as my mother called it, and I knew my aunt loved to hear him use the caressing words to her. He had risen, not quite from the ranks it is true, but if ever a gentleman came ready born into the world it was Robert Dorland, upon whom at our home everyone seemed to look down.

"What will you do, Edlyd?" asked Mr Carrison; "you hear what your uncle says, 'Give up the enterprise,' and what I say; I do not want either to bribe or force your inclinations."

"I will go, sir," I answered quite steadily. "I am not afraid, and I should like to show you—" I stopped. I had been going to say, "I should like to show you I am not such a fool as you all take me for," but I felt such an address would be too familiar, and refrained.

Mr Carrison looked at me curiously. I think he supplied the end of the sentence for himself, but he only answered:

"I should like you to show me that door fast shut; at any rate, if you can stay in the place alone for a fortnight, you shall have your money."

"I don't like it, Phil," said my uncle: "I don't like this freak at all."

"I am sorry for that, uncle," I answered, "for I mean to go."

"When?" asked Mr Carrison.

"Tomorrow morning," I replied.

"Give him five pounds, Dorland, please, and I will send you my cheque. You will account to me for that sum, you understand," added Mr Garrison, turning to where I stood.

"A sovereign will be quite enough," I said.

"You will take five pounds, and account to me for it," repeated Mr Carrison, firmly; "also, you will write to me every day, to my private address, and if at any moment you feel the thing too much for you, throw it up. Good afternoon," and without more formal leavetaking he departed.

"It is of no use talking to you, Phil, I suppose?" said my uncle.

"I don't think it is," I replied; "you won't say anything to them at home, will you?"

"I am not very likely to meet any of them, am I?" he answered, without a shade of bitterness—merely stating a fact.

"I suppose I shall not see you again before I start," I said, "so I will bid you goodbye now."

"Goodbye, my lad; I wish I could see you a bit wiser and steadier."

I did not answer him; my heart was very full, and my eyes too. I had tried, but office-work was not in me, and I felt it was just as vain to ask me to sit on a stool and pore over writing and figures as to think a person born destitute of musical ability could compose an opera.

Of course I went straight to Patty; though we were not then married, though sometimes it seemed to me as if we never should be married, she was my better half then as she is my better half now.

She did not throw cold water on the project; she did not discourage me. What she said, with her dear face aglow with excitement, was, "I only wish, Phil, I was going with you." Heaven knows, so did I.

Next morning I was up before the milkman. I had told my people overnight I should be going out of town on business. Patty and I settled the whole plan in detail. I was to breakfast and dress there, for I meant to go down to Ladlow in my volunteer garments. That was a subject upon which my poor father and I never could agree; he called volunteering child's play, and other things equally hard to bear; whilst my brother, a very carpet warrior to my mind, was never weary of ridiculing the force, and chaffing me for imagining I was 'a soldier'.

Patty and I had talked matters over, and settled, as I have said, that I should dress at her father's.

A young fellow I knew had won a revolver at a raffle, and willingly lent it to me. With that and my rifle I felt I could conquer an army.

It was a lovely afternoon when I found myself walking through leafy lanes in the heart of Meadowshire. With every vein of my heart I loved the country, and the country was looking its best just then: grass ripe for the mower, grain forming in the ear, rippling streams, dreamy rivers, old orchards, quaint cottages.

"Oh that I had never to go back to London," I thought, for I am one of the few people left on earth who love the country and hate cities. I walked on, I walked a long way, and being uncertain as to my road, asked a gentleman who was slowly riding a powerful roan horse under arching trees—a gentleman accompanied by a young lady mounted on a stiff white pony—my way to Ladlow Hall.

"That is Ladlow Hall," he answered, pointing with his whip over the fence to my left hand. I thanked him and was going on, when he said:

"No one is living there now."

"I am aware of that," I answered.

He did not say anything more, only courteously bade me good-day, and rode off. The young lady inclined her head in acknowledgement of my uplifted cap, and smiled kindly. Altogether I felt pleased, little things always did please me. It was a good beginning—half-way to a good ending!

When I got to the Lodge I showed Mr Garrison's letter to the woman, and received the key.

"You are not going to stop up at the Hall alone, are you, sir?" she asked.

"Yes, I am," I answered, uncompromisingly, so uncompromisingly that she said no more.

The avenue led straight to the house; it was uphill all the way, and bordered by rows of the most magnificent limes I ever beheld. A light iron fence divided the avenue from the park, and between the trunks of the trees I could see the deer browsing and cattle grazing. Ever and anon there came likewise to my ear the sound of a sheep-bell.

It was a long avenue, but at length I stood in front of the Hall—a square, solid-looking, old-fashioned house, three stories high, with no basement; a flight of steps up to the principal entrance; four windows to the right of the door, four windows to the left; the whole building flanked and backed with trees; all the blinds pulled down, a dead silence brooding over the place: the sun westering behind the great trees studding the park. I took all this in as I approached, and afterwards as I stood for a moment under the ample porch; then, remembering the business which had brought me so far, I fitted the great key in the lock, turned the handle, and entered Ladlow Hall.

For a minute—stepping out of the bright sunlight—the place looked to me so dark that I could scarcely distinguish the objects by which I was surrounded; but my eyes soon grew accustomed to the comparative darkness, and I found I was in an immense hall, lighted from the roof, a magnificent old oak staircase conducted to the upper rooms.

The floor was of black and white marble. There were two fireplaces, fitted with dogs for burning wood; around the walls hung pictures, antlers, and horns, and in odd niches and corners stood groups of statues, and the figures of men in complete suits of armour.

To look at the place outside, no one would have expected to find such a hall. I stood lost in amazement and admiration, and then I began to glance more particularly around.

Mr Garrison had not given me any instructions by which to identify the ghostly chamber—-which I concluded would most probably be found on the first floor.

I knew nothing of the story connected with it—if there were a story. On that point I had left London as badly provided with mental as with actual luggage—worse provided, indeed, for a hamper, packed by Patty, and a small bag were coming over from the station; but regarding the mystery I was perfectly unencumbered. I had not the faintest idea in which apartment it resided.

Well, I should discover that, no doubt, for myself ere long.

I looked around me—doors—doors—doors I had never before seen so many doors together all at once. Two of them stood open—one wide, the other slightly ajar.

"I'll just shut them as a beginning," I thought, "before I go upstairs."

The doors were of oak, heavy, well-fitting, furnished with good locks and sound handles. After I had closed I tried them. Yes, they were quite secure. I ascended the great staircase feeling curiously like an intruder, paced the corridors, entered the many bed-chambers—some quite bare of furniture, others containing articles of an ancient fashion, and no doubt of considerable value—chairs, antique dressing- tables, curious wardrobes, and such like. For the most part the doors were closed, and I shut those that stood open before making my way into the attics.

I was greatly delighted with the attics. The windows lighting them did not, as a rule, overlook the front of the Hall, but commanded wide views over wood, and valley, and meadow. Leaning out of one, I could see, that to the right of the

Hall the ground, thickly planted, shelved down to a stream, which came out into the daylight a little distance beyond the plantation, and meandered through the deer park. At the back of the Hall the windows looked out on nothing save a dense wood and a portion of the stable-yard, whilst on the side nearest the point from whence I had come there were spreading gardens surrounded by thick yew hedges, and kitchen-gardens protected by high walls; and further on a farmyard, where I could perceive cows and oxen, and, further still, luxuriant meadows, and fields glad with waving corn.

"What a beautiful place!" I said. "Garrison must have been a duffer to leave it." And then I thought what a great ramshackle house it was for anyone to be in all alone.

Getting heated with my long walk, I suppose, made me feel chilly, for I shivered as I drew my head in from the last dormer window, and prepared to go downstairs again.

In the attics, as in the other parts of the house I had as yet explored, I closed the doors, when there were keys locking them; when there were not, trying them, and in all cases, leaving them securely fastened.

When I reached the ground floor the evening was drawing on apace, and I felt that if I wanted to explore the whole house before dusk I must hurry my proceedings.

"I'll take the kitchens next," I decided, and so made my way to a wilderness of domestic offices lying to the rear of the great hall. Stone passages, great kitchens, an immense servants'-hall, larders, pantries, coal-cellars, beer-cellars, laundries, brewhouses, housekeeper's room—it was not of any use lingering over these details. The mystery that troubled Mr Garrison could scarcely lodge amongst cinders and empty bottles, and there did not seem much else left in this part of the building.

I would go through the living-rooms, and then decide as to the apartments I should occupy myself.

The evening shadows were drawing on apace, so I hurried back into the hall, feeling it was a weird position to be there all alone with those ghostly hollow figures of men in armour, and the statues on which the moon's beams must fall so coldly. I would just look through the lower apartments and then kindle a fire. I had seen quantities of wood in a cupboard close at hand, and felt that beside a blazing hearth, and after a good cup of tea, I should not feel the solitary sensation which was oppressing me.

The sun had sunk below the horizon by this time, for to reach Ladlow I had been obliged to travel by cross lines of railway, and wait besides for such trains as condescended to carry third-class passengers; but there was still light enough in the hail to see all objects distinctly. With my own eyes I saw that one of the doors I had shut with my own hands was standing wide!

I turned to the door on the other side of the hall. It was as I had left it—closed. This, then, was the room—this with the open door. For a second I stood appalled; I think I was fairly frightened.

That did not last long, however. There lay the work I had desired to undertake, the foe I had offered to fight; so without more ado I shut the door and tried it.

"Now I will walk to the end of the hall and see what happens," I considered. I did so. I walked to the foot of the grand staircase and back again, and looked.

The door stood wide open.

I went into the room, after just a spasm of irresolution—went in and pulled up the blinds: a good-sized room, twenty by twenty (I knew, because I paced it afterwards), lighted by two long windows.

The floor, of polished oak, was partially covered with a Turkey carpet. There were two recesses beside the fireplace, one fitted up as a bookcase, the other with an old and elaborately caned cabinet. I was astonished also to find a bedstead in an apartment so little retired from the traffic of the house; and there were also some chairs of an obsolete make, covered, so far as I could make out, with faded tapestry. Beside the bedstead, which stood against the wall opposite to the door, I perceived another door. It was fast locked, the only locked door I had as yet met with in the interior of the house. It was a dreary, gloomy room: the dark panelled walls; the black, shining floor; the windows high from the ground; the antique furniture; the dull four-poster bedstead, with dingy velvet curtains; the gaping chimney; the silk counterpane that looked like a pall.

"Any crime might have been committed in such a room," I thought pettishly; and then I looked at the door critically.

Someone had been at the trouble of fitting bolts upon it, for when I passed out I not merely shut the door securely, but bolted it as well.

"I will go and get some wood, and then look at it again," I soliloquized. When I came back it stood wide open once more.

"Stay open, then!" I cried in a fury. "I won't trouble myself any more with you tonight!"

Almost as I spoke the words, there came a ring at the front door. Echoing through the desolate house, the peal in the then state of my nerves startled me beyond expression.

It was only the man who had agreed to bring over my traps. I bade him lay them down in the hall, and, while looking out some small silver, asked where the nearest post-office was to be found. Not far from the park gates, he said; if I wanted any letter sent, he would drop it in the box for me; the mail-cart picked up the bag at ten o'clock.

I had nothing ready to post then, and told him so. Perhaps the money I gave was more than he expected, or perhaps the dreariness of my position impressed him as it had impressed me, for he paused with his hand on the lock, and asked:

"Are you going to stop here all alone, master?"

"All alone," I answercd, with such cheerfulness as was possible under the circumstances.

"That's the room, you know," he said, nodding in the direction of the open door, and dropping his voice to a whisper.

"Yes, I know," I replied.

"What you've been trying to shut it already, have you? Well, you are a game one!" And with this complementary if not very respectful comment he hastened out of the house. Evidently he had no intention of proffering his services towards the solution of the mystery.

I cast one glance at the door—it stood wide open. Through the windows I had left bare to the night, moonlight was beginning to stream cold and silvery. Before I did aught else I felt I must write to Mr Carrison and Patty, so straightway I hurried to one of the great tables in the hall, and lighting a candle my thoughtful link girl had provided, with many other things, sat down and dashed off the two epistles.

Then down the long avenue, with its mysterious lights and shades, with the moonbeams glinting here and there, playing at hide-and-seek round the boles of the trees and through the tracery of quivering leaf and stem, I walked as fast as if I were doing a match against time.

It was delicious, the scent of the summer odours, the smell of the earth; if it had not been for the door I should have felt too happy. As it was—"Look here, Phil," I said, all of a sudden; "life's not child's play, as uncle truly remarks. That door is just the trouble you have now to face, and you must face it! But for that door you would never have been here. I hope you are not going to turn coward the very first night. Courage!—that is your enemy—conquer it."

"I will try," my other self answered back. "I can but try. I can but fail."

The post-office was at Ladlow Hollow, a little hamlet through which the stream I had remarked dawdling on its way across the park flowed swiftly, spanned by an ancient bridge.

As I stood by the door of the little shop, asking some questions of the postmistress, the same gentleman I had met in the afternoon mounted on his roan horse, passed on foot. He wished me goodnight as he went by, and nodded familiarly to my companion, who curtseyed her acknowledgements.

"His lordship ages fast," she remarked, following the retreating figure with her eyes.

"His lordship," I repeated. "Of whom are you speaking?"

"Of Lord Ladlow," she said.

"Oh! I have never seen him," I answered, puzzled.

"Why, that was Lord Ladlow!" she exclaimed.

You may be sure I had something to think about as I walked back to the Hall—something beside the moonlight and the sweet night-scents, and the rustle of beast and bird and leaf, that make silence seem more eloquent than noise away down in the heart of the country.

Lord Ladlow! My word, I thought he was hundreds, thousands of miles away; and here I find him—he walking in the opposite direction from his own home—I an inmate of his desolate abode. Hi!—What was that? I heard a noise in a shrubbery close at hand, and in an instant I was in the thick of the underwood. Something shot out and darted into the cover of the further plantation. I followed, but I could catch never a glimpse of it. I did not know the lie of the ground sufficiently to course with success, and I had at length to give up the hunt—heated, baffled, and annoyed.

When I got into the house the moon's beams were streaming down upon the hall; I could see every statue, every square of marble, every piece of armour. For all the world it seemed to me like something in a dream; but I was tired and sleepy, and decided I would not trouble about fire or food, or the open door, till the next morning: I would go to sleep.

With this intention I picked up some of my traps and carried them to a room on the first floor I had selected as small and habitable. I went down for the rest, and this time chanced to lay my hand on my rifle.

It was wet. I touched the floor—it was wet likewise.

I never felt anything like the thrill of delight which shot through me. I had to deal with flesh and blood, and I would deal with it, heaven helping me.

The next morning broke clear and bright. I was up with the lark—had washed, dressed, breakfasted, explored the house before the postman came with my letters.

One from Mr Carrison, one from Patty, and one from my uncle: I gave the man half a crown, I was so delighted, and said I was afraid my being at the Hall would cause him some additional trouble.

"No, sir," he answered, profuse in his expressions of gratitude; "I pass here every morning on my way to her ladyship's."

"Who is her ladyship?" I asked.

"The Dowager Lady Ladlow,' he answered—"the old lord's widow."

"And where is her place?" I persisted.

"If you keep on through the shrubbery and across the waterfall, you come to the house about a quarter of a mile further up the stream."

He departed, after telling me there was only one post a day; and I hurried back to the room in which I had breakfasted, carrying my letters with me.

I opened Mr Carrison's first. The gist of it was, "Spare no expense; if you run short of money telegraph for it."

I opened my uncle's next. He implored me to return; he had always thought me hair-brained, but he felt a deep interest in and affection for me, and thought he could get me a good berth if I would only try to settle down and promise to stick to my work. The last was from Patty. O Patty, God bless you! Such women, I fancy, the men who fight best in battle, who stick last to a sinking ship, who are firm in life's struggles, who are brave to resist temptation, must have known and loved. I can't tell you more about the letter, except that it gave me strength to go on to the end.

I spent the forenoon considering that door. I looked at it from within and from without. I eyed it critically. I tried whether there was any reason why it should fly open, and I found that so long as I remained on the threshold it remained closed; if I walked even so far away as the opposite side of the hall, it swung wide.

Do what I would, it burst from latch and bolt. I could not lock it because there was no key.

Well, before two o'clock I confess I was baffled.

At two there came a visitor—none other than Lord Ladlow himself. Sorely I wanted to take his horse round to the stables, but he would not hear of it.

"Walk beside me across the park, if you will be so kind," he said; "I want to speak to you."

We went together across the park, and before we parted I felt I could have gone through fire and water for this simple-spoken nobleman.

"You must not stay here ignorant of the rumours which are afloat," he said. "Of course, when I let the place to Mr Carrison I knew nothing of the open door."

"Did you not, sir?—my lord, I mean," I stammered.

He smiled. 'Do not trouble yourself about my title, which, indeed, carries a very empty state with it, but talk to me as you might to a friend. I had no idea there was any ghost story connected with the Hall, or I should have kept the place empty."

I did not exactly know what to answer, so I remained silent.

"How did you chance to be sent here?" he asked, after a pause.

I told him. When the first shock was over, a lord did not seem very different from anybody else. If an emperor had taken a morning canter across the park, I might, supposing him equally affable, have spoken as familiarly to him as to Lord Ladlow. My mother always said I entirely lacked the bump of veneration! Beginning at the beginning, I repeated the whole story, from Parton's remark about the sovereign to Mr Carrison's conversation with my uncle. When I had left London behind in the narrative, however, and arrived at the Hall, I became somewhat more reticent. After all, it was his Hall people could not live in—his door that would not keep shut; and it seemed to me these were facts he might dislike being forced upon his attention.

But he would have it. What had I seen? What did I think of the matter? Very honestly I told him I did not know what to say. The door certainly would not remain shut, and there seemed no human agency to account for its persistent opening; but then, on the other hand, ghosts generally did not tamper with firearms, and my rifle, though not loaded, had been tampered with—I was sure of that.

My companion listened attentively. "You are not frightened, are you?" he enquired at length.

"Not now," I answered. "The door did give me a start last evening, but I am not afraid of that since I find someone else is afraid of a bullet."

He did not answer for a minute; then he said:

"The theory people have set up about the open door is this: As in that room my uncle was murdered, they say the door will never remain shut till the murderer is discovered."

"Murdered!" I did not like the word at all; it made me feel chill and uncomfortable.

"Yes—he was murdered sitting in his chair, and the assassin has never been discovered. At first many persons inclined to the belief that I killed him; indeed, many are of that opinion still."

"But you did not, sir—there is not a word of truth in that story, is there?"

He laid his hand on my shoulder as he said:

"No, my lad; not a word. I loved the old man tenderly. Even when he disinherited me for the sake of his young wife, I was sorry, but not angry; and when he sent for me and assured me he had resolved to repair that wrong, I tried to induce him to leave the lady a handsome sum in addition to her jointure. 'If you do not, people may think she has not been the source of happiness you expected,' I added.

"Thank you, Hal," he said. "You are a good fellow; we will talk further about this tomorrow."

And then he bade me goodnight.

"Before morning broke—it was in the summer two years ago—the household was aroused by a fearful scream. It was his death-cry. He had been stabbed from behind in the neck. He was seated in his chair writing—writing a letter to me. But for that I might have found it harder to clear myself than was in the case; for his solicitors came forward and said he had signed a will leaving all his personalty to me—he was very rich—unconditionally, only three days previously. That, of course, supplied the motive, as my lady's lawyer put it. She was very vindictive, spared no expense in trying to prove my guilt, and said openly she would never rest till she saw justice done, if it cost her the whole of her fortune. The letter lying before the dead man, over which blood had spurted, she declared must have been placed on his table by me; but the coroner saw there was an animus in this, for the few opening lines stated my uncle's desire to confide in me his reasons for changing his will—reasons, he said, that involved his honour, as they had destroyed his peace. 'In the statement you will find sealed up with my will in—' At that point he was dealt his death-blow. The papers were never found, and the will was never proved. My lady put in the former will, leaving her everything. Ill as I could afford to go to law, I was obliged to dispute the matter, and the lawyers are at it still, and very likely will continue at it for years.

When I lost my good name, I lost my good health, and had to go abroad; and while I was away Mr Carrison took the Hall. Till I returned, I never heard a word about the open door. My solicitor said Mr Carrison was behaving badly; but I think now I must see them or him, and consider what can be done in the affair. As for yourself, it is of vital importance to me that this mystery should be cleared up, and if you are really not timid, stay on. I am too poor to make rash promises, but you won't find me ungrateful."

"Oh, my lord!" I cried—the address slipped quite easily and naturally off my tongue—"I don't want any more money or anything, if I can only show Patty's father I am good for something—"

"Who is Patty?" he asked.

He read the answer in my face, for he said no more.

"Should you like to have a good dog for company?" he enquired after a pause.

I hesitated; then I said:

"No, thank you. I would rather watch and hunt for myself."

And as I spoke, the remembrance of that 'something' in the shrubbery recurred to me, and I told him I thought there had been someone about the place the previous evening.

"Poachers," he suggested; but I shook my head.

"A girl or a woman I imagine. However, I think a dog might hamper me."

He went away, and I returned to the house. I never left it all day. I did not go into the garden, or the stable-yard, or the shrubbery, or anywhere; I devoted myself solely and exclusively to that door.

If I shut it once, I shut it a hundred times, and always with the same result. Do what I would, it swung wide. Never, however, when I was looking at it. So long as I could endure to remain, it stayed shut— the instant I turned my back, it stood open.

About four o'clock I had another visitor; no other than Lord Ladlow's daughter—the Honourable Beatrice, riding her funny little white pony.

She was a beautiful girl of fifteen or thereabouts, and she had the sweetest smile you ever saw.

"Papa sent me with this," she said; "he would not trust any other messenger," and she put a piece of paper in my hand.

"Keep your food under lock and key; buy what you require yourself. Get your water from the pump in the stable-yard. I am going from home; but if you want anything, go or send to my daughter."

"Any answer?" she asked, patting her pony's neck.

"Tell his lordship, if you please, I will 'keep my powder dry!'" I replied.

"You have made papa look so happy,' she said, still patting that fortunate pony.

"If it is in my power, I will make him look happier still, Miss—' and I hesitated, not knowing how to address her.

"Call me Beatrice,' she said, with an enchanting grace; then added, slily, "Papa promises me I shall be introduced to Patty ere long," and before I could recover from my astonishment, she had tightened the bit and was turning across the park.

"One moment, please," I cried. "You can do something for me."

"What is it?" and she came back, trotting over the great sweep in front of the house.

"Lend me your pony for a minute.'

She was off before I could even offer to help her alight—off, and gathering up her habit dexterously with one hand, led the docile old sheep forward with the other.

I took the bridle—when I was with horses I felt amongst my own kind—stroked the pony, pulled his ears, and let him thrust his nose into my hand.

Miss Beatrice is a countess now, and a happy wife and mother; but I sometimes see her, and the other night she took me carefully into a conservatory and asked:

"Do you remember Toddy, Mr Edlyd?"

"Remember him!" I exclaimed; "I can never forget him!"

"He is dead!" she told me, and there were tears in her beautiful eyes as she spoke the words.

"Mr Edlyd, I loved Toddy!"

Well, I took Toddy up to the house, and under the third window to the right hand. He was a docile creature, and let me stand on the saddle while I looked into the only room in Ladlow Hall I had been unable to enter.

It was perfectly bare of furniture, there was not a thing in it—not a chair or table, not a picture on the walls, or ornament on the chimney-piece.

"That is where my grand-uncle's valet slept," said Miss Beatrice. "It was he who first ran in to help him the night he was murdered."

"Where is the valet?" I asked.

"Dead," she answered. "The shock killed him. He loved his master more than he loved himself."

I had seen all I wished, so I jumped off the saddle, which I had carefully dusted with a branch plucked from a lilac tree; between jest and earnest pressed the hem of Miss Beatrice's habit to my lips as I arranged its folds; saw her wave her hand as she went at a hand-gallop across the park; and then turned back once again into the lonely house, with the determination to solve the mystery attached to it or die in the attempt.

Why, I cannot explain, but before I went to bed that night I drove a gimlet I found in the stables hard into the floor, and said to the door:

"Now I am keeping you open."

When I went down in the morning the door was close shut, and the handle of the gimlet, broken off short, lying in the hall.

I put my hand to wipe my forehead; it was dripping with perspiration. I did not know what to make of the place at all! I went out into the open air for a few minutes; when I returned the door again stood wide.

If I were to pursue in detail the days and nights that followed, I should weary my readers. I can only say they changed my life. The solitude, the solemnity, the mystery, produced an effect I do not profess to understand, but that I cannot regret.

I have hesitated about writing of the end, but it must come, so let me hasten to it.

Though feeling convinced that no human agency did or could keep the door open, I was certain that some living person had means of access to the house which I could not discover. This was made apparent in trifles which might well have escaped unnoticed had several, or even two people occupied the mansion, but that in my solitary position it was impossible to overlook. A chair would be misplaced, for instance; a path would be visible over a dusty floor; my papers I found were moved; my clothes touched—letters I carried about with me, and kept under my pillow at night; still, the fact remained that when I went to the post-office, and while I was asleep, someone did wander over the house. On Lord Ladlow's return I meant to ask him for some further particulars of his uncle's death, and I was about to write to Mr Carrison and beg permission to have the door where the valet had slept broken open, when one morning, very early indeed, I spied a hairpin lying close beside it.

What an idiot I had been! If I wanted to solve the mystery of the open door, of course I must keep watch in the room itself. The door would not stay wide unless there was a reason for it, and most certainly a hairpin could not have got into the house without assistance.

I made up my mind what I should do—that I would go to the post early, and take up my position about the hour I had hitherto started for Ladlow Hollow.

I felt on the eve of a discovery, and longed for the day to pass, that the night might come.

It was a lovely morning; the weather had been exquisite during the whole week, and I flung the hall-door wide to let in the sunshine and the breeze. As I did so, I saw there was a basket on the top step—a basket filled with rare and beautiful fruit and flowers.

Mr Carrison had let off the gardens attached to Ladlow Hall for the season—he thought he might as well save something out of the fire, he said, so my fare had not been varied with delicacies of that kind. I was very fond of fruit in those days, and seeing a card addressed to me, I instantly selected a tempting peach, and ate it a little greedily perhaps.

I might say I had barely swallowed the last morsel, when Lord Ladlow's caution recurred to me. The fruit had a curious flavour—there was a strange taste hanging about my palate. For a moment, sky, trees and park swam before my eyes; then I made up my mind what to do.

I smelt the fruit—it had all the same faint odour; then I put some in my pocket—took the basket and locked it away—walked round to the farmyard—asked for the loan of a horse that was generally driven in a light cart, and in less than half an hour was asking in Ladlow to be directed to a doctor.

Rather cross at being disturbed so early, he was at first inclined to pooh-pooh my idea; but I made him cut open a pear and satisfy himself the fruit had been tampered with.

"It is fortunate you stopped at the first peach," he remarked, after giving me a draught, and some medicine to take back, and advising me to keep in the open air as much as possible. "I should like to retain this fruit and see you again tomorrow."

We did not think then on how many morrows we should see each other!

Riding across to Ladlow, the postman had given me three letters, but I did not read them till I was seated under a great tree in the park, with a basin of milk and a piece of bread beside me.

Hitherto, there had been nothing exciting in my correspondence. Patty's epistles were always delightful, but they could not be regarded as sensational; and about Mr Carrison's there was a monotony I had begun to find tedious. On this occasion, however, no fault could be found on that score. The contents of his letter greatly surprised me. He said Lord Ladlow had released him from his bargain—that I could, therefore, leave the Hall at once. He enclosed me ten pounds, and said he would consider how he could best advance my interests; and that I had better call upon him at his private house when I returned to London.

'I do not think I shall leave Ladlow yet awhile,' I considered, as I replaced his letter in its envelope. 'Before I go I should like to make it hot for whoever sent me that fruit; so unless Lord Ladlow turns me out I'll stay a little longer.'

Lord Ladlow did not wish me to leave. The third letter was from him.

'I shall return home tomorrow night,' he wrote, 'and see you on Wednesday. I have arranged satisfactorily with Mr Carrison, and as the Hall is my own again, I mean to try to solve the mystery it contains myself. If you choose to stop and help me to do so, you would confer a favour, and I will try to make it worth your while.'

'I will keep watch tonight, and see if I cannot give you some news tomorrow,' I thought. And then I opened Patty's letter—the best, dearest, sweetest letter any postman in all the world could have brought me.

If it had not been for what Lord Ladlow said about his sharing my undertaking, I should not have chosen that night for my vigil. I felt ill and languid—fancy, no doubt, to a great degree inducing these sensations. I had lost energy in a most unaccountable manner. The long, lonely days had told upon my spirits—the fidgety feeling which took me a hundred times in the twelve hours to look upon the open door, to close it, and to count how many steps I could take before it opened again, had tried my mental strength as a perpetual blister might have worn away my physical. In no sense was I fit for the task I had set myself, and yet I determined to go through with it. Why had I never before decided to watch in that mysterious chamber? Had I been at the bottom of my heart afraid? In the bravest of us there are depths of cowardice that lurk unsuspected till they engulf our courage.

The day wore on—the long, dreary day; evening approached—the night shadows closed over the Hall. The moon would not rise for a couple of hours more. Everything was still as death. The house had never before seemed to me so silent and so deserted.

I took a light, and went up to my accustomed room, moving about for a time as though preparing for bed; then I extinguished the candle, softly opened the door, turned the key, and put it in my pocket, slipped softly downstairs, across the hail, through the open door. Then I knew I had been afraid, for I felt a thrill of terror as in the dark I stepped over the threshold. I paused and listened—there was not a sound—the night was still and sultry, as though a storm were brewing.

Not a leaf seemed moving—the very mice remained in their holes! Noiselessly I made my way to the other side of the room. There was an old-fashioned easy-chair between the bookshelves and the bed; I sat down in it, shrouded by the heavy curtain.

The hours passed—were ever hours so long? The moon rose, came and looked in at the windows, and then sailed away to the west; but not a sound, no, not even the cry of a bird. I seemed to myself a mere collection of nerves. Every part of my body appeared twitching. It was agony to remain still; the desire to move became a form of torture. Ah! A streak in the sky; morning at last, Heaven be praised! Had ever anyone before so welcomed the dawn? A thrush began to sing—was there ever heard such delightful music? It was the morning twilight, soon the sun would rise; soon that awful vigil would be over, and yet I was no nearer the mystery than before. Hush! what was that? It had come. After the hours of watching and waiting; after the long night and the long suspense, it came in a moment.

The locked door opened—so suddenly, so silently, that I had barely time to draw back behind the curtain, before I saw a woman in the room. She went straight across to the other door and closed it, securing it as I saw with bolt and lock. Then just glancing around, she made her way to the cabinet, and with a key she produced shot back the wards. I did not stir, I scarcely breathed, and yet she seemed uneasy. Whatever she wanted to do she evidently was in haste to finish, for she took out the drawers one by one, and placed them on the floor; then, as the light grew better, I saw her first kneel on the floor, and peer into every aperture, and subsequently repeat the same process, standing on a chair she drew forward for the purpose. A slight, lithe woman, not a lady, clad all in black—not a bit of white about her. What on earth could she want? In a moment it flashed upon me—*the will and the letter! She is searching for them.*

I sprang from my concealment—I had her in my grasp; but she tore herself out of my hands, fighting like a wild-cat: she hit, scratched, kicked, shifting her body as though she had not a bone in it, and at last slipped herself free, and ran wildly towards the door by which she had entered.

If she reached it, she would escape me. I rushed across the room and just caught her dress as she was on the threshold. My blood was up, and I dragged her back: she had the strength of twenty devils, I think, and struggled as surely no woman ever did before.

"I do not want to kill you," I managed to say in gasps, "but I will if you do not keep quiet."

"Bah!" she cried; and before I knew what she was doing she had the revolver out of my pocket and fired.

She missed: the ball just glanced off my sleeve. I fell upon her—I can use no other expression, for it had become a fight for life, and no man can tell the ferocity there is in him till he is placed as I was then—fell upon her, and seized the weapon. She would not let it go, but I held her so tight she could not use it. She bit my face; with her disengaged hand she tore my hair. She turned and twisted and slipped about like a snake, but I did not feel pain or anything except a deadly horror lest my strength should give out.

Could I hold out much longer? She made one desperate plunge, I felt the grasp with which I held her slackening; she felt it too, and seizing her advantage tore herself free, and at the same instant fired again blindly, and again missed.

Suddenly there came a look of horror into her eyes—a frozen expression of fear.

"See!" she cried; and flinging the revolver at me, fled.

I saw, as in a momentary flash, that the door I had beheld locked stood wide—that there stood beside the table an awful figure, with uplifted hand—and then I saw no more. I was struck at last; as she threw the revolver at me she must have pulled the trigger, for I felt something like red-hot iron enter my shoulder, and I could but rush from the room before I fell senseless on the marble pavement of the ball.

When the postman came that morning, finding no one stirring, be looked through one of the long windows that flanked the door; then he ran to the farmyard and called for help.

"There is something wrong inside," be cried. "That young gentleman is lying on the floor in a pool of blood."

As they rushed round to the front of the house they saw Lord Ladlow riding up the avenue, and breathlessly told him what had happened.

"Smash in one of the windows," be said; "and go instantly for a doctor."

They laid me on the bed in that terrible room, and telegraphed for my father. For long I hovered between life and death, but at length I recovered sufficiently to be removed to the house Lord Ladlow owned on the other side of the Hollow.

Before that time I had told him all I knew, and begged him to make instant search for the will.

"Break up the cabinet if necessary," I entreated, "I am sure the papers are there."

And they were. His lordship got his own, and as to the scandal and the crime, one was hushed up and the other remained unpunished. The dowager and her maid went abroad the very morning I lay on the marble pavement at Ladlow Hall—they never returned.

My lord made that one condition of his silence.

Not in Meadowshire, but in a fairer county still, I have a farm which I manage, and make both ends meet comfortably.

Patty is the best wife any man ever possessed—and I—well, I am just as happy if a trifle more serious than of old; but there are times when a great horror of darkness seems to fall upon me, and at such periods I cannot endure to be left alone.

Vaila

by M. P. Shiel

— E caddi come l'uome cui sonno piglia —
Dante.

A good many years ago, a young man, student in Paris, I was informally associated with the great Corot, and eye-witnessed by his side several of those cases of mind-malady, in the analysis of which he was a past master. I remember one little girl of the Marais, who, till the age of nine, in no way seemed to differ from her playmates. But one night, lying a-bed, she whispered into her mother's ear: "Maman, can you not hear the sound of the world?" It appears that her recently-begun study of geography had taught her that the earth flies, with an enormous velocity, on an orbit about the sun; and that sound of the world to which she referred was a faint (quite subjective) musical humming, like a shell-murmur, heard in the silence of night, and attributed by her fancy to the song of this high motion. Within six months the excess of lunacy possessed her.

I mentioned the incident to my friend, Haco Harfager, then occupying with me the solitude of an old place in S. Germain, shut in by a shrubbery and high wall from the street. He listened with singular interest, and for a day seemed wrapped in gloom.

Another case which I detailed produced a profound impression upon my friend. A young man, a toy-maker of S. Antoine, suffering from chronic congenital phthisis, attained in the ordinary way his twenty-fifth year. He was frugal, industrious, self-involved. On a winter's evening, returning to his lonely garret, he happened to purchase one of those vehemently factious sheets which circulate by night, like things of darkness, over the Boulevards. This simple act was the herald of his doom. He lay a-bed, and perused the feuille. He had never been a reader; knew little of the greater world, and the deep hum of its travail. But the next night he bought another leaf.

Gradually he acquired interest in politics, the large movements, the roar of life. And this interest grew absorbing. Till late into the night, and every night, he lay poring over the furious mendacity, the turbulent wind, the printed passion. He would awake tired, spitting blood, but intense in spirit—and straightway purchased a morning leaf. His being lent itself to a retrograde evolution. The more his teeth gnashed, the less they ate. He became sloven, irregular at work, turning on his bed through the day. Rags overtook him. As the greater interest, and the vaster tumult, possessed his frail soul, so every lesser interest, tumult, died to him. There came an early day when he no longer cared for his own life; and another day, when his maniac fingers rent the hairs from his head.

As to this man, the great Corot said to me:

"Really, one does not know whether to laugh or weep over such a business. Observe, for one thing, how diversely men are made! Their are minds precisely so sensitive as a cupful of melted silver; every breath will roughen and darken them: and what of the simoon, tornado? And that is not a metaphor hut a simile. For such, this earth—I had almost said this universe—is clearly no fit habitation, but a Machine of Death, a baleful Vast. Too horrible to many is the running shriek of Being—they cannot bear the world. Let each look well to his own little whisk of life, say I, and leave the big fiery Automaton alone. Here in this poor toy-maker you have a case of the ear: it is only the neurosis, Oxyecoia. Splendid was that Greek myth of the Harpies: by them was this man snatched—or, say, caught by a limb in the wheels of the universe, and so perished. It is quite a grand exit, you know—translation in a chariot of flame. Only remember that the member first involved was the pinna: he bent ear to the howl of Europe, and ended by himself howling.

Can a straw ride composedly on the primeval whirlwinds? Between chaos and our shoes wobbles, I tell you, the thinnest film! I knew a man who had this peculiarity of aural hyperæsthesia: that every sound brought him minute information of the matter causing the sound; that is to say, he had an ear bearing to the normal ear the relation which the spectroscope bears to the telescope. A rod, for instance, of mixed copper and iron impinging, in his hearing, upon a rod of mixed tin and lead, conveyed to him not merely the proportion of each metal in each rod, but some strange knowledge of the essential meaning and spirit, as it were, of copper, of iron, of tin, and of lead. Of course, he went mad; but, beforehand, told me this singular thing:

That precisely such a sense as his was, according to his certain intuition, employed by the Supreme Being in his permeation of space to apprehend the nature and movements of mind and matter. And he went on to add that Sin—what we call sin—is only the movement of matter or mind into such places, or in such a way, as to give offence or pain to this delicate diplacusis (so I must call it) of the Creator; so that the 'Law' of Revelation became, in his eyes, edicts promulgated by their Maker merely in self-protection from aural pain; and divine punishment for, say murder, nothing more than retaliation for unease caused to the divine aural consciousness by the matter in a particular dirk or bullet lodged, at a particular moment, in a non-intended place! Him, too, I say, did the Harpies whisk aloft."

My recital of these cases to my friend, Harfager, I have mentioned. I was surprised, not so much at his acute interest—for he was interested in all knowledge—as at the obvious pains which he took to conceal that interest. He hurriedly turned the leaves of a volume, but could not hide his panting nostrils.

From first days when we happened to attend the same seminary in Stockholm, a tacit intimacy had sprung between us. I loved him greatly; that he so loved me I knew. But it was an intimacy not accompanied by many of the usual interchanges of close friendships. Harfager was the shyest, most isolated, insulated, of beings. Though our joint ménage (brought about by a chance meeting at a midnight séance in Paris) had now lasted some months, I knew nothing of his plans, motives. Through the day we pursued our intense readings together, he rapt quite back into the past, I equally engrossed upon the present; late at night we reclined on couches within the vast cave of an old fireplace Louis Onze, and smoked to the dying flame in a silence of wormwood and terebinth. Occasionally a soirée or lecture might draw me from the house; except once, I never understood that Harfager left it. I was, on that occasion, returning home at a point of the Rue St. Honoré where a rush of continuous traffic rattled over the old coarse pavements retained there, when I came suddenly upon him. In this tumult he stood abstracted on the trottoir in a listening attitude, and for a moment seemed not to recognise me when I touched him.

Even as a boy I had discerned in my friend the genuine Noble, the inveterate patrician. One saw that in him. Not at all that his personality gave an impression of any species of loftiness, opulence; on the contrary. He did, however, give an impression of incalculable ancientness. He suggested the last moment of an æon. No nobleman have I seen who so bore in his wan aspect the assurance of the inevitable aristocrat, the essential prince, whose pale blossom is of yesterday, and will perish tomorrow, but whose root fills the ages. This much I knew of Harfager; also that on one or other of the bleak islands of his patrimony north of Zetland lived his mother and a paternal aunt; that he was somewhat deaf; but liable to transports of pain or delight at variously-combined musical sounds, the creak of a door, the note of a bird. More I cannot say that I then knew.

He was rather below the middle height, and gave some promise of stoutness. His nose rose highly aquiline from that species of forehead called by phrenologists 'the musical,' that is to say, flanked by temples which incline outward to the cheek-bones, making breadth for the base of the brain; while the direction of the heavy-lidded, faded-blue eyes, and of the eyebrows, was a downward droop from the nose of their outer extremities. He wore a thin chin-beard. But the astonishing feature of his face were the ears: they were nearly circular, very small, and flat, being devoid of that outer volution known as the helix. The two tiny discs of cartilage had always the effect of making me think of the little ancient round shields, without rims, called clipeus and peltè. I came to understand that this was a peculiarity which had subsisted among the members of his race for some centuries. Over the whole white face of my friend was stamped a look of woeful inability, utter gravity of sorrow. One said 'Sardanapalus,' frail last of the great line of Nimrod.

After a year I found it necessary to mention to Harfager my intention of leaving Paris. We reclined by night in our accustomed nooks within the fireplace. To my announcement he answered with a merely polite "Indeed!" and continued to gloat upon the flame; but after an hour turned upon me, and said:

"Well, it seems to be a hard and selfish world."

Truisms uttered with just such an air of new discovery I had occasionally heard from him; but the earnest gaze of eyes, and plaint of voice, and despondency of shaken head, with which he now spoke shocked me to surprise.

"À propos of what?" I asked.

"My friend, do not leave me!"

He spread his arms. His utterance choked.

I learned that he was the object of a devilish malice; that he was the prey of a hellish temptation. That a lure, a becking hand, a lurking lust, which it was the effort of his life to eschew (and to which he was especially liable in solitude), continually enticed him; and that thus it had been almost from the day when, at time age of five, he had been sent by his father from his desolate home in time sea.

And whose was this malice?

He told me his mother's and aunt's.

And what was this temptation?

He said it was the temptation to return—to fly with the very frenzy of longing—back to that dim home.

I asked with what motives, and in what particulars, the malice of his mother and aunt manifested itself. He replied that there was, he believed, no specific motive, but only a determined malevolence, involuntary and fated; and that the respect in which it manifested itself was to be found in the multiplied prayers and commands with which, for years, they had importuned him to seek again the far hold of his ancestors.

All this I could in no way comprehend, and plainly said as much. In what consisted this horrible magnetism, and equally horrible peril, of his home? To this question Harfager did not reply, but rose from his seat, disappeared behind the drawn curtains of the hearth, and left the room. He presently returned with a quarto tome bound in hide. It proved to be Hugh Gascoigne's Chronicle of Norse Families, executed in English black-letter. The passage to which he pointed I read as follows:

> *'Nowe, of thise two brethrene, tholder (the elder), Harold, beying of seemely personage and prowesse, did goe pilgrimage into Danemarke, wher from he repayred againward hoom to Hjaltlande (Zetland), and wyth hym fette (fetched) the amiabil Thronda for hyss wyf, which was a doughter of the sank (blood) royall of danemark. And his yonger brothir, Sweyne, that was sad amid debonayre, but far surmounted the other in cunnying, receyued him with all good chere. Butte eftsones (soon after) fel sweyne sick for alle his lust that he hadde of Thronda his brothir's wyfe. And whiles the worthy Harold, with the grenehede (greenness) and foyle of yowthe, ministred a bisy cure aboute the bedde wher*

Sweyne lay sick, lo, sweyne fastened on him a violent stroke with swerde, and with no lenger taryinge enclosed his hands in bondes, and cast him in the botme of a depe holde. And by cause harold wold not benumb (deprive) hymself of the gouernance of Thronda his wif, Sweyne cutte off boeth his ere[s], and putte out one of his iyes, and after diverse sike tormentes was preste (ready) to slee (slay) hym. But on a daye, the valiant Harold, breking hys bondcs, and embracinge his aduersary, did by the sleight of wrastlyng ouerthrowe him, and escaped. Nat-with- standyng, he foltred whan he came to the Somburgh Hed not ferre (far) fro the Castell, and al-be-it that he was swifte-foote, couth ne farder renne (run) by reson that he was faynte with the longe plag[u]es of hyss brothir. And whiles he ther lay in a sound (swoon) did Sweyne come sle (sly) and softe up on hym, and whan he had striken him with a darte, caste him fro Samburgh Hede in to the See.

'Nat longe hereafterward did the lady Thronda (tho she knew nat the manere of her lordes deth, ne, veryly, yf he was dead or on live) receyve Sweyne in to gree (favour), and with grete gaudying and blowinge of beamous (trumpets) did gon to his bed. And right soo they two wente thennes (thence) to soiourn in ferre partes.

'Now, it befel that sweyne was myndede by a dreme to let bild him a grete maunsion in Hialtland for the hoom-cominge of the ladye Thronda; where for he called to hym a cunninge Maistre-worckman, and sente him hye (in haste) to englond to gather thrals for the bilding of this lusty Houss, but hym-self soiourned wyth his ladye at Rome. Thenne came his worckman to London, but passinge thennes to Hialtland, was drent (drowned) he, and his feers (mates), and his shippe, alle and some. And after two yeres, which was the tyme assygned, Sweyne harfager sente lettres to Hialtlande to vnderstonde how his grete Houss did, for he knew not the drenchynge of the Architecte; and eftsones he receiued answer that the Houss did wel, and was bildinge on the Ile of Vaila; but that ne was the Ile wher-on Sweyne had appoynted the bilding to be; and he was aferd, and nere fel doun ded for drede, by cause that, in the lettres, he saw before him the mannere of wrytyng of his brothir Harold. And he sayed in this fourme: 'Surely Harolde is on lyue (alive), elles (else) ben thise a lettres writ with gostlye hande.' And he was wo many dayes, seeing that this was a dedely stroke. Ther-after, he took him-selfe back to Hjalt-land to know how the matere was, and ther the old Castell on Somburgh Hede was brek doun to the erthe. Thenn Sweyne was wode-worthe, and cryed, 'Jhesu mercy, where is al the grete Hous of my faders

becomen? allas! thys wycked day of desteynye.' And one of the peple tolde him that a hoost of worckmen fro fer partes hadde brek it doun. And he sayd:

'who hath bidde them?' but that couth none answer. Thenne he sayd agayn; 'nis (is not) my brothir harold on-lyne? for I haue biholde his writinge'; and that, to, colde none answer. Soo he wente to Vaila, and saw there a grete Houss stonde, and wharm he looked on hyt, he saye[d]: 'this, sooth, was y-bild by my brothir Harolde, be he ded, or bee he on-lyue.' And ther he dwelte, and his ladye, and his sones and hys sones sones vntyl nowe. For that the Houss is rewthelesse (ruthless) and withoute pite; where-for tis seyed that up on al who dwel thcre faleth a wycked madncss and a lecherous agonie; and that by waye of the eres doe they drinck the cuppe of the furie of the erelesse Harolde, til the tyme of the Houss bee ended.'

I read the narrative half-aloud, and smiled.

"This, Harfager," I said, "is very tolerable romance on the part of the good Gascoigne; but has the look of indifferent history."

"It is, nevertheless, genuine history," he replied. "You believe that?"

"The house still stands solidly on Vaila."

"The brothers Sweyn and Harold were literary for their age, I think?"

"No member of my race," he replied, with, a suspicion of hauteur, "has been illiterate. "But, at least, you do not believe that mediæval ghosts superintend the building of their family mansions?"

"Gascoignc nowhere says that; for to be stabbed is not necessarily to die; nor, if he did say it, would it he true to assert that I have any knowledge on the subject."

"And what, Harfager, is the nature of that 'wicked madness,' that 'lecherous agonie,' of which Gascoigne speaks?"

"Do you ask me?" He spread his arms. "What do I know? I know nothing! I was banished from the place at the age of five. Yet the cry of it still reverberates in my soul. And have I not told you of agonies—even within myself—of inherited longing and loathing…"

But, at any rate, I answered, my journey to Heidelberg was just then indispensable. I would compromise by making absence short, and rejoin him quickly, if he would wait a few weeks for me. His moody silence I took to mean consent, and soon afterward left him.

But I was unavoidably detained; and when I returned to our old quarters, found them empty.

Harfager had vanished.

It was only after twelve years that a letter was forwarded me—a rather wild letter, an excessively long one—in the well-remembered hand of my friend. It was dated at Vaila. From the character of the writing I conjectured that it had been penned with furious haste, so that I was all the more astonished at the very trivial nature of the voluminous contents. On the first half page he spoke of our old friendship, and asked if, in memory of that, I would see his mother who was dying; the rest of the epistle, sheet upon sheet, consisted of a tedious analysis of his mother's genealogical tree, the apparent aim being to prove that she was a genuine Harfager, and a cousin of his father. He then went on to comment on the extreme prolificness of his race, asserting that since the fourteenth century, over four millions of its members had lived and died in various parts of the world; three only of them, he believed, being now left. That determined, the letter ended.

Influenced by this communication, I travelled northward; reached Caithness; passed the stormy Orkneys; reached Lerwick; and from Unst, the most bleak and northerly of the Zetlands, contrived, by dint of bribes to pit the weather-worthiness of a lug-sailed 'sixern' (said to be identical with the 'langschips' of the Vikings) against a flowing sea and a darkly-brooding heaven. The voyage, I was warned, was, at such a time, of some risk. It was the Cimmerian December of those interboreal latitudes. The weather here, they said, though never cold, is hardly ever other than tempestuous. A dense and dank sea-born haze now lay, in spite of vapid breezes, high along the waters enclosing the boat in a vague domed cavern of doleful twilight and sullen swell. The region of the considerable islands was past, and there was a spectral something in the unreal aspect of silent sea and sunless dismalness of sky which produced upon my nerves the impression of a voyage out of nature, a cruise beyond the world. Occasionally, however, we careered past one of those solitary 'skerries,' or sea-stacks, whose craggy sea-walls, cannonaded and disintegrated by the inter-shock of the tidal wave and the torrent currents of the German Ocean, wore, even at some distance, an appearance of frightful ruin and havoc. Three only of these I saw, for before the dim day had well run half its course, sudden blackness of night was upon us, and with it one of those tempests, of which the winter of this semi-polar sea is, throughout, an ever-varying succession. During the haggard and dolorous crepuscule of the next brief day, the rain did not cease; but before darkness had quite supervened, my helmsman, who talked continuously to a mate of seal-maidens, and waterhorses, and grulies, paused to point to a mound of gloomier grey in the weather-bow, which was, he assured me, Vaila.

Vaila, he added, was the centre of quite a system of those rösts (dangerous eddies) and cross-currents, which the action of the tidal wave hurls hurrying with complicated and corroding swirl among the islands; in the neighbourhood of Vaila, said the mariner, they hurtled with more than usual precipitancy, owing to the palisade of lofty sea-crags which barbicaned the place about; approach was, therefore, at all times difficult, and by night fool-hardy. With a running sea, however, we came sufficiently near to discern the mane of surf which bristled high along the beetling coast-wall. Its shock, according to the man's account, had oft-times more than all the efficiency of a bombing of real artillery, slinging tons of rock to heights of several hundred feet upon the main island.

When the sun next feebly climbed above the horizon to totter with marred visage through a wan low segment of funereal murk, we had closely approached the coast; and it was then for the first time that the impression of some spinning motion in the island (born no doubt of the circular movement of the water) was produced upon me. We effected a landing at a small voe, or sea-arm, on the western side; the eastern, though the point of my aim, being, on account of the swell, out of the question for that purpose. Here I found in two feal-thatched skeoes (or sheds), which crouched beneath the shelter of a far over-hanging hill, five or six poor peasant-seamen, whose livelihood no doubt consisted in periodically trading for the necessaries of the great house on the east. Beside these there were no dwellers on Vaila; but with one of them for guide, I soon began the ascent and transit of the island. Through the night in the boat I had been strangely aware of an oppressive booming in the ears, for which even the roar of the sea round all the coast seemed quite insufficient to account. This now, as we advanced, became fearfully intensified, and with it, once more, the unaccountable conviction within me of spinning motions to which I have referred. Vaila I discovered to be a land of hill and precipice, made of fine granite and flaggy gneiss; at about the centre, however, we came upon a high table-land sloping gradually from west to east, and covered by a series of lochs, which sullenly and continuously flowed one into the other. To this chain of sombre, black-gleaming water I could see no terminating shore, and by dint of shouting to my companion, and bending close ear to his answering shout, I came to know that there was no such shore: I say shout, for nothing less could have prevailed over the steady bellowing as of ten thousand bisons, which now resounded on every hand. A certain tremblement, too, of the earth became distinct. In vain did the eye seek in its dreary purview a single trace of tree or shrub; for, as a matter of course, no kind of vegetation, save peat, could brave, even for a day, that perennial agony of the tempest which makes of this turbid and benighted zone its arena. Darkness, an hour after noon, commenced to overshadow us; and it was shortly afterward that my guide, pointing down a precipitous defile near the eastern coast, hurriedly set forth upon the way he had come. I frantically howled a question after him as he went; but at this point the human voice had ceased to be in the faintest degree audible.

Down this defile, with a sinking of the heart, and a most singular feeling of giddiness, I passed.

Having reached the end, I emerged upon a wide ledge which shuddered to the immediate onsets of the sea. But all this portion of the island was, in addition, subject to a sharp continuous ague evidently not due to the heavy ordnance of the ocean. Hugging a point of cliff for steadiness from the wind, I looked forth upon a spectacle of weirdly morne, of dismal wildness. The opening lines of Hecuba, or some drear district of the Inferno, seemed realized before me. Three black 'skerries,' encompassed by a fantastic series of stacks, crooked as a witch's fore-finger, and giving herbergage to shrill routs of osprey and scart, to seal and walrus, lay at some fathoms' distance; and from its race and rage among them, the sea, in arrogance of white, tumultuous, but inaudible wrath, ramped terrible as an army with banners toward the land. Leaving my place, I staggered some distance to the left: and now, all at once, a vast amphitheatre opened before me, and there burst upon my gaze a panorama of such heart-appalling sublimity, as imagination could never have conceived, nor can now utterly recall.

"A vast amphitheatre" I have said; yet it was rather the shape of a round-Gothic (or Norman) doorway which I beheld. Let the reader picture such a door-frame, nearly a mile in breadth, laid flat upon the ground, the curved portion farthest from the sea; and round it let a perfectly smooth and even wall of rock tower in perpendicular regularity to an altitude not unworthy the vulture's eyrie; and now, down the depth of this Gothic shape, and over all its extent, let bawling oceans dash themselves triumphing in spendthrift cataclysm of emerald and hoary fury,—and the stupor of awe with which I looked, and then the shrinking fear, and then the instinct of instant flight, will find easy comprehension.

This was the thrilling disemboguement of the lochs of Vaila.

And within the arch of this Gothic cataract, volumed in the world of its smoky torment and far-excursive spray, stood a palace of brass... circular in shape... huge in dimension.

The last gleam of the ineffectual day had now almost passed, but I could yet discern, in spite of the perpetual rain-fall which bleakly nimbused it as in a halo of tears, that the building was low in proportion to the vastness of its circumference; that it was roofed with a shallow dome; and that about it ran two serried rows of shuttered Norman windows, the upper row being of smaller size than the lower. Certain indications led me to assume that the house had been built upon a vast natural bed of rock which lay, circular and detached, within the arch of the cataract; but this did not quite emerge above the flood, for the whole ground-area upon which I looked dashed a deep and incense-reeking river to the beachless sea; so that passage would have been impossible, were it not that, from a point near me, a massive bridge, thick with algæ, rose above the tide, and led to the mansion. Descending from my ledge, I passed along it, now drenched in spray. As I came nearer, I could see that the house, too, was to half its height more thickly bearded than an old hull with barnacles and every variety of brilliant seaweed; and—what was very surprising that from many points near the top of the brazen wall huge iron chains, slimily barbarous with the trailing tresses of ages, reached out in symmetrical divergent rays to points on the ground hidden by the flood: the fabric had thus the look of a many-anchored ark; but without pausing for minute observation, I pushed forward, and dashing through the smooth circular waterfall which poured all round from the eaves, by one of its many small projecting porches, entered the dwelling.

Darkness now was around me—and sound. I seemed to stand in the very throat of some yelling planet. An infinite sadness descended upon me; I was near to the abandonment of tears. "Here," I said, "is Kohreb, and the limits of weeping; not elsewhere is the valley of sighing." The tumult resembled the continuous volleying of many thousands of cannon, mingled with strange crashing and bursting uproars. I passed forward through a succession of halls, and was wondering as to my further course, when a hideous figure, bearing a lamp, stalked rapidly towards me. I shrank aghast. It seemed the skeleton of a tall man, wrapped in a winding-sheet. The glitter of a tiny eye, however, and a sere film of skin over part of the face, quickly reassured me. Of ears, he showed no sign. He was, I afterwards learned, Aith; and the singularity of his appearance was partially explained by his pretence—whether true or false—that he had once suffered burning, almost to the cinder-stage, but had miraculously recovered. With an expression of malignity, and strange excited gestures, he led the way to a chamber on the upper stage, where having struck light to a vesta, he pointed to a spread table and left me.

For a long time I sat in solitude. The earthquake of the mansion was intense; but all sense seemed swallowed up and confounded in the one impression of sound. Water, water, was the world—nightmare on my chest, a horror in my ears, an intolerable tingling on my nerves. The feeling of being infinitely drowned and ruined in the all-obliterating deluge—the impulse to gasp for breath—overwhelmed me. I rose and paced; but suddenly stopped, angry, I scarce knew why, with myself. I had, in fact, found myself walking with a certain hurry, not usual with me, not natural to me. The feeling of giddiness, too, had abnormally increased. I forced myself to stand and take note of the hall. It was of great size, and damp with mists, so that the tattered, but rich, mediæval furniture seemed lost in its extent: its center was occupied by a broad low marble tomb bearing the name of a Harfager of the fifteenth century; its walls were old brown panels of oak.

Having drearily observed these things, I waited on with an intolerable consciousness of loneliness; but a little after midnight the tapestry parted, and Harfager with hurried stride, approached me.

In twelve years my friend had grown old. He showed, it is true, a tendency to corpulence; yet, to a knowing eye, he was, in reality, tabid, ill-nourished. And his neck protruded from his body; and his lower back had quite the forward curve of age; and his hair floated about his face and shoulders in a disarray of awful whiteness. A chin-beard hung grey to his chest. His attire was a simple robe of bauge, which, as he went, waved aflaunt from his bare and hirsute shins, and he was shod in those soft slippers called rivlins.

To my surprise, he spoke. When I passionately shouted that I could gather no fragment of sound from his moving lips, he clapped both palms to his ears, and thereupon renewed a vehement siege to mine: but again without result. And now, with a seemingly angry fling of the hand, he caught up the taper, and swiftly strode from the chamber.

There was something singularly unnatural in his manner—something which irresistibly reminded me of the skeleton, Aith: an excess of zeal, a fever, a rage, a loudness, an eagerness of walk, a wild extravagance of gesture. His hand constantly dashed the hair-whiffs from his face.

Though his countenance was of the saffron of death, the eyes were turgid and red with blood—heavy-lidded eyes, fixed in a downward and sideward intentness of gaze. He presently returned with a folio of ivory and a stylus of graphite hanging from a cord about his garment.

He rapidly wrote a petition that I would, if not too tired, take part with him in the funeral obsequies of his mother. I shouted assent.

Once more he clapped palms to ears; then wrote: "Do not shout: no whisper in any part of the building is inaudible to me."

I remembered that, in early life, he had seemed slightly deaf.

We passed together through many apartments, he shading the taper with his hand. This was necessary; for, as I quickly discovered, in no part of the shivering fabric was the air in a state of rest, but seemed for ever commoved by a curious agitation, a faint windiness, like the echo of a storm, which communicated a gentle universal trouble to the tapestries. Everywhere I was confronted with the same past richness, present raggedness of decay. In many of the chambers were old marble tombs; one was a museum piled with bronzes, urns; but broken, imbedded in fungoids, dripping wide with moisture. It was as if the mansion, in ardour of travail, sweated. An odour of decomposition was heavy on the swaying air. With difficulty I followed Harfager through the labyrinth of his headlong passage. Once only he stopped short, and with face madly wild above the glare of the light, heaved up his hand, and uttered a single word. From the shaping of the lips, I conjectured the word, "Hark!"

Presently we entered a very long black hall wherein, on chairs beside a bed near the centre, rested a deep coffin, flanked by a row of tall candlesticks of ebony. It had, I noticed, this singularity, that the foot-piece was absent, so that the soles of the corpse were visible as we approached. I beheld, too, three upright rods secured to the coffin-side, each fitted at its summit with a small silver bell of the kind called morrice pendent from a flexible steel spring. At the head of the bed, Aith, with an appearance of irascibility, stamped to and fro within a small area.

Harfager, having rapidly traversed the apartment to the coffin, deposited the taper upon a stone table near, and stood poring with crazy intentness upon the body. I too, looking, stood. Death so rigorous, Gorgon, I had not seen. The coffin seemed full of tangled grey hair. The lady was, it was clear, of great age, osseous, scimitar-nosed. Her head shook with solemn continuity to the vibration of the house. From each ear trickled a black streamlet; the mouth was ridged with froth.

I observed that over the corpse had been set three thin laminæ of polished wood, resembling in position, and shape, the bridge of a violin. Their sides fitted into groves in the coffin-sides, and their top was of a shape to exactly fit the inclination of the two coffin-lids when closed. One of these laminæ passed over the knees of the dead lady; another bridged the abdomen; the third the region of the neck. In each of them was a small circular hole. Across each of the three holes passed vertically a tense cord from the morrice-bell nearest to it; the three holes being thus divided by the three cords into six vertical semicircles. Before I could conjecture the significance of this arrangement, Harfager closed the folding coffin-lid, which in the centre had tiny intervals for the passage of the cords. He then turned the key in the lock, and uttered a word, which I took to be, "Come."

At his summons, Aith, approaching, took hold of the handle at the head; and from the dark recesses of the hall a lady, in black, moved forward. She was very tall, pallid, and of noble aspect. From the curvature of the nose, and her circular ears, I conjectured the lady Swertha, aunt of Harfager. Her eyes were red, but if with weeping I could not determine.

Harfager and I, taking each a handle near the coffin-foot, and the lady bearing before us one of the candlesticks, the procession began. As we came to the doorway, I noticed standing in a corner yet two coffins, inscribed with the names of Harfager and his aunt. We passed at length down a wide-curving stairway to the lower stage; and descending thence still lower by narrow brazen steps, came to a portal of metal, at which the lady, depositing the candlestick, left us.

The chamber of death into which we now bore the coffin had for its outer wall the brazen outer wall of the whole house at a point where this approached nearest the cataract, and must have been deep washed by the infuriate caldron without. The earthquake here was, indeed, intense. On every side the vast extent of surface was piled with coffins, rotted or rotting, ranged upon tiers of wooden shelves. The floor, I was surprised to see, was of brass. From the wide scampering that ensued on our entrance, the place was, it was clear, the abode of hordes of water-rats. As it was inconceivable that these could have corroded a way through sixteen brazen feet, I assumed that some fruitful pair must have found in the house, on its building, an ark from the waters; though even this hypothesis seemed wild. Harfager, however, afterwards confided to me his suspicion, that they had, for some purpose, been placed there by the original architect.

Upon a stone bench in the middle we deposited our burden, whereupon Aith made haste to depart. Harfager then rapidly and repeatedly walked from end to end of the long sepulchre, examining with many an eager stoop and peer, and upward strain, the shelves and their props.

Could he, I was led to wonder, have any doubts as to their security? Damp, indeed, and decay pervaded all. A piece of woodwork which I handled softened into powder between my fingers.

He presently beckoned to me, and with yet one halt and uttered "Hark!" from him, we traversed the house to my chamber. Here, left alone, I paced long about, fretted with a strange vagueness of anger; then, weary, tumbled to a horror of sleep.

In the far interior of the mansion even the bleared day of this land of heaviness never rose upon our settled gloom. I was able however, to regulate my levées by a clock which stood in my chamber. With Harfager, in a startingly short time, I renewed more than all our former intimacy.

That I should say more, is itself startling, considering that an interval of twelve years stretched between us. But so, in fact, it was; and this was proved by the circumstances that we grew to take, and to pardon, freedoms of expression and manner which, as two persons of more than usual reserve, we had once never dreamed of permitting to ourselves in reference to each other.

Down corridors that vanished either way in darkness and length of perspective remoteness we linked ourselves in perambulations of purposeless urgency. Once he wrote that my step was excruciatingly deliberate. I replied that it was just such a step as fitted my then mood. He wrote:

"You have developed an aptitude to fret." I was profoundly offended, and replied: "There are at least more fingers than one in the universe which that ring will wed."

Something of the secret of the unhuman sensitiveness of his hearing I quickly surmised. I, too, to my dismay, began, as time passed, to catch hints of loudly-uttered words. The reason might he found, I suggested, in an increased excitability of the auditory nerve, which, if the cataract were absent, the roar of the ocean, and bombast of the incessant tempest about us, would by themselves be sufficient to cause; in which case, his own aural interior must, I said, be inflamed to an exquisite pitch of hyperpyrexial fever. The affection I named to him as the Paracusis Willisii. He frowned dissent, but I, undeterred, callously proceeded to recite the case, occurring within my own experience, of a very deaf lady who could hear the fall of a pin in a rapidly-moving railway-train.* To this

* Such cases are known, or at least easily comprehensible, to every medical man. The concussion on the deaf nerves is said to be the cause of the acquired sensitiveness. Nor is there any limit to such sensitiveness when the concussion is abnormally increased.

he only replied: "Of ignorant persons I am accustomed to consider the mere scientist as the most profoundly ignorant."

Yet that he should affect darkness as to the highly morbid condition of his hearing I regarded as simply far-fetched. Himself, indeed, confided to me his own, Aith's, and his aunt's proneness to violent paroxysms of vertigo. I was startled; for I had myself shortly before been twice roused from sleep by sensations of reeling and nausea, and a conviction that the chamber furiously spun with me in a direction from right to left. The impression passed away, and I attributed it, perhaps hastily (though on well-known pathological grounds), to some disturbance in the nerve-endings of the 'labyrinth,' or inner ear. In Harfager, however, the conviction of wheeling motions in the house, in the world, attained so horrible a degree of certainty, that its effects sometimes resembled those of lunacy or energumenal possession. Never, he said, was the sensation of giddiness wholly absent; seldom the feeling that he stared with stretched-out arms over the verge of abysmal voids which wildly wooed his half-consenting foot. Once, as we went, he was hurled, as by unseen powers, to the ground; and there for an hour sprawled, cold in a flow of sweat, with distraught bedazzlement and amaze in eyes that watched the racing house. He was constantly racked, moreover, with the consciousness of sounds so very peculiar in their nature, that I could account for them upon no other hypothesis than that of tinnitus highly exaggerated. Through the heaped-up roar, there sometimes visited him, he said, the high lucid warbling of some Orphic bird, from the pitch of whose impassioned madrigals he had the inner consciousness that it came from a far country, was of the whiteness of snow, and crested with a comb of mauve. Else he was aware of accumulated human voices, remotely articulate, contending in volubility, and finally melting into chaotic musical tones. Or, anon, he was stunned by an infinite and imminent crashing, like the huge crackling of a universe of glass about his ears. He said, too, that he could often see, rather than hear, the parti-coloured whorls of a mazy sphere-music deep, deep, within the black dark of the cataract's roar. These impressions, which I ardently protested must be purely entotic, had sometimes upon him a pleasing effect, and long would he stand and listen with raised hand to their seduction; others again inflamed him to the verge of angry madness. I guessed that they were the origin of those irascibly uttered "Harks!" which at intervals of about an hour did not fail to break from him. In this I was wrong: and it was with a thrill of dismay that I shortly came to know the truth.

For, as once we passed together by an iron door on the lower stage, he stopped, and for several minutes stood, listening with an expression most keen and cunning.

Presently the cry "Hark!"escaped him; and he then turned to me, and wrote upon the tablet: "You did not hear?" I had heard nothing but the monotonous roar. He shouted into my ear in accents now audible to me as an echo heard far off in dreams: "You shall see."

He lifted the candlestick; produced from the pocket of his garment a key; unlocked the door.

We entered a chamber, circular, very loftily domed in proportion to its extent, and apparently empty, save that a pair of ladder-steps leaned against its wall. Its flooring was of marble, and in its centre gloomed a pool, resembling the impluvium of Roman atriums, but round in shape; a pool evidently deep, full of an unctuous miasmal water. I was greatly startled by its present aspect; for as the light burned upon its jet-black surface, I could see that this had been quite recently disturbed, in a manner for which the shivering of the house could not account, inasmuch as ripples of slimy ink sullenly rounded from the centre toward its marble brink. I glanced at Harfager for explanation. He signed to me to wait, and for about an hour, with arms in their accustomed fold behind his back, perambulated. At the end of that time he stopped, and standing together by the margin, we gazed into the water. Suddenly his clutch tightened upon my arm, and I saw, not without a thrill of honour, a tiny ball, doubtless of lead, but smeared blood-red by some chymical pigment, fall from the direction of the roof and disappear into the centre of the black depths. It hissed, on contact with the water, a thin puff of vapour.

"In the name of all that is sinister!" I cried, "what thing is this you show me?"

Again he made me a busy and confident sign to wait; snatched then the ladder-steps toward the pool; handed me the taper. I, mounting, held high the flame, and saw hanging from the misty centre of the dome a form—a sphere of tarnished old copper, lengthened out into balloon-shape by a down-looking neck, at the end of which I thought I could discern a tiny orifice. Painted across the bulge was barely visible in faded red characters the hieroglyph:

'harfager-hous: 1389—188'

Something—I know not what—of eldritch in the combined aspect of spotted globe, and gloomy pool, and contrivance of hourly hissing ball, gave expedition to my feet as I slipped down the ladder.

"But the meaning?"

"Did you see the writing?"

"Yes. The meaning?"

He wrote: "By comparing Gascoigne with Thrunster, I find that the mansion was built about 1389."

"But the final figures?"

"After the last 8," he replied, "there is another figure, nearly, but not quite, obliterated by a tarnish-spot."

"What figure?"

"It cannot be read, but may be surmised. The year 1888 is now all but passed. It can only be the figure 9."

"You are horribly depraved in mind!" I cried, flaring into anger. "You assume—you dare to state—in a manner which no mind trained to base its conclusions upon fact could hear with patience."

"And you, on the other hand, are simply absurd," he wrote.

"You are not, I presume, ignorant of the common formula of Archimedes by which, the diameter of a sphere being known, its volume may be determined. Now, the diameter of the sphere in the dome there I have ascertained to be four and a half feet; and the diameter of the leaden balls about the third of an inch. Supposing then that 1389 was the year in which the sphere was full of balls, you may readily calculate that not many fellows of the four million and odd which have since dropped at the rate of one an hour are now left within it. It could not, in fact, have contained many more. The fall of balls cannot persist another year. The figure 9 is therefore forced upon us."

"But you assume, Harfager," I cried, "most wildly you assume! Believe me, my friend, this is the very wantonness of wickedness! By what algebra of despair do you know that the last date must be such, was intended to be such, as to correspond with the stoppage of the horologe? And, even if so, what is the significance of the whole. It has—it can have—no significance! Was the contriver of this dwelling, of all the gnomes, think you, a being pulsing with omniscience?"

"Do you seek to madden me?" he shouted. Then furiously writing: "I know—I swear that I know—nothing of its significance! But is it not evident to you that the work is a stupendous hour-glass, intended to record the hours not of a day, but of a cycle? and of a cycle of five hundred years?"

"But the whole thing," I passionately cried, "is a baleful phantasm of our brains! An evil impossibility! How is the fall of the balls regulated? Ah, my friend, you wander—your mind is debauched in this bacchanal of tumult."

"I have not ascertained," he replied, "by what internal mechanism, or viscous medium, or spiral coil, dependent no doubt for its action upon the vibration of the house, the balls are retarded in their fall; that is a matter well within the cunning of the mediæval artisan, the inventor of the watch; but this at least is clear, that one element of their retardation is the minuteness of the aperture through which they have to pass; that this element, by known, though recondite, statical laws, will cease to operate when no more than three balls remain; and that, consequently, the last three will fall at nearly the same moment."

"In God's name!" I exclaimed, careless what folly I poured out, "but your mother is dead, Harfager! You dare not deny that there remain but you and the lady Swertha!"

A contemptuous glance was all the reply he then vouchsafed me.

But he confided to me a day or two later that the leaden balls were a constant bane to his ears; that from hour to hour his life was a keen waiting for their fall; that even from his brief slumbers he infallibly startled into wakefulness at each descent; that, in whatever part of the mansion he happened to be, they failed not to find him out with a clamorous and insistent loudness; and that every drop wrung him with a twinge of physical anguish in the inner ear. I was therefore appalled at his declaration that these droppings had now become to him as the life of life; had acquired an intimacy so close with the hue of his mind, that their cessation might even mean for him the shattering of reason. Convulsed, he stood then, face wrapped in arms, leaning against a pillar. The paroxysm past, I asked him if it was out of the question that he should once and for all cast off the fascination of the horologe, and fly with me from the place. He wrote in mysterious reply: "A threefold cord is not easily broken" I started. How threefold? He wrote with bitterest smile: "To be enamoured of pain—to pine after aching—to dote upon Marah—is not that a wicked madness?" I was overwhelmed. Unconsciously he had quoted Gascoigne: a wycked madness! a lecherous agonie! "You have seen the face of my aunt," he proceeded; "your eyes were dim if you did not there behold an impious calm, the glee of a blasphemous patience, a grin behind her daring smile." He then spoke of a prospect, at the infinite terror of which his whole nature trembled, yet which sometimes laughed in his heart in the aspect of a maniac hope. It was the prospect of any considerable increase in the volume of sound about him. At that, he said, the brain must totter. On the night of my arrival the noise of my booted tread, and, since then, my occasionally raised voice, had caused him acute unease. To a sensibility such as this, I understood him further to say, the luxury of torture involved in a large sound-increase in his environment was an allurement from which no human strength could turn; and when I expressed my powerlessness even to conceive such an increase, much less the means by which it could be effected, he produced from the archives of the house some annals, kept by the successive heads of his race. From these it appeared that the tempests which continually harried the lonely latitude of Vaila did not fail to give place, at periodic intervals of some years, to one sovereign ouragan—one Sirius among the suns—one ultimate lyssa of elemental atrocity. At such periods the rains descended—and the floods came—even as in the first world-deluge; those rösts, or eddies, which at all times encompassed Vaila, spurning then the bands of lateral space, shrieked themselves aloft into a multitudinous death-dance of water-spouts, and like snaky Deinotheria, or say towering monolithic in a stonehenge of columned and cyclopean awe, thronged about the little land, upon which, with converging débacle, they discharged their momentous waters; and the loebs to which the cataract was due thus redoubled their volume, and fell with redoubled tumult. It was, said Harfager, like a miracle that for twenty years no such great event had transacted itself at Vaila.

And what, I asked, was the third strand of that threefold cord of which he had spoken? He took me to a circular hall, which, he told me, he had ascertained to be the geometrical centre of the circular mansion. It was a very great hall—so great as I think I never saw—so great that the amount of segment illumined at any one time by the taper seemed nearly flat. And nearly the whole of its space from floor to roof was occupied by a pillar of brass, the space between wall and cylinder being only such as to admit of a stretched-out arm.

"This cylinder, which seems to be solid," wrote Harfager, "ascends to the dome and passes beyond it; it descends hence to the floor of the lower stage, and passes through that; it descends thence to the brazen flooring of the vaults, and passes through that into the rock of the ground.

Under each floor it spreads out laterally into a vast capital, helping to support the floor. What is the precise quality of the impression which I have made upon your mind by this description?"

"I do not know!" I answered, turning from him; "propound me none of your questions, Harfager. I feel a giddiness..."

"Nevertheless you shall answer me," he proceeded; "consider the strangeness of that brazen lowest floor, which I have discovered to be some ten feet thick, and whose under-surface, I have reason to believe, is somewhat above the level of the ground; remember that the fabric is at no point fastened to the cylinder; think of the chains that ray out from the outer walls, seeming to anchor the house to the ground. Tell me, what impression have I now made?"

"And is it for this you wait?" I cried—"for this? Yet there may have been no malevolent intention! You jump at conclusions! Any human dwelling, if solidly based upon earth, would be at all times liable to overthrow on such a land, in such a situation, as this, by some superlative tempest! What if it were the intention of the architect that in such eventuality the chains should break, and the house, by yielding, be saved?"

"You have no lack of charity at least," he replied; and we returned to the book we then read together.

He had not wholly lost the old habit of study, but could no longer constrain himself to sit to read. With a volume, often tossed down and resumed, he walked to and fro within the radius of the lamp-light; or I, unconscious of my voice, read to him. By a strange whim of his mood, the few books which now lay within the limits of his patience had all for their motive something of the picaresque, or the foppishly speculative: Quevedo's *Tacaño*; or the mundane system of Tycho Brahe; above all, George Hakewill's *Power and Providence of God.* One day, however, as I read, he interrupted me with the sentence, seemingly à propos of nothing: "What I cannot understand is that you, a scientist, should believe that the physical life ceases with the cessation of the breath"—and from that moment the tone of our reading changed. He led me to the crypts of the library in the lowest part of the building, and hour after hour, with a certain furore of triumph, overwhelmed me with volumes evidencing the longevity of man after 'death.' A sentence of Haller had rooted itself in his mind; he repeated, insisted upon it: "*sapientia denique consilia dat quibus longævitas obtineri queat, nitro, opio, purgationibus subinde repetitis*..."; and as opium was the elixir of long-drawn life, so death itself, he said, was that opium, whose more potent nepenthe lullabied the body to a peace not all-insentient, far within the gates of the gardens of dream. From the Dhammapada of the Bhuddist canon, to Zwinger's Theatrum, to Bacomi's Historia Vitæ et Mortis, he ranged to find me heaped-up certainty of his faith. What, he asked, was my opinion of Baron Verulam's account of the dead man who was heard to utter words of prayer; or of the leaping bowels o' the dead condamné? On my expressing incredulity, be seemed surprised, and reminded me of the writhings of dead serpents, of the visible beating of a frog's heart many hours after 'death.' "She is not dead," he quoted, "but sleepeth." The whim of Bacon and Paracelsus that the principle of life resides in a subtle spirit or fluid which pervades the organism he coerced into elaborate proof that such a spirit must, from its very nature, be incapable of any sudden annihilation, so long as the organs which it permeates remain connected and integral. I asked what limit he then set to the persistence of sensibility in the physical organism. He replied that when slow decay had so far advanced that the nerves could no longer be called nerves, or their cell-origins cell-origins, or the brain a brain—or when by artificial means the brain had for any length of time been disconnected at the cervical region from the body—then was the king of terrors king indeed, and the body was as though it had not been.

With an indiscretion strange to me before my residence at Vaila, I blurted the question whether all this Aberglaube could have any reference, in his mind, to the body of his mother. For a while he stood thoughtful, then wrote: "Had I not reason to believe that my own and my aunt's life in some way hinged upon the final cessation of hers, I should still have taken precautions to ascertain the progress of the destroyer upon her mortal frame; as it is, I shall not lack even the minutest information." He then explained that the rodents which swarmed in the sepulchre would, in the course of time, do their full work upon her; but would be unable to penetrate to the region of the throat without first gnawing their way through the three cords stretched across the holes of the laminæ within the coffin, and thus, one by one, liberating the three morrisco bells to a tinkling agitation.

The winter solstice had passed; another year opened. I slept a deep sleep by night when Harfager entered my chamber, and shook me. His face was ghastly in the taper-light. A transformation within a few hours had occurred upon him. He was not the same. He resembled some poor wight into whose unexpecting eyes—at midnight—have glared the sudden eye-balls of Terrour.

He informed me that he was aware of singular intermittent straining and creaking sounds, which gave him the sensation of hanging in aerial spaces by a thread which must shortly snap to his weight. He asked if, for God's sake, I would accompany him to the sepulchre. We passed together through the house, he craven, shivering, his step for the first time laggard. In the chamber of the dead he stole to and fro examining the shelves, furtively intent. His eyes were sunken, his face drawn like death. From the footless coffin of the dowager trembling on its bench of stone, I saw an old water-rat creep. As Harfager passed beneath one of the shortest of the shelves which bore a single coffin, it suddenly fell from a height with its burthen into fragments at his feet. He screamed the cry of a frightened creature, and tottered to my support. I bore him back to the upper house.

He sat with hidden face in the corner of a small room doddering, overcome, as it were, with the extremity of age. He no longer marked with his usual "Hark!" the fall of the leaden drops. To my remonstrances he answered only with the words, "So soon! So soon!" Whenever I sought I found him there. His manhood had collapsed in an ague of trepidancy. I do not think that during this time he slept.

On the second night, as I approached him, he sprang suddenly straight with the furious outcry:

"The first bell tinkles!"

And he had hardly larynxed the wild words when, from some great distance, a faint wail, which at its origin must have been a most piercing shriek, reached my now feverishly sensitive ears. Harfager at the sound clapped hands to ears, and dashed insensate from his place, I following in hot pursuit through the black breadth of the mansion. We ran until we reached a mound chamber, containing a candelabrum, and arrased in faded red. In an alcove at the furthest circumference was a bed. On the floor lay in swoon the lady Swertha. Her dark-grey hair in disarray wrapped her like an angry sea, and many tufts of it lay scattered wide, torn from the roots. About her throat were livid prints of strangling fingers. We bore her to the bed, and, having discovered some tincture in a cabinet, I administered it between her fixed teeth. In the rapt and dreaming face I saw that death was not, and, as I found something appalling in her aspect, shortly afterwards left her to Harfager.

When I next saw him his manner had assumed a species of change which I can only describe as hideous. It resembled the officious self-importance seen in a person of weak intellect, incapable of affairs, who goads himself with the exhortation, "to business! the time is short—I must even bestir myself!" His walk sickened me with a suggestion of ataxie locomotrice. I asked him as to the lady, as to the meaning of the marks of violence on her body. Bending ear to his deep and unctuous heard, "A stealthy attempt has been made upon her the skeleton, Aith."

My unfeigned astonishment at this announcement he seemed not to share. To my questions, repeatedly pressed upon him, as to the reason for retaining such a domestic in the house, as to the origin of his service, he could give no lucid answer. Aith, he informed me, had been admitted into the mansion during the period of his own long absence in youth. He knew little of the fact that he was of extraordinary physical strength. Whence he had come, or how, no living being except Swertha had knowledge; and she, it seems, feared, or at least persistently declined, to admit him into the mystery. He added that, as a matter of fact, the lady, from the day of his return to Vaila, had for some reason imposed upon herself a silence upon all subjects, which he had never once known her to break except by an occasional note.

With a curious, irrelevant impressement, with an intensely voluntary, ataxic strenuousness, always with the air of a drunken man constraining himself to ordered action, Harfager now set himself to the ostentatious adjustment of a host of insignificant matters. He collected chronicles and arranged them in order of date. He tied and ticketed bundles of documents. He insisted upon my help in turning the faces of portraits to the wall. He was, however, now constantly interrupted by paroxysms of vertigo; six times in a single day he was hurled to the ground. Blood occasionally gushed from his ears. He complained to me in a voice of piteous wail of the clear luting of a silver piccolo, which did not cease to invite him. As he bent sweating upon his momentous futilities, his hands fluttered like shaken reeds. I noted the movements of his muttering and whimpering lips, the rheum of his far-sunken eyes. The decrepitude of dotage had overtaken his youth.

On a day he cast it utterly off, and was young again. He entered my chamber, roused me from sleep; I saw the mad gaudium in his eyes, heard the wild hiss of his cry in my ear:

"Up! It is sublime. The storm!"

Ah! I had known it—in the spinning nightmare of my sleep. I felt it in the tormented air of the chamber. It had come, then. I saw it lurid by the lamplight on the hell of Harfager's distorted visage.

I glanced at the face of the clock. It was nine—in the morning. A sardonic glee burst at once into being within me. I sprang from the couch. Harfager, with the naked stalk of some maniac old prophet, had already rapt himself away. I set out in pursuit. A clear deepening was manifest in the quivering of the edifice; sometimes for a second it paused still, as if, breathlessly, to listen.

Occasionally there visited me, as it were, the faint dirge of some far-off lamentation and voice in Ramah; but if this was subjective, or the screaming of the storm, I could not say. Else I heard the distinct note of an organ's peal. The air of the mansion was agitated by a vaguely puffy unease.

About noon I sighted Harfager, lamp in hand, running along a corridor. His feet were bare. As we met he looked at me, but hardly with recognition, and passed by; stopped, however, returned, and howled into my ear the question: "Would you see?" He beckoned before me. I followed to a very small window in the outer wall closed with a slab of iron. As he lifted a latch the metal flew inward with instant impetuosity and swung him far, while a blast of the storm, braying and booming through the aperture with buccal and reboant bravura, caught and pinned me against an angle of the wall. Down the corridor a long crashing bouleversement of pictures and furniture ensued. I nevertheless contrived to push my way, crawling on the belly, to the opening. Hence the sea should have been visible. My senses, however, were met by nothing but a reeling vision of tumbled blackness, and a general impression of the letter O. The sun of Vaila had gone out. In a moment of opportunity our united efforts prevailed to close the slab.

"Come"—he had obtained fresh light, and beckoned before me—"let us see how the dead fare in the midst of the great desolation and dies iræ!" Running, we had hardly reached the middle of the stairway, when I was thrilled by the consciousness of a momentous shock, the bass of a dull and far-reverberating thud, which nothing conceivable save the huge simultaneous thumping to the ground of the whole piled mass of the coffins of the sepulchre could have occasioned. I turned to Harfager, and for an instant beheld him, panic flying in his scuttling feet, headlong on the way he had come, with stopped ears and wide mouth. Then, indeed, fear overtook me—a tremor in the midst of the exultant daring of my heart—a thought that now at least I must desert him in his extremity, now work out my own salvation. Yet it was with a most strange hesitancy that I turned to seek him for the last time—a hesitancy which I fully felt to be selfish and diseased. I wandered through the midnight house in search of light, and having happened upon a lamp, proceeded to hunt for Harfager. Several hours passed in this way. It became clear from the state of the atmosphere that the violence about me was being abnormally intensified. Sounds as of distant screams—unreal, like the screamings of spirits—broke now upon my ear. As the time of evening drew on, I began to detect in the vastly augmented baritone of the cataract something new—a shrillness—the whistle of an ecstasy—a malice—the menace of a rabies blind and deaf.

It must have been at about the hour of six that I found Harfager. He sat in an obscure apartment with bowed head, hands on knees. His face was covered with hair, and blood from the ears. The right sleeve of his garment had been rent away in some renewed attempt, as I imagined, to manipulate a window; the slightly-bruised arm hung lank from the shoulder. For some time I stood and watched the mouthing of his mumblings. Now that I had found him I said nothing of departure. Presently he looked sharply up with the cry "Hark!"—then with imperious impatience, "Hark! Hark!"—then with rapturous shout, "The second bell!" And again, in instant sequence upon his cry, there sounded a wail, vague but unmistakably real, through the house. Harfager at the moment dropped reeling with vertigo; but I, snatching a lamp, hasted forth, trembling, but eager. For some time the high wailing continued, either actually, or by reflex action of my ear.

As I ran toward the lady's apartment, I saw, separated from it by the breadth of a corridor, the open door of an armoury, into which I passed, and seized a battle-axe; and, thus armed, was about to enter to her aid, when Aith, with blazing eye, rushed from her chamber by a further door. I raised my weapon, and, shouting, flew forward to fell him; but by some chance the lamp dropped from me, and before I knew aught, the axe leapt from my grasp, myself hurled far backward. There was, however, sufficiency of light from the chamber to show that the skeleton had dashed into a door of the armoury: that near me, by which I had procured the axe, I instantly slammed and locked; and hasting to the other, similarly secured it. Aith was thus a prisoner. I then entered the lady's room. She lay half-way across the bed in the alcove, and to my bent ear loudly croaked the rales of death. A glance at the mangled throat convinced me that her last hours were surely come. I placed her supine upon the bed; curtained her utterly from sight within the loosened festoons of the hangings of black, and inhumanly turned from the fearfulness of her sight. On an escritoire near I saw a note, intended apparently for Harfager: "I mean to defy, and fly. Think not from fear—but for the glow of the Defiance itself. Can you come?" Taking a flame from the candelabrum, I hastily left her to solitude, and the ultimate throes of her agony.

I had passed some distance backward when I was startled by a singular sound—a clash—resembling in timbre the clash of a tambourine, I heard it rather loudly, and that I should now hear it at all, proceeding as it did from a distance, implied the employment of some prodigious energy. I waited, and in two minutes it again broke, and thenceforth at like regular intervals. It had somehow an effect of pain upon me. The conviction grew gradually that Aith had unhung two of the old brazen shields from their pegs; and that, holding them by their handles, and smiting them viciously together, he thus expressed the frenzy which had now overtaken him. I found my way back to Harfager, in whom the very nerve of anguish now seemed to stamp and stalk about the chamber. He bent his head; shook it like a hail-tormented horse; with his deprecating hand brushed and barred from his hearing each recurrent clash of the brazen shields.

"Au, when—when—when—" he hoarsely groaned into my ear, "will that rattle of hell choke in her throat? I will myself, I tell you—with my own hand!—Oh God…" Since the morning his auditory inflammation (as, indeed, my own also) seemed to have heightened in steady proportion with the roaring and screaming chaos round; and the rales of the lady hideously filled for him the measured intervals of the grisly cymbaling of Aith. He presently hurled twinkling fingers into the air, and with wide arms rushed swiftly into the darkness.

And again I sought him, and long again in vain. As the hours passed, and the slow Tartarean day deepened toward its baleful midnight, the cry of the now redoubled cataract, mixed with the throng and majesty of the now climactic tempest, assumed too definite and intentional a shriek to be longer tolerable to any mortal reason. My own mind escaped my governance, and went its way. Here, in the hot-bed of fever, I was fevered; among the children of wrath, was strong with the strength, and weak with the feebleness of delirium. I wandered from chamber to chamber, precipitate, bemused, giddy on the up-buoyance of a joy. "As a man upon whom sleep seizes," so had I fallen. Even yet, as I approached the region of the armoury, the noisy ecstasies of Aith did not fail to clash faintly upon my ear. Harfager I did not see, for he too, doubtless, roamed a headlong Ahasuerus in the round world of the house. At about midnight, however, observing light shine from a door on the lower stage, I entered and found him there. It was the chamber of the dropping horologe. He half-sat, swaying self-hugged, on the ladder-steps, and stared at the blackness of the pool. The last flicker of the riot of the day seemed dying in his eyes. He cast no glance as I approached. His hands, his bare right arm, were red with new-shed blood; but of this, too, he appeared unconscious. His mouth gaped wide to his pantings. As I looked, he leapt suddenly high, smiting hands, with the yell, "The last bell tinkles!" and galloped forth, a-rave.

He therefore did not see (though he may have understood by hearing) the spectacle which, with cowering awe, I immediately thereupon beheld: for from the horologe there slipped with hiss of vapour a ball into the torpid pool: and while the clock once ticked, another! and while the clock yet ticked, another! and the vapour of the first had not utterly passed, when the vapour of the third, intermingling, floated with it into grey tenuity aloft. Understanding that the sands of the house were run, I, too, flinging maniac arms, rushed from the spot. I was, however, suddenly stopped in my career by the instinct of some stupendous doom emptying its vials upon the mansion; and was quickly made aware, by the musketry of a shrill crackling from aloft, and the imminent downpour of a world of waters, that a water-spout had, wholly or partly, hurled the catastrophe of its broken floods upon us, and crashed ruining through the dome of the building.

At that moment I beheld Harfager running toward me, hands buried in hair. As he flew past, I seized him. "Harfager! save yourself!" I cried—"the very fountains, man,—by the living God, Harfager"—I hissed it into his inmost ear—"the very fountains of the Great Deep…!" Stupid, he glared at me, and passed on his way. I, whisking myself into a room, slammed the door. Here for some time, with smiting knees, I waited; but the impatience of my frenzy urged me, and I again stepped forth. The corridors were everywhere thigh-deep with water. Rags of the storm, irrageous by way of the orifice in the shattered dome, now blustered with hoiden wantonness through the house. My light was at once extinguished; and immediately I was startled by the presence of another light—most ghostly, gloomy, bluish—most soft, yet wild, phosphorescent—which now perfused the whole building. For this I could in no way account. But as I stood in wonder, a gust of greater vehemence romped through the house, and I was instantly conscious of the harsh snap of something near me. There was a minute's breathless pause—and then—quick, quick—ever quicker—came the throb, and the snap, and the pop, in vastly wide circular succession, of the anchoring chains of the mansion before the urgent shoulder of the hurricane.

And again a second of eternal calm—and then—deliberately—its hour came—the ponderous palace moved. My flesh writhed like the glutinous flesh of a serpent. Slowly moved, and stopped:—then was a sweep—and a swirl—and a pause! then a swirl—and a sweep—and a pause!—then steady industry of labour on the monstrous brazen axis, as the husbandman plods by the plough; then increase of zest, assuetude of a fledgeling to the wing—then intensity—then the last light ecstasy of flight. And now, once again, as staggering and plunging I spun, the thought of escape for a moment visited me: but this time I shook an impious fist. "No, but God, no, no," I cried, "I will no more wander hence, my God! I will even perish with Harfager! Here let me waltzing pass, in this Ball of the Vortices, Anarchie of the Thunders! Did not the great Corot call it translation in a chariot of flame? But this is gaudier than that! redder than that! This is jaunting on the scoriac tempests and reeling bullions of hell! It is baptism in a sun!"

Recollection gropes in a dimmer gloaming as to all that followed. I struggled up the stairway now flowing a steep river, and for a long time ran staggering and plunging, full of wild words, about, amid the downfall of ceilings and the wide ruin of tumbling walls. The air was thick with splashes, the whole roof now, save three rafters, snatched by the wind away. In that blue sepulchral moonlight, the tapestries flapped and trailed wildly out after the flying house like the streaming hair of some ranting fakeer stung gyratory by the gadflies and tarantulas of distraction.

The flooring gradually assumed a slant like the deck of a sailing ship, its covering waters flowing all to accumulation in one direction. At one point, where the largest of the porticoes projected, the mansion began at every revolution to bump with horrid shiverings against some obstruction.

It bumped, and while the lips said one-two-three, it three times bumped again. It was the levity of hugeness! it was the mænadism of mass! Swift—ever swifter, swifter—in ague of urgency, it reeled and raced, every portico a sail to the storm, vexing and wracking its tremendous frame to fragments. I, chancing by the door of a room littered with the débris of a fallen wall, saw through that wan and livid light Harfager sitting on a tomb. A large drum was beside him, upon which, club grasped in bloody hand, he feebly and persistently beat. The velocity of the leaning house had now attained the sleeping stage, that ultimate energy of the spinning-top. Harfager sat, head sunk to chest; suddenly he dashed the hairy wrappings from his face; sprang; stretched horizontal arms; and began to spin—dizzily!—in the same direction as the mansion!—nor less sleep-.embathed!—with floating hair, and quivering cheeks, and the starting eye-balls of horror, and tongue that lolled like a panting wolf's from his bawling degenerate mouth. From such a sight I turned with the retching of loathing, and taking to my heels, staggering and plunging, presently found myself on the lower stage opposite a porch. An outer door crashed to my feet, and the breath of the storm smote freshly upon me. An élan, part of madness, more of heavenly sanity, spurred in my brain. I rushed through the doorway, and was tossed far into the limbo without.

The river at once swept me deep-drowned toward the sea. Even here, a momentary shrill din like the splitting asunder of a world reached my ears. It had hardly passed, when my body collided in its course upon one of the basalt piers, thick-cushioned by sea-weed, of the not all-demolished bridge. Nor had I utterly lost consciousness. A clutch freed my head from the surge, and I finally drew and heaved myself to the level of a timber. Hence to the ledge of rock by which I had come, the bridge was intact. I rowed myself feebly on the belly beneath the poundings of the wind. The rain was a steep rushing, like a shimmering of silk, through the air.

Observing the same wild glow about me which had blushed through the broken dome into the mansion, I glanced backward—and saw that the dwelling of the Harfagers was a memory of the past; then upward—and lo, the whole northern sky, to the zenith, burned one tumbled and fickly-undulating ocean of gaudy flames. It was the aurora borealis which, throeing at every aspen instant into rays and columns, cones and obelisks, of vivid vermil and violet and rose, was fairily whiffed and flustered by the storm into a vast silken oriflamme of tresses and swathes and breezes of glamour; whilst, low-bridging the horizon, the flushed beams of the polar light assembled into a changeless boreal corona of bedazzling candor. At the augustness of this great phenomenon I was affected to blessed tears. And with them, the dream broke!—the infatuation passed!—a hand skimmed back from my brain the blind films and media of delusion; and sobbing on my knees, I jerked to heaven the arms of grateful oblation for my surpassing Rephidim, and marvel of deliverance from all the temptation—and the tribulation—and the tragedy—of Vaila.

Xélucha

by M. P. Shiel

He goeth after her... and knoweth not..."
— (From a diary)

Three days ago! by heaven, it seems an age. But I am shaken—my reason is debauched. A while since, I fell into a momentary coma precisely resembling an attack of petit mal. "Tombs, and worms, and epitaphs"—that is my dream. At my age, with my physique, to walk staggery, like a man stricken! But all that will pass: I must collect myself—my reason is debauched. Three days ago! it seems an age! I sat on the floor before an old cista full of letters. I lighted upon a packet of Cosmo's. Why, I had forgotten them! they are turning sere! Truly, I can no more call myself a young man. I sat reading, listlessly, rapt back by memory. To muse is to be lost! of that evil habit I must wring the neck, or look to perish. Once more I threaded the mazy sphere-harmony of the minuet, reeled in the waltz, long pomps of candelabra, the noonday of the bacchanal, about me.

Cosmo was the very tsar and maharajah of the Sybarites! The Priap of the détraqués! In every unexpected alcove of the Roman Villa was a couch, raised high, with necessary foot-stool, flanked and canopied with mirrors of clarified gold. Consumption fastened upon him; reclining at last at table, he could, till warmed, scarce lift the wine! his eyes were like two fat glow-worms, coiled together! they seemed haloed with vaporous emanations of phosphorus! Desperate, one could see, was the secret struggle with the Devourer. But to the end the princely smile persisted calm; to the end—to the last day—he continued among that comic crew unchallenged choragus of all the rites, I will not say of Paphos, but of Chemos! and Baal-Peor! Warmed, he did not refuse the revel, the dance, the darkened chamber. It was utterly black, rayless; approached by a secret passage; in shape circular; the air hot, haunted always by odours of balms, bdellium, hints of dulcimer and flute; and radiated round with a hundred thick-strewn ottomans of Morocco.

Here Lucy Hill stabbed to the heart Caccofogo, mistaking the scar of his back for the scar of Soriac. In a bath of malachite the Princess Egla, waking late one morning, found Cosmo lying stiffly dead, the water covering him wholly.

> 'But in God's name, Mérimée!' (so he wrote), to think of Xélucha dead! Xélucha! Can a moon-beam, then, perish of suppurations? Can the rainbow be eaten by worms? Ha! ha! ha!' Laugh with me, my friend: '*elle dérangera l'Enfer*'! She will introduce the pas de tarantule into Tophet! Xélucha, the feminine Xélucha recalling the splendid harlots of history! Weep with me—*manat rara meas lacrima per genas*! expert as Thargelia; cultured as Aspatia; purple as Semiramis. She comprehended the human tabernacle, my friend, its secret springs and tempers, more intimately than any savant of Salamanca who breathes. Tarare—but Xélucha is not dead!
>
> Vitality is not mortal; you cannot wrap flame in a shroud. Xélucha! where then is she? Translated, perhaps—rapt to a constellation like the daughter of Leda. She journeyed to Hindostan, accompanied by the train and appurtenance of a Begum, threatening descent upon the Emperor of Tartary. I spoke of the desolation of the West; she kissed me, and promised return.
>
> Mentioned you, too, Mérimée—'her Conqueror'—'Mérimée, Destroyer of Woman.' A breath from the conservatory rioted among the ambery whiffs of her forelocks, sending it singly a-wave over that thulite tint you know. Costumed cap-à-pie, she had, my friend, the dainty little completeness of a daisy mirrored bright in the eye of the browsing ox. A simile of Milton had for years, she said, inflamed the lust of her Eye: 'The barren plains of Sericana, where Chineses drive with sails and wind their cany wagons light.'

I, and the Sabæans, she assured me, wrongly considered Flame the whole of being; the other half of things being Aristotle's quintessential light. In the Ourania Hierarchia and the Faust-book you meet a completeness: burning Seraph, Cherub full of eyes. Xélucha combined them. She would reconquer the Orient for Dionysius, and return. I heard of her blazing at Delhi; drawn in a chariot by lions. Then this rumour—probably false. Indeed, it comes from a source somewhat turgid. Like Odin, Arthur, and the rest, Xélucha—will reappear.'

Soon subsequently, Cosmo lay down in his balneum of malechite, and slept, having drawn over him the water as a coverlet. I, in England, heard little of Xélucha: first that she was alive, then dead, then alighted at old Tadmor in the Wilderness, Palmyra now. Nor did I greatly care, Xélucha having long since turned to apples of Sodom in my mouth. Till I sat by the cista of letters and re-read Cosmo, she had for some years passed from my active memories.

The habit is now confirmed in me of spending the greater part of the day in sleep, while by night I wander far and wide through the city under the sedative influence of a tincture which has become necessary to my life. Such an existence of shadow is not without charm; nor, I think, could many minds be steadily subjected to its conditions without elevation, deepened awe. To travel alone with the Primordial cannot but be solemn. The moon is of the hue of the glow-worm; and Night of the sepulchre. Nux bore not less Thanatos than Hupuos, and the bitter tears of Isis redundulate to a flood. At three, if a cab rolls by, the sound has the augustncss of thunder. Once, at two, near a corner, I came upon a priest, seated, dead, leering, his legs bent. One arm, supported on a knee, pointed with rigid accusing forefinger obliquely upward. By exact observation, I found that he indicated Betelgeux, the star 'a' which shoulders the wet sword of Orion. He was hideously swollen, having perished of dropsy. Thus in all Supremes is a grotesquerie; and one of the sons of Night is—Buffo.

In a London square deserted, I should imagine, even in the day, I was aware of the metallic, silvery-clinking approach of little shoes. It was three in a heavy morning of winter, a day after my rediscovery of Cosmo. I had stood by the railing, regarding the clouds sail as under the sea-legged pilotage of a moon wrapped in cloaks of inclemency. Turning, I saw a little lady, very gloriously dressed. She had walked straight to me. Her head was bare, and crisped with the amber stream which rolled lax to a globe, kneaded thick with jewels, at her nape.

In the redundance of her décolleté development, she resembled Parvati, mound-hipped love-goddess of the luscious fancy of the Brahmin.

She addressed to me the question:

"What are you doing there, darling?"

Her loveliness stirred me, and Night is bon camarade. I replied:

"Sunning myself by means of the moon."

"All that is borrowed lustre," she returned, "you have got it from old Drummond's Flowers of Sion."

Looking back, I cannot remember that this reply astonished me, though it should—of course—have done so. I said:

"On my soul, no; but you?"

"You might guess whence I come!"

"You are dazzling. You come from Paz."

"Oh, farther than that, my son! Say a subscription ball in Soho."

"Yes?… and alone? In the cold? On foot…?"

"Why, I am old, and a philosopher. I can pick you out riding Andromeda yonder from the ridden Ram. They are in error, M'sieur, who suppose an atmosphere on the broad side of the moon. I have reason to believe that on Mars dwells a race whose lids are transparent like glass; so that the eyes are visible during sleep; and every varying dream moves imaged forth to the beholder in tiny panorama on the limpid iris. You cannot imagine me a mere fille! To be escortcd is to admit yourself a woman, and that is improper in Nowhere. Young Eos drives an *équipage à quatre*, but Artemis 'walks' alone. Get out of my borrowed light in the name of Diogenes! I am going home."

"Near Piccadilly."

"But a cab?"

"No cabs for me, thank you. The distance is a mere nothing. Come."

We walked forward. My companion at once put an interval between us, quoting from the Spanish Curate that the open is an enemy to love. The Talmudists, she twice insisted, rightly held the hand the sacredest part of the person, and at that point also contact was for the moment interdict. Her walk was extremely rapid. I followed. Not a cat was anywhere visible. We reached at length the door of a mansion in St. James's. There was no light. It seemed tenantless, the windows all uncurtained, pasted across, some of them, with the words, To Let. My companion, however, flitted up the steps, and, beckoning, passed inward. I, following, slammed the door, and was in darkness. I heard her ascend, and presently a region of glimmer above revealed a stairway of marble, curving broadly up. On the floor where I stood was no carpet, nor furniture: the dust was very thick. I had begun to mount when, to my surprise, she stood by my side, returned; and whispered:

"To the very top, darling."

She soared nimbly up, anticipating me. Higher, I could no longer doubt that the house was empty but for us. All was a vacuum full of dust and echoes. But at the top, light streamed from a door, and I entered a good-sized oval saloon, at about the centre of the house. I was completely dazzled by the sudden resplendence of the apartment. In the midst was a spread table, square, opulent with gold plate, fruit dishes; three ponderous chandeliers of electric light above; and I noticed also (what was very bizarre) one little candlestick of common tin containing an old soiled curve of tallow, on the table. The impression of the whole chamber was one of gorgeousness not less than Assyrian. An ivory couch at the far end was made sun-like by a head- piece of chalcedony forming a sea for the sport of emerald ichthyotauri. Copper hangings, parnlled with mirrors in iasperated crystal, corresponded with a dome of flame and copper; yet this latter, I now remember, produced upon my glance an impression of actual grime. My companion reclined on a small Sigma couch, raised high to the table-level in the Semitic manner, visible to her saffron slippers of satin. She pointed me a seat opposite. The incongruity of its presence in the middle of this arrogance of pomp so tickled me, that no power could have kept me from a smile: it was a grimy chair, mean, all wood, nor was I long in discovering one leg somewhat shorter than its fellows.

She indicated wine in a black glass bottle, and a tumbler, but herself made no pretence of drinking or eating. She lay on hip and elbow, petite, resplendent, and looked gravely upward. I, however, drank.

"You are tired," I said, "one sees that."

"It is precious little than you see!" she returned, dreamy, hardly glancing.

"How! Your mood is changed, then? You are morose."

"You never, I think, saw a Norse passage-grave?"

"And abrupt."

"Never?"

"A passage-grave? No."

"It is worth a journey! They are circular or oblong chambers of stone, covered by great earthmounds, with a 'passage' of slabs connecting them with the outer air. All round the chamber the dead sit with head resting upon the bent knees, and consult together in silence."

"Drink wine with me, and be less Tartarean."

"You certainly seem to be a fool," she replied with perfect sardonic iciness. "Is it not, then, highly romantic? They belong, you know, to the Neolithic age. As the teeth fall, one by one, from the lipless mouths—they are caught by the lap. When the lap thins—they roll to the floor of stone. Thereafter, every tooth that drops all round the chamber sharply breaks the silence."

"Ha! ha! ha!"

"Yes. It is like a century-slow, circularly-successive dripping of slime in some cavern of the far subterrene."

"Ha! ha! This wine seems heady! They express themselves in a dialect largely dental."

"The Ape, on the other hand, in a language wholly guttural."

A town-clock tolled four. Our talk was holed with silences, and heavy-paced. The wine's yeasty exhalation reached my brain. I saw her through mist, dilating large, uncertain, shrinking again to dainty compactness. But amorousness had died within me.

"Do you know," she asked, "what has been discovered in one of the Danish Kjökkenmöddings by a little boy? It was ghastly. The skeleton of a huge fish with human—"

"You are most unhappy."

"Be silent."

"You are full of care."

"I think you a great fool."

"You are racked with misery."

"You are a child. You have not even an instinct of the meaning of the word."

"How! Am I not a man? I, too, miserable, careful?"

"You are not, really, anything—until you can create."

"Create what?"

"Matter."

"That is foppish. Matter cannot be created, nor destroyed."

"Truly, then, you must be a creature of unusually weak intellect. I see that now. Matter does not exist, then, there is no such thing, really—it is an appearance, a spectrum—every writer not imbecile from Plato to Fichte has, voluntary or involuntary, proved that for good. To create it is to produce an impression of its reality upon the senses of others; to destroy it is to wipe a wet rag across a scribbled slate."

"Perhaps. I do not care. Since no one can do it"

"No one? You are mere embryo—"

"Who then?"

"Anyone, whose power of Will is equivalent to the gravitating force of a star of the First Magnitude."

"Ha! ha! ha! By heaven, you choose to be facetious. Are there then wills of such equivalence?"

"There have been three, the founders of religions. There was a fourth: a cobbler of Herculaneum, whosc mere volition induced the cataclysm of Vesuvius in '79 in direct opposition to the gravity of Sirius. There are more fames than you have ever sung, you know."

"The greater number of disembodied spirits, too, I feel certain."—"By heaven, I cannot but think you full of sorrow! Poor wight! come, drink with me. The wine is thick and boon. Is it not Setian? It makes you sway and swell before me, I swear, like a purple cloud of evening—"

"But you are mere clayey ponderance!—I did not know that!—You are no companion! Your little interest revolves round the lowest centres."

"Come—forget your agonies—"

"What, think you, is the portion of the buried body first sought by the worm?"

"The eyes! The eyes!"

"You are hideously wrong—you are so utterly at sea—"

"My God!"

She had bent forward with such rage of contradiction as to approach me closely. A loose gown of amber silk, wide-sleeved, had replaced her ball attire, though at what opportunity I could not guess; wondering, I noticed it as she now placed her palms far forth upon the table. A sudden wafture as of spice and orange-flowers, mingled with the abhorrent faint odour of mortality over-ready for the tomb, greeted my sense. A chill crept upon my flesh.

"You are so hopelessly at fault—"

"For God's sake—"

"You are so miserably deluded! Not the eyes at all!"

"Then, in heaven's name, what?"

Five tolled from a clock.

"The Uvula! the soft drop of mucous flesh, you know, suspended from the palate above the glottis. They eat through the face-cloth and cheek, or crawl by the lips through a broken tooth, filling the mouth. They make straight for it. It is the deliciæ of the vault."

At her horror of interest I grew sick, at her odour, and her words. Some unspeakable sense of insignificance, of debility, held me dumb.

"You say I am full of sorrows. You say I am racked with woe; that I gnash with anguish. Well, you are a mere child in intellect. You use words without realization of meaning like those minds in what Leibnitz calls 'symbolical consciousness.' But suppose it were so—"

"It is so."

"You know nothing."

"I see you twist and grind. Your eyes are very pale. I thought they were hazel. They are of the faint bluishness of phosphorus shimmerings seen in darkness."

"That proves nothing."

"But the 'white' of the sclerotic is dyed to yellow. And you look inward. Why do you look so palely inward, so woe-worn, upon your soul? Why can you speak of nothing but the sepulchre, and its rottenness? Your eyes seem to me wan with centuries of vigil, with mysteries and millenniums of pain."

"Pain! but you know so little of it! you are wind and words! of its philosophy and rationale nothing!"

"Who knows? I will give you a hint. It is the sub-consciousness in conscious creatures of Eternity, and of eternal loss. The least prick of a pin not Pæan and Æsculapius and the powers of heaven and hell can utterly heal. Of an everlasting loss of pristine wholeness the conscious body is sub-conscious, and 'pain' is its sigh at the tragedy. So with all pain—greater, the greater the loss. The hugest of losses is, of course, the loss of Time. If you lose that, any of it, you plunge at once into the transcendentalisms, the infinitudes, of Loss; if you lose all of it— "

"But you so wildly exaggerate! Ha! ha! You rant, I tell you, of commonplaces with the woe—"

"Hell is where a clear, untrammelled Spirit is sub-conscious of lost Time; where it boils and writhes with envy of the living world; hating it for ever, and all the sons of Life!"

"But curb yourself! Drink—I implore—I implore—for God's sake—but once—"

"To hasten to the snare—that is woe! to drive your ship upon the lighthouse rock—that is Marah! To wake, and feel it irrevocably true that you went after her—and the dead were there—and her guests were in the depths of hell—and you did not know it!—Though you might have.

Look out upon the houses of the city this dawning day: not one, I tell you, but in it haunts some soul—walking up and down the old theatre of its little Day—goading imagination by a thousand childish tricks, vraisemblances—elaborately duping itself into the momentary fantasy that it still lives, that the chance of life is not for ever and for ever lost—yet riving all the time with under-memories of the wasted Summer, the lapsed brief light between the two eternal glooms—riving I say and shriek to you!—Riving, Mérimée, you destroying fiend.—She had sprung—tall now, she seemed to me—between couch and table.

"Mérimée!" I screamed, "—my name, harlot, in your maniac mouth! By God, woman, you terrify me to death!"

I too sprang, the hairs of my head catching stiff horror from my fancies.

"Your name? Can you imagine me ignorant of your name, or anything concerning you? Mérimée! Why, did you not sit yesterday and read of me in a letter of Cosmo's?"

"Ah-h…," hysteria bursting high in sob and laughter from my arid lips—"Ah! ha! ha!"

"Xélucha! My memory grows palsied and grey, Xélucha! pity me—my walk is in the very valley of shadow!—senile and sere!—observe my hair, Xélucha, its grizzled growth—trepidant, Xélucha, clouded—I am not the man you knew, Xélucha, in the palaces—of Cosmo! You are Xélucha!"

"You rave, poor worm!" she cried, her face contorted by a species of malicious contempt.

"Xélucha died of cholera ten years ago at Antioch. I wiped the froth from her lips. Her nose underwent a green decay beforc burial. So far sunken into the brain was the left eye—"

"You are—you are Xélucha!" I shrieked; "voices now of thunder howl it within my consciousness—and by the holy God, Xélucha, though you blight me with the breath of the hell you are, I shall clasp you, living or damned—"

I rushed toward her. The word "Madman!" hissed as by the tongues of ten thousand serpents through the chamber, I heard; a belch of pestilent corruption puffed poisonous upon the putrid air; for a moment to my wildered eyes there seemed to rear itself, swelling high to the roof, a formless tower of ragged cloud, and before my projected arms had closed upon the very emptiness of insanity, I was tossed by the operation of some Behemoth potency far-circling backward to the utmost circumference of the oval, where, my head colliding, I fell, shocked, into insensibility.

* * * * *

When the sun was low toward night, I lay awake, and listlessly observed the grimy roof, and the sordid chair, and the candlestick of tin, and the bottle of which I had drunk. The table was small, filthy, of common deal, uncovered. All bore the appearance of having stood there for years. But for them, the room was void, the vision of luxury thinned to air. Sudden memory flashed upon me. I scrambled to my feet, and plunged and tottered, bawling, through the twilight into the street.

The Medici Boots

by Pearl Norton Swet

For fifty years they lay under glass in the Dickerson museum and they were labeled "The Medici Boots." They were fashioned of creamy leather, pliable as a young girl's hands. They were threaded with silver, appliqued with sapphire silks and scarlet, and set on the tip of each was a pale and lovely amethyst. Such were the Medici boots.

Old Silas Dickerson, globe-trotter and collector, had brought the boots from a dusty shop in Florence when he was a young man filled with the lust for travel and adventure. The years passed and Silas Dickerson was an old man, his hair white, his eyes dim, his veined hands trembling with the ague that precedes death.

When he was ninety and the years of his wanderings over, Silas Dickerson died one morning as he sat in a high-backed Venetian chair in his private museum. The Fourteenth Century gold-leaf paintings, the Japanese processional banners, the stolen bones of a Normandy saint—all the beloved trophies of his travels must have watched the dead man impassively for hours before his housekeeper found him.

The old man sat with his head thrown back against the faded tapestry of the Venetian chair, his eyes closed, his bony arms extended along the beautifully carved arms of the chair, and on his lap lay the Medici boots.

It was high noon when they found him, and the sun was streaming through the stained-glass window above the chair and picking at the amethysts, so that the violet stones seemed to eye Marthe, the old housekeeper, with an impudent glitter. Marthe muttered a prayer and crossed herself, before she ran like a scared rabbit with the news of the master's death.

Silas Dickerson's only surviving relatives, the three young Delameters, did not take too seriously the note which was found among the papers in the museum's desk. Old Silas had written the note. It was addressed to John Delameter, for John was his uncle's favorite, but John's pretty wife, Suzanne, and his twin brother, Doctor Eric, read it over his shoulder; and they all smiled tolerantly. Old Dickerson had written of things incomprehensible to the young moderns:

"The contents of my private museum are yours, John, to do with as you see fit. Merely as a suggestion, I would say that the Antiquarian Society would snap up many of the things. A very few are of no particular value, except to me. One thing I want done, however. The Medici boots of ivory leather must either be destroyed or be put for ever under glass in a *public* museum. I prefer that they be destroyed, for they are a dangerous possession. They have gone to the adulterous rendezvous celebrated in the scandalous verses of Lorenzo the Magnificent. They have shod the feet of a murderess. They were cursed by the Church as trappings of the Devil, inciting the wearer to foul deeds and intrigue.

"I shall not disturb you with all their hideous history, but I repeat, they are a dangerous possession. I have taken care to keep them under lock and key, behind plate glass, for more than fifty years. I have never taken them out. Destroy the Medici boots, before they destroy you!"

"But he did take them out!" cried Suzanne. "Uncle was holding the boots when—when Marthe found him there in the museum."

John reread the note, and looked thoughtfully at his young wife. "Yes. Perhaps he was preparing to destroy them right then. Of course, I think the poor old fellow took things a bit too seriously—he was very old, you know, and Marthe says he practically lived in this museum of his."

"And why call a pair of old boots dangerous? Of course, we all know the Medicis were plenty dangerous, but the Medici boots—that's ridiculous, John. Besides—"

Suzanne paused provocatively, her red lips pouting. She looked down at her trimly shod feet. "Besides, I'd like to try on those Medici boots—just once. They're lovely, I think."

John was frowning thoughtfully. He scarcely heard her suggestion. He spoke to Eric, instead, and his voice seemed a bit troubled.

"I believe that Uncle *was* getting ready to destroy those boots that very morning he died; else why should he have taken them from their case—after fifty years?"

"Yes, I believe you're right, John, because that note is dated fully a month before Uncle's death. I think he brooded over leaving those boots to one he cared for. Poor old man!"

"I wouldn't call him so, Eric. He had his dreams of adventure realized more fully than most men. I—I think I'll do as he says. I'll destroy the Medici boots."

"If you'd feel better about it," assented his brother. But Suzanne did not speak. She was looking at her shoe, pursing her lips thoughtfully, seeing her feet encased in the gay embroideries of the Medici boots.

John seemed relieved by his decision. "Yes, I'd better do it. We'll be getting back to town in a few days. Old Erskine, you know, Uncle's lawyer, is coming down this afternoon. Then soon we'll be on the wing, Susie and I—Vienna, Paris, the Alps—thanks to Uncle."

"Maybe you think I'm not thankful for my chance at a bit more work at Johns Hopkins," said Eric, and they did not again speak of the Medici boots.

The deaf old lawyer of the Dickerson estate arrived, and Suzanne, with the easy capability that was part of her charm, saw that he was made comfortable.

At seven there was a perfect dinner served on the awninged terrace outside the softly lit living-room. The stars aided the two little rosy lamps on the table, and swaying willows beside a stone-encircled pool swung the incense of the garden about them.

As dinner ended, John took from the pocket of his coat a small, limp-leather book. He pushed back his dessert plate and laid the book on the table, tapping it with a finger as he spoke.

"This is the history of the Medici boots. It was in the little wall-safe in the museum. After all Uncle said of the Medici boots, shall we read it?" And turning to the old lawyer, he told of Silas Dickerson's letter concerning the boots.

Erskine shook his head, smiling. "Most collectors get an exaggerated sense of the supernatural. Read this, by all means—it should prove interesting."

"Yes, read it, John." Suzanne and Eric spoke almost together.

So, in the circle of rosy light at their little table, John read the story of the Medici boots. It was not a long story and it was told in the language of an anonymous translator, but as John read on, his listeners were drawn together, as by a spell. They scarcely breathed, and the summer night that was so mildly beautiful seemed to take on a sense of hovering danger.

'In the palace of Giuliano de' Medici I have lived long. I am an old woman now, as the years are reckoned in this infamous place, though I am but fifty and three.

'Separated from my betrothed, duped, sold into the marble labyrinth of this hateful palace, it was long before my spirit broke and I went forth, bejeweled and attired in elegance, among the silk-clad Florentines. I was labeled the most beautiful mistress of any of the Medici. I was smirked at, fawned upon for my lord's favors, obscenely jested about in the orgies that took place in the great banquet hall of the palace.

'But in my heart always lay the remembrance of my lost love, and in my soul grew black hatred for the Medici and all their kind. I, who had dreamed only of a modest home, a kind husband, black-haired, trusting little children, was made a tool of the Medici infamy.

'In time, I almost felt myself in league with the Devil. Secretly, and with a growing sense of elation, I made frequent rendezvous with a foul hag whose very name was anathema to the churchly folk of Florence. In her hole of a room in a certain noisome street, she imparted to me those terrible secrets of the Black Arts which were deep in her soul. It was amusing that she was paid in Medici gold.

'The corruption of the Medici bred in them fear; in me a sort of reckless bravery. It was I who poisoned the wine of many a foe of the Medici. It was I who put the point of a dagger in the heart of the old Prince de Vittorio, whose lands and power and palaces were coveted by my lord, Giuliano.

'After a time, bloodshed became an exhilaration to me; the death agonies of those who drank the poisoned cup became more interesting than the flattery of the Medici followers. Even the ladies of the house of the Medici did me the honor of their subtly barbed friendliness.

'Through this very friendliness, I conceived my plan of sweet revenge upon the monsters who had ruined my life. With so great a hatred boiling in my soul that my mind reeled, my senses throbbed, my heart rose in my throat like a spurt of flame, I cursed three things of exquisite beauty with all the fervor of my newly learned lessons in devilish lore.

'These three beautiful objects I presented to three ladies of the house of

Medici—presented them with honeyed words of mock humility. A necklace of jeweled links—I pledged myself to the Devil and willed that the golden necklace would tighten on the soft throat of a lady of the Medici while she slept, and strangle her into black death. A bracelet of filigree and sapphires—to pierce by its hidden silver needle the blue vein in a white Medici wrist, so that her life's blood would spurt and she would know the terror that the house of the Medici gave to others.

'Last, and most ingenious, a pair of creamy boots, pliable, embroidered in silver and silks, encrusted with amethysts—my betrothal jewels. In my hatred I cursed the boots, willing that the wearer, as long as a shred of the boots remained, should kill as I had killed, poison as I had poisoned, leave all thoughts of home and husband and live in wantonness and evil. So I cursed the beautiful boots, forgetting, in my hate, that perhaps another than a Medici might, in the years to come, wear them and become the Devil's pawn, even as I am now.

'In my life, the Medici will have the boots, of that I feel sure; but after that—I can only hope that this bloody history of the boots may be found when I am no more, and may it be a warning.

'I have lived to see my gifts received and worn, and I have laughed in my soul to see my curses bring death and terror and evil to three Medici women. I know not what will become of the golden necklace, the bracelet, or the boots. The boots may be lost or stolen, or they may lie in a Medici palace for age on age, but the curse will cling to them till they are destroyed. So I pray that no woman, save a Medici, will ever wear them.

'As I live and breathe and do the bidding of the lords of Florence, the accursed Medici—I have told the truth. When I am dead, perhaps they will find this book, and, in hell, I shall know and be glad.

MARIA MODENA DI CAVOURI.
Florence, 1476.

"Whew!" said old Erskine.

John laughed. "I don't suppose this charming history would have been any more thrilling if I had read it from the original book, in Italian, of course. Wonder where Uncle got it! There was no mention of it being in the library—but there it was."

"Now, will you destroy those boots?" asked Eric, and he was not entirely in jest.

But Suzanne said, laughingly, "Not before I find out if the Medici lady had a smaller foot than I! Are they still in the museum, John?"

"Never you mind, my dear. They're not for the likes of you."

"Oh, don't be silly, John. This is 1935, not the Fifteenth Century." And they laughed at Suzanne's earnestness.

The book that held the story of the Medici boots lay on the white cloth, looking like a book of lovely verse.

Suzanne, a small white blur against the summer dark, sat quietly while the men talked of Silas Dickerson, his life, his mania for collecting, his death that had so fittingly come to him in his museum. It was nearly twelve when Suzanne left the men on the terrace and with a quiet "good-night" entered the living-room and crossed to the long, shining stairs.

The men went on with their talk. Once, John, looking toward the jutting wing that was the museum, exclaimed, "Look at that, will you? Why—I'd swear I saw a light in the museum."

"You locked it, didn't you?" asked Eric.

"Of course; the key's in my desk upstairs. H-m. I'm probably mistaken, but it did seem as though a light shone there just a moment ago."

"Reflection from the living-room window, I think. Country life is making you jittery, John." And Eric laughed at his brother.

The men sat on, reluctant to leave the beauty of the night, and it was almost two o'clock when they finally went inside.

John said, "I think I'll not disturb Suzanne." And he went to sleep in a wide four-postered bed in a room next to his wife. Eric and the old lawyer were in rooms across the hall.

The still summer night closed about the house of Silas Dickerson, and when the moon lay dying against the bank of cloud, puffed across a sky by the little wind that came before dawn, young Doctor Eric Delameter awoke, suddenly and completely, to a feeling of clammy apprehension. He had not locked his door, and now, across the grayness of the room, he saw it slowly opening.

A hand was closed around the edge of the door—a woman's hand, small and white and jeweled. Eric sat straight and tense on the edge of his bed, peering across the room. A woman, young and slender, in a long, trailing gown, came toward him smiling. It was Suzanne.

With a gasp, Eric watched her approach till she stood directly before him.

"Suzanne! You are asleep? Suzanne, shall I call John?"

He thought that perhaps he should not waken her; there were things one must remember about sleep-walkers, but physicians scarcely believed them.

Eric was puzzled, too, by her costume. It was not a night-robe she wore, but an elaborate, trailing dress upon which embroideries in silver shone faintly. Her short black curls were bound about three times with strands of pearly beads, her slim white arms were loaded with bracelets. The pointed toes of little shoes peeped beneath her gown, little shoes of creamy leather. An amethyst gleamed on each shoe.

The sight of these amethystine tips affected Eric strangely, much as though he had looked at something hideously repulsive. He stood up and put out a hand to touch Suzanne's arm.

"Suzanne," he said, gently. "Let me take you to John. Shall I?"

Suzanne looked up at him, and her brown eyes, usually so merry, were deeply slumberous, not with sleep, but with a look of utter abandon. She shook her pearl-bound head slowly, smilingly.

"No, not John. I want you, Eric."

"Mad! Suzanne must be mad!" was Eric's quick thought, but her caress was swifter than his thought. Both jewel-laden arms about his neck, Suzanne kissed him, her red lips pouting warmly upon his.

"Suzanne! You don't know what you're doing." He grasped both her hands in his and with a haste that would have seemed ludicrous to him had he viewed the scene in a picture-play, he hurried her out of his room and across the hall.

Eric opened her door softly and with no gentle hand shoved Suzanne inside her room. She seemed like a little animal in his grasp. She hissed at him; clawed and scratched at his hand. But when he had shut the door, she did not open it again, and after a moment he went back to his own room.

His mouth set in a firm line, his heart beating fast, Eric locked his door with a noiseless turn of the key. It was almost dawn, and the garden lay like a rare pastel outside his window; but Eric saw none of it. He scarcely thought, though his lips moved, as if chaotic words were struggling for utterance.

He looked down at his hand, where two long red scratches oozed a trickle of blood. After he had washed his hand, he lay down on his bed and covered his eyes with his arm, against the picture of Suzanne. Above all else there stood out the gleaming tips of her little shoes, as he had glimpsed them through the dim light of his room when she came toward him.

"She wore the Medici boots! The Medici boots! Suzanne must have taken them from the museum!" Over and over he said it—"The Medici boots! The Medici boots!"

Eric rather dreaded breakfast, but when he came down at eight, to the terrace where a rustic table was set invitingly, he found John and the lawyer awaiting him. John greeted his brother affectionately.

"Morning, old boy! Hope you slept well. Why so solemn? Feeling seedy?"

"No, no. I am perfectly all right," Eric replied hastily, relieved that Suzanne was not present. He added with a scarcely noticeable hesitation, "Suzanne not coming down?"

"No," replied John, easily. "She seemed to want to sleep awhile. Sent her regrets. She'll see us at lunch."

John went on. "I certainly had a nightmare last night. Thought a woman in a long, shining dress came into my room and tried to stab me. This morning I found that a glass on my bed-table was overturned and broken, and, by George, I'd cut my wrist on it."

He showed a jagged cut on his wrist. "Take a look, Doctor Eric."

Eric looked at the cut, carefully. "Not bad, but you might have bled to death, had it been a quarter of an inch to the left. If you like, I'll fix it up a bit for you after breakfast."

Eric's voice was calm enough, but his pulse was pounding, his heart sick. All morning he rode through the countryside adjoining the Dickerson estate, but he let the mare go as she liked and where she liked, for his mind was busy with the events of the hour before dawn. He knew that the slash on his brother's wrist was made by steel, not glass. Yet when the ride was over, he could not bring himself to tell John of Suzanne's visit.

"She must have been sleep-walking, though I can't account for the way she was decked out. I've always thought Suzanne extremely modest in her dress, certainly not inclined to load herself with jewelry. And those boots! John must get them today and destroy them, as he said. Silly, perhaps, but—" His thoughts went on and on, always returning to the Medici boots, in spite of himself.

Eric came back from his ride at eleven o'clock, with as troubled a mind as when he began it. He almost feared to see Suzanne at lunch.

When he did meet her with John and Mr Erskine on the cool, shaded porch where they lunched, he saw there was nothing to fear. The amorous, clinging woman of the hour before dawn was not there at all. There was only the Suzanne whom Eric knew and loved as a sister.

Here, again, was their merry little Suzanne, somewhat spoiled by her husband, it is true, but a Suzanne sweetly feminine, almost childish in a crisp, white frock and little, low-heeled sandals. Their talk was lazily pleasant—of tennis honors and horses, of the prize delphiniums in the garden, of the tiny maltese kitten which Suzanne had brought up from the stables late that morning and installed in a pink-bowed basket on the porch. She showed the kitten to Eric, handling its tiny paws gently, hushing its plaintive mews with ridiculous pet names.

"Perhaps I'm a bigger fool than I know. Perhaps it never happened, except in a dream," Eric told himself, unhappily. "And yet—"

He looked at the red marks on his hand, marks made by a furious Suzanne in that hour before the dawn. Too, he remembered the cut on John's wrist, the cut so near the vein.

Eric declined John's invitation to go through the museum with him that afternoon, but he said with a queer sense of diffidence, "While you're there, John, you'd better get rid of the Medici boots. Creepy things to have around, I think."

"They'll be destroyed, all right. But Suzanne is just bound to try them on. I'll get them, though, and do as Uncle said."

Eric remained on the terrace, speculating somewhat on just what John and Suzanne would do, now that the huge fortune of Silas Dickerson was theirs. Eric was not envious of his brother's good luck, and he was thankful for his share in old Silas' generosity.

At five o'clock he entered the hall, just as Suzanne hurried in from the kitchen. She spread our her hands, laughingly.

"With my own fair hands I've made individual almond tortonis for dessert. Cook thinks I'm a wonder! Each masterpiece in a fluted silver dish, silver candies sprinkled on the pink whipped cream! O-oh!"

She made big eyes in mock gluttony. Eric forgot, for a moment, that there ever had been another Suzanne.

"You're nothing but a little girl, Suzie. You with your rhapsodies over pink whipped cream! But it's sweet of you to go to such trouble on a warm afternoon. See you and the whatever-you-call-'ems at dinner!"

"They're tortonis, Eric, tortonis."

Suzanne ran lightly up the stairs. Eric followed more slowly. He entered his room thinking that there were some things which must be explained in this house with the old museum.

Twenty minutes before dinner Eric and John were on the terrace waiting for Suzanne. John was talkative, which was just as well, as he might have wondered at his brother's silence. Eric was torn between a desire to tell his brother his reluctant suspicions concerning the Medici boots and Suzanne and his inclination to leave things alone till the boots could be destroyed.

He said, diffidently, "John, has Suzanne those—those boots?"

John chuckled. "Why, yes. I saw them in her room. Do you know she went down to the museum last night and took those boots? It*was* a light I saw in the museum. It was her light. Suzanne has ideas. Wants to wear the boots just once, she says, to lay the ghost of this what's-her-name—Maria Modena. Suzanne says she couldn't sleep much last night. Got up early and tried on those boots. Well, I think I'll destroy 'em tomorrow. Uncle's wish, so I'll do it."

"Tried them on, did she? Well, if you should ask me, I'd say that history of the boots was a bit too exciting for Suzanne. It *was* a haunting story. Uncle must have swallowed it, hook, line, and sinker, eh?"

"Of course. His letter showed that. But Suzanne lives in the present, not the past, as Uncle did. I suppose Suzanne will wear those boots, or she won't feel satisfied. I don't exactly like the idea, I must confess."

Something like an electric shock passed through Eric. He said, somewhat breathlessly, "I don't think Suzanne ought to have the Medici boots."

John looked at him curiously and laughed. "I never knew you were superstitious, Eric. But do you really think—"

"I don't know what I think, John. But if she were my wife, I'd take those boots away from her. Uncle may have known what he was talking about."

"Well, I think she's intending to wear them at dinner, so prepare to be dazzled. Here she is, now. Greetings, sweet-heart!"

Suzanne swept across the terrace, her gown goldly shimmering, pearls bound about her head, as Eric had seen her in the dim hour before dawn. Again the rows of bracelets were weighting her slim arms. And she wore the Medici boots, the amethyst tips peeping beneath her shining dress.

John, ever ready for gay clowning, arose and bowed low. "Hail, Empress! A-ah, the dress you got in Florence on our honeymoon, isn't it? And those darned Medici boots!"

Suzanne unsmilingly extended her hand for him to kiss.

John arched an eyebrow, comically. "What's the matter, honey? Going regal on me?" And retaining her hand, he kissed each of her fingers.

Suzanne snatched away her hand, and the glance she gave her husband was one of venomous hauteur. To Eric she turned a look that was an open caress, leaning toward him, putting a hand on his arm, as he stood beside his chair, stern-lipped, with eyes that would not look at John's hurt bewilderment.

The three sat down then, in the low wicker chairs, and waited for dinner—three people with oddly different emotions. John was hurt, slightly impatient with his bride; Eric was furious with Suzanne, though there was in his heart the almost certain knowledge that the Suzanne beside them on the terrace was not the Suzanne they knew, but a cruelly strange woman, the product of a sinister force, unknown and compelling.

No one, looking on Suzanne's red-lipped and heavy-lidded beauty, could miss the knowledge that here was a woman dangerously subtle, carrying a power more devastating than the darting lightning that now and then showed itself over the tree-tops of the garden. Eric began to feel something of this, and there shaped in his mind a wariness, a defense against this woman who was not Suzanne.

"No *al fresco* dining tonight," said John, as the darkening sky was veined by a sudden spray of blue-green light. "Rain on the way. Pretty good storm, I'd say."

"I like it," replied Suzanne, drawing in a deep breath of the sultry air.

John laughed. "Since when, sweet-heart? You usually shake and shiver through a thunderstorm."

Suzanne ignored him. She smiled at Eric and said in a low tone, "And if I should lose my bravery, you would take care of me, wouldn't you, Eric?"

Before Eric could reply, dinner was announced, and he felt a relief and also a dread. This dinner was going to be difficult.

John offered his arm to his wife, smiling at her, hoping for a smile in return, but Suzanne shrugged and said in a caressing voice, "Eric?"

Eric could only bow stiffly and offer his arm, while John walked slowly beside them, his face thoughtful, his gay spirits gone. During dinner, however, he tried to revive the lagging conversation. Suzanne spoke in a staccato voice and her choice of words seemed strange to Eric, almost as though she were translating her own thoughts from a foreign tongue.

And finally Suzanne's promised dessert came, cool and tempting in its silver dishes. Eric saw a chance to make the talk more natural. He said, gayly, "Johnny, your wife's a chef, a famous pastry chef. Behold the work of her hands! What did you say it was, Suzanne?"

"This? Oh—I do not know what it is called."

"But this afternoon as you were leaving the kitchen—didn't you say it was almond something or other?"

She shook her head, smiling. "Perhaps it is. I wouldn't know."

The maid had placed the tray with the three silver dishes of dessert before Suzanne, that she might put on them the final sprinkling of delicate silver candies. Daintily, Suzanne sifted the shining bubbles over the fluff of cream. Eric, watching her, felt very little surprize when he saw Suzanne, with almost legerdemain deftness, sift upon one dish a film of pinkish powder which could not be detected after it lay on the pink cream.

Waiting, he knew not for what moment, he watched Suzanne pass the silver dishes herself, saw her offer the one with the powdered top to John. And it was then that their attention was attracted by the entrance of the maltese kitten. So tiny it was, so brave in its careening totter across the shiny floor, small tail hoisted like a sail, that John and Eric laughed aloud.

Suzanne merely glanced down at the little creature and turned away. The kitten, however, came to her chair, put up a tiny paw and caught its curved claws in the fragile stuff of Suzanne's gown. Instantly, her face became distorted with rage and she kicked out at the kitten, savagely, and with set lips. It seemed to Eric that the amethysts on the Medici boots winked wickedly in the light of the big chandelier.

The kitten was flung some ten feet away, and lay in a small, panting heap.

John sprang up. "Suzanne! How could you?" He took the kitten in his arms and soothed it.

"Why its heart's beating like a trip-hammer," he said. "I don't understand, Suzanne—"

As the kitten grew quiet, he took a large rose-leaf from the table-flowers and spread it with a heaping spoonful of the pink cream from his dessert. Then he put the kitten on the floor beside it.

"Here, little one. Lick this up. It's fancy eating. Suzanne's sorry. I know she is."

The kitten, with the greed of its kind, devoured the cream, covering its small nose and whiskers with a pinkish film. Suzanne sat back in her chair, fingering her bracelets, her eyes on Eric's face. John watched the kitten, and Eric watched, too—watched tensely, for he sensed what would happen to it.

The kitten finished the cream, licked its paws and whiskers and turned to walk away. Then it spun around in a frantic convulsion, and in a moment lay dead on its back, its tiny fed tongue protruding, its paws rigid.

Outside, the storm glowered, and in the chartreuse light of the forked lightning, the great chandelier was turned to a sickly radiance. Thunder rolled like muffled drums.

Suddenly Suzanne began to laugh, peal after peal of terrible laughter, and then, after a glare of lightning, the big chandelier winked out. The room was plunged into stormy darkness, and they could hear the rain lashing through the garden to hurl itself against the windows.

"Don't be frightened, Suzanne." It was John's solicitous voice, and it was followed by a quick movement from Suzanne's side of the table.

A sheet of blue-green light illumined the room for an instant, and Eric saw Suzanne struggling in her husband's arms, one jeweled arm uplifted and in her hand a shining dagger.

With a bound that was almost involuntary, Eric reached them and struck at the knife in Suzanne's hand. It clattered to the floor. And as though the fury of the storm and Suzanne's madness both were spent, the slashing rain and the lightning stopped abruptly, and Suzanne ceased to struggle.

"Light the candles, Eric—quickly—on the mantel to your right! Suzanne is hurt!"

In the candle-light, palely golden and swaying, Eric saw Suzanne slumped limply in John's arms. The hem of her golden dress was redly wet and one cream-colored little shoe was fast becoming soaked with blood from a slash across the instep.

"Let's get her over to the window-seat, Eric. Do something for her!—Oh, sweet-heart, don't moan like that!" There was no question or reproach in John's voice, only compassion.

Eric took off his coat, rolled up his sleeves. His mouth was grimly set, his hands steady, his voice crisply professional. "Take off those shoes, John. She'll—be herself, then. I mean that she'll be Suzanne—not a murderess of the Medicis. Take them off, John! They're at the bottom of this."

"You mean—" John's voice was breathless, his lips trembling.

"I mean those hellish boots have changed Suzanne from a sweet and lovely girl to—well, do as I tell you. I'll be back with gauze and some things I need."

When Eric hurried back, there were three servants grouped at the dining-room door. He spoke to them bruskly and they left, wide-eyed and whispering. Eric closed the door.

While the wet leaves tapped against the windows and stars struggled through the clouds, Eric worked, silently, expertly, grimly, by the light of a flashlight held in John's unsteady hands and the light of the flickering candles. The house lights were all snuffed out by the storm.

"There," Eric gave a satisfied grunt. The brothers stood looking at Suzanne, who seemed asleep. Her golden dress glimmered in the candle-light and the pearls were slipping from her dark hair. The Medici boots lay in a limp and bloody heap in a corner, where Eric had flung them.

"When she awakes, I shouldn't tell her about any of this, if I were you, John."

"There are things you haven't told me, Eric, aren't there? Things about—the Medici boots?"

Eric looked steadily at his brother. "Yes, old fellow; and after I've told you, those boots must be destroyed. We'll burn them before this night is over. We mustn't move her now. We'll go out on the terrace—it's wet there, but the air is fresh. Did you smell—something peculiar?"

For, as they passed the corner where the Medici boots lay slashed and bloody, Eric could have sworn that there came to him a horrid odor, fetid, hotly offensive—the odor of iniquity and ancient bloody death.

The Thing from—Outside

by George Allan England

They sat about their camp-fire, that little party of Americans retreating southward from Hudson Bay before the on-coming menace of the great cold. Sat there, stolid under the awe of the North, under the uneasiness that the day's trek had laid upon their souls. The three men smoked. The two women huddled close to each other. Fireglow picked their faces from the gloom of night among the dwarf firs. A splashing murmur told of the Albany River's haste to escape from the wilderness, and reach the Bay.

"I don't see what there was in a mere circular print on a rock-ledge to make our guides desert," said Professor Thorburn. His voice was as dry as his whole personality. "Most extraordinary."

"*They* knew what it was, all right," answered Jandron, geologist of the party. "So do I." He rubbed his cropped mustache. His eyes glinted grayly. I've seen prints like that before. That was on the Labrador. And I've seen things happen, where they were."

"Something surely happened to our guides, before they'd got a mile into the bush," put in the Professor's wife; while Vivian, her sister, gazed into the fire that revealed her as a beauty, not to be spoiled even by a tam and a rough-knit sweater. "Men don't shoot wildly, and scream like that, unless—"

"They're all three dead now, anyhow," put in Jandron. "So they're out of harm's way. While we—well, we're two hundred and fifty wicked miles from the C. P. R. rails."

"Forget it, Jandy!" said Marr, the journalist. "We're just suffering from an attack of nerves, that's all. Give me a fill of 'baccy. Thanks. We'll all be better in the morning. Ho-hum! Now, speaking of spooks and such—"

He launched into an account of how he had once exposed a fraudulent spiritualist, thus proving—to his own satisfaction—that nothing existed beyond the scope of mankind's everyday life. But nobody gave him much heed. And silence fell upon the little night-encampment in the wilds; a silence that was ominous.

Pale, cold stars watched down from spaces infinitely far beyond man's trivial world.

Next day, stopping for chow on a ledge miles upstream, Jandron discovered another of the prints. He cautiously summoned the other two men. They examined the print, while the women-folk were busy by the fire. A harmless thing the marking seemed; only a ring about four inches in diameter, a kind of cup-shaped depression with a raised center. A sort of glaze coated it, as if the granite had been fused by heat.

Jandron knelt, a well-knit figure in bright mackinaw and canvas leggings, and with a shaking finger explored the smooth curve of the print in the rock. His brows contracted as he studied it.

"We'd better get along out of this as quick as we can," said he in an unnatural voice. "You've got your wife to protect, Thorburn, and I,—well, I've got Vivian. And—"

"*You* have?" nipped Marr. The light of an evil jealously gleamed in his heavy-lidded look. "What you need is an alienist."

"Really, Jandron," the Professor admonished, "you mustn't let your imagination run away with you."

"I suppose it's imagination that keeps this print cold!" the geologist retorted. His breath made faint, swirling coils of vapor above it.

"Nothing but a pot-hole," judged Thorburn, bending his spare, angular body to examine the print. The Professor's vitality all seemed centered in his big-bulged skull that sheltered a marvellous thinking machine. Now he put his lean hand to the base of his brain, rubbing the back of his head as if it ached. Then, under what seemed some powerful compulsion, he ran his bony finger around the print in the rock.

"By Jove, but it is cold!" he admitted. "And looks as if it had been stamped right out of the stone. Extraordinary!"

"Dissolved out, you mean," corrected the geologist. "By cold."

The journalist laughed mockingly.

"Wait till I write this up!" he sneered. "'Noted Geologist Declares Frigid Ghost Dissolves Granite!'"

Jandron ignored him. He fetched a little water from the river and poured it into the print.

"Ice!" ejaculated the Professor. "Solid ice!"

"Frozen in a second," added Jandron, while Marr frankly stared. "And it'll never melt, either. I tell you, I've seen some of these rings before; and every time, horrible things have happened. Incredible things! Something burned this ring out of the stone—burned it out with the cold interstellar space. Something that can import cold as a permanent quality of matter. Something that can kill matter, and totally remove it."

"Of course that's all sheer poppycock," the journalist tried to laugh, but his brain felt numb.

"This something, this Thing," continued Jandron, "is a Thing that can't be killed by bullets. It's what caught our guides on the barrens, as they ran away—poor fools!"

A shadow fell across the print in the rock. Mrs. Thorburn had come up, was standing there. She had overheard a little of what Jandron had been saying.

"Nonsense!" she tried to exclaim, but she was shivering so she could hardly speak.

That night, after a long afternoon of paddling and portaging—laboring against inhibitions like those in a nightmare—they camped on shelving rocks that slanted to the river.

"After all," said the Professor, when supper was done, "we mustn't get into a panic. I know extraordinary things are reported from the wilderness, and more than one man has come out, raving. But we, by Jove! with our superior brains—we aren't going to let Nature play us any tricks!"

"And of course," added his wife, her arm about Vivian, "everything in the universe is a natural force. There's really no super-natural, at all."

"Admitted," Jandron replied. "But how about things *outside* the universe?"

"And they call you a scientist?" gibed Marr; but the Professor leaned forward, his brows knit.

"Hm!" he grunted. A little silence fell.

"You don't mean, really," asked Vivian, "that you think there's life and intelligence—Outside?"

Jandron looked at the girl. Her beauty, haloed with ruddy gold from the firelight, was a pain to him as he answered:

"Yes, I do. And dangerous life, too. I know what I've seen, in the North Country. I know what I've seen!"

Silence again, save for the crepitation of the flames, the fall of an ember, the murmur of the current. Darkness narrowed the wilderness to just that circle of flickering light ringed by the forest and the river, brooded over by the pale stars.

"Of course you can't expect a scientific man to take you seriously," commented the Professor. "I know what I've seen! I tell you there's Something entirely outside man's knowledge."

"Poor fellow!" scoffed the journalist; but even as he spoke his hand pressed his forehead.

"There are Things at work," Jandron affirmed, with dogged persistence. He lighted his pipe with a blazing twig. Its flame revealed his face drawn, lined. "Things. Things that reckon with us no more than we do with ants. Less, perhaps."

The flame of the twig died. Night stood closer, watching.

"Suppose there are?" the girl asked. "What's that got to do with these prints in the rock?"

"*They*," answered Jandran, "are marks left by one of those Things. Footprints, maybe. That Thing is near us, here and now!"

Marr's laugh broke a long stillness.

"And you," he exclaimed, "with an A.M. and a B.S. to write after your name,"

"If you knew more," retorted Jandron, "you'd know a devilish sight less. It's only ignorance that's cock-sure."

"But," dogmatized the Professor, "no scientist of any standing has ever admitted any outside interference with this planet."

"No, and for thousands of years nobody ever admitted that the world was round, either. What I've seen, I know."

"Well, what *have* you seen?" asked Mrs. Thorburn, shivering.

"You'll excuse me, please, for not going into that just now."

"You mean," the Professor demanded, dryly, "if the—hm!—this suppositious Thing wants to—?"

"It'll do any infernal thing it takes a fancy to, yes! If it happens to want us—"

"But what *could* Things like that want of us? Why should They come here, at all?"

"Oh, for various reasons. For inanimate objects, at times, and then again for living beings. They've come here lots of times, I tell you," Jandron asserted with strange irritation, "and got what They wanted, and then gone away to—Somewhere. If one of Them happens to want us, for any reason, It will take us, that's all. If It doesn't want us, It will ignore us, as we'd ignore gorillas in Africa if we were looking for gold. But if it was gorilla-fur we wanted, that would be different for the gorillas, wouldn't it?"

"What in the world," asked Vivian, "could a—well, a Thing from Outside want of *us?*"

"What do men want, say, of guinea-pigs? Men experiment with 'em, of course. Superior beings use inferior, for their own ends. To assume that man la the supreme product of evolution is gross self-conceit. Might not some superior Thing want to experiment with human beings?

"But how?" demanded Marr,

"The human brain is the most highly-organized form of matter known to this planet. Suppose, now—"

"Nonsense!" interrupted the Professor. "All hands to the sleeping-bags, and no more of this. I've got a wretched headache. Let's anchor in Blanket Bay!"

He, and both the women, turned in. Jandron and Marr sat a while longer by the fire. They kept plenty of wood piled on it, too, for an unnatural chill transfixed the night-air. The fire burned strangely blue, with greenish flicks of flame.

At length, after vast acerbities of disagreement, the geologist and the newspaperman sought their sleeping-bags. The fire was a comfort. Not that a fire could avail a pin's weight against a Thing from interstellar spacs, but subjectively it was a comfort. The instincts of a million years, centering around protection by fire, cannot be obliterated.

After a time—worn out by a day of nerve-strain and of battling with swift currents, of flight from Something invisible, intangible—they all slept.

The depths of space, star-sprinkled, hung above them with vastness immeasurable, cold beyond all understanding of the human mind.

Jandron woke first, in a red dawn.

He blinked at the fire, as he crawled from his sleeping-bag. The fire was dead; and yet it had not burned out. Much wood remained unconsumed, charred over, as if some gigantic extinguisher had in the night been lowered over it.

"*Hmmm!*" growled Jandron. He glanced about him, on the ledge. "Prints, too. I might have known!"

He aroused Marr. Despite all the jourelist's mocking hostility, Jandron felt more in common with this man of his own age than with the Professor, who was close on sixty.

"Look here, now!" said he. "*It* has been all around here. See? It put out our fire—maybe the fire annoyed *It*, some way—and *It* walked round us, everywhere." His gray eyes smouldered. "I guess, by gad, you've got to admit facts, now!"

The journalist could only shiver and stare.

"Lord, what a head I've got on me, this morning!" he chattered. He rubbed his forehead with a shaking hand, and started for the river. Most of his assurance had vanished. He looked badly done up.

"Well, what say?" demanded Jandron. "See these fresh prints?"

"Damn the prints!" retorted Marr, and fell to grumbling some unintelligible thing. He washed unsteadily, and remained crouching at the river's lip, inert, numbed.

Jandron, despite a gnawing at the base of his, brain, carefully examined the ledge. He found prints scattered everywhere, and some even on the river-bottom near the shore. Wherever water had collected in the prints on the rock, it had frozen hard. Each print in the river-bed, too, was white with ice. Ice that the rushing current could not melt.

"Well, by gad!" he exclaimed. He lighted his pipe and tried to think. Horribly afraid—yes, he felt horribly afraid, but determined. Presently, as a little power of concentration came back, he noticed that all the prints were in straight lines, each mark about two feet from the next.

"*It* was observing us while we slept," said Jandron.

"What nonsense are you talking, eh?" demanded Marr. His dark, heavy face sagged. "Fire, now, and grub!"

He got up and shuffled unsteadily away from the river. Then he stopped with a jerk, staring.

"Look! Look a' that axe!" he gulped, pointing.

Jandron picked up the axe, by the handle, taking good care not to touch the steel. The blade was white-furred with frost. And deep into it, punching out part of the edge, one of the prints was stamped.

"This metal," said he, "is clean gone. It's been absorbed. The Thing doesn't recognize any difference in materials. Water and steel and rock are all the same to It.

"You're crazy!" snarled the journalist. "How could a Thing travel on one leg, hopping along, making marks like that?"

"It could roll, if it was disk-shaped. And—"

A cry from the Professor turned them. Thorburn was stumbling toward them, hands out and tremulous.

"My wife—!" he choked.

Vivian was kneeling beside her sister, frightened, dazed.

"Something's happened!" stammered the Professor. "Here—come here—!"

Mrs. Thorburn was beyond any power of theirs, to help. She was still breathing; but her respirations were stertorous, and a complete paralysla had stricken her. Her eyes, half-open and expressionless, showed pupils startlingly dilated. No resources of the party's drug-kit produced the slightest effect on the woman.

The next half-hour was a confused panic, breaking camp, getting Mrs. Thorburn into a canoe, and leaving that accursed place, with a furious energy of terror that could no longer reason. Up-stream, ever up against the swirl of the current the party fought, driven by horror. With no thought of food or drink, paying no heed to landmarks, lashed forward only by the mad desire to be gone, the three men and the girl flung every ounce of their energy into the paddles. Their panting breath mingled with the sound of swirling eddies. A mist-blurred sun brooded over the northern wilds. Unheeded, hosts of black-flies sang high-pitched keenings all about the fugitives. On either hand the forest waited, watched.

Only after two hours of sweating toil had brought exhaustion did they stop, in the shelter of a cove where black waters circled, foam-flecked. There they found the Professor's wife—she was dead.

Nothing remained to do but bury her. At first Thorburn would not hear of it. Like a madman he insisted that through all hazards he would fetch the body out. But no—impossible. So, after a terrible time, he yielded.

In spite of her grief, Vivian was admirable. She understood what must be done. It was her voice that said the prayers; her hand that—lacking flowers—laid the fir boughs on the cairn. The Professor was dazed past doing anything, saying anything.

Toward mid-afternoon, the party landed again, many miles up-river. Necessity forced them to eat. Firs would not burn. Every time they lighted it, it smouldered and went out with a heavy, greasy smoke. The fugitives ate cold food and drank water, then shoved off in two canoes and once more fled.

In the third canoe, hauled to the edge of the forest, lay all the rock-specimens, data and curios, scientific instruments. The party kept only Marr's diary, a compass, supplies, fire-arms and medicine-kit.

"We can find the things we've left—sometime," said Jandron, noting the place well. "Sometime—after *It* has gone,"

"And bring the body out," added Thorburn. Tears, for the first time, wet his eyes. Vivian said nothing. Marr tried to light his pipe. He seemed to forget that nothing, not even tobacco, would burn now.

Vivian and Jandron occupied one canoe. The other carried the Professor and Marr. Thus the power of the two canoes was about the same. They kept well together, up-stream.

The fugitives paddled and portaged with a dumb, desperate energy. Toward evening they struck into what they believed to be the Mamattawan. A mile up this, as the blurred sun faded beyond a wilderness of ominous silence, they camped. Here they made determined efforts to kindle fire. Not even alcohol from the drug-kit would start it. Cold, they mumbled a little food; cold, they huddled into their sleeping-bags, there to lle with darkness leaden on their fear. After a long time, up over a world void of all sound save the river-flow, slid an amber moon notched by the ragged tops of the conifers. Even the wail of a timber-wolf would have come as welcome relief; but no wolf howled.

Silence and night enfolded them. And everywhere they felt that *It* was watching.

Foolishly enough, as a man will do foolish things in a crisis, Jandron laid his revolver outside his sleeping-bag, in easy reach. His thought—blurred by a strange, drawing headache—was:

"If *It* touches Vivian, I'll shoot!"

He realized the complete absurdity of trying to shoot a visitant from interstellar space; from the Fourth Dimension, maybe. But Jandron's ideas seemed tangled. Nothing would come right. He lay there, absorbed in a kind of waking nightmare. Now and then, rising on an elbow, he hearkened; all in vain. Nothing so much as stirred.

His thought drifted to better days, when all had been health, sanity, optimism; when nothing except jealousy of Marr, as concerned Vivian, had troubled him. Days when the sizzle of the frying-pan over friendly coals had made friendly wilderness music; when the wind and the northern star, the whirr of the reel, the whispering vortex of the paddle in clear water had all been things of joy. Yes, and when a certain happy moment had, through some word or look of the girl, seemed to promise his heart's desire. But now—

"Damn it, I'll save *her*, anyhow!" he swore with savage intensity, knowing all the while that what was to be, would be, unmitigably. Do ants, by any waving of antenna, stay the down-crushing foot of man?

Next morning, and the next, no sign of the Thing appeared. Hope revived that possibly It might have flitted away elsewhere; back, perhaps, to outer space. Many were the miles the urging paddles spurned behind. The fugitives calculated that a week more would bring them to the railroad. Fire burned again. Hot food and drink helped, wonderfully. But where were the fish?

"Most extraordinary," all at once said the Professor, at noonday camp. He had become quite rational again. "Do you realize, Jandron, we've seen no traces of life in some time?"

The geologist nodded. Only too clearly he had noted just that, but he had been keeping still about it.

"That's so, too!" chimed in Marr, enjoying the smoke that some incomprehensible turn of events was letting him have. "Not a muskrat or beaver. Not even a squirrel or bird."

"Not so much as a gnat or black-fly!" the Professor added. Jandron suddenly realized that he would have welcomed even those.

That afternoon, Marr fell into a suddenly vile temper. He mumbled curses against the guides, the current, the portages, everything. The Professor seemed more cheerful. Vivian complained of an oppressive headache. Jandron gave her the last of the aspirin tablets; and as he gave them, took her hand in his.

"I'll see *you* through, anyhow," said he, "I don't count, now. Nobody counts, only you!"

She gave him a long, silent look. He saw the sudden glint of tears in her eyes; felt the pressure of her hand, and knew they two had never been so near each other as in that moment under the shadow of the Unknown.

Next day—or it may have been two days later, for none of them could be quite sure about the passage of time—they came to a deserted lumber-camp. Even more than two days might have passed; because now their bacon was all gone, and only coffee, tobacco, beef-cubes and pilot-bread remained. The lack of fish and game had cut alarmingly into the duffle-bag. That day—whatever day it may have been—all four of them suffered terribly from headache of an odd, ring-shaped kind, as if something circular were being pressed down about their heads. The Professor said it was the sun that made his head ache. Vivian laid it to the wind and the gleam of the swift water, while Marr claimed it was the heat. Jandron wondered at all this, inasmuch as he plainly saw that the river had almost stopped flowing, and the day had become still and overcast.

They dragged their canoes upon a rotting stage of fir-poles and explored the lumber-camp; a mournful place set back in an old 'slash,' now partly overgrown with scrub poplar, maple and birch. The log buildings, covered with tar-paper partly torn from the pole roofs, were of the usual North Country type. Obviously the place had not been used for years. Even the landing-stage where once logs had been rolled into the stream had sagged to decay.

"I don't quite get the idea of this," Marr exclaimed. "Where did the logs go to? Downstream, of course. But *that* would take 'em to Hudson Bay, and there's no market for spruce timber or pulpwood at Hudson Bay." He pointed down the current.

"You're entirely mistaken," put in the Professor. "Any fool could see this river runs the other way. A log thrown in here would go down toward the St. Lawrence!"

"But then," asked the girl, "why can't we drift back to civilization?" The Professor retorted:

"Just what we *have* been doing, all along! Extraordinary, that I have to explain the obvious!' He walked away in a huff,

"I don't know but he's right, at that," half admitted the journalist. "I've been thinking almost the same thing, myself, the past day or two—that is, ever since the sun shifted."

"What do you mean, shifted?" from Jandron, "You haven't noticed it?"

"But there's been no sun at all, for at least two days!"

"Hanged if I'll waste time arguing with a lunatic!" Marr growled. He vouchsafed no explanation of what he meant by the sun's having "shifted," but wandered off, grumbling.

"What *are* we going to do?" the girl appealed to Jandron. The sight of her solemn, frightened eyes, of her palm-outward hands and (at last) her very feminine fear, constricted Jandron's heart.

"We're going through, you and I," he answered simply. "We've got to save them from themselves, you and I have."

Their hands met again, and for a moment held. Despite the dead calm, a fir-tip at the edge of the clearing suddenly flicked aside, shrivelled as if frozen. But neither of them saw it.

The fugitives, badly spent, established themselves in the 'bar-room' or sleeping-shack of the camp. They wanted to feel a roof over them again, if only a broken one. The traces of men comforted them: a couple of broken peavies, a pair of snowshoes with the thongs all gnawed off, a cracked bit of mirror, a yellowed almanac dated 1899.

Jandron called the Professor's attention to this almanac, but the Professor thrust it aside.

"What do *I* want of a Canadian census-report?" he demanded, and fell to counting the bunks, over and over again. His big bulge of his forehead, that housed the massive brain of him, was oozing sweat. Marr cursed what he claimed was sunshine through the holes in the roof, though Jandron could see none; claimed the sunshine made his head ache.

"But it's not a bad place," he added. "We can make a blaze in that fireplace and be comfy. I don't like that window, though."

"What window?" asked Jandron. "Where?"

Marr laughed, and ignored him. Jandron turned to Vivian, who had sunk down on the 'deacon-seat' and was staring at the stove.

"Is there a window here?" he demanded. "Don't ask me," she whispered. "I—I don't know."

With a very thriving fear in his heart, Jandron peered at her a moment. He fell to muttering:

"I'm Wallace Jandron. Wallace Jandron, 37 Ware Street, Cambridge, Massachusetts. I'm quite sane. And I'm going to stay so. I'm going to save her! I know perfectly well what I'm doing. And I'm sane. Quite, quite sane!"

After a time of confused and purposeless wrangling, they got a fire going and made coffee. This, and cube bouillon with hardtack, helped considerably. The camp helped, too. A house, even a poor and broken one, is a wonderful barrier against a Thing from—Outside.

Presently darkness folded down. The men smoked, thankful that tobacco still held out. Vivian lay in a bunk that Jandron had piled with spruce boughs for her, and seemed to sleep. The Professor fretted like a child, over the blisters his paddle had made upon his hands. Marr laughed, now and then; though what he might be laughing at was not apparent. Suddenly he broke out:

"After all, what should It want of us?"

"Our brains, of course," the Professor answered, sharply.

"That lets Jandron out," the journalist mocked. "But," added the Professor, "I can't imagine a, Thing callously destroying human beings. And yet—"

He stopped short, with surging memories of his dead wife.

"What was it," Jandron asked, "that destroyed all those people in Valladolid, Spain, that time so many of 'em died in a few minutes after having been touched by an invisible Something that left a slight red mark on each? The newspapers were full of it."

"Piffle!" yawned Marr.

"I tell you," insisted Jandron, "there are forms of life as superior to us as we are to ants. We can't see 'em. No ant ever saw a man. And did any ant ever form the least conception of a man? These Things have left thousands of traces, all over the world. If I had my reference-books—"

"Tell that to the marines!"

"Charles Fort, the greatest authority in the world on unexplained phenomena," persisted Jandron, "gives innumerable cases of happenings that science can't explain, in his *Book of the Damned*. He claims this earth was once a No-Man's land where all kinds of Things explored and colonized and fought for possession. And he says that now everybody's warned off, except the Owners. I happen to remember a few sentences of his: 'In the past, inhabitants of a host of worlds have dropped here, hopped here, wafted here, sailed, flown, motored, walked here; have come singly, have come in enormous numbers; have visited for hunting, trading, mining. They have been unable to stay here, have made colonies here, have been lost here.'"

"Poor fish, to believe that!" mocked the journalist, while the Professor blinked and rubbed his bulging forehead.

"I *do* believe it!" insisted Jandron. "The world is covered with relics of dead civilizations, that have mysteriously vanished, leaving nothing but their temples and monuments."

"Rubbish!"

"How about Easter Island? How about all the gigantic works there and in a thousand other places!—Peru, Yucatan and so on—which certainly no primitive race ever built?"

"That's thousands of years ago," said Marr, "and I'm sleepy. For heaven's sake, can it!"

"Oh, all right. But *how* explain things, then!"

"What the devil could one of those Things want of our brains?" suddenly put in the Professor. "After all, what?"

"Well, what do we want of lower forms of life? Sometimes food. Again, some product or other. Or just information. Maybe *It* is just experimenting with us, the way we poke an ant-hill. There's always this to remember, that the human brain-tissue is the most highly-organized form of matter in this world."

"Yes," admitted the Professor, "but what—?"

"*It* might want brain-tissue for food, for experimental purposes, for lubricant—how do I know?"

Jandron fancied he was still explaining things; but all at once he found himself waking up in one of the bunks. He felt terribly cold, stiff, sore. A sift of snow lay here and there on the camp floor, where it had fallen through holes in the roof.

"Vivian!" he croaked hoarsely. "Thorburn! Marr!"

Nobody answered. There was nobody to answer. Jandron crawled with immense pain out of his bunk, and blinked round with bleary eyes. All of a sudden he saw the Professor, and gulped.

The Professor was lying stiff and straight in another bunk, on his back. His waxen face made a mask of horror. The open, staring eyes, with pupils immensely dilated, sent Jandron shuddering back. A livid ring marked the forehead, that now sagged inward as if empty.

"*Vivian!*" croaked Jandron, staggering away from the body. He fumbled to the bunk where the girl had lain. The bunk was quite deserted.

On the stove, in which lay half-charred wood—wood smothered out as if by some noxious gas—still stood the coffee-pot. The liquid in it was frozen solid. Of Vivian and the journalist, no trace remained.

Along one of the sagging beams that supported the roof, Jandron's horror-blasted gaze perceived a straight line of frosted prints, ring-shaped, bitten deep.

"Vivian! Vivian!"

No answer.

Shaking, sick, gray, half-blind with a horror not of this world, Jandron peered slowly around. The duffle-bag and supplies were gone. Nothing was left but that coffee-pot and the revolver at Jandron's hip.

Jandron turned, then. A-stare, his skull feeling empty as a burst drum, he crept lamely to the door and out—out into the snow.

Snow. It came slanting down. From a gray sky it steadily filtered. The trees showed no leaf. Birches, poplars, rock-maples all stood naked. Only the conifers drooped sickly-green. In a little shallow across the river snow lay white on thin ice.

Ice? Snow? Rapt with terror, Jandron stared. Why, then, he must have been unconscious three or four weeks? But how—?

Suddenly, all along the upper branches of trees that edged the clearing, puffs of snow flicked down. The geologist shuffled after two half-obliterated sets of footprints that wavered toward the landing.

His body was leaden. He wheezed, as he reached the river. The light, dim as it was, hurt his eyes. He blinked in a confusion that could just perceive one canoe was gone. He pressed a hand to his head, where an iron band seemed screwed up tight, tighter.

"Vivian! Marr! Halloooo!"

Not even an echo. Silence clamped the world; silence, and a cold that gnawed. Everything had gone a sinister gray.

After a certain time—though time now possessed neither reality nor duration—Jandron dragged himself back to the camp and stumbled in. Heedless of the staring corpse he crumpled down by the stove and tried to think, but his brain had been emptied of power. Everything blent to a gray blur. Snow kept slithering in through the roof.

"Well, why don't you come and get me. Thing?" suddenly snarled Jandron. "Here I am. Damn you, come and get me!"

Voices. Suddenly he heard voices. Yes, somebody was outside, there. Singularly aggrieved, he got up and limped to the door. He squinted out into the gray; saw two figures down by the landing. With numb indifference he recognized the girl and Marr.

"Why should they bother me again?" he nebulously wondered. Can't they go away and leave me alone?" He felt peevish irritation.

Then, a modicum of reason returning, he sensed that they were arguing. Vivian, beside a canoe freshly dragged from thin ice, was pointing; Marr was gesticulating. All at once Marr snarled, turned from her, plodded with bent back toward the camp.

"But listen!" she called, her rough-knit sweater all powdered with snow. "*That's* the way!" She gestured downstream.

"I'm not going either way!" Marr retorted. "I'm going to stay right here!" He came on, bareheaded. Snow grayed his stubble of beard; but on his head it melted as it fell, as if some fever there had raised the brain-stuff to improbable temperatures. "I'm going to stay right here, all summer." His heavy lids sagged. Puffy and evil, his lips showed a glint of teeth. "Let me alone!"

Vivian lagged after him, kicking up the ash-like snow. With indifference, Jandron watched them. Trivial human creatures!

Suddenly Marr saw him in the doorway and stopped short. He drew his gun; he aimed at Jandron.

"*You* get out!" he mouthed. "Why in — can't you stay dead?"

"Put that gun down, you idiot!" Jandron managed to retort. The girl stopped and seemed trying to understand. "We can get away yet, if we all stick together."

"Are you going to get out and leave me alone?" demanded the journalist, holding his gun steadily enough.

Jandron, wholly indifferent, watched the muzzle. Vague curiosity possessed him. Just what, he wondered, did it feel like to be shot?

Mart pulled trigger.

Snap!

The cartridge missed fire. Not even powder would burn.

Marr laughed, horribly, and shambled forward. "Serves him right!" he mouthed, "He'd better not come back again!"

Jandron understood that Marr had seen him fall. But still he felt himself standing there, alive. He shuffled away from the door. No matter whether he was alive or dead, there was always Vivian to be saved.

The journalist came to the door, paused, looked down, grunted and passed into the camp. He shut the door. Jandron heard the rotten wooden bar of the latch drop. From within echoed a laugh, monstrous in its brutality.

Then quivering, the geologist felt a touch on his arm.

"Why did you desert us like that?" he heard Vivian's reproach. "Why?"

He turned, hardly able to see her at all.

"Listen," he said, thickly. "I'll admit anything. It's all right. But just forget it, for now. We've got to get out o' here. The Professor is dead, in there, and Marr's gone mad and barricaded himself in there. So there's no use staying. There's a chance for us yet. Come along!"

He took her by the arm and tried to draw her toward the river, but she held back. The hate in her face sickened him. He shook in the grip of a mighty chill.

"Go, with—you?" she demanded.

"Yes, by God!" he retorted, in a swift blaze of anger, "or I'll kill you where you stand. *It* shan't get you, anyhow!"

Swiftly piercing, a greater cold smote to his inner marrows. A long row of the cup-shaped prints had just appeared in the snow beside the camp. And from these marks wafted a faint, bluish vapor of unthinkable cold.

"What are you staring at?" the girl demanded. "Those prints! In the snow, there—see?" He pointed a shaking finger.

"How can there be snow at this season?"

He could have wept for the pity of her, the love of her. On her red tam, her tangle of rebel hair, her sweater, the snow came steadily drifting; yet there she stood before him and prated of summer. Jandron heaved himself out of a very slough of down-dragging lassitudes. He whipped himself into action.

"Summer, winter—no matter!" he flung at her. "You're coming along with me!" He seized her arm with the brutality of desperation that must hurt, to save. And murder, too, lay in his soul. He knew that he would strangle her with his naked hands, if need were, before he would ever leave her there, for *It* to work Its horrible will upon.

"You come with me," he mouthed, "or by the Almighty—!"

Marr's scream in the camp, whirled him toward the door. That scream rose higher, higher, even more and more piercing, just like the screams of the runaway Indian guides in what now appeared the infinitely long ago. It seemed to last hours; and always it rose, rose, as if being wrung out of a human body by some kind of agony not conceivable in this world. Higher, higher—

Then it stopped.

Jandron hurled himself against the plank door. The bar smashed; the door shivered inward.

With a cry, Jandron recoiled. He covered his eyes with a hand that quivered, claw-like.

"Go away, Vivian! Don't come here—don't look—"

He stumbled away, babbling.

Out of the door crept something like a man. A queer, broken, bent over thing; a thing crippled, shrunken and flabby, that whined.

This thing—yes, it was still Marr—crouched down at one side, quivering, whimpering. It moved its hands as a crushed ant moves its antennæ, jerkily, without significance.

All at once Jandron no longer felt afraid. He walked quite steadily to Marr, who was breathing in little gasps. From the camp issued an odor unlike anything terrestrial. A thin, grayish grease covered the sill.

Jandron caught hold of the crumpling journalist's arm. Marr's eyes leered, filmed, unseeing. He gave the impression of a creature whose back has been broken, whose whole essence and energy have been wrenched asunder, yet in which life somehow clings, palpitant. A creature vivisected.

Away through the snow Jandron dragged him. Marr made no resistance; just let himself be led, whining a little, palsied, rickety, shattered. The girl, her face whitely cold as the snow that fell on it, came after.

Thus they reached the landing at the river.

"Come, now, let's get away!" Jandron made shift to articulate. Marr said nothing. But when Jandron tried to bundle him into a canoe, something in the journalist revived with swift, mad hatefulness. That something lashed him into a spasm of wiry, incredibly venomous resistance. Slavers of blood and foam streaked Marr's lips. He made horrid noises, like an animal. He howled dismally, and bit, clawed, writhed and grovelled! he tried to sink his teeth into Jandron's leg. He fought appallingly, as men must have fought in the inconceivably remote days even before the Stone Age. And Vivian helped him. Her fury was a tiger-cat's.

Between the pair of them, they almost did him in. They almost dragged Jandron down—and themselves, too—into the black river that ran swiftly sucking under the ice. Not till Jandron had quite flung off all vague notions and restraints of gallantry; not until he struck from the shoulder—to kill, if need were—did he best them.

He beat the pair of them unconscious, trussed them hand and foot with the painters of the canoes, rolled them into the larger canoe, and shoved off. After that, the blankness of a measureless oblivion descended.

Only from what he was told, weeks after, in the Royal Victoria Hospital at Montreal, did Jandron ever learn how and when a field-squad of Dominion Foresters had found them drifting in Lake Moosawamkeag. And that knowledge filtered slowly into his brain during a period inchoate as Iceland fogs.

That Marr was dead and the girl alive—that much, at all events, was solid. He could hold to that; he could climb back, with that, to the real world again.

Jandron climbed back, came back. Time healed him, as it healed the girl. After a long, long while, they had speech together. Cautiously he sounded her wells of memory. He saw that she recalled nothing. So he told her white lies about capsized canoes and the sad death—in realistically-described rapids—of all the party except herself and him.

Vivian believed. Fate, Jandron knew, was being very kind to both of them.

But Vivian could never understand in the least why, her husband, not very long after marriage, asked her not to wear a wedding-ring or any ring whatever.

"Men are so queer!" covers a multitude of psychic agonies.

Life, for Jandron—life, softened by Vivian—knit itself up into some reasonable semblance of a normal pattern. But when, at lengthening intervals, memories even now awake—memories crawling amid the slime of cosmic mysteries that it is madness to approach—or when at certain times Jandron sees a ring of any sort, his heart chills with a cold that reeks of the horrors of Infinity.

And from shadows past the boundaries of our universe seem to beckon Things that, God grant, can never till the end of time be known on earth.